GEM

First Edition Design Publishing

GEM
Copyright ©2013 Naida Reynolds
ISBN 978-1622872-62-6 PRINT
ISBN 978-1622872-61-9EBOOK

LCCN 2013932202

January 2013

Published and Distributed by
First Edition Design Publishing, Inc.
P.O. Box 20217, Sarasota, FL 34276-3217
www.firsteditiondesignpublishing.com

Cover Art – Deborah E Gordon

ALL RIGHTS RESERVED. No part of this book publication may be reproduced, stored in a retrieval system, or transmitted in any form or by any means — electronic, mechanical, photo-copy, recording, or any other — except brief quotation in reviews, without the prior permission of the author or publisher.

Chapter One

He was usually a much more observant man. He had noticed when she sat at the table next to his, but she had kept her head down, reading papers she took from a large brown portfolio. If it hadn't been for the American tourists, he might have passed the time at the café without fully seeing her.

"Gem! Gem! Why it is you!" the taller of the two men said excitedly.

Wyatt sharpened his focus on the young woman. Gem. Perhaps! However, it was a common nickname.

Gem looked up, shading her eyes with her hand to locate the voice in the bright morning sunlight beyond the café's canopy. As she lowered her hand, Wyatt realized the true meaning of the phrase 'blind luck'. He hadn't known where to begin searching for her. She travelled quite often, James had said; she could be anywhere in the world.

Wyatt saw the extraordinary deep violet eyes fringed with sooty black lashes; the luminous skin caressed by the pale green, tailored silk blouse; the crème coloured ballerina length silk skirt rustling in the breeze, revealing lovely legs. A dab of powder, a hint of lipstick; no other cosmetics were needed for this natural beauty. Her pale blonde hair, artfully woven in an intricate braid extended well past her shoulders; tendrils, tousling in the early August breeze, framed her sun-kissed cheeks.

Breathtaking! Nature had bestowed its finest artistry to her, exquisite beauty, lacking nothing - except a soul.

He had studied the photos hour after hour. He saw her in his nightmares. It was indeed her.

Gem groaned inwardly as she looked blankly at the handsome young couple.

"Hello," she said tentatively, forcing a bright smile.

Wyatt continued to observe her. The same lovely smile- perfect straight, white teeth.

Gem set down her tea cup. She should have taken a table inside the café, but it was a shame to be indoors on such a lovely day.

"T and J-" the taller man offered.

"Tad and Jeff - remember? - San Francisco," the other man, nearly a head shorter than his partner, filled in the unspoken questions.

Gem nodded, still smiling. "Of course, San Francisco!" Blast! When was San Francisco? Last spring? No, that was the broken arm. No, February was the broken arm. A year ago? What have I landed myself with? There's so much I don't know - or don't recall. And why should I have to know everything? She usually didn't have 'unknown' situations in London. London had always been her base.

"You're in London! How lovely!" Please don't ask me to be your guide, she sent a silent plea. But that offer would never have been suggested - she would never have made that offer! Not for London!

"Only for an hour or so," the taller one replied. He pointed to his partner. "Tad insists on hitting every castle possible in two weeks."

"Ah!" Gem mentally relaxed. "Where to first?"

"We've done the 'Palace'," it had to be Jeff speaking- process of elimination; he used air quotes around palace. "Off to Warwick now. Super!"

"We didn't stop to think, couldn't imagine bumping into you in Merry Olde England! You are always grabbing a jet, always travelling. So ubiquitous!"

"And we never did get your cell number when you were in good old S.F. Another of your whirlwind jaunts," Jeff lightly scolded.

Gem nodded. "Of course." They certainly wouldn't have a mobile number. Mobile numbers were only for family. A ring at an inopportune moment might be a massive headache - a lost mobile was a scorching one, and possibly a cog that could slip. And international mobile rates were crippling. She had heard that complaint more than once or twice the past few years. - Flat numbers, perhaps, but no mobile number! No cogs that could slip!

"Well, Gem, old dear, it's been fab!" Jeff grinned. "But we're off to see knights in shining armour."

"They are a dying breed these days, I believe," she mused.

"There's that British sense of humour we love so much, Gem!" Tad waggled a finger at her. "Hugs all around!"

She was pulled from her chair and thoroughly hugged by both men. Then more farewells and promises were extracted from her to 'look them up' next time she was in good old S.F.! She knew where to find them!

"Who actually says farewell?" Gem chuckled, as the lads went on their way.

"Apparently tourists from good old S.F.," came an amused reply from the next table.

Gem turned to her left, her eyes meeting the gaze of a strikingly handsome man. His hair was lush dark, nearly black, his eyes light grey with a faint rim of blue around the irises. Wow! He could be a magazine advert for a shining knight - sans armour! He was impeccably dressed. Savile row, no doubt, or a personal tailor -elegant black suit, sparkling white shirt, so subtle grey tie that perfectly matched his eyes. The suit, so perfectly tailored, indicated what she knew would be a smashing body.

He smiled at her, and her heart flip-flopped. So corny, but so true! She blushed, took a step backward, then with her usual lack of grace, knocked her papers off the table.

"Blast!" Gem sighed.

He was quickly beside her. He was tall. Very tall! And perfection!

He scooped up the papers as Gem nervously, and again true to nature, managed to tip over her tea cup. She wondered desperately if this devastatingly gorgeous man was someone she should know.

"Blast!" Blushing furiously, she mopped up the tea with a serviette.

"One of those days?" he chuckled.

"One of those years. Not much sleep last night," she admitted, clattering the tea cup against the saucer. "Blast! Not a good day to pick up babies," she sighed.

She glanced at him. The muscles of his jaws tightened. The smile seemed to fade a bit.

"You have an infant?" he asked smoothly, handing her the papers he had collected.

"Oh - no - no," Gem waved her hand, papers and all, in protest. "No children. No pets. Free. Untethered."

"Ah!" The smile returned.

Lord! What beautiful teeth!

Gem snapped to her senses. Control! Always be in control of yourself! No blathering, she warned herself.

"May I?" He indicated a chair at her table.

"Yes," she managed a calm tone - or hoped it sounded calm, watching as he drew out her chair for her, before seating himself.

"Wyatt Grantham," he extended his hand, "no children, no pets, also free and untethered." Did she recognise the name? He studied her face.

Gem relaxed. He didn't seem to expect her to know him. Lovely, she thought happily. His handshake was firm, but not crushing, his touch causing another flutter to her heart. "Congratulations - being untethered," she offered half-humorously, half-questioningly, completely inanely.

"Untethered - for now," he grinned, "but a man should marry. Home, family, the ultimate goal." He arranged her papers in a neat pile as he spoke.

My gosh! He is so - so - so - Gem's vocabulary failed her.

"And you are?" he prompted with a smile.

"Completely lacking social graces," Gem blushed. "Gem Forrester. Ah - Gemimah - Forrester."

"A lovely name. It suits you - Gemimah," Wyatt stressed her full name.

Gem laughed. "I haven't been called Gemimah in so long. I nearly forgot it was my name. I'm called Gem."

It was HER!

Game ON!

He glanced down at the papers. Sketches of churches, some of the drawings were of very fine detail. "You are an artist," he observed.

"Not really. I studied art history. I'm writing a book about medieval cathedrals - history and architecture." Please let me speak coherently and say something interesting!

"Coffee table book?"

"More or less. I'm expanding my thesis."

"Master's?"

"Doctoral."

His eyebrows rose. "Very impressive."

"Last year. So glad that's in the past. But I'm obsessed with cathedrals."

"Last year," he repeated, nodding his head. "Very interesting, indeed."

Oh good! It's interesting! Gem smiled.

"And you?" she coaxed gingerly, hoping not to sound prying.

"I admire churches, but they are not an obsession with me," he said lightly. "Oh - work. Business." He paused. Would she trip to the name now? "Grantham Enterprises International."

"Oh," Gem said politely.

Wyatt again closely studied her face. The name hadn't registered with her. He would stake his life on that.

Game definitely ON!

And bless James for refusing to trade on the Grantham name, insisting on adopting Smythe, their grandmother's maiden name. The Game would play smoothly.

Wyatt's gaze fell upon her right hand.

"What a fascinating ring," he murmured, tracing the object with his finger. "Wherever did you find such a treasure?"

She watched his finger, circling, circling hypnotically, mesmerizing her.

Gem's thoughts drifted back.

Gemmy had been hastily packing for the flight.

"Gem," Gemmy hesitated, then smiled. "You must see this!" She held up a ring that gleamed in the bright ceiling light of their bedroom. "This ring is over two hundred years old! It was crafted in London!"

Gem's eyes opened wide at the sparkling jewel. "Stunning! Wherever did you find it?"

"Barcelona! Lovely, lovely Barcelona! Magical Barcelona! Oh, how I dearly love Barcelona!" Gemma sang and danced around the room. She stopped dancing and lowered her voice conspiratorially. "I cashed in my stocks and bonds. I am going to purchase the loveliest flat you have ever seen! In lovely Barcelona! You will love Barcelona as much as I do, Gem. You must come visit. Ever so often!"

Gem laughed at her sister's joyous mood. "Barcelona is lovely, I hear!"

Gemmy winked at her. "I'll tell you a secret, dearest sister in the entire wide, wide world." Gem nodded encouragingly. "You know, love, how thrilled I am to go on this trip, but when it's over - when mum and dad and I come home - I am retiring from the Agency. Good and truly retiring - permanently!" She dramatically lowered her voice. "I'll tell mum and dad on the plane - and soon the dear Agency and I will be parting company - forever!"

Gem gasped in astonishment. "What! You! You who loved to travel so much you wanted your passport bronzed!"

Gemmy giggled. "Bronze is, after all, third place. I am going to be first place! I'm going to live in Barcelona forever! No more quick flights for the Agency! No more gruelling cross-country hopping, six countries in two days to finish my blasted thesis! It is finally, finally finished. And now it's Barcelona forever!" she sighed happily. "And NO MORE AGENCY! Do you know that Harry is still grumpy about that passport I lost last month?"

Gem smiled, shaking her head. "I can't imagine why! Lost - one extremely sensitive, especial government passport bearing your photograph!" Gem laughed. "But - still - more power to you, dear heart. At last I shall always know where to find you. Barcelona, wasn't it?"

"Yes. I shall always be there!" Gemma smiled at her sister, then at the ring. "This is a very, very old, very important ring, my dear sister," she said, holding out the ring to Gem. "Take care of it for me while I am away. It's priceless. It is one of a kind!"

Gem gingerly accepted the ring, admiring it as she held it in the palm of her hand. The centre stone was a medium size, square cut diamond; it was encircled by smaller, square cut diamonds - all woven together in an intricate, almost embroidered web of fine sterling silver - the work of a great artisan.

"A lovely thesis completed gift for yourself, dear Gemmy. You deserve it!"

Gemma laughed at her sister. "Gem! You are so funny!"

Then it was a flurry of activity. Knapsacks grabbed, hugs, kisses, and Gem's family was off to catch the plane.

"I'll be seeing you," their father said to Gem, as he always did when he bid good-bye to his daughters.

"Wherever did you find it?" Wyatt was repeating his query, and frowning. She was certainly lost in her thoughts. The lovely violet eyes had an odd, clouded look.

Gem shook herself, realizing he was speaking to her. Back to the present! The painful memories. The painful past. The painful present.

"Barcelona," she cleared her throat. She forced a bright tone. "It's over two hundred years old. It was crafted in London, I was told."

"Quite lovely. It is a treasure," Wyatt murmured.

"Congratulations gift on a thesis finally completed - a - very - long effort," Gem said with a faint smile. There was nothing else to say. She couldn't tell him the truth.

"Hmm, yes, quite a treasure," Wyatt repeated. He scowled slightly. "Gem - I am being forward - I realize- but as you have already had tea, may I coax you to be my guest for lunch?"

He gazed at her, and Gem found her breath catching in her throat. She could get lost in his eyes! She glanced at her watch. "It's half ten. A bit early for lunch perhaps," she said hesitantly.

"Long stroll?" he coaxed. "Mull which restaurant? Window shopping?"

She opened her mouth to decline. She didn't even know him - other than his name. And then his mobile rang.

Wyatt glanced at the number. "I am sorry to be rude, but I must take this call. Minor fracas this morning at the company, now escalating to major."

Gem nodded understandingly.

"It was an error, Manton. Don't dwell on it." He paused, listening to the man at the other and of the line. "No, you may not dismiss him. You've been much more flexible with other new employees." He winked at Gem, shaking his head. She could hear the voice ranting from the other end of the line. "The issue will be resolved, it's nothing critical." He paused again, holding the mobile away from his ear for a moment. "No. No. Listen - no listen. You terrify him. He's terrified of disappointing you." Another pause. He shook his head again at Gem. "Listen, Manton - I am attempting to persuade a delightfully charming, exquisitely beautiful woman to have lunch with me, and I am not going to continue to ignore her·to listen to you rant." She blushed at his compliments. He was momentarily distracted. How could she possibly still be able to blush!

Wyatt scowled and spoke firmly into his mobile. "Send Peter to Greece and get off the lad's back. And raise his allowance. His starting pay won't cover much spending money for Athens' night life." He snapped the mobile closed. "Forgive me," he grinned at Gem. "Manton is Director of our London office but is currently at the Paris office. I hired his son as his assistant. The lad is brilliant, over-eager, and drives his father to great distraction. Peter overreached on a project, caused a minor flap, and now Manton is out for his blood's blood."

Gem laughed. The man was so suave! So polished! So commanding!

"As you heard, Peter is going to the Athens office immediately. Manton, however, would prefer to dispose of his son in the middle of the ocean."

The smile left Gem's face.

"I have offended you," he said abruptly, gently touching her hand.

Gem shook off the remark and forced a smile. "No, not at all." Careless words, but only to her. She began to slip the papers into the portfolio.

"Stroll? Lunch?" he gave a slight frown, concerned that he had somehow ruined his chance at the Game.

Gem reflected for a moment. Damn the ocean. Damn all the oceans! All the seas! They might torture her at night, rob her of her sleep, but they would not steal this lovely day from her with this smashing man!

"Yes, thank you," she smiled.

He took the portfolio from her hands, tucking it under his left arm, taking her left hand in his right.

The day had been perfect, Gem reflected as she sorted the jumble of papers on her desk. There had not been the slightest awkward pause, or lapse of conversation, from the moment they left Oscar's Café until they had parted hours later. She had been extremely careful of her remarks; however the effort had been unnecessary. The conversation had floated from university studies - Oxford and the Sorbonne for him, Cambridge for her; family: Wyatt, none; her - Gem had felt a stabbing pain of guilt as she replied the same: none.

They had walked for miles, and at one point he had insisted on purchasing a straw hat for her to wear as the August sun beat down on them. They had eliminated restaurants along the way, finally deciding on the White Rose Pub, a new venue for both.

And fortunately for Gem, she was not recognized by anyone she did not know along their walk. After all, London had been her base. Tad and Jeff were, hopefully, an aberrant episode, not an incident to become commonplace. She could relax in her own country. And she was thrilled to be in the company of the staggeringly handsome, attentive, Wyatt Grantham.

Lord! She couldn't recall the last time she had been out with a man! She had been so busy! There had been that one lad - was his name Eli? No matter; that was eons of months ago.

Wyatt had actually asked about her study of cathedrals - not merely a polite query, but question after question on the subject of which she was extremely well versed. "Medieval cathedrals," he had mused. "Good heavens! That's some nine hundred fifty years to study! Very ambitious! The book will be huge! Italy alone will be a massive section."

"Italy shall be a separate volume. If I ever finish the first one," Gem had laughed.

"Indeed! Where does one begin on such an epic work?"

"Ireland, Scotland, Britain, Volume I. Europe Volume II. Italy -"

"Volumes III, IV, V, and VI," he had chuckled.

Gem had laughed again. "I have photos of many cathedrals, but I have to re-shoot quite a few, including Elgin, Fortrose, Durham, Winchester, and Carlisle, I think. I do know at least the first two. What I view through the lens does not always translate to quality final product," she explained.

"Or the weather wasn't as conducive as it seemed to be on a particular day," he had suggested.

"Precisely," Gem had smiled. "Fortrose and Elgin photos were ruined by a scratched lens - which I didn't realize was damaged until I had returned to London and had the photos processed."

She had tried to direct the conversation to chat about him, but he redirected her thoughts to European cathedrals, restaurants, and disastrous dining in various cities; his travels mainly related to business, however he did not elaborate on that subject.

Their stroll past shops, after the pub lunch, surprised Gem. She didn't realize that men window shopped - or window hopped as she and Gemmy had titled the process. Wyatt's taste in window shopping was of a much higher calibre than hers, but Gem couldn't find fault with his excellent style.

She sorted, arranged, and entered architectural statistics into her computer. Handsome Wyatt Grantham teased her thoughts as she worked, causing her to do a major proof-reading of facts.

He had asked to see her again when they parted at the bus stop. He had wanted to drive her home, or escort her in a taxi, but Gem had politely declined. She had easily agreed to join him for tea at nine o'clock the following morning - again at Oscar's Café. She didn't worry about sleeping through her alarm. She now had an unforgiving internal clock – always waking at seven in the morning; tomorrow would be no different.

Gem smiled to herself. He certainly was delicious! She could not put Wyatt Grantham from her thoughts. Such a lovely day! When was the last time she had had an outing - with anyone? Work, study, work, the heart wrenching search that nearly drove her to desperation!

Gem shut down the computer, having accomplished very little of what could only very loosely be termed work. She took a shower and immediately fell asleep as her head touched the pillow.

Hours later Gem wakened. She didn't need to check the time. It was precisely two o'clock in the morning. It was always precisely two o'clock. Brisbane or London, it was always two o'clock. The moon shone faintly on the quiet street below the windows of her flat. She shook her head to focus her eyes and her brain, then slid from her cosy bed, pulled on her dressing gown, and switched on her computer. She clicked on the top folder in her computer files - the Pacific

Ocean, and reached over to press the start button on the cd player. Vera Lynn's voice sang to her every morning at this time - I'll Be Seeing You - her parents' favourite song. The songs of the Second World War. Gem kept the volume low so as not to disturb the other residents in the building.

Pacific Ocean: 165,241,241.439 square kilometres; 10,914.888 meters at its greatest depth.

But I am only interested in a relatively small part of you, she informed the massive body of water. The Timor Sea. Or perhaps the Arafura Sea.

Gem paced the floor, retracing her steps to the computer to stare at the screen that seemed to mock her night after night on end. Perhaps it just seemed endless, for she had only recently started her own search. Until a few weeks previously, she had worked assignments. Worked until she could no longer bear to board a flight. She could no longer cross bodies of water by air or by ship. She could no longer travel through the Chunnel. She was trapped in England and would be so until she had resolved her search. Or until the Agency had resolved its search. They were all working together - brainstorming, searching for details, for clues, for glitches. For any information, no matter how minute or illogical. Anything. Absolutely anything.

Six hours out of Brisbane. Flying dead reckoning? Or instrument panel?

Gemma and Gemimah. They were only 'Gem' - interchangeable - or both at the same time - from the time they could first remember. Twins - so identical that only a careful scan of fingerprints could differentiate Gemma from Gemimah. Identical deep violet eyes, same black lashes, skin tones, and teeth.

Gem and Gem. Friends didn't get them confused - they had had few friends, didn't need them - they always had each other. Their home outside Brisbane had few neighbouring houses, few and far between.

There was one difference between the sisters, Gem self-edited. To give the girls some identity separation, their parents had bestowed upon the girls different surnames. Gemma had their mother's surname, Gemimah their father's.

Gemma Louisa Lawson. Gemimah Louisa Forrester.

The surname difference was also a hope of protection for some day in their future, if necessary, due to their parents' careers. Margaret Lawson and Gerald Forrester wrote and published little known travel guides.

Margaret mainly pursued the travelling while Gerald remained at home to write the books.

A lovely story, Gem mused silently. Actually mum was a courier for the British government and dad was a master cryptographer.

There had been no formal private or public schooling for Gem and Gem; they had been parent educated. The girls hadn't been forced to study; they had devoured books, and no subject limits had been imposed by their parents. Possessing near photographic memories was also an ace in the hole for the sisters while they pursued their course work.

The sisters had been separated when they were twelve. Margaret Lawson's courier assignments more and more involved European countries; Gemimah had moved with their mum to England, basing out of Auntie Jane's cottage in the country; Gemma had remained in Brisbane with their father.

Constant e-mails, phone calls, and then texting, had kept the sisters intimately tuned to one another. Month long visits three times a year to Australia had kept the family unit solid.

Gem was still amazed when she thought of the exciting offer to Gemmy and herself when they had reached their eighteenth birthday. Harry Breckett, long time family friend, and Director of the Agency - a wholly separate department of British Intelligence - had offered the twins courier positions with the Agency. Harry believed that no one would ever suspect the two young sisters were government couriers. Receiving no parental objections, Gem and Gem had pursued the required training; Gemimah had been posted to London, continuing her studies at university, while Gemma had been posted to and studied at Melbourne.

The sisters had worked diligently, followed the rules to the letter, and enjoyed travelling - sometimes at the drop of the proverbial hat - with special government passports, micro-chipped to allow them nearly free passing at airport customs counters all over the world.

Their paths rarely crossed, but they were perpetually linked by phone and computer, meeting at least once a month - usually in Europe. Gemma rarely set foot in London, Gemimah retreating to Australia only for the designated family reunions.

Gemimah's immediate government supervisor was Mrs Brown, who had been employed by the Agency for many years, first as a courier, then as an agent, and finally as one of the Directors; she was now retired to courier assignment supervisor, which allowed her more time for her precious gardening. Gemma was connected to Eric Portermann, Agency agent and government pilot.

On assignment, names on passports aside, the sister couriers were known to Agency personnel as 'Gem'. No differentiation. Which was helpful when Gemimah had flu, or when Gemma had broken her arm skiing late last winter; they covered each other's assignments without missing a beat.

Gem paced the floor as the minutes ticked by. She crossed to the computer, enlarging the section of the Timor Sea. 480km wide, covering approximately 610,000 square k, some 3300 meters deep. Wide and deep enough in which to lose a prop plane.

Flying under radar? If so - why? To what purpose? No contact. No SOS. No Mayday.

"No nothing!" Gem said bitterly.

What was the flight plan? Her father had sent it by code to Harry, but Harry had been unable to decipher the message, Mrs Brown had carefully explained to Gem the day the plane was lost. "We don't know where the plane went down, my dear. Without the flight plan we can only begin with guess work."

"Harry can't break dad's code," Gem had caught the older woman's point.

"He is in your father's league with codes, trust me on that. But there was a sort of glitch in the receiving code computer. The only letter that was deciphered was the letter D. Harry sent the preferred flight plan to Mr Portermann. Your father was to confer with Portermann, and confirm by code 'as stated' or indicate alternative plans, then confirm by code at the last possible minute before leaving the house for the airstrip. He was then to destroy the file, and shut down his coding computer."

"My father never made coding errors, and only he knew how to use his code computer," Gem had insisted.

Gem knew there were three Agency sending/receiving code computers in the world. One in the States, one in France, and her father's in Brisbane. The main frame was in London in Mr White's Agency computer lab. Harry could send and receive coded messages from the other code computers, but the three computers could not transmit to each other unless Harry sent a code to connect a relay.

"Nor does Harry make errors," Mrs Brown had firmly insisted.

"A computer glitch. But which computer?" Gem had groaned with frustration.

"Harry is continuing to work on the problem with Mr White," Mrs Brown had attempted to console her. "Planes are searching the waters off the coast of Australia, however there have been no signs of debris."

"But no on knows where to search," Gem had protested helplessly. "And how does one coordinate a search when the flight was 'unscheduled'? Take-off from a private airstrip, no flight plan was filed with a commercial airport. And the flight never existed. It's like piecing together a picture puzzle while wearing a blindfold."

"Pilots logging flight hours for 'new' Australian government requirements," Mrs Brown had explained. "Harry pulled a lot of strings to get this process in the works."

Gem shut down the computer and crawled into bed. It was only half four. Too early to sleep. The dark hours wouldn't be over for another half hour. She had to wait it out.

I'm trying, Gemmy!

For the past two months, Gem's thoughts had been so confused; she had existed to complete courier assignments, and to re-adjust her life to her non-existent family. Her life was a waking nightmare. The insomnia had started that night. 30 May. She couldn't sleep during the day. She had insisted on working until mid-July. Until she realized she could no longer trust her concentration - her judgment - and the latter was what had disturbed her the most. Now she was having trouble focusing on anything but Gemmy and the missing plane. Nor could she board a plane or bear to look at large expanses of water. She was in an emotional stupor, dragging herself through each day, forcing herself to work on her book, desperately attempting to find a starting point to search for the plane - for Gemmy, for mum, for dad, for Mr Portermann.

And then there was Barcelona.

As the hands moved to five on the clock face, Gem closed her eyes, her thoughts again drifting back to Wyatt Grantham. Much more pleasant thoughts. She wanted to gaze into his eyes - and to shut down her brain.

Chapter Two

Gem had been correct; she did not need an alarm to waken her two hours later. She was awake when her mobile rang at seven o'clock.

"Good morning, my dear," Mrs Brown's voice greeted her.

"Morning ma'am," Gem stifled a yawn as she replied.

"You sound tired, my dear. Still the insomnia?" Mrs Brown's voice sounded concerned.

"Yes," Gem swept a curtain of hair back from her face.

"Are you napping during the day?"

"No, I am working on my book."

"You will exhaust yourself. Would you please ring Dr Hallowell?" Mrs Brown urged, as she had the previous week.

"I am fine, ma'am. I can manage. I don't want to take pills - they might cloud my brain."

"Hypnosis then. I've heard it is often successful for various ailments."

"I am not ailing," Gem declined the suggestion.

"Very well, my dear. Please perform your morning ablutions and join me for tea at nine o'clock," her supervisor crisply ordered.

Blast! "Could we please meet at eight?"

There was never any fuss with Mrs Brown. Eight it was!

Gem was out of the door within a half hour. She knew her skirt and blouse complimented her - they had come from Gemmy's wardrobe, and her sister had had flawless taste in clothes. Gem's own style was to dress comfortably for walking - her favourite exercise.

A quarter hour walk would take her to the café Mrs Brown had designated, conveniently located across the intersection where she would meet Wyatt. Her heart skipped at least three beats just thinking of his name. White clouds tinged with pale blue warned of weather - hopefully later in the day. She could take a bus back to her flat if rain moved in earlier than forecasted.

She methodically weaved through the pedestrians ahead of her. It would not do to keep Mrs Brown waiting; it simply was not done.

As she walked, the silk of Gemmy's blouse stroked her skin. The coordinating skirt and blouse of soft blue had been one of her sister's favourite outfits, the skirt just grazing her ankles. Gem had Gemmy's clothing and jewellery, but nothing more from the family.

Mrs Brown had been gentle, but firm, as the two women had sorted the possessions in the house outside Brisbane the morning the plane was lost. "No one can know the plane is missing. We cannot allow information to be released until the location of the plane has been discovered. If it was sabotage, we need to learn who had information that cost the Agency the lives of two couriers and two agents."

Gem had only replied, "Understood. Standard procedure."

"All records were immediately sealed. Gemma, your parents, Portermann, never existed. Reply to all inquiries, if any occur, that your parents passed away years ago. No siblings. And that it is only a means to protect you in the event it was sabotage - no links to you. You were raised by your Auntie Jane, who is also now deceased."

Which was true, Gem had reflected.

"All information has to be sealed until the crash site is discovered," Mrs Brown had reiterated, "and any information or records on the plane are reviewed."

"I understand." Gem had looked around the living room, knowing that she might never again see any memories of her family.

"The packers will be here soon. Your family possessions will be sent to the Agency warehouse in London. A couple will be moving in here within the week. They will only reply to queries that they heard the owners had relocated to the States. You girls and Margaret travelled so often you never related much to anyone in this area." So true, Gem had reflected. "I am very sorry to say that you will all be quickly forgotten by people who barely knew you. Low profile. Very important. Very necessary."

"Gemmy worked so hard to complete her thesis, and it may never be appreciated." Gem had brushed her fingers across the cover of the manuscript. Even she had not read it, and now she might never have the chance to do so.

"The search will continue. It must. We do not forget our own," Mrs Brown had soothed.

"I don't understand why the black box hasn't sent a signal. There was one on the plane?"

"I should hope Portermann had one, but it has not been confirmed."

"Blast!"

"Precisely, my dear. Harry said you may take Gemmy's jewellery and her clothing. However, all other items must be sent to the warehouse. All computers will be sent to the Agency for monitoring."

The first boxes packed were the ones Gem would take with her back to London. She smiled wistfully at the eclectic selection in her sister's jewellery box. Gemmy had loved jewellery, although few of her pieces were what others would consider quality. Gem had nicknamed her sister 'Crow' for her attraction to shiny objects.

The ring! The lovely two hundred year old ring. That had been the last time they were together. Gemmy packing for the flight to Singapore; their mum had also had an assignment to the same city; their father was travelling with them as a cover - to write a travel magazine article: A Family Holiday in South East Asia.

Gem had arrived home a half hour before her family was to leave for the airstrip. She had been completely exhausted after three weeks of flying to one assignment after another. She had longed for a long bath and a long sleep after the interminable flight from Athens to Brisbane. Her family would return in three days' time, and they would then enjoy a month long holiday together.

Gemmy had been glowing with excitement; her last assignment, thesis complete, the planned move to a lovely new flat in Barcelona. Gem had begun to despise the name of that city in Spain.

Mrs Brown had packed Gemmy's clothes as Gem had lifted the ring from the jewellery box; the ring Gemmy had handed to her for safekeeping. She had put the ring on her third finger, right hand. It had fit perfectly. She would never take it off.

Her family had left to meet Mr Portermann at the private airstrip. Gem had kept her eyes open that night until nearly midnight, unpacking her luggage, taking a bath, washing her hair. Then she had fallen into bed and into a sound sleep.

She had been jolted awake at two o'clock in the morning. Clear as a crystal bell she had heard Gemmy's voice calling to her: 'Gem! Where are you? Where are you? Help - please, dear God! Gem!'

And Gem had instantly realized that her family was gone.

She had immediately rung Mrs Brown and Harry who were in Sydney for conferences of the South East Asia Network - the Agency's bureau in that part of the world. They had arrived shortly before four o'clock. Harry had checked with all the airports from Brisbane to Singapore; and no unidentified planes had been on radar from Port Moresby to the Caroline Islands to Singapore. No Maydays had been issued. Mr Portermann's prop plane, the Pilos, had not responded to any Agency over-ride directives demanding immediate flight coordinates.

At five o'clock that horrible morning - 30 May - the Agency declared the plane missing and presumably crashed.

Gem had known at two o'clock that morning that all on board on perished. No one attempted to dispute her pronouncement.

The early morning crowd had thinned at the café by the time Gem arrived to claim a table. She chose one under the canopy; their backs would be to a wall; the other sides had clear visibility of other patrons. Gem carefully read the scene.

Mrs Brown was two minutes behind her. She surveyed the seating arrangement and approved. "You look drawn, my dear," Mrs Brown observed.

"I can manage," Gem again assured her. "I will have to wait this out."

"You are obstinate," Mrs Brown shook her head.

The waiter took their order and Mrs Brown reserved further comment until tea and toast were served. The young woman and the older woman casually surveyed the area for listening ears, and seeing none, Mrs Brown spoke again.

"You may have to manage for quite some time, my dear," Mrs Brown said gently.

"No new information?" Gem asked with a faint tinge of hope.

"No information period, my dear. Harry is walking on eggshells with all assignments, keeping an ear to the ground, debriefing every courier after even the most routine trip. There is no current connection anywhere to 30 May. Ships are on practice manoeuvres in the area but -"

"We aren't certain of the area," Gem finished. "I am sorry, rude of me to interrupt."

"Not in the least, my dear. But you are correct regarding the area," Mrs Brown accepted the apology with a gracious nod. "Ships' personnel are experimenting with a new, more definitive sonar device, extremely clear imaging. However, they have not been instructed to look for specifics. What is discovered is discovered - new debris amongst old, already confirmed wreckage of planes and ships."

"In a graveyard of World War II wreckage of planes and ships," Gem muttered. Why would you search for a plane if you weren't specifically instructed to look for a plane?

"Harry is still working with Mr White on the code computers."

"Without success," Gem said bitterly.

"Eat your toast, my dear. It may put some colour into your cheeks this morning." She brushed the young woman's hair back so she could see her face. "You braided your hair yesterday. I like the crimped look it leaves when your hair is down."

Without consciously doing so, Mrs Brown oft times slipped into 'mother mode' with Gem. It was a habit of knowing the twins from the day of their birth, although over the years she had come to know Gem a bit better than her sister since Gemimah was London based.

"It has been weeks," Gem moaned softly, obediently taking a bite of toast.

"Everything that can be done is being done, I assure you. We must tread very carefully. We do not know why, we do not know who, we do not know how this happened."

"Blast!"

"Gordon White has reviewed the computer programs step by step, repeatedly. He has literally spent days and nights, going without sleep, living on coffee and cigarettes. He's disassembled and reassembled Harry's code computer, and your father's computer, at least a half dozen times searching for the most minute trace of dust, a bent connection, anything that could be affecting the computers. Your father's message was sent. It was logged by Harry's computer as being immediately received. No failure of any kind was noted by Harry's computer."

"It doesn't make sense," Gem groaned again, forcing herself to take another bite to finish the toast.

"Gordon is heartsick that he has failed you, my dear. He's flown to the States, to France, to check the other code computers in hopes that the transmission that went awry somehow logged in correctly into the other computers. He simply can't find any discrepancies."

"And he's a wonk," Gem murmured.

"The best B.I. has ever had in our ranks. He helped design the current code computers, and our communications computers."

Gem had met Gordon White on numerous occasions during the six years she had worked for the Agency. She knew he was intensely passionate of his field. And the day Gem 'retired' as a courier, the last day she had entered the Agency building to sign her temporary leave papers, Mr White had stopped in Harry's office to extend his sympathy once again to her. She could clearly still see the stricken look in his eyes as he voiced his sorrow to her of the loss of her family - and of Eric Portermann, who had long been known to Gem and to Gemmy. Gem had quickly signed the temporary release papers that day, designating that she was 'retired', and had then sought out Mr White to pick at his expertise.

"We'll find them, Gem," his voice had cracked. "If at all possible, we will find them," he had assured her, echoing the sentiments of the other Agency employees who had been apprised of the lost plane; it was a very limited list - only Need To Know.

"Is there anyone else who could be called in, someone - somewhere - anywhere - to give a different view?"

She hoped she hadn't offended his pride, but he had not appeared offended. "Aren't all computers manufactured in China these days? Perhaps there's an expert in China who could be called in," she had grasped at straws.

"An excellent idea, Gem," Gordon White had validated her suggestion. "However, I build all Agency and B.I. computers. We know them inside and out." He hadn't added 'no pun intended'.

"But B.I. and Agency computers can be hacked - all computers can be hacked," Gem had thought aloud.

"Technically yes. There are people capable of circumventing even the most protected devices, but our computers are checked constantly during the day, every single day of the week, to make certain our protection is current and completely unaffected," he had assured her.

"But it's still a possibility," she had protested.

Gordon White had grudgingly - very grudgingly conceded, "It's a possibility - extremely unlikely. And we do not want a foreign country in our computer system," he had reminded her.

"Good point," Gem had given over to that argument.

"Well, I do appreciate his efforts," Gem remarked to Mrs Brown. "Everyone has been so kind. It is simply so frustrating. No progress. Barely even a start."

"It has to take time. We must be very careful," Mrs Brown reminded her. "We do not know if this is connected. If it is, and that is a definite possibility, we must tread very carefully, indeed. Connected - or for another reason - that is currently untraceable."

She didn't have to say connected to what exactly. Gem knew the reference.

"We lead such cryptic lives," Gem sighed.

"So we do. Your life should be less cryptic," Mrs Brown mused, "since you are 'retired'." A small smile traced her lips. "However, we all are aware of the Agency's retirement program."

"No one ever truly retires from the Agency," Gem actually smiled. "Retirement is a word ill defined by the Agency. Or rather it is not defined by the Agency."

"Precisely," Mrs Brown nodded. "And retired as a courier, perhaps, but not from searching for the Pilos. You are still on the payroll, my dear. Do whatever you can to help us." She took a last sip of her tea. "Now, my dear, you must get on with your day, and I with mine," she patted Gem's hand.

"Yes, ma'am," Gem replied. She sat a few minutes, pondering the conversation as the older woman left the café. She knew Mrs Brown had been completely honest with her. Her supervisor, and Harry, had included Gem in the investigation from day one.

She watched Mrs Brown proceed down the pavement. She knew the woman to be in her mid-fifties, but Gem couldn't say Mrs Brown had aged a day in all the years she had known her. Mrs Brown's hair had gone prematurely grey when she was in her late twenties; she had always been a touch stout, always wore suits in various shades of brown, with gold blouses and amber beads around her neck; she always carried a small brown handbag, and wore a small brown hat to match her outfit. She easily melted into a crowd: a virtually non-descript woman.

Get on with your day. Your beloved sister, parents, and a dear family friend are at the bottom of an ocean, trapped in a plane for over two months, and no one can openly search for them because they disappeared on a secret mission.

Her family. They had disappeared as if they had been placed in a Witness Protection program - except it was the witnesses who were dead.

Where was James Bond when you needed him? Blast! He wasn't real either.

Gem shook off the ennui. She had but a few minutes to meet Wyatt. Well, her day would definitely be improving after all!

She saw him approaching Oscar's as she waited at the corner to cross the street. Her heart lifted measurably. He took her hand as she reached him. He smiled down at her, and she was immediately as enamoured with him as she had been the previous day. He was strikingly handsome in a black pinstripe suite, again a snowy white shirt, today an ebony black tie. He quite literally took her breath away.

She was barely aware they had taken a table, had given their order; the world dissolved around her. Gem fought to gain control of her senses. She laughed easily as he related the latest of Peter's escapades: throwing his father a Thank You party the previous evening for sending him off to the Athens office and endless days of sun.

Gem glowed beneath Wyatt's admiring gaze, his hearty laugh, as she told him how she had managed to lose three cameras on three different trains in a single day in Italy.

"Most expensive day of my life!" she admitted, laughing.

"You should have received a Thank You party from the camera manufacturer," he laughed, choking as he drank his tea.

Wyatt sat back, and gently shook his head. "Gem," he said, suddenly thoughtful. "I wondered -"

She looked at him questioningly as he paused.

"Grantham Enterprises is sponsoring a school art fair this evening," he began tentatively. "Students sell their artwork with half the profit of the sale going to the student and half to the school," he frowned slightly. "I hope that you will consider being my guest at the event this evening - despite such poor notice."

"Lovely," Gem instantly accepted. "I would be delighted." He smiled that beautiful smile at her reply.

" Excellent! May I call for you at five o'clock?"

Call for her. That was a bit uncomfortable. She had always been so careful. Agency training. Such a private life.

"Could we meet at the show? - Errands - very busy day," she hedged.

Wyatt graciously agreed, a trifle surprised at her suggestion. Women weren't usually so reticent in revealing their addresses - in his experience. He wrote the name and location of the school on the back of his business card, tucking it in the side pocket of her shoulder bag. "And now, I am extremely sorry to have to rush off, but I have a meeting at the office in a few minutes. Peter's faux pas is dominoing."

He covered her hand with his. "Five o'clock," he gently reminded her.

After he had gone, Gem chided herself. So what if he knows where I live! I am a regular human being now. Well - semi-regular. This is everyday life now. The courier career had been fascinating, exciting, thrilling at some points. It had actually been the stuff of Agatha Christie novels, Foreign Correspondent, and hundreds of spy novels.

And it was deadly dangerous if one of the damned cogs slipped.

She and Gemmy had realized the seriousness and danger of their service. But how they had enjoyed it! And how careful they had been to avoid trivial relationships - not that there had been much time for such. They had had to be cautious, careful, circumspect, and prudent - to alleviate the alliteration, Gem laughed to herself.

But now she was 'retired' from the agency - which was a huge joke among Agency staff. No one ever truly retired from the Agency, as she had remarked to Mrs Brown. Mrs Brown had 'retired' three years ago. There was still an office with her name on the door, and she still used that office. And she was still on salary because her expertise and her dedication was still of great demand. Perhaps Agent Emeritus was a better description than retired. Gem was 'retired' from her job as a courier, but her salary would continue until she no longer served the Agency. If required she would have Agency protection and medical services. She was a member of the Agency Family and always would be.

However, Gem was now inclined to throw caution to the wind. Outside sources could not connect her to the Agency. Being a courier had oft times been a lonely life. Be careful, be circumspect, move on with a small part of my new life, while my past is in a perpetual holding pattern, she sharply regained reality.

Wyatt Grantham!

Oh, how I want to be with this man! He was a new part of her new life!

She walked for miles, pondering the conversation with Mrs Brown. Two months and no progress. She appreciated Mr White's endeavours, but the lack of results frustrated her. Without a flight plan, searches were another waste of time, effort, and cost. There had to be a better starting point. She had done little herself other than to stare at the computer and attempt calculations of flight hours and kilometres per hour.

Her thoughts drifted from Mrs Brown to Wyatt Grantham. She was very pleased of the invitation, accepting it as a compliment, for a man as smashing as Wyatt Grantham would have many female admirers.

Bless Tad and Jeff and their farewells! They had been the catalyst of her meeting Wyatt, for she hadn't seen him sitting at the next table until he had replied to her careless jest at the American tourists' departure. - And why do Americans always hug everyone? She wondered of that habit.

A catalyst.

That was precisely what Gem needed. Where did it begin? When did it begin?

She continued walking, unaware of the people hurrying past her on the crowed pavement.

Connected. Was it connected?

Or was it a matter of pilot error? It was difficult to imagine that a pilot as experienced as Mr Portermann would have made an error in his flight check. He had been a pilot for B.I., and then the Agency for decades. Could a routine flight check become so routine that he simply missed a detail? Something one had seen or checked countless times had been perceived by the mind's eye as correct when it was not?

A possibility. But one Gem doubted.

Giving Mr Portermann the benefit of the doubt, what would be the next logical idea to pursue?

The Project.

Connected to the Project?

Big Ben's pronouncement of time jerked Gem from her mental processes.

One o'clock. Time to finish tasks that would produce results! She tackled errand after errand: pick up photos, purchase computer paper, purchase a new mouse - they did not survive repeated bumps off her desk - but they did bounce, replenish shampoo, replace Elgar cd - cds are not proper coasters for hot beverages, home by half three, shower, wash hair, flag a taxi. Cutting time way short; home by half two. And she refused to think of any subject other than Wyatt Grantham. She needed to clear her brain so that she could think clearly during the dark hours.

She was out of the door with time to spare. Gemmy's periwinkle blue sundress with the thin straps, mid-calf length, and her own sand coloured sandals would hopefully suit the occasion; mobile, matching shoulder bag, keys, taxi fare, and credit card. She took deep breaths to calm a flair of nerves.

He was waiting for her when the taxi drew up to the school, taking her hands to ease her from the vehicle.

"Perfect," Wyatt smiled at her. "Breathtaking. Perfect."

"Thank you," she said a bit shyly. "You look perfect yourself." Because you are!

He had showered, his hair still a touch damp; yet another black suit, pearl grey shirt, dark grey tie. He certainly didn't lack for wardrobe selection. Intricate silver cufflinks gleamed in the late afternoon sun as he took her hand to escort her into the school building.

If attendance was indication of success, the art show would rake in a sizeable profit that evening. Student art hung on walls of the wide corridors on both sides of the spacious entrance. Each student had a generous sized area in which to display their projects. Two tables near the entrance were staffed by volunteers ready to accept payment for purchases.

A stunning brunette - not much shorter than Wyatt - and he was very tall - greeted the guests with a warm smile as they entered the school. Wyatt introduced the woman to Gem as Ms Emma Holton.

"Ms Holton is the lead Research and Development Manager at our London office," he explained to Gem. "She also directs all company volunteer projects."

Gem felt overwhelmed by the statuesque woman - perfectly groomed in a white linen suit and a buttercup yellow blouse. She had little time for more than a brief greeting with Ms Holton as Wyatt guided her along the path of the exhibits.

"We must not tie up Ms Holton. It's her responsibility to put the customers in the proper purchasing spirit," Wyatt winked at Gem. "This will hopefully be an excellent fund-raiser for the school and the students, and the concept was Ms Holton's idea. She's on pins and needles that this evening won't be an embarrassment for GEI."

"GEI?" Gem repeated.

"Grantham Enterprises International," Wyatt explained.

"Oh, right," Gem winced. His company. "It's a wonderful idea," she ventured, glancing at the various exhibits. "Ms Holton must be a very capable person."

"Indeed!" Wyatt said firmly. "She has a brilliant future ahead of her. Hopefully it will always be with GEI."

Wyatt directed the conversation to the art displays. He placed his hand at the small of her back to guide her through the crowd. Gem was impressed with the various mediums the students had used. At least a dozen paintings of various subjects already bore green 'SOLD' tags. One item in particular caught Gem's eye: a five foot modern sculpture of a man, comprised of square metal pieces welded to a wire form.

"That would be striking in a garden," she mused. "How very clever. Excellent form."

"Have you a garden?" Wyatt queried, a note of surprise in his voice.

"No," Gem laughed. "It was simply a thought."

He was constantly at her side, interested in her every comment, and speaking encouragingly to the students at each exhibit. They wandered the corridors for over an hour, and Gem was impressed with Wyatt's easy manner with the young artists. She was drawn to an exhibit of watercolours; the artist was a girl of perhaps sixteen, so shy she had difficulty speaking to the people who stopped to view her paintings. Gem carefully studied each of the paintings, the subjects varying from an elderly man scraping the bottom of a boat, to gardens bordering ponds. Not Monet, but beautifully restful, the execution showing definite talent in Gem's opinion. She found four paintings of various sizes that she particularly admired; scenes of gardens without water features; the colours were softer hues of blues and greens, as opposed to touches of yellow reflected in the ponds of the other watercolours.

"Have you plans to attend university?" Gem asked the artist.

The girl shyly met her eyes. "I hope to," she said softly. "I'm not sure."

Gem took a slip of paper from her shoulder bag, wrote her name in one corner, and the name and phone number of one of her former professors below. "Ring this number. Talk to Professor Fulken's secretary, give her my name, and she will set up an appointment for you with the Professor. He will review your paintings and perhaps that will help you decide if you want to pursue university or art school."

The girl's eyes opened wide as she took the slip. She managed an eager nod.

"I'll ring the Professor's office tomorrow to tell them to expect to hear from you," Gem advised, gathering the paintings she had selected to purchase.

"Do you think she has talent of note?" Wyatt asked as they moved through the crowd.

"I do," Gem replied, "however my opinion is dust. Professor Fulken is the person to ask."

Wyatt reflected on her words and of her motive for offering to assist the young artist. And what was her game? "I believe we have seen everything here. Dinner?" he casually suggested.

Gem nodded, not wanting the evening to end. She paid for her purchases, although Wyatt had offered to so. When his interest drifted to another woman, Gem didn't want a gift of the watercolours to be a painful memory of the time she had spent with him.

Dinner was excellent, the restaurant a bit stuffy for Gem's tastes, but she revelled in Wyatt's company. He drove her home in his car, a stunning, sleek white 1960 Jaguar XK-150FHC that had a black top and interior. It was as heart stopping gorgeous as its owner! And it totally suited him. Wyatt walked her up the steps of the building, but did not suggest seeing her to her flat.

"I have to go to Paris for a few days," he said, frowning.

"Peter again?" she grinned.

"Problems running rampant," Wyatt groaned. "Manton is chewing my - nerves," he quickly altered his choice of words. He pulled his mobile from his pocket. "May I have your phone number? I shall need to call you for sane conversation."

And she gave him her number without a moment's hesitation. It was an Agency mobile, but she could use it for personal use henceforth. Harry had approved so.

"You must have my number," he insisted.

She took her mobile from her purse. "Allow me," he took the phone from her hand, his fingers flying over the keyboard. "My mobile number, office, and flat numbers. Ring me when you are desperate for scintillating conversation of art, cathedrals, favourite museums, music, when you desire a stroll or a pub crawl."

He smiled down at her and her heart melted. How could Ms Holton manage to work for the man and not be hypnotized by him?

"You look very tired, Gem." He kissed her gently and Gem's lips tingled. "Ring me any time day or night. But please, get some sleep." He slipped her mobile back into her shoulder bag.

Gem ran her fingers through her hair. "Insomnia," she found herself admitting to a man she had met only a little more than twenty-four hours ago.

"Chronic?" he frowned.

"Lately. But I'm fine - really," she insisted.

"I do hope it eases. When I finish in Paris - if Paris doesn't finish me first, and it might," he chuckled, "I want to spend a great deal of time with you, Gem."

"I'd like that," she said softly, and smiled into his eyes. Oh those eyes - what a trap they could be!

Another kiss and she entered her building. She looked out the living room window and saw that he had waited until she had turned on the light in her flat. He raised his hand in a brief salute, got in his car and drove off.

"My heavens!" Gem whispered. "This is good!"

At two o'clock in the morning reality once again set in. She turned on the cd player. 'I'll Be Seeing You' was the first song to play. "Oh, how I wish," she said sadly as she listened to the lyrics.

The computer screen stared back at her. Again the Pacific Ocean. The Timor Sea. The Arafura Sea. The Caroline Islands. Singapore. Vietnam. China. Jakarta. Gem swept the new mouse across the screen, clicking on the South China Sea.

Xisha Island.

Of the Paracel Island group. Uninhabited. Wildlife paradise beneath the sea. Possession of the People's Republic of China. Or the possession of the Socialist Republic of Vietnam. Possession still under debate.

Project CSU.

The HMS Coventry - missing January 1945, no firm date, 74 crew missing

The USS Seahawk - missing 5 January 1945, 76 crew missing

U-1408 - perhaps 30 crew on board. Last seen 2 January 1945, Hong Kong shipyards

It was highly unusual for couriers to be apprised of Special Projects, but the Gems were well versed on Project CSU - Coventry Seahawk U-1408. The sisters' inclusion was due to their father's obsession of the Second World War; he read book after book on the subject, and passed them on to his daughters to read. Margaret Lawson also read everything her daughters and husband read, so she also had been informed of Project CSU.

The pilot who had first sighted and photographed the sunken submarines was Eric Portermann. That had been over a year ago. It had taken months of work enlarging the photographs to obtain probable identification of the vessels, and to research old records for information - records not available on computers; records in storage in the U.K., the U.S., and Germany; months of cutting through diplomatic red-tape - very sensitive red-tape, two Allies, one former Axis power; sensitive to avoid the hew and cry of the media. Extremely sensitive red-tape as Eric Portermann had been violating the air space of two foreign countries at the time he had shot the photographs; and the two foreign countries still in dispute of the territorial possession of Xisha Island - off which the submarines lay two miles to the southeast - on the ocean floor. Extremely sensitive as Eric Portermann had been testing a new, extremely high powered, sonar/camera device - Eric Portermann- a British agent.

Reams of World War II and U.K. documents had been delivered to Gerald Forrester in Brisbane. He had locked himself in his office for months, sifting through the paperwork. Success came as he, blurry-eyed, discovered the documents of the HMS Coventry. Secret Mission UKC-1-1945-A-2-SEA: United Kingdom Coventry January 1945 Australia 2 South East Asia. Gerald Forrester, reviewing additional corresponding information, concluded the mission of the HMS Coventry was to dispatch two Australian officers to the coast of southern China to assist the Chinese guerrilla fighters working their teams south to Hong Kong.

Information from the U.S. government stated the mission of the USS Seahawk was to dispatch two US guerrilla warfare experts to the same location. German documents regarding the U-1408, simply stated that the U-boat had been in South East Asia during the war. There was no additional information; the lack of information was perplexing; complete records of U-1408 should have survived the war - unless perhaps they had been destroyed when the submarine was listed as missing; similar problems were noted of two other U-boats lost - one off the coast of South America, and one off the coast of Mexico.

The Gems had read the paperwork at Harry's office the previous winter, as had their mum.

The total number of persons involved with Project CSU was fourteen: three couriers, Gem, Gem, Margaret Lawson; Gerald Forrester, Agent; Harry, Agency Director; Mrs Brown Agency Director-'retired'; Agent1; Eric Portermann, Agent; and one government official from Britain, Australia, Germany, Vietnam, China, and the U.S.

Who actually knew what information had been disseminated in the various government offices of said nations? Need-To-Know-Only had been stressed, but at times that was a crap shoot. The goal of Project CSU was to investigate the site and then have the area designated as a memorial to the fallen Allied sailors; the fate of U-1408 was in flux. Good luck!

Diplomacy certainly could get a workout when so many countries were involved.

Gem searched her mind for any clue in the information of Project CSU. Gemmy's Singapore assignment - her last assignment - had been to deliver a message to a counter-courier from Vietnam; their mum's assignment had been to deliver a message to a counter-courier from China. Gemmy's message was coded in Vietnamese, mum's into one of five major family languages for the Chinese official. Gem's own message had been verbal, and had been delivered to Agent 1 in Athens - in code - so sensitive it could not be committed to paper, for if found in Agent 1's possession he might not have survived another day.

Gem's mind swirled with facts, kilometres, a hundred unanswered questions. She went to bed as the dark hours finally ended for the morning; the sun would soon be rising and she had work to accomplish that day. She fell asleep as the time on the clock slipped to 5:00.

Chapter Three

Wyatt rang at least twice a day from Paris.
"Did you lose your camera today?" he teased the first morning of his trip.
"I am not in Italy. I have not boarded any trains," Gem laughed.
"Are you out for a walk?"
"I am. White cloud day. You?"
"Dreary meetings. A spot of rain. We are enjoying a ten minute break," he sighed.

The first day passed quickly for her. She spilled tea on her notes and had a devil of a time reading the smeared handwriting. Keying the information into the computer was very frustrating, requiring referring to computer files for accurate specific building facts of Winchester.

The dark hours were long: hours of searching for a connection between Project CSU and the Pilos. The only connection she could find was Eric Portermann. He had been a fixture in the Lawson-Forrester household for decades. Was it known to the Project CSU diplomats that the pilot who had taken the photos was a British agent? She had to refer the query to Mrs Brown - but not at four o'clock in the morning.

The second morning Wyatt was away, Gem was sitting at Oscar's Café having tea when he rang.
"Please save me from all lads named Peter!"
"No end in sight?"
"I'm thinking of transferring him to Siberia, but the Russians are balking at the idea."
"You have an office in Siberia?" Gem teased.
"No, but that's a minor detail compared to Peter's folly," Wyatt laughed. "Are you by any chance having tea at our café?"
"I am." Gem said lightly. 'Our café'! That was a pleasant thought!
"Don't talk to strange men at the next table!" Wyatt ordered.
"No one here looks particularly strange," she countered.
"You never know. Did you remember to call your professor friend yesterday?"
"Yes. Are you surviving French cuisine?"
"As long as I don't ask what is on my plate!"
Gem laughed. "It is usually preferable not to know."
"You sound tired. Are you sleeping?"
"No, I'm chatting to you."
"Very amusing," he said dryly. "At night," he clarified.
"I am doing very well. And you?"

"Late meetings every night. Manton is working me too hard."
"Pull rank on him!"
"I'll give that a try, but I don't have high hopes for it."
The second phone call was very brief.
"Have you ever had frog legs?"
"No."
"Good. Don't!"
"I should think frogs would prefer to keep their legs."
"Right you are!"
"Avoid food. Drink champagne!"
He rang again that evening.
"It's raining here."
"It's raining here," she replied.
"I'm starving. Paris should have Brit pubs," Wyatt declared.
"There are quite a few good ones - you have to search for them," she nearly tripped over the word 'search'.
"Manton won't let me out of his damned meetings long enough to locate one!"
"Didn't you pull rank on him then?" Gem teased.
"I did."
"How did he react?"
"He completely ignored me. I was talking to air."
"Give a person power and you have to live with the results," Gem observed.
"You don't know how right you are, Gem. Go to sleep," he urged.
"Five minutes."
"I'll ring you tomorrow. Make me laugh when I do, please," he ordered.
"Good night," Gem laughed.

The dark hours were wrenching. She wakened as usual, feeling so lonely she wept for hours. Even thoughts of Wyatt didn't ease the pain. Mrs Brown, Harry, the Agency staff, were all kind to her, but she couldn't complain to them about her loneliness. This was her problem and she had to fight through it, alone and lonely. Loneliness wasn't the worst of it; but she couldn't bear to think of the worst of it.

Wyatt's voice the next morning was a soothing balm.

"I miss you, Gem! I'm coming home tonight. Save the weekend for me! We'll invade a cathedral."

"You can carry the camera equipment," she agreed.

"I believe when you invade you should brandish weapons," he protested, "not cameras."

"Very technical of you. How is Manton this morning?"

"He'll be happy to see the back of me. I believe he is in my hotel suite at this very moment packing my bags for me."

"Is he pulling rank on you?"

"Indeed. He usually does. 'Twill be a long time before I again set foot in Paris - strange food and insubordinate management!"

Gem was gazing at the Thames when he rang that afternoon. "Nine o'clock tomorrow morning too early for you?"

"Just about right," she moved away from the river, knowing it would be her luck to drop her mobile into the drink. Harry would pitch a fit if Gem lost an Agency mobile. "What shall I wear?"

"Clothes. Manton is drawing a finger across his throat. I'd best go. - Something comfortable!"

Gem shook her head, laughing, as she pocketed her mobile. She forced herself to go home to work on her book. She would not accomplish anything tomorrow.

She should ring Mrs Brown regarding her query of Mr Portermann. She had intended to ring yesterday, but she had been distracted by a realization that she had violated Agency SOP. All her family's computers had been sent to the Agency for monitoring. When Gem had returned to London in early June, she had sent all the e-mails she had received from her family to Gemmy's computer, per Mrs Brown's request - actually her gentle, but firm, order. Gem had also forwarded all the family photos that were in her computer files.

All the photos except four; photos of the sisters at various ages - her most favourite - the one of them at their eighteenth birthday party: Gem and Gem, side by side, their arms around each other's shoulders. Gem had stared at the photos the previous day, but she could not bear to hit send and purge the file. She had decided to bury the file and had spent hours creating passwords to protect the photos. She felt guilty violating Mrs Brown's order, but she simply could not give up the photos. Only she had access to her computer. Well, a hacker could hack it, but she was absolutely certain the photo file could not be breached. Please God! I hope I am not wrong. She needed to keep Gemmy close as long as she could - in any way she could.

She pulled up the file again after returning from her walk. She hadn't written down the passwords - error there - write, read, burn, but she did manage to access the file; she did then write, read, burn. She again buried the file and rang Mrs Brown.

"It was a moot point," Mrs Brown informed her. "As the legal possession of the island is still in dispute, neither country pressed the issue of the pilot's identity. It was a can of worms the officials declined to open. Harry was quite staggered with relief, I can tell you."

"I can only imagine," Gem replied in awe.

"Have you anything for me, my dear?" Mrs Brown queried hopefully.

"No," Gem admitted, catching her bottom lip between her teeth. "Just gathering information."

"Very well. Are you sleeping?"

"Not at this moment," Gem replied lightly.

Mrs Brown chuckled, pleased to hear a spark of humour from the young woman. And why would that be? she mused. "I will chat to you soon then, my dear."

Gem turned her attention to the question of something to wear the following day. Comfortable. Quick check of the weather forecast: warm and sunny. She decided on an Indian print mid-calf skirt, free flowing and bright, with a white tee, and beige canvas shoes.

Gem then fell back on her routine, working on the text for Winchester Cathedral, cross referencing, fact checking, reviewing the photos; two views needed re-shooting and she wanted to expand the section to include three additional snaps. The interior shots were excellent; the detail drawings of the interior were complete. A day trip would be required, car rental; for proper light the photos should be re-shot this month. Perhaps next week - or soon - before the month slipped away unnoticed as they had tendency to do.

Months slip away. Months she had not known about. How many months would it be now? A fortnight. She had known now for a fortnight and thinking about it made her sick to her stomach. It was always there, at the back of her mind, begging to be acknowledged. Too heart- breaking to be acknowledged.

She sank into the cosy over-stuffed chair - Auntie Jane's chair. A fortnight. Another of the reasons she had retired: forced to decide between completing an assignment and saving a link to Gemmy.

She stared at the ring on her finger. Gemmy's beautiful ring. How idiotic Gem had been that last night at the house in Brisbane.

There were only two of them now who knew. Gem and the young man at the Barcelona airport. It had happened so quickly.

Her flight from London had been delayed leaving Heathrow. The Barcelona airport had been extremely crowded. The minute she had stepped into the building she had keyed a number code into her mobile to access clearance via satellite to the Agency's computer. An airport official had arrived immediately. Her passport had been stamped and she had hurried in the direction of the check-in counter for her connecting flight to Milan; she had had less than ten minutes to make the flight. If she had missed the flight someone would likely be assassinated in Africa the next morning.

She had heard her name called, had jerked around, scanning for a familiar face, but there was none in the crowd. A handsome, young man about her age had caught her arm. His face was ashen, his eyes horrified. He had stepped back, staring at her.

"What did you do? Where have you been?" he had demanded. "You said a few weeks; you've been gone over two months! What did you do to our baby?" he had choked. "God in heaven! How could you! You still have my ring, but you killed our baby!"

"Oh no!" Another nightmare! Gemmy! The ring! Barcelona! Lovely, lovely Barcelona!

The Milan flight call was last notice.

"Listen to me!" Gem had grabbed his arm. "I need desperately to talk to you, but I have to catch the Milan flight. I promise you, on my life, I can explain this staggering situation! Please, please," Gem had pleaded, "trust me! Meet me here, noon, tomorrow. Will you please?"

His eyes had filled with tears, but he had nodded.

Impulsively she had hugged him. "I am so sorry. I have to go. Trust me!" This young man was the reason Gemmy had intended to move to Barcelona! She didn't love the city! She loved this man! Gem had given him a quick kiss on the cheek. "Trust me!" she had said one last time. Then she literally had to run to catch the plane.

Gem rested her head on the back of the chair, tears trickling down her cheeks. It wasn't until she was on the jet that she had realized she hadn't asked his name.

Gemmy had been pregnant, the young man was the father of her child, and Gem was so incredibly stupid she hadn't asked his name!

But he had thought she was Gemmy! It was a blessing she hadn't asked. He would have thought she was insane! He hadn't known Gemmy was a twin - or he likely would have guessed she was not Gemmy.

Gem had reached Milan, message delivered, assassination averted. And then the fog had moved in. She couldn't get to Barcelona until two days later. She had roamed the airport, waiting, for ten hours. She never saw him again. All she knew then, as now, was that he was nicely dressed, and he was British. And he didn't know that Gemmy and their child were dead. She had gone to the local newspapers to put notices in the personal columns: 'Milan flight delayed! Please ring me!' She had included her flat number.

She had to return to London. It was her last assignment. She had gone directly to Harry's office to give her report, then had taken a taxi to Heathrow. She had purchased a ticket to Barcelona. And then had frozen. She couldn't get on the plane. She couldn't bear to think of flying across the Channel, or travelling in the Chunnel. And that had ended her career as an Agency courier.

She walked the streets of London, hoping the young man had, on impulse, come to this city. She didn't see him. A fortnight. It still didn't seem real. Nothing seemed real any more. She wore the ring now hoping someone would recognize it - and connect it to someone. She had gone to a few fine jewellers to ask if designers could give her information about the style and artist who had crafted it, but only received shaking heads in reply. She had never received a phone call regarding the newspaper notices, although she had paid for the adverts to run for a fortnight.

She had started going to Oscar's Café every morning for tea. It had been Gemmy's favourite café for tea on the rare visits she had made to London on Agency business. Perhaps by some incredible spin of fate the young man would stop by Oscar's. The first day she stopped at Oscar's, she had met Wyatt. At least that was a blessing.

And if she did see the young man again, what would she have said to him? She didn't know. But she would have told him as much of the truth as she could.

Gem stared at the ring. Gemmy's lovely engagement ring from the man she had loved.

Gem had chosen the flight over the young man's desperation. She wasn't capable of making prudent, responsible decisions. She was no longer capable of being a courier. She was heart sick for the young man.

If the Pilos was found - no, it had to be found - then Gemmy would again exist. A notice would be put in newspapers, and hopefully the young man would eventually learn what had happened to the woman who had loved him, and whom he had loved.

Could life get more confusing? My life is so askew, Gem moaned softly. And sitting, feeling morose, was a waste of time.

She made a cup of tea.

Concentrate. She had worked and slept for the past two months, trying to deal with her emotional pain. She had expected by now that the Agency would have made progress on the search. Mr White had made no progress on the code computers. Nor had Harry been able to resolve the issue. Planes and ships were searching the waters of South East Asia to no avail. Her family's possessions were in an Agency warehouse. And had likely been catalogued by now - Agency SOP.

Nothing. Nothing. Nothing.

She had spent hours researching cathedrals for her books. Perhaps now research would help her trip on to a lead to the Pilos.

She had read many, many books about the War.

Project CSU.

Time to do more research. Her previous readings had been over-all views. Now she would concentrate on areas August 1944 to 1945, submarines, U-boats, and Germany. Gem switched on the computer and made a list of sites to study. When her mobile rang that evening, she was delighted that it was Wyatt's voice she heard. But then, who else would it be other than Mrs Brown - now her main Agency contact.

"Do you miss me?" he teased.

"Absolutely!" she sighed.

"I'm back in London!"

"Are you dining on proper food?" she teased.

"Too tired to think of food. I will see you in twelve hours!"

"Perfect!" she said happily.

"Until then, pleasant dreams."

"And to you," Gem said breathlessly, then frowned because she could no longer remember her dreams.

She felt better having talked to him. He was the one bright point in her life these days. These days! She had met him a scant five days ago, yet he had become a shining point in her days!

She switched off the computer and went to bed - with a notepad and pen in case she couldn't turn off her brain as easily as she had the computer. Good point she did. She turned on the bedside lamp to scratch notes: Submarine Museum, Imperial War Museum. Hong Kong. Why the U.S. sub and a British sub? Why not just one to transport the guerrilla experts?

She started reading web sites again at two o'clock when the dark hours arrived, and finally shut down the computer three hours later.

Wyatt rang at ten minutes to nine - on his way. She grabbed her constant companion - her camera, slipped her mobile into her skirt pocket, grabbed her shoulder bag and flew down the front steps to meet him, eager to shut down her brain for a few hours.

As he pulled the Jag to the kerb, she started giggling, marvelling how easily he could unfold his tall frame from the small vehicle. "This car was not designed for a person of your height," she laughed.

"Don't I know!" he admitted dryly. "How tall are you?"

"Tall enough for me," she teased.

"Tall enough for me too," he laughed. "You'll fit fine. You did the other night." Then he frowned. "You'll need a hat. Hot sun day. Best fetch it."

Gem thought to protest - it wasn't, after all, the hot Australian sun - but he leaned against the Jag, apparently not brooking any dissension. "Sunglasses!" he called as she retraced her steps to her flat.

After grabbing both items, they were on their way, Wyatt settling her in the car before folding himself in.

"And we are off!"

"Destination?" Gem queried happily. "Am I suitably dressed?"

"Are you comfortable?"

"Indeed."

"Then you are suitably dressed. I like the skirt. Very feminine."

"And cool and comfortable."

"Most suitably attired! We are off to Kenilworth."

"Kenilworth? Is there a cathedral to storm at Kenilworth?" she asked in surprise.

"Have you ever stormed a cathedral?"

"No," she admitted, shaking her head.

"Nor have I. Best we practice storming a castle ruin," he winked at her.

"Lovely," Gem grinned, settling back to enjoy the drive.

He reached over briefly to clasp her hand, then returned his attention to driving. "Did you miss me while I was away?" he asked curiously.

"Yes," Gem replied, a bit startled by the query. Very much, she admitted only to herself. "Did you miss me?" she said lightly. He probably hadn't thought of her beyond the brief phone calls.

"Couldn't get you out of my mind," he said firmly, glancing at her.

Gem was even more startled by his reply. "When would you have time to think about me, between frog legs and Mr Manton?" she kept her voice light. She was so likely heading to a broken heart.

"During deadly boring meetings. At night in my hotel suite," he replied evenly, keeping his eyes on the tarmac. "Tell me, how did you keep yourself amused for the past few days?"

Gem shrugged. "Work, errands, nothing exciting." Looking for a missing plane, my dearest friend, my family, my past. My present, my future. "So Peter is in Athens then?"

"Indeed," Wyatt shook his head. "The lad is - unusual. But work is over for the week! Tell me - all the cathedrals you spoke of this past week, you never once mentioned Salisbury. I web surfed medieval cathedrals this week -"

"No!" Gem laughed.

"Indeed," Wyatt acknowledged with a nod. " I should think Salisbury is one of the most interesting cathedrals in England."

"I haven't visited it in years, however it is on my list," Gem replied.

"We should do a day trip - if you like - that is. Keep it in mind," he suggested casually.

"Oh, I shall," Gem agreed. Beyond today! Lovely!

"Tell me about Fortrose," he requested.

"You can't possibly want to hear anything more about cathedrals," Gem protested.

"I want to hear your voice. Manton droned on and on for three days."

Gem had to concentrate on what he was saying; he looked so handsome that he was completely distracting.

"You're not wearing a suit today - you look different," she ventured. Stone washed jeans, a blue denim shirt over a black t-shirt.

"Good different or bad different?"

"Just less formidable," she decided.

"Good then, I should think," he accepted her words. "Did you go to Oscar's every day?"

"Yes." A futile endeavour each day, she silently mused.

"Were you out walking every day? Napping? You look tired."

"I can't sleep during the day." She wanted to take the conversation away from her. "Did you resolve young Peter's crisis?"

"To the best of our ability," he nodded.

"You're very patient with him."

"The lad is brilliant, dedicated, and honest, not a combination easily found these days."

"In business."

"In humans," Wyatt frowned. "We simply have to add capable to Peter's abilities and he will be a proper asset to the company."

They turned off the carriageway and Wyatt directed the car along winding country lanes.

"Do you ever race the Jag?"

"No, indeed," Wyatt denied. "It is a treasure to me - as your ring is to you, I imagine."

"Hmm. Yes it is," Gem agreed solemnly, looking down at the ring on her finger, the diamonds glinting in the bright morning sunlight.

"On your left," Wyatt indicated, "grape vines. Did you know there are quite a few wineries in England?"

"I didn't," Gem replied, turning her eyes to the view. She fell silent, trying to force out thoughts crowding into her mind. Gemmy, the young man, their baby - all linked to the ring Wyatt so casually mentioned. Even Oscar's Café tugged at her thoughts; it had been Gemmy's café - the place Gem had met Wyatt. Odd coincidences life threw at us sometimes, she mused. And when life threw - there was never a warning to duck, when ducking might have been of the utmost necessity.

Wyatt didn't interrupt her reverie. He couldn't demand to know all her thoughts. And quiet was appreciated; he couldn't abide women who chatted so incessantly he could quite literally feel his ears start to bleed from the constant pounding attack of verbosity.

After another twenty kilometres it was he who broke the silence. "What research have you been studying this week?"

Gem was so startled by the sound of his voice, so lost had she been in her thoughts that she replied without thinking. "World War II."

"Why?" Wyatt demanded curiously, surprised by her reply.

Control fool! Gem chided herself. No slipped cogs! She carefully chose her words. "It - it wasn't unusual for cathedrals to be damaged by bombs," she said evenly.

"Of course! Such horrific destruction," he mused. "One wouldn't immediately consider the historical impact, the necessary reconstruction required, the funding required repairing damage let alone managing routine maintenance of cathedrals."

"Precisely," Gem agreed. "So often the funding simply isn't available. That is usually the case more often than not. And visitors to cathedrals often don't consider those issues when they tour cathedrals and forget to leave a decent donation."

"Perhaps Ms Holton should put her inestimable fund-raising talents to the issue," Wyatt suggested. "I'll speak to her."

"That would be lovely!" No slipped cogs and perhaps something beneficial would come of her remarks.

"If you owned this car would you race it?"

Gem laughed that he had harkened back to her query of a good half hour earlier. "Certainly not! It's very old isn't it?"

"A bit younger than our combined ages," he nodded.

"And how would you know my age?" she asked curiously.

"You are considerably younger than I, but not so young as a relationship would be arresting," he teased.

"Well said," Gem laughed.

"Do you enjoy picnics?"

"Indeed."

"Before Kenilworth then," he replied.

"How old am I?" Gem was curious about his thoughts.

Wyatt pondered his reply. "You are extremely brilliant, so I imagine you breezed through university. Teaching. Thesis," he mused. "Twenty-four. Just."

Gem's eyes widened in surprise, not only at his overly generous compliment but also at his stunning accuracy.

"You are amazing. A natural talent?"

"Oh - I have a few," he drawled.

"How old are you?"

"Thirty-four. Too old for you?" he gave her a steady gaze before returning his eyes to the road.

"No," Gem replied. "A long as I don't bore you."

Wyatt firmly shook his head. "I doubt you shall ever bore me, Gem. I believe we are quite the perfect match. Quite perfect," he repeated.

Gem felt butterflies fluttering inside her heart.

"You are a very confident man, aren't you?" she marvelled, smiling faintly.

"I am, Gem, and you may rely on that," he said firmly. "Don't ever forget that."

"I won't," she said, relaxing at his remarks.

"Excellent," he said, his voice still firm.

He managed everything with such ease, and found a perfect secluded picnic spot in a meadow beyond the village of Kenilworth. The picnic hamper was filled with sliced meats, cheeses, grapes, cubed melons, sliced tomatoes, cucumbers, biscuits, slices of cheesecake, and bottles of an enviable wine - all which they spread upon striped blankets he had thought to pack. Gem sat on the grass beneath a beech tree, Wyatt stretched out alongside her.

"Not up to pub grub standards, but an acceptable repast," he teased Gem. "I realize the restaurants I frequent are not to your liking."

"I never said that," Gem protested blushing.

"Monday we vetted twenty restaurants, bistros, and pubs - your face lit up at every pub we passed. Your eyes glazed at every restaurant," he teased.

"So untrue," she reached across the blanket to snag a biscuit to sail at him.

Wyatt deftly caught the missal, reaching up at the same time to catch her around her waist, pulling her down against him. His lips teased hers before bestowing a resounding kiss on her mouth.

"Save your energies for future battles," he warned lightly.

"What?" Gem puzzled at his remark.

"Kenilworth. Time to storm a castle!" He set her aside, sat up and reached for the hamper.

She had removed her hat while the tree branch sheltered them from the sun. Wyatt plopped it on her head. "A parasol would be more appropriate for Kenilworth," he teased.

"Storming a castle, holding a parasol!" Gem said crisply. "I would prefer a sword."

"Nay lass. I shall never permit thee to carry a weapon!" he firmly shook his head. "Parasol or naught."

Kenilworth was fascinating, and they wandered the grounds for hours. Gem shot two rolls of film within a half hour of their arrival. They toured every bit of the new red sandstone structure open to the public.

"Construction began a hundred years before building began on Salisbury Cathedral," Wyatt mused to Gem.

"Staggering!"

Gem took photos of Wyatt in the ruins of John of Gaunt's Great Hall. She instructed him on the use of her camera and he took shots of her in the Elizabethan gardens. She changed film and continued shooting the twelfth century gatekeep, the ruined state apartments, the fourteenth century Oriel Tower - magnificent ruins of the structure that had been built over a span of several centuries.

"Immense," Wyatt marvelled.

"Stormed only by Parliamentary forces," Gem sighed.

"And your camera," Wyatt teased.

Gem was not comfortable as they wandered down to the man-made lake, the ingenious defence of Kenilworth centuries past.

"Imagine the construction effort," Wyatt marvelled at the water defence. "The inspiration of moats."

Gem stared at the lake. It was not an ocean, she reminded herself; yet it was just as deadly. She stared at the water, horrified at what it represented: five loved ones dead – she included Gemmy's baby - and the complete alteration of her own life.

"Gem. Gem." Wyatt caught her hand. "It's mesmerizing isn't it?" he observed.

"Yes," she gasped, tearing her eyes away from the lake.

"You haven't taken any photos of the lake," he reminded her.

Gem complied, snapping a half dozen shots, then turned quickly away to face the castle. Gazing at the Thames did not bother her, but the lake was causing her pulse to race, and her head to ache. "I believe I missed a shot I wanted in the gardens," she said to Wyatt.

"One can never have too many photos of gardens," he said firmly.

And once back at the gardens he found a guide staff member to take photographs of them together. And away from the lake, Gem regained her equilibrium. Wyatt swept the hat off Gem's head as the guide focused the camera on them.

"Have you read Sir Walter Scott's novel Kenilworth?" Wyatt whispered in Gem's ear as the guide adjusted her position and shifted the camera.

"I have not," Gem replied, looking up at him, and Wyatt kissed her as the woman snapped the shot.

"Perhaps we should read it together sometime," he murmured, capturing her eyes with his gaze, kissing her again. "I'll take doubles of these photos," he murmured, finally drawing back from her. "In fact, I'll take the film for developing."

"Okay," Gem said breathlessly.

They chatted about Kenilworth the duration of the drive back to London; Wyatt insisted on a pub dinner before taking Gem back to her flat.

"Would you like to come in for a cup of tea?" Gem asked as he walked her to the door of her building.

"Thank you, but no. I must stop at the office," he replied. "I requested the entire weekend with you," he reminded her of his phone call from Paris. "I planned today. What do you wish to do tomorrow?"

"It will depend on the weather," she said firmly.

"Nine o'clock? Tea at Oscar's first?"

"Yes. Shall I meet you there?"

"No," he firmly shook his head. "I shall call for you here. Hat! Sunglasses!" He gave her a quick kiss. "On your way then! Sleep!"

Again he waited until she turned on the lights in her flat.

The day in the fresh air had made Gem sleepy, shower, bed, and awake at two o'clock. She read until five o'clock, concentrating on the Allied Forces in Europe in the fall of 1944. Read, focus; she actually felt she had begun research that might eventually provide a clue to her search for the Pilos. Yet, again, she might simply be fooling herself.

Wyatt rang her at eight o'clock. "Attire for today?" he asked crisply.

"Comfortable," she replied.

"In an hour then."

Brief, but sweet.

Wyatt frowned, puzzled, when Gem stated that today was cloud day. He quickly warmed to the idea, discovering the event consisted of finding a park and lying on the grass to look for creature formations in the fluffy white clouds wandering across the bright blue August sky.

At first they lay side by side, but Wyatt soon pulled Gem against him to lie with her head braced on his shoulder. She had worn her hat - he had sent her back to her flat again to fetch it. Their sunglasses altered the hue of the clouds to further assist in projecting fancifully into the cloud formations. Their location in the park was so perfect they were joined in their game for quite some time by youngsters eager to join in the cloud search. Wyatt braced himself on an elbow to snap shots of the cloud watchers arrayed on the grass around them. "This will be an interesting photo for your albums - of which no doubt, you have many," he teased.

"No - not actually," Gem replied carefully. Her albums, preserving family members, childhood memories, had been sent to the Agency warehouse in early June. She had files of work and travel photos and that was it.

"No?" Wyatt was surprised. A photographer who had few albums of her work? "We'll start one. Kenilworth will easily fill an entire album."

The children were eventually called back to their parents, and dark clouds began to invade the horizon.

"Pub lunch," Gem announced, noting the increasingly threatening sky.

"You choose, I'll drive," Wyatt quickly agreed.

After lunch they spent the rainy afternoon at the British Museum. Gem thought Wyatt might be bored with the suggestion, however he was an avid companion. After dinner at Oscar's, where she surreptitiously looked for the young man, Wyatt took her home. She didn't suggest he come up for tea, nor did he remark of it; he was going again to the office to work.

"Do you work every night?" she asked curiously.

He chuckled. "I have reports to review from this past week. And a meeting tomorrow evening. Would you have lunch with me tomorrow?" he asked as he kissed her goodnight.

"When and where?" Gem nodded.

"Denby's - do you know it? More pubish than modern," he teased. "Half noon?"

She nodded and went into her flat. She watched from the window as the Jag drove off.

It was sweet of him to spend the weekend with her when he had work on his desk. It wasn't late by any means. Not too late to ring Mrs Brown. Reading of the War had prompted a query regarding her father's ambition to crack old Nazi war codes. Mrs Brown, however, did not answer her mobile- which was unusual. On impulse, Gem rang Mr Cawley, Mrs Brown's second in command. He had been Assistant Agency Director until the plane. Now Mrs Brown, reactivated to full time, was AD, and Mr Cawley was the Agency Liaison Officer - a new position created to field everything arising from the search that Harry and Mrs Brown did not have time to pursue. Positions changed sometimes from day to day, depending on if Harry or Mrs Brown were in country or out. Everyone just did what needed to be done.

"Yes, Gem," Cawley answered her call.

Gem believed the man slept even less than she.

"I rang Mrs Brown. No answer," Gem said succinctly.

"Mrs Brown is on holiday. How can I help you, Gem?" he said crisply.

"Holiday? - Or holiday holiday, or -?" Gem asked, frustrated. On holiday? Really?

"Or - naturally," Cawley replied firmly. "We ARE in crisis mode."

Gem felt relieved. Work under the guise of a holiday.

"How can I help you, Gem?" he repeated encouragingly.

"It was just a thought I had," Gem shrugged. "It can wait."

"We are a team, Gem. Clue me in please," he pressed.

Gem sighed. "My father was working on breaking old Nazi codes from the War. I wondered how many, if any, he had managed to crack."

"Good question. I will follow up and relay the results to you," he replied. "Are you sleeping better?"

"The same," she conceded. "How is Mr Choate? Mr White? I feel rather lost on the moors, not working," she admitted.

"You are working, Gem. Just not at your former position, and you are not reporting to the office. Mr Choate has been reassigned. He is in training - no questions, please. Mr White is writing new programs to search the code computers for errors. The couriers are quite busy, and we might not hire for awhile. Harry is not certain it's a proper idea while the search is still an open file. That decision may be revisited, if needs be."

"I understand," Gem murmured. "I appreciate any information you can give me."

"I'll get right on it. Keep brainstorming, Gem," he ordered before he rang off.

Odd that. Mrs Brown going on holiday. And Mr Choate in training. And for what position? Was he still with the Agency? The Agency was under siege with work and she couldn't offer any assistance as a courier. They were down three couriers. And they were down two agents. Mrs Brown was out in the field. Everything was topsy-turvy.

Gem started reading. She read for two hours then planned Monday - take the watercolours to the framers, meet Wyatt for lunch, then spend the afternoon at the British War Museum. It would be the first of many visits there, she now knew. Read, review, mentally sort until there was a flash of a clue. She had no idea how long it would take Mr Cawley to process her request. He didn't have to wait for Mrs Brown's return to go through channels, however. He was Liaison. He was clearing channels.

A few hours of sleep and she was back at the computer. Add visit to bookshop for Monday afternoon. She would prefer to read in bed or in Auntie Jane's comfy chair rather than stare at a computer screen for hours. She scanned the computer for book titles referencing Eisenhower, Mountbatten, Patton, Bradley, the Ardennes Forest, a.k.a. Battle of the Bulge.

And it would be so lovely to see Wyatt in the morning - just a few short hours away now. He took her mind off the turmoil swamping her brain.

Chapter Four

Gem started each morning at Oscar's Café, varying the times, watching for Gemmy's young man. The concept was beginning to seem fruitless; however the hours spent over cups of tea proved worthwhile, for she was making great progress on her reading list of World War II books. Wyatt joined her three days for morning tea following the weekend they visited Kenilworth. She had lunch with him that Monday, Tuesday, and Thursday, dinner the other evenings. He had her family's intense work ethic, yet he made time for her, and she did not feel neglected by his meetings and long work hours. He sent her flowers, took her to pubs and cafés of her choice, and on long walks on the evenings he did not have to work.

Friday he set aside the entire day for a drive to Salisbury Cathedral. He fetched a pub lunch and read reports while Gem shot photos and spent hours sketching outside and inside the cathedral. She quite enjoyed the fact that Wyatt's classic Jag seemed as much a draw to visitors as did the cathedral. It touched her heart that he contributed to each and every fund raising box they passed when they first toured the complex. Then he left her to work and found a place to stretch out to read the reports he had brought from his office.

Gem spent her quiet evenings reading, and on the nights Wyatt had to work at the office he rang her to chat for a few minutes. She spent the dark hours reading, her mind often reeling at the staggering suffering that rose from the pages of the books. And more than one night she spent pacing the floor, agonizing over her heartless decision that horrid day to fly on to Milan instead of staying to talk to Gemmy's sweetheart - her fiancé. But what choice had she had that day - really? It was the damned if you do, etcetera.

So another week passed. Mr Cawley had made a brief phone call to her while she was at the British War Museum the day after she had made her query to him. He had referred her query to Harry who had assigned Mr Cawley the task of researching Gerald Forrester's computer files, but Mr White had to first break Gerald Forrester's passwords to allow access to search for any hidden files.

It would be a long process to obtain the reply to Gem's query. If only her father had sent backup files to Harry! SOP would have required that action, had her dad been originally assigned the Word War II code breaking as a project. However, he had not. It had not been a current subject of immediate concern. It had been a subject of historical interest to her dad. And his findings would have been of interest to the Agency; it simply was not of vital necessity at this time in this new century. But now because of Project CSU, it could now be of vital interest to the Agency - or rather it could in Gem's mind. Blast! Additional frustration for Gem to accept.

Yet, it should have been of vital interest months ago, specifically because of Project CSU!

And her father would have known that! Even without having been required to send backup files to Harry, her dad would have done so! And Harry would know his computer files backwards and forwards! Gem needed to talk to Mrs Brown as soon as she returned from her 'holiday'.

Somewhere there were backup files! Or backup files had existed at one time. Did the backup files still exist? Had her father sent them to someone else at the Agency? Or to someone at B.I.? But would he have done that? Gem thought probably not. It wasn't something that would be considered of importance to B.I.

Too many questions! But Gem knew she was right. Backup files existed. Or had existed.

Gem sighed. Thank heavens for Wyatt Grantham! He was a sweet interlude in her life. And the only part of her life that made sense to her.

Saturday was the drive to Abingdon.

"Why Abingdon?" Gem asked curiously when he called for her that day.

"A wealth of pubs for your selection, one for lunch, a stroll along the Thames, and through the gardens, a second pub for dinner," Wyatt suggested, as he plopped the wide brimmed woven hat on her head. "Leave this one in the Jag," he had teased, "so you don't have to run back to your flat each time you need it."

Sunday was a visit to the Tower of London as neither of them had been there in years.

"My treat," Gem insisted. "All inclusive, lunch, dinner, the works."

"Absolutely not!" Wyatt point blank refused.

"Wyatt, I am not a destitute writer living in a garret," Gem protested.

"Indeed you are not, as your address clearly indicates," Wyatt agreed, nodding to the building. "However, I am old fashioned in regards to courting protocol."

"Courting," Gem murmured.

"Indeed. An archaic term perhaps, yet a proper one. Do you think I regard you as a passing interest, Gem?" he asked, his tone serious.

Gem was speechless.

"Tell the cat to release your tongue," he teased. "Oh, my dear, you so amuse me." He put the car in gear. "Relax and enjoy the day - you have been working yourself into exhaustion." And to what end? Wyatt silently mused.

His words stabbed her thoughts. She had the flat thanks to Gemmy. Gemmy who had been an absolute wiz at the stock market. Within two years' time, Gemmy had guided Gem's investments into a tidy sum. The flat had also been Gemmy's suggestion, at which time she had liquidated certain stocks to enable the purchase of the flat for Gem.

Gem was not a pauper; although she was not wealthy, her finances were secure. She also had inherited her parents' finances and the money Gemmy had set aside for the flat in Barcelona. Harry had arranged the banking transfers. - There were no strings he could not finagle. However, it was not Harry's abilities which consumed her thoughts. It was Wyatt Grantham's thoughts.

Gem shook her head doubtfully. "There are millions of women in the U.K. and Europe alone. Why me?"

"There is only one you, Gem. You are unique. Amusing. Fascinating. Brilliant. And a rare beauty," Wyatt said smoothly.

Whoa! Only one of me! Now! How close he had come to the truth!

"I am confused," Gem said aloud.

"Then don't ask why," Wyatt suggested. "Just enjoy the day," he urged again. "No pressure, no demands, just assurance of the same. If you feel I am pressuring you in any way, say the word, and I will back off." And begin again until the end.

Truth to tell, Gem did not feel pressured. She felt immense relief. He made it so easy for her to enjoy being with him. No demands of her, simply requests to share her time. She turned to look at him, an act which still took her breath away. He glanced at her, winked, and returned his attention to the traffic.

Throughout the day her thoughts drifted back to his words. He would hold her hand, or slip his arm around her waist, yet his touch was guiding, not possessive. And when she was with him, she didn't feel lonely, or alone, or lost in her life, and he was encouraging of her work.

Sunday ended with a request from Wyatt. "Do you enjoy craft fairs?" he scowled.

"Yes," she replied hesitantly at his look. "You do not?"

"Can't say I have ever been," he admitted. "However, I am required to attend a jumble and craft fair Saturday."

"Who issued the requirement?" Gem laughed at his obvious discomfort.

"Ms Holton. Another of her fund-raisers. I have no idea to whose advantage this time," he sighed. Avoid all staff employees if any happen to attend - aside from Ms Holton - she was too difficult to avoid without giving offence.

"A definite yes," Gem agreed happily. "It won't be so bad," she tried to assure him.

Wyatt rang her that evening. "Apparently I am off to Germany in the morning. I will be away most of this week," he informed her.

"Excellent food in Germany. And excellent beer," she advised.

"Excellent indeed," he agreed. "I'll ring you lest you chance to forget me!"

"Is Mr Manton meeting you in Germany?" she chuckled, recalling Wyatt's remarks of the man of the Paris meeting.

"I am travelling solo. I would invite you along, but this isn't a day trip," he replied. "It's just long days at the office, so to speak."

"What do you do at the office?" Gem asked. Really, she didn't know much about him if she put her thoughts to the facts.

"Basically I watch other people work, and tell them if they are doing something wrong - or tell them they are doing a proper good job. I watch other people work, and then I read their reports," he said lightly.

"And you go to meetings."

"Yes. Many, many meetings."

"What is your business? I don't know very much about you. You actually seem a bit mysterious to me," she admitted.

"Mysterious? No. You could check out GEI on the inter-net." He couldn't imagine she hadn't already done so. Or had she? Fishing expedition? "Very well,

GEI acquires businesses, streamlines them, then either sells or continues to operate them."

"Ah," Gem nodded, settling in Auntie Jane's comfy chair. "International sounds very impressive," she said hesitantly.

"Everything sounds impressive when international is in the title. It's supposed to sound impressive. Part of taking the upper hand in negotiations at the onset."

"Sounds very formidable," she said warily.

Wyatt chuckled. "It goes with the suits."

"And you travel quite often."

"I have been known to travel frequently," he agreed. "And you?"

"I have also been known to travel frequently - but not much lately," Gem replied.

"Tired of airports?" he teased, attempting to draw her out.

Gem took a deep breath, steadying her thoughts. Control! "I travelled to do research, to shoot photos - a holiday here or there," she carefully coached her words.

"A proper holiday is a luxury at times in my world," Wyatt observed. "I plan to remedy that in the near future. The day trips with you have been much appreciated."

"And by me also," Gem agreed quietly.

"Most excellent to hear that! I'll manage a free day on Friday, if that is a good day for you."

"Perfect!" she sighed happily.

"I suggest Bath Cathedral. What say you?" Wyatt coaxed. "A long day trip, but doable."

"You'll tire of cathedrals," she warned.

"I won't. It's the company I shall be keeping that's important, Gem. I intend to purchase the first copy of your book - hot off the press," he insisted. "Now I have to pack. You need sleep."

Sleep was not on Gem's agenda. Shower, reading, then sleep, and more reading.

Her mobile rang again, and Gem was pleased to read Mrs Brown's number on the screen.

"Lunch tomorrow, my dear?" her supervisor suggested, which of course, was more a declaration of fact than an invitation.

"When and where?" Gem asked eagerly.

"Noon at Charley's," Mrs Brown suggested a long owned Agency business.

"It's closed. I heard a fire," Gem frowned.

"It is and it was. However, Charley is Family, and we needn't worry about privacy. He will come through for us."

Gem sat at Oscar's for two hours the following morning, drinking cups of tea, and frequently glancing up from her book to scan the area for Gemmy's young man. Thank heaven the weather was warm and sunny so she did not have to bide her time inside the café. She did not wear a blasted hat or sunglasses. If he appeared he should easily be able to see her. However it was another futile attempt.

She stopped at the framers to check the progress of the watercolours. Two were finished, perfectly matted, the frames complimenting, not detracting from the artist's work. She paid the bill and collected the finished pieces; the remaining two paintings would be available the following week.

She dropped off the rolls of film she had taken at Abingdon at her usual photography shop, checking also for photos she had possibly forgotten to collect. Salisbury. Wyatt had waited so patiently at Salisbury. She had spent so much time on her work at the cathedral they hadn't had time to visit Stonehenge. Another excursion Wyatt promised for the weeks ahead. She scanned the photos and was very pleased with of a number of shots she had taken of Wyatt in blue jeans and a t-shirt, sitting on the ground, leaning against the door of the Jag, as he read reams of reports. She would have the photos matted and framed for him for a surprise - once she had decided which shots to use.

He rang as she thought of him.

"Are you taking your daily constitutional?" he teased.

"Is that what it is?" Gem laughed "I just thought I was enjoying the outside world."

"No, definitely a constitutional," he insisted. "Habitual walking definitely deserves a title."

"Are you lunching?"

"On my way and greatly looking forward to beer," he chuckled. "What did you read last night?"

"Starting on the Battle of the Bulge - as the Americans called it," Gem replied.

"Ah! The Ardennes. Mountbatten, Patton, Eisenhower -." And cathedrals? Wyatt thought perplexed.

"Bradley," Gem added, amazed at Wyatt's remarks. Well read! "Are you a student of history?"

"Insatiable. Which prompts the question - which cathedral should I visit here - time permitting?"

"Aachen Cathedral. Charlemagne is buried there. It's magnificent!"

"I'll make a point of it then," Wyatt promised. "I hired a car. The drive will be relaxing."

"A relaxing drive in Germany? I don't believe so! Where are you?"

"Berlin. I have to ring off now, but if you need me, give me a ring. You never have, you know! I have three telephones - and never a ring from you!"

"I shall!" Gem blushed at his comments.

"You're blushing aren't you?" he teased.

"You have to ring off now!" she protested, embarrassed that he knew she was blushing.

She could not believe his phone calls made her feel so happy. And despite the gravity of her meeting with Mrs Brown, Gem arrived at Charley's Pub with a light heart.

Destruction from the recent fire was still evident on the pub's facade.

Charley himself, greeted her at the door - he was smoking a pipe. He welcomed her with a hearty smile and a huge hug, planting a big kiss on each of Gem's cheeks.

"She's not here yet," he informed her. "It's a bit of a mess still but we'll do a proper lunch for you."

"When do you open again?" Gem gazed at the smoke stained exterior of the building.

"Month - two," his eyes followed her gaze.

"What happened?" Gem asked in awe of the damage.

"Struck by lightning, wouldn't you know! From God to my soul," he shook his head, still amazed at the wondrous event.

"Staggering!"

"It'd be done for weren't for the Family," he admitted, rolling his eyes.

"Family Pub," Gem nodded.

It was an Agency owned pub, but it was open to the public - one of the many London scenes for 'ears and eyes'. Charley was 'retired' - as retired as one could be being Agency Family. He managed the pub and siphoned accrued information to the Powers-That-Be. Other such establishments were scattered across the U.K., and other countries: self-supporting businesses in their own right, yet viable for government intelligence. Such institutions were frequented by Agency Family for relaxation and for immediate cover, if necessary. Gem had frequented Charley's with Gemmy now and then when they had an Agency meeting in London. They had always gone to Charley's for relaxation, never needing the pub or other businesses for cover - fortunately.

Charley ushered her into the pub, the interior draped in canvas, save for a large round table in the centre of the room. Oak ceiling beams had obviously been cleaned and re-stained to a brown so deep it appeared black in the dim light filtering in from the small windows fronting the street. The bar had been restored but was bare of product. It would be a sad sight were it not for the progress of the restoration work.

"Well now, the experts are definitely putting in best effort," Mrs Brown announced her arrival. "Even Thor couldn't destroy Charley's!"

"Gave it a damn good try," Charley protested. "Wait - I thought he was god of thunder," he countered.

"Thunder, lightning, storms, oak trees, god of strength, protector of human kind. A very busy god," Gem rattled off as sometimes happened when her memory kicked in full blast.

"There are also references regarding fertility and healing, I believe," Mrs Brown turned her gaze to Gem. "You need more sleep, my dear. Perhaps you should have a chat with Thor."

"I'll consider that," Gem sighed, hoping the meeting would not include a litany of her sleep - or rather - not sleep habits.

Mrs Brown set her purse on a chair near their table, then turned around slowly, reading the pub's interior for suitable restoration progress. They could hear metallic rumblings beyond the bar counter. "Charley is preparing our lunch," she announced. "Why don't you bring me up to date on your progress, my dear."

Gem sat down and Mrs Brown took the chair opposite.

"Even in this light I can see no progress in your sleeping habits," she studied the young woman's face. "But moving on," she said crisply, noting Gem's frown. "You made an inquiry to Mr Cawley."

"The codes from World War II," Gem began. "Dad would have known they might relate to Project CSU. He would have sent backup files of the codes he had successfully deciphered," she didn't bother pre-thought; Mrs Brown would easily get her drift with the Cawley message relay.

Mrs Brown considered the remarks. "It would have been a habit of your father's to send the backup," she nodded.

"Yes," Gem said firmly.

Mrs Brown pursed her lips, pondering the situation. "Then," she thought aloud, "did Harry receive the transmissions?"

"Exactly," Gem nodded. She admired her supervisor's expertise in sizing up situations. Experience! There was no substitute for it!

"And if he did not, why not?" Mrs Brown fell silent.

Charley unobtrusively delivered a pint to each diner, of which there were in this case, only the two.

"Previous transmissions problems, of which no one was aware," Mrs Brown concluded.

"Or did he send to someone else? But why would he?" Gem scowled. The beer was good! Charley's best!

"I will confer with Harry. I would definitely conclude that this is a Question," Mrs Brown shook her head. "I won't speculate at this time. Excellent work, my dear."

"And what new information have you - if any?" Gem said hopefully.

"A perplexing issue," Mrs Brown frowned. "Thank you," she said aside to Charley as he served them burgers and chips.

"What?" Gem eagerly prompted.

"The Vietnamese contact," Mrs Brown continued to scowl as she selected a chip.

"What?"

"It appears he went missing - three weeks ago," Mrs Brown shook her head. "His body was discovered washed up on shore - southern coast of China."

"No!" Gem nearly choked on her burger. "Was he on assignment to China?"

"No. A trifle diplomatic disarray there," Mrs Brown said uneasily. "It is difficult to obtain exact dates of his most recent courier assignments, travel connections. Dealing with a citizen from one country, deceased found in another country. Both countries in dissension over Xisha," Mrs Brown sighed audibly. "And perhaps, now, codes gone missing."

"Oh dear," Gem caught her bottom lip between her teeth. "Mysteries compounding."

"So it would seem," Mrs Brown continued to frown. "And unfortunately a second counter-courier has gone missing. A courier from China."

"Another!" Gem, caught mid-sip, slammed her mug to the table. "Blast! Mrs Brown! What the devil is happening?"

The other woman shook her head. She fell silent again, doing her duty to Charley's burger.

Gem followed suit. Something was greatly amiss. Total now: four couriers, two agents. - And Gemmy's baby.

A cog had slipped. Perhaps two. Or more. But definitely one. Where? How? And who had let the damned cog slip?

Mrs Brown finally was ready to continue the conversation. "The identities of the missing couriers are not being made known. There are too many lives to protect - couriers, agents, counter-couriers. If I thought specifics would be of assistance to you, I would state names. However, I firmly believe silence is of the utmost importance at this time."

"I completely agree," Gem mused. One other family now suffered the pain she felt. Hopefully the most recent missing counter-courier would not also be a victim - nor would his family. "Perhaps he has gone underground for his own safety," she pondered aloud.

"Perhaps," Mrs Brown nodded. "And that is all I am able to present to you at this time," Mrs Brown concluded. "However, as we both are aware, events may swiftly change. We might meet of necessity tomorrow or not for weeks. We will all continue working on our goals. And continue to share our gleanings."

Gem nodded.

Charley reappeared, bearing plates of cheesecake.

"Charley! All my favourites today!" Mrs Brown gave the publican a warm smile.

"And Gem's," he returned the smile.

Mrs Brown then shook Gem to her core.

"You are keeping company with Wyatt Grantham," the woman announced mildly.

Keeping company? More archaic than courting - or was it vice versa? mused Gem.

"Yes," she slowly admitted. "Is that a problem?"

Mrs Brown appeared to consider the query. "Not as such," she reflected. "He is - a very wealthy - very powerful man, you know," she advised. "Grantham Enterprises International. Grantham Charities. Grantham Hall."

"I really hadn't thought of particulars," Gem was stunned by her supervisor's remarks.

"No, you wouldn't, my dear. Your head has never been turned, nor would it be, by flashy cars, yachts, weekends in the south of France, villas in Rome."

Gem laughed. "That sounds like a 1950's film."

Mrs Brown chuckled. "I do not own Givenchy, or shop Rodeo Drive, but I know elite when I see it. Perhaps I am out of my depth here."

Gem acknowledged the remarks with an understanding nod. "I am out of my depth with Wyatt Grantham, you mean? What does he see in me?"

"I know what he sees in you, my dear," Mrs Brown said firmly. "You are a rare flower - forgive me the garden reference - I do know flowers. You are a rare blue rose. You are an innocent where men are concerned. And Wyatt Grantham is like no other man you have ever met or shall ever meet again."

Gem took a deep breath. "Do you think he's dangerous?" she asked shakily.

"My dear, we may all be dangerous - if pushed hard or far enough - especially to protect someone we love," she shook her head. "I am afraid," she sighed, "that he might break your heart, my dear. Some men pick a flower, shred its petals and then crush what's left beneath their feet."

Gem rubbed her forehead. "I am out of my league," she admitted with a sigh.

"You have virtually no experience with men, have you?" Mrs Brown asked, but actually already knew the answer.

Gem shook her head, resting her chin on her hand. "You don't trust him, do you?"

Mrs Brown carefully considered the query. Margaret Lawson should be here to advise her daughter; or Gemma, chattering, exchanging girl chat with her sister. Gem was not her responsibility, but she greatly worried about the young woman she had known since birth.

"I have never met the man," Mrs Brown admitted. "I have never heard a word said against him in the business world. His ethics in that area are unquestionable. As far as women are concerned, he has been extremely discreet. I believe him to be a man of his word, if that is of any assistance to you."

Gem listened, hanging on every word the woman spoke. Was it of any assistance? Perhaps.

"Gem, he is a man of thirty-four. To say that Wyatt Grantham is a man of the world is a serious understatement. You may be twenty-four, but compared to other women he has known, you are the equivalent of a little girl dressed in a starched pinafore. You might be adept at the mechanics of espionage, but you are clueless with men."

Rather blunt. "Okay," Gem considered the remarks. "He won't even come to my flat for a cup of tea," she volunteered the information.

"As it should be," Mrs Brown nodded. "You live in a Jane Austen World, my dear. Wyatt Grantham lives in a Shark-Infested, Gritty Business World."

"My current world contains mounds of grit!" Gem mildly flared a protest.

"Your soul is Jane Austen," Mrs Brown countered. "Wyatt Grantham's is grit. Perhaps it has to be for him to survive in his cutthroat world."

"Okay," Gem nodded again. "It's early days yet. I only met him a few weeks back." She had heard every word the woman had spoken. She closed her eyes to think, and he invaded her mind. His scent, his eyes, his smile that sent butterflies coursing through her body, his voice gently teasing, laughing, his generous attention to her likes and dislikes. He was interested in her! Was that so difficult to believe? "It's early days yet," she repeated.

"Oh dear. I am too late," Mrs Brown studied Gem's face. "You are in love with him."

What! She had just met him! Absurd! Gem stared at the other woman. "Yes, I am!" she admitted to herself for the first time. "Oh my!" More butterflies! It felt like a migration this time!

Mrs Brown sighed. "If you were my daughter, Gem, and I know I am speaking out of turn here," she admitted, "go slowly. You must follow your heart, of course, and I hope and pray for the best. That your heart has made a wise decision."

"Thank you for your concern. Going slowly is excellent advice." Gem appreciated being able to talk to someone about the subject. "Wait -" she puzzled. "How did you know - about Wyatt?"

"An agent on assignment just happened to see you and Wyatt together in a pub. Neither the agent nor I shall speak of your relationship to anyone else. You certainly deserve to live your life as you wish. Your Agency Family only wishes for your happiness. And truth to tell," Mrs Brown chuckled, "were I your age, I wouldn't be able to tear my eyes from Wyatt Grantham. But go slowly. However, I doubt that I would be able to do so myself."

"Oh my! He is mesmerizing," Gem shook herself. "He makes me laugh. I can forget my life when I'm with him. I feel I am myself again."

"He makes you happy," Mrs Brown nodded. "I had that once - with Mr Brown," she confided. Mr Brown had never before been mentioned to Gem. "To be with that certain person who accepts you as you, and allows you to be yourself. And who enjoys that particular you. It puts a rainbow in the sky."

"Yes," Gem wholeheartedly agreed.

Mrs Brown glanced at her watch. "Time, my dear. We must be at our duties. And please, Gem, try to get more sleep. Wyatt Grantham has put a bit of a spark back in your eyes. I would like to see the full sparkle I had always seen before -" she didn't finish the statement.

Gem nodded, knowing what her supervisor did not wish to say.

They gathered their purses and Gem her paintings.

"And I approve of the no tea at your flat," Mrs Brown gave another opinion. "And no brandy, no wine, no nightcaps of any kind. Don't easily put away that pinafore."

"Take that advice, Gem," Charley gave an emphatic nod. "You go slow, girl."

"Charley!" Gem turned, gasping.

"My lips are sealed, Gem," he said firmly, "but I got three daughters, and I want them in pinafores as long as possible. Don't give that man what he can get by just walking down the street." He pounded the bar counter for emphasis.

"Blast!" Gem declared as she and Mrs Brown exited the pub. "Charley!"

"He'll hold his tongue, as he said," Mrs Brown chuckled. "We are Family and we do not give up our own. Always remember that, my dear."

Definitely words to remember. We do not forget our own. We do not give up our own.

"One last word, my dear," Mrs Brown frowned. "I waited at the car park, watching you chat with Charley earlier. You did not see me. Your habits are becoming a bit rusty perhaps? Keep your skills sharp," she warned. "Now take care, my dear. You have my number if you need me."

Gem walked home, a long walk of well past an hour. Her thoughts first concentrated on Wyatt - and redoubling her effort to be aware of her surroundings. Wyatt. She was in love with him! She had never been silly over film stars or male students at university. Nor had Gemmy been obsessed in their youth with callow lads; however, Gemmy had been stunned by Renoir and Chopin, and Gem by Willkie Collins and Johann Strauss - the Younger.

They had not been sheltered in their lives; they had just led different lives than their peers. Yet while Gem was still in a pinafore, Gemmy had discovered haute couture!

Mrs Brown hadn't spoken ill of Wyatt Grantham, BUT she had made it clear that Wyatt and Gem were of two different worlds. Wyatt was of the shark-infested, gritty world of business, but - and this was a HUGE but - Gem had, over the past six years, carefully and scrupulously, delivered courier messages that had brought down a sadistic dictator, disrupted gun runners and drug dealers, sealed alliances between warring factions in two small countries, rescued hostages in a war-torn nation, settled oil-lease disagreements, prevented assassination, and furthered negotiations of many other situations. She was not a novice in her career.

Yet, she was confused. Wyatt kissed her passionately, loosened a flurry of butterflies within her, set her blood racing with such fury her fingers and toes tingled. His smile left her without the power of clear thought and speech. And although she was very capable of opening doors for herself, he insisted on doing so, settling her into the Jag, refusing to allow her to contribute financially to wherever they went.

He treated her beautifully, kindly, thoughtfully, gentlemanly. He had not assumed an invitation to her flat because he had taken her to lunch or dinner, or a day in Salisbury. He hadn't suggested a weekend away - quite the opposite - he didn't ask her to accompany him to Germany because it wasn't a day trip. She could not have gone on the trip, naturally, because she could not leave terra firma. Yet he didn't know of her crippling inability to travel by air or across water - or beneath it, for that matter. He had not asked her because it was a business trip - and it encompassed a number of days.

He never pushed her for more. Gem laughed wistfully. She actually did feel that she was being courted. Old fashioned. Archaic. No matter. She was enjoying being courted.

She appreciated that Wyatt did not ask questions about her childhood, her family, her past life. She only had her current life. He asked NO questions she could not answer. She had to live in TODAY, and he allowed her to do that.

She liked that he was interested in her work. She more than enjoyed his attention, his phone calls. A small, pleased smiled touched her lips. He was pursuing her, and knowing that filled her with awe. Gem was, as Elizabeth Bennet had said, 'greatly diverted'.

Diverted from the main strain on her brain. Gem shuddered, thinking of the evening, and the night ahead of her.

Her brain shifted gears. Nazi codes. Wasn't it likely that the German government had the code translations? Why not request said translations? Germany was a major world power. True there were skin-heads and neo-Nazi groups in Germany, but the groups were all over the world. Gem would have to put the query to Mrs Brown. Why not ask the German government for the translations to the old Nazi codes? Period.

Gem thought of stopping at Oscar's Café for dinner, but decided she had enjoyed enough freedom away from the flat for one day. Best attend to work.

She pushed the start button on the cd player to listen to Vera Lynn. Atmosphere for the Battle of the Ardennes Forest. Mountbatten, Eisenhower, Patton, Bradley - and the Darling of the Armed Forces singing songs made famous during the war.

Not the German government. There may still be Nazi sympathizers in the government, age notwithstanding. People of any age could still be enthralled by the psychotic babble of the infamous psychopath Hitler. A closed mind simply didn't have the intellectual capacity to process reason, logic, or compassion.

Gem settled in Auntie Jane's comfy chair with her book of the night. Impulsively, she set aside the book to reach for her mobile. It rang as she flipped it open.

"Are you reading?" Wyatt's voice melted her heart.

"Actually, I was just going to ring you," Gem laughed.

"Excellent. Please do!"

Call ended.

Gem scrolled down her contact list, laughing and shaking her head.

He answered immediately. "Imagine my startled look of surprise," he teased. "You found my mobile number!"

"Very droll! Germany must have a pleasant quality Paris lacks," she said pertly.

"I like the food! I haven't spoken to you for hours and I get sass!" Wyatt laughed.

"Indeed! Where in Germany? Still Berlin?"

"Side trip to Brandenburg. Can you hear the concertos?"

"You are clever!"

"It's a whacking distance from here to Aachen!" Wyatt observed.

"Germany being an immense territory," Gem teased.

"First phone call, all sass!"

"How is Germany?" Gem laughed.

"Wondrous! Land of bratwurst and mega beers! Polkas!"

"Beer garden?"

"Yes, but I don't see a single flower!"

"You shall sleep well tonight!"

"Up early, long meetings," he replied. "Do I hear Vera Lynn in the background?"

"You know music," she said admiringly.

"The Darling of the War? Everyone knows her voice. What are you reading?"

"Battle of the Ardennes Forest."

"I hope the International Federation of Cathedrals appreciates your dedicated research," he teased.

"Including International because it sounds impressive," she teased back. "The Federation would indeed be impressed - if it existed."

"We have Strauss here - junior."

"The Younger."

"You know music," he shot back. "Do you miss me?"

"I find I do," she smiled.

"I find same," he chuckled.

Gem heard voices in the background.

"I have to get back to the staff outing. I'm getting looks and my beer is getting cold."

"Have one for me!"

"I did two hours ago. Did you enjoy it?"

"My first phone call and I get sass!" Gem mocked.

"Women sass, men banter."

"How erudite of you. And a bit chauvinist."

"Now you're just showing off," he laughed. "And I admit I am - a chauvinist. Second phone call tomorrow, that's an order. Give my regards to General Eisenhower!"

"Goodnight," she laughed.

"Sleep!" he ordered.

Gem wished she was at the beer garden. What fun she and Gemmy had had in Munich! A week of beer gardens! Every night a different venue. It was rather amazing she was still in a pinafore after that week! Control!

And back to Vera Lynn and the War. 'I'll Be Seeing You' was playing. Oh, dad! Her heart ached suddenly, remembering her parents dancing to the music their last Christmas together - last year.

Gem paced the floor. Oh how she hated the dark hours. It was there - something in the back of her mind. She knew it, yet it eluded her. Hitler. Hitler knew he was going down…marshalling his forces for a last surge…drawing forces and equipment away from other fronts…draining future protection away from Berlin.

She knew there was a connection to the U-boats with the missing records. A connection to the U-boats and the undeciphered codes. U-1408.

Gem consulted the inter-net for information on U-boats, crew complement. Nothing jumped out at her.

Back to the book. She crawled into bed and read until her eyes finally closed. Five o'clock.

The week passed quickly. Reading, reading, fetch the photos of Salisbury, Oscar's Café, phone calls to Wyatt, phone calls from Wyatt, flowers from Wyatt delivered; another night sitting in the comfy chair, thinking only of Gemmy, their parents, and Mr Portermann. Gemmy and her fiancé - and their baby. Five souls had died in the plane crash. One counter-courier was dead, another missing. Gem's head ached from thinking, her eyes ached from weeping.

Gem dragged through each day, but each day was brightened by the phone conversations with Wyatt.

She was cleaning the cooker on Thursday when he rang.

"Are you dressed?" he demanded.

"At three o'clock in the afternoon? Of course I am dressed!" she laughed.

"Walk and dinner? One hour?"

"You're in London!"

"One hour," he prompted.

"Yes!"

A stroll along the Thames, and dinner at the White Rose, live music all evening, and no thinking for hours! Gem sat revelling in the music until Wyatt caught her attention and drew her from her seat. She gave him a curious look until she saw him motion to an elderly couple to take the chairs she and Wyatt had just vacated. He led Gem back to the wall, his arms slipping around her waist to hold her; she leaned back against him, resting her head against his shoulder.

She could feel his heart beating, his strong arms around her. Nothing else existed for her except Wyatt and the music.

He had a gift for her when he drove her home. An elaborately carved beer stein.

"I purloined it from a beer garden in Dresden," he winked at her.

"You did not!" she laughed.

"Gift shop in Aachen. Bath tomorrow?"

"Yes," she smiled.

"Long drive. Eight o'clock?"

"Yes. The stein is lovely. Thank you," she said shyly.

"You are most welcome, my dear," he replied lightly.

And Bath. They discussed the Battle of the Ardennes Forest, music, Aachen Cathedral, on the long drive the following morning. Wyatt read reports while Gem shot rolls of film of the cathedral. He carried her camera tripod and camera bag, fetched pub grub, asked how she determined the shots she desired, and he again read reports while she discussed the cathedral with the clergy. He was completely engrossed in his own work when she finally returned to the Jag, photos shot, drawings completed. He was so engrossed in the report he was reading that he didn't see Gem approach; she slipped out of his view and took front and driver's side shots of the Jag. If the snaps were useable she would have them matted and framed along with the photos she had taken of him at Salisbury Cathedral.

"Mission accomplished?" he queried when she leaned down to kiss his cheek.

"Done," she firmly nodded.

"Unless a lens is cracked."

Gem's eyes opened wide in horror. "Don't curse the work, please!"

He winced in regret. "Celebratory pint?"

"Perfect!" And he was perfect!

Bath by day, dinner at Oscar's Café, and a new book to read that night. The point at the back of her mind was still elusive. She scanned web-sites for possible references to U-1408, and other U-boats in South East Asia during 1944 through V - J Day. Nothing jumped out at her; lists of personnel, missions, sunk, returned to Germany, scuttled, personnel lost. Nothing that tripped Eureka to help her reach that lost thought at the back of her mind.

The next morning she and Wyatt were off to Aylesbury for the jumble/craft fair.

Wyatt had avoided staff at the school art show, and he would avoid all he could at Aylesbury. If he and Gem arrived early enough they could leave and be on their way back to London before late rising staff had a chance to cross their paths. He respected his staff's privacy and he expected the same in return.

There was no avoiding Ms Holton, accompanied by her husband and their three children. Ms Holton was the sole of tact, and was the event coordinator. Wyatt saw the Holton family at the entrance to the crafts area, and turned and noticed that Gem had wandered off. He located her at a table piled high with blue jeans and worn shirts. She was chatting with the woman at the till who was stuffing items into a faded tote.

Gem, grinned at Wyatt when he reached her side.

"Jumble clothes?" he frowned.

"Perfect for scrubbing floors and potting plants," she replied.

"Do you have many plants?"

"None," Gem laughed. "However, I have been considering purchasing a few. I might like to have plants."

"Ah," he looked at the tables overflowing with used garments, and winced.

"Not your idea of a shopping spree," Gem teased. "We could look for the Savile Row section."

"Amusing," he replied dryly.

"Ah, bird boxes!" Gem hared off, weaving her way through the crowds.

Wyatt shook his head and followed. This was not going to be a daylong event! He watched her eagerly scrutinizing every bird box on display: wood, metal, wood and metal, canvas, glass, plain, decorated, painted, varnished, carved, and woven. He watched as she studied each bird box until she found one that she thought suitable. She was delighted with a metal cylindrical style with a painted roof, but thought the metal might retain too much heat for a bird's comfort. She finally selected a painted wood bird box with metal trim.

"Have you a bird?" Wyatt teased as she paid for the item, absolutely refusing his money.

"I have a friend who is a gardener. It could also be a garden ornament," Gem ran her fingers over the gaily painted wood.

"Your professor friend?" Wyatt asked smoothly.

"No," Gem glanced up, shaking her head. "A cathedral friend. She's more Renaissance than medieval."

"Is she also writing a book?"

"No," Gem chuckled. "Her first and only passion is gardening." And national security, she did not add. Gem gave Wyatt a bright smile.

"Shall we deliver it to her later?" Wyatt suggested, wondering of a 'cathedral friend'.

"No. I'll meet her for tea one of these days." Hopefully she will have some good news for a change!

"When she comes out of her garden?" Wyatt took the bird box from her hands.

"Gardens," Gem laughed, "many, many gardens." Or so she had heard. She didn't even know where Mrs Brown resided. Nor had Mrs Brown been to Gem's flat. It was a security measure according to Agency guidelines.

Gem was rescued from further questions regarding her gardener friend when Ms Holton saw them approaching. Ms Holton's husband was a bit taller than his wife - and she was tall; their children, Gem surmised, were tall for their ages. Wyatt introduced Gem to Stuart Holton. Ms Holton introduced Gem to the children: Liam 4, Jane 7, and Ella 2. While the men briefly chatted, Gem and Ms Holton wandered with the children to the games area. The two oldest children played splat the rat, while Ella fiddled with the tiny bows on her dress, and did pirouettes to make her skirt swirl. Liam smacked his finger instead of a rat, and Ella twirled into a heap on the pavement. While Emma consoled her son, Gem scooped up the youngest of the brood, jollying her out of her tearful wail, gently tickling her tummy and directing her attention to the bows.

"Ella's pretty bows," Gem said softly, using a quiet voice to attract the child's attention. "Ella the beautiful fairy tickles the bows."

The child puffed out her cheeks then suddenly chortled, "Fairy bows, fairy bows, fairy bow," she chanted.

"You've done it now," Jane sighed. "We'll hear fairy bows 'til she naps."

"Preferable to crying," Emma Holton laughed.

Liam was back to the rat and Ella stretched her arms out to her mum. Gem handed her over, then cheered the other children in the rat splatting contest as Emma Holton watched the young woman encouraging her children, and stored the scene in her memory.

A few minutes later the men joined them, and Wyatt eased Gem away after congratulating Ms Holton on another successfully organized event. Gem shook hands with each child, and then she and Wyatt continued their stroll around the fair grounds.

As they walked away, Emma Holton was bemused that the worldly Wyatt Grantham was interested in the lovely, unpretentious, down to earth young woman. And if so, was he savvy enough to realize that Gem was indeed a very special young woman?

"Did you have a pleasant chat with Ms Holton?" Wyatt asked casually.

"We didn't chat," Gem laughed. "We watched the children. Liam splatted his finger instead of a rat, and howled. Ella twirled into a heap on the pavement and wailed, and Jane bashed every rat! I can't imagine how Ms Holton manages a career, the children, and her husband!"

"Not all husbands require managing," Wyatt chuckled, relaxing.

"Well, I think she's amazing!"

"What woman isn't," Wyatt observed. "You're amazing."

"I manage me, not a great accomplishment compared to Ms Holton," Gem replied. And I am currently failing miserably. "But thank you for the compliment. Does Ms Holton manage you at the office?" she teased.

"What do you think?" Wyatt raised an eyebrow.

Gem replied, crisply enunciating each word. "I don't think she would dare to do so."

"Good answer," Wyatt said dryly, but with a smile.

They stopped at each craft stand reviewing the wares, and spent an hour sorting through stacks of books at the last jumble table. Wyatt selected a half dozen books: histories and architecture; Gem found a two volume set: World War II, the Pacific Theatre.

"Are there many medieval cathedrals in the Pacific Theatre?" Wyatt queried wryly over her shoulder.

"I'll let you know after I read the books," Gem replied with a laugh.

"More sass!" He brushed his lips against the top of her head. "Shall we lug our purchases to the car, then search out lunch?"

"Lovely!"

"I'll take the books, you take the bird bath and your new fashion statements. We'd best store them in the boot lest Calvin Klein tries to steal them."

"Sass!" Gem accused.

"Banter!" Wyatt countered.

Lunch and a walk around Aylesbury. Dinner in London. A lovely, lovely day.

Sunday was a drive to Hitchin, a stroll around the shops, a picnic on the river bank, and dinner at a pub on the drive home.

And reading at night for Gem. She switched off between the War in the European Theatre and the War in the Pacific, reading until her brain felt numb. The dark hours were still dark but she could focus her thoughts.

Gem felt divided between two worlds, and she only enjoyed one of the worlds. The one in which Wyatt ruled her thoughts. He was in Belgium on Monday and Tuesday. Wednesday they drove to Saffron Walden to become immersed in Victorian times at the Bridge End Garden, and Audley End House. During the weeks with Wyatt, Gem toured more of England than she had for years. She went through rolls of film and the photo shop was on the top of her errand list each week.

'One rainy afternoon we'll put the photos in albums,' Wyatt had promised when he had given her the photos of Kenilworth.

But that day was still in the future. Gem stored the photo packs in a large box, waiting for that rainy afternoon.

He rang from Belgium during the day and she rang him at night.

"How are you spending your evening?"

"I'm south of Iwo Jima."

"You are very focused for you age," Wyatt observed.

"My age! Are you so elderly then?" Gem teased.

"No. However, I do feel old this evening - one meeting after another today. Perhaps I have been settled so long in business I lost track of my daily life."

"I do understand! I have been consumed for years with studies and work. I tend to let the rest of the world survive without me."

"Work?" Wyatt puzzled about that remark.

"My book," Gem said quickly, hopefully not too eagerly.

"Yes, of course."

"Until lately. Since I met you, I feel more attuned to daily life," Gem admitted.

"Diversion is the spice of life. Unfortunately, I shall be diverted to Edinburgh Thursday and Friday. Wednesday and the weekend I want to be diverted by you."

"Sounds excellent!"

Wyatt brought her chocolates from Belgium. Wednesday they took a stroll around Oxford, and had lunch and dinner together.

And while Wyatt was away Gem spent hours at the British War Museum, staring at the displays, hoping for a spark to ignite what she knew was at the back of her mind - but which she couldn't grasp. It was there - a connection between the Pilos and the War. What the hell was it?

She rang Mrs Brown Wednesday evening to request the use of an Agency vehicle to drive to the Royal Navy Submarine Museum at Gosport. A Range Rover was waiting for her at Charley's Pub at eight o'clock Thursday morning. She hadn't driven a vehicle since early July, but she knew the rules of the road; and once a year for the past six years, Mr Critchley had put her through a defensive driving course. She made good time to the coast, dreading seeing the expanse of water, however what better place to put a submarine than at a harbour!

The HMS Alliance was a World War II era submarine. It had been launched in 1945, and hadn't participated in the War, but it was reference material of the age. Gem had tea at the tea shop, then took the forty minute tour of the Alliance three times. She toured the submarine from the forward torpedo compartments to the control room, the galley, the engine room and the after torpedo compartment. She learned of submarine navigation, diving, the very important resurfacing, and also the very important part of how to escape from the vessel. She soaked up the information for future reference.

Another cup of tea, then a stop at the gift shop. More reading ahead: she purchased two books; and viewings: she purchased a copy of each dvd available of submarine warfare, British and Allied submarine operations, Atlantic convoys, and one of U-boat wrecks.

Wyatt didn't ring and she deferred ringing him until that evening. She focused on the road on the drive back to London, declining to think of the War, following Mr Critchley's defensive driving rules: complete concentration on driving and only that!

Gem returned the vehicle to Charley's Pub, scouted a bookshop for Operation Drumbeat, a book referenced on a web-site of U-boats, and took a bus home. A long fact filled day was followed by a shower, and then she rang Wyatt, catching him briefly between meetings.

"Busy day?" she queried, deftly avoiding setting a hot cup of tea on the dvd of U-boat wrecks.

"Very. You?" he replied.

"Errands. Shops. The usual."

"Clothes, nails, hair?"

"Bookshops, dvds. Is there something wrong with my hair?" her voice faltered.

"I was filling in the shop blanks," Wyatt was quick to soothe. "Your hair is lovely. You are lovely."

"Okay," Gem said hesitantly.

"Don't dwell on careless words, my dear. I find it charming that you spend hours in bookshops, rather than hair or nail salons. Your fine mind is extremely intriguing."

My dear! How lovely to hear those words.

"I rather like being intriguing!" she laughed, his earlier words quickly forgotten.

"I have another meeting, sweetheart. Pub hopping tomorrow night."

"That will be intriguing," she feigned a whispery, mysterious voice.

"Sass!"

"Goodnight."

"Goodnight, sweetheart."

Sweetheart. Twice.

Thinking of Wyatt's voice and his words carried Gem through her long evening. She watched all the dvds twice. The scenes of SS officers struck a chord. It was there. SS officers. And missing U-boat records. She just couldn't seem to get her mind clear enough to reach the thoughts trying to break out to be noticed.

Mrs Brown rang to suggest meeting for tea in the morning.

Gem was burned out from reading about the War. She switched on the computer and pulled up the file on Salisbury Cathedral; an hour of editing text would be refreshing.

When the dark hours began, she was still in need of a break from her reading list of the past week. She wondered how late Wyatt's meeting had lasted into the evening. Oh how she longed to see him! It had been a long week and she had only seen him on Wednesday. How fortunate she had been at Oscar's Café that specific morning. And how cruel fate had been to Gemmy and her baby, mum, dad, and Mr Portermann on that one particular flight to nowhere.

Gem returned to the first part of her search - the work she had done the week she 'retired'. Mr Portermann's plane was a single engine jet turboprop; maximum flying altitude 30,000 feet, maximum speed 270 knots, 500K per hour; it had satellite navigation.

It had sat nav!

She went to a web-site to review the flight checklist of the plane: Pre-Flight 10 items, Before Engine Start 4 items, Engine Start 11 items, Before Take Off 7 items, After Take Off 3 items, Climb 6 items, Descent 2 items, Approach 3 items, On Final 4 items, After Touch Down 6 items, Shut Down 10 items. A staggering 66 items on the checklist.

Did Mr Portermann miss something? This was not his first flight, not the first plane he had ever flown! He had been a pilot for decades.

What was the flight plan? There could be so many combinations: Brisbane to Darwin, Darwin to Jakarta, Jakarta to Singapore, was the most logical concept to her.

Gem was not a mathematician, but from what she understood from perusal of information was that the Pilos would have to refuel after approximately 2500 nautical miles. She read that most nations use nautical miles for air flights as did sea going vessels. She couldn't recall - perhaps it was China and Russia who did not use nautical miles, she mused silently. And if she couldn't recall then her brain was very tired.

Again, not being a mathematician, she attempted to compute the nautical miles likely on the flight plan. Brisbane to Darwin 1537.240NM, divide by 270 knots, would equal a flight time of 5.589964 hours. Darwin to Jakarta, 1477.321NM, flight time 5.4715592 hours. Brisbane to Jakarta 3014.561NM. Had to refuel at Darwin. Brisbane to Jakarta was approximately 11.061523 hours, approximately again, because she had not read math.

The flight left the landing strip at 20:00 hours that night; eight o'clock. Gem was shocked awake six hours later. There was a time zone change, but six hours out was still six hours out. It wouldn't change total hours of flight.

Gem felt herself getting punchy.

The plane did not land at Darwin for refuelling. It did not land at any airports, nor request landing permission at any airports in Australia. Brisbane to Port Moresby was not a logical flight plan. Nor was the airport at Port Moresby contacted by Mr Portermann's Pilos.

No SOS.

No Mayday.

It simply was not logical to fly beyond Darwin without refuelling. Were they off course? That would put the Plane over the Timor Sea or the Arafura Sea then. Mr Portermann would not have risked his passengers' lives.

Mr Portermann would not have decided on a flight plan from Alice Springs to Jakarta. It wasn't logical. It would add too much time to the flight. Agents and couriers were not frivolous with time requirements when on assignment. On time, or early and looking casual was acceptable; late was never even a consideration. A late courier or agent processed reports in some lost little government cubical until retirement. A missed time requirement slipped cogs and cost lives.

Gem shut down the computer and turned off the cd player, and secured her notes in the touch pad combination locked file box. She had committed the notes to memory but sometimes it was a comfort to have the written page accessible.

Bird box for Mrs Brown was her last conscious thought as she closed her eyes at five o'clock.

The meeting was at a coffee shop at Charing Cross Road, or Heaven as Gem designated the street lined with bookshops. Mrs Brown was delighted with the bird box; it would be a centrepiece of her new garden she declared. The coffee shop had few customers, but the two women read the room and spoke in subdued tones.

"Does Harry have any new ideas?" Gem pressed earnestly.

"One possibility," her supervisor frowned. "Hijacking at the airstrip."

Gem firmly shook her head. "It is fact that Gemmy sent the all clear at take-off," she protested.

"She could have been forced to do so."

"Air pirates." Gem reflected seriously on the suggestion. "At any rate they were alive until two o'clock. I know that for certain. I just know it."

Mrs Brown patted Gem's arm. "I do not doubt you on that, my dear. Nor does Harry. We use two o'clock as our base."

In other ways Gem might doubt herself but not in this instance. "Who would hijack the plane then?"

"We have no idea. It has just been suggested a possibility. We must consider all possibilities. Drug runners, arms dealers, there are enumerable subversive groups in this world, known and underground."

"Another passenger - unknown to you and Harry, joining the flight at the last minute?" Gem suggested.

"Someone Mr Portermann trusted," Mrs Brown conceded.

"Someone would have texted that fact, Gemmy, mum, dad." Gem didn't feel the idea was logical.

"Someone forced their way onboard."

"Someone with a death wish?" Gem scowled.

"Parachuted out," Mrs Brown countered.

"Forced the plane down," Gem said, her heart in her throat. "Or simply took the plane and killed everyone," she forced herself to say the words. "Air piracy."

"Possibly. Change the numbers on any plane, fiddle the registry, and the plane is clean and gone. There's no lack of islands in that part of the world where one might hide a plane."

"It could be anywhere in the world. Rather outrageously widens the search area," Gem said grimly. "Who is working on this theory?"

"Agent 1. He has had his ear to the ground for some weeks now, but has yet to find a hint of a hijacker. However, we must examine all possible theories."

"Where was the plane kept? The Brisbane airport?"

"Private airport outside Brisbane - not the airstrip of the last departure."

"B.I."

Mrs Brown nodded.

"Why did Mr Portermann fly from one airstrip to another for take-off that night?"

Mrs Brown gazed at her.

"Right." Answer your own query, Gem mused. She stared out the windows, gazing at Foyles Bookshop across the street, but her eyes did not see the building. "Private airport - accessible use for small private plane owners to defray cost," she glanced at Mrs Brown who nodded. "Spring here - winter in Australia - nothing in that." Gem threw up her hands in resignation. "Busy night in Brisbane, small planes diverted to B.I. Airport - use another airstrip for immediate departure at 20:00 hours."

"That's the gist of it, clear and simple. Too many eyes on the skies otherwise."

"B.I. airport personnel see anything unusual that night? Anything at all?" Gem pressed.

"Higher than usual landing requests due to the high traffic at Brisbane. That happens in spurts - no rhyme or reason."

"No one around who shouldn't have been around?" Gem was mentally flailing.

"Personnel noticed nothing unusual. They are well-trained. People are not allowed to simply wander around that airport. They would alert B.I. Security."

"Someone earlier - from another flight - a seemingly legitimate excuse for being at the airport - no reason to alert airport personnel?" Gem thought aloud.

"Possibly," Mrs Brown nodded. "Records are being scrutinized. There will be the necessary investigation of all pilots and passengers for all flights that day. Harry requested all flights from the previous fortnight investigated - under the auspices of major restructuring of the airport facility - 'How can we better serve you?' That line of query."

"A shot in the dark," Gem raked her fingers through her hair, "but everything is a shot in the dark with this search. It is so blasted frustrating!"

Mrs Brown nodded agreement. "Made more frustrating by the complete lack of progress. Constant information gathering is very important. Not a single clue. Two o'clock is our only lead."

"It leads nowhere," Gem sighed. "But I know I am right," she insisted again.

"As do I. It is a start, my dear. A very tiny one." She glanced at her watch. "Further thoughts? Queries?"

"One. To whom does Agent 1 report?"

"Harry first. I am second if Harry is unavailable."

"No one else?"

"Absolutely not!"

As they parted on the pavement outside the coffee shop, each woman had more thoughts than they believed their brains could sort.

"A word of warning, my dear," Mrs Brown said.

Gem sighed inwardly. Go slow with Wyatt Grantham, she waited to hear.

"Do NOT enter Foyles. You will be in there for days."

Gem burst out laughing. "Avoid the chance to peruse every book ever written? Harsh!"

Mrs Brown gave her a warning look before she turned and walked away.

Gem took the warning at full value. Wyatt would be back in London soon. He was the ONLY reason she did not cross the street.

Wyatt brought her a gold Luckenbooth Holyrood brooch from Scotland. Gem was speechless.

"That cat's got your tongue again," he teased.

"Oh-no," she gasped. "It is so exquisite, Wyatt!"

"As are you, my dear," he smiled that smile that sent butterflies flying free inside her.

"Truly you shouldn't have, Wyatt," Gem murmured. "I can't accept such an expensive gift." Auntie Jane had once purchased such a brooch in Scotland and said it had set her back more than three months wages.

"I knew I should have purchased that book for you- Hiking in Scotland. It included a cd," he teased. "Wear the pin. Enjoy it."

"I would be frightened I would lose it!" she protested.

"Trifles can be replaced. People can't," he gazed into her eyes.

"This is not a trifle!" she insisted.

"It is compared to your lovely ring, and you take good care of that. I am certain you shall not lose the pin. Now give me a kiss and put it on. We have pubs to storm and pints to hoist!" he ordered with a smile.

The kiss, the pin was worn, and Wyatt shifted the Jag into gear.

The mention of her ring briefly froze her heart, but Gem took a deep breath and ordered herself to enjoy the evening. But she would spend hours that night thinking of Gemmy and her sweetheart.

They spent Saturday and Sunday visiting museums in Oxford, a picnic lunch on Saturday, a pub dinner, a pub lunch on Sunday, and a picnic dinner in a park.

Wyatt frowned slightly as he poured the wine at the picnic early Sunday evening.

"May I ask you a personal question?"

A phrase which could only raise warning flashes in a person's mind - as it did in Gem's. She took a deep breath, wary of the query. Hopefully it wasn't about her family. "Yes," she nodded.

Wyatt wondered at the lengthy pause before a simple yes or no reply. "Have you ever been married?"

"No," Gem replied, relieved and startled at the query. "You?"

"No," Wyatt shook his head. Well he should have expected that. Only fair to return the question. "Engaged?"

"No. You?"

"No," he replied, looking deep into the wine glass in his hand. Then he raised his head to study her eyes. "I have wondered, to be blunt, if there is someone from your past in your thoughts - in your heart. Do I have - residual competition?"

"Interestingly phrased," Gem smiled. "No, to all your queries. And I doubt you would ever be in competition with any man for any woman," Gem said with all honesty.

"A kind remark, thank you," Wyatt frowned. The responses were as he expected. The Game would continue.

Gem was relieved by the questions, and greatly flattered by his remarks about 'residual' competition. He didn't pursue other such queries, and the conversation drifted on to the museums they had visited that day.

She enjoyed his arm around her waist when they walked, and how he held her hand when they listened to music in pubs, or when he assisted her out of the Jag. He gazed into her eyes when they chatted; he was affectionate, not pushy, and when he kissed her she didn't want him to stop.

"Are you in London this week?" she asked as they packed the remains of the picnic.

"Oslo on Tuesday, Madrid Wednesday. I'm not going into the office tomorrow. Shall we check out the haunts in Pluckley?" He pulled her close for a kiss.

"Ah, ghost hunting?" Gem tried to think clearly; his hands were resting on her shoulders; she was getting lost in his eyes.

"We'll have wine and sandwiches at the Pinnock Bridge with the Watercress Woman, shall we?" And there was another kiss. "I have neglected you lately. Madrid is the last meeting for some time. We will have proper time together in the future."

"I haven't felt neglected," Gem protested. "You are an extremely busy man. I understand that."

"Too busy as of late, but for a purpose. I travel now so I needn't be away for the coming months," he murmured.

"That sounds lovely."

"Pluckley?"

"Watercress sandwiches and wine."

It didn't matter to her what they did, or where they went. She simply was delighted to be with him. He was so easy mannered. She was impressed by him when they were in shops and pubs. He did not expect, he did not demand special service or treatment from staff. He waited patiently to be served the same as any customer. A proper gentleman he was.

Mrs Brown's words were in her mind as he accompanied Gem up the steps to her building.

"Would you like to come in for a glass of wine?"

Wyatt frowned. "I pay a great deal of money to have my name kept out of the media. I do not want our relationship to be compromised, my dear, so I shall decline."

"I understand," Gem replied. Her life had long been lived trying to avoid drawing attention to herself. Mrs Brown would certainly approve of Wyatt's statement, Gem reflected. Wyatt had the perspective of a mature man, and it greatly pleased Gem.

Gem could take a day from working on her book, but she could not take an evening off from her search.

She wondered if there could have been any reason that Mr Portermann had not used the satellite navigation on the plane that night. Had it been working? Had North Korea been jamming GPS flight signals that night? That was a question that would only ever be answered by denials, if any reply was ever made. It had been raining that night, but from the information Gem could pull up on the inter-net, precipitation did not affect GPS.

Mr Portermann would have managed quite nicely, thank you, without GPS. Thus GPS was an item to eliminate for consideration. But! If GPS had been a flaw that night, could there have been other flaws? Keep GPS on the written and mental lists, as a reminder.

Gem knew that Wyatt had a most excellent mind and she wished she could tap his intellect. However, that was so far out of the question as to enter the realm of the impossible. One simply did not step outside of the Agency. Wyatt was a civilian. One did NOT involve civilians. Cogs slipped and civilians could be put in danger. Agency SOP: Do Not Involve Civilians.

Wyatt was a very private person, she mused. He had as much his own separate world as she had hers. To have her own private world she had to allow him his. And work was definitely his private world. She had offered three times to meet him at his office on days when they met for lunch, but all three times he had refused the offer, meeting her instead at a café or pub. Conversely, when he asked about her day, he did not demand details of her every waking moment.

Back to work. She couldn't involve Wyatt. She needed to stay focused. What next to consider regarding the flight? Flight distance and times - approximates for both; flight checklists; weather; mild temperatures, rain, no wind to speak of - no haboobs. Nothing unusual.

She would ring Mrs Brown in the morning to inquire if any private or commercial flight reports indicated any problems in the area that night. Flights from Australia to South East Asia. No doubt someone had already processed that information. Check for anomalies.

The computer screen glared back at her. Timor Sea. Arafura Sea. Gulf of Carpentaria was deep enough to hide a plane. 1450.323NM, flight time 5.371567 hours, from Brisbane to the coast off Burketown. Six hours would put the plane in the Gulf of Carpentaria.

Gem pushed the start button on the cd player again. Vera Lynn's voice soothed.

Query Mrs Brown of search planes and vessels regarding the gulf. However, the Pilos should have been fine flying over the gulf to Darwin. - She thought. Still query to Mrs Brown.

Mrs Brown's replies in the morning to Gem's questions did not bring satisfaction.

"I will put your queries to Harry, my dear. I have nothing in my reports of flight anomalies regarding 29 or 30 May. I should think an investigation was ordered. I will refer the suggestion of the Gulf of Carpentaria to Harry. It is a logical theory, and perhaps one that has already been addressed, however not yet reported to me."

"I appreciate you speaking to Harry," Gem said.

"Keep working, my dear, your queries are well though-out," Mrs Brown replied. "Are you still wearing a pinafore, my dear?"

Gem's jaw dropped at the blunt, unexpected question. "Err-yes," Gem rolled her eyes.

"As it should be," Mrs Brown said firmly and rang off.

Well, it was a pleasant thought that Mrs Brown was concerned about her, Gem sighed.

Pluckley, with all its haunting tales was a delightful visit. Gem and Wyatt indeed ate watercress sandwiches and sipped wine at the Pinnock Bridge, but were disappointed they weren't joined by the ghost - the Watercress Woman. They rambled lanes, climbed over styles, strolled through the village, but did not meet any apparitions or feel visited by spirits. Perhaps a second visit some time would be more eventful.

Wyatt rang from Oslo and Madrid. Gem returned to her Second World War reading at night, worked on the layout for the Bath Cathedral during the day, and ran errands. She finally remembered to pick up the two remaining watercolours, dropped off rolls of film shot at Pluckley and Saffron Walden.

Mrs Brown rang to arrange a meeting for Thursday lunch, again at Charley's Pub.

The outside of the pub showed considerable improvement as did the interior. Charley served them each a pint, then went off to prepare their lunch while Gem and Mrs Brown surveyed the change in the pub room. "A fortnight - perhaps a bit more, and this place will be rocking again," Mrs Brown declared.

"Rocking!" Gem laughed. "Where did you get that term?"

"I have witnessed pub nights here," Mrs Brown replied sagely. "Charley's son has a band that quite lifts the roof off this building at times."

"You on a pub night! That I should like to see!"

"Agency businesses must be reviewed from time to time. Now could you see Harry at a pub night? He never drinks any beverage stronger than water, and loud music makes him squirmy," Mrs Brown expounded. "Now sit down, my dear, you look exhausted as usual. Is Wyatt keeping you out late evenings?"

"No, ma'am, he is not," Gem defended her dream man.

"The onerous then is still your insomnia and your work, which cannot be helped at this time."

"Yes, ma'am. What news have you for me?"

"Harry is on holiday, as of today. I shall also be going on holiday."

"How long?"

"Harry will be away an indeterminate time. I shall return in three weeks, perhaps a month. Cawley will be available for queries. Neither Harry nor I will be in contact with the Agency."

"Mr Cawley is in charge."

"Indeed."

Charley appeared with burgers, chips, and salads.

"Is the band area encroaching too far onto the table area, Charley?" Mrs Brown indicated the section where the floor was squared off with red-tape.

"Not according to the band, ma'am," Charley chuckled. "Equipment takes space."

"I understand. It was merely a thought. Do you think more light fixtures should be installed?" Mrs Brown counted the current fixtures, finding the number sorely lacking.

"The customers prefer low lights. More conducive to snogging."

"I shouldn't think lighting would be a considering factor for that with your patrons."

Gem ate quietly, her eyes blinking at the conversation.

"Enough light for snogging, too much light for sex," Charley announced.

Gem choked on a chip.

"Excellent point. Thank you, Charley," Mrs Brown concluded the remarks.

Charley wandered back to the kitchen.

"There you have it, my dear. You may come to Charley's for pub night and still go home wearing your pinafore."

Gem set down her fork, shaking her head. "I simply cannot believe the conversation here today," she laughed.

"You were raised in a hothouse, Gem," Mrs Brown said not unkindly.

"I was not!" Gem protested.

"A mental hothouse. You did not run wild."

"I never had the time."

"You never took the time. - Fortunately for the Agency."

They fell silent, focusing on their food. It was Mrs Brown who finally broke the silence.

"The Gulf of Carpentaria had been considered, but no evidence was found to warrant a search. However, it is quite deep, and a submarine will go on manoeuvres to do a proper search next week. The vessel is currently in the Arafura Sea."

"Thank you. The flight anomalies?"

"An ongoing process according to Harry. A number of airlines have been slow to supply the information. It has been requested for a study of flight anomalies in South East Asia, January through June of this year. One cannot demand immediate response without drawing excess attention to the request," she replied. "I believe Charley is using more spices in his burgers."

"Fresh chives," Gem observed. "He didn't use them last time we were here."

"Pronounced difference."

Two queries answered, Gem reflected as she walked home. She stopped at the shop for the Pluckley and Saffron Walden photos, and naturally could not pass her favourite bookshop without stopping in. It had the appeal and the disorder of Foyles, smelled equally musty and fusty, but was of a much smaller size. She rummaged about for an hour, and was rewarded by literally stumbling over a book of the history of the Etruscans. She thought Wyatt might enjoy reading it, knowing his passion for history.

Once home, she quickly showered and dressed, sorting the photos, waiting for Wyatt to ring her. She did not have to wait long.

"Dinner one hour?" he asked.

"Yes!"

She had time to wrap the book - white paper, tied with a blue ribbon.

And he had gifts for her. "Wyatt! You shouldn't have!" Gem protested. But she was delighted with the brightly coloured scarf from Madrid, and a beautiful off-white and ice blue zippered cardigan from Oslo. She caressed the soft wool, shaking her head.

"A thank you and a kiss will suffice nicely," he ordered, which she gladly gave.

"I have a surprise for you," Gem gave him the book.

Surprise indeed! Gem was startled by his silent reaction as he unwrapped the book and opened the cover to the title page. "Well," he grinned. "Perhaps I should go away more often! This is a wonderful gift."

"A thank you and a kiss," Gem said, to which he complied.

"Dinner and an early night," he said a few minutes later. "I have a big day planned for us tomorrow."

"Don't you have to work?" she protested. "You have been away from your office most of the week."

"I worked five days into three," he said firmly. "Tomorrow is our time."

"Where are we going?"

"Cotswold Way. Picnic, hiking, relaxing beneath the largest tree we can find."

"So be it!"

Gem listened to the cd and paced the floor, going over in her mind the conversation she had had with Mrs Brown at Charley's Pub. A submarine would be in the Gulf of Carpentaria next week. She had no idea how long the search would take. She was so tired. She refused to think and read for the duration of the dark hours that morning. Absorb material, use it later, when her brain felt refreshed. But when would that be?

It was a heavenesque day: the temperature was balmy, the sky bright late August blue with puffy white clouds. Gem raided Gemmy's clothes for hiking and decided on a blue tee and stone-washed jeans. To her surprise Wyatt was dressed the same.

"We match!" she laughed when she ran down to meet him.

"Oh, my dear, we certainly do," he said firmly.

On the drive to the Cotswolds, he told her of his days in Oslo and Madrid.

"And where to next?" she queried.

"Randwick Woods. Hiking with you."

"I mean business trips!" she laughed.

"On hold for awhile."

"Ah -nice. Randwick Woods. Sounds lovely!"

"Indeed. We are going off the beaten path."

"Oh yes?" Gem said curiously.

"Yes. I intend to kiss you a great deal."

"Oh yes! I'll quite like that!"

"Oh, my dear, you will."

Their lunch was in knapsacks, one for each of them, easier than carrying a picnic basket. Wyatt wore the blanket around his shoulders. They hiked the trail for a time and turned off through the woods. There were quite a few hikers on the trail, but Wyatt managed to find them a secluded spot under a very large tree.

After lunch and wine, Wyatt stretched out beneath the tree, drawing Gem down beside him. Between the wine and his kisses Gem ached for him, eager to say farewell to the pinafore.

It was Wyatt who pulled away first. He held her face in his hands. "Slow down, Gem," his voice was husky.

Her heart was pounding, her body reeling from the passion that had abruptly been shut down. She was stunned as he stood up and walked away to stare off into the trees. All around them was silence, the worst of it a thick, invisible wall between Wyatt and her.

Gem crawled to her feet, bewildered, her breath coming in shallow bursts; she blushed, embarrassed now for responding with a complete abandonment that shocked her.

Wyatt gazed at the horizon, forcing his thoughts over the past month and a half. And the past weeks with her. It had all been so easy. And so it would continue. He turned slowly to look at her.

Gem sighed. I am not in your league, am I? Why are you with me? Or was he? She couldn't meet his eyes, so she turned away. Still the pinafore. And how many other women were there in his life that he didn't pull away from? Mrs Brown was correct. Gem though in dismay of crushed petals and a broken heart.

Gem sighed inwardly as he walked towardss her. He took her left hand.

"You are a brilliant young woman, my dear," he said quietly.

Gem's heart sank as he spoke. It was over then, while still in early days.

"This had to be properly done. I do not want an affair. I want you to spend the rest of your life with me," he said firmly, drawing a small box from his pocket.

Gem stared at him, unable to believe what she had just heard.

The ring was magnificent.

"I didn't want to overshadow your other ring, so I had this designed in a similar style," Wyatt said quietly. "The setting is platinum. It shall last a lifetime."

It was a medium size square cut diamond encircled with smaller diamonds in a spider-web weave. The clarity of the diamonds was brilliant.

"Does that cat have your tongue again?" he teased.

Gem nodded.

"Is that a yes - and a yes?"

She nodded again. "Yes!" she replied ecstatically, finally finding her voice. "Yes!" Without a moment of hesitation.

He slipped the ring on her finger, sealing the proposal with a very long kiss.

The sat beneath the tree, each with a glass of wine, and her hand in his.

"You have no family. I have no family," Wyatt said tentatively. "Would you mind a small, quiet wedding?"

"Not at all," Gem agreed. Whom would she invite?

"Registrar's office?"

Gem nodded.

"Friday - noon?"

Gem started. "So soon?"

"Have we reason to wait?"

"There's so much to do - there's my flat," she replied.

"I can hire a crew to pack for you. There's no lack of space for your possessions at the Hall."

"The Hall?"

"Grantham Hall. My home. Our home to be. It's at Ticking Bottom," Wyatt explained, "a quiet village. There's a pub, the Yellow Crow - excellent pub grub."

"Ticking Bottom! An unusual name," Gem laughed.

"Milton Keynes. Whiterashes. Mockbeggar. Wightwizzle, Spital-in-the-Street," he laughed. "Ticking Bottom isn't so outrageous. You might greatly enjoy living in the country. Constant new subjects for you camera."

"It sounds wonderful," Gem rested her head on his shoulder. They would be a family. Our home to be - he had said.

"As for your flat, I'll pay off the lease," Wyatt offered.

"I own my flat."

"Sell it. Pad your bank account. Do whatever you like with the money," he suggested. "Settle the flat, select a dress. I have selected your wedding ring. However, if it is not to your liking you shall have any you wish."

"And your ring or are you not inclined to wear one?" she asked hesitantly.

"I shall," he said firmly. "May I surprise you with the honeymoon trip? No long travelling time - just peace and quiet."

"Sounds lovely," Gem sighed happily.

"Tomorrow morning then, rings, and I shall contact a removal company for you."

"I'll do the packing. However I shall need cartons," Gem decided.

"You shall have them. Cartons and sealing adhesive," he stood up, pulling Gem to her feet. "We have a bit of a hike ahead of us now. And a proper dinner - pub, your choice. And you are not to exhaust yourself. If you need help you shall have it."

Everything had been settled so quickly that afternoon. Gem thought to ring Mrs Brown, but remembered her supervisor was on holiday. As was Harry. She rang Mr Cawley to leave a message with him for her superiors.

"I am delighted for you, Gem!" Mr Cawley replied in astonishment. "Grantham is a very lucky man, indeed! He's no fool to let you slip through his fingers! And in that vein, you must remember to be extremely careful," he warned.

"I realize that," Gem replied.

"He's a civilian. He cannot know anything about the Agency."

"I understand. No slipped cogs," she sighed. Years of preventing cogs from slipping.

"You'll do fine. Backup is always available to support you if you feel you've misspoken. Files can be altered - you know the routine. It's not easy, but again it's not terribly difficult. I've been married for fifteen years and my wife still completely believes I'm an accountant."

"That's encouraging," Gem laughed.

"Where are you going on your honeymoon?"

"It's a surprise."

"Oh. Did you happen to mention no flights or large bodies of water?" Cawley said abruptly.

"Wyatt said peace and quiet and no long travel."

"Hmm. Perhaps you should ring Hallowell for a prescription - something light - to take the sting off in the event you find yourself on a plane."

"I'll be fine. Wyatt has travelled quite a bit the past few weeks. I don't think he's interested in the hassles of travel."

"Very well. Still you might discuss the issue of flying."

She rang off soon after that. Asking Wyatt what clothes to pack might give her an indication of whether or not flight or water or both were involved.

As she looked about her flat that night, she decided to sell it. Leasing would be a headache; she didn't wish to be a landlord. She was starting a new life. There would be no purpose in keeping the flat. She would be residing at Grantham Hall at Ticking Bottom - that so unusual name!

As soon as she had cartons she would start packing. Her computer and lap-top, and World War II research would be among the last items packed. She could take time off from the book, but not from her research. She did not fool herself that the insomnia would disappear when she married Wyatt. She had enough material in her mind to mentally sort and review during the dark hours. A time to sort what had so far been accumulated.

She brewed a cup of tea and relaxed in Auntie Jane's comfy chair. What a day she had had! She still could not believe that Wyatt had proposed! In those moments of dismay she had thought he was going to end their relationship. She had thought he had suddenly concluded that she was a mistake. But she was the one who had been in error. A very extremely happy error!

At least she could share her happiness with Mr Cawley. Agency Family.

If only 30 May had not happened. If only she and Gemmy could both be as happy as Gem was this night. Happy! And impossibly sad her family was not with her.

There was so much she could not share with Wyatt. Her family. The Agency. Her search efforts for the plane, the reason it went missing. Actually she could not share most of her life with him. She would be divided in half. - Well, as most people are! Most people had their family life and their work life. Wyatt would have his marriage and his work life. And it was just a part of her work life that did not exist. And her family. Oh, the thoughts!

I can do this! I love Wyatt Grantham! I want to be his wife! I will be a great wife! A loving, supportive wife! I want him to be happy and content in our marriage! And I will not fail my family and the Agency! It will all work out. She would make it work!

Now sleep. And then work. And tomorrow she would purchase a wedding ring for Wyatt.

She pressed the start button on the cd player. Vera Lynn's voice and hours of reading. The blasted dark hours. So much information to gather. She still couldn't reach that errant thought. But she knew it had to do with SS officers.

Pacing, cup after cup of tea. Press the start button on the cd player.

Wyatt rang at eight o'clock to tell her cartons would be delivered at nine o'clock, and he would call for her an hour after that. The delivery was precisely on time: two cases of flattened cartons and a case of sealing adhesive. She would start packing that very evening.

Jeans were fine for hiking but Gem dressed with care to shop with Wyatt, intricately braiding her hair into a tidy plait. Shopping with Wyatt for books at a jumble sale was an entirely different matter than shopping for a wedding ring. She insisted on platinum to match her rings. He insisted diamonds and elaborate designs were not acceptable, finally selecting a wide band, plain finished with a bevel edge. He reached for his credit card and Gem protested.

"You simply cannot pay for your own wedding ring. It simply isn't right."

"Well you're not paying that price!" he protested.

"I am not a pauper, Wyatt. This is the one time you simply must step back," Gem refused to concede the issue. To her surprise and relief he finally relented and let her pay for the ring.

"Lunch now," he suggested, still slightly vexed by her tenacity over his ring. "And then wedding dresses."

"No," Gem firmly shook her head. "I will find my dress. Alone."

"I'll see it Friday when I drive us to the registrar's office," he countered.

"I shall take a taxi on Friday. Properly done!" she reminded him of his words at Randwick Woods.

"So be it. Flowers?"

"Sorry. Still my list."

"Your list will be too long for you," it was his turn to protest.

"If I need help I will ask."

"Well then, a long lunch and lots of beer," he concluded.

"Well said!"

Gem judged lunch to be the time to carefully ask about the honeymoon.

"I don't know what to pack," she told him as they settled in a dark corner at the White Cat Pub. She chose the dark corner, remembering the conversation at Charley's. Not too dark, but dark enough. And still possible to scan the room, recalling Mrs Brown's words to sharpen her skills.

"Casual, comfortable, perhaps something a bit dressy in the event I can coax you beyond a pub one evening."

"Not much help," she frowned slightly.

"One hint then," he conceded. "We will not be leaving the U.K. Good enough?"

"Most excellent! I shall manage quite nicely then." Thank heavens - no flights or water! "Peace and quiet. Lovely!"

"And what else is on your mind today?" he teased. "Any other queries?"

And suddenly she did have one. An extremely important one. "We didn't discuss -" she hesitated.

"Yes?"

"Wyatt, do you want children?" she asked, catching her bottom lip between her teeth.

He was stunned by the query. "Certainly," he replied, trying to keep an edge from his voice. "You?"

"Yes. How many?" she asked curiously.

He pondered the question, while the waiter served their food. "Since I won't be the one carrying them for nine months, I shall leave that decision to you. One, a dozen, some number in between - your choice." But will it really matter?

"Good answer," she said admiringly.

"Thank you. Remember my reply when you are in labour the first time," he teased. "Ah - I can see you blushing even in this light."

"Just eat your food," Gem mumbled, wishing she could control that reaction.

Halfway through lunch Wyatt's mobile alerted a text message.

"I can see you frowning, even in this light," Gem murmured. "Office?"

"The Hall," he chuckled as he keyed in a response. "I have to cut our afternoon short, I am sorry to say. There's a bit of a dispute between the estate manager and the gardener."

"Wouldn't the estate manager have the final decision?"

"Not if one wants gardens," Wyatt replied, chuckling.

"Well I have packing to do," Gem smiled.

"And we have tomorrow. Lunch and a stroll along the Thames?"

"Weather permitting. Rain in the forecast."

"We'll take umbrellas."

"Actually that sounds quite romantic. Strolling in the rain."

"We have time for a stroll now. A bit of window shopping?"

"Not the dress."

"I need a new suit. I'm getting married Friday."

"Ah! Shall I help you select a suit?"

"No! You can't see it until Friday," he teased.

Wyatt had to be at the Hall in late afternoon, thus Gem was home with plenty of time to start the arduous task of putting together boxes and then filling them. She stripped the bed, washed the sheets and clothes that had accumulated in the hamper, and packed cartons while machines did their work. Friday she would do laundry and pack what would not be needed on her honeymoon. What a lovely word: honeymoon!

Books and non-essential kitchen items were packed by the time Wyatt rang in early evening.

"Do you still have an estate manager?"

"Yes indeed," Wyatt chuckled, "and a gardener!"

"Ah, to have the upper hand!"

"Keeping the upper hand is the important rule," Wyatt said smoothly. "Have you an umbrella?"

"I do," she replied.

"Save that for Friday," he teased.

When Wyatt rang off, Gem took a break from packing; tea and comfy chair were needed. Gem admired the ring on her left hand. Stunning! It never occurred to her that she would ever have such a beautiful ring.

Marriage! To Wyatt! She had never truly thought of getting married. Well, to be honest, it was a bit of a handicap never really having time to date. And Gemmy had never been serious about any of the chaps she had dated - until that young man in Barcelona. It had always been studies and work. At the very least marriage had been a fuzzy image in the very distant future.

Staggering! Now she was getting married! And to the most handsome man imaginable - now that Cary Grant was no longer amongst us. Gem laughed out loud, feeling wondrously happy.

And then she slammed back to earth. She only had Mr Cawley with whom to share her delight. Gemmy would have shrieked with joy for her and hugged her to pieces. Mum and dad. Mum would have sparkled like all the stars in the northern hemisphere - or southern - depending on where she was at the time of the announcement.

She had the Agency, and no other family. No friends. She had never had time for them so none existed. She had needed only Gemmy. Enough self-dissection! She had packing to do!

Gem decided to keep two books out that she hadn't had a chance to read. She packed all her dvds except the copy on U-boats; cds would also be packed last, along with the linens she would need this week. She wouldn't need the bed. Leave it for new flat owners or donate. Auntie Jane's comfy chair, settee, desk, and the chest of drawers would definitely go with her.

Clothes were sorted for the week ahead, then the honeymoon, and if necessary she would purchase on the trip; Gemmy's strapless, black tea-length dress, black heels, evening bag, and Gemmy's 'diamond and black onyx' earrings would be for a dressy evening. Bless Gemmy! Always with me, Gem murmured. Two shoulder bags, tights, stockings, frillies. She should have made a packing list. Kitchen items would not be needed, she realized, locating the cartons and marking them for donation.

It was nearly midnight when she went to bed. Then there was the reading during the dark hours until dawn.

Wyatt rang just a few short hours later, but as usual she was awake at seven o'clock.

"I'll apply for the marriage license tomorrow. Only one of us need be there and you have a long list of must do's," he offered.

"Another item off our list then," Gem agreed.

"I shall need your birth certificate. Can you bring it along when I call for you for lunch?"

"Birth certificate," she said slowly. Blast! Her parents' names were on it, so the certificate was at the Agency warehouse. A new one could be arranged but that process was Harry's bailiwick. This was a backup Mr Cawley could not accomplish. Only Harry could process altered documents.

"A passport would suffice," Wyatt suggested at her vague response.

"I have that at hand," Gem replied, greatly relieved. No explanations needed for a missing birth certificate!

Lunch was at the British Museum, and the stroll along the Thames was beneath umbrellas. Gem gave Wyatt the passport, and another step towards their marriage would be managed the following day. He had arranged for the removal van to arrive Thursday afternoon with a second call for items at nine o'clock Friday morning. More packing, more reading, and another day had been checked off the list of the Friday wedding deadline.

Gem rang an estate agent, who quickly came round to view the flat. Then Gem sorted through photo packs to find the shots of Wyatt and the Jag she had taken at Salisbury and Bath. She took them to the shop to be matted and framed as a wedding gift for Wyatt. It took a bit of pleading with the shop owner but he promised the photos would be available Thursday morning.

The estate agent rang to arrange a viewing of the flat that same day, so Gem used that time to make a round of the shops to look for a wedding dress, which she found in the third shop she entered; she also found a pair of shoes to suit the dress. The dress had to be taken in a bit, but it would be delivered Thursday morning. Thursday would be a very busy day! She stopped at a flower shop and ordered a small bouquet of six white roses to be delivered Friday morning at ten o'clock. Six white roses: one each for Gemmy, her fiancé, their baby, mum, dad, and Mr Portermann.

Dinner with Wyatt was very romantic. She had suggested Italian instead of pub food much to Wyatt's surprise, and he selected a cosy, dimly lit restaurant with excellent food; the wine flowed freely.

"Oh, do you have my passport?" Gem asked as their dessert was served. It was, after all, a very especial government passport.

"It's at the Hall. We won't need passports on our trip, so I thought it best to keep them together. You needn't worry about misplacing it while you pack," he traced his finger lightly on her arm.

Misplacing a passport jarred her thoughts. She wouldn't need it for some time in the future. Best leave it where it was. She would be moving to the Hall after their honeymoon.

"How long will we be away?"

"Eleven days - the last a travel day. I thought perhaps we would have a weekend trip in October, if that suits you then," he said, his voice silky. "We'll have a lot of changes in our lives, adjustments to make, but life will be very interesting for us, I promise you."

"I am eager to see Grantham Hall," Gem said dreamily. Her new home!

"And you shall, but not until after the honeymoon. One step at a time."

Gem looked about the restaurant, sighing contentedly. "This is a lovely place. We should come here again."

Wyatt teased, "Tired of pub grub?"

"Never! But you must be."

"I have many breakfast and lunch meetings each week, so I enjoy a variety of dining experiences," he shook his head. "Have you shopped for a dress?"

"I found it. Your suit?"

"Done."

"What progress we have made in three days!"

Packing and another long night of reading and listening to Vera Lynn singing. She was growing tired of concentrating on the War.

Her flat sold on Tuesday for half again as much as she had originally paid for it, making Gem a very tidy profit. The new owner would take the bed. Wyatt rang to say he had to schedule a late meeting that day so their honeymoon would not be interrupted by work. Gem arranged for removal of the donation boxes - to be managed the following day.

Suddenly she felt overwhelmed from the activity of the past few days, and the demands of the next two days. She grabbed her camera and went walking, stopping at Oscar's Café for lunch, then continued aimlessly walking until late afternoon. She watched the dvds of the British and Allied submarines, marvelling at the disparity in size compared to the smaller U-boats. She started reading Operation Drumbeat, astounded by the U-boats massive successful destruction of Allied shipping off the U.S. Atlantic Coast in the early years of the War.

A physical break from information gathering for eleven days would be a much appreciated holiday. A mental break would be easily come by.

And where the devil were Mrs Brown and Harry? Both away for over a fortnight! Unavailable for contact. Had they both gone underground? Gem was Need-To-Know, but even she wasn't in the loop on this situation. Whatever it was it was beyond NTK. Blast!

Wednesday morning, with a very deep pang of nostalgia, Gem signed the papers, accepted a check, and agreed to vacate the flat by midnight Friday. The shop rang to say her dress was ready for a fitting. Wyatt rang to ask her to lunch and to dinner. The dress fit perfectly. Gem was exhausted by the time she joined Wyatt for lunch at the White Cat Pub.

"Well done!" he murmured in surprise when she announced the sale of the flat. "But it must be difficult for you," he signalled the publican for two pints.

"It's been my home for a few years now," she nodded, gulping back her emotions. She would save the tears to flow freely that night. "Oh, I'd best deposit the check after lunch."

Wyatt choked on his beer. "Good lord! You're carrying it around with you?"

"I got distracted by phone calls," she admitted.

"I'll take you to the bank immediately after lunch," he insisted. "You do have the check with you?"

Gem checked her shoulder bag. "Yes," she sighed with relief.

"You need a caretaker," Wyatt shook his head in amazement.

"Applying for the position?" she teased.

"Well someone should! Eat. You are looking a bit peaky," he ordered as their food was served.

He insisted on taking Gem to the bank in a taxi, and when he returned to work she went shopping for nightgowns and dressing gowns; her pyjamas would not be suitable for a romantic honeymoon. She was casting off the pinafore whole heartedly. The framing shop rang - her order was ready. Everything was falling into place. She made a quick trip to the shop, then enjoyed a peaceful walk back to her flat.

They had Chinese food for dinner at Gem's suggestion. As she perused the menu she had a stabbing thought. Had the Chinese courier been found? She read the room, frowning. Mental note: ring Mr Cawley when she returned to her flat.

Wyatt saw the lovely violet eyes cloud as he watched her surreptitiously look about the dining room. What or whom was she looking for in the restaurant? He sought to capture her attention.

"I have arranged for a car to take you to City Hall on Friday," he said, signalling the waitress for another pot of tea.

"Oh yes?" Gem mentally shook off her thoughts of Agency business.

"The driver will take you to the registrar's office and then take your luggage to -" he stopped, winking at her.

"To-?" she took the bait.

"Another destination," he laughed. "Now, still on your list?"

"My dress will be delivered tomorrow."

"May I suggest tomorrow is a day each on our own to complete our tasks and do what relaxing is possible?"

Gem easily agreed. She had neglected to purchase film and, no doubt, some other errand would pop up which would catch her attention.

"I have the rings," Wyatt reminded.

"And a new black suit," she teased.

"Sass! Haven't heard that for some time," he grinned.

"I hardly saw you last week!" she laughed.

"That will change very abruptly in about forty-eight hours," he glanced at his watch. "Let the countdown begin!" He leaned over to kiss her.

"So be it!"

Gem sat in Auntie Jane's comfy chair, sipping wine, and gazed about the room. For four months she had looked at flats in a dozen different sections of London. It had taken her two years to decorate the flat. Now the walls were bare, the bookcases empty, the kitchen spartan. She would pack the computer equipment tomorrow, the lap-top on Friday morning. All service connections would be severed Friday at midnight.

She had moved from the family home in Brisbane to Auntie Jane's cottage in Lincolnshire. Auntie Jane had died when Gem was at university. The cottage had been sold, and mum had been relocated to Paris, and Gem to London three years ago. Another move. And the last one!

It would be too easy to wallow in memories and self-pity. She had work to accomplish. She poured another glass of wine and reached for the book she had started the previous night. Wyatt rang to say good night, and she continued reading. And she read again during the dark hours.

Thursday flew by. Gem packed the computer equipment, the dress arrived, the removal van, the cartons disappeared, as did the furniture save for the bed and the comfy chair. She sought fresh air at Oscar's Café. How often would she frequent this café once she and Wyatt lived at the Hall? She had first come here to look for Gemmy's sweetheart. She had to come back. She had neglected to ask Wyatt if there was a rail station at Ticking Bottom. Impulsively she texted the query to him. He responded immediately to the affirmative, and inquired as to what she was doing.

'Lunch at Oscar's.'

'Don't talk to any strange men wearing black suits.'

'All the men here look quite normal.'

'Sass! Order a glass of wine for me. Five minutes away.'

So much for not seeing each other that day!

Chapter Five

Friday morning couldn't have gone more smoothly. The bouquet arrived wrapped in a wide, white satin ribbon. The removal van cleared out the remaining cartons and furniture. Gem felt a brief moment of panic when the computers went out the door. Eleven days without a computer for reference! Would she be able to manage? During the day she would be with Wyatt, but in early morning - during the dark hours - she would be on her own.

She jumped as her mobile rang.

"Everything going smoothly?" Wyatt asked mildly.

"Perfectly," Gem replied, surprised herself there had been no problems.

"The car will arrive at eleven o'clock."

"I shall be ready," she said confidently.

It was a bit tricky to manage the zipper on her dress, but it was a lovely dress: A-line, strapless, tea-length; the soft white fabric of the skirt was beautifully embroidered, and hints of beading glinted in the sunlight flowing in through the windows; a satin bow tied at the waist, draped down the skirt; a lace overlay extended two inches past the hem of the skirt.

She settled a soft white shawl around her shoulders. She had wound a thin satin ribbon through her French braid. The square cut cubic zirconium earrings and necklace from Gemmy's jewellery box perfectly complimented the dress.

She was ready.

Wyatt rang again to inform her the driver had arrived. Gem buzzed the driver through the security door. Not a hired driver, but a proper chauffeur! He carried her cases down to the car. Gem reached for her bouquet. She was definitely ready!

She took one last walk through the flat.

Off with the old, on with the new, she sighed, then locked the door.

The chauffeur was standing beside a stunning white Rolls-Royce Phantom V. Gem knew a bit about the Rolls-Royce line as Mr Critchley was a devotee of English classic vehicles, and liberally spoke of them during breaks when Gem renewed her defensive driving course.

Traffic was heavy, but the chauffeur deftly guided the vehicle through the streets. The windows, including the one between Gem and the driver, were smoked. She felt cocooned in the plush white interior.

Wyatt was waiting at the kerb as the Phantom arrived at City Hall.

"You look splendid, my dear," he smiled. "You sparkle in the sunlight." He gently touched the necklace at her throat. "The jewellery graces your beauty."

She turned around so he could see the dress. "Not too much?" she asked with a questioning smile.

"You are stunning." Wyatt nodded to the chauffeur that he could leave. "He'll return for us."

"You look wonderful!" Gem admired her fiancé. Black suit, crisp white shirt, and a steel grey tie that set off the grey eyes that mesmerized her. Control! Think! Don't look at his eyes, or you won't be able to move! "New suit?" she teased.

"Impulse purchase. You know how that is," he chuckled, then smiled. "The countdown is over." He escorted her into the building.

The ceremony was lovely, and before Gem could believe it she was Gemimah Forrester Grantham!

The Phantom V was again waiting at the kerb.

"Wyatt, this car is absolutely smashing!" she marvelled as they settled in the vehicle.

"I thought it suited the day. A wedding day should sparkle. As you do."

Gem looked in awe at her wedding ring: a band completely circled in diamonds. "Yes. But you have spent too much money on me," she protested, touching the ring.

"A wedding ring is a symbol of eternity. Remember that, Gem. And whatever I purchase is well worth the price," he said firmly.

"Well, thank you," she gazed into his eyes. She could look at him for simply hours at a time!

He slipped his arms around her, his kiss long, teasing. "Hmm, a wedding lunch, and then the honeymoon," he murmured.

"Yes," Gem said softly. When he drew back, she reached her hands up to his face to draw him back to her.

It was a few minutes before Gem realized the Phantom V was again parked at a kerb.

"We have arrived," Wyatt said softly.

The Cumbria. A very elegant London restaurant.

"Not of your choice, I am certain," Wyatt said smoothly, "however, the occasion wants a bit more than a pub lunch."

"Yes," Gem agreed, looking around the restaurant.

A bit more indeed: elegant cherry wood panelling, blinding white starched table linen, crystal and sterling silver glinting beneath frosted globed chandeliers.

"A quiet lunch day," Gem murmured as they were seated at their table.

"I reserved the Cumbria for us," Wyatt said quietly.

He fell silent as the waiter poured champagne into gilded flutes. Even the staff was elegant, Gem marvelled: crisp white shirts, black bow ties, black trousers, each man as impeccably groomed as Wyatt.

Gem suddenly felt very self-conscious, out of her element, and very shy. Wyatt's world: of which she must now be a part. She felt very alone, and suddenly very aware she had married a man she barely knew.

"This is so very strange," she said softly. "I was alone this morning and now I am married. It's rather like walking into a cloud." Or off a cliff, she thought uneasily.

Wyatt handed her a flute, taking the other. "Oh, I promise you, Gem, you shall never be alone again," he said firmly. "We shall have many, many years together to remember this day. To our future, Gem. Forever is a very long time." He tapped his flute against hers.

Their lunch was served immediately to Gem's surprise; steak and salad. Wyatt had obviously ordered the menu when he had booked the restaurant.

The Cumbria's staff was extremely discreet, appearing only to serve and remove tableware, and to present a very small white wedding cake, decorated with white roses across the top and cascading down one side.

Wyatt had thought of everything, Gem observed; he was a man of details.

"Now may I ask our honeymoon destination?" she teased, forcing herself to relax, champagne tickling her senses as Wyatt refilled the flutes.

"Yes you many!"

"Where are we going?" She laughed at his stalling.

"It's a surprise. You may ask but I shall not tell," he chuckled.

"Very clever. Banter," she gave him an exasperated smiled.

"I was expecting some sass by now. Are you feeling inhibited by your surroundings?" Wyatt teased.

"Yes," she admitted, "and I am not dressed for sass," she added lightly.

"No more wedding dresses for you then," Wyatt teased. "Drink your champagne, relax. Don't let your steak cool."

Gem was careful with the champagne, wary it would be more potent than her regular brew. Control. She did not want a cog to slip. The cake was cut, served, eaten, the remaining section boxed for the honeymoon dinner at their destination.

She nestled against Wyatt as the Phantom V drew into traffic for the next leg of their journey.

"This is luxury," Gem sighed happily.

"Do you enjoy luxury?" Wyatt slipped his arm possessively around her waist, holding her close.

"A taste of it might be pleasant, but any more than that could be overwhelming."

"Diamonds, furs, a private jet, designer fashions, a private yacht," Wyatt murmured, his lips brushing her hair.

"I have enough diamonds, truly," she said, holding up her hands. "I don't wear fur. Designer fashions are over-priced, and I don't pay for names."

"Ah," Wyatt listened, tracing a finger across her throat.

"And you don't own a private jet or a yacht. Do you?" she sat up suddenly, turning to look at him, frowning at the thought of flight and oceans.

"No, I do not," he shook his head. "A waste of money."

"Indeed!" she settled back against him. Thank heaven! No flight or oceans!

Wyatt frowned, perplexed at the satisfaction with which she had accepted his reply. Enough diamonds, indeed! And they all belonged to him!

"I do not own this car," he said matter-of-factly.

"The Jag suits you."

"I do own that," he admitted.

"Mmm, lovely." Gem fell silent, enjoying each moment as it came.

A half hour later she was no longer relaxed, as the Phantom V turned into the car park of a private airport, continuing through a gate to the runway. She stared in dismay as the classic car drew to a stop alongside a helicopter.

The chauffeur opened the door and before Gem found her voice to protest flight, the luggage was transferred to the helicopter.

Wyatt introduced the pilot to Gem; she managed a handshake and before she could speak, Wyatt had her belted into a seat. Her head pounded, blood rushed to her ears. She realized Wyatt was speaking to her over a headset she didn't realize she was wearing. They were airborne.

"What?" she tried to concentrate on his voice, forcing her breathing to a slow, steady rhythm, concentrating on not losing her lunch.

He was pointing to the Tower of London, Big Ben, Parliament, as the helicopter circled the city beneath them.

Damn and Blast! Why hadn't she listened to Mr Cawley! Anxiety pills would be greatly appreciated! She hadn't told Wyatt of her dread of flying; she had put herself in this position. She hated the sound of the helicopter blades, the view of only sky and clouds that met her eyes. What had Gemmy, their parents, Mr Portermann seen as the Pilos left the sky that night? She was shivering; she pulled her shawl tight around her shoulders. Her head ached. Wyatt was pointing at something again. The helicopter dipped, circling Stonehenge, then climbed again. Blast! Next, the coast, she feared.

Count to twenty. Again. Again. Control. The private landing strip. Count to twenty. Do not faint!

Wyatt's voice drifted to her ears. "Is this your first flight in a helicopter?"

Was It? Yes! Gemmy greatly enjoyed helicopters. She had wanted to take flying lessons. She always sat in the co-pilot seat when she flew with Mr Portermann. She would have been in the co-pilot's seat that night. She would have seen the water, the waves, rising up to meet the Pilos as it slammed into the sea.

Gem's head ached. The blasted helicopter blades drummed into her brain. Answer Wyatt!

"No," she shook her head. "No." She also had to be Gemmy.

Wyatt was pointing out the window to her left.

Green. Trees. Grass. And then finally the helicopter was landing.

Lovely, Gem thought in dismay. An island. A helicopter and water. Flight and a massive body of water!

Wyatt's hands were on her waist swinging her down to earth. She felt inclined to drop to her knees to kiss the grass beneath her feet, but that action would require an explanation.

As the helicopter took flight once more, Gem steeled herself to view their destination. She saw water.

"Gem!" Wyatt was holding out his hand to her. Behind him was a white multi-story cottage with balconies, flowering trellises, a huge green expanse spreading down to the water. And water as far as she could see.

"Where are we?" she asked, dazed by her surroundings.

"Isle of Wight. Short walk to Ventnor." He coaxed her around the corner of the building and into the cottage. "This is Marigold Cottage."

"Marigold. A very pretty name." She could relax now and not look out the windows at the view. The English Channel. Might as well be the Pacific Ocean.

Wyatt gave her a quick tour. The cottage was very large, the interior cosy with overstuffed chairs and sofas, likely accumulated before the Second World War by the looks of the style; built-in bookcases lined what originally would have been called a drawing room; framed original oil paintings hung above the bookcases which overflowed with hardcover and softcover books. Her eyes were drawn to the paintings, but Wyatt guided her along through a dining room, modern kitchen, laundry alcove, covered porch and sitting room, maid's room, cook's room, and finally back to the main hall and to the staircase.

At the top of the stairs a wide hall ran the length of the house, a half dozen closed doors on each side led to bedrooms and separate baths.

"The master suite." Wyatt opened the last door on the right.

It had a sitting room, comfortably furnished with overstuffed chairs, a sofa, and tables. Double doors led to a balcony overlooking the Channel. To the right of the sitting room was the bedroom, two separate bathrooms, and dressing rooms; there were chests of drawers and a lowboy. The rooms flowed one into the other, giving the area a spacious feel.

"Wander about while I fetch the luggage," Wyatt suggested. "We are on our own here. No staff, however the caretaker stocked the fridge. There are excellent restaurants and pubs on the island, and Ventnor is only a ten minute walk down the lane.

"Perfectly private," Gem mused.

"Precisely," Wyatt smiled.

He brought her cases and left her to unpack.

"What about your luggage?" she queried, confused.

"I brought it over earlier this week when I checked on the arrangements. Oh- your bathroom is the one with the pink towels."

Gem unpacked; there was more than enough space for her clothes. She changed from her wedding dress into a long skirt and sleeveless tee, leaving the earrings and necklace on the lowboy, then she went to find her husband. Husband! A musical sound! Wyatt had planned this surprise for her and she was damned well going to enjoy their honeymoon! She was just going to avoid water. And she was not going to think of the return journey to London!

He was in the kitchen checking the contents of the fridge.

"Let's find a pub," he winked at her. "Celebrating more to suit you."

"You are a tad overdressed," she teased.

"Five minutes," he promised.

When he came downstairs, Gem handed a package to him - the five photos she had had matted and framed.

"When did you take these shots?" he queried, stunned by the gift.

"At Bath and Salisbury. Do you like them?" she asked shyly.

"Very much indeed," he kissed her, then handed her a small box.

"It's lovely!" Gem gasped at the silver pendant on a chain. Or was it platinum? It appeared to match the rings he had placed on her finger.

"It's a watch." Wyatt hooked the chain around her neck then showed her how to open the pendant.

Gem enjoyed the stroll to the pub; she did not have to look at the water. They had a pint, pub grub, and a half pint before walking back to the cottage. The evening air was warm, and a light fog was stealing in to obscure the Channel waters. Wyatt's arm was around her shoulders; he stopped to kiss her, his fingers stroking her cheek. How long would it be before she would be able to look at him without having to fight for breath and control of her desires? Lord! He was smashing!

"I'll check the weather forecast for tomorrow," he said when they entered the cottage.

"Yes," Gem replied breathlessly. Breathless from his kiss and his silent suggestion.

She took a quick shower, deciding on the green nightgown and the matching dressing gown; they were a bit fancy for her, but well suited the 'occasion' - tossing away the pinafore.

Wyatt was waiting for her as she stepped from the bathroom; the duvet and sheets were folded back on the bed. The room was dark save for the moonlight streaming in the windows. And the light behind her.

Wyatt walked towardss her, supremely handsome in his dark dressing gown. He untied hers, letting it slip to the floor.

"Why do women wear nightgowns?" he murmured. He reached up to pull the band from her braid, his fingers gently combing through her hair to remove the satin ribbon.

"Because they are beautiful?" Gem suggested, her breath catching in her throat at his sensual touch.

"Women or the nightgowns?"

"Both?" she queried faintly.

"Unnecessary."

"Women or nightgowns?" Gem countered, her heart beating wildly.

He reached behind her to switch off the bathroom light, leaving them as shadows in the moonlight.

"Nightgowns," he said firmly.

"For warmth then?"

"Unnecessary." He drew her over to the bed.

Gem was the proverbial nervous bride, but she was more than willing. He tossed the duvet to the floor, following it with their clothing.

"I'll keep you warm," his voice was husky.

She could only let him lead the way. His hands caressed her flesh, stroking, his lips teasing hers, then roaming, enticing, sending shivers through her entire body. She met his kisses with a passion heretofore unsummoned from her soul. His fingers stroked her thighs, then moved, gently commanding.

He spun a magical web, overwhelming her senses. He led the way, lowering his body on to hers; her mind teased that this was the time the camera drifted to the sky in films. The pinafore was about to be tossed. He murmured in her ear, shredding her mind as his body tore hers with pain.

"Well met, Gemma! I know who you are!"

As Gem gasped in pain, her body and mind reeling, he pulled back. The look on his face instantly changed from triumph to shock, then to fury.

"Damn you! What have you done, you conniving, vicious bitch!" he rasped.

He grabbed his dressing gown, dragging it on, then threw Gem's at her.

She clutched it to her breasts, staring at him, speechless, her mind spinning out of control, her stomach churning.

Gemma! Stars exploded in her brain as if he had struck her.

Chapter Six

With fingers numb and shaking, Gem pulled on her dressing gown; her brain was shutting down.
Gemma!
She buried her face in her hand. She couldn't think! Had she somehow slipped into an alternate universe?
Wyatt snapped on the lights, blinding Gem with the brightness.
"How did you convince James you were pregnant, damn you?" he spat out. "Did you give him drugs? Get him drunk? He fought for years to get clean and sober, you conniving bitch!"
Gemma! James! He thought she was Gemma! James had to be the young man in Barcelona!
"Oh my God!" Gem groaned. What did they have to do with Wyatt? "I don't understand," she shook her head in bewilderment.
Wyatt grabbed her right hand, dragging her from the bed.
"This ring! James gave it to you! It had been in our family for over two hundred years! Do you think the design of your engagement ring was a coincidence? You told him you were pregnant! He took the ring to propose to you, you accursed bitch! Pregnant!"
Gem's hand flew to her mouth. 'Our family!' "I don't understand - your name?" Gemmy would have recognized the surname.
"He used Smythe - his middle name - our grandmother's maiden name. James wanted to succeed on his own merits - not because of the Grantham name," Wyatt said harshly. "He had lived in my shadow too many years."
Gem helplessly shook her head. She couldn't defend Gemmy or herself. She couldn't bear to look in his eyes.
"James loved you! You were the first woman he ever loved! He wanted to marry you. To raise a family with you! Did you get him drunk, then tell him later he had made love to you? God what a liar you are!"
Gem felt his glare burning her flesh.
"You told him you had to go to Australia to finish your PHD thesis. But you had completed it last year - so you told me!" he ground out the words. "Another lie!"
"He was so proud of you! He wanted to keep you his lovely secret until you could announce your wedding plans. He purchased that flat you insisted was perfect for the THREE of you! It took nearly every cent he had! You rang him every day for a fortnight and then nothing! Not a word from you for nearly two months."

Gem's blood ran cold. She knew why there were no more phone calls, but she couldn't tell Wyatt. Tears began to trickle down her cheeks.

"You deserted him and you were carrying his child! Ha! He haunted the airport in Barcelona, waiting for you to come back to him! Praying every day you would magically come back into his life!"

It would have to be magic, Gem thought miserably. How could this possibly become worse?

"And then there you were! At the damned airport! You walked straight past him! When he caught up with you he said you looked at him as if he were a stranger!"

Wyatt shook his head in revulsion. "Have you played so many men that you don't even remember them?"

Gem groaned. "I promised him I would return the following day. I had to go to Milan." Someone would have died if I hadn't taken that flight. "But then Milan got fogged in. I couldn't fly to Barcelona for two days. I waited at the airport for ten hours, hoping he would come," she said helplessly.

"Why the hell didn't you ring him from Milan? You could," he said slowly, "have gone to his old flat. Why didn't you look for him?"

Gem couldn't admit she hadn't known James's name.

"You couldn't give him ten minutes at the airport! What was so damned important in Milan that you couldn't give ten minutes to your fiancé," he spat out the last word, "whom you had not seen in months? He thought you had killed his child. The child that had never existed! What was so damned important? A cathedral? Another mark?"

Gem stood numbly. She could not reply.

"You still wore the ring he had given to you." Wyatt waited for her to speak, but she remained silent. "Cat got your tongue, Gemma?" he demanded.

His speaking her sister's name stung more than his sarcasm.

"You waited for him for ten hours and he never came. Shall I tell why that was so? James waited for you for five hours. Then he went to a bar and got drunk. Sober for six years and he crumbled. - Because you had deserted him and killed his baby. He was stumbling through the streets. He stepped in front of a lorry!"

And so much worse, Gem moaned.

"I flew to Barcelona to hold his hand while he lay dying, pouring out his heart about his beautiful Gem who had deserted him. How he had loved you so! How you had deserted him once and when he found you again you had destroyed his child. Then you deserted him again without any explanation!"

Tears streamed down Gem's cheeks. All her thoughts of Gemmy's sweetheart, waiting at Oscar's, hoping he would appear - and all that time he was dead.

Wyatt threw up his hands in disgust. "You killed James as neatly as if you had driven a knife into his heart."

She still couldn't explain. She could offer no defense. She couldn't defend dear Gemmy, nor ease Wyatt's pain at the loss of his brother.

Wyatt smiled grimly. "I wanted to hunt you down but I didn't know where to begin. I didn't even know what you looked like. James only called you 'Gem'. His Gem!"

He angrily paced the floor. "But then I discovered a treasure trove while I was clearing out James's flat. The flat he purchased for you! Photos of you. I still had no name other than Gem, but I had the photos!"

"Photos," Gem said warily. Their family had always strenuously avoided having their photos taken by anyone outside of their family.

"James was so right. You are beautiful. Exquisitely beautiful! I was planning to search for you, but then miraculously you appeared right before my eyes. And two Americans were kindly hailing you as Gem - whom they had met in good old San Francisco."

Wyatt gave a sardonic chuckle. "And the rest was so easy. For being such a cunning woman, you were a remarkably easy target. And so began the Game. Always think of my Game with a capital G, my dear."

"How clever of you," Gem said, bitterly devastated. She felt hollow. She had truly, foolishly, believed he loved her. Instead she had a stunningly handsome, fascinating husband who hated her! If dreams crashing were audible, the heavens would have been staggered by the thunderous clamor coming from her heart.

"Well, you certainly have won your game then, haven't you," she said numbly. How could she possibly feel more hollow than she had the weeks after the Pilos went down? But she did. She didn't think she could ever hurt as deeply as she did now.

Her pinafore. Her Jane Austen world. His shark-infested, gritty world of reality.

Oh! Mrs Brown! How right you were! Definitely out of Wyatt Grantham's league!

"I thought you loved me," Gem could barely catch her breath. How incredibly foolish she had been!

"I never spoke a word of love to you. I said I wanted you to spend the rest of your life with me," he said curtly.

"So very clever of you. Game over," she said softly, fighting to control her nerves. She refused to let him see he had succeeded in destroying her.

She had thought Wyatt the Perfect Man. He was still perfect. The Perfect Monster! How many women had married their Dream Man only to discover he was a grisly nightmare?

She struggled to keep her voice steady. "I am more sorry than I can say about James. It was my fault that he died," she said softly. She had saved one life and lost another.

A slipped cog.

'A courier's job seems innocuous, easy...but remember ladies, always think as carefully as you can...one slipped cog and someone could die...you or someone you love, or someone whose death you will never hear of...but one slipped cog is death for someone', Mrs Brown's words of the Gems' first training day stung Gem's brain.

And this time it had been James.

"You needn't concern yourself with the annulment," Gem said flatly. "I'll have the formalities started as soon as I return to London."

She wanted to be angry, but even that emotion had been lost to her for weeks. Gem pulled the rings from her fingers, handing them to Wyatt.

"Annulment!" Wyatt jeered. "Oh no, Gem!" he dragged out the words. "There will be no annulment. There will be no divorce. You are my wife, and you will remain my wife. You will wear the rings I gave you as a constant reminder that you are legally bound to me for life. You will wear the ring James gave you as a constant reminder of the vicious, selfish game you played on him." He laughed haughtily. "You've had your fun playing games with men, Gem, but now the tables have been turned. I own you now. You are going to be the most dutiful, devoted wife a man could ask for. You are going to jump when I snap my fingers. You are going to give me your utmost, undivided attention. No other men will exist for you now. I don't know for whom you were saving your virginity, but as we both now know, I captured it. And you."

Gem's jaw dropped as he spewed out his vile words.

"You expect me to 'pretend' to be your wife?" She couldn't believe his words.

"No pretense. You are my wife," his voice became dangerously silky. "And heed my words, Gem. Don't ever try to play me for a fool. You cross me just once and I will make your life miserable. I am going to enjoy your brilliant mind. I am going to savor your exquisite body in my bed, day after day, night after night. I promise you, you will be kept too busy to wander. I am going to enjoy training you to please me in every sense of the word. I do really and truly own you now."

And then the anger returned. Gem exploded.

"You have lost your mind, Wyatt Grantham, if you think I am going to remain in your presence for any longer that it takes me to get the hell out of this house," she spat out the words.

She stalked to the lowboy, wrenching open the drawers, grabbing her clothes.

Wyatt strode to her and tossed the items in her hands back into the drawers, then slammed them shut. He leaned against the lowboy, arms folded across his chest. A sardonic smile came to his lips. Gem backed away, wary of his confident attitude. He couldn't legally force her to stay, she reminded herself.

"As I said, my dear wife, I have photos."

What photos could possibly give him this unshakeable confidence?

"What ph-photos?" she stammered. What could he possibly have that he believed trapped her to him?

"Photos of you in Barcelona. You were wearing the ring, by the way. Photos of you in a city garden. Do you recall the day? You were having a conversation with a quite world famous - or shall I say infamous - criminal. I don't believe I need to mention his name, do I? Or perhaps I do. Tell me, my dear, how many notorious, elusive master criminals do you know?"

Gem stared at him, dreading the point of his remarks.

"Does the name John Staunton mean anything to you, darling?" he drawled the last word out in a nasty tone. "James apparently snapped the photos without your knowledge. Perhaps he was a shade too early to meet you one morning?"

How could matters possibly keep getting worse? Gem groaned inwardly. Another slipped cog. Photos! It couldn't get any worse. Could it?

It could.

With three words.

"Gemma Louisa Lawson," Wyatt said silkily.

Gem sank to her knees, wrapping her arms around her shoulders.

"I found a passport in a magazine in James's flat."

Curses! Damn! Blast! The damned passport Gemmy had lost last spring! That's why Wyatt had called her Gemma! That hadn't clicked before in the maelstrom of thoughts spinning out of control in her brain.

The lost passport. A very especial passport. The micro-chip in the binding. The passport Harry had nearly had a stroke over when he had to replace it. He had grudgingly flown to Spain to hand the replacement passport to Gemmy.

"Damn, damn, damn!" Gem groaned painfully, rocking back and forth on her knees.

Gemmy didn't exist. Wyatt had a passport for a non-existent person!

"An illegal passport, bearing a very striking photo of you, my dear wife, and all your vital statistics," Wyatt laughed heartily. "I can tell by your - uneasy - reaction that I have won another Game. Photos - Game Won. Passport - Game Won. Owning you, Gem - Game Won."

He reached down, gripped her wrist and pulled her up from the floor.

"I wonder, Gem, Gemma, Gemimah," he teased, "what would be the legal consequences of a forged passport AND the incriminating photos?"

"God! I shudder to think," Gem admitted, feeling more desperate that she had said her words aloud. "Wyatt, please! Please give me the passport and the photos! I can't tell you how important they are to me!" she tearfully pleaded.

"I can only imagine," he said dryly.

"Oh no, I promise you, you can't possibly imagine," she countered plaintively.

"More promises from beautiful Gemma," he chuckled bitterly. "Game Over, my dear. NO further games of your devising. I hold all the rules to all future Games. The passport and the photos are in a very secure place and only I am aware of that place. If you step one foot out of bounds of the rules, photos and passport go to the tabloids. You linked with John Staunton in the public eye. Might make things a bit difficult for you. The press has an insatiable thirst for scandal on any level. I repeat: your games are over, my dear."

A safe? - no doubt at his home, office, bank? It could be any of the three, or at some other site? He travels so often. Germany? France? Belgium? Norway? Scotland? Spain? Those were just the countries he had traveled to since she had met him. It could be anywhere in the world. Damn international travel!

Gem was trapped. The passport could not be explained away. The photos would be the end of a brilliant British agent - Agent 1, who masqueraded as a notorious, extremely elusive master criminal. Paul Andriani was Agent 1. John Staunton did not actually exist.

One phone call to Mrs Brown or to Harry could put Wyatt Grantham in solitary confinement somewhere in the world where no one would ever find him. Or he could be accused of trumped up charges of treason - not so trumped up, actually, since he had items in his possession he SHOULD NOT HAVE. But Harry and Mrs Brown were not available.

Oh, the Agency was good! But slipped cogs happened. And one slipped cog now and all the undercover work searching for the Pilos could leak, setting off a domino effect causing problems in other countries - for couriers, agents, and governments.

Harry battled every day to protect Agency security in a world that simmered just beneath the surface with hate, terrorism, blind distrust, and pure greed. A cog slipped just for a moment in one small corner of the world and God only knew what would occur; political explosions could kill halfway around the world. Resurgent Nazi groups, skin-heads, terrorists - were just a few of the ticking time bombs Harry tried to monitor.

And what domino affect would the sudden disappearance of Wyatt Grantham have in the world? Mr Cawley would possibly have the authority to put the brakes on Wyatt, but what cogs would slip if he did disappear? Disappear on his honeymoon. And Gem would be the suspect! Oh Lord! Gem's brain was so confused.

Wyatt watched Gem, wondering what she was processing in her brilliant mind. She did so fascinate him.

Gem stood staring uneasily out the window.

She couldn't defend herself. Wyatt had convicted Gemmy of James's death.

Gemmy was dead and out of Wyatt's reach. She no longer existed on paper anywhere - except for the blasted passport.

The photos were a side item as the likeness perfectly matched Gem.

Yet Gemma Louisa Lawson wasn't dead. She existed to Wyatt as Gem - still very much alive. (Only dead inside).

And again: Gem had admitted to Wyatt that she had known about the missing passport. She couldn't brush that off.

Had Gemmy known about the photos she would have destroyed them. Alas, that chance was gone.

Gem had the ring James had given to Gemmy.

Gem knew about the meeting at the airport in Barcelona. She had been there.

Gem had promised to meet James - and had acknowledged the promise.

Gem had spoken of HER thesis to Wyatt - there was a discrepancy of a year - but still it had been mentioned.

Gem had traveled a great deal - had chatted to Wyatt about her travels.

Just a trifling bit of facts Gem could not deny or dispute that she was not, indeed, Gemma Louisa Lawson, the woman with whom James had fallen in love. The woman who had deserted James - and destroyed their baby - well, lies according to Wyatt.

Thus she - Gem - was the woman who had 'tricked' James - lied to him about being pregnant - but Gem now knew that Gemmy had been pregnant when she went on her last flight.- Gem could not explain that to Wyatt.

Wyatt knew Gem hadn't been with a man before him. Which made Gem again a liar?

Thus Gem had lied to James, deserted James, stolen from James - the ring. She was the only Gem who now existed.

She couldn't tell Wyatt the truth. Agency SOP. Do not involve civilians. Wyatt wouldn't believe her anyway, unless the Agency backed her up. And they would.

And Wyatt would be furious that hiding Gemmy's death had caused James's death. He certainly wouldn't keep quiet about that. He would go to the tabloids - cogs would slip and explode all over the world.

Gem's head ached from trying to sort the jumbled mess of her thoughts.

What would happen to the employees of GEI if Wyatt suddenly disappeared from the face of the earth - if he was accused of treason? Could the Agency make treason charges stick? What kind of power did Wyatt hold in the U.K.? Internationally?

Gemmy had loved James. James had died because of Gem's decision. It had been his choice to drink that night, but her actions at the airport had affected him. She was not going place blame on someone in the throes of dark despair. Wyatt loved his brother as Gem loved Gemmy. He did not know the truth. And could not know it until the Pilos was found, and information discovered and sorted.

'We do not forget our own. We do not give up our own,' Mrs Brown had said.

Civilians. Caught in Agency SOP.

In Wyatt's eyes Gem (Gemmy) had played James, and Wyatt had served the final, winning volley.

She had no choice but to agree to Wyatt's terms.

"Are you planning my demise?" Wyatt queried sardonically. "Just a word of warning, Gem. Manton has a letter to be opened in the event of my death. And don't involve your friend Staunton in our marriage."

A slipped cog and Gem could bring down Paul Andriani. She could bring down the Agency.

Gem felt like she was selling her soul to protect the Devil - Wyatt - to protect her heart - to protect her secret life. And to regain her soul, she had to find the Pilos; and discover why seven people had lost their lives; she included James, the baby, and the Vietnamese counter-courier. And what had happened to the Chinese counter-courier? Had he been found?

Eleven day - ELEVEN DAYS - before she could contact the Agency. She couldn't ring Mr Cawley with Wyatt in her orbit.

She couldn't afford a possible distraction, an overheard phone call - possibly another slipped cog. Damn! Cogs were slipping like autumn leaves blowing in a windstorm.

A squall! Could a squall have blown up and taken down the Pilos?

Damn! Focus!

Wyatt had won! He had to win! Gem had no choice but to lose this game of his.

'You'll never be alone again,' he had said at the restaurant that day. That hadn't been a promise from Wyatt. It had been a warning. Or a threat.

The hollow feeling coursing through her body was eating her.

"Have you finished mulling over the agreement?" Wyatt demanded dryly.

"Just because you are wealthy and powerful doesn't mean you have the right to treat women this way!" she shot back.

"Women like you target wealthy, powerful men. Did you wonder why I didn't accept your invitations to your flat or invite you to mine? James wasn't your match, my dear, but I am. Was his lack of wealth the reason you ejected him from your life? If so, that was a big mistake on your part. At the age of twenty-five - today - in fact, he would have received his inheritance. He would have been a very wealthy man. Your error, my dear. Was the person- man in Milan - in your sites as a replacement for James? Or was Staunton? He is a very dangerous man, it is said. And James - he would have given you everything your greedy heart desired. I, however, am not so inclined."

She couldn't protest his challenges.

"Unfortunately for you, my dear Gem, while James was a generous, sensitive soul, I am not. Your cloying remarks that I spend too much money on you will not be uttered by you again."

"Would James approve of what you have done to me?" she demanded wretchedly.

"Let's ask him, shall we? No - wait - we can't - he's dead," Wyatt said in icy tones. "James can offer no opinions."

Gem could see the aura of Wyatt's full fury directed at her.

"You can't stop me from getting an annulment," she tried once more in desperation.

"Actually, Gem, I have two passports for you - under two different names," he reminded her. "How very interesting. Next challenge?"

Blast! The marriage license! Her passport!

"How can you do this to me? Don't you have any conscience?" she demanded plaintively.

"A conscience!" The steel in his voice matched the steel in his eyes. "Have you any concept of what you did to James? You destroyed him without a single qualm - didn't you? You were so 'thrilled' to become engaged! You loved James so much! A lovely small family wedding in Barcelona, you promised. The family you don't have!" He glared at her, seething distaste. "Have you no concept of James's feelings when you not only deserted him, but you disappeared with the family heirlooms he had given you? He was devastated - believing he had broken my trust - as you had destroyed his faith in you," Wyatt's words scalded.

Heirlooms? Plural?

"James was entitled to the heirlooms, but he took them without my knowledge. I was away on a business trip when he met you. I wouldn't have minded him giving you the jewellery had you been worthy of his love. You chose an excellent mark in James - he was so trusting. Unfortunately for you he was not an only child."

Gem was exhausted. She couldn't take much more of his rage.

"I know, of course, precisely what he gave you." Wyatt reached into the pocket of his dressing gown, withdrawing the necklace and earrings she had worn with her wedding dress. "You carelessly left these on the lowboy earlier. Over seventy K, my dear. This ring," he held up Gemmy's engagement ring, "is another thirty K. You are quite the thief, Gem!"

Gem gasped at the knowledge.

"I'm rather surprised you hadn't already sold or pawned them by now. As you are my wife now, you will be permitted to wear these items, but they shall remain in my safekeeping. You shall continue to wear the ring, as I previously said, but I own it."

Gem's eyes glistened with tears. She had no fight left in her. She didn't care about the jewels. Gemmy would have loved the jewellery because James had given it to her.

Her dreams, the hope for a family - shattered.

"Vengeance," she said, blinking back tears.

"Payback. Justice for James. And making certain you never forget what you did to him. And making sure you never have the opportunity to destroy another man or his family," Wyatt said coldly. "Am I stepping on your toes? Had you already selected your next victim? Bury one, go on to the next? Was I to be your next mark? If so - poor you! You are not worthy of being the kind of woman a man would die for."

Lovely. He's marked me as a Black Widow. "I didn't know James had died," she shook her head sadly.

"A bit late to show concern or sympathy for him," Wyatt said coldly.

Gem raked her fingers through her hair. Her mind was shutting down again, the feeling of hopelessness gnawed at her heart.

"You have stalled long enough," Wyatt said crisply. "My patience with you is wearing thin."

"You win," she said miserably. "Game. Set. Match."

"Imagine my surprise," Wyatt said dryly.

"Your behavior is archaic," Gem said bitterly. "Your ethics are scandalous."

"I do not consider you a worthy judge of either my behavior or my ethics. Now cease your fussing and come to bed. Dealing with you the past weeks has been aggravating and exhausting. And save any tears you might decide to use. They do not impress me."

Gem stared at him in shock.

"Come to bed," he repeated.

"No," she sidestepped out of his reach.

"For God's sake, I am not going to hurt you," he exhaled sharply.

"You already have!" she said bluntly.

"You started your game, Gem. But I won it."

"I don't mean that," she blushed.

"Ah - that was unfortunate, and completely unexpected, as you now realize. However, if you had warned me, I wouldn't have believed you," he admitted honestly.

"I'm not sleeping in that bed with you," she insisted.

"We have a half dozen others we can use," he said bluntly. "For better or for worse. You just hit the start of the worse part. I own the Game now. But soon it will be better for you."

He slowly walked towardss her, cupping her chin in his hand, lifting her face up so her eyes would meet his.

"You're shaking, Gem. I promise I'll try not to hurt you." He flicked off the lights.

"It won't always be like this," he said gently, "holding her in his arms. He stroked her hair. "You have great passion within you. Give in to it and welcome the magic I shall give to you."

He had been very gentle, persuasive; she hated herself for succumbing to the mastery of his touch.

"I don't want magic," she said flatly. "I want an annulment."

"I think technically you now want a divorce," he chuckled. "Request denied. Apparently we will revisit our previous discussion about terms. But not tonight."

He fell silent and Gem prayed desperately that he would go to sleep, leaving her alone to her thoughts. But he did not sleep. His caresses took her breath away, leaving her malleable in his hands, and making her despise herself again for letting him cloud her mind yet again.

"Already an improvement," Wyatt murmured. "You wear me out."

Gem pushed away from him, hoping his comment was possible. "Is that a promise?" she sighed wearily.

"For tonight," he caught a lock of her hair and wound it around his finger. "Perhaps."

Gem reached to the foot of the bed for her dressing gown, and pulled it on. "I am going to shower - to wash your scent off me," she snapped, irritated at his cavalier attitude. She grabbed a fresh nightgown from the drawer.

"You should be used to the scent. It's the cologne you gave to James. Very expensive. Did you get the cash to purchase it from your last mark before James?"

Gem glared at him. "You are a horrid person!"

"Look in a mirror, Gem," Wyatt laughed. "Don't keep me waiting too long. And I would suggest a bath instead of a shower. Soak a bit."

To her dismay Gem noticed the bathroom door did not have a lock. She gave a sigh of relief when she heard water running in the other bathroom. She did decide on a bath, scrubbing her skin until it was bright pink. Then she washed and dried her hair. She could hear him moving about in the bedroom. Her mind was dull, but she decided she was not going to run frightened from him. And she was going to avoid looking into his eyes as much as possible. Her brain was tired. She couldn't sort information.

A beautiful day! All shot to hell! A lie! The past weeks with him! All lies! His clever, devious Game! Was there ever a greater fool in the world than she had been? There couldn't possibly be!

SS officers. Submarines.

Blast! Her brain was short-circuiting. She felt like a robot in a science fiction film.

She cleaned her teeth. The wedding dress hanging on the bathroom door reflected in the mirror, mocking her. She stuffed it in the bin liner, hanger and all, knocking the soap on the floor in the process. Blast! She picked up the soap, and it slipped from her grasp twice before she could set it back on the sink. The blasted nightgowns would also go in a bin liner when she could get her hands on pyjamas. The waste of money on the nightgowns! She could always use the dressing gowns.

He tapped at the door and called her name.

SS officers. World War II. SS officers. How the hell could they bring down a plane nearly seventy years after the end of the War?

He called her name again. Damn!

She flung the door open to meet him with a scalding look. She started as he placed a full goblet of wine in her hand. She quickly drained it and was handed another.

"Actually, this is a sipping wine, not a pain killer," Wyatt said in a light tone.

Gem looked past him, refusing to meet his eyes. She saw that the bedclothes had been straightened. The sheets previously blue, were now white. She could hear a washing machine filling downstairs.

She glanced at him, blushing, knowing why he had changed the sheets. And she was sorry she did look at him. His eyes were the flame and she was the dim-witted moth to be scorched. She shook herself, refusing to be trapped.

He was the enemy now, not the mesmerizing, handsome man with whom she had fallen in love. He came towardss her; she side stepped away but that was as far as she got.

"A lovely presentation, all for me. Thank you, my dear. I am impressed," he frankly admired her.

"I'd tell you what I think of you but I don't use that sort of language," she said caustically.

He laughed. "Be careful of the wine. It is very strong."

"The better to block you out of my mind."

"I can help you block your mind," he teased, tracing a finger from her throat to the top of the lace covering her breasts.

"I'd rather have my fingernails pulled out." Her breath caught in her throat at his touch.

"I'll wager you didn't enjoy the first few mugs of coffee you drank."

"A faulty argument. I enjoy coffee now. I detest you."

He ignored her words. "You are very passionate, Gem. Relax. Welcome the sensations I give to you."

"I would rather welcome them from other than you," she seethed.

"Rubbish! You have no experience with which to make that decision. You began to blossom our last time."

"You manipulate me!"

"Yes." His eyes smoldered. "And you are very welcome. Now, stop chattering and start relaxing."

He took her left hand and slipped the wedding and engagement rings on her fingers. "I've done this twice now today, and that is enough. Do not remove them again." He took the wine glass, setting it aside, then slipped the heirloom ring on the third finger of her right hand. "Do NOT lose this ring," he ordered firmly. He took a long sip from the wine glass then wrapped her fingers around the bowl. "Finish your wine. I would like to get some sleep tonight."

"I'm not stopping you," she retorted bitterly.

"Simply looking at you derails my need to sleep to quench other desires," he chuckled.

She glared at him and he laughed.

"Relax, Gem. It's time to sleep."

Gem drank the wine and followed him to the bed. She longed for sleep. It was nearly midnight.

"I sleep on the left," he informed her. "Scoot over."

"Arbitrary," she retorted.

"Knights have to keep their sword hand free. We're a dying breed," he replied.

His words smacked her back to the thoughts she had had when she first saw him.

"You, sir, are not a knight," she said coldly.

"And you, Gem, are no longer a maiden," he said smoothly, placing a long, leisurely kiss on her lips.

Huffily she turned her back to him, moving to the far side of the bed. He pulled her back, wrapping his arms around her. She didn't push him away. She was only too glad to finally sleep.

Gem's eyes opened slowly. Still early morning. Of course. The dark hours.

Two hours of sleep only. But her brain was already sorting.

The sound of Gemmy's voice came crystal clear to her mind: 'Gem! Where are you? Where are you? Help- please dear God! Gem!'

She knew it was only her sub-conscious now looking for her sister. Her twin - her other half.

Wyatt's arm encircled her waist. As stealthily as she could, Gem slowly eased out from under his arm, away from his body, and off the bed. She searched in the dark for her nightgown or dressing gown, finally finding the nightgown on the floor at the foot of the bed.

The moon streamed through the glass doors leading to the balcony. She carefully, soundlessly, opened the doors, stepping out into the cool night air. Pebbles of moonlight dotted the Channel waves.

A lovely choice for a honeymoon, Gem thought bitterly. Actually, it was rather ironic as the honeymoon was a sham. Like her marriage.

Not a marriage. An agreement. Not a honeymoon. A nightmare journey. As if she needed another nightmare!

The Channel. The helicopter. Two items from her own private hell to torment her. Wyatt hadn't known of her fear and hatred of flying and massive bodies of water. She had to concede that if he now knew, he would probably have been very pleased to know his choice of destinations cut her deeply. The Channel was not an ocean, but it certainly had the appearance of one.

She shivered. The night air was cool, but she still felt the heat from Wyatt's hands on her skin. His scent, or rather James's, was again on her flesh and in her hair.

If she had a mind to make the concession, she would admit he had been extremely gentle with her. She blushed furiously at the memory of his fingers, his enticing kisses seductively working his charms on her body. How do men learn to do what they do to a woman?

Blast! She hated him! He had broken her heart! And it ached from the reality of his cruelty, and the love she had felt for him. But her body did not hate him and his masterful technique. How could her body betray her heart!

"Damn me!" she whispered bitterly at the thought of his smile, and lowered eyelids as he had finished his seduction of her.

The pinafore had been exchanged for a waking nightmare.

'You need to be kissed much more often, my dear,' Wyatt had murmured, stroking her hair, holding her close against him.

'My dear'! Gem thought bitterly. God! How I wish he would choke on his words!

'Marry in haste, repent the rest of your life' she paraphrased.

How he had played her! The phone calls, the interest he had shown in her book, the visits to cathedrals, museums, the picnics, the strolls, the pub lunches, the dinners, the gifts! Oh, my God! And now he manipulated her in bed!

Damn him! When he touched her she wanted to protest, then moments later she couldn't think. He would trap her in the spell he wove. How many other hearts had he broken weaving his magic? How many women in the world were with her wanting to put a knife in his back?

The thought shocked Gem. She couldn't think like that! That wasn't her, any more than Gemmy was the bitch Wyatt thought her to be.

Gemmy! And James! Lost from each other!

Gem couldn't bear to think of the pain James had suffered those months and then to have her leave him in despair at the airport.

I am as horrid as Wyatt believes me to be.

That damned night that had ruined so many beautiful lives!

My God, Gemmy! We could be apart for weeks on end and you always knew when I was troubled about something. And I knew when you were troubled or angry. We had our own personal radar. Why can't I feel that now? Why can't I just feel where you are?

And why didn't my radar work to sense why you were so happy that last day? Had I known about James I could have gone to him! His heart would have been broken, but he would still be alive!

Find the Pilos. Find Gemmy, mum, dad, Mr Portermann. Tell Wyatt Grantham the truth and get the hell away from him. He could go away and break someone else's heart.

Where are you, my dearest friend? Tears for her family, for James, for herself streamed down her cheeks. Yesterday morning - now - so long ago - she had felt happy again. Now she was again in the abyss of despair. She was back to 30 May, two o'clock in the morning. One day - perhaps next month, a year from now, or four years, the Pilos would be found. Then Gem might find some peace.

Gem stared across the water, the waves hypnotically willing her mind to the South Pacific. Perhaps one day she would indeed have peace. But she knew now that she would never again be happy. She was lost and would always be as lost as Gemmy and the others. And alone. She would always be alone.

The tears continued to flow. And when the last of the tears ceased, Gem knew there would be no more. She had no more tears; they were spent; and so was she. And as the tears ended, her heart grew cold. And her mind cleared.

Nazis. SS officers. U-boats. What she couldn't retrieve from the back of her mind: U-1408. The U-boat had last made port at Hong Kong. For repairs? For provisions? For -? How could files of certain U-boats be missing - but not others? Specific U-boats. No. The files weren't missing. The files had not been misplaced. The files had purposely been destroyed. To hide the missions? Why?

Her head ached. Champagne, beer, wine, tears.

Was the answer in the Pilos or because of its flight mission? Was the answer on the U-boat, because of its mission, or the messages the crew had transmitted back to Germany? After nearly seventy years anything on the U-boat would have rusted, wouldn't it? Messages received, coded or not, would have long ago disintegrated. However, coded messages transmitted to Germany would likely have survived. Intercepted codes her father had been trying to decipher. The book of intercepted, yet undeciphered codes her father had been working on was massive - a thousand or more pages. How many codes had he broken? Only Harry would know. And where the Blast! was Harry?

A breeze stole by, ruffling the trees brushing against the balcony. There was an almost infinitesimal hint of morning light in the sky.

Gem heard a rustle of sound behind her.

"How long have you been out here?" Wyatt asked softly.

"I don't know," Gem lied, realizing for the first time that lying to Wyatt would now be a great necessity.

He touched her hand. "You're cold," he frowned. "No dressing gown?"

"I'm fine," she insisted.

"No slippers?"

"No." She didn't own a pair.

She didn't feel the cold; she didn't feel anything. She stared at the Channel waters. Damn the oceans! Damn the seas! They kept their secrets, rarely and grudgingly giving back that which was not theirs' to keep.

"Come back to bed before you take a chill. It's nearly five o'clock."

"I don't want to go back to bed," she protested.

"Come back to bed - to sleep." He lifted her easily in his arms, carrying her through the sitting room. He set her down on the bed, rubbing her feet to warm them before tucking the bedclothes around her. He slid in beside her, warming her body with his.

"Go to sleep," he murmured, enfolding her in his arms.

Her eyelids closed; it was five o'clock her mind told her. She could sleep now.

Chapter Seven

Gem awakened at seven o'clock - her mind's current natural clock dooming her to start a new day. She started to stretch; her hand grazed Wyatt's shoulder and he stirred slightly. Blast! She had forgotten he was beside her. She tried to slip away from him, but he tightened his hold around her waist. She tried to push his arm away but his hold was unbreakable.

"Don't you ever sleep?" he murmured against her ear.

"I rise at seven," she grumbled. She was awake; she might as well get out of bed.

"We're on holiday," he nuzzled her neck. "Our honeymoon."

"Your honeymoon," she spat out the words. "I'm in a nightmare vortex stuck in a time warp."

"You are also neatly trapped," he chuckled. "If we must be awake, let us explore the art of intimacy."

"Why don't you take a cold shower!" Gem snapped.

"Water conservation. Now don't speak. Listen to your body"

It seemed like hours before she regained her thoughts. She finally escaped him for a shower, taking extra time to braid her hair, delaying as long as possible before she had to once again endure his company. She had no idea what his plans were for the day, so she put on a ballet length camel coloured skirt and white tee.

Wyatt had dressed in casual slacks and a shirt, and had made the bed.

"Tea." He pointed to a cup on the lowboy and his gaze wandered her from head to toe. "Well worth the wait."

She ignored him, picked up the cup and walked down the stairs. The cottage was immaculate, understated, yet its subdued tones spoke of old money. The furniture was over-stuffed, the type you sank into on a rainy day, with your favourite book and a cup of hot chocolate. The kitchen was updated but great pains had been taken to retain the period feel of the cottage - early 1920's, Gem guessed. The dryer was in use - the sheets from last night - and she felt colour rising to her cheeks. She turned to discover Wyatt watching her.

"No need to feel embarrassed," he said quietly, seeing the flush on her cheeks. "If I had known last night I would have handled the situation differently."

"I doubt that," Gem said bitterly. "You wouldn't have believed me."

He considered her accusation. "Perhaps you are correct," he conceded. "But I would have listened to you."

Wyatt took the cup from her hand, rinsed it and set it in the sink.

"We'll walk to the inn at Ventnor for breakfast. I'll sport you pub grub for lunch and dinner, but I insist on a change once a day."

"I'm not hungry," Gem refused.

"Perhaps I didn't make myself clear last night," Wyatt said evenly. "Your world no longer revolves around you. It revolves around me."

Gem glared at him. This was going to be a tortuous day.

"Stop fussing and get your hat and walking shoes."

"I didn't pack a hat. And you said comfortable clothes. There was no mention of hiking."

Wyatt shook his head. "We'll visit the shops after breakfast." He stroked her cheek. "Your complexion is too perfect to be ruined by sun." She jerked her head away, bringing a laugh from him.

Gem was lost in thought as they walked to the village.

"You're very quiet this morning," Wyatt observed casually.

"I have nothing to say to you," Gem shrugged.

"Really. You were quite chatty when I courted you."

"I didn't hate you then. And you didn't court me, you were stalking me," she snapped.

"Game well played on my part, for we are wed. And please watch your tone," Wyatt said evenly. "I won't tolerate public displays of temper. And you don't hate me, sweetheart. You are in love with me."

"What an ego! You must be so proud of yourself!"

"Satisfied would be the word I would choose. Satisfied by the win and satisfied by you," he winked, his eyes roaming her body.

"Vengeance is mine sayeth the great Wyatt Grantham," she needled.

"Were you this witty with James?" he chuckled sardonically. "I would say he was over-matched. He was the artistic, sensitive brother. Did you grow weary of his gentle soul while you played your game? How foolish of you."

Gem clamped her lips together, wary of what she might blurt out in anger.

"And again speechless," Wyatt taunted. "No witty reply?"

"I do hate you," she insisted grimly.

"Oh, I am going to have such fun with you, my dear," he said dryly.

Love him! Well if love was akin to hate, then she would take the hate.

"You are the most arrogant man I have ever known," she marveled.

"Ah, sweetheart, I am the only man you have ever known," he returned pointedly. "You simply used the others as I am using you. You have finished your games while mine have only begun."

Gem fell silent again. She had had hours of target practice, was quite adept using a pistol. Why did one never have a pistol when one wanted one? She was quite certain Mrs Brown and Harry would have her back in such a situation. After all, couriers never really retired. And she was Agency Family. Ah, what a lovely thought. A gun!

"Planning my demise again?" Wyatt queried loftily.

Gem stumbled over a stone and Wyatt caught her arm to steady her.

"Yes, planning to cooperate?" She gave him a mock sweet smile.

"Ah, I thought so," he looked at her, but there was no smile on his face. "Now seriously, my dear, you truly must watch your step."

Double entendre? she wondered.

The inn was very attractive, posh, Gem frowned. Hopefully the breakfast menu wasn't fussy. Flowers were everywhere, on tables, in corners of the room, the maître d's desk. It reminded her of Auntie Jane's funeral luncheon at her cottage.

To add to her discomfort she and Wyatt were seated at a table overlooking the Channel waters.

"Yer early, so yer get the best view," the waitress bubbled. "This table is a favourite of our patrons." She was very eager to please, and it was easy to see why. She couldn't have been more than eighteen but she couldn't take her eyes off Wyatt. Gem doubted the girl had ever seen a man as handsome as Wyatt - except, perhaps, in films. Well, she too had been fooled - beyond belief!

And because of handsome Wyatt their service was excellent, but Gem's attention was drawn to the view. As it had been in the dark hours, she was hypnotized by the water. The waves swashing against the sandy beach was a knife straight into her heart.

"Gem," Wyatt endeavored to direct her attention from the view beyond the window to the menu. "A bride is supposed to give her undivided attention to her groom," he successfully distracted her for a moment.

"What? - Oh - a garden omelet and water, thank you," she said, turning to stare again at the Channel.

Wyatt watched her with bemused patience, wondering what she found so captivating of the view. Channel waters to the horizon. He didn't honestly believe she was purposely ignoring him. Her violet eyes held a puzzled look, as if she was confused by the waves gently breaking on the sandy shore.

When their order arrived she barely noticed the food, picking absently with her fork at the omelet.

The waitress appeared, expressing concern at his companion's lack of interest in her food, but Wyatt told her all was well.

Gem had had very little sleep the past night. It was a wonder she was even awake now. It had been a long night for both of them, Wyatt mused. She fascinated him. She seemed such the innocent - well actually, physically, she had been until last night, he scowled at the memory of his shock. How she had managed her games in the past without ending up in some man's bed was beyond him. However, he would wear her down and get the answers to all his questions.

It had all been so easy! She had been caught off guard as completely as he had intended. But then he had begun the Game knowing what she was, while she hadn't known that this time she was the mark. If only she was as innocent mentally as she had been physically. Had she been, his lack of scruples would greatly trouble him.

When her appetite returned there was food at the cottage to prepare.

Gem stared at the water, again only seeing the Pacific Ocean. How many islands were there in South East Asia? No doubt thousands. She would have to check the computer. Perhaps the Pilos had missed Darwin for some unknown reason. Instrument panel failure? GPS jammed? The plane could have crashed on an island and not into one of the seas. Still there would be no survivors had the Pilos crashed into a mountain. She knew there were no survivors.

"Where are you, Gem?" Wyatt queried softly.

"Athens again! Can you believe it! Where are you?" came a laughing reply. Gem gasped in shock. Her hand flew to cover her mouth. "Oh no!" She shot up from her chair, bolting from the table and out of the inn.

By the time Wyatt settled the bill, soothed the staff and finally caught up with Gem, she was at the shore staring blankly at the horizon.

'Where are you, Gem?' Gemma had queried.
'Rome, I think! Where are you Gem?' Gemimah had laughed.
'Washington D.C., I think!' Gemma had laughed.

It was a catch phrase the sisters had shared when their assignments had been so solidly back-to-back-to-back, jet lagged and constantly wondering what was the currency and rate of exchange wherever they had found themselves.

'Where are you, Gem?' Gemma had asked.
'Athens again! Can you believe it! Where are you?' Gemimah had laughed.
'Brisbane! Waiting for you!' Gemma had laughed.

'Where are you, Gem?' It was Gemmy's final desperate plea the night the Pilos went down. The same pleading cry that seared Gem's brain every night at the beginning of the dark hours. The plea that coursed through her mind while she paced the floor, searched the computer, searched the books, the dvds, searched everything for an inkling – the slightest clue!

Where are you? Gem thought desperately, staring at the cold, soulless water.

A joke between the sisters that had become a desperate cry for help.

So confounded by Gem's frantic behavior was Wyatt that he approached her slowly, not wishing to startle her. He had found her early that morning on the balcony staring at the Channel waters, as she did now. From the moment they had been seated at the table, Gem couldn't drag her eyes from the water.

Why? he scowled, dumbfounded.

He gently put his hands on her shoulders, turning her to face him. Her violet eyes had a veiled, haunted look. The look, so strange, bewildered him.

It took a moment for Gem to become attuned to reality.

"I'm sorry. Poor manners," she said dully, and gave no other explanation.

Wyatt nodded slowly. "Let's find a hat for you," he said gently.

He put his arm around her shoulders, walking her away from the water. The lane wound through a grove of trees, and with the water out of her sight, Gem could shake off the flashback.

She waited for a scolding, some recrimination from Wyatt, but he did not refer to her outrageous behavior at the inn. She regained control. There would be words later, no doubt, in the privacy of the cottage, but she would deal with that when it occurred.

Ventnor was a lovely island village; the shops were charming and well-stocked, catering to tourists, the shopkeepers friendly.

Gem tried on hats beneath Wyatt's appraising gaze.

"Which one?" she asked

"Which one do you like? Or shall we take one of each?"

"I only need one," she protested. "This one," she decided on the last one she had tried on. She reached into her shoulder bag for cash, but Wyatt sharply shook his head and paid the bill.

Outside, hat now on her head, Gem protested, "I will pay for my purchases."

"You are my wife. Your financial necessities are my responsibility," he said firmly, "however, I do not refer to extravagant purchases."

"Ridiculous," she quietly seethed. "I don't want anything from you. And stop referring to me as your wife! I detest the thought of being married to you!"

"What a difference twenty-four hours makes," Wyatt said coolly. "Hiking shoes, slippers," he directed her into another shop.

Gem courteously suffered the shop assistant's attention, and Wyatt's appraisal of available choices of hiking shoes, then slippers. She wore the hiking shoes, and the ones she had worn into the shop and the slippers were put in a bag; Wyatt again paid the bill.

"We'll drop the package at the cottage. Fetch your camera, then we'll put your new shoes to good use."

Within a quarter hour they were walking across a lush meadow, Wyatt carefully steering her away from water views.

"We shall now have a pleasant chat," he said firmly, "no histrionics."

If he was referring to the inn, Gem was not going to discuss the matter. She was weary of him, of his constant presence at her side. She was weary of him running her life and she had only been with him for less than twenty-four hours - as he had mentioned earlier. How was she ever going to bear living with him day in and day out?

"I've already said I have nothing to say to you," Gem said flatly. "I have no desire to chat with you, nor to share your company."

"This is going to be a very unusual marriage," he said dryly.

"It is not a marriage, it is a prison sentence."

"Well said! However, that is not a proper attitude to have on a honeymoon. Relax, enjoy the fresh air. You enjoy walking in London every day. Just look at this beautiful view," he waved his hand towards the emerald expanse.

"You don't listen, you simply do not listen," Gem retorted.

"I will listen to you when you quit sulking."

Gem turned to snap at him, but he held up a hand to silence her retort. She bit her lip to hold her tongue.

"Now do you have a current driver's license?"

"Yes."

"We will start there." He linked her arm with his, guiding her still further away from the coast. This was after all an island and water was again likely to come into view. "You will need a vehicle to visit cathedral sites. You will have lunch and dinner with me in the city quite often. Then there is shopping you will need to do -"

"Lunch, dinner? No. I refuse to pretend that this is a real marriage."

"Think about the vehicle you would like -"

"I don't want a vehicle! I just want to go home!" she said sharply.

"The Hall is not quite ready in the housekeeper's opinion. She wishes to 'spiff it up' for you - her words, not mine."

"I refer to my flat!"

"I was under the impression that you had sold your flat," Wyatt drawled. "Your home is now Grantham Hall."

Gem shook her head in dismay and frustration. "My home is now hell," she said bitterly.

"Early days yet," Wyatt said easily. "Many marriages have problems at the beginning. I'll sort you out."

His remarks further increased her agitation, but she refused to be goaded into another round of verbal combat. They walked for over two hours, not speaking, each drawn into their own private world of reflection. The wide brim of her hat obscured him from her view, which suited Gem perfectly; she could pretend she was walking alone across the green expanse of the island. The air and sun were reminiscent of the climate of the Mediterranean.

She thought of James. He had been 'clean and sober' for six years. Had Gemmy known he was in recovery? She had loved him. She wasn't a judgmental person; she would have been very supportive to James. And Gem had no doubt Wyatt had offered his best efforts to James during those difficult years.

Her thoughts wandered, ping-ponging from the Pilos to the devastating clash of the previous night, agonizing over a different choice of words. If she had thought more clearly, more circumspectly, would the result have been different?

Wyatt glanced at his watch. She had had time to calm, and he had had time to think, but no amount of reflection could explain her reaction at the inn to his simple query. 'Where are you, Gem?' 'Athens again! Can you believe it! Where are you?'

Gemimah's passport had been stamped in Athens at the end of last May. Between the two passports there were a half dozen stamps from Athens. She had laughed! To whom had she been replying: 'Where are you?' The reply to his query had been so completely automatic - it had been second nature to her. 'Where are you?' Was she replying to a query from Staunton? To her friend? - The recipient of the bird box?

She had been shocked at her reply to his query. Why? Shocked! But she had given no explanation. Nor would she, he decided. She had withdrawn into a shell and he knew it would be extremely difficult to draw her out again. What secrets she held she would not easily share. At any rate, not while she had her guard up. But that could be worn down. It would be a challenge. And it would be accomplished.

Gem realized they had been walking in a giant circle as Ventnor's Victorian architecture once more came into view.

"The Ventnor Botanic Gardens are spectacular," Wyatt crisply informed her. "You have had time to walk off your temper. We shall have lunch at the Royal Garden Café, then tour the gardens and the greenhouse."

Gem nodded, feeling peckish after the long walk, and very little breakfast. The view of the gardens from their table was extraordinary. The food was excellent, the island brewed beer delicious.

The conversation, however, was not to Gem's liking. Wyatt read to her from a brochure of the gardens and made pointed remarks and queries to her.

"The Australian and Mediterranean gardens may be familiar to you as your passports reflect your travels to those areas," he gave her a studied look.

"A rhetorical remark, passports," Gem said coolly.

"I don't believe you've been to New Zealand."

"Same."

"Shall we fly to Jamaica or the Seychelles?"

"No!" she said startled by the query.

"Why not?" Wyatt drawled.

"I don't want to go," Gem forced her voice low.

"Why not? I'll accept a valid reason."

"It is expensive and a waste of money."

Wyatt shrugged. "You can afford the trip. You sold your flat. You insist you have funds."

"I don't have a passport," she gave him a mock sweet smile. Why oh why had she sold her flat? Now she had no home! The Hall was his home!

"Not what I hear," he winked at her. "Finish your salad. The gardens await. Or would you rather return to the cottage for a nap?"

"No, thank you," she said firmly.

"You look very tired. You didn't sleep well last night."

"I'm fine," she insisted, growing weary of people nagging her of her lack of sleep. "And I am finished with my salad."

Wyatt frowned at the salad remaining on her plate. "Someone made the effort to prepare your lunch. Eat it," he leaned back in his chair, motioned for the waiter for two beers, folded his arms across his chest, and fixed Gem with a stern gaze.

The gardens were spectacular as Wyatt had stated, Gem agreed as they strolled from the Palm Gardens to the South African Terraces. Gem shot two rolls of film before they reached the herb garden.

"Staggering!" she gasped in a hushed voice as she snapped a photo of a fig tree that was over a hundred years old.

"Becton would give his teeth for this tree," Wyatt chuckled. "We mustn't tell him about it or he'll insist on building a greenhouse to grow giant fig trees. Becton is the gardener at the Hall," he explained to her.

"Oh," she nodded, wincing at the mention of the Hall. She wondered if the tour of the gardens was supposed to be a reminder to her of the gardens in Barcelona. She didn't trust him now. She could never trust him again.

"The gift shop will close soon, if you want to purchase a souvenir," Wyatt took her hand and directed her out of the herb garden.

"Why should I want a souvenir?" she said coolly.

"A memory of our honeymoon," he raised her hand to his lips.

Gem ignored the kiss and glared at him. "No, thank you! I don't want memories of this travesty, this journey through the netherworld. I'm certain this time with you will be seared into my brain."

"Sweet of you to say so," Wyatt laughed.

He insisted on holding her hand as they walked the lane back to the cottage.

"A lovely day," Wyatt observed. "Are you enjoying our honeymoon so far?"

Gem shot him a nasty look, pulled out of his grasp and stalked away. In three strides he caught up to her, took her arm, keeping her at his side.

"Temper, my dear," he taunted quietly. "Do you like the cottage?"

"It's lovely," she said curtly. "It would be perfect if you didn't come with it."

"Would it have been lovely if James was with you? It was his - part of his inheritance - that is. He would have owned it outright as of yesterday. Our wedding day. The date of all our future wedding anniversaries."

Gem gasped, rounding on him. "My God! You are hateful! Bringing me here!"

"Ah, you don't enjoy the irony? The flat in Barcelona, this cottage, a quite sizeable bank account. What he wouldn't have given you! He only wanted you to be happy, to take care of you. And now that's my job."

Gem gasped at his devious mind - and the fact that he felt no guilt or remorse for his actions. Gemmy's face swirled in her mind. She had been happy - nearly bursting with joy. "You are despicable!"

"I am a good match for you, aren't I," he smiled coldly.

When they reached the cottage, Gem only wanted to shower and change her clothes. Wyatt had other ideas. He won. Yet again.

Gem finally showered and dressed, retreating downstairs while Wyatt was in his bathroom. Retreat was perhaps a poor choice of words for nearly every room had a view of the Channel.

The cottage was cosy, homey, and she hated being there. She stood in the sitting room at the rear of the house, leaning her head against the window. The waves came lazily towardss the island; clouds were forming on the horizon, and a light fog was filtering in. She slipped out the door leading to a covered porch.

Water. The Timor, Arafura, Carpentaria, the port of Hong Kong, the South China Sea. Hong Kong. SS officers. It was there. Somewhere. Why couldn't she reach that thought?

Wyatt watched her from the balcony. Again the water. He watched her for half an hour; she just stood there on the grass, staring out upon the water. He reached into his trouser pocket for his mobile and rang the office.

When he joined her the look was again in her eyes. Haunted. Guilt? No. That word was not in her vocabulary.

"Gem," he moved to stand directly in front of her, blocking her view.

"What?" she started.

"We're walking to a pub for dinner. Fetch a windcheater."

"I don't need one," she shrugged.

"It's getting foggy, the air is cooling."

"I'm fine. If we are going let's go," she turned away from him.

He caught her arm. "Listen, my dear wife, I am not your nanny. Use some common sense."

"Please stop calling me that!" Gem said testily.

"Wife, wife, wife. Legally and in every other sense off the word," Wyatt said smoothly.

"I am a fly trapped in a spider's web," she said bitterly.

"The worm has turned. The shoe is on the other foot. Hoisted on your own petard," he countered. "Enough cliché word play. Windcheater. I am waiting."

The fog was quite thick by the time they reached the village. The pub was quiet, but there would be live music later, they were assured by the barkeep, and business would then be brisk. They both ordered the cottage pie, a pint of one of the island's famous brews, and Gem also ordered a salad, her appetite growing a touch.

"The greengrocer at Ticking Bottom will be thrilled to have you as a customer," Wyatt chuckled.

"Does Mr - your gardener," she couldn't remember the man's name, "plant a vegetable garden?"

"Becton. Yes, but we give the greengrocer as much business as possible."

"Oh," Gem nodded, sipping her beer.

She fell silent and Wyatt watched her, refusing to force conversation. Other customers began to drift in, two other couples, both elderly, and two young men, obviously of the island and regulars at the pub.

Gem looked around reading the room - the scene. She was not going to be rusty as Mrs Brown had suggested. The old habit was a comfort now. She had let down her guard when she met Wyatt. And now more than ever she needed to be sharp. She had to guard against the enemy. And Wyatt was now an enemy.

The elderly couples were tourists, retired probably, judging by their age. Not wealthy, comfortable; the two young men were neatly dressed, and would have felt right at home in good old San Francisco. As she was reading the room, Wyatt went to the jukebox, putting in one coin after another, no doubt selecting romantic music simply to annoy her. At least the music might still him from talking. And, of course, she soon realized, Wyatt, in the guise of a gentleman, selected songs that would not offend the elderly couples. Sinatra was first, a recording droning on and on about love drew pleasant nods from the other customers.

Gem, let her mind drift, absorbing the atmosphere of the pub; very typical - dark woodwork, prints of Ventnor's historic buildings on the walls. A dart board, a worn flag on the wall, likely from the War against U-boats.

The song crept into her mind: 'I'll Be Seeing You', Vera Lynn's voice caressed the words; a lump stuck in Gem's throat, her thoughts pulled back months to that night halfway around the world; her father speaking the words as he kissed her cheek, then one last hug.

Wyatt watched Gem, startled by her total emersion in the music. She stared at her beer, the look in her eyes the same as when she stared at the Channel waters. As the song ended he laid his hand on hers.

"That song seems to captivate you," he said gently.

Gem started at his touch, suddenly aware of the sounds of life around her.

"It's a lovely song," she replied numbly.

"I heard it in the background when we chatted on the phone one night," he murmured.

"Yes. One night a hundred years ago," Gem said, taking a long drink of her beer. It was more than likely he had heard the song for it was usually in her cd player.

He let her reply pass without adding a remark of his own. The water, and now this song. Another mystery of Gemma or Gemimah or Gem, whatever name she chose to go by.

Chapter Eight

Fog completely obscured the water and seemed to envelope the cottage. There were no city street lamps to reflect in the white swirling mass; however Gem could see a faint glow from a lighthouse down the coast. She had closed the doors behind her so the night air wouldn't drift in to wake up her own personal dictator.

A fog horn would have completed the mysterious atmosphere of the dark hours. How many thousands of ships had passed the island during the War years? Destroyers, tankers, submarines, U-boats.

Japan had control of Hong Kong. Had SS officers been sent there for meetings? Roosevelt, Churchill and Stalin had met at Yalta in February, 1945. Had there been a similar Axis meeting in Hong Kong the previous month?

Ardennes Forest battle. Hitler's last major surge.

Hong Kong.

Had anyone at the Agency been posted to the British Embassy in Hong Kong before it reverted back to China in 1997?

Aside from their parents! She had nearly forgotten their parents had met at the British Embassy in the early 1980's, when both had minor diplomatic postings to Hong Kong. That was two from the Agency! And how many in addition to the Lawson-Forresters? Her parents had moved from Hong Kong to England, where she and Gemmy were born - then to Brisbane, then mum and Gem back to England.

Harry, Mrs Brown, Mr Cawley, Mr Choate, and Agent 1- Paul Andriani, even Mr White, were all of an age where Hong Kong could have been in their past. And Mr Critchley. - All who could be considered the crème de la crème of Agency staff. And to what profession had Paul Andriani belonged before he went undercover? And had he had a previous profession would he have made the transition to the criminal element to which he now 'belonged'?

Nine days remaining of her torture tour with Wyatt Grantham. The name alone grated on her nerves.

The fog had been extremely dense when they left the pub. Gem had a faint hope she could lose Wyatt in the mist but he had kept her close to him. No such luck that he would wander into the Channel, to disappear forever. Oh, but there was the letter to Mr Manton.

Hong Kong. Mexico, Coast of South America. What was the connection with the U-boats, missing files and those specific areas of the world? South America. Which country? She searched her mental files.

A fog horn truly was needed to match the eerie lighthouse beam washing, washing through the fog.

Brazil.

Brazil. Mexico. Hong Kong. Three specific targets.

Gem heard the snick of the lock as the doors opened behind her.

Again the water, Wyatt mused. And yet she couldn't even see the water from the balcony. However, the muffled sounds of waves could faintly be heard.

"Are you thinking of jumping?" he said calmly, yawning.

"I'm too much of a coward," Gem replied flatly.

"I can think of many words to describe you," Wyatt began. Gem flinched at a forthcoming litany of sarcasm, as he slid his arms around her shoulders. "But coward is not one of them. Raging insomniac perhaps, but never coward. It's five o'clock."

He took her hand, led her inside and locked the doors.

"You have a dressing gown and slippers. Why do you not wear them?" he demanded, yawning again.

"I couldn't find them in the dark," Gem shrugged.

"Turn on the damned light then." He tucked the sheet and duvet around her.

"I am not a child. Stop hounding me," she protested.

"A child would have more sense," he said, snuggling her body against his. "Now I am cold," he shivered.

She was already asleep.

Instantly asleep? How could she fall asleep so quickly? Was she programmed mentally to do so? And when did she awaken at night? What hour until five o'clock in the morning? And then awake again two hours later?

He yawned again. Hopefully the long hours walking on Saturday, and the fresh air would keep her asleep now until a decent waking hour.

It didn't. Wyatt looked at his wrist watch as she tried to get out of bed.

Seven o'clock.

"Don't you dare move for at least another hour," he ordered.

"You sleep. I'm getting up," she persisted. "I'll prepare breakfast for you," she offered, attempting again to escape his arms.

"I'm in no mood to be poisoned," he growled. "Sleep!"

He didn't relent, and although he did fall back to sleep, he did not loosen his hold on Gem. She sorted through her brain, attempting to gather information from years of reading, to find some connection to the three U-boats.

Wyatt prepared breakfast, Gem discovered when she had showered. He had slept another hour, then neither of them had slept. He was putting the food on the plate when she reached the kitchen. The fragrance of the food cooking tempted her appetite. And Wyatt, standing in his black silk dressing gown, was quite literally smashing to look at. Damn butterflies! They were back! They should have flown away and have been long gone by now!

He glanced at her and she knew he could read her thought. Damn him!

"Later," he winked at her.

"You're disgusting," she muttered.

"Am I just! Sit," he indicated a chair at the kitchen table. "You reminded me that you are not a child," he drawled, setting the plate in front of her. "Thus I need not have to remind you to clean your plate."

Scotch eggs and steak.

"Steak for breakfast," Gem murmured. "Quite odd."

"No salad. I do not prepare salad."

"You should be capable of the job," she said coolly, "as you appear to be trainable."

"That I am not, so get that thought out of your lovely brain. Eat," he ordered. "While I shower you may do the washing up, strip the sheets from the bed and gather your laundry."

"Yes, your Dictatorship!" she retorted with mock humility. He had put the sheets on the bed two nights past and now wanted them changed? A demanding man! His housekeeper at the Hall must either be a harridan to be able to work for him, or a mouse frightened of her own shadow.

"Ah, the sass returns. Lose the edge, my dear. Is the steak to your liking?"

Gem nodded. It was the best cooking she had had since arriving on the island. A comment she most assuredly would not share with him.

Wyatt studied her as she ate. "You appear enamored with the Channel," he observed.

"I hate it," Gem said sharply. "The Channel, the oceans, the seas, I hate it all!"

Wyatt was startled by her vehemence, but did not address the strength of her reaction.

"Then you will not be disappointed our walk today will be in the opposite direction."

"Not at all disappointed," Gem agreed, quieting her temper. "Where to today?" Probably walking across the entire island, which was preferable to being alone in the cottage with him.

"There's a cycle race from Ryde ending at Ventnor. I thought we would walk until we find a location suitable for you to take photos."

Gem nodded agreement. Thoughtful of him to think of something that might interest her. She could not help wondering what was the catch. He was a man of ulterior motives. Still, it would be interesting to see what shots she could manage.

They walked for over an hour, finding an excellent location where the cycling trail curved through a grove of trees. Gem got off a half dozen quick shots. Then was struck by a thought.

"You should take up cycling. That would wear you out," she gave Wyatt the sweetest mock smile she could manage, her voice dripping sugar.

"How touching is your concern for my health. Cold showers, cycling. What next?" he drawled.

"Hang gliding? Parachuting?" She trained her camera on the curve of the road as it disappeared into the trees.

"Without a parachute, no doubt."

"Good idea that. However, I would be willing to pack one for you." She shot frame after frame, hoping the clarity would be sharp. A bit of aberrant fog seemed to waft in from the shore. She followed the next cyclist with the camera as he swept past her. Focus right, click, click, click, click, she loved the sound of the noise as she trained the camera in a steady swerve, following the racer as he rounded the curve to the left of the path. She liked the rhythm of the flow, the speed of the cyclists, the vivid colours of the sport clothes the men wore.

Gem turned to her right to re-start the motion, shooting the next group, then gasped as Wyatt snatched her by the waist, swinging her back and away from the road, her camera flying from her hands as a racer cut a wide swath onto the grass where she had stood a minute earlier.

"You almost flew yourself - without a parachute," Wyatt held her tightly against him.

Gem could feel his heart racing. "Ah - thank you!" She was shaking. "Lord! He could have been seriously hurt!" The thought shook her to her core.

"You'd have come out on the wrong side yourself," Wyatt said hoarsely.

"My error. I got lost in the moment," she sighed, still unnerved by the thought of what might have happened.

"Precisely how you should be when we are in bed," he slowly released her, reaching down to retrieve her camera. "Is it damaged?" he asked, handing it over to her.

She focused on the last cyclists, snapping three shots. "Appears to be working."

"Less expensive than Italian trains then," he chuckled, regaining his composure. He looked at his watch. "Time to go."

Go where? Back to the cottage, it would seem as they retraced their steps. They did not speak as they walked, until Marigold Cottage appeared through the trees.

"The helicopter will be here in two hours. Put the laundry into the dryer, give your bathroom a quick clean. I'll prepare lunch. Do you eat fish?"

"I dislike it intensely," Gem shuddered. "Can't stand the smell of it, fresh or cooked."

"Oh - something else you dislike aside from me," he teased. "Bangers and mash then."

"Where are we going?" she asked hesitantly, and very eager to leave the island, lovely as it was.

"Wash, bathroom, pack," he reminded her.

"You're very practiced at giving orders," Gem said smartly.

"I am. You seem to need direction."

"You are too critical and impatient."

"Time is money, Gem. We are going back to London and we are not going to keep the pilot waiting."

London! Yes! There is a lovely, lovely God! Gem nearly burst with excitement. She would be on familiar territory again. She checked off his list quite quickly. And she could pack on ten minutes' notice; she and Gemmy had practiced the art of immediate departure for years.

One more helicopter flight was the price she had to pay to be quit of Marigold Cottage. And once more on terra firma she would flat out refuse ever again to leave it!

The blasted wedding dress could finally be disposed of in a bin liner. She would rather squash Wyatt Grantham in a bin liner, tie a knot in the top and put him out in the refuse bin - and burn the wedding dress.

He had saved her from a nasty accident that morning. But she wouldn't have been at the race in the first place if it had not been for him! Or in this cottage! Or on this island - waiting to escape! She knew she would never return to Wight. There were too many painful memories invading her mind. She did not want to add this island to her list.

She carried the bin liner downstairs, then her luggage.

"Bathroom clean, packed. Shall I clean your bathroom?" she offered, eager to return to London.

"Done this morning." Wyatt was amused to see her energy and at least a token of her former spirit.

Gem scowled as he lifted the bin liner, then opened it.

"Your wedding dress," he scowled.

"I won't be wearing it again," she said curtly. "I thought to donate it to a Used-A-Bit shop, but it's obviously now cursed."

"It's a lovely dress."

"Perhaps you would like to add it to your collection," she said smartly. "Photos, passports, dress."

"Your - " he left the word unsaid, and she blushed.

"Cad."

"No doubt it was your wit that drew James to you. Pack that," he indicated her dry laundry. "Lunch shortly."

Again a meal well prepared.

"You could apply for a job as a chef," Gem observed coolly.

"I shall add that to my list of future endeavors," he said dryly. "Did you appreciate James's cooking?"

"Hence the dress being in the bin liner," Gem sought a no reply reply. To her surprise Wyatt laughed heartily at her comment.

"You do amuse me, Gem!"

She did the washing up, he took out the bin liners. While Wyatt packed, Gem tossed the remains of the wedding cake and her bouquet into a bin liner and put it out with the trash. Once those memories had been dispatched she wandered the rooms. Gemmy would have adored Marigold Cottage, Gem mused. Gemmy would have filled the cottage with warmth and laughter. And more books! She and James would likely have shared the cottage with their child on holidays, and when the heat of Barcelona became oppressive.

Gem studied the paintings on the wall in the parlor. Many were pastoral scenes, arresting for the unusual delicacy of light and shadows; however, she was most drawn to a painting of an elderly couple seated at an outdoor café, a bottle of wine on the table before them, each holding a glass of wine in a toast to each other, while they held each other's hand.

"That was James's favourite painting," Wyatt said, his voice without emotion. "That was how he pictured the two of you many decades later in your lives. He painted it after you left for Melbourne to finish your thesis. There the two of you would be- holding hands, content to let the world drift by, content and still in love with one another after a lifetime together."

James was an artist; wanting to succeed in life without the Grantham name. And Gem knew he would have been successful. Save for a lost plane.

She felt cruel not replying to Wyatt's remarks, although they were obviously intended to wound.

"It's beautiful. It holds his heart," was all she could say.

When he finally spoke again it was not to reply to her remarks.

"The bird is ten minutes out. Everything in order? We will not leave work for the caretaker."

"Food in fridge," Gem said tentatively.

"For the caretaker. It will last a few days."

She reached for her luggage but he picked up the cases. Gem turned for a final look at the painting. "I'm sorry James. I'm sorry Gemmy," she whispered the words so quietly Wyatt could not hear them, but then even a normal tone would have been lost as the noise of the helicopter blades drowned out all other sounds.

The bird - as Wyatt had called it - waited on the rise above the cottage. Gem turned and stared at the Channel waters as Wyatt stowed the luggage aboard the helicopter.

As he took her hand to assist her aboard Gem balked, pulling back, her heart beating wildly in her chest as she stared at the whirling blades. Wyatt said something she couldn't hear, then with an arm around her waist, another under her arm, he lifted her aboard.

He put the headphones over her head and adjusted the seat belt.

"Close your eyes," his voice came clearly to her. "I'll tell you when to open them again." He took both of her hands in his.

She did as he said.

"When was the Cologne Cathedral constructed?" his voice asked smoothly.

"I don't know," Gem protested. The helicopter blades whined. It was lifting off the ground.

"Construction began in the fifteenth century," Wyatt stated.

"Thirteenth." Gem shook her head.

"I'm certain it was the fifteenth."

"The spires were completed in 1880."

"Six hundred years to complete one cathedral? Someone was lax on the job. Brits would have finished it in a third of the time! Charlemagne is buried there," Wyatt suggested.

"Aachen Cathedral."

"He died in 481."

"814," Gem laughed.

"I believe you are incorrect there. I'm certain the suite number was 481. Westminster Abbey and Westminster Cathedral are one and the same," Wyatt stated.

"False."

"Know-it-all," he teased. "There are no cathedrals in Ireland."

"False."

"I'll agree to 814," Wyatt conceded. "If you text too much on a mobile phone your fingers will fall off."

"Correct," Gem grinned.

"There are no Catholic churches in Italy."

"True," Gem giggled.

"False. There's at least one. The Pope has to go somewhere on Sundays. Pope Leo III consecrated Winchester Cathedral in 1805."

"Aachen Cathedral in 805," Gem laughed.

"Winchester Cathedral is really a song not a cathedral."

"One of each."

"Cows can be trained to stand on their heads, but only on Thursdays."

"True," Gem nodded.

"False. Only on Tuesdays. Thought you would know that one for sure!" Wyatt teased again. "If you stand every cathedral in the world side by side they would stretch to the moon."

"You would only need the Catholic churches to reach the moon."

"Possibly. The Salisbury Cathedral is built on the remains of Stonehenge."

"False."

"It was constructed upside down."

"True," Gem laughed.

"False. Cameras were invented because mirrors had gone out of fashion."

"True."

"False. Try checking your hem in a camera," Wyatt quipped. "Create a sentence using the words bunnies, cat, hop."

Gem thought for a moment. "Bunnies hop, cats cannot."

"Acceptable," Wyatt decided. "But probably inaccurate."

"Inaccurate was not one of the words," Gem teased.

"It is now. Reconstruct the sentence."

"Bunnies hop, cats hop inaccurately," she grinned.

"Lax. You must have worked the original construction crew at Cologne. Cary Grant was born in Finland."

"False."

"Queen Elizabeth was born in Finland."

"Which one."

"Both," he squeezed her hand.

"False."

"Ringo Starr and Dylan Thomas were both born in Finland."

"False."

"Count back from one hundred silently and slowly."

Gem had reached fifty when Wyatt squeezed her hand again. "We are down. Open your eyes."

Her eyes flew open. "Thank heavens," she leaned back in her seat and sighed deeply.

The Phantom V and its driver were waiting for them.

"Do you need traveling supplies?" Wyatt asked, while the luggage was loaded into the boot of the Rolls.

"Traveling? We just returned," Gem protested.

"Wight was the first leg of our journey," he informed her. "Shops?"

"Where are we going?"

"Surprise."

"I don't know if I need anything as I am unaware of our destination," she frowned. Plane, ship, boat? If Mr Cawley ever again made the slightest suggestion to her, she would listen to it! Well, one thing she did need. To get rid of the nightgowns!

"Marks and Sparks," Gem conceded, and Wyatt informed the driver.

Shopping was delightful. Wyatt's mobile rang as they entered the store. Gem shopped as Wyatt listened to the phone conversation, scowling frequently. Gem purchase pyjamas, plush zippered dressing gowns and slippers. There was no argument from Wyatt about who would pay the bill since he was still engrossed on his mobile, and she waited patiently for him to finish the call.

He had surprised her many times that afternoon: the consideration of leaving the cottage in order for the caretaker, his comments to her of James's painting were not sarcastic, the near accident with the cyclist, and his distracting her on the helicopter flight was kindness itself. He was an unusual man. And a frightening one. He could be considerate. He was also very devious. He had warned her to watch her step, and she must do so.

She watched the shoppers: families, mums with their children, young couples flirting, people deciding purchases, arguing over selections, waiting in queue. All going home eventually to their real lives. And she was going God only knew where.

"I am sorry, my dear," Wyatt finally pocketed his mobile. "Did you manage to find what you needed?" He guided her through the exit doors.

"Yes, perfectly. Peter?" she queried, flashing back to what was for her a happier, if unreal, time.

"No, fortunately. We are on the clock now. An early dinner, I think," he said, signaling the driver to pull to the kerb.

The White Rose. Another painful memory. She would rather he had chosen another pub, but then there didn't seem to be any point in expecting that he would understand or care that going to this particular pub would distress her. At the very least she was again on familiar territory, if only temporarily. Familiar surroundings, familiar food, familiar faces, usual regular crowd, Gem read the room.

"The helicopter was not a pleasant mode of transport for you," Wyatt observed as they ate their dinner.

"No."

"Was it the helicopter or do you now have an aversion to flying?"

"I prefer not to fly," Gem ran her fingers through her hair. Hopefully the next leg of their journey did NOT involve flight!

"Did you suffer a frightening flight experience?"

How was she supposed to reply to that? She hadn't been in the Pilos. She had flown nearly two dozen times after the prop plane was lost. Then came the day she couldn't set foot on a plane. "Just burned out," she shrugged. Her eyes wandered the room, avoiding his gaze.

"Flight. Seas, oceans, the Channel, large bodies of water. To what else do you have an aversion? Not cars. Trains, lorries, motorcycles?"

"No."

"When did the burn out begin?"

"Awhile back."

Wyatt leaned across the table and spoke very quietly. "When you speak to me, look at me, my dear."

Gem took a deep breath and raised her head to meet his gaze. She wanted to avoid his eyes! "What?" she said, irritated.

"We shall leave in a quarter hour." The look was there again, Wyatt noted, then it was gone.

Gem nodded.

"No aircraft or vast bodies of water shall be involved," he informed her.

"Thank you," Gem said quietly.

The Phantom V was again at the kerb waiting for them.

"Excessive flight burn-out," Wyatt picked up the thread of the earlier conversation. "It's not surprising. At least two or three flights a week. You're fortunate the government didn't suspect you of trafficking drugs."

"I don't have anything to do with drugs," Gem protested heatedly.

"You slipped something to James, so you can stop denying your innocence. He wasn't a fool."

"You seem to think he was," she could have bit her tongue for that remark.

"He was your cat's paw," Wyatt said coldly. "I'll discover your game sooner or later, my dear."

She thought to challenge him, then thought better of the idea. He had his game. She would have to develop her own. Who had said about chess: in chess and in life, don't play the other person's game, play your own?

The Phantom V stopped and Wyatt stepped out of the vehicle for a few minutes, returning with a selection of magazines.

"Long ride ahead," he informed Gem, sliding various fashion magazines into her lap while he held a handful of car magazines. She would prefer to trade her issues for his.

The next stop was the last stop: Euston Station. A Caledonian Sleeper?

Gem's jaw dropped. "To-?"

"Inverness."

Not the Chunnel to Paris! Wonderful!

"I don't think you will be very comfortable," Gem said doubtfully. "The berths - the - there'll be sharing a loo."

"Not if one reserves a number of compartments," Wyatt said smoothly. "A tad over twelve hours. We'll manage."

With 'a number of reserved compartments' there was no lack of space. What one could do when one had the ready, Gem shook her head. Wyatt used one compartment for his cases, Gem had one for her luggage, leaving one compartment for sleeping. The lower berth was a double but would not be large enough for Wyatt, she reflected. But it had been his decision. There was a large basket of cheeses, meats, three bottles of wine, and glass flutes.

"Why Inverness? - Oh - you must have a cottage there," she said bluntly.

"The company owns a cottage. It's a retreat for staff and their families. Or for sensitive business meetings," he replied. "Your photos of Elgin and Fortrose do not meet your needs for your book. Perhaps the light will be acceptable this week."

Again, thoughtful of him. And why? Just part of his game, she decided. No doubt he had some insidious purpose; perhaps James had painted murals on the interior walls of the cottage or some such thing. It did grate on her to be beholden to him for anything. Whatever his reasons, she would deal with them as she must.

"Thank you," she said as courteously as she could manage. He gave her a curt nod.

Where was the man who had held her hands, spoken so gently on the helicopter? Oh - yes - that was part of his game somehow - to confuse her, to keep her off balance.

"There's a lounge. Decent enough. Shall we have a drink?"

Gem quickly agreed. They had arrived early at the station and had settled in their 'suite' while the other passengers were still arriving for the journey north, thus they had the lounge all to themselves for a few minutes.

Gem smiled at the young bartender as he served their half-pints. Wyatt gave her a mocking smile.

"You'd destroy the lad in less than a week," he said pointedly.

"I simply smiled at him," Gem protested in a hushed voice.

"You can't be unaware of your effect on men. You know how beautiful you are - what men are thinking when they look at you."

"All women are beautiful," Gem scoffed. "Men are simply too ignorant to realize that."

"Touché. Your fair sex has a great champion in you. That does not preclude the fact that that lad hasn't a clue to the real you. Praying mantis comes to my mind," Wyatt shook his head. "My lovely lying, cheating, bride," he whispered.

Gem flushed at the cold remarks. She drank down the rest of her beer, left her chair and walked to the bar.

"Excellent service, thank you," she smiled at the young man, shook his hand, and walked slowly out of the lounge.

Wyatt threw back his beer, tipped the bartender and caught up with her outside the lounge.

"Temper, my dear," he said evenly, escorting her to their compartments, and firmly closing the door.

"I am not a cheat," she snapped, rounding on him.

"A discriminating siren then," he said loftily. "You do not deny being a liar."

Gem counted to twenty four times. She fought the urge to protest, but she could not deny being a liar. She was lying for self-preservation and for the time being she would have to add lie upon lie. She would not do so without qualms, however, and prayed it would not become second nature to her. A secret career for the Agency was one matter; a life of perpetual deceit was not in her true nature. How did Paul Andriani manage to survive constantly living a life of lies?

"As you say," she replied, looking him straight in the eyes.

Wyatt gazed at Gem. It was part of his job to read people. But he couldn't read her. Acquiring information from her could be a long process.

"Why don't you slip into something more comfortable, or slip out of everything," he held her gaze.

And she did as he suggested; she slipped into a comfy pyjama set and one of the zippered dressing gowns.

"Do you intend to join a monastery?" he scowled.

"Why I do believe this was on my shopping list," Gem smiled.

"A shopping binge well wasted."

"Hardly a binge. I am not a spend-thrift."

"Not with your money. I am aware of that. Your most expensive possession appears to be your camera. Or was that a gift from an admirer?"

Gift from my mum and dad last Christmas. "I don't accept gifts from men," Gem said crisply.

"Aside from a small fortune in jewels that you took from James - and gifts from me. You do have a discerning taste in jewellery."

Gem ignored him.

"Why do women wear clothing to bed?" Wyatt's comment paraphrased his query of the 'wedding night'. "The Venus de Milo had only a swath of cloth around her hips. She didn't appear to actually wear clothing - much less to bed - no pun intended."

"The climate of Greece is perhaps a shade milder than England or Scotland." Gem smiled prettily and insincerely.

"You know it is. You have been there many times - as Gemimah twice, I believe, and as Gemma four times."

I can't remember all Gemmy's assignments - and holidays! Gem was caught up short. Assigned countries varied from year to year. Gemmy had traveled frequently to India, the South Pacific, to the States, to South Africa, to Japan, and to many other countries. Of that lot, Gem had traveled to the States and to Greece. Gem couldn't possibly know every stamp that was in her sister's passport. Oh dear! And Blast!

"What?" Wyatt demanded.

"What?" Gem parroted, startled.

"The look in your eyes. You look as though someone just walked over your grave," he murmured.

"A hideous expression," she replied distastefully.

She reached into her shoulder bag for her hairbrush to cover the fact that she dare not meet his eyes.

Wyatt continued to study her. "I will accept the nightgowns. It is as warm in here as Athens. If you become cold I will keep you warm. Toss those other things away," he ordered.

"I will not!"

"Then keep them out of my sight. They are annoying."

"I can't imagine how your employees can bear to tolerate you," she shot back.

"They are paid very handsomely to do so," Wyatt drawled.

The nightgown didn't last long, coming apart in Wyatt's hands.

"Damn things!"

"I don't recall asking you to remove it," Gem snapped. "Why don't you take up knitting to keep your hands busy!"

"Yarn makes me itch," he suddenly chuckled. "Now you're shivering. I'd best keep you warm."

Gem sat in a chair in her luggage suite. Lightning flashed through the room and lit up the sky beyond the compartment windows.

The dark hours. She was so tired. She had been for weeks. She drew her feet onto the seat of the chair, resting her head on her knees. She didn't mind his touch; she welcomed it. But she would never admit that to him.

Sort. Sort. She raked her hands through her hair.

SS officers. James. Gem's head snapped back. James? How the Blast did he enter into the correlation? James?

She rested her head on her knees again. Damn nightgowns. She was chilled. Thunder. And then rain pelted the windows. She enjoyed thunderstorms. Perfect weather for cuddling in the comfy chair, a mystery in hand, a cup of tea on the table at her elbow. But that had not been her habit for months.

James! What would James have to do with SS officers? She was more tired than she realized.

Wyatt was stirring. She prayed he would not waken. Prayers were always answered, yet not as she wished on this night.

He was beside her, stroking her hair.

"I didn't mean to waken you," she said sincerely, no hidden meaning.

"You didn't. Your side of the berth is empty. That awakened me."

"I don't think the berth is large enough to have sides," she observed candidly.

"True. Come back to bed." She had wakened every night so far. How could she manage to stay awake as she did each day with so little sleep?

"I'm not going to sleep. And I don't want to keep you awake," Gem protested.

"I am certain you do not want to keep me awake," Wyatt chuckled. He drew her off the chair and to the berth, switching on the light and reaching for the stack of magazines on the table.

"Let's do a bit of reading. We are on our honeymoon and are expected to spend a great deal of time in bed - perhaps not reading magazines, but so be it," he grinned.

He settled in the berth, pulling her over to lean back against his chest. "Relax," he ordered gently, "I'm not going to touch you."

"You already are," she refuted his comment.

Wyatt brushed her hair to one side, blew on her neck and nipped her ear with his perfect teeth. "But I'm not touching any of the really fun parts," he teased. His arms went around her, holding a magazine open for both of them to view. "Vogue. Let's see if we can find some clothes for you."

"You don't like my clothes," she said stiffly.

"I didn't say that."

"As good as," she was nettled by his words.

"The pale green skirt set, the lily watercolour skirt, the dress you wore to the art fair were quite fine. The Indian print skirt was very striking."

Gem sighed inwardly. So far every item he mentioned had come from Gemmy's wardrobe.

"I'm merely suggesting you might wish to expand your wardrobe. You would look lovely in black. It would shimmer against your skin," he stroked her arm.

"I'm a liar, a thief, and I have terrible taste in clothes," Gem said coolly.

"I didn't say that about your clothes," Wyatt said smoothly.

"As near as."

"Add a bit overly sensitive over minor issues."

"Black? Hmmm. Perhaps I should become a widow. Then I would wear black at all times," she muttered. She had brought Gemmy's black dress with her.

"Another clever remark," Wyatt said dryly. "Often too overused by disgruntled wives. How long have we been married - remind me? Ten years? Reading magazines in bed! Now pay attention," he suddenly teased, "or I will find other ways to amuse me with you."

Gem got the hint. "That's a lovely dress," she said a tad overly sweet.

She was bored very quickly with the magazine from the first page. Style was not of interest to her, but supposed it was of interest in Wyatt's 'league'. By the third magazine she was praying he would fall asleep or that the magazine would suddenly self-combust in a massive ball of flames.

"Wouldn't you rather read your car issues?" Gem suggested. She wanted quiet to sort thoughts.

"What kind of car do you want?" he tossed the style magazines and reached for one of cars. "Porsche, Ferrari. Lotus, McLaren, Interceptor, red, black, yellow?" he flipped through the pages.

"No," Gem suddenly laughed.

"Alfa Romero?"

"No. Not a sports car."

"Mercedes, Volvo, BMW? The Phantom V?" he teased.

"The Phantom V was lovely, but no."

"Panda?"

"No," Gem laughed again

Wyatt tossed magazine after magazine off the bed.

"Classics? Morgan?"

"Lovely, however not practical."

"Oh practical! Land Rover, Range Rover," he continued to suggest vehicles.

"Range Rover. Defender."

"That's a place to begin."

"Black. 1990." And perhaps that would be the end of the car chatter. His directing her life was irritating her.

"So be it. Manual or automatic?"

"Manual," she shrugged.

He fell asleep soon after that, propped against the pillows and Gem did not try to move away from him; she would risk waking him and that might give him ideas.

Had she thought James because of Gemmy? - Some kind of transference? Was there someone in the Agency named James? No, not as far as she could recall. Then what had triggered James in her mind? The cottage? Barcelona? No.

Barcelona had been in her mind too often since 30 May. Flashback from being at the cottage? SS officers. Hong Kong. James.

The continental breakfast arrived at seven o'clock; the train arrived at Inverness an hour later. Wyatt was met at the rail station by a delivery person holding a large manila envelope and keys to a white Land Rover.

They had breakfast at an inn then drove to the cottage beyond the outskirts of the city. Once the luggage was unpacked, Wyatt insisted they sleep for a few hours. Gem lay awake, fighting a rising temper. Do this, do that; he had been at her side nearly every single minute since the wedding ceremony. Day after day after day. She played her gaze around the bedroom. It was a loft with a single bathroom, a double wardrobe, two highboys, two wingback chairs on either side of a table used as a dry bar. The staircase led down to a decent size lounge that was open to the kitchen; another staircase led up from the kitchen to a second loft. There were two additional bedrooms and bathrooms downstairs, but Wyatt insisted on using this particular loft because of the view of the forests at the rear of the property.

"You should be sleeping," Wyatt murmured.

"I can't sleep during the day," she shrugged.

"You can't sleep at night either. You are very tired."

"I'm tired of you telling me what to do," she snipped.

"Oh," was his only reply to her comment. "Put on your hiking shoes, we're going for a walk." He pulled her from the bed.

"Let me guess, we're walking to Inverness for lunch," she groused.

"You are very cross," Wyatt lifted an eyebrow.

"Do you wonder why? I want to be away from you!"

"What is your learning curve, Gem? I have already informed you that is not going to happen."

"I hate you!"

"That may be. However you chose your lot. Now deal with your decision."

"You lied to me! You cheated me!"

"I held you to a promise you made to James. However, you will not run off on me. Toe the line, my dear, and we shall have some peace and quiet in our marriage. Fight me every bit of the way and I will crack down on you. Now swallow your nasty temper and let's go. Hat, shoes, camera!"

The view from the loft was only a tiny part of the wonders of the property- the ducks on the river, hares darting across the countryside, a fox disappearing across a berm. And there were pheasants aplenty being flushed out by the sound of a twig breaking, or a call of another bird in the distance.

"Over there," Wyatt said softly, pointing far beyond the creek. "Do you see it?"

"What am I looking for?" Gem whispered.

"A flash of bright blue."

"With an orange breast!" Gem murmured, adjusting her lens, shooting, shooting, one snap after the other. "What is it?"

"Kingfisher. Back over there now," he turned her to her left. "Osprey."

And snow grouse.

Gem scanned the landscape, shooting, turning slightly to her left, snapping, repeating.

"Any cyclists coming?" she asked with a tinge of humour to her voice.

"Not yet," Wyatt chuckled.

They continued to climb the rise. Gem shot three additional rolls of film before Wyatt called a halt.

"Time to start back. We have dinner booked for this evening in Inverness," he urged her along.

"Posh?" Gem frowned.

"A bit."

"You are quite the arranger. The helicopter, the sleeper car, the picnic basket, the Land Rover, dinner," she observed.

"Ms Clover Wexton," Wyatt replied. "Executive Assistant Extraordinaire."

"Why don't you sleep with her, and leave me alone?" Gem needled. Perhaps he did! That could be a bright spot in her life!

"Ms Wexton has a partner," Wyatt returned smoothly. "Good old San Francisco. They are quite happy, host marvelous parties. They have a horse ranch in Sussex."

"Oh," Gem nodded. Check Ms Wexton off the list.

"Do you ride, my dear?"

"I fall off more than I ride."

"Oh," he mimicked her tone.

"How convenient to have minions constantly at your beck and call."

"She is being groomed for a highly responsible position with the company."

"Highly responsible. Yes, Mr Grantham, No Mr Grantham. Whatever you say, Mr. Grantham."

"In the real world people need to know how to problem solve, they need to know how to get things accomplished NOW."

"A pity you can't groom her to be your mistress."

"No need for one. I have you at my beck and call. Yes, Mr Grantham. No, Mr Grantham. Whatever you say, Mr Grantham," he said loftily.

Gem shot him a look which he ignored.

She showered, put on Gemmy's black tea-length dress, her own stockings and shoes, and put her mobile, compact, and lipstick into her black evening shoulder bag. She braided her hair to show off Gemmy's black onyx and diamante earrings. Crow! Gem thought affectionately. Where are you my dear Crow? I will find you, I promise! Gemmy's wide black scarf would do for a shawl.

"Very modest, no cleavage," Wyatt said coolly appraising her.

He was breathtaking in the inevitable crisp white shirt, open at the throat, no tie, and the suit he had worn to the wedding. Perhaps she could figure out a way to get rid of that reminder. He must have dozens of black suits. Would he notice if one was missing? Probably. What didn't he notice!

Gem gazed at him. If she hadn't already foolishly done so, she could have lost her senses over him. But he seemed in a bit of a temper. His eyes had been light gray when they were hiking that day; now they had deepened to a dark steel grey. It was going to be a dreary dinner and a long evening, she realized in the

Land Rover as they drove to Inverness. He was silent, but she preferred his cold silence to forced conversation.

The restaurant was overbooked, the hostess embarrassed that their table was not immediately available.

"We'll wait in the pub," Wyatt graciously informed the woman, guiding Gem through the door at their right. He knew his way around the restaurant and had obviously been there many times before this evening. Gem could well imagine that the hostess was embarrassed that Wyatt Grantham's table was not available.

But Gem was impressed that Wyatt hadn't demanded better service, hadn't demanded a table should be ready for him. He waited at the bar for two glasses of wine then managed to find them a table in the crowded bar.

"I don't imagine you are frequently asked to wait for a booked table," Gem observed quietly.

"I'm not all powerful Zeus. I don't mind waiting," Wyatt said calmly.

They had barely sat down when Gem heard her name called. Blast! Scotland! Really? She steeled herself for a bad turn. She didn't know anyone in Scotland, much less Inverness.

A young couple approached the table. She was blonde, he had darker hair, but not as dark as Wyatt's. Gem had an excellent memory for faces, but she had never seen these people before.

"I told Greg it was you," the pretty young woman said with a soft smile.

Americans, Gem could tell by their accent. How many Americans had Gemmy known? A slipped cog waiting to happen? Tread carefully, she warned herself.

Wyatt stood and shook hands with the couple, watching Gem out of the corner of his eye. Her smile was frozen. "I'm Gem's husband, Wyatt Grantham," he said pleasantly.

"Greg Henley, my wife Cheryl - from Curtis Wisconsin, USA," the stranger replied.

"Your husband," Cheryl said warmly to Gem. "I knew that was an engagement ring," she took Gem's hands. "Look how beautifully the rings complement each other."

Gem was speechless, not daring to look at Wyatt. She knew his eyes would hold a query for her - one she could not or would not answer.

Greg took up the conversation where his wife had left off. "We met Gem in Geneva last May. She was waiting for a flight to Brisbane. Did you finish your dissertation?" He looked at Gem and she nodded.

Americans were always so friendly! And so blasted chatty! And they hugged! Why was Gemmy in Switzerland? Switzerland was Mr Choate's itinerary. Or it had been until the Pilos went missing.

"We were staying with our son, Jonny, he was having treatments," Cheryl's voice cracked as she looked at Wyatt.

"Leukemia. He was only six. There wasn't hope for him, really, but we wanted to try. To give him a chance."

Gem nodded slowly. This was so very sad. The couple was speaking to Wyatt and she didn't look at him.

Greg patted his wife's arm. "We had Jonny out for the day and we saw Gem sketching at a café. Jonny was captivated by her sparkly, purple eyes, as he called them. She sketched the three of us, all together, and Jonny was laughing - she was telling him about the 'roos and koala bears in Australia. We hung the portrait in his room, and he talked about you every night - and koala bears and the 'roos- before he went to sleep."

That was Gemmy. So kind! So sweet! And much more adept at quick sketching people than I, Gem mused.

I am so sorry," Gem said gently. "So young and so sweet." She said it for Jonny and Gemmy.

The hostess appeared to inform the Henley's their table was available. Mr Henley invited Gem and Wyatt to join them, but his wife intervened.

"No dear," she smiled, "they're on their honeymoon, aren't you?" she added to Gem.

"Yes," Wyatt replied quickly. "But thank you. And our deepest condolences."

Gem hugged both of them. They were among the last people to speak to Gemmy. "Are you in Scotland for long?"

"Until Friday," Greg said. "We go back to Wisconsin, then can't bear being there without Jonny. We sold our house and just go where the wind blows us. When we're ready we'll settle somewhere, start over again. We're going to Ireland next."

The hostess reappeared and coaxed the Henley's along, then returned to inform Wyatt and Gem a table was available for them.

Once seated, Wyatt remained silent until the waitress had taken their order and brought wine and flutes.

"Do you still sketch?" he asked. "Aside from details for your book?"

"No," Gem shook her head.

And why the hell was Gemmy in Switzerland? She would have to ask Mrs Brown if Gemmy had had an emergency assignment. But Gemmy would have mentioned it that last night. - Perhaps she was waiting for a more advantageous booking to Brisbane. Still she might have mentioned that.

Or had she gone to Geneva to purchase a gift for James? That was possible. But Gem couldn't remember anything at the house that raised a question - who did this belong to etcetera - that Gem couldn't answer. Oh dear - was a gift ordered but never called for? Or had a gift been sent to James in Barcelona?

"The village stationer would have supplies if you would like to sketch while we are here," Wyatt finally spoke.

Gem hadn't sketched for pleasure since the last time she was on holiday with Gemmy. Other sisters went shopping. Gem and Gemmy sketched and chatted hours on end. Gemmy's sketch pads were at the Agency warehouse; it would hurt too much to sketch now - except for detail work for the book.

"I'm not interested in sketching these days," she sipped her wine.

"You sketched James - quite often," Wyatt said bluntly.

"Did you toss the sketches?" Gem held her breath.

"No," he shook his head. "You signed them G.L."

"Gem Louisa," Gem lied. Her sketches were signed G.F. She would have to make certain that Wyatt never saw the sketches for her book. They were signed.

This was another cog ready to slip. Gemmy's sketches of James that could be traced back to Gemmy if Gem was not careful. Mrs Brown would not be pleased if she knew about James. Harry would pitch a fit. Wyatt had the photos, passports, and now sketches of James by Gemmy. How many more pitfalls would she hit? She didn't worry about the Henley's portrait; they already accepted her as Gemmy.

Her brain was so tired.

Wyatt ventured little conversation during dinner, short comments asking if the food was to her liking, did she wish for more wine?

He was extremely polite, but Gem knew there was something behind his facade that was going to set her on edge. The strain of the last few days was eating her nerves.

It was late when they left the inn. The waitress had suggested they stay for the music in the pub. Another time Wyatt had smoothly replied, his arm firmly around Gem's shoulders. On the return drive to the cottage Gem could feel the storm brewing.

The storm indeed broke as they entered the cottage. Gem started up the staircase to change but Wyatt stopped her.

"I'll take the earrings now," he said coldly.

Gem clamped her lips together. Apparently not 'onyx and diamante'. She removed the earrings and handed them to him.

"And where is your other passport?" he said dead quietly.

And there it was! She had missed that point!

She had never been to Switzerland and Wyatt knew that from reading her passport. Mr Choate was courier to Switzerland and he had never missed an assignment, needing a replacement. Gemmy's passport stamped Switzerland was with her - on the Pilos. Gemmy had been wearing the ring in Switzerland. Had she been to Switzerland before last May, the stamp would have had a date previous to last April. - Not for a layover to Australia in mid-May.

"Neither of your passports have been stamped in Switzerland," Wyatt read her thoughts. "Where is your third passport?" He caught her hand, holding it gently, but firmly.

She had no idea as to the other passport.

"Where is it? Is it under Gemimah?"

"No," Gem admitted. "I don't know where it is," she said miserably. "God's truth. I've been looking for it for months. I don't know where it is," she shook her head. "I swear, if I had it, I would gladly give it to you. I can't find it."

He let go of her wrist. "How careless you are with your passports. Did someone steal it?"

Gem walked to the staircase and sank to the bottom step.

"No," she buried her head on her knees. "It's just lost."

He stood looking down at her, puzzled by her dejection. He threw his hands up in the air, then sat down beside her, putting his arm around her shoulders, pulling her against his chest.

"Fallen into an abyss?" he said gently.

"Yes. Precisely. An abyss."

"You lie to me," he said bluntly.

"Yes - but - and you won't believe me - I have never in my life committed an illegal act," she said sincerely.

"Other than having two forged passports, consorting with a known criminal, and you ran off with the jewellery James had given to you. You lie to me. You are going to continue to lie to me, aren't you?" he said quietly.

Gem counted to twenty. "People have pasts. I never asked you about yours."

She pulled away from him, and began to pace the floor. Then she stopped and turned to face him. "You tricked me into this marriage. I am truly sorry about what happened to James. If I could change that, I swear I would. Our lives are on the opposite side of the spectrum - your life is in the light, mine is in the dark. But I need my life back! Give me a divorce, please! If you won't then - yes, if I feel I have to lie to you, I will lie to you."

Wyatt gazed at her, frowning. He accomplished take-overs, fought international industrial espionage; he directed an international company, employed nearly two thousand employees. Yet this fragile beauty, a liar, a thief, a woman with a brilliant mind, confounded him; she sketched a portrait of a dying child; then weeks later drove a man to his death without remorse. At times the violet eyes blazed with anger; at other times they were veiled and haunted. What had she done to earn the haunted eyes? Who else had she destroyed? How many men?

She was fascinating! He could not deny that fact. No wonder James had been love struck, then devastated when she had deserted him.

She was sorry, she felt responsible for James's death. But there had been no words of love for him - not even lies of having loved him. His death wasn't a personal tragedy to her. How could she be so cold?

His eyes narrowed as he watched her. She was so close to unraveling. And what would he learn when she did? Close, but still there was a bit of steel in her that held her back from the brink. No. He wasn't finished with her yet. Not by a long shot. Not until she had stepped off the edge. Not until she was broken. Not until she could truly feel the pain and the loss of the life she had destroyed. Her eyes were pleading, so seemingly sincere. Her life was on the 'dark side of the spectrum'. Indeed. Her own pitiful dirge. The acting was very credible.

Wyatt stood up, keeping his voice even. "So convincing, my dear wife. I am impressed. I applaud you," he sharply clapped his hands. "No divorce. It has been a very long day. Time for bed."

He stepped aside, sweeping his hand towards the staircase.

Gem stared at him, completely disheartened. Why had she thought she could reach him? He wasn't going to change. The battle would continue. She had to gird herself with resolve.

She was so tired. How long could her mind continue to function, split in so many directions?

"Think long and hard about that passport, my dear. And choose your lies carefully. I am a man of limited patience where you are concerned."

Gem slumped into a chair. This round of the battle had completely gone nowhere. She had said as much as she dared say. More than she should have said. He wouldn't listen but she was not ready to simply exist on his terms.

This evening was certainly a disaster. And the Blasted earrings! What else had James given to Gemmy? This Blasted situation was always going from bad to worse. Would the law of averages ever begin to turn in her favor?

Wyatt took her hand to draw her from the chair and lead her to the stairs.

"I am not tired," she protested.

"Good. We won't sleep then. Opt for the dressing gown - the rest is a waste of time," he pointedly suggested.

She delayed in the bathroom as long as she could. Nightgown and dressing gown. She wasn't about to tell him what to wear so she would expect the same courtesy from him. He was sipping a glass of Scotch, looking out the window at the night sky. His hair was damp from a shower, so apparently he had used another bathroom while she had dawdled. The duvet and top sheet were pulled back on the bed.

"You look stunning, my dear. Positively bewitching," he smiled. He finished his drink and stretched his hand out to her.

"Stop the terms of endearment. The words are lies," she said tersely. "I have no love for you, nor you for me. I am not your sweetheart, or your dear anything."

"Such words are more proper to use - especially in public than say - Bloody Mary," the smile left his face. She was waging another battle. "However, I cede the point to you that you are the authority on lying."

"I shall only reply to you when you use my name," Gem retorted, her temper rising.

"Which name would that be? Gemimah? Gemma? Perhaps Gemmy? Gem?" She glared at him when he spoke the name Gemmy. "Or shall I decide myself which name you should use? Indeed, are there perhaps other aliases from other passports of which I should know? Tell me, my dear, what other names do you hide?"

Gem ignored his sarcastic queries. "Call me Gem, please."

"Is that the name on your driver's license? Your birth certificate? And how many of those do you have?"

"One." Which was true for both queries? It just happened that her birth certificate wasn't readily available.

"So you say. You really have no reason to be annoyed with my queries. You admit yourself that you lie to me," he shrugged. "Now come to bed. You are extremely owly tonight. You need sleep."

"Sleep is not on your mind!"

"It will be eventually," he chuckled. "Come to bed."

"No! I hate it when you touch me! You make my flesh crawl."

"Yes, I do. And you are most welcome for that!" Wyatt grinned.

"That's not what I meant!"

"I'll accept it nonetheless," he outright laughed at her.

"How does one get through your thick skin?"

"One doesn't. Save your energies and cease trying."

"You make me feel like a whore!" Gem seethed.

"Nonsense! I'm not paying you."

"I hate talking to you!"

"Then we won't talk. It certainly isn't required," he moved towardss her.

"I am not in the mood!" Gem stalked past him to the staircase. "There are other beds in this cottage!"

At the top of the step, Gem's slipper heel caught in the hem of her nightgown, pitching her forward; she clutched at the railing but couldn't catch it. Wyatt bolted across the floor, reaching out to grasp her arm, pulling her back hard against his chest. He wrapped his arms around her, crushing her against him, his breath sharply exhaling.

Gem started shaking, gasping for breath.

"You could have broken you neck!" Wyatt's voice was hoarse with shock.

"I know," she gasped, her words muffled by the fabric of his dressing gown.

"Did I hurt your arm?" he slowly released her.

Gem shook her head numbly, swaying on her feet.

"Do you feel faint?"

"No," she shook her head again.

He pushed her into a chair, reached for the Scotch, splashing some in a glass and thrust it into her hands. Gem threw it back and held out the glass for another shot. Wyatt refilled her glass then poured one for himself. He tossed it back, set the glass on the dry bar, then strode across the room to the highboy where Gem had put her nightwear. He rummaged through the top drawer, finding, then pulling out a set of the pyjamas she has purchased the previous day. He handed them to her.

"These are probably more - suitable for you after all," he said, his voice raspy. "And perhaps a parachute wouldn't be out of the question."

"Thank you," Gem managed to gasp out, still stunned and shaking from the near accident.

Wyatt muttered something but she didn't understand his words. He went into the bathroom; she heard running water, then he came out and got into bed. Gem went to the bathroom to exchange the dressing gown and nightgown for the pyjamas, and cleaned her teeth. She turned out the lights and slipped between the sheets.

She laid her head on his shoulder, resting her left hand on his chest. "Thank you - for catching me," she said softly.

"You are welcome. Go to sleep," he said quietly.

Gem sighed deeply and closed her eyes, grateful for sleep.

She fell asleep almost immediately, the top of her head tickling his chin. He exhaled sharply, then folded his arm around her shoulders.

Wyatt lay quietly, unable to sleep, still shocked by the sight of Gem starting to plunge down the staircase. He made a mental note to add safety precautions to the already growing list regarding her. Keeping her in hand was one matter, but he did not want to see her dead. Her death was not part of his Game.

Gem paced the kitchen floor. She had slept soundly until the dark hours arrived. She was still stunned by Wyatt's remarkable reflexes earlier. And thankful. She could be dead by now if he hadn't saved her from falling headlong down the stairs. However, she wouldn't have been in that situation if it hadn't been for him! She wouldn't be in this cottage! She would be in her flat in London, working as she should be working now.

There were bookshelves in the lounge. She quickly scanned the spines of the books for any possible references to the War. Gardening, wild birds, wildflowers, guide books to Scotland, guide book to the Orkney Islands. Not a single book that would be of help to her.

SEVEN DAYS left until she would have the use of her computers. There was a computer on a desk by the bookshelves, but she didn't dare try to use it.

James. Why had she thought of James - other than the obvious?

He would have been twenty-five on their wedding day. Wedding Day! The words made her cringe!

James. Twenty-five. He had been involved with drugs and alcohol when he was young, very young. Clean and sober six years which would have put him at eighteen or so. Prior to that. Very young. Youth. Hitler's youth movement? She sorted her mental files. No.

She paced, dragging her fingers through her hair. Gemmy where are you?

Gemmy and the Henley's son, Jonny. The poor little boy.

Geneva. Barcelona.

Why was Gemmy talking to Paul Andriani? Geneva. Barcelona. Both were Mr. Choate's territory. Where had Gemmy met James? And I'm supposed to know that, of course! When would Wyatt bring up that subject for nasty comment?

Why, indeed, would Gemmy be talking to Paul Andriani? Why would he be in Barcelona? Why would an undercover agent be speaking to a courier in a public garden? A little too open for a meeting. No doubt they had read the area. But they had missed James taking photos! And why hadn't he told Gemmy? If he had, the photos would have been destroyed. Or had she said she had been talking to a stranger about the gardens? How had she managed it if James had mentioned the photos? No. She had been unaware of the photos. Because they had existed for Wyatt to discover.

So many questions. And no answers.

Chapter Nine

It was easier to slip out of the bed in the dark hours than when the sun had risen.

What was the purpose of pyjamas or dressing gowns if one could never locate either of them? Gem wrapped the sheet around her body and reached over the foot of the bed to scrounge the duvet for the first item resembling clothing.

"Why bother?" Wyatt teased. "Only the two of us here."

"One more than I would like," Gem shot back. "Don't let me stop you, go ahead, take your shower."

"You're plucky this morning," Wyatt said loftily, reaching into the wardrobe for his clothes.

"No, I'm just very angry," Gem said irritably.

"Well, that's every morning, as far as I can tell."

"Do you wonder why?" She found her pyjamas at the foot of the bed between the sheets.

"Naturally bad tempered?" he reached a hand down to ruffle her hair as she pulled at the duvet on the floor.

"You're standing on my dressing gown!" She jerked at the fabric.

"Yes, I am," Wyatt laughed.

"Blast! I hate you!" Gem seethed.

Wyatt reached down to retrieve the dressing gown. "That's not what you were thinking a few minutes ago," he lifted her from the bed setting her on her feet, then draped the cloth around her shoulders. "You can't resist me." He traced his finger down between her breasts.

"You're a Blasted Svengali," she brushed his hand away.

"Look into my eyes Trilby and deny that I made you sing just a very few sweet minutes ago."

His eyes trapped hers, his lips teased hers; his hands slid beneath the folds of her dressing gown, stroking her, coaxing her to respond, and she did. Then, suddenly he pulled the fabric closed. "Later, Trilby." He grabbed his clothes and walked to the stairs. "I'll shower elsewhere."

Gem glared at him "Seducer!" she accused in a parting shot.

Wyatt turned to stare at her. "And again, you are most welcome!"

The ego that man has! Gem fumed. He touched her and instantly her self-control disintegrated. After this morning she could certainly understand Trilby. He simply hypnotized her! And yes, she had sung. Blast! She needed a cold shower!

And it was as unpleasant as she thought it would be. One minute and she switched to hot water.

She could smell breakfast cooking as she dressed. Wyatt had selected jeans and a sweater, and she followed his lead, not knowing what today would bring.

Sheets of paper lay on the table by his plate.

"If you have work to do I can go for a walk," she offered.

He scanned the papers. "Ms Wexton faxed weather forecasts for this week," he handed Gem the sheets, "as well as trip notes. Today and Thursday sunny. Wednesday, Friday possible showers. Saturday questionable. Do you prefer morning or afternoon light?"

"Both actually. Ms Wexton is certainly thorough," Gem reviewed the forecasts.

"Indeed. She would like a promotion and a rise in salary. Something about an addition to the stable, I believe," he tapped her plate with his fork. "Eat."

She put down the papers. He certainly could manage in the kitchen.

"Approximately 76K to Elgin, 34 to Fortrose. Where did you stay your last trip?"

"Aviemore." The last time she was in Scotland to shoot photos. Her most recent trip was a courier assignment which Wyatt was not going to know.

"More driving distance from there, naturally. What say we drive to Fortrose, backtrack to Inverness to Elgin. You will have both cathedrals morning light. We'll lunch in Elgin, then you shoot Elgin afternoon light and we'll backtrack to Fortrose. Drop off the film for developing late afternoon, call for it tomorrow. If the photos don't suit we will re-do the process Thursday - weather holding, of course."

"That is quite a bit of driving for one day," Gem mentally computed the kilometers.

"We'll share the driving," Wyatt took the folder and sheets. "We'll do the washing up, then be on our way."

The Land Rover was similar to the Range Rover she had borrowed from the Agency for the drive to Gosport weeks back. Wyatt had suggested she drive the first leg of the journey, no doubt to criticize how she managed the vehicle, but he did not refer to her driving abilities, as she had expected. He said very little, actually, speaking only to point out views he thought might interest her.

Fortrose was easily managed; she had the interior photos and drawings from the Aviemore trip. She shot two rolls of the exterior, confident the light would develop properly crisp this time.

Wyatt drove the distance to Elgin. Gem again shot two rolls of film. It was a quiet working morning for her. Aside from the drive she was able to forget he was with her.

"Pub lunch? Or Chinese?" Wyatt queried as she tucked her camera into its case.

"I'm not really hungry," Gem replied. "Whatever you decide."

He decided on a pub, ordering two specials of the day and two half-pints.

"I'm not hungry," Gem insisted.

Wyatt placed his hand over her beer mug.

"No lunch, no beer," he said firmly. "You need to eat."

Gem glared at him. He was again telling her what to do! "As you say," she gave him a mock sweet smile.

"James would have been quite surprised by this side of your personality," he said dryly. "He said you were 'so sweet' to him. Try to assume some proper public manners. One of the characters in your extremely well practiced repertoire must be able to project some social graces. Try at least to pretend you are a lady."

"I'll try," Gem replied, her voice sweetly tinged with sarcasm. "However, I shall not be of your caliber 'acting' the role of 'proper gentleman'."

Wyatt's eyes narrowed. "Do you prefer my role as lover?" he drawled. "You enjoyed it this morning."

His words silenced her.

"Choose your battles carefully, my dear. But as I warned you before, I shall win each and every one."

Gem ate slowly, thoroughly chewing every bite to prevent the ability to speak to him.

"What happened to the charming character I courted? You did her quite well," Wyatt observed as he drove the Land Rover back to Elgin Cathedral.

"Hunted." Gem crisply corrected him.

"Ah, yes. I won that Game. However did you manage to curtail your nasty temper all those weeks?"

"How ever did you manage not to let your facade drop?" she returned with sarcasm.

Wyatt laughed. "You are so quick, my dear. It will be interesting to see how long you can keep up with me."

For the love of Gemmy and James, for the Agency, for everyone aboard the Pilos, the dead Vietnamese counter-courier, the missing Chinese counter-courier, Gem bit her tongue. Elgin afternoon photos finished, Wyatt assumed the role of chauffer to Fortrose for the last shooting of the day.

The light was perfect. Gem shot two rolls of film. She knew she had excellent shots, but she used the camera as a buffer between Wyatt and her. She mentally checked off the cathedrals she had on film, and the ones left to shoot. Lord only knew when she would get to the remaining ones being tethered now and at Wyatt's mercy.

Cathedrals. SS officers. James. Hong Kong. U-1408.

James.

James.

Not his youth!

He was an artist!

Stolen European art!

Stolen by the Nazi's as they conquered one country after another in their psychotic attempt to rule the world!

Gem lowered the camera, and stared at the cathedral.

Stolen European art! Lost for decades!

Still lost!

SS officers. Hong Kong. U-1408. Stolen European Art.

"Eureka!" Wyatt said triumphantly.

"What?" Gem frowned, confused. His voice shook her out of her thoughts.

"Eureka!" he repeated. "The look on your face just then was the visual equivalent of Eureka."

"Oh!" Gem was astounded. She could imagine he was very well correct.

"You must have got what you wanted," Wyatt observed.

"I think I did," Gem said firmly.

Eureka indeed!

SS officers. Hong Kong. U-1408. Stolen art treasures. How it intertwined was still the question. And what could it all possibly have to do with the Pilos?

Wyatt drove back to Inverness. A photo shop was still open and promised development of the film by the following afternoon. Wyatt insisted on visiting the shops. He was welcome to it. Gem drifted along beside him, deep in thought.

Could she risk a text message to Mr Cawley? Damn. She hadn't charged her phone in days. In fact the charger was neatly packed in with her lap top. How could she have been so daft as to not have her charger with her? The Agency wouldn't be worried if they couldn't get ahold of her: she was on her honeymoon. In fact, they wouldn't even consider ringing her.

Still SEVEN DAYS remaining! When you wanted days to go slowly they zipped past, when you wanted days to fly they dragged on, seemingly carrying the entire weight of the world.

He was there, interrupting her thoughts, handing a sweater to her.

"Try this on. It should fit," he ordered, a look in his eyes warning her not to protest. "You could probably wear a child's size, you are so thin."

Gem ignored the critical comment. Aryan sweater. Luscious; a rich crème colour. Of course it fit. Wyatt Grantham was probably never wrong on such matters. His taste was flawless. Very irritating.

Gem stared at herself in the mirror. How many times had she stared into a mirror seeing two of her? How many times had she peered around a doorjamb to look directly into her own face? Since 30 May, when she saw her reflection it was always only her.

She handed the sweater to Wyatt.

"Did it fit?" he asked, patience thinning.

She nodded, then turned again to her own thoughts. She did not give attention to what he was doing other than to try on a dress, or a skirt, or a blouse, another sweater he handed to her. His every choice fit.

Had Mrs Brown returned from holiday? - Or was that the end of this week? And Harry?

On to another shop, then another. She wandered around the racks, seeing yet not seeing.

"You are worse than a child - constantly wandering off," Wyatt murmured in her ear, putting his arm around her waist. "Dinner. Pub or Chinese? Italian?"

"Chinese," she replied automatically. She looked at him, surprised to see he carried two shopping totes. The crème coloured sweater and one in a deep blue. Thank heavens he hadn't purchased any of the other clothes he had insisted she try on.

Chinese and wine. Wyatt had stored the sweaters in the Land Rover so they were burden free.

"Inverness has many, many excellent art galleries and museums. Would that be of interest to you for this evening?" he asked while they ate their food.

"Yes, very nice," Gem agreed.

Wyatt leaned back in his chair, projecting a relaxed air Gem no longer felt in his presence. "Where did you study photography?"

"I didn't," she shook her head, taking a sip of wine to delay her response. Harry had studied the subject and he had guided her. "I talked to other photographers."

"Your photos of the Jag are very striking. Perhaps you have a natural talent."

"At the very least a natural interest." She did set not down the wine glass, holding it as focal point.

"A natural instinct," he nodded.

For photography perhaps. Not for men.

"Tell me, why did you tell James your PhD thesis was of medieval art glass? Why not medieval cathedrals? Did you decide art glass because he was an artist?" he asked curiously, yet with no underlying tone - for a change.

"Whatever I say, you won't believe me, will you?" Gem said quietly, looking about her, reading the room.

"I might," Wyatt replied. "Tell me, why do you scan the area wherever we go? The gardens at Wight, the shops today, pubs, restaurants, cathedrals, museums."

The shops today? She hadn't even realized she was reading. If there had been something to notice would it have snapped through her thoughts to register?

"Are you looking for past marks? Future marks? Someone else who might recognize you as did the Henley's? If you are hiding from someone, you're not doing a proper job of it. Your hair colour is natural, your eye colour. Hiding in plain sight?"

He certainly was observant. He had been watching her read. He knew she was doing it.

Gem shook her head. As she spoke she looked him directly in the eye. "A natural instinct. And no, I am not in hiding. Nor have I ever been in hiding. Were I suddenly to do so it would only be to hide from you."

"Fascinating. The natural instinct remark was a lie. You've long made a practice of your habits. The rest was the truth," he observed with a nod.

Gem ignored his remarks about her lies. "However, there would be no point trying to hide from you, I realize that," she said calmly.

"Also not a lie," Wyatt pursed his lips.

They didn't make it to the museums or galleries, instead, stopping into a second-hand bookshop that appealed to both of them. Wyatt watched as Gem's eyes lit up at the sight of the stacks of books piled on shelves, long tables and on the floor.

Gem found a number of books about the War - campaigns in Europe, a paperback on fleet type submarines, and a book on the Nazi invasion of Europe. Wyatt selected a handful of books also relating to history but not of the War. Gem held back the copy of the Nazi invasion and Wyatt arranged to have the other books shipped to the Hall.

Gem dreaded returning to the cottage, concerned there would be another argument. However, to her delight, Wyatt's mobile rang as they entered the cottage and he became deeply engrossed in a conversation for over an hour. He went up to the bedroom to take the call in private. Gem took a beer from the fridge and settled in the lounge to read of Hitler's psychotic troops chewing their way across Poland in early September 1939. The Dictator of Evil had devoured Warsaw at the end of September, when Wyatt walked down the stairs.

Gem was so engrossed in the book she didn't realize Wyatt was in the room until he set a beer down on the book in her lap.

"Why the War?" he asked.

"What?" Gem frowned blankly at the query.

"The books you selected this evening all relate to the Second World War. Are you considering writing at thesis on the War?"

He lounged in a chair across from her, focusing his mesmerizing eyes on her.

Don't look in his eyes, she warned herself or you will be lost! Blast Trilby! Blast Svengali!

"I find the subject interesting. The history you don't know will repeat," she replied with a shrug.

"How long have you been researching the War? And please look at me when you speak to me."

"Reading, not researching," she replied, looking at him only when she spoke, keeping guard on her senses. Did he know the affect his eyes had on her? He had to know. He had to be using them as weapons against her self-control.

"The books you bought at the jumble sale were War history. You must have quite a library accumulating," he observed mildly, noting the lie in her eyes - definitely not reading for enjoyment. She was researching.

"As have you," she countered.

"Of various historical subjects." He watched her, wondering if her interest was professional interest or some kind of gambit. "The library at the Hall has many, many volumes on the War. You might find them of interest to you."

"Oh - thank you." She felt her pulse quicken - because of him - not the books.

"Which leads me to another matter. I must attend a meeting Monday at the office, so that is no longer a travel day for us."

Gem quickly looked up.

"Yes, I thought that would please you. You have a choice - a flight to London or we'll drive down."

Her face went ashen when he presented the first option. "You would prefer to drive," he decided.

"Yes. It's a very long drive," Gem winced, knowing the option was probably not his first choice.

"A bit over nine hours. We'll share the driving. You are competent behind the wheel."

"Competent?" There was an edge to her voice. Mr Critchley thought her more than competent!

"Acceptable then," Wyatt conceded. "You'll improve."

"You are so arrogant and condescending!" she retorted.

Wyatt laughed. The colour was back in her face. "I just wanted a reaction. Now plans for tomorrow. Check the photos and there are a great many sites to visit here. The Aviation Museum, the Culloden Battlefield, the Clava Cairns, the Floral Hall Gardens. There's also hiking, museums. What would you like to do?"

"All of it," Gem decided.

"And there is John O'Groats. Have you been there?"

She paused a bit too long to his thinking.

"Yes," she nodded, looking away from him.

"When?"

Really! What business was it of his? She could refuse to reply, or she could just lie.

"After you deserted James, then," he said smoothly, but there was an edge to his voice. "Brisbane by way of Geneva and John O'Groats. My, my, what a butterfly you were. A very busy few weeks while you were supposed to be in Brisbane. Brisbane - Geneva, John O'Groats. Was that also when you stayed in Aviemore to photograph the cathedrals we drove to today?"

Last week of May. Gem had stepped in to cover assignments for a courier who went down with appendicitis. John O'Groats was a make-shift delivery site. Then on to Paris, Andorra; then her own assignments to Genoa, Florence, Athens, and finally to Brisbane.

"Cat got your tongue again? Pesky little creature it is," Wyatt pressed. "Gemimah's passport had quite a few stamps. Gemma's passport didn't have any stamps after mid-April. Ah! There again is the third passport," Wyatt was thinking aloud to needle her into an admission of some kind.

Guard every word. One battle at a time. Perhaps one day she would actually win a battle - aside from the one of pyjamas - sooner or later- a win? Blast the word later! It was gaining too much power and prominence in her life.

"Do you ever tire of being evil?" she demanded, smarting from his words.

"Do you?" He couldn't fathom how her brain worked.

Wyatt stood up, took their beer bottles to the kitchen then returned to lift Gem from the chair, letting her book drop to the floor.

"Word play is over for this evening. Time for another amusement." He stroked her cheek, gazing into her eyes. "Time for a song, Trilby."

Nazi troops chewed through Poland, Gem read on, Britain and France declared war on Germany. Germany continued chewing through Denmark and Norway the following spring, Belgium in early April, then the Netherlands, Luxembourg, and France.

Gem sorted through her mind, recalling stories she had heard of - people secreting family art treasures in hidden cellars and vaults. But the Nazi's pillaged galleries, museums, private homes of art of every medium. Some of the art was found after the War. Still much of the art had never been recovered. Lost to families, nations, and the world.

What did the Nazi's do with the artwork still missing? Where did they hide it that it had not yet been found? Hong Kong? South American? Mexico? U-boats diverted from war missions to transport stolen art? Nazi officers transporting the pillaged art across oceans?

Gem read until her head ached, slipping back into bed at half four. Wyatt folded her in his arms and slept. Gem stared into the dark, her brain intertwining the War and the Pilos, until the hour slid to five o'clock.

The clerk immediately recognized Gem when she walked into the shop.

"Ten packs for Forrester," he said smiling, as she and Wyatt walked to the counter. "Correct?"

Gem smiled. "Excellent. And eight rolls of film, please." She had a half dozen rolls in the camera bag, but always purchased additional rolls when she picked up photos that had been processed.

Wyatt handed a credit card to the clerk before Gem could take one from her shoulder bag. She turned to protest but saw the steel in the gray eyes that stared at her.

When they returned to the Land Rover, Wyatt did not immediately engage the engine.

"Forrester?" he said curtly.

"What?" Gem gave him a blank look.

"Your surname is Grantham. Gemimah Louisa Forrester GRANTHAM."

Gem winced at his remark. "Habit," she said simply. "But the marriage is as much a farce as this 'honeymoon'," she continued with frustration.

"This marriage is not a farce, it is real," Wyatt said sternly. "Courting is subtle, the honeymoon is the beginning, marriage is discovery and the growth of the relationship."

"Your courting was a sham! The honeymoon is a sham. You can't base a marriage on lies!"

"Ha! It is done all the time," Wyatt coldly laughed.

Gem dragged her fingers through her hair. "I am so tired of the arguments."

"Stop arguing then," he engaged the engine. "We are now going to shop for a vehicle for you. Mind your attitude - and don't wander off!"

At the car dealer, Wyatt introduced himself to the manager, then introduced Gem as Mrs Grantham, who was in need of a vehicle. Gem bit her tongue and saved a glare for Wyatt when no one was looking in her direction. The sales manager prattled on to Wyatt, asking questions of models and needs and particulars. Gem sighed inwardly, following the men from car to car - she had no choice - Wyatt's arm was around her waist, trapping her again. At one point Wyatt leaned down to whisper in her ear, telling her to smile. She pasted a small, forced smile to her lips.

"Are you interested in test driving any of these cars, my dear?" Wyatt smoothly inquired.

"I can't tell one from another," she admitted. "Different colours, other than that they look alike."

Wyatt chuckled. "You can recognize a Range Rover," he teased.

"And a Panda, and a Mini, and a Volvo," she shrugged.

"Mrs Grantham generally prefers hiking boots to tires," Wyatt informed the manager.

Mrs Grantham again!

"A Range Rover would likely be ideal for you, sweetheart. Do you agree?"

"Sure," Gem lifted her hands helplessly.

"Colour preference?" the manager queried.

"Black is fine," Gem replied. "A 1990 would be very acceptable."

The manager blinked at Wyatt. "Excuse me for a moment."

"Are you being difficult?" Wyatt whispered in Gem's ear.

"No, seriously, I am not," she insisted sincerely. "New vehicles have GPS systems already installed. I find them considerably annoying. Don't you?" she asked Wyatt.

"Quite," was his only response. Then, "Range Rover any year sans GPS?"

"Yes, but a Range Rover Defender," Gem decided firmly.

The manager returned with a small white card which he handed to Wyatt. "This man is not a dealer, but if there is a black 1990 Range Rover out there he will know where it is."

They thanked him for his assistance and were walking back to the hired Land Rover when Wyatt's mobile rang.

"I have to take this," he said to Gem, frowning.

"I'll look through the photos," she nodded, settling in the vehicle, hoping the phone call would occupy him for quite some time.

The light the previous day had proved to be perfect. She easily had enough photos for the chapters of the Elgin and Fortrose Cathedrals. The photos from the cycling race were crisp and colourful as she had hoped they would be. She would likely never use them, but it had been an interesting exercise in camera detail. Only that. She winced as she saw the photo taken just before Wyatt had pulled her back from the road. On the far right side of the photo was the tiniest spot indicating the racer who had swung wide and would have struck her had Wyatt not had cat-like reflexes to rescue her.

The photos of the gardens at Ventnor were striking and Gem thought she would like to have a few of them matted and framed. She didn't know where she would hang them, then she thought again. Why would she want to see any of the photos again? She would put them in the box with the photos she had taken on the excursions with Wyatt before their absurd marriage. There would be no rainy Saturdays with Wyatt, putting photos in albums as he had once promised. Sad memories she would push permanently from her thoughts. When she got her hands on those photos she would shred them. Stupid! Stupid! Stupid! - But then she should keep photos of historical sites, and she would make certain Wyatt was not in the photos.

Wyatt finally returned to the Land Rover. "Black 1990 Range Rover Defender will be delivered Wednesday next.

"I thought you were talking to your office," she replied in surprise.

"I did. Then I made a phone call."

"Truly amazing," she mused. "You purchased a vehicle on your mobile, that easy!"

'He is a wealthy, powerful man', Mrs Brown had said to her. Gem should have listened to the warning.

"I imagine you can have absolutely anything you wish," she said flatly.

"Including you, my dear. You were so easy." Then he shook his head. "Really, Gem, no one can have anything they want. There is a limit."

"If one has ethics perhaps. I doubt you are troubled by such trifles," she said curtly. He was echoing her thoughts from moments earlier.

"Are you referring once again to our marriage, my dear?" he said loftily. "I'll remind you, Gem, that you wanted me. And now you are paying the price for getting your wish. You didn't know your mark. Your error."

"You are a cad."

"James was a gentleman. Perhaps you should have committed to that marriage," he said coolly.

"That wasn't possible," Gem retorted, then gasped slightly, realizing she had spoken aloud.

"Why not, pray tell? Spin a tale to explain your deception. Amuse me. I'm interested in all your clever ruses."

"You wouldn't understand," she said bitterly.

"Perhaps I would. Perhaps not. Talk and we shall see."

"I can't," she replied simply.

"You won't," he said crisply.

"Have it your way," Gem shrugged.

"Oh, my dear, I intend to. We will revisit this subject often. There are many years ahead of us, my dear wife, many years for you to regale me with stories of your, shall we say, sordid past?"

Gem cringed every time he uttered the word 'wife'. It grated on her every nerve.

How could he be so gentle, so considerate and kind in bed, and yet be such a monster out of it!

Wyatt insisted Gem drive to the Highland Aviation Museum. GPS worked splendidly, but she was very adept at reading a map, and the satellite system irritated her. She could read signs as well as the next person. Find the Inverness airport; find the aviation museum. Rely too much on computer systems and lose your brain power.

The Highland Aviation Museum display room was well presented; the commitment and the diligence of the staff were overwhelming. History preserved by the dedication of a few.

There were a dozen aircraft that had been restored or were in the process of being restored.

Gem and Wyatt could actually walk inside a Valiant V-bomber. It was post the Second World War, but nonetheless fascinating. They viewed the cockpit of the Valiant and a Buccaneer - also not of the War, and the cockpit of a Lightning - designed and built in the States, and provided during the War to train RAF pilots.

She shot rolls of film; she didn't count the number. She was captivated by the cockpit of the Lightning.

"One could have become quite claustrophobic in here," she mused. "I would be. And all the dials. How could one learn so much?"

"I imagine a claustrophobic would have been assigned elsewhere," Wyatt murmured.

The sorting came unsummoned. The blitz, night after night, the scores dead night after night. She felt like a robot or a computer; however, either would have been more efficient that her brain; probably easily succeeding in solving her queries in a more timely fashion than could she with her mental capacities.

"I can't imagine the courage of the people. I'd have been frightened witless every moment," she said in awe.

"Staggering," Wyatt replied softly. "But they were of the land of Boadicea. They saved the country and then with the Allies they saved the world. God who made thee mighty -"

"Indeed," Gem nodded.

The aviation museum greatly inspired Gem, although she had had to sort to find Boadicea. Twelve years studying in Australia had put her a bit behind in the early history of England, but she had read voraciously once she was transplanted.

Next was the Culloden Battlefield; more inspiration. She was British by birth; she had to have acquired some courage by genes or osmosis. She steeled herself to broach a subject on the hike from the battlefield to the Clava Cairns.

She had shot a roll of film at the battlefield, her energy building. The skies were broody, promising an infliction of rain to come. And she decided to face another battle of her own. She scanned the area around them. There was no one in sight. The landscape was clear. Trees bordered their right, a field on their left, but there no voices to be heard, no ears to overhear; no sounds but that of nature.

Gem stopped and turned to face Wyatt, summoning every ounce of courage in her body.

"I want a divorce - immediately," she demanded firmly, her eyes meeting his.

Wyatt stopped mid-stride, meeting her defiant challenge. She had spunk.

"Nonsense, my dear. It's rude to demand a divorce while on one's honeymoon. It ruins the ambiance. I expect proper manners from you," he replied. He put his arm around her shoulders. "The cairns are just ahead. You'll probably want to use at least two rolls of film."

Gem broke away from him and continued to glare at him.

"You are so vile! Send me a postal card from Hell when you get there!" she steamed.

"I have already been - at least twice," he drawled. "Send me a long letter when you arrive. Postage due, if you wish."

"I have also already been! I am still there!" she shot back, completely incensed.

Wyatt stared at her. She could not imagine the feelings, the intensity of such words!

Gem flailed the air with her arms, turning her back to him, then turning again to face him, desperate to appeal to some part of his mind that would hear her plea.

"Dear God! I loved you!" she moaned.

"How sad for you - you lost your touch reading your mark," Wyatt responded coldly. The lovely, pleading violet eyes were a masterpiece of acting.

"Have you ever been in love?" Gem pleaded, her heart aching from his deceit - of the past few days living with his hatred for her, his scorn, his words filled with revulsion. She tried to reach one iota of compassion within him.

Wyatt coldly observed her impassioned plea, already weary of this argument. This would only be the first of many battles. Yet he had to have control and continue to do so. Her word games were interesting, amusing. But once home, and at work he would have little time for verbal amusements. He had few days remaining to impress upon her the fact that his word was the new law, as far as she would know, now and in the future. He had set the terms of their relationship. The terms would not change. Nor would she. But she would, by God, live by his terms.

Once he returned to work, she had to be in order. GEI required his undivided attention. He had wasted the entire month of August on the Game. Subsequent Games would be at his leisure, for his amusement. He would waste no additional time upon bending her to his rules.

Wyatt turned the full intensity of his disgust upon her. "Have I ever been in love? No," he said coldly. "Have I ever loved someone? Yes. James. Perhaps you remember my brother."

"You are so cruel," Gem shivered despite the warm day.

"Am I? You should have remained with James. He was, literally, the kindest person I have ever known. Oh - but then you would eventually have destroyed him - no wait, you did," Wyatt ground out.

Gem turned away from him. He simply wouldn't understand until she could explain about Gemmy.

"He told you how he had fought back from the depths of despair. He trusted you. And you threw him back to that abyss."

Gem sadly shook her head. "That's not how it was," she protested helplessly.

"Tell me then, how it was," Wyatt demanded.

"I can't." She shook her head again.

"You won't," Wyatt denied her reply.

"As you please," Gem murmured, losing the battle. "You are going to destroy me," she moaned.

"Rubbish! You are tough as nails! You've simply never been on this side of your game before. Qualis vita, fini ita: as is the life, so is the end."

"How clever you are! You studied Latin," she said scornfully.

"Italian restaurant menu," his voice lost a bit of sting. "Don't lose your sense of humour, my dear. Soon it will be all that you have left."

"Fluctuat nec mergitur," Gem said coolly.

Wyatt frowned. "She is tossed by the waves but she does not sink. You studied Latin," he observed.

"I read it in a book," she shrugged.

"Oh, my dear, you do so amuse me," Wyatt chuckled.

"I hate you."

"Soto la bianca cenere, sta la brace ardent: under the white ash, the glowing embers lie."

"Another Italian menu?" she snipped. "That is fallacy. No glowing embers."

"The embers glow between the sheets," Wyatt laughed. "That, Trilby, you cannot deny!"

Gem turned and stomped away, cheeks burning. When they returned to - wherever - she would triple her focus on the search for the Pilos. She would escape this horrid beast!

Gem paced the kitchen floor, sorting, sorting. Something about the plundered art was at the back of her mind. Years of reading her father's books, histories, mysteries of the War.

Wyatt watched her, standing at the railing of the darkened loft. He had wakened when she slipped from his arms. Two o'clock. He was aware she returned to bed some two and a half, three hours later each night. Her pattern. She did not sleep between two and five o'clock in the morning. The pacing here at the cottage, the staring at the coastal waters on Wight. He had stopped the clocks in the cottage. Would she notice? Would it make a difference in her lack of sleep pattern? Sleep! Fresh air, late hours, hiking hours every day did not wear her out sufficiently to alter her perplexing sleep pattern. Lack of sleep problem. Aberrant was not the proper word. Hers was an extremely regular sleep cycle. Awake from two to five o'clock in the morning. She could not or would not sleep past seven o'clock in the morning. He decided 'could not' rather than 'would not'. She insisted she could not sleep during the day.

He had searched her luggage, handbag, through the wardrobe, drawers, the pockets of her clothing. He was convinced her sleep problem - insomnia - was not caused by drugs. Insomnia. He would have to address the issue. She needed more sleep. He couldn't understand how she could manage to exist through each day on the little sleep she had each night. He had twice the hours of sleep she had had, and he was exhausted. There were sleep specialists in London. An appointment for her with one of the physicians would be at the top of his agenda when they moved to the Hall. She was mentally functional, but how long would that continue?

He could use that to his advantage. But it would colour the Game. The final win might be less satisfying.

And what was she thinking about each night?

Gem paced the floor. Sorting. Sorting. The Psycho Band of Lucifer's Nazis had started pillaging art in 1933. Sorting was brilliant! Yet, how much more additional information could her brain absorb before content began replacing former reference content? Would that happen? It hadn't before - to her knowledge.

The evil Nazi machine pillaged from 1933 until the end of the war in Europe - 8 May 1945. Twelve years of rounding up millions of brilliant, innocent people, exterminating them, stealing lives and possessions, bombing and pillaging other countries. Twelve years of attempting to eliminate the beautiful diversity of the world for a mad man's psychotic dream.

Twelve years of pillaged art. SS officers. Mexico. South America. Hong Kong. The Pilos. Breaking World War II German codes. U-boats. Missing files. The HMS Coventry. The Seahawk. U-1408.

Planet Earth was a very large world in January, 1945. It was a much smaller planet today.

Gem flipped off the lights downstairs and carefully climbed the staircase to the loft. Wyatt slipped into bed only a few short minutes before Gem slid her body between the sheets. He reached over, pulling her against him. She would awaken in two short hours. Two short hours of sleep for both of them.

Before she closed her eyes Gem thought of Wyatt's comment along the walk to the cairns. He said he had been to Hell at least twice. The battle to get James clean and sober. James's death. Had there been a third time? And if so, what had been the third time?

Gem agonized over breakfast the next morning. Trilby was one matter; living with the man was quite another. She would gladly exchange Trilby this very moment for a future without Wyatt Grantham. But she could easily get used to Trilby. However, Wyatt Grantham could not continue to be part of the equation.

"You are frowning. Why?" Wyatt said conversationally.

"I don't think I can bear to be in a car with you for ten hours," Gem sighed, referring to the planned drive back to London that coming weekend.

"Much less than ten. I have a heavy foot on the pedal," Wyatt chuckled.

"Speeding tickets?" Gem gave him a curious look.

"A few. You'll have your book to read when you're not driving. We'll stop at that bookshop to select another book for you for the drive."

"You'll criticize and irritate me when I drive," Gem protested.

"Only when you speed," Wyatt said firmly, but then he winked at her.

Gem couldn't help but laugh.

He started clearing the table; Gem gathered her plates, watching how efficiently he managed the washing up. He seemed so relaxed, in good humour. Why couldn't he always be this way? There were flashes of the man with whom she had fallen in love. But the flashes were false, for that man had never existed.

Gem felt like screaming. She would like some sanity in her life instead of this constant confusion, and the constant bickering. Perhaps if she held her tongue he wouldn't have fodder with which to taunt her. It was a good thought, but Gem didn't know how long she could manage that concept.

"Hat, hiking shoes, sunglasses," Wyatt finally spoke again. "Floral Hall Gardens today, Mrs Grantham."

She resisted the urge to respond by look or word to his taunt, quietly following his command.

Wyatt parked the vehicle in a city car park, suggesting they walk to the Floral Gardens. He carried the camera case as they strolled along the West Bank of the River Ness. It was a good thirty minutes before they reached the gardens, but the weather was pleasant and Gem could focus on her surroundings and clear her mind a bit.

Wyatt suddenly turned to her frowning. "I neglected to inquire," he scanned the clear blue sky. "Were the photos of the cathedrals the quality you require, or do we take another drive to Elgin and Fortrose?"

"The photos are excellent, thank you," Gem replied courteously.

Wyatt nodded. "We needn't rush our tour of the gardens then."

One could easily spend the entire day touring the Floral Hall Gardens. It was a veritable sub-tropical paradise in two glass houses. Gem and Wyatt followed the curving paths, listening to the tour guides, but wandering at their own pace. Wyatt read aloud the brochure information as Gem shot frame upon frame of the tropical plants.

"I think we should invest in palms for the Hall," Wyatt suggested.

"They would require quite a bit of maintenance," Gem murmured as she removed the roll of film from her camera, inserting another.

"We have a gardener," Wyatt replied.

You have a gardener. The Hall is your home not mine, Gem did not voice her thought.

"Perhaps you should have banana trees and orchids," Gem referred to the other items catching Wyatt's interest.

"Very much too involved for the Hall," he shook his head.

It was a pleasant morning for Gem, despite the company. Wyatt was amused by the koi pond and Gem found watching the fish relaxing.

"A definite must, but no doubt it will cause great dissension between Mr Becton and Mr M."

"Mr M?" Gem repeated as a matter of courtesy, indicating she was listening, if not interested in his remarks.

"Mr Macinski, the estate manager."

"Ah." Hopefully she would not be required to be involved in the management of the estate, or the house. Wyatt's estate, Wyatt's home - her prison, no doubt. He tainted the pleasure of the morning with his remarks at the waterfall.

"A striking scene for a wedding ceremony. Tropical paradise, the palms, the cascading water," he observed.

"I suggest you celebrate your next marriage here," Gem replied with a mock sweet smile. "Please make it soon."

"The subtle sarcasm of a brilliant mind," Wyatt drawled.

"Were I brilliant, I would not be in this situation," she failed to bite her tongue.

"You were outwitted," he replied. "And you are becoming crabby. I suggest lunch in the coffee shop and then we'll tour the outdoor gardens."

The coffee shop was quite comfortable. They decided on panini sandwiches and tea, and while they awaited the order Wyatt viewed the artwork on the walls. The brochure indicated the art was produced by local artists and was available for sale. Wyatt requested Gem's suggestions in choosing a number of the paintings.

"For the Hall?" she queried. Not having seen his home, she did not feel adequate to make suggestions.

"For the Berlin office. It's one of GEI's busiest offices. I think sending artwork from Inverness would be a proper, subtle invasion, don't you?"

"Indeed," Gem agreed solemnly.

Wyatt approved all her suggestions, purchasing and arranging shipping to Germany.

The extensive outdoor gardens occupied them the entire afternoon. Wyatt requested Gem to shoot various views of the outdoor pond, suggesting they have double prints developed so that Mr Becton would have a set for his perusal.

"You need not share the photos of the banana or coffee trees, nor those of the orchids and begonias with Mr Becton. His budget is, after all, somewhat limited," Wyatt informed her. "However, the pathways, the garden walls, the ponds, waterfall and the fountain might be of interest to him, and won't cripple the Hall's finances."

In spite of the half hour stroll back to their vehicle, they were able to drop off the film at the photo shop for pick up the following day. Dinner at a pub was delightful, for the food and the live music. Gem was not really hungry but had to eat due to Wyatt's edict: no food, no brew.

"You have been on your feet for eight hours. You have walked for hours today. Did you not eat before you met me, Mrs Grantham?" Wyatt frowned as she picked at her food.

"Will you please stop calling me that!" Gem said irritably.

"I want to impress the fact upon you that that is your new name. You shall be addressed as such now. Do you need assistance leaning to spell your new surname?"

Berk, Gem silently retorted. "I shall manage the spelling," she said evenly. "Perhaps you should eat more salads. More greens might cause you to be less disagreeable."

Wyatt laughed; that was not the reaction he had expected.

Gem ate every bit of her dinner. She could not make conversation with her mouth full. She was amused by the young waitress serving their table. She watched Wyatt's face for reaction as the young blonde bent over a good deal more than was necessary, bestowing an ample view of her décolletage when she served Wyatt's order to him. Wyatt, however gave no visible reaction, directing his attention instead to Gem. His lack of response to the waitress did not dim the young woman's bid for his attention.

"You had best leave her a good tip for her show tonight," Gem teased Wyatt, as the waitress moved her display to the bar for another round of beer for her most handsome customer and his companion.

"I tip for service not for views," Wyatt said dryly.

"If you need more spice in your life, I can easily manage the drive to the cottage on my own tonight," she teased.

"I do not require outside spice in my life, sweetheart. I still have a lot to teach you. Perhaps another lesson this evening," he replied calmly.

Gem sent him a veiled glare.

"I see I win again. Now relax and enjoy the music. Pub groups are one of the many jewels of this city. We should purchase cds before we leave Inverness. We should have souvenirs of our honeymoon. You need a remembrance."

"I don't need souvenirs to help me remember this nightmare. I need something to help me forget it," she retorted, again only prompting laughter from him. Again that thick skin!

He pulled her chair close to his, draping his arm across her shoulders as they listened to a local band.

"Must we sit so close?" she protested, irritated by his proprietary behaviour.

Wyatt leaned over to whisper in her ear. "Indeed. There are many men in this room looking at you. Lovely to look upon; however, they do not realize you are dangerous to know. You are still not worthy of being the kind of woman a man would die for."

Gem stiffened, and before she could make a scathing reply he again whispered. "Listen to the music, drink your beer, while I reflect on a lesson for you for tonight, Trilby."

Gem sat at the kitchen table, gazing through the window, her chin resting on her hand. The dark hours were to search for the Pilos, not to reflect on the Blasted Svengali. Thank heavens he was asleep! How did men learn what they knew?

Argentina. Add Argentina to the list, for it was well documented that Nazi's had escaped to that country during the ensuring chaos in the spring of 1945. Allied Forces continued their advance across Europe while Adolph the Evil's troops were decimated - Thank God!

Romantic music on satellite radio, candles, murmured whispers, the gentlest touch. Gem's cheeks flamed as the memory flooded her thoughts. Blast!

He needed a mistress!

She sorted, retrieving a reference of hundreds of thousands of art objects stolen by the Evil Monsters. The art had been stored at various locations in Paris and in Germany until Allied Forces started the heavy bombing of Europe. Art objects had been moved by the Evil Empire to salt mines for preservation, and many thousands of the items had been recovered. But not all; and many items recovered had not yet been returned to the original owners by the end of the first decade of this new century. The scales of justice needed to be greased or kicked in the pants.

Art objects moved to Mexico, South America, Hong Kong. Who had been on the receiving end? It was, admittedly, just a theory, but it would be the theory of her focus. She turned off the light in the kitchen, looking out at the stars.

The theory and then the finding of a trail to lead to the Pilos.

There didn't seem to be a single hope for a divorce from Wyatt. He wouldn't even give proper consideration to the concept. He referred to their marriage as a Game! His Game. His rules.

The Timor Sea. The Arafura Sea. The Gulf of Carpentaria. Three days. THREE DAYS, remained before she could charge her mobile and reconnect to the Agency. Hopefully progress had been made in her absence. Hopefully Mrs Brown and Harry had gleaned information or fresh insight into this drama on their 'holiday'.

Four o'clock, Wyatt glanced at his watch. Stopping the clocks had made no difference. She hadn't even noticed the time pieces no longer indicated the correct time. He pulled on his dressing gown. Perhaps disrupting the time frame would alter the situation.

Gem started as the lower level suddenly flooded with light. Wyatt walked down the stairs, drew her from the kitchen chair, and wordlessly led her back to bed. Gem didn't resist; there was no point in doing so. His Game. His rules.

Wyatt silently held her in his arms, her breathing revealing she lay awake and so then did he, finally closing his eyes as her breathing became steady, shallow. And she slept. He turned his wrist to check his watch. Five o'clock. Again two o'clock to five o'clock. A time pattern not seeming to alter. Again, he knew, she would waken in only two short hours.

"I believe Loch Ness is out of the question for sight-seeing," Wyatt ventured at breakfast. "It is a lake and a very deep one."

"Pass," Gem said without considering the attraction.

"A picnic and hiking in the hills then, away from any bodies of water larger than a stream?" he suggested.

"Yes," Gem agreed quietly. At least at times he did listen to her.

She needed colour in her cheeks, Wyatt reflected. Sparkly, purple eyes. He hadn't seen sparkle in her eyes since their wedding day. Perhaps she was actually reacting to no longer being in control of her life. She would never change. But she could be controlled.

Gem descended the stairs, ready for the day. Wyatt regarded her without expression.

"Hat," he said crisply. Why did she require repeated instructions for such a simple item? Was it so very difficult to see the sun was shining in a cloudless sky?

Gem glared at him, then wordlessly retraced her steps to get the blasted chapeau.

France. Stolen art stored in museums in or around Paris.

She shook herself to stop the automatic sorting. How often she and Gemmy had remarked of the fact of unbidden information suddenly dredging up from mental recesses at the most unexpected times. A word, a look, an object during their day, sending flashbacks of reading material to their brains.

Gem hadn't had the automatic sorting flow this much since 30 May. Perhaps it was her anger towardss Wyatt that had released a temporary block. To be honest, she hadn't realized the automatic sorting had been a bit blocked. What else had been blocked of which she was unaware?

"It's only a hat," Wyatt called from the foot of the stairs. "Did you misplace it?"

Gem realized she had been standing in the centre of the room, hat in hand, completely unaware of her surroundings. She quickly cleaned her teeth, then met him at the cottage door.

"Teeth," she offered an explanation.

"Okay," was his only reply.

He had already packed a basket for lunch, including two bottles of wine. He set down the basket, reaching to a chair for the crème coloured sweater he had purchased in Inverness.

"I don't want it," Gem said coolly. "I shall purchase my own clothes."

Wyatt tied the sweater around her waist despite her protests. "My error," he said firmly. "I stated comfortable clothes. I neglected to mention something for cool days. I merely remedied an error."

He was very striking in the deep blue sweater he had purchased the same day for himself.

"Oh," Gem replied, accepting his explanation. She had nothing other than the shawls and a thin windcheater. "Thank you then," she said with quiet effort.

They cut across the cottage property, right, then up into the hills. Very shortly they were deep in the forest, following a path indicating years of use. Within an hour they were in a clearing, lush green, and over the rise Gem sighted a crumbling crofter's cottage. The stone walls surrounding the cottage and the neglected field were in better condition than the cottage.

The play of light and shadows on the walls and cottage kept Gem busy for hours, capturing a shot, working different angles, waiting for the sun to move across the sky to the next hour, silently waiting for a pheasant to take flight.

Wyatt stretched out on his side in the field watching her work. She was amazing, working so smoothly, visualizing the shot, patiently waiting for a cloud to pass, camera held firmly, immobile as stone to capture a red squirrel in the vacant window of the cottage.

As she moved into the trees beyond the cottage, Wyatt quietly followed, stealthy as was she, alert to every movement in the shadows. Gem sensed him beside her, grateful that he moved when she did, stopping as did she. His almost inaudible whisper alerted her to the red deer straight ahead of them, immobile, head alert, ears pricked for danger. Gem clicked the shot, the sharp sound of the camera sending the deer fleeing through the trees. They walked on as one, moving silently as possible deeper into the forest.

"There," Wyatt mouthed, pointing to a fallen log.

Gem nodded, getting the shot before mouthing a reply, "What was it?" of the small, thin creature, dark, the tail long, ears short, resembling a squirrel, crème coloured patches below its ears.

"Pine marten."

"I thought it was a squirrel," Gem murmured.

Their presence was felt and no other wild creatures came forth to be immortalized on the film in Gem's camera. They retreated to the sun to talk about the wildlife she had photographed.

"Lunch," Wyatt announced, setting out the meal beneath a shade tree.

"I don't think I've ever heard of a pine marten," Gem mused.

"It's like the history you don't know repeating itself," Wyatt nodded. "Creatures you have never heard of become extinct without your knowledge."

Gem reflected on the seriousness of his observation.

"Do you hunt?" she asked, sipping a glass of wine. "Aside from me," she added a sting to her words.

"That's my clever girl," Wyatt raised an eyebrow. "Aside from you. No. I do not. You?" he turned the query back to her. "Aside from marks - and with your camera."

"No," she flashed him a glare.

"No reason to be nettled," he said smoothly. "You initiated the subject. And you know what you've done." *And I will find out every sordid detail - eventually.*

Gem ignored his words. She looked up at the sun, enjoying its warmth, and that of the sweater. She had to admit the sweater was an excellent suggestion, despite the sun and the mild breeze.

Wyatt watched her survey the view from their position beneath the tree. The sweater, a perfect fit, delicately accentuated the curves of her breasts. He set down his wine glass, taking hers from her hand. He teased her lips with his, easing her back and down to the blanket, his fingers slowly sliding down the zipper of her sweater.

Gem's breath caught in her throat, his kisses long, teasing, coaxing, his hands slipped beneath her tee to caress her- "No, no," she turned her head, "not here."

"Merely a prelude, my dear," he murmured.

Even his preludes were dangerous, Gem reflected, changing the film in her camera. They had hiked for hours, returning to the cottage as the sun was setting. Wyatt had made dinner, cottage pie and chips, then he had insisted on an early night. The early night did not involve sleep, but rather another lesson.

Two days. TWO DAYS. Then access to her mobile, her computers, and the Agency! Gem paced the kitchen floor, her brain too tired to sort, her thoughts drifting back to 30 May. She reviewed every minute of her conversation with Gemmy, the abrupt awakening at two o'clock, Mrs Brown and Harry arriving, the packing at the house.

Mrs Brown and Harry had been in Australia. Where was Paul Andriani that night? South East Asia was often his territory of operations. But he could also be in South America, Africa, he could be anywhere in the world actually at any given time.

But! But he had met Gemmy in Barcelona in mid-May. What had they discussed? What were the chances of Mrs Brown arranging a meeting for Gem with Paul Andriani?

Saturday was the day of errands, calling for the photos, a visit to the bookshop, purchase of cds, pub lunch, cleaning the bathroom, bedroom, kitchen and lounge, washing clothes, and the final packing.

Again an early night - not only for sleeping.

Wyatt went back to sleep as Gem eased out of his arms. Someone had to be awake in the morning to do the majority of the driving - all of it, if Gem seemed unable to focus completely behind the wheel.

Gem paced through the dark hours. She had no idea what to expect of her coming life at Grantham Hall. If she had to manage staff she would be completely unprepared for that duty. The Lawsons and Forresters had never had staff.

She had lived in England, Australia, England again, at university, at her flat. For the past six years her life had revolved around traveling. It would seem so strange to be situated in one location. Her daily life and routine would be at Wyatt's whim. Still, she would have to carve out time for her search; the book would be secondary. She dragged her fingers through her hair. Her stomach churned at the thought of the battles to come, the need for privacy to work. Phone calls to the Agency were one thing. But she needed access to meetings with Mrs Brown. However she had to manage it, she must be able to meet Mrs Brown.

Gem's internal alarm clock struck as usual at seven o'clock. Wyatt's side of the bed was cold. His luggage, set by the railing the previous night, was gone. She could hear sounds in the kitchen, then suddenly he was sitting on the bed alongside her.

"Good morning," he gave her a brief kiss, "quick shower, breakfast is on the cooker. We'll be on the road as close to eight as possible."

And he was gone.

Five minute shower, ten minutes to dress. He reappeared to take her luggage downstairs and out to the Land Rover. By eight o'clock, breakfast finished, kitchen clean, they were indeed on the road.

Gem was assigned the task of the cd player. And as he had said, Wyatt did have a heavy foot on the pedal, but managed not to get stopped on the road - or snapped by a camera – to Gem's knowledge.

They stopped for a pub lunch but Gem had lost track of their location. She read for two hours and Wyatt was thankfully silent. She drove for two hours then relinquished the wheel at Wyatt's insistence. He quit the dual carriageway, and cut cross country on roads and lanes, leaving Gem completely confused of the directions to Ticking Bottom.

"How long have you been troubled with insomnia?" Wyatt asked suddenly, turning down the volume of the music.

"I am not troubled by it," Gem countered. "It's just there."

She saw the muscle in Wyatt's jaw tighten.

"How long have you had insomnia?" he rephrased the query.

"Awhile," Gem shrugged.

"Awhile as in months, years?"

Gem raked her fingers through her hair. "Awhile. Just that. Simply that," she said edgily.

"Have you consulted a physician?"

"I don't need to see a doctor. I am fine. It will pass eventually." When the Pilos is found. She was unaware of the sigh that escaped her lips.

"You need more sleep. I am older than you, and I definitely require more than I have managed the past nine nights in bed next to you," he said firmly.

"Stay on your side of the bed then," she said simply. "I have no desire to keep you awake at night."

"You're lying to yourself now, my dear," he drawled. "That certainly is a novel change."

"You are the most arrogant man I have ever met!" Gem said, amazed.

"That is quite a remark when one imagines the possible length of the list of men you have indeed met," he nodded. "Do not confuse arrogance with self-assurance, sweetheart," he advised.

"I am not your dear or sweetheart," Gem retorted.

"That discussion is long over. Do not return to it again," he ordered.

He did not speak again for a few minutes. Gem was about to return to her book, when he returned to the original subject of their chat.

"Regarding your insomnia," he began, and Gem groaned audibly. "I have informed the Macinskis of your problem, so that they will not be concerned to see lights on at the Hall at all hours of the night."

"Thank you." Mr Macinski was Mr M, she recalled, the estate manager.

Chapter Ten

"Where is Ticking Bottom then?" Gem asked, thinking to gain control of a hopefully civil conversation.

"Somewhere between Bedford and Cambridge," Wyatt said obliquely.

"Is the location a secret?" she queried, a bit teasingly.

"Not as such. It's a rather small, forgotten village secluded in lush forests."

"You let the world swirl around you, yet not allow it to influence your lives?"

"So to speak," Wyatt nodded. "Watch for four beech trees on your left," he ordered.

A few minutes later, Gem saw the beeches prominently in front of a stand of trees that stretched along the side of the lane.

"There!"

"Watch for four beech trees," he repeated the instructions. "Count to ten slowly."

Gem counted and watched. "There!"

"Count to ten again, and look for four beeches."

Gem nodded. "There!"

"And turn left," he said, as he directed the Land Rover onto another lane.

"The lane isn't marked," Gem observed.

"No. From the opposite direction, as in driving out from London, four, four, four, turn right."

"Not properly marked for emergency vehicles," Gem frowned.

"T.B. is on the list. There's no concern in that area."

"T.B.," Gem mused.

"Abbreviation used by the villagers."

Gem's eyes wandered over the countryside. Meadows and fields lined the lane, thick forests stretched behind, all the way to the horizon. Wyatt turned onto another lane. Gem was losing track of the route from the first turn by the first set of beeches. There was an old stone bridge, and then she thought another turn, and another old stone bridge. The lanes meandered, winding, until she was completely lost. Then Ticking Bottom came into view. Stone cottages with thatched roofs, and stone shops, also with thatched roofs, bordered the narrow cobblestone lane.

Wyatt slowed the Land Rover, allowing Gem to absorb first impressions of the village.

"No speeding allowed in T.B.," he said firmly. "Don't want any locals crunched beneath wheels."

"It's perfect," Gem marveled. "In which cottage does one Miss Marple reside?"

"Last one on the right, just beyond the chemist's shop," Wyatt chuckled.

Wyatt slowed the vehicle to a crawl, pointing out the bookshop, pub, gift shop, chemist, doctor's office, greengrocer, the Mercantile, bakery, a dentist's office, the rail station on the left, the smithy.

"A blacksmith?" Gem remarked in surprise.

"Also does carpentry and thatching."

"It looks like an artist's conception of the proper English village," Gem chuckled.

"Quite so."

"No school," Gem mused.

"Next village but one," Wyatt replied.

He directed the Land Rover across yet another old stone bridge, following the narrow cobblestone lane to wind up towards a green, park-like expanse. At the base of a hill Wyatt pressed the brake.

"Grantham Hall," he quietly announced.

It was completely unlike what Gem would have imagined if she had made the effort to imagine Grantham Hall. It was charming; mullioned, leaded glass windows peaked through masses of ivy creeping up the walls and over the roof. Grantham Hall was a long grey stone structure of three stories, yet it was not immense in the category of the considerable sized estates of which the U.K. was famous.

"It's lovely," Gem said quietly. "Not what I expected."

"It is not a baronial palace," Wyatt cocked a brow. "Were you expecting Pemberley?"

"Hardly, since you are no Mr Darcy," she said coolly. "I wasn't criticizing. It's not - too - much. I had expected overpowering, very grand." Hopefully there wouldn't be a large staff to face every day.

He drove the Land Rover up the long cobblestone drive to the right of the Hall, parking just short of a side entrance door. As they unloaded the luggage from the boot, a man of about fifty, dressed in jeans and denim shirt, Grantham Hall embroidered on the left side pocket, appeared from the rear of the house.

"Mr M - may I present my wife, Gemimah Forester Grantham," Wyatt said smoothly.

"How do you do, it's a pleasure to meet you," Gem extended her hand.

The man, a bit taken back, pulled off his woven hat and firmly grasped her hand. "Amos Macinski, ma'am," he replied with a wide grin.

"Mr M is the estate manager and constant adversary of our gardener, whom you will meet another time. Sunday is Mr Becton's day to peruse the countryside for plant traders. Mr M is the man to speak to if you want something altered, walls demolished, bathrooms retiled, curtains hung, walls painted, and what have you."

"Thank you," Gem nodded awkwardly. She had no intention of requesting any such changes, her only wish being to survive each day with some remnants of sanity.

"Mrs M is our housekeeper and must be around here somewhere," Wyatt began.

"Right behind you." A woman matching Mr M's age stepped around Wyatt. She had a friendly smile, bright blue eyes, and short brown hair that was losing a battle with gray. "I was just starting your dinner. Mind you! Inverness to the Hall by this time. Did he garner a speeding notice then?" she winked at Gem, who shook her head and choked back a laugh.

"Mrs Ada Macinski, my wife, Gem Grantham," Wyatt dropped the effort of a formal introduction.

"Welcome to your new home, ma'am," Mrs M smiled, startled as was her husband when Gem shook her hand.

"It's a pleasure to meet you," Gem smiled. The M's were friendly, if their employer was not.

Blast protocol. Whatever it would be in this circumstance. Gem wasn't raised in a home with staff and she didn't put on fussy airs.

"The kettle is on. Or would you prefer a glass of wine?" Mrs M queried to Gem, as Mr M unloaded the remaining luggage, carrying it to the side door.

"Wine would be lovely," Gem murmured, starting to follow the estate manager.

"Mr W, take your bride inside properly then," Mrs M crisply ordered.

To Gem's bewilderment, Wyatt led her across the long cobblestone walk to the formal double doors at the front of the Hall.

"We rarely use this entrance," he unlocked the door, pushed it open, then swept Gem up in his arms. "The bride must be carried over the threshold of her new home," he said with a decided drawl.

Once the threshold was crossed, he kissed her slowly. And cameras clicked, startling the couple. Mrs M and Mr M each held a camera to Gem's dismay. Wyatt set her down, shaking his head at his staff.

"We'll unpack, then I have phone calls to place. Mrs M will give you a tour of the house when you are ready," Wyatt said firmly.

Gem quickly looked about her as the men ferried the luggage in from the Land Rover. The double door entrance opened onto a wide main hall. Directly opposite the double doors was a wide staircase. The walls and staircase were a deep, highly polished cherry wood. The gray stone floor echoed the exterior of the house.

Mrs M watched the young woman's gaze wander the area. A very young woman, the housekeeper mused.

"Living room," Wyatt indicated the double doors to the left of the main hall, "library, den, study, sitting room," he waved a hand down the hall past the living room. "Kitchen over there," he waved his hand to the right of the main hall.

Mrs M shook her head. "Come down when you are ready, Mrs Grantham," she smiled at Gem, then shook her head at the Master of the Hall.

Double doors at the top and to the left of the staircase opened to the master bedroom suite: a cosy sitting room with deep blue walls, a rich wine upholstered settee, two blue, crème, and wine striped wingback chairs, coffee table, lamp tables, and a fireplace to the right.

"Master bedroom through here," Wyatt led Gem around the far side of the fireplace wall. A bank of windows extended from the sitting room across the bedroom wall. Gem peeked through the curtains at the view of the gardens and a

151

sprawling green lawn boasting very large oak and beech trees. A window seat with cushions extended below the stretch of windows.

There was a very large, canopied four poster bed of intricately carved cherry wood, marble topped bedside tables, two wingback chairs and another coffee table. The bedroom colours were the same as those in the sitting room and there was also a fireplace facing the bed.

"My dressing room and bath are in here," he pointed to an open door to the left of the bed. Yours is around here," he led her to the far right side of the bed. He scowled when he saw that her dressing room was not empty. "Apparently Mrs M thought to unpack the boxes sent from your flat. You will thank her, of course. Mrs M is not your personal maid. We do not run to such niceties here. This is a country home not a five start hotel. Mrs M is the Hall Manager. She cooks, cleans, and manages the house. Do not make demands of her."

"I won't," Gem quickly assured him.

"See that you don't. The Macinskis are very kind people. They are not to be victims in any clever plans you might think to plot. And I will not tolerate you using the Macinskis as a buffer between us, my dear. You attempt that and I will properly deal with you.

"Very put in my place, aren't I?" Gem said coolly. "Thank you for a lovely welcome to your home."

Wyatt ignored the remarks. "I have work to do."

He carried his luggage into his dressing room, then Gem's bags into hers. She set about unpacking, and noticed the bathroom door had a lock. She twisted it to make sure it worked, unaware that Wyatt was watching her.

"Doors can be replaced. Locks can be removed," he said dryly, then left her alone in her dressing room.

Berk. I hate him, I hate him, I hate him, Gem practised her new mantra.

Unpacking took Gem a total of five minutes. She quickly showered, changed to a mid-calf, blue skirt and matching jumper, putting her trip worn clothes in the hamper. She would sort out the laundry issues later. She heard the shower running in the other bathroom, and made a quick escape from the master suite.

Gem retraced her steps down to the main hall and towardss the direction where Wyatt had indicated the kitchen to be, following a long wide hall, with closed doors on the right and left. At the end of the hall was the kitchen.

Mrs M was working at a large island counter, a wine glass in front of her.

"Mrs G, come in, come in," the housekeeper waved a knife in a beckoning motion. "Wine?" she smiled.

"Yes, please," Gem said gratefully.

"I prefer ice in mine. You?" Gem nodded. Mrs M produced a wine glass and a bottle of wine. She filled the glass, handing it across the counter to Gem, then indicated a breakfast stool. "Sit yourself down and relax. Traveling can be so exhausting."

"It was a long drive," Gem conceded - and with a less than ideal companion!

Gem sat on the stool, facing the housekeeper and sipped the wine, and looked around the kitchen. The kitchen was white; white bead board cupboards below the white, large tile counters, glass front white cupboards above the counters, white fridge, white cooker and hood, white sink, white back splash; the cupboards and drawers below the island counter were also white.

"Wine glasses cupboard to the left behind you, wine bottles lower cupboard behind you," Mrs M smiled.

Gem nodded. The kitchen would appear quite sterile were it not for the gray stone floors, colourful dishes and glasses behind the glass-front cupboard doors, and the hanging plants above the kitchen sink; windows above the sink overlooked the span of the front lawn.

"Long drives are wearying, but dinner will perk you up a bit. I'm just going to pop it in the cooker then, be ready in an hour."

"Thank you," Gem nodded, noticing the housekeeper's glass need refilling, so she added more ice and wine, and handed it to the older woman.

"Thank you, dear," the housekeeper managed to hide her surprise.

"You are welcome, ma'am," Gem nodded. "This is a very bright kitchen," she observed.

"It's a good working one. Mr M did the remodel last year. The windows used to be tiny, and there was no island. The Mister had old windows at the carriage house and he managed to fit them in here. A good proper job he did. He'll paint or change out anything here that doesn't suit you," Mrs M assured her.

"I should think the kitchen should entirely suit the cook," Gem replied. "I find the room very comfortable."

"You're seeing the cook," Mrs M chuckled, "and it does suit me. That's settled then. Mr W has specific food requirements, and you must tell me yours."

"I will eat whatever you prepare," Gem said, then jumped up from the stool at the sound of the voice behind her.

"No." Wyatt had entered the room to take a beer from the fridge. "She detests lamb, mutton, veal, and anything that lives in water," he said crisply. "Mrs Grantham would exist on pub grub if at all possible," he added to Gem's dismay, causing her to feel that she was a difficult person for whom to cook.

"So noted," Mrs M nodded. "Have either of you clothes for the wash?"

"No," Wyatt replied.

"And thank you for unpacking my clothes for me," Gem said sincerely. "It was very kind of you to do so."

"You are welcome, Mrs G," the housekeeper replied, "not that it took more than five minutes," she said, looking at the timer on the cooker. "Plenty of time. I'll show you to your office."

"Office?" Gem's brows knit in surprise.

"Mr W called last week to say you required an office," she looked at Wyatt. "He thought to re-do his old study for you as he prefers to work in the library." She shook her head. "The study would be a bit dreary for you. I thought the old solarium," she informed Wyatt. "It hasn't been used much for years. Bright and sunny, good size, and it looks over the gardens."

Gem didn't dare look at Wyatt. What power did Mrs M have that she could countermand the head of the house without requesting to do so?

Wyatt shrugged as Mrs M led the way through the kitchen door Gem had entered, down a short hall to the right and through another door.

"Gosh!" Gem's eyes grew wide at the long, wide room. The long interior wall would be excellent for hanging art, and opposite it was a bank of windows running the entire length of the room. Below the windows was a long, dark cherry wood counter with open shelves and cupboards below. The windows overlooked lavish gardens and a sprawling rear lawn. On the right wall was an exterior door leading directly out to the gardens. Her desk had been placed against the short, far left wall. Auntie Jane's comfy chair, settee and chest of drawers were against the long interior wall.

The boxes of books, computers, stationery supplies, cd player, television, and dvd player, from her flat were at the centre of the room; her swivel chair was at her desk.

"Mr M painted the walls white to clean them up a bit. You choose the colour you prefer and he'll do a proper paint job for you. Mr M built the counter and the shelves. You'll likely want a rug or two on the floor for comfort," Mrs M suggested.

"And curtains. It's a bit draughty in here in winter. Tell Mr M what you decide and he'll arrange it," Wyatt interjected. "You were correct," he gave the housekeeper a nod. "Much preferable to the study. Dinner?"

"Half six as usual," the cook said firmly.

"Very well," Wyatt nodded to the women and left the room.

Mrs M continued the tour of the office. "Along here," she led Gem the length of the room, past the desk, "is a bathroom," she opened a door on the right, then the opposite door, "and back to the hall."

"It's lovely, thank you for all your good thoughts and work," Gem sighed happily, as they walked back across the room. She had a perfect place to escape from Wyatt.

"Oh dear," Mrs M frowned, looking out the windows to the garden. "It appears that the Mister is a bit agitated."

Gem followed her eyes and saw the estate manager staring at a wide staked area in the rear yard.

"Mr Becton, the gardener, insists on installing a pond system come spring. Mr M wishes to install Mr Becton in the Thames!"

Gem choked on her wine, laughing. "A Thames art installation."

Mrs M chuckled. "Oh, Mr M wishes to know if you want the garden door removed to allow additional wall space."

"No!" Gem quickly refused. It would be a quick escape from Wyatt when necessary!

Mrs M continued the tour through the door opposite the bathroom. "The great room, as Mrs Senior used to call it," she advised, opening the double doors across the hall.

Gem liked the room; it was very large: huge fireplace, overstuffed chairs, two black button back chesterfield sofas, coffee tables, other tables of various heights, reading lamps; the fabric colours were mainly of burgundy and greys; apparently the flag stone floors extended throughout the entire ground floor. Gem knew without looking at the signature of the paintings on the walls that they were James's work. Mrs M led her back towards the kitchen; the next set of double doors opened to a formal dining room: twelve guests could easily be seated around the long, oval, mahogany table; the chandelier sparkled, antique vases reposed on elegant side tables, three china cabinets were filled will lovely porcelain dishes. Perhaps selected by Mrs Senior, Gem silently mused.

"It's a very lovely room," Gem said quietly. She wouldn't want to touch the fine china for fear of breaking it.

"A proper waste of space," Mrs M announced. "This room is rarely used; the breakfast room being much cosier." She led Gem to a room off the formal dining room, which was also accessible to the kitchen and to a long butler's pantry situated between the kitchen and the dining room.

The breakfast room was a good size, square, and had floor to ceiling windows on two sides. Every bit of space that wasn't windows was covered in small mosaic tiles, crème coloured, painted with white daffodils, pink hollyhocks, red roses, and leaves and trailing vines in various shades of green; three small stain glass chandeliers hung over a dark green wrought iron table which would seat six, however only four chairs were present. Baskets of trailing ivy hung in front of the windows.

"This room is perfect," Gem said breathlessly. "I could live in this room!"

"It's like eating in a garden," Mrs M nodded. "Mr W prefers it for meals when he is here - which has been a rarity for many, many years. But now you'll both be living here!" she smiled warmly.

In separate worlds as much as possible, Gem hoped.

Mrs M sniffed the air. "Back to diner prep. Look about on your own, my dear, or I can show you about tomorrow."

"I'll unpack in the office," Gem decided. She felt awkward wandering around the house on her own. It was Wyatt's domain, not hers, and she would feel like an intruder, which, actually, she was.

Her office was a straight shot from the breakfast room through the immaculate butler's pantry and across the hall.

Mrs M appeared in the office, filled Gem's glass with ice and wine, and then returned to her work in the kitchen. Gem quickly set about making the old solarium into a haven. Within fifteen minutes she had her computer hooked to the cables at the centre of the counter, the printer printing, the telly, cd player, dvd player, and radio unpacked and working at the far right corner of the counter. She put the combination lock file cabinet on a bottom shelf at the far left by her desk - hopefully it was unobtrusive to Wyatt's eyes.

The computer was humming as she unpacked reams of printer paper, dictionaries, thesaurus, paper cutter, paper shredder - to destroy many now unwanted photographs - rulers, shears and the remaining office paraphernalia.

Rugs would definitely suit the room and add a bit of colour. She made a quick list for the shops - for whenever that trip would be occurring. She was living by Wyatt's rules now. He called the shots. But not forever, she silently assured herself, and not when she could ease out of them whenever possible.

One nail protruded from the wall, perfect for the flower clock she had purchased years ago in Venice. The elaborate design was out of place in its new environment, but then so was she. And the clock was a lovely memory of her first holiday with Gemmy in Italy. Gemmy had, as usual, purchased jewellery as a souvenir of the trip - a delicate silver filigree bracelet, currently nestled in Gem's jewellery box, somewhere in one of the cartons still to be unpacked.

And when she found the carton she must look for other pieces of jewellery that James might have given to Gemmy. She couldn't very well give Wyatt the box and suggest he look through the jewellery. What if she had already given him all the Grantham family heirlooms? He would think her horrible for not recognizing the gifts from James - as though men had given her gifts of jewellery for years. Let him just think she was hoarding the heirlooms, as, no doubt, he already did. - Or perhaps he would ask for a specific item and she could find it to give to him. Diamonds versus cubic zirconium. CZ's were fashioned to give the impression they were diamonds, weren't they?

She would look for the jewellery box during the dark hours. Then thought better of it. Wyatt was working in his library; Mrs M was in the kitchen. Gem shifted cartons, looking at the computer generated labels she had affixed to the top of each box. Second carton from the bottom of the second pile of boxes. It was marked 'frippery' - their dad's term for all things that glittered - of interest to the women in his life.

Gem slipped the bracelet from the box. Her sister had worn it constantly - except when she was on assignment. Neither of them wore jewellery when on assignment, Gem smiled to herself, then shook off the thought.

Perhaps if she wore the bracelet it would help her focus on finding Gemmy when other distractions might attempt to derail her. The clasp of the bracelet was tricky, but she managed it, wearing it on her right wrist so it would not became tangled with her watch band and ruined.

She set the jewellery box on a shelf under the counter, and started unpacking her books. How kind of Mr M to have so properly fitted the office with ample storage space. She would have to find gifts for the Macinskis for their thoughtfulness to her.

"Very efficient," Wyatt drawled from the doorway. "Quite computer savvy aren't you. One of your numerous talents."

"Just read the instruction manual when you first install," Gem replied, trying not to sound as defensive as she felt.

"Good memory," he complimented.

You have no idea! Gem silently replied. "Actually I have an excellent memory," she said with a saccharin smile. "And you?"

Wyatt nodded. "You will discover that I also have an excellent memory, my dear," he said, his voice quiet, emotionless.

He stepped towards her, slipping a finger between the bracelet and her wrist. "A gift from a past admirer?" He lifted her wrist to his lips and kissed her palm, his eyes boring into hers.

"No," she kept her voice low, not wishing Mrs M to hear the squabble.

"Did James give it to you?" he whispered.

"No," she hissed. Gem knew exactly when and where Gemmy had purchased the bracelet.

"This is the first time you have worn it since I met you."

"Am I required to have your approval of the jewellery I wear?" she glared at him.

"We'll do that later, my dear, I promise you."

A definite warning. But why?

He seemed to read her mind. "You shall not wear jewellery other men have given you." With each word he lowered his lips to hers for a firm kiss. "Mrs M is serving dinner," he said in a normal speaking voice.

Romantic Mrs M had set the table with crystal, fine china, sterling and a vase of small sweetheart roses.

"Very beautiful, thank you," Gem said to the housekeeper, "but it was so much trouble for you."

"Not a bit, dear. Your first dinner in your new home must be special. Now leave all washing up, I'll do it in the morning," she advised.

"No Mrs M," Wyatt said firmly. "House rules prevail. Sunday is not your work day and we have troubled you enough. The washing up is ours to do."

Mrs M was hesitant, but Wyatt brooked no dispute. "Good night. Have a lovely evening," she warmly wished them with a pleased smile.

Gem watched from the breakfast room as the housekeeper picked up a large picnic hamper and left the kitchen by the side door.

Wyatt watched Gem watch the housekeeper. "Mrs M cooked enough for the four of us. The hamper has their dinner. It's efficient and she needn't cook another meal after a long day at work."

"Very practical," Gem murmured.

Wyatt held out a chair for her. Mrs M had placed the dinner settings very close together and Gem moved her chair slightly away from Wyatt's. Sham romance she did not need. She had already had enough of that!

"Washing up?" she said casually, wondering at Wyatt's remarks.

"Plain and simple. We do the washing up. As I said, Mrs M already has put in a day's work. And this," he indicated the tableware does NOT go in the dishwasher."

"Certainly not," Gem agreed. She wouldn't know how to work a dishwasher if it was an option. Her family had always done the washing up by hand.

"You are suitably handy with a dish towel, as you showed at the cottages. Perhaps you read an instruction manual on the subject at one time."

"Dinner, as delightful as usual," Gem said caustically. "At least the food is delightful if not the company."

"Wine seems to give you courage. Sass is preferable with humour, my sweet, not sarcasm. Tread carefully. The honeymoon is over," Wyatt said dryly.

The honeymoon never happened, Gem thought bitterly.

"Where do the Macinskis live?" she struggled for a subject that would hopefully not raise his ire.

"The old carriage house, beyond the gardens, opposite the stables where we now garage vehicles."

"Oh." Gem was out of conversation. She turned her attention to her dinner. Mrs M had prepared a roast, small potatoes with gravy, asparagus with cheese sauce, and a delicious salad. She was quite the chef.

"I will be at the office tomorrow, however I will return for lunch and then work from here in the afternoon. I expect you to mind your manners with the M's whenever I am not home to watch you. No games, no whinging that the frightful man trampled on a lovely, delicate flower, and hurt her feelings. Do not attempt your games with any men in Ticking Bottom. The women here would cut you to shreds. No one, including the M's, are aware of your involvement with James, nor anything else about you. Step out of line, my dear, and the world will know all about you."

Play your own game, not his, Gem reminded herself.

"Cat got your tongue again?" he said dryly. "You really should put that creature on a lead."

"Why should I speak? To what purpose? I have nothing to say to you, and I am decidedly disinterested in anything you might have to say to me."

"You are behaving like a petulant child."

"No! I am behaving like a woman who is furious! You may issue orders to your employees - staff - however you refer to them. But I am not used to taking orders." Except from Mrs Brown and Harry. And that was my career.

"The woman scorned. How droll. I AM used to giving orders, as you stated. GET used to taking them."

Nigel! She silently slammed him, doubting anyone could bear his company for any length of time.

Mrs M had prepared an apple pie, but it tasted like ashes in Gem's mouth. "I'll do the washing up, shall I? You can return to your work then," Gem offered. "Or don't you trust me with your precious crystal and china?"

Wyatt considered her words. "No I do not," he replied.

Gem sighed with relief when she could finally escape to her new haven. Washing up completed, Wyatt was again in his office. She couldn't bear to endure battles with him day after day. She had lost her resolve to no longer do verbal battles with him. Resolved again: do not let him bait you, she urged herself.

Gem organized her cds, putting one after another into the player while she unpacked and sorted books. First Paul Horn, perfect for attempting a calm mental state, then the Hothouse Flowers for her soul.

She stepped back to survey her work. The soothing, framed watercolours were propped against the skirting board - to hopefully be hung at some future time. The boxes of worthless photos - of her time with Wyatt playing tourist before their ridiculous marriage - were dumped in a box and shoved to the back of a cupboard. She would shred them in the morning.

A tickle at her brain confused her. Something she needed to do. What was it? She dragged her fingers through her hair, sorting, sorting. So very important. Gem nearly had the thought when she heard footsteps outside her door.

"It's time for bed," Wyatt said, breaching her haven.

Gem looked at the clock on the wall. "It's nine o'clock," she protested. "If you're tired, can't you go up to bed? I'll be along soon."

"I don't enjoy going to bed alone," Wyatt held out his hand.

Gem fumed as she shut down the computer, the printer and turned off the cd player. She chaffed at his constant orders. She had been too shocked at first to realize what his terms of their relationship would be, but now the confinement was setting in as status quo, and she didn't like it one bit!

She felt grimy from unpacking the boxes and a shower lulled her into a false sense of peace. When she emerged from the dressing room she saw that Wyatt had started a crackling fire in the fireplace.

Wyatt gathered her into his arms, whispering against her ear. "I want to make mad, passionate love with you."

Gem pulled back. "You don't love me. I don't love you," she said coldly. "It's just sex."

He slipped off her dressing gown. "Pyjamas. Really," he shook his head. "Just sex is too clinical. It tarnishes the finesse," his hands stroked her shoulders, "the delicacy," his hands roamed to her hips, "the poetry of two bodies surrendering to the mysteries, the art of passion," his eyes held hers captive.

Gem narrowed her eyes, holding the gaze, and said bluntly, "You are so full of _."

"Watch you language, sweetheart," Wyatt chuckled. "Vulgarities should not escape such lovely lips."

Gem booted the computer, giving a long sigh of relief that at least one part of her life had finally returned to normal. She was reconnected with her world. She remembered the important thing she had to do: charge her mobile! Hopefully it would be charged by morning. Hopefully she would be able to get a signal in Ticking Bottom!

At least the dark hours would be a bit less lonely. And she could think again. She couldn't understand how Wyatt could wipe away her ability to have conscious thought. How many women in his past had reacted as she did? No doubt hundreds of them. Handsome men like Wyatt cut a swath wide and deep into the female population. She shook off the image. Other women were welcome to him. Hopefully he would soon become bored with her and direct his attention elsewhere. She might miss the singing, but Trilby survived without Svengali.

Files. The photos. What were the passwords? She had written the codes and memorized them. It seemed like a lifetime ago. She hadn't worried of the files at the flat. She wasn't concerned that the Macinskis would use her computer - she trusted them - oddly enough, since she had only met them that day. However, while Mrs Brown considered Wyatt Grantham a man of ethics, Gem no longer could. He was the enemy. The enemy could not be trusted.

One password. Another. The computer processed slowly, waiting, delaying, as Gem had instructed the program to do; a misstep and the computer would deny access and lock the file.

Her thoughts drifted to Paul Andriani. Barcelona. Gemmy had worn the ring. She was not on assignment. Why had Paul Andriani approached a courier not on assignment - and in a public place? Had Gemmy simply made an error wearing the ring? Excited about being engaged, had Gemmy let a cog slip? But Barcelona was not her territory. And she hadn't worn the ring to Singapore.

Gem was desperate to contact the Agency. Mrs Brown, and possibly Harry, had to have returned by now. Either of them could answer the questions regarding Barcelona.

At any rate, when the file of the photos was sent to Gemmy's computer at the Agency warehouse, Mrs Brown and Harry would be alerted. And Gem would likely get a phone call from the Agency.

Gem couldn't research on the computer while the passwords were responding. She gazed about the office. A very fine temporary haven for her use until she could get the Hell out of Ticking Bottom. Her next haven would be in the flat she would purchase once she got rid of Wyatt Grantham. And what a lovely day that would be! Please God! Don't let it be too far in the future!

Done. Passwords entered. The file. Gem sat in the swivel chair, gazing at the photos. The last time for who knew how long that she would see the snapshots. The two sisters, grinning at the camera, front teeth missing; rail-thin in bikinis at the family pool when they were nine years old; bikinis properly filled out a few years later.

The faces staring back at her had been so happy, so confident, so sure they could handle what the world threw at them. When the world had thrown Wyatt Grantham at her she was so foolish she had neglected to duck. And now she wasn't confident that she could handle crawling out of bed in the morning to bear his scorn and anger.

Gemmy's face smiling at her. Depending on her. Calling out to her for help. The last desperate plea - a plea to her sister.

Goodbye. I love you, Gemmy! Gem took a deep breath. She keyed in Gemmy's e-mail address. Another deep breath and she tapped the enter key to send.

The screen went blank.

Gem buried her face in her hands, resting her elbows on the counter; then slid her fingers up, dragging them through her hair as she stared at the blank screen.

Then she saw his reflection in the night darkened windows. How could her reflexes be so static?

"How long have you been standing there?" she queried, forcing a calm tone to hide her anxiety.

He took a deep breath before speaking. "Long enough to know you destroyed something you desperately wanted to remain hidden. Not long enough to know what exactly it was."

Gem breathed an inner sigh of relief. Had Wyatt seen anything he would be demanding answers to a hundred questions.

"You're finished for the night. It's nearly five o'clock," he said firmly.

"Aren't you going to demand that I tell you what exactly I destroyed?" she said bitterly.

"I am becoming reconciled to the fact that you are quite similar to an artichoke. Many layers. I may never know all the layers that form you. But I do intend to pull back layer by layer to do my damndest to solve the mysteries of you. You are, indeed, a fascinating woman. No wonder James was mad about you. Come to bed, sweetheart," he said firmly. "Time to sleep."

Gem could have fainted with relief that he hadn't seen the file. She had to redouble her efforts to keep her guard up against Wyatt Grantham! So far she was failing miserably!

Chapter Eleven

Wyatt dropped another rule on Gem at breakfast.

"The Defender will be delivered Wednesday. I have arranged for you to take a defensive driving course this week."

A defensive driving course? She didn't need that! "I don't believe I need the course," she protested quietly, since Mrs M was in the kitchen. The housekeeper was watching a program on the telly that hung over the counter across from the cooker; Gem didn't want the woman to become uncomfortable if she and Wyatt had a row.

Wyatt lowered his voice, watching Mrs M through the door between the breakfast room and the kitchen. "No course, no keys to the Defender. You'll be at the mercy of the rail line then. That does not suit me," Wyatt said quietly.

Freedom of a sort from him. "Very well, the course," Gem nodded.

"Four hours this afternoon, four Wednesday, four hours and finish the course Thursday."

Twelve hours. Same as the Agency course with Mr Critchley.

Wyatt's mobile rang and to her delight he took the call. Less time for forced chat. She didn't bother to listen to the conversation, and was rather surprised that he didn't leave the table for privacy. Gem savored her breakfast: eggs, bacon, toasted muffin. Mrs M was a fine cook.

"I stand corrected," Wyatt remarked, dropping his mobile into his pocket.

Gem looked up as he spoke. Lord! he was handsome in his business suit. He must have dozens of white shirts - this one with a very subtle pearl stripe - and he must have just as many suits. She had to mentally shake herself to listen to his words as he spoke.

"The Defender will be delivered today half noon. I will be home for lunch an hour before that. Your instructor will arrive at one o'clock. I have a manual for you to study while you are taking the course."

Probably similar to the one in my brain. "Yes, Sir," she gave him a mock sweet smile.

Wyatt gave her a lofty gaze. "Perhaps I can delay my meetings this morning," he murmured to her, "or would you like to retract that particular sass?"

"Yes. Retracted," she immediately replied. However, a stirring of butterflies suggested otherwise. She took a long sip of tea to gain time to connect her mind to her body. She truly would prefer him to be out of the house.

"Come to the library then." Once there he gave her the course book and showed her the shelves with the books relating to the Second World War. "You may borrow whatever you like here, but I would appreciate books being returned to their proper places."

"Understood. Thank you," Gem replied sincerely.

He gave her a kiss that started the butterflies fluttering again, then left.

Gem shook herself to squelch the feelings he created within her. It was ridiculous! Her mind couldn't stand him, but her body couldn't get enough of him! Well! She was going to control that battle as much as possible!

The defensive driving course book was the exact same manual used by the Agency. Gem gave it a quick skim and was confident she had the information readily available in her mind for that afternoon's session.

Mrs M!

Gem hurried to the kitchen. "I am so sorry! I meant to help you with the washing up," she apologized to the housekeeper.

Mrs M smiled at the new Missus. Mrs Senior would help with the washing up, but she never expected Mr W to marry a woman who would. His taste in women had drastically improved over the years. "All set in the dishwasher, dear. Tea?"

"Indeed," Gem easily agreed.

"Then we'll do a tour of Hall or did you do that last evening?"

"I didn't" Gem replied. "I was too engrossed in settling my office. It's lovely - the counter, the shelves. It will be an excellent work space."

"Splendid," the housekeeper nodded.

The tour was at a leisurely pace, Mrs M straightening a curtain here, flicking a piece of dust off a table there. The Hall was clean and very well maintained. Gem was not surprised by that fact. The M's were obviously dedicated people, and Gem sensed the Hall was as much Mrs M's home as it was Wyatt's. And Wyatt would naturally see that his family home was properly tended.

"This is the living room, drawing room, lounge, parlor - whatever you wish to call it," Mrs M stated. "It's really not used - much as the dining room."

Another fireplace, Gem mused silently. "The chimney sweep must love getting this appointment each year," Gem said aloud.

"Indeed," Mrs M chuckled. "Put bands on all his children's teeth the Hall has."

Gem was drawn to a photo on the fireplace shelf.

"That's Mr J, James, Mr W's younger brother," Mrs M said with a catch in her voice. "He's told you about Jamie, of course - that's what the Mr and I called him. He was a very good lad. It broke Mr W's heart when Jamie died. Ours too."

"Yes," Gem nodded, not daring to say anything that might tip her hand to the housekeeper. That would rile Wyatt if she did.

"Jamie, what a spirit he had. Did you hear about the story of the day he insisted on preparing tea for everyone? Must have been ten, no eleven at the time. He was proud as punch when he served everyone their afternoon cup." She shook her head laughing. "Didn't let on he'd poured a bit of vinegar into every cup first!"

Gem started laughing. She was going to enjoy being at the Hall with Mrs M!

"Oh the sour faces that day! He was a trickster." She sobered, the smile leaving her face. "Such a good boy. And so sad it was." She wiped away a tear with the hem of her apron. "Must move on, we must."

They only took a quick look into the library. "Mr W's domain," then moved on to the study, pleasant but on the dull side. A sitting room overlooking the back yard, a den- also a bit dull, and back to the main hall.

"The family mainly gathers in the great room," Mrs M explained.

"Master suite, as you know," the tour continued at the top of the stairs. "Five bedrooms, some sharing a bath," she led Gem down the hall. The rooms were clean, well decorated, and obviously, from their pristine state, had not been used in years. "Jamie's room," Mrs M did not open the door as she had to the other bedrooms. "It had been Mr W's room before - well - until he moved into the master suite."

Before their parents died, Gem decided. James's room was immediately to the left of the master suite. Gem would like to look in there! Perhaps she might find something indicating why Gemmy had the stopover in Geneva.

"Mr W brought Jamie's things home from Spain. He unpacked the boxes. I go in to dust and hoover once a week or so, but I doubt Mr W can bear to go in there now."

She continued the tour down the hall past the master suite. On the wall opposite the master suite was a single door.

"Stairs to the second floor - or attic you could call it. Used to be a huge playroom for the children. It's a steep climb, and one I don't make but twice a year when Mr M and I clean up there - spring and fall. It's organized and quite a history now of the generations of Grantham Hall residents. Attics can tell so many stories of families. One story at the top of that flight of stairs is that no Grantham ever discarded furniture, books, photographs. There are trunks full up there. When you are at odds and ends, you'll want to go up for a look at the treasures of the past. Oh - and there's a bit of Jamie's furniture up there from his last flat." She shook her head. "Dear me. I sometimes think if he hadn't gone off to paint over there, well, he'd be still alive today. Take a torch when you go up, and mind the steps. They aren't well lit."

"Yes, ma'am," Gem agreed.

Mr J would likely be alive today if he hadn't met Gemmy. (Was that in Barcelona?) And I wouldn't be here NOW, Gem mused. She felt as sad as Mrs M, and for many of the same reasons. Still, even if James had never met Gemmy, her loved ones would still have been on the Pilos on 30 May. The flight to nowhere.

Gem wasn't going to pump Mrs M for information about James. If it got back to Wyatt that she had, then he might decide to let a slew of cogs slip: passports, photos. Oh dear! However, Gem was not adverse to allowing Mrs M to talk to her heart's content on any subject of her choosing. And, indeed, Gem would like to explore the attic - when she was in the house alone. No one around to tell Wyatt that she had been up there. Gem wondered if there was anything of Gemmy's in the attic or in James's room. Something that Wyatt had overlooked, or had thought to be James's.

"I'd best be about my work then," Mrs M announced as they walked down the stairs to the main floor.

"Is there any way I can be of assistance to you?" Gem asked.

"Heavens no, child, you have your book to write. Cathedrals, is it, I believe Mr W said?"

"Yes," Gem nodded.

"We'll have a cup later. Oh- Mr M will be installing an inter-com in your office this week," she advised Gem.

"Inter-com?" Gem hesitated.

"Yes. There's one at the stables, the carriage house, where the Mr and I live, the master suite, kitchen, library, great room, study. It's quite convenient. If you'd like me to bring you a cup when you're working, you just buzz the kitchen inter-com, and I'll be along."

"Okay," Gem nodded. "Or I could simply walk to the kitchen," she smiled. Margaret Lawson would pitch a fit if one of her daughters thought she was too good to get her own cup of tea!

Mrs M chuckled. "However you wish, dear," A very sweet girl, the woman decided. But was she strong enough to stand up to Mr W when he needed to be put in his place? Only time would tell, she mused, as she returned to the kitchen.

The office was lovely; the morning sun wavered through the banks of mullioned lead glass windows to play light and shadow chase across the opposite wall.

Very pleasant, indeed, Gem admired her new haven. The gardens were still vibrant with colour, beckoning her to grab her camera; she hadn't used all the rolls of film in her camera bag. She alerted Mrs M to her plans.

"Wear a hat," Mrs M reminded her.

Blast! Gem sprinted up the stairs to her dressing room, then retraced her steps and exited the Hall by the garden door in her office. So convenient! Her own personal escape hatch!

It was the most pleasant few hours she had spent for days and days. Sun, flowers, no Wyatt. Perfection.

The gardens swept in a long half-moon shape from the door of Gem's office across the green lawn. To the left of the gardens was a massive aged oak tree, and beyond that to the left another sweeping curve of flowers. The carriage house was barely visible down and to the right of the yard, partially hidden by a screen of beeches that bordered the entire backyard and around again to the far left side of the Hall. At one time someone had been very fond of beech trees, Gem mused. Beyond the beech trees was a forest ranging as far as Gem could see.

She finished a roll of film that she had started in Scotland, put in another, shooting various angles of the trees, gardens and zooming in to catch a butterfly on a single rose, a bird box framed by long stemmed buds Gem didn't recognize, and a bird bath half in sun, half in shade.

When the roll was finished, Gem glanced at her watch. Eleven o'clock. Definitely time for tea.

Gem cut carrots and chatted with Mrs M about menus while the housekeeper prepared chips and roast beef sandwiches for lunch.

Wyatt walked in the kitchen door as Gem finished setting the table in the breakfast room. It was obvious that the kitchen door was the preferred choice over the formal entrance to the Hall. Mrs M soon departed, carrying the picnic hamper to the carriage house for the M's lunch.

Gem noticed over lunch that Wyatt's eyes were steel gray. She doubted that he had had a pleasant morning at the office.

"Did Mrs M give you the grand tour of the Hall?" he asked, his tone edgy.

"Yes," Gem replied politely, wary of his temper.

"What else did you do this morning?"

"I took photos of the gardens."

"Did you even glance at the driving manual?" he scowled.

"Yes, I did."

Question, a reply, question, reply. It was a ping-pong conversation. At least the food was delicious, if the atmosphere was stilted and unpleasant.

"What did you discuss with Mrs M?" Wyatt gave her a steady, commanding look.

"The inter-com system. Very little actually." She point blank refused to be grilled by Wyatt about her chats with the housekeeper.

They had barely finished eating and clearing the table when the Defender was delivered. Mrs M returned from her lunch to assume the washing up chores while Wyatt and Gem looked over the vehicle. A black 1990 Range Rover Defender in mint condition. Gem found it amusing to look at the classic vehicle behind the classic Jag. A second vehicle drove up the drive, to pick up the driver who had delivered the Defender. Gem looked over Wyatt's mobile phone purchase while Wyatt chatted with the men.

"Well?" Wyatt queried when they were alone again.

"It's smashing!" Gem smiled. "Amazing what you can do when you have a mobile phone."

"See that smashing is an adjective, not a verb," Wyatt chuckled, ignoring the rest of her comment.

Gem actually laughed. At times he did have a sense of humour. He smiled at her and her heart did a flip-flop. Not again! The other Wyatt Grantham did NOT exist. This man is the ENEMY! You must NOT forget that! Gem reminded herself.

Yet another vehicle drove up to the Hall.

"Your instructor," Wyatt said, taking her arm, escorting her to a recent model, blue Range Rover.

"Range Rovers are very popular," Gem murmured, frowning a touch. The vehicle looked very familiar.

The driver parked behind and to the right of the Jag, and stepped down from his vehicle.

"Shall I park here or on the lane?" The man approached the couple.

"Right there is fine," Wyatt replied. "Mr Critchley?"

"Yes. David Critchley."

"Wyatt Grantham, and my wife, Gem Forrester Grantham," Wyatt remarked, shaking hands with the man. As did Gem.

Gem smiled politely at the instructor. She fought to keep her face impassive.

"My wife," the words nettled Gem as Wyatt spoke them, but she kept smiling, "is an excellent driver and no doubt will be an apt student for your course. My dear, do you need your book?"

"I already read it," Gem replied.

"I gave it to you this morning," Wyatt frowned. "How could you possibly have read it in so short a time?"

David Critchley gave a slight frown at the discussion.

"Speed reading course at university," Gem said smoothly, which was an actual fact; both she and Gemmy had taken the course.

"Splendid. My wife took a similar course. Doesn't use the ability for pleasure reading though," David Critchley informed them.

"Nor do I," Gem smiled.

"Shall we begin? It is best to proceed in the vehicle you will primarily use."

Wyatt handed the Defender keys to Gem.

"It just arrived," Gem smiled at the course instructor. She eagerly crossed to the driver's side while David Critchley climbed in the passenger side.

Wyatt took his brief case and a stack of books from the Jag while Gem looked over the interior of the Defender. There was no point for him to remain outside. He had work to do in the library. She had been warned. Hopefully she would heed his words, otherwise this would indeed be a brief marriage for both of them. And God only knew what would happen to her if he carried out his threats - which he would easily do without regret.

When Wyatt entered the Hall, Mr Critchley turned to look at Gem. "Well hello, Mrs Grantham," he chuckled.

"Well hello, Mr Critchley," Gem laughed.

"Mr Grantham is unaware of your most excellent reading memory," he observed quietly.

"A woman has to have some secrets," Gem chuckled, completely relaxing in the presence of the man she had known for six years. "And I couldn't really explain why I had already read the manual," she added.

"True enough. He doesn't know of your previous, yet current career," still an observation not a query.

"Does Mrs Critchley know of your previous career?" Gem raised a perfectly groomed eyebrow to the man who was a British agent when she was still trying to fill out a bikini.

"European buyer for a leather goods shop? Naturally," he smiled.

"How do you account for your current job?" Gem laughed. "You are obviously an instructor in the public eye then."

"Took the course years ago, also naturally. Leather goods samples are extremely valuable, and I did drive all over Europe."

"As you say," Gem laughed. "Very plausible. I hadn't heard that you had retired from the Agency."

"Do NOT assume, Gem. Remember your training. And don't ask questions - SOP," he replied crisply.

"Yes, Sir," Gem replied quickly. Moving in the public sector, yet still employed by the Agency, she realized by his comments. And one never truly retired from the Agency.

"You look exhausted, by the way. Still the insomnia?"

"Does everyone know?" Gem sighed.

"Your contacts do. And I am one of them, for twelve hours this week. You passed last spring, but you are registered for this course, and you must complete it - again. You will pass because you have been well-trained, but you are a student, nonetheless."

"Yes, Sir," Gem knew - SOP.

"All right then, let's take this beauty out and see what she can do. Really, Gem! A classic Defender! Interesting choice. And excellent - GPS has been installed."

The better for Wyatt to track me! Gem thought bitterly. Blast him! Blast Wyatt Grantham!

Four hours on the road with Mr Critchley was exhausting as usual. Total concentration driving on roads she had never before driven on. She would have been quite lost without the GPS, but still she hated it - specifically because it had been installed precisely against her wishes.

After Mr Critchley left, Gem returned to the house, suppressing her anger to Mrs M, but ready to face the lion in his den -the library. However Mrs M informed her that Mr W was taking a shower.

Gem took the steps two at a time, shutting the master suite door sharply. Wyatt was dressing when she stormed into the bedroom.

"You had GPS installed on the Defender!" she snapped out the accusation.

"Keys," Wyatt held out his hand.

"It's to track me, isn't it?" she demanded.

"Certainly it is. You are my wife. Your safety is my concern. Does that surprise you?" he ground out.

"You're so concerned about my safety! Who's going to protect me from you?"

"Absolutely no one," Wyatt said loftily.

Gem glared at him. That reply was the dead truth! She returned to her original complaint of the conversation. "The GPS is just another way for you to control me."

"Calm down," he demanded. "All Hall estate vehicles have GPS. You'll still be able to keep your secret life secret from me." For the time being. "Simply stretch your mental faculties, your brilliant mind, and you'll be the same vicious little bitch you have been all along. Keys."

Gem glared at him, flipped the keys to him and stalked to her dressing room.

Wyatt pocketed the keys, reflecting on the fact that Gem had not denied having a secret life. Well, there was progress there.

A shower did nothing to alleviate her frustration. To compound her frustration she had neglected to inquire of Mr Critchley as to whether or not Mrs Brown or Harry had returned from holiday. Mobile! Her mobile! Was it charged?

Yes! Gem discovered when she reached her office. Her mobile worked! A thought was teasing her mind. She could hear Mrs M in the kitchen, preparing dinner.

"Do you need any help?" Gem asked the cook

"No dear, thank you," Mrs M pointed a butcher knife at the fridge. "Wine is chilling, if you'd like a glass."

"Maybe later," Gem frowned. "Where is Mr W?"

"The library. Knock before you enter, dear, he may be on the telephone."

"Yes ma'am," Gem replied. She would do so, but only to please Mrs M.

A muffled "Come in" replied to her tap at the door. He was sitting at his desk, scowling at the computer, and transferred the look to her. "Close the door," he said crisply, eyebrows rising as she smartly pushed it shut.

Gem strode over to stand across the desk from him. "Did you install GPS on my phone?" she demanded sharply, her eyes narrowed in a fierce glare.

"Lower your voice," he said sternly. "You ARE capable of having a civil conversation."

"Did you?" Gem repeated, her voice now quietly seething.

"Yes."

"How dare you!"

"I dare a great many things, darling," he said curtly, leaning back in his chair. His face showed no emotion.

"When did you do it?" She had always had her mobile with her, except when it was charging this morning. When had he had the opportunity to install the GPS?

"The night of the art show," he replied, his voice cold, his eyes nearly black with temper.

The memory came to her mind. "You entered your phone numbers. Damn! You are insidious!" she accused heatedly.

"Are you just realizing that, sweetheart? And I take your words as a compliment from one so practiced in deceit such as yourself," Wyatt nodded. "Consider the GPS protection."

"You are not protecting me! You are still hunting me! Protecting the world from me!" she scoffed.

"The protection works both ways then, doesn't it." It was not a query but rather a statement of fact.

"I hate you!"

"Not original. Growing tiresome," he replied, folding his arms across his chest, as she continued to glare at him. "I'm waiting for an adjective."

"Contemptuous!"

"Weak," he scoffed, shaking his head.

"Despicable!"

Wyatt considered her suggestion. "Acceptable." He turned his gaze to his computer screen. "If that's all - I have work to do," he said, curtly dismissing her.

"Rhinoceros hide," Gem gave a parting shot as she put her hand on the doorknob. The sound of his laughter followed her all the way to her office. When she had calmed down she sought out the glass of wine.

Mrs M's glass was nearly empty. Gem took the cook's glass, filled it with ice and wine, then repeated the process for herself.

"I'll set the table," she offered.

"Thank you, dear," Mrs M smiled to herself.

Where had Mr W met this young woman? The previous women whom he had brought on occasion to the Hall only acknowledged staff to demand service. In fact, Mrs M had been relieved when Mr W had stopped bringing his women friends to the Hall. He had shown good judgment however in marrying Mrs Gem. Hopefully she could hold her own against Wyatt Grantham; when he was in a mood he could truly be a difficult person to deal with. Ada Mancinski smiled approvingly of Gem Grantham, very approvingly, and she was certain the Senior Granthams would have been delighted with their son's bride. And Jamie would have adored her for her easy natural manner.

"Done," Gem announced, returning to take a seat on a kitchen stool. "Did you have a pleasant day?"

"Very pleasant, thank you dear, and again for setting the table," Mrs M nodded. "Was your driving lesson satisfactory?"

"I believe so. It's a great deal to remember," Gem replied. "Mr Critchley is a very severe taskmaster."

"He must be. People put their lives in his hands," Mrs M said firmly.

"Indeed," Gem agreed. Eight more hours and she would have the keys to the Defender, and at least a bit of freedom from Wyatt Grantham.

Gem dreaded another meal with Wyatt. She reminded herself to hold her tongue when he irritated her. Eat, do the washing up, work in the office. Her evening could be salvaged.

"Mr Critchley was very impressed with your session today," Wyatt observed when they sat down for dinner in the breakfast room.

"Good," Gem said quietly.

"So impressed with your progress, in fact, that he said you should complete the course at your Wednesday session."

"What?" Gem was stunned. "What?" She couldn't believe her ears. "It's a twelve hour course!"

"Indeed," Wyatt observed the expression on her face. "Mr Critchley said you were remarkably attentive, and quite literally tore through eight hours of the course in four."

A brilliant compliment from Mr Critchley! She knew he hadn't skipped any phases of the course; he simply would not do that. Perhaps she did so well because of the refresher course she had taken a few months earlier.

Closer to keys!

"He is an excellent instructor," Gem said. "I'm surprised you didn't insist on being in the back seat this afternoon. Doesn't Mr Critchley need to be protected from me?" she said, then instantly regretted the jibe.

"Some people cannot be corrupted," Wyatt replied. "And I would say Mr Critchley is no fool to fall to your wiles."

Wiles! I have wiles! Gem could only scoff at the idea.

Corruptible. An interesting thought.

"So you really believe that? That some people are uncorruptible - incorruptible?" she frowned at choosing the correct form.

"Either is correct," Wyatt resolved the puzzle for her.

"Thank you," she frowned. "Then - do you believe that? That not everyone can be corrupted?"

"Indeed. Some people are corrupted because they are weak, or extremely pressured against their will. It's a question of ethics and morals. Some people simply cannot or will not be corrupted. They refuse to succumb to pressure."

"Go on," Gem urged when he paused.

"I am waiting for a sarcastic comment," Wyatt replied.

"Oh - none," Gem waved the air with her fork. "Go on."

"What's the query?"

Gem stared at him. "Actually, I'm not quite sure. Perhaps there isn't one." She was certain no one in the Agency could be corrupted. A thought to store away for now. There was too much information gathering and sorting yet to do.

Wyatt accepted the comments without further pursuing the subject. "I want you to drive to the city with me tomorrow morning, Gem. You can shop, then meet me for lunch at the White Rose. I'll be leaving the office at five o'clock. I will ring you a few minutes before I leave the office and I will drive you home," he said firmly.

Not my home, Gem mused to herself. What would she do in the city all day? Drop off rolls and rolls of film to be processed, visit the war museum, bookshops.

"Yes I will go," she nodded. Freedom! London! An entire day in London, suffering only lunch with Wyatt! It was a trade-off she could tolerate.

Wyatt frowned. "It wasn't a suggestion. It was an order," he said dryly, drawing a chilly look from her.

Still, a day in the city was a day in the city, Gem mused, holding any further comments she might think to snap at him.

As they were clearing the table Wyatt's mobile rang.

"I'll do the washing up," Gem volunteered. Much better to work alone than to have to share the kitchen in argument or cold silence.

Wyatt accepted the offer. He had reams of reports to read, neglected during the days on Wight and in Scotland.

Gem did the washing up then took a glass of wine to the office to savor while she sorted photos of their excursion to Salisbury Cathedral. Three stray shots of Wyatt were in the cathedral pack. She studied the photos she had snapped of him reading his reports. He was stretched on his side, resting on the grass in the afternoon sunlight.

His lies were an arrow straight into her heart. His accusations burned into her mind. To look at him, reading so intently, oblivious to his surroundings while Gem had pursued her photos- he looked so handsome, so deceptively human. Cold. Vicious, calculating. How could she have been so easily fooled? How could he walk beside her, sit across from her at the table, sit beside her in the car, sleep beside her in bed, so calm, so unconcerned, so uncaring that he had smashed her heart to bits? How could he carry on through each day as if their lives, their relationship was 'normal' - while she walked remotely through each day, completely shattered? How could he ratiocinate what he had done to her without an iota of guilt? She was sleepwalking through her days and nights, trying to force her mind not to fret about this new life of hers. She was trying to survive each day without losing herself, without falling into an abyss from which she could never escape. And each day for Wyatt went on as usual!

Gem pushed the photos one by one into the shredder, listening with satisfaction as the teeth chewed up at least a bit of her 'past' with Wyatt.

She forced herself to concentrate on work. Vivaldi on the cd player was a mood relaxer. Then reaching for a Puccini cd she knocked over the glass, spilling wine into the empty Vivaldi cd case. So much for Vivaldi soothing her nerves. The mess was finally cleaned up, she was ready to focus on Salisbury when Wyatt walked into the room. Concentration was a very remote possibility for the evening.

"This is for you," he handed a credit card to her.

"What is it?" Gem asked, confused.

"It's a credit card," Wyatt stated the obvious.

"For what?"

"For your use. Balance is two thousand. When you need additional funds let me know."

Gem stared at him as he turned and walked out of the office.

Blast! She shook her head, reached for the shears and cut the plastic into four pieces. It would jam the shredder so she put the pieces in her combination lock file box. She didn't need or want his money, Blast him!

Cutting up the credit card was very therapeutic, allowing Gem to retrieve concentration to work on the Salisbury photos. Three interior shots were excellent, three exterior shots were brilliant. She read her research notes of the cathedral, then the text she had written, heavily editing entire paragraphs.

Chopin followed Puccini, then Haydn. All were followed by Wyatt.

"Time for bed, my dear," he announced from the doorway.

Gem glanced at the clock; only a bit past nine o'clock.

"Why don't you have an affair with Ms Holton? She seems like a lovely person," Gem protested, frustrated by his clock watching.

"She's too tall," Wyatt replied crisply.

"What?" Gem demanded. Wyatt was taller than Ms Holton. What did height have to do with the suggestion?

"Her husband would shoot me. Remember, married with three children?" He walked to the computer, clicked save, closed out the screens, shut down her computer and switched off the cd player.

"What! Now you have ethics?" she scoffed. "Did you somehow happen to accumulate them in the past few hours?"

He took her hand, leading her from, the room. "Come Trilby, sing a song for me," he said smoothly.

Gem curled up in Auntie Jane's comfy chair and read Operation Drumbeat, during the dark hours. What a difference there was in size of the Allied submarines and the Nazi U-boats, which stored provisions in every part of the vessel. Wyatt appeared in the office shortly before five o'clock and wordlessly led her back to bed.

London! Beautiful London! Gem was home if only for the day. Wyatt let her off at a fabric shop so that she could look for curtains for her office.

"White Rose, noon," he said firmly.

"I could meet you at your office," Gem suggested.

"White Rose, noon," he replied, his eyes deepening with a bit of steel. "Have you your mobile?"

"White Rose, noon," Gem parroted, holding up her phone.

She looked at fabric for a half hour, deciding to wait on the curtains until she selected a paint colour for the room. She would check paint colours after lunch. Now it was time for tea and a phone call or two.

Mrs Brown did not answer her mobile, nor did Harry. Third choice was Mr Cawley and he answered immediately.

"Welcome back, Gem," he said casually. "Did you have a safe journey?"

Ah! The lovely sham wedding and the hideous honeymoon.

"Indeed," she replied. Well, she had been safe the entire time she was away, safe from everything except Wyatt. "However I feel I have been out of the loop for months," she interjected, hopeful to detour further questions about her 'marriage', and her monumentally poor judgment regarding Wyatt Grantham. "Have Mrs Brown and Harry returned from holiday?"

"Negative, Gem," Mr Cawley replied crisply.

"Any new information whatsoever?" she asked faintly.

"Not to my knowledge."

"When is Mrs Brown due to return?" she pressed.

"Unknown."

"Can you find some information for me? I want to know if Gemmy ever had assignments to Barcelona or Geneva."

Mr Cawley paused, and Gem could envision him frowning. "I will check. Mr Choate was Barcelona and Geneva, but I will check records."

"Thank you, Mr Cawley. I would appreciate the information."

"Other queries?"

"Not at this time," Gem said quietly

"Glad to have you back, Gem," he said before he rang off.

Twelve days and no new information. Where the Blast was Mrs Brown? And Harry?

Gem rang Mr Cawley again.

"Yes, Gem?"

"The Chinese courier?"

"No word."

Mr Cawley added a comment. "Your file was received by Gemmy's computer."

"I should have sent it months ago," Gem admitted ruefully.

"Taken care of now. Don't fret about it. You've had a bit on your mind as of late," he said matter-of-factly.

The subject was closed - to Gem's relief.

Nothing! No progress! So extremely disappointing! Twelve days and nothing!

She dropped off the film for developing and managed to stop at two bookshops before she met Wyatt at the pub. It was grinding to see him again after the lovely hours when he hadn't invaded her life.

"Books," Wyatt chuckled after they had given their order. He insisted no beer or wine for them today and Gem thought that a bit odd since he had often had beer and then had returned to his office. Tea was fine after all. Wine and Mrs M were waiting for her at the Hall. "No fabric samples?"

"Not yet," Gem admitted. "Perhaps this afternoon." Then she thought again about a beer. "I would like a half-pint," she said, scanning the room.

Wyatt shook his head. "I don't want you alone in London with alcohol on your breath." Why was she looking about? For whom was she searching?

"You didn't mind that weeks ago," she pressed the point.

"Things are different now, aren't they, sweetheart," he said easily.

Gem's guard went up but she didn't lose her temper. Play her game, not his.

Wyatt didn't rush their lunch, but he did glance at his watch from time to time.

"Do you need to return to your office now?" Gem queried.

"Shortly," Wyatt pursed his lips. "You'll need to clear your shopping for the afternoon."

"I beg your pardon?" Gem frowned.

"I have made an appointment for you with a physician, Gem, a specialist in sleep disorders. Hopefully he will be able to help you with your insomnia," Wyatt said quietly.

Gem saw red. Control. She counted to twenty three times.

"I see," she said much more calmly than she would have without the counting. Wyatt paid the bill. "I'll walk you there."

Stay calm, Gem, she urged herself. She could not allow him to win this battle!

A specialist? She might easily handle this situation. She had referenced specialists in insomnia in late July. One in particular had very impressive credentials. It all depended on the office location.

"Who is the physician?" Gem asked as they left the pub.

"Jenkins," Wyatt said casually. "Your appointment is for half one."

That was the one. Play it very carefully. "I've heard he's excellent," Gem nodded.

Dr Jenkins would insist on a physical. Gemmy had broken her arm. Gem had not. It had been a serious break, necessitating a cast for over two months. Early February, cast until late April. Likely Gemmy was wearing the cast when she had met James. Had James mentioned the broken arm to Wyatt? Patient confidentiality. No. She did not trust the physician not to give Wyatt a report. The man got whatever he wanted! And if Wyatt had known about the broken arm he would have mentioned it to Dr. Jenkins. They would compare notes and there would be more demanding queries from Wyatt. And he had no right to make an appointment for her! She was completely capable of doing so for herself. She had a personal physician.

It was the office building that was a decisive factor. It was a skyscraper. It was the perfect building!

At the entrance of the office building Wyatt stopped. "Shall I walk you to the office?"

"I can find it," Gem said calmly.

"Seventh floor, office seven four two."

"Seven four two, Dr Jenkins," Gem repeated.

"Very well. Give me a ring when you're finished here. For now, give me a kiss goodbye," Wyatt ordered.

Gem dutifully gave him a quick kiss.

"I require a better offering than that sorry attempt." He kissed with a message that telegraphed his desire for her and started the blasted butterflies swarming. "We shall work on goodbye kisses tonight," he teased. "Ring me when the appointment is over and I will take you home. Now off you go."

Gem nodded. I don't have a home, I sold it, she did not say. She entered the building and walked directly to the bank of lifts. She knew he was watching her as she stepped into the lift and pushed the button for the seventh floor. People crowded in about her and pushed buttons for other floors. Absolutely perfect. She stepped off the lift on the third floor with two other women. She knew this building, having delivered a courier message to an office a year ago. She walked around the bank of lifts to the second bank, took a lift down and exited the building on the opposite side of where she had entered less than ten minutes earlier. Wyatt would be furious. What a pity. She turned off her mobile and started walking. When she did not appear at the appointed hour, the doctor's office would ring Wyatt and he would ring her. And she would not be available. She had won this part of the battle. The next part of this battle was going to be a scorcher, she knew.

Cathedrals were out. If he actually left his office to look for her - she couldn't decide yes or no on that one - he would not find her. Take her home indeed. She no longer had a home thanks to his deceit. And he had betrayed her again! Tricked her into going to a physician. She could decide that for herself!

She walked past shops, zigzagging across the city, avoiding museums and bookshops; wandering, until she spotted a brilliant outfit in a small shop window: an ankle length brown and turquoise skirt, brown tee, with a scarf of the same colours as the skirt. And she found it to be a perfect fit. She paid the bill and wore the outfit out of the shop, her own clothing in a shopping bag. At another shop she bought a pair of brown lace up boots, a brown hat with a wide brim and sunglasses. She pinned her hair up and pulled on the hat, then went out to stroll the pavement, comfortable in the knowledge that if Wyatt was looking for her, he would be looking for her in the clothes she had worn into the office building. However, more power to Wyatt if he did see and recognize her.

For a few hours she felt truly like herself. She and Gemmy had done a few quick changes when they had had constant assignments, sometimes two in a city on the same day and they didn't want to be obviously recognized. She walked, feeling completely free. She couldn't permanently manage to hide this way, but it was fine for one day. She checked her watch and found a public phone, rang rail stations until she discovered where she would be able to catch the train for Ticking Bottom; the train left at quarter past four and would arrive in Ticking Bottom at half five.

Wyatt slammed his mobile shut. He shouldn't have been surprised that Gem did not arrive at Jenkins' office. He had known he couldn't trust her. What was she hiding that would prevent her from going to the doctor? Or was it merely because he insisted she do so? More likely that. She was extremely stubborn. He would have to rid her of that trait. He alerted Ms Holton that he would be out for the remainder of the day, then he strode out of the office. He was now wasting additional time on Gem. Where the hell was she? In the lift he rang her mobile. No reply. Naturally she would have turned off her phone. He drove around for hours. She was not at Oscar's. He thought back for references she had previously made of her favorite shops. Marks and Spencer. Other than that he drew a complete blank. Cathedrals. Too obvious. He drove to the park where they had picnicked and watched clouds. The Thames?

She wouldn't have been foolish enough to bolt. He was convinced she believed he would turn passports and photos over to the tabloids. And he would. He wasn't concerned the Grantham name would be blackened. She would be at fault. He would be another of her victims; the onerous would be on her.

He repeatedly checked his mobile GPS, but he couldn't spot her as he drove along streets. He stopped at a few bookshops before deciding Gem would avoid the obvious. Except for the most obvious. She was still in London. She had to return to Ticking Bottom. Her only recourse was the train. One hour.

He stopped for petrol, wine, and beer. On the drive to Ticking Bottom he planned the next course of action.

He was furious. In all the weeks he had known her, he could find no trail of Gemma Louisa Lawson. Information on Gemimah Louisa Forrester had university and teaching references; nothing more. Other than the passports and the photos, she had covered her tracks with expert artistry. Who had she been prior to her current aliases? What damage had she done to other people? Whatever she was concealing, she was very accomplished at hiding it.

Gem half expected Wyatt to be at the rail station when she boarded the train. He was not. He would be at Ticking Bottom when she arrived. She put her sunglasses in her shoulder bag, her hat in the shopping bag. She had won a few hours, but would decidedly lose the remainder of the day. But it had been worth it. She had won one battle. She was still very tired from lack of sleep, but she had felt very much like Gem for those few hours - and very much like Gemmy - who would definitely approve the new clothes! She sat back, relaxed, and savored the ride to T.B., storing up her energy for the coming battle. She had had a day of freedom from Wyatt Grantham. A day for her heart not to ache. She refused to think of the price she would pay for the freedom. But whatever the price, it had definitely been worth it!

Wyatt was leaning against the Jag, arms folded across his chest, as Gem stepped off the train. He walked towardss her. His eyes were nearly black. Very, very angry, she mused to herself. He took the shopping bag from her hand, firmly grasped her arm above her elbow and steered her to the Jag. He put her in the car, snapped the seatbelt around her, closed the door and clicked the key chain to lock the door. He put the bags in the boot, unlocked the driver's side door, and climbed into the Jag. He did not speak and Gem did not utter a word, or so much as a sigh.

Very pointed, Gem observed. He did not unlock the passenger door until he was ready to open it; she could have unlocked the door from the inside, but he was making a point: Supreme Control. So she let him make his point. The real battle was ahead.

Mrs M cheerfully greeted them as they entered the kitchen door. "My you are early! Dinner hasn't been started. Shall I make tea, a few appetizers?" she smiled. Mrs G had been shopping! Good! Her wardrobe was pitifully small.

"No, thank you, Mrs M," Wyatt said smoothly, steering Gem through the kitchen. "We do not wish to be disturbed."

"No, thank you, Mrs M," Gem called sweetly. I would love it if we were disturbed, she sighed inwardly.

"Yes, Mr W," the housekeeper chuckled, closing the door between the kitchen and the hall.

Gem groaned inwardly, knowing Mrs M was imagining a romantic interlude for the newlyweds. A battle royal was more like it. With each step Gem dreaded the storm that was to break when they reached the master suite. Wyatt firmly closed the door behind them, leading her through the sitting room to the bedroom. He tossed the shopping bag on the bed, finally releasing her.

When he turned her to face him, Gem was actually frightened by the fury in his eyes.

"What the hell do think you were playing at today?" he demanded furiously. "Don't you ever - ever! - again turn off your mobile! For a brilliant woman your actions today were dangerously brainless!"

It was a medical appointment! Gem stared at him opened mouth, speechless.

"Get this into your lovely, foolish head, Gemimah Grantham! I am a very wealthy man! You are my wife! I don't want to frighten you, but you MUST use any single thread of common sense you possess to be careful!"

Gem's temper flared; she was sick to death of his tirades. "How dare you -"

"Hush!" Wyatt fought to control his fury. "I couldn't contact you today! How was I to know you hadn't been abducted? Was I simply to wait for a ransom call? When I ring you, you damn well better answer! Do you understand?"

Gem nodded. He truly was concerned for her safety.

"Yes!" Wyatt demanded, incensed. "Say the word!"

"Yes, I understand. I am sorry," Gem said slowly and sincerely. "And I will be careful. I promise. And I will answer my mobile when you ring. I promise."

His eyes were clearing to a medium gray. Gem could tell his temper was abating - a bit.

Wyatt took a deep breath. "Good!" he finally said, his voice controlled.

End of one storm, Gem held her breath, the beginning of the next storm.

"You missed your doctor's appointment this afternoon," Wyatt forced a measured tone to his voice.

Gem slowly edged away from him. "Oh, did I? Was that today?" she forced an extremely casual tone to her voice. "It must have slipped my mind. Busy times, busy day."

Wyatt gave her a steady look and Gem tried to avoid his eyes.

"I rescheduled the appointment," he said evenly.

"I won't go," Gem shook her head.

Wyatt took a step towardss her. "I will take you by the hand and lead you to Dr. Jenkins' office. I will sit right beside you while you wait. I will escort you into the examination room."

"He can't examine me without my permission. Not everyone needs eight hours of sleep a night," Gem countered.

"Do you ever even have five hours of sleep a night? If you continue along this path you will soon be one of the walking dead!"

"My won't that be embarrassing to you! There you will be - the Great Wyatt Grantham - lunching with a zombie! Marry in haste, repent forever," she quipped, sounding more courageous than she actually felt.

Wyatt threw up his hands in frustration. "In heaven's name! For what possible reason will you NOT seek medical advice?" he demanded.

"He can't help me!" Gem insisted fervently, her nerves fraying from fatigue and the constant battles with him. "Stop pressuring me!"

"The doctor can give you a prescription. Be sensible about this, Gem!" Wyatt refused to relent, completely stymied by her persistent unreasonable protests.

"Don't speak to me about being sensible. If I was sensible, if I had one speck of common sense, I wouldn't be in this house! Or this village! I would be in my own flat! My home! I would be happy!" she fumed.

"You weren't happy when I met you!" Wyatt countered.

"You didn't meet me! You trapped me! You tricked me! And I'm not happy now! You can't force me to go to the doctor. He can't examine me without my permission and I won't give it!" He can't discover I never broke my arm! Control! I can't find it! "I refuse to discuss this further!"

"You need more sleep! God knows I need more sleep," Wyatt's temper rose.

"Then leave me alone at night! Go to sleep! I didn't ask to be here! Leave me alone, Mr Wyatt Grantham!" She was so close to the edge she could see the line.

"Damn it! I'll remind you that I make the rules in this marriage and you damn well know why!" he ground out his words. "I should have you sectioned! Get a lovely tranquilizer for you! Then we would both get some sleep!"

Gem snapped. "Ha! Sectioned! That you CANNOT do! You try it and damn everything! I will bring you down! I will bring you to your knees! Crash! You will be done!" Gem snapped her fingers at him. "Finished!" she laughed, shaking her head. One phone call!

Wyatt stared at her coldly. "And there you are! What secrets do you have, what information in your twisted, vicious mind, Gemma?" Was she threatening him with John Staunton?

Gemma! Gemma!

Gem flew at him, striking at him blindly. "I am not Gemma! Don't ever call me that!" she shrieked.

Wyatt's head jerked back, he clutched one of her wrists, then the other as she flailed at him. He forced her wrists behind her back, holding them in one hand, holding her tight against his body with his free arm around her shoulders.

"Hush, hush, hush," he whispered gently. "Hush, Gem," he repeated the words again and again until she began to calm.

He released her wrists, his hand moved up to gently stroke her hair, his voice soft, soothing. Gem fought to catch her breath.

Wyatt's mind reeled in astonishment. He was confounded that she had reacted so violently at the mention of the name Gemma. She astounded, confounded, and constantly confused him. Her presence in his life invaded his every waking hour, and consumed his dreams.

What in her secret life, her persona of Gemma produced such anguish within her? Or again, was it an act? Was this how she lured men into her vicious world?

Finally she was quiet, leaning against him, exhausted. He could swear she wasn't using drugs. He was weary of searching, but he would do so again. Slowly he released her.

Gem covered her face with her hands.

"I'm sorry, I'm sorry," she moaned. That was one edge. She couldn't bear another. She didn't know what she might say. What cog she would cause to slip. Her mind was swirling too fast to sort. What had she said? Slowly, slowly she regained her thoughts. She hadn't said anything except not to call her Gemma. Wyatt would have to regard that as he would. "I'm sorry. I have never struck anyone before - ever," she said helplessly. Hopelessly.

Gem raised her eyes to look at him. His face was blank of expression. He stepped a pace back from her.

"Did I hurt your arm?" he asked in an odd tone Gem had not heard before in his voice.

"What?" she asked, bewildered by the query.

"Your right arm. That was the one you fractured last winter - February, wasn't it?" he frowned. "James mentioned you were wearing a cast when he met you."

"Oh," Gem caught her breath - finally. She had to think as though she was looking in a mirror. Gemmy's right arm. He knew! What the HELL had James said that Gem had no way of knowing? "Yes. Skiing in Germany." Where the hell in Germany? Where were the details when she needed them? Blast that lovely couple from good old San Francisco! They had turned her life from one living hell to another!

"It's fine," she murmured. "I am sorry," she said again.

He hadn't hurt her. At least not physically. "Well - not a bad attempt - for a novice," Wyatt said smoothly, attempting to lighten the nearly sparking atmosphere in the room. "Your blows missed the target. However, I suggest you refrain from future further attempts. You're stronger than you appear to be," he ventured a gentle tease.

Gem nodded. "If you refrain from future alliteration, I shall consider your suggestion."

Wyatt gave a short chuckle, then grew serious. "Perhaps you should rest until dinner, Gem," he emphasized her name. "You've had a trying day. I'll ask Mrs M to delay dinner until seven."

Before she could reply he walked out of the suite. Gem sank down on the bed, playing the scene over, her mind whirling, smacking with the threat she had made. Sorting was improving a bit.

Whatever had possessed her to threaten him? Damn! A slipped cog! She could bring him down! But to what avail? And what had Wyatt made of her words? Likely he had thought she was referring to Paul Andriani - a.k.a. John Staunton! The days ahead would be one land mine after another!

She wanted desperately to talk to someone. Someone in whom she could confide. She wanted her best friend. Her most trusted confidante. She wanted Gemmy!

Gem pulled herself off the bed. I need a shower, she decided. I need a walk in the garden. I need a glass of wine. How well did sound travel down to the kitchen? - she wondered, turning on the water in the shower.

She felt a bit refreshed; showered, favorite crème skirt and blouse. She would love to pull on a pair of jeans and a tee, but at the Hall? She didn't know what was considered proper - for regular daily wear or for dinner.

Mrs M gave her a cheery nod when Gem walked into the kitchen and fetched the wine bottle from the fridge. "Glass on the counter for you, dear. Mr W is in the library. Dinner will be a bit still."

Thank you for the warning about Wyatt! Gem nodded. "I'm going out to the garden - or do you need my help?"

"No, dear, everything is set. You go on," the cook urged. Mrs G was so tired. Insomnia was a battle, she knew; her sister had suffered it years back.

The flower blossoms nodded on the gentle, early evening breeze. The gardens were heaven, Mr Becton a master of his craft, his work reflecting his artistic soul. Gem watched the evening sun play off the bright colours of the blossoms against the various spikes of ornamental grasses. She had read a number of gardening books a few years back and with very little effort she could sort, then name all the items in the gardens. However, she was too tired to make the effort.

"I suppose a stroll in the gardens would be considered a form of rest," Wyatt's voice came from behind her.

Gem turned to see him approaching, carrying a wine bottle in one hand, a beer in the other. "Mrs M thought you might be ready for a refill."

Gem accepted the offer. "Did Mrs M overhear our - discussions?" she asked uneasily.

"I'd say not," Wyatt grimaced, shaking his head. "She is still speaking to me, and I didn't receive any scowls from her." He poured wine into Gem's glass. "Are you sure you couldn't try a nap?"

"I can't sleep during the day," Gem protested as she had another time to him. Was it on Wight? In Scotland? She couldn't remember.

"Or all night," Wyatt said quietly.

Gem steeled herself for another battle.

"Sometimes it's simply difficult to turn off one's brain," he set the wine bottle down on a rock. "Here, if you want more," he pointed to the bottle. He slipped his arm around her waist, a practise Gem was becoming used to, and guided her along the path.

Wyatt pointed to the horizon beyond the gardens. "Do you see the top of the tallest tree, way off?"

"Yes," Gem nodded.

"That is the edge of the estate. And as you turn," he eased her around, "the estate extends as far as you can see."

Except for Ticking Bottom, Gem mused.

"There's a stream above the stables that winds down and through the village. It's on Hall property but all the villagers can fish it."

"You don't mind?" she was surprised.

"Stay out of my stream declared the lord of the manor?" Wyatt chuckled. "Archaic and miserly."

"Do you fish?"

"Never had the time," Wyatt shook his head. "Mr M fishes, catch and release. The Missus refuses to prepare fish, doesn't like the odours it leaves on her hands or in the house. If you ever do desire fish you'll have to order it at a pub," Wyatt chuckled.

"Mrs M rules," Gem said firmly.

"To some degree," Wyatt nodded. "Mrs M was here long before I arrived. But she isn't set in her ways, surprisingly. And you are now the lady of the Hall. If you want changes, make them known to Mrs M."

"And Mr M will carry them out?" Gem added, laughing.

"True," Wyatt agreed. "And now, down here," he steered her past the massive oak tree to the left, to the far side of the grounds, "Mr Becton is planning to expand the gardens and install a pond or waterfall next spring."

"What about the staked area?" Gem inquired.

"Garden art, I have heard."

"Lovely!"

"Don't hold your breath. Mr M refuses to allow any of the projects," Wyatt laughed.

The Project CSU.

Gem pushed the thought from her mind, trying to concentrate on Wyatt's words.

"Wouldn't that be your decision?"

"Mr M was here long before -" Wyatt started to say, then laughed again.

"Mr Becton should speak to Mrs M. Perhaps she would tell Mr M -" Gem stopped and laughed.

Sometimes Gem saw flashes of the man with whom she had fallen in love - what seemed now a lifetime ago.

Gem read on through Operation Drumbeat. The success of the Nazi U-boats was terrifying. No wonder the German Psychopath believed he could conquer the world! That was still a terrifying thought in the twenty-first century. The book was fascinating; however Gem wasn't certain the information would be of value to her search. She was lulled into a state of solace by the quiet of the house, the only sounds the hum of her computer and the deep ticking of the long case clock in the main hall. Thus she was greatly startled by the soft ping indicating a text message on her mobile. The ping was a signal programmed into Agency mobiles by Mr White to alert the staff member of a text message from another Agency staff member. All other text alerts were the first few bars of Land of Hope and Glory.

Gem bounded out of the comfy chair to grab the mobile sitting by its charger alongside the computer. Mr Cawley.

'Chinese courier found. Dead. Thai courier dead.'

The text ended. Gem deleted the message.

Chinese counter-courier. Thai counter-courier. Vietnamese counter-courier. Gemmy. Mum. Two couriers, three counter-couriers. Dad. Mr Portermann. Two agents. Total seven.

SEVEN!

The tiny hairs at the nape of Gem's neck prickled. Were couriers being hunted, the agents collateral damage? Was the hunt because of Project CSU? Or were the couriers being disposed of simply to disrupt the International Network between certain nations? The U.K Network. The South East Asia Network. Agents again, collateral damage? Gem's brain was overloaded. Sorting became difficult.

Or was the International Network being hunted: couriers and agents?

Or-. The Thai courier. Was that a red herring? Thailand was not involved in Project CSU.

Gem texted a query to Mr Cawley.

'Was the Thai courier on assignment?'

'Information currently unavailable.'
'Who was the Agency contact?'
'Blank.'
'Thanks!'
'Get some sleep!'
'Eventually.'
Blank. Paul Andriani. Agent 1.
And where in the world was Paul Andriani?
Barcelona.
Thai counter-courier.
Where was Paul Andriani on 29/30 May?

Gem made sure all messages were deleted, then slipped the mobile into her dressing gown pocket. Wyatt was correct. She always needed her mobile turned on and in her pocket. She glanced at the clock. Half four. She shut down the computer and went up to bed. She could ponder Mr Cawley's text messages while the clock ticked to five.

Wyatt pulled her close to him, stroking her hair. Gem lay awake. His hand was gentle, soothing, not coaxing or a prelude.

"It's five o'clock," he finally murmured. "Go to sleep, Gem."

She was asleep before the clock struck the fifth chime.

Gem ate breakfast in the kitchen with Mrs M; Wyatt had a breakfast meeting to Gem's delight. He had left the keys to the Defender with her, and Gem simmered a bit, feeling the school girl getting the keys from daddy for the family vehicle. Still, to her joy, he would not be at the Hall for lunch! Free day away from THAT MAN!

"Another muffin, dear?" Mrs M queried.

"No, thank you. Shall I help you with the dishes?"

The housekeeper shook her head. "I'll just take a cup out to the men, then put the dishes in the dishwasher."

"I'll take the tea out to them," Gem volunteered.

The estate manager and gardener were arguing when Gem approached them with mugs of tea. Mr M introduced Gem to Mr Becton, who tipped his hat to her, as did Mr M, who was wearing a sport cap instead of his usual straw hat Gem had seen him wearing the past few days. Gem admired the gardens to Mr Becton, then returned to the house, hearing the men resume their argument as she reached the kitchen door.

The garden flowers were so beautiful Gem put a query to Mrs M. "Do you think Mr Becton would mind if I cut flowers to put in the office?"

"He would take no offense if you filled the house with flowers. You are the lady of the Hall now. You do as you wish then," Mrs M advised her. "I'll text the Mister to fetch flower baskets." Then she showed Gem to a door off the kitchen. It was a mudroom with a washing machine, dryer, racks for hanging clothes to dry, shelves for hats, wellies, and a cupboard that held gardening shears and gloves. "I'll get down a few vases."

Mr Becton seemed gratified that the new Missus wanted flowers from his gardens. He was silent, however, when Mr M appeared with a huge wicker basket in each hand, passing them over to Gem without acknowledging the gardener. The estate manager tipped his hat to Gem and walked back towards the carriage house.

Gem selected the blossoms she wished for her office; Mr Becton cut the stalks then filled the baskets with his own suggestions, providing Gem with a smile with every flower he gave to her care. When the baskets were full, he tipped his hat to her, inviting her to refresh the flowers whenever she wished.

Half a dozen vases were waiting for Gem on the kitchen counters. Mrs M took one look at the overflowing baskets and retrieved additional vases from the butler's pantry.

Mrs M and Gem worked side by side, chatting easily as they arranged the vases with vibrant floral masterpieces.

"I thought a cottage pie for dinner. Will that suit you?" the cook inquired of Gem.

Gem nodded. "And a salad perhaps?"

"Indeed. Mr W does not eat enough greens."

Which could account for his perpetually surly attitude, Gem amused herself. She enjoyed the housekeeper's company, and felt less awkward at the Hall when she was with Mrs M.

"It is lovely to have people in the house again," the housekeeper smiled. "The Mister and I have been mainly on own here since Mr J went off to university. Mr W found it best to be at the London flat. Truth to tell, aside from being with his brother, Mr W lived more at his office than at his flat. And he traveled a great deal the past few years. But Jamie and Mr W were always close, best of friends despite the difference in their ages. Wyatt always looked out for Jamie," Mrs M slipped into very familiar names.

Mrs M was obviously without a clue to Wyatt's suspicions of James and Gem. Thank heavens, or Gem would not be able to live at the Hall.

Gem made a subtle flower arrangement of pinks and yellows for her office, saving the more vibrant colours for vases for other rooms in the house.

Mrs M nattered on. "Back in the days when the Senior Granthams were here the house was always filled with guests, parties, and young people. The Mister and I always had our hands full," she recalled wistfully.

"It must have been great fun," Gem tried to imagine the nearly silent house as a hive of activity.

"So it was! Jamie was a magnet to young ones. Mr W, being a good ten years older, kept a sharp eye on Jamie and his friends. No shenanigans allowed - he was more strict than the Senior Granthams. But Jamie was his responsibility after their parents died, and Mr W only being twenty-four at the time of the plane crash. It was an overwhelming time for both the lads and Jamie just into his teen years."

"Devastating for both of them," Gem murmured, trying to ward off a flashback of her own.

"Tragic. You won't be putting me on an airplane. But you young people are all jet-setting people these days," Mrs M shook her head.

"I detest flying," Gem admitted.

"Keep your feet on the ground," Mrs M nodded.

Once the vases were filled, Gem helped ready the kitchen for lunch, then as Mrs M prepared sandwiches and put crisps in a bowl, Gem carried the vases to the great room, main hall, her office, master sitting room, with the one remaining vase for the master bedroom.

Mr Critchley was punctual, naturally, for the driving course. Four hours of his orders, questions, nitpicking procedures, and Gem was mentally exhausted. However, she would now be able to find Ticking Bottom from every possible route from London to Thrapston.

At the end of four hours, Gem parked the Defender on the Hall drive.

"Well done as usual, Gem. You receive a certificate this time - framed," Mr Critchley smiled. Her previous certificates had been placed in her Agency file.

"Why eight hours instead of twelve?" Gem asked curiously.

"You hit all the marks, no repetition needed. He patted the dashboard. "This is an excellent vehicle. She'll take care of you. Good sharp responses. A classic yet! Not a Lamborghini, hmmmm."

"Yes, that would be so me," Gem laughed. "Would you trade your Silver Dawn for this Defender?"

"Ah-no. Never," he laughed. "She'll be at one or two car shows in November, if you want to come visit her. I'll let you know the dates."

"I hope to be there," Gem replied smiling.

"Keep in touch, Gem. I'll tell Mr Grantham that you are road ready. Be alert."

"I will," Gem assured him.

"Try to get some sleep," he advised. "You look worse than you did on Monday."

"Lovely compliment. Thank you," Gem winced.

"It was the truth. Keep in touch."

"I shall."

She waved him off, then dashed into the kitchen, tossing the keys to the Defender into the air, catching them neatly, and grinned at Mrs M.

"That is the look of success!" Mrs M smiled.

"Indeed!"

"Congratulations! Wine?"

"Shower first. I have vased flowers and driven the entire countryside today," Gem laughed.

"Whenever you say then," Mrs M chuckled.

Thank heavens Mrs M wasn't temperance! Gem giggled, dashing up the steps to her bathroom.

The water stinging her flesh completely refreshed her. But was she ready to take on Wyatt again? Perhaps. At any rate, she had the keys to the Defender. It would be London again tomorrow - on her own terms this time.

Wyatt.

Nothing could have shocked Gem more than Mrs M's words that morning. Wyatt and James's parents had also died in a plane crash. They had so very much in common, and they were so far apart. The tragedies should have brought them together instead of dividing them. But then, Wyatt was unaware of her side of their story. Perhaps one day they could at least be civil to one another - and be sincere about it.

Gem had finished dressing when Wyatt walked into the bedroom. He straightened an aster blossom, tucking the stem further down into the vase Gem had placed on the coffee table.

"Do you mind the flowers? Mr Becton wasn't adverse to thinning his flower beds," she said hesitantly. "Mrs M and I put the arrangements together."

"Mr Becton wouldn't object. The gardens are Hall property. The two of you were certainly well occupied today."

"It was very pleasant. Mrs M is very kind." Gem watched him remove a damaged petal from a blossom. "Mrs M is very happy to have people in the house again. She-she mentioned your parents - that they died in a plane crash." Saying the words tore at Gem's heart, her mind flashing to two o'clock 30 May. "So devastating," she said gently, wishing she could tell him she could deeply understand how he felt about the accident.

Wyatt's eyes narrowed. "My, my, Mrs M was chatty today," he said coldly.

"I'm sorry," Gem flushed. "I didn't intend to cause her trouble with you."

Wyatt glared at her. "You can't possibly understand about the accident. I'll thank you not to mention it again. My annoyance isn't with Mrs M. Do not play the Macinskis, Gem. I will not permit you to hurt them as I have already warned you about your games. Drop the innocent, caring persona. It grows tiresome."

Gem's cheeks flamed at his open hostility towardss her.

"In the future, address your queries of a personal nature directly to me. Do not wheedle information from the Macinskis or others."

"I didn't, truly," Gem protested. "We were simply chatting."

"Spare me your protests," he dismissed her with the wave of his hand. "I'm going to shower."

Gem walked very slowly down the stairs, still smarting from his words. She counted to twenty over and over again until she reached the kitchen, wordlessly filling a glass with ice and to the top with wine.

"Mr W said the flowers added much needed colour to the rooms," the housekeeper said, then noted the young woman's face. She sipped her wine and said quietly. "He's in a mood tonight. Don't take it to heart, dear. Mr W has lost everyone dear to him. He has been running on empty for months. Losing Jamie was so shocking, so blindingly unexpected after everything else. He has you now and he will be himself again in a short time. He's a very good man. And the Mister and I are delighted you are here."

Gem gave Mrs M a short smile. So - so unaware of everything. "He has you, and Mr M also. And Mr Becton."

"Yes," Mrs M nodded.

"I'll set the table and then do you need help with anything else?"

"No, dear, thank you." The housekeeper's heart went out to the girl, but she knew the first weeks of marriage were often difficult. She could speak to that from her own experiences. Loving a man was a lot different when you were actually living with him.

The wine was cold and delicious, but it could not numb Wyatt's stinging remarks, Gem mused, as she went to her office. She knew exactly how he felt - about his parents - and James. She had the same pain, but she couldn't console him, or share her pain.

Gem shook herself. What was she thinking? She didn't want to share her pain with him! She didn't want to talk to him or to even see him. She had to force herself to tolerate his presence and that was the extent of the consideration she would give to Wyatt Grantham!

And another dinner to endure.

Gem reached for the framed certificate Mr Critchley had given to her. It would be a comfort seeing her name in print except Mr Critchley had used Grantham as Gem's surname. But then, why wouldn't he have done so? She and Wyatt were the only two who knew their marriage was a sham. Mr Critchley was a kind man. He was part of her real family: the Agency - the only family she had now.

"Congratulations," Wyatt said from the doorway. "Mr Critchley said you were an exceptional student."

"Did he," Gem smiled to herself. It wasn't a question. She knew she was. "He is an exceptional instructor."

"Dinner," Wyatt informed her, and walked away.

"We'll take a walk after dinner," Wyatt stated as Gem suffered through the tedium of dining with him.

Another order. It was not an invitation or a suggestion, but merely a statement of fact.

"Salad?" he frowned.

"Mrs M said you need more greens in your diet," Gem murmured.

"Indeed," Wyatt scowled

Gem noticed he ate the salad but obviously did not enjoy doing so.

How could his employees bear to be around him? Oh - yes - highly paid. They would have to be to tolerate his attitude.

The washing up completed, Wyatt insisted Gem put on her hiking shoes purchased on Wight. He showed her the converted carriage house, and then the stables.

"Use the first garage for the Defender," he told her.

The Jag was already in the next garage, then two estate Land Rovers; two other spaces were vacant, the last held a vehicle under a heavy made-to-measure cover.

Wyatt opened all the garage doors with a button on the Jag's key chain.

"Very handy," Gem murmured, as he then closed all the garage doors at the same time by again pressing the key.

"There's a button on the Defender key chain that will open your garage, but not the others," he said crisply. He held up another key chain. "I also have a set of keys for the Defender."

Naturally. Control. He always had control.

"There is a third set, however, please try not to lose your keys. I don't have time to rescue you if you're stuck God knows where from your own carelessness. And Mr M doesn't have time to drive all over the countryside to fetch you home."

"Yes, Sir," Gem, said smartly.

Wyatt let the remark pass. They continued to walk past the end of the drive and across the patchwork quilt of fields Gem had seen the past Sunday, when she saw Ticking Bottom for the first time. She couldn't believe it had only been a few days; it seemed like an eternity. It was less than two weeks since she had moved out of her London flat. That also seemed like an eternity ago.

As they crossed a stream, Gem could see that the course of the water divided into brooks to flow beneath the three stone bridges of Ticking Bottom. She saw a man walking in the distance at the edge of the tree line. He was carrying a shot gun. She stopped to stare at him.

"You allow hunting on the estate?" she looked at Wyatt.

"Hunting is a fact of life," Wyatt followed her eyes to the figure in the distance. "If you walk in the woods wear a bright yellow scarf or shirt. You'll be safe. No one will shoot you. And inform Mrs M when you do go for a walk beyond the tree line, or if you are going for a walk around Ticking Bottom proper. Common courtesy to her. She needs to know if you're out shopping, out working on a cathedral shoot - whether or not you will be in for lunch."

"Of course," Gem replied.

They walked for another few minutes then Wyatt said he had reading to do that evening.

"Put your vehicle in the garage," he said.

He waited while she did so to make sure the buttons on the key chain worked as they should.

When they entered the kitchen, Wyatt took a beer from the fridge, holding it out to her.

Gem shook her head.

"Do you plan to go into the city tomorrow?"

"Yes," Gem replied, feeling a bit of a thrill that she now was able to do so without having him direct her activities.

Wyatt nodded. "You'll have lunch with me. The White Rose. Noon." He walked down the hall towardss the library.

Not and invitation; an order. So much for him not directing her activities, she muttered to herself as she settled in front of her computer. It nettled her that she couldn't have the following day to herself without him intruding on her time. Her irritation grew; she made errors on the text she composed, spending more time correcting errors than she did on actual writing. The work finally began to flow and she glanced up to Wyatt's reflection in the windows, the dark night made a perfect mirror of the glass.

"Come to bed," he said crisply.

Gem looked at the clock on the wall. "Half eight! I thought you had work to do?" Her temper began to rise.

"I set it aside."

"Well, I don't want to set mine aside," she protested.

He stood silently, waiting.

"I detest you!"

"Not my concern," he shrugged.

"You are a nightmare," Gem snapped.

"And you, my dear, are stunningly adept at sleight-of-hand - a nightmare disguised as a luscious daydream," he reached out to take her hand.

Much later he stroked her cheek.

"How many men's souls have you tortured?" he murmured, trailing his finger down her throat.

"You obviously needn't worry," Gem gasped, catching her breath as his finger continued to wander. "You don't have a soul."

"We are so perfectly matched, my dear, are we not," he nuzzled her ear. "You exhaust me."

"Go to sleep," she murmured. "You're exhausted."

"Not completely - not yet."

And he wasn't, Gem was soon to realize. Nor was she.

Gem set aside the book she had been reading and reached for a note pad and pen, writing a list to soak into her brain.

Were the couriers being hunted?

Why the Thai courier - Thailand not being associated with Project CSU?

Agents collateral damage?

Thai courier on assignment? Possible accidental death?

Couriers hunted to disrupt international agencies?

International Network being hunted?

Why Geneva?

Pick up the photos - no that one was for morning.

Have collage of photos matted and framed for Mr Becton - no, also for morning.

She paced the floor.

Who in the Agency had been posted to Hong Kong before it reverted to China?

Gem reached for her mobile, texting the last point to Mr Cawley.

He quickly replied.

'Shall check for information. Sleeping any better?'

'No. Thanks for checking.'

Gem returned to writing her list.

Did Gemmy ever have a courier assignment to Barcelona or Geneva?

Gem paced again. There was something tickling the farthest reaches of her memory. She couldn't immediately access all information. She wasn't a computer. SS officers. But there was so much sorting to do. How had Mr Memory managed to so quickly access storage in his brain? Probably word association.

Gem read her list again, cut it into sections then shredded the sections.

Ping.

Mr Cawley was still working!

'Brown, Harry, Blank, Portermann, White, M Lawson, G Forrester, Denton -retired-died 4 July this year.'

'How did Mr Denton die?'

'Fishing. Portsmouth. Slipped off bank. Hit head. Drowned.'

'Thanks for information!'

'Sleep.'

'And back to you!'

Denton! She hadn't heard that he had died. However, the first week in July she had had courier assignments to Norway, Finland, Germany, France, Italy and

Denmark. She had had her assignments and that of another courier who was covering Gemmy's territory to Japan, Hawaii, Washington D.C., and Adelaide.

Gem dragged herself upstairs meeting Wyatt at the landing. Wordlessly he tucked her into bed and into his arms.

"Sleep," he whispered, and she closed her eyes, ending the dark hours for that morning.

Chapter Twelve

Gem picked up the photo packs and a dozen rolls of film, intending to hike through the woods on the weekend. She also hoped to shoot some distance shots of Ticking Bottom: meadows, fields, the captivating stone bridges, thatched cottages. She would select the photos to be matted and framed for Mr Becton. There was still the matter of paint and curtains for the office. She didn't enjoy decorating, but the idea of a finished work environment did appeal to her.

Tea at Oscar's Café also appealed to her. She read the area, thinking of the hours she had waited, drinking tea, watching for Gemmy's young man. And if she hadn't done that, she wouldn't have met Wyatt. Dreadful memory that one. But he had been hunting her. Perhaps he would have seen her elsewhere and the result would have been the same. Thinking of Wyatt put a damper on the morning, and a damper on selecting paint, curtain fabric and rugs. That shopping was more effort than she could manage today.

Leaving the Hall that morning had been a trial with Wyatt's list of reminders. Mobile - first and foremost, hat, lunch, noon, White Rose. Do you know the route to Ticking Bottom? - Yes - she had assured him. He had followed the Defender into the city until he had to turn off to the office car park. That was the moment that Gem again tasted a bit of freedom.

And now it was time for lunch. She was half way to the White Rose when her mobile pinged. Mr Cawley.

'Location?'

'White Rose Pub. Lunch with Wyatt.'

'Okay.'

She would ring Mr Cawley once she was on her own again.

Wyatt was waiting for her.

"I'm sorry, am I late?" Gem glanced at her watch.

"I am early, my dear," he kissed her forehead, then seated her at the table. "Did you have a pleasant morning shopping?"

"Yes, thank you," Gem said politely. She set the bag of photo packs on the floor beside her chair, and Wyatt picked it up as she scanned the room. There were a few customers, generally the regular crowd.

"Honeymoon memories?" he queried.

Gem gave a slight shake of her head, knowing he used the phrase because it would irritate her.

"I would like you to be home by three o'clock this afternoon," he said. "Will you be finished with your shopping to make that time possible?"

And his control of her continued.

A shadow blocked the light coming in the windows of the pub and Gem looked up, expecting to see a waitress coming to ask for their order. She was stunned instead by the face smiling down at her.

"Mrs Brown!" Gem said, surprised and absolutely delighted to see an extremely welcome face.

No slipped cogs, Gem's mind snapped into focus. Let her supervisor lead the way, Gem quickly decided.

"Hello, my dear," Mrs Brown smiled warmly. "How lovely to see you again." She turned her smile to Gem's companion." And you are Wyatt Grantham," she nodded to him.

Wyatt stood up, the ultimate gentleman, Gem mused sourly. Always the consummate actor, she had come to realize.

"May I?" Mrs Brown indicated a chair and Wyatt moved smoothly to seat her, his action receiving another smile and a nod from the older woman for his always excellent manners - excellent when anyone else, other than she was on the receiving end, Gem silently fumed. "I am Mrs Brown. Gem and I are old acquaintances. Quite often we meet each other at cathedrals. Gem is captivated by their structure and history, while I seek the beauty of the colours of the art glass."

"It is a pleasure to meet a friend of my wife," Wyatt said graciously, offering his hand, which Mrs Brown briefly shook.

Gem felt like kicking him beneath the table. But no doubt he would want to meet her 'friends', another way of gleaning information about her, perhaps hoping to forge another link to the chain binding her to him.

"And it is a pleasure to meet the man who won Gem's affections."

"Thank you," Wyatt smiled, and Gem just knew he enjoyed the word 'won' - a word innocuous to Mrs Brown, but one that was a sharp slap to Gem of his vicious Game - which he had won.

"It is reassuring to know that Gem will be well cared for," Mrs. Brown said firmly.

"I will, indeed, do my best," Wyatt said smoothly.

He was setting Gem's teeth on edge with every word he spoke.

"My dear," Mrs Brown turned her attention to Gem. "You look exhausted. Still the insomnia?"

"I'm fine," Gem automatically replied, as always.

"Wyatt, you simply must try to get Gem to sleep more."

"I assure you, Mrs Brown, I do indeed try, but she can be a bit difficult to convince," Wyatt shook his head, smiling at Gem. "She works too much, and coax as I do, she fights rest."

"You must insist she nap during the day."

"I don't believe there are any indications that I have any influence with Gem. She does as she pleases," he said smoothly.

"She usually does," Mrs Brown chuckled.

Am I invisible here! Gem silently screamed.

"Well I must be off. So many errands today. I live in the country," Mrs Brown informed Wyatt, "but I try to come to London once or twice a week - if necessary. Perhaps we might meet for tea or lunch soon, Gem. Perhaps next week."

"Lovely," Gem nodded. Perhaps we might accomplish some work on two very damned important projects!

"Take care of your jewel, Wyatt," Mrs Brown patted Gem's shoulder.

"I'll guard her with my life," Wyatt smoothly assured the woman.

"Indeed. See that you do," Mrs Brown nodded, standing. "And, my dear, try to rest. You don't want to make yourself ill," she ordered Gem. "You don't want to lose time working on your project - your lovely book." She smiled again at Wyatt and then left the pub.

Gem wanted to stab Wyatt with a fork, but she didn't have one since a waitress hadn't even appeared yet to take their order.

"Guard me!" Gem quietly seethed. "You beast!"

"Simmer down, my sweet," Wyatt said lazily. "You are a precious jewel in need of guarding. Even Mrs Brown believes so."

"I suppose you will insist on joining us when I meet Mrs Brown for lunch."

"There's no need. You won't breathe a word of our arrangement," he stroked the ring on her right hand. "Will you, my dear?"

His action was much more effective than his words.

Gem sighed, passports and photos coming to her mind. "No. I certainly shall not."

Find Gemmy, her parents, Mr Portermann. Solve the conundrum of the Pilos and the mounting courier deaths. Then she would be free. She stared at the ring on her right hand, and felt the weight of the rings on her left hand. Damn eternity! It was not going to claim her chained to Wyatt Grantham!

The waitress finally appeared to take their order, apologizing that they were very short staffed that day.

"What would you like, my sweet?" Wyatt stroked Gem's hand.

"Burger, salad and tea, please," Gem replied. Wyatt ordered the same. "And put arsenic in his," she murmured as the waitress walked away.

"Out such thoughts from your brilliant mind, my dear," Wyatt said softly. "If I can't trust you, you shall have to spend every minute of every day with me. Is that your desire?"

Gem shook her head.

"I didn't hear you, my dear," Wyatt insisted.

"No arsenic," she murmured.

"Appreciate the freedom you have then."

"My insidious husband," Gem muttered.

"I believe that is the first time you have referred to me as your husband. Imagine my surprise!" Wyatt said softly.

"I said it only because it goes so well with insidious."

Wyatt chuckled." Sarcastic sass. You are becoming quite proficient at that verbal skill."

"You inspire me," Gem gave him a saccharin smile.

"Another compliment from you," Wyatt grinned. "I am honoured."

Gem shook her head, thankful to receive her food so she could eat and leave the pub. She didn't want conversation, but Wyatt was interested in the quick meet with Mrs Brown.

"Mrs Brown seems quite fond of you," Wyatt observed. "How long have you known her?"

Gem frowned, wondering how to reply, then mentally shrugged off concern. "A number of years." She would have to take each of his remarks on their own.

"And you share a passion for cathedrals."

Blast! Is he attempting to finagle information of Mrs Brown or herself? "Yes."

"An odd passion to share. I should think most people tour cathedrals then forget them."

"There are also those who fight to preserve them for their beauty and history," Gem suggested. She tried to alter the direction of their discussion.

Wyatt however declined the redirection. "Is Mrs Brown retired?"

"Yes." Sometimes.

"Is she a widow perchance?"

"I believe so. I have never met a Mr Brown. She has never mentioned a husband to me." Well, that wasn't exactly quite true.

"She has the manner of a very capable woman. Was she in business?"

"I don't really know," Gem said vaguely. "I do know she has a passion for gardening, goes on and on about tulips. There must be a thousand varieties of those. Colours, frills, plant in clumps, protect planted bulbs from vermin," Gem prattled off from a gardening book she had once read.

"She bends your ear a bit on tulips," Wyatt chuckled.

"Never, ever mention the word to her. Do not ask her how her tulips are, or were, this year. You will fall asleep long before she has finished her recitation. This year compared to last year, compared to four years ago, compared to seven or ten years ago. Quality of blossoms, coffee grounds mixed in the soil appears to give a better boost to blooming plants than do eggshells to the fritillaries - or some such flower."

"I'll remember the warning," Wyatt grinned and Gem hoped the subject of Mrs Brown was put to rest. "You didn't invite her to our wedding."

"She was on holiday," Gem said coolly, hating the reference to the abominable occasion. "Purchasing tulip bulbs in Denmark or Belgium or someplace." Who knew where Mrs Brown had been when Gem had signed away her life. "And we had decided no guests," she reminded him.

"Mrs Brown couldn't have rescued you, you realize. Your fate was sealed when James died. And don't expect her to rescue you now," he said very quietly.

Oh, but she could, Gem reflected silently. But at what cost? What cogs would slip? What chaos would ensue if -?

"You might, however, invite her to the Hall for tea," Wyatt suggested.

Gem looked at him in surprise." Not likely," she said firmly. She wanted to keep Wyatt away from the Agency. And Mrs Brown would not accept such an invitation. Not safe to fraternize too much. "Fall planting is a major undertaking. Mrs Brown is expanding her gardens next spring, laying out curves, composting, selecting garden ornaments and so forth. Then she will likely be on holiday touring cathedrals and gardens in warmer climates."

"Very unlikely then," Wyatt observed. "But she did insist you need more sleep," his tone became lighter. "There would be an afternoon nap for you, tea and tulips with Mrs Brown."

Gem considered the remark. "Actually, that was a tad clever of you," she gave a nod of concession.

"Just a tad?" Wyatt mocked being affronted.

"You are lucky you received that much," Gem raised her eyebrows.

Home by three o'clock. Orders! Orders! Orders! Gem mused as they parted after lunch. Wyatt's reminder rang in her ears. He siphoned off what little joy she had in her life. She returned to the Hall and started working on her book. Mrs M had left a note on the kitchen counter that she and Mr M were at the shops, but she would return within time to prepare dinner. Since Gem didn't know when the M's would return she didn't feel safe searching James's bedroom. She retraced her steps to the Defender and put it in the garage. She put the Vera Lynn cd on the player, wanting to listen to it at the Hall during the daytime for a change. The rolls of film should immediately go into the camera case so they would be available when she needed them. Gem stacked the rolls carefully, thereby discovering a problem. There was too much space in the camera case for the film. She emptied the case, counting lenses. Blast! She was missing a lens. Perhaps she had misplaced it. She didn't recall packing it in her luggage - she only ever returned the lenses to the camera bag after she had used them. Well, she had unpacked boxes and set up her office in a bit of a hurry her first evening at the Hall. No doubt she would find the lens in a box under the counter.

She sorted photo packs. All photos having to do with Wyatt and Scotland went into a box at the back of the cupboard, save for the photos of Elgin and Fortrose Cathedrals. Memories of the previous week were still too raw to deal with. Mr Becton's gardens had photographed beautifully, the colour was brilliant, the light was subtle. Garden photos set aside, Gem laid out all the Elgin shots to the left of her computer, Fortrose to the right of it. A few shots of each were immediately discarded, then Gem switched on the computer to pull up the texts of both cathedrals. She selected five photos of Elgin, restructured then edited the text, and wrote captions for the photos and sketches. She added three sentences which would necessitate again restructuring the paragraph.

It was difficult working on the book when her thoughts truly wanted to wander to Mrs Brown and her surprising appearance at the White Rose, which was obviously the result of the text from Mr Cawley. Why hadn't Mrs Brown sent the text? The only reason would be that she wanted to give Gem a pleasant surprise.

The sound of the kitchen door opening and closing snapped her thoughts back to the Hall. A moment later Wyatt walked into her office.

"We are going to the pub for a pint," he informed her.

"I'm in the middle of a paragraph. I need to restructure it," Gem protested. "Can't you go alone?"

"Let me rephrase - we are going to the pub for a pint, we means you and I. It's chilly. You'll need a sweater or a windcheater."

"Blast! I didn't accomplish any work for over a week -"

"You have the photos of Fortrose and Elgin. You worked on our honeymoon."

Gem remained seated, holding her ground. "Your honeymoon. My journey through adversity."

"Your first journey to that destination. There will be future such journeys,"

Wyatt gazed at her. Another bit of spirit was returning which would make the Game more interesting. "Now that we have established that your journey has just begun, get your wrap. We'll walk. Don't keep me waiting."

Lord, he has beautiful eyes, Gem mused. Blast! Lose a battle, lose another battle. She tore her eyes away from his. Guard up, eyes down. She fetched a windcheater and a sweater, but choosing neither of the two sweaters Wyatt had purchased for her. Those would remain unworn in her dressing room as would the scarf from Spain and the pin from Scotland. The beer stein had been stuffed in a box in the cupboard with all the photos she wouldn't keep.

Ticking Bottom proper was a ten minute walk from the Hall, but was visible from all the windows facing the village. Walking along the curving cobblestone lane down across the old stone bridge was like walking into a pastoral painting.

"How has Ticking Bottom escaped development?"

Wyatt chuckled. "Development companies have yet to find Ticking Bottom."

"It is rather out of the way, as in You-Can't-Get-There-From-Here - no matter where 'Here' is."

"Precisely!"

Gem looked for particular shots she would like to get the following day: the thatched cottages, the cobblestone lane itself, the shops with the swinging signs perpendicular to the stone buildings, the Pink Horse Gift and Curio Shop, the Yellow Crow designating the pub, the Killingstoke Inn.

The air was indeed cooling; dark clouds scudding across the sky promised rain, and Gem was grateful she had also selected the windcheater. Chimney smoke lingered on the breeze, autumn colours tinged leaves in the distant forest. If Wyatt didn't come with the package, she would look forward to living in Ticking Bottom, Gem mused, watching the sun streaks filter through the clouds to dapple the cobblestones at their feet.

"I want you to limit your purchases in London to only the items you are not able to find in our village shops. Grantham Hall is loyal to our local merchants," Wyatt said firmly.

More orders from him. "Very well," Gem agreed.

The Yellow Crow was quite large inside; the windows of red and blue art glass cast colour stains across the old wood plank floor; there was a huge fireplace in the corner opposite the bar, flames licking at hefty logs immediately took the chill off the patrons entering the establishment; the bar itself stretched across the entire room to the left of the entrance to the pub; a band-set up was in another corner; a lift-up counter gave access to the kitchen, and the aromas emanating from that area tickled Gem's appetite; old hunting and fishing prints hung on the walls. It was a cosy atmosphere, Gem decided, and no doubt a central attraction to the locals.

There were only five people in the pub; the publican behind the bar and four other men sitting at the counter.

Wyatt introduced Gem to the men and she shook hands with each of them: Mike Morgan, the publican; Miles Lyndon, village doctor; Royce Harwood, village dentist; Daniel Whitney, village chemist, and the greengrocer, Bert Shaw.

The dentist and doctor were semi-retired and spent many of their days fishing, according to Bert Shaw.

"It's rather quiet in here," Gem said, gazing about the room.

"It will liven up soon," Wyatt replied. "A pint, my dear?"

"Half-pint, and dark, please," Gem smiled at Mike Morgan.

Wyatt said the same, slipped an arm around her waist, and led her to a table by the fireplace.

"You might find this a bit strong for you, my sweet," Wyatt advised skeptically, when Mike brought over the beers.

"Ah, you know the beer gardens," Gem replied softly, giving him a sweet smile, knowing the other men were glancing their way. "Oktoberfest. Oh, the memories. Surprising how much German one can learn in a week," Gem said with a faint smile.

"Secrets and mysteries," Wyatt leaned over to whisper in her ear, a very cosy scene for the watching patrons and barkeep. "How fascinating you are," he stroked her cheek, "how passionate, sensual -"

"How consummately irritating you are," she whispered in return. "Contemptuous, calculating, supercilious -"

He cut off her words with a kiss. "I stole the rest of your words, my dear," he murmured, a warning edge to his tone. "Now you may use your lips to drink your beer."

One by one the men came over to sit and chat about fishing, local business, and a reforestation project for Ticking Bottom. Gem listened attentively, gleaning that Ticking Bottom was a very close-knit community, and that Wyatt had considerable influence in the village, although he didn't push his opinions above those of the other men seated at the table.

As Mike turned up the lights in the pub, the party at the table broke up. Mike handed an umbrella to Wyatt as he and Gem left the pub. Raindrops splashed and puddled on the cobblestones as Wyatt and Gem walked across the old stone bridge and up the curving lane to the Hall.

"We're going to get soaked," Wyatt grinned, tucking her arm through his as the wind shifted, driving the rain beneath the umbrella.

Gem laughed, slipping her free hand into her pocket to cover her mobile, not wishing to have to put a request for a new phone to Mrs Brown or Harry - wherever he was.

It was such a relief to have Mrs Brown back from 'holiday'. Perhaps her supervisor had new information for Gem's search.

Wyatt distracted her thoughts. "Very romantic, a stroll in the rain," he observed as a crack of lightning split the sky.

Actually it was rather a romantic atmosphere, Gem mused, remembering their walk along the Thames in the rain before their wedding day. "We already had that romantic lie," she said tonelessly. She had kissed a prince who had turned into a frog.

Mrs M shooed them upstairs for showers and dry clothes. "Dinner at half six," she reminded them.

Wyatt caught Gem's hand as she shed her windcheater and sweater, setting her mobile on the coffee table. "I'll wash your back for you," he teasingly offered.

"Wash your own back," Gem turned her wrist and slipped from his grasp. "Why don't you get a mistress," she suggested crisply.

"A man may have a mistress or a wife. To have both at the same time is just greedy," Wyatt observed firmly.

"Go ahead, be greedy," Gem insisted, pulling off her soaking shoes.

"I intend for you to have all my attentions. We have so much in common." He caught her waist. "Lord, you are damp," he frowned as her skirt clung to his trousers.

"You'll ruin your suit," she warned.

"Shower, five minutes," he demanded, taking her garments into her bathroom to drop into the laundry hamper.

"I'm going to help Mrs M with dinner," Gem protested.

"Five minutes," he ordered, lowering his head to hers.

"Fifteen," she bartered, turning her head to avoid his lips.

"Very well," Wyatt agreed. "Fifteen minutes."

Gem sprinted to her bathroom, stripped off her wet frillies, showered, towel dried, grabbed a skirt, frillies, a tee, and dressed in less than ten minutes; she grabbed her mobile and bolted down the stairs while Wyatt was still in his bathroom.

One game won!

She was in the kitchen, scrubbing potatoes in the sink when Wyatt walked into the room.

"Good evening, Mrs M," Wyatt said smoothly.

"Good evening, Mr W," the cook smiled.

Wyatt took the potatoes out of Gem's hands, set them in the sink, then took her hand, leading her out of the kitchen, down the hall, up the stairs and into the master suite. He pulled her down on the bed.

"Very amusing," he leaned over her, his voice husky.

"I thought so," Gem said smartly.

He lay down beside her, pulling her against him, wrapping his arms around her.

"The men you met today, Gem, are your contacts in the event you cannot reach me or the M's. If you're out hiking and twist your ankle, if you run out of petrol, or have a puncture, or have engine trouble. I will give you their mobile numbers, and you must enter them into your phone," he said, his voice serious.

"All right," Gem replied, staring into his eyes. A special meeting arranged by Wyatt. Apparently he was VERY concerned for her safety. She had heard his words, and now the butterflies were beginning to swarm.

He kissed her and the butterflies flew wildly. "Later," he said, then left her lying alone on the bed.

That was it? Gem was stunned as he walked out of the suite. Had his initial intention of the post shower tease been merely to discuss the visit to the pub? Or was he merely usurping her win? She decided on the latter; he could have told her about the men at dinner. She returned to the kitchen to help Mrs M with dinner preparation.

Mrs M was surprised by the young woman's quick reappearance, but Mrs G was not frowning so all must be well this evening with the young couple.

"Wine, dear?" Mrs M smiled.

Gem shook her head. "I had a half-pint at the Yellow Crow. I'll just have a cup of tea."

As Wyatt and Gem were doing the washing up after dinner, he informed her that he would be on the phone for hours that evening, and that the list of phone numbers was by her computer. He didn't encourage further conversation. Gem entered the phone numbers into her mobile, and with Wyatt occupied in the library, she took the advantage to text Mrs Brown, unconcerned that she would be interrupted by Wyatt.

'Did Gemmy ever have an assignment to Barcelona?'
'No.'
Mrs Brown was certainly quick to reply!
'Geneva?'
'No.'
Gemmy had only been in Barcelona to see James then.
'Why the query?'
'Just sorting.'
'Very specific sorting. However I leave you to your own processes.'
'Harry returned?'
'No.'
'When?'
'???'
'Okay.'

Gem paced the floor. Where was Harry? She could ask but no reply would be forthcoming.

Where had Gemmy met James? Gem could ask Mrs Brown of Gemmy's assignments from the day she had broken her arm until 29 May, however that information would not give her the destinations of her sister's travels on her own time. And Gem certainly could not create a query to Wyatt of how James had met Gemmy. She was Gemmy to him and she should know how and when she had met James.

Blast! If only she hadn't gone to Oscar's the day she met Wyatt! There were countless café's, pubs, restaurants, tea shops in London, and he had been at Oscar's that particular day! If she hadn't met him then, if perhaps she had met him weeks later, she might have been thinking more clearly and more cautiously. She might have had the brains to run away from him, instead of straight into his trap.

Gem paced the floor, sorting. Sorting the obvious, she chided herself.

Gemmy's favorite London café! Wyatt. James. Gemmy had to have met James at Oscar's. Gem would stake her life on that. She would wager that Wyatt had learned about Oscar's from James. Gem had gone to Oscar's looking for Gemmy's young man. Wyatt had gone to Oscar's hunting for Gemmy.

Last time Gemmy had been in London? First week of March. She had stayed at Gem's flat while Gem had completed a series of Gemmy's assignments. The cast had hampered Gemmy's manual dexterity; also the cast was very noticeable and would have drawn attention to the courier. The cast had been removed in mid to late April. Gem wasn't properly aware of Gemmy's exact travels in March; she had been country hopping, working on her thesis, recording her work to later transcribe to her computer. Gem did know that Gemmy had met their mum for a long weekend in Paris in late March. Other than that, Gemmy could have been in London or Barcelona. They didn't ask the 'Where are you' query when they weren't on assignment. Wyatt knew exactly where Gemmy had been until she lost her passport and received a new one in late April.

Gem didn't resent Gemmy for not speaking of James. Her sister certainly had deserved a private life - as did everyone. But - oh - the cause and affect fallout to Gem because she hadn't known about James!

No assignments to Barcelona. No assignments to Geneva. James was the only reason for Barcelona. Still the query of Geneva, since she hadn't been covering for Mr Choate.

Gem reached for her mobile to text Mrs Brown.

'Cause of death of Thai courier?'

'Knife.'

'On assignment?'

'Still unknown.'

'How many German codes had dad deciphered?'

'Still no answer.'

Gem paced, raking her fingers through her hair. She pushed the start button on the cd player. She needed Vera Lynn's voice for comfort. Wyatt had Gemmy's passport. Gem could ask to see the passport but she knew he would deny that request. If their positions were reversed she would refuse the request.

Paul Andriani was a man of disguises. Why hadn't he been wearing a disguise in Barcelona? Why was he in Barcelona as himself - a.k.a. John Staunton? Wyatt was extremely astute to have recognized John Staunton, for although it was well known that Staunton was a 'criminal', his name was much more famous than his face. John Staunton's avoidance of cameras was legendary. Gem would definitely like to know how Wyatt had managed to recognize Staunton. Whoa! Think of the sarcasm that request would draw from Wyatt - and another verbal battle.

Ping

'No backup knowledge to date. Perhaps lost in decoding computer glitch. White trying to recover. Little if no hope of that, I would say.'

'No paper copy?'

How could Harry not have a print copy?

'Shall try to track down.'

'Possibility of checking with Harry?'

'No.'

'Okay.'

It was a long shot. Not everyone makes paper copies these days. Some people wanted less paper in their lives. Foolish not to have print copies for records and files. And honestly. The Agency? One would think the Agency would have paper on every damn thing! She would trust Mrs Brown to come up with the information. Gem just knew it had to exist.

'Paper on any codes?'

'Shall check.'

'Thanks!'

'You're tired. Go to bed.'

'Soon.'

Gem cleared all messages and charged her mobile. Long day. City. Lunch with Wyatt. Saw Mrs Brown. Pub. Dinner. Sorting. She dragged her fingers through her hair. She was exhausted.

"It's later," Wyatt announced from the doorway. Then he switched off the cd player.

Gem paced the floor of the office, listening to the lyrics: 'I'll Be Seeing You'. When? Gem groaned. And then she made notes.

Hong Kong: Margaret Lawson, Gerald Forrester, Eric Portermann, Mrs Brown, Harry, Mr White, Paul Andriani, Mr Denton.

Dead: Gerald Forrester, Agent; Eric Portermann, Agent; Mr Denton, Agent

Dead: Gemma Lawson, Courier; Margaret Lawson, Courier; Vietnamese Counter-courier, Chinese Counter-courier, Thai Counter-courier

Dead: James Smythe and baby - heartbreaking collateral damage

Five and three. Agency and SEA Network

Gem made a cup of tea, then pressed the start button again on the cd player.

Mr Denton. Drowned while fishing. Not an unusual cause of death. Was there the slightest hint of suspicion in Mr Denton's death?

Portsmouth. Near the submarine museum Gem had toured in August.

Had Mr Denton retired to Portsmouth or to a nearby village?

If his death was suspicious, he could be connected to the Pilos and to Hong Kong. If his death was accidental, then of course, there was no link. The Agency cadre, formerly of the British Embassy in Hong Kong, may not be a link to the deaths. But there were too many coincidences.

Or not too many coincidences. Well-trained embassy officials, dedicated, loyal to the U.K. It would not be an unusual transition to recruit them to B.I. Or the Agency: couriers and agents 'retire' or are recruited by yet another branch of the government. You need replacements, you recruit people you know and trust before you go outside to 'unknowns'.

Questions for Mrs Brown or Mr Cawley:

Did Mr Denton retire to Portsmouth or was fishing that day a special trip? Was he alone?

Any indications of foul play in Mr Denton's death?

Update on the Thai courier's death. On assignment?

Gem read the notes three times, cut them into sections, and shredded the pieces.

She paced the floor. She would ask Mrs Brown if there were any updates on the search for the Pilos. How could a plane be missing for over three months without a single sign of it?

Gem turned at the sound of footsteps - to see Wyatt. He switched off the cd player, lifted her over his shoulder and turned out the office lights.

"What are you doing?" she demanded.

"Firefighter's carry," he yawned. "Bed time. Again."

Gem opened her eyes. Something was different. She stretched her arms - and -nothing! She turned over; Wyatt's side the bed was empty. Lovely!

Thank heavens, he was already up! Force brain to work, she urged herself. Bathroom! Before he comes out of his. She swung her legs to the floor, brushing sleep from her eyes - not that much could have accumulated in two hours.

She heard his bathroom door open; he stood beside the bed, towel around his waist

Lord! he's breathtaking! Her eyes were drawn to his body, his skin still glistening from the shower.

"Try to sleep a bit longer," Wyatt urged.

"I can't," Gem sighed, searching for her dressing gown. "Shower," she muttered.

"I have time. I'll join you for a proper long shower. I'll wash your back for you," he tossed her dressing gown to her.

"No, thank you! Water conservation - remember - your words," Gem shot back.

"My word woman! - you are distracting," he leaned down to kiss her.

"And you are irritating," Gem slipped around him and off the bed.

"Same thing," Wyatt chuckled.

"I am going to buy you a dictionary," Gem walked into her dressing room, sliding hangers on the pole, deciding what to wear.

"We'll read the S's together - in bed," he followed her. "Sexy, seductive, sensual, sate, satiate, skin, saucy, savor."

"Saber rattling, sarcastic," Gem selected a skirt, "sacker, sacrifice, sacrilege, seducer, surfeit, satire, scamp, scalawag, scapegrace, scrounger, seething," she pulled a tee off a hanger.

"Shrewd, shrew, sagacious," Wyatt took the garments and tossed them over his shoulder. "Did you memorize a dictionary?"

"Yes," Gem smiled smugly. "Did you?" She swiped the fabric off his shoulder and hung the garments on a hook on the back of the bathroom door. She slipped around him to pull open a drawer to look for frillies.

"Sage, sanguine, sahib - cross word puzzles," he took the frillies.

"Sahib! In your dreams," Gem scoffed. "Sap, sardonic, sneering." She put her hands on his chest to press him backwards and out of her dressing room.

"Sass, smart aleck." He slipped his hands to her waist.

"Ha! Reduced to slang! Salacious, savage."

He closed the door to the dressing room with his foot, drawing her back towardss the bed. "Sanguinary, sassy, satisfy, scathing, scorch, satisfying."

Gem pushed his hands from her waist. "Satan, satyr, scoundrel, scourge, Scratch," she said frowning at his irritating persistence. She wanted to take a shower and get away from him this morning. She pushed open the door to the dressing room, ignoring his advance.

"Scorn, smack, stinging, scandal, strip, scuttle, sear, secret, seize, sensitize, subjugate," he continued from behind her, "subject, subdue."

"Subtle," Gem turned to look at him. She hadn't missed the warning. "You win," she gave him a cold look.

"It's a definite draw," Wyatt conceded with a gracious nod. "Yours was a remarkable performance."

"As was yours. Excellent vocabulary. As I said, you win," she turned towardss her bathroom.

"I say we call a truce. I already instructed Mrs M to delay breakfast," he said quietly.

Gem rinsed the shampoo from her hair, standing under the streaming water and muttering to herself. "Stupid, scapegoat, self-wrong. Svengali." But truth to tell, she didn't really mind losing the game this morning. But heavens! she was tired. The shower was barely reviving her.

After Wyatt left the Hall, Gem tried to focus on cathedrals, but she couldn't decide which one to work on. She started on Fortrose, switched to Elgin, then to Salisbury, spreading the photos across the counter, looking for inspiration but finding none. It was pathetic when one could not find inspiration from a cathedral.

She texted Mrs Brown hoping to get answers to ponder.

'Did Mr Denton retire to Portsmouth?'
'Yes.'
'Why?'
'Fishing. Fishing. Fishing.'
'Any indications of foul play?'
'No.'
'Agency reviewing police report?'
'B.I.'
'Why B.I.?'
'Agency shorthanded.'
'True.'

Gem couldn't disagree with the issue, nor offer assistance by returning to her former career.

'How many witnesses?'
'None.'
'Red flag.'
'Possibly, but B.I. confirmed police analysis.'
'That's good.'
'Indeed.'
'Is Harry in danger?'
'Very likely. Part of the job.'
'True.'

And it was, Gem sighed.

Four and three. Four Agency dead, three SEA Network. Delete Mr Denton from eight.

No revelations.

Books, dvds. Gem picked up each and set them down again. Her brain was too full of the War. She paced the floor, trying to sort, but she couldn't concentrate. Her mind was too tired to sort.

The Defender. London. Too much effort. She didn't want to have to concentrate on the driving, Mr Critchley's style - absolute total concentration, not a single thought unrelated to driving was allowed.

Tea. She went to the kitchen. Mrs M gave her a frown. "You need a bit of fresh air, dear," the housekeeper suggested as she handed Gem a cup." Have a proper walk before lunch."

"Yes," Gem agreed.

"Mr M will be in soon to install the inter-com in your office," Mrs M informed her. "Is there anything else you need him to do?"

"No," Gem shook her head and drank her tea. "I'll just fetch my camera and be off."

"Hat, mobile," Mrs M reminded her. "If you'll be walking in the woods, wear something yellow."

"Yes, ma'am." Gem changed to a yellow tee and went to her office for her camera. She had a full roll with which to work, and sorted through the camera bag to quickly organize it. The missing lens. Blast! She had used it in Scotland. But where? Another lens! A trip to London on Monday.

Phone. Yellow. Hat. Camera. She felt as if she was going on a minor expedition.

Mr M, wearing a battered fedora, was entering the kitchen as Gem was leaving the house. He doffed his hat to her and Gem flashed him a grin. Sport cap, fedora, not the straw hat he had worn earlier in the week. The man had a collection of chapeaus!

Gem walked through the gardens, across the lawn to skirt the woods, looking for a path. She didn't intend to wander about alone in the forest; she felt confident as long as she could see the Hall. She focused the camera up through the canopy of branches to shoot the sun streaking through the leaves. She wasn't looking for a particular subject, allowing the lens to capture the pristine seclusion of her surroundings. She wandered along the tree line, down around the meadow, shooting the stone bridge, then a long shot of Ticking Bottom shops. She should have brought another roll of film; the Hall was only minutes away, but she decided against returning just yet; instead she sat on the bank of the brook, and watched it trickle past her, the water dappled by the sun. It was very quiet. There was the sound of birds chatting to one another, the lapping of the water against stones in the brook.

It was a few minutes before she noticed the fish in the brook. Not having ever read a book about fish she had no means to identify them, but they darted past her so quickly she wouldn't have had time to get a proper look at them. Wyatt would know the kind of fish; no doubt he knew every bit of Ticking Bottom. She pushed him from her mind. She didn't want to think about anything. She needed to clear her brain so that she could again start sorting information.

How long could she bear to live at the Hall?

The Hall. Wyatt. Project CSU. The Pilos. The Search. Her book. Her brain was on overload. A hat. Mobile. Yellow. The men at the pub. Lord! Wyatt was moody! He was constantly giving her orders. She was used to Agency rules and SOP. She had expected to make adjustments in her life when she married Wyatt, but she had expected a proper marriage, not an agreement based solely on his terms.

The fish were swimming downstream with the current. Gem was swimming upstream against the current in every aspect of her life.

Why had Gemmy gone to Switzerland? Gemmy in Switzerland was an anomaly. It could be an important clue. Or had she flown to Geneva to purchase a gift for James? A purchase would have a receipt. Would it be in her purse on the Pilos? Or had she left it behind in Brisbane, in which case it would be at the Agency warehouse. Mr Cawley could obtain information from the warehouse.

She glanced around the area. There was no one in sight. Gem pulled her mobile from her skirt pocket.

'Receipt from Geneva in Gemmy's effects at the warehouse?'

It took a few minutes for the response. She wasn't sure of Mr Cawley's scheduled hours, but she doubted that he was ever away from his mobile.

'Will send query.'

The Agency warehouse staff was meticulous in their cataloguing. The information would be readily available.

Another question rose in her thoughts.

'Last courier assignment to Geneva prior to 30 May?'

She could have put the queries to Mrs Brown, but these were relatively minor points to tie up her time. Mrs Brown would likely delegate such queries to Mr Cawley.

Ping

'3 May, Choate.'

'Counter-courier Swiss?'

'Yes.'

A simple direct delivery. At various times a neutral country could be a delivery location, but that was not the case on 3 May.

'Neutral delivery to Switzerland prior to 30 May?'

'No.'

She needed to search James's room at the Hall. She felt like a spy. But a spy needed opportunity.

Ping

'No receipt.'

'Thanks.'

'Ideas?'

'Still gathering information.'

'Keep in touch.'

'I shall.'

The bedroom search was a must.

Gem cut across the meadow, returning to the Hall via the cobblestone lane.

Mrs M was leaving the house as Gem approached the kitchen door.

"There you are dearie," the housekeeper breathed a sigh of relief. "Mrs Moody is feeling a bit under the weather. I'm going to sit with her this afternoon. I've called Mr W to tell him so. I made you a sandwich and a salad and there are crisps for your lunch. Your dinner is in the slow cooker. I will see you Monday. You have a lovely weekend, dear."

"Monday?" Gem said puzzled.

"I have weekends off. Didn't you know?" Mrs M frowned. Didn't Wyatt tell his young bride anything of the workings of the Hall?

"Yes, of course," Gem smiled. Had Wyatt told her of Mrs M's schedule? Blast! Weekends alone with Wyatt! That brought a shudder to her soul.

Gem glanced at her watch. Nearly one o'clock. She hadn't realized it was so late. Hopefully Mrs M had had her lunch before she went to sit with Mrs Moody. Wyatt would be annoyed with her if he thought she had ignored his rules about Mrs M and lunch.

And when would the Master of the Hall deign to make an appearance? Since she had met him he never seemed to have a regular schedule at his office. Had he meetings that day that would keep him in the city until late afternoon? She didn't know; he hadn't mentioned meetings at breakfast; mainly he had questioned her on her plans for the day - which had been to work on her book - of which she had accomplished absolutely nothing.

Gem watched from the breakfast room as Mrs M walked down the cobblestone lane towardss the village proper. She was alone, so apparently Mr M was still occupied somewhere on the estate. But then Mrs Moody wouldn't need Mr M also to sit with her.

Inter-com! She hurried to the office, sandwich in hand to view the object of Mr M's morning activity. There it was - on the wall to the left just inside the doorway. So that could be an indication that Mr M would not be in the house for the remainder of the day. She knew the sound of the Jag's engine and would have to listen for it. And be quick about her business in James's room. But she had to quickly eat the lunch Mrs M had prepared for her. She didn't want Mrs M to think that she had wasted her efforts trying to please Gem.

The door to James's bedroom was unlocked, and she left it open, the better to hear the Jag if Wyatt did not spend the afternoon at his office. She didn't touch or move anything that might draw attention to the fact that someone had entered the room. Framed paintings hung on the walls; there were other paintings, framed, some not yet framed, and unfinished canvases stacked on a table to lean against the wall. There was a large four poster bed, similar to the one in the master bedroom. Books were neatly shelved, sharing space with carved wood boxes. An empty easel, two artists' pallets, blank canvases, dvds, cds, boxes with paints and brushes.

Gem gently slid open drawers in the highboy: clothes. There was a dressing room, more clothes. A desk with six drawers held folders of sketches, and photo albums. Gem quickly scanned one album for photos of Gemmy, but found none. She pulled out another album and quickly flipped through the plastic pages: photos of James and Wyatt with a handsome couple; there was a striking resemblance between the men, so Gem decided the older man was their father; their mother was lovely, but Gem didn't see much visual resemblance of her in her sons; there were photos of the M's, of young people with James - likely the multitude of friends Mrs M had mentioned. Wyatt and James standing by the Jag, Wyatt's arm was around his brother's shoulder - a mate photo. There was a photo of James standing in front of a green convertible that Gem thought to be a Morgan, but she couldn't see a clear view of it. Was that the car under wraps in the last garage stall?

There were so many photos of the brothers at parties, lounging on the grass, chatting, hiking - Gem thought possibly in Scotland - at Marigold Cottage on the shore overlooking the Channel, at the Colosseum of Rome, the Parthenon, and the Acropolis in Athens; so many photos; they had certainly traveled a great deal together.

Gem returned the album to the drawer; she hadn't ever made a dent in the first album and the drawers held stacks of them. She read the room to make sure it was undisturbed from her minor search and then gently closed the door behind her. She felt a twinge of guilt trespassing in James's room, but it had been for a good cause. She would like to do a proper search one day when she was more certain about Wyatt's whereabouts. He would be furious if he knew she had entered James's room.

The Hall was still, save for the clock ticking in the main hall. She went down the steps and read the study Wyatt had used before making the library his office - according to Mrs M. There were no family photos in the study. Gem did not open the desk drawers or the cupboards. This was just a preliminary reading of the rooms. The sitting room was also void of family photos and personal items. The paintings on the walls in the sitting room and study were James's art.

The next room was the living room/parlor/lounge. Gem decided it was the living room - Mrs M had said it was her decision what to call it - so living room it was. It was a formal room for formal entertaining; the furniture was excellent quality. The only personal items in the room were James's paintings and the framed photo of the young artist on the fireplace shelf; there was a very strong resemblance between the brothers and the man in the photo album in James's room - so obviously their father.

Why were the doors to all the rooms kept closed? Naturally she would expect the doors to the library to remain closed because it was Wyatt's office. But why the other rooms? Was it simply habit or a DO NOT ENTER warning? She opened all the doors, except for the library and would watch to see what happened when Wyatt or Mrs M was in the house. In her opinion the Hall seemed cheerier - less oppressive - when she could see the sunlight streaming in through all the windows when she walked past the open doors.

The great room was much more comfortable than the living room; Gem would enjoy curling up on one of the chesterfields in this room on a rainy day, book in one hand, mug of hot chocolate in the other. The beautiful handmade cupboards in the corner to the left of the fireplace hid the telly, dvd equipment, and an elaborate sound system. She hadn't heard Wyatt listening to music, so perhaps it wasn't equipment he used very often. And yet again, the only family items in the room were James's paintings.

Gem wandered back to the living room to look at the photo of James. She thought of the Grantham family as she looked into the eyes of the man Gemmy had loved for so brief a time. A lovely family of four reduced to one survivor. The same as Gem's family. She and Wyatt were indeed a match in that way.

Gem noted that James had his mother's green eyes, Wyatt his father's grey eyes. She wondered if the Senior male Grantham's eyes had turned to steel when he was angry. Or perhaps he had not had the same temper his son possessed.

"Have you decided yet that you made a terrible error in judgment, marrying the wrong brother?"

Gem spun around, shocked at the sound of Wyatt's voice. Why hadn't she heard the Jag coming up the driveway? Was she so lost in her thoughts that it blocked out everything else?

"If so, it's too late, my dear," he said dryly.

Wyatt stood watching her. Did she often think of James? Did she ever think of him now? Had she conveniently put him from her mind when she had deserted him last spring? Had she a shred of feeling for the young man she had destroyed?

"There's that rascally cat again, holding your tongue," Wyatt said casually, watching the wary expression on Gem's face.

"I'm not in the mood to argue with you," Gem said hesitantly.

"Excellent. I didn't come home to argue with you," he said pointedly.

As he walked towardss her Gem eased to her left, putting the sofa between them.

"You certainly have a flexible schedule, leave the office any time you please," she said dryly.

"I'm the boss. I can do that. I worked and now it's time to relax. With you."

"I'm going to my office to work," Gem turned her back and walked out of the room.

"No."

Always demanding! Always his terms!

He easily caught up with her in the main hall, folding her arms around her, pulling her back against his chest.

"Why don't you leave me alone?" she demanded, as he smoothed her hair to the side and kissed the nape of her neck.

"You don't really want me to. I know that and you know that. And good Lord, Gem, why would I leave you alone? Look in the mirror, woman! You make my blood boil!" he teased.

As he turned her around to face him she slipped from his arms and walked down the hall to the kitchen. "Take a cold shower!"

"There's not enough cold water in the world. You know that," he leisurely followed her.

Gem took the lid off the slow cooker and stirred the stew Mrs M had prepared for their dinner.

"Why don't you go golfing?' she suggested, as he slowly walked around the island.

"Gave it up. Too many fees, too expensive."

"I'll pay the fees," she insisted.

He took the spoon and lid from her hands, setting the lid on the slow cooker, the spoon in the sink, then his hands on her waist.

"I'll take up golf again when I'm eighty and our grandchildren are ferrying you around to cathedrals."

Gem flung herself away from him. "I'm not having your children!" she declared heatedly.

"Now my dear wife," Wyatt advanced again with measured steps, "whose children do you think you shall have if not mine?"

"Any other man's - but not yours!"

"Nonsense," Wyatt continued, slowly backing her into the corner where the counters met. "You know I would never allow that."

"Perhaps you are too sure of yourself," Gem said bluntly.

"We shall see, my dear," Wyatt drawled, neatly pinning her against the edge of the counter.

"Yes, we shall," Gem lifted her head confidently, crossing her arms across her breasts. She would find the Pilos and get the Hell out of Grantham Hall and away from him!

"Sass. You're very spirited this afternoon. It's very sexy."

"You think everything is sexy!"

"Only where you are concerned," he murmured, taking her arms and wrapping them around his waist, beneath his suit coat.

Elgin Cathedral completed. Fortrose Cathedral completed. Two chapters completed, photos, drawings, texts. The cathedrals reminded her of her missing camera lens. She had always been so careful with this camera and the attachments. She sat in Auntie Jane's comfy chair, eyes closed, thinking back to the last time she had used the lens. Inverness. The Culloden Battlefield. She and Wyatt had had a verbal battle - yet another one. She had shot nearly two rolls of film - photos of the battlefield and then the last shot - the battlefield in the foreground, the roofs of Inverness at the edge of the field, the past and the present meeting in a stunning composition.

"You are the grimmest bride, I have ever seen," Wyatt had scowled at her as she had removed one lens from her camera and had attached another.

"What do you expect?" Gem had snapped.

"I expect the great actor in you to show some talent! Smile!"

"You are the great actor, the writer, the director, the producer of your own horror film!" Gem had snapped.

There had been a bitter silence between them as they walked along to the Clava Cairns - the four thousand year old Bronze Age Cemetery. Gem had used both lenses at the cairns, shooting a roll of film with each lens.

Wyatt had offered to carry the camera bag but Gem had declined. He had stood watching her as she photographed the Standing Stone, the Paired Standing Stone, but had wandered a bit away as she shot the SW Passage Grave - all with the missing lens. Had it been weeks earlier she would have wanted Wyatt in the frame as she shot the photos. Now she just wanted him shot period.

He had taken the camera bag from her shoulder as they walked the distance back to the battlefield and the Land Rover.

"You're quite pale. Aren't you feeling well?" he had asked.

"You hound me to wear a blasted hat in the sun, then complain that I am pale," Gem had snapped.

"I am inquiring if you are ill?"

I am devastated! Humiliated! My heart aches, my stomach is tied in knots. I want to scream, to tear out my hair, to rage against you every waking minute of the day!

"No," she had replied. "I am not ill."

Gem cringed remembering the scene. She still felt the way she had that day at the battlefield. She was still devastated. Wyatt was still horrid.

And that was the last time she could remember using the missing lens. She had repacked the camera case so many times during those hideous days - at the GEI cottage, at the crofter's cottage the day they had had the picnic.

Blast!

She had unpacked her luggage hurriedly the day they had arrived at the Hall. Gem went up to her dressing room to check her luggage in case she had become distracted by one of Wyatt's nasty comments, and had absent-mindedly put the lens in the luggage instead of the camera case. Not there. She checked pockets of sweaters, her windcheater, jeans. Nothing. She went back to her office and started pulling out boxes from beneath the counter, pulling out photo packs, stationery items; she went through the drawers of her desk.

Blast! No lens!

She was completely frustrated with herself by the time Wyatt entered her office an hour later, the room in complete disarray, drawers pulled out, boxes dumped on the counter, books pulled off shelves. Gem raked her fingers through her hair.

Blast!

"Are you by any chance looking for this?" Wyatt pulled the camera lens from his pocket.

Gem stared in astonishment. "Wherever did you find it?" she demanded.

"In a box. It must have come in the post today. Mrs M put it on my desk." He carefully handed the lens to her. "Mrs Godwin, the caretaker at the cottage at Inverness found the lens under a chair in the lounge. The cottage hadn't been used for a month prior to our stay, so she assumed it belonged to one of us, and posted the lens here. Well packed and well insured." He handed her the box Mrs Godwin had posted.

"Bless her heart!" Gem sighed with relief. "I'll send her a note, a check for postage and her time, and -" she gave him a questioning look for a suggestion.

"The postage and insurance were charged to the cottage account. A box of chocolates would be appreciated. Mrs Godwin is partial to anything chocolate," Wyatt advised. "Fortunately not as expensive as Italy," he said with a faint smile.

"No," Gem shook her head. She would do errands on Monday, thrilled she wouldn't be purchasing a replacement lens that day.

Wyatt looked around the shambles that earlier had been Gem's office. "Do you need help organizing?" he offered, surveying the wreckage.

"No, thank you," she replied. "I made the mess, I shall set it back to rights."

"I'll be in the library then."

She heard him in the kitchen, then he walked back into her office, silently handed her a beer, then stepped over the muddle in the centre of the room and walked out the second door at the far end of the room, his actions drawing a chuckle from her.

It took Gem the remainder of the evening and a second beer, also delivered by Wyatt, to sort the mess. She played cds, then switched on the telly, wondering what had happened in the world the past fortnight when her mind and life were in a muddle. And she was beginning to feel that by living in Wyatt's strange world, she was in danger of losing touch with reality. Gem was drawn back to his world at the end of the newscast when Wyatt made his nightly Town Crier appearance to announce bedtime.

"You should clang a bell when you do your nightly tour," Gem said, yawning.

"I'll consider that suggestion," he smiled.

And as usually happened, Gem became lost in his smile.

Chapter Thirteen

Gem stared at the computer screen, the Pacific Ocean, wondering if it would be worth the effort doing the flight time and nautical miles to the Caroline Islands. Mr Portermann couldn't have been that far off course! It was only the faintest possibility but one that Gem was not ready to pursue.

Mr Cawley would be awake. She often wondered when he slept and what were precisely his work hours - he was always at the other end when she rang or texted. And what of Mrs Cawley? Did she ever see her husband? Gem reached for her mobile.

'Update on Timor, Arafura, Carpentaria?'

'No new information on your queries. Search extended to Banda and Coral seas.'

'Banda too far.'

'Possible tail wind.'

'Grasping at straws.'

'Indeed. Sometimes they pay out.'

'Do you ever sleep?'

'7.5 hours/day. You?'

'Goodnight!'

The Coral Sea. Waste of time. That was in the opposite direction of his destination! Mr Portermann should have been flying out of the rain that night. He would have quickly solved an error like that!

Unless.

Unless the Agency was still considering the air piracy theory. That sent a chill through her blood. Or they thought Mr Portermann had been disoriented.

Banda Sea was a long shot. By Gem's calculations the Pilos would have been out of fuel before it reached the Banda Sea.

Gem pushed the button to re-start the cd. She prepared a cup of hot chocolate, settled in the comfy chair with Operation Drumbeat and the crew of U-123, and Vera Lynn providing the music atmosphere.

U-boats, crews, guests, agents. The latter were two SS officers.

Ping

'Philippine agent missing.'

'Last location?'

'Unknown. Missing four days.'

'Ever posted to Hong Kong?'

There was a very long pause. Gem waited, hoping a reply would come before five o'clock. She was desperate for sleep. Vera Lynn was singing about the last time she saw Paris when Gem's mobile pinged.

'No.'

'Age?'

'32.'

'Possible to check of parents and Hong Kong?'

'Will take days. Shall do. Unlikely to get information.'

'Thanks!'

'Clues?'

'Still gathering information.'

'Bonne chance!'

'Merci!'

Gem cleared her text messages, and closed the book. She had had her fill of Madmen for the night.

She made another cup of hot chocolate.

Agents Dead: dad, Mr Portermann, Mr Denton.

Missing Agent: Philippine agent.

Couriers: five

Nine total now

Eight. She was including Mr Denton. The hairs at the nape of her neck prickled.

She texted again.

'Mr Denton no accident.'

'Evidence to contrary.'

'Evidence be damned!'

'Will forward your thoughts to Mrs Brown.'

'I know I'm right.'

'Don't doubt you for a nano-second, Gem. How can I help you?'

'Keep replying!'

'Day or night. Promise!'

'Thanks!'

'Family, Gem. Forever!'

'Night.'

'Night.'

She cleared the messages. Gosh! Mr Cawley's words were comforting! His words actually gave her confidence and touched her heart. Mrs Brown and Harry would be on holiday, but never Mr Cawley. He was her main link to the Agency! He was always there when she needed him. Odd there. He was the Agency person she saw the least. Perhaps four times in the past six years. She had spoken to him as many times in as many years. But since the first of August he had always been there when she needed him.

She finished her hot chocolate and let Vera Lynn finish Land of Hope and Glory. There was perhaps still a bit of the Second World War that had yet to end.

Wyatt was walking down the stairs as Gem was starting up to bed.

"It would be hope and glory for me if I could sleep past seven o'clock," he yawned, draping his arm around her shoulders.

"Sleep as long as you like," Gem suggested, feeling peaceful after the messages from Mr Cawley.

"I swear if you get out of bed during the next three hours, I will keep you there until noon," Wyatt murmured.

"Let me think about that," Gem murmured, actually half-seriously. It would be her decision then, wouldn't it! Hours to think.

His words echoed in her mind when Gem's eyes opened two hours later. Her game. Not his. She closed her eyes and refused to move even so much as a toe until he stirred.

Her thoughts wandered to Mr Cawley. He was an excellent example of the proper Agency employee. Constantly available, constantly researching answers for God only knew what mad queries other staff might put to him. He was indeed Family.

And since Wyatt had come up a myth, the Agency was still the only Family she had.

The missing agent. Where had he gone missing? Who was his contact?

She thought of every lost agent and courier and their families. Neither Gemmy, nor their mum or dad, or Gem had ever ignored the danger of their jobs. But by following SOP and specific directives they had eliminated every single possible slipped cog that could have been prevented.

AND NO ONE HAD A HANDLE ON THIS PROBLEM!

Not true.

Everyone possible was working on every situation. The Agency staff members were working 24/7. But people did need sleep. They needed opportunity to step back, to clear their brains, to clear perceptions.

The people lost would be found. There would be answers, there would be resolution. There would be justice. It might be silent Agency justice, but there would be justice.

How did Mr Cawley manage to have a marriage? Gem mused.

Wyatt groaned, stretching, glancing at his watch. "Nine o'clock!" he rubbed his eyes.

"You are most welcome," Gem announced, stretching, pushing back the bedcovers. "I won!"

Wyatt shifted, pinning her to the bed by moving his leg across hers. "You played your game well," he conceded.

"I won! Shower!"

"Not yet."

"I won!" Gem protested.

"It's not yet noon," he replied.

"You don't play fair!" Gem protested again.

"And in this instance you will be pleased that I don't. I need to thank you for letting me sleep undisturbed. And then we will both have won."

"But I won!"

"Yes you did. And you shall win again."

And she did.

Rain splooshed from every eave on the Hall roof, every branch, every leaf, hour after hour. Fog shrouded the gardens; even the brightest lights from the carriage house were invisible.

Absolutely perfect atmosphere to solve a murder mystery. Unfortunately that was what Gem was attempting to do. It was not an Agatha Christie book that she reading. This was real life. And it was driving her to distraction.

What would James Bond do? Or Miss Marple? Or conceding the greatest detective - Sherlock Holmes. What would he do?

The M's did not work the weekend. So Gem and Wyatt were alone. Together. And alone. No buffer.

If only Miss Marple would come into the office, sit in Auntie Jane's comfy chair, pick up her knitting, and suggest to Gem that she ring Mrs Brown to arrest -

In this case - no one.

Gem paced the office, the dining room, the breakfast room, through the butler's pantry, into the kitchen and around the island, and into the mudroom. Vera Lynn's voice followed her even into the mudroom.

Laundry. Blast!

Gem grabbed a laundry basket and walked down the hall, stopping short when she saw Wyatt in the great room. He was stretched out on the chesterfield facing the hearth, stacks of ring binders in front of him on the coffee table, the wingback chair seats, and on the floor.

"Laundry?" Gem politely queried. It would be churlish of her not to ask since the task must be done.

Wyatt glanced up frowning. "Done," he replied dismissively, returning to his reading.

Really! She was pleased she wasn't expected to do his laundry, but he could have been more polite replying to her offer. She brushed off her mild resentment; she found enough in her hamper in her bathroom to make a load of wash, and once it was in the machine she wandered back to the great room.

"Heavens!" she looked at all the binders. "Have a problem deciding what to read?" she asked lightly.

"A few second quarter reports," Wyatt glanced up again. "They all must be read."

"How many companies comprise GEI?" her eyes grew wide.

"I don't see that's any of your business," Wyatt said curtly. Fishing for information for a future game? "GEI has nothing whatsoever to do with you."

Gem gave a slight gasp at the stinging remark. He had been in a decent mood when they had breakfast; in fact his mood had been almost pleasant - for him. She turned to walk back to her office, to let him stew on his own when a thought struck her like a thunderbolt. Wyatt Grantham was a very wealthy man.

"Why didn't you demand I sign a pre-nup?" she queried.

"You just realized that?" he raised an eyebrow, sighing impatiently at the interruption. "Pre-nups deal with the legalities of divorce and death," he said loftily. "There will be no divorce. Perhaps you recall that we have already discussed that subject."

Gem stared at him, her temper rising to equal his own mood. Could the man be civil for more than a few minutes each day?

"And should I die before you, I do have a will. GEI shall still not be your concern. I set a trust fund for you, the yearly amount of which shall keep you in film, but very little else."

"That must have tweaked your solicitor's interest," Gem said coolly. She didn't need his money.

"That is also none of your business."

"I imagine your solicitor expects all sorts of odd issues from you - and your revolting manners and practises," she snipped.

Wyatt's eyes narrowed, the grey colour darkened." Another display of your waspish temper. Do you wish to reference a specific issue, my dear?" he said coldly. "Perhaps an interesting subject for a change instead of your usual whinging."

"No wonder you've never been married before! You're a monster!"

"Again, we are well matched," Wyatt replied sardonically. "And for your information I chose previously not to marry."

"No - much better to blackmail women into sleeping with you!"

Wyatt laughed harshly. "You don't believe that. And really, Gem - I could have had you in bed the first day we met."

"That's not true!" Gem gasped incredulously.

"Oh, but it is, my dear," Wyatt scoffed. "You were so easy. You still are. No resistance. I'd give you a demonstration, but I have work to do, as you can see. Now you have a brain, use it to find something to amuse you. Off you go then." He turned his attention back to the report he was reading. If she stood there much longer the hostility in her eyes would set him ablaze.

Without uttering another word, Gem walked to her office, pocketed her mobile, grabbed her wellies and mac from the mudroom and went out into the rain. Rain and fog were indeed preferable to being in the house with that ogre. Ogres should actually live under a bridge - not in houses with humans! The extraordinary ego that man had! No wonder Wyatt never wore hats. He wouldn't ever be able to find one large enough to fit his big head!

The fog was so thick lights couldn't cut through the white mass; Gem stayed to the side of the cobblestone lane, conscious of the fact that a vehicle would be upon her before she or a driver would realize the confrontation: human versus mechanical beast - human 0, beast 1. Gem slogged through the rain, the only sound reaching her ears was plopping: raindrops plopping on the cobblestones, the trees, the leaves. Steady. Plopping.

The fog thinned a bit as she crossed the old stone bridge below the Hall. Gem walked through the village, noting the faint glow of light from the shops; she passed no one on the lane; T.B. residents appeared to be settled into their own lives inside their homes. She walked as far as the second bridge entering Ticking Bottom, then backtracked as far as the rail station and crossed the tracks to see what was hidden from view by the Yellow Crow Pub. Ah! Something was hidden that she hadn't seen from the windows of the train the day she had escaped Wyatt's underhanded medical plot. There were cottages and shops behind a grove of trees that backed the pub. Gem followed the lane - still of cobblestones - to discover a butcher shop, plumbing and heating contractor, a family-style restaurant, a hair salon/barber shop, a clothing shop - catering more perhaps to women of Mrs M's generation - and a bank. The fog shifted and drifted, but Gem estimated approximately forty stone and thatched cottages she hadn't known existed in Ticking Bottom. Every cottage appeared - at least through the fog - to be surrounded by a dry stone wall and neat country gardens. Ticking Bottom seemed to be a quite sufficient village except for providing a church and a school.

Gem mentally tallied the cottages she had seen in T.B. the past week - perhaps twenty-three - and now she had discovered forty more. Quite a sum of homes in a village someone would have great difficulty to find - unless one actually knew the village was there - nestled, or perhaps more appropriately, lost, somewhere between Cambridge and Bedford.

The Pilos lost somewhere between Brisbane and -

Wyatt tossed the report to the table. Harsh. He had been too harsh with her. She had made two queries and he had gone for her jugular. Hell! For the most part she didn't annoy him; well she did, but he should be able to tolerate her more than just in bed. He had to get over the fact that just looking at her reminded him of James; he had to become used to her presence. He usually had great patience with people, but he had very little with her - without having to constantly force himself to concentrate to be civil, to force himself to smile at her, to remember some semblance of manners or social graces. Hell! He rubbed his eyes, weary of reading the never diminishing stack of reports. It had been a frustrating fortnight for both of them. He could give her a bit of slack. It would certainly keep her off balance. Which was how he preferred her to be for his Game.

He sniffed the air. The chicken he had put in the cooker after she left the Hall was a reminder of lunch.

The long case clock chimed half past the hour. Wyatt looked at his watch. Half twelve already and binders more to read that afternoon. He reached for his mobile on the coffee table to text Gem.

'Lunch. Half hour.'

He peered out the window; dead thick fog, then went from room to room turning on the lights, so that she could find her way back to the Hall.

Land of Hope and Glory - outside text. The Ogre of the Hall, no doubt, Gem muttered to herself. She read the text and thought precisely of what he could with his lunch. But texting that message would only draw his fire, and she had had enough of that for one day. She forced herself to turn in the direction of the Hall. It had been a very interesting walk. The fog settled in again, so thick Gem had to fix her eyes on her shoes as each step she took met the cobblestones. She knew she should be able to find the Hall as the lane curved up the hill. A wistful smile came to her lips when she saw the faint light piercing the fog and then the outline of Grantham Hall. Wyatt had turned on all the lights on the ground floor so that she could find her way back to the house.

His eyes now held less steel, she noticed, when she entered the kitchen. The room was cosy warm from the cooker and scented with the aroma of roasting chicken.

She shed her mac and wellies in the mudroom; the dryer was humming; her skirts and tees had been hung to air dry.

"Thank you for taking care of my laundry," she said quietly.

Wyatt gave her a perfunctory nod. "Chicken, potatoes, corn bread, for lunch. You have time to prepare a salad if you wish to have one."

"No," Gem replied.

"Will you fetch the wine and glasses?" he said, his tone more a request than an order, for a change.

Gem did as he asked. "I'll set the table," she offered.

"We'll eat here. Lazy weekend," he replied, setting the roasting pan on the island counter. "Did you have a pleasant walk?" he asked as he carved the fowl.

"I did," Gem nodded, sipping wine. "I discovered another section of Ticking Bottom - behind the Yellow Crow."

"Ah, that's where it is!" Wyatt chuckled. "I thought there used to be more shops and cottages in this village."

He was in a less difficult mood, Gem mused. "No school. No church."

"No school," he had mentioned the day she came to T.B. "The church and cemetery are behind the inn. You can't properly see it for the oak grove." Wyatt served her plate to her. "The vicarage is rented. The vicar lives in Crispin, but the church is available for weddings, funerals, and the W.I. meetings. No available clergy for T.B. to have its own vicar."

"Oh," Gem replied, savoring the chicken. "You are actually an excellent chef," she repeated a comment she had offered in Inverness. "Did Mrs M instruct you in the culinary arts?"

"Self-taught. You only taste the results of many disasters. James was a much better cook, and Mrs M did teach him."

Gem didn't want to touch his last remark. "Were you too stubborn to listen to Mrs M?" Gem queried, directing the conversation away from James.

"A bit too impatient to follow recipes," Wyatt replied. "I don't appreciate being told what to do, as you may well imagine."

"Indeed," Gem murmured.

"You are quite the same, it would seem," Wyatt reflected, pausing his fork in mid-air.

Gem nodded. She had to tread warily, never knowing what remark of hers might irritate him. "Being ordered about irritates me."

"Especially if the order comes from me."

"Naturally," Gem nodded again.

Wyatt fell silent for a moment. Then he said, "I was caustic to you earlier. I do apologize for that. You asked perfectly reasonable questions, however my replies were unreasonable. I have a great many reports to read every week."

An Apology. Hell must be cooling off a bit. "As you said, GEI is none of my business. I was simply astonished by the amount of paperwork that involves your time."

"I understand," Wyatt nodded, then frowned. "My reply to your second query stands."

"Yes." His money did not concern her for she had her own funds. And one day she would have her freedom from him. End of story. "You made everything quiet clear."

"Yet you do not always listen."

"I always listen. I simply ignore what I choose to ignore."

"And your point is -?" Wyatt said bluntly.

"Sometimes I must concede to you. But I shall not always do so."

He refilled their wine glasses, then stood and leaned against the cooker, his arms crossed against his chest.

"Concede or not, you shall always lose, my dear," he gazed at her. "You shall always lose, Gem."

"No," Gem firmly shook her head.

Wyatt pondered her words. "Do not play your opponent's game, but rather play your own," Wyatt said smoothly.

"Yes!" Gem gasped, blushing. Blast the man! "The gloves are off!"

"Well, my sweet, as far as I am concerned, the gloves have been off since the day I met you. You should have realized that by now. I have tried to make that clear to you for a fortnight."

"Indeed, you have made it very clear."

"The only way you will win this Game is over my dead body."

"That won't actually be necessary," Gem shook her head. There were already too many dead.

Wyatt gazed at her, then smiled. "You are so confident, my love, so mysterious. So out of your depth."

"So it would seem," Gem agreed. She drained her glass. "I'll do the washing up. You should get back to your reading."

"I'll clear up. Leftovers for dinner," he reached for the plastic food containers.

What to do next? Book? Photos? Read. Sort and shred photos? Books, Gem decided, as she washed the dishes.

She approached Wyatt in the great room where he was again stretched out on the chesterfield; a report binder was in his hands, another one lay open, face down on his chest. He looked so deep in concentration that she wondered if she dared interrupt him.

"Yes, sweetheart?" he looked up from his book after she had waited a few minutes, deciding whether or not to speak.

"How does that word not stick in your throat?" she shook her head.

"I practise saying it. See, you don't listen," he teased.

"Ha, ha," Gem laughed dryly.

"Yes, sweetheart?" he repeated, his eyes twinkling.

Gem sighed, tolerating his sense of humour - or what he considered humour. "Do you mind if I look at the books in your library?" she asked politely.

"Whenever you like, my dear, unless I am speaking on the phone when I am in there. Have at it."

"Thank you."

He nodded and continued reading.

Gem knew the location of the books regarding World War II, since Wyatt had pointed them out to her earlier in the week, but she took the time to browse the shelves looking at the names of the authors; there were complete collections of Dickens, Robert Louis Stevenson, Mark Twain, Voltaire, James Hilton, Shakespeare, George Eliot, Winston Churchill, and on and on. There were other shelves of Aristotle, Dante, Socrates, Kant, Gray, Dryden, Dumas. Gem would continue browsing later. She was here to look at the section on the War - Second World War; she differentiated because there were at least two dozen volumes on the War to End All Wars. She settled on the floor, scanning the titles before her, counting thirty-thee titles. Her dad would have enjoyed perusing the subjects on Wyatt's library shelves: the British capture of U-570, Churchill's speeches, the Royal Marines, the R.A.F., the Royal Navy, R.A.F. bombing raids, Hawker Hurricanes, D-Day, the Battle of Britain, Pearl Harbor, seven books on submarines; famous battles: Midway, the Coral Sea, the Philippine Sea, Guadalcanal, the OSS. Now that had a ring to it: the Office of Strategic Services. Gem tried sorting, but couldn't find a source in her mind.

Whatever the reason, it struck a chord; it was the book she had to read. She crossed her legs, leaned back against the bookcase and opened the cover, wondering if her father had heard of the book. If she hadn't previously read it, then likely neither had he. She read the first chapter slowly, then closed her eyes, mentally reading it from the first page. Halfway through the first chapter she was satisfied, and she opened her eyes. Wyatt was standing in the doorway.

"I thought you might actually be sleeping," he sounded disappointed as he walked over to her.

She would have been caught if he recognized the procedure she and Gemmy had practised from the time they had first learned to read. "Resting my eyes a moment," she repeated the excuse she and Gemmy had used for years.

"Oh," he gazed down at her. "You ARE permitted to sit on the furniture in here," he smiled. "And you may take books to your office."

"Right," Gem moved to rise to her feet, but he reached down and lifted her clear off the floor.

"You are light as a feather," he chuckled.

"Hardly that," Gem protested, as he set her on her feet. She straightened her skirt and tee, feeling his eyes on her.

"What say we pop down to the pub for a pint?"

"Excellent!" she gladly agreed. There were buffers down there, which meant more time that day they would not argue.

Fog swirled around them, so dense it couldn't be cut by their torches.

"It's as if we're walking through cotton wool," Gem mused.

"Or a cloud - but there are no images to see," Wyatt referred to their cloud gazing day in August.

A deluded day, Gem frowned at the reference, however Wyatt apparently didn't note her pointed silence. He seemed to accept their pre-marriage days as point of fact, while Gem thought of them as a knife to her heart.

The Yellow Crow was bursting at the seams. A couple moved to vacate their chairs for the owner of Grantham Hall, but Wyatt waved them back down to their seats; he and Gem sat on the ledge to the side of the fireplace.

He doesn't throw his weight around here either, Gem observed. She read the room; the crowd was relaxed and genial. The band didn't play until eight, but anyone who wanted to perform could take the floor. That saved Gem from having to talk to Wyatt, as she gave her attention instead to the music, currently being provided by a young couple getting experience before they applied for jobs with a local band. Wyatt, apparently not in a proprietary mood, refrained from putting his arm around her waist or shoulders as he often did in pubs. Gem let her mind wander to the music, cringing inwardly at the romantic songs that seemed to mock her; she much preferred the couple's traditional humorous drinking songs.

"Dinner here or at home?" Wyatt leaned over to murmur in her ear.

"Here," Gem smiled. The Hall could be oppressively quiet with only the two of them there. "Leftovers leftover until tomorrow."

And as their dinner was served, Wyatt quietly ordered a round for everyone. Mike Morgan announced a round had been bought but did not say by whom; the crowd gave a roar of approval, and a few nods were quietly sent to Wyatt.

"Not a frightfully rowdy crowd," Gem observed.

"Not when the publican is a constable," Wyatt grinned. "And you always know where he is if you need him."

Gem read on through the book about the OSS. OSS. Burma, China. Whoa! South East Asia. Coventry. Seahawk. South East Asia.

Mr Cawley was awake. Gem didn't think he referred to this time as the dark hours. She pulled her mobile out of her pocket.

'Were OSS agents on the Coventry and Seahawk?'

'Will try to obtain information on that query.'

U-1408. OSS. OSS. OSS.

ODESSA.

That was the thought she couldn't reach previously.

The Organization for Former SS members.

U-1408, Hong Kong. U-1050, Mexico. U-1100, South America.

U-boats transporting Odessa members into hiding in early 1945? Battle of the Ardennes Forrest. Hitler's Maniacal Machine starting to crumble. Some rats leaving the ship early? Or going underground to keep the Nazi Machine alive? Neo-Nazis, skin-heads. Not all Odessa members had been tracked down over the decades since the War.

Destroy the files of the U-boats. No records to delineate which Odessa members went into hiding, or the locations to where they had been dispatched. Members and their families. U-boat staffs, guests, agents. A hell of a ship's complement.

She had to meet with Mrs Brown!

Odessa members could have been quite young in 1945. They could easily still be alive today! Decades ago, 1970? - terrorists claiming to be Odessa members killed anti-Nazi members.

Destroy the files of the U-boats. Send coded messages back to Germany after safe arrivals. Codes that likely couldn't be deciphered for decades. Or had been set aside while the world's attention had been diverted to Korea and the Cold War - spies, agents, couriers, double-agents. The Nazi codes had been bound into a very thick book, but had received only sporadic attention over the years. And decade after decade things go by the by. Old codes should be broken, but politics change, funding is cut, politics change again; a quiet, non-descript job deciphering half-century plus old codes loses its importance. - Unless - one simply can't let go of a part of history. Her dad had picked up the gauntlet dropped by lack of interest and funding.

And someone knew Gerald Forrester was making progress decoding the old Nazi ciphers. Finding names. Names would have changed, but there is always a trail, human, if not paper.

And how does one survive relocating to another part of the world to go into hiding? One needs funds to support oneself, one's family.

Art. Stolen. Pillaged from European homes and museums, from galleries and private collectors. Not all the stolen art had been tracked down.

Gem's head began to ache. There was so much to sort and to keep straight in her mind.

Black Market 1945. Black Market. Still thriving today.

Ping

'Information will take weeks or months for reply.'

'No surprise.'

'Keep in touch.'

'Yes.'

Oh, Dad! Had your passion, your genius for deciphering, opened an old can of worms that would actually bring down the Pilos?

And if so - how?

Gemmy, mum, dad, and the rest. So many lives because of virtually dead codes?

Or my theory could be completely wrong, Gem groaned. And then where would I start again on the search?

Oh Gemmy, Gemmy. Where are you? Mum, dad, Mr Portermann. Now the Philippine agent.

One last text for the dark hours.

'Philippine agent contact?'

'Blank.'

Lord! Paul Andriani. Again! Thai counter-courier. Philippine agent.

'Thank you. Goodnight.'

'Goodnight.'

Four on the Pilos. Vietnamese counter-courier. Chinese counter-courier. Thai counter-courier. James. The baby.

Mr Denton, Gem was certain. The Philippine agent missing. Gem had no hope he would be found alive. A grim total of ten - and one missing.

Thank heavens she had Mr Cawley. He was her dark hours link to the world. She didn't think she could bear all the horrible things happening if she was alone every night. It was bad enough being alone during the rest of her waking hours.

Chapter Fourteen

Sunday morning was a repeat of the previous morning. Gem let Wyatt sleep. Her brain was too tired to sort, so she stared out the window that overlooked the gardens. Either the fog was still thick or someone, overnight, had painted the mullioned windows white. Had to be fog: Mr M was off weekends.

Fog. She did not mind the fog, but it trapped her in Ticking Bottom with the Ogre of Grantham Hall. It certainly wasn't safe to attempt to drive when one couldn't see beyond the windscreen. She was eager to talk to Mrs Brown, however that wouldn't be prudent with Wyatt in the house.

She wondered if Mr Cawley was sleeping. 7.5 hours a day! However did he manage that? Well, the obvious - no insomnia. Also he did not mention consecutive hours of sleep.

Where was Harry? On holiday week after week after week? In high profile meetings? Was he in the U.K.? The States? Most likely in South East Asia. Or Australia? It was very possible that his holiday had nothing to do with the Pilos. He could be at any hot spot or simmering spot anywhere in the world.

Wyatt's arm lay across her stomach. She was trapped. Gemmy was trapped.

Was the Philippine agent still alive? She highly doubted it.

Perhaps the deadly issues in the SEA Network had nothing to do with the Pilos. Perhaps someone was simply trying to interrupt the International Network.

Her head began to ache. Clear the mind, she silently urged herself.

Another entire day at the Hall with Wyatt.

A long walk would be extraordinarily necessary. Perhaps she could get lost in the fog.

Blast! He was waking.

Well, at least she wouldn't have to think about anything for a while. - He was indeed a powerful man!

"Gem, you are the desire of my dreams," he murmured, his hand starting to roam.

"You are the villain of my nightmares," Gem replied wearily.

"Really? - How long have you been dreaming of me?" he teased,

"You are incorrigible!" Gem pushed his hand away from her breast.

"You won't be repeating that," he laughed. "And you are most welcome - in advance."

Gem scanned the photos again; two were perfect, the rest of the prints were unusable. The light was a shade off on one snap, the other two were not as crisp as she demanded.

"Another trip to Hampshire," she muttered. "Blast!" She had photographed Winchester early last May, and had thought a return trip unnecessary. Wrong, wrong, wrong.

"The photographer or the camera?" Wyatt queried from the doorway.

"Not the camera," Gem replied, gathering the photos into a file folder.

"The shots were not to your standards, so why keep them?"

"The composition is what I wanted, so I will use these photos as a guide," she shrugged.

"How many shots do you take of each cathedral?"

"Usually three or four dozen. But I ran out of film at Winchester, then the weather moved in, so the rest of that day was lost. My error. Never run out of film. Thus back to Hampshire."

"How often do you misplace your camera and lenses, aside from Italian rail excursions?"

"Not very," Gem replied casually. One lens lost in Cherbourg, camera and case stolen in Hamburg - that was planned - a courier delivery - and the loss didn't count as it wasn't her camera; a camera stolen in Paris, but it was one of lesser quality than her current camera. "Not very."

"Ah ha," Wyatt observed her thought processing, counting the times she made a slight grimace. "I'll arrange for an insurance adjuster to appraise your equipment then set a policy for you. Once it's in effect, you will have to inform the agent when you lose, damage, or acquire additional equipment."

"That won't be necessary, I can manage on my own," Gem protested.

"I haven't seen any indication so far that you can manage a single aspect of your life," Wyatt drawled. "But as you wish. Your camera equipment is your responsibility," he conceded.

"Why don't you go back to your reading?" she scowled at him.

"Lunch," he advised.

"Oh." Will this day ever pass? At least his mood was an improvement over yesterday's snarls.

The text for Winchester was composed and would suit the next set of photos. Hopefully there would be a chance to get proper light yet this fall, weather permitting. If she had to wait until spring then she would. The cathedral had welcomed people for over a thousand years; eight months would be well worth the wait to do justice to Winchester.

Gem needed a diversion. If she still lived at her flat she would go to a café or for a walk to the shops, to a museum.

She put her laundry away. Wyatt was reading as she walked past the great room to the staircase. He was in the exact position when she came down the stairs an hour later.

"How do you remember all that you read?" Gem asked quietly. She and Gemmy couldn't discard all the information they absorbed.

"Intense concentration," he looked up from the book in his hand.

"Sorry. I shouldn't have interrupted," Gem apologized.

"That wasn't meant to be a cut, just a statement," he stood, stretching, and Gem tried not to look directly at him. The man was electric! "Shall we see if we can get lost in the fog? Pint at the Crow?"

"Yes," she nodded. Fresh air to dispel her thoughts.

Wyatt stopped outside the kitchen door.

"What?" Gem puzzled.

"We are waiting."

"Why?"

The M's materialized through the fog.

"I thought they would like to join us this afternoon," Wyatt murmured.

"Lovely!" Gem smiled. Back with humans!

Gem chatted with Mrs M, Wyatt with her Mister, as they strolled to the pub.

"A new hat?" Gem nodded at the estate manager's head, a fishing hat with hooks hanging from the brim.

Mrs M leaned over to whisper. "His straw hat has become a planter," she suppressed a smile. "The Mister hasn't found a new hat he likes."

Hence the sports cap, the fedora, now the fishing hat. "A garden installation," Gem murmured, and the two women laughed hilariously. The men turned to stare at them, but Mrs M and Gem gave them an innocent look and kept on walking down the cobblestone lane.

At the Crow, Wyatt watched Gem chatting with the M's. She was such a difficult person to read. He saw a flash of a genuine smile and a laugh at one of Amos's jokes, and the light of her smile had actually reached her eyes - but only briefly.

He expected a wary look in her eyes when she was alone with him. He wanted her to know he would not tolerate any of her games. But it was the haunted look in her eyes - when she didn't know he was watching her - that puzzled him. That odd haunted look. Was it fear? If so, it wasn't fear of him, for he had seen that look, sometimes fleeting, sometimes prolonged, during the days they spent together in August. Was it guilt? Remorse for some previous game she had played to ruin another man? James hadn't mentioned that look in her eyes. He was an artist; if the look had been there when she was with James, his brother would have noticed it - and he would have remarked of it as he lay dying in that hospital in Barcelona. The look that had been fleeting, or a bit longer a few times, in August was now a common occurrence; the look was in her eyes more often than not since their wedding night.

Whatever had happened to cause the haunted look had occurred between the time Gem had deserted James and had met Wyatt. What had Gem done to earn that expression? What was haunting her? Could she actually feel guilty for her past actions? Could she feel regret? The reserved person she presented to Wyatt was not the easy going, lively Gem, James had so heartbreakingly described to Wyatt. The only time she dropped the reserve was in bed. And wasn't she a quick learner there!

Gem glance at Wyatt and blushed, reading his mind and drawing a chuckle from him.

Gem sorted photos, choosing five of Mr Becton's gardens to be matted and framed. The frame shop had a collage frame that would perfectly suit the photos. So the photos for Mr Becton, a straw hat for Mr M. and perhaps then a blouse for Mrs M; and the chocolates to be sent to Mrs Godwin. Her list was made for morning.

When she was in the city she would call Mrs Brown to arrange a meeting. Now that she had the Defender, she would make use of it! - As long as Wyatt didn't disrupt her plans with unreasonable demands. And that would always be a likely possibility.

She finished reading the book on the OSS, and would return it to the library in the morning. She didn't want Wyatt to think she was invading his 'office' in the dark hours. He'd probably think she was searching for the passports and photos. That would be a fruitless search. He wasn't a careless man to put them in a place easily discovered. There very likely was a safe in this house and also likely he had one at his office in the Grantham building. If she was Wyatt, she would put the passports and photos in the safe at his London office.

Ping

'Malaysian agent missing.'

Blast!

'Contact?'

'Blank.'

Paul Andriani again! Thai c-courier, Philippine agent. Malaysian agent!

'Where is Blank?'

'???'

'Update on Philippine agent?'

'No indication parents were ever connected to Hong Kong in anyway - per your recent query. That is only new information.'

'What the blast is going on?'

'???'

'Okay. Keep in touch.'

"I shall, Gem.'

The South East Asia Network, if not the entire International Network. Malaysia, Thailand, Philippines. None of the countries were involved in Project CSU. China, yes. Vietnam, yes. Pilos: two couriers, yes, cryptanalyst, yes, agent/pilot, yes. Statistics would indicate an attack on the International Network, not on Project CSU. The SEA Network as the main target was iffy. The International Network was the most likely theory for now. She pulled out her mobile.

'All other agents and couriers accounted for?'

'As of midnight.'

Gem glanced at the clock. Four hours ago. Okay. That was a bit reassuring. She deleted the messages.

Who? Or what group, would want to disrupt the Networks? And why? Why throw down this gauntlet? Why challenge the Agency and the SEA Network? This was not a minor challenge to a powerless entity. And for now, other couriers and agents would step in to replace the fallen. Procedures would be reviewed and tightened, new safety measures directed, security increased.

Did Mrs Brown know Harry's location? Was Paul Andriani in touch with the Agency on a regular basis or was he just out there?

Vera Lynn's voice stopped singing, and Gem pushed the start button on the cd player. Then she paced the floor. Sorting was difficult again. There was so much information. And now the new information from Mr Cawley.

And she was so very weary.

Gem couldn't shake off the feeling of fatigue.

Odessa.

Perhaps it wasn't logical to focus on Odessa in the 21st century, but Gem was not going to discount that group.

When would answers start replacing questions? Day after day there were more and more questions. Few answers came and they only brought more queries.

Mr Denton's death doubly troubled her. He was a fine man. And while not wishing to cast aspersions against the police and their investigation, or against B.I., and its investigation, she thought Mr Denton's death to be an anomaly. His death was no accident. And with all the deaths so far of agents and couriers, there could be no justification in accepting any decision other than murder.

And that was unsettling. It brought the hunting to this soil. What was equally, if not more unsettling, was as to how couriers and agents were being targeted. Their identities were scrupulously protected. Someone had infiltrated the Agency Network, and the SEA Network. Or someone had given up the Networks to - ?

It had to be the former. She simply refused to believe someone in the Network would give up their own. A spy had infiltrated the Network. In South East Asia. But how Mr Denton then? And how the Pilos?

Gem turned off the cd player. Her thoughts were going nowhere.

Monday morning. Hopefully the fog would lift. Hopefully she could go to London, escape from Wyatt for a few hours, and have what she could only - hopefully consider - a normal day.

Once out of the shower and dressed, Gem texted Mrs Brown requesting a meet for lunch that day. Wyatt was waiting for her in the bedroom to go down with her to breakfast.

"Are you going to the city today?" he queried.

"Yes," Gem nodded, very thankful the sun was shining for a change.

"Good. Lunch, one o'clock, Cantonese House," he said crisply as he tied his tie.

"Oh," Gem frowned, slipping her mobile into her skirt pocket. "I texted Mrs Brown to ask if she would like to have lunch with me today."

"Indeed?" Wyatt gave her a brief nod. "I will yield to Mrs Brown."

A reply came as they reached the breakfast room.

Ping

'Wednesday noon. Charley's.'

Blast!

'Okay.' Gem texted back, frowning that she had to wait two more days to talk her supervisor.

"Disappointment?" Wyatt asked.

"Wednesday," Gem sighed. At least she would have the day in the city.

"Lunch then," Wyatt declared. "Would you prefer a pub?"

Gem shook her head. "Cantonese House is fine."

Wyatt again followed her into London, and again Gem smiled to herself as he turned off to the car park, and she could then focus her thoughts on her errands.

The framed photos greatly pleased her, and were ready in a matter of minutes as the mattes were pre-cut for the collage frame, simply requiring the removal of the back of the frame to slip in the snaps. Next on the list was the sweets shop; she wrote a quick thank you note to Mrs Godwin, slipped it into the package, and the shop would manage the shipping of their product. Gem was off then to purchase a straw hat for Mr M. One would think it a relatively easy task with the multitude of shops in London; it was not easy. She went to at least a half dozen shops before literally stumbling upon a garden nursery that had an abundant stock of straw hats. A black hat seemed the most suitable for Mr M. She hadn't paid close attention to time and she was ten minutes late, meeting Wyatt at the restaurant, hampered by the difficulty of finding a parking space.

His eyes were steel grey when he pulled out the chair to seat her at their table.

"I am very sorry," Gem rushed to apologize. "There was a dearth of parking spaces available. I am sorry you had to wait," she flushed.

"A man always has time to wait for a beautiful woman," Wyatt said smoothly. "Did you accomplish your errands?"

"A few," she nodded. "I sent the chocolates to Mrs Godwin. The box should keep her well stocked for a week."

"Excellent," his eyes lightened a touch and he gave her a brief smile.

Gem glanced about, reading the room. Odd. She was having Asian cuisine while her thoughts were so occupied with South East Asia. Odd. She looked at the faces of the other patrons. Any of them could be an agent or a courier. She heard a smattering of languages, Spanish, German, and one she thought was Bantu. In this restaurant or in any other restaurant or pub or café in London there could be an agent watching. Well, she was proof of that wasn't she? Not perhaps as an agent or a courier any longer, but she was of the Agency.

After the waitress took their order, Gem glanced around the room again, and saw two women at a nearby table openly staring at Wyatt.

"They're staring at you," she murmured.

"And there are men gazing at you," Wyatt replied quietly. "You have a bit of colour in your cheeks, for a change. Have you been rushing about all morning?"

"Yes," she smiled. "It's lovely to be out of the fog." Her smile faded. "It was very rude of me to be late. I am sorry."

Wyatt put his hand over hers. "Apology accepted, Gem, don't dwell on it."

Oh those eyes, Gem sighed inwardly. They should come with a warning label 'Dangerous. Avoid at all Costs.'

Wyatt slipped his fingers beneath the silver filigree bracelet to stroke her wrist. Gem's breath caught in her throat at his light, sensual touch. Blast him! He knew what he was doing to her!

"What are you thinking?" he murmured.

"That you should return to your office," she said pointedly, drawing a pleased chuckle from him.

"We could go to my flat," he softly suggested.

"You could go to your office," Gem repeated her remark.

"Later then," he countered.

"A warning or a threat?" she murmured.

"A promise," he lifted her hand to kiss the flesh his fingers had stroked.

Wyatt did return to his office and Gem pursued her quest for a surprise for Mrs M. She window shopped for an hour before stumbling, not literally this time, upon a new shop, so new its sign was being hung; a placard in the window stated the shop was 'Now Open'. There were still boxes to be unpacked inside the shop, but Gem found a blouse on a hanger that quite delighted her. She had first thought the fabric was suede, but it was actually cotton, the gold dyed fabric shifting in the light to light gold and dark gold reflecting a non-existent suede texture.

"Brilliant!" Gem flashed a smile at the shop assistant.

"I dyed it, not knowing what would be the result. I'm very pleased with the look," the young woman said eagerly.

Talented. "Do you design the clothes?"

"My sister is the designer, we both sew. We make all the clothes, and most of the jewellery."

Gem quickly decided on the blouse for Mrs M, and used her credit card, still in her maiden name, to pay the bill. She would not be using Grantham any longer than she had to; she hadn't changed her name in her own mind, and would never do so.

As she was walking to the Defender she saw a flat hat in a shop window, purchasing it on impulse for Mr M. Of the two hats, he might approve of one. At least they would add to his collection until he found one that suited him.

The drive to Ticking Bottom was pleasant, perfect down time for relaxing before she once again entered Wyatt's realm. Lord of the Manor, wasn't he just! The cobblestone lane through Ticking Bottom was scarce of villagers. Perhaps they were already beginning to gather at the Yellow Crow for a late afternoon pint.

Mr M met her on the drive when Gem parked the Defender in the stable garage. He always seemed to know when she was arriving and broke from his routine to query if she had bags for him to tote into the kitchen for her.

She handed the bags holding the hats to him. "To tide you over until you find the one which perfectly suits you," she explained, as he pulled the hats from the bag. "For work," she pointed to the black straw hat, "for fun," she pointed to the flat hat.

His face split into a wide grin as he tried on the straw hat, changing to the flat hat, and doffing the latter to her.

"Both shall do quite brilliantly, Missus," he smiled. "Thank you. I shall give them both a work out!"

She didn't need his assistance with the rest of her bags, so he walked back to the carriage house. Gem greeted Mrs M, then took her bags to her office. Mr

Becton was in his gardens, so Gem used the garden door, and slipped out to give him his surprise gift.

"You shouldn't have," he protested softly. "But I'm right happy you did," he grinned at her. "I'll be pleased to hang this in my cottage."

Mrs M remained. As the housekeeper handed Gem a glass of wine, Gem handed her the blouse. Mrs M was at first speechless, but gave her a wide smile.

"Child, you shouldn't have!" she protested, but was delighted and pleased with the gift. "Isn't it beautiful!" she beamed. "Pub night with the girls - and my denim skirt!"

"Lovely," Gem laughed. Mrs M clicked her wine glass against hers, and Gem claimed a kitchen stool, to sit and listen as the housekeeper filled her in on the other participants of the girls' pub night.

"Ellie Hornsby's eldest, Willow, is expecting again. She no longer fits her name after five little ones. She should try running away from her husband, instead of running after her little ones all day," Mrs M said bluntly, causing Gem to laugh and choke on her wine.

"Still, Willow is a good mum, and all the children have their dad's green eyes, thank the Lord! Willow was a bit of a run-around in her younger days. She can't run now," Mrs M winked at Gem. "Willow was a great concern to her parents for many a year. Now George, being Willow's husband, is hard working and a good father, and not one to chase other skirts, if you understand my meaning. They live over at Crispin."

"Doesn't sound like he has time to do extra-curricular chasing," Gem laughed.

"Wouldn't be a secret in T.B. if he was, not the way Ellie Hornsby tells all to anything with ears," Mrs M said firmly, refilling their glasses. "There were doubts now when he wed Willow. She being a bit wild, and he just on the re-bound from Marigold Weston who had run off with Douglas MacDougall."

Gem sipped wine and let the other woman's words flow over her. Mrs M's chatty tones held Gem's brain devils at bay - if only for a short time. She was back to reality when the housekeeper looked at the clock on the wall.

"Mr W will be home shortly," Mrs M observed.

Gem wondered if Mrs M knew she was a buffer between the young couple - although Wyatt had warned Gem not to use the M's as such. And if Mrs M did realize she was a buffer what did she think of the need of such?

What did Mrs M think of Gem as Mrs Wyatt Grantham? - A label Gem personally abhorred, but one which the housekeeper would view as a great honour to any woman. The M's obviously thought the world of Wyatt Grantham, yet they accepted Gem into the picture without showing any obvious reservation. And that was too bizarre, as Gem herself knew that she was a misfit for the 'Lord of the Manor'.

"Shower!" Gem announced, draining the wine glass.

Mrs M thanked her again for the blouse and Gem impulsively hugged her.

A parting comment from Mrs M nearly overwhelmed Gem. "Perhaps when you have a lull in your day we might do the shops in T.B."

"Perfectly lovely! Pick any day except Wednesday," Gem grinned and headed upstairs. She would definitely miss the M's when she could finally separate herself from Wyatt and Grantham Hall.

Gem luxuriated beneath the pounding water, then selected a cosy tee and fleece skirt, intending to help Mrs M with dinner preparations. She stopped short when she walked out of the dressing room.

Wyatt had entered her wine soothed sphere. He shed his coat and tie, pinning her in her tracks with a dark, cold stare. "Gifts for the M's - and Mr Becton?" he demanded, his voice icy.

"It's my money," she protested firmly.

"I already warned you about tricks, Gem. Don't use the M's!"

"Good evening to you," Gem said pointedly. "And as you have said, I don't listen to you,"she brushed past him, fed up with his nasty temper.

Wyatt grabbed her upper arm, his fingers digging into her flesh. "No games, my dear wife!" he warned. "Don't hurt them or I swear to God, Gem, I will -"

Gem gasped. "You're hurting me," she winced painfully.

Wyatt immediately released her, looking down at the angry red marks on her flesh. He bent his head down to brush the marks with his lips. "My apology, sweetheart," he murmured, then strode into his dressing room.

The marks on her arm began to turn blue. Gem scowled then went to her dressing room to change into a jumper with long sleeves. Mrs M need not see the marks.

She retreated to her office, too upset to attempt a pleasant chat with the housekeeper. She turned on her computer, and pushed the start button on the cd player. Vera Lynn's voice would give her some courage. She would go for a walk to escape the Hall, but she didn't want Mrs M to think she had to set dinner back for her. And Wyatt would be displeased at that. Do not aggravate his already tenuous mood.

She clicked on the Pacific Ocean screen saver, taking a glimpse of it, then clicked on a screen with the Cologne Cathedral. She was sick to death of cathedrals. Of books. Of Wyatt Grantham.

My world is so bizarre, she sighed inwardly, crossing her arms and putting her head down to rest upon them on the counter. She couldn't seem to grasp control of one single aspect of her life. Each day only seemed to go from bad to worse. Wyatt hated her, his attitude towardss her was unrelenting. She couldn't make any progress on finding the Pilos. She was physically and mentally exhausted. Her life was as much a jumble as her brain.

If only I could talk to Gemmy. Have a giggle with her. Just to see her once more - without having to look into a mirror to do so.

She looked up to see Wyatt's reflection in the window. He couldn't help but notice she now wore a long sleeve sweater instead of the tee she had on earlier.

Wordlessly he drew her from her chair, pushing up the sweater sleeve to look at the bruises on her arm. Wyatt put his arm around her shoulders, pulling her against his body, and resting his cheek against the crown of her head.

"I am truly sorry," he said quietly. "I swear to you, Gem, it shall NOT happen again. Although I don't expect you to believe that."

She sighed deeply. And it would not happen again, she knew. Whenever he called her by her name, she knew he was deadly serious. The intensity of his soft voice shocked her."I believe you," she murmured.

He held her, not speaking, until Mrs M entered the office to announce that dinner was served.

Dinner began quietly as Mrs M set the dishes on the table in the breakfast room. Minutes later she was out the kitchen door, picnic hamper in hand, leaving Gem and Wyatt alone for the evening as usual.

Wyatt cleared his throat and Gem glanced up. "Mr M is very pleased with his new hats," he gave her a short smile. "He believes he looks the complete roué in the flat hat. In fact he stated that were it not for Mrs M, he would retire to France to live a life of complete and delightful debauchery."

Gem pondered the vision. "I dare say he could pull it off. He could switch to the straw hat when he desired to only be partially debauched," she gave Wyatt a wary smile.

Wyatt nodded, his smile widening to the one that mesmerized Gem. "The photos you had framed for Mr Becton were very striking. You do lovely work, my dear."

Gem nodded her appreciation of his remark, relieved to see that his eyes were light grey.

Wyatt gave an unexpected chuckle. "Mrs M is going to lord it over the ladies at girls' pub night, that the 'new Missus at the Hall treats her like the Queen herself'. Mrs M is the only girl under sixty-five mind you."

"Is that a good thing?" Gem said warily.

"Indeed. Mrs Hornsby is the one most often lording it over the others, with her eight or nine grandchildren," Wyatt said smoothly.

"Six," Gem corrected. "Six grandchildren."

"Five and a half," Wyatt countered.

Heavens! He certainly was aware of the local gossip of Ticking Bottom! She shouldn't really be surprised at that.

"Well, Mrs M will now be the Queen Bee at the pub for a while," Wyatt concluded.

"They are all so kind to me," Gem quietly ventured an explanation of the gifts, hoping she wouldn't draw Wyatt's fire for her remarks.

"I understand," Wyatt replied tentatively. "I also need you to understand my concern for them."

"I promise I do," Gem said sincerely.

"Very well then, we shall consider the issue settled," Wyatt replied. "Tell me about your day, excluding the nasty bit when I came home from the office," he grimaced.

I tried to spend the day not thinking, Gem did not say.

"Shopping, driving, lunch with you, wine with Mrs M. Not terribly eventful," she said simply. "You?"

"Meetings. Manton is on another tirade with his son."

"Another Peter domino effect?"

"Young Peter Manton has apparently fallen in love with his supervisor. Her husband is less than thrilled," Wyatt wearily shook his head, and at the same time tried to suppress a grin.

"Siberia?"

"Toronto. He can cool his heels in snow piles come winter."

Dinner was a bearable segment of Gem's evening that day. She volunteered to do the washing up, remembering the deluge of reports Wyatt had to read. Once again in her office, she noticed the book of the OSS she had meant to return to Wyatt's library. The door was open, he was leaning back in his chair, feet propped up on his desk when she tapped at the doorjamb.

"Come," he waved her in.

"I wanted to return your book," she explained the intrusion. "It was very interesting. Thank you for letting me borrow it."

"Which one did you read?" he read the title as she turned the book's spine towards him. "Yes, a very interesting book."

"You've read it?" she asked in surprise.

"I've read most of the books here - at one time or another," he nodded. "The past few years I've been reading these 24/7," he held up the report binder in his hand, his fingers covering the title of the report. "Did you want to take another book?"

Gem shook her head. "Not now, thank you. I'm sorry I disturbed you," she wandered back to her office.

She was at loose ends. She stared at the Cologne Cathedral. And wondered if Mr Cawley had any new information. She didn't dare text him in case Wyatt stopped in the office on his way to the kitchen for a beer.

She scanned the photos on her computer. One cathedral after another. Click, click, click, she played the mouse. She pulled up the text of each cathedral, proof reading, adding a comma, transposing two sentences. She marveled at the incredible beauty of Winchester Cathedral, the genius of gifted architects who designed such magnificent structures for the ages - unforgettable beauty - versus people who thought they were architects, but were without vision and designed hideous concrete hotels, office buildings, and museums; perhaps the ones who lacked vision had been raised in concrete bunkers.

What was Paul Andriani thinking at this moment? - her mind drifted, as it was wont to do. Was he wondering if he was next on the list of agents to go missing? Was he next? It would be terrifying to have that worry in one's mind. But Paul Andriani was a master of his career; a master of living undercover.

Gem clicked on the Salisbury Cathedral. What a lovely day that had been, the drive with Wyatt in the Jag, the lunch. Bath. Blast! How charming he had been! She sat in the comfy chair, drew her feet up to the cushion and rested her forehead on her knees. If she was in her flat she could text or ring Mrs Brown or Mr Cawley, instead of worrying that Wyatt would walk in on her mid-conversation.

"Do you have a headache?" Wyatt asked quietly.

Gem shook her head without raising it. "No," she gave a muffled reply.

"At loose ends?" he queried, getting a nod this time as a reply. "Come for a walk in the gardens with me then," he took her hand, coaxing her from her chair.

"Did you finish your reading?" she asked.

"I never finish," he gave a half-laugh.

He didn't hold her hand as he usually did when they walked - his proprietary claim on her. She put her hands in the pockets of her skirt, enjoying not being attached to him.

"Do you feel your mind all a jumble, all the facts and statistics drifting one into another?" she asked curiously.

"Now and then," he admitted, "hence the break. And you with your book?"

"No," Gem shook her head.

"No?" Wyatt said surprised. "Never?"

"Well, they're all cathedrals, aren't they," Gem hedged, "not apples and constellations," she pointed at the sky.

"I see," Wyatt nodded.

It was so difficult to be in his company. Specifically because she didn't want to see him, to talk with him. To spend any time with him whatsoever. How could he stand being with her? It was a constant strain on her nerves, and must be also on his. They were two people with an invisible wall between them. Yet they had so very much in common - a fact that only she knew.

Wyatt didn't press conversation. He was still annoyed with himself for bruising her arm that afternoon. The Game was a mental exercise, not a physical challenge. He had to step back from the situation. This was his Game. He had to tolerate her presence as best he could; and when he could no longer bear her presence, he would have to stay away from her until he had his temper under control.

Paul Andriani. Barcelona. The Thai c-courier. The Philippine agent. The Malaysian agent.

Mr Cawley was awake with her.

'New information?'

'No.'

'No Harry?'

'No Harry.'

'Thanks.'

'Keep in touch.'

'I shall.'

Is Harry with Paul Andriani? No. Harry was on holiday. Gem was certain she would have been told if Harry had gone underground. She was NTK. Wasn't she? She pulled out her mobile again.

'Am I still NTK?'

'Absolutely!'

'Other couriers/agents accounted for?'

'Yes.'

Gem pushed the start button on the cd player, and cleared the text messages on her phone, slipping it back into her pocket.

The map of South East Asia filled the computer screen.

Gem pulled out her mobile again.

'Banda Sea report?'

'Not yet.'

'Coral Sea?'

'Same.'

The Agency was treading water. No pun intended.

Was Harry restructuring the Network? Mr Choate had been reassigned. The Agency Network would not take weeks to restructure, but the International Network certainly would take weeks, if not months, to do. There would be meetings with other Network Directors of all participating countries. And the three latest missing couriers/agents would again require Network restructuring. Just reading and approving the profiles of the 'applicants' would be incredibly intensive and grueling. And if necessary, Mrs Brown would be called in to assist in the process. Perhaps that was what she had been doing on 'holiday' when Gem made the incredibly foolish error of marrying Wyatt.

If Harry was restructuring he would have to meet with Paul Andriani in safe territory. Australia. Probably Sydney. Or the private airstrip outside of Brisbane. Wherever the meeting, it would be damned secure.

Gem had asked Mrs Brown if Harry was in danger, and the reply had been 'very likely'. Why? Basically, because he was traveling in the world of espionage, or because Mrs Brown suspected that Agency staff or the Network was being hunted? Hunted? Or red herrings? Project CSU or the Pilos? Odessa?

Gem made a cup of hot chocolate and paced the floor of the office. 'I'll Be Seeing You' wafted on the air. Oh! how many times she and Gemmy had watched their parents dancing to the song!

She was so tired. And weary of waiting for some solid answers to her queries to help her with her search.

She washed the cup and hot chocolate pot, then sat in the comfy chair listening to the long case clock in the main hall tick away the minutes. She closed her eyes, willing herself to sleep. But sleep did not come. Gem shut down the computer, switched off the cd player, and went up to bed.

Wyatt stirred, wrapped his arms around her, his right hand gently stroking her arm until she fell asleep; the clock downstairs yet again striking five chimes.

Gem decided not to go to the city. Rain was pounding down on Ticking Bottom and Gem knew the driving would be tedious; and she really had no reason to go to London. She would work on her book and clear out photos from her files.

She groaned at the memory of Wyatt promising they would spend a Saturday putting photos in albums. When had he said that? After Aylesbury? Bath? Pluckley? She couldn't remember. And she didn't care.

She sorted the photos of Kenilworth. Wyatt was in so many of the snaps, smiling, so unbearably handsome. And there were the photos he had taken of her. I looked so happy, Gem mused painfully. One by one she slipped the photos into the shredder. Aylesbury was next, then Pluckley. She had the cathedral photos of Bath and Salisbury, the other snaps went into the shredder. One by one the photos were chewed then spit into the bin liner.

All the negatives went into a pack marked negatives. She would give them to Wyatt the day she walked out of the Hall for the last time, free and clear of Wyatt Grantham. Then he could have his memories. And she could forget everything. It was petty to think of giving him the negs, but she would still enjoy doing so.

She didn't shred the photos of Wight and Inverness. Wyatt wasn't in a single shot and the photos were excellent. However, she would never wish to frame them. But it was painful to think of shredding the photos. Shred? Yes? No? Keep? Gem tossed the packs into the box and shoved it back under the counter. They could be chewed another day.

She cleaned the office, her bathroom, had lunch with Mrs M, then tried to focus on cathedrals, and lost that challenge. There was no point going over all the Agency information in her brain until she had some answers to her current questions, and had feedback for her theories.

She changed the water in the flower vases and cut more, dodging the raindrops with an umbrella, then reorganized the cupboards in the butler's pantry while Mrs M did the same to the kitchen cupboards.

Finally at a loss to occupy her time, Gem pulled on her wellies and her mac, and tamped along the forest line, across the brook, around the meadows and fields, then down along the upper lane of shops, down past the rail station and across the old stone bridge below Grantham Hall.

The purr of the Jag's engine reached her ears as Gem walked through the kitchen door. She flashed Mrs M a smile, stealing herself to be polite to Wyatt as she ducked into the mudroom. She started to shed the mac when it was deftly slipped off her shoulders. Wyatt gave it a good shake and hung it on its hook.

"Sit," he ordered, easing her on to a stool, then pulled off her wellies. "You need a hot shower."

"Mmmm," Gem nodded, aware that Mrs M, in the kitchen, could hear them through the open door.

Wyatt gently lifted her off the stool, setting her on her feet. "Go. Shower," he whispered. "Evening, Mrs M," he said, following Gem through the kitchen door.

"Evening, Mr W," the housekeeper called after them. Should she set dinner back an hour? She glanced at the inter-com. He would let her know.

"You're here early," Gem remarked as he closed the master suite doors behind them. She went through to the bedroom, flipping on light switches.

"I am home early," Wyatt corrected, distinctly enunciating the word 'home'.

"As you say," Gem shrugged.

"It is your home too, my dear," Wyatt reminded her, removing his suit jacket, pulling off his tie.

"It is not my home. It will never be my home," she snapped, rubbing her neck. "To you it's a home. To me it's a trap."

"You are cranky because you are cold and exhausted," Wyatt drew her hand away to gently massage her neck and then her shoulders. "You need more sleep."

"I need to get away from you," she turned to glare at him.

"That is not going to happen. Lord! You are pale, Gem," he scowled. "Take your shower. I'll get you a cup of tea to help take the chill off you."

"Don't bother," she shut the bathroom door, grasping for at least a modicum of privacy.

The hot water pounding down upon her felt wonderful, but it didn't ease her nagging thoughts. She was no longer at loose ends. It was worse than that. She couldn't get her brain started. She had refused to focus on ideas or facts of any kind while she had walked the perimeter of Ticking Bottom proper. When she had crossed the old stone bridge, she had decided to sort only facts pertaining to the Pilos. But she couldn't sort. All she could think of was Gemmy.

Then Wyatt had reached the Hall at the same time as she, leaving her feeling trapped between Gemmy and him.

She sighed deeply as she turned off the tap, wrapping her wet hair in a towel; she towel dried her body and slipped into a plush dressing gown.

As she combed out and loosely braided her hair, it occurred to her to tell Wyatt she was feeling ill, that she did not want dinner, wishing only to rest a few hours in bed. She could pull the blankets over her head, hide in the darkened room and escape from him for a time. It would be a lie, and one he would likely believe. She may as well lie to him for he so often accused her of doing so.

She pulled on frillies, a skirt and warm jumper, brushing away the thoughts of lying. Forge ahead Gunga Din, she urged herself.

There was a cup of tea on the coffee table; the tea was still steaming, but the suite was quiet. Wyatt had gone downstairs. Gem enjoyed her tea alone and in peace.

Her home also. Ha! Quite the fantasy world in which Wyatt Grantham ruled! He was very wealthy, Gem shrugged. He could afford any world in which he chose to live.

Mrs M had dinner well in hand, so Gem set the table in the breakfast room, took a cup of tea and sought refuge in her office. She charged her phone, hoping to get some text answers during the dark hours that loomed ahead of her. She was eager and anxious to meet Mrs Brown the following day, and for the dark hours she had Mr Cawley.

Wyatt was cordial at dinner, but the meal was as everything else, a time to endure his presence.

"Did you work on your book today?" he frowned as he stuck a fork in his salad. No doubt the greengrocer was pleased at the increase business from the Hall. But really! Salad again! Every dinner!

"No," Gem murmured, savoring Mrs M's succulent lemon chicken.

"Still a bit at loose ends?"

"A bit," she admitted aloud. Completely - she admitted to herself.

"Mrs M said you reorganized the butler's pantry today. Why? Mrs M can hire a girl from the village when she needs assistance," he informed her.

"I enjoyed doing the task," Gem tossed her head defiantly. "It's an autumn tradition here apparently. The summer plateware is moved to the upper shelves, the autumn colours are moved to within reach for everyday use."

"It sounds like a huge waste of time to me," Wyatt frowned.

"Apparently tradition is very important to Mrs M," Gem countered.

"That may be so," Wyatt conceded, "but you needn't follow traditions just to please Mrs M. Use what plates you wish when you wish to do so."

"It suits Mrs M," Gem insisted. "And why should I wish to change anything? Let your next victim change whatever she wishes to change."

"Your sour mood hasn't improved, I see," Wyatt's eyebrows raised slightly.

"Well, don't expect it to improve while I am here. You want my mood to change? Then give me a divorce!" she snapped, leaning her head down, and pressing the back of her neck with her hand.

Wyatt set down his fork, stood and walked over to Gem. He put his right hand on the back of her neck, his left on her forehead.

"Do you suffer migraines?" he asked softly.

"No. It's just a stiff neck," she muttered.

"Quite a knot," Wyatt massaged her neck for a few minutes, then drew her from her chair. "Lie on the sofa for a bit." He settled her on the chesterfield across from the fireplace in the great room. "Close your eyes."

A few minutes later he gently lifted her head to slip a warm pack under her neck.

"Rest for a while, my dear," he murmured.

Gem heard him doing the washing up, then he returned to replace the warm pack with another. There was a third warm pack and then she slept.

Gem wakened at two o'clock, to face the dark hours as usual. She had slept so soundly she hadn't realized that Wyatt had carried her up to bed. He was sleeping soundly. She quietly changed into pyjamas and a dressing gown and went down to her office. Her neck pain was gone and she could think again. Thinking about the search was one thing. Understanding Wyatt's gentle and thoughtful manner to her earlier was quite another thing altogether.

Mr Cawley would be awake. Gem pulled out her mobile.

'News?'

'Thai courier knifed.'

'In Thailand?'

'Jakarta.'

'Courier destination?'

'Singapore.'

'Didn't arrive Singapore?'

'No.'

'Departure Jakarta?'

'Thailand.'

The courier had departed Thailand on assignment to Singapore, but somehow was diverted to and killed in Jakarta.

'Explanation?'

'None.'

'Network did not redirect him?'

'No.'

'Philippine agent?'

'No new information on Philippine or Malaysian agents.'

'Mr Denton's effects?'

'Warehouse.'

'Catalogued?'

'Yes. No red flags.'

The Agency had gone through all Mr Denton's possessions but nothing unusual had been found.

'Still listed accidental death?'

'Yes.'

'Disagree.'

'Put to Mrs Brown at lunch.'

'I shall.'

'Information from you?'
'Want to run past Mrs Brown first.'
'Okay.'
Gem turned on the computer and the cd player. Vera Lynn sang her heart out as Gem stared at a map of South East Asia. And she reached again for her mobile.
'Left Thailand?'
'Bangkok.'
'Where Philippines?'
'Manila.'
'Malaysian?'
'Jakarta.'
'Searching Jakarta for Philippine agent?'
'Yes. And also Malaysian.'
Three of Paul Andriani's contacts were missing or dead. Gemmy's counter-courier was dead. Mum's counter-courier was dead.
'Everything else copasetic?'
'For now.'
'Harry?'
'???'
Gem stared at the map on her computer. By a small stretch of the imagination, one could draw a triangle from Bangkok to Jakarta to Manila to Bangkok. A rough diamond from Hong Kong to Manila to Jakarta to Bangkok to Hong Kong. All areas held by the Japanese during the Second World War. A diamond or a triangle.
And what would Mrs Brown think of Gem's theory? She pulled out her mobile again.
'Where Blank?'
'???'
'Just a long shot query.'
'No kidding!'
Triangle. Mr Denton was not part of the triangle or the diamond. He had been in Portsmouth, half a world away from South East Asia.
'Mr Denton's last 6 assignments?'
Gem paced, waiting for a reply, and pushed start on the cd player. While she was waiting she cleared her mobile of the text messages.
Chinese c-courier knifed. Thai c-courier knifed.
'Cause death Vietnamese c-courier?'
'Thought you knew. Knife.'
All knifed.
'Someone has a busy knife!'
'Indeed!'
Gem made a cup of hot chocolate and paced. And cleared messages.
Wyatt had been so kind earlier. Dr Jekyll and Mr Hyde. Wonder if he has ever been diagnosed with a split personality? Gem muse dryly.
Ping
'Moscow, Washington DC, Turkey, Washington DC, Toronto, Iceland.'
'Thanks!'

Nonspecific cities could mean a counter-agent receiver or a neutral delivery, not specific to Iceland or to Turkey. But not in Gem's South East Asia diamond or triangle.

Perhaps Mr Denton's death was accidental after all. Could mean there were no red-herrings. A ploy then, to disrupt the SEA Network, and only that Network. No connection to Project CSU or the Pilos.

Brain is working again, Gem mused, but it is so very tired. She needed a holiday. A proper honeymoon would have been a much needed and much appreciated holiday. Instead she got a journey through Hell with Dr Jekyll. How appropriate; Robert Louis Stevenson was Scottish.

Wyatt stirred when she slipped into bed.

"How is your neck?" he murmured.

"Fine. And thank you," she whispered.

"Good," he kissed her shoulder and put his arm around her. "Go to sleep sweetheart."

As Gem opened her eyes Wyatt tugged gently on her braid.

"How is your neck?" he repeated his query of two hours earlier.

Gem turned her head to the right and to the left. "Still fine."

"You're lunching with Mrs Brown today?"

"Yes."

"Do you feel up to the drive into London? If not, you could ride in with me and Mr M could drive you home. He has errands in the city this morning," Wyatt suggested.

"I'll drive," Gem replied. "I feel fine, truly."

"Excellent," Wyatt murmured, his voice growing husky. "And since you are awake and well-"

Dr Jekyll, Mr Hyde, and Svengali, Gem mused, and the latter was voracious!

Mrs Brown was on time as usual, as was Gem, eager to have her theory heard, and to have answers to her queries.

Charley's Pub was renovated, the reconstruction completed, and lights low enough for snogging, even in the daytime.

Mrs Brown looked at the lights, turned to Charley and received a shrug in reply.

"Limit Agency staff on alcohol, Charley," she warned. "No slipped cogs."

"Yes, ma'am," he chuckled. "Should we limit fraternization with civilians also?"

Mrs Brown considered the query. "Use your best judgment there."

"Yes, ma'am," he nodded firmly.

I wish I had not been allowed any fraternization with civilians, Gem muttered to herself.

The women appreciatively tucked into the food and half-pints Charley provided.

"Mr Cawley said you have a theory," Mrs Brown gave Gem an encouraging look.

Gem slowly but succinctly outlined her theory of the three U-boats, Mexico, South America, Hong Kong, the stolen European art and Odessa. Her supervisor listened patiently.

"Thus, surviving member of Odessa, somehow or other, obtained information of Project CSU, your father's decoding of World War II Nazi codes, and felt threatened they would be discovered and routed out of hiding," Mrs Brown frowned.

"Hiding in plain sight."

"Without a doubt in some cases," Mrs Brown agreed. "But to take down the Pilos, my dear," she shook her head. "I just don't see a connection. North Korea jamming satellite signals, yes, but how else the plane, I just don't know."

Hours and hours of sorting, reading, useless, Gem groaned inwardly. But Mrs Brown's next remarks surprised her.

"Well, I certainly will not discount any of your theory, my dear. Odessa is a fact, the U-boats, most logical. Why else destroy the files? Who would think Nazi codes unbroken for decades would be deciphered? U-1408 was one of the subs with missing files. Nazi's are still a scourge today." She took a long pull on her beer. "There was no supportive evidence that North Korea jammed GPS signals 29 or 30 May. However that doesn't mean they didn't do so. We simply cannot use it as fact in our investigation."

Gem held her breath. Validation!

"However," Mrs Brown continued, "we also have the problem of the dead and missing counter-couriers and agents. Do you propose to tie them into your theory?"

"What is their history connection to Hong Kong?" Gem thought aloud. "You, Harry, Mr White, mum, dad, Mr Portermann, Blank, were all posted at one time or another to Hong Kong. And Mr Denton." She grimaced that she had forgotten to include him.

"Hong Kong has always been an extremely busy embassy," Mrs Brown nodded. "It was a regular posting for all new British diplomats and junior staff. Staff were regularly assigned, trained, recalled, transferred."

"Mum, dad, Mr Portermann and Mr Denton."

"However, there were hundreds of staff at the embassy over the years. It was a very important embassy. It still is very vital for the U.K."

Gem nodded. "Any information on the Thai courier? The Philippine and Malaysian agents? Oh, and the Chinese and Vietnamese counter-couriers. Any of them ever attached to Hong Kong in any way?" she pressed.

"It would be very likely that they all had assignments to Hong Kong at one time or another," Mrs Brown acknowledged. "But there is a great deal of red tape to cut before accessing information from their countries. The Network is currently extremely fragile. As you well know, one simply does not put out an advert in a tabloid to read 'Now Hiring Couriers and Spies'. Candidates must be vetted by their country of origin and by the Agency. Six countries are now in the throes of searching for and or replacing trusted, loyal - and courageous staff. The same countries are putting a great deal of faith in other Network countries. Procedures are being checked, questioned, verified, and altered where necessary. Checking, double checking. Information is coming in piece meal."

"So that's what has occupied Harry. He's vetting isn't he?" Gem mused aloud.

"In all probability, yes," Mrs Brown nodded.

"And restructuring the Network - at least South East Asia."

"Which may filter down to other countries - if necessary," Mrs Brown patted her lips with her serviette. "Charley," she called to the publican. "Most excellent burger. Would it be possible to obtain the recipe?"

"Indeed," he reached for paper and pen. "You too, Gem?"

"Yes please, Charley," she grinned, then turned back to her companion. "The South East Asia Network is being hunted," she grimaced.

"It would appear so. Is it related to the Pilos? We do not know."

"Is the SEA Network being hunted, or the entire Network? Entire Network could include the Pilos," Gem frowned.

"Related? Unrelated? Neo Nazis? Odessa? It could take months, my dear, before we have a solution."

Gem frowned. "Mr Denton was murdered." She still felt that was a fact.

Mrs Brown's eyebrows raised slightly. "The police and B.I. investigations state accidental death."

"That is incorrect," Gem shook her head.

Mrs Brown reflected on her companion's remarks. "We shall leave the file on Mr Denton open for a while," she gave Gem a small nod.

Charley served cheesecake with strawberry topping for dessert.

"Most excellent," Mrs Brown heartily approved. "Still only one dessert selection."

"Yes, ma'am," Charley gave her a huge smile.

"Why only one dessert?" Gem queried.

"I only like cheesecake," came the simple reply and the removal of the lunch dishes from the table.

Gem mentally sorted for a few minutes. "The investigation at the private airport - contacting passengers regarding seeing anything unusual at the airport prior to 30 May."

"The investigation is complete, the information is being compiled," Mrs Brown replied.

"The pre-flight and flight checklist for the Pilos was very detailed. Do you think Mr Portermann rushed the pre-flight?" Gem hesitated even to offer the suggestion.

"Highly unlikely, I should think," Mrs Brown actually scowled. "The Pilos was Mr Portermann's 'child'. Nor would he risk his passengers lives so carelessly."

"But if one does the check list time after time, it would become almost automatic - seeing something or not seeing something - because it was always previously correct."

"I do not wish to believe that, my dear."

"Crash statistics attributed to pilot error is very high," Gem countered.

"Yes. It must be a consideration," Mrs Brown slowly agreed.

"The Banda Sea? The Coral Sea?"

"Both searches unsuccessful. Submarines are now on training missions around the Caroline Islands; however, there is no dearth of World War II vessels in the Pacific Ocean. - So many battles were fought in the Pacific Theatre. Guadalcanal, Midway, Coral Sea, to name a few."

"Carpentaria?"

"Unsuccessful. It is a process of elimination."

"Were there OSS officers on the Coventry and the Seahawk?"

"Very likely," Mrs Brown nodded. "Confirmation for that will take months, but I do not see how that would relate to the search for the Pilos or to Project CSU."

"The OSS was in South East Asia. I wondered if the OSS was infiltrated by double agents, someone the officers trusted - but were betrayed by unknowingly."

"Someone who, by extension, could be in the SEA Network today," Mrs Brown mused. "It's possible."

"Had the Coventry and Seahawk completed their missions?"

"No."

"Could the missions have been discovered, and U-1408 dispatched to scuttle the subs?"

"You think your dad discovered such information in old Nazi codes?" Mrs Brown fell silent to reflect on the suggestion. "Yes. Possibly."

"Dad would have printed backup reports of the codes he deciphered," Gem said firmly.

"Indeed. He would have sent the translations by code to Harry, and consequential material would have also been sent on paper to Harry at the Agency."

"But the decoding computer glitched," Gem winced.

"I'm not quite certain that is a verb," Mrs Brown frowned. "I will check again on the paper backup. Perhaps steps were missed. Or perhaps your father was instructed to send the paper other than to Harry. Perhaps to B.I. for review. However, I must warn you that it is not easy to contact Harry at this time. Your query may go unanswered for some time."

Gem took the last bite of her cheesecake and pushed away the plate. "I won't be able to manage another bite of food the rest of the day," she sighed contentedly.

Mrs Brown surveyed her with a critical eye. "You're a bit on the thin side. Doesn't that husband of yours ever feed you?"

"Yes, and quite often," Gem said firmly.

"He is remarkably handsome, isn't he?" Mrs Brown reflected pensively.

"Quite," Gem said agreeably. She certainly couldn't refute her supervisor's words. "Devastatingly handsome."

"And you are a remarkably beautiful women, my dear, when you aren't a wreck from lack of sleep," Mrs Brown said bluntly.

"Kinder words have never been spoken," Gem said, shocked at Mrs Brown's frankness.

"Tut, tut, my dear, don't be offended. I am merely concerned that you will soon make yourself quite ill if you don't take better care of yourself." Mrs Brown would never attempt to take Margaret Lawson's place with her daughter, but words had to be said. "Our processes are still grinding slowly. You will be of no assistance to the Agency if you suffer a collapse. Try not to think of anything we discussed just now for at least a few days. As difficult as it is, I want you to try to step away mentally from the investigation whenever possible."

"Yes, ma'am," Gem nodded respectfully. But a thought did trouble her. "Harry could be in dangerous situations, couldn't he?" she frowned.

"Very much so."

"He's hunting for the hunter, isn't he?"

"Possibly."

Mrs Brown was the Agency Director before Harry. She had been involved in the SEA Network as thoroughly as Harry currently was.

"Are you in danger, ma'am?" Gem asked with great concern.

"I do not believe so," Mrs Brown smiled gently. "Sweet of you to be concerned. And I do not believe you are in danger."

"I am retired," Gem agreed. "Well as much as -" she didn't bother to finish the remark.

"Indeed."

They picked up the recipe copies from Charley, and chatted for a few minutes outside the pub.

"You will walk a bit before you drive, my dear," Mrs Brown reminded Gem.

"I shall do a bit of window shopping," Gem assured her.

"Excellent. And you have my mobile number. Call me as often as you like. And give my regards to your handsome husband," Mrs Brown patted Gem's arm, before crossing the street to her vehicle.

Gem indeed walked. Wyatt would be furious if he knew she had had a beer with her lunch then contemplated driving. So walking would be good. And she would have a stiff cup or two of coffee before she got behind the wheel of the Defender.

She walked for a quarter of an hour looking at window displays, a bit dismayed to see summer clothes replaced by winter woolens, but nonetheless mentally reviewing her wardrobe and what she should shop for in the next few weeks.

She was trying to decide whether or not she wanted to stop at the shop where she had purchased the blouse for Mrs M, when she first noticed him. He ducked back quickly but she knew he was there.

Wing mirrors. Mr Critchley's pet peeve: drivers never fully utilized their mirrors. There was a chemist's shop on the next street; the windows usually displayed make-up and various sizes of mirrors to utilize while applying cosmetics.

She walked slowly, stopping to look in each shop window she passed, so when she did stop at the chemist's shop it was not unexpected. There were two mirrors, plus the reflection in the window. He ducked back again.

She was indeed being followed.

Gem moved to the dividing wall between the chemist's shop and the draper's shop next door.

She turned her back to the wall, scanning from left to right, reading the area as she drew her mobile from her pocket and scrolled her contact list.

"Yes, my dear," Mrs Brown's voice said crisply.

"I'm being shadowed," Gem kept her voice low.

"Yes, my dear."

"You put a shadow on me?" Gem was surprised and nervous. "Why?"

"No, my dear, I did not," Mrs Brown said calmly.

"But you knew!"

"Yes, my dear. I saw him when we left the pub."

"You didn't ring to tell me," Gem accused, bewildered by the woman's placid attitude of the issue.

"You are a professional, my dear. Are your abilities getting rusty? At any rate, I had complete confidence you would make him sooner or later. Couldn't have been very difficult for you."

"Why am I being shadowed?" Gem persisted.

"I am not the one to ask, my dear."

"But who -"

Mrs Brown, against habit, interrupted. "Who are your choices, my dear? Now, I am confident you will get this situation under control. Give my regards to your handsome husband."

Gem stared at her phone. Mrs Brown had rung off!

She was being shadowed! Mrs Brown was aware of the fact. But the Agency had not ordered the job. Yet Mrs Brown was completely unconcerned about the matter. What the blazes!

Not the Agency. Private. A private detective!

Give my regards to your handsome husband! Mrs Brown had repeated her earlier remark.

How dare he!

Curse him! Curse, Wyatt Grantham!

Get the situation under control! Indeed! I hope the man enjoys walking, Gem steamed. And walk she did. Three hours of walking, leading him through lingerie and perfume shops, then back out onto the pavement, and into other shops catering to women's needs or interests. Finally, weary herself, of walking, she made a wide circle back to the Defender.

Wing mirror check. He got into his vehicle. Since Wyatt was going to receive a report, Gem made damn sure her driving was absolutely brilliant. Her shadow kept back on the road, but she knew he was there. He was behind her, in fact, until she drove the Defender across the second old stone bridge leading into Ticking Bottom proper. Gem continued on to the Hall, but her shadow had disappeared.

Wyatt's Jag was on the driveway.

Chapter Fifteen

Gem said a quick cheery greeting to Mrs M, who was in the kitchen watching her telly while she prepared dinner.

"Would you like a glass of wine, dear?" the housekeeper queried.

"Perhaps later," Gem smiled, fighting to control her anger. It wouldn't do to let Mrs M see that she was furious. She remembered the beer at the pub, realizing she didn't dare let Wyatt smell alcohol on her breath since she had driven back from London, so she dashed up the stairs to her bathroom and gave her teeth a good cleaning. Prolonging confronting Wyatt made her temper rise even more. She had a full head of steam when she reached the library, bursting in the door to stand and glare at him. He was sitting behind his desk reading, his feet propped up on the edge of his desk.

"Close the door," Wyatt ordered, his eyebrows raising.

Gem complied, slamming it shut.

"What?" he demanded, more than slightly annoyed by her show of temper.

"You put a shadow on me! A tail!" Gem snapped, quickly altering her wording. Shadow was too distinctly an Agency word. No slipped cogs wanted now!

Wyatt's jaw dropped. "Well, apparently he isn't very adept at his job," he observed loftily. "And lower your voice unless you want Mrs M to know what kind of a bitch you really are." He swung his feet down from the desk but he did not stand.

The remark stung Gem, but she was too angry to be derailed by his words. "Oh, your man is quite capable," Gem shot back, but she did lower her voice, not wishing to upset Mrs M. "And how long exactly has he been following me?" she demanded.

"Since last Thursday."

Not too bad then.

"How did you know?" Wyatt demanded curiously.

"Reflection in a reflection," Gem offered carefully. She didn't want to give away her training.

"Why would you even be aware of that?" he demanded sharply.

Not another slipped cog please! "Mr Critchley." She hoped to make this work. And Mr Critchley would back her up if Wyatt checked with him on her explanation. "Defensive driving - just a trick. Always check mirrors. Reflections." Wyatt visibly relaxed and Gem hoped that he had accepted her words.

"Why the hell are you having me followed?" she demanded, her temper rising again. "It frightened the hell out of me!"

"I'm sorry," Wyatt replied, surprised by her reaction. "I didn't think you would ever notice Choate was following you."

Choate! He's losing his touch, Gem laughed scornfully, yet silently. A courier spotted by a 'retired' courier. Or perhaps my skills are still reasonably sharp, Gem congratulated herself. She knew they had been lax of late.

"Choate? That's his name, eh?" She didn't want to tip her hand. "So why did you hire him?" she demanded, still extremely angry.

Wyatt rose from his chair and walked around the desk to lean against it, arms folded across his chest.

"You are the wife of a very wealthy man, as I have stated a number of times," he said smoothly. "You apparently do not listen. It's not unusual to hire protection under such circumstances."

"You don't actually think for a moment that I believe that explanation, do you?" she scoffed.

"Very clever," Wyatt shot back in return. "Very well, my dear. To put it bluntly, your behavior is suspicious. Hiding computer files, verbal self-editing to hide what you might accidentally have let slip. How many times have I seen your eyes cloud, knowing that your clever, wicked little mind has shifted to one of your countless secrets? To John Staunton perhaps? You are hiding something, my dear. You do not fool me for a moment. I saw those photos of Barcelona. I do not know what is going on in that brilliant mind of yours -"

"And you won't!" Gem curtly interrupted. "You can force me to remain in this absurd relationship, but you can't get into my brain!" Damn! He was so observant! He hadn't forgotten John Staunton-Paul Andriani - and he wouldn't!

"You might be extremely surprised, my dear Gem, of what exactly I am capable of," he said harshly. "Whatever your game is this time, I promise you I will find you out. Despite the terms of our marriage," he emphasized the last word, "you have had unlimited freedom, by my choice. I made it crystal clear to you there will be no more victims for your twisted schemes. If necessary, I will have a bodyguard with the soul of Bloody Mary stick to you like a leech."

"Bloody Mary didn't have a soul!" Gem shot back.

"You'll be a perfect match then won't you? Oh, you play so innocent, sweetheart, but you lie, you connive, you leech the soul from men. You are as dangerous as Pandora," he said contemptuously.

Watch your step, Gemimah, she warned herself, using her own personal code word to fight off her own fury.

"I am confounded that Mrs Brown, a seemingly astute woman, would even consider having something like you for a friend," Wyatt ground out his words.

'Something!' Gem closed her eyes for a moment to stop from reaching for anything to throw at him. 'Something'!

She saw his face sharply alter. Mrs Brown! She couldn't permit him to become suspicious of Mrs Brown. Gem couldn't afford that slipped cog. She had talked fast, taken great pains at the pub last week, to put forth Mrs Brown as a retired, innocuous acquaintance. And that persona of Mrs Brown must remain intact.

"Mea culpa. You win," Gem said, suddenly defeated. "I concede. I promise. No more pitched battles. Your terms. Your Game. Set. Match. Win. Winner takes all," she said penitently; another warning, indeed, to think of his Game with a capital 'G'.

"Good Lord!" he mocked her with a laugh. "Sack cloth and ashes."

"Yes," she nodded. "Whatever you say. I swear."

Wyatt gazed at her, still scornfully. "More lies? We shall see, won't we, my dear." She hadn't given up her battles. This was simply a new tactic for her.

Gem met his gaze. Not any lies she could possibly avoid. "No lies," she said, ironically, as truthfully as she could manage.

Wyatt stood staring at her, assessing her words and deciding whether or not to believe her. He did not. He would not. She would continue to lie. He would play her game for a while. For his own amusement. She was still the mouse. He was still the cat.

"Very well," he said with disgust. "I will accept your promises," he did not keep the scepticism from his voice. "Now go. I have work to do."

Gem smarted at his curt dismissal of her. She went to her office and collapsed in her swivel chair. Automatically she turned on the computer and pulled up the photos of cathedrals, clicking on Winchester. A thousand years of comfort to others; she should make a visit to the cathedral. Perhaps she could find some comfort there.

Blast the photos of John Staunton! Blast Barcelona! Naturally Wyatt didn't realize the man in the photos was a British agent. And Blast Paul Andriani! Why had he been in Barcelona? Why had he met Gemmy there? My poor Gemmy! And mum and dad. Lord! How appalled they would be with the mess Gem had made of her life! Appalled and fearful for her.

But Gem wasn't physically frightened of Wyatt. The bruises on her arm were fading. He had been shocked by the black and blue marks. She knew there would be no more. However, she was greatly concerned that he would get inside her head and leave her unable to think clearly, that she would then make an error she couldn't correct. He couldn't discover there had been two Gems, not just one.

She rested her chin on her hand, looking away from the computer and out at Mr Becton's gardens. The gardens of Grantham Hall. Mr Wyatt Grantham. Of Grantham Enterprises International. The wealthy and powerful Wyatt Grantham!

Oh dear!

How stupid of me! How very, very stupid! Grantham Enterprises International!

Of course Wyatt would be concerned about the photos! James, Wyatt's dear brother, had been in love with a woman who 'consorted' with an international 'criminal'. Wyatt had no idea that John Staunton - Paul Andriani - was a British agent in shark skin camo. Wyatt was worried that Gemmy's involvement with John Staunton could threaten the security of his business empire!

He considered her the cause of James's death. And also a threat to GEI.

Gem gasped. I would have had me shadowed the second we returned from Scotland!

Gem's blood ran cold. Was a shadow there before their marriage? Had there been someone before Mr Choate? She groaned silently, mentally reviewing her actions from the day she had met Wyatt at Oscar's. There were meetings with Mrs Brown.

I am so tired, Gem whispered.

She searched the furthest reaches of her mind. Going to shops, Gosport, picking up the Agency Range Rover at Charley's pub. She had let down her guard when she retired, when she met Wyatt. Yet - yet. She still had read rooms, her surroundings. She thought she was still practised enough to spot an anomaly. Save for Wyatt. He had certainly duped her, but why should she have been expected to catch that flaw?

Mrs Brown. If Gem had unconsciously let down her guard, Mrs Brown never let down hers. No words were ever spoken when ears and eyes were nearby. She and Mrs Brown constantly, casually, observed their surroundings.

Mrs Brown hadn't been concerned today when she realized Gem was being followed. And Mr Choate! Of all people! Confusing! Mr Choate had been reassigned, Mr Cawley had said.

Gem took a steady breath. She was certain she was in the clear, and had been since she met Wyatt.

Wyatt's comments regarding Mrs Brown, however, did greatly trouble Gem. She had to take great pains to prevent him from becoming suspicious of Mrs Brown. She didn't want Wyatt to attempt to cut Mrs Brown out of her life.

She was so lost in her thoughts that she jumped when Wyatt's voice spoke behind her.

"Mrs M is ready to serve dinner," he quietly informed her. She had been so deep in thought he had startled her, Wyatt observed. And what, pray tell, was going on in that brilliant mind? he wondered.

Gem saw in his eyes that he was still very angry with her. He did not trust her. She realized he never would trust her.

I'll just wash my hands then," she murmured, walking quickly to the bathroom off the office.

She shouldn't be surprised or concerned that he didn't trust her, even after her earlier promise. The tap water was soothing; her thoughts continued to wander.

He had told her exactly what he thought of her that horrible night at Marigold Cottage. Often enough he had accused her of being a liar. Then there was her point blank refusal to see a physician about her insomnia. Naturally he would think she was hiding something there. Then her hysterical outburst when he had called her Gemmy.

"You will wash away your skin," Wyatt interrupted her thoughts. He saw that she refused to meet his eyes in his reflection in the mirror.

Is he going to constantly be watching me? she silently worried, as he watched her eat her dinner, or more accurately push the food around her plate.

"Not hungry, my dear?" he asked pleasantly, knowing Mrs M was still within earshot in the kitchen.

"Not very," she forced a smile and a sweet tone to her voice.

"A late lunch with Mrs Brown?"

"It was quite a large lunch actually," she heard the kitchen door close behind Mrs M. Now he would take the gloves off.

"A pub lunch?" he kept his words measured in a casual tone.

"Yes."

"Did you shop today? Any purchases? Lingerie? Perfume?" Wyatt lifted an eyebrow.

"No. And Mrs Brown paid the lunch bill," Gem replied. Or rather the Agency paid the bill. Blast Mr Choate! He had already reported to Wyatt about her activities that day.

Gem nearly gasped with relief. No! No! Bless Mr Choate! He had been a stellar courier! He would literally die before he gave up an agent or a courier to a civilian. Not even to a client of Wyatt Grantham's status and power. Wyatt was a civilian. Mrs Brown and Gem were Agency. Family!

Mr Choate was a blessing in disguise. If she had clearly seen him that afternoon, she wouldn't have been so furious at Wyatt for having her shadowed. And Mr Choate still had it! She hadn't placed him!

And perhaps she wasn't as clever as she thought she was! That's why Mrs Brown had said it couldn't have been difficult for Gem to make her shadow!

Mr Choate had given himself up to Gem! He had wanted her to know that he was shadowing her!

Mr Cawley had said Mr Choate had been reassigned. That implied that Mr Choate was still very much active in the Agency. How could he have been hired by Wyatt Grantham to shadow Gem? And what did Mr Choate think of Wyatt Grantham hiring someone to tail his wife? She definitely had to have a chat with Mr Choate! And she was damned certain anything said between the two of them would not be reported to Mr Wyatt Grantham!

Gem actually laughed out loud - to Wyatt's surprise. And her appetite returned.

"What precisely is so amusing, my dear?" Wyatt said in a smooth voice, wondering of her prolonged silence. He wondered if her brilliant mind was calculating as quickly as a computer.

"Mrs Brown," Gem smiled. "She mentioned twice today how remarkably handsome you are. I believe you quite take her breath away."

"A high compliment indeed," Wyatt gave a small nod of acknowledgement. "And did she also remark that you are looking particularly exhausted today?" he said with a frown.

Gem winced. "She did. Her words were not as kindly for me," she admitted.

"I am not taking proper care of you, am I?" Wyatt said thoughtfully.

"Mrs Brown would never say that," Gem protested. "She would never criticize you."

"I'm sure she would not. I am certain you would never give her reason to do so," Wyatt countered. "The words were mine. We must remedy the situation. A wife's health is always of concern to her husband."

"Very pointedly said," Gem observed politely. She had promised no more pitched battles, but she hadn't promised to completely hold her tongue.

"Clever, my dear," Wyatt chuckled. "Very adroit."

"I wouldn't be here if I were clever," Gem shook her head.

"Oh, my dear, you are so clever. And yes, you would still be here. My Game," he chuckled gently. "Remember? Always and forever."

Gem smiled at him. The last laugh would be hers.

They had started washing up when Wyatt's mobile rang.

"I'll finish here," Gem insisted. She needed time to compose herself, whether or not she liked the fact, she had to apologize to Wyatt for her attitude that afternoon. It would, hopefully, keep him off balance. Her game.

He didn't return to the kitchen so she decided to face him in his lair.

When she tapped at the library door she heard him say "Come," so she opened the door. He was on the phone; Gem started to back out of the room, but he beckoned her forward, then held up a finger to indicate a minute.

"I'm sorry. I didn't realize you were still on the phone," she said when the call ended.

"The business was concluded," he replied, waiting expectantly for her to speak.

Gem took a deep breath. She did not enjoy the taste of crow. "I overreacted earlier. And I apologize for my temper," she said with complete honesty. If she had to have a shadow, Mr Choate would definitely be her choice.

Wyatt pursed his lips as she talked. Let her play her game, he decided.

"I truly understand why you felt the necessity to hire someone to follow me. And I promise in the future, that I shall not lead that - Mr Choate - was it? - on a wild goose chase all over London. I wager the poor man is soaking his feet at this very moment." Gem knew that Mr Choate had painful bunions which he soaked nightly. Mr Choate's bunions had been an Agency joke for years.

What an odd day, Gem mused as she finished her apology, not wishing to seem over eager regarding Mr Choate, or Wyatt might become suspicious, fire Mr Choate, and hire someone else.

Wyatt digested her words; her angle was not obvious; perhaps it would become clear at another time.

"Apology accepted, my dear." He leaned forward across the desk to hand her a slip of paper. "Choate's mobile number. If you go into the city when I do in the morning, I will notify him. However, if you leave the Hall after I do, then you must ring him. You must give him a half hour notice before you leave Ticking Bottom."

"Yes, Sir," Gem nodded.

"Was that attitude?" Wyatt scowled.

"No-Sir," Gem had the grace to grimace. "It all sounds so serious. So -"

"Headmaster, not husband?" Wyatt grinned faintly.

"Just so," Gem nodded, returning his grin.

"I understand. Now if you will excuse me, my dear, I have work to do," he said, keeping his tone patient.

Gem went to her office. Apparently Mr Choate was still on the job. And Gem would be going into the city to have a chat with him in the morning. Her life was definitely taking a turn for the better. She had Mr Cawley during the dark hours and Mr Choate when she left Ticking Bottom.

She turned on the telly to watch the international news, backing it up with news on the web. Nothing was startling, which was most excellent for the Agency. Harry could work in relative peace and, hopefully, little danger.

Ping

Gem fairly jumped at the sound. She glanced about. Wyatt was not in the room.

'Entrenched.'
'What?'
'Repeat. Entrenched.'
'Why.'
'???'
'How long?'
'???'
'Okay.'

Entrenched. In her six years with the Agency, this was the first time Entrenched had been declared. No information would be dispersed by phone or text. Information could be transmitted to the Agency, however, no questions would receive replies.

What had happened since Gem and Mrs Brown had lunched at Charley's? What indeed?

It was rather unnerving. And definitely frustrating. And who had given the order? Not that it mattered. There was no option but to accept the Entrenched order. Don't waste time making queries that would receive no replies. Couriers and agents were to remain static until notified one by one to return to the Agency. Was someone missing - or was this a routine check?

Ping

'Routine check.'

'Great!'

'Mrs Brown says to take a holiday. Relax. Don't think about work.'

'Take a nap?'

'Said that suggestion was pointless.'

Gem had to laugh at that text as she cleared the messages. She looked up to see Wyatt's reflection in the dark windows.

Gem smiled at him. "Mrs Brown," she could say with some veracity. "Said it was pointless to tell me to take a nap," Gem explained. She slipped the mobile in her skirt pocket, hoping Mr Cawley had had his final say until the dark hours.

"Finish what you are doing," Wyatt said firmly without replying to Gem's remarks.

Gem looked at the clock on the wall. "It's only eight o'clock," she protested. "It's the shank of the evening."

He waited silently.

Gem pulled her fingers through her hair. She had promised no more battles. Of course that was not possible, especially since most of his remarks to her irritated the Hell out of her. Blast! This simply could not go on forever! "I'm finished," she shut down the computer and turned off the telly.

"Eight o'clock," she muttered, as he took her hand and led her up the stairs.

"As I said previously, you are younger than I. I need more sleep and so do you. How ever do you manage each day with so little sleep? And you walked across London today!"

"Perhaps you do need more greens in your diet as Mrs M suggested," Gem said lightly, trying to control her frustration at her evening being cut so short.

"Sass! Haven't heard that for a while," Wyatt chuckled.

Gem groaned inwardly as she awakened. So much for going to bed early. Actually, she had to admit she had had a bit more sleep than usual. Wyatt grunted softly as she slipped out from beneath the arm that was always around her waist as she slept.

There had been no further texts from Mr Cawley after the messages alerting of the Entrenched order. Since the Agency was Entrenched she would likely not receive any texts unless Mrs Brown or Mr Cawley had questions for her.

Take a holiday! That was rich! Don't think about work! Again rich!

And what had Mrs Brown truly thought of Gem's theories? She hadn't completely dismissed Gem's ideas. And where did one go from here? How could Odessa members bring down the Pilos? If they had somehow put a bomb on the plane -. No. Not a bomb. Gemmy wouldn't have had time to send Gem a plea for help. Air pirates? Yes. No. Gem had known instantly that they were all dead. It was a crash.

Gem dragged her fingers through her hair. She was so tired.

Pilot error? That was possible. Probable. But Gem wouldn't accept that. She couldn't deny that no one was infallible. But in this instance she did not believe that applied to Mr Portermann.

But someone was hunting the Network. And why? And who had access to the Network, other than Network staff? Yet, within the other Network agencies, cogs could slip. A 'friend', a relative could have tripped to a courier or agent's job. One drink too many? A lost mobile? Mr White had the expertise to instantly destroy a lost mobile anywhere in the world. Did other Network agencies have the same technical capabilities? Did the Agency share out such technology?

Gem would worry about Gemmy's lost passport if she hadn't known it was now absolutely 'safe'. She had to trust Wyatt that the passport was safe for she certainly couldn't ask him if he could guarantee that no one else could get hands on it.

Mr Choate. Why was he playing private detective? It was difficult passing the dark hours until morning, waiting to speak to him. She could text him; he would reply, but just because she was awake didn't mean everyone else in the Agency also had to be awake.

Actually Mr Choate was too vital an Agency employee to be detailed to shadow her. What a waste of training and expertise.

Ping

Someone was awake!

'How goes the war?'

'No end in sight.'

'I disagree. I think you put a bee in Mrs Brown's bonnet.'

'In what way?'

'Can't say.'

'Oh right. Entrenched.'

'Yes. Keep thinking!'

'I shall.'

'Remember - I'm always here!'

'Thank you.'

'Goodnight.'

'Goodnight.'

Entrenched or not, Mr Cawley was still there for her. That gave her a great lift!

Gem pushed the start button on the cd player. 'I'll Be Seeing You'... Gem had hope.

A bee in Mrs Brown's bonnet! Whoa! That was a stupendous feeling! Which bee, she didn't know. But it was a good thing. And where to go next?

'How' would be a good starting point. But she truly hadn't a clue. Perhaps Mrs Brown was correct. Perhaps she should take a mental holiday. Let her thoughts wander and see if another Eureka would strike her.

She made a cup of hot chocolate and sat in Auntie Jane's comfy chair, looking at the office. She should select a paint colour, curtains, rugs. She had boxes of photos she could have framed to hang on the wall. The thoughts made her wince. Why decorate the office? She didn't intend to be at the Hall a minute longer than was necessary. But the room was so sterile. Perhaps if it had a more finished appearance, was completely her own room, it would be more conducive to sorting. Gemmy would have splashed colour around the room. Gem preferred a more subtle decorating style. However colourful rugs would be pleasant. She closed her eyes, trying to will herself to sleep. It didn't work.

She let her thoughts wander. Unfortunately they wandered to Wyatt. A fool's slip to promise not to battle with him. No matter how much she tried, she knew she would not succeed keeping that promise. And he would have that to throw back at her. His terms. Blast! The list would no doubt be endless. She had to keep working. Keep thinking. Find the Pilos. Find Gemmy and the others!

Chapter Sixteen

Wyatt handed Gem a list of rules at the breakfast table.

Gem gulped hard. Actually making a list of his terms? Dr Jekyll was at the forefront! She read the list with dismay until she realized the guidelines had been prepared by Mr Choate: walk close to shops, do not abruptly alter plans if at all possible, do not let the Defender's petrol gauge fall below a quarter tank, never turn off mobile, never wear new garments out of a shop unless first alerting Choate, etcetera, etcetera. She quickly memorized the list, then tucked it into her skirt pocket.

"Clear enough for you?" Wyatt said firmly.

"Indeed," Gem nodded, greatly looking forward to spending time with the former Agency courier.

"Will you be going into the city today?" Wyatt asked.

"Yes. I shall leave when you do," she replied politely. She might just be able to bear Wyatt Grantham for awhile - but not too long.

Wyatt nodded, then rang Choate.

Gem's first stop was at the photo shop. She purchased two rolls of film; she did have quite a supply already, but planned to go out and about at Ticking Bottom with her camera. She continued down the street to a coffee shop, ordering one tea white, and one coffee black to go, knowing Mr Choate preferred coffee. Back out on the pavement, she held up a cup to Mr Choate and he walked up to join her.

"Morning Mr Choate," she handed over the cup.

"Morning, ma'am," he accepted the cup with a nod.

Gem had known the man since the day she and Gemmy had started their Agency training. He was non-descript, slightly balding, medium height, medium build, brown eyes, brown shirt, brown trousers, brown shoes; his appearance never varied.

"Gem," she insisted and he nodded again.

They started walking, ending at a small deserted green space between buildings two blocks away from the coffee shop. They both scanned the area, keeping their backs to one of the buildings.

"Were you shocked that Wyatt wanted to have me followed?" she jumped directly into conversation.

"Mr Grantham wants to protect you, Gem. We all do."

He wants to control me, Gem did not say.

"How in heaven's name did I draw you? Mr Cawley said you had been reassigned."

"I was. Assigned to Technical Operations - The Eyes and Ears of Britain."

"I've never heard of it," Gem frowned.

"Agency sub-division. What better way to know what's going on in everyday life in this country than to have a private investigation operation," Choate said firmly.

"Well! Stun me with a gun!" Gem shook her head in surprise.

"I'm head of the division now. It was Portermann's territory."

"Ah, the Agency is amazing," she marveled. "And Wyatt just happened to call Technical Operations?"

"Mr Grantham mentioned to Mr Critchley that he might be interested in protection for you."

"And as they say, the rest is history," Gem giggled. "What a set up!"

"T.O. is known in some circles as the best in the business," Choate said calmly.

"And I drew you - the head of the division," Gem said pointedly. "Why not a lesser operative?"

"We have civilians. But you are special. Not only to Mr Grantham. And I could not assign a civilian to shadow Agency staff. It would make daily reports a headache. I would have to edit the reports at times, then relay the reports to Mr Grantham."

"A civilian might include TMI."

"Precisely. And a civilian would question my editing. I shall edit on foot, so to speak," Choate grinned as he sipped his coffee.

Gem sighed. "It's embarrassing that Wyatt hired your company."

"Not at all, Gem. It was extremely convenient that Mr Grantham rang us up. The Agency had recently considered putting a shadow on you."

The Agency meaning Mrs Brown and Harry, Gem interpreted the words.

"I asked Mrs Brown if she thought I was in danger, but she said no," Gem protested.

"The Agency investigation regarding-" he searched for a sensitive choice of words.

"The Pilos," Gem said bluntly.

"Yes. The more we discover that we are making no progress, the more questions we have. We're in limbo."

"And Entrenched."

"That's only temporary."

"The Agency is in limbo. The Pilos is in limbo. I am in limbo," Gem sighed.

"Indeed. And now with network counter-couriers and agents missing and dying, we aren't sure who exactly is in danger. Whatever the deal is, it involves the Agency Network. Not B.I. The Networks are separate in our contacts."

Gem was partially appeased. "It's still embarrassing," she persisted.

"The Agency was most pleased that Mr Grantham insisted on providing protection for you," Choate repeated.

It's not protection, it's absolute control over me!

"It's not an unusual situation, Gem. Many men in Mr Grantham's position provide protection for their loved ones."

'Loved ones' nearly made her choke on her tea. She redirected the subject.

"You're a P.I. - must get seamy at times," she teased. It was so very cheery to be with Family.

Choate laughed. "We don't do divorces, Gem. Our level of operations is directed at espionage in Mr Grantham's level of the international business world. His life is very cutthroat. But I doubt he would ever put that concern on your shoulders. You are probably the only - and a most appreciated - breath of fresh air and sanity in his life."

How little you actually know - and better for all of us - what you don't know.

"I am guilty of TMI, but you need to be reassured of the necessity in Mr Grantham's mind to protect you."

"You know a great deal about him, don't you?" Gem mused. A great deal more than I know!

"Extremely little actually," Choate informed her. "Your husband is so extraordinarily private a man that only his family would really ever know him."

And I shall never know him, Gem mused.

"He's cutthroat then," she said warily.

"No, Gem. I did not say that," Choate protested emphatically. "His business life can be cutthroat."

"Is his world dangerous?"

"For him, I imagine, quite dangerous, financially speaking. He is the sole owner of Grantham Enterprises International. It's a staggering responsibility. And there are always people who want to take down someone as successful as he. However, it would take someone better than him to take down Wyatt Grantham. I'm not certain that person exists."

I wonder that myself. Could I? Or couldn't I? she mused. If she intended to - which she had to admit she truly didn't - but still was the possibility out there?

"That would be a battle to see," Choate continued. "Bloody - and to the death. He's an empire builder. And his empire involves a great many employees all over the world. Wyatt Grantham wouldn't permit the destruction of his empire without the ultimate war. And - he would be dangerous. Not an adversary I'd wish to face. Imagine your worst nightmare - well beyond your current one of the Pilos - horrifying as that one is."

I am living it right now. One nightmare after another.

"I enjoyed our chat, Mr Choate, and may we have many more of them," Gem tapped her cup against his.

"And I rested my feet," he grinned. "Other queries?"

"The Philippine and Malaysian agents."

"I can't, Gem. I can't violate SOP even with you," Choate said firmly.

Gem grinned. "I had to try."

"I respect that."

"Are all couriers and agents in danger?"

Choate hesitated. "They always have been. Remember your training. Any other questions?"

Gem shook her head.

"You have my mobile number. Ring me, text, anytime. Day or night," he urged. "Now, Mrs Grantham, carry on with your day."

Gem smiled, took his empty cup, and they parted: she to lead and he to shadow. Her life was drastically improving!

Gem's main purpose to go to London that day was to chat with Mr Choate. She didn't have any errands to accomplish, but stopping at a bookshop was always a good way to pass time.

Mrs Brown had suggested that Gem take a holiday, according to Mr Cawley, but holidays had been seized here and there with Gemmy; a weekend in Paris, four days in Chicago; a weekend in the Seychelles. An actual holiday was not part of her usual routine.

But Mr Cawley had urged her to keep thinking.

She purchased four mysteries, a book about the Royal Pavilion at Brighton, and a guide to English Villages. She was walking past an art supply shop when the American couple caught at her thoughts. How long had it been since she had sketched other than   cathedrals? Pencils, sketch pads, a box of pastels, another of charcoal sticks and Indian rubbers, and she was onto the next shop, wondering if Mrs M had ever tasted chocolate wine. The weekend was looming; another unbearable, long weekend with Wyatt. She had the shop assistant carry a case of mixed wines to the Defender's boot. A case of mixed brews also wouldn't go amiss.

She had lunch at Oscar's, sitting at a table next to Mr Choate's, then drove to the park where she and Wyatt had watched clouds; however she refused to have those memories lingering in her mind, appreciating only the fact that it was a very large park and afforded a great deal of privacy.

A grove of trees to her back gave privacy from anyone looking over her shoulder - unless someone climbed one of the trees. She opened the sketch book, took out pencils and began sketching from memory. Gemmy was first. One might think Gem was sketching a self-portrait; however she wasn't looking into a mirror, but rather into the past. She looked up frequently to scan the area. Mr Choate stood under a tree directly ahead of her. He was on alert so she could relax.

Next was a sketch of mum with her mop of short, wild curls. Their mum's curly hair was the reason the twins so often wore their hair in braids - the braids tamed the curls and provided crinkled hair which was easier to manage than a main of corkscrew curls. Margaret Lawson was beautiful, her husband handsome - not as handsome as Wyatt, Gem had to admit, but few men in the world were.

Their dad had started greying a few years earlier; his eyes were lined with crow's feet, but they had always held a twinkle for his wife and daughters. Gem was breaking Agency rules, but she could not still her hand and her thoughts. Two hours later she packed up the drawing materials and walked across the green expanse to Mr Choate.

"Do you have a fireplace or paper shredder?" she asked.

"One of each," he said with a slight frown.

"Then please take these," she tore the pages from the sketch book.

He looked at the drawings, his eyes showing alarm. "You shouldn't have," he said sternly.

"I had to," Gem replied simply. "If I didn't, I swear I would go mad."

He nodded slowly. "If you sketched in the park for a time, you must have something to show for your efforts," he counseled.

Gem gave him a frown and returned to her position beneath the tree. Since she had to have something to show for her time, she sketched the roofs of the houses beyond the edge of the park, and then a young couple with a toddler who were sitting under a distant tree; quick studies, but done.

She had taken advantage of Mr Choate, but would not do so again. She was fighting to keep her equilibrium, and that was chancy at best.

Her chat with Mr Choate had been very interesting to say the least. The poor man was deluded that Wyatt had only hired Mr Choate to protect her. That was a great laugh, Gem scoffed. Mr Choate had said he didn't know much about Wyatt, and perhaps that was true about his private life, but he certainly seemed to know a great deal about Wyatt Grantham the businessman. And from Mr Choate's remarks, Gem decided her husband - she winced at the word - was not an adversary with whom she wished to tangle, regarding their 'marriage'. She would not involve the Agency, but she couldn't stop hoping that the relationship would end even before the Pilos was found.

And she was less than comfortable with the fact that Mr Choate thought Wyatt could be a dangerous business adversary. Dangerous was indeed a frightening word.

Mrs M approved of the chocolate wine and took four bottles to the carriage house along with the M's dinner, and Gem decided the wine might be a tasty substitute for hot chocolate during the dark hours. Dinner was the usual exercise in discomfort; Wyatt as usual seemed to think there should be proper conversation at the dinner table, and Gem had nothing to say to him on any subject.

"Did you have a pleasant day in the city?" Wyatt queried.

"Fine. It was fine," Gem made her usual comment about her day. "And your day?" She felt required to return the query. "Business as usual?"

"Business is never usual," Wyatt replied cryptically, and did not elaborate on the remark.

"Oh."

"Did you complete your shopping list?"

"Yes."

"Did you spend the entire day in the city?"

"Didn't you get a report on my activities from that Mr Choate?" Gem said, keeping her tone light, but her words were pointed.

"I did indeed. You have resumed sketching, I hear," Wyatt said smoothly.

"Yes," Gem replied. Mr Choate would have destroyed her first drawings as soon as he had had a chance to do so.

Wyatt frowned, watching as the haunted look clouded her eyes; her hand holding her fork rested on the table as she became lost in her thoughts. And for what reason?

"Mrs M mentioned you purchased a supply of wine," he decided to change the topic of conversation.

"What?" Gem frowned.

"Wine. Beer. Mrs M mentioned you purchased some interesting beverages."

"Ah, yes. Chocolate wine and a few special brews," Gem nodded.

"Perhaps we might share a glass later," he suggested.

'A breath of fresh air and sanity in his life', Mr Choate's words came to her mind. An extraordinarily private man. He seemed to spend most of his waking hours working. - Except when his mind was in the bedroom.

"You don't go out very often do you?" Gem observed. A few visits to the pub the past week, but other than that he was always working.

"No. It's not my habit to do so. Why? Do you want to go somewhere - to a film - or -?" he put out a hand to suggest she continue her thought.

"Not especially," Gem mused. "I just meant that - well - people like you usually go to - events - charity things - fund raisers - don't you?"

"People like me?" Wyatt smiled. "People like Me? Do you mean men?"

Gem gave him an exasperated look. "Wealthy people," she tried again. "Important people."

"Oh, I'm important now, am I?" he chuckled. "A compliment from you."

"I'm sorry I spoke," Gem stabbed at the pork chop on her plate.

"No. My apologies, my dear," Wyatt said, still the humorous edge to his voice. "I am so rarely treated these days to your conversational style that I didn't recognize it this evening."

"Perhaps you don't receive event invitations because you are so sarcastic," Gem said sweetly.

"Perhaps. That is a reasonable deduction. Or perhaps I pass the invitations on to staff who might enjoy the events more than I."

"Oh," Gem said simply. That possibility hadn't occurred to her. "That's a lovely idea," she admitted.

"In the future I shall have Ms Wexton send the invitations to you to choose what events would interest you," he declared formally.

"That's not what I meant either," Gem said helplessly. "I just meant that you are here every evening - working."

"I am home every evening," he corrected her choice of words. "And you would rather I was somewhere else?"

Gem simply decided to ignore his remarks. There was no point attempting a conversation with the man! And yet another lovely dinner hour! she thought sarcastically.

Wyatt read the defeated expression on her face. "That was apparently not your thought either," he forced a patient tone. "I haven't lived here for many years. After James was established at university, I started working 29/7 - as he probably told you. When he needed me - I was there to lend aid - otherwise I was at the office. I moved to the London flat, but I was rarely there. And basically I held that schedule until I met you."

"And you can no longer work 29/7 at the office and keep your watch on me," Gem said coolly.

"Actually," he said pausing for a drink of wine, "Ms Holton has taken over a substantial amount of my work load. I enjoy being home - and I definitely enjoy you," he winked at her.

"Your mind is always in the bedroom," Gem said a trifle sharply.

"Yours is there also - more often than you are willing to admit," Wyatt said firmly.

"I don't know why I attempt to have a conversation with you," Gem said completely frustrated.

"You realized you needed the practise. Apparently people don't often chat with you. It must be your abrasive personality," Wyatt said dryly.

"I can't talk to you!"

Wyatt leaned back in his chair and turned his stunning gaze upon her. "You do not converse with me, Gem. You chat with Mrs M. You chat with Mr M. You chat with Mr Becton. You talk at me."

Gem fell silent, staring at the pork chop on her plate; it gave her no advice. "Perhaps a fair point," she conceded grudgingly, "however your point works both ways."

Wyatt reflected on her statement, then gave her a nod of concession. "Touché."

Gem studied her carrots, then looked at him. "How was your day at work?" she forced a pleasant tone to her voice.

"Tolerable. Basically tolerable," he said offhandedly.

"Did you battle winged monkeys?" she asked, searching for something to say.

"Winged monkeys?" Wyatt searched for a reference point. "Ah! No," he chuckled. "I dispatch Ms Holton to deal with them. She's quite fearsome in her power suits."

So are you! Gem wanted to say, then realized she was getting trapped again in his eyes. She focused on her food, savoring her carrots, and the sound of his voice. "You have a high regard for Ms Holton, don't you then?" she ventured.

"Indeed," he firmly nodded.

"It's good to have someone on your side," Gem said softly, more to herself than to him.

"I didn't hear you," Wyatt replied; but he had heard every word.

"It's good that she's dependable - reliable," Gem self-edited her words for his ears.

"Quite," he agreed. "How was your day with Choate," Wyatt turned the subject.

"Mr Choate?" Gem looked at him in surprise. Where was this question going?

"Do you find his presence unsettling?" Wyatt explained.

That question she could handle. "Not in the least," she assured him. "It's quite heartening actually to know he is behind me." You take that your way, and I shall take it mine. "I quite forget that he is there at times, in fact." Not at all true. And even if he wasn't there, he was still on her side.

Gem sipped a glass of wine, mentally reviewing her day, as she started her computer; the chat with Mr Choate, lunch at Oscar's, sketching in the park. Add that she had lunch 'alone' at Oscar's. Wyatt hadn't insisted she join him for lunch. Perhaps he had had a lunch meeting that day. His day was 'basically tolerable'. He worked so many hours every day. He spent most of the past weekends reading reports.

She had been surprised that he hadn't become angry with her at dinner for reneging on her promise of the previous day - not to battle with him. She couldn't seem to manage to keep that promise.

She was in her office; he was in the library - his office. They were married three weeks ago tomorrow. It seemed like an eternity already - and also like it never happened. She was living in an alternate world - Wyatt's World.

Hothouse Flowers was on the cd player, as she opened the cover of the book of the Royal Pavilion at Brighton; the book was beautifully done with stunning photography and interesting, well written text.

What would she do tomorrow? How could she fill the hours of the day? Work on her book? She could use a few photos of Winchester, but she had photos and sketches of Bristol Cathedral, of Carlisle, and Canterbury. Canterbury would be next, she decided.

Canterbury Cathedral; fifteen photos were perfect, detail sketches, notes on paper, and many more on the computer. She cross checked dates and every other fact in her research notes, checked and rechecked sources, then started writing the text, studying the photos, attempting to correlate the text to specific photo details. She hoped she didn't decide to change photos as she refined the text.

Hothouse Flowers gave way to Edith Piaf, and she in turn to Paul Horn.

Gem studied the photos again, searching for the perfect photo, the perfect perspective.

She stopped, stunned as the office was plunged into darkness, the only light glowing from the computer screen. She spun her chair around to see Wyatt with his hand at the light switch. Even in the light from the computer screen Gem could see the scowl on his face.

"What happened?" she demanded, startled. "Did the flying monkeys get Ms Holton?" she queried, alarmed at his stern look.

"What?" he demanded, puzzled.

"You look so cross. I thought something might have happened at your - office."

The music ended as Wyatt switched off the cd player. "Something did NOT happen. He walked over to her, clicked save to files and shut down the computer.

"What are you doing?" Gem demanded.

"It is eleven o'clock! You should have been in bed hours ago." He reached down to pull her out of her chair.

"I am not a child!" Gem protested, as he led her by the hand from her office.

"You are a chronic insomniac who refuses to listen to reason," he said sternly. "Who refuses to visit a physician. Who refuses to rest during the day." He propelled her up the staircase.

"When I go to bed early you won't let me sleep," she retorted.

"I relax you, so don't start on that," he said, his voice still stern. "You're the one who insists on waking at seven o'clock every morning - including on our honeymoon."

It was not a honeymoon, it was a nightmare! "It's a habit," she lied, searching her drawers for a set of pajamas.

"Habits can be broken. I truly have to reform you," he declared, pulling back the duvet and top sheet.

"Dictator!" she shot back from her dressing room.

"Adventuress," Wyatt replied.

"That's not true!" Gem said defiantly, pulling off her clothes, pulling on her pajamas.

"Flighty insomniac then," Wyatt called from his own dressing room.

"Back to the drawing board with that one," she rolled up a towel, skirted the bed and sailed the missal at him.

"Clytie!" he chuckled.

"You are conceited," Gem darted out of the bathroom, toothbrush in hand. "You are not Apollo, and I am not pining for you!" she darted back into her bathroom.

Not Daphne! he mused silently, but aloud said, "Euphrosyne or Aglaea."

Gem came out of the bathroom, brushing her hair, to stare at him. A reference of grace and beauty.

"Thank you for that," she said quietly.

Wyatt slipped his arms around her waist. "You're amazed I could pronounce the names, aren't you?" he teased.

"I would be amazed if anyone could pronounce them," she said in an admiring tone.

"Sorbonne."

"Ah."

He tossed the hairbrush in the direction of her dressing room, then led her to bed.

"Grace and beauty will diminish with exhaustion. Go to sleep," he ordered, leaning down to give her a brief kiss.

Gem pushed the start button on the cd player, listening to the one memory of her family that she could have with her.

Ping

'Good day?'

'Very interesting.'

'Surprised of Choate?'

'Pleasantly.'

The reference to Mr Choate made her smile.

'How goes the Entrenched?'

'Plodding. Choate cleared you today for Agency access when Entrenched ends.'

'He has that authority now?'

'He's a Director.'

'He is wasting his time shadowing me.'

'Choate and Agency think differently on that than you.'

'What do you think?'

'I agree with Choate and Agency. Don't second guess.'

'Do you have a shadow?'

'We all do for a week or so. Just a precaution. Yours is permanent due to Mr G.'

She was singled out because of Wyatt. Blast! But she did want Mr Choate with her. Easy way to get Agency information PDQ.

'When do you sleep?'

'I am a night owl. Mrs B is a lark.'

Gem wanted to ask him about his wife, but didn't want to step out of bounds.

'Are you clearing couriers?'

'No. Processing ones that have been cleared. Take care.'

'You too. Goodnight.'

'Goodnight, Gem.'

She smiled. Mr Cawley's nightly texts cheered her. She cleared her messages.

What next? What for tomorrow? Go into the city? If she did, she would tie up Mr Choate from more important work than shadowing her. She could stay at the Hall, work on Canterbury. But she would be at the Hall all weekend - alone with Wyatt! If she went to the city on Saturday, he would probably insist on going with her since he would not be at the office.

The war museum - any one of the many of them. She hadn't visited the IWM for weeks. It would probably be a fruitless trip, being mainly a link to her theory. The next concentration for her was logically the British Embassy in Hong Kong.

'Can one obtain information on the British embassy-Hong Kong prior to 1997?'

'Likely when Entrenched is lifted. Shall forward request to Mrs B.'

'Thank you!'

'You are most welcome! Keep thinking, Gem!'

The embassy was likely B.I. Access could be denied to Agency staff; however, she had access to Mrs Brown and her knowledge. Only Mrs Brown. Mum, dad, Mr Denton, Mr Portermann were all gone.   - Paul Andriani. But where the Hell is he? And Harry. Same as last query. Where the HELL IS Harry? - Oh, Mr White. But she couldn't go to the Agency to chat with him. She would have to be reactivated to full status to enter the Agency building. She couldn't be reactivated if she couldn't accept assignments. No. She would have to access information from Mrs Brown.

And what information did she wish to acquire?

What was embassy SOP regarding interaction with civilians prior to 1997? Was there much fraternization with local residents? And if so, did the fraternization have to be vetted? Did embassy staff reside in the embassy or in private housing? If private housing, was house staff British or local residents?

Gem wrote the list, read then shredded it. She reached for her mobile and texted the queries to Mr Cawley to forward to Mrs Brown.

Her parents had been posted to Hong Kong before their daughters were born: England, Hong Kong, England; pre 1987. Then the family went to Australia, then mum and Gem back to England.

And what of the others? She pulled out her mobile again from her pyjama pocket.

'When were Brown, Harry, Blank, Denton, White, Portermann, posted to Hong Kong embassy?'

'Will put query to Mrs Brown. Will take time of course.'

'Yes.'

After the Entrenched was lifted.
'Will not obtain information on Blank.'
'Of course not. My error to include him.'
'Information a.s.a.p.'
But not at all possible tonight.
London or not? She thought not.

Paul Andriani was a curious soul. Barcelona. Hong Kong. Where was he on 29/30 May? Would she be able to get that information from Mrs Brown? She wondered if he was ever in Geneva. Why WAS Gemmy in Geneva? That was likely another query that would never be answered. How long had she been there? A day? Two? Her last stop before Australia?

Gem paced the floor, wondering about Geneva. Did she meet someone there? Was it simply a personal break day before she went back to finish her thesis? If so, why Geneva?

It was so frustrating having so many questions that couldn't be answered. Or having answers on hold.

Gem worked all morning on Canterbury Cathedral. Mrs M was chatty over a cup of tea, then was called to sit again with Mrs Moody, whose care girl had been scheduled in error for another job that day. Gem made herself a sandwich for lunch, then decided to walk to the Mercantile to look at paint samples for her office. Only basic colours were available; if she wanted a variety of colours for choice or a colour match to an item she would have to go to a paint shop in London. Basic would do fine if she could only decide on a colour!

Half one. She should have remained at the Hall and searched the attic in case something else of Gemmy's had been left in James's flat - aside from the damning photographs. Obviously Gemmy hadn't left any clothes behind or Wyatt would have scorched her by now with that fact. Gemmy had taken all her possessions and the Grantham jewellery. Possessions - really only travel clothes for a week or so. But the jewellery. That certainly did not look good for Gemmy's defense. Perhaps there was something she had left at James's flat that Wyatt wouldn't discern as belonging to Gemmy. There was nothing in James's bedroom - that Gem had seen at quick glance that one time she had entered the room. Well then. Perhaps the attic.

Blast ! Mrs M likely had texted Wyatt that she was leaving early that day - and why. Would he return early as he had last Friday when Mrs M had gone to sit with the elderly woman?

Gem was halfway up the attic stairs, torch in hand when she heard the Jag on the drive. Blast! She hurried to her office, stashed the torch in a desk drawer, and clicked on the Canterbury file.

She heard him walk through the kitchen then straight down the hall to the library, back to the kitchen, and then he walked into her office. The long weekend with Wyatt was starting very early, she mused silently.

"Mrs M had to leave early," she informed him, knowing however that he had already been apprised of the situation.

"Very convenient," Wyatt drawled.

"For whom?" she glanced up from the computer screen, pretending she was preoccupied with her work.

"For us. A long quiet afternoon," he set a glass of wine next to her computer.

"That's why you came back early," Gem shook her head.

"Why I came HOME early. Still having trouble with that word are you?"

His tone was even but Gem heard a slight edge to it. She took a sip of wine, then looked at him. Medium grey eyes.

"Remember, my dear, 'home is where the heart is' - as they say," he sipped his wine, gazing at her over the rim of his glass.

"How do those words not stick in your throat?" She gave him a mock smile.

"They come from a place of power. You have a bit of attitude this afternoon," he observed dryly.

"As do you," she nodded.

He reached out his free hand to stroke her cheek. "I'll temper it for a while, just for you, shall I?" he spoke very softly.

And he did.

His mood was back by the time they sat down to the roast Mrs M had left in the cooker for their dinner. As Wyatt served the food, Gem slipped into the office to put a Puccini cd on the player. Perhaps music would soothe the savage ogre, she paraphrased.

Wyatt lifted an eyebrow as the strains of music wafted quietly into the breakfast room. At least dinner wouldn't be completely silent tonight.

"An excellent idea, sweetheart," Wyatt gave Gem a nod, but his face was still grim.

She pondered whether she should just sit quietly, of if she should attempt a chat as they had discussed the previous night. And it made her uneasy not to know the root of his dark mood.

"Did you have a difficult day?" she gingerly asked him, expecting him to snap at her.

"It was difficult," he agreed. "I ordered an employee of the London office to be dismissed."

"Incompetence?" she queried.

"Yes. He was a spy. Since he was detected that would suggest incompetence to a certain degree," Wyatt scowled.

Gem choked on her tea. "A spy?" she gasped. That was a shocking remark. Of all the replies with which he could have responded this one hit too close to her.

"It is called industrial espionage. It does exist you know."

"Yes - certainly," Gem's voice quavered. Mr Choate had used that word during their chat the previous day.

"I detest spies," Wyatt ground out.

"You do?" Gem said faintly.

"Spies are cowards."

"Aside from James Bond," Gem murmured.

"Bond is fantasy fiction," Wyatt scoffed.

"Yes," Gem conceded. "Did your - spy - do a great deal of industrial damage to your company?"

Wyatt shook his head. "No. New employees go through a weeding out process. Unbeknownst to them all their assignments are dummy projects."

"You tracked his project leak," Gem suggested.

"Yes," Wyatt ended the subject. She did not need to know any further details nor was he prepared to divulge additional information. "Forgive me, my dear, I have put a damper on our evening."

"What did the employee say when he was found out?" Gem pressed on, not really hearing his last remark. "Did he admit to being a spy?"

Wyatt relented on his decision and replied to her query. "He was released for poor performance, and is unaware that his ruse was discovered."

"Oh, very good indeed," Gem nodded admiringly. "Have you caught many spies?" she queried and caught her lower lip between her teeth.

"A number of them over the years."

"Using the same method?"

"Various methods."

"Such as?" Gem urged him to continue.

"The methods are not for public knowledge," Wyatt said curtly.

Blast! Gem felt like she had been splashed with a bucket of cold water. "Oh," she said a bit coolly.

Wyatt watched her expression change from avid interest to very affronted. "Were you considering implementing the methods into your next game, my dear?" Wyatt demanded curiously.

Gem glared at him for a moment, then rose from her chair, stacked her dishware, carried the pile into the kitchen and put the items into the dishwasher. And still without saying a word, she walked to the mudroom, took her windcheater off its peg and walked out the kitchen door. She shrugged on the windcheater as she walked down the drive to the cobblestone lane. Her mobile was in her skirt pocket; it was dark so she didn't need the blasted hat Wyatt always insisted she wear.

Was there any cash in her pocket? She rummaged first in one, then the other. Easily enough for a pint. She didn't give a damn what the locals would think of her going to the Yellow Crow on her own. She couldn't bear to be in the Hall one minute longer with that OGRE.

The pub was rocking - as Mrs Brown would say. Gem ordered a half-pint then weaved her way through the crowd to stand near the fireplace with her back to the wall. She read the room, a mixed crowd of young and older patrons. Mike Morgan - publican and constable - had nodded to her when she ordered her brew, but he was too busy to chat, much to her relief. He seemed a bit surprised that she had paid in cash, but she refused to have it entered to Wyatt's account.

The band was popular with the patrons, drawing wild applause, the customers singing along with most of the songs. Gem continued reading the room and was about to fetch another half-pint when Wyatt entered the pub. He saw her immediately, ordered a pint for himself and a half for her, then threaded his way through the crowd to her side. He took the empty mug from her hand and set it on the fireplace shelf, and handed over the full one. Gem set it alongside the empty mug and pulled her mobile from her pocket.

'If you say a single word to me you will be wearing this beer.'

She sent the message, picked up the mug, held it up to him and slipped her phone into her pocket. Gem took a long, refreshing drink of her brew as he checked his text message, then gave her a nod of concession. She continued to subtly read the room, smiled at people who glanced at her, and let her mind go blank of concentrated thought.

She knew there would not be another beer, and when Wyatt took her empty mug, handing it to the waitress, Gem knew they would be leaving the Crow. And she knew she would have to eat the same when they returned to the Hall. Wyatt took her hand and led the way through the crowd, and Gem watched as the heads of all the women in the pub swiveled appreciatively in Wyatt's direction. She wished she could wrap him up in a big bow and hand him over to any one of them.

She walked alongside him on the way back to the Hall, but when he tried to put his arm around her shoulders, she slipped out of his reach.

Wyatt locked the kitchen door behind them. Gem went to her office, but he was right behind her. As she switched on the office light he switched it off.

"It's late," he said, taking her hand to lead her out the door.

"Lord! you have a one track mind!" she snapped, hanging back.

"Early days yet. You're still a new toy," he said loftily, still annoyed with her haring off to the pub on her own.

Gem gasped. "Is that how you regard women?" she demanded heatedly.

"That's how I regard you. As you regard men - no doubt. I'm astounded that you can ever pretend to be offended."

Gem stared at him dumbfounded. "How can you be so cruel?"

"Oh don't play the victim card tonight, my dear wife. You neatly victimized others, now it's your turn."

"Toy or wife! How charming! How disgusting!" Every word he said incensed her.

"You are my consort then, - a convenience. A ready partner for my amusement, a pleasant companion when I dine. You were lacking in being amusing and pleasant this evening, by the way. You - who so prettily promised just the other night that there would be no more battles. Did you not make that promise?"

"King of your own little word, aren't you!" Gem, refusing to move, gave him a mocking smile.

"It's quite a large world actually."

"Those women tonight at the Crow," she said with disgust. "They were fairly undressing you with their eyes. You must have to beat off women with a stick. Go annoy them!"

Wyatt laughed. "I don't have to beat them off. You are my deflector. I don't have the inclination or time to pursue relationships with other women. I don't have to woo you, or shower you with attention, flowers, gifts. You are available when I want you and you disappear when I no longer wish amusement."

"Get a mistress, get a dog -"

"They both would require more attention than I wish to give."

"You are so cold, positively evil," Gem said wearily, "so uncaring, so brutal."

"And what were you to James, my dear? Were you the woman James had thought you to be, I would have been extremely jealous of my brother's great fortune in loving you. Yet - you are who you are. I could so easily have destroyed you when we met, Gem. That was my first inclination. I took the option of having you about as a convenience, but you are extremely irritating. However, you are correct in one aspect. I have no feelings where you are concerned. As I have said before, you and I are a match. You are ruthless and I can be more frightening than you can imagine. I have tolerated three weeks of your sulking, whinging, and self-pity. Cease playing the victim and start adapting to our relationship. I have no more patience to deal with you."

Wyatt's mobile rang. He looked at the number then said," Go to bed now!" He went into the library and closed the door behind him.

Gem stared at the closed door, then trudged up the stairs. She took a shower, put on pyjamas, and crawled wearily into bed. She was asleep before Wyatt walked up the stairs to join her.

Gem's mood was not improved by sleep. The dark hours loomed before her.
Gemmy, where are you? She moaned, pacing the floor of her office.
Ping
'Embassy staff posting dates denied by B.I.'
'Not really surprised.'
'Considered a privacy issue. May be possible to find some references on computer.'
'Will try that suggestion. Thank you.'
'Fight the good fight as they say, Gem.'
'I am trying. And losing the battle.'

Gem made a cup of hot chocolate and pushed the start button on the cd player. Vera Lynn was singing about the White Cliffs of Dover, as Gem paced the floor. She hadn't really expected the request to be honoured if B.I. was involved. She was Agency (retired) not B.I.

Perhaps another tactic. She pulled her mobile out of her pyjama pocket.
'Information possibly obtained from Mrs Brown?'
'Will pass on request.'

Mrs Brown was a lark. Reply would not be until morning, unless her supervisor was working on Entrenched SOP.

Blast! Mrs Brown couldn't go against B.I. SOP! She was the Acting Director of the Agency since Harry was on 'holiday'.
Ping
'Request denied. Sorry.'
'Long shot. Thanks anyway.'
Agency. B.I. Couriers. Agents. Spies!

Blast! She wished Wyatt had told her the other methods GEI used to root out industrial spies. It might have given her an inspiration for her work. There had to be a spy in the Network. Or a mole. Or a sleeper.

Someone had to know the identities of the Network couriers and agents. It wasn't just random 'luck' killing people, for robbery, whatever, and just happening to kill Network personal.

She was so tired.

Had there been a way to subtly wheedle the information from Wyatt? She didn't think so; he didn't trust her as it was; John Staunton didn't help there - the infamous master criminal: the photos. I wouldn't trust me either, Gem mused.

A mole. Or a sleeper. She pulled out her mobile again.

'Agency investigating Agency Network for mole or sleeper?'

'Yes. Investigation complete. Neither discovered.'

'Outsider then.'

'Perhaps.'

Gem cleared the messages from her mobile.

Harry was very busy! Or did Paul Andriani - Undercover Agent 1- do that type of investigation? There was absolutely no point to make that query. She wondered if Wyatt had ever discovered a mole at GEI? That was another query that would go unanswered. The query could not be put forth in an innocuous manner. He would immediately suspect she was planning her next targeting method.

Ping

'Making any progress regular search?'

'No.'

'Okay. Goodnight.'

'Goodnight.'

She had to survive the weekend with Wyatt and chat with Mr Choate on Monday in London. Just chatting with him might help her to stay sane.

She didn't have the energy, mental or physical, to attempt a web search on the British Embassy that night. Arguing with Wyatt had taxed her mental capabilities. At least she had had more sleep than usual before the dark hours began. She wondered who had rung him. She wondered who she could thank for keeping him on the phone for so long that night.

She paced, listening to Vera Lynn's music, letting her mind wander, as the dark hours ebbed away.

Gem sighed as her brain insisted she waken. Six hours of sleep total; that was a blessing.

If I was the woman James had thought me to be, Wyatt would have been jealous of his brother. Gemmy was! Wyatt would care for her if...! Gem groaned inwardly, feeling hollow - but how could her heart ache so when she felt hollow? Wyatt was killing her.

He stirred and kissed the nape of her neck.

"No!" Gem pulled away from him. "I am not in the mood! Leave me alone!" she demanded.

Wyatt drew back. "Awake less than five minutes and already peevish. What has set you off now?" he scowled.

Gem pulled on her dressing gown. Were all men so thick brained? She sank to the edge of the bed. "You!" she raked her fingers through her hair. "I can't believe what you did! I simply can't believe it!" she groaned in dismay.

"What precisely have I done?" Wyatt asked impatiently.

Gem threw up her hands in exasperation. "You tricked me into this horrid relationship!"

"Marriage," he corrected, exhaling sharply. "Why are you on about this again? It is over, done with, settled. Stop fretting about it."

"Fretting! My God, you are cold! How could I ever have loved you!"

Wyatt rubbed his face, then pushed himself up to lean back against the pillows behind him. "You speak as if you are the only person who has ever fallen in love and suffered a disappointment. Remember James, my dear? He also was in love," Wyatt mocked her. "Oh wait! He was in love with you, wasn't he? And you broke his heart. Your turn. Now we have an agreement, you and I. Abide by the terms, and we shall get along smoothly. Ignore the terms and, oh dear, things will get very sticky for you. End of story," he advised, his gray eyes growing darker.

"The terms are all yours!" Gem snapped, pacing the floor, her temper rising, pain gnawing inside her.

"Yes. You had a poor negotiator," Wyatt replied dryly. "Who was it? - Ah, yes - it was you. Words of advice for the future, my dear: hire a better negotiator next time. No- there won't be a next time, will there? Now get over your snit. No doubt your poor little heart will mend soon. Perhaps tomorrow. From now on, my dear, you may whinge and moan as much and as often as you like, but I will no longer listen or reply to your self-created misfortune."

Gems stared at him in astonishment. "How did you ever become so jaded?" she asked in pained awe.

Wyatt frowned at her. "An odd query from the likes of you." He got out of bed and pulled on his dressing gown. "Alright, Gem, you are not in the mood. I'm going to shower and start breakfast," he said to her surprise. "Dress warm; we have a long day ahead of us."

Gem went through the motions: shower, skirt, shirt, braid hair; another day with that ogre.

The radio was on in the kitchen when she went down for breakfast. There was a pile of Wyatt's reports on the counter along with plates of omelets, bacon and toast. Wyatt limited the conversation to a reply of either tea or coffee. As always his cooking was excellent. Gem wondered fleetingly if he was still thinking that she would poison him if she prepared their meals. Or perhaps he merely enjoyed cooking. Either way, she didn't care. She was shutting down again emotionally, Gem realized. He was winning again.

Dishwasher filled and running, he ordered, "Camera, hat, sunglasses, windcheater."

"Where are we going?" she asked curiously.

They were using one of the Hall's Land Rovers.

"Winchester Cathedral. You said you needed additional photos. No clouds today, should be good light."

"Just a minute please," she ducked back into the house to fetch the photos she wanted to re-shoot of Winchester, and her sketch pad and pencils.

There were two ways to consider his plans for the day: thoughtful or controlling. Gem refused to decide which, hoping only to survive the day. She saw a stack of reports on the back seat of the Land Rover; Wyatt would not waste the day waiting for her.

"Do you have enough film or shall we stop at the chemist's shop?" he queried as they crossed the old stone bridge on the curve below the Hall.

"I have more than enough," Gem assured him.

"Alright, then we are off," Wyatt murmured.

Those were the last words spoken between them until they reached the cathedral. Wyatt put on a Beethoven cd, then the radio; anything was preferable than forcing a chat, Gem sighed inwardly - and thankfully.

They had Chinese for lunch, then Gem spent the afternoon with her camera and sketch pad while Wyatt sat in the Land Rover and read reports. She shot a dozen photos, changed lenses and shot a second dozen of every angle she thought would be advantageous for her final selection of photos for her book. If she used a digital camera she could immediately review the shots and know then and there if she likely had what she wanted; but she had tried digital cameras, and they were not a 'fit' that suited her. She liked the pursuit of using her instincts and the waiting to know if her instincts had been correct.

Once the exterior shots were accomplished, Gem moved inside the cathedral, and managed to shoot another two rolls of film in between the visitors straggling through the sanctuary. Wyatt had not mentioned a time limit, so she spent an hour sketching the West Doors, the ceiling in the North Presbytery Aisle and the Holy Sepulchre Chapel. Wyatt didn't make an appearance in the cathedral telling her it was time to go, so she went through roll after roll of film shooting what she had sketched, hoping to have some of the photos and her sketches framed for her office.

After four hours she decided she was probably pushing her luck with Wyatt's patience and she returned to the Land Rover. He got out of the vehicle to open the passenger door for her.

"Finished?" he queried, setting the report he had been reading on the rear seat.

"Yes, thank you. And you?"

Wyatt thumbed through the stack of binders on the seat behind her. "Seven. That's a start," he engaged the engine. "It's a long drive home. What say we stop at the Crow for dinner, my dear?"

"Okay," Gem nodded. The less time alone with him, the better for her nerves.

My dear! Give it up! He was a businessman; perhaps she could strike a bargain with him. And be a better negotiator this time. She held her tongue while he manoeuvred the vehicle into traffic. It was Mr Hyde who had planned the day. Hopefully he would remain long enough to negotiate new terms with her.

"How was the light?" he asked casually, glancing from the windscreen to her. She seemed unsettled.

"Fine - very good actually. Thank you for coming here today. It was a successful shoot, I believe," Gem said politely.

"How many photos did you take?"

Clouds were following them on the drive back to Ticking Bottom; there would likely be a storm that night, and hopefully during the dark hours to give some spice to the early morning.

"My dear?"

"What?" Gem frowned, studying the sky. Clouds. She would do a series on clouds.

"Did you take a great many photos?" Wyatt asked.

"Eighty or more, I should think," Gem shrugged.

"Did you sketch?"

"Some." Conversation or control - demanding to know what she had done?

"I would like to see some of your sketches. Your newer ones."

"If you wish," she replied. "They are only sketches."

"You are quite talented. I'm interested in your work."

As long as it only involves the book and a few other sketches, Gem mused silently. The sketches of her family had been destroyed by Mr Choate, she sighed.

"That was quite a deep sigh," Wyatt remarked. "Is something troubling you, my dear?"

"Only the usual," she said, purposely cryptic.

"Oh." He didn't inquire as to the nature of her troubles, assuming she was referring to him.

She watched the traffic going and coming, wishing she was in any other car on the road. She dragged up the courage to broach the subject that irritated her constantly.

"Would it be possible to negotiate a change of terms?" Gem frowned.

"Regarding?" Wyatt glanced at her.

"My dear, sweetheart, all the nauseating drivel. Blast! I'll pay you to stop using those disgusting words!" she said desperately.

"Not necessary to pay me, Gem," Wyatt said calmly. "Did you decide on Bloody Mary then?"

"I hate you more than I can say!" she snapped.

"Keep saying that, my dear. You might actually convince yourself that you do," he said dryly.

"It is impossible to talk to you!"

"Why don't you try saying something I want to hear for a change then?"

"Which would be?" she demanded.

"Tell me about James," he glanced at her again.

Gem stiffened. She could fairly hear cogs begin to shift. "He was your brother," she said coolly. "You knew him better than anyone."

"How did you convince him you were pregnant? Did you get him drunk and watch him pass out? Or did you use drugs? How long were you with him?" Wyatt said dead quietly. "Why did you choose to play James? No doubt your friend Staunton could connect you to men more affluent at the time than was James. Someone more exciting - another player - like you. Or do you only go after innocents like James?"

Gem considered his queries and fought the desire to verbally strike back. Gemmy would never have hurt anyone.

"I want answers," Wyatt pressed demandingly.

Gem held her ground. "I am not going to give you any," she said firmly, staring straight ahead at the red lights of the cars ahead of them. "Your time to ask questions was before you trapped me into this relationship. I won't answer your questions, and I won't talk to you about James." She had called his bluff so to speak. It would be easy to pump Mrs M for information, but that would get back to Wyatt in one way or another. And she would not use Mrs M despite what Wyatt thought she would do. She couldn't reply to his queries of a man whom she had barely met. All she could do was protect Gemmy. "Forever how long I must be with you is how long I shall refuse to discuss James with you."

"Eternity then, my dear wife," he replied calmly.

Gem refused to speak to him for the duration of the drive to Ticking Bottom. Eternity be damned! She would not be with him that long!

Wyatt enjoyed the quiet drive. She had had her say enough the past twenty-four hours, and that would be the end of that! And eventually he would have the information he sought from her regarding James; next week, next month, next year; eventually it would come. And she would damned well regret him knowing what he learned from her.

The M's met them at the Crow and Gem enjoyed a pleasant dinner for a change, chatting with Mrs M while her Mister chatted with Wyatt. The evening, however, was not drawn out, because Wyatt was attuned to his watch and he drove Gem home for an early night as usual; but not an early night of sleep.

Gem sipped a cup of hot chocolate as she snuggled in Auntie Jane's comfy chair. As angry as she was with Wyatt, she had to admit she was relaxed.

She had promised him no further battles, but she couldn't stop arguing with him. He said he would no longer listen or reply to her arguments. Oh, she hated him! He could deny her words but she wouldn't deny her feelings. He made her so angry she couldn't think straight. She had barely survived three weeks with him. How could she bear to survive no end in sight?

He had mentioned Staunton again. There could have been humour in that situation except for the tragedy. Poor Paul Andriani was making Gem's life miserable, through no fault of his or hers.

She simply had to hold her tongue and not give Wyatt any more ammunition for his caustic remarks. Bloody Mary indeed!

Paul Andriani. While John Staunton had a nefarious personality, Paul Andriani was a proper gentleman. She and Gemmy had had infrequent courier assignments to Paul Andriani, he, of course, being in disguise other than that of Staunton. They had also seen him at various times at the Agency; his smile was always so warm, he was so sweet and kind, his sense of humour was articulate, his manner continental and suave. And he was very good-looking, if not stunningly handsome as was Wyatt. When you were chatting with Paul Andriani, he would give you his undivided attention, making you feel very special. If Paul Andriani hadn't been so very focused on his profession it could have been so easy to fall in love with him. He was a very sexy man. So charming.

Gemmy had had more courier assignments to Paul Andriani than had Gem. And while others were confused by the twins at times, Paul Andriani always knew which Gem he met. And those times at the Agency, it seemed that Gemmy and Paul Andriani had almost had a secret code going between the two of them. Gem had wondered a number of times if there was 'something' between her twin and the master agent, but it had never really seemed an actual possibility.

Or was that another secret Gemmy had had? Had Gemmy had feelings for Paul Andriani? And he for her?

That certainly wasn't a fact Gem could check. One could not simply contact the master agent and ask him questions of any kind. Even Harry and Mrs Brown couldn't contact Paul Andriani when they wished to do so. He contacted the Agency at his discretion. Courier assignments to him were at his designation to the Agency, not vice versa.

Had Paul Andriani known about James? He had obviously known Gemmy was in Barcelona. Did HE know why Gemmy had gone to Geneva? What did he know about anything? How long had Paul Andriani existed as John Staunton? How long had John Staunton lived on the periphery of human existence?

And what was Mr Cawley doing this morning? Gem pulled her mobile from her pocket. She had to remember to charge it before she went back to bed.

'Blank ever posted to Hong Kong?'

'???'

'How long PA been JS?'

'Are you pissed????'

'No!'

However she wouldn't really mind a beer at this moment.

'Are you smoking something?'

'No!'

'You aren't lucid if you actually expect answers to those ridiculous questions!'

'Ouch!'

'Indeed!'

'Had to try.'

'Please immediately delete queries/replies.'

Gem followed orders. Was Mr Cawley grumpy this morning?

'Done.'

'You need a mental holiday, Gem!'

'How do I manage that?'

'Meditation. Extended honeymoon.'

Continuation of a nightmare? She was already living that. She could work on her office.

'How goes Entrenched?'

'Possibly winding down.'

'Couriers/agents accounted for?'

'Cannot reply to query.'

A bolt of lightning split the sky, flashing brilliant light into the room. The heavens opened to pound the Hall with rain. The lightning was rampant, and Gem watched, mesmerized, at the trees and bushes in the garden bending in the sudden fierce wind.

'Storm here.'

'Also here.'

'Do you work every night?'

'Yes. Same as you.'

That made Gem grin. Mr Cawley. Her link to the sane world.

'Back to work.'

'Give it a rest for a few days.'
'Can't.'
'Please, please try. Must refresh your brain.'
'Okay. Will try. Goodnight.'
'Goodnight, Gem.'

She searched the computer for information of the British Consulate General, but could find no pertinent information other than the name of the current British Consul-General to Hong Kong and Macao, and a list of his predecessors going back to 1997. Her parents were pre-1997. How about the others?

Another night of no proper information. Gem stopped the music, rinsed her hot chocolate cup and went up the stairs to bed.

Wyatt awakened two hours later when Gem's internal clock brought her awake. He FINALLY went back to sleep when she showered and dressed for the day. She didn't waste time preparing breakfast because she knew he wouldn't eat what she had touched; she ate a cup of yogurt in her office while she taped paint chip samples to the long wall. Did the colour really matter as long as it wasn't puce or black?

The world beyond the office windows was drenched; a heavy mist entwined with fog, making the day very dark indeed. Without sunlight, it was not the day to decide paint colour. She checked the weather forecast on the computer, learning that the view beyond the windows was as good as the weather would be that day; quarantined again in Ticking Bottom with Dr Jekyll and Mr Hyde. Likely the former. She worked on Canterbury refining and expanding the text, becoming immersed in the magnificence of the cathedral.

She was so pleased with the photos! Late April sunlight, just before she had met Gemmy in Florence for a three day weekend. A happy time! Had Gemmy known that weekend that she was pregnant? Gem would never know. Unless she found something among James's personal effects that would refer to Gemmy. She would like to do a more thorough search of James's bedroom - and then there was the attic. Perhaps this week if the M's went to the shops. However when Mrs M left early, Wyatt would come back to the Hall early.

Gem wasn't left alone at the Hall. Either Mrs M or Wyatt or both always seemed to be here. And now when she was away from Ticking Bottom, Mr Choate was shadowing her. At least he was a blessing because he was a friend and a contact to the Agency. Gem slumped in the comfy chair, drawing up her legs to rest her forehead on her knees. She felt like a criminal suspect from the telly. Couriers and agents were being hunted while she was sequestered. Well, she had already been hunted; she just was very unlikely to be murdered. In this case, Dr Jekyll, she was quite certain, was not lethal. He simply had an extreme case of fury.

Where was Paul Andriani? Had any couriers or agents disappeared during the Entrenched? Where was Harry?

"Gem."

And the Philippine and Malaysian agents? Had they been found?

"Gem."

Perhaps Mr Choate would have a bit of information tomorrow, despite the Entrenched SOP.

Wyatt touched her shoulder, startling her. He knew she wasn't sleeping. What had taken her thoughts so deep she hadn't heard him?

"What?" she queried, lifting her head, puzzled at her surroundings.

He saw the haunted look in her eyes. She had been in her secret world again.

"Pub breakfast this morning," he replied, handing her her mac.

"I had breakfast," she protested.

"I see," he nodded at the yogurt cup and spoon on the counter. "Hardly substantial. No protests now. You'll need your wellies."

At least she would be out of the house with him. The Crow was surprisingly busy, serving a massive brunch buffet, and tea, coffee, apple cider, and hot chocolate. The M's were again waiting for them, Mr M wearing the flat hat Gem had given him. The publican sat with them for a while and the chemist stopped by for a chat. Eve, the owner of the gift shop stopped at their table to show off her new baby girl, who Mrs M immediately took in her arms for a cuddle. Gem felt a stabbing pain in her heart. She hadn't thought often of having children, only fleeting thoughts in the past of 'someday' - until she had put the question to Wyatt days before their wedding. And now the thought was irrelevant. Their marriage wasn't real. They would never be a proper family. Perhaps sometime in the years to come, when she was free of Wyatt, perhaps she would meet a man who was only Mr Hyde.

Gem smiled as Mrs M handed the baby to her; she couldn't remember the last time she had held a baby; back at university perhaps. Smiling, Gem glanced up at Mrs M, her peripheral vision catching Wyatt as he chatted with the baby's father. His eyes were nearly black despite his smile and easy tone of voice. She knew instantly that he was thinking of James. Her thoughts went back to his queries of the previous day. She desperately hoped that was a conversation that would not be repeated that day.

Gem stroked the baby's cheek with her finger, then with a wistful smile handed the child back to her mother.

"She's brilliant," Gem said softly. "Congratulations."

To her surprise, Wyatt did not suggest they immediately leave, and while his eyes remained the very dark colour, he appeared relaxed as other locals stopped by the table to chat. The customers grazed the buffet throughout the morning, and Gem, accompanied by Mrs M, wandered back a number of times herself. It was on their final pass that Gem learned of the reason for the continued feast.

"Is this some kind of a special event?" she murmured to the Grantham Hall housekeeper.

"Goodness no," Mrs M replied. "One Sunday a month. Of course Mr W wouldn't have mentioned the situation to you. He pays for the spread from nine to noon, once a month - has for years, but he rarely attends - hates the Lord of the Manor look of it."

"Oh," Gem murmured. A man of many surprises.

"He does the same across GEI once a month. Gets people together to chat and relax, he says. He hosts family events twice a year at GEI - winter holiday in December, and a summer picnic at the end of July." She lowered her voice. "He missed attending the picnic this year as it was just after Jamie passed away, dear lad. He was handling the business with Jamie's flat in Barcelona."

"It's very thoughtful of him," Gem murmured.

"To be sure. You couldn't have married a finer man," Mrs M said firmly. "He's moody as of late, a side I've not seen in him for quite some time. He's still grieving, naturally, but I know having you now will be a great comfort to him."

Oh Lord! That was the last thing their relationship was doing for Wyatt. Did he ever feel as hollow inside as she felt? Somehow Gem couldn't believe he did.

Bar service was finally open. Gem went to the bar and ordered a round for the customers, putting it on her credit card, taking the first half-pint for herself. This was turning into a wickedly difficult day for her. And to her embarrassment Mike Morgan announced that she had purchased the first round for the house.

They walked back to the Hall with the M's, splitting at the drive as the older couple walked on to the carriage house. Gem steeled herself for a tirade from Dr Jekyll but none came. Wyatt announced he had work to do in the office and Gem was alone for the rest of the afternoon.

She put her laundry in the washing machine, not bothering to ask Wyatt about his; he was completely capable of managing his own needs. The paint samples caught her eye and she wavered between a crème and a subtle green, but the deep stone grey would set off framed photos. Black and white film. She hadn't used that for a few years. B/W film went on her list for Monday.

Ping

'Malaysian counter-agent dead.'

'How?'

'Knife.'

'Entrenched lifted?'

'No. Burn messages and replies.'

Burn! He was in a new mode. Gem quickly cleared as requested.

Mr Cawley was blatantly violating Entrenched SOP! He could be dismissed for releasing the information to her! What was he thinking?

'Done.'

She assured him.

'Later, Gem. Keep thinking!'

'Get some sleep!'

'Soon.'

Mr Cawley violating Agency SOP greatly concerned Gem. And of course she would never let it be known to anyone that he had done so.

Wyatt tossed the report he was reading to his desk. He couldn't erase from his mind the image of Gem holding the baby. It was the perfect vision of his dreams: his exquisitely beautiful wife holding their child. His beautiful wife: the love of James's life. How natural Gem had looked with a baby in her arms! She never ceased to amaze him. Brilliant, witty, extremely sexy, passionate, mysterious, extraordinarily beautiful, and irritatingly feisty!

And what of the insomnia? He was no closer to understanding the cause of that. She had suffered from it before their marriage. It had nothing to do with James's death. He was certain she hadn't known about James's death until their wedding night.

She refused to talk about James. Guilt? Did she simply not remember him? Was James just a vague memory to her? If so, she would never forget Wyatt. He would make damned sure of that!

Gem gazed at the colour chips until they started to blur together like the fog and the mist beyond the office windows.

There were no additional messages from Mr Cawley. Perhaps he was sleeping. Had it been lack of sleep that had prompted the SOP violation? Unlikely. Mr Cawley was too consummate a professional to easily disregard rules.

The crème colour, rich as it was, was a bit on the bland side. The grey was definitely growing on her.

What was with Wyatt? She had expected to draw his fire when they reached the Hall, but he hadn't said a word regarding what had made him so angry at the Yellow Crow. And he had definitely been angry; his eyes had clearly declared his mood.

And Mrs M's words in confidence about the monthly pub parties and those at GEI. Wyatt was an enigma! Or was it simply that she was the only person in his circle who was in his target sight?

The Malaysian counter-agent! Knifed! Thai, Chinese, Vietnamese, Malaysian, counter-couriers and counter-agents. All knifed. And what of the Philippine counter-agent?

Plane = four. Knifed = four. Mr Denton, James, the baby, the missing Philippine counter -agent= four. Twelve.

She was so weary. Was she even thinking clearly anymore? Were there two killers? The Pilos and the knifings? How to account for Mr Denton? Were there more than two killers?

Gem hung her clean laundry, put the rest in the dryer, looked through the book on the Royal Pavilion, and read for a half hour of various English villages. A walk was an inviting notion but as she decided to take that option, the heavens opened to send more pounding rain down upon the Hall.

Biscuits. The computer yielded hundreds of recipes; peanut butter, she decided; hopefully Mrs M wouldn't mind Gem puttering in her kitchen. She was removing the third dozen from the cooker when Wyatt walked into the room.

"Delicious," he snagged a biscuit from the baking sheet. "Stunningly beautiful - and you can bake," he observed, sinking his perfect teeth into moist goodness.

Gem ignored his compliment. "It might be poisoned," she nodded at the biscuit in his hand.

"Wouldn't you be in trouble then!" he chuckled, but there was an edge to his tone. "My, my. Quite domestic aren't you? Cleaning, laundry, baking, holding babies. The domestic side of Gemimah Forrester Grantham - indeed, quite the proper picture of my lovely wife."

And there it was, Gem mused silently. "I do so regret not adding the poison," she said wistfully, slipping the biscuits from the metal sheet to the cooling racks.

Wyatt burst out laughing. He took a handful of biscuits, a beer from the fridge and walked back to his office.

Gem stared opened mouth at his retreating back. That was hardly the response she had expected!

Gem paced the floor. She had made it through Sunday without having an argument with Wyatt. After dinner Wyatt had returned to his office, leaving Gem to do the washing up at her insistence since he had prepared their meal. She had spent the evening working on the Canterbury chapter.

Hour after hour. Day after day. Living in this house was going to drive her mad! Gem sank into Auntie Jane's comfy chair. Mrs M was good, cheery company. But when Gem and Wyatt were alone at the Hall, she was so lonely. It wasn't that she wanted his companionship; when they were in the same room together their conversation usually ended in an argument. But at her flat she had had the freedom to ring Mrs Brown or Harry - until he went on prolonged holiday - or Mr Cawley, whenever she chose to do so. But here at the Hall, she had to constantly be careful of communicating with the Agency.

Ping

'How is early morning going?'

'Long. Yours?'

'Same. What are you doing?'

Feeling sorry for myself. But she couldn't say that. She had worn herself out in June and July, so much so she slept and worked with little time remaining to think. August had been spent with Wyatt. Now she had nothing but work. What was her focus? Oh, the embassy. But that work was stymied because she couldn't get answers.

'Wondering what dad's position was at the embassy in Hong Kong.'

She texted the message for lack of a reply to Mr Cawley's query.

'Cryptanalyst. Same as with Agency.'

'Mum's?'

'Events coordinator: galas, receptions, that sort of thing. Knowing who was who and why.'

'Thank you.'

He had done it again!

'How can you reply if still Entrenched?'

'Just happened to know answer.'

'How "just happened to know"?'

'Don't ask too many questions, Gem.'

Again he was violating SOP for her.

'I don't want you to damage your position at Agency for me.'

'Quickly delete messages then.'

Gem's fingers flew over the keys of her mobile.

'Done!'

He was certainly putting his neck on the chopping block for her. The visual made her cringe. Bloody Mary. Blast Wyatt! (She hadn't set anyone on fire!) And there was no connection, she had to reassure herself. She was gathering information to solve a mystery; she was NOT using Mr Cawley for nefarious reasons. And her mother's position at the embassy would have been common knowledge if she worked in the public eye in Hong Kong. And just as naturally, her father's position at the embassy would not have been public knowledge; and he had held the same position at the Agency.

Ping

'You must go to London this morning.'
'Will do. Have you ever been to Hong Kong?'
'No. You?'
'No.'
'Is it raining in Ticking Bottom?'
'Yes.'
'Raining here. Back to work. Goodnight.'
'Goodnight.'

Gem deleted the messages, then charged her mobile. Interesting. Someone at the Agency wanted her to be in London that morning. That certainly caught her interest. So brilliant having Mr Choate as a direct connection to the Agency!

She was exhausted when she crawled into bed. Wyatt stroked her arm until she fell asleep.

A day without a battle, Wyatt observed before he fell asleep. But there could have been many - if he had chosen to call her on any of her actions or her remarks.

Chapter Seventeen

Since she was going to the city, Wyatt 'suggested' lunch at the White Rose. Gem could have said she was returning to the Hall after her few errands, but that would probably have irritated him. And she would have had to follow through for Wyatt would receive a report from Mr Choate. And chatty Mrs M might casually mention to Mr W the hour of Gem's return. Gem knew Mrs M wasn't spying on her, but she might mention facts, and why not? Why shouldn't Mrs M feel free to chat with Mr W?

Gem dropped off the rolls of film at the photo shop, then window hopped, wondering if she wanted to spend time at the British War Museum. If she was inside she could take off the blasted hat Wyatt had insisted she wear because of the clear, sunny day.

And when was someone going to tell her why Mr Cawley told her to go to London this morning? She didn't have long to wait for that answer.

Ping

'Coffee/tea.'

Mr Choate! Gem back tracked two blocks to a coffee shop. He followed her into the shop but stepped in front of her at the counter, ordering and paying for both their beverages. They were quickly back on the street then, walking until they reached the small green space where they had had their previous chat. Gem raised her eyebrows in query as they read their surroundings.

Mr Choate reached inside his coat and pulled out a sheet of paper, handing it to Gem. She gave him a curious frown then focused on the paper. Name and dates.

Brown 1985-1997
Harry 1984-1997
Denton 1983-1997
Lawson 1983-1985
Forrester 1983-1985
Portermann 1983-1999
White 1983-1999

Gem set the information in her memory bank then handed the sheet back to Mr Choate, who immediately returned it to the inside pocket of his coat.

"Is the Entrenched lifted?" she asked, her breath catching in her throat.

"No."

"Why would you give me this information?" she asked nervously. The information would have been available to both of the Agency Directors, but why had they both violated Agency SOP to give the information to her?

"Mrs Brown sends her regards, Gem. She will ring this week regarding a possible meeting," Mr Choate said in reply to her query.

Mrs Brown had given up the information to Gem! Good heavens! All three of them were violating Agency SOP! All three of them laying their careers on the line for her! And Mrs Brown had ignored B.I. SOP! Gem took a deep, steadying breath. Violating directives!

"Why?" she repeated breathlessly.

"Don't ask too many questions, Gem," Mr Choate advised, his face blank of expression.

They all did it for her. For Family.

"Tightly knit," Gem murmured.

"Just so. We don't forget our own, Gem," he replied firmly and solemnly. "We'll find them," he added the promise.

And hopefully they would find the Pilos before being married to Wyatt Grantham drove her mad!

"Where to Lady Grantham?" he asked in a professional manner.

"Tosh," Gem said briskly.

"Mr Grantham doesn't use his title, but still it is there," Choate informed her.

What? A man of many mysteries. She certainly knew very little of Wyatt! But then, he didn't want her to know him well, did he?

"Why doesn't he use the title?" Gem queried. Mr Choate didn't seem surprised there was knowledge she didn't have of her 'husband' - that word still made her inwardly cringe. He must think the Grantham's marriage was an odd one. Which it most definitely was!

"Apparently he is not easily impressed by such matters. And he prefers to live a very quiet private life."

Perhaps Mr Choate wasn't surprised that she knew very little of Wyatt. The Agency had obviously been keeping tabs on Gem, for Mrs Brown had known Gem was seeing Wyatt in August, and Gem had not informed her supervisor or anyone at the Agency of the relationship. And how much could she have known of the man she had married after knowing him for a month?

Mr Choate or someone at the Agency must believe that Gem should have information of her 'husband' - there was that awful word again! They were looking out for her apparently. Like friends and family do when one of their members does something remarkably stupid as to marry a person who is nearly a complete stranger!

"Where to Mrs Grantham?" Choate queried again.

She thought for a moment. "London War Museum," she finally decided.

"Very good, ma'am," Choate formally replied.

"Cut the guff, Mr Choate," Gem grinned. "Only Gem will reply to you from this moment on."

He grinned. "War museum it is then."

At the museum Mr Choate was sometimes behind her, sometimes beside her so they could discuss the displays.

"Are you searching for anything in particular, or simply absorbing?" Choate asked at one point.

"Absorbing. There's a question at the back of my mind, but I can't put my finger on it," she replied. After a half hour she did have a query for her shadow. "Do you think that after so many years," she formulated the query as she spoke, hesitating, "that - that there could be information of the War that has been lost in records?" She paused again before continuing and her companion allowed her to process as she spoke. "Such as the Nazi codes dad was still deciphering?"

"Undoubtedly," Choate nodded. "However, one would have to have a starting point. Allies. Axis Powers. Branch of service - such as the OSS."

"Oh," Gem nodded. "Mrs Brown ran that by you to ask if it was a request worth pursuing?"

"Not for that reason. Mrs Brown considered it a reasonable request in the event your search relates to Project CSU. I submitted the query to channels, but I do fear it could be many months before it is even considered for processing."

"Oh," Gem murmured, disappointment evident in her voice.

"Were I you, I would assume the reply was to the affirmative and carry on from there."

"I don't really know if it would lead anywhere," Gem hedged.

"Then store it mentally as affirmative in the event it would be useful in a theory," he suggested.

They were silent for a time when a vexing thought prompted another query from Gem.

"Mr Choate," she began, frowning, "what do you state in reports to Wyatt about my activities?"

"Destinations and times," he replied. "London War Museum, time in and time out. Photo shop, time in and time out."

"Not very detailed," Gem frowned, puzzled.

"Reference points."

In the event I am abducted, Gem decided. Lovely thought.

They stopped at the coffee shop for beverages to go, then exited the building, stepping to the side of the entrance. It was not a busy customer day at the museum, so they could speak freely without being overheard by the public entering and exiting the building.

"You said last week that Wyatt could be a dangerous man," Gem mused aloud.

"Indeed," Choate nodded. "Mr Grantham could ruin a person with one word or one stroke of a pen."

Not comforting words, Gem thought uneasily.

"And you are a crack shot," Mr Choate ventured," which would make you a dangerous woman to some people. Although you are likely a touch out of practice," he conceded.

A gun is quite different than a word or a pen!

"He had a brother," Gem said, not knowing why she mentioned the fact, other than she was so pleased she could talk to Family.

"James," Choate nodded. "Deceased. Mid-July this year."

Curiosity got the better of her. "Do you have profiles on Wyatt and James?"

"Technical Operations has files on many noteworthy people," Choate freely admitted. "Would you like to see the files on Wyatt Grantham and James Grantham Smythe?"

"You couldn't do that! You work for Wyatt!" Gem gasped.

"I am employed by the Agency first," he shook his head. "As are you. And you are NTK. If you want the files - just say the word."

Gem's eyes widened in astonishment. Spying on Wyatt ! Lord! If he discovered that she couldn't imagine his outrage. His fury on Wight would be miniscule compared to learning that Gem had spied on him - and on James. And oh how Wyatt hated spies!

Wyatt's likely rage aside, no she didn't want to see any files. James was dead. And there was no way possible that he was involved in Project CSU, or the disappearance of the Pilos and his beloved Gemmy. Wyatt certainly was not involved - otherwise he would know she was not Gemmy.

"No," Gem said firmly. "I do not wish to see the files. Ever!" At the very least she had to respect Wyatt's contract with Technical Operations.

"A wise decision," Choate agreed. "A person should not investigate a spouse without cause. I don't believe Wyatt Grantham has ever been a playboy. His reputation is stellar. As is yours," Choate complimented his companion. "Ethics. Morales. You two are quite the pair."

"Not a playboy per se," Gem observed. "But he does have a past."

"Good Lord, Gem, the man is thirty-four years old. Did you think he was a monk or a saint before he married you?" Choate's eyebrows lifted skeptically.

"No," Gem protested, more than a little embarrassed that she was having this conversation with anyone - especially Agency Family.

Choate finished his coffee and crushed the container in his fist. "I suggest this subject would be better discussed with ah - a woman - perhaps Mrs Brown, if you need an ear."

Gem shook her head. "Mrs Brown said weeks ago that I was out of Wyatt's league."

"I'm sure that was not a criticism of you, Gem," Choate replied with a small smile. "Nor is it necessarily a bad thing. I would say you are the perfect mate for Wyatt Grantham. He is a man who could properly appreciate having a 'Gem'," he winked. "And you will have a proper family again - not only the Agency."

Oh, you are so deluded about Wyatt and me, Gem sighed inwardly. Wyatt and a family. No, I do NOT think so.

"Chat over, Gem?" Choate inquired. "Where to next?"

"Oh! Lunch!" Gem looked at her watch. Half an hour. She'd best not be late again! "White Rose, with Wyatt."

"You'll make it," Mr Choate advised. "Don't speed!"

Gem arrived at the pub with two minutes to spare. She had kept him waiting once, she did not dare do so again. She was pleased that Wyatt arrived after her, yet on time.

"You are flushed, my dear," Wyatt observed, kissing her gently.

"I lost track of the time," she admitted. "I was at the war museum."

"Fascinating," Wyatt murmured, gazing down at her.

"It is," Gem agreed.

"I was referring to you," he said softly, holding her gaze as he leaned down to kiss her again. "My lovely wife spent the morning at the war museum," he chuckled. "My, you look luscious, sweetheart. Did you have an informative time at the museum?"

"Indeed," she murmured, noting that, as usual, he drew out her chair for her. His manners were always polished, even if his temper was not.

As Gem studied the menu, a notion struck her. "Latin phrases on an Italian menu?" she demanded. "Wouldn't the phrases have been in Italian?"

Wyatt laughed heartily. "I wondered when you would finally trip to that!"

The waitress took their order, then Gem pressed the issue. "Where did you learn the phrases?"

Wyatt shrugged. "I read Latin at school."

"Of course you did," she sighed. He was an accomplished man.

"It's so useful in everyday life," he said drolly, bringing a smile to her face.

"Why Latin?"

"It was a challenge."

"And you like challenges," Gem replied. Another fact she now knew about him. What did she know about Wyatt Grantham? He was vindictive, a great actor, his thoughts were rarely out of the bedroom, he pursued challenges, he was an excellent businessman, he read a great deal, he was a good cook. She would have to make a list when she got home. She should know her adversary - other than just physically.

As the thoughts streamed through her mind, Gem read the room, noting the women stealing glances at Wyatt. She wasn't the only person to note the glances. The male companions of the women in question, also noticed the looks directed at Wyatt. And their waitress, not the usual one at the pub, was just as obnoxious in her attention to him.

Wyatt had been sitting across the table from her, but he moved to the chair next to her to whisper in her ear. "Caeca invidia est."

"What?" Gem queried softly.

"Envy is blind."

"Ah."

"Amantes amentes. Lovers are lunatics," he lifted her hand to his lips and kissed her fingers.

Gem laughed. He was laying it on thick for the other women.

"What are your plans for this afternoon?" he inquired as their order was served.

"Unsure. You?"

"Meetings. All afternoon," Wyatt yawned.

Gem yawned also, as all yawns are communicative.

"You need more sleep at night," Wyatt declared.

"So do you," she lowered her voice to a whisper. "I suggest separate bedrooms."

Wyatt laughed so hard he nearly choked.

"Oh, my dear, you do amuse me!" His eyes twinkled. "I am tempted to cancel the meetings."

Know thy adversary. She couldn't wheedle information out of the M's because Wyatt would be furious. She refused to request the Agency files on Wyatt. That left the information gathering to her.

"We could walk along the Thames," she suggested.

The remark surprised Wyatt. What play was this? "Tempting, my sweet, but I must decline. Perhaps another day." She hadn't sought his company since before their wedding. A ploy for sure.

"Indeed," Gem accepted the rejection she had hoped would come.

She didn't know how to pass the afternoon, but she realized she did not want to immediately return to the Hall. Her reluctance was no reflection on Mrs M, but of her own frustration of feelings of confinement there.

She retraced her route to the photo shop, remembering she hadn't purchased film on her stop there that morning. A large paint shop was six blocks away so she included that on her list to select a dozen paint chip samples to stick to the wall in her office. And as she walked to the paint shop, she reflected on her chat with Mr Choate. Lord Wyatt Grantham. Well, it stood to reason. The man did have a Hall. She knew so little about him. She didn't even know if he had a colour preference- other than black for his suits. She knew his food dislikes. He preferred beer to wine, but would drink either; he preferred tea to coffee, but drank both; he had a tendency to speed when he was behind the steering wheel of a vehicle. He did not hunt or fish - but then when did he have time for either? - he always seemed to be working. He was used to giving orders. He seemed patient with everyone but her.

As usual, Gem could not pass a bookshop, wandering to the section on travel books. South East Asia. Mr Choate followed her, giving her a frown.

"Information on computer," he said in a low voice.

"Thought a book might spark something," Gem scowled. "Ah!" She back tracked to the war section and found two books on World War II in South East Asia.

"Good choice," Choate murmured.

She selected another on the history of the War in Australia. Mr Choate handed her one on the Philippines, another on the Japanese invasion of Hong Kong in December 1941.

Ping

Gem reached for her mobile then realized it was Mr Choate's mobile receiving a text.

"Entrenchment lifted," he murmured to her.

That was an afternoon brightener! However her quick smile faded as she saw a troubled look crease his forehead.

Ping

Her mobile this time. A text from Mr Choate.

'Philippine counter-agent dead- knifed.'

Gem looked at him, shaking her head.

'All other agents/couriers accounted for.'

'Okay.'

'Clear messages.'

She looked at him and nodded.

Feeling very subdued, Gem made her way to the counter and paid for her purchases. Mr Choate's time was too valuable to be tied up shadowing her. She texted him that she was returning to the Hall. He followed her to the second old stone bridge at Ticking Bottom, then turned his vehicle around and drove back to London.

Mrs M was preparing dinner. Gem set the table and cut up carrots for the stew that would simmer in the slow cooker until it was ready to be served. Gem poured wine for the housekeeper, a cup of tea for herself, and listened to Mrs M chat about the new barber joining the staff at the hair styling/barber shop, the new pizza cooker at the pub, and the new Christmas items arriving at the gift shop. Mrs Moody's health was deteriorating; it was only a matter of time.

"She's had a good life," Mrs M said firmly. "She raised her children right, all a credit to Mrs Moody and her late Mister. He was a fine man, he was. Her children are scattered all over the globe, save for Sam - he has the plumbing shop here in T.B.," she informed Gem. "Mr M says he does a right fine job of it. Sam did the alterations at Marigold when Mr W wanted the cottage improved before Jamie inherited. The housekeeper's eyes took on a sad look when she spoke of the younger Grantham. "It was to be a surprise for him."

Gem held her breath, feeling her presence was intruding on the other woman's thoughts. She was wary of making a comment lest it was thought she was pumping Mrs M for information.

The housekeeper shook off the sad thoughts and gave Gem a smile.

"Did you enjoy your day in the city, dear?" she queried.

"Yes. We had lunch at the White Rose," she felt she should supply some contribution to the chat. "Oh, and I got some more paint chip samples. I can't decide on a colour for the office wall."

"Live with the colours for a bit and one will catch your fancy. Unless you want to have stripes or perhaps a wall covering. The Mister is a dab hand at wallpapering."

"I hadn't considered paper," Gem admitted, but that seemed too much of a choice to make with her already crowded thoughts.

It was time for Mrs M's favorite telly program, so Gem excused herself to take a shower, a lengthy process as she washed and braided her hair in an intricate French braid which she hadn't worn in weeks.

Wyatt was in the bedroom when she finally left her bathroom, still wearing her dressing gown. He had obviously just finished his shower. And he was waiting for her.

"A beautiful respite to a long day," he said slowly, capturing her eyes with his.

"Mrs M has dinner prepared," Gem parried.

"I've sent the M's to the Crow for dinner. The stew is in the slow cooker," he advised as he walked around the bed to her.

Lord he was magnificent! Gem gazed at him as he slipped his hands inside her dressing gown.

Gem curled up in Auntie Jane's comfy chair to read the book on Australia during the War. Vera Lynn was soothing her with music, and Gem had a cup of hot chocolate on the table at her elbow. She took a deep breath as she opened the cover of the book, and caught the scent of Wyatt's cologne that lingered on her skin.

Well, she hadn't expected Wyatt was a saint or a monk when they married. But she couldn't help wondering how he had learned everything he knew. She had never had dinner served to her in bed before - except for the time she had flu - and that was only tea and toast served by her mum. Wyatt, dinner, and Wyatt again. She would imagine he was the definition of the word libido. Just thinking of the evening hours let the butterflies loose inside her.

Concentrate on work! Not on Wyatt! She would think of him during the day however. Wyatt and cathedrals were an odd mix.

Name and dates of the Agency staff at the Hong Kong embassy.

Mrs Brown, Harry and Mr Denton had all left the embassy when Hong Kong had reverted to China in 1997. Mum and dad had left years earlier. Mr White and Mr Portermann had both remained at the embassy until 1999.

Gem was curious of the dates when the seven had begun working for the Agency. And Mr Cawley would have his mobile beside him. She texted the query and made another cup of hot chocolate while she waited his reply.

Ping

'Mrs Brown 1997, Harry, Denton same. Lawson, Forrester 1985. White, Portermann 1995.'

They had all immediately started at the Agency directly after leaving the embassy, except for Mr White and Mr Portermann, who had worked for the Agency while still being posted to Hong Kong.

'Why White and Portermann both with Agency and embassy to 1999?'

'White setting up new computer systems Agency and embassy. Portermann setting up security Hong Kong and revamping Agency same.'

'Spread rather thin.'

'Lawson, Agency Security First Assistant 1985-1990. Forrester, Agency Computer Security Analyst 1985-1999. Forrester Agency cryptanalyst 1985 -. Lawson courier 1990-.'

Information Gem had not known previously of her parents until this moment. Dad had been an Agency computer security analyst and a cryptanalyst for fourteen years, while still living in London and then through the move to Australia.

Bless the lifted Entrenched!

Her parents had gone from the embassy to the Agency.

'White embassy Computer Communications Director 1983-1999, Agency Computer Communications Director 1983-. Portermann embassy Security Director 1983-1999, Agency Security Director 1983-.'

There was a short pause then another text.

'Denton embassy courier 1983-1997, Agency agent 1997- 'retired' this year. Read and destroy all messages.'

Gem scrolled, reading and committing the messages to memory, then deleted all.

'Done. Agency spread thin over years?'

'Once had twenty couriers. Procedures refined, staff reassigned.'

"Reassigned?"

'Charley's Pub, camera shop, nightclubs, airports. Part of Eyes and Ears of U.K.'

She thought she would give another query a shot. It could only be refused.

'Blank ever posted to Hong Kong embassy?'

There was a long pause. Gem returned to her book and a third cup of hot chocolate, and pushed the start button on the cd player yet again.

Ping

'Yes.'

Gem nearly dropped her mobile. Mr Cawley violated serious, MOST SERIOUS Agency SOP!

'Delete query and reply immediately!'

Gem's fingers shook as she cleared the messages.

'Done!'

She could scarcely breathe. Why had he given her a fact reply instead of the regular ??? or DO NOT ASK scolding?

Had his reply been cleared by Mrs Brown or was he putting his neck on Bloody Mary's chopping block again?

Ping

'Mrs Brown sends regards.'

'And mine to her!'

Gem cleared the screen. Mrs Brown, the Lark, had cleared the query at four o'clock in the morning!

Chills coursed through Gem's body. The Acting Director of the Agency had violated VITAL Agency SOP for Gem! This was a frightening issue!

The most important question was why had Mrs Brown done so?

Gem was NTK. But she wasn't cleared to receive information on Paul Andriani!

What was going down at the Agency or - and - the Network that persuaded Mrs Brown to act as she had?

'Why did you send last data?'

'So ordered. You are NTK.'

'Since when does NTK include Blank?'

'For this one query apparently.'

'Many thanks!'

'Delete messages!'

'Immediately.'

'Goodnight, Gem.'

'Goodnight.'

Gem started pacing, then made still another cup of hot chocolate to take off the chill the text messages had caused.

Ping

A message from Mr Choate! At this hour of the morning!

'Tea/coffee. Half ten.'

'Okay. Why are you up at this hour of the morning? Do Agency staff ever sleep?'

'Look who's asking the question! Go to bed, Gem!'

'And you!'

'Clear all messages!'

'To be sure!'

What the hell was going on? Had the Entrenched and then the lifting of it crashed an Agency information dam?

The activity this morning had pushed the Philippine counter-agent's death from her thoughts. She couldn't allow that to happen again.

Gem washed her cup, turned off the office lights, cd player, and went to bed. She was exhausted and hopefully she could shut down her brain and recharge for two hours.

"Do you ever think about anything other than -" Gem started to say, but his lips interrupted her query.

"You didn't complain last night," Wyatt murmured.

"An observation is not necessarily a complaint you -"

"Observation noted, now hush," he again cut off her words.

Gem was relaxed by the time she and Wyatt went down to the breakfast room.

It was Gem's turn to fetch the beverages that morning, then she and Mr Choate walked down the block from the coffee shop to the green space where they had previously chatted.

"Why were you asking about Gemmy having assignments to Barcelona?" Choate asked, his face serious.

Not a routine query. Be careful. Let no cogs slip, Gem urged herself. "Gemmy told me - that- that - night-"

"I understand," Choate said quietly.

Gem took a deep breath. She hadn't talked about that night to anyone since the last debriefing in early June.

"She told me she was going to retire. She was going to purchase a flat in Barcelona. I was simply curious about Barcelona - if she had had recent assignments there."

"Barcelona was my turf."

"I realize that. I wondered if she had covered any of your assignments - or if she had ever been there on neutral ground," Gem said hesitantly. "Just searching for any information about her."

Choate nodded. "As close as the two of you were, there are things she didn't know about you or you about her."

Gem nodded, sighing. His words were so true.

"I can't imagine how deep is the pain you suffer. I don't know if you will ever have all the answers to all your questions. But I hope you will," Choate said quietly.

"We'll find them," Gem insisted.

"Indeed. Then you will have your family's items from the warehouse. Perhaps then you'll have other answers."

They each reflected on the conversation. Then Choate spoke again.

"Now, why the queries of Geneva?"

Gem explained the incident of meeting Jonny's parents at the pub in Inverness.

"Damn! That was a shocker! Split moment thinking with Mr Grantham present," Choate exhaled sharply. "Fortunately you also sketch. Difficult to explain if you couldn't draw a straight line."

"Indeed," Gem agreed, pausing while a couple stopped in the green space to tuck a pink blanket on a baby in her pram.

"Only I can't understand why Gemmy was in Geneva. Definitely a puzzler," Choate frowned. "There's no information at the Agency connecting Gemmy and Geneva."

"And her passport is - with her."

"The replacement passport."

Gem nearly choked on her tea. "Just so." And wasn't that a stabbing reminder of her frustrating daily life with Dr Jekyll!

Wyatt was right. She was adept at lying. And she was lying to Mr Choate - Family.

Mr Choate didn't continue the topic so Gem took the lull in the chat for her own purposes.

"What is happening, Mr Choate? You know of my query to Mr Cawley." She didn't need to be specific. She could only be referring to the one of Paul Andriani.

"And the reply," Choate said crisply.

"But why? Such information has never been released to me on NTK."

"Anomalies happen. But only very rarely, be advised," he warned firmly.

"But why? Agency SOP!"

"There is that," Choate conceded. "Mrs Brown has the authority to over-ride SOP and in this instance she chose to do so. She advised me she was doing so."

"I shouldn't have put forth the query so early in the morning," Gem said guiltily.

"It wasn't a problem. We were in a meeting," Choate replied.

"At that hour?"

"It was later in Singapore."

"Oh yes. Much later," Gem agreed. About noon then.

They held their conversation again as an elderly woman stopped near them to adjust her girdle.

"We need a meeting place," Gem murmured.

"Charley's. Camera shop."

"Camera shop. I don't know about meeting at a pub at this hour of the morning. It would look rather badly on your report to Wyatt," Gem grimaced.

"Howard's Bookshop then," Choate suggested.

A bookshop - lovely! "I don't know about a Howard's Bookshop."

"A very recent addition to our Agency retail line. He's not really ready for customers yet, but he'll let us in. Use the bookshop staff parking area."

"I am meeting Wyatt for lunch at noon. Shall we go to Howard's after that?" she suggested.

Choate nodded and Gem started walking to the restaurant - Chinese today - Wyatt had suggested at breakfast that morning. She was nearly at the restaurant when her mobile rang. It was Wyatt saying that his meeting was running over and he would not be able to make their luncheon date. It was a cheery call for

Gem. She texted the information to Mr Choate and altered her route to the bookshop, stopping at the photo shop first to pick up the Winchester photos.

Howard welcomed them through the door, offering tea, coffee, and fresh rolls from a bakery down the street. Gem and Mr Choate accepted the beverages and rolls and settled at the rear of the shop on a large sofa. They didn't have to read the area since Howard was the only other person in the shop and he was 'retired' Agency.

"The Philippine agent," Gem said softly.

"Found in Hong Kong. He was identified by his fingerprints."

"Similar to the others?"

"Stabbed in the heart," Choate responded.

"All knifed from the front? They all saw their attacker then?" Gem murmured.

"Yes."

"Same knife?"

"It is believed so. None of the bodies were in very good condition by the time they were found," Choate winced.

"And what else?"

"Identification missing. Killed where they were found, usually abandoned buildings."

"All had the same Agency contact?"

"Yes."

Paul Andriani.

"Do you know where the contact is then?"

"No. He's been out of touch for a fortnight.

"He wasn't cleared then. Why was Entrenched lifted if he wasn't cleared?"

"Harry cleared him," Choate said with a shrug.

Another violation of Agency SOP.

"Why did Harry to that?"

"I can't speak for Harry."

Gem was out of questions for the time being.

She strolled through the shop checking the selections of the various sections. The front of the shop had new stock, used books lined the shelves at the rear of the shop where customers would be able to settle in chairs and sofas to read or chat, and enjoy the beverages Howard planned to provide. Gem found a well-thumbed book of birds, another of flowers. It would be a good read, and then she would be able to identify all the birds and flowers she could see from her office window.

As he had previously, Mr Choate followed the Defender to the second old stone bridge, then turned his vehicle about and left Ticking Bottom.

Gem had reached the Hall when she realized that Mr Cawley had provided information on all Agency/Embassy staff members except for Mrs Brown and Harry. She would request that information during the dark hours the next morning.

She didn't have any reason to go to the city for the remainder of the week but it was tempting to think of driving in just to fill the hours of her days. She could only haunt so many bookshops a week, and she couldn't think of any books she needed or wanted; she already had many to read on the War - and she should be concentrating on them.

Dozens of photos of Winchester Cathedral, and rolls of film, colour and black and white, would occupy some of her hours during the day and evening. She had reading and sorting to do in the dark hours, and Mr Cawley to text if she had queries.

Mrs M was leaving the Hall as Gem walked from the garage to the kitchen door. "Today is Sam's day to sit with his mum," she explained to Gem, "but he got called to an emergency plumbing disaster. Mr W knows I'm going to sit with Mrs Moody. Dinner is in the fridge, instructions on the counter. Mr W will be late for dinner, just keep his food warm in the cooker for him."

"Yes, ma'am," Gem nodded politely.

The housekeeper walked down the drive, then turned back to wave to Gem.

Lovely! Wyatt wouldn't be back for hours, she thought eagerly. The house was hers to explore alone! The photos and books were left on the office counter. Gem dutifully read the dinner instructions, then climbed the stairs.

Mr Choate's queries of Barcelona and Geneva spurred Gem to again search James's bedroom. She didn't have to listen for the Jag this time which was very helpful since the windows of the Hall were now closed to the chill of the autumn days.

The door knob turned easily in her hand. She was rather surprised that Wyatt didn't keep the door locked. The room needed a good dusting, indicating that Mrs M hadn't recently breached the sanctity of James's room to dust and hoover.

The bathroom was empty of personal items. Clothes filled the dressing room to the left of the bathroom and the door to the hall; clothes that had obviously belonged to James as they would be too small for Wyatt's frame; clothes obviously to be worn in a warmer climate, shorts, tees, four pairs of sandals, three windcheaters. Gem searched the pockets of the garments, but all were empty, bearing not so much as a scrap of paper.

Gemmy's clothes and those of their parents had been searched the morning the Pilos had gone missing; Gem recalled the packers using clear zipper-lock plastic bags for all personal items, including books and clothing; hundreds of clear bags, now stored at the warehouse, safe from dust and deterioration; protected inventory that hopefully would one day be returned to her.

James had a large collection of art books and Gem skimmed each, hoping she would find a note or receipt that might provide a clue to Geneva. She replaced every book in its proper place, and a bit dust-free, however the dust would soon return to cover her search.

The shelves held unfired pottery objects - pots, small figures, empty frames; perhaps work from art classes from years ago. The paintings and sketches on the walls had been beautifully matted and framed. Gem wondered if James had had the art framed, or if Wyatt had done so after his brother's death. The framed art was signed and dated by the artist. Oh what talent James had had!

Gem had started at the bathroom working her way to the left and thus was startled to come upon a distressed wood cabinet that had not been in the room the first time she had searched it. The cabinet was wide and deep with fourteen shallow drawers. The cabinet looked to be an antique, sturdily built of worm wood. Wyatt must have put the cabinet in the room one day when she was out for a walk, she decided, because she would have heard him moving the piece of furniture had she been in her office. Or perhaps he had moved it the night she had had the stiff neck and had fallen asleep on the chesterfield in the great room.

The drawer handles of the cabinet were of pounded metal, cold to the touch as she slid open the top drawer. Sketches. She pulled out, scanned the contents, then closed each of the drawers. She started with the top drawer again, gently lifting the large top sheets of drawing paper to see James's subjects, checking each drawer carefully, looking for sketches of Gemmy. There were no sketches of her. Wyatt had said Gemmy had sketched James. Where were those sketches? Perhaps Wyatt had only been looking for a reaction.

Either James was a person who did not accumulate possessions, or if he did they were stored somewhere else. The desk, she remembered, held photo albums. Apparently James had been well traveled if he had taken many of the photos in the albums, Gem mused. Bavaria, Austria , France, Germany; a number of shots Gem was certain had been taken outside of Copenhagen, Florence, Rome, the Seychelles, Cairo, Crete, on and on.

It was near the end of the fifth album that Gem found a photo that shook her nerves.

The photo had been taken in what appeared to be a courtyard, an excellent night shot, the glow of light from an open window, and Gemmy's full profile: the black dress Gem now wore, the onyx and diamond earrings clearly visible, her hair braided as Gem usually wore hers. Gemmy was gazing at something beyond the left edge of the photo.

Gem slipped the photo from the album sleeve turning it around, hoping to see a date and place notation. There was a date and she had to decipher the words; James had written it by hand - it had to be James because it was not Gemmy's excellent script: 14 May, My Beloved Gem.

Blast! Wyatt had not mentioned this photo - only the ones of Gemmy and Paul Andriani/John Staunton in the gardens - whichever ones they were in Barcelona. Had Wyatt even seen this photo? If Gem took it, would he know that it was missing? Had he ever paged through the albums?

Gem sniffed the air- a faint scent of James's cologne - the scent Wyatt said Gemmy had given to James. The cologne Wyatt wore everyday - to annoy Gem. She hadn't noticed the scent when she had entered the room. And now she had a horrid, sinking feeling. As she set the album on the desk, Wyatt spoke from the doorway, his voice brittle as thin ice.

"Did you find what you were searching for, my dear?" He walked across the room to stand behind her.

Count to twenty. Control. Count to twenty. Control, Mrs Brown's suggestions rang in her ears. She had reached eighteen on her second count when Wyatt took the photo from her hand.

"A most brilliant photo, sweetheart," Wyatt turned it over and read the words aloud in a cutting tone. "The day prior to 'Beloved Gem' flying to Australia to finish her thesis. Or was it flying to Geneva to - what?" He slipped the photo into the pocket of his suit coat, then placed his hands on her shoulders, holding her against him. "Were you searching for the other photos perhaps? Or for your passports? But that would be foolish wouldn't it? You know they are all locked away."

His breath was hot on her neck, his body rigid with anger.

"Or perhaps you were missing James all of a sudden, wanting to feel close to him." He slid his hands down her body to rest upon her waist, resting his cheek against hers. "You obviously don't miss his love-making. You can't miss that which you never had."

Gem successfully pushed away his hands but he folded his arms around her shoulders, resting them across her breasts.

"Were you looking for the lovely nude sketches he did of you? I'm having the sketches matted and framed for our bedroom. They were going to be my wedding gift to you, but the framers simply don't seem to want to return the portraits to me."

"You bastard!" Gem pulled away, spinning around to face him, her eye blazing. What had Gemmy been thinking!

"Touchy," Wyatt said dryly, then his tone became brusque. "James couldn't understand why you refused to have photos taken of you, or to let him sketch you. You were such a private person that way. Aside from the passport and the snaps of you with Staunton, this was the only photo he had of you," he patted his coat pocket. "He didn't think you knew that this photo existed."

Gemmy hadn't known, because the photo still existed outside of the Agency warehouse. She breathed a sigh of relief, but she was still furious with Wyatt's jest about the nude sketches of Gemmy. Wyatt knew about Gemmy and James's relationship. Gem only knew what she had heard from Wyatt. She had to tiptoe through a minefield every time Wyatt mentioned James - and his relationship with 'her' - Gemmy - so Blasted confusing!

"Whom did you torture before you met me? You're so accomplished at your insidious methods," Gem demanded heatedly.

"Hmm," Wyatt mocked her. "James dated Ashley, charming girl who usually had her head in the clouds, but she was very sweet. Celia - pretty, considerate. She realized she cared for Deborah - I believe her name was Deborah - more than she cared for James. We attended their wedding - a lovely couple. Francie, vivacious, excellent tennis player. Polly, a bit of a know-it-all, but still also considerate and very polite. Lucy, perky, a chatterbox, but very kind. James parted friends with all those lovely young ladies."

Gem glared at him, wishing the Agency had permitted her to keep her pistol.

"And then you entered his life. No. - No. There was no one before you. You sow, you reap, you clever girl you," he finished dryly. "Want to continue this discussion or shall we move on to the next? Whom did you torture before James? How many men? How many since James - but you might not have had time for many before you met me."

Before she could find her voice to verbally scald him, he pulled her over to and down on the bed.

"Now you're cranky! Shall I relax you? This isn't after all, the bed you didn't share with James. That is still in the flat at Barcelona. We could go there for a second honeymoon, perhaps in early November. Would you like that, my dear? To go see the flat again - the one you just had to have for the three of you?" He leaned down to kiss her, but Gem scrambled up and off the bed; he caught her wrist in a firm grip.

"If you tell me what you were searching for, Gem, perhaps I could help you find it," Wyatt said quietly, then released his hold on her.

He watched as the violet eyes changed from fury to the haunted look.

Without saying a word, Gem fled the room, seeking solace in her office to control her temper.

Lord! he could get vicious, Gem shuddered as she paced the floor. But she had chanced his temper by entering James's room. And she had been searching the room. She couldn't very well deny that fact. She had violated James's possessions in Wyatt's home, and she had no right to be in there. She understood Wyatt's anger; and perhaps she should feel guilty of her actions - but she didn't. She now knew that there was nothing in the room that indicated the reason Gemmy had gone to Geneva. And she had found that snap of Gemmy. Which was now no longer in James's room; she knew it wouldn't be returned to the photo album. She wished she could have kept the photo. ONLY SHE knew it wasn't a photo of her. She could have had it for a remembrance.

That man positively brought out the worst in her! She had never had a temper! Nor had Gemmy. Having a temper was not an advisable trait for a courier. How many times had she heard Mrs Brown or Harry say those same words to couriers who had reacted poorly in a frustrating situation. Lose your temper, lose your advantage, was a well-worn phrase at the Agency. Having spirit was one thing; having a temper was a different matter.

Gem stopped pacing and sniffed the air of the office. Chicken. Wyatt had pre-heated the cooker and put in the pan of chicken. He had been at the Hall for at least a quarter of an hour before she realized he was in the house. And how long had he watched her searching through the photo albums in James's room?

Blast! She went to the kitchen to check on the bird. It had a while yet to bake. She made a cup of tea, sipping it as she put out the tableware; and once the table was set, she would put Dvorak on the cd player, hoping the music would calm her jangled nerves.

Gem had neglected to hang her windcheater in the mud room. She took the Defender keys from a pocket, tossed them to the counter, and gasped as the keys hit the computer scanner and sailed against and then through a pane of glass and out into the garden. She whirled about as Wyatt chuckled from the doorway.

"You could try to do that a hundred times and you would miss every time."

"I'm sorry!" Gem said helplessly.

"Let's hope that was your best shot of the day," Wyatt grinned. "It's nothing, my dear, other than extremely amusing. Mr M will fix the window tomorrow. We'll stuff a towel in the space for tonight."

"I'll pay for the glass," Gem insisted.

"Nonsense. Mr M has stacks of glass panes in his workshop. Becton has kicked up many a rock through these windows over the years with his lawn mower. You check on dinner, I'll clear away the broken glass, find something to plug the hole and then locate your keys. Looks like rain tonight," he glanced out the window. "We don't want you taking on water over night."

Very decent of him, Gem reflected as she opened the cooker door. And bless Mr Becton and his lawn mower for setting precedence breaking windows.

She heard the strains of Elgar shortly before Wyatt entered the kitchen to carve the chicken. Elgar; a calming choice, Gem mused.

They spoke very little during dinner, but Wyatt didn't mention her search of his brother's bedroom, nor did he refer to the photo Gem had found in the photo album.

They had nearly completed the washing up after dinner when Wyatt's mobile rang, as it did so often at that time of day.

"Go," Gem mouthed to him.

She made a cup of hot chocolate to drink as she sorted through the photos of Winchester Cathedral. Over sixty shots were crisp, the lighting exactly what she wanted. Gem organized the snaps by specific views, and exterior and interior. It would take hours deciding exterior shots alone. But! She definitely had choices this time. And she knew she would have some framed for the office wall.

Gem emptied the dishwasher, eliminated four exterior photos from the group of snaps and put Edith Piaf on the cd player. She was thinking of making a cup of tea when Wyatt walked into the office, mobile to his ear. He handed her a slip of paper with three words on it: GO TO BED! He stepped out of the office, waiting and watching until she shut down her computer and turned off the music.

Nine o'clock! she groaned peevishly as she climbed the stairs and he returned to the library. She grumbled through her shower, "Ogres belong beneath bridges." At least her day was ending. It was the dark hours she had to face next. She lay awake for a few minutes, thinking back to Wyatt's horrid manner that afternoon. He had calmed down rather quickly. He had a very short fuse where she was involved. And he had been very kind and helpful when she had broken the window pane in her office. He certainly puzzled her, she yawned, and closed her eyes.

First query on her mind. Mrs Brown. And Harry! Gem pulled her mobile out of her dressing gown pocket. Mr Cawley would be awake!

'Mrs Brown, embassy post to 1997? Agency post 1997-? Harry embassy post to 1997? Agency post 1997-?'

Hot chocolate and Vera Lynn time while she waited for a reply. She either had to purchase another tin of hot chocolate mix or drink more tea. However, she was beginning to prefer hot chocolate; perhaps she could find the mix in T.B. - Now when had she started thinking of the village in local vernacular?

Ping

'Brown, embassy courier 85-88, embassy agent 88-94, SEA net supervisor 94-97, Agency Dir 97-2008. Retired - HA! Agency Acting Dir current. Read and delete.'

And so she did.

'Done.'

'Harry, embassy courier 84-85, embassy agent 85-95, SEA net supervisor 95-97, Agency First Assist Dir 97-2008, Agency Dir 2008-. Read and delete.'

'Done.'

An Agency Director and an Agency Acting Director concurrent. Curious that.

That took care of the postings to the embassy and same current staff at the Agency.

'All couriers and agents accounted for as of now?'

'No.'

'Who is missing?'

'Unclear.'

'Worrisome.'

'Possibly. Don't lose any sleep over it. Could be an error. Has been known to happen.'

'Okay.'

'Sorting?'

'Gathering information.'

'Okay. Goodnight.'

'Goodnight.'

Gem deleted the messages and reached for her book. Australia. The War years. Were there any chocolate biscuits in the kitchen? she suddenly wondered. She searched the cupboards but couldn't find any, so she added the item to Mrs M's shop list.

Australia, Vera Lynn, hot chocolate, and no chocolate biscuits.

Ping

'Couriers/agents accounted for.'

'Thank you!'

'An error, thank Heaven!'

Gem deleted the messages.

Harry, Mrs Brown, mum, dad, Mr Denton, Mr White, Mr Portermann. They all must have known each other extremely well, considering how long they worked in the same two circles. She wanted to ask the dates and job descriptions of Paul Andriani, but that was a bit pushy since she did get an SOP violation answer on the embassy posting for him. She would wait awhile before she pushed her luck again.

She read for an hour, then set aside the book to allow her memory a break from concentrating.

Paul Andriani. What a fascinating, clever, creative man! She wanted so much to know more about his Agency and embassy activities. What kind of undercover network did he have? John Staunton was known in unsavory circles worldwide. How extensive his private network must be! Four courier and agent contacts of his were dead. I wouldn't wish to continue being one of his contacts, Gem shivered. Establishing the replacement couriers and agents was Harry's job but - a BIG BUT - Paul Andriani would have to approve Harry's decisions, for it was he who ultimately was placing his life in their hands - and their lives in his hands.

The photo of Gemmy. Was there any way Wyatt could use that snap against her? She didn't think so, but she couldn't afford to underestimate him. He did have it as a means to torment her. Had he actually missed seeing that photo in the album when he cleared James's flat? Had he seen the photo and not recognized Gemmy? Had the snap been put in the album as a trap for her? If he had known the photo was there, and then had discovered it to be missing, he would have known Gem had been in James's room. Thus she had searched the room - for whatever reason. Which was what had happened. Only she was caught in the act - this time.

Bed. Sleep. Rest brain, she moaned, as she climbed the stairs to the master suite.

Chapter Eighteen

Wyatt was very relaxed that morning, Gem thought dryly a few short hours after the dark hours had ended. But he was always relaxed at breakfast, except for the past Saturday morning when simply waking beside him had made her grumpy.

Mrs M was her usual cheery self and tutted about the broken window in the office, assuring Gem that the Mr would fix it right as new, and that Gem had a ways to go to meet the gardener's score for broken windows at the Hall.

Gem fled to her office after breakfast as Wyatt prepared to leave for the city.

"You aren't driving in today?" he asked from the doorway.

"No," Gem shook her head, slipping photos from the shop packet. He was still there, she sighed, grudgingly turning around to face him.

"We have theatre tickets for Friday evening," he informed her. "You'll need a dress - do not wear the black one again."

She should have seen that order coming.

"Formal, semi-formal?" she queried reluctantly.

"Somewhere in between. And no cleavage," he warned.

"I don't have to worry about that," Gem muttered, turning back to her photos.

"Nonsense," he said smoothly. "You have a perfect figure. And exquisite legs."

"Thank you," Gem said hesitantly.

"You are welcome, my dear. Now. Are you driving to the city?"

"I had best," Gem conceded. She had no idea what he expected her to wear.

"I'll alert Mr Choate. Hat, phone," he reminded her. "You have your credit card. I have meetings today, but if you need additional funds, ring me and I will arrange to cover your purchases."

Gem nodded as she slipped the photos back into the packet. "Thank you." There was no point in repeating that she didn't want his money. She would manage perfectly well on her own.

She went to the shop where she had purchased the blouse for Mrs M, and explained her needs to the shop assistant.

"Colour?" the young woman queried.

"I haven't a clue," Gem admitted.

"How tall is your husband?"

"Very."

The shop assistant smiled and went through a door at the back of the shop, returning a minute later with another young woman, who studied Gem from head to toe. The second woman then, wordlessly, left again through the same door, returning with a long gown draped over her arms. Obviously this was the sister who was the designer. The shop assistant wore her black hair long and straight with a chopped fringe. The designer wore her black hair styled in a dramatic angular cut coming to points at her cheeks, a long V in the back and a sleek fringe about her eyes. They were obviously sisters and seemed to communicate to each other with looks rather than words.

The gown, a knit fabric, was a blue - so deep it was nearly black; it had a high collar, wrist length sleeves, and it would cling to every inch of Gem's body.

"Oh my," Gem said doubtfully.

"Try it on," the designer insisted. "What size shoe?" and nodded at Gem's reply, as the assistant led Gem to an alterations room.

The gown was lined with a wispy net which would prevent embarrassing static cling to Gem's legs when she walked, Eda, the shop assistant explained. Her sister, Ora, was very careful about preventing such situations when one was dressed to impress. Ora appeared with a pair of shoes dyed to match the fabric of the gown. Gem frowned slightly at the three inch heels, but agreed with the designer that the heels were a must.

Ora walked behind Gem showing her how to wear her hair, braiding half-way down each side then tucking into a smooth horizontal roll above the nap of her neck. Eda grabbed shears and slightly styled Gem's fringe. Then Ora left the room and returned with stud earrings.

"Light rose lipstick," Ora advised, producing a small clutch shoulder bag to compliment the gown.

"Brilliant!" Gem smiled. This was the place to shop! She waved Mr Choate into the shop for a man's opinion.

"Family friend," she whispered to the young women.

"What do you think?" Gem slowly turned around so he could view the entire effect.

Mr Choate studied her as Ora had. "It's killing a fly with an elephant rifle." He nodded. "Yes."

He remained in the shop while Gem changed into her skirt and tee, and called Eda over to a display stand, arguing with the shop assistant until Gem and Ora emerged from the alteration room.

"Why are you two arguing?" Gem asked, as Eda came to the counter to process the sale, including frillies dyed to match the gown.

"The prices should be at least double what they are," Choate declared firmly.

Gem looked at the tags on the items she was purchasing. "Oh, dear yes," she murmured, thinking of the quality of items she and Gemmy had purchased in Rome and Paris. "At least double," she agreed reaching for a pen to correct the prices on the tags.

Ora handed Gem a hair slide, indicating she put it above the centre of the roll when she arranged her hair.

Choate then led Ora to the front of the shop, suggesting she put the more expensive items towards the rear of the shop.

He's stuck in detective mode, Gem chuckled to herself. He must be so bored shadowing me every day.

Eda had placed the gown in a long zippered garment bag with the shop's name stenciled down the side. "Thank you," she beamed at Gem, thrilled at the now very prosperous sale. "You'll come back," she urged.

"Most definitely," Gem nodded, leaving the shop, coaxing Mr Choate to resume his paid profession.

"They'll do fine if they make a few adjustments," Choate nodded.

"Indeed," Gem agreed. "I am finished for today, Mr Choate, except for a tin of chocolate biscuits, and hot chocolate mix."

"Shop down the street," he pointed to their right.

Gem set aside the book, gently rubbing her eyes. The Aussies were brilliant, and the book on Australia during the War was fascinating. She closed her eyes, leaning her head back against the chair. The reading. All she had read and what good was it? It didn't bring her any closer to Gemmy, their parents and Mr Portermann. The reading was transference - filling her mind with information as she procrastinated on the original search. The books had been a balm, an excuse to prevent her from admitting she was as lost in her search as the Pilos was lost in the world.

The books were a balm to help her bear her relationship with Wyatt

She needed to get back to sorting. She didn't know where to start.

Hot chocolate and chocolate biscuits, Vera Lynn's music, and pacing.

Why was Paul Andriani in Barcelona last May? Well, the obvious - he was working. And Gemmy was there because of James. Why would an undercover agent and a courier acknowledge each other in a public place when they weren't on assignment? Gemmy couldn't have contacted him; Paul Andriani had to have instigated the contact. And she couldn't ask the Agency if he had been in Barcelona. If the Agency knew that he was in that city - and if Gem asked the query, the Agency would want to know the reason she posed the question. He could have been anywhere in the world and she would have asked of that specific city. No- she couldn't go that route.

Barcelona was Mr Choate's previous territory, and she couldn't ask him if he knew if Paul Andriani was in Barcelona last May. The date on the snap from the album was 14 May. Wyatt had said 'Gem' had left James the next day. So when had James taken the photos of Gemmy and John Staunton? Gemmy had her passport with her, so even the Agency might not have been apprised of the date Gemmy had gone to Barcelona. And the Agency wouldn't have known when she had left that city to travel to Australia.

And Geneva. Geneva was a definite clue.

Because -

Gem made another cup of hot chocolate. Since when had she switched from tea to hot chocolate?

Because - There was no reason for Gemmy to be in Geneva. But she had been there. So there had to be a very important reason for her to be in Geneva.

It had to be 15 May. Was she there only that day? There had been no receipts from Geneva in the Agency warehouse. If she had stayed overnight there would have been a hotel receipt - that could still be in Gemmy's handbag - on the Pilos.

Gem couldn't very well ring hotels in Geneva checking on a receipt because Gemmy Lawson no longer existed. She didn't want to put a name in the air that could only be verified as an alias traced now to Gem - as Wyatt assumed Gemma Lawson to be - Gem's alias. - There was logic in that thought somewhere.

Was the missing Pilos linked to the deaths of the SEA counter-couriers and counter-agents? She texted a thought to Mr Cawley.

'Any suspects in SEA courier/agents deaths?'

Gem pushed the start button on the cd player. It was now habit to do so.

'No.'

'Okay.'

'What do you have for us Gem?'

'Sorry. Can't think of a single thing.'

'Still sorting?'

'Yes.'

'Good.'

'Any new information of any kind?'

'No. Go back to work!'

'Night.'

'Night.'

She made a cup of tea, regretting having done so, because it wasn't hot chocolate.

She paced the floor, letting her mind wander, trying to shake lose some of her thought processes.

Ora and Eda's shop was brilliant! The gown was gorgeous. The shop had been the highlight of her day, and then she had shopped for the hot chocolate and biscuits, and come directly back to T. B., to free up Mr Choate for more important work for T.O. and the Agency.

Mrs M had insisted on making a sandwich and hot chocolate for Gem. The window in the office had been repaired, and Gem had spent the afternoon sorting snaps of Winchester Cathedral, eliminating five exterior photos. There was no point reworking the text until she had selected the final photos she would use for the chapter.

Wyatt had spent the evening working in the library while Gem had stayed in her office. He had delivered another note to her at nine o'clock, while he listened to whatever was happening at the other end of his mobile line. The man was rarely ever away from work.

Why disrupt the SEA Network? If one had MADE the couriers and agents, why not use that knowledge to disrupt the Network rather than kill the staff? Naturally the staff would be replaced, so the disruption would only be temporary.

Gem pulled her mobile from her pocket again.

'Murder Network staff to sneak in a mole or sleeper? Or there is a mole or sleeper already in the SEA Network.'

She had to stop eating the chocolate biscuits or she wouldn't fit the dress come Friday night.

'Interesting thought. Will pass along to Mrs Brown and Choate.'

'Harry still unavailable?'

'To everyone but Mrs B and Choate.'

At least he was available to someone in the Agency. She had no need to contact Harry directly.

Wyatt's late hours did not diminish his appetite, Gem mused a few hours later as she showered. He was exhausting.

"Are you going to London today?" he called to her from his dressing room while she was smoothing the bedcovers.

"Not today," Gem replied. She would give Mr Choate a break - a concept she would not share with Wyatt.

He was tying his tie as he walked into the bedroom. "If your plans change alert Mr Choate," Wyatt said abruptly.

Lord! he looked so very handsome! Gem stared at him, butterflies flying free inside her, and she had to fight the impulse to -

"Really, my dear," Wyatt gave her an amused look. "Shall I delay my meeting this morning?"

"Certainly not," Gem blushed. "You're already running late because - well because -"

"Yes," he nodded, his voice suddenly husky. "I neglected you again last night. I shall try not to make that a habit." He took a step towardss her.

"I just finished dressing," she protested, shaking her head. "Have your breakfast. Go to work."

"I'll delay work for you, but not for breakfast," he teased, giving her a long kiss.

"Your mind is always in bed," Gem accused.

"And where was your mind just now?" He gave her a quick second kiss. "Later!" he promised.

Gem ate her breakfast in the kitchen while Mrs M did the washing up. The housekeeper wasn't pleased that Mr W had rushed off without breakfast, but she could imagine why he was behind schedule that morning, seeing the dreamy look in the young woman's eyes. The honeymoon continued, the housekeeper smiled to herself; she was certain being married to Gem was helping to ease Mr W's pain of losing Jamie.

"What are your plans for today, dear?" Mrs M queried, finally drawing the young woman's attention.

Gem stirred from her reverie. What was wrong with her? She couldn't get her mind out of the bedroom! She shook herself. "Nothing eventful," she replied. "Would you like some help with the housework?"

"Dusting or hoovering?"

"We'll flip a coin," Gem suggested, drawing the latter, which included dusting mopping the stone floors as well as hoovering the rugs. Mrs M started the dusting and Gem followed her from room to room, wondering if they would include James's room. She rather doubted it but the room did need cleaning.

When the ground floor was finished they broke for lunch, then started the first floor. Gem cleaned the master suite while Mrs M continued dusting the other bedrooms. The dusting was finished before the floors, freeing Mrs M to plan for dinner.

"Shall I clean James's room?" Gem asked the housekeeper.

Mrs M shook her head. "Best not yet - not for a time," she finally decided. "Mr W goes in there now and then as of late, and I don't want to disturb the room if he is sorting Jamie's things."

"Yes, ma'am," Gem replied, losing her chance to check the photo albums - with a legitimate reason for being in the room. She didn't dare risk going against Mrs M's decision. She didn't want Mrs M to know she was snooping in James's room. There would be another opportunity and it wasn't as if she needed the photo; she wanted to see if Wyatt had put it back in the album.

Gem paced the floor; the office nearly sparkled; she had cleaned the room while Mrs M had finished preparing dinner. Wyatt had spoken very little during the meal and had frowned a great deal. Actually, it had been a pleasant dinner, quiet with no arguments, Vivaldi in the background.

Gem had spent the evening eliminating a dozen exterior photos of Winchester, two of the interior. And there had been another hand delivered note at nine o'clock. At least she was actually getting a bit more sleep at night before the dark hours began, Gem mused as she made a cup of hot chocolate and pressed the start button on the cd player.

What did Paul Andriani know about - everything?

Gem thought of the quiet chats between Gemmy and Paul Andriani the times during the past three years when all Agency staff had attended the quarterly meetings. What had the two chatted about? Paul Andriani - charming, average height, brown hair, hazel eyes, a chameleon able to blend into a crowd - a great advantage for his profession. Gem had always enjoyed his company as much as Gemmy had. Had there been anything between Gemmy and the undercover mastermind? Had Gemmy been involved with Paul Andriani before she met James? Gemmy could have been involved with Paul - and not told Gem about the relationship.

It was just so unusual that Gemmy could have kept so many secrets from her. James, Gem could understand; but Gemmy was going to tell the family when the Pilos returned from Singapore. - Gem was certain of that. - Otherwise Gemmy wouldn't have mentioned Barcelona. The ring was an engagement ring - to be a secret until the family was together in Brisbane. Gem was certain of that.

But a fling with Paul Andriani - a time of experiments? A lost weekend? A passion that quickly flamed, then just as quickly burned out?

How could Gemmy have a relationship with a man who travelled the world in disguise? A man who disappeared for months on end. That simply didn't seem like a relationship that Gemmy would fancy.

What didn't I know about her - besides James and Geneva?

Where was Paul Andriani and what did he know about Barcelona and Geneva?

As Security Director of the Agency, Mr Choate might know of Paul Andriani's whereabouts.

Gem pulled her mobile from her pocket. Mr Cawley was awake.

'Does Mr Choate know location of Blank?'

'Wondered where you were tonight. Extremely doubtful. Mrs B rarely knows.'

'Thanks.'
'Still sorting?'
'Yes.'
'Storm brewing. Should hit T.B. in a half hour. Thunder/lightning.'
'Thanks for the warning!'
Gem had a silly query for her dark hour's companion.
'If you are an accountant - why do you work at night?'
'Flexible hours, so I can sleep when the kids are at school, be awake when they get home. My wife works days. We have every evening together - now and then - insert chuckle.'
Gem laughed at his direction.
'Sounds lovely.'
'It's a sweet life - now and then - never dull.'
I envy you. Wanting to spend every evening with your family, Gem silently mused.
'Take care!'
'And you, Gem!'
Not that she wanted to spend a single moment longer with Wyatt than she had to - but it would be pleasant to spend an evening with someone - other than him.
A very sweet life for Mr Cawley, indeed.
Just don't ever let your family get on a plane without you! But Mr Cawley had probably already thought of that idea.
The storm broke as Gem climbed the stairs to bed.

What Wyatt neglected at night he made up for in the morning, Gem thought as she dressed.
"City today?" he inquired as he helped her pull the bedcovers into shape.
"No."
"Very well, Be ready at six o'clock this evening. Wine and hor d'oeuvres served from seven to the eight o'clock curtain time."
"What play will we be seeing?" Gem asked.
Wyatt shrugged. "I have no idea. It's some charity function - save the spotted school or education for hedgerows - some such thing."
Gem nodded. "Sounds impressive - and fun," she smiled. "Do you enjoy attending plays?"
"Depends on the play," he glanced at his watch. "I have to dash. Be ready when I get home this evening."
"Yes," she called to his back as he left the suite.
Mrs M was more than a little displeased that Mr W had again missed breakfast.
"He's working too hard again," the housekeeper frowned. "It will kill him one day."
And I'll probably be blamed for that, Gem thought sourly, then slapped herself mentally. Her mum would have been shocked at that remark. Truth to tell, Gem was shocked she had thought so callously.

"He must enjoy his work," she managed a reply to appease the housekeeper. "Perhaps he has a breakfast meeting."

"Perhaps," the other woman grumbled.

Gem sought to change the subject. "Cleaning today?" she suggested.

"Oiling the wood," Mrs M shook her head, still annoyed with the Master of the Hall.

"And what does that entail?" Gem queried doubtfully.

It entailed ladders, wood oil, buffing cloths and a tremendous expenditure of energy. Gem insisted on using the taller ladder, while Mrs M concentrated on the lower sections of the cherry wood panelling.

Lord! what an effort, Gem sighed, standing back to admire the gleaming cherry wood in the main hall. The woodwork was beautiful but would painted plaster walls have been such a faux pas when the house was built?! It would have been easier to simply paint every bit of the ground floor walls. They managed the main hallway, butler's pantry, and main hall by the end of the morning, then took a lunch break. The great room took most of the afternoon to finish even with both of them working on the same room.

Gem took a shower - thankful she had worn gloves when she had applied the wood oil - washed and dried her hair, then had tea, muffins and cheese at Mrs M's insistence.

"Hors d'oeuvres are not a proper diet," the housekeeper scolded.

"I had a proper breakfast and lunch, and this is as good as dinner. Your muffins are very nearly a full course," Gem tried to please the woman.

"All I can say is Mr W had better take you out for a proper dinner after the play."

"Very likely," Gem assured her, not really having a clue to Wyatt's actual plans.

She was ready on time, smiling with pleasure as Mrs M praised the designer of the gown and admired how lovely Gem looked. Ora had been correct on the hair style she had suggested. The housekeeper insisted on running to the carriage house for her camera, deciding that Gem's was too difficult to quickly learn to get a proper picture of the Missus. Gem felt foolish standing patiently in the main hall while Mrs M took enough photos to make sure she 'got a good' one.

"You be careful walking in those shoes then," the older woman warned.

"I shall," Gem assured her as she heard the kitchen door open and close.

Mrs M hurried to the kitchen to let the couple have a few minutes of privacy before they left for their special evening away from the Hall.

"Appropriate?" Gem smiled hesitantly as Wyatt approached her. She wanted Ora's creation to be appreciated. She turned around slowly so Wyatt could get the entire view of the gown.

"Indeed," he frowned.

"What?" Gem said a trifle anxiously.

"I have a phone conference this evening. I donated the tickets to a theatre class," he informed her, then went to the library, closing the doors behind him.

What? What!

Gem was stunned. She stared at the double doors, expecting him to reappear. But he did not.

That was IT? His only comments?

Speechless, she slowly walked into the kitchen and poured hot water from the electric tea kettle into a mug of hot chocolate mix.

"You'll spill on that dress," Mrs M warned.

"It doesn't matter. Well, yes, it does matter. We're not going. He has a phone meeting tonight," Gem murmured.

"No!" Mrs M's eyes glinted. "Don't spill that on your dress," she ordered, marching out of the kitchen.

Gem could hear the woman fairly stomping down the hall. "No, ma'am," Gem called politely. She walked to her office, set her shoulder bag on the counter, turned on her computer and slipped Vera Lynn into the cd player.

She didn't truly mind not going to the theatre, but she was disappointed that Ora's gown didn't get a night out; and the young women had made such an effort putting Gem together for the evening.

Gem clicked the mouse on the Winchester file; she'd work on it after she changed to pyjamas - she had had enough clothing changes for the day.

She didn't hear Wyatt enter the room, only realizing he was there when the music abruptly ceased. Wordlessly he shut down her computer and handed her her evening bag.

"Come," he said taking her arm.

"Where?" Gem demanded, confused.

"Out," he said crisply, leading her through the kitchen, out the door and to the Jag.

"Your meeting," she protested as he shut the passenger door.

"Manton will take the conference," he replied curtly, as he slid into the vehicle, smartly closing the door and engaging the engine.

"Why?" Gem frowned.

"Because he is not married, he lives alone, and because I have a wife with a new gown. I also have a very irate housekeeper!"

"You gave away the tickets," Gem quietly reminded him.

"That is so. However, there is a new art gallery opening in London. Then dinner at the Cumbria. You are a tad over dressed for the White Rose."

The Cumbria. What a nasty memory, Gem held her tongue. Oh this would be a lovely evening, she sighed inwardly.

"Apparently I have been neglecting you, working too many hours to give my bride the attention she so dearly deserves," he said dryly. "I have a responsibility to you now, to make you properly happy and content. I got a scalding earful from the president of your fan club."

Whoa! Mrs M hadn't done Gem any favours this evening. "I have never said a single word of complaint to Mrs M," Gem said quietly in her own defence.

"I am inclined to believe that," Wyatt said coolly. "You seem to have no trouble directing your every complaint to me - as it should be."

Gem fell silent, letting him grouse - not wishing to add fuel to the fire. And would it be such a terrible thing for him to be away from his work for a few hours? Perhaps it would be, if the meeting was very important. And why had he taken notice of his housekeeper's remarks? He was the Lord of the Manor after all!

"You're going to receive a speeding notice," she suggested quietly, as the Jag tore up the tarmac.

"I'll add it to the pile for this month," he shrugged.

"How many do you have?" Gem gasped slightly

"A few," Wyatt admitted, easing up on the pedal. "It is a sports car, after all." He glanced over at her. "You look absolutely smashing, by the way."

"Thank you," Gem replied politely.

"Women and their need to show off a new gown," Wyatt muttered.

"This evening was not my idea," Gem quietly pointed out the fact. "We'll just make the worst of it and get through the evening."

The unexpected remark struck Wyatt as extremely humorous. "Well said!" he laughed.

Gem massaged her toes. Very high pumps punished toes. Ouch! She had always lived in a world of loafers, not arch achers. The evening had wandered on decently once Wyatt's temper had eased. The art gallery was impressive, the building a bit too modern for her taste, all metal and glass - one of those cold, almost futuristic structures supposedly designed to suggest good taste - to the uninitiated perhaps, Gem frowned. The art displayed was another matter altogether: impressive, spirited, extremely original, the work of four artists, including a brilliant sculptor.

"Who sculpted your gown?" Wyatt had murmured as they sipped champagne at the gallery.

"A new designer," Gem had replied. "Ora of Ora and Eda's Design Shop. Ora is brilliant."

"Indeed she is. No doubt she appreciates your business. Do you need additional funds in your account?"

"I do not," Gem had declined the offer, bringing a frown from Wyatt.

The Cumbria was the same as it had been on their 'wedding day'; subtle elegance, exceptional service, excellent food, and less personality than was to Gem's liking. She enjoyed the relaxed, amiable atmosphere of pubs, as had Gemmy.

"Perhaps next time you shop you'll find something that shows off your lovely legs," Wyatt had suggested.

"Perhaps," Gem had replied, greatly hoping that she would not have to shop again anytime soon.

They had returned late to the Hall and Gem was very tired. Wyatt had 'relaxed' her, and now at the dark hours she was exhausted. Hot chocolate, pacing, and Vera Lynn for company. 'I'll Be Seeing you'. When? When?

Mr Cawley was awake.

'Any comment on a mole or sleeper in SEA Network?'

'Logical theory per Mrs B and Choate. Harry will review suggestion.'

'Okay.'

If the mole/sleeper was already in the Network, then the obvious choice would be Paul Andriani - but that would be extremely obvious since he was the contact of four dead Network staff. Red herring? Go with the obvious to throw the investigation off path? And if Paul Andriani was the mole/sleeper, had he been all along - since he started working for the British government? Or was he a turncoat - a traitor? She had a difficult time thinking of Paul Andriani as a traitor.

She would prefer to think the mole/sleeper was an unknown entity.

'Who was Mr Portermann's main contact in SEA Network?'

'I don't know. Perhaps only Portermann and Harry would know. Doubt Harry would say. Will put query to Mrs B. My opinion - Blank.'

'Okay. Thanks!'

And then what?

'How long have you been with the Agency?'

'Been wondering when you would ask about me. 2003-.'

'Position?'

'2nd Assistant Director 2003-08. First AD 2008-'

And Acting Director when Mrs Brown and Harry were on 'holiday'.

'Previous to 2003?'

'1993-2003, agent SEA Network.'

Whoa!

'Why didn't you mention that earlier?'

'The obvious.'

'I didn't ask.'

'Precisely.'

'Do you think there is a mole/sleeper? Did you know any of the murdered SEA agents/ couriers?'

'All after my time. Know other current/past. Don't believe any moles/sleepers.'

'What of Mr Choate? How long Agency courier?'

'2002-past June.'

'Previous to that?'

'Records sealed.'

What? What?

'What?'

'Records sealed.'

'I got that! Why?'

'If I could tell you why the records wouldn't be sealed, would they then?'

'Very humorous!'

'You offered the query!'

For what possible reason would an Agency staffer's records be sealed?

'Are other Agency staff records sealed?'

'Think!'

'Aside from the Pilos.'

'Yes.'

'Is this a frequent occurrence?'

'Define frequent.'

'Are you playing cat and mouse with me?'

'No.'

'Once a year?'

'No.'

'Twice a year?'

315

'No.'
'Only when absolutely necessary?'
'Yes.'
'Are you going to give me any other information about Mr Choate?'
'No. Records sealed.'
'Right. I got that.'
'Then stop asking. I am on holiday next two days.'
'Where are you going?'
'B&B in Penzance.'
'Lovely!'
'Then I am on holiday for a fortnight.'
'Mediterranean cruise?'
'No. Holiday.'
'Agency holiday?'
'Yes.'
On assignment then.
'I will miss you!'
'Same here. Choate will be your contact. Keep sorting.'
'I shall.'
'Night.'
'Night.'
'Possible Storm brewing.'
Gem looked out the window.
'Clear here.'
'Not reference to weather.'
'Okay.'
Thus the upper case S Gem realized.
'Take care, Gem!'
'You also!'

Storm brewing. What storm? At the Agency? SEA Network? The entire Network? Had it started with the Pilos? With Project CSU? Or was it a matter of disrupting the Network? Or was it all of her questions?

Another query for Mr Cawley popped into Gem's brain.

'Who is Director of SEA Network?'
'Now - Harry. Temporarily.'
'Previously?'
'Portermann.'
'Thanks! Safe trip!'
'Thanks!'

Mr Portermann had been the Director of the SEA Network. Another point to the idea of disrupting the SEA Network.

Gem's head started to ache. It was only four o'clock, but she went to bed.

Wyatt raised up on one elbow. "It's only four o'clock," he yawned. He propped the pillows behind him, leaning against them. "Come here," he coaxed.

She lay in Wyatt's arms, her cheek resting against his chest, as she pondered Mr Cawley's warning. A Storm brewing. And what would happen when it broke?

Where was Mr Cawley going on holiday? Why was he going on holiday? He had been a SEA Network agent!

And Mr Choate! His records were sealed! Was Mr Choate his proper name or was that an alias or a new assumed name - which technically, was an alias. Right?

The more Gem learned, the more she realized she had known nothing for years. Well, of course. Pre-CSU she wasn't NTK - because it hadn't been necessary. She had been a courier, and NTK was rarely accorded to couriers.

My brain is over-loaded, Gem mused.

"And why precisely is that?" Wyatt yawned again.

Blast! "I said that aloud?" Gem gasped.

"Yes. And you are not talking in your sleep, because it isn't five o'clock yet. Why is it always two o'clock? Why is it always five o'clock? What happened at two o'clock in the morning? What ended at five o'clock in the morning? Why can't you sleep past seven o'clock in the morning?" he queried, yawning again.

"You should go to sleep," Gem replied quietly.

"I should get some answers."

"That is not going to happen."

"Why don't you tell me? You can trust me."

Gem pulled away, but he pulled her back, close against him. "The hell I can trust you! I trusted you once! That's why I'm in this mess!"

"Marriage," Wyatt corrected her. "And our marriage has nothing to do with your insomnia."

Insomnia. Mr Cawley wouldn't be available to text for a fortnight! She couldn't text Mr Choate during the dark hours, could she? He would need to be awake during the day to shadow her and to work at T.O. The dark hours would be so lonely! Mr Cawley had been her only link to the world outside the Hall during the wee hours of the morning. But someone would have to be covering Mr Cawley's job during those hours. Would Mr Choate get any sleep during the coming fortnight?

"You've drifted into your other world, haven't you?" Wyatt muttered.

My other world. I am trapped in two worlds.

"It's an escape from this one," Gem said coolly.

"You're not happy there."

"I'm not happy here!" Gem protested.

"That's of your own choosing."

She couldn't believe she had admitted to another world. She was so tired she wasn't thinking straight! No slipped cogs!

"You don't understand."

"No, I do not, Gem. Talk to me."

He wanted to pump 'Gemmy' for information about her life 'before' James - and the months after Gemmy 'returned' to Australia.

"No."

Note to self: do NOT waken Wyatt when you go back to bed, Gem ordered herself.

Wyatt didn't speak again. Gem wasn't easily going to give up any answers. He would simply have to keep chipping away at the facade. One day she would crack. He would make sure that she did.

Gem walked through the fields, thankful she had pulled on her wellies. There were dry sections interspersed with areas so mucky each step threatened to pull her feet from her wellies. She finished the roll of colour film and replaced it with black and white, then changed the lenses to a wide angle zoom. She had no particular subject in mind, other than wishing to escape the silence at the Hall. Wyatt was in the library reading another mountain of reports that he had lugged from the boot of the Jag that morning after breakfast.

He hadn't referred at breakfast to their conversation at the end of the dark hours, much to Gem's relief. Perhaps he would eventually cease asking her questions that she would continually refuse to answer.

No doubt Mr Cawley was on his way to the B&B in Penzance. Then after that - where? She would likely never get a reply if she asked about his Agency 'holiday'.

Mr Choate was awake! She wondered if he was rotting the day away at his office. She texted the query.

'At your office?'

'No. Problem?'

'Just wondering if you were at your office. Just curious.'

And desperate for a friendly chat.

'At the shop.'

'Camera? Book?'

'Ora and Eda's shop.'

What?

'Why?'

'They needed an infusion of cash. I bought 30% of the business. Silent partner.'

'Seriously?'

'Yes. Re-arranging shop this morning.'

Gem laughed. What next!

'You are an amazing man, Mr Choate!'

'You are an amazing woman, Gem! And how are you expending your time this day?'

'Snapping T.B in b/w. I will stop at the shop next week.'

'Please do.'

'Mr Cawley is away.'

'Yes. I am available when you need me, Gem.'

'Thank you! Mark up those prices!'

'Indeed.'

'Chat later.'

'Yes.'

She would not take additional time from him. He deserved time for himself.

Ticking Bottom would be interesting to view in black and white. She switched to a telephoto lens, experimenting, just for the heck of it, and what was rubbish would be shredded. Gem wandered for hours, shooting two rolls of black and white film, and would have continued the wander had Wyatt not texted that lunch was in twenty minutes, a time frame that would just fit her trek back to the Hall.

Cottage pie and chips. Gem made a salad but Wyatt declined her offer to prepare one for him.

"Who oiled the wood?" he asked as they ate, lunching in the kitchen as had become their weekend habit.

"Mrs M and I worked on it yesterday," Gem replied. His cottage pie was a bit better than Mrs M's, but Gem would never state that comment to either of them.

"Why did you help her? I told you she can hire a girl from the village," he frowned.

"Why shouldn't I help Mrs M?" Gem protested. "What do women in your circle do all day, go shopping and lounge at spas?"

"My circle? And which one would that be?" he queried dryly.

"The la-di-da, lord of the manor circle," she said crisply.

"Ah. Well, many women in my circle are quite often professional women who own, and or manage, highly respectable and lucrative businesses," he said pursing his lips. "Lovely attitude, I might say, from a young woman who attended university, taught a few courses, travelled the world, and is writing a book about cathedrals. What serious work have you ever accomplished, my dear, to lay claim to a legitimate work ethic? Or perhaps you have professional career experience through unknown positions with that rogue Staunton. What did you do in that secret world of yours? Something that apparently needed an alias - perhaps more than one?"

Gem held her tongue, mentally reviewing the countless assignments she had completed while attending university, teaching, and writing her thesis.

"Oh - I neglected to mention writing your thesis. However, that was last year. What have you accomplished this year? A second thesis was it? I haven't seen the first have I, thus I am rather unimpressed by your second effort. Perhaps you would like to share either one with me one of these days," he suggested smoothly. "What was your thesis - medieval cathedrals or art glass?"

Dr Jekyll. Perhaps Mrs M was correct. Perhaps he was worn out from working so many hours for GEI.

"Don't misunderstand me, my dear. When you are bored with your bookshops, traipsing around with your camera, working on your book, listening to your music, if you do desire to help Mrs M, it is perfectly alright with me. I don't have to pay you wages," he said loftily. "I am simply wondering of how you think to use this ruse to your advantage - and to the detriment of others. You needn't try so hard to get into Mrs M's good graces. You conned her almost as soon as you first set foot in this house, which is surprising because she is usually an extremely perceptive person where women are concerned."

Gem, for a change, kept her temper in check as he spoke, mollified to know that she had proper facts of which he was unaware - and had to be kept unaware.

"So the la-di-da lord of the manor remark rankled you perhaps?" she said politely when he finally finished speaking. "Or perhaps Mrs M was correct - you need more greens in your diet."

She cleared her dishes, putting them in the dishwasher, as Wyatt sat staring at her.

"Truth to tell," Gem said quietly, "I don't fit into your circle, and you don't fit into mine. I don't expect people to jump at my orders, or wither beneath my criticism, and I don't expect to be waited upon, or to have people do for me."

"And precisely what is your circle, my dear? Crooks, thieves, basic run-of-the-mill felons?" he said pensively.

Gem declined to reply to his query." Have you finished with your lunch? May I have your dishes?"

He slid the plates over to her. Fascinating woman! What a game she played!

Gem put the remaining dishes in the dishwasher, the leftover cottage pie in the fridge, then wordlessly walked to her office.

It would be easy enough to show Wyatt her thesis, 'The Power, Politics, and Art of Building Medieval Cathedrals', printed in four-colour, bound in leather. She was damned proud of it. Three dozen copies had been printed, three of which were at the Agency warehouse with her family's possessions, fifteen were in various libraries, Harry, Mrs Brown, Mr Portermann, and Professor Redmond each had copies - Mr Portermann's copy was probably in his possessions at the Agency warehouse. The remaining copies were in the combination locked file box. And they would remain there.

Gem switched on the telly to monitor international news for a hot spot that would be taking Mr Cawley from his office at the Agency. Mr Choate, of course, would inform her if anything in particular was steaming - she was NTK. But she might get an inkling of her own before he alerted her. She didn't trip to anything, but left on the telly for company and switched on her computer.

A storm was moving in as she spread the Winchester photos on the counter to continue eliminating snaps she would not use. Great splotches of rain pelted the windows as the sky blackened, turning early afternoon into evening dark; so dark in fact, that her mind slipped into dark hours thoughts; but she shook them off as too taxing mentally to cope with when Wyatt could walk into the office at any moment, and startle her into a verbal faux pas, or slipped cog. She washed her laundry, then returned to the snaps, eliminating nine exterior shots and all but five of the interior photos.

The storm eased in late afternoon and to Gem's relief, Wyatt suggested they tramp through the wet to the Crow for dinner and a brew. The M's were there to ensure a pleasant evening for Gem despite Wyatt's presence.

The dark hours were exceedingly lonely without Mr Cawley's nightly texts of replies to her questions. She had never visited Penzance, but would have to put the city on her list of sights to see when she regained her freedom from Dr Jekyll.

Her circle! The only circle she had was the Agency. Lord! he was suspicious of her! And if doing household tasks was a ruse, she should find chores that were less taxing physically!

Mr Choate! Purchasing thirty percent of Ora and Eda's shop! An interesting escape from the intense life of the Agency. And it was an available cover, if cover was ever required - aside from that of managing a detective agency. All Agency staff had a cover. Gem and Gem had had their covers as art students, then the work of their individual dissertations.

Gem paced hour after hour, sorting, yet not retrieving, specific information that was of aid to her search. Hot chocolate, chocolate biscuits, Vera Lynn's music and pacing, hour after hour, and sorting. Perhaps Mrs Brown was correct. Perhaps Gem needed a mental holiday from the search. But she had the dark hours to pass. And she would not return to bed early this morning, refusing to have another frustrating discussion with Wyatt.

Sunday was a repeat of Saturday. Wyatt was so preoccupied with his reports he barely spoke to her at meals, which suited Gem perfectly.

The sky once again struck Ticking Bottom, this time with a monsoonal rain that continued throughout the day. Gem finished the chapter of Canterbury Cathedral, then expanded the text, and selected the final snaps of both the exterior and interior of Winchester; the sketches were finished and she could concentrate on the text of the cathedral.

She vaguely heard noise in the kitchen, confident of Wyatt fetching a beer and then returning to the library and his reports, so she was rather surprised when he entered the office to hand her a cup of tea.

"You need a break," he suggested.

Gem accepted the offering. "I don't need a break," she protested. "You're the one with masses of reports to read."

"Precisely why I need a break. And you are it. Comes with the terms of our agreement. Remember?" he lifted an eyebrow.

Gem flushed angrily. "For your information Mr Grantham, men do not own women," she chipped the words out of icy tones.

"Nonsense. Trophy wives. Perfect examples."

"Other husbands neglect their wives! Why can't you? You never really wanted me!"

"Again, my dear, nonsense. You so amuse me. And any man with a grain of sense wants you. You already know that. You can't possibly miss the longing glances you draw from anything with an Adam's apple," Wyatt sipped his tea and chuckled.

"What I do see is how women look at you! Why don't you have an affair!"

"It's a fortunate man who has such a generous wife," Wyatt drawled. "Giving me your permission to have an affair! I don't need your permission, sweetheart!"

"Then have an affair! Perhaps a tall red-head. Find one you like and I will introduce her to you!"

Wyatt choked on his tea. "You're offering to procure women for me? There's a term for such a person!"

"How dare you! "Gem's cheeks flamed.

"Good Lord! You're offended? Have some decency woman! You are my wife, NOT a madam! Or was that a former profession of yours? Shall I introduce you in the future as my wife, Gemimah Forrester Grantham, author, and former madam?" Gem stared at him, speechless at his anger. "It has a certain tone to it, doesn't it, sweetheart. Shall I also include confidant of a master criminal? My God! Is that what you did for Staunton? Procure women for him?" Wyatt glared at her.

The reference to Paul Andriani clamped her tongue.

"And shall I then extol your other virtues to all, my dear? Lying, tangled webs of deceit? That you're a man hunter?"

"Stop," Gem said softly.

"Then cease the constant battles which you promised recently - and so plaintively - you would do."

Gem stared at him bitterly. "You always win, don't you?"

"Yes, and I always shall, as I have always informed you. When are you going to accept that truth?" he said grimly. "You should have been wiser at choosing your adversary."

"I should have been wiser choosing a husband," Gem said bitterly.

"Another truth, sweetheart. You didn't choose. I made that decision! Live with it! And do NOT speak again of affairs and mistresses. It's all proper rubbish!" He strode from the office and Gem heard the library door slam.

Gem was astonished by Wyatt's outrage. What a bizarre moral code the man possessed! And he was angry with her! As if she had offended his reputation! Or honour! What a joke!

Trophy wives! And it wasn't as if he introduced her to anyone other than the locals in T.B. - and Ms Holton! Truly - all the man did was work! Every evening, nearly every weekend since the disastrous trips to Wight and Inverness. Not that she was whinging. The time he spent working was less time that she had to endure his presence.

Gem stewed for a couple of hours, then started feeling peckish. The left over cottage pie had been lunch that day, but there remained enough for two for dinner if supplemented with muffins and salad. She heated the food, set the table, then texted Wyatt that dinner was ready.

'Pass.'

And that was it? Let him stew then, Gem decided. She finished off the cottage pie, and returned to her office, concentrating on the text for Winchester. She wrote, checked facts, studied each photo judiciously for details stated in the text, deleted the entire text and began again. She rewrote, reread, edited and tweaked the text until she was satisfied with the final draft. She stood, stretched and glanced at her watch. Eleven o'clock!

Well! No note tonight! She had to get some sleep before the dark hours began. She turned off the office lights, leaving the ones lit on the staircase for Wyatt so that he wouldn't stumble and break his neck on the stairs.

A table lamp was left burning in the sitting room, and to Gem's surprise she saw that Wyatt was already in bed - sleeping. Well, the man could hold a grudge.

She slipped into bed, trying not to disturb him; he stirred but did not waken, and he did not reach out for her. Better still.

Two o'clock came very quickly, and Gem groaned inwardly as her brain clicked on. She kept her eyes closed, but could not win the fight for sleep.

The second night without Mr Cawley. She hoped he was enjoying his stay in Penzance before embarking on his assignment. She wondered now if she had asked of the assignment would he have told her? Perhaps Mr Choate would tell her when she saw him midmorning.

Gem made a cup of hot chocolate and sat at the kitchen island - in the dark - dark hours - dark room. The music from the cd player drifted in to fill the room with memories.

She hadn't realized how much she had come to rely on Mr Cawley's nightly texts to keep up her spirits. A Storm was brewing. Was that a fact, or was it Mr Cawley's feeling?

Mr Cawley had told her to 'take care', but that was not a particular warning. Mr Choate hadn't indicated any cryptic messages in his texts from the shop. No. Not a fact, she decided. Mr Cawley was projecting a feeling of things to come. A Storm brewing was not unusual considering the Agency's involvement in the International Network. A brewing Storm could be a squall or a hurricane. She considered that Mr Cawley was voicing an opinion.

Where are you Gemmy? Where are all of you?

Ended - another weekend with Wyatt Grantham. Begun - another week with Wyatt Grantham. Day after day with that man! Week after week!

He had called her a man hunter! That couldn't be further from the truth! She was two people now, and neither of them had been man hunters!

And oh! how it worried her when he mentioned Staunton!

She was hopeless at finding the Pilos. Finding Gemmy. Mum. Dad. Mr Portermann.

Gem sat in Auntie Jane's comfy chair, sipping hot chocolate, listening to the music. She pulled her feet up onto the cushion, resting her head on her knees. She was at loose ends again. She had the information about the Agency staff. Dates. Embassy. Dates. Agency. But she didn't know what to do with the information - if anything. Everything was self-explanatory - except for Mr Choate. And that could be explained away as an undercover agent needing a new identity. Odd he had switched to a position as courier - if that was the case. But the new identity could have been a precaution and later discovered to be unnecessary. Or it could be a matter of hiding in plain sight. Either way, Gem didn't think Mr Choate's past had anything to do with the Blasted screwed up equation Gem was sorting. At least she hoped it didn't.

Hello! If the secrecy of Mr Choate's former identity or occupation was of such importance, he wouldn't be working for the Agency.

Misthought. It wasn't his identity that was in question. It was his records that were sealed prior to 2002. Some kind of covert work, no doubt.

And that was that!

She would add Mr Choate into the equation again, if necessary.

Her brain had stopped clicking. No sorting. She felt like a robot with a bad circuit.

It was raining again. She could hear distant thunder.

Mr Cawley told her to keep working. But she was at an impasse. She had given the Agency all she could think of - for now. There wasn't anything more. She could finish reading the books about the War, but it would be a history lesson from now on - not a path to the Pilos.

There were flashes of lightning.

Gem raked her fingers through her hair.

Geneva. Geneva was important. There was no way to find out WHY Geneva. Geneva was as mysterious as the disappearance of the Pilos.

Gem made another cup of hot chocolate, turned off the office lights and sat staring out the office windows at the lightning strikes darting from one cloud to another, as if playing hide and seek with the thunder. She pressed start on the cd player, keeping the loop going of Vera Lynn's voice.

She repeated 'Gemmy' over and over and over as a mantra, hoping for a clue to click in her mind. And then she dragged herself up the stairs to bed.

Gem awakened at seven. Alone in bed. She heard the shower running in Wyatt's bathroom. He was up early. More sleep would be lovely, but her mind would not allow it.

She was still deciding what to wear when Wyatt walked out of his dressing room, shrugging into his black suit coat.

"Are you going to the city today?" he queried abruptly.

"Yes," Gem replied, hesitating to watch him. His demeanour was so cold!

"Ring Mr Choate then three quarters of an hour before you leave the Hall. He will meet you at the bridge below the village. I won't be home for dinner."

And he left the suite.

Whoa! Still angry.

Mrs M was preparing breakfast, and scowling when Gem entered the kitchen.

"Has he been in that temper the entire weekend?" she queried, very displeased.

"Not quite," Gem admitted.

"Did he work most of the weekend?"

"Yes, ma'am. Thank you," she replied as the cook set her food in front of her.

"Did he have that attitude throughout the weekend?" Mrs M repeated her query.

Gem formulated a response. "We had words," she admitted. "And he's angry." We had many, many words!

"Doesn't excuse that attitude," Mrs M refused to relent. "He will kill himself if he continues to work himself into the ground."

The housekeeper's irritation hadn't eased by the time Gem left the Hall, and Mrs M would have to deal with Wyatt on her own terms. Gem was not going to get between the two of them.

She dropped off film at the photo shop and purchased a dozen rolls of film, four of black and white, the rest of colour, and then she walked to Ora and Eda's shop; Mr Choate walked in behind her.

"Brilliant," Gem smiled, as she looked around the shop. It was much better organized.

"Did your husband approve of the gown?" Eda asked eagerly.

"Very much so," Gem assured her.

She purchased a few fall clothes, mid-calf shirts, jumpers, ignoring Wyatt's remarks about showing off her legs. His next wife could show off hers.

She and Mr Choate had lunch at Charley's Pub.

"Where is Mr Cawley?" Gem asked curiously.

"That query must be put to your supervisor," Mr Choate replied firmly.

"Off to an accounting seminar, no doubt, and will be rewarded with a certificate and a rise in pay," she grinned.

"I believe that is the usual result of courses and seminars," Choate nodded. "Likely a small rise."

"Government accounting board," Gem laughed.

"Do you want this pub on the report sheet?" he asked as their order was served.

Gem pondered the query. Wyatt would probably be livid if she went to a pub on her own. "Best say a take-away sandwich - chicken- that restaurant by the photo shop."

"As you wish, Gem," Choate agreed.

"All couriers and agents accounted for?" she asked hopefully, sipping her tea.

"As of midnight."

"Blast! Twelve hours."

"We can't require staff to report every four hours, unless we are in a crisis. But SEA is reporting every six hours. I get the next reports of regular couriers at midnight."

"And you sleep when?"

"More than you do, Gem. You're looking extremely tired today. You have to take better care of yourself."

"I'm not making any progress. The Agency isn't," Gem said dismally. "30 May. This is October now. How many more months?"

"No one has that answer, Gem," Choate shook his head.

They fell silent for a time, concentrating on Charley's burgers and chips. Gem was the first to break the silence. "Oh, and congratulations on the shop. It's brilliant!"

Choate nodded. "I'm cash and an advisor. Solely that. The partners were happy that you came in today."

"Mr Choate's girls," Gem murmured.

Choate scowled at her. "That sounds improper," he said sternly.

Really? "As in daughters," Gem tried to appease him.

"I do not have daughters, I have partners," he firmly corrected her.

"Indeed, Mr Choate," Gem replied chastised.

Touchy man!

"You're a lady, Gem, remember that," he advised firmly. "Now where to this afternoon? Bookshops, shopping?"

"I don't know."

"Imperial War Museum?"

Gem considered that suggestion. "Indeed. IWM."

"So be it."

As Gem walked back to the Defender, she noticed magazines on a newsstand. Tabloids, film mag rags; who was cheating on whom, who was sleeping with someone's husband, wife, who was caught with a call girl, hooker.

Huh, Gem thought silently, reflecting on Wyatt's disgust of her comments the previous day. She certainly wouldn't want her face and name splashed over the news rags. She didn't have the strength to endure that humiliation. And she wouldn't be able to bear Gemmy and Paul Andriani's photos glaring at her from the newsstands - and specifically linked to her. And Gem didn't doubt for a moment that Wyatt would carry out his threat of the photos and the passports. Wouldn't that just send the Agency into a tizzy, and Mrs Brown, Harry and Mr Choate into severe apoplexy!

She truly had to curtail her temper with Wyatt when it was possible to do so. He just had the uncanny ability to set her teeth on edge!

Gem stared at the computer screen and it stared back at her. She had clicked on the Pacific Ocean, then on a map of Indonesia. Hopeless. She shut down the computer, pushed start on the cd player yet again, and slumped in Auntie Jane's comfy chair.

She and Mr Choate had spent three hours at the IWM, viewing all the displays; then she had returned to Ticking Bottom, the Hall, and a very quiet Mrs M, who invited Gem for dinner at the carriage house. Gem had politely declined, eating her dinner in her office while she had watched the international news – fortunately not seeing any hot spots that would be of Harry's jurisdiction in SEA. Hopefully the Network still could account for its entire staff.

Wyatt had come back late and had gone directly to the library. She had heard him but had not seen him. She had focused on the text of Winchester and time had slipped away again. It was nearly midnight before she had realized the time, and had gone to bed. Wyatt was again in bed, sleeping, and staggeringly handsome in the moonlight streaming in the bedroom windows.

She let her mind wander, then focused on her mantra of continually repeating Gemmy's name. The desperate hours of 30 May stabbed at her mind, and Gem fought to catch her breath as the pain consumed her heart.

Every day there was no new information. No progress was a step closer to the Pilos remaining lost forever.

Gem raked her fingers through her hair, agonizing through the dark hours.

The week continued. Every day was a repeat of Monday. She saw Wyatt for a few minutes each morning; he was up before she awakened at seven o'clock, and left when she was in the shower, or even before that. Mrs M was exceedingly annoyed by Mr W's behaviour, and Gem felt guilty that the housekeeper solely blamed Wyatt for his attitude.

Gem helped Mrs M finish the project of oiling the woodwork, worked on her book, drove into the city, walked along the Thames, watched a group of Morris dancers, and window shopped.

The Winchester Cathedral Chapter was finished. She started on Bristol Cathedral, which was progressing steadily until she shredded the snaps she wanted to use instead of the ones she had decided to discard. That error necessitated a drive into the city to order reprints, and a return trip to fetch the snaps.

The dark hours drained her. She couldn't sleep when she went to bed. Wyatt was in bed each night before she finally put away her work for the evening. Her mind wandered and she would completely lose track of time. The text of Bristol did not progress smoothly, and she had to struggle to find words, a problem she had never before suffered.

One thing she did sorely miss was the butterfly gathering. She was glad that she didn't have to see Wyatt much each day, because the butterflies inside her were rampaging. The thought of him made her fair want to rip off his clothes. Obviously she was exhausted - and clearly losing her mind if she had those thoughts of Wyatt!

Gem paced the floors during the dark hours, wondering where Mr Cawley was, and hoping that he was safe. Her nerves were fraying, her hope for the Pilos was flagging. She drank cup after cup of hot chocolate, spilling it twice on the office counter and bathing the Vivaldi cd in brown liquid.

Gem was thrilled on Friday morning when her mobile rang with a call from Mrs Brown, suggesting lunch at Charley's, an acceptable pub lunch for Mr Choate to report to Wyatt as Mrs Brown was a lunch companion.

Mrs Brown was exceedingly concerned when she saw Gem. "My dear, you simply must get more sleep. You cannot continue to go on as you are now. I had hoped your marriage to Wyatt would be of some comfort to you, or be at the very least a happy distraction. I am at a loss for words seeing you in this condition. I must say I am disappointed that Wyatt isn't taking better care of you."

"I'm just going through a bad spell," Gem protested. "It will all even out."

"I do hope so." Mrs Brown frowned.

Gem savoured a half-pint, heedless of Wyatt's previous remarks of not wanting her to drink alcohol beverages when she would be driving the Defender. She would do a good bit of walking and have coffee before she drove the Defender back to Ticking Bottom.

"Is Mr Cawley okay?" Gem queried as Charley served them the special of the day.

"He is, as is Harry," Mrs Brown informed her. "They are the subject of this meeting. Mr Cawley and Harry are in Indonesia." She briefly patted Gem's hand. "An Australian charter pilot out of Darwin, notified air traffic control that he had spotted plane wreckage on an Indonesian island. The wreckage is on the side of a mountain."

"Which island? There are over eighteen thousand islands in Indonesia," Gem frowned.

"The name is being withheld until there is credible information. The island is uninhabited. Mountains, forests, swamps, but it is well within the flying distance of the Pilos's fuel supply," Mrs Brown paused to have a bite of her lunch.

Gem waited patiently, but she felt all pins and needles in her body. She forced herself to eat, nerves jangling.

"Harry and Mr Cawley were flown in by sea plane from Darwin this past Tuesday. They have a local guide, but the search will be quite arduous due to the geography of the island. It is an extremely remote area, a good deal of the island is rain forest, and there are swamps. It will be sometime before we have a report of any kind from the expedition."

"Wow!" Gem said breathlessly.

"I don't want to raise your hopes, but Mr Choate and I felt you should be apprised of the situation."

"Thank you," Gem said, forcing herself to remain calm. She reflected on the information. "Mr Cawley is on holiday for a fortnight. What if the expedition takes longer than that?"

"Mr Cawley's 'seminar' is in Melbourne. Once the seminar is completed, and if time demands an extension, he shall be invited to tour Australian government accounting offices. It is rather an 'honour' to receive such an invitation," Mrs Brown smiled.

"Sounds dreadfully boring," Gem grinned.

"Not to an 'accountant seeking a promotion' - and thanks to you - a decent rise in pay." Mrs Brown gave her a pointed look.

"Right," Gem nodded, chagrined. "It should please Mrs Cawley."

"Indeed," Mrs Brown smothered a smile. "Ah, lovely," she added as Charley served his excellent cheesecake. "I must stress, my dear, that this journey may be a wild goose chase, but nonetheless, the sighting must be investigated. Harry will text a brief report every evening, but information will be suppressed until we have concrete answers regarding the sighting."

"I understand, SOP," Gem replied, savouring the dessert. "Do you think there is any hope of wheedling this recipe out of Charley?"

There was every hope and Gem decided she would prepare the dessert the following day. Hot chocolate and cheesecake for the weekend!

Gem remembered to mention the subject of personnel at the Hong Kong embassy circa the 1990's.

"Staff had quarters in the embassy compound. We were at liberty to fraternize with locals during our off time, however there was very little opportunity to do so," Mrs Brown replied. "Couriers and agents, naturally, had their own residences – as is the current situation."

There didn't appear to be any useful information there, Gem decided. And she knew for a fact that couriers and agents had little free time to call their own.

Mrs Brown had parting remarks for Gem along the same line as her greeting. "Will you please take a break from your search work? Rest. I have little hope this expedition will ease your insomnia, but perhaps you could use the hours in a restful pursuit," Gem's supervisor urged.

Gem nodded firmly. "I will try," she promised.

The promise did not preclude going to Howard's Bookshop for reference books of Indonesia, which drew a frown from Mr Choate. He had lunched at Charley's but at another table, checking via his mobile with Technical Operations. She took up a great deal of his time but he was too professional to state that fact. And she was Family, looking for Family.

Another dreaded weekend with so many hours to fill. There was the cheesecake recipe to prepare, the bird and garden books to read, the pastels to use, and her camera. Hopefully rain and fog would not mar the weekend. Gem remembered to pick up the photos she had had reprinted; she returned to Ticking Bottom, shopping at the Mercantile and greengrocer's instead of London shops, to free Mr Choate to his more important duties.

Mrs M was in a more placid mood than she had been all week. "Mr W is bringing Chinese dinner home this evening," the cook informed Gem.

Hopefully he would eat in the library, Gem mused silently.

Mrs M left the Hall as Wyatt walked into the kitchen, his arms full of photo albums and bags of Chinese take-away.

Gem was drinking a cup of hot chocolate and nearly choked when she saw the photo albums. There was a row in the making!

They ate in the kitchen; Wyatt set out the plates. Gem got the silverware and could have used one of the knives to cut the silence between them.

"Do you have any plans for the weekend?" he asked coolly.

"I don't know. Have I?" Gem replied quietly. "I don't generally know my weekend plans until you tell me what they are. You make the rules, after all, Mr Grantham."

"Shall I rephrase the query, my dear? Tread warily and remember I could so easily destroy you."

He was still very angry with her. Gem took a deep breath. "I have no plans," she said stiffly.

Wyatt took a beer from the fridge for himself, and refilled her cup with hot chocolate. "Perhaps we should use the time to put all the photos in albums," he suggested.

"Photos," Gem stalled the brewing Grantham storm.

"Wight, Inverness, Kenilworth, Aylesbury, Randwick Woods, etcetera," he carefully explained.

Mentioning Randwick Woods was a slap in the face as far as Gem was concerned.

"Oh," she said quietly, not volunteering that most of the photos no longer existed.

"How is the work progressing on your book?"

"Fine," Gem controlled her voice, remembering how he had mocked her book earlier that week.

"You've been working too hard. You look very tired."

"I lose track of time," she shrugged.

"Perhaps it is time for you to see a physician about your insomnia."

"No."

"Consider my suggestion."

"I don't believe I shall," she picked at her food.

"Get more sleep then. You wear a wrist watch, there is a clock on the wall in your office, there is a clock on your computer, and I gave you a pendant watch - which you do not wear, by the way. You have no excuse to be so lax about time."

Time. What time was it in Malaysia? How far had the expedition climbed up the side of the mountain in four days' time? What time was it on the island? Much of Indonesia was in the same time zone as Hong Kong - eight hours plus London time. Approximately two o'clock in the morning.

Mrs Brown had already had reports since Harry texted her every night; but Mrs Brown wasn't sharing yet. How long would it take a person - well a few people - to hike up a mountain in a rainforest? Mrs Brown had also mentioned swamps. Lord! What a trial for Harry and Mr Cawley!

Wyatt watched her face and wondered at the puzzled frown that marred her beautiful brow. She was again in her secret world. Had she escaped to her private world because he had mentioned time?

He had loosened the reins this week to see how she would react. She looked as worn out as she had the day he met her. And there was the haunted look again in her eyes. What had she done that she was hiding? Whatever the issue, it had not been resolved. And again a visit to a war museum this week. According to Choate's report she spent three hours there the other afternoon.

"How was the food at Charley's Pub?" Wyatt asked casually.

Blast! Mr Choate's report. Well, Charley's was open to the public for lunch - just not today.

"Decent enough," she kept her voice even. "I had lunch with Mrs Brown." It nettled her to be followed - no offence to Mr Choate, and she didn't want to laud the pub or Wyatt might suggest they lunch there together.

"And how is Mrs Brown?"

"Quite well."

"Did Mrs Brown suggest you needed more rest?"

"Yes," Gem admitted grudgingly.

"Perhaps you will heed her words if not mine."

Gem continued to push her food around on her plate. "Perhaps."

"If you are finished eating, I'll do the washing up," Wyatt volunteered, weary of the effort of conversing with her.

She went to her office, realizing that she had to be conscientious to keep her mobile charged in the slight event that Mrs Brown or Mr Choate relented and decided to text her of news of the expedition during the dark hours.

Gem pulled out the black and white photos and colour snaps she had picked up at the photo shop. The thatched cottages were stunning in black and white, and definitely worth framing. She turned to look at the wall, pondering how she would hang the photos, once framed - once the wall was painted. She had to decide on a paint colour. Relax, Mrs Brown had urged. Gem enjoyed painting. She decided on a grey/green colour; it was a darker colour, but it should be suitable with the stone floor. Light coming in the bank of windows would prevent the room from feeling too dark.

One decision made. Photo frames would be a brown-black. Mattes would be heavy crème.

Elgar this evening, Gem decided - oh! - two decisions already in one evening! - she teased herself, as she pulled up the Bristol Cathedral file on her computer. She composed text, edited text, and edited again, growing frustrated with her inability to concentrate on the cathedral; her thoughts were captivated by the image of Harry, Mr Cawley and their guide hacking their way through primeval rainforest growth. Bless them! Searching for, hopefully, the Pilos. The side of a mountain. My God, how horrible it would be to see a mountain looming straight ahead in the early morning hours. Had the mountain just appeared in a split second?

Gem jerked back in horror, burying her face in her hands. Had it been over just that quickly? Her heart started pounding so hard she thought it would burst out of her chest.

She glanced at her mobile. Charged! How she would dearly love to text Mr Cawley that night. Two o'clock Ticking Bottom time would be wending on to mid-morning on the mountain.

Bristol Cathedral stared at her from the computer screen. Gem shook off the thoughts of the mountain and the Pilos, to concentrate on the medieval cathedral. She pushed the start button on the cd player, opting to listen to Elgar again, over the mentally exhausting decision to select another composer. - How many times would she misspell Bristol this evening? And finally, despite the misspellings, the text began to flow.

What did the wildlife consist of on the island? In the rainforest? Snakes? Monkeys? Sloths? She had always been fascinated by sloths. The name alone delighted her.

Cathedrals! Focus. Concentrate!

She jumped when Wyatt's reflection loomed over her in the window.

"No!" she groaned.

"You are entirely incapable of taking care of yourself," he said firmly. "Computer off," he ordered, pushing the stop button on the cd player.

Ten o'clock.

Frustrated, Gem clicked SAVE and shut down the computer.

Apparently his anger had waned. She soon learned his libido hadn't.

Gem hadn't used Mrs M's kitchen for much other than the biscuits she had baked, and preparing the odd sandwich for herself a few times. Locating cooking utensils, measuring cups and the like was more time consuming than she had expected it would be. Preparing the cheesecake and doing the washing up took most of the dark hours - and four cups of hot chocolate, and many times of slipping into the office to press the start button on the cd player; she could hear Vera Lynn's voice quite clearly in the kitchen. When at last the kitchen was restored to order, the cheesecake in the fridge, Gem picked up a reference book on Indonesia and stretched out on Auntie Jane's settee.

Facts on the number of islands comprising Indonesia greatly conflicted, listed sometimes as 13,000 to 16,000 to over 18,000. And surprisingly, despite the extraordinary population of Indonesia, there were many uninhabited islands. Where-or-where in Indonesia were Harry, Mr Cawley, and their local guide?

Gem scanned one book, laid it on the floor, reached down for another, scanned that, then a third, switching back and forth, two on the floor, open, face up, one in her hands.

Unrest was not unusual in the islands, considering the vast diversity of religions and cultures. Each of the books had considerable historical references and Gem opened each to the sections on the Second World War. Considering the vast expanse Indonesia covered, one might certainly decide it was a prime area in which a plane or a person could easily disappear. Especially if a person had been brandishing swastikas and insanely murdering innocent people for years. One wouldn't need an uninhabited island in which to disappear; one could simply manage to do so in the extremely populated cities. Lay low, melt into the population and simply, and completely, disappear.

Gem yawned. Were the men taking a lunch break by now? Starting their climbing early each morning, resting during the heat of the day? She yawned again.

Gem rubbed her eyes, dragged her fingers through her hair, and rubbed her neck. Something was different. Slowly she opened her eyes.

Oh-oh.

Wyatt was standing at the end of the settee, staring down at her. She had fallen asleep reading the reference books.

He bent down to retrieve the books from the floor, then took the one from her lap.

"I expect you to sleep in our bed," Wyatt bit out the words. He glanced down at the open pages. "What is it with you and the War?"

Gem flung herself off the settee to grab the books from his hands.

"Are you writing a book on the War?" he demanded. "The submarine museum at Gosport, the IWM, the British War Museums, your dvds of U-boats and submarines, your books on the Battle of the Bulge, the book of the OSS."

"What business is it of yours what I read and where I go?" Gem demanded, raking her fingers through her hair.

"Temper, temper," Wyatt said dryly.

"I am so tired of you being apprised of my every waking hour outside this house," she snapped. "You are in control of me, I get that," she held up her hands to emphasize her words. "I am so sick of you spying on me! You actually had the audacity to hire someone to spy on me!"

"Yes," he acknowledged, "you are my wife."

"That doesn't give you the right to spy on me!"

"It gives me the responsibility to see to your protection."

"That's only an excuse for you!"

"It's a fact, Gem."

She slammed the books down on the counter. "Spying! You detest spies. You said so yourself!"

Wyatt exhaled sharply. "Habits, patterns," he said firmly. "Choate knows habits and regular patterns are safety hazards. He tells you what routes to drive into the city."

Cover. No slipped cogs. "Yes," she agreed. She knew from Agency training to vary driving patterns, and so she did without being told to do so by Mr Choate. And Mr Choate would naturally back her up on that if asked by Wyatt. Mr Critchley also taught that procedure in his defensive driving course.

"Choate is doing his job - which is to protect you."

"Including telling you every little thing I do every day. Where I go, whom I speak to," she snapped again. Save for her lunch with Mr Choate at Charley's the other day.

"Yes. It may never be necessary to use the information, my dear, but the information is on file if we ever need it," he explained calmly. "To be blunt -"

"I get it," Gem scowled and backed down, knowing he was referring to abduction. "Still ! It's spying on me. You are spying on me!"

"Take it as you wish," he shrugged.

"You're spying on me because you don't trust me!"

"You know I don't. I was very blunt on that subject at Marigold Cottage. Nothing has changed. Did you think it had?"

Well, it wasn't always at the front of her mind. That was taken up with the Pilos, and gathering information, and wondering of Harry, and Paul Andriani, and when she could focus on it - her book.

"Don't ever fool yourself, my dear. Nothing has changed in our relationship," Wyatt repeated without emotion. "Did you think it had or would?"

Gem shook her head. She was simply trying to survive each day. "I try to force it out of my thoughts," she said wearily.

"Your error," he exhaled sharply. "Breakfast half an hour."

Not the best start to the day. She had to get the Hell away from Wyatt. He certainly wasn't going to change on the control issue, she sighed as she showered. The past week had been nearly pleasant with him ignoring her. Now the plague that was Wyatt Grantham was beginning again.

Wyatt fumed while he prepared their meal. Slipping out of bed early every morning was one matter. Sleeping on the settee in her office would not become a habit!

Damn! She got under his skin! He was not used to having his orders or decisions questioned. He did not tolerate obstructions to his goals. He was not going to tolerate defiance from least of all her!

Her research. The War interest. Indonesia. John Staunton. Geneva. The third passport. The locked file box. He could insist she open that. But he wouldn't. Not yet, not until something surfaced in whatever plans she was formulating, to indicate it was necessary to search her file box. With Choate following her, she could not leave the U.K., even with the third passport she denied having. And the GPS on her mobile, and on the Defender, gave him instant updates on her location. Trust her! He had obviously corrupt business adversaries he trusted more than he trusted Gem!

Damn! He couldn't read her. Still! After all these weeks! Astute judge of character that he was, he couldn't read her - yet! And how had she so cleanly escaped the inter-net? No family. No trace of a Jane Forrester or a Jane Lawson - the supposed aunt. Education facts, honours graduate, teaching assistant. That was it! People in witness protection programs had longer dossiers than had Gemimah Forrester Grantham! She covered her tracks well!

Gem did the washing up as Wyatt retired to the library when his mobile rang. Hopefully he would be there for hours. The photo albums on the kitchen counter were a glaring warning of the battle to come this weekend.

After she had learned of his deceit, she had thought the promise of the albums was a part of his Game. And he raged again that she couldn't be trusted! Ogre!

Gem stared out the kitchen window. The sun was shining in a cloudless sky. It would be a lovely day to sketch or to use the pastels set she had purchased weeks ago.

Half eight o'clock in the morning in Ticking Bottom. Coming to late afternoon on an uninhabited island in South East Asia. She would check the computer to see what weather the searchers would be wrestling with this weekend.

Wyatt had not returned by the time Gem had finished the washing up, so she took the opportunity to do the weather check. Her heart sank in sympathy for Mr Cawley and the others. Monsoonal rains for the next three days. Mr Cawley would not likely make it back to London in the scheduled time frame of his 'seminar'. That meant someone would have to prep him on Australian government accounting procedures. Or perhaps he had studied that before he left England. Probably had. The man was a wonder of detail.

What staggeringly wonderful men, including the local guide! Mr Cawley flying half-way around the world to climb a mountain in a rainforest to search for Gemmy, mum, dad, Mr Portermann. Lord! The courage the three men had! - All for the passengers of the Pilos! Bless them!

Gem gathered her sketch book, pencils, and the pastels set. Wellies were probably a must and although it hadn't rained for a few days, the fields might still have those mucky areas. She would take her camera along to shoot what she sketched in the event she didn't finish drawing. She was putting the items in a medium portfolio when Wyatt walked into the office.

"Shall we start on the photo albums?" he said casually.

"I was going out to sketch," Gem hedged. He didn't reply and his steady gaze warned her that he was not going to brook refusal. "Fine," she conceded, and pulled out the box of photo packs taken at Wight and Inverness. "Have at it," she shrugged.

Wyatt slipped the snaps from the first pack, scanning the photos, then did the same with the second pack. "Where are the other photos? Pluckley, Bath, Randwick Woods, etcetera?" he demanded.

Gem stared at him. "I shredded them," she said crisply.

Wyatt stared at her, startled by her reply. "Why? Why would you destroy your work?" he shook his head, puzzled.

Gem crossed her arms and leaned against the counter.

"Why would I destroy the photos of your clever lies? Your clever Game - Games?" she said coldly. "I don't need photos to remind me of your lies. I live your lies every single minute of every single day. You want photos of YOUR honeymoon, then take them, revel in them," she grabbed her portfolio and brushed past him. Forget the wellies and the windcheater. Her thick jumper would have to do. She strode out the kitchen door and was half-way down the drive when Wyatt called to her.

"Gem!"

She turned to glare at him, just in time to catch the hat he tossed to her. He turned and went back inside the Hall.

Humph! she muttered in surprise. She pulled on the hat and continued down the drive to the cobblestone lane, and across the meadow to sit by the brook.

She caught her breath as she pulled the sketch pad and pastels from the portfolio. Control. Control, she soothed her frayed nerves.

She had won the first round of this battle, but she knew he would not easily give up a fight on this issue. She had thwarted him and she knew that would rankle Wyatt Grantham to his core.

Still, winning the first round felt great!

The pastels felt good in her fingers. It had been years since she had used them. She took colour photos of the thatched cottage in the distance, then concentrated on the sketch pad and the pastels.

Climbing in a monsoon would be better than climbing in a typhoon? Right?

And if the plane was the Pilos?

Oh my God! It would all be over! She could explain everything to Wyatt! She would have her family again - her memories. They would 'exist' again. She could get a divorce. She would never have to see Wyatt again! She would be free!

Gemmy! Gemmy! Gemmy! She moaned. After so many months! Mum! Dad! Mr Portermann!

Gem sat motionless, staring, unseeing, at the cottage across the field. It would all be over. After nearly four and a half months. Four and a half months of emptiness. So many lonely, painful months.

If it was the Pilos - it wouldn't be connected to the murders of the SEA Network counter-couriers and counter-agents. They would be a separate issue.

But they couldn't be separate. It was too coincidental that the two counter-couriers - the Vietnamese courier Gemmy was to meet, and the Chinese courier mum was to meet - were murdered - considering how many counter-couriers there were in the SEA Network - and in the International Network - and the murdered SEA Network counter-agents. It couldn't be a coincidence. The Pilos and the SEA Network murders were connected. How? Would that be answered by finding the Pilos?

And if it wasn't the Pilos? Mrs Brown had cautioned her against getting her hopes up. Gem had to constantly remember that warning! But it was the first hope she had had since 30 May. The only hope she had had.

And if it wasn't the Pilos - the search would continue.

She had to push the thoughts from her mind. Her nerves were no longer fraying; they were shredding. - Horrid thought! Photos! Albums! She also pushed those thoughts from her mind.

The light was shifting, the sun was high in the sky. She took another photo of the cottage to note the progression of shadows. And now smoke drifted up and away from the chimney.

Ping

Gem grabbed her mobile from her skirt pocket.

'Text when communication is safe.'

Her fingers flew over the keys.

'Now.'

'Torrential rains trapped expedition in mountain cave.'

'Lucky to find a cave!'

'Found by Cawley when he dropped his torch.'

'Bless Mr Cawley!'

'Indeed. You holding on okay?'

'Yes. Thank you.'

'Will update you half two tomorrow morning.'

'Thank you Mr Choate!'

'Are you trying to rest?'

'Trying to relax.'

'Okay. Bye for now.'

'Bye.'

Bless his heart! Her Agency Family was so good to her!

Conversely. If her family hadn't worked for the Agency, all would likely still be alive.

But! And a BIG one! The Forresters and Lawsons had always been aware of the possible dangers of their jobs. And that fact had never been a consideration in joining and remaining with the Agency.

Land of Hope and Glory. A text message from Wyatt.

'Lunch half hour.'

She glanced at her watch. Lovely. The next battle.

Sighing heavily, Gem packed up her art supplies in the portfolio, slung the camera bag over her shoulder, and steeled herself for a dismal lunch.

She would like to count down the days until the expedition reached the plane on the mountain as a hope to a divorce. But since that joy was definitely far from an immediate fact, she had to remain circumspect and accept that there still was no end in sight for her current situation. Blast!

Wyatt was preparing lunch when she walked into the kitchen. She put the portfolio and camera case in her office and taking a deep breath, returned to the kitchen to take the tableware from the cupboard.

"The table is set," Wyatt informed her, noting her efforts. "Breakfast room."

That was a change from weekend meals. He was the one who had first set the eating in the kitchen rule when Mrs M wasn't preparing the food. Easier, less effort, Wyatt had stated.

Gem watched, surprised, as he removed a ham from the cooker. He had prepared mashed potatoes, gingerbread, and a bowl of mixed vegetables.

"Beer - in the fridge, unless you prefer wine," he suggested, glancing over his shoulder at her.

Beer for him, Gem fetched a bottle, then made a cup of tea for herself.

And what was his present Game? She would have to take each moment as they came so as not to allow him to throw her off balance. While Wyatt sliced the ham, Gem carried the beverages and side dishes to the breakfast room.

"I made a cheesecake for dessert," she hesitantly volunteered.

"So I noticed. I defrosted strawberries for topping."

"Aren't you afraid the cheesecake might be poisoned?" she said pointedly.

"May we please have any battles or arguments after lunch?" Wyatt said dryly. "They are counter-productive to processing food."

Counter-productive? Gem had to ponder that statement. "Oh dear. Do you suffer from indigestion?" Gem's brows knitted in a frown. She hadn't noticed that he suffered from health problems.

"No. I am a carrier. I give indigestion."

Gem nodded thoughtfully. "I imagine you do."

"I refer to you. You pick at your food. You rush away from the table before you finish eating. Lack of sleep is a serious issue, and combined with poor diet it will lay you low very quickly," Wyatt observed firmly.

"And why should you care?" Gem said bitterly.

"I don't have time to defend my care of your health to Mrs Brown or to Mrs M," Wyatt replied crisply.

"Mrs Brown called you?" Gem asked in shock.

"No, but I have the feeling she will if you start wasting away. And Mrs M is never quiet about you." Nicely feigned concern of his possible indigestion. He should have a BAFTA statue fashioned for her: Best Actress in a Continuing Vixen Role/Series.

He left the kitchen and shortly thereafter, Gem hear the Hothouse Flowers cd playing in her office. Gem frowned. She couldn't get a handle on this particular Game of his. And this was adding to her shredding nerves. She couldn't mentally process the expedition, the Pilos, Gemmy, and Wyatt's sudden new Game.

And why would Wyatt be in any way concerned about Mrs Brown holding him responsible for her health? He had only met the woman once. Mrs M was another matter altogether. She knew Wyatt inside and out - had for years. And no doubt she had a familiarity with him that precluded such niceties as 'minding your own business'.

Lunch was an extremely polite affair. Wyatt asked her of her walk. Gem replied that she had been sketching - using oil pastels, she corrected herself. She asked him if he had managed to accomplish the reading of any reports in addition to preparing lunch - which she complimented him as excellent. He returned the compliment with a remark of a brilliant cheesecake recipe.

"Family recipe?" he casually inquired.

"Inter-net," she lied just as casually.

He didn't start the next step of the Game until after the washing up, which he did not desert for a phone call - for a change.

When the last item had been placed in the dishwasher, Wyatt leaned against the counter and stared at Gem speculatively, as he drank a second beer.

"Did you shred the negatives as well as the snaps?" he demanded quietly.

Blast! Why had he thought of the negs? She had wanted to use them as a final, nasty, parting shot when she walked out of the Hall for the last time - on her way to a divorce solicitor - and to a new life.

"No," she grudgingly admitted.

Wyatt accepted her words with a curt nod. "Have the photos reprinted then. We will work on the albums next weekend."

Again with the albums! And his lies!

"I am not interested in the albums!"

"Not surprising, considering the effort you put into hiding your past. That practice is over. From now on you shall have a past - although the most substantive part might only date from the day we met," he informed her with a pointed look. "Have you found your third passport?"

Ouch! So that was his Game! He was trying to track her past - and Gemmy's - of course. Of course, he would try to track her.

Stay calm. Count to twenty. Naturally it was not surprising that he wanted information on her. She was 'connected' to James. And to 'Staunton'. And she wasn't giving him any information about either men.

"Have you found the third passport?" he repeated his query.

"No," she admitted truthfully. Perhaps the passport was in a plane crashed into a mountain in the middle of a rainforest. On an uninhabited island in a 1,919,440 square kilometre area of Indonesia.

"No," she sighed wearily.

Wyatt scowled. That damned haunted look was in her eyes again.

"You're reading about Indonesia. Have you ever been to South East Asia?" he asked casually.

Still hunting her. "No. Have you?"

"Yes."

"Have you offices there?" she asked curiously, then regretted the query. GEI was none of her business.

"No."

He didn't elaborate, and she didn't press the subject. Could she move on now to the remainder of the afternoon? Had he covered all his issues?

"I would like to read your thesis," Wyatt said.

"Why?" Gem queried cautiously. Cathedrals, not art glass. She was in trouble.

"To see your work."

She was done. Gem walked to her office. The reason Gemmy had returned to Australia. The lie. But not a lie.

She had had enough with the chat. She took cash from her shoulder bag, stuffed it in her pocket, picked up her camera case and walked out the kitchen door.

The sky was on her side. Clouds drifted in, wispy at first, and then slowly building. She burned the colour roll then switched to black and white, switching lenses, covering the entire sky in sections. She like the views she was seeing: the old stone bridge below the Hall, a close-up of the cobblestones in the lane, a single surviving meadow flower stark against the fall worn rubble around it. Stark reality. Oh! so similar to her life, Gem thought sarcastically. The rail station would be striking in black and white. She finished the roll and started another.

Gem glanced at her watch as the sun slid lower in the sky. Four o'clock. Midnight in a cave in a rainforest, on a mountain side, on an uninhabited island somewhere in the waters of Indonesia. Harry would be checking in with either Mrs Brown or Mr Choate. She pulled out her mobile to text Mr Choate.

'Safe to receive.'

Hopefully he had new information.

It was nearly a quarter of an hour later that she received a reply.

Ping

'Still in cave. Cawley worried about explaining jungle rot to his wife from possibly touring Australian government accounting offices.'

Gem burst out laughing. The pressure the men were under, the perils they were facing - and Mr Cawley offered humour! What a dear heart!

'Brilliant! Thanks for the laugh!'

'Chat later.'

'Yes!'

She was still chuckling when she wandered into the old cemetery. Although the church no longer held services, it was well maintained, as was the cemetery. Generally, in the old cemeteries she visited, stones were askew as if fighting to escape the ground. Ticking Bottom cemetery headstones were straight to the sky, the graves neatly, lovingly tended. The interred were not forgotten, nor neglected. Gem finished the second roll of black and white film, and switched to colour to capture the fall colour of the serene setting.

She had neatly framed the stain glass church windows overlooking the cemetery when the hairs on the back of her neck prickled.

Wyatt.

Gem snapped the shot, then dragged her fingers through her hair. The next battle.

"Yes?" she swung around to face him with studied patience.

"Beer? M's? Crow?" he suggested mildly.

Gem considered the suggestion that had been stated with neutral attitude.

"Indeed," she agreed. However hot chocolate was more appealing than beer.

Gem simply could not summon the flow of the previous night with the Bristol text. Writing hadn't been a problem when she had prepared her thesis. Now it was a grind, each sentence was a struggle, a cohesive paragraph was an alien concept. She studied the photographs, searching for inspiration. If one couldn't find inspiration from studying a cathedral what hope was there for the Bristol chapter? Inspiration. Peace. Quiet. Resolve. Hope. Contentment. Wisdom of the ages. Faith. Unbending. Unquestioning. Amazing thoughts.

The captions beneath the photos flowed. Progress, she smiled, reaching levels of resolve and contentment.

And then the fly fell into the ointment.

"Come to bed, sweetheart," Wyatt said from the doorway.

"You've smashed my thoughts!" Gem groaned, dropping her head to rest on the keyboard.

"You're tired," Wyatt coaxed. He crossed the room and began to massage her shoulders, his hands sliding down to her waist, resting his cheek against hers, rubbing gently.

Gem sighed, melting to the strength of his arms.

"You know you want to," he whispered in her ear. "You always want to."

His arrogance ignited her shredded nerves. "You always want to!" Gem flung back. "What I want doesn't matter!"

"Now you're simply being snappish," Wyatt replied. "You need more sleep. And more lovemaking."

Gem escaped from the chair, rounding to face him. "You are so insufferable! It's always you, isn't it. Always what you want!"

"Of course it is, Gem. You know that. And you benefit yourself!" Wyatt retorted.

"Blast ! You are driving me mad!"

"Fortunately for you it shall be a one way trip," he countered.

"How do I despise you, let me count the ways," Gem fumed.

Wyatt scoffed. "Gem! You are too brilliant a woman to purloin and butcher a great poet's words. Put that devious mind of yours to work and find your own words. I expect better from you than that pitiful trifle."

"You are a beast!"

"No creativity!"

"Dark Lord!"

Wyatt reflected on the retort. "I do actually favour that. You may address me as such from now on," he chuckled. "The Dark Lord commands you to come to bed. You will be awake again in a few hours, and I would like to admire you before I sleep."

He jested about her insomnia, but while she denied the problem, refused to seek a solution, he worried about the drawn look on her face. The haunted look in her lovely violet eyes was there usually more often than not these days.

Gem sighed wearily, grudgingly giving up the battle for it was obvious Wyatt was not going to relent. She took a quick shower, pulled on pyjamas and climbed into bed.

Wyatt drew her over to him, wrapped his arms around her and gently kissed her. "Go to sleep, sweetheart," he murmured. As much as he wanted to keep her awake, her need of sleep overruled his need of her.

Gem was startled by his words. And she was grateful for them. She was exhausted, and sleep was a sweet desire.

Gem stared out the windows over the sink as she did the washing up; she had volunteered for the task since Wyatt had, as usual, prepared breakfast. And that was an agreeable arrangement as he was a far better cook than she. Apparently he wasn't actually worried that she would poison him, for he had enjoyed the cheesecake the previous night.

The dark hours had been so bleak again without Mr Cawley's texts. Mr Choate had texted at half past two, as he had promised to do, but could only inform her that the expedition team was still in the cave, waiting out the torrential rainfall. Their guide advised against proceeding in the rain, as it was very difficult to avoid the wildlife. One did not wish a sun bear to drop out of the tree tops without a bit of warning.

Gem had researched the sun bear on the inter-net, and was very uneasy after learning the animal was one of the fiercest bears in the world. Mr Choate had promised again to text an update at half past two Monday morning.

I must make it through this day. I must make it through this day, Gem said over and over.

"Is that your daily mantra?" Wyatt queried dryly.

Gem started, unaware that he had walked up behind her. And she was also unaware that she had spoken aloud. Did she do that often? She had to watch her step on that in the future.

"One of them," she shrugged.

"How heart-warming," Wyatt observed, his tone still dry. "As much as I would like to hear your other mantras, I have to postpone that delight. I'm going to the office for a few hours. Are you comfortable staying here alone or shall I ask Mrs M to come over to stay with you? Or you could walk over to the carriage house and have a chat with the M's."

What an odd query. "I am perfectly comfortable being alone here," she insisted. "I have my work to do."

"As you wish then. Shall we meet at the Crow for lunch at one o'clock?"

"Indeed," Gem easily agreed. Alone at the Hall for the entire morning! Perfectly perfect! "One o'clock it is."

She watched from the kitchen window as the Jag disappeared down the cobblestone lane and across the old stone bridge. She would wait twenty minutes, then begin her search of the Hall. As backup to her plans she booted up her computer, pulled up the file on Bristol, sorted the photos, and put a cup of tea on the counter next to her scanner.

Gem retrieved her torch from her desk drawer. She had neglected to turn off the torch the last time she had used it; the batteries were dead. She searched the mudroom for a torch, as Mrs M had insisted she not climb the attic stairs without one. Usually three torches sat on the shelf above the wellies, but the torches were gone. Every single one of them. Blast! It wouldn't be smart to disregard Mrs M's order. If she took a tumble on the steps there could be holy hell to pay with Wyatt. He wouldn't allow her to be alone at the Hall ever again.

The attic search was off then for that day. So it was back to James's room, and another proper search of the photo albums. The photo of Gemmy was gone, as Gem had suspected it would be. And there were no other photos of Gemmy. But there were dozens of Grantham family photos she had only glanced at the last time she was in James's room - the day Wyatt had caught her in there. She was rather surprised actually that Wyatt hadn't locked the door to the room; it was possible to do so as the door had a key lock.

Gem studied the photos of the Senior Granthams. Mrs Grantham was very tanned, blonde, and stunningly beautiful. Mr Grantham was nearly as handsome as his eldest son, and had an aura of being strong and virile - also like Wyatt. Gem hadn't noticed any photos of the elder Granthams in any of the rooms at the Hall. Perhaps there were photos at Wyatt's London flat, since he had mainly resided there for years.

There were photos of James and young ladies - perhaps the girlfriends Wyatt had so sarcastically referred to in his tirade that day. And in the last album, the one she had barely glanced at that other day, there were photos of Wyatt and women. Stunning women, tall, beautiful, exquisitely groomed. Three of the women were film actresses, three were models, two were minor royals; she didn't recognize the other women in the photos, but they certainly were smashing.

Wyatt had certainly 'dated' in his league. And had certainly married out of it. Gem was definitely relieved that she didn't have to, or have a desire to, compete with the women for Wyatt's affections. She would have been a major disaster in that competition! Perhaps one of the women would return to reclaim his attentions when Gem escaped her 'marriage' to him.

Search completely completed of James's room. She went on to the other bedrooms in the event something had been 'accidentally' placed in another room. She had hoovered and dust mopped the other bedrooms, but had not searched them with Mrs M working in the same vicinity with her. The bedrooms had obviously not been used for years. Not so much as a hairpin was to be found in drawers, dressing rooms, or bathrooms. All the rooms looked picked clean.

The study and the den held books and stationery supplies. Nothing else. How could a house be so void of personal items? Had Wyatt made it so to keep her from knowing anything about him other than what he specifically wanted her to know? To keep her in the dark? And there was nothing more of James, save for his framed artwork on nearly every wall in the Hall. He certainly had been a prolific artist for his young age!

The library. The doors were not kept locked when Wyatt wasn't at the Hall. But the desk drawers were locked, as was the panelled cabinet behind the desk.

Was she looking for something specific or was she just snooping? The attic. Give it a try, she reconsidered. The steps were dark. Dangerously so.

Land of Hope and Glory. Text message from Wyatt.

'One o'clock.'

Gem looked at her watch. She just had time to freshen up and walk to the pub. And she would purchase two torches in London tomorrow when she dropped of the blasted negatives for reprints.

She was out the kitchen door before she realized she had neglected to close the library doors, and that would not do. Wyatt must not know that she had been snooping around the Hall again. It had been a waste of time, except for seeing the snaps of Wyatt's past amours. If nothing else, she was neat and clean. She took another quick scan of the library before closing the doors. Was the snap of Gemmy in one of the locked desk drawers, the locked cabinet, or in a hidden safe? A safe was possibly behind the cabinet. She decided the photo was with the passports and other photos. But she was certain it was completely beyond her reach.

Monday morning the dark hours were even drearier. Monday, mid-morning Indonesia, and still monsoonal rains. The expedition remained in the cave. Mr Cawley was certain he had spotted a White-Handed gibbon and two Siamangs, according to Harry via Mr Choate. No progress on the uninhabited island somewhere in the waters of Indonesia.

What was Gem to do with her time while she waited for news of the plane on the mountain? She had thought of shredding the negatives, but what was the point since Wyatt knew they still existed? Gem reached for one of the references books on Indonesia and decided to read it cover to cover.

The assistant at the photo shop winced when she saw the stacks of negatives Gem produced for reprints. The staff had worked four weddings over the weekend and those contracts took precedence over reprints. That information did not disturb Gem in the least. She asked for the prints to be ready by Friday and was assured that would not be a problem. She would have the photos for the weekend and Wyatt's insidious ramble down his 'memory lane'.

She prepaid the bill and was reminded Friday was a half-day and then the shop would be closed until the following Monday.

The days dragged by. The expedition finally left the cave Tuesday morning, and Mr Cawley sent word he had seen a number of Komodo Dragons, and wild orchids that would make Mrs Brown's eyes spin. Gem finished reading one reference book and started a second book. Bristol Cathedral text stalled because Gem couldn't focus on anything but a plane crash sighted on the side of a mountain.

Gem changed her paint colour selection from the green/grey to a deep taupe and then back to her first choice. She finally had the paint mixed on Thursday and would begin painting on Monday. Mrs M stated that Mr M would do the painting, but Gem insisted on doing the work herself. It would fill her time and ease her feeling of being at loose ends.

Wyatt was in the library every evening but he was in control again of her 'bedtime' which frustrated Gem to nearly losing her temper every night. She would relent each night because the look in his eyes indicated there was no chance of argument. And truth to tell, she didn't want to argue that particular subject. He still left for work before breakfast every morning and Mrs M continued to voice her disappointment to Gem as well as to Wyatt. His mood was a bit distant all week, but his libido wasn't.

Gem prepped the office walls and window trim on Thursday. She had purchased the paint, brushes, rollers and tarps to protect the floor; she could just imagine Wyatt's scornful look if she upset a can of paint on the stone floor.

It was an odd week for Gem. She lost her hat in one shop, her sunglasses in another, and when she backtracked to find the items both were gone. She didn't miss the blasted hat, but the sunglasses were a favorite pair she had purchased in Florence two years earlier. She had accidentally caught a Bach cd in a pile of snaps to be destroyed and had damaged the shredder - which she had to replace. Gem actually looked forward to painting, deciding to start on Friday, remaining at the Hall, and thereby not losing and hopefully not breaking anything else.

Chapter Nineteen

Friday dawned a perfectly beautiful day. As had been his habit that week, Wyatt left early for a meeting at his office. Gem had a quick breakfast at the kitchen island, chatting with Mrs M, and then changed to the clothes she had bought at the jumble sale - they were in perfect condition for painting - and for nothing else. She put her hair in a loose braid, moved the furniture to the centre of the room, and spread the tarps on the stone floor. She cut in carefully at the ceiling and at the woodwork, up and down the ladder, up and down the ladder until the basics were finished. Thank heavens for the jumble sale clothes, she sighed as she dropped the brush a half dozen times, the third time while she was on the ladder. And again thank heavens the paint would wash out of her hair and off her skin.

Gem glanced at her watch. Eleven o'clock. Friday. What was Friday? Blast! she groaned. The photos! She had an hour to get to London to pick up the photos. She grabbed her mobile and the keys to the Defender. Mrs M was upstairs hoovering, so Gem left a quick note stating she was out on an errand and would be back soon. The last thing she needed was another battle with Wyatt about not having the photos for the weekend. She had enough on her mind just thinking of the expedition in Indonesia, without having Wyatt railing at her for not listening to him - about anything. How long did it actually take to climb a mountain in a rainforest? Apparently longer than a fortnight!

The London traffic was horrid, people leaving early for a long weekend, traffic diverted due to a lorry accident. Gem reached the photo shop five minutes before it closed. She fetched the photos, and walked out with the staff as they left the shop for a series of weekend wedding shoots. Seventeen packs of photos! That should keep Wyatt amused for the entire weekend while Gem painted her office. She frowned, realizing that painting would probably not be a good excuse to take her away from 'Photo Album Weekend'.

Keys. Keys, she searched her pockets for the Defender keys.

Blast! They were still in the ignition. She glanced at the shops on either side of the photo shop. Blast! Half-day. All the shops were closed.

Blast! Mr Choate! She had neglected to call him! Gem pulled out her mobile. Dead. She hadn't charged the phone since when? No money. She couldn't use a public phone. And having money wouldn't have helped. She couldn't recall any of the phone numbers in her mobile contact list. She had always just scanned down the list, never really glancing at the corresponding phone numbers.

If she had a wire hanger she could probably unlock the Defender - if she had left the window cracked. Blast!

Double Blast! She had never before locked keys in a vehicle! She stood glaring at the Defender. Where was the defence now? She stood glaring at the vehicle, then tried every door, then the boot. Gem scowled, wondering what to do, when a police officer walked up to her.

"Is there a problem, Miss?" he asked politely.

"Keys locked inside," Gem said, fuming with frustration.

The officer looked at her and Gem could read his mind. She was certainly not dressed like someone who owned a very expensive classic vehicle such as a 1990 Defender in mint condition.

"Your vehicle, Miss? Do you have any identification?"

Oh sure! In my shoulder bag at Grantham Hall, Ticking Bottom. That sounded farfetched even to her.

"No, officer, not with me," she admitted.

"Is there perhaps someone you could call?" he suggested politely.

My Shadow, who is actually Director of Technical Operations - a private detective agency under the guise of a secret government Agency. Or my wealthy, powerful husband, Wyatt Grantham. I am obviously married to someone like him. Does any of this sound logical? Even remotely plausible? Of course it doesn't, Gem inwardly sighed.

"No officer. Thank you," she started to walk along the pavement. Photographic memory be damned! When her mobile was charged she would memorize every Blasted number on the Blasted contact list!

Bite the bullet. She had no other choice. She had to go to Wyatt's office. He would be furious with her! No working mobile, no money, no keys, and she looked like something even a cat would refuse to drag into a house.

The Grantham Building was eight blocks away and she Blasted herself every step of the way. This was not one of those situations she would look back on one day, share with friends, and laugh hysterically.

Gem stood on the pavement, staring at the stately new red sandstone structure bearing the dignified brass plate 'Grantham Building'. No 'Enterprises' or 'International' was indicated anywhere on the building. The building, ten stories tall, stood on a half block area. Across the street from the building was a lush, fenced-in square block park with mature trees and lavish gardens. No doubt Wyatt Grantham had a penthouse office with windows over-looking the park, which likely might be considered one of the loveliest office views in the entire city.

The interior of the building was old marble floors and handsome aged dark wood panelling. The Grantham Building fairly breathed: Tradition. Old Money. Stability.

Gem was startled to see the metal statue that had been stickered SOLD at the school art show in August. And it wasn't the only stickered item in the lobby that Gem remembered from the art show. She easily recognised eight paintings from the show and thought another three or four were also from the school fund-raiser. Apparently GEI, or more pointedly, Wyatt Grantham, supported the causes for which Ms Holton raised funds. Gem saw the well groomed front desk receptionist watching her; the young woman forced a polite smile as Gem approached her desk.

"May I help you?" the receptionist queried, still with a smile.

Gem noted the silver name plate on the desk. "Ms Jones," Gem nodded. "Wyatt Grantham's office, please," she said, summoning every ounce of courage she could muster not to spin emotionally out of control.

Ms Jones's eyes widened imperceptivity. "Eighth floor," she replied politely, indicating the first of the bank of three lifts.

"Thank you," Gem replied, her nerves shredding to non-existence. Wyatt was going to be furious with her!

As she entered the lift, Gem saw the receptionist pick up the receiver of the phone on her desk.

No doubt ringing ahead to warn of the vagrant soon to arrive, Gem groaned.

Was Wyatt's office truly on the eighth floor - or would Gem step off the lift into the hands of building security?

She sighed, looking about her. Even the whisper quiet lift spoke of elegance with its beautiful wood panelling.

Yes. Probably security - hence Ms Jones pointing to the first lift. - Likely direct access to armed personnel.

As the lift doors opened, Gem looked about in surprise. More elegant panelling. And a second receptionist as equally well-groomed as Ms Jones. Impressive staff so far. Of course - it was Wyatt's staff - and what one would expect of his business world.

The silver name plate identified the eighth floor receptionist as Ms Carton, who was obviously awaiting the interloper's arrival.

"May I help you?" Ms Carton inquired with a frozen but polite smile.

"Mr Grantham's office," Gem quietly requested.

The receptionist gave a slight frown. "Mr Grantham is in conference today. He is unavailable for appointments."

She was very polite, Gem mused. I wouldn't allow me to go a step further either.

"Ms Holton then," Gem took a deep breath.

The receptionist smiled. "Along the corridor, second door on the right, Research and Development. Just walk right in."

Good decision, Gem observed. 'Whatever' it was that wanted Wyatt Grantham would never get past Ms Holton. Gem replied with a thank you and a nod, and followed the receptionist's instructions.

The second door on the right opened onto a very spacious room with seven desks - computer systems, printers and blocks of wood filing cabinets at every desk work centre. Emma Holton was standing at a desk towardss the rear of the room in front of impressively carved double doors. She was apparently holding court, and four women and three men hung onto her every word. All seven of the young staff members were as well-groomed as the receptionists. Ms Holton was striking in her black power suit. Wyatt Grantham's 'wife' was the dregs of society compared to his impeccable staff.

It was Ms Holton who first noticed Gem. And the woman did not miss the slightest of proverbial beats, nor bat the proverbial eyelash. She immediately walked to Gem, extending her right hand.

"Mrs Grantham. How lovely to see you again," Emma Holton smiled warmly. The last time she had seen Mr Grantham's wife was before their marriage, when the young woman had scooped up the youngest wailing Holton to comfort the child.

Ms Holton immediately seized control of the situation. "You are here to see Mr Grantham, of course."

"Thank you, yes," Gem could have fallen through the floor with humiliation.

Ms Holton crossed the room to a far desk, reaching for the telephone; Gem quickly followed her. "One of those days?" Emma Holton softly and sympathetically queried.

"Yes," Gem admitted ruefully.

"I usually have them on my busiest days when there is not a single extra minute to correct an error," Ms Holton said softly and with a gentle smile.

Despite Ms Holton's kindness Gem agonized. This was not going to be good. Perhaps she should just use the phone to ring Mr M to come to London to fetch her. She was certain Ms Holton would have the Grantham Hall estate manager's phone number at the ready.

Ms Holton spoke into the phone receiver. "Delia, put Mr Grantham on the line," she said crisply, impatiently tapping a pencil against the desktop.

"You're very tall," Gem murmured. "Oh! I said that aloud!"

"It's very handy," Ms Holton chuckled," for power meetings with Good Ole Boys from other companies. Intimating. However height is very annoying when I'm trying to buy clothes. Not much choice out there."

Gem grinned at her. She liked Ms Holton. Gem set the bags of photos on the desk, and reached for a pen and piece of paper, writing down the name and address of Ora and Eda's shop for the generous spirited Ms Holton. "Shop here," she whispered. "You won't regret a visit to this shop."

Ms Holton mouthed a grateful reply, then she spoke crisply into the phone again. "Delia, I realize Mr Grantham is extremely busy today. Now put him on the phone or you will be extremely unemployed in approximately ninety seconds." She winked at Gem. "Mr Grantham, Mrs Grantham is here to see you." Emma Holton frowned. "Certainly I am sure it's Mrs Grantham," she insisted firmly.

Gem surreptitiously read the room, noting that the young staffers had returned to their desks, busying themselves while also watching Ms Holton and 'Mrs Grantham'.

Gem forced herself to remain calm, outwardly, but she felt totally inadequate and incompetent compared to the industrious young staffers, all of whom were probably at least a year younger than she.

There were twenty-four hours in a day. How could a day go so wrong so quickly? Blast!

Wyatt walked through the double doors at the rear of the office. He was scowling, greatly aggravated by the interruption of the meeting, but his look changed to one of amusement when he saw Gem. Paint stained: shirt, jeans, face, there was even paint in her braid. He stopped dead in his tracks.

"Oh darling. Are you having a difficult day?" His scowl disappeared and he fought back a grin. "Ms Holton, please take the meeting," he glanced beyond Gem to his properly groomed assistant.

Emma Holton quickly nodded and entered the doors from which Wyatt had just appeared.

"Go ahead and laugh," Gem sighed as Wyatt put his arms around her and dropped a kiss on her lips.

"I wouldn't think of it," he shook his head.

"I am so sorry," Gem blushed furiously. "I locked the keys in the Defender. My mobile is dead. I don't have any money. And I'm a dreadful sight."

"You look beautiful," he chuckled. "Is there actually any paint on the walls?" he teased.

"Well, I probably won't get the coverage I had expected," Gem conceded with a frown, drawing a huge laugh from Wyatt.

"I'm not sure about the colour," he teased again, sliding his fingers through her hair to smooth her fringe and brush it out of her eyes.

"It will work," Gem insisted.

"Let's go to Jake's for lunch and a half-pint and you can tell me all about your morning," Wyatt whispered in her ear.

"Okay," Gem whispered her reply, eager to get away from the seemingly unwatchful eyes of Wyatt's super groomed staff.

"You have the photos," Wyatt said approvingly, noting the huge shopping tote on the desk.

"The cause of the list of errors of this morning," Gem nodded.

Her escape from the office was not immediate for Wyatt slipped his arm around her waist, guiding her to each desk to introduce her to the staff of Research and Development.

"Relax," he whispered in her ear.

Gem shook a paint stained hand with each employee, and managed a polite smile.

There was more than one dropped jaw in the office as the impeccably groomed Wyatt Grantham introduced his wife to his staff.

At the last desk he issued an order to a Ms Ames, who was still trying to make her jaws meet. "Please inform Ms Holton that I am out of the office for the remainder of the day." He reached for the bag of photos.

"Yes, Sir, Mr Grantham," the young woman immediately snapped to attention.

Gem knew her face was bright pink by the time they left the R&D office.

She groaned inwardly as Wyatt added humiliation to humiliation when he introduced her to the eighth floor receptionist as they waited for the lift. Ms Carton gave a very polite and patently startled look as she shook Gem's hand.

As the lift doors closed, shutting out the eighth floor Gem groaned audibly. "How could you embarrass me like that?" she demanded in dismay. "Truly I am sorry I came here. I didn't have any other choice. Isn't there a single Blasted back door to this building - opening out onto a lake into which I can throw myself?"

Wyatt pushed the button on the instrument panel to halt the lift, and then he gave her a firm kiss.

"I introduced you to everyone to show them I was not embarrassed by your appearance. It took great nerve to come here today, I realize that. You had to face the vicious lion in his den. I was the last person you wanted to ask for help. I realize that also. Now smile, my dear. There's still a bit of the gauntlet to run. Where is Mr Choate, by the way? Didn't he have his set of keys to the Defender?"

"I didn't call him," Gem admitted sheepishly. "It was just a quick trip in for the photos before the shop closed for the weekend. I forgot I had to pick them up today. I only had an hour - I just didn't think."

Wyatt frowned. "Don't fret about it," he said gently. "We'll get it all handled. Is your hat in the Defender?"

"I lost it the other day. And my sunglasses," she sighed.

"Oh dear. They were brilliant sunglasses," he sympathised. "Perhaps we can find another pair like them. And we'll get you a stack of hats to keep in the Defender," he decided, giving her braid a quick tug. He pushed the start button and the lift descended to the ground floor.

"Now smile, sweetheart," he urged, as they exited the lift, and he led her to the main reception desk.

Ms Jones's eyes grew wide as they approached her. Gem could almost read her mind: Mr Wyatt Grantham escorting a scourge from the streets back out to the pavement.

Wyatt introduced the women then added, "Please chat for a few minutes." He stepped away to use his mobile. "Perhaps Ms Jones can talk you out of that paint colour," he teased Gem.

Gem sighed. "The colour is fine," she said to Ms Jones, whose eyes were still wide in disbelief. "One of those days," she admitted.

"That's every day for me," Ms Jones giggled. "I've been here for three months and I can't believe I haven't destroyed the building yet. Ever have a water tap come off in your hands? Water everywhere! But everyone here is so patient and helpful. This is the best company to work for in London. But I still have to finish that awful defensive driving course. Failed three times - and the company pays for it. It's considered very important here," Ms Jones confessed in a conspiratorial voice.

"Mr Critchley?" Gem lowered her voice.

"Yes," Ms Jones said sadly.

"Tip," Gem leaned over the desk. "Mr Critchley won't pass you if you aren't ready - but remember to watch your mirrors, stay calm, concentrate every minute. You'll pass."

"Thank you, Mrs Grantham," the receptionist brightened considerably. "I'll remember."

Wyatt joined them, raising a brow at Ms Jones's enthusiasm.

"Girl talk," Gem explained with a pert smile.

"Hmmm. Why do I sense trouble?" Wyatt replied cautiously.

"Oh no, Mr Grantham," Ms Jones said seriously.

"Did you talk about the paint? No? Then I am stealing away my wife now," Wyatt gave a nod to his employee.

Gem saw the stares as they walked down the street, his arm around her waist.

"Blast!" she cringed. "You stepped out of GQ and I fell out of the rubbish bin."

"You look very sexy. Paint on your face, your hair in a braid, your clothes from one of England's finest jumble sales - and I might say, promising every centimetre a delight to uncover."

"Is your brain ever out of the bedroom?" Gem sighed.

"Not with you, sweetheart," he leaned down to kiss the top of her head.

"Those young women in that office thought if they were married to you, they would always be beautifully groomed," Gem grumbled.

"They quite likely would be. They would be at the shops constantly. I would never see them. We would have nothing to discuss. And they certainly wouldn't be as much fun as you are. There's no humour in pseudo perfection."

"We don't discuss, we argue. And I think you enjoyed seeing me humiliated today," Gem fretted.

"Hush. Absolutely untrue. You are my wife and I wouldn't purposely humiliate you in public." He stopped walking, briefly, to kiss her.

Gem was slightly mollified. Yet even at Jake's Pub the server looked askance at Gem.

"My wife and I will each have a half pint," Wyatt crisply ordered, then reached for Gem's hand and kissed her fingers. "Shall we have the specials, sweetheart?" His eyes directed hers to the menu board.

Gem quickly agreed. "But I can't have beer if I'm driving."

"You are coming home with me," he said firmly.

"But the Defender -"

"Mr Choate shall take the Defender to the Hall, Mr M will see him back to the city."

"Mr Choate is too busy a man to run such errands," Gem protested uneasily.

"It wasn't a problem for him. Mr Choate has business to see to near Ticking Bottom."

"Oh," Gem frowned, then accepted Wyatt's remarks at full value. She would chat with Mr Choate later, she knew, because he would be upset that she hadn't rung him when she rushed out of the Hall that morning. She hadn't got a ticking off from Wyatt for her actions, but she would from Mr Choate.

"How did you manage - oh, - the phone call," Gem concluded. "Very organized."

"Precisely," Wyatt nodded.

The waitress brought their order, eyeing Wyatt with obvious appreciation. She moved to the next table, ostensibly to clean it, but keeping an ear to their conversation.

Wyatt clicked his beer mug against Gem's, stating clearly to listening ears, "Now, my dear bride, tell me the battles you have been fighting without me this day."

Gem leaned over to whisper to him. "You are laying it on a bit thick."

"Just seizing the opportunity for a civil conversation," he whispered in return, "and enjoying teasing the hell out of you!"

Gem conceded with a rueful smile. "It all started with the photos -oh no- no - where are the photos?" she gasped.

"Under the table. I took them off Ms Ames's desk."

Gem hadn't even noticed he had carried the bag from the Grantham building to the pub. "I don't what is wrong with me today! I can't concentrate for a single minute. - No comment please!"

"Damn! And I had a good one!" Wyatt laughed.

"I just bet you did!" Gem also laughed, and described her morning. "And, yes, my mobile was dead. I forgot to charge it. I'm sorry. And I think the police officer thought I was trying to steal the Defender," she shuddered.

"No doubt he did," Wyatt agreed.

"I know you never wanted me to go to your office. It was appalling of me to show up today - "

"Heavens, sweetheart, what other choice did you have," he said kindly. "Again, I was not embarrassed. It's not that I don't want you to come to the office. I simply want home separated from business. The Hall is my sanctuary - no stress."

"Oh yes, stress free," Gem said dryly. "You work constantly - and then - the Battling Granthams appear nightly!"

Wyatt gave her a lofty gaze. "I can control the battles, if and when I like. However, our battles of wit keep me mentally sharp. You are quite the verbal adversary."

Gem frowned. "Yes," she replied slowly, "although you always have the upper hand."

Wyatt reached over to tickle her ear. "Don't go all pouty on me now and destroy this pleasant, if temporary, truce," he said lightly. "Save the battles for home."

Gem relented. It was a pleasant, if temporary, truce. "Okay. You do work too hard however, according to Mrs M."

"I'll take that observation under advisement," Wyatt nodded.

When the waitress brought the bill, Wyatt handed it to Gem "Did you want to pay this today? - Oh wait - no money!" he teased.

"Ha-ha-ha," Gem retorted, suppressing a smile. "You are too clever by far." She swirled the mug of beer, watching the golden liquid form a maelstrom. "You just - left work today. You were so busy," she said guiltily.

"I'll fire myself on Monday," he quipped, then grew a bit serious. "Ms Holton stepped in. It should have been her meeting to begin with, but she had just concluded a very impressive deal for the company minutes before you walked into R&D. Her stepping in for me today fosters her credibility with the suits at the conference table."

"But what about your credibility? You left the conference table at an important meeting because your wife locked her keys in her car?"

"I will be the shining white knight, you - my featherheaded maiden," Wyatt teased.

"Thank you most unkindly Sir Knight," Gem retorted.

Wyatt stayed silent for a moment. "To be perfectly honest, Gem, there is a photo of you on my desk."

Oh! My God! A photo of me? Or of Gemmy? "What photo?" she said hesitantly, paling.

Wyatt's eyes narrowed. Why would a photo be so disconcerting? "You're wearing clothes, if that is of concern to you." He ordered a half pint for each of them, but Gem changed her order to a cup of tea. "A photo I took of you at Fortrose. You are most serenely studying the cathedral. And you look stunning."

Gem wasn't aware that Wyatt had taken a photo that day - she wasn't even aware that he owned a camera. But relief flooded her. Thank heavens it wasn't another photo James had taken of Gemmy that Gem wasn't aware existed. "Oh," she forced a casual tone. "Then I didn't have broccoli in my teeth or some such thing."

Such a mysterious woman: distressed over a photo, Wyatt mused. And why would that be? "No broccoli," he shook his head.

"And thank heavens I was wearing clothes - you don't have any -"

"No, my dear, I do not," Wyatt assured her, with a slight smile. "Curse my luck." Then he chuckled. "The men at the meeting today could not help but notice your photograph. None of them would have questioned for a moment why I left the office when you arrived."

Gem blushed. "Thank you. That was very kind of you to say."

And she could still blush! Such a very unusual woman!

"Your staff was quite wide-eyed when I entered the building today," she told him. "But Ms Holton didn't miss a beat. She was very kind."

"You are my wife, therefore you are of great importance to Ms Holton. She is the consummate employee. And she is very happy that I married you," Wyatt said smoothly.

"Why?"

"Because," he said bluntly, "her husband is no longer concerned of her working for me."

"Ah! I am a buffer."

"And a damned fine one," Wyatt acknowledged.

Gem smiled knowingly. How did he keep women at bay? "Ms Holton threatened that Delia when she rang through to tell you I was there to see you. She's quite commanding. I'd be wary of her, if I worked with her - or for her."

"Power struggle between the two. Delia will be offered a position at one of the offices in Germany. Manton and I agree that she needs to have her attitude adjusted," Wyatt nodded. "She'll be gone in a week or two."

"Ms Holton wins!"

"Absolutely. No question about it."

"She hangs on to your every word," Gem observed.

"Indeed. And because of that, in six months she will be promoted to Managing Director of the London Office. And she deserves the promotion. She pays attention. But don't tell her about the MDLO position - that is still under wraps."

He trusted her with that information? Odd. "I doubt I shall soon see her again. But I am very appreciative that she was there today."

"Ms Holton likes you," Wyatt patted Gem's hand.

Gem stared at him pointedly. "A backhanded compliment. 'She' likes me."

Wyatt shook his head. "Way too easy, my dear. We are at truce - remember? If only for this one brief afternoon."

Gem nodded her head, accepting the remark. "You can be fun," she replied.

Wyatt dramatically clutched his chest. "A compliment! From my featherheaded maiden no less!"

"It's the beer talking. Don't get used to it."

"Thank you. I am so underwhelmed," he laughed. "I won't get used to it. You'll soon be back to your normal, independent, sparring self," he smiled, winking at her. "Finish up, my dear, we should be off soon."

"Should you drive? You've had a bit of the brew - and with your propensity to have a heavy foot -"

"Hmmm. Let's go to the flat," he smiled. "You've never been there."

"Again the one track mind," Gem sighed.

"Come darling," he laughed, "we have shops to visit."

"Why?"

"We are on a mission. Hats and sunglasses!"

"Oh."

As they walked to various shops, the odd looks continued from their divergent appearances.

"You should dress like that more often, darling. You make me look good," Wyatt teased.

"My sole purpose for going to your office today," Gem gave him a mock sweet smile.

"And all this time I thought your visit was to entice me home."

"How much did you have to drink?" Gem shot back.

"Oh, how I miss these quiet afternoons together when I am at the office," he teased in a mock wistful tone.

"Ahuh. Perhaps I should drive back to the Hall."

"I'd sooner take a taxi back to T.B."

"Ouch!"

"Precisely!"

"I'm a good driver! Ask Mr Critchley!"

"I'll accept his opinion when he owns a classic Jag!"

"Tosh! Mr Critchley has a 1951 Silver Dawn Rolls," Gem said loftily.

"How do you know that?" Wyatt stopped suddenly.

No slipped cogs! Please! Mr Critchley would always have her back. "Hour upon hour with him in the Defender. Driving course - remember?"

"Really," Wyatt said skeptically.

"Truly. Ask Ms Jones. No doubt he has mentioned it to her." Twelve hours once a year the past six years!

Wyatt seemed to accept her explanation, so they continued walking and started shopping - to the tune of two pairs of very acceptable sunglasses and four hats - to remain in the Defender - not to be taken into the Hall.

"May I drive this car?" Gem asked seriously when Wyatt settled her in the Jag.

Wyatt paused, sucking in his breath sharply. "Not today," he said firmly. "If you wish, you may drive it - but not without me beside you," he finally relented.

Gem considered the remark. "Thank you. I won't ask again. And I won't drive it."

Wyatt stared at her, frustrated. "Then why the hell -"

"Don't get all disagreeable now and ruin a civil conversation," she paraphrased his earlier words.

Wyatt laughed heartily. "Please, please, my dear - in the future - lock your keys in your car at least once a week. No need to dress to impress, just come to the office in distress."

"You're a poet! A very bad one!" Gem teased. "Watch your driving," she warned, suddenly frowning at the traffic.

"Do you want to sit on my lap? No? Then stop driving, love," Wyatt laughed.

Mrs M met them at the door, a look of concern in her eyes.

"I was so worried when that man delivered your car," she tut-tutted to Gem.

"Everything is fine, Mrs M," Wyatt assured her, then pointed to Gem. "Don't give her any wine. She's already had beer today."

"As have you!" Gem shot back.

"Shower, clean clothes, dinner," Wyatt commanded. "I am not dining with Michelangelo tonight."

"Nag, nag, nag," Gem mocked, started down the hall towardss the staircase.

Wyatt winked at Mrs M. "Can't hold her liquor."

"Beer!" Gem called over her shoulder.

"Nag, nag, nag," Wyatt laughed, quickly following her to the master suite. "Dinner will be late, Mrs M! Take the Mister to the Crow on my bill," Wyatt called over his shoulder.

"Indeed," Mrs M observed mildly, and turned the cooker dial to low.

Mr M had finished painting the long wall in Gem's office while she was in the city. It was a sweet thought and he did a proper job. Curtains and rugs next - and hanging her art - including the watercolours she had purchased at the school art fair in August. The watercolours made her think of the art hanging in the Grantham Building. She realized after she had left the building with Wyatt that there had been additional student art on the corridor walls on the eighth floor. It had been very generous of Wyatt to have GEI purchase and display the students' artwork. He was an unusual man. He was a mystery.

What an odd day. The first truly pleasant one she had shared with Wyatt since before their wedding. And he had actually dropped everything to help her. No scolding, no recriminations of any kind. He had been her knight-in-shining-armour, rescuing her in her time of distress; or at least a knight in a smashing black suit, sparkling white shirt and steel grey tie. So like the man she had met at Oscar's Café so very long ago- at least it seemed a long time ago.

Brick wall!

Refocus!

The Wyatt today was an aberration. He was not the man who had trapped her in the sham relationship, she reminded herself.

How sad. Today was the best time she had spent with him since before Marigold Cottage; teasing, laughing, smiling, non-demanding.

He was certainly a force to be reckoned with, she shuddered. Even the formidable Ms Holton addressed him as Mr Grantham. There had been no informality between Wyatt Grantham and his staff at GEI. It was extremely intimidating to know that Gemmy's secrets were in his powerful grasp.

He was a man she would never have known had it not been for Gemmy and James. If only she had listened to Mrs Brown's warning. No, she wasn't in his league. He had the entire world at his fingertips. She didn't even have a world. In fact she and Wyatt weren't even in the same universe.

Today was simply a glitch in some whacked-out time/space continuum.

Focus.

Ping

'Should reach plane by Monday morning. Progress again delayed by rain.'

'Okay.'

'Keep mobile charged!'

'Yes, Mr Choate. Sorry you were inconvenienced today driving Defender to Hall.'

'I was driving this way already. Never again forget to ring me!'

'No, Mr Choate.'

'Defender excellent drive.'

'Indeed.'

'Will text tomorrow. Good night.'

'Good night.'

Mr Choate had reacted with considerable restraint. She had deserved a reprimand for her carelessness. It could NOT happen again.

Gem turned to survey the painted wall, a smile teasing her lips, as she recalled the first time she had seen the finished work - when she had completed the washing up after dinner. She had entered the office, Wyatt had followed her.

"Well, I like the colour," Gem had firmly announced.

"My comments to Ms Jones were in jest," Wyatt had insisted. "She still has new employee jitters. But the colour is quite adequate," he had conceded.

"Adequate?"

"Adequate is acceptable. It's adequate. Come to bed and we're argue about it."

"No," Gem had given him a saccharin smile.

"Come to bed and we won't argue about it."

"No," Gem had repeated. "I'm not tired."

"I'll make you tired then."

"We just got out of bed."

"Two hours ago!"

Gem had gasped as he slung her over his shoulder and carried her up the stairs.

"You'll ruin your back!" she had warned.

"Well worth it, my dear. Well worth it."

Gem had no doubt Wyatt would soon return to his normal persona, as he had said she would. More battles were in the near future.

Gem sighed. Hot chocolate, Vera Lynn on the cd player, and chapters on the wildlife of Indonesia.

Her thoughts wandered back.

"We forgot to turn off the lights," Gem had protested.

"You'll be going down in a few hours. Turn them off at five. You did charge your mobile, didn't you?"

"Yes," she had replied as he set her down on the bed. "Are you tired yet?"

"You are in a mood today," Wyatt had said, puzzled.

"I know. And I don't know why. It's just there."

"Keep it up," he had kissed the tip of her nose. "This way you are nearly bearable."

"Oh, so funny!" she had reached back above her head, grabbing a pillow to slam against his head.

And then he had make her tired.

Gem sighed again. "Bizarre," she murmured at the memory, and returned to her reading.

Gem studied the newly painted wall, visualizing placement of the art. She had drawn a schematic; she needed a hammer and nails; she had borrowed those items from Mrs Brown when she had hung art at her former flat. No doubt Mr M would loan her whatever she needed when she actually was to the point of pounding nails - and probably her fingers.

The end walls had to be painted, and the wood trim around the windows. She could stand or kneel on the counter to paint around the windows, which she would do when her paint clothes came out of the dryer. The paint tin, brushes and tarps were in the corner ready to be used.

Wyatt wandered into her office, a coil-bound report in his hand.

"I suggest a beadboard ceiling," he said, surveying the old plaster above them. "Three or four light fixtures."

"Too much work," Gem protested, reflecting that once she had left the Hall permanently, he could do whatever he wanted to finish off the room. "I just won't look up." The paint on the ceiling was a stark white and would suit her just fine.

"Mr M and Matt could complete the work in three days. You would have to select the light fixtures. We could drive to Cambridge to visit some shops."

"You have your reading."

"I can spare the time. Pub lunch?" he suggested.

Why not? She had hours to fill.

And it took hours. They shopped, lunched, shopped again, but could not find a lighting fixture that suited the room. They returned to T.B. to have dinner with the M's at the Crow, first driving to the Hall to garage the Jag.

Wyatt put the project to Mr M who called over a customer at the bar, introducing him to Gem as Matt, the local blacksmith and carpenter. Matt listened to the discussion at the table, pulled a notepad and pen from his pocket, and sketched a wrought iron light fixture that would suit the age of the Hall.

Gem approved; Wyatt suggested three for the size of the room. Mr M and Mrs M concurred. That matter was quickly settled.

It was all set, but the project made Gem uneasy, being included in the decision, in the project, when she didn't really belong at the Hall. She belonged at the Agency. That was the only place she belonged now.

And once the Pilos was found, when Gemmy and mum, dad, and Mr Portermann again existed, perhaps she could work again as a courier. She pushed the thought to the back of her mind to fully consider when she was alone in her office, or during the dark hours.

Wyatt watched Gem's eyes, aware immediately when she had drifted to her other life. It was only for a few moments, and she was again mentally at the table at the Crow in Ticking Bottom. But where had she been - and with whom? - Staunton? Or whomever she was with after she left James? Had she been with Staunton? And why? It obviously had not been a physical relationship the two had shared.

It was decided that Gem should use the study while the ceiling and light fixtures were installed in her office. Lovely. But still not of concern to Gem.

Mrs M suggested Roman shades for the windows and exterior door and Gem agreed. Perhaps the room should become an office for the housekeeper when Gem no longer resided at the Hall.

Gem was relieved when the band started playing and discussion of the office finally ended. Wyatt spirited her away a short time later, and they walked back to the Hall alone, the M's deciding to stay a bit longer to listen to the music.

"If you don't want the changes in your office, I'll let Mr M know of your decision," Wyatt offered. "It is your office after all. You should have only what you desire."

Truth was, she didn't care. "Very good ideas. It will be brilliant," Gem voiced approval. "But I think it is all an unnecessary expense," she frowned.

"That's not an issue," Wyatt said firmly.

And the matter was settled.

Gem! Where are you? Where are you? Help? Please dear God! Gem!

Gem bolted upright in bed. Wyatt jerked awake as she pulled out of his arms.

It had been clear as a bell - as clear as it had been that night!

Gem's heart pounded, she fought for breath. She couldn't breathe! She couldn't catch her breath!

"Gem," Wyatt sat up, pulling her gently into his arms. He heard the long case clock strike two. What the hell is it with this hour?

Gem counted to twenty over and over. Why not simply count to one hundred, she puzzled, trying to catch her breath.

Gemmy couldn't breathe! She was gasping for breath! Gem knew it! Gemmy was drowning!

"Shallow breaths. Slow, Gem, breath slow, steady," Wyatt soothed gently.

She nodded, concentrating.

It was over so quickly, so quickly, Gem knew. They had been lost in seconds.

"I'm sorry I woke you," Gem murmured when she could breathe properly again.

"Shocked the hell out of me," he admitted.

"I doubt that," Gem sighed, "but it would be an improvement."

"Sass! You're feeling better," Wyatt decided. "Bad dream?" he asked gently, releasing her.

"Bad reality," Gem shook her head. "Go back to sleep," she urged, reaching to the foot of the bed for her dressing gown. "It's the middle of the night for you."

"And what is it for you then?" Wyatt asked curiously, rubbing his face with his hands.

Gem pulled on her dressing gown. "The dark hours," she replied, shaking her head wearily as she walked out of the suite.

She was desperate for hot chocolate, and once the cup was in her hands, Vera Lynn on the cd player, she started to pace.

It's not the Pilos. The plane had hit water.

Gem checked her mobile. She had missed a text from Mr Choate. She quickly finished her hot chocolate and concentrated her thoughts.

'Should reach plane by early afternoon Monday.'

Gem texted a reply.

'It's not the Pilos.'

A reply came in minutes.

'How do you know?'

'I felt Gemmy gasping for breath. She was drowning.'

'Can you talk now?'

'Too risky.'

'Call me later. Anytime.'

'I shall.'

'I'm here, Gem.'

'Thank you!'

He didn't text good night. He would wait awhile, Gem knew, in case she would text again.

The insidious hollow feeling inside her swallowed her heart.

If the Pilos was in water, what waters then? Timor Sea? Banda Sea? Gulf of Carpentaria? Coral? Arafura. South China Sea? Out of range? If the Pilos had refuelled it would be logical to expand a sea search. But the Pilos had not refuelled.

Gem buried her face in her hands.

It would not soon be over. They were not a single step closer to finding the Pilos. And it put everything else back into play. The murdered counter-couriers and agents. And Mr Denton had drowned. It was all back in play.

Another cup of hot chocolate. Gem paced the floor. She pushed start again on the cd player. 'I'll Be Seeing You'. The words ripped at her heart.

Logically: for some reason Mr Portermann had got off course - we don't know the flight plan. Was he off course? Did the Pilos have a fuel reserve because of tail winds?

Wyatt pulled on his dressing gown. What the hell was that all about? Not a bad dream. 'A bad reality', Gem had said. A flashback of some sort? The shock had taken her breath away.

The Dark Hours. Gem had actually named the insomnia pattern!

She confused the hell out of him. She woke in shock, gasping for breath and then within minutes had shot a clever quip at him. How could she so quickly compartmentalize what had just happened to her? Had it happened before to her?

Perhaps her compartmentalising was not so surprising. She easily brushed off her relationship with James, still steadfastly refusing to even talk to Wyatt about him - as steadfastly as she refused to show any, except a brief passing remorse, for James's death. She was extremely reserved unless she was arguing with him. He had seen sparks of life in her after her visit to his office, but even she couldn't explain her mood of Friday. Likely it was only relief that her frustrating situation had been resolved.

Gem laughed wryly as a thought struck her. She could have walked to Howard's Bookshop or to Charley's Pub! Either of the men would have connected her to Mr Choate. She could have avoided the humiliating visit to Wyatt's office. Her mind was a muddle. Was there intelligent life somewhere in her brain?

She heard the soft padding of slippers across stone floor. Wyatt! She felt a flash of relief that she hadn't rung Mr Choate.

"I wanted to be certain you were still breathing," he said lightly.

"I am, thank you," Gem smiled faintly. "You should be in sleeping."

"Goodnight," Wyatt nodded.

How many hours a night did she pace the floor? Wyatt scowled. And the same cd night after night. World War II songs. Was it one particular song that she listened for, or was it the cd in general? World War II. What specifically about it held her attention? The same cd every night. The books, the dvds. And now Indonesia. Neither passport he had of hers had been stamped in South East Asia. Perhaps the third one - the missing passport - was the one she had used to travel in that part of the world. But she had denied ever having travelled to South East Asia. Was that another lie?

Was it a past game of hers? The reason for the haunted look, her connection to Staunton? Or was it a game she was plotting for the future? If that was the case it would never come to fruition. He had made certain she would never get out of England without him.

Now he could sleep. The other pieces of the puzzle known as Gem, or Gemma, or Gemimah, would eventually fall into place.

To Gem's relief, Wyatt slept in on Sunday morning. He had glanced at his watch when she slipped out of bed, had lifted a hand in a slight wave, turned over and went back to sleep. Gem quickly dressed, grabbed her mobile and left the Hall, walking down to the creek where she had a good read of 360 degrees of her position. She regretted ringing Mr Choate so early in the morning but she couldn't be certain she would have another chance to talk to him without other ears being around.

Mr Choate answered immediately, listening to her remarks without interrupting her.

"I know it sounds foolish," Gem said helplessly, "but that's what I feel," she concluded.

Mr Choate cleared his throat; Gem knew the connection was still made, but he paused for a time before speaking. "I will inform Mrs Brown then," he said at last. "We'll hear from Harry tonight. Tomorrow we'll start a new search. Beyond Banda, I would suggest. However, Mrs Brown is in charge of directing the searches, and she may have ideas of her own."

"Thank you for believing me," Gem said gratefully.

"You knew the time the plane left the air, Gem. I'm not about to start doubting you now," Choate said firmly. "Anything else on your mind this morning?"

"No," Gem winced, "other than the fact that I should have gone to Howard's or Charley's with the fiasco the other day."

"It won't happen again," Choate said succinctly.

"No, Sir, it won't," Gem replied sincerely.

"I will text you at two o'clock tomorrow morning."

"Okay, bye."

"Goodbye, Gem."

Wyatt slept until breakfast became brunch, and then he read reports in the library the remainder of the day. Gem painted the short walls in her office and started the trim around the windows. She was exhausted, and stiff from kneeling on the counter when Wyatt appeared and suggested dinner at the pub with the M's.

Gem tried to work on the Bristol chapter during the evening, but it still wouldn't work; she couldn't concentrate on the text. Just thinking about starting the search again was mentally exhausting. She didn't know where else to go with the search, she mused, sipping her third cup of hot chocolate. She had to purchase another large tin of the chocolate mix in the morning. She stared at the text, deleting a paragraph, set her cup on the counter, and knocked her scanner to the floor.

Blast! Add another scanner to the shop list. The scanner, her hat, the sunglasses, the shredder, the Bach cd in the shredder. What next!

Next was Wyatt, standing, waiting in the doorway.

"The colour is improving," he stated as she shut down the computer; she was too tired to argue with him that night.

"Better than adequate," she smiled confidently, waiting to hear him eat his words.

"One step up from adequate."

"So are you," she grinned.

"You'll change your words soon," Wyatt smiled.

Oh that smile! He was wickedly handsome!

Wyatt looked beyond her to the counter. "Where is your scanner?"

"Bin. I knocked it off the counter," Gem sighed.

Wyatt gazed at her quizzically. "Hat, sunglasses, scanner. Is that a new shredder?"

"Apparently shredders don't appreciate Bach cds," Gem threw up her hands in frustration, and started to walk out of the office.

"Keys, mobile -"

"Blah, blah, blah," Gem grumbled, flipping the light switch to leave him standing in the dark.

Gem stared at the computer screen. She simply could not imagine where the Pilos went down.

Hot chocolate. Vera Lynn. Pacing. She was exhausted. She couldn't get her brain started sorting.

Ping

'Climbing slow this morning. Mrs Brown will contact you later this morning.'
'Thanks!'
'Any new thoughts?'
'No. Brain is dry.'
'Needs sleep.'
'Needs a plane.'
'Indeed. Goodnight.'
'Goodnight.'

Gem started shivering. The room was a trifle cold. She switched off the computer. Four o'clock. She would go to bed and think until the last dark hour ended for this morning.

Wyatt glanced at his watch. Four o'clock. "Why so early, my love?" he yawned.

"I'm cold," she shivered.

"Come here," he gently coaxed, tucking the duvet and his arms around her.

He returned to his slumber, while Gem nestled in his arms, grateful for the warmth of his body - and his strong arms. She sighed contentedly.

Wyatt stirred for a moment and kissed her shoulder.

Gem had to admit she would think of this moment fondly when she was again in a flat of her own.

Where was the Pilos? Where was Gemmy? South China Sea could be a logical starting point. There weren't any other starting points - logical or illogical. She decided she would suggest the SCS to Mrs Brown. The hour dragged as Gem wondered of the progress of the men on the mountain – somewhere - on an island - in Indonesia.

Chapter Twenty

To Mrs M's satisfaction, Wyatt stayed for breakfast Monday morning.

"City today?" he queried Gem. "Or painting?"

"City. New scanner," Gem grimaced.

"Purchase two. Be prepared," Wyatt smiled.

Oh that smile again! Gem sighed inwardly. It was a lethal weapon. She shook herself, fighting off the butterflies threatening to swarm again.

As they cleared the table Gem's mobile rang.

"Mrs Brown," she said to Wyatt.

"I'll clear for Mrs Brown," he smiled, nodding to her to take the call.

"Good morning, my dear," Mrs Brown's cheery voice greeted her. "Would it be possible for you to join me this morning on a shopping errand? I would appreciate your opinion of a camera I am considering purchasing."

"Yes, ma'am. What time would be convenient for you?" Gem tried to conceal her excitement at the invitation. New information!

"Ten o'clock," Mrs Brown replied. "Camera Shop."

"Yes, ma'am," Gem replied, and the conversation quickly ended. She slipped the mobile into her skirt pocket. "Mrs Brown needs advice about a camera," she explained to Wyatt, as he finished clearing the table.

"I have conference calls all day. Enjoy your visit with your friend. Mind your P's and Q's," he kissed her forehead. "I'll notify Choate and then follow you into the city."

"Yes," Gem replied. Was the reference to P's and Q's a warning not to speak of their relationship to Mrs Brown?

Ten o'clock London time, evening in Indonesia. Mrs Brown HAD information, Gem decided. A face to face meeting, not a simple text Yes or No about the plane. But then Gem already knew the answer on that issue.

The Camera Shop had been an Agency shop since before Gem was a courier, and it was a fully functioning shop. Film developing was available, but she preferred the shop she usually frequented, because she didn't want every aspect of her life to include the Agency. - Although now nearly everything about her life - including Wyatt - seemed to revolve around the Agency, even if the Agency was unaware of that fact. It had been Gem's decision to accept the relationship with Wyatt - but that decision had been influenced by her commitment to the Agency.

Gem was two minutes late to the meeting, but Mrs Brown patiently accepted her apology.

"Nonsense, stuff and bother," Mrs Brown replied calmly. "Newlyweds are often distracted and quite often late. And they lock their keys in vehicles and forget to charge their extremely necessary mobiles," she said pointedly. "New responsibilities, two schedules to mesh now."

Mrs Brown studied Gem.

"Still not sleeping well, I see," she observed crisply. "Not resting in the afternoon. I thought your charming new husband was going to insist that you nap each afternoon."

"I assure you he hounds me to rest," Gem replied, "but the project, the book -"

"Wyatt," Mrs Brown interjected, browsing a selection of cameras on the counter.

"Yes." Gem couldn't deny that Wyatt consumed more of her time than pleased her. "And there are so many cathedrals in this country."

"Indeed. Accomplish what you can now, my dear. Once you start your family your free time will be miniscule."

"Do you have children, Mrs Brown?" Gem impulsively asked a personal question. She had known the woman all of her life, but her own knowledge of Mrs Brown's private life extended only to gardens.

"Mr Brown and I never had children. He passed away shortly before our sixth wedding anniversary," the woman confided without self-pity. "A slipped cog."

"Oh," Gem said faintly.

"Those pesky cogs are so very important, my dear." Gem nodded.

"However, I do feel that my couriers and agents are my children - of a sort. When you need me, Gem, you know I will help. Whatever the problem or issue."

"Yes, ma'am," Gem said gratefully. It was a tempting offer, but the results of a request could be disastrous in Gem's current situation.

Mrs Brown selected a camera, frowned at it, set it down, and picked up another, focusing it on the street beyond the windows of the shop. She walked along the counter, repeating the process with each camera on display.

"On to business, my dear," Mrs Brown turned to Gem. "Your phone chat yesterday with Mr Choate was extremely interesting. If you are confident of your thoughts of the other night, then I hope you are not disappointed that the plane was not the Pilos."

Mrs Brown's words were not unexpected, but they still stung Gem.

"What was it?" Gem asked quietly.

"A U.S. PBY lost in 1943."

"The Aussie pilot couldn't distinguish a PBY from a modern prop plane?"

"It was a jungle, my dear. Amazing the pilot saw the plane at all."

"I realize that," Gem apologized. "I'm sorry. It's just that I am so frustrated."

"We all are, my dear," Mrs Brown agreed.

Gem looked about the room. The commercial photo displays were strikingly colourful: sandy beaches, panoramic shots of snow-covered mountain ranges.

"There was a crew of nine on the PBY," Mrs Brown said quietly.

Gem nodded. "Well - at least someone is finally going home. I hope there are people who still remember them."

"There will be family - and the US Air Force."

"Back to the old drawing board - as 'they' say," Gem sighed. "And where do we go from here?"

GEM

"To water," Mrs Brown replied. "I will coordinate another search, expanding to the South China Sea. Again using training manoeuvres to map wreckage. Our only choice is to expand the search."

Mrs Brown's trust in her was overwhelming. Gem's connection with Gemmy. Two o'clock in the morning. 30 May. And this past Saturday night.

"I could be mad you know," Gem said quietly.

"Oh, my dear, we are all a bit mad," Mrs Brown chuckled. "If we weren't, we would have proper jobs." She again started examining cameras.

Mrs Brown trusted her. Wyatt did not. Sometimes there was no logic in life.

Mrs Brown put each camera to her eye, again focusing on the street beyond the shop windows. Gem reached behind the counter to snag a Nikon FM-10 with a zoom lens, shooting frame after frame, getting the feel of the camera.

"This is a fine one," she handed the camera to her supervisor, then reached for a Canon EOS-IV with auto focus. Another very fine camera! Gem liked the feel of it!

Mrs Brown selected another Canon - a digital. "You're wasting imaginary film," Mrs Brown chuckled. "What am I looking for? Digital? 35 millimetre?"

"I have no idea," Gem replied patiently. "What will be your subjects? Flowers? Your gardens? People?"

"Mainly flowers."

"Digital then. Simplicity itself to use, excellent photos," Gem advised.

Mrs Brown cleared her throat. "I believe I prefer this one. What is your opinion?" she queried as the shop assistant appeared from the back of the shop to unlock the front door.

Gem looked at the camera in question. "I would suggest one of higher quality. The Nikon might suit you, and the price is reasonable."

"Good heavens!" Mrs Brown blinked rapidly at the price.

"No? The Vivitar then?"

"A bit better," Mrs Brown shuddered, and reached for the Canon Gem had set down. "I like this one."

"Good choice. You could purchase that camera - or use the money to take a fifteen day cruise to the Caribbean," Gem laughed.

Mrs Brown looked at the price then quickly set the camera on the counter. "The Vivitar," she decided.

They looked at four other cameras, and Mrs Brown returned to her last choice.

Gem picked up the Canon, handing it to the shop assistant.

"You're taking that one?" Mrs Brown asked, shocked.

"I've had my eye on one of these for months. And there is no way I'm going to the Caribbean!"

"Thank you for delaying your opening time, Ms Tanor," Mrs Brown said to the shop assistant.

"No problem, Boss," the young woman grinned. "Not often I have such splendid sales when the shop is closed. Nice to see you, Gem."

"I can't believe you bought that camera," Mrs Brown shook her head as they left the shop.

"Staff discount," Gem reminded her. "I'm curious to use the auto focus."

"Are you returning to Ticking Bottom now?"

"I have a bit more shopping to do," Gem replied, noting Mr Choate in her peripheral vision. "You will coordinate now," she said cryptically. "What shall I do?"

"I don't really know, my dear. Just carry on as you have been doing," Mrs Brown frowned as she considered the query. "And go about your daily life. When we have new information perhaps we'll be able to resolve some of our issues. Until then, keep sorting and hoping for more - whatever it is you - feel - or divine," she concluded briskly.

A new scanner, first on the shopping list, four rugs for the office. Blast! She had forgotten to bring the photos she wanted matted and framed.

She was at loose ends again. What sorting was there to do? She had no ideas. Odessa. Black market. Hong Kong. The U-boats. No more ideas came to mind. She had to wait on the submarines mapping logical areas of the South China Sea. Once Harry was off the mountain, perhaps he would be able to obtain new information about the SEA Network.

A stop at Howard's Bookshop was never amiss, and a thorough review of the shelves provided two books on the occupation of the Japanese in South East Asia during the War. Mr Choate had a long chat with Howard, during which time he was able to prop up his feet and at the same time keep his watch on his charge.

Ora and Eda's shop increased Gem's wardrobe with a mid-calf chocolate brown skirt, matching long cardi, crème coloured turtle-neck sweater, and the name of a shop that would have lace-up chocolate brown boots to finish her outfit. Mr Choate suggested a long brown, orange and white scarf graced with gold butterflies, and a tortoise shell slide for Gem's hair. It only took three people to put her together today.

When Gem returned to the Hall she showered, put away her purchases and joined Mrs M in the kitchen for wine, tea for Gem, and the news that Willow and her husband had decided on the names Victor or Parmella, depending on which name would be required for their new baby-to-be.

"Parmella for a girl?" Gem queried hesitantly. "Unusual."

"Paternal family name," Mrs M offered. "Never was as common as Marigold or Clementine. You don't hear the name Gemimah much these days. Old family name?" Mrs M asked.

Gem was rescued from replying by a delivery from Sam's Plumbing and Heating.

"Wyatt insisted these be delivered today," Sam informed the women, as he carried in two medium sized electric fireplaces. "For Mrs Grantham's office." He had the items unpacked, plugged in and heating the office in a matter of minutes.

Gem took a second cup of tea into her toasty warm office and hooked up her new scanner; it worked perfectly. She loaded film into her new camera, anticipating using it the following day, weather permitting. She was very curious to see the snaps the Canon would produce in comparison to the professional camera her father had given to her.

She sorted the black and white photos for framing, deciding to add three colour shots of clouds she had taken at Ticking Bottom.

And she felt his presence. She turned to give Wyatt a finger wave.

"Thank you for the fireplaces," she smiled, still surprised he had remembered her early morning remark when she had slipped into bed.

"Can't have you coming down with chilblains," he smiled.

"Ooh, sounds painful," Gem agreed.

"So I hear. New scanner," Wyatt observed

"Yes, they just don't properly bounce." Oh! He had such animal magnetism! She shushed her thoughts that were drifting to the master bedroom.

"Did you have a pleasant day?" he queried casually.

"Lovely, thank you. Yours?" she replied, glancing away from him so as not to be trapped by his eyes. Mrs M would soon have dinner ready.

"Quite successful, thank you," he nodded, noting the new camera and reaching for it. "It better have been profitable if you're going to purchase scanners and Canons," he whistled as he inspected the camera. "You buy clothes at jumble sales and then purchase this," he lifted an eyebrow.

"There is nothing wrong with shopping at jumble sales," Gem insisted firmly. "That's how one has funds to buy that camera. I paid for it," she clipped out. "I have my own finances."

Wyatt put the camera to his eye and snapped a shot of Gem. "Very nice," he admired. "The camera and you."

"You know your cameras, apparently," she moderated her tone, hoping to avoid an argument.

"A passing knowledge," he stepped to his left, snapping another photo of her. "I was teasing, my dear, about the camera. You have your credit card. I'll transfer additional funds into your account."

"That's not necessary," Gem protested.

Again she didn't want money in her account, Wyatt mused. What is this game? "Did Mrs Brown find a camera to her liking?"

"It must be sometime since she'd purchased one. She choked on the prices," Gem remembered with amusement.

"What did she select?"

"A quite acceptable Vivitar. A sixth of the price of the Canon - if you're wondering," Gem said crisply. "It should suit her needs - photographing flowers."

"Gem, I was teasing," Wyatt insisted.

She looked at him shaking her head. "I don't always know when you're teasing. I don't know you."

"Except in the biblical sense - a joke," he smiled. "You certainly blush a lot!" He picked up the camera again, focusing on her, and snapped the shutter. "Pub night tonight - live music - Rock-a Billy. Are you interested?"

"Absolutely!" Gem agreed. "You're wasting my film," she laughed, as he moved around the office snapping shot after shot of her. Gem fumed as he held the camera aloft when she tried to take it from him, but she ended up laughing, as he continued to snap photos of her. Finally she was able to wrestle the camera from him.

"I will take doubles of each of those," Wyatt requested.

"I don't think so. Oh! You used the entire roll of film," Gem sighed.

Wyatt took the camera, removing and pocketing the film. "Put a roll on account at the chemist. Two rolls if you feel frivolous."

"Do either of you understand the concept that dinner has been served?" Mrs M appeared at the doorway, a stern frown creasing her brow. She gave a pointed look to Wyatt.

"I forgot," he winced at Gem. "Mrs M sent me to announce dinner. She's getting cross," he gave a stage whisper to Gem, and she laughed.

Rain fell all day Tuesday and Wednesday. Gem was at a stalemate with her search for the Pilos. No news came from the Agency, other than a brief text from Mr Choate early Wednesday morning that the expedition was quickly reaching the base of the mountain. Mr Cawley would return to London by the weekend. Gem and Mrs M cleaned the house, and Gem was surprised to find the photo albums Wyatt had purchased, and the photos in the study. She hadn't thought of the items since what was becoming known in her mind as 'Paint Day'. Hopefully he had set aside his intentions that they would organize the photos in the albums.

The dark hours were extremely wearing on Gem. She had no new thoughts of the location of the Pilos, and its passengers. She hoped for another feeling from Gemmy, but none came. She filled the dark hours reading the books of the Japanese occupation of SEA during the War. It was additional information for her already too full memory bank, but did not offer a single clue to resolving her frustrating situation.

Thursday dawned dark and gloomy and the rain fell in sheets. Mrs M frowned a great deal, sighed and muttered mild oaths and dire prophecies of forty days and forty nights of rain. Gem could swear she heard the housekeeper grumbling about looking on the computer for building plans for a vast boat to be constructed of wood.

The Bristol Cathedral chapter was finished by noon Thursday. Carlisle Cathedral would be next, but Gem needed a short break. She would need to fill hours over the weekend, and Carlisle would more than fill empty time.

Mrs M was called to the Moody cottage while she and Gem ate lunch. Gem quickly volunteered to do the washing up and to prepare dinner, deciding to serve Burgers a la Charley, chips, and Charley's cheesecake. Dinner, however, was many hours in the future. And! Gem would be alone in the house for hours! She watched from the kitchen window as Mrs M trudged down the cobblestone lane, umbrella in hand, bobbing with every step. Gem had offered to drive the housekeeper to the Moody cottage, but Mrs M had refused, grumbling that she had to walk off her mood before it strangled her soul.

Gem was alone in the house! And this time she had two torches. One should do the trick, she decided; torch in hand, she climbed the steps, breathing a sigh of relief that the door to the attic was not kept locked. The space was huge, running the full length and width of the Hall. The space was extremely well organized - a job well done, no doubt, by Mr M - since the Missus said she steadfastly refused to climb the staircase but twice a year.

The furniture appeared to be grouped by generation of previous Hall residents. Gem had no clue of the history of Grantham Hall; whether it had always been in the family or if the Hall had previously been known by a different name.

Many of the furniture pieces were choice antiques that would look smashing downstairs; however the rooms were already well furnished with other antiques. Scrapbooks and photo albums were neatly stacked on shelves which were also ladened with books, likely acquired over decades by previous family members. Gem would have put the books in the library. She would relish spending an afternoon going through every title on the shelves.

The attic was comfortably warm, but not overly so to dry out the furniture, or the family memories; the air was stuffy and Gem was tempted to open the windows, then thought better of the idea. That would be Mr or Mrs M's decision.

Neither the Lawsons nor the Forresters were large families, and had not accumulated the great amount of possessions displayed before Gem, from being handed down from generation to generation. Her family however had been close-knit even when separated by thousands of miles and numerous continents.

The attic was another reminder that she was in limbo. She and Wyatt were not a family, nor would they ever be a family. Perhaps once she was through this mess of confusion, when she started her life over again- perhaps she would adopt a child and have a proper family of her own.

Gem moved from one generation grouping to another: Jacobean, Rococo, Art Deco - the art alone was stunning, and if it was her decision it would be in every room of the house downstairs. She traced a finger lovingly over a table set in a small grouping away from the other generations: pewter base, glass top mosaic tile of flowers, deep rose petals, dark green leaves set in a medium blue background; Italian, Gem decided. And she knew - she simply knew - that Gemmy had selected the table.

Great grandparents, grandparents, Gem could guess at all the groupings - parents - and Gem knew, the furniture James and Gemmy had selected for their future home in Barcelona. James and Gemmy had selected striking, original works for their flat, the designs simple, completely expressing the heart and soul of the creative geniuses who had wrought the furniture.

James and Gemmy had already started building their lives together. Wyatt hadn't realized that - but then he didn't have a chance to be apprised of that information. And, still, all in all, Gem could not spot anything Gemmy would have purchased in Geneva and would have had sent to Barcelona.

And logically, if Gemmy had sent James a gift or an item for their flat, he very likely would have told Wyatt - while he was dying - that Gemmy had taken the time to post 'such and such' from Geneva - but then why had she deserted him?

No. There was nothing here to explain Geneva.

Blast! Gem stopped suddenly - hearing the unmistakable revving of the Jag's engine! She flew across the attic floor, dashed carefully down the steps and out the door, making sure the attic door was firmly closed.

Why was he at the Hall? She glanced at her watch - nearly two o'clock. She darted into her bathroom to wash dust from her hands, to make sure she wasn't wearing any on her face to rival the paint stains of the past Friday. Her clothes looked neat, not streaked with dirt or any traces of her excursion into the attic.

She stuffed the torch in a drawer, covering them with frillies, feeling like a spy. Speaking of spies - or agents - where the Hell was Paul Andriani the night the Pilos disappeared from the sky, its passengers from existence.

She didn't want Wyatt to know she had been in the attic for it would only be natural for him to refer to the furniture from the Barcelona flat. She knew the items were Gemmy's taste, but NO she wasn't able to remember when or where the furniture had been purchased. She wouldn't be able to tell Wyatt how 'she' and James had paid for the items - or who had specifically selected each item.

Gem sat on the bed, counting to twenty three times to gain control of her thoughts and attitude. Do not be jumpy from the surprise of Wyatt arriving early at the Hall that afternoon!

She was still counting when Wyatt walked into the bedroom, interrupting her thoughts.

"Here you are! Have you been hiding?" Wyatt chuckled.

"No indeed," Gem said calmly. "Having an early day?" Thank heavens the Jag was a sports car and proudly proclaimed its power.

"Ms Holton had our meeting well in hand. I came home early to see you," he sat beside her on the bed.

Gem sighed inwardly. One track mind. She was in charge of dinner and it would be late this evening.

"I thought we might brave the elements and walk to the pub for a beer," he suggested to her surprise.

"Lovely!" Gem happily agreed. "Pints on me!" She jumped up from the bed heading towardss the door.

"No!" he followed. "I pay the bills in this house. However, you can drive us to Brighton on Saturday."

"What's at Brighton?" Gem queried uneasily. Another villa or GEI cottage?

"Lunch at the Pavilion. I thought it would be pleasant to spend the day out and about," he slipped his arm around her waist as they walked down the staircase.

"Indeed!"

"Tea on the balcony - if the weather is with us, however it is a bit late in the season," he suggested.

What a lovely idea! And how had he thought of it? Perhaps it had been a suggestion from Mrs M - or also likely - Ms Holton.

Gem stopped at her office to shut down her computer. There was a gift bag on the counter.

"What is this?" she queried, frowning at Wyatt.

"Open it," he said lazily.

Cds: Dvorak, Offenbach, Liszt, Verdi, Sibelius, Debussy, Queen, Schubert, Glenn Miller, Susan Boyle, and so many more. Twenty-one cds total.

"Your music library is pitifully small," Wyatt drawled. "Mrs M and I decided you needed a larger selection."

"Glenn Miller?" Gem asked curiously.

"He was here to entertain the troops during the War," Wyatt nodded. "All original recordings."

Gem nodded, touched that he thought it would be of interest to her because of her reading.

"Queen?"

"Brilliant!" Wyatt grinned.

"Indeed! Thank you," she smiled, completely delighted. "A very impressive library." She was a bit daunted by the gift, stunned that he had spent hundreds of pounds on music for her. And then the electric fireplaces, which she knew were top of the line.

"Wellies and mac or you will get soaked," Wyatt led her to the mudroom. "The M's will meet us in an hour. I thought we would do the shops to pass the time."

Gem was pleased that the M's would be joining them. She did wonder however if they ever considered that Wyatt and Gem were not exactly the proper portrait of a romantic young couple. In fact, they were an accurate portrait of people who should not be on the same continent at the same time.

The shops were busy, but the couple from the Hall was cheerfully greeted as soon as they stepped in the door wherever they went. Wyatt knew everyone who greeted them; not unusual Gem realized - he had been of the Hall since his birth; but she was amazed at how easily he related to the locals of Ticking Bottom. The locals were not of his 'league' but it didn't matter to them, and they seemed very fond of Wyatt. Most called him by his first name, others addressed him as Mr W, but the familiarity was there nonetheless. Gem 'read the room' wherever they went, as usual, and relaxed in the completely non-threatening atmosphere of T.B. shops.

And she was always aware of the stunning grey eyes rimmed in blue, and of the smashing smile that everyone received from the Lord of Grantham Hall. Gem had to take a deep breath at times so she was not overpowered by the charisma Wyatt exuded.

Among the people of Ticking Bottom that day, the Wyatt whose company she shared, was the man with whom she had fallen in love. He still existed with other people. But aside from 'Paint Day' and the cds, this man was now a stranger to her. And when she watched him chatting with the locals, her heart ached with loneliness. She longed to be loved as she had thought she would be.

And at the Crow, Wyatt's aura and the atmosphere around him was the same as it had been in the shops. Had she not realized this quality in him in their other visits to the pub? Had her thoughts and emotions been so clouded that she hadn't been completely aware of this atmosphere around Wyatt? Or was he changing his manner?

He smiled at her; the smile that loosened the butterflies. She returned the smile, yet felt wistful inside, knowing she was on the fringe of his attention - she was only in Ticking Bottom because of James and Gemmy. She was receiving the glancing rays of the charm that flowed to the others at their table and in the pub.

And she didn't want the charm and attention of this man. He was real in the world of Ticking Bottom. His world. He was not real in her world. Wyatt Grantham was a real person in his world, yet he was a figment of her imagination in her world. She was an outsider in Ticking Bottom. She would always be an outsider.

Gem had to redouble her effort to find the Pilos, but she didn't know where to start. She was exhausted from the pain and loss of her family. She couldn't think of a single way to find them. As full as her memory was, all the facts and figures in her brain seemed useless to her. She had started at nothing and she was still at nothing. If she was building a rocket ship to the moon, she would be further along than she currently was searching for a prop plane in the realm of her world.

Gem awakened before the clock struck seven. Her brain was weary. She had paced for hours just two short hours ago.

There had been no newsy, welcome text from Mr Choate since the plane discovered had not been the Pilos. There was no new information from the Agency, so Mr Choate could enjoy a few more hours of sleep a night instead of spending time contacting personnel on one of the most remote islands in the world.

The man who had charmed Ticking Bottom the previous night was not waking and turning those charms upon Gem. She had to admit Wyatt's expertise in bed was a rare welcome aspect to their relationship.

And then he did waken. And he did weave his charm around her.

"A day of doom and gloom," Wyatt announced sometime later, reaching for is dressing gown, and glancing out the window. "Are you going to the city today?"

"Hadn't intended to, and why the prophecy of D&G? Horrid meetings today?" Gem asked curiously, wrestling with the duvet to convince it to surrender her dressing gown to her hands.

"Mrs M," Wyatt replied, yawning. "She can manage three days of rain, but not four in a row," he cautioned. "Her mood will be D&G, as you say."

D&G it was. Wyatt ate a hasty breakfast to Gem's amusement, and made a quick break for the peace of his London office, making his escape through the front entrance   - completely not his habit.

Gem giggled as she watched him escape. She cleared the table, carrying the dishes to the kitchen where Mrs M was sighing and playing Russian roulette with the telly remote.

"Not a thing on the telly," the housekeeper sighed again. And again.

It was the same programming that had held her enthralled the previous morning.

"It's a perfect day," Gem said lightly.

"Perfect? Perfect? The rain never stops! Might as well live in a rainforest!" Mrs M grumbled.

"Too many boa constrictors," Gem suggested easily. "Let's put on some music and dance until our feet ache."

Oh! That drew a sour look!

"I am too old for that nonsense. There is work to do. What would Mr W think if I spent my days dancing about the Hall like a mad woman?"

"He'd probably have hysterics," Gem teased. Ouch! That was a vitriolic glare. "Okay! What say you get your mac and umbrella and we'll head to London for the day? M&S. Check out the sales, try on outrageous clothes, have lunch, go to a film, art museum. Whatever you like," Gem ventured.

A light sparked in the housekeeper's eyes, then immediately flamed out. "I don't think that would be at all proper. There's housework to be done," Mrs M protested.

"That wasn't a suggestion. Let's go!" Gem insisted, quickly texting Mr Choate that the two of them would be leaving the Hall immediately. He would have to meet them outside London.

Ping
'10 minutes.'
'What? Where are you?'
'Inn. Ticking Bottom.'
'How long have you been there?'
'Saturday morning. End or it will be 15.'

Interesting! Gem mused, then looked at Mrs M. "Go! Hand bag, Mac! Umbrella," Gem ordered the housekeeper, then ran to fetch her own mac and shoulder bag; her mobile was already in her skirt pocket.

Mrs M was huffing and puffing in the Defender. "I don't think Mr W will appreciate this," she frowned.

"He won't mind a bit," Gem said confidently. No D&G allowed today!

Mr Choate pulled out behind them as the Defender passed the inn.

Parking in the city was frustrating as usual, but Mrs M had already begun to relax and did not venture a single grumble.

"I can't remember the last time I was in London on a lark," she fairly glowed.

"Way too long then! What's better than starting a day at M&S! Behold!" Gem swept a hand before them. "It's all at your feet! Enjoy!"

"If you were here more often your dressing room would be a good sight fuller," Mrs M said pointedly, looking about the store.

"One can look, but one need not necessarily buy," Gem replied.

"Well you should," Mrs M flung back at her. "Any girl your age should have ten times the clothes you do. You need to shop, girl."

"Then let's shop," Gem laughed.

Two hours later Mrs M had as three new dresses, two pairs of jeans, two twin sets, a new hat and a huge handbag she insisted she could take on a week's holiday in the Seychelles. At least a fortnight, Gem silently advised.

Gem held back on her purchasing for Ora and Eda's shop which was next on their list.

It was in perfumes at M&S where Gem spotted Mrs Brown smiling at her from the opposite counter. Gem glanced warily at Mrs M, but Mrs Brown walked over to join them.

"Gem, how delightful to see you again," Mrs Brown smiled warmly.

"Mrs Brown is a cathedral compatriot," Gem explained as she introduced her supervisor to Wyatt Grantham's house manager.

After a brief polite exchange, Mrs Brown went into Agency mode. "I thought perhaps you might meet me for lunch on Monday," she suggested to Gem, who recognised an order when she heard one. Gem quickly accepted the invitation.

As they parted Mrs M whispered to Gem," You should invite Mrs Brown to the Hall for lunch one day," she urged.

"Oh," Gem chuckled, "Mrs Brown is a whirlwind. Quick lunch in London, quick errands, and she is on her way home to her gardens. She must have to fetch something on Monday and I'm included in her free time." She hoped the remark didn't sound brusque.

"Family friend?" Mrs M inquired. "She seems so comfortable with you, as if she's known you for a long time."

Watch for cogs to slip, Gem warned herself.

"No, not really," Gem said hesitantly. Too close to the truth. 'Family' - and family friend.

"I thought perhaps she was a family friend," Mrs M stumbled over what might be an awkward moment. "You - just - never mention family - I didn't know - if it had been - a long time," she gave up trying to find the correct words.

"It seems like yesterday, and then it seems like forever," Gem murmured, as she selected a bottle of fragrance, hoping Mrs M would not pursue the subject.

Mrs M accepted the remarks at face value. Was it ever easy for anyone to chat about past sadness?

"You should have a light scent, Lily of the Valley perhaps," she suggested to the young woman, handing another bottle to Gem. "You should be with friends your own age today, instead of spending the day with me, or lunching with Mrs Brown on Monday."

Nothing like putting someone on the spot, Gem winced.

"Studying, work, travel," Gem shrugged helplessly. "One loses contact with friends." Lost planes, non-existent families, your best friend in the entire world 'disintegrated' by the government.

"And then they have their own families and move on," Mrs M said softly. "It does happen so often these days."

"Yes," Gem said, at a loss for other words.

Mrs M nodded, listening between the words. She would have to speak to Mr W. Everyone needed that one special friend who would always listen - and not judge you.

Gem decided on the Lily of the Valley scent. Mrs M decided to go racy and selected a heady passionate fragrance, which raised Gem's eyebrows and drew a smothered fit of giggles. Mrs M drew herself up to her full height, assumed a stern demeanour then immediately dissolved into a hearty laugh.

Mrs M was delighted with Ora and Eda's shop. She assured the designer how thrilled she was with the blouse Gem had purchased for her at the shop. She added to her wardrobe as did Gem, who purchased a long denim skirt, denim jacket, a crème gauze blouse, and a shoulder bag. Mr Choate remained outside the shop, truly being a silent partner that day.

Lunch was at the White Rose Pub, a pint for Mrs M, hot chocolate for Gem, then they took a side trip to the shops on Oxford Street instead of seeing a film. Mrs M found a new blouse for the next girls' pub night, and Gem bought a long black knit skirt, long black cardigan sweater, a black turtle neck sweater, and long lace-up black boots. And for no reason that she could think of other than it matched his eyes, and against her better judgment, Gem purchased a charcoal grey Aran sweater for Wyatt. He wouldn't like it she decided, but there it was. She could return it on Monday before she had lunch with Mrs Brown.

Then it was back to Ticking Bottom, wine and a chat with Mrs M as they prepared dinner. Gem took a long shower, pleased that Mrs M was now watching the telly in the kitchen and humming to herself.

Gem longed to spend the rest of the day in snugly pyjamas and her flannel dressing gown, but this was Grantham Hall, and one should be suitably dressed for dinner. She hung her purchases in her dressing room, and laid the grey sweater on the bed. She pulled out a fresh skirt and jumper, and was sipping her wine as Wyatt walked into the room.

Oops! She could tell by the look on his face that he had checked on dinner with Mrs M upon arriving at the Hall. He hadn't used the front entrance. Brave of him to enter through the kitchen considering the haste in which he had left the house that morning.

His bemused look said everything and Gem swallowed a mouthful of wine and giggled, covering her mouth with her hand. When his eyebrows shot up she collapsed on the bed in a fit of giggles, and Wyatt moved quickly to rescue the wine glass as she fell.

"What the hell happened today?" he demanded, puzzled.

"D&G was replaced by SLSW - shopping, lunch, shopping, wine," Gem laughed.

"A good day was had by all by the looks of it," Wyatt chuckled. "How much wine have you had?"

"Not that much," Gem recovered control, but still she smiled. "Mrs M needed a day of escape."

Wyatt reached a hand down to pull her to a sitting position and placed the glass in her hand. "Indeed," he said, smothering a smile.

"Don't be cross with her, please," Gem smiled hesitantly. "It was my idea."

"I'm not cross," he informed her. "In fact, I am very pleased. She rarely gets out of T.B. for a fun day. You were most excellent today, my dear." His gaze caught the sweater on the bed. "What is this?"

"It matches your eyes - when you're angry," Gem said lightly, throwing her head back, her hair flowing down to touch the duvet. "You'll hate it. I'll return it on Monday."

"I do not hate it," he said slowly, frowning a bit at the reference to the colour of his eyes and his temper. He slipped out of his suit coat and pulled the sweater over his head. "Perfect fit," he leaned down to kiss her cheek. "A perfect fit. Thank you."

"You're going to take it off now," she said rhetorically, as he took the wine glass from her hand, setting it on the coffee table.

"Yes. Everything. For you also," he stroked her cheek. "Mrs M already knows dinner will be late this evening. She and the Mister will dine at the Crow."

"Hmmm, again," Gem observed. "Why do I ever bother getting dressed every morning?"

"Damned if I know!"

"I should only wear pyjamas and a dressing gown."

"Skip the pyjamas," he suggested. "Thank you for the surprise."

"You've already worn it too long." Where did those words come from? she wondered, reaching up to wrap her arms around his neck.

"How many glasses of wine have you had?" he repeatedly curiously.

"Just this one - on lots of ice. Shall I get a glass for you?" she sighed, rubbing her cheek against his.

"Later," he murmured against her ear.

Her office was toasty warm, the multi coloured rugs on the floor brightened the office. The ceiling work would start on Monday, and Gem would work in the study for a few days. It would only be work on her book; she was making no progress on the search. She hadn't had opportunity to chat with Mr Choate while she was in London with Mrs M. And she was very curious as to what Mrs Brown would have to discuss at lunch on Monday.

Gem's brain was a dry, dusty file of information that would not yield the clue that she needed to bring her family home. She stared at the pages of her book, still South East Asia and Japan. Page after page of information entered into the dry well. She sipped hot chocolate, cup after cup of it, and listened to Vera Lynn's legendary voice.

The excursion to Brighton was very pleasant. Wyatt was relaxed and Gem was pleased to spend the day with Mr Hyde. She hadn't seen Dr Jekyll for a while, but he would return she knew. The weather was perfect for the long drive, and the mild temperature allowed for lunch on the balcony of the Royal Pavilion. They spent the entire visit inside the museum, not venturing the short walk to the coast to view the Channel. Gem had seen enough of that on Wight, and she was glad that Wyatt did not suggest a stroll on the Pavilion grounds.

Gem had hoped she would receive a text from Mr Cawley during the dark hours on Saturday, but it did not happen, and she was alone to pass the dreary time, reading, drinking hot chocolate, and listening to Vera Lynn.

Wyatt moved her office furniture to the great room on Sunday afternoon, to clear the room for the ceiling work the following day. Gem insisted on moving her office equipment, telly and cd player on her own. She was used to managing and organizing her equipment and Wyatt had reports to read. The study offered little working space in comparison to her office, and Gem was uneasy sharing a wall with the library. She already felt spied upon, and working in the room next to Wyatt's office made her wary of her privacy. She saved some space by putting the framed watercolours in the den.

Pacing the floor was impossible in the study. When she needed to pace she did so in the kitchen. Otherwise she curled up with a book, Vera Lynn and hot chocolate in a wingback chair in the study. There was still no text from Mr Cawley, and the hours dragged with each excruciating tick of the long case clock in the main hall.

Chapter Twenty-One

"You look worse than you did last Friday," Mrs Brown frowned at Gem as the former courier entered the pub. "Do you ever sleep?"

"Certainly I do," Gem insisted, sliding onto a chair at the table the older woman had selected.

"Perhaps you should see Dr. Hallowell."

"No, I am just fine," Gem pulled her fingers through her hair.

"Perhaps I should give your husband a ring," Mrs Brown said pensively.

"If you talk to Wyatt I shall go underground," Gem said a trifle coolly.

Mrs Brown pursed her lips at that remark, and held her silence while Charley approached their table.

The publican smiled at each woman. "You look like hell, Gem. Ever think about going to a doctor?" Charley said bluntly.

"If one more person suggests I see a doctor I shall scream," Gem said sharply, raking her hair with her fingers again.

"Well, I beg your pardon I'm sure, Princess," Charley clipped out. "What is your pleasure today?"

"I'm sorry," Gem said, suddenly penitent. "I had a very long night."

Mrs Brown ordered a pint.

"Hot chocolate, please," Gem requested politely.

Both women ordered the daily special and Charley quickly disappeared into his kitchen.

"I am truly sorry," Gem repeated to her supervisor. "I'm just so frustrated that there's no progress. No new leads. Nothing!"

Mrs Brown nodded sympathetically. "Perhaps there are no new leads -"

"There never have been any leads," Gem countered. "We have been working in the dark since 30 May. I'm sorry - I interrupted you."

Mrs Brown drew on her patience. The Agency had lost many staff members in the past five months. Gem had lost the most personally. "You are quite right, my dear. So we have. But it would appear that situation is changing."

Gem gasped slightly. "What? What has happened?"

"Another SEA agent was knifed and left for dead," Mrs Brown said slowly. "Her assailant had taken her mobile, not realizing that she had been carrying two. She managed a one word text."

"What?" Gem demanded breathlessly.

"Skinhead," Mrs Brown enunciated pointedly. "The agent's body was found two days later in a swamp."

"Skinhead!" Gem shivered. "Nazi!" She was stunned by the agent's death.

"Indeed my dear."

"Where?" Gem pressed.

"Singapore."

"Counter-agent?"

"Our Number One Agent."

Again Paul Andriani!

"We are awaiting autopsy reports to ascertain if the evidence in this death is similar to that of the other couriers and agents."

"And if it is?" Gem queried breathlessly.

"Then your suggestion of Odessa becomes extremely interesting," Mrs Brown gave her a cryptic smile. "And very disturbing."

Gem nodded, pausing to eat some of her burger. "Who knows of the suggestion of Odessa?" she queried hesitantly.

"Mr Choate, Harry, Mr Cawley, Number One, myself," Mrs Brown replied. "And, of course, you, my dear."

"I clear myself," Gem shook her head.

"We have all been cleared, my dear," Mrs Brown said firmly.

"And Charley," Gem suggested. "We discussed Odessa here," she reminded her superior.

"He wears ear plugs when we discuss business, my dear," Mrs Brown informed her.

Gem's jaw dropped. "He does? I never noticed."

Mrs Brown shook her head. "I am not surprised."

"I certainly have lost my touch," Gem admitted, disappointed in herself.

"You have had many, many issues to divert your attention as of late, my dear," Mrs Brown patted her hand. And very likely more to come, she was not quite ready to suggest.

Gem fell silent while she finished her burger, cogitating Mrs Brown's remarks. Finally she drew a conclusion.

"There is a mole in the SEA Network."

"Very possibly," Mrs Brown nodded slowly.

"Harry is working on that theory?"

Mrs Brown leaned back in her chair, her fingers toying with her fork. "Harry went underground," she finally admitted.

"Underground? Why?" Gem demanded.

Mrs Brown hesitated. "I am unsure," she admitted quietly. "I am hoping to receive a message. He arrived in Hong Kong Saturday evening. He sent me a brief text stating he was disappearing. I have not heard from him since."

"Staggering," Gem murmured. "And now what?"

"I do not know, my dear," Mrs Brown admitted pensively. "I am working in a fog. I cannot contact Harry, or Number One. The new Acting Director of the SEA Network has no information to offer. I'm afraid this is a matter of sit and wait."

"One thing after another," Gem mused.

"In addition to all of this, the SEA Network staff has been called in and is incommunicado - completely isolated - for their own safety."

"And Agency staff?" Gem pressed.

"Reporting in every four hours."

"Mr Cawley? Is he back in London?"

"Indeed. Mrs Cawley is very pleased with her husband's pay rise," Mrs Brown lifted her eyebrows. "No doubt he will be thanking you for your influence there."

Gem smothered a smile. She thought it was only natural that a wife would expect her husband to be compensated for being required to travel halfway around the globe to attend an intensive accounting course.

"He must be exhausted," Gem murmured.

"He has mentioned being so, and seems to have a rather annoying and lingering case of jet lag. He returns to his Agency post this evening. Watch the international news channel this evening," Mrs Brown suggested. "I won't ruin the news item for you."

The lunch concluded with Charley's signature cheesecake, and as Mrs Brown strolled away from the pub, Gem nabbed Mr Choate for a chat in Charley's car park. They leaned against the building and constantly read the area.

"Did you move to the Killingstoke Inn because of my careless jaunt to London that Friday?" Gem asked bluntly.

"No indeed," Choate firmly shook his head. "While you were jaunting carelessly, the block of flats where I lived went down in flames."

"Oh Lord! Mr Choate! Were you injured?" Gem asked worriedly.

"No. All the tenants made it safely out of the building."

"Did you lose everything?"

"Damn near - well, yes - everything," he admitted.

"I am so sorry."

"I'll manage, but your concern is appreciated. When Mr Grantham called to tell me you had had a spot of trouble, he heard the sirens over his mobile. He immediately arranged for me to have suite of rooms at Killingstoke inn. Very considerate of him to offer," Choate said reflecting on the incident.

"Indeed," Gem agreed, nodding. It did so sound like Wyatt. He could be a very considerate person. Or the gesture was part of some Game of his. Time would tell on that. "And that's the reason you were going to be in the T.B. area that day."

"Yes," he straightened up. "Where to now, Gem, shopping?"

"Back to T.B. I'm too tired to shop today," she admitted.

"You'll need a bit of a walk first if you had beer," he warned.

"Hot chocolate," she replied.

The afternoon weather was perfect for a walk to the creek. Gem had recovered her energy on the drive to the village, so she passed two hours with the pastels set and her sketch book.

The ceiling in the office was rapidly progressing and would be finished by the end of the day. The new lighting fixtures would be hung Tuesday morning, so she could move her equipment back in that afternoon. A matter of inconvenience of only two days. Mr M and Matt were excellent at their professions.

Mrs M was still smiling from her Friday outing and the sunny day kept her cheery mood consistent.

Wyatt was a bit pensive at dinner, and Gem caught him frowning at her.

"What?" she demanded. "You're staring at me."

"Am I?" Wyatt replied, startled. "I didn't realize I was. How was your day, my dear?"

"Quite pleasant, thank you," Gem ventured. "I had lunch with Mrs Brown."

"Indeed," Wyatt said smoothly. "Did she compliment you on how well you look?"

Gem gave him a sweet smile. "Yes, she did. How was your day?"

"Much as usual," he replied. "Your office is taking shape."

"Indeed."

"Did you select the paint colour for the ceiling?" Wyatt queried.

Gem shook her head. "Mr M's decision. I quite like it. The pearl grey compliments the walls and window trim."

"He'll change the colour if you prefer another," Wyatt suggested, frowning.

"I don't. Would you prefer a different colour?" Gem said doubtfully.

"It's your work space, my dear," Wyatt countered. "I really have no opinion on the matter. I just didn't want you to have to live with a colour not to your taste."

Much ado about paint colour, Gem sighed inwardly. He didn't want her to have to live with a paint colour she didn't want, yet he was forcing her to live with a husband she didn't want. There was no logic to his thinking, she silently groused.

Wyatt offered to do the washing up, suggesting Gem sit and relax for a while. At least he didn't mention seeing a physician. If he had and she had screamed – as she had declared she would do at Charley's - he wouldn't have grasped her reason for doing so. She went to the study and the thought of screaming reminded her to turn on the telly for the international news. She watched, taking a trip to the bathroom twice then finally settled in. An hour later Wyatt walked into the room, to bring her a cup of hot chocolate.

"Thank you," she said, startled by the gesture.

He leaned against the desk. "Would like a chocolate biscuit?"

"Thank you, no," Gem said warily, keeping an eye on the telly.

"Not much room in here for you," he murmured. "We'll put your office back to rights tomorrow evening," he suggested.

"Thank you," Gem was puzzled by his attention to her.

Then the news item appeared on the telly. Gem held her breath as she watched: a charter pilot out of Darwin, Australia, had spotted a plane that had crashed into the side of a mountain on a small, uninhabited, Indonesian island. The site was investigated by an experienced local guide from Timor Island, who discovered a U.S. PBY that had gone missing in 1943, with a crew of nine. The Indonesian government, with the assistance of the Australian government and U.S. servicemen, was recovering the remains of the airmen, which would be returned immediately to the United States for internment.

Wow! Gem was stunned by the respect given to the news story.

"Remarkable," Wyatt said quietly. "Nearly seventy years later."

"Yes," Gem said breathlessly. It was not the Pilos, but the crew was going home.

"Coincidence that," Wyatt said in a curious tone.

"What?" Gem demanded.

"You've been reading about Indonesia and South East Asia for weeks. Perhaps you had a premonition," he said quietly.

Only that! "No indeed," Gem firmly shook her head. "I read. Simply that. You read," she shrugged. I wish to heaven I had a premonition. Or was the feeling of Gemmy drowning a premonition? She shook off the thought; with Wyatt in the room, her thoughts had to be guarded.

"I'm going to read for an hour," Wyatt informed her. "Would you like another cup of hot chocolate before I go to my office?"

Gem hesitated, puzzled by the query. "No," she shook her head. "But thank you for offering."

"Very well," Wyatt replied and left the study.

Why the solicitous manner? Because she look tired, as Mrs Brown and Charley had so pointedly remarked? At least Wyatt had been less blunt than Charley.

She was exhausted. She finished her hot chocolate, took the cup to the kitchen to rinse it, and then she went to bed. She was suddenly desperate for sleep. It had not been the Pilos. There was so much work to do and she know didn't where to start. She was desperately tired.

Wyatt's scowl quickly disappeared when he finally found her in bed and sound asleep. It was only eight o'clock. Even in her sleep her face bore the strained look of complete exhaustion. He went back down to his office, turned off the lights and soon joined her between the sheets. He slipped his arms around her, cradling her as she slept. He was no closer to putting together the pieces of the puzzle that was Gem. And was there an additional piece to the puzzle?

Mr Cawley had returned and Gem actually looked forward to the dark hours that morning. She texted as soon as she had made a cup of hot chocolate.

'Thank you for climbing a mountain for my family, for me.'

The reply was awhile in coming.

Ping

'You are welcome. I am sorry it wasn't the Pilos. You 'knew' before we did according to Choate.'

'Yes. Are you rested?'

'No! Thanks for the pay boost! Didn't expect that. Put Mrs B in a tizzy. LOL.'

'You are welcome. Glad to have you back!'

'Glad to be home.'

'How was Harry?'

'Extremely puzzled.'

'What next?'

'Ball in Harry's court.'

'Okay. Goodnight.'

'Goodnight.'

She had finished reading the reference books of Indonesia. She couldn't read another book. Her brain was too full of information that was useless to her for searching for Gemmy; for the Pilos. She couldn't sort the information. She was exhausted mentally and physically.

Gem wandered into her office. The roman shades would be ready early next week. The light fixtures were striking: elongated hexagonal lanterns fashioned from old wavy glass and wrought iron. She wandered into the study, then out again, finally settling in the kitchen to watch the news until half four, when she decided to go back to bed. She forced all thought out of her mind and snuggled in Wyatt's arms.

Gem cropped the photos of Carlisle Cathedral that she intended to use in the chapter: cropped snaps on left pile, snaps to be shredded on the right pile. And unfortunately a full cup of hot chocolate spilled across the top and down, seeping through each stack of snaps. The leakage continued across the desk top, over the edge and down to the rug; not a single photo could be salvaged. At least the negatives were safe and dry in an envelope.

Blast! The Nazi's didn't bomb Carlisle, but I destroyed it with hot chocolate, she muttered. Reprints.

As she cleaned up the mess, a notion struck her. Lunch with Wyatt. She would go to his office, and this time she would not be a paint splattered, bedraggled mess. Her new chocolate brown outfit with the white turtleneck, chocolate boots, and the butterfly scarf. Appropriate - chocolate had necessitated the excursion to London. She took a quick shower, and French braided her hair, leaving face framing tendrils. She approved the mirror's image. Much better than paint day! Negatives, keys, mobile, new shoulder bag. Money! She was all set and organized this time. Hopefully she wouldn't screw up, blow a tire, get covered with grease and have to regroup. However if she did make an appearance covered in grease, Wyatt would probably find it amusing.

She stopped in the kitchen to inform Mrs M that she would be out for lunch. "Hot chocolate and photos don't mix well. I need reprints," Gem gave a chagrined smile.

"Yes, dear," the housekeeper returned the smile, knowing an impromptu lunch was in the offing. "Earrings, necklace," she patted her throat.

Blast! Gem retraced her steps, opting for delicate gold filigree earrings and a matching necklace she had purchased in Florence the year after she had purchased the clock. Gemmy had found a pewter hair slide that same holiday; it sat in Gem's jewel box looking forlorn.

We're still searching, Gemmy! she whispered, then set out again on her mission.

"I'm out Mrs M," she grinned, dashing out the kitchen door.

"See you when I see you," the housekeeper called after her. Photos, indeed. She hoped the London flat was clean and tidy!

Gem found a parking space by the photo shop and ordered double prints in the event another set of snaps could not swim in chocolate. Finding a parking space at the Grantham Building would be hit and miss so she decided to walk. The same police officer was at the same corner. Gem gave him a polite smile and wave as she crossed the street. He wouldn't remember her, but she remembered him. He smiled back, glancing at the Defender. He did remember! she chuckled to herself.

Gem didn't personally care what people thought of Gemimah Forrester; she was her own person; however she didn't want Mrs Wyatt Grantham's persona to be one of ridicule. She was playing a role for Gemmy's sake. And play it she would! Mrs Grantham on the outside, Gem Forrester on the inside!

Ms Jones was delighted to see her. "Oh! Mrs Grantham! I did it!" the receptionist bubbled. "Mr Critchley passed me!" she dashed around the desk and hugged Gem. "Excellent mirrors he said!"

"Our little secret!" Gem laughed.

"You can go up, ma'am," Ms Jones smiled. "I'll ring that you're coming."

"Please don't bother," Gem replied, desiring the element of surprise. She was pleased she had worn the long chocolate brown sweater; it was chilly in London.

"Yes, ma'am."

Gem waited patiently for the lift to rise to the eighth floor.

Ms Carton did a double take as Gem stepped from the lift. "Mrs Grantham, good day," the eighth floor receptionist said respectfully.

"Good morning," Gem smiled. Much better, she mused.

"I believe Mr Grantham is in R&D. Just walk in."

Gem nodded her thanks. This visit she noticed the brass sign on the door leading to the Research and Development office. All eyes turned to her when she entered the room. It was obvious she had walked into a meeting. Wyatt was at the centre of the room. Ms Holton, standing by the double doors at the rear of the room, gave Gem a small finger wave and a smile, and Gem returned the gestures.

Wyatt turned around. When he saw her his face split in a wide grin. "Darling! I didn't recognize you sans paint stains," he chuckled as he walked over to her. "To what do I owe this pleasure?" He kissed her, resting is hands on her waist.

"Still laying it on a bit thick," she blushed and whispered in his ear.

"The pleasure is all mine," he teased back, also whispering. "Civility, my sweet."

"I spilled hot chocolate on Carlisle," she admitted as he released her.

"God bless hot chocolate and Carlisle Cathedral. Don't worry, my dear. The church Father's will clean up the mess and send me the bill," he teased.

"I needed reprints," Gem laughed. "Do you have time for lunch?"

"I am all yours, sweetheart. Are you buying?"

"You are," she smiled sweetly.

"The pleasure is still all mine."

"The office staff has their eyes stuck to us," Gem observed in a whisper.

"I only see you, sweetheart," he murmured.

"You are too much," she protested softly.

"As are you," Wyatt teased.

"Do you have loose ends to tie? I can wait downstairs with Ms Jones," Gem queried.

"Hmmm," Wyatt said, his voice husky. "Your perfume is wonderful. Lily of the Valley."

"Still thick," Gem whispered.

"Loose ends, Ms Holton," Wyatt informed his assistant.

"Yes, Mr Grantham," Ms Holton replied crisply.

Wyatt nodded to Gem, slipping his arm around her waist again. "Keys, mobile, money?" he teased, guiding her out of the room.

"All accounted for today," she laughed, blushing. She could hear laughing as Wyatt closed the door behind them.

"Let's resume, shall we," she heard Ms Holton say firmly just before the door was completely closed.

Gem watched the numbers on the panel count down as the lift descended. "You are quite the actor," she remarked with a slight grin.

"As are you, my dear. BAFTA's for both of us," Wyatt chuckled. "You certainly arrived dressed to impress today." He pushed the stop button on the lift panel.

"And not in distress. But again you were in a meeting," she said ruefully. "Again poor timing."

"Not poor timing as far as Ms Holton is thinking. She again was delighted with your timing, and has become your number one fan at GEI. If you continue to come to the office, Ms Holton will be Managing Director, London, in a few weeks rather than months, and then Director of London Operations. Manton and I are currently clarifying her status with other branch offices."

"Are you currently the Director of London Operations?" Gem asked. It was amazing her lack of knowledge of GEI!

"President and CEO of GEI. Manton, despite his location at the Paris Office is DLO. Promotion for Ms Holton and Manton will be CEO. And he will be doing the travelling I generally do."

"That will cut your power."

Wyatt laughed. "I own GEI outright. No stockholders. The power will always be there."

"Oh," Gem nodded, reaching out to press the start button on the lift panel, but Wyatt drew back her hand.

"Not yet. I haven't seen you for hours," he murmured.

"Here comes Svengali," Gem replied softly.

A few minutes later he murmured, "Oh Trilby, I wish it was evening."

"Mmm," Gem leaned against his chest. "I am amazed you ever accomplish any work."

"It's a struggle," he chuckled. He brushed her fringe back across her forehead. "I mussed you a bit."

Gem repaired her lipstick, and straightened her sweaters and skirt.

"Better," he nodded, then pushed the start button. "Damn! I wish I hadn't rented the flat! We could have postponed lunch! Hotel?"

Gem laughed. "You are completely incorrigible!"

"I don't recall completely or even basically being incorrigible before I met you." he replied as the lift doors opened. "The wife is always blamed, you know, my dear," he whispered in her ear, as they stepped from the lift.

Gem giggled, blushing again. She had forgotten what fun he could be! - this Wyatt - who was not of her real world.

"Carry on, Ms Jones," Wyatt said crisply as they passed the receptionist's desk.

"Yes, Sir, Mr Grantham," she bubbled, winking at Gem, and Gem winked back.

"I saw that," Wyatt raised his eyebrows as they left the building. "What was that all about."

"Girl stuff," Gem said simply.

"Hmmm," Wyatt mused, but let the matter drop. "Jake's?"

"Indeed," Gem agreed.

The same waitress waited on them as had on Paint Day, her behaviour was a bit more professional.

"You clean up nicely, it appears," Wyatt chuckled as the waitress left with their orders, tea for Wyatt, hot chocolate for Gem. "Is your pride assuaged then?"

"I am not that silly," Gem protested.

Wyatt shook his head in response. "No, you are not," he said knowingly. "This office visit was to take the sting off me. That was very sweet of you, my dear, but was highly unnecessary. And on your next visit, please wear a black bin liner, tied at the neck," he smiled.

"For heaven's sake why?" Gem demanded.

"Mr Palmer and Mr Westley could barely keep their eyes in their sockets," Wyatt leaned over, keeping his voice quiet.

"I am suitably presentable today," Gem insisted in protest.

"What you present, my dear, no matter how suitable is a tease to a man's imagination."

Gem laughed. "Good one! You almost sound like a jealous husband!"

"I am a jealous husband," Wyatt said quietly. "You had best believe that, my sweet. What you have is only for me, Gem," he said with a stern look.

Gem felt her skin grow warm. His aura was so very intense. "I haven't given you any reason to think that I have been -" she searched for the word, losing her thoughts in his penetrating gaze.

"Unfaithful," Wyatt supplied the word. "You haven't. But, as I have said, my sweet, you have no idea of the affect you have on men."

"It's all in your mind," Gem whispered. "And you! The waitress still can't take her eyes of you. I dare say the women at your office drool over you daily. The hearts you break! Or don't break," she said suggestively.

Wyatt chuckled, reaching out to stroke her cheek. "Do I detect a note of jealousy? Graphically speaking, sweetheart, do you really think I have anything left to share with another woman after spending each morning and night with you?"

Gem gasped. "Graphic indeed!" she murmured. "And I am not jealous, if that is what you are thinking!"

They fell silent as their order arrived.

"I won't go to your office again," Gem murmured, as the waitress moved away from their table.

"Please do feel free to come to the office," Wyatt insisted, "but be aware that you are turning heads. And no doubt you have long before I met you. If you are unaware of that fact you should be - thus I am warning you."

Gem nodded, taking a bite of the cottage pie in front of her.

"Where is Mr Choate, by the way?" Wyatt puzzled.

"Mr Choate? Oh -" Gem replied faintly.

"Why isn't he with you today?"

Gem flushed. She had done it again! "I forgot to ring him," she admitted sheepishly.

"Again," Wyatt scowled. "You have his mobile number."

"Yes," Gem nodded. I've had it for years!

Wyatt pulled out his mobile and sent a text message. "Not again, my sweet," he said very sternly. "No more outings without Mr Choate. Agreed?"

Gem nodded. "Yes," she replied penitently.

How could she have been so foolish again?

"However, if he had been with you that Friday, I would have suffered an entire dreary day at the office," he said more gently.

"Oh - and thank you for that remark about the paint stains - you nearly didn't recognize me," Gem relaxed and teased in return.

"You blushed. To your toes I'd wager!"

"But you can't blush!" Gem felt her colour rising again.

"I don't believe I ever could," Wyatt admitted. "Manton, however, turns positively red when he's angry. Becomes absolutely apoplectic," Wyatt murmured. "I've never seen anything like that before."

"How IS Peter?" Gem laughed, relieved that the conversation had shifted away from Wyatt and her.

"I haven't heard lately. Manton is refusing to speak his name."

"Not a good sign," Gem said doubtfully.

"Add to the fact that Manton is having a devil of a time finding a flat in Paris."

"Paris is difficult. I think Rome is worse, however," Gem bit into a chip. "These are very good chips," she observed.

"You had a flat in Paris? And in Rome?" Wyatt said smoothly.

"A few years back," Gem, admitted. Watch for slipped cogs. Assignments had been so frequent in Europe for a brief six month period that she and Gemmy had both had temporary flats. Gem to Paris and then Rome. Gemmy to Berlin, as Gem's German was fractured at best.

"Interesting," Wyatt casually observed.

"Not really. Student days. Summer studies and research," Gem smiled pleasantly. Oh how adept she was becoming at lying. A liar, Wyatt had called her. And, now, so she was.

Wyatt saw the violet eyes start to cloud.

"Perhaps you could offer Manton advice," Wyatt said, carefully watching her eyes. She so rarely offered information about her 'past'.

"Move back to London!" Gem laughed. "That is my advice."

"I doubt his supervisor would agree to that solution at this time."

"You!" Gem laughed.

And the clouded look in her eyes was gone, Wyatt noted. So quickly this time.

"Guilty!"

"How is he managing the food?"

"Better than I do." Wyatt glanced at his watch.

"You have to go back - to your office," Gem reached for her shoulder bag.

"I do, but not quite yet," he nodded. "Phone conference with Manton and the Berlin office."

"How is your German?"

"Excellent. Yours?"

"Only fit for ordering at a beer garden," Gem admitted. Hopefully Gemmy hadn't impressed James with her talent at that particular language. "If one doesn't use a foreign language it has a tendency to rust."

Wyatt nodded. "What has Mrs M on the menu for dinner this evening?"

"BBQ. Shiskabobs, I believe. Mrs M thought an autumn picnic would be pleasant."

"Oh Lord! Pray for rain," Wyatt groaned. "Pineapple and beef - I do not understand the concept of that combination."

"Be kind," Gem coaxed. "Mrs M tries so hard to please."

Wyatt shrugged. "How is the wine stock at the house?"

"Diminishing," Gem admitted. "Shall I stop for a few bottles on the way to T.B.?"

"A case or two. Save at least one glass for me," he teased. He glanced up as the door to the pub opened. "Here is your escort," Wyatt rose as Choate entered the pub. "No protests now."

"No, Mr Grantham," Gem parroted his staff, but was chagrined that she had again forgotten to ring Mr Choate.

"Sass! Isn't it a bit early in the day for that?" Wyatt's eyes twinkled. He leaned over to whisper in her ear. "Save it for the sheets. Oh! There it is! The blush!"

"Sir," Choate greeted Wyatt. "Mrs Grantham," he gave Gem a stern look - and not only for Wyatt's benefit.

To Gem's surprise, Wyatt did not immediately rush off.

"Is the flat readied for your friend?" he inquired of the private investigator.

"Yes, Sir. Most suitable. Thank you for your assistance," Choate replied formally.

"Good." Wyatt soundly kissed Gem. "Keep an eye on her, if you would please, Mr Choate."

"With my life, Sir," Choate said firmly.

It was not a casual reply, Gem knew in her heart. Family.

"She is displaying a tendency to go rogue," Wyatt said dryly.

"Indeed, Sir," Choate gave Gem another stern look.

"Don't go rogue again, please," Wyatt ordered Gem, dropping a quick kiss on the tip of her nose, as they left the pub.

Wyatt walked towards the Grantham Building. Gem walked to the end of the block, Choate a few steps behind her. The route to the Defender was straight ahead. Gem glanced back over Choate's shoulder; Wyatt was barely visible on the crowded pavement.

She reached the corner, abruptly turned to her left and continued walking to a park a few blocks ahead, where she could chat with Mr Choate without being overheard.

"I'm sorry you were dragged out on such short notice," she apologized.

"I'm on call 24/7, Gem."

"I realize that but -"

"Do not push him, Gem. I cannot stress enough that Wyatt Grantham is a force to be reckoned with. He is serious about your protection. His attitude was calm just now, but he was furious. Behind all that polished manner is a steel barracuda, and I'm not sure you fully understand that." Choate routinely scanned the area as he spoke. Gem resumed the same SOP.

You're telling me! "Okay," Gem tried to appease her Agency co-worker.

"No more leaving Ticking Bottom without me," Choate said severely.

"Yes, I promise," she nodded. She was being fenced in as effectively as she had been on Wight and at Inverness. Not only Wyatt, but now an unrelenting Mr Choate. "But honestly, Mr Choate, do you think I need protection?" Gem pressed the issue.

Choate reflected on the query. "Perhaps not from an Agency point of view - that I am aware of. Outside the Agency, in the civilian world, Wyatt Grantham's orders are law. He pays the bill and he is not - I repeat - not a man to be crossed."

I do know that! Now, she wondered again, if I did cross him, could even Harry, Mrs Brown, or Mr Choate battle Wyatt Grantham? Doubt gave her a sinking feeling. It had always been a backup hope, but that now seemed blatantly futile. Just exactly how far did Wyatt Grantham's power truly stretch?

"Are we on the same page?" Choate queried.

"Yes," Gem nodded.

"Good. And your reason for this chat?"

"Sidebar," Gem reverted to the previous remarks. "How did Wyatt Grantham get to be so powerful?"

"Money is power. Conversely, power is money. He flies under the radar, Gem. He isn't ostentatious. He doesn't throw his weight around - unless he has to - and then watch out! He is silent power. Grantham Enterprises International is a huge company. But his power stretches way beyond GEI."

"I can't believe all you know," Gem exhaled sharply.

"GEI has existed for over a hundred years. Your husband inherited and expanded at an astonishing pace. All under radar."

Gem reflected on his words. "Mrs Brown said she considered Wyatt to be ethical."

"Yes."

"Is Wyatt's power common knowledge - or so at least in the business world?"

"One of the best kept secrets in any world."

A bit more in-depth than their last chat about Wyatt. Wyatt could trump the Agency, Gem was beginning to believe.

"Okay, okay," Gem processed and stored the information.

"Now?"

"His flat? What about the flat?"

"I leased it for a neighbour who can't find a place to live. All my neighbours were burned out. Rebuilding the block will continue for months - perhaps a year before occupancy is available."

Of course! The fire! It had slipped her mind.

"Next query?"

"None really," Gem shrugged. "However, I am rather surprised that Wyatt - that we -" she self-edited, "live at Ticking Bottom - at Grantham Hall, instead of a gated community."

Choate stared at her in amazement. "I am concerned about your training, Gem. Or perhaps you simply have so very much on your mind."

"What?" Gem said, confused. What didn't she see?

"Ticking Bottom."

"Yes, Ticking Bottom," she repeated.

"Gem," Choate was nearly speechless. "Ticking Bottom is a gated community. You don't see the gate, but it's there."

Gem stared at him in disbelief. "Do the locals know that?" she couldn't grasp the truth of his words.

"Some do," he concluded. "Do you ever see locals out hunting with rifles?"

Gem nodded.

"Your protection. The publican, the chemist -"

"The doctor," Gem nodded, remembering the men she had met the first time Wyatt had taken her to the Yellow Crow.

"They are the backbone of T.B. The 'hunters' are hired security who live in T.B. proper. The village is not on any map - a village time 'forgot'. That's why it's so difficult to find. Wyatt Grantham owns all the cottages, all the shops, and Mr M is the estate agent, who rents out the cottages, and the shops to businesses."

Shivers ran up Gem's spine. "It's like that old telly series - The Prisoner," she said in awe.

"One of my favourites. I have the dvd set if you would like to borrow it."

Apparently I'm living the series, Gem mused silently. "It is such a different world," Gem said totally astounded by Mr Choate's revelation.

"Gem, you have never lived in the real world, have you." It was not a question. "This is just a different different world. You'll adapt. You always have."

"It's too much to process," she said shaking her head. "What else does GEI own, aside from Ticking Bottom?" she wondered aloud.

"Eight other gated communities around the world, golf courses, ski resorts, island resorts, factories, a shipping line, two air charter lines, vast amounts of land. I can't recall what else offhand."

"Okay," Gem said faintly.

"I have your secrets and now you have some of mine," Choate advised her. "Remember, Gem, Family."

"Always," she nodded.

"Are we finished then?"

"Yes," she nodded again. "Yes."

Her mobile played Land of Hope and Glory - a text message from Wyatt.

'Shall I stop for the wine?'

'I shall stop.'

'Excellent. Later, my love.'

'Indeed.'

"Do the M's know - about Ticking Bottom?" Gem asked Choate before she led and he followed back to their vehicles.

"He does. I don't know about Mrs M," Choate replied.

Gem fetched the wine which Mr Choate loaded into the Defender. She put the information she had learned to the back of her mind as she drove to Ticking Bottom. If she mulled information while she drove she would more than likely steer the Defender right up a tree.

Mr M carried the wine into the kitchen, much to Mrs M's smiling approval. Her smile disappeared when she looked at Gem's face.

"Dear, you are dead white! Sit!" she pushed Gem down on a kitchen stool.

Gem stared at the woman, wondering. Do you know about Ticking Bottom?

"Are you ill?" Mrs M queried.

Gem shook her head. "Headache. I'm going to lie down."

Mrs M insisted on seeing Gem to bed, covering her with a blanket, then she closed the curtains.

"Shall I ring Mr W?" the woman worried.

"No. I just need an hour and I'll be fine. Please don't ring him. I'll come down in a bit," she smiled at Mrs M.

Gem didn't bother closing her eyes. She wouldn't sleep. She almost wished Mr Choate hadn't told her what he knew. Obviously he had thought that she should know - perhaps believing it would convince her of Wyatt's reasons for wanting to make certain Gem was safe. And Mr Choate was Family protecting Family.

Gem had wondered of Wyatt's ability to control her since that Blasted night on Wight. Yet she had always thought there was a loophole - a way she could end the relationship with Wyatt when the Pilos was found - and Gemmy, and mum, dad, Mr Portermann could once again exist. And now she wasn't so certain about that. When she could finally explain ALL to Wyatt, how would he react? How would a steel barracuda react? The lies, the deceit - even though her reasons for doing so were extremely valid. Or rather, were valid in her opinion.

James had died needlessly because an obituary had not been published. If she had told Wyatt the truth that horrid night on Wight, instead of compounding the lies and deceit, he wouldn't have believed her. Games. She played games - to Wyatt's way of thinking. And this was another one. Playing a game in which he was the unknowing - dupe? Victim? She didn't know how he would designate himself.

Good heavens! Even Mr Choate was wary of Wyatt Grantham. What chance did Gem have against a steel barracuda? The Prisoner, indeed!

Blast! Find the Pilos and get the Hell as far away from Wyatt Grantham as possible! She had never had to go underground before. But there was always a first time for everything.

He had been so different since 'Paint Day'. Oh, that charm! He threw her completely off balance when he was pleasant - and Blast it! - kind!

For the first time she was truly frightened of him. How did one deal with a steel barracuda? And more than that - Wyatt Grantham was a vengeful man. Hence their 'marriage'. And he had said not so very long ago that their relationship had not changed. It was the same as it had been on Wight and at Inverness. She had to ask him what he had meant about P's and Q's the day she had met Mrs Brown.

No! Blast him! Blast Wyatt Grantham! She wasn't a steel barracuda, but she wasn't a coward! Wilting like day old flowers wasn't Gemimah Louisa Forrester!

Resolve! Tough it out. Keep your head up, your chin in, and your nose clean - or some such thing. And hopefully the mystery of the Pilos would be solved.

Gem threw off the blanket, took a quick shower and changed into a skirt and jumper. She pulled out her braid, shaking her hair free - and clearing her brain a bit. She had to look beyond the restraints imposed by Wyatt, because Mrs Wyatt Grantham did not exist! Gemimah Louisa Forrester did!

Mrs M started when Gem appeared in the kitchen. "Not resting, dear?"

"I am much better, thank you," Gem reached for the wine glass and the bottle from the fridge. "Did you have a pleasant day?" The housekeeper nodded, smiling. "Oh, let me help you," Gem volunteered, watching Mrs M cut up vegetables for the shiskabobs.

"Potatoes." Mrs M slid a knife and cutting board across the island to her. "And your day?"

"Good," Gem said slowly, concentrating so as not to cut off a finger instead of a potato slice. Then she reached for a piece of pineapple off Mrs M's cutting board.

"Not wise," the cook shook her head, "not with wine." She offered a slice of green pepper instead. "Did you have lunch?"

"Jake's Tavern. Good food."

"Not as good as mine!"

"Never!" Gem agreed, laughing.

"Did you get your snaps?"

"Tomorrow. Double prints this time - margin for error," Gem said ruefully.

Mrs M chuckled. "You need one of those spill proof mugs."

"I usually tip those down the front of my clothes," Gem giggled, reaching for the wine bottle to re-fill the housekeeper's glass. "Oh ! You need more ice," she declared fetching the tray from the freezer.

Mrs M studied her young companion, deciding to speak frankly. "You know, dear, you are quite different than what I had expected," she said thoughtfully, "when Mr W said he was marrying. Just said it out of the blue one day. 'I'm getting married Mrs M' he said, 'at noon today. My wife and I will be living here. We will return Monday next'. That was all he said."

"Surprise!" Gem winced, sipping her wine, careful not to spill it.

"Am I speaking out of turn?" Mrs M said cautiously.

"No, ma'am. May I have some more green peppers, please?" Gem asked politely, continuing to slice the potatoes, and eating every green pepper strip the cook sliced. "Lovely peppers!"

"From the kitchen garden." Mrs M slid the green peppers over to Gem and took back the potatoes, finished slicing them, watching as the bride sliced and ate the peppers. She chuckled to herself as she started slicing onions. "These are very mild - they shouldn't upset your tummy," she pointed at the onion on her cutting board.

"Onions never bother me," Gem assured her.

"Ah, fine then. Where was I?"

"That was all he said," Gem nodded sagely.

"You have a good memory."

"Indeed I do. More green pepper please?"

"You'll make yourself sick," the cook warned.

"Not on green peppers," Gem grinned at her, then frowned slightly. "Eggs sound rather gruesome, however."

"Hmm," Mrs M nodded, then looked at the ceiling, gathering her thoughts. "We - the Mister and I - well, we expected someone more -" she searched for words.

"Sophisticated," Gem nodded easily.

"Err - yes."

Not a lamb to the slaughter, Gem mused silently. "Not someone so completely awkward and out of her element. A total embarrassment to Wyatt Grantham," Gem said bluntly. "He married in haste," she munched another strip of green pepper. "Oh my! Did I say that out loud? The oddest things have been popping into my mind lately! I don't know whether I am coming or going. I just don't know. I'm sorry."

"I understand, dear. There have been so many changes for you the past weeks. And more to come, I would say. Shall I make you a cup of hot chocolate or tea?"

"Hot chocolate would be lovely," Gem replied. "And honestly, Mrs M, you will never know how right you are. So many changes."

Mrs M chuckled. "My dear, I was a young bride too once, many years ago. You are too critical of yourself. Mr W obviously thinks the world of you or he wouldn't have married you."

He hates me. He thinks I killed his brother. I did. But it was an accident. And this isn't a marriage. It's a Game of revenge. Wyatt Grantham wants my head on a platter.

Mrs M as a young bride. Did Mr M seduce her with his eyes? Did he possess a smile that churned butterflies through her insides? Did he possess a touch that would drive all coherent thoughts from her mind? Or melt her every resolve to stay away from him - with exquisite kisses? Gem couldn't imagine Mr M to be as 'talented' as Wyatt.

"I think you are still a bride," Gem said softly. "Mr M thinks so. I see it in his eyes when he looks at you."

"Thank you, dear," Mrs M smiled. "The Mister makes me feel that way." She emptied the onions into a bowl. "I was worried about Mr W marrying so quickly," she admitted, setting the cup of hot chocolate in front of Gem.

"Marry in haste," Gem nodded sagely. Oh how she had learned that to her own heartbreak. She topped off her companion's wine glass.

"For some perhaps. But Mr W couldn't have chosen better," Mrs M said firmly. "Mrs Fiona, the lads' mum, would have taken you right to her heart."

Not if she had thought I had killed James!

"She had no time for putting on airs and fancy attitudes, I can tell you."

Gem smiled wistfully at the older woman. Mrs M was so kind. And so deluded about Wyatt Grantham's marriage.

"You've eaten all the green pepper!" Mrs M suddenly laughed.

"Delicious!" If only the M's weren't a package deal with Wyatt and Grantham Hall! "I'll fetch some from the garden."

"Ask the Mister. He's firing up that BBQ machine." She nodded her head to the fridge. "Take him a beer, would you, dear."

Mr M was indeed firing up the BBQ 'machine'. He was attired in a chef's coat, and was wearing the flat hat Gem had given him. "Thank you, dear," he accepted the beer in barter for three green peppers.

The garden table was set for two with fine linen, crystal, and candles. And white fairy lights twinkled in the garden.

Very romantic, Gem groaned silently, hoping the dining arrangements were for the M's and not for Mr W and his 'bride'. That word still grated on Gem's nerves. It was so sweet of the M's - and so much effort.

Mr M cocked his head. "Jag coming up the lane," he informed the young Missus.

Gem's nerves jangled. She was so tired.

"Green peppers," Mr M reminded her.

Gem slipped back into the kitchen, washed the peppers, and was slicing one by the time Wyatt walked into the kitchen.

"Good evening, ladies," Wyatt said casually.

Gem glanced up, reaching for a second pepper at the same time, and managed to tip over her wine glass sitting next to the cup of hot chocolate. "Oh, dear!" she gasped, hurriedly fetching a wet cloth from the sink to mop the mess.

Wyatt set the glass upright. "No harm done, nothing broken," he said smoothly, taking the cloth to finish wiping clean the counter.

"Wine on the green pepper," Gem apologized.

"Flavour for the shiskabobs," he suggested, kissing the nape of her neck.

Mrs M took the cloth from Wyatt's hand. "I'll finish with the dinner prep. You two run off then. Dinner is still a time off," she dismissed the young couple.

The last thing Gem wanted was to be alone with Wyatt. She didn't know now how to react to him. The trap seemed so infinite now.

"Look at your office, dear," Mrs M called from the kitchen, as Wyatt drew Gem down the hall towards the staircase.

"Yes!" Gem said eagerly. She had forgotten the ceiling project was to be finished that day.

Wyatt patiently backtracked to her office with her. It was lovely: the pearl grey beadboard ceiling, the antique looking light fixtures; even the roman shades had arrived and were hung above the bank of windows.

"A very proper office for you, my dear," Wyatt declared. "We'll hang your art when your photos are back from the framers."

"I forgot to pick them up," Gem sighed.

"So much on your mind, my sweet. Perhaps you need a relaxing shower," he suggested.

"I had a shower earlier," Gem protested. "I'd best help Mrs M," she turned to walk back to the kitchen.

Wyatt caught the back of her jumper. "She said she could manage without you," he said quietly. "I cannot," he coaxed her down the hall and up the staircase.

Upon reaching the bedroom, Wyatt noticed the drawn curtains and blanket on the bed.

"Did you actually nap today?" he asked, surprised.

"I had a bit of a headache," Gem replied.

Wyatt frowned. "Are you ill?" He touched the back of his hand to her forehead. "You are a bit warm."

"I am perfectly well," Gem replied. "Was your conference call - successful?" She folded the blanket easing around Wyatt to set it on the window seat across the room. She avoided his eyes, not wanting to be captivated. She was so confused.

"Quite successful," he watched her, amused, trying to decide why she was manoeuvring to elude him.

"You have time for a shower before dinner," she suggested.

"You know perfectly well that is the last thing on my mind," he said smoothly, again catching her jumper, and drawing her back to him. "Unless you join me," he slipped his arms around her waist, holding her against his body. "You are teasing."

"No, I am not," Gem replied, a catch in her voice.

"You're trying to avoid me."

"No," she denied futilely.

The jumper was the first thing to go.

I still think pineapple and beef is an odd combination," Wyatt suggested as he moved the furniture back into Gem's office.

"I thought the combination was delicious," Gem disagreed.

"I have no actual opinion," Wyatt chuckled. "You ate all my pineapple - and yours."

"Thank you very much," Gem nodded, hooking up the scanner to the computer. In an hour her office was organized and she was out of the study.

Wyatt leaned against the counter, drinking a beer as Gem hooked the printer to the computer, then made sure all the connections were complete.

"I wasn't aware you are so fond of pineapple," Wyatt observed.

Gem frowned. "I'm not. I suppose it was just the moment," she shrugged. Nor was Gemmy particularly fond of that fruit. Thinking of her sister brought a query to her mind. "What did you mean the other day when you told me to mind my P's and Q's? - When I was meeting Mrs Brown," she added for clarification.

"What do you think I meant," Wyatt tipped up the beer bottle to drain the rest of the brew down his throat.

"I'm asking you," Gem insisted. "Was that a threat?"

"You decide," he replied cryptically, and walked out of the office.

And what was that supposed to mean? Gem scowled. She had best take it as a threat. Things were not going to change, no matter how thoughtful and kind he might be at times. This was the Wyatt Grantham of her world. And beyond the bed in the master suite, he did not like her.

Gem gazed around her office. It would suit her very nicely, as it had before. And it was warmer. She did raise two of the roman shades to bring in some of the night. The fairy lights no longer twinkled in the garden. Gem could not imagine why the M's had gone to so much effort to plan a romantic evening for Wyatt and her. It was so thoughtful; and so unnecessary. Wyatt had reacted graciously to the M's dinner preparations; Gem had hid her embarrassment. She certainly hoped Wyatt didn't think she was involved in the planning of the 'romantic' trimmings.

Imagine Ticking Bottom being a gated community! Wyatt owned every building! Gem had refused to look at the Agency file on Wyatt, but Mr Choate was siphoning information to her. To Gem, it was clearly a warning. Mr Choate had no knowledge of the basis of Wyatt and Gem's marriage, yet Mr Choate was warning her of her husband's power. Whoa! Don't push Wyatt. Don't push Wyatt - because you can't win.

Push him out of your mind!

Gem made tea and cut up the last of the green pepper. Mr Cawley! So nice to have him back in the dark hours! She pulled her mobile out of the pocket of her dressing gown.

'SEA agent. Same knife?'
'Still unknown.'
'Country of origin?'
'China. Based out of Hong Kong.'
'Where is Harry?'
'Amusing, Gem.'
'How are you feeling?'
'Exhausted. You?'
'Same. But I didn't climb a mountain.'
'You are still climbing your mountain, Gem.'
'No news?'
'None that I know of for now.'

Did Harry go underground to hunt for a killer? Did he go underground to study the mechanics of the SEA Network? To look for flaws?

'SEA Network still sequestered?'
'Yes.'

Unless Harry came up with new information, the Agency would continue to be at a stalemate.

'Searching the South China Sea?'
'Orders in channels, no pun intended.'

No information forthcoming from that area.

Gemmy, Gemmy, Gemmy. Give me a clue!

Please!

Gem made another cup of hot chocolate. And another. Vera Lynn sang to her while Gem paced.

She couldn't believe she had rushed off again to London without first ringing Mr Choate. He was employed by Wyatt, and she was thwarting him. That could not happen again! She had said that on Paint Day.

Wyatt. Sleeping. And sleeping within his arms was heavenly. Whether he was Dr Jekyll or Mr Hyde, he was a fascinating man. And he was in a warm, cosy bed. Gem switched off the electric fireplaces and went to join him.

Gem groaned as her eyes opened. She raised her head off the pillow then sank back down.

"Stay in bed and rest, sweetheart," Wyatt murmured in her ear. "If you can't sleep then rest quietly."

He held her for half an hour; Gem tried, but she could not sleep. - And then she didn't want to sleep. Nor did Wyatt.

"Are you going to London today?" he queried, later.

"Yes," Gem nodded.

"Shall I ring Mr Choate or will you?" Wyatt asked.

"I'll drive in when you do," Gem decided.

She fetched the Carlisle photos and the framed snaps. There was nothing else for her to do in the city so she returned to Ticking Bottom. The clouds were striking, fluffy white blending with steel grey. She garaged the Defender and dashed inside the Hall for her camera.

"Don't forget your hat! There is sun out there," Mrs M called as Gem started out the kitchen door again.

Gem halted and turned, plunking the camera down on the island.

"Why is everyone always reminding me to wear a Blasted hat?" she demanded in frustration.

Mrs M looked at her in astonishment. "Mr W hasn't told you? I don't know what that man thinks at times." She squared her shoulders and pursed her lips. "Mrs Fiona had cancers of the skin. She and Mr Jack were flying to Zurich for her medical treatments when the plane crashed. Jamie was with them that day. He was the only survivor of the crash. He was in hospital nearly a year."

Gem nodded, knowing what was coming. "Yes," she said quietly, nodding.

"It wasn't surprising he couldn't get off the pain medications. And then he started drinking," Mrs M said sadly.

Gem listened quietly, believing the woman needed to talk about Jamie more than she was explaining hats. And while Mrs M talked, Gem made tea. She didn't ask questions, she didn't pry into Wyatt's life; she simply let the information come to her: the months James was in hospital, the physical therapy, the drug and alcohol addictions, the rehabilitation.

Gem made more tea, and Mrs M talked for two hours, finally ending with the remark, "Mr W hounds people to wear hats to protect from sun damage."

"He doesn't wear hats," Gem said simply.

"He wears screening lotions," Mrs M explained. "Hats give Mr W migraines."

After the conversation, Gem put her camera in her office. The sky was grey now, threatening rain, and was no longer of enough cloud diversity to interest Gem to capture the sky on film. She sorted the Carlisle Cathedral snaps, packing one complete set in a box and setting it in a cupboard below the counter. From now on she would always order duplicate sets of her cathedral shots. She stared at each photo, trying to imagine the dedicated effort it took to conceive the idea of building the cathedral a thousand years ago. One thousand years! It was a staggering thought!

Another staggering thought was the information Gem had just heard from Mrs M: Wyatt and the reason of his obsession that she should wear hats. At least it was a thoughtful protection from him, instead of just another issue of control over her. Lord! Wyatt had had a difficult past ten years! She knew he had fought hard to help his brother in one recovery process and then the next session. Wyatt had been a very good brother to James. All that effort to help James, and still he had lost him.

If Gem discovered that someone had caused the Pilos to crash - would she feel as vengeful as did Wyatt? She could definitely understand the quest for revenge. But could she act on that desire?

Wyatt listened, growing irritable as the meeting dragged on. It was a basic take-over: employees would retain their positions, wages and benefits; however he refused to award financial compensation to directors who had, through greed and neglect, driven the business into arrears. GEI staff would have the company operating at profit in ninety days. Clear and simple.

The directors were wheedling, whinging, crudely diverting blame to anyone but themselves.

Wyatt wondered what Gem was doing. She was presumably at the Hall, for Choate had reported her return two hours ago. Perhaps she was working on her book; she had said recently that she was making progress on the project - when she wasn't destroying her photos with hot chocolate. Mrs M had frequently remarked to him how hard working Gem was.

Gem. She was exceedingly frustrating. Why was it so damned difficult to figure her?

Ms Holton was countering one of the director's remarks. Wyatt quickly shifted his focus to the meeting, then again let his mind drift when it was obvious his assistant had complete control of the situation.

He couldn't get the sensation of Gem's exquisite skin from his mind, her passionate response to his touch. She was so easy to manipulate, but she was never boring.

Wyatt calmly, dispassionately, observed the conniving directors. He had seen their kind so many times over the years, and he was weary of the all-consuming effort he had put into GEI, especially over the past decade.

And despite the effort, nay even before, he had had his fair share of interludes with women. There were memories that touched his thoughts. Yet none of the other women captured his thoughts as did Gem. He had never been of the mind that one woman was the same as the next; it had not been his habit to take women for granted. However, past relationships had been solely for mutual pleasures - no ties - no commitments - well understood on both sides.

And he had tied himself to Gem with good reason - power on his side; none on hers. She had insisted it was revenge. A description he could accept. He had control over her. Complete control. Yet he was all at sea. Aside from the passion between the sheets, or when he had raised her ire, there was no life in her. She met his physical passion equally. And just as equally shut him out of every other aspect of her life. And she had shut James out of her private life, promising to share everything when she had returned from Australia. But theirs had not been a physical relationship.

And what the HELL was that all about?

He should have insisted on an autopsy. He should have demanded to know what drugs James had been given - or had taken. But the injuries were the result of the accident. Wyatt's questions of drugs hadn't surfaced until that night on Wight. It hadn't occurred to him that drugs had again had a hold on James.

He knew every inch of Gem's body and there were no indications she had ever used drugs. There were none in her possession. Choate gave a detailed report of her activities and there were no indications that she could be buying or using - that Wyatt could suspect from the reports. Mrs Brown was a possibility but Choate's reports only ever stated the most innocuous meetings.

Wyatt scowled, lost in questions. The demands of GEI were of no interest to him these days. He was grooming Ms Holton to move up and she was exceeding his and Manton's expectations. He had no difficulty promoting women over men; he didn't tolerate barracudas or sharks; logic, ethics, common sense, humanity, were the qualities he expected in staff. - The same qualities he had also desired in the women with whom he had had intimate relationships. Yet he was fascinated by a woman who did not possess any of those qualities.

He was beginning to believe Gem was quite scatter-brained. Logical? Not to his observations of her - constantly switching thoughts, or losing track of conversations. Ethics? He could not see any indication she possessed any. Common sense? Locking keys in the Defender, losing camera lenses, cameras, shredding cds, losing fake passports, becoming involved with John Staunton. Humanity? Sketch a dying child; and then what she had done to James.

He couldn't stop thinking about her.

Wyatt narrowed his eyes on Ms Holton standing at the opposite end of the conference table.

"We are finished here," he interrupted the protests of the soon-to-be-former president of the manufacturing company in Birmingham. "Ms Holton has given the details of the offer. It's final," he announced, then walked from the room.

All eyes of the seven men remaining at the table swivelled from Wyatt to the tall brunette now at the head of the conference table. Ms Holton smiled inwardly, and sent a silent Thank You to Gem Grantham. Since Gem Grantham had entered the picture, Emma's power at GEI had tripled. She knew Wyatt Grantham's vision for the company for the next two decades, and she and Manton could bring it all home. Wyatt Grantham had given her opportunities for career growth in the past six years that she wouldn't have had at other companies. She wanted to take over London operations and send Wyatt Grantham home to his bride. If he didn't cut his work schedule he'd be dead in five years from stress. And she wasn't about to let that happen. She and her family had a beautiful home in the country thanks to Wyatt Grantham. He was generous to all his employees and their loyalty to him was unshakeable.

"There is no further discussion," Ms Holton said firmly. "This is not a Take-It-Or-Leave-It situation. You are all finished here. I will have your signatures now." Celebration steak and wine dinner this evening. Ring Stuart to alert him, she mused, keeping her gaze steady and cold as she faced down the men at the table.

Gem heard the Jag on the cobblestone lane.

"I thought you were at the office all day," she acknowledged his presence without taking her eyes off the photos on the computer screen.

"I couldn't get you out of my mind," Wyatt said casually.

Gem glanced back at him, then back to the computer screen, and when she turned around he was gone. "That was short lived," she shrugged. He had a tendency to be mercurial.

Wyatt frowned as he changed into jeans and a denim shirt. Where was the cheery young woman who James had said had made him roar with laughter? She was never moody, her eyes sparkled, the girl with the infectious smile, James had sighed weakly. But Wyatt had never seen that young woman. He had perhaps seen a fleeting glimpse of her in August, but he had never seen the woman James had so lovingly described. How could Gem be so different in so few months' time?

Gem carefully cropped the snaps, then scanned them into the computer.

The hairs at the nape of her neck tingled. Right. He was there again.

Wyatt silently watched her work. James had said she was wildly romantic. But Wyatt had never seen that in Gem. She was always so reserved and quiet.

Gem turned around. "What?" she queried, dragging her fingers through her hair.

Ah! He had seen that gesture enough times to recognize it. She was frustrated.

"I'm enjoying watching you," he said lazily. "You bite on the end of your pen when you're concentrating," he observed.

A reference from James of Gemmy? We both shared that habit; a habit that always drew a frown from their mum. They had inherited the habit from their dad.

"Yes," she admitted, yawning.

"You're tired. Perhaps you should lie down for awhile," Wyatt suggested.

"And there it is," Gem grumbled, tossing her pen to the counter. "The legendary sexual prowess of Wyatt Grantham!"

"You think I'm legendary? Thank you, sweetheart - a lovely compliment," Wyatt chuckled. "Actually I wasn't thinking of letting you seduce me - just yet," he said slowly. "As I said, I was thinking of you."

Gem stiffened. This couldn't be good. "What?" she said bluntly.

"You bewilder me, Gem. I can't figure you out," he admitted.

"You don't know me," she shrugged. And you never will!

"Two different people."

"I'm a Gemini -"

"James spoke of your vitality. Your spirit. The sparkle in yours eyes. He said you laughed all the time. Your joie de vivre."

Gem and Gem. We laughed constantly. Our parents would shake their heads and leave the room - to escape us. Mrs Brown once said the only way she could keep her sanity was to keep us on separate continents - which she did as often as she could. Gem and Gem, laughing until the tears streamed down our faces.

Wyatt watched the haunted look cloud her eyes. And where was she now?

"There is no joy in our relationship," Gem said bluntly. "I don't recall that you specified terms regarding my personality in the 'agreement'."

Wyatt shook his head. "No," he regarded her carefully. "There's a difference. The difference between night and day. The difference between the you in the photos with Staunton and - you," he pointed a finger at her. "The woman in the passports had an aura about her. Like two different people. Alike in appearance, but there is now no aura."

"You try being married to you," Gem said coolly. "You try maintaining an 'aura' when you're followed wherever you go, when you're controlled every single day. You try being married to someone who loathes you - and then we'll check your aura! The person in that passport photo, in the other photos, does not exist."

"Did that person ever exist?" Wyatt queried softly.

"Yes," Gem sighed. "A very, very long time ago. But she no longer exists." I'm sorry Gemmy.

"Do you prefer wine or beer?" he still probed. The haunted look remained.

This was a cinch. "Whatever is offered, but not at the same time." That was one of their jokes. Gemmy had learned one or the other - drastically learned that - on a whirlwind three day holiday in NYC. "What are you offering?"

"From which parent did you inherit your smart mouth?" Wyatt asked dryly.

Gem's eyes glittered. "Both." Gemmy obviously hadn't told James anything about their parents. How had she managed to hold back information? "From which parent did you inherit your cruel streak?" She folded her arms across her chest, and glared the challenge.

"Touché," he nodded. He looked at his watch. "Where is Mrs M?"

"The M's are at the shops. They'll return about four o'clock, Mrs M said," Gem replied. "Ah! Your one track mind!" Where did he get his sexual energy?

Wyatt studied her face. What was she hiding? It would be good to keep her off balance. "Let's walk to the pub for a beer."

"Okay," Gem said, startled.

"Don't you ever wear jeans?" Wyatt waited while she closed out of her computer screens. He put up both hands in concession. "Not a criticism. You just never dress what I would consider comfortably casual."

"I didn't know what Mrs M would consider proper to wear here," Gem replied hesitantly.

"Your choice, Gem," Wyatt frowned. "We don't stand on ceremony here. Have you ever known more casual staff than the M's?"

"They are rather surprising," Gem agreed.

"Go - change," he crisply ordered.

Lovely! Jeans! Gem took the steps two at a time while Wyatt leaned against the banister. Five minutes tops, she was in jeans, a turtleneck sweater and a pullover, and her favourite loafers.

Mrs M had dinner prepared by the time they returned from the pub. Gem had opted for tea instead of beer, and hot chocolate for dinner; beer just didn't sound appealing, she winced as she thought of the brew.

Wyatt had ceased his annoying questions - for the time being; Gem knew he wasn't completely finished fishing about her past. To divert his attention at dinner, she asked of Ms Holton.

"She is quite well, I believe," Wyatt replied, suppressing a smile as she tried to direct the conversation away from herself.

Gem suddenly frowned. "Ms Jones mentioned that she passed the defensive driving course. Why would a receptionist be required to take that course?"

"Advancement prep."

"What does a receptionist advance to at GEI?"

"Depends on the employee. Ms Holton was the front receptionist six years ago."

"What! Well, that was quick advancement on her part, wasn't it just," Gem murmured. GEI must have an extremely observant supervisory staff to recognize staff potential. She knew that Mrs Brown and Harry had observed Gem and Gem for years, regarding possible hiring by the Agency.

"Ah, what?" Wyatt demanded, setting down his fork and staring pointedly at Gem. "You had best not be implying there was other than a proper working relationship between Ms Holton and me!"

"No-no," Gem quickly protested. "I wouldn't think that of Ms Holton. She seems very capable."

"But you would think that of me?" Wyatt said sternly. "For your information, Ms Holton is very capable. And I do NOT play sexual politics with staff. And anyone who tries that at GEI is out of the company!"

Gem had obviously stepped on his toes. She held her silence so as not to further aggravate him.

"And for some outlandish reason I cannot fathom, Ms Holton genuinely likes you. So don't even dare to speak ill of her," he warned harshly. "She has only thought of you with kindness and consideration."

"I don't think ill of Ms Holton," Gem protested. "I only meant to suggest that someone must have carefully observed her at work to realize her full potential. She wasn't pigeon-holed to a particular position."

"I see," Wyatt replied dryly. She seemed to be speaking sincerely, but he was never certain with her.

Gem thought for a moment. "How would one decide Ms Jones was prepared to advance to another position?"

"Her judgment. Ms Jones is the first person to greet visitors to the Grantham Building. She decides who is directed to the various departments, or if one should be sent to the information office on the first floor."

Gem frowned, thinking out loud. "I told Ms Jones I wanted to see you. She directed me to the eighth instead of the first floor. My appearance would have suggested she advise me to leave the building."

"Which she would not have done," Wyatt replied. "First floor, or ring security if she thought that action was necessary."

"Was she reprimanded for sending me to the eighth floor?"

Wyatt sipped his wine before he spoke. "Ms Jones is apparently a very intuitive person. She judged the situation and made a correct decision to send you on. When a position is available she will be transferred to R&D."

Gem was stunned by his reply. "And Ms Carton?"

"She will be partnered with Ms Jones when a second position is available. It will be interesting to see if they work well together. It appears they have similar judgment skills."

"Perhaps they both suffer from poor judgment," Gem countered.

"You are the only person without an appointment who has accessed the eighth floor in the past four months. They have shown excellent judgment."

Gem ate a bit of her dinner, and then offered another query. "Your office is on the eighth floor." Wyatt nodded. "I should think the view would be better from the twelfth floor."

"Lovely view," Wyatt nodded. "It's a remarkable incentive for employees to earn an office on the top floor. And added incentive to work very hard to retain that office."

"Very clever of you," Gem conceded admiringly.

"I do have a few good ideas," Wyatt smiled.

Gem's heart flip-flopped. Oh that deadly smile!

Gem frowned again thoughtfully. "It's rather surprising that GEI isn't in a modern office building."

"The Grantham Building - London - is historic. It was built by my great-grandfather. I prefer traditional structures to metal and glass. Such structures are often too harsh on the eyes and lack true architectural style. All Grantham office buildings are historic buildings, restored by GEI, if necessary."

"All? More than just the London building?" Gem said, surprised.

Was she fishing for information? If so, it was public knowledge. "Eight office buildings in as many countries."

"Oh," Gem said faintly. Quite impressive, but then most aspects of Wyatt Grantham were impressive. And she shouldn't be surprised, as Mr Choate had informed her of just some of the properties of GEI.

The information about Wyatt was definitely interesting, but she wouldn't be pleased if she was a private citizen whose entire background was in a special government file. Well, hers was. - And she accepted the fact that her file was held by the Agency - but that was an employee file.

As he did ninety-nine percent of the time, Wyatt spent the evening in his library. Gem completed the chapter of Carlisle Cathedral, and sorted through the snaps of Chichester Cathedral - one of her favourites because of the bell tower.

She popped a Dr Who dvd into the player, wishing she was Rose forty thousand years in the future. Would it take forty thousand years to find the Pilos?

All the snaps of Chichester were perfect. She had been on holiday when she had taken the photos. Mum and dad had been in New Zealand on a week's holiday, Gemmy had been in - was it Washington D.C.? Actually where they had been then wasn't important. Where they were now was. Gem stopped working to gaze at the telly and the smashing Dr. She HAD to purchase more of the series. It was perfect escapism for her.

"Do you travel in time?" Wyatt asked half-teasing.

She hadn't been aware that he was standing behind her.

"Time isn't relevant in my life," Gem tossed off the remark without thinking. She had already been in limbo for months.

"As I have noticed. You confuse waking and sleeping hours," he said more seriously. "You also confuse fact and fiction."

My life is fiction. "In your eyes perhaps," Gem sighed. "I am too tired to argue."

"I'm not here to argue, my dear. It's time for bed, and as you say, you are exhausted. End of discussion."

"Dark Lord," Gem muttered, and Wyatt chuckled at her remark. She went along quietly.

Mr Cawley was again the joy of the dark hours.
'Any news?'
'Not sure. May have some next few days.'
'Harry?'
'Not sure.'
'Something happening?'
'Not sure. Mrs B frowned all day. Very uncommunicative.'
'Autopsy reports?'
'Not available yet.'
'SEA Network?'
'Still sequestered.'

Gem made a cup of hot chocolate, and pushed the start button on the cd player. Vera Lynn. Gem's constant companion of the dark hours.

What was on Mrs Brown's mind? Mr Cawley was being cagey. Something was happening. Or had something already occurred? Something that troubled or puzzled Mrs Brown. That something could be any number of things. It could the SEA Network isolation or Harry going underground. Or the fact that so many of the murdered counter-couriers and agents were connected to Paul Andriani. Odessa? Waiting for the autopsy report?

Mrs M had included green peppers with the shopping. Green peppers and hot chocolate. Lovely!

Gem paced, listening to the cd. The music and her memories were the only links she had to her parents. And to Gemmy. She snuggled in Auntie Jane's comfy chair, leaning her head back, eyes closed, trying to sleep. It was best that she didn't win that battle. Wyatt had been very perturbed when she had fallen asleep on Auntie Jane's settee. She had heard the five chimes that morning, but had waited a few minutes too long before getting up off the settee. No. She couldn't win the battle of sleep this morning. And she admitted again that until the Pilos was found, the dark hours would continue.

Gem dusted the furniture, while Mrs M hoovered and mopped the floors. The unused bedrooms were off the list for this week. Gem cleaned her bathroom in the bedroom suite and the one off the office. After lunch with Mrs M, she was at loose ends and concentrated on the text of Chichester. She cross-checked her notes with other historical reference material, checked for spelling errors, refined, then expanded the text, marvelling at Bishop Stigand's devotion to the construction of the cathedral. - How did one have the vision, the insight, how did one find the desire of commitment to begin a project of such immensity as the building of a cathedral? Staggering!

Again she sensed his presence before she saw him.

"It is fascinating to watch you work," Wyatt said, leaning against the doorjamb. "You become so immersed, so focused, that you become oblivious to your surroundings. You were in your own world just now, as you are those three hours every morning. And in those hours you seem to be at the nethermost part of your private world."

Gem stiffened, waiting for a caustic shot from the intruder into her private world.

"That was not a criticism," he explained as he seemed to do frequently as of late. "I find it intriguing to observe your level of concentration - your ability to close off the rest of the world. You seem more accessible during the day however, than you do when you are in your netherworld."

Netherworld was more accurate than Gem wanted to admit. Her day life and her night life. She was weary of trying to keep the lives separate. She was weary of being drawn into the netherworld that drained her energy and provided no answers to her unending queries.

"You are two people," Wyatt said quietly. "You lead two lives, and both, I believe, are in quiet desperation."

Gem didn't dare look at him, knowing her eyes would acknowledge the truth of his words.

"You are two people," he repeated, frowning as he pondered his remark. "And two questions remain. How long have you been two people? And why are you two people?"

Gem still refused to look at him. She didn't want her eyes to give away her secrets or to confirm his suggestions.

"Your silence informs me that I have to solve the mysteries of Gem without any assistance from you."

And I shall hinder you at every opportunity to solve the mysteries! Gem continued her silence.

"I am not as mysterious as you make me out to be," Gem said, forcing her voice to be steady.

"Rubbish," Wyatt laughed. She was never boring. "I'm going to have a shower then a glass of wine. I won't disturb your work any longer. However, if you care to join me, I shall be in our sitting room. Mrs M has yet to begin dinner prep," he added softly, smiling at her.

A shower and wine did sound heavenly. Blast! She was lost after he smiled at her.

Wyatt's lips curved in a satisfied smile as he heard the water running in Gem's shower. What would be the first step to break through to Gem's private world? He still had made no progress in obtaining information of the Gemma whom James had loved.

Gem slipped into a dressing gown. She had seen the wine bottle and glasses on the coffee table in the sitting room. Flames were licking at the logs in the fireplace. Wine and a crackling fire. He had certainly set the mood. There was no purpose in dressing. As she entered the sitting room, Wyatt took her hand and seated her on the settee, then he filled two glasses before settling beside her.

"How was your day, my dear?" he asked casually.

"Long," she sipped the wine. And it's far from over, she observed silently. "You had another short day."

"One of the perks of having an excellent staff. Is your book progressing to your satisfaction?"

She winced recalling the smarting remarks he had made of her book and thesis weeks back.

"Yes, thank you," she said hesitantly, wondering the angle of this cosy arrangement. Unless it was a variation on the obvious: his one track mind.

"Sadly remiss of me, but I have never asked - do you have a publisher for this volume?"

"One of my former professors is associated with a small London publishing house. They published my thesis." She did not give any names that he could use against her.

"I still would like to read your thesis," he said smoothly. "Where might one obtain a copy?"

There was nothing in the book that referred to her family. "It's available in a number of libraries," she grudgingly admitted.

"Of course you have copies," Wyatt suggested.

"I do," Gem nodded.

"May I read a copy or must I track one down and purchase it?" Wyatt teased at her reluctance.

He didn't believe the thesis existed.

"Let me think about that," Gem replied reluctantly. "Mm. This is excellent wine," she murmured. "Subtle, fruity, mildly sweet. I can't place it."

He lifted the bottle suggesting a refill.

"Not yet," she shook her head. "Are you going to ply me with wine and then seduce me, Wyatt?" she teased, relaxing with the combination of the fire, the wine, and that smashing smile.

He nearly dropped the bottle. It was the first time she had addressed him by name since their wedding night.

"I hadn't actually considered seducing you now," he replied.

Gem studied him. "You are so smooth. It's ingrained in you, isn't it? The intensity of your gaze, the finesse of your touch. Women are putty in your hands, aren't we?" she mused frankly.

Watt shook himself. "Who is seducing who?" he said lightly. "I wanted you to taste the wine. Manton wants GEI to purchase a winery in Hampshire. Ms Holton suggested I ask your opinion, as she prefers a dry wine."

"I'm not qualified to express an opinion. I don't drink expensive wines," Gem protested. "Purchasing a winery is an enormous decision."

"A very simple decision actually. This is a reasonably priced table wine. Would you purchase it? Yes or no?"

"What is reasonable to you may not be to me," Gem countered.

"Same price per bottle you paid the other day when you bought the wine." he smiled.

The butterflies were threatening. "Yes," Gem took a deep breath, "I would buy this wine." She reached up a hand to stroke his cheek.

"I am definitely purchasing that winery!" Wyatt murmured, sometime later. "I'll call Ms Holton after dinner."

Gem blushed, covering her face with her hands. "I swear I am losing my mind," she sighed.

Watt laughed. "You're embarrassed!"

"Of course I am!"

"Why? Because you wanted me?" he teased.

"Don't gloat!"

"I'm not. I'm remembering with great enjoyment your unbridled spontaneity."

Gem snapped the sheet trying to untangle her legs. "I'll pay for this forever, won't I," she sighed. She pulled on her dressing gown. "It won't happen again!" she stomped to the bathroom. She slammed the bathroom door to shut out his laughter.

What is wrong with me? she scolded herself. I can't blame the wine. I did want him! I wanted him so badly my teeth ached!

Must be lack of sleep. It must be! Shower! Dinner! Work! Concentrate! A very, very cold shower!

Wyatt reached for his mobile. "Ms Holton. Purchase the winery! And send me a case of the wine!" He rang off. He listened to the water running again in her shower. She had called him by his name. She had initiated the love-making. Was it time for another Game? It was as far as he was concerned; he was growing tired of this Game.

Gem couldn't decide tea or hot chocolate, so she made a cup of each. Even hours later she still couldn't account for her aberrant behaviour that afternoon. And now absurdly, she wanted to go upstairs and wake him up. Her teeth were starting to ache again. She paced the floor, listening to the cd, wondering what it was about that man that drove her mad!

Ping

'Autopsy inconclusive, but could be same knife.'

'Agency going on theory killer is the same person?'

'Yes.'

'Storm still brewing?'

'Yes.'

'SEA still sequestered?'

'No.'

'Harry still underground?'

'Yes.'

'How is your jet-lag?'

'Horrid!'

'Tell Mrs Brown you need a proper holiday.'

'After the pay rise? Not going to happen.'

'Are you sleeping well?'

'No. You?'

'Same. Where is Harry?'

'Tokyo.'

'Really?'

'I have no idea, Gem.'

'Does Mrs Brown know?'

'I doubt it.'

'Is this ever going to come right?'
'Yes. It will Gem.'
'Okay. Good night.'
'Good night.'

She wished she could believe Mr Cawley. But she was losing hope. And she was so Blasted exhausted.

Chapter Twenty-Two

Someone was shaking her.

"Gem…Gem…"

She pushed the hand away. She had to sleep!

"Gem! Mrs Brown is on my mobile. You didn't answer yours."

"What? Oh," Gem groaned. "It must be -" she tried to sort her sleep starved brain. "What time is it?" she murmured. "Office."

Gem rubbed her eyes.

"Here," Wyatt placed his mobile in her hand.

Gem tried to force her eyes open.

"Yes?" she said groggily.

Mrs Brown's voice was cheerful as usual. "Good morning, my dear. I am sorry to waken you so early but I would like you to join me for tea at half eight."

"Yes," Gem replied automatically. Could one die from lack of sleep? "Half eight."

"I am dreadfully sorry, my dear, to ring you on Wyatt's mobile. I couldn't reach you on yours. I've landed you with explaining how I happened to have his number. Goodbye."

Damn! Explain that one away!

"Yes ma'am," Gem groaned. Half eight. Explain that!

She tried to brush the sleep from her eyes, wanting only to pull the duvet over her head and hide from the world.

"How the hell did Mrs Brown happen to have my mobile number? It's a blocked number," Wyatt demanded curiously.

I must get up, Gem tried to marshal her mental functions. Mrs Brown probably had the mobile number for the President of the United States. The PM was likely on her speed dial.

Gem forced herself to sit up, carefully avoiding eye contact with Wyatt.

"Mrs Brown purchased a new mobile last week. She had to re-enter the numbers into her contact list." Did this sound anywhere near a logical or possible truth? "I must have given her your number instead of mine. I never ring my phone and rarely ring yours. I must have confused the numbers."

"Ah ha," Wyatt said dryly.

Gem reached for her dressing gown and swept her hair back. He didn't believe her, and she couldn't fault him. It was a feeble story. She glanced at him warily. Bless peripheral vision.

He was stretched out on the bed staring at her. Damn! He took her breath away!

"You don't actually think for a moment that I believe that explanation, do you? I don't object to Mrs Brown having the phone number," he drawled, "but I don't understand why you are lying to me." He reached out a finger to stroke a line down between her shoulders.

Well, that went well, didn't it? she mused sarcastically. Well, damn! Mrs Brown just has her ways of doing things, hasn't she? Could she possibly avoid the rest of this conversation?

"Can a person actually die from lack of sleep?" Gem mused aloud.

"I'll ask the doctor you refused to see, shall I?" Wyatt drawled. "I think one would likely land in hospital before actually dying."

Gem shook her head helplessly. "Mrs Brown is my friend. She has your mobile number. May we please leave it at that?" she sighed.

Wyatt paused before replying. "For the time being we may." He glanced at his watch.

"What is the time, please?"

"Half six. If you are going to meet her at half eight, you'd best get a move on it, sweetheart," Wyatt suggested crisply.

Mrs Brown had neglected to mention their meeting place. Gem rang her when she reached London.

"Croyden Café, my dear," Mrs Brown said briskly and immediately rang off.

Gem arrived at the appointed time but Mrs Brown was already seated and had ordered breakfast for both of them.

"You look more tired than usual, my dear, if that is possible," her supervisor stated.

"Long night," Gem murmured, pushing food around the plate in front of her. Looking at the eggs made her wince.

"No appetite, dear?"

"I just feel a bit queasy," Gem said faintly.

"Hmm, yes," Mrs Brown replied and signalled to the waitress. "Please bring tea and dry toast, and remove this plate," she gestured to Gem's breakfast.

"Any news about Harry?" Gem queried a few minutes later, scanning the café as did her supervisor.

"None," Mrs Brown replied. "We do not -" she paused as her mobile rang.

Gem waited patiently while the other woman listened quietly to the phone call – and frowned. The toast was definitely preferable to eggs and bacon.

"I'm sorry, my dear," Mrs Brown announced as she rang off, "but I must leave. Might you be able to meet me for lunch at Charley's? - Noon, shall we say?"

"Yes, ma'am," Gem nodded quickly, and her companion hurried from the café.

She finished her tea and toast, paid the bill for herself and Mrs Brown, then joined Mr Choate on the pavement. He gave her a quizzical look but Gem could only shrug at Mrs Brown's hasty departure.

Since she had no plans for the hours until noon, Gem suggested they visit the Imperial War Museum. Once inside, they went their own ways, but Gem was never out of Choate's sight. She added to her World War II reference collection with three dvd sets on the Blitz, the R.A.F. and the third on Allied campaigns in Europe.

They arrived at Charley's Pub a quarter of an hour early and Gem ordered a glass of wine while she waited.

"You have a new dart board, Charley," she observed.

"Second new one this week. You couriers do get a bit rowdy when you're pissed, don't you," he remarked with a disdainful sniff. "One bloke wore the last board out of here - around his neck. Concussion I'd say."

Mrs Brown arrived precisely on time. She studied Gem as she sat down at the table, then took the wine glass from the young woman's grasp.

"No more of that for you, my dear," she said firmly, ordering Charley to bring tea for herself and apple juice for Gem.

"I detest apple juice, and that was only my first glass of wine," Gem protested.

"Learn to love the juice, my dear," Mrs Brown ordered.

"Very high-handed of you," Gem pursed her lips.

"When needs be," Mrs Brown said crisply. "Oh, my dear, I am going to have my hands full with you, I can see."

Gem frowned. "You voiced that same opinion the day we started at the Agency."

"I did indeed. However, I didn't realize that day I was making a lifelong commitment to you. Couriers do come and go, but I see now that you and I shall always be together. I will be here for you when you need me, my dear," Mrs Brown patted Gem's hand. "Now drink your juice and tell Charley what you wish for lunch," she instructed while the publican stared from one woman to the other.

"Steak and chips," Gem replied, puzzled by her supervisor's remarks. Mrs Brown ordered the daily special, cottage pie and chips.

"Now my dear, I am most frightfully sorry you had to explain to Wyatt how I managed to obtain his mobile number. Was he quite put out? I realize it was a blocked number."

Gem told of the new mobile phone patter she had fed to Wyatt.

"I am sorry you had to lie to him, my dear. I shall acquire a new mobile as soon as possible," Mrs Brown decided. "Thus the lie will be minimal. The time was also rude as I interrupted his sleep."

"His sleep!" Gem said sharply. "His sleep!"

"And yours naturally, my dear," Mrs Brown continued smoothly. "I apologize for cancelling our meeting so abruptly this morning."

"News about Harry?" Gem queried hopefully.

"Unfortunately no. His communications are brief and rare." Mrs Brown frowned. "I fear we won't be hearing from him again for some time."

"The SEA Network is again full force," Gem ventured the information she had learned from Mr Cawley during the dark hours.

"Indeed. However, the new couriers and agents are extremely uneasy with all the recent tragedies in that sector. One sometimes lowers defences when 'business' runs smoothly for years. Then all of a sudden one disaster after another occurs and SOP's are challenged and then repeatedly altered. Everyone becomes unsettled for a bit."

Charley served their orders then disappeared again into the kitchen.

Gem waited patiently for her supervisor to broach the subject of this meeting at her own pace. The steak was settling in much better than would have the eggs earlier.

Mrs Brown finally spoke again after she had tasted Charley's cottage pie and deemed it extremely savoury.

"Paul Andriani has disappeared," Mrs Brown announced abruptly. The sudden remark so jolted Gem that her knife and fork clattered to the table.

"What! When? Where?"

"It was confirmed this morning - the reason I had to leave so abruptly at breakfast. Where? We do not know. He was to meet an Agency courier in Athens. He did not make the appointment."

"Is Paul Andriani much involved in Project CSU?" Gem asked.

"No. Project CSU is a historical project, a matter of red tape and diplomacy. But he is an advisor when factions get a bit heated."

"Harry. Paul Andriani. You're not going on 'holiday' soon are you?" Gem queried warily. She pushed away her plate. The food was excellent but her appetite had simply disappeared.

"If I go on holiday, I will inform you ahead of time. And thank heavens I don't have to worry about you."

Gem chuckled. "I have Mr Choate. How convenient that Wyatt hired him - of all people!"

"Nothing convenient about it," Mrs Brown replied firmly. "Wyatt had mentioned to Mr Critchley that he was considering protection for you when you were out and about on your own. Mr Critchley suggested Technical Operations."

"I just don't believe I need to tie up Mr Choate," Gem protested, deciding after all to finish her steak; the taste was so tempting.

"You have had excellent training, my dear, but it's possible your observation powers and reflexes might be a touch dull with too much occupying your mental processes. You must take advantage of Mr Choate's time whenever necessary."

And now she had Paul Adriana's disappearance to sort. Undercover was one matter. Underground or completely disappearing was a completely different issue. Would he contact anyone? Had he contacted Gemmy in Barcelona - unbeknownst to the Agency - to anyone, other than James's camera? However, if there had been vital information that he had shared with Gemmy, would he have turned to someone else with the vital matter when she had disappeared? Had what Paul had shared with Gemmy - if anything, Gem had to self-edit - could that have caused the disappearance of the Pilos? Or had it been something so vital to an operation that he could not pass the information on to the Agency? Something so sensitive? Perhaps a reason Gemmy had gone to Geneva? Damn! She needed to talk to Paul Andriani! And that surely wouldn't happen now!

"If you are contacted by Paul, would you tell him I really want to talk to him?" Gem queried hopefully.

Mrs Brown nodded. "However, do not hold your breath, my dear. I don't believe he will surface for quite some time, very likely months. We have had Agency undercover agents who have permanently disappeared after a single parting message."

"How can you be certain it was his idea to disappear?" Gem puzzled.

"He contacted the Agency courier, requesting a meeting at the Acropolis. She saw a man standing thirty yards away. When she looked at the man, he held up a hand in a form of a salute, then disappeared into a crowd of tourists. When Paul Andriani did not meet her, the courier contacted me with the information I have just relayed to you."

"When did this happen?"

"Saturday last. It was Paul's habit to contact me every Friday morning at half eight. That has been his pattern since the Pilos was lost. He did not contact me Friday last. This morning at half eight, as you know, my mobile rang. There was no one on the line. I went to the Agency to see if Mr White could trace the number on my mobile. He could not. It was a disposable mobile in his opinion, and Paul only uses disposable mobiles these days." Mrs Brown paused to sip her tea. "I conclude that Paul was alerting me to the fact that he was still alive."

"Does anyone else know that Paul rang you every Friday at that time?" Gem pressed.

"No. You now know. I shall inform Mr Choate, and no one else," Mrs Brown said firmly.

"The Three Musketeers," Gem mused. "We certainly could use a proper D'Artagnan right now."

"Indeed. Or perhaps a soothsayer," Mrs Brown looked pointedly at Gem.

"Not likely," Gem protested unhappily. "My brain has stopped working."

"And with good reason, my dear, but it will soon sort itself out. I believe we must skip dessert today," Mrs Brown announced. "I have scheduled an appointment for you with Dr Hallowell."

"I do not need a doctor," Gem protested, dragging her fingers through her hair.

"Oh, my dear, I believe you do. No more wine or beer for you," Mrs Brown rose from her chair. "Come," she urged Gem from her chair. "It might be too soon, but it may be possible that Dr Hallowell will be able to tell you today if you are carrying twins."

"What?" Gem gasped and was quickly shushed by the older woman who guided Gem out of the pub. The shock sent Gem into horrified silence.

"Pregnant," Gem said finally in disbelief.

Mrs Brown put Gem into the Agency Range Rover.

"You poor dear," Mrs Brown tsk-tsked, as she engaged the engine. "Lack of sleep, the stress you've been under these many months, it's no wonder you haven't been thinking clearly enough to recognize the symptoms."

No kidding! A major understatement! If I had been thinking clearly I wouldn't be married to Wyatt Grantham! And I certainly would NOT be pregnant!

Dr Hallowell's private clinic was in an Agency building; his office was on the left side of the building, a tea shop was on the ground floor to the right, a dress boutique was above that.

An hour later Mrs Brown escorted Gem from the building. Gem was two months along. Blast Wight! - or Inverness! It was too early for Dr Hallowell to confirm twins. But he was edging to that decision with her extreme fatigue and weight gain - which she hadn't noticed - for she was still a bit under a proper weight; but not as underweight as she had been since the Pilos went down.

Mrs Brown drove Gem back to the pub where Gem had left the Defender.

"Everything is copasetic for now," Mrs Brown said firmly. "Would you like to stop for tea at Charley's?"

Gem shook her head. "I need to walk for awhile."

"Just so," Mrs Brown agreed. "I will not say a word to anyone until you and Wyatt have made the announcement. You have my mobile number. Contact me anytime you wish. Day or night."

Gem nodded. She needed to talk to Mr Choate immediately. She cupped her hand to draw him around the side of the building.

"Yes, Gem?" he queried, his face blank.

"For your report today, please, Mrs Brown and I went into a building at that address. There are offices, a dress shop and a tea shop," she said firmly.

"Yes, Gem," Choate replied. This was her issue and did not relate to T.O. If Wyatt Grantham at some time in the future inquired pointedly about this date's report that would be handled at that time."

"I need to walk, Mr Choate," Gem said distractedly.

"Lead on, Gem."

Gem couldn't get control of her thoughts. Pregnant! She had never thought of birth control! That had been for sometime in the future - when she had time for a relationship! Meeting Wyatt - he hadn't even suggested an intimate relationship, and then suddenly they were married! He had never asked if she was taking birth control pills. He probably assumed she was.

She was pregnant! And literally TOO VERY STUPID to be a mum!! Twins! She couldn't wrap her mind around that at this moment. Carrying twins would indicate the same in her family background. It was a possibility - and Dr Hallowell had said a strong possibility. But it wasn't currently a fact. And twins or not! - she would not let children permanently bind her to Wyatt Grantham!

She couldn't bear to tell him. How would he react? No doubt with a sarcastic reference to James and a 'fictitious' pregnancy - that only Gem now knew was NOT 'fiction'.

How could she be so COMPLETELY STUPID! She wasn't going to tell Wyatt - not for a few weeks, if possible. She needed to be able to handle the situation in her own mind first. Blast!! Had she ever been so desperately alone? Gemmy, mum, dad. Married to a man who hated her. Pregnant. What next?

A child would be another weapon with which Wyatt could threaten her. His money, his power, his child. Add that to the photos and the passports. She could never fight Wyatt for custody of a child. Find the Pilos, Gemmy, mum, dad, Mr Portermann. Tell Wyatt the truth. Divorce him. Lose the child to him. Or children. He would take everything from her.

Gem walked in a daze. The trap was even stronger now. Would she ever be able to get away from him?

Now she was pregnant. Gemmy had been pregnant. The pain of that thought tore at her heart.

She continued walking until Mr Choate texted, advising of the time. In the length of time it took her to walk back to the Defender, then drive to Ticking Bottom, she was cutting it very short for a much needed quick shower before Wyatt arrived at the Hall.

Just thinking about the man raised her ire!

What would he think of her pregnancy? She had asked him before their marriage if he wanted children and he had replied yes. But that was when he was playing his insidious Game at her expense. Did he really want to be a father? If not, perhaps there wouldn't be a custody battle when Gem was finally able to divorce him.

She let the warm water of the shower cascade down her face, her eyes closed. She could see his smile - it was burned into her brain. His eyes gazing at her with that intensity that freed butterflies as easily as did his smile. She could feel his touch on her skin -

Blast! Well, now at least she had a reason for the desire for him that had begun recently to consume her thoughts. Hormones! The wicked little devils! Good hormones. Bad hormones. Out of control hormones. But now she knew and she could control her impulses!

Wyatt quickly left her mind as she dressed - jeans, blue jumper - and Paul Andriani quickly consumed her thoughts. She glanced at her watch. Half four. Wyatt would probably be leaving his office about now if he wanted to shower before dinner. She had time to ring Mrs Brown with a quick question. Her brain had been dry for a time now, no doubt filled with too many of the blasted hormones. But she could process a few thoughts.

She grabbed her mobile, told Mrs M she was going out for a bit of fresh air, then hastened down the drive and turned left onto the cobblestone lane. She could see the Jag when it passed the rail station - a clear unobstructed view, but she couldn't be overheard by anyone for the open fields and meadows provided no hiding places for eavesdroppers.

"Yes, my dear," Mrs Brown answered immediately.

"My mind is clearing a bit - too many hormones, I think," Gem said breathlessly. "Why did Paul Andriani disappear?" she queried.

"Slipped cog perhaps. I believe he was made."

"I don't believe that any more than I believe dad sent an undecipherable code. No! There has to be a mole. Or a sleeper. Has to be!"

"There is no evidence of either, my dear," Mrs Brown said firmly. "A slipped cog is the most likely cause. It was bound to happen, sooner or later. He had extremely dangerous assignments in an extremely dangerous world. One misstep in the criminal underground is one's last step. The wrong look or slip of the tongue in that element, the wrong read of a person, a single moment of hesitation. He was too good for too many years. The level of concentration is excruciating. It was bound to happen, my dear. It often has with undercover agents, and Paul was well aware of that fact. An agent is made and that is it."

"Didn't he have a code word - something to give you that would undeniably indicate he had gone underground - disappeared?" Gem countered.

"No. There was only the phone call every Friday."

"Perhaps he's sleeping, and John Staunton will resurface," Gem suggested, scanning her surroundings.

"Possibly. At any rate, I wanted you to be aware of the situation in the event - the very unlikely event - he contacted you, so that you wouldn't inadvertently give him away. He is very likely in dire straits."

"Harry doesn't know," Gem mused aloud.

"I shouldn't think so. It's a damn cat and mouse game, and we are already spread too thin. Now no Harry, and no Paul."

"And I certainly can't be re-activated," Gem sighed.

"Indeed not. Pregnant and paralysed by fear of water and flying."

"I can't help," Gem said sadly.

"Oh, my dear, you can. Use that marvellous brain of yours. I need your perspective. You have to see what the rest of us can't see - or feel - that which is eluding the rest of us."

"I'm trying," Gem replied, frustrated. "Wait - why would you think Paul Andriani might contact me?"

"The suggestion is only a shot in the dark, my dear. Paul always seemed to be so comfortable with you and Gemmy at the office conferences."

"More Gemmy than me," Gem conceded.

"Perhaps in your mind, but not in mine."

Barcelona.

"But yours would be the more accurate perception because it is yours. And perhaps at those conferences I mistook one of you for the other," Mrs Brown acknowledged ruefully.

"To be honest, if Gemmy and I really tried we could confuse - if only temporarily - mum and dad," Gem admitted.

"And perhaps Paul," Mrs Brown suggested.

"I hadn't thought of that," Gem agreed. But that was neither here nor there.

Gem rang off then, and walked slowly back to the Hall. Wyatt would be back soon. And she was beginning to be very angry with him. He had never asked if she was using birth control!

Blast! She was pregnant! She still couldn't wrap her mind around that fact. She was going to have a baby. Next May. Thank heavens not 30 May! She couldn't tolerate her marriage, she couldn't find the Pilos, and she was going to add a baby - possibly two - to what now seemed a completely fictional life. She had a family that did not exist. She was in a marriage that was not truly a marriage. Why not add a baby or two?! And what else? She shook her head as she walked up the drive. Rose had a fantasy life travelling in time and space with the Dr. I'd trade her a nightmare fantasy life in a second, Gem sighed. The thought irritated her no end, she silently fumed as she entered the house.

"Wine, my dear?" Mrs M queried.

Gem shook her head. "Hot chocolate," she smiled faintly. Now she really wanted a half-pint, no a pint, no a keg! She took the cup of hot chocolate to her office.

A sham marriage, finding the Pilos, finding Gemmy, a baby - let's leave it at that for the time being. I'm going to go off the rails, Gem sighed as she started her computer. I'm going to go stark raving mad before this mess is all settled!

Chichester Cathedral. She pulled up the file.

Her thesis. Should she give Wyatt a copy? That would only confirm to Wyatt that 'she had lied' about the reason 'she' had returned to Australia - to finish her thesis.

Gem shook herself. That was Gemmy - not her! Yet, giving Wyatt a copy of her thesis would be proof in his eyes that 'she' had lied to James when she had left Barcelona. Let him find a copy if he truly wanted to read it. If she gave him a copy would that make her less of a liar?

Damn! Why did he always make everything so difficult!

Mrs M stuck her head in the office to announce the Mister had rung to say he was taking her out to dinner.

"Go, go," Gem smiled. "I'll handle dinner here," she assured the cook. "Have a lovely weekend!"

"We'll see you Sunday at the Crow," Mrs M reminded her. "Sunday buffet."

"Perfect!" Gem smiled. Less time for her to spend alone with Wyatt!

She was deep in thought as she set the table. This should be one of the happiest days of her life. A celebration.

How was she going to manage? She couldn't begin to imagine what kind of a father Wyatt would be. A child would likely have his own Mr Choate. The thought made her groan.

"Tired?" he said from the doorway.

She hadn't heard the Jag! Blast! She had to focus!

"A bit," she forced a casual tone to her voice. "You?"

"Not overly. Mrs M off already?" Wyatt queried, his manner relaxed.

"The Mister is taking her out to dinner," Gem replied. "Dinner will be ready shortly."

"Have I time for a shower?"

"Absolutely," Gem nodded. She paced finishing the dinner prep so the chicken would still be piping hot when it was served. Potatoes, broad beans, Mrs M's freshly baked rolls, salad for Gem. A perfect celebration dinner. She made a pot of tea for herself; there was beer in the fridge for Wyatt.

He helped her serve the plates, querying, "Wine, beer, sweetheart?"

"I'll have tea - it's warming," she replied.

"Shall I adjust the heat? Are you cold?"

"I'm fine. Tea just seems perfect tonight." Gem assured him.

Wyatt casually studied her as they ate. She was in a mood.

"Did you have a pleasant visit with Mrs Brown today?"

"Yes. Mrs Brown remembered at breakfast that she was supposed to be someplace else, so we met for a long lunch." That was true - in a fashion.

"Did you do any shopping?"

"Mr Choate has already given you a report of my day," Gem said politely.

"I didn't ask that." He did not refute her remark.

"Breakfast, the IWM, lunch," Gem pointedly reviewed. "I went to a dress boutique and took a long walk. And you?"

"Business meetings," he summed up in two words. "The Imperial War Museum again?"

"It's fascinating," she replied.

"The staff must know you by name, you're there so frequently," Wyatt remarked. "Did you purchase anything at the dress boutique?"

"Wasn't that included in the report? I did not." I didn't purchase anything today - except pre-natal vitamins, but I'm not ready to tell you that. "Oh - I did purchase dvd sets at the IWM. If that interests you."

"You're touchy tonight," Wyatt raised an eyebrow. "Calm down."

"I am so tired of you constantly telling me what to do," Gem retorted in frustration.

"What does that matter - you rarely listen," Wyatt frowned.

"But it's the idea that you expect me to! You are unreasonable and demanding!"

"You are obstinate and irritating," Wyatt countered. When precisely had he lost control of their relationship? - he wondered silently. For he surely had.

"No arguments at dinner," Gem said quietly.

"Quite," Wyatt nodded. "Thank you for remembering."

Gem tried to focus on appropriate dinner conversation, a difficult effort since her thoughts were diverted in so MANY ways.

"Did you purchase a winery today?" she asked politely.

"I did," Wyatt replied with a grin. "Ms Holton will finalize the purchase. We'll take a drive down one day, but after GEI has it well in hand. Perhaps early in the new year."

"But don't you want to see it before you purchase the business?"

"I drove down today. I would have invited you along, but Mrs Brown seemed so eager to share your company."

"Oh," Gem nodded. She did NOT want to pick up the thread of THAT conversation. "What did you think of the winery?"

"It's definitely a growing concern. The owners wish to retire. As you know the product is excellent. Management is reliable. I doubt GEI will change much other than sprucing the place up a bit."

"You won't go in with a new broom?" Gem queried.

"Don't mess with what works," Wyatt said firmly. "Basically we need to work on salaries, and as I said appearance of the property. I will suggest wine tasting events to draw more notice and appreciation of the product. Ms Holton believes a spring fund-raising event is needed for the local animal rescue centre. Apparently that will be one of the first projects for Ms Jones and Ms Carton."

"Ms Holton is quite into fund-raising then, isn't she? The school art fair, the jumble and craft sale," Gem recalled.

"Keeping in touch with the community," Wyatt nodded.

Sunday buffets at the Crow once a month, Gem mused. Not only Ms Holton. Yes, indeed, a fascinating man; for he was the person who ultimately had to approve Ms Holton's suggestions. The Mr Hyde part of Wyatt Grantham.

Since Gem put the food on the table, Wyatt took the washing up chores, and she settled in her office to do a bit of work on Chichester, selecting Queen for the cd player.

Chichester would have progressed more smoothly had Gem been able to concentrate on the cathedral - instead of her conversation that day with Mrs Brown regarding Paul Andriani. He constantly battered at her brain, demanding attention.

"Excellent choice of music," Wyatt stated as he walked into her office, a gift tote in his hand.

"What's that?" Gem said warily. Beware of Ogres bearing what looked like gifts.

Wyatt handed over the bag. "Frillies, I believe you call them."

Gem blushed furiously. "Did you send Ms Holton out shopping for you?"

"Yes I did. She purchased a winery," Wyatt retorted. "However, I am capable of shopping for my own wife's delicates!"

Gem counted to twenty. He had purchased frillies for her!It was a feat, she had to admit, and one her own father would never have dreamed of attempting for Gem's mum.

"Thank you," she managed, startled by his remarks.

"You are welcome. You have gained a bit of weight and I thought you might be more comfortable in this size," Wyatt suggested.

"Gained weight!" Gem gasped.

"Just a bit," Wyatt soothed. "It's a more proper look for you. You were way too thin when we met."

"You knew I had gained weight?" Gem said uneasily.

"I know every bit of your body, my sweet, and the pleasure has been all mine," Wyatt grinned.

If he was so astute she couldn't keep her secret for long. "Thank you," Gem said with a smile. "It was very thoughtful of you." And a timely warning of information.

"You are most welcome, sweetheart," Wyatt replied. "Now I'll leave you to your work, shall I?"

Gem was exhausted. Now she was not sleeping for two. Dr Hallowell had assured her that even resting quietly each day would be beneficial. He didn't want to give her pills to help her sleep, and she wouldn't have taken any.

She pushed the start button on the cd player, made hot chocolate, and paced the office.

Paul Andriani. He got MADE! It was simply so difficult to believe. He was the master of undercover agents. He had been undercover longer than any other such agent in Agency history. And there was a starting point for queries. She knew very little about the history of the Agency. She wanted a long chat with Mr Choate. Information culling, of course, because the history of the Agency has nothing to do with Gemmy and the Pilos, Paul Andriani, or Project CSU.

Gem knew two things for certain: the disappearance of the Pilos was not pilot error - she simply wouldn't believe Mr Portermann had made an error; and Paul Andriani did not get made because of a slipped cog. Someone caused the Pilos to disappear, and someone gave up Paul Andriani - made sure it was his contacts who were murdered. But why? Again red herrings? Or to take the master agent out of his work for the Agency - because he might find a mole or a sleeper?

A sleeper. Gem had to get more rest. Perhaps she should go back to bed at four o'clock every morning. She could sort her thoughts in bed. Lord only knew how Wyatt would hound her about sleep when he learned that she was pregnant.

Where would Paul Andriani go to disappear? India. Get lost in the masses. New York City. Rio. Rome. Barcelona?

Barcelona. Had he been in Barcelona to set up a 'sanctuary' in the event he needed to disappear? That certainly wouldn't have been a reason to - she couldn't believe that idea. Paul Andriani wouldn't have harmed Gemmy, their parents, Mr Portermann, to save himself, if he had thought Gemmy had known about a possible sanctuary. On the contrary, he would have known such a secret was safe with Agency Family. And he would have given his life to save everyone on the Pilos! - Unless he had turned. Gone rogue. Bought off by the other side of the Black Market - any of them.

No! She would never believe that!

She made another cup of hot chocolate, pushed the start button on the cd player, and reached for her mobile.

'What news have you Mr Cawley?'

He was slow to answer. Gem kept pacing.

She would have to walk a great deal from now on. It would be a waste of time for Mr Choate to have to follow her around London simply because she needed exercise. She had become lazy since the Defender was delivered to the Hall. Her route would be the cobblestone lanes of Ticking Bottom, and she would no doubt come to know the village as well as Watt claimed to know her body.

Ping

'No news you don't already know.'

'Okay.'

'Long night.'

'Indeed. Do you ever get weary of long nights?'

'No. However they are my choice. But not yours, Gem.'

'True.'

'What do you know, Gem?'

'Not a thing.'

'Keep sorting.'

'I shall. Goodnight.'

'Goodnight.'

Gained weight. What else was Wyatt aware of that she didn't know? she pondered as she climbed the stairs. It was certainly more comfortable to think, lying in a warm bed, and in a strong embrace.

Where was Paul Andriani?

"I'm going for a walk," Gem informed Wyatt as they finished doing the washing up after breakfast. "I need fresh air."

"Do you want company or would you prefer to be alone?" he queried.

"Haven't you reports to read?" Gem was surprised by the question.

"Always."

"Sure," Gem replied. She couldn't figure out this Game of his. Or was it merely a walk? If he annoyed her, she would simply turn and walk away from him. "Wellies and macs - it's starting to mist."

They didn't talk much for the first half hour. Wyatt pointed out two magpies arguing, and Gem quickly caught the birds on film. She laughed, watching the two birds, beak to beak, shrilly vocalizing.

"Mr M and Mr Becton?" Gem queried, teasing.

"Perfect description," Wyatt laughed, "but don't you dare quote me!"

After an hour of walking along the cobblestone lanes winding through Ticking Bottom, Wyatt frowned, turning to look at Gem. "Aren't you tired?"

"I am always tired," Gem shrugged.

"Why the long walk? Is it because I said you had gained weight? It was not my intention to offend you," he assured her.

"I need exercise. I walked every day when I lived in London." *And I am going to continue to gain weight. How long before you notice that?* she sighed inwardly.

"You are beautiful, you know," Wyatt again assured her.

Tell me that in four or five months. Especially if there are twins! I'll be larger than the Hall! "Thank you," Gem said quietly, not a bit reassured.

"Shall we stop at the Crow for a half-pint?" Wyatt suggested.

Gem nodded, but ordered hot chocolate, and to her surprise Wyatt had a cup of tea.

"Would you like to take a drive?" Wyatt asked.

"Where?"

"Just a drive in the country."

"Yes," Gem nodded. "Are you tired of reading?"

"Indeed!" he said so vehemently that Gem had to laugh.

They used one of the estate Land Rovers, and as Wyatt had suggested, just took a drive; lunch was at Thrapston, dinner at Mildenhall. They chatted infrequently about the landscape they passed, the villages they drove through, stopping frequently when Gem wished to take photos.

Gem appreciated the drive as it diverted thoughts from her mind of the baby(ies) - she mentally added the ies - she was carrying, of Gemmy and her baby, and all the other troubling issues of her life.

But once back at the Hall, when Wyatt retired to his office to read, the thoughts flooded Gem's brain.

How far along had Gemmy been when the Pilos was lost? Perhaps two months? If so, it would be March to November - perhaps she would have been due very soon. This was compounding in an extraordinarily sad way. Gem would have to tell Wyatt she was pregnant while he still believed she had lied to James about the same condition. She realized she was going to face a new intensity of his anger and sarcasm.

Instead of heating water in the hot pot she made a pitcher of hot chocolate to last for an hour. She paced the floor in her office, her anxiety building.

Day after day, week after week, month after month, everything I do turns to acid, Gem moaned. *Lot's wife had the proper idea: turn into a pillar of salt.*

How do I get out of this situation? Did I take my vitamin this morning? She took the pill vial out of the combination locked cabinet and quickly counted the pills. She hadn't. She took the vitamin, returned the vial to the cabinet and cleared the lock key pad to zero. Unless someone knew the exact date she started with the Agency, then her secret was safe.

Gem turned on the telly and decided she would just as easily change lives with Amelia Pond as with Rose. Living with the Dr had to be easier than living with Dr. Jekyll.

As she decided whether or not to make another pot of hot chocolate, she sensed Wyatt standing in the room. Her radar was certainly improving. She washed out the pot. His thoughts, she knew, were not on beverages.

She was so tired. Had she ever been so exhausted in her life? Not even the week Gemmy had died - when Gem had had the extra assignments and flights.

"What are you thinking?" Wyatt had asked earlier.

"What?" Gem had replied faintly.

"Precisely. It would seem you are not in the mood, as you once previously stated," he had observed.

"I'm tired," Gem had sighed.

"Go to sleep then, sweetheart," he had replied gently, tucking the duvet and his arms around her.

Sleep! She was desperate for it!

Mr Cawley was awake! She texted him as soon as she had a cup of tea. She would have hot chocolate later.

'News?'

'No.'

'Blank?'

'Somewhere in the world. Your guess as good as mine - or Mrs B's.'

'Harry?'

'No.'

'You?'

'Flummoxed. You?'

'Same.'

'Then we are all flummoxed, Gem. Start sorting. You've got the brain.'

'I'm stymied.'

'My wife says baking a cake helps her think. Has to be from scratch.'

'I'll think about that.'

She hadn't baked a scratch cake in years, Gem chuckled. She glanced at her watch. Quarter past two; well, she certainly had the time.

Mrs M's kitchen was so well organised, Gem had the ingredients ready very shortly. Sifting the flour, combining the ingredients was a basic exercise in thought. The aroma of the cake baking was a definite feeling of accomplishment. As she did the washing up, she thought of James, and Fiona and Jack Grantham. Where were they buried? The logical reply was the cemetery by the Ticking Bottom Church. She hadn't properly looked at headstones when she had visited the church weeks past. She had been more interested in the structure of the church and the art glass windows.

She was struck by her insensitivity. She should have visited James's grave soon after she arrived at the Hall - for Gemmy, for their baby. She would go in the morning when Wyatt was reading in his library.

As the cake cooled she prepared the icing - and wondered of Paul Andriani. Where was he on 30 May? Mexico? South America? Africa? South East Asia? She had to ask Mrs Brown. But the Acting Director of the Agency would likely refuse to answer that question.

She reached for her mobile.

'Where was Blank on 30 May?'

She already knew what Mr Cawley's reply would be.

'You must put that query to Mrs B. Did you bake a cake?'

'Yes. White on lemon.'

'Love lemon cake. From scratch?'

'Yes.'

'Good. Sleep well.'

'And you.'

Gem iced the cake, had a cup of tea as she did the last washing up, then trudged up to bed shortly before five o'clock.

It was brunch at the Crow Sunday. Gem had to put off her visit to the cemetery until that afternoon. She looked for Mr Choate, but he did not make an appearance that morning. No doubt he was at his office at T.O.

As was their usual habit, Gem and Wyatt shared a table with the M's. Eve, from the gift shop, stopped at the table as she had on Brunch Sunday in October, and again she had baby Erin with her.

"Such a lovely name, Erin," Gem smiled at the baby. Shivers prickled the nape of her neck. Eve was so relaxed with her baby, and Gem was too stupid to be a mum.

"Her brother, when he arrives, will be Ellis," Eve said confidently. "Then there will be Ella and Eaton. Two boys and two girls."

"That's quite some planning," Gem marvelled.

"I've been deciding on the names since I was a little girl. Haven't you?" Eve gave Gem a look suggesting she was daft if she hadn't already planned and named at least four children at her age.

This was territory Gem didn't want to approach.

"Always the boy names first. Men always think the first one will be a boy, don't they Wyatt?" Eve chatted along.

Gem was wondering if the young woman had an off-switch she could press.

"It's a possibility," Wyatt said graciously.

Gem glanced at his eyes; light grey; apparently Eve didn't perturb Wyatt, but she herself had had enough talk of babies and names.

"What name would you like for a baby, my dear?" Mrs M asked casually.

Gem gave a slight frown, not wishing to be put on the spot. What was Mrs M thinking asking such a question? "I have no idea," she put up her hands in protest.

"What about you, Wyatt?" Eve pushed the query.

"James for a boy, Jamie for a girl," Wyatt replied easily. He patted Gem's hand. "What say you, my dear?"

Only Gem knew how pointed was his query to her.

"Very nice," she gritted her teeth as she forced an approving smile to him. Absolutely not! And this was simply conversation! When it got down to facts, she would be dealing with Dr Jekyll, not Mr Hyde, and not Wyatt.

"Or perhaps Gemmy, after you, my dear," Wyatt suggested, his voice as smooth as butter, his eyes darkening a bit.

A lovely lunch buffet turned into another nightmare. If he suggested Gemma, she would walk out of the pub.

"Hot chocolate, sweetheart?" Wyatt queried attentively.

Gem shook her head. She was ready to escape the pub, but Wyatt was obviously settled in for a time yet. Eve finally took her 'special' cheer and moved on to another group at the far end of the room. The M's stayed on when Gem and Wyatt finally left, fortunately for Gem, because she was in no mood for additional cheery conversation. Wyatt however, ignored her silence.

"You're in a sour mood," he observed dryly.

"You were taunting me," she said bitterly.

"You're being overly sensitive. Probably lack of sleep."

"Don't start."

"I won't, if you will at least try to rest this afternoon," he parried.

Gem refused to answer at first, then had to admit to herself that Wyatt's suggestion was the same Dr Hallowell had made.

"I will," she agreed. *After a walk without you.*

To appease Wyatt, Gem curled up on Auntie Jane's settee, the book of birds in her hands; he went to the library to read one of his many reports. She waited a half hour, to make certain he was settled, then she grabbed her windcheater from the mudroom and slipped quietly out the kitchen door. His reports usually occupied him for hours on end on weekends, so she should be able to steal away for a half hour.

It was only a brisk ten minute walk to the church, but finding the Grantham family section took a bit of doing. Many of the headstones were so old it was nearly impossible to read the inscriptions. And there were so many headstones to read - stretching across an area of a city block.

Think logically, Gem urged herself, as she wandered through the grove of trees, taking quick glimpses of the headstones. Grantham Hall was at least a century old. The church itself was older still. Search along the older looking stones closest to the church and then work out from there. The idea worked, but it still took Gem another quarter of an hour to find the Grantham family plot. It was sadly easy to find James; his was the newest headstone amongst the Grantham family relatives:

> James Grantham Smythe
> Beloved Son of Fiona and Jack Grantham
> Beloved Brother of Wyatt Grantham

James had changed his name to find his own identity, and Wyatt had seen to it that the name would remain his own for eternity.

Gem kneeled and gently touched the chiselled words. "If only I had known," she said quietly, "I would have told you everything."

"And what would everything be?" Wyatt said quietly behind her.

Gem jumped to her feet, whirling around to face him. She certainly hadn't sensed his presence this time!

"How often do you come here?" he demanded.

Gem stared at him, refusing to answer, but directly meeting his cold, dark gaze.

"You want rid of me, Gem?" Wyatt queried bluntly.

"How?" she demanded without hesitation.

His eyes narrowed to cold steel glints as he studied her. She was so beautiful. The haunted look clouding the lovely violet eyes was as deep as he had ever seen it. She looked so slight, almost frail, her long blonde hair blowing back from her face in the brisk November wind.

The next part of the Game.

"Tell me everything about Gemimah Louisa Forrester Grantham, from the moment you were born, until this very minute," he said coldly.

Gem helplessly shook her head. "I can't," she said plaintively.

"You can, but you won't," Wyatt denied her reply.

Gem dragged her fingers through her hair. "Have it your way. You always do," she said defencelessly.

"And I always shall." Wyatt gave her a curt nod.

He hadn't honestly expected her to tell him what he wanted to know. But also, he wouldn't have released her from their agreement - even if she had told him everything she had just said she would have told James.

"You need to rest," he held out his hand to her.

Gem shook her head, sighing, as she walked towards him.

One day she would tell Wyatt everything. When she found Gemmy and the Pilos. And he would be just as angry that day as he was at this moment.

They did not exchange a single word as they walked back to the Hall.

Gem again settled on Auntie Jane's settee, attempting to study the birds in the bird book, but while they flew on the page they did not land and remain in her brain.

Beloved brother of Wyatt Grantham. She had thought of that before; that Wyatt had loved James as much as she had loved Gemmy. James had survived the plane crash that had killed their parents. Gem lost Gemmy, the baby, and their parents in the Pilos. Gem knew everything that Wyatt did not to know. Including the very basic fact that she was pregnant.

She was every bit the liar Wyatt accused her of being. She felt tormented by him - yet she held all the information that would torment him as much as had James's death.

Blast!

And still she wasn't going to tell him the truth. Not yet. No civilians. She held him at fault for everything - their relationship, her frustration at his control over her; the baby(ies). She should have been in control since the day they met! But she hadn't been because she had been so distressed by losing Gemmy. And mum, and dad, and Mr Portermann. But her deepest grief was for Gemmy. As Wyatt's deepest grief was for James.

As if he had been summoned by her thoughts, Wyatt entered the office.

"Steak and potatoes for dinner?" Wyatt casually asked.

"Steak, please, pass on the potatoes. I'll make a salad," Gem replied with a soft smile.

"I'll pass on the salad."

"Right," Gem nodded.

It was probably hormones doing her thinking for her, but for the first time since Wight, she was seeing Wyatt in a different light. However, she wasn't quite sure what that light was at this moment. Mr Hyde - gentle, thoughtful, bearable company. Dr Jekyll - cold, calculating, sarcastic - her greatest enemy.

No!

Her greatest enemy was the person who brought down the Pilos!

Dr Jekyll was the person she purposely kept in the dark. Her adversary of her own creation.

Gem returned the bird book to the shelf under the counter, and went to the kitchen to assist with their dinner prep. Wyatt was watching the news on the telly.

"Breakfast room or here?" she asked politely.

Wyatt gave her a cursory glance. "Your choice," he shrugged, wondering of her quiet demeanour. How often had she visited James's grave? And why had she done so? Did she actually have feelings for his brother? Had she ever had feelings for James? Or was it guilt? Or regret for her foolish decisions that had put her under his control?

Gem decided on the kitchen for dinner. She watched the news as she shredded lettuce, and cut vegetables, preparing a bit more than usual in the event that Wyatt would like to share; if not, she would have the left-overs during the dark hours. Food value and not weight - if she watched the dressing. She stiffened as a name and photo appeared on the telly screen. Emerald. The vivid red-haired actress. Husband seeking divorce after only a year of marriage - infidelity - hers.

Wyatt glanced at Gem. "She's quite attractive isn't she?" he said smoothly, turning the steaks over on the cooker.

"Quite," Gem nodded.

"Very tall. And very," he paused pointedly, "talented."

"Is she," Gem said, a statement not a query. She could imagine the purpose of the pause, and his definition of the word 'talented'.

"Did you want to ask me about her?" Wyatt queried, still the oh-so-smooth tone to his voice.

"Why should I?" Gem replied evenly.

"Because you saw the photos of her in the album in James's room."

"You have your past, I have mine," Gem replied coolly.

"Indeed," Wyatt chuckled sardonically. "No doubt yours was as interesting as mine - but in different ways."

"Truly," Gem nodded in agreement.

"What would you tell James?" Wyatt queried softly.

"What I won't tell you."

"About John Staunton?"

Gem shook her head and remained silent.

Gemmy and Paul Andriani. What was there between the two of them? Although Mrs Brown sometimes might have confused Gem and Gem, Paul never would have. Would he? Gem had seen the private chats between Gemmy and Paul. What was that about? Had Mrs Brown known all the times the sisters had covered for each other? Perhaps. But it was only from necessity they had done so.

The Gem's had covered for each other in courses - taking notes, which was only in extreme crisis in scheduling - not an easy thing to do when their universities were half way around the world in location. They never, even once, covered an examination for the other, which would have easily been possible since they were reading such similar courses. But it was never done! Covering an assignment because of flu was one matter; covering an exam was a lie.

Had there been something between Gemmy and Paul Andriani? Not from Gemmy's side, Gem was certain of that. Gemmy had accepted James's engagement ring. There was no disputing that fact. Gemmy had loved James. But what of Paul Andriani? Had he loved Gemmy?

"About Staunton?" Wyatt repeated firmly.

"No," Gem replied, drawn from her reverie. Gemmy had loved James. But was Paul in her sister's past? Perhaps Gemmy had had more secrets than Gem had known. But try as she might, Gem could not believe there had been anything between Gemmy and Paul - at least not from Gemmy's side.

"Tell me one thing about James that isn't a lie from your lips," Wyatt asked quietly.

"He was," Gem began, then paused, reliving that now horrendously sad few minutes she had spent with Gemmy in their bedroom in Brisbane, 29 May. "He was a wonderful man," she replied, reaching out to Gemmy's heart. "And I wish everyone would have known that." Everyone meaning their mum and dad. Hopefully Gemmy had had a few minutes on the Pilos to share her short lived joy with their parents. He had to have been wonderful. Gemmy had loved him.

"Did you ever love James?" Wyatt asked bluntly.

"One thing, you asked," Gem replied, "and I answered that."

"Why won't you tell me more?"

"Because I simply can't," Gem said easily. "It's not that I won't tell you. I can't tell you," she turned to look him straight in his eyes. "I can't."

Not won't. But can't, Wyatt reflected deeply on her words.

"If you could tell me, you would?" he asked, puzzled.

"Yes," Gem said without hesitation, "I would." To set you free. To set me free. Yes, I would.

"Did Staunton threaten you? Is that why you left James?"

"No," Gem replied without thinking. Blast. No more answers to Wyatt!

He didn't press the subject further. He didn't know her world, but he did know she was beginning to crack. And that satisfied him for the time being. He would accept her words - temporarily.

Was there any point in texting Mr Cawley? Yes, for sanity's sake.
'What news have you?'
'Rain tomorrow. You?'

'Rain tomorrow, I hear.'
'Amusing, Gem.'
'Blank?'
'Still blank. Won't surface until he is ready to do so.'
'If ever.'
'Quite.'
'Jet lag?'
'Horrid!'
'See Dr Hallowell.'
'You should say!'
'Tropical diseases. They exist. Seriously. Perhaps something you didn't see, saw you, and bit you.'
'Interesting suggestion. Hadn't thought.'
'Do.'
'Will consider. Sorting?'
'Of a sort.'
'Amusing.'
'How's the family?'
'Which one?'
'Both.'
'Both copasetic.'
'SEA okay?'
'For now. Keep sorting.'
'Too tired.'
'Same.'
'Goodnight.'
'Goodnight.'

Too tired. Hormones? Baby - whoever you are, are you exhausting me? Gem groaned.

She would spend the time baking a cake, but cake remained. Wyatt had complimented her effort of the previous night, requesting next time white on chocolate cake. She would consider that.

He hadn't referred again to James while they ate dinner. And after the washing up he had returned to his library while Gem had tried again to study birds without much success.

It had been such a very long day.

Hot chocolate. Pacing. Gemmy. Paul Andriani. What was there? Anything? She was too tired to think of that question. She pressed the start button on the cd player for the fifth time that morning. I'll Be Seeing You... Ever? Gem groaned.

Chapter Twenty-Three

Gem stirred at the sound of a mobile ringing. Not hers, she decided. The ringing ceased and she felt Wyatt's arms leave her.

"What time is it?" she asked groggily.

"Six. Go back to sleep, sweetheart," Wyatt whispered in her ear.

She felt him slip from the bed.

"Where are you going?"

"To play golf. Go to sleep."

"You don't golf."

"I'll learn."

Gem turned over to see him threading his tie beneath his collar. How could he dress so quickly? Why did he dress so quickly?

"Are you a doctor then? Making a house call at this hour?" she attempted a feeble tease.

"Yes. Sorbonne. I wasn't just a tourist you know. Go to sleep."

Gem sighed. She didn't know he actually had degrees. He had never mentioned. Wealthy son. Accomplished businessman. Of course. He had made his own way. "Two doctors in the house. No waiting," she murmured, drawing a chuckle from him. "At least one of us should advise a proper breakfast. I'll make it for you," she pulled back the sheet. He pulled it from her fingers, tucking it around her.

"Neither of us is medical. And I don't have time, but thank you for the offer, darling," he leaned down to give her a gentle kiss. "Damn it, Gem, go back to sleep, or I swear I'll have Choate come sing you lullaby's until you do!"

Gem heard his firm words, but his voice was soft. "He has a lovely voice. He used to sing in a rock band - sounds similar to Art Garfunkel," she murmured.

"How the blazes do you know that?" Wyatt jerked back to stare at her.

"I made it up," she admitted, then became uneasy. "Winged monkeys?" His empire?

"Don't worry about the monkeys," Wyatt chuckled "I can handle them. Go to sleep!"

"Yes."

She heard him close the door. It was odd being in bed without him - except for the week when he was furious with her. - Because of her suggestion that he should take a mistress. She closed her eyes, but she couldn't sleep. Early meeting at the office? He hadn't mentioned it last night. No - the phone call. Her mind was still foggy.

Emerald. Divorce. She had cheated on her husband. Had she cheated on Wyatt also? More the fool she! Gem hadn't had any experience before Wyatt but she knew enough to know that...she knew...Perhaps that's why Emerald had cheated on her husband. Because he wasn't Wyatt? If memories of Wyatt had been the reason for Emerald's infidelity, then Gem could understand that – he would be some competition for any man. Unless...Wyatt was the reason! Infidelity.

Where was he going? To a deposition? Because of a divorce? Or was he just going to Emerald? Because he had heard last night on the news she was going to be free again?

No. No. No.

Wyatt and Emerald? Was he the reason a husband was divorcing a wife?

Oh!

Gem grabbed her mobile, her fingers quickly flying over the keys. A way out for her? Divorce?

'Are you having an affair with Emerald?'

Wyatt stopped the Jag to check the message.

'What?'

'Are you?'

'I don't have time for nonsense. If you won't sleep then bake a cake. White on chocolate. Back late. Paris.'

Oh. Gem felt a moment of relief. But it was pushed aside for a moment of dismay. No divorce - at least not for her. Poor Emerald. But she likely had a pre-nup. Her poor husband. He had been slammed!

Gem dragged herself from bed. She would be up soon at any rate.

She had finished her shower and dressed when the Agency texted.

'Viral infection. Thanks for suggestion. Hope text doesn't cause problem for you at this hour. Might sleep now.'

'Not a problem. Family.'

'Damn right!'

'Pleasant dreams!'

'Thanks! Bye.'

'Bye.'

A lovely day brightener! Bless Mr Cawley! Family!

Mrs M was already in the kitchen taking breakfast items from the fridge.

"Good morning, dear," the cook smiled at her. "Eggs, bacon?"

"Good morning, Mrs M. Semolina, I believe," Gem replied, her attention caught by the telly.

Emerald was on the morning news. Gem certainly wouldn't want her photo and name splashed on the telly every half-hour. Emerald's husband's face and name shared the screen.

Photos, passports. Would Wyatt want his photo and name on a split screen along with her name? The only answer could be a resounding NO! Well, not Mr Hyde; she was never sure about Dr Jekyll.

"Marriage, divorce, move on to the next," Mrs M shook her head in disgust. "Why do some people bother getting married in the first place?"

"I should imagine most people hope that their marriage will last," Gem replied faintly. Not her marriage, of course. She didn't want it to last. "I suppose some marriages simply don't work."

"That Emerald," Mrs M said disdainfully. "She was here once with Mr W - for dinner," she couched her words.

Dinner and - Gem could well imagine.

"She sure acted like she was some sort of princess. I can't imagine what Mr W saw in her," Mrs M sniffed.

"She's gorgeous," Gem laughed. "That's certainly enough."

"Pretty is as pretty does, as the saying goes," Mrs M raised her eyebrows. "As I said she was only here once."

Mrs M seemed to be reassuring her. There was the London flat, Gem mused. It was more easily accessible than the long drive to Ticking Bottom - and it likely didn't come with a sharp-eyed housekeeper.

Gem was happy when the news reader moved on to the next story. Chat of Emerald and semolina did not mix well.

"Are you going to the city today, dear?"

"I hadn't intended going. Do you need an errand run?" Gem offered.

"No. I thought you might be having lunch with Mr W."

"He's in Paris," Gem replied. She hadn't had lunch with him in London since the last time she had gone to his office. Perhaps he had found another luncheon companion as of late. - Emerald? "What are you plans for the day?"

"Bit of dusting, deciding menus for the week, a walk to the greengrocer and chemist. Or would you prefer to do the menus?" the house manager queried.

"No thank you. It's your expertise, not mine," Gem refused the task. "What say I do the dusting, we'll have lunch at the Crow, then do the errands?" Gem suggested.

"Done!" Mrs M smacked the counter top with her hand. "I do detest dusting."

"I'll start the dusting, you start the menus," Gem laughed.

Mrs M thought again that the young woman should be ringing her friend, Mrs Brown, for lunch, but perhaps that would be another day. Today would be their day to do the shops.

Wyatt texted while Gem was dusting the great room.

'How late did you sleep?'

'Noon.'

'Sass! Actual time?'

'Six.'

'Then rest later! Going to London?'

'No. Village.'

'Alright. Later.'

'Monkeys?'

'Jogger.'

'What?'

'Later, sweetheart.'

Gem and Mrs M were on their walk to the village by half eleven, lunch first, then the shops. As they entered the Crow Wyatt texted again.

'Working on your book?'

'Lunch at Crow w/Mrs M.'
'You paying?'
'You are. LOL. Lunch with jogger?'
'Perhaps. Later sweetheart.'

Mrs M's burger and chips looked delicious, but Gem exercised control and limited herself to salad. Just by looking at the housekeeper's burger, Gem could feel herself gaining weight. And she would have tea more often than hot chocolate!

"Have you thought, dear, of what changes you would like to make at the Hall?" Mrs M queried as they ate.

"I can't think of any," Gem replied. Such decisions were not up to her.

"You'll want to add your own touches, to make the Hall your home," the house manager insisted.

Gem shook her head. "It should suit Wyatt. The Hall is his refuge from work and the city."

"Very well, dear," Mrs M let the subject drop. She would mention the matter to Mr W.

At the Mercantile Gem judiciously avoided the baby clothes, actually avoiding anything to do with babies. She bought a set of deep blue towels for the all-white bathroom off the office. She was probably going to be spending more time in there in the next few months.

"I'll put it on your account, Mrs Grantham," the shop assistant said helpfully.

"Cash," Gem insisted. Wyatt paid for lunch, but this was her purchase.

"Yes, ma'am," the employee said politely.

The greengrocer would deliver the order and after Mrs M's errand at the chemist, the women strolled back to the Hall. Exhausted as she was, Gem had energy from nerves to work off, so she put the towels in the bathroom, and informed Mrs M that she was going for a long walk.

She walked to the cemetery to visit James's grave, assured she would not be interrupted by Wyatt this time. She would like to know how he had discovered her the previous day, but it didn't really matter. She had to survive each day, one at a time, and yesterday was a thought that was too aggravating to ponder.

What emergency, if that was the correct word, had taken Wyatt so abruptly to Paris that morning? He had been in a hurry, but his manner towardss her had been light and patient. His reply to her text regarding Emerald had also been patient. He could have replied that her query was none of her business. It was odd thinking of Wyatt being involved in a relationship with the stunning actress. His past. He had not been a saint. And she certainly was not jealous!

She wandered the lanes of Ticking Bottom, wondering when she would have to tell Wyatt about the baby(ies). Finally, unable to come to a definite decision, she pushed frustrating thoughts from her brain to allow her mind to wander as her feet were doing.

Paul Andriani. And where was he then? Mr Cawley had a virus. She wouldn't text him during the dark hours of Tuesday morning, for it was likely he would still be resting.

Resting. She was supposed to rest. Sighing heavily, she returned to the Hall to follow Dr Hallowell's suggestion. It would be the bird book again.

Gem insisted she would prepare her own dinner, so Mrs M left early to do the same at the carriage house for herself and the Mister. Gem made a salad and ate in her office as she watched the early evening news. There was more chat of the lovely Emerald. Gem turned off the telly and pressed the start button on the cd player. Wyatt was probably eating at a restaurant and frowning at the food.

Since she was alone in the house, Gem turned on her computer and gazed at the Pacific Ocean, and the South China Sea. Had the new team - aka - submarines or whatever arrangements Mrs Brown had made - begun their search? Gem had a strong feeling the Pilos would not be found in the South China Sea. If only she could get a strong feeling of the correct area to search!

Wyatt texted.

'Go to bed!'

'Fine!'

'Home late.'

'Apparently.'

'Goodnight sweetheart.'

'Goodnight, Dark Lord.'

She turned off her office lights, leaving on the kitchen, hall, and staircase lights for Wyatt, then snuggled luxuriously in the spacious, empty bed. It did seem strange going to bed without Wyatt beside her. Alone or not, she quickly fell asleep, exhausted by baby(ies) and walking.

Wyatt eased into bed, trying not to wake Gem, but the weight of his body on the mattress alerted her to his return.

"What time is it?" she queried sleepily.

"Midnight. Go to sleep, love," Wyatt whispered.

"Why Paris?"

"Manton was struck by a car."

Gem sat up in bed. "What happened?" she demanded, concerned for the man whom she had yet to meet.

"He was jogging and was hit by a car," Wyatt replied, pulling her down and slipping his arms around her.

"And?" Gem pressed.

"Broken arm. Lost a shoe, which greatly upset him - rather pricey shoes, I understand."

"Do you have to go to Paris again tomorrow?"

"Ms Holton will travel there for this week. She will practice her French and learn to pretend to eat frog legs. Did you miss me today, my sweet?" he nuzzled her neck.

Gem started to mentally review the day.

"Well, that is my answer then," he said crisply.

"It was a busy day," Gem protested. "I dusted, walked to the village with Mrs M, had lunch, shopped, replied to your text, went for a long walk, replied to your other texts -"

"All of which took a matter of seconds."

"I thought of you then. I worked in my office until your final text - at which time I went to bed. I did wonder if you had dinner," she added. "So I thought of you today a number of times."

Wyatt leaned back against the pillow. "I will accept that. Go back to sleep, my dear."

She wouldn't text Mr Cawley. He was likely still sleeping off the viral infection. Tea, cd, then what?

Mr Manton. Frightening! She had never been in an accident. Gemmy had broken her arm skiing, but Gem had never broken a bone.

Ping

Mr Cawley was awake!

'How goes the sorting?'

'Frozen. Search in SCS?'

'It has commenced. No news yet.'

'How are you feeling?'

'Battling. A bit better. Why are you frozen?'

'I don't know where to start. Stalemate.'

'Start at the beginning. Did you miss something?'

Start from the beginning. 30 May.

'Too painful.'

'Yes. But give it some thought in the event SCS is a loss.'

'Okay.'

'Also new search in Arafura and Timor Seas per Mrs B.'

'Okay.'

'Back to work.'

'I'll try same here.'

But she couldn't force herself to recall every detail of the first dark hours. Reliving every moment in sequence. It was difficult enough getting the random imagines that tormented her.

She reviewed the math of flight nautical miles and fuel estimates and came up with the same result: Gulf of Carpentaria, Arafura Sea, Timor Sea; Banda Sea and South China Sea both seemed out of range.

Paul Andriani. Barcelona. She needed a chat with Mr Choate. Barcelona had been his territory. Perhaps he could give some insight which would, in turn, give Gem a clue to Gemmy and the photos of her with Paul Andriani.

Tea, cd player, pacing. She looked about her office, realizing she still hadn't hung her art work.

One more text to Mr Cawley.

'Any word from Blank?'

'No.'

'SEA Network still complete?'

'Yes.'

'Okay. Goodnight.'

'Goodnight, Gem.'

Tea, cd, pacing. Three hours at any other time of day did not seem as long as the hours between two and five o'clock in the morning, Gem observed.

"Waking at seven does have its advantages," Wyatt murmured as Gem forced open her eyes. If her eyes refused to open why did her brain insist on waking?

"And there you are again. You complain of the hours I keep! Why don't you go back to sleep for a few hours," she tried to reason with him.

"Ha! Not a chance. You're awake. I'm awake. I'll gladly trade off sleep and keep you in bed awhile," he smiled at Gem.

And the butterflies flew freely. And were then gathered.

"Are you going to the city today?" Wyatt asked Gem at breakfast.

"I have a bit of shopping to do," she nodded. Viewing - not purchasing yet. She hadn't a clue of babies, the caring for, the tending of same. She could read at Howard's Bookshop for an hour or so, commit the information to memory and peruse it at her leisure on her walks - before she told Wyatt - and then she could read the books openly. "I am going to ask Mr Choate to lunch," she added.

"Mr Choate?" Wyatt frowned.

"He has so many rules," Gem explained. She needed to pump his brain, more accurately. "Where I may park - or not - walk close to buildings, how to enter or exit a shop. How to cross streets for heaven's sake. I want to get the rules clear." She pulled a small note pad from her pocket. "Shop list and for clarifying Mr Choate's rules."

"I gave you a list of his rules," Wyatt still frowned.

"Oh, you did indeed. I must have shredded it with text sheets for Chichester, because I simply cannot find it. And I need clarification on driving routes. Mr Choate does not accept excuses."

"Indeed. Nor should he," Wyatt agreed.

Mr Choate was wary of the lunch invitation when Gem approached the subject at the bookshop. He finally agreed when Gem assured him that Wyatt had been apprised of the chat. Then, as Mr Choate wandered the bookshop and chatted with his old mate, Howard, Gem settled on the sofa at the rear of the store with a book on baby's first year: feeding, nappies, illnesses, sleeping habits - apparently that depended much on the infant - clothing, prams, and on and on. It all sounded routine enough - until one was up against it proper.

Ora and Eda's shop was next on the list. Gem employed Gemmy's practiced eye as best she could for skirts and jumpers. She had shopped so often with Gemmy over the years she could now discern her sister's style which was, she had to admit, preferable to hers - and as it seemed, appreciated by Wyatt to Gem's taste. Ora and Eda approved Gem's selections without suggesting a substitution or alternate choice. When Gem began to 'expand' she would ask Ora to design some clothes for her. But that would have to wait until she had had 'that chat' with Wyatt.

Mr Choate selected a quiet café where, he said, the food was good, but the service was sparse once orders were served. They sat at a table, away from other diners, keeping their backs to the wall. They casually, but constantly, read the room.

Gem quickly discussed rules with her co-worker so as not to completely lie to Wyatt regarding the lunch. A rule was added: she could not enter a shop without Mr Choate's expressed approval. They reviewed driving routes, altering one because of frequent traffic congestion.

Well done then! On to the real reason for the chat.

They both knew nothing was off the table between them since the Pilos went down. Only Mrs Brown reserved the right to retract Gem's NTK.

"And the reason we are here?" Choate queried bluntly.

"When was the last time you saw Gem?" she asked, keeping her voice just above a whisper.

"May."

"Where?"

"Barcelona."

"Barcelona!" she fought to keep her voice low. Gemmy had not been on assignment to Barcelona in May. Or ever. "Were you on assignment?"

Choate shook his head. "A proper holiday."

"Why that particular city?"

"Habit. Every May, Barcelona. It's quite a pleasant city."

"What did Gem say to you?" she pressed.

"We didn't speak."

"You didn't?"

"I saw her and she saw me. That was it."

Gem puzzled for a moment. But it was only logical. It was not an assignment. Then she nodded her understanding of the encounter. "Did you see Gem with anyone?" Hopefully not - or NOT, at least, James.

"Yes."

Never say more than was necessary - if possible - Agency SOP.

"Do you know who was with her?"

"Yes."

The exchange was wearing on her. "Who was with Gem?"

"Blank."

They fell silent as the waiter delivered their order. Choate looked approvingly at his chicken wrap. "This looks a treat."

Gem picked at her salad. Oh how she would love an order of chips and a huge burger! Gem shook off the food longings.

Mr Choate's reply made her frown. It was not the one she had wanted to hear, yet it certainly confirmed Wyatt's claim to the possession of photos. Not that she had thought his claim a lie. It was simply clarification.

"Was he on assignment?" Gem murmured.

Choate nearly choked on his food. He frowned at her in reply.

"Right," Gem muttered. One did not make queries of Paul Andriani's assignments unless one was Harry or Mrs Brown. "I wish I knew what they had discussed."

"You would have to ask Blank," Choate shrugged.

Gem ate silently for a few minutes. Mr Choate was being very frank and she knew she was prying into his holiday.

"Did you chat with him while you were in Barcelona?"

"Yes, but - oh hell - we didn't mention Gem," he volunteered the next reply to what would certainly be her forthcoming query. "I saw them at one of the city gardens," he admitted, ignoring Agency SOP. "They spoke for a few minutes. That's all I know."

"But why did they meet in the first place?"

"To be honest, it looked like they quite literally bumped into each other," Choate remarked. "They both appeared very startled to see each other."

"You never saw her again?" Gem asked sadly.

"No. Sorry, Gem. I can't help you with Barcelona."

Gem pondered the chat as she chewed lettuce and carrots. She could easily go off carrots if she had much more of them.

"You were assigned to Switzerland," she mused aloud. She already knew the answer.

He nodded, polishing off the wrap and then the chips.

Gem sighed. "Gemmy. Geneva. I just don't understand."

Choate frowned. "Why would she be in Geneva? There were no assignments to Geneva that time in May. 3 May only; that was it."

"I know. I checked," Gem added.

"If an assignment had come up, I would have taken it, then returned to my holiday," Choate insisted.

Gem nodded. "Then why was Gem in Geneva? Why? Why? Why?" She reflected for a few minutes. "Switzerland. Watches. What else?"

"Cuckoo clocks."

"Chocolate."

"One can order it all over the inter-net," Choate protested, "and have it shipped all over the world." He paused, drumming his fingers on the table. "Post in Brisbane is still checked every day. Nothing arrived after -"

"Yes," Gem knew how the sentence would end - 30 May.

"Nothing was shipped to that address."

"No."

"That couple in Inverness - did they say she was with someone?"

"No. They thought I was Gem so - well -"

"Indeed, I can keep up here," Choate reminded her. "Did you feel it was implied that she - you were with someone in Geneva?"

"No," Gem shook her head.

"If they had seen the two of you together, they still wouldn't have noticed that your eyes are the faintest shade darker than hers."

Gem nodded. "The difference was minute. But the Agency needed to know - it's in my file. Even mum had to put on her specs to see the difference. Dad could tell us apart by our accents."

"I never could tell the difference there," Choate admitted ruefully. "You two were so practised at matching your diction, pronunciation, accent."

"That was our idea. Dad helped train us, so he likely would notice the slightest difference. Toned down accents for both countries. Our own accent basically."

"An amalgam. I dare say most people would think your speech pattern had been altered of influences by much world travel."

"That was precisely the point."

"Mr Grantham has muted tones also - no doubt from his travels. For some people it is the structure of their tongue, jaws, teeth," he lapsed into professional studies of his field of investigation.

Gem nodded. "We digress. No information on Switzerland - or the chat in Barcelona."

"Only he knows," Choate concluded.

"Where is he?" Gem bluntly queried. "Where is Paul Andriani?"

"Wouldn't everyone like to know that answer," Choate nodded, his brows lifting.

Gem frowned and reached for the bill, paying over Mr Choate's protests. "My idea to meet like this," she insisted. "You can pay when you are no longer my shadow."

"Hopefully, for your sake, that will end soon. When this mess is sorted you will have a T.O. company shadow," he advised her.

When this mess is over I will no longer need a shadow. I will no longer be legally attached to Wyatt Grantham, Dr Jekyll, or the almost bearable Mr Hyde. When I am free, Gem mused silently, I will quietly disappear and start living my life on my own terms again.

Oops! Except, now a spanner had been tossed in the works. A little she or he or, dear heavens, they.

"One day indeed," Gem nodded, as they left the café.

As Gem walked back to the Defender, she had to admit to herself that there was one aspect of the relationship with Wyatt that she would miss - and it greatly astounded her that she would admit the fact even to herself. The man could entice magic. And although she would not admit it to Wyatt - she no longer wished he would take a mistress. While their relationship existed, she did NOT want to share him. He might be too tired for her. And she would NOT like that at all!

Once she returned to the Hall, she chatted for an hour with Mrs M in the kitchen, then set out for a walk. She realized that she needed rest, but defined that as the time she spent reading at Howard's Bookshop that morning. She walked for two hours, returning to the Hall only when approaching black clouds threatened to erupt into a deluge, for her wellies and mac were in the mudroom.

Gem had had her time to herself for the day and offered her assistance to the housekeeper for dinner prep. Mrs M offered hot chocolate while they worked, Gem opted for tea. When the food was in the cooker, she set the table, then retired to her office to browse the inter-net, and watch the international news. There were no red flags in the simmering hot spots that would be causing headaches for Mrs Brown.

She contemplated asking her supervisor to meet her for lunch this week, so she could put a question to Mrs Brown. Where was Paul Andriani the night of 29/30 May? Only Mrs Brown could now give or deny that information, since Harry was unavailable.

Gem jumped when Wyatt spoke from the doorway.

"Did you get your facts clear with Mr Choate, my sweet? I'm sorry I startled you," he chuckled. "You were so very deep in thought then, were you?"

"A tad distracted," Gem smiled uneasily. Thank heavens you can't read my mind! "I did indeed. Mr Choate will give me a revised list of rules the next time I see him - or rather he sees me."

Wyatt studied her. "You seem comfortable now with this situation of Mr Choate," he observed.

"I am," Gem agreed. "Mr Choate isn't annoying - not like a governess - err governor - whatever the male title is for a governess - if there is one. He's there, but is not obtrusive."

Her words seemed to be agreeable to Wyatt.

He was quiet as Mrs M served dinner that night, and after the housekeeper left the Hall, Gem drifted to her past thoughts, as she wondered just how many women a man like Wyatt had in his past. And who had trained him so well to do what he did - so beautifully?

"What?" Wyatt asked sharply.

"What?" Gem asked, startled from her thoughts.

"You were staring at me with an extremely odd expression in your eyes. What were you thinking?" he demanded frowning.

Gem flushed scarlet, and gasped. "Nothing!" She was acutely embarrassed. Again, thank heavens, he could not read her mind!

But apparently he could do so. He whistled softly. "Good Lord!" he chuckled, his frown disappearing. "We shall chat about this later - no we shall definitely not chat," he said, his eyes glinting. "There's no need to be embarrassed, love. You know where my thoughts usually are."

"But - that's you!" Gem replied bluntly. "You're a man!"

"Fortunately for both of us I am," he laughed heartily. "Again, fortunately for both of us, you are not."

"Dinner is going to be unendurable," Gem sighed, still blushing.

"I whole heartily agree, my dear. How quickly can you finish your dinner?" he teased.

Gem scrunched up her face, wadded her serviette and aimed it at his head. He had the good grace not to duck, catching the square of linen to hand back to her.

"A flag of truce until we finish here," he winked at her.

A very unendurable dinner. How quickly could she finish her food? - But she didn't want to encourage his ego.

"I wasn't thinking about what you were implying," she protested. "I was thinking about a related issue."

"Well, I'll accept that - with pleasure - whatever made you blush so beautifully. Care to explain?" he teased.

"I care to dine alone in the kitchen," she retorted with a mock smile.

"Don't ever lose the moment, my sweet," he still teased. "Don't ever lose the moment."

"I believe I already have," she sighed, conceding defeat, unable to voice her query of the other women and - she pushed those thoughts from her mind.

Wyatt generously changed the subject, to her relief. "Did you manage your shopping today?" he asked casually.

"Indeed. I purchased a few items - skirts, jumpers."

"Perhaps you can put them on to show me - later," he winked again. "And I can help you out of them."

"Perhaps you can eat your hat!" Gem retorted.

"I don't believe I actually own such an item," Wyatt chuckled. He relaxed, enjoying her sass. "You had a pleasant day, then," he observed.

"Very," Gem acknowledged. "And your day? How is Mr Manton?"

"He is steadily improving, and I survived another Tuesday at the office."

"Monkeys?"

"Meetings," he frowned, and to Gem's surprise actually spoke of the office. "Ms Holton is having a problem with a subordinate. I dislike office politics."

"Not that Delia?" Gem asked.

Wyatt nodded. "Ms Margordy."

"I thought she was going to Germany?"

"Ms Holton wants to ship her out, but I don't believe Ms Margordy's German is proficient for the foreign office."

Gem pondered the quandary. "Ms Holton is exceptional?"

"Indeed."

"Then let her have her power," Gem suggested. "Give Ms Holton free reign to manage, and Ms Margordy will sink or swim in Germany."

Wyatt considered the suggestion, then pulled out his mobile. He gazed at Gem as he spoke into the phone. "You are in charge. Ms Margordy is your decision," he said crisply, snapping his mobile shut.

"I hope this doesn't backfire," Gem had second thoughts.

"Trust your instincts, sweetheart," Wyatt said firmly. "We'll see how it all plays out."

Gem was quiet as they did the washing up. Paul Andriani was never far from her thoughts. What was the chat about between Gemmy and Paul Andriani? Mr Choate had said it appeared the two had simply run into each other. But he saw the incident from a distance. Or was the incident arranged to look accidental?

Three of them had been in Barcelona on the same day - in the same city garden. A coincidence? Difficult to believe. Mr Choate was on a proper holiday, so he was clear. But Gemmy and Paul Andriani. - Or Paul Andriani. Gemmy wouldn't have had the undercover agent's mobile number, but Paul Andriani could have had her number - in his memory. He had the mobile numbers of specific agents and couriers in the event he had to transfer information to the closest agent or courier. Paul Andriani could have arranged a special meeting with Gemmy, unbeknownst to anyone in the Agency. Hopefully he would contact Mrs Brown.

Wyatt watched her as they tidied the kitchen. What was she thinking now? Earlier, during dinner, it was obvious she had been thinking of sex - or as she had said, something related to the subject - close enough then to cause her to blush furiously.

And where was she now? The haunted look was in her eyes. Her secret world caused the insomnia, her inability to sleep past seven o'clock in the morning. It was almost as if those hours had been programmed into her mind.

His fascination with her grew every day. She grew more exquisitely beautiful every day. How could she be the same woman who had destroyed James? Yet she had never denied that fact. Seemingly sweet, seemingly thoughtful, actually brilliant. According to Choate's reports she never set a foot over the line. Which Gem was she? My God! she was a finer actress than the much praised Emerald!

What was she working on, what plan was she devising?

Gem - what a difference between a brilliant woman and one who thinks I.Q. refers to herself in a line: I queue where?

Did she ever think of James other than going to his grave? Was it James who haunted her? Wyatt could not believe that James had had a single clue of the woman who had stolen his heart.

She accepted the M's as family - or appeared to do so. He had given that credit card to her two months ago, yet she had never asked to have the balance increased.

Who the hell was this woman he had married? He hadn't a clue. Gemimah Louisa Forrester. Gemma Louisa Lawson. Why keep the same middle name? Was that a clue of sorts? A family name?

Whoever she was, Gem, James's Gem, was driving him mad with unanswered questions! No wonder James had lost himself in her. He himself could have so easily fallen under her spell - if he hadn't known of her true nature when he met her. And still knowing, he was mesmerised by her practiced, artful magic.

The kitchen was clean and in proper order for Mrs M.

"How about that fashion show?" Wyatt slipped his hands to her waist.

Gem nodded with a frown. Her brains needed a rest but no doubt Wyatt would make at least one snide comment regarding her taste in clothes. But to her surprise he did not.

"Very complimentary, my dear, the clothing perfectly suits you. The designer is excellent, and I believe the same one that designed your lovely gown that did not attend the theatre."

"Yes," Gem concurred.

"Very inconsiderate of me," Wyatt smiled apologetically.

His mobile rang, and as always he had to take the call. "Excuse me, my dear," he whispered and left the bedroom.

Gem put the clothes away, changed into her pyjamas, and went down to her office. He would likely be on the phone for hours. No doubt his work load increased with Mr Manton out of the Paris office, and Ms Holton out of the London office this week.

It was days since she had truly concentrated on her book. Chichester still needed much work. She had so much to think about! She pulled up the file; if she couldn't concentrate on it, at least having it on the computer screen would be a blind if Wyatt walked into her office while she was on mental tangent.

Sleeper. Mole. It had been days since she had thought of either. But that was likely what Harry was ferreting out. Either could explain everything from the Pilos to the murders of the SEA Network. Could Paul Andriani be a mole or a sleeper? She had to talk with Mr Choate again. She needed to pick his brains about the history of the Agency. A courier could be a mole, or a sleeper. A double-courier - as in a double-agent. A double-agent.

"Stuck in thought?" Watt said, causing Gem to jump in her chair.

"I thought you were on the phone," her hand flew to her breasts as she tried to catch her breath.

"I was - having a chat with Mr M who pays the estate bills," Wyatt said dryly. "You have not been using the credit card I gave you."

"No," Gem said firmly.

"May I have it please?" he held out his hand.

Gem hesitated, pulled out and opened the combination-lock file box, shielding the combination from his eyes. She gathered the plastic shards and put them in his hand.

"Why the devil do you refuse to use the funds?" he demanded scowling. "You weren't adverse to taking jewellery from James. How much money did he give you?"

"He didn't give me money," Gem protested. Gemmy wouldn't have asked James for money. She had her own more than adequate funds.

She couldn't very well admit she hadn't examined the jewellery when she had packed Gemmy's items. 'She' should remember – know - the pieces James had given her. Gem had thought the pieces to be costume jewellery.

"I am not versed in jewellery. I didn't know it was valuable," Gem countered. But no doubt James had told Gemmy the items were family heirlooms. Gemmy simply hadn't had the time to mention that fact to her sister. "You have the jewellery now. I have my own funds. I eat your food. I live in your house. I drive your Defender. But I pay for my own purchases!"

Wyatt scowled. Perhaps James had not given her money; he had not mentioned doing so, therefore Wyatt could not argue the point. He seriously doubted her remarks about the family jewellery.

"The vehicle is in your name, you own it," he countered.

"No I do not. You can tell me what to do, when to do it, where to go, and when. I may have to follow your orders, but you do NOT own me, despite what you said on Wight!" she declared, her nerves tingling, on alert for battle. She had seen his fury at Marigold Cottage, but she was not going to back down.

Wyatt stared at her and Gem could see his eyes darken to steel grey. His temper was rising. "You are the most thoroughly exasperating, vexing woman I have ever known," he scowled.

"Thank you," Gem replied calmly. "I am extremely pleased to know that fact."

Wyatt exhaled sharply and glanced at the plastic shards in his hand. He fought to keep his voice even. "I won't be concerned then that you will go over your account limit," he gazed at her.

"I shall not," Gem said quietly.

He shook his head, put the shards in his pocket, turned on his heel and left the room.

Gem sank down in Auntie Jane's comfy chair. This battle was won - hopefully more than a temporary win, and that the subject of money would not come up again.

She realized that she was shaking. Tension, still the underlying tension. Mr Hyde again supplanted by Dr Jekyll, but at least he hadn't been as nasty as he might have been. She was running on nerves and adrenaline. Gemmy, the Pilos, Wyatt. The baby(ies). She was physically exhausted, her brain was toast, and everything was at stalemate.

Perhaps if she cleared her brain again, did not think of anything pertaining to her current life, she could start sorting again in a few days. She read about birds, and flowers, made tea, and listened to the cd - that was the only concession she made to the search. She could not bear the dark hours without hearing Vera Lynn's voice.

By the time the dark hours ended she was familiar with birds, flowers, and a number of plants that attracted birds and butterflies. She missed texting Mr Cawley, but she was too tired to even think of the Agency. Wyatt welcomed her back to bed, tucked her in and gave her a gentle kiss, his lips undemanding of hers. "Go to sleep, sweetheart," he murmured.

Chapter Twenty-Four

Wyatt's mobile rang as he stepped out of the shower. Gem hastily dressed and went downstairs to allow him privacy for his call. He looked absolutely smashing with the towel around his waist. Gem took deep breaths as she walked past the great room. Wyatt had already gathered the butterflies that morning, but they were ready to fly again. Must be the Blasted hormones!

The M's were walking in the kitchen door as Gem entered from the hall. Mr M didn't usually accompany the Missus in the morning. If he was here to see Wyatt he might have a bit of a wait, Gem mused before she saw the box in his hands.

"Well, there you are, and just in time," Mrs M gave Gem a wide smile, folded back the flaps on the box, and reached inside to lift out an extremely fluffy tabby cat.

"Isn't she brilliant!" Gem exclaimed as the housekeeper handed over the bundle.

"What have you there?" Wyatt queried as he walked into the room.

"It's a cat," Gem teased, snuggling her cheek against the feline's head. "Opposite of a dog - well, sort of. Do you mind?"

"Not at all," Wyatt scratched the cat behind its ears. "Keep him inside or he'll eat Becton's birds. Gruesome sight to be sure."

"She's a she," Gem corrected. "Look at her face."

"Mrs Moody is moving to a care centre today," Mrs M stated," and she can't have her kitty there."

"What's her name?" Gem asked.

"Mrs Macgillicudy."

"Who in their right mind names a cat Mrs Macgillicudy?" Wyatt frowned.

"You don't have to be in your right mind to name a cat," Mrs M cooed to the feline. "That's the only explanation for all the felines named Fluffy and Bootsie."

"Mrs Mac or Mrs Gill," Wyatt suggested. "Macgillicudy is too long for the cat to learn to spell when she starts school."

Gem burst out laughing. "Ridiculous!" she charged. "I've never had a cat before," she said softly. "She is perfect."

"She came with accessories," Mr M announced. "Wyatt - help me carry in the stuff. Instructions, litter pan, food."

Mrs M turned on the telly as was her habit before she started to prepare breakfast. "Litter pan goes in the mudroom," she declared.

Mr M left after the cat items were in the house.

"You don't mind having the cat in your house?" Gem asked quietly as Wyatt filled the litter pan.

"Home, Gem, 'our home'," Wyatt said very quietly. "You seem to have difficulty remembering those words. Mrs M said you needed a friend. Now you have one," he glanced at his watch. "I don't have time for breakfast this morning. I will be 'home'," he stressed the word, "in time for dinner, sweetheart." He gave her a quick kiss, patted the cat's head and left.

"Mr W isn't staying for breakfast?" the cook queried with a frown.

"No. He had a phone call earlier," Gem explained. "Perhaps he has an early meeting."

"I rang him," Mrs M informed her, "to let him know we were fetching the cat this morning, so he didn't have to make the trip to Mrs Moody's house."

"I'm surprised he doesn't mind having a cat in the house," Gem observed. "Oh, Mrs M, just tea and a muffin this morning, please."

The cook's eyebrows lifted a touch but she gave a short nod. "Mr W doesn't mind pets." Then she laughed. "But he hates snakes. Jamie had a pet snake when he was a lad. He had it in the backyard one day, walking it, he said, but it got away from him. He was so devastated Mr W went out and bought him another one. It was always getting loose around the house. Mrs Fiona finally asked the lad to move the snake to the stable, because Mr W used to swear a blue streak when the snake was lost in the house. Mrs Fiona didn't hold with her son's swearing, but Mr W wouldn't stop the curse words until the snake was found. I nearly hoovered it a time or two," she wiped laughter tears from her eyes. "Between you and me, I think Jamie let the snake loose to rile his brother to cursing."

"I wouldn't want a snake loose in the house either," Gem laughed. "Did Wyatt help search for the snake?" She shuddered at the thought of doing so herself.

"Indeed. It was harmless, of course, but it didn't like the cold stone floors."

"What happened to it? - the second snake."

"Slithered away on another walk one day. Jamie was older by then and he switched his interest to girls."

"What were the snakes' names?"

"Homer the Roamer, the First and Second," Mrs M chuckled. "Mr W named them, and that tickled Jamie. Now set down the cat and eat your breakfast. She needs to wander about and find her own way. Are you going to London today?"

Gem wanted to chat again with Mr Choate, but the drive to the city sounded exhausting. It could wait one day. She would try to finish Chichester today. And rest. "Not today," she replied. "More likely tomorrow."

"I have to leave at 4 o'clock. My club starts meeting again today; we don't meet during the summer. I'll start dinner before I leave," Mrs M stated.

"I can prepare dinner," Gem assured her.

"No, you have your work," the cook insisted.

Gem started her computer, but before she pulled up the cathedral file she checked the inter-net for information on cat care and medical information. She jumped as a streak of fur leaped to the top of the counter to investigate whatever caught her fancy.

"On the prowl, eh?" Gem chatted to the cat. "As you will Mrs Mac."

The cat padded across the counter, sniffed everything that caught her eye, nudged a window shade, then turned abruptly and shot off the counter and out of the room in a complete blur. Gem found herself laughing at the remarkable spirit roaming the house. Yes. Much preferable to a snake!

The work on Chichester went more smoothly that Gem expected. She took a break for lunch with Mrs M, then completed the chapter in early afternoon. After sitting for hours she needed a walk in the crisp early November air. When she left the Hall the cat was sleeping on the cd player in Gem's office.

The walk was refreshing and she stayed out for two hours, letting random thoughts drift into her mind. She was still amazed that Wyatt so easily let Mrs M bring the cat into this house. And Mrs M, telling Wyatt that Gem needed a friend. So very odd. Well, a cat was as good a companion as any other, and much better to her way of thinking than a snake named Homer the Roamer - first or second.

Gem actually giggled as she imagined Wyatt swearing as he searched the Hall for a missing snake. And to actually have purchased a second snake for James when the first one was lost! That was brotherly love to the ultimate! Definitely Mr Hyde and not Dr Jekyll.

Mrs Moody would no doubt miss her furred companion. Perhaps the care centre would allow visitation of Mrs Mac to Mrs Moody. Mrs M might know if that was a possibility. Losing a friend. Losing a brother. Too many loses.

Gemmy swept into her thoughts. Gem couldn't think of the next step in the search for the Pilos. Was there a next step or was it a matter of waiting for reports of the search of the seas in South East Asia? She did want to know more of the history of the Agency. She would go to London to chat with Mr Choate tomorrow. Still, it was possible that he would not reply to her queries because the Agency was extremely covert. And the history of the organization was not pertinent to the current situations of this particular government department.

Another thought struck her. The Pilos would be found. It had to be found. And when it was, when she left the Hall, never to return - what would she do? She would have to live in London because Wyatt would have visitation to their child - unless he got custody - his money, his power. What a fight that would be! And once that was sorted, perhaps she could obtain a teaching position. Or perhaps she would live in Oxford or Cambridge - still convenient to the Hall for visitation for Wyatt. She would be a single mother. If that wasn't a completely frightening thought, what was! At least she would not be troubled by finances; but the divorce would be costly; she could imagine that Wyatt would have the best possible legal team in the country on his side of the bargaining table. And this time she would not be her own negotiator! Mrs Brown or Mr Choate would be able to suggest excellent legal advisors. Perhaps Mr Cawley would have a suggestion.

Suddenly Gem was completely exhausted. She slowly walked back to the Hall, wondering, as she walked, if Wyatt ever thought of Emerald and the other women in his past. Very likely every day, she frowned.

Mrs M was a reading a cookery book when Gem reached the Hall; there was a shelf full of the books in the kitchen and Gem took one with her to read while she rested on Auntie Jane's settee. Perhaps she could find recipes to help her stave off gaining weight in addition to hours of daily exercise.

Mrs Mac was apparently not a shy cat for she leaped onto the settee and snuggled on Gem's lap. The warm, purring ball of fur was very conducive to relaxing.

The long case clock in the main hall struck four chimes. Gem set the cat on the settee cushion and went to the kitchen. Mrs M appeared entranced by the cookery book before her on the counter.

"Time, Mrs M," Gem caught the woman's attention.

The house manager looked up, startled, then glanced at the clock on the wall. "Oh my. I did lose track of time."

"I'll prepare dinner. What am I cooking?" Gem smiled.

"Roast, potatoes, snow peas," Mrs M hurriedly gathered her belongings.

"Of you go then," Gem nodded. "And thank you for Mrs Mac. She's a wonderful cat!"

"Indeed," Mrs M agreed as she made a hasty exit, causing Gem to wonder of the club. It certainly held Mrs M's devotion.

Gem switched on the telly, per Mrs M's habit to view the international news as she started dinner. She could do a roast and potatoes blindfolded. When was the last time she had prepared a roast? Last Christmas? No. New Year's Day in Brisbane. It had been incredibly hot and the idea of a roast seemed foolish, but the family had voted and so it was. Swimming in the pool, a hike, the roast, potatoes and cauli. Mrs Brown and Harry were there. Mr Portermann was there. And Paul Andriani, but not as John Staunton. Who had Paul been that day? Gem mused with a wry smile -ah -a university mate of Gemmy's from Melbourne.

The food was in the cooker. Gem cleaned the counter, finishing wiping as Mrs Mac sailed up to land neatly on the island top.

"No, no, Mrs Mac," Gem said in dismay. She scooped up the feline, stroking her between the ears.

"She'll be on the counters when no one is around," Wyatt observed from the kitchen door. "Just frequently wipe the counters. Trying to keep her down will be a losing battle," he suggested.

I'm already fighting many of those concurrently, Gem thought. No point in adding another one to the list. As if responding to Wyatt's words, Mrs Mac escaped from Gem's arms to the top of the counter. Gem scooped her up again and held her.

"Oh! I forgot to ask Mrs M," Gem murmured.

"Ask her what?" Wyatt reached into the fridge for a beer, holding it out to Gem who shook her head.

"What?" Gem frowned. "Ah - Mrs Moody will miss this beauty. I wondered if the care facility would allow Mrs Mac to visit Mrs Moody."

Wyatt popped off the beer cap. What a thought! And why would Gem be concerned about the elderly woman? She had never met Mrs Moody to his knowledge. "It can be arranged," he replied. "They'll likely both want to see each other," he agreed.

"Okay," Gem nodded, again setting the cat on the floor. She wiped the counter, rinsed the cloth, then checked on the roast and potatoes before rinsing the snow peas, and checking the bread box to count the dinner rolls.

"You look competent in the kitchen," Wyatt remarked.

"Competent? That implies adequate. I am efficient!" Gem replied confidently. "You have time for a shower," she suggested. Mental review of the cat list that came with Mrs Mac: time to feed her.

"Your family didn't have pets when you were growing up?" Wyatt said casually, watching her scoop cat food into the feline's bowl.

"I don't have a family," Gem said automatically. What cogs were going to slip if she wasn't careful?

"You don't have a past either," he continued in the same tone. "How can one not have a past these days with computers and government documentation?"

Because of government clearing! Gem refused to be drawn into the conversation. "Would you like a salad with dinner?" she skirted his query.

"False identities, forged documents -"

"Would you like dinner rolls or gingerbread?" Gem interrupted, turning to look him straight in the eyes.

Wyatt returned the stare. "Dinner rolls, no salad," he replied at length.

"Fine," Gem clipped out the word. "I'm going to take a shower," she announced, leaving him in the kitchen, eager to duck any further comments he might decide to make.

Mrs Mac, having finished dining, scooted along with Gem up the stairs. Wyatt paused for a moment then turned the dial on the cooker down a few degrees.

"You are a voyeur Mrs Mac," Wyatt remarked to the cat as he took the roast from the oven. The feline stared at him then blinked her eyes. "Most silent cat I've ever known," he looked at Gem.

"She's new. You don't know her," Gem replied, setting plates on the island top.

Wyatt acknowledged the comment with a nod. Now there were two females in the house he didn't know. It would be easier to understand the cat than her human.

"I forgot," he pulled a collar from his pocket and hooked it around the cat's neck.

"Mrs Mac," Gem read the name tag. "Good guess."

"It was the most logical of the two."

"Does it have a tracking chip?" she queried loftily.

"Naturally," Wyatt replied.

Gem studied him via her peripheral vision as he sliced the roast. She made a pot of tea for herself and fetched another beer for him. Was Mrs Mac another part of his Game? She wouldn't know, would she? - Until he sprang some sort of trap. The man was devious - she certainly knew that!

While they ate dinner Mrs Mac prowled, often bursting into spurts of speed, racing through the kitchen into the hall, then darting back to the mudroom.

"You look exhausted, sweetheart," Wyatt frowned.

"I am tired," Gem conceded. In fact she was so weary it was an effort to hold her fork.

"I'll do the washing up. Why don't you go to bed - and rest."

"I was just in bed," she said lightly, "and I didn't get any rest."

"I have a report to read. Go to bed, read a book. I promise I won't tempt you to exert yourself - in any way - until morning."

The suggestion was tantalizing and it only took a minute for Gem to agree. She drank her tea. "Thank you. I'm going to bed." She made a detour to her office to pick up her copy of Pride and Prejudice to read if she could keep her eyes open. Mrs Mac padded silently behind her. And once in pyjamas and snuggled against the pillows, Gem gave a sigh of relief. Perhaps two hours of walking was too much. She opened the book and succumbed to her world of Jane Austin - her world according to Mrs Brown. Mrs Mac leaped onto the bed, curling next to Gem.

Wyatt amazed her again by bringing her a cup of hot chocolate. "Mrs Mac seems content with you," he smiled, tickling the cat's ears.

"She's lovely," Gem smiled. "Thank you for allowing her in the house."

"You are most welcome, sweetheart," Wyatt leaned down to gently kiss her.

He left then to read in the library. Gem drank her hot chocolate, and read half a chapter of her book before she fell asleep.

Gem had had nearly seven hours of sleep but was still exhausted when the dark hours began. She thought to stay in bed and let her mind wander, but her wakefulness might disturb Wyatt. She dragged herself down the stairs to her office, Mrs Mac scooting down the steps ahead of her.

Gem made tea, and for the first time, she wasn't physically alone during the dark hours. Mrs Mac was in the kitchen, the office, the mudroom munching kitty crunchies, and back in the office to nestle on Gem's lap in Auntie Jane's comfy chair.

Ping
'I missed you last night.'
'Brain was too frozen to think.'
'Better tonight?'
'A bit. I have a cat now.'
'Name?'
'Mrs Mac.'
'Perhaps she will help thaw your brain.'
'Perhaps. What news have you?'
'Timor Sea is clear.'
'Where next?'
'Arafura.'
'Are you feeling better?'
'Yes.'
'Any news of Blank?'
'None.'
'Harry?'
'None. Good luck thawing your brain.'
'Thanks. Goodnight.'
'Goodnight.'

Mrs Mac stretched lazily, then slid to the floor.

Gem cleared her text messages and paced. Mrs Mac settled on the cushion of the comfy chair.

"You can sleep anytime, anywhere, can't you, my beauty," Gem said to the cat. "How I envy you. However do you manage that then?'

"She knows her boundaries and is content with her life," Wyatt said from the doorway.

His voice startled Gem "You should be sleeping," she frowned.

"Indeed. Would you like another cup of tea?" he asked, taking the cup from the counter.

"Yes, please," Gem got up and followed him to the kitchen. "Why are you awake?"

"Why are you?" he replied casually, filling the kettle and setting it on the cooker.

Gem watched silently as he took cups from the cupboard.

"Tea or hot chocolate?"

"Tea, please."

"Your insomnia and your secret world," he looked up at her as he scooped tea into the teapot.

"Are you baiting your hook or just casting into the wind?" Gem murmured.

"Clever you," Wyatt acknowledged her words with a brief nod. "Are you going to the city this morning?"

"Why? Are you going to have me followed? Oh wait - you already do," she accepted the cup of tea he handed to her. To her surprise he merely chuckled.

"You should be concerned, my dear, if no one was behind you," he advised, sipping his tea.

"What do you mean?" she queried edgily.

He drained his cup, rinsed it and set it in the sink. "That would mean I was allowing you to become a target, my dear. The Game would be over," he replied loftily and walked out of the kitchen.

The dark hours and a cup of tea with Dr Jekyll.

The Game would be over: passports, photos to the tabloids. A threat or a warning? A threat: toe the line or -. A warning: from the beginning the Game was never open ended as Wyatt had said on Wight. The Game was always intended to end with the tabloids.

It wasn't a cat and mouse game. The mouse wasn't being hunted by a cat, but by a machine gun.

Gem paced the floor. Mrs Mac sat on the counter, her bushy tail around her, her eyes closed. Gem pushed the start button on the cd player again. The abyss was getting deeper. She had to find Gemmy, the Pilos, or she had to ring Mrs Brown and skewer Wyatt. Not that skewering Wyatt wasn't tempting! She dragged her fingers through her hair. She was so tired. And Wyatt was frightening. He was the steel barracuda.

The music stopped. Gem stopped pacing and looked at the cd player. Wyatt was standing next to it.

He walked to her, taking her in his arms. "My words were a harsh rejoinder, my dear, for which I apologize. I was not threatening you," he gently assured her.

"This time you weren't," Gem sighed wearily.

"Touché," Wyatt admitted. "Come to bed. It's half four."

Mrs Mac raced up the stairs ahead of them.

"Keep an eye on her so she doesn't trip you down the stairs," Wyatt warned.
"Indeed," Gem firmly agreed. She certainly did not need a fall!

Wyatt followed The Defender into the city; Choate was in his vehicle behind the Jag. Gem sighed as the Jag turned off to the GEI car park, and she continued on to Wakefield Tower. It was close enough to Traitor's Gate to match her mood. She was still exhausted. She had had a total of nine hours of sleep since last night, but it didn't touch her fatigue. She parked the Defender and walked to the wall, keeping her back to the Thames. She texted Mr Choate.

'Chat.'

With their backs to the wall they could watch for ears and eyes not of Mr Choate's department.

"Yes, Gem," Choate stood beside her, scanning the scene in front of them, as did she. He glanced over at her. "You look like hell by the way. Do you ever sleep?"

"Yes," Gem replied grumpily. "Well, not enough, I guess." She yawned and then broached the subject of their chat. "Who vetted current Agency staff?" she murmured. The walkway was more crowded with tourists than she had expected it to be at that hour of the morning.

"Eric Portermann."

"This is likely a foolish question. Are applicant's backgrounds checked for possible ties to Nazis?"

"Rigorously. Applicants, spouses, children, if there are any, parents, grandparents, in-laws, cousins, aunts, uncles, friends."

"If a connection is discovered?"

"Applicant is rejected and names go on a Watch List."

"Does Technical Operations vet applicants for private businesses?"

Choate held his reply as a young couple stopped nearby to check each other's tonsils.

"Someone got out of bed too soon this morning," Choate suggested dryly, eliciting a giggle from Gem.

"True love," Gem said, trying to keep envy out of her voice.

"True lust," Choate muttered. As the couple finally deigned to move on, Choate replied to Gem's last query. "We have many requests for vetting private business applicants."

Gem nodded, pondering the reply. "Thus the prospective employer would be apprised of requested information and that report would become part of T.O.'s data bank."

"The reports would be available to the Agency and B.I., yes."

"Who in the Agency has access to the T.O. data bank?"

"Harry, Mrs Brown, Mr Cawley, and the T.O. Director."

"Currently you."

"Yes."

She reflected back to Mr Cawley's remarks of Mr Choate's file, which was less than complete. "Mr Portermann vetted you?" she glanced at her companion.

"He did indeed," Choate nodded.

"How far back in the applicant's life does the vetting process extend?"
"To birth."
"Mr Portermann vetted you back to your birth?" she pressed the query.
"He did."
"Including your previous employment history?"

Choate glanced down at her. "I receive reports of all your requests to Mrs Brown and to Mr Cawley, Gem," he said dryly. "Your NTK only extends so far." He crossed his arms.

They held their conversation as a family of five, including three young children in t-shirts emblazoned 'California', dawdled past, the children attempting to scale the wall, to their parents' obvious consternation.

"We shall be here all morning," Choate said grimly.

It was nearly a quarter of an hour before they could again speak freely.

"Is this chat in regards to my past?" Choate queried bluntly.

"No, not really," Gem admitted to her failed attempt to pry that information from him.

"Good. Otherwise it would be a waste of your time. Next question."

Gem thought for a moment. She didn't think her other queries would be beyond her NTK.

"How long has the Agency existed?"

"Hundreds of years, perhaps a thousand - as long as there have been spies in England. It predates B.I. Former agents and couriers were not always a respectable lot. Whoever paid the highest price usually received the information - or it was given over during torture."

"Lovely," Gem shuddered at the image. "There must be thousands of files."

"Indeed."

"Have you read all of them?" she teased.

"Only the files since 1900. I have only been director for a few months, you know," he reminded her.

Speed reading. Gem assumed.

Another family again delayed conversation. It was not a wise decision to select Wakefield Tower for a location for discussion.

"How long has T.O. been tracking Nazis?" Gem finally had a chance to continue her queries.

"Winter '32-'33. Churchill hounded the Agency that Germany needed to be watched. I'm certain you already know of his early concern about Hitler," he conceded her ability to retain read material. "The Agency Director at that time began to thoroughly document staff, family members, businesses, personal contacts. That which T.O. currently compiles."

"How long has T.O. existed?" Gem realized she had no idea of that department of the Agency.

"Since 1910. And the answer to your next question - there is no indication, not even the slightest, that any Agency staff member is a Nazi or a Nazi sympathizer. We are extremely thorough, you know."

"That was my next question. One might wonder about a mole or a sleeper. T.O. files must be immense," Gem reflected.

"No indication of moles or sleepers. The files are immense, but we are tracking possible terrorists, Gem, not all U.K. residents."

"You have files on Wyatt and James," she pointed out.

"V.I.P. files. Every government maintains such files," Choate crisply informed her. "However, we do not peep into windows."

"I'm so pleased to hear that," she returned his tone. "I am in the file," she mused. "And my family - Mr Portermann?"

"Removed to a temporary file - at the warehouse. Only temporary, Gem."

"And B.I.? Everything similar to the Agency?"

"Same procedure, everyone thoroughly scrutinized."

"There's nothing there then. Not a scrap of anything?"

"Nothing that we can see. We've all been over all our information many times."

"But a mole is obvious. Or a sleeper," Gem insisted.

"Possibly. But one first must have the equation," he frowned.

"One plus one equals how many deaths, one after the other," Gem said grimly. "Eleven by my count." Plus James and the baby.

"You're including Denton," Choate frowned.

"I am," Gem nodded firmly.

"Well, we don't know how many do we? - Hopefully no more than we already have. We certainly cannot say at this time," Choate conceded.

"Paul Andriani?" she kept her voice very low. "Where is he?"

"You tell me, Gem," he shrugged. "If you can't figure out the answer, others won't be able to do so. Then he will be safe where he is."

"I wouldn't know where to start looking for him," she shook her head.

"That's your mobile," Choate alerted her.

"Oh!" She hadn't heard the music. It would be Wyatt with that text ring tone.

'Lunch possible?'

She had to eat.

'Where? When?'

'Noon? Jake's?'

'Yes.'

'Later then, sweetheart.'

'Later, Dark Lord.'

Once again in the Defender, Gem rang Dr Hallowell's office about her fatigue. He would see her anytime that afternoon - just walk in. Mr Choate would have to report the tea shop; she wouldn't purchase clothes at the boutique; she would only shop at Ora and Eda's shop as they needed her business more than a fancy boutique.

She had time to stop at Howard's Bookshop before she met Wyatt. She purchased three travel books, four about cats - one a six hundred page encyclopaedia that should occupy her a few weeks - or years. Normally she would have walked to Jake's but she couldn't manage the walk today.

Wyatt was waiting for her at the tavern so Choate took his leave of them.

"Darling, you look dead on your feet," Wyatt scowled, "what have you been doing this morning? Walking all over London?"

"Looking at books mainly. I went to Wakefield Tower and watched the Thames flow for an hour," she sighed, grateful to sit down.

"What did you purchase?" Wyatt asked after the waitress had taken their order and drooled the entire time over him.

"A few books on cats, a couple of travel books," she replied.

"Are you planning a holiday?" Wyatt said smoothly.

Gem shook her head. "I thought I would read about the countries I've already visited. Too many whirlwind jaunts, one cathedral after another."

"How is your book progressing?" he stroked her hand, and studied her eyes. The haunted look was not there, but her eyes reflected her fatigue.

"I think Chichester is finished. I don't know what I will do next," she frowned.

Gem quickly drank her tea, feeling a bit revived, and ordered another.

"You're a bit pale," Wyatt frowned. "Shall I have Mr Choate drive you back to the Hall after lunch?"

"Oh, I can manage," Gem insisted. "I have another few errands to do this afternoon."

"For heaven's sake pace yourself then," Wyatt said firmly.

"I shall," Gem promised. "How is Mr Manton progressing?"

"He's on the mend. I'll tell him you were asking of him."

"And Ms Holton? Is she surviving Paris?"

"Remarkably well. Ms Holton packed Ms Margordy off to Germany. Ms Holton is flourishing, Ms Margordy is very subdued - according to the Berlin office manager. Berlin is very inflexible, efficient, and completely humourless."

"It sounds horrible," Gem shuddered.

"It's the perfect office to adjust attitudes," Wyatt replied succinctly. "If Ms Margordy can survive Berlin for a year she'll continue with GEI, otherwise she will be looking elsewhere for a position."

"Make or break," Gem nodded.

"Indeed. And enough business chat," he declared as their order was served. "There's a classic car show in Northampton on Saturday. Shall we drive over for the day?"

"Yes!" Gem said eagerly. "I believe that's the show Mr Critchley mentioned in September. He'll have his Silver Dawn Rolls there. I bet it's positively smashing!"

"Saturday it is then." Wyatt smiled, setting butterflies free again, Gem sighed. "Now eat your lunch."

Gem was frustrated when she left the doctor's office. Her blood was fine, but she had again gained weight. Mr Choate waited for her on the pavement.

"I had tea at the shop," she said with a sigh.

"Indeed," Choate nodded.

Dr Hallowell was not comforting. His conclusion for the severe exhaustion and the weight gain despite the exercise, and carefully watching her diet, was the conclusion she dreaded at this limbo stage in her life. Most probably twins. Rest as much as possible, moderate exercise, drink plenty of warm water.

Errands. She had mentioned errands to Wyatt. There was not a single item she needed to purchase so she would have to invent something. She bought film for her camera, black and white and colour, a rug and towels for her bathroom - either one - and while she was deciding on the colour of the towels she pondered how she was going to tell Watt she was pregnant. How? And when? As she walked to the Defender she passed a tobacconist's shop. Why not? She entered the shop and purchased a very expensive cigar. She would lock it in the file cabinet in her office until she could muster the courage to tell him this particular fact of his life.

But she was not going to mention twins. Not until Dr Hallowell confirmed that. And even then she would hold off telling him as long as was possible to do so. By the time she had to tell him about twins, be that the case, hopefully the Pilos would have been found. If the Pilos wasn't found she could admit her mum was a twin; Auntie Jane was not a figment of Gem's imagination. Likely that would be the best way to go. He could try if he wanted, to find information of Auntie Jane, but Gem had never mentioned her auntie's surname, and simply wouldn't. Still, she didn't want him thinking twins at all! And now thinking was giving her a headache.

She engaged the engine, cleared her mind and drove the peaceful drive back to Ticking Bottom. Mrs M was washing windows. So many windows in the house.

"I'll do the windows upstairs," Gem volunteered, taking a bottle of window cleaner and a paper towelling roll.

"You should rest," the housekeeper frowned. "I'll do those windows tomorrow."

"I rested on the drive here," Gem protested. She could rest later. She took the kitchen step-stool with her.

The bedrooms each had two large windows, then there was a window in each of the three bathrooms, not including James's room - she wouldn't go in there again. The master suite had a bank of windows and the window overlooking the back gardens, plus the windows in the bathrooms. The suite could wait a day or so.

She fought through her fatigue. Work had to be done, so it was done. She pushed thoughts from her mind, giving her attention only to the views beyond the windows. The Hall Park and gardens must be lovely in the spring. The beech tree on the front lawn had been expertly placed when first planted, she decided; it didn't crowd the Hall nor dim the sunlight streaming in the windows. She started with the first bedroom on the left, working around to pass the suite; the last window to be cleaned was at the other end of the hall, to the left of the attic door. Bless Mr M for cleaning the attic twice a year. That was off the list.

As she stepped off the stool, Wyatt's voice sounded behind her, dripping acid.

"This is what you consider pacing yourself?"

"Yes. I'll do the suite tomorrow," Gem replied.

He took her elbow and steered her into the sitting room, kicking the door closed with his foot. "Cleaning windows is not your responsibility!"

"Mrs M can't do all the chores here," Gem protested.

"She can hire help from the village," Wyatt said angrily.

"I'll just sit on the settee than and demand tea and crumpets, shall I?" Gem scoffed. "Bitch Lady of the Manor, wait on me hand and foot because I'm too lazy to do a spot of work!" she seethed. "That's your league, your Lordship! I can get my lily white hands dirty!" She put her hands on her hips, bracing for a withering Dr Jekyll excoriation.

"What is this lordship rubbish?" he demanded curiously.

Information from Mr Choate. Do not allow cogs to slip. Damn! Time to lie.

"A reference to the Hall. Lord of the Manor rubbish," she said hesitantly. "I was striking back at you."

"Damn! Gem, you are exasperating!" he shook his head, his anger waning. "Will you please rest before you have to go to hospital for exhaustion?"

She considered his words, staring him in his eyes. "Yes," she nodded, handing over the cleaning bottle and towelling.

Dr Jekyll disintegrated by Mr Hyde, Gem mused, opening the door.

"I sent Mrs M home," Wyatt called after her.

"You are in charge of dinner then," Gem shot back over her shoulder as she walked down the stairs to her office.

She turned on the telly and settled in the comfy chair with a cup of warm water to hydrate herself. Within seconds Mrs Mac was snuggling on her lap. "It's you and me against the world," Gem whispered to the ball of fur. And Harry, and Mrs Brown, and Mr Choate, Mr Cawley. Where the HELL was Paul Andriani on 29 May?

The international news didn't provide any obvious issues of fomenting hot spots. The sky, however, was definitely fomenting. She carried the cat to the counter, raised the shades to watch the sky, and returned to the chair, cat settling again on her lap.

"I do love you," she whispered in Mrs Mac's ear. The feline ignored her words, as Gem had read on the inter-net, that cats do; yet they hear your words and they listen; cats simply do not feel the necessity to respond, as they assume you know what they are thinking - since you SHOULD know what they are thinking.

Gem concentrated on the news. Emerald was no longer the word of the day - bless the gods of actors' agents and the agents. Not that Emerald had a place in her thoughts!

The model, Thia, in one of the other photos in an album in James's room didn't come to her mind. Gem relegated Emerald to Thia's non-entity status.

"What?" Wyatt entered the office and noticed her scowl.

"Emerald! Really!" Gem sniffed with a slightly haughty tone.

Wyatt reached down to take her hand, drawing her to her feet, and at the same time shifted Mrs Mac to the back of the chair. "Everyone has a past, sweetheart," he said clearly, "even you. Unfortunately for some of us - there are photos," he added wryly. "Dinner is ready. And then you go to bed."

Mrs Mac followed Gem everywhere. She definitely was the sunshine of the dark hours. The window shades were still raised; the cat sat on the office counter and watched the night beyond the windows.

"You will love the gardens in the spring," Gem assured the feline, "I'm sure they will be beautiful. She did not voice the sudden thoughts that she hoped not to be at the Hall herself come March and April, when the gardens would come to life with flowers, birds and butterflies. Within forty-eight hours she had come to realize that wherever she went Mrs Mac would also go. And that would be another battle with Wyatt.

Ping

'Mrs Brown requests your company at lunch - noon today.'
'Lovely! Perfect!'
It had been Gem's plan to ring her supervisor to request a meeting.
'Done then. How is your cat?'
'Mary Poppins.'
'Practically perfect etc. That's a cat. How are you?'
'Fine. You?'
'Rubbish! How are you?'
'Exhausted.'
'Still brain freeze?'
'Not really. What news have you?'
'None. You?'
'Same. Nothing.'
'Bake a cake. We need something to go on, Gem.'
'SCS?'
'Nothing from subs.'
'Blank?'
'Same.'
'Harry?'
'You are putting me to sleep. You've got the damned brain! Use it! Sort!'
'Thanks! I don't have enough pressure!'
'Life or death?'
'No.'
'Then get to work! Make a cup of tea. Bake a cake. Bake a dinosaur for God's sake. Put your brain to work!'
'I am exhausted!'
'Who isn't? White hasn't slept in nearly six months! Harry is out of the picture. Do you need a reminder of the body count so far?'
Gem nearly dropped the phone after reading the last text.
'Back Off!'
'No! You already have! You're exhausted. Sit in a f...... chair and think!'
Gem counted to twenty. Again. And again.
'Stop counting to twenty!'
'I don't know where to start!'
'At the beginning!'
'No!'
'Family!'
'Stop!'
'Gemmy!'
'Stop!'
'Never give up. Never give up. Never, ever, ever give up!'
'W.S.C.'
'He had guts. So do you.'
'I'm too tired.'
'You can rest when it's over Gem. Please!'
'Okay.'
'Goodnight.'

'Goodnight.'

Gem cleared the messages.

She pushed the start button on the cd player.

She refused to start at the beginning. She would rather think about Emerald, and Thia. What were the other names? - Yes - Jorgan Kalla - the other model, twelve ounces dripping wet; and the actress - from the horrid re-make of P&P - Elyse Rindahl; every human had thirty-two teeth - she had what ? - sixty-two? What producer did she sleep with to get the role of Elizabeth Bennett? The entire production was illiterate! Really!

30 May

No!

There was nothing there! She had relived that night every day and night from 30 May until the day she had met Wyatt! She knew every single minute from two o'clock to five o'clock that morning. From the instant Gemmy came to her until Mrs Brown had put her to bed. Why the Hell would she want to start there? - Yet again! Again! Again!

No!

She heard footsteps in the hall.

Wyatt.

Had the man forgotten how to sleep?

He strode into her office, took the cat from her lap, setting Mrs Mac on the floor, lifted Gem from the chair and started carrying her out of the office.

"I can walk," Gem protested.

"It is four fifty-three. Not another word from you," Wyatt ground out his words.

Gem put her face as close to the shower spray as possible, without having to worry that her eyes would blow back into her head to flow out her ears.

The butterflies were calmed. The man was mesmerizing! And she was not in the frame of mind to suggest he ring up Elyse Rindahl for a friendly lunch.

The blasted butterflies! She should name all of them Hormonia! She pulled on a towel, remembered to turn off the shower and padded, dripping wet out through her dressing room, around the bed, and for the first time into Wyatt's dressing room. He was standing, towel around his waist, scripping hangers across the rod holding his shirts.

"What?" he frowned, perplexed that she had entered the room. "Ah," he murmured, gazing into the deep violet eyes. He reached for his mobile and sent a quick text.

'Breakfast late.'

He did not add, 'apparently raging hormones' to the message. He had to have a chat with Gem. But now was not the moment.

As usual, Mrs Brown was precisely on time. And blunt as usual.

"Neat as a pin! The mark of a cracker-jack courier," Mrs Brown said crisply. "Unfortunately you look like you just stepped out of Hell!" she quickly scanned her young companion.

"Such first kind words," Gem smiled sweetly. "However, the rest of your remark was less than a usual gracious greeting."

"What do you expect, my dear?" Mrs Brown said pointedly. "You look like hell. Is Wyatt biting and swallowing his tongue, or is he actually being honest with you of your appearance?"

"He's nagging me to rest," Gem paraphrased his recent comments.

"I suppose I need to request a daily report from Choate on your health."

"Good. Then everyone can spy on me every day," Gem sighed. "The housekeeper, Wyatt, Mr Choate, you. Who else shall we add to the list?"

Mrs Brown's eyebrows raised so high they disappeared into the brown hat atop her grey hair. "Tea, my dear?" she asked calmly.

"Yes please, ma'am," Gem immediately settled down.

Mrs Brown nodded to Charley who quickly served a half-pint and a cup of tea to the Agency staff. He suggested a lunch order and Gem relented to the thought of his pub burger and chips, Mrs Brown assenting to the same.

"Is Wyatt eagerly anticipating your new arrival?" Mrs Brown queried, taking a long drink of her beer. This was going to be a very long gestation period.

Gem squirmed in her chair. Blast! She would love a beer. "I haven't told him yet," she admitted.

"Why?" Mrs Brown gently queried.

"It could be twins," Gem sighed. "I can't explain twins. I have no family. Thus no history. No past."

Mrs Brown leaned back in her chair. Had the Agency ever had such a problem? She pondered her time at the Agency and then back to Hong Kong. No. Only the Agency was the question.

Gem sipped her tea then left the table to go to the kitchen to request a hot chocolate when Charley could manage the order. When she resumed her seat Mrs Brown was ready to speak.

"If necessary," the older woman began, then paused, taking a deep breath. "If necessary, tell Wyatt everything."

"What?"

"Tell Wyatt everything," Mrs Brown repeated calmly.

"No!" Gem gasped. "I won't do that! I can't!" It was not easy, she realized, for Mrs Brown to come to that decision, but Mrs Brown did not know all the facts. "He's a civilian," Gem hedged. And I have put my soul on the line for the Agency! You cannot abruptly invalidate what I have done! Gem groaned inwardly. But Mrs Brown didn't know about Gemmy. And James. And John Staunton. And Paul Andriani. "No!"

"My dear, tell him if you must. About Gemmy, your parents - it was an accident."

"An accident which can't be verified. No public information. People who never 'existed'."

Charley served their food and a cup of hot chocolate. Gem eagerly tucked into meat and potatoes. She would have to walk it off at Ticking Bottom that afternoon - no use wasting Mr Choate's time walking across London. And there were the windows to clean. That should be some exercise.

"Tell Wyatt everything," Mrs Brown repeated.

"A missing plane. Dead agents, couriers." Wyatt hated spies! "It's too unbelievable!"

"Still, it's true," Mrs Brown said quietly.

Your brother died because - . Wyatt was still too raw. The photos, the passports. Wight.

SHE was still too raw. She had a job to do! Find Gemmy! The Pilos! Mrs Brown didn't know about the passports and the photos. She didn't know about Wight. The 'marriage'.

Explaining everything without proof? It was a fantasy! It was her life! Her past! Everything! Give it over to Dr Jekyll! That would be giving in! Conceding! Hormones? Was she thinking clearly? She was so tired.

No she was NOT going to explain to Wyatt! She was NOT going to concede to Wyatt and hope that he would believe her.

She had to have proof. She was going to succeed. She would solve the mystery of the Pilos. And then she would tell him!

"No," Gem said firmly. "It's not over."

"Lord, girl," Mrs Brown grumbled. "There are extenuating circumstances -"

"Not for me," Gem protested. It was an odd badge of honour for which she would grasp. I am not a bitch, or a liar. I am not a game-player. I want vindication. "If I have to - explain everything," she decided firmly, "then I shall. But only when I am ready. And it has to be my decision. Only my decision."

Mrs Brown could not read the young woman's thoughts. But considering what she had suffered the past months, the decision could only be hers. "As it should be," Mrs Brown relented. "On your own time. It shall be your decision, and your decision only."

"Thank you, ma'am," Gem said softly. But her thoughts were anything but soft. Blast you Wyatt Grantham! Why couldn't you be the man I thought I had married! I'm not going to give anything more than I wish to give! My decision, indeed!

"This isn't the reason for our meeting." Gem suddenly realized they had become sidetracked. And oh, the burger was absolute heaven after all the salads she had consumed lately.

"No," Mrs Brown agreed.

Gem met the other woman's eyes. "You're going on 'holiday' then, aren't you?"

Mrs Brown nodded slowly. "Yes."

"A tad late in the season for gardening items."

"Yes."

"I am to contact Mr Cawley or Mr Choate with queries or other issues."

"Yes."

Charley appeared with his Agency famous cheesecake and after refreshing their beverages, disappeared again into his kitchen. When they were alone again, Gem broached the question that had been nagging her.

"Mrs Brown," she began tentatively, then struck with a full blade. "Where was Paul Andriani on 29 and 30 May?" she said, her eyes steadily meeting those of her supervisor.

Mrs Brown wiped the corners of her mouth with her serviette, then set it on the table. "My dear," she tsked-tsked, "you know I can't give you that information."

Gem dragged her fingers through her hair. "I know," she conceded. "I had to ask."

"I understand," Mrs Brown replied, her fork poised above the luscious dessert. "My dear," she said pensively, "have you ever been to Hong Kong?"

"No, ma'am," Gem replied with a shake of her head. Then she looked at the other woman who held her eyes with a steady gaze. "No indeed, ma'am," she repeated.

"Enjoy your dessert, my dear," Mrs Brown smiled pleasantly.

Paul Andriani had been in Hong Kong that horrid night! He had been in South East Asia. Much to think about!

"How long will you be on holiday?" Gem asked.

Mrs Brown grimaced. "A matter of weeks perhaps."

"Will you be in contact with Mr Cawley or Mr Choate?"

"Possibly."

"Sounds intriguing," Gem said thoughtfully.

"When isn't our work intriguing?" Mrs Brown chuckled candidly.

"So true," Gem agreed. "I suppose when one does the job day in, day out, it simply becomes a regular job. But it is rather an unusual career - wrapped in a veil of normalcy."

"Indeed. And it is never dull, is it, my dear?"

Gem shook her head. And although she was no longer in the field, her connection to the agency assured her that her life was still not dull. "When do you leave?"

Mrs Brown looked at her watch. "Two hours' time. Is there anything else you need to discuss?"

Gem shook her head. Other queries could be put to Mr Choate during the day or to Mr Cawley during the dark hours. "No, ma'am."

"Very well. Now remember, my dear, what I said about having a chat with Wyatt. He would be a great comfort to you." Mrs Brown picked up her hand bag and stood, preparing to leave.

"It's not SOP," Gem refused to consider the suggestion.

"It is not. But he has no idea the tragedy you suffered, the pain you have been enduring the past months. He has also suffered a great loss recently. He will understand your pain better than others could," Mrs Brown said sympathetically. "You must have planned to tell him something when the Pilos is found," she looked curiously at Gem.

"Yes," Gem nodded, "but – oh - it's such a mess right now, ma'am." Wyatt's loss was precisely why Wyatt would NOT understand her pain. The truth of the Pilos would only cause Wyatt's pain to deepen, and his fury to increase.

"Indeed it is. I can't recall such a domino effect or crises in the history of the Agency, or B.I., for that matter. But it isn't fair to you to have such a cloud hanging about you, sorrow you can't share with your husband. These are extraordinarily unusual circumstances for you. And Wyatt is an extremely unusual man. We can trust him."

Not truly. He is extremely unusual. And extremely devious. I do NOT trust him, Gem thought in a flash. Comfort would be the last emotion Wyatt would extend to her.

"Please consider my suggestions, my dear. You have my permission to share the information - but only with Wyatt."

"Yes, ma'am, thank you," Gem said dutifully.

After Gem parted from her supervisor she stopped at her favourite dress shop, hoping to find skirts with elastic bands; she found three in her size and with Eda's assistance selected fabric for four more which Ora would have ready for her in a week's time.

Gem cleared her mind, then drove to Ticking Bottom. She was very weary, yet determined to clean the windows in the master suite. Wyatt could wash those in his dressing room and bathroom. Mrs Mac assisted Gem with the project, watching the cleaning chore with a practised cat eye.

When the task was complete, Gem sought Auntie Jane's settee, taking a glass of warm water and three books to read as a cover device so that her thoughts could drift to Agency business. Mrs M offered to make her a cup of tea or hot chocolate, but Gem declined, instead heeding her physician's advice.

Mrs Mac curled on Gem's feet, appropriately - as Gem opened a book about cats - and promptly became caught up in her lunch discussion with Mrs Brown.

Paul Andriani had been in Hong Kong that fateful night. Mrs Brown and Harry had been in Sydney. It was possible that Paul Andriani had said he was in Hong Kong, but he had been undercover - so who could confirm his words as fact? Actually, it would have been a rare occasion if his whereabouts had been or could have been confirmed. Bless Mrs Brown for breaking an iron-clad Agency rule to give Gem the information, but she would not accept it as fact. And why had Mrs Brown violated another Agency rule for her?

Paul could have travelled undercover to Brisbane from Hong Kong. He could easily access the private airport without calling any attention to himself. And Gem just knew that Paul Andriani was aware of the location of the private airstrip. Paul had passports under various assumed names, unknown even to Harry and Mrs Brown. Paul Andriani wrote his own ticket with the Agency - he had to for his own security. And precisely because of that 'ticket' he could currently be anywhere: South America, Russia, the States, Barcelona.

Gem had always believed Paul Andriani was completely loyal to the Agency - to Family. It would be difficult to question that loyalty. Honestly! Would James Bond turn traitor? Never!

John Staunton, black marketeer, was a notorious ladies' man. But was Paul Andriani? Had the warmth in his voice when he spoke to Gemmy hidden a secret passion for her? Gem had no idea the answer to that question. She was no judge of men was she! That had been made crystal clear to her when she had fallen victim to Wyatt's charms.

Paul Andriani was the perfect suspect as a mole in the SEA Network - and the Agency. He could travel at will, no one ever knew his location, unless he provided that information. He could be John Staunton one moment, God only knew who else the next moment. He had met Gemmy in Barcelona. He could have met her in Geneva unbeknownst to anyone save Paul and Gemmy.

And no one knew where the HELL he currently was! Just disappear and not be accountable to anyone regarding your location!

Now that was Power!

How did he have access to funds? Credit cards? A secret bank account? Well obviously! And wasn't that just handy! How much money had John Staunton had in banks around the world? An I.D. code, password, and unlimited access to his funds - no doubt untraceable bank accounts. What a clever man!

Enough thinking. She would let the thoughts ferment unattended in her brain, and see what the process produced later.

Gem set aside the book and studied the cat at her feet. Mrs Mac was striking! The unbelievably long fur, the thick mane encircling her neck, the long, exquisitely beautiful, bushy tail. She slipped off the settee, trying not to disturb the dozing feline, and fetched her camera. Of course her movement wakened the cat and Mrs Mac stretch languidly, veritably posing for Gem, before jumping down to the floor to stretch full length on her back, again posing.

"You are quite the show off," Gem laughed, following the cat, snapping shot after shot as Mrs Mac leaped to the counter, snapping shots until a roll of film was finished. "You certainly must be framed," Gem declared.

Gem finally set the camera aside and turned her attention to the next cathedral. Durham Cathedral with its smashing nave, and the astonishing drum columns; the arches, the vaults, the flying buttresses. Staggeringly inspiring! Medieval genius! It certainly put to shame vulgar, modern glass and steel structures.

Her snaps were excellent but could any photo ever do justice to the beauty of the ages?

No, Gem decided, but she had tried her best. She used a black marker to indicate crop lines which also gave her the idea of how the photos would look in black frames - if she decided to add to her wall art. Her detail drawings were finished to her approval. The text did not yet exist, however she had twenty pages of notes of dimensions and historical material. Simply looking at the photos of Durham was inspiring.

She worked carefully, adjusting crop lines minutely. Music would be a pleasant addition to her work but Mrs M had the telly in the kitchen at a high volume as she routed out pans and pots from the cupboard. If an interview on a chat show or a favourite news reader was on air, the housekeeper sometimes increased the volume; the more her interest, the higher the volume. Gem chuckled at the other woman's viewing habits, keeping her ear trained for any interesting news alerts.

"Do you realize you just marked ink streaks all over your forehead?" Wyatt chuckled as he entered her office.

Gem grabbed a tissue and rubbed at her skin." Makes my day just perfect," she muttered. "What is this?" she demanded, at the black ink smudged on her fingers.

"Leaking pen," Wyatt said calmly. "Here let me." He dipped a tissue in her water glass and gently wiped her forehead. "Bad day?"

"Fascinating," Gem looked up, trying to watch his fingers as he carefully brushed aside her fringe. She caught herself before she said something she shouldn't. His touch made her ache for him. She shook off the feeling as best she could. "Errands. Lunch with Mrs Brown."

Wyatt turned his ministrations to her fingers. "Sound a horrible day," he teased, tossing ruined tissues and wetting clean ones.

"Not really," Gem sighed. "I was simply irritated with the ink."

"Understandably so," he murmured. "Lord, my dear, you have lovely skin."

"Result of wearing damned hats," she muttered.

"A bit grumpy are you then?"

"No," Gem protested. She wished dinner could be put back. Butterflies were swarming.

"Did Mrs Brown tell you how lovely you look?"

"You mean haggard?" she replied edgily, her tone reacting to his question and his touch.

"Not quite that," he said smoothly.

"I am too tired to argue with you," Gem sighed wearily, fatigue stealing into her muscles.

"I don't recall asking you to argue with me. So don't," Wyatt ordered. He tossed the last wad of sodden tissues, then reached for more to dry her fingers.

"Mrs Brown has a high opinion of you." Gem was captivated by his gentle touch.

"Has she?" he glanced to her face, watching her watching him.

"But of course she doesn't know the real you," she said, her tone turning crisp. He tossed the tissues and stroked her fingers with his.

"Ouch," he replied wryly. "Your verbal foreplay is certainly beginning early this evening."

"What!" his words shocked her. Gem blushed furiously. "Foreplay!"

"You are either choking or speechless. I think speechless," he grinned. "Another amusing battle this evening then?" He gently squeezed her fingers. "Best wash off the ink residue so it doesn't irritate your skin," he advised.

Dinner began pleasantly enough, but quickly deteriorated, beginning with one query from Wyatt.

"Would you like to make alterations to the dining room?" he asked as Gem sliced the steak Mrs M had beautiful grilled.

"Why?" she replied, puzzled by the query.

"To suit your taste. The dining room hasn't been refurbished in twenty years," he countered.

"I am not an interior designer," Gem shied away from the subject.

"You are an artist," he suggested.

"That doesn't qualify me to design a dining room," she frowned.

"You decorated the Barcelona flat."

Blast! Gemmy 'just threw things together' - her words - stain glass effect - colour, colour, colour. A great difference from studying the structure and history of cathedrals. And Gem went for comfort always, and style - well, that wasn't her interest.

"James was the artist," she protested, then wished she could bite her tongue to retract the remark.

Wyatt studied her as the discussion progressed.

"But you made the flat a home," he countered, watching her eyes as they clouded to the haunted look.

Gem set down her fork and knife. What was the purpose of this conversation? She did not want to draw swords this evening against Dr Jekyll.

"Don't hare off," he said firmly. "Eat your dinner." He lowered his gaze. "I merely thought you might like to have the walls a different colour - lighter - darker - a different style of furniture. The attic is full of it. Or perhaps you would prefer to consult a professional designer. This is not a major issue, my dear, merely a query."

Gem darted glances at him while he ate. She didn't leave the table. Perhaps his query was innocuous. Mrs M had also suggested Gem might wish to make changes at the Hall. Mrs M had put the suggestion to Wyatt since Gem had not been interested in the subject, she decided.

"We don't use the dining room. Why make changes?"

"Would the room suit you for entertaining - perhaps a dinner party?" He was surprised that she didn't seem eager to do such a project.

"Whom do you wish to entertain?" Gem asked, puzzled. She had met a few members of the GEI London office staff. She had met locals at the pub. But she had never met Mr Manton or any of his friends, or family members, if any other family still existed.

"In theory," he suppressed a frown. Whom do you wish to entertain? No reference to a suggestion that she would wish to have a dinner party, to invite friends for a social evening.

Mrs M had said that Mrs Grantham needed a friend. Had Gem friends, other than Mrs Brown? Choate had not indicated in reports that Gem had met anyone other than the one woman for lunch or tea - or the visit to the camera shop.

She was twenty-four years old. In all those short years she must have had other friends - but none currently other than Mrs Brown? Or John Staunton? Did she have no family? Wyatt could find no trace of any. How could a person be so alone?

"In theory, I feel the dining room is fine for entertaining," Gem shrugged.

"Adequate?" Wyatt suggested, suddenly teasing.

The paint colour in her office was adequate to him. She liked the colour. "Indeed," she smiled briefly. "Adequate."

Gem had rested after dinner - at Wyatt's insistence again, he had done the washing up; she had spent time in her office in the comfy chair, and then she had gone to bed. She was sleeping longer before the dark hours, yet she was desperately exhausted.

Mrs Mac had followed Gem down to the office. To the right of her computer was a thermos and a cup. She removed the thermos cap - hot chocolate. Gem filled the cup, wondering again what was Wyatt's ploy?

Where was Mrs Brown? Meeting Harry? Or - perhaps Paul Andriani? Meeting with the director of the SEA Network ? Which should be Harry, but was not now. Or was Mrs Brown on an unrelated mission?

Mr Cawley would be awake, she mused, studying the liquid in the cup. She was virtually certain Wyatt had not sprinkled arsenic into the thermos. It would be too obvious: a thermos or cup and arsenic; no matter how thoroughly washed, traces of the poison would likely remain. She sipped the beverage without trepidation; it was still very hot and very good. She sighed and pushed the start button on the cd player.

Ping.
'Classic car show tomorrow, Northampton.'
'Yes. Will be there. You?'
'Yes. Critchley will have Silver Dawn. Choate going with you?'
'No.'
'Will be circumspect then.'
'Yes. Word of Harry or Blank?'
'No. Sorting?'
'In fits and starts.'
'What do you have to share?'
'A weary brain.'
'Not good enough.'
'I'm trying!'
'Try harder!'
'Stop pushing!'
'Start putting your brain to good use then!'
'I will!'
'Tomorrow then. Goodnight.'
'Goodnight.'

Mr Cawley pushing was frustrating. Did he expect her to pull a solution from thin air? She didn't have all the information. She didn't have all the facts. How was she supposed to reach a solution that escaped everyone else at the Agency?

Gemmy! Where are you?
I can't do this any longer.

But she had to - or Wyatt would win. And she was NOT going to spend the remainder of her life with that man! Not even with Mr Hyde - and certainly not with Dr Jekyll!

And why the HELL should she care about the dining room? It was his house - not hers! If he wanted changes made, he could jolly well hire a designer and do the house up just the way he wished it to be.

Another cup of hot chocolate, but no pacing. Mrs Mac however did a bit of it. And leaping - up and down, pussyfooting across the back of the settee, across the back of the comfy chair, across the counter, the desk, then the feline eyed the hanging ceiling lights.

"Don't even think it," Gem hastily warned.

The fixtures were sturdily made, but how ever would she retrieve Mrs Mac from that height without waking the Dark Lord?

Mrs Mac finally curled into a ball on top of the printer. To sleep so easily, anywhere, Gem mused. What a gift!

Paul Andriani. Her thoughts constantly returned to him. Paul Andriani and Gemmy in Barcelona. Was Gemmy in Geneva because of him? She could only learn about Geneva by talking to Paul and she couldn't talk to him until he surfaced. If he ever did. If some agents went underground 'forever', it was possible Paul Andriani would be one of them. If he didn't return it could be considered an admission of guilt - Gemmy, the Pilos the murdered counter-couriers and agents. And if he didn't return, without information only he might have - would the Agency ever be able to solve this mystery? Very possibly not.

What did Mr Cawley think she could do? Solve a mystery without all the information - all the facts? She repeated the query, and shook her head wearily.

She finished the hot chocolate, washed the thermos and cup, and turned off the cd player. "Let's go to bed, shall we, Mrs Mac?" Gem issued the invitation. In a matter of a few days, the feline had decided her choice sleeping spot was stretched out alongside Gem. Wyatt on her right, cat on her left, Gem was quite boxed in as she slept.

Mrs Mac was a voyeur! She was also more curious that Wyatt appreciated her being, especially when she decided to put a paw or two in at an inappropriate time.

"She needs her claws clipped," Wyatt groaned as he grabbed his dressing gown.

"It's only one scratch," Gem tried to squelch a smile. "Although it does run all the way down your back. Best clean it with antiseptic," she suggested.

"And how do you suggest I manage that?" he demanded.

"Your hands are very talented when you wish them to be - for your advantage," Gem said flippantly.

"And when you wish them to be - which is - daily," Wyatt retorted bluntly.

Gem blushed, but she managed to feign a weary sigh. "I'll get the bottle and cotton wool. You'll have to expect scratches now and then when you have a cat," she firmly warned.

"Well that was the worst timing I can imagine," Wyatt grunted, as Gem gently applied the antiseptic to the wound. "You could kiss it and make it better," he suggested.

"None of that now. You must learn some self-control," she insisted.

"Not bloody likely! It's Saturday and we have all day," he reached behind him to grab her, but Gem neatly backed out of his reach.

"Car show today," Gem crisply reminded him.

"You'd rather go to a car show than spend the day in bed with me?" he demanded.

"Naturally," Gem retorted, pressing the saturated cotton wool along the quite deep scratch.

"Ouch!"

Gem jerked her hand away. "Did I hurt you?"

"Just my ego. Your words stung."

"Is that all? Then you're done," she said pertly. "I'm for a quick shower."

"Excellent idea. I'll wash your back for you !"

"Alone," she firmly insisted.

The shower was quick but then she decided to wash and dry her hair. She pulled on a denim skirt and couldn't decide on a jumper. Ah! The blue twin-set had been Gemmy's favourite, and Gem had never worn it before.

She had taken so long in the bathroom, Wyatt had cooked and served breakfast by the time she reached the kitchen. As Gem reached for her tea cup she saw Wyatt glaring at her.

"What?" she asked, startled by his harsh look.

"I should think you would get rid of that twin-set," he said caustically.

Gem looked at the sweater set. "What is wrong with it?" she queried, confused.

"It's the set you are wearing in the photos."

"Blast!" Gem groaned. Gemmy's favourite set. "Excuse me," she said quietly, and walked quickly from the kitchen to hurry down the hall and up the staircase. Blast! Blast! Blast! Her face flamed with embarrassment. The faux pas would probably land her at the mercy of Dr Jekyll for the entire day - without any relief from Mr Hyde. She pushed the twin-set to the back of a drawer in her dressing room. She refused to put it in the rubbish bin. One day she would wear it again - when her life was once again hers.

She pulled a white turtleneck sweater over her head and slipped on a pumpkin coloured jumper, smoothed her hair and went down the stairs to breakfast. She counted to twenty over and over until she entered the kitchen. When she sat at the island, Wyatt refreshed her tea.

"If your food is cold, I'll heat it a bit in the cooker," he said, his voice quiet, and there was still an edge to it.

Gem took a bite of the eggs; they could stand a bit of warming but she didn't want to waste a moment longer than necessary with him over breakfast. "It's fine, thank you," she said politely. "I apologize for wearing the twin set."

"You didn't recall that you wore it that day," he said with a stiff nod.

"I don't recall what I wore yesterday," she said honestly; her words drew a faint smile to his lips. "But you wore a black suit," she ventured a smile.

"A wild guess?" His smile grew a bit wider.

"Yes," Gem replied, still smiling. He always wore a black suit. And yesterday he had worn a smashing white shirt with a faint pearl strip; and a grey tie so dark it was nearly black. And he had looked so handsome!

Wyatt's mood improved. He managed the washing up while Gem braided her hair, fetched her camera, and a denim jacket; the jacket was at Wyatt's suggestion as the temperature might be slow to warm that day. Gem left the shade up in the office so that Mrs Mac could look out the windows to watch for birds.

"Be a good kitty while we are away," Wyatt tickled the cat's ears. "No wild parties," he added as if in afterthought, drawing a chuckle from Gem.

He could be fun, she had to admit.

"Are you managing to keep up with reading all your reports?" Gem queried as he steered the Jag down the cobblestone lane.

He nodded. "Ms Holton is taking a few of the thinner ones home with her to read on weekends. They usually are returned to the office stained with marmalade."

"Does that irritate you?"

"Not in the least," he said easily, slowing down so as not to crunch locals as they drove past the Yellow Crow.

"Ms Holton is ambitious, isn't she?" Gem observed.

"Indeed."

"Is she a barracuda?" Gem thought of Mr Choate's description of Wyatt.

Wyatt glanced from the road to her. "Do you think she's a barracuda?" he was surprised at the question.

Gem reflected on his query. "No," she finally replied. "I think she simply thrives on challenge."

Wyatt nodded acceptance of her remark. "Am I a barracuda?" he queried, shifting, smoothly changing lanes.

"Yes," Gem said firmly, voicing her own opinion as well as Mr Choate's. "By nature and by inclination for power," she stated her own personal thoughts.

"Indeed?" he replied, startled by the firmness of her words. "Your thoughts or Mrs Brown's?"

"Mine. Mrs Brown said you are of the world of grit and reality," Gem replied honestly. She saw no reason not to repeat the wiser woman's remarks. Mrs Brown had not indicated Gem should not repeat her comments to Wyatt.

"And how did Mrs Brown describe the world you are of?" Wyatt asked smoothly, realizing she was in an unusually relaxed, chatty mood.

"The world of Jane Austen," Gem replied without thinking.

Jane Austen? More likely Mata Hari! How could Mrs Brown confuse the two? She obviously didn't know Gem very well. Or she didn't choose her friends wisely. But he wanted information from Gem, and perhaps he would get some today.

He reached a hand over to gently tug her braid. "What do you call this braid?" he asked.

"French braid."

"It's very becoming," Wyatt complimented. "James loved to watch you braid your hair. He said you elevated the dexterity of effort to an art form."

Gem sighed inwardly, wary of the direction of the conversation. At least she could match Gemmy strand for strand on braiding.

"Your hair is very sexy when you release it from a braid."

"Ah," Gem replied, unsure how to reply to the remark. "Your words, or James's?" She could have bit her tongue for not biting her tongue!

"Mine. And your hair is very sexy in an intricate design created by the same fingers that -" he didn't finish the remark.

"Is there a point to this discussion?" Gem said a touch coolly, blushing as she spoke.

Wyatt chuckled. "I'm attempting to correlate how sexy you are with a Jane Austen world. Jane Austen," he held out his left hand. "Bloody Mary," he held out his right hand.

"Mr Critchley would cite you for careless driving," Gem observed dryly, ignoring his remarks.

"He had Ms Jones terrified," Wyatt shifted the subject, "until you had a chat with her," he said pointedly.

Gem suppressed a smile. "Really? How interesting," she said, not deigning to offer words to explain Ms Jones's change in attitude towardss the defensive driving instructor.

"What did you say to her?" Wyatt asked bluntly.

"You missed the turn," Gem smiled to herself. "Girl chat," was all she would reply to his query. "You're speeding," she grinned.

Wyatt eased up on the pedal. "What was the first vehicle you drove?" he glanced at his mirrors, and Gem smiled again to herself.

"Land Rover. They're virtually indestructible," Gem replied. "You? Bet not the Jag."

"Land Rover also. It seemed indestructible at the time."

Gem turned to stare at him. "You wrote off a Land Rover?"

"Not entirely," he cleared his throat." I did learn that not all Land Rovers are swimmers. Didn't James tell you the tale?" he glanced at her. "It was one of his favourites."

How much time had James had to talk that last night? She simply had to take the chance. "No."

"No, he didn't mention me did he?" Wyatt confirmed and Gem flashed back to Wight. James hadn't mentioned his family to Gemmy. He wanted his anonymity until they planned their wedding.

"You missed another turn. Are we going to Northampton?" she giggled.

"Do you wish to drive?" Wyatt chuckled, teasing. "You distract me!"

You're trying to entrap me! she mused confidently. "You'll manage, sooner or later," she ventured. "Or later than sooner. Or just late. I imagine the car show also runs tomorrow."

"I take you for a relaxing morning drive and I get sass!"

"I didn't know I needed luggage for a drive to Northampton."

"You drive then."

"You'll get a ticket if you pull over here!" Gem laughed.

When they finally arrived at the car show, Gem was astonished at the scene that met her eyes. Classic cars, stretching nearly to the horizon, filled the meadow. Banners announcing the models flapped in the wind, enabling the visitors to immediately locate the vehicle section of their dreams.

"Don't wander off now," Wyatt ordered as he took a straw hat from the boot and plopped it on her head. "White cloud day."

"But it's November," she feebly protested.

"It's still daylight," he refused to listen to her protest.

Gem decided there was no point in arguing the issue. She looked at the banners, finally spotting the flag for Rolls Royce at the far end of the meadow. They walked past the banners of Mercedes - a half dozen models ranging from a 1957 300SL roadster to a smashing 1955 300SL gullwing coupe; then past Ferraris - and a brilliant 166 Inter; past a 1948 and a 1955 Porsche 356.

Wyatt stopped to look at a 1953 MGTF Midget, and Gem pointed to a 1950 MGTD Midget.

"I don't think you could get into either of those," Gem laughed.

"I might get in but I would never survive climbing out," Wyatt chuckled.

The vehicles stretched on and on, a 1930 Duesenberg, a 1929 Cord, a white 1932 Auburn speedster alongside a red 1935 Auburn Phaeton Sedan.

"Dream cars," Gem sighed breathlessly, as they passed over a dozen Jags and some twenty Bentleys, Triumphs, Alpha Romeos. A Spider and a Spider Junior were parked side by side, drawing a huge crowd of petrol heads.

"I can't believe there are so many cars here," Gem gasped.

"A lead-in to the show in Birmingham later this month," Wyatt replied.

"And all the proud owners!" Gem breathlessly admired the vehicles. "I've never seen a Sunbeam Tiger before. What's the year?"

Wyatt read the detail card on the windscreen. "1966." A 1935 Sunbeam was just beyond the Tiger.

"Spectacular," Gem murmured, wandering along, speechless until she gasped again. "Look! A 1919 Silver Ghost!" she whispered.

"How do you know the model and the year?" Wyatt asked in surprise.

"I read a book once about Rolls Royce models. 1955 Silver Cloud," she nodded to her left, "1949 Silver Dawn and Mr Critchley with his 1951 Silver Dawn," she held up a hand to wave to Agency Family.

Critchley, chatting with another couple, joined them a few minutes later, shaking hands with Wyatt, and tipping his fedora to Gem with a respectful "Ma'am." Gem shook hands with him.

"A pleasure to see you again, Mr Critchley. Your Silver Dawn is brilliant! How many years has it owned you?"

"Twenty-eight," a voice piped up from behind the Silver Dawn's owner.

"A wedding gift from my bride," Critchley introduced his wife, Abby, to the Granthams.

Wyatt whistled, "That's what I call a gift!"

Abby wandered off then to chat with another couple viewing the Rolls, and Gem started asking the defensive driving instructor about his vehicle, starting with the bonnet. As they began discussing the engine, Wyatt stepped back, surveying the field of vehicles from afar. When he looked back at the Silver Dawn, Choate had joined the discussion beneath the bonnet and the threesome moved to the driver's side of the vehicle.

Abby Critchley walked over to join Wyatt. "I am chatted out," she sighed. "Classic car owners are a lot unto themselves," she said wearily. "He can go on forever."

Gem moved to her left as another person joined their small enclave at the Rolls boot.

"Ed Cawley," he introduced himself, shaking hands with Gem and the two men. "Staggering car," he admired.

"You should see the interior," Gem eagerly suggested. "Absolutely elegant!"

"Did you see the Simka?" Cawley interjected.

"A death trap," Critchley pronounced crisply. "Think of driving in London rush hour in that bit of metal!"

"Did you see the Morgans? I'd like that '36 open tourer," Choate marvelled. "Can you imagine putting out the money for one of those?"

"I like the '52 Morgan Plus four, and the '53 MGTF Midget," Gem sighed.

"Rougher ride than this Rolls," Critchley countered. "Did you see the 1964 ½ Ford Mustang? Everything original! And the '68 Charger?"

"Trade either for your Rolls?" Gem teased.

Critchley shillyshallied on that query.

Abby observed the small group. "Mrs Grantham seems very interested in classic cars," she ventured to Wyatt.

"She has a '90 Defender," he said smoothly. "She appreciates the historical side of many subjects."

Wyatt watched Gem chatting about the Silver Dawn and the other classic models around them. There was sparkle in her eyes, and she chatted and laughed easily. There was not a single bit of the reserve he had seen in her since the day he had met her. As Critchley pointed to the far end of the field, Gem craned her neck to look where he indicated and Wyatt saw that she absolutely glowed. The spirit James had mentioned.

"I do not get the obsession," Abby Critchley said helplessly. "It's some kind of magic, I suppose," she shrugged.

"Indeed," Wyatt nodded firmly. Magic. That joi de vivre. Vivacious. Animated.

The small group wandered over to the '55 Silver Cloud, their heads turning as the two owners chatted and pointed to specific aspects of each vehicle, but Wyatt remained apart from them, watching his wife. At the Hall with the M's, at the Crow, wherever he had been with her over the past three months he had not seen Gem as he saw her now.

This was the Gem with whom James had fallen in love.

Apparently being surrounded by men ignited a spark within her. This was the woman he had seen in the photos with John Staunton.

Abby Critchley walked to her husband's side, he looked down at her, smiled, and put his arm around her shoulders.

Wyatt doubted that Critchley would succumb to Gem's wiles as easily as had James. Yet older men could turn themselves into fools over a beautiful woman. Choate? Highly unlikely. He was safe from Gem. The other man who had joined the group? He was wearing a wedding ring. Did Gem target married men? None of the three men seemed affluent enough to capture the interest of a man-eater.

Choate had been a perfect solution to keeping tabs on Gem - and for her protection. Yet she was completely lacking of concern for her own safety. She couldn't be less concerned for her safety, in fact.

And she hadn't mentioned the photos since their wedding night. He had - and the passports, but she had not. Apparently she was convinced she could not gain access to them. Which she could not.

And despite many dust-ups between them, Gem was not violating the terms Wyatt had set of their relationship. When he had spoken of the twin-set that morning she had immediately changed her clothing - and had voiced an apology to him for her first choice of jumpers.

Yet she hadn't settled into their marriage. She seemed to live each day as if their relationship was but a temporary one. For some reason, in her mind, she believed there was a way out for her.

John Staunton? Was she in contact with him? Staunton had his underground network. Wyatt had his own. And there were no hot spots on Wyatt's network radar influenced by Staunton. In fact, in some circles it was thought that Staunton had disappeared - or had been eliminated, the latter being the most likely situation. Wyatt's network had only been able to produce one photo of the man - taken three years earlier. Wyatt had a dozen recent photos of Staunton. Gem knew, but also must now be convinced she couldn't obtain them. She had searched the Hall at least twice, to his knowledge, but there was nothing at Grantham Hall that she would be able to obtain for her use - even with explosives.

She wasn't worried for her safety - or being hunted. She was doing the hunting - no - she was searching.

Was she searching for Staunton? She had been searching for something since she moved into Grantham Hall. And likely before that. Had the search to do with the passport he had found in James's flat? Or the one stamped Geneva? Had she met Staunton there?

'If I could give it to you, I would gladly' - or some words to that effect. The whereabouts of the passport had obviously concerned her as much as discovering its existence had infuriated him. Gemma Lawson. A person who did not exist. Was Gem concerned the existence of the third passport would come back to haunt her?

Was it possible - without involving the government to trace the use of a passport? It was a matter too delicate to involve Choate's agency. Too delicate to involve the computer wonk at GEI. Hacking airline files…There were lines even he couldn't cross.

Wyatt gazed at Gem, chattering, laughing, as if she had walked out of a dark cloud into brilliant sunshine.

She accused him of controlling her; the GPS, Choate; yet he truly controlled very little of her life. He controlled what he intended to control: her ability to destroy another person's life, and he would not permit a divorce. Very little control actually. Divorce. An interesting concept…Was it a thought? It would easily enough be accomplished, if he wished to end the relationship.

The reason for the alias, the search. He could only obtain the information he sought from one source: Gem. And she was silent as stone of her past; of herself.

Yet, there were ways…to breach her cloak of anonymity. It would not be easy. So far he had failed. She hated him. She distrusted him. That would have to change.

A take-over. He had heretofore never lost a take-over fight. He would not lose this one. He had to redouble his effort of the allusion of concern and interest in her; he would have to rearrange his schedule to spend more time with her. Events such as today's were an acceptable way to share her company without having to spend a great deal of time alone with her. He wasn't, however, adverse to spending more time with her between the sheets; that was the only time he didn't have to feign interest in her.

And whatever happened in the future would depend on knowledge he gained of her.

For now, it was back to work. He had won her heart once. He would do so again.

Choate gave a salute to Wyatt, which he acknowledged with a nod and a brief smile. The other man wandered off as did Choate. Wyatt walked slowly to Gem who was listening to Critchley as he spoke to a couple of Rolls enthusiasts.

GEM

"Might I entice you away for lunch?" he murmured to Gem. "You must be a bit peckish. It's been hours since breakfast."

"Yes," she grinned. "Decidedly peckish."

"Shall we stop at the food tent first? If there's nothing there that appeals to you, we'll find a pub somewhere. Or shall we start at a pub?" he smiled.

"The food tent should be fine."

Wyatt again shook hands with the Critchleys, as did Gem, then he slipped his arm around her shoulders to guide her through the crowds.

"Are you chilly, my dear?"

"No," Gem shook her head.

"Food tent, ahead and left," he grinned at her," smells like burgers and chips. How does that sound to you?"

"A definite yes," Gem agreed.

Gem sat in Auntie Jane's comfy chair, cat on her lap, cup of hot chocolate in her hand, cd playing. There had not been a thermos of hot chocolate waiting for her. The dark hours were a bit brighter this morning. She relaxed just thinking of the day at the car show. It had been smashing to spend time with Agency Family. Of course no business could have been discussed, but it was sheer joy to be with familiar faces, people who knew her and cared about her. And she now knew a great deal about the Rolls called Silver Dawn and Silver Cloud.

Lunch had been a great time. Without referring to his brother, Wyatt had explained how he had learned while on a fishing trip with friends that some Land Rovers cannot swim.

"Speed was definitely a factor," Wyatt had admitted ruefully, "speed, a sharp curve, and stupidity," he had winced.

"A very bad day for you," Gem had grinned.

"The vehicle could probably have managed the water, if not for the boulders at the bottom of the lake."

"Were you injured?" she had asked concerned.

"No."

"Very fortunate for you!"

"Those were my mother's words."

"And your father?" she had asked gingerly. This was the first time he had every mentioned his mother.

"'Thank God you weren't hurt. No Jag for you until you're twenty-one'," Wyatt had chuckled, shaking his head. "It was supposed to be mine on my eighteenth birthday."

"Ouch! - Still, a classic Jag at twenty-one! Not too painful," she had grinned.

"Waiting the three years was a lesson," Wyatt had nodded. Then he grinned, admitting, "It was a very painful lesson."

"You still speed," Gem had reminded him.

"Not as much as I once did."

"You're impatient."

"I am actually working on that," Wyatt had replied. "Progress is slow, you may have noticed."

"Mmm," Gem hadn't been able to think of a polite reply. One poorly chosen word and Mr Hyde would have become Dr Jekyll.

"Not an unexpected reply," Wyatt had chuckled softly. "More hot chocolate?" Gem had declined. "Tea then?"

"No, thank you."

They had spent an additional three hours looking at the classic cars, talking to the owners, until Wyatt had decided Gem looked exhausted.

"Tea and then home," he had insisted firmly.

He had prepared dinner, insisting she rest for an hour. "Read, watch the telly, just rest," he had ordered. And she had. And after dinner he had insisted she go immediately to bed. She had been distracted for a while by Elizabeth Bennett and Mr Darcy. She would have traded Wyatt for Mr Darcy in an instant. Wyatt would have liked Lizzie; she hadn't killed his brother.

Would the dark hours ever end? Not if she continued flailing at jumbled masses of information.

She knew there had been at least one traitor in B.I. - Kim Philby, who had defected to Moscow in the '60's. B.I. was one matter. People knew B.I. existed. Philby's defection had been known by the public. The Agency was a non-existent government department. A traitor or mole or sleeper, had there been one, and was routed out, would be an Agency secret. Definitely a query to put to Mr Choate.

Ping

'Good show!'

'Good grief! Lots of cars!'

'Did you buy a Morgan?'

'Wishful thinking! You?'

'On my salary? Good one! Are you working?'

'Yes.'

'Then stop texting! Goodnight!'

'Goodnight!'

Gem deleted the messages.

A mole. Actually it was an absurd idea. Mr Portermann was no novice at his profession. Mr Choate had detailed to her the Agency's rigorous investigation of applicants. But it could be in the SEA Network: counter-couriers and agents. That was the most logical place. She would have to have a chat with Mr Choate on Monday.

Gem dragged her fingers through her hair. Paul Andriani. It always came back to him.

Gem heard a tapping. "What?" she looked up. Wyatt, a knit throw across his arms, had knocked on the doorjamb.

"I was concerned that you might be chilly down here," he said, handing the throw to her.

"Thank you," she replied startled, of the gesture, and that he was again awake at this hour.

"Do you need another electric fire - or larger ones?"

"No. These are quite -"

"Adequate?" he interrupted with a grin.

"Quite - helpful," Gem smiled.

"Okay. Shall I make you a cup of hot chocolate before I go up? I forgot the thermos earlier," he admitted.

"I thought I would make a cup of tea," Gem started to get out of the chair.

"Sit," he waved her back down. "I'll get it for you." As he left the room he pushed the start button on the cd player.

Gem shook her head, puzzled. It had been an odd Saturday, and Sunday was starting out the same way.

He brought her the tea, kissed her gently on her lips and went back upstairs to bed.

"Very odd indeed," Gem shook her head again.

Mr Hyde was on overtime apparently.

Paul Andriani. Blast! Where was that man? Perhaps Mr Choate would have information by Monday morning. And Mrs Brown. What was she up to? And Harry? The Agency was quickly diminishing in its ranks.

She would like to go back to work; save for being unable to fly, or cross large bodies of water - or being pregnant - oh - and being trapped by Dr Jekyll or Mr Hyde, depending on who was the warden of the day.

Sunday. He would be at the Hall all day. Perhaps he would spend the entire day reading in the library. She could work on Durham.

When was she going to tell him? How much longer could she put it off? He knew every - well he knew her body - and soon he might figure it out for himself. It was not a decision she would make right now.

Paul Andriani. Geneva. Barcelona. Mole.

Mrs Mac stretched and jumped down from her lap. Gem looked at her mobile. Quarter to five. Was Mrs Mac learning to tell time?

Chapter Twenty-Five

"There are times Mrs Mac cannot be in our bedroom," Wyatt pronounced firmly. "This is one of those times. She is too curious!"

Gem giggled. "She lived in a cottage with an elderly woman. I am sure there is much here to catch her interest."

"We'll get mice in for her to catch then." He scooped the cat from the bed, setting her on the floor. "Stay," he crisply ordered the feline.

"Dogs stay, cats don't listen," Gem grinned as Mrs Mac leaped onto the bed again.

"Damn!" Wyatt muttered, pulling the sheet over their heads. "How many dogs have you owned?"

"None. However I have seen them in parks," she murmured, just before he completely diverted her thoughts. "Well, apparently Mrs Mac didn't injure you - again," she teased.

"Hush, too much talking."

"What shall I prepare for your breakfast, my dear?" Wyatt queried much later.

"More like brunch," Gem murmured.

"A proper Sunday brunch then," he agreed.

"Semolina and tea," Gem shook her head. Breakfast was not currently her favourite meal of the day.

"So be it," he nodded. "Bacon?"

"Oh that sounds wonderful."

"Shall I serve you in bed?"

"You already did," she teased.

"Then you are most welcome."

Troubling thoughts returned to Gem as she showered, then increased as she dressed. She could barely button her jeans. This was not good! Exercise, watching her diet; she was still gaining weight too quickly. It likely was twins, as Dr Hallowell believed. She should be happy. But she wasn't. And she felt horrible that she wasn't happy. She knew Wyatt would use the pregnancy against her. How? She didn't know. But he would.

He had made semolina, toast, tea, and bacon for her. The food was tasty, but something was off.

"You're frowning. Is something wrong with your food, my dear?"

"I was just thinking," Gem murmured.

It was his attitude, his manner. She couldn't put her finger on what was bothering her, but it was definitely something about Wyatt.

"Cats or cathedrals?"

"Cathedrals," Gem fudged a reply.

"Is there a problem with your photos?" he frowned.

"No. I was thinking about the text."

"Are you having difficulty with the structure?"

Gem shook her head. "No. I was just composing, so to speak, in my mind."

He seemed to accept her explanation. "Tea, my dear?"

Gem shook her head again. "I'll do the washing up," she offered. "Thank you for preparing breakfast."

"My pleasure, my dear. I'll do the chores. I'm avoiding reports," he winked at her. "No arguments now, run along to your cathedral."

The words were slightly dismissive - as an adult might say to a child - and while there was a ten year difference in their ages, Gem was not a child. His words momentarily irritated her, but she brushed off the annoyance; there were too many important subjects to think about to focus on a casual remark.

Gem turned on the telly, keeping an ear to the international news while she waited for her computer to come to life. She left the computer, drawn to the telly by the news report of riots in Indonesia. Unrest was a fact of life in that area of the world. Still, it was unsettling to see the riots with the recent murders clouding the SEA Network. Also unsettling because it was very likely that Harry was in that area. And perhaps Mrs Brown. Heaven only knew the location of the ubiquitous and mysterious Paul Andriani.

Gem folded her arms as she studied the map on the telly of the major sections of unrest. There was film of entire neighbourhoods that had been set on fire, armed militia chasing rioters in the streets, the protesters pelting soldiers with whatever was at hand - rocks, bottles, bricks, it appeared. The SEA Network staff would be frightfully busy, couriers with messages being instantly rerouted; agents in the field would be trying to discover the leaders of the insurrection to advise the SEA Network Director of the most feasible means to diffuse further violence, and attempt negotiations between factions. It was a thankless, dangerous job that would only manage a shallow peace for a few months before other factions were spurred to additional violence. And the master underground agent had disappeared into thin air as opposed to simply hiding in it.

A hot spot, but one that always simmered just below the surface, to erupt, be quelled for a time, to again simmer, to again erupt. Not an extraordinary hot spot at this time. She dragged her fingers through her hair before crossing her arms again. The news reporters didn't have much information to add other than the count and names of the major cities involved, and the suspected group names of the insurrectionists. There were two groups involved this time whose names Gem did not recognize. Yes. Mrs Brown was at SEA Network HQ, meeting with that Director.

Gem shook her head, frowning, worrying of the fate of the agents in the field. This was the danger the Agency feared most: the unknown leaders of the new entities. Could they actually be reasoned with, or were the leaders fearless, brainwashed zealots with an intensity, and so complete a lack of regard for human life, that only their own deaths could bring some relative calm to the hot spots? And hopefully the death or deaths would not make martyrs of the leaders.

Wyatt watched her from the doorway. Indonesia. Again. The reference books. Now she was completely mesmerized by the newscast of the rioting in that area. Gemma Louisa Lawson's passport in his possession had been stamped Tokyo, as well as Australia, the States and a number of European countries. Gemimah Louisa Forrester's passport had never been stamped in any countries of South East Asia, but bore stamps of Australia. Combine the two passports, Gem had travelled extensively around the world, travelling to some countries - Australia, Greece, Europe, the States, actually much of the U.K., Scandinavian countries, on both passports. Neither passport had stamps in any city in China, or countries in South America. What stamps did the third passport bear other than Barcelona and Geneva?

Gem finally noticed him, and when she became aware of him, he handed her a cup of tea. He saw the haunted look in her eyes.

"Thank you," she said quietly, her gaze wandering back to the telly.

"I'll be in the great room reading," he murmured.

"Okay," she replied distractedly. And when the news reader moved on to the next story, she checked the computer for more information regarding the crisis in Indonesia. Perhaps Mr Cawley would have updated information by the time the dark hours arrived.

When there was no more current information to glean, she pulled up the Durham computer file, but her thoughts were only on the Agency and her staff Family.

Blast Paul Andriani for disappearing!

He was MADE. Mrs Brown had stated that reason for his disappearance. Was that the truth? Had whoever murdered the SEA counter- couriers and agents made Paul Andriani? Or had he disappeared because he was worried evidence would be discovered linking him to the murders? Or indicating he had in some way been involved with the killer - or killers?

Paul Andriani.

Her head started to ache. She needed fresh air. She shut down the computer, turned off the telly, and took the tea cup to the sink.

"Are you restless?" Wyatt queried behind her.

"I thought I would go for a walk."

"Do you mind company or would you rather be alone?"

How was she supposed to react to that query? She couldn't rudely state that she would rather not have him with her.

"Company would be very nice," she said politely, simply unable to think of a gracious way to refuse his suggestion of joining her.

They walked up the lane, past the dormant meadows and fields. The air was brisk, bracing, driving nagging thoughts from Gem's mind.

Wyatt didn't invite conversation and Gem didn't appear interested in chatting, which suited him perfectly. He concentrated on projecting the manner he had in August, suppressing the intense dislike he felt for her.

His mobile rang. "It's Ms Holton," he said to Gem. "I have to take this call."

"Go ahead," she nodded.

They continued walking and Gem watched the smoke curling from the chimney of a cottage in the distance. It appeared to be a working farm. Rather unusual, wasn't it, she thought, to have a working farm in a gated community?

She saw a 'hunter' walking at the edge of the meadow just outside the line of trees. From the gait and carriage of the 'hunter' she realized the person was a woman. She wondered if she had seen the woman at the Crow. A possibility. Would she have recognized her as a security officer? She was losing her touch reading. She was losing her Agency training.

"Yes? Really!" she heard Wyatt responding, clearly surprised by Ms Holton's side of the conversation. Gem watched him, curious at the smile that came to his lips. She tried not to listen to his words, but it was rather difficult not to hear what he was saying because Wyatt did not turn away or hang back for privacy.

"Have they met all the terms? Really!" His smile grew wider, as he listened. "Indeed! Then sell! The factory is theirs!"

He slipped his mobile into his pocket.

"You look very pleased," Gem observed.

"I am indeed pleased," Wyatt replied.

"You sold one of your factories?"

"I did. I sold it to the employees."

"For an excellent profit no doubt," Gem suggested.

"An acceptable profit," he conceded. "That word, by the way, is not blasphemy," he explained, thinking to build a bit of a 'bridge' between them. "Four years ago the employees wanted to purchase the factory when the owner decided to sell. However they could not afford the asking price and he wouldn't lower it. The employees asked GEI for a loan to close the sale. I assigned a researcher to the project. She concluded that the employees were not ready to manage the factory successfully at that time. So GEI purchased the business. It was viable. The project researcher took over as manager to assist the staff to set up a business plan, and to streamline operations. If the staff could run to a profit for two years, and afford to purchase the factory, I would sell to them."

"For a profit," Gem repeated.

"Naturally," Wyatt concurred. "They had to want the company. I wouldn't 'give' it to them. They had to work for it. And they did."

"They met your terms, and you made a profit," Gem glanced over to watch the 'hunter' walking the perimeter of the forest.

"I repeat 'profit' if not a curse word, my dear. I recovered the price I had paid and the salary GEI paid the project manager - and a bit more than that."

"Oh," Gem reflected on his remarks. Her nose was getting cold as the wind increased. She watched the wind shred the chimney smoke at the distant cottage.

"The employees reached the goal, the researcher successfully completed her assigned project, and I have one less report to read each month," Wyatt said with a grin.

"Well, congratulations then," Gem said sincerely.

"Thank you," Wyatt accepted her words with a nod.

"And Ms Holton will handle the sale?"

"Yes. She contributed her own terms. The employees have to have a yearly fund-raising project, and they also must maintain the village park and community gardens."

"And congratulations to Ms Holton."

"I'll pass your words on to her."

One less report to read each month. An interesting remark. "Do you enjoy being an empire builder?" she asked curiously.

Wyatt laughed at her words. "My grandfather was the empire builder. He built Grantham Enterprises. My father expanded the company. I inherited wealth. What should I have done? I don't play golf or polo. I don't have James's artistic talent. I have business acumen. I expanded Grantham Enterprises to the international level. That's what I do. I do business."

"What would you rather do?" Gem glanced up at him, rather surprised at his words. He so rarely spoke of business.

"Own a pub," he grinned.

"You could open a chain of pubs," Gem suggested.

"One pub. Only one," he countered.

"One report to read each month," Gem smiled. He looked so handsome. His eyes were soft grey; he was smiling the smile that set butterflies loose.

"Precisely." He put his arm around her shoulders, drawing her close. It was getting chilly.

"Perhaps one day you shall own a single pub."

"Perhaps I would hire you as a barmaid," he teased, "hair pulled back in a sexy French braid."

Gem caught the tone in his voice.

"A pub! Rubbish," she shook her head. "You enjoy - no - you thrive on the power of GEI."

"The money isn't bad either," Wyatt remarked candidly.

"Is money power or is power money?" she asked curiously.

"Well, they often go hand in hand," Wyatt observed.

"Which would you rather have?" she pressed.

"Both," Wyatt said firmly. "I had the money to purchase that factory in the Midlands, and the power and money to sell the factory back to the employees at a price they could afford."

"Do you do that often?" This was definitely a side of Wyatt Grantham she had not before seen.

"Now and then. I own a golf course which is open to the public. The staff wanted to purchase the business and privatise it. I refused to sell and replaced the manager with a GEI project researcher."

"Why?"

"There are too many private golf clubs, too few available to the public."

"No - why fire the previous manager?"

"He was huffy that I would not sell. I do not tolerate attitude."

"I have noticed," Gem replied bluntly.

"Oh! - As if that stops you!" Wyatt laughed, clutching her tightly against him. "Now, sweetheart, enough exercise and fresh air for you. I really think you should have an appointment with Dr Lyndon," he suggested, turning her about to guide her back to the Hall.

"I have a physician," Gem protested.

"You have? Then for heaven's sake make an appointment for a physical. You look like walking death!"

"Oh, how charming you can be," Gem gave him a mock sweet smile.

"Oh, how foolishly stubborn you can be," Wyatt said firmly. "I want you to rest now. I'll make a pot of hot chocolate for you and a grilled sandwich, and you will rest."

"You are very bossy," Gem frowned.

"It's power," he said smoothly.

"Yes," Gem said quietly. "And it's irritating."

"Get used to it, love," Wyatt said firmly "I have the power. You do not."

Gem bit her tongue. She couldn't argue with his words. Not yet, at any rate. But hopefully soon she would be able to do so.

Gen ate the sandwich, drank the hot chocolate, and rested. And she watched the news unfolding in Indonesia. But her thoughts were distracted from the news to Wyatt. He had said he would be reading in the library. He was Mr Hyde today. Perhaps she should take the advantage and tell him about the baby - only one - for now. She would rather deal with Mr Hyde than his evil counterpart.

He was very considerate today; and amusing with his 'pub humour' earlier. She had thought for a moment that he actually was serious about owning a pub, but really, how could one give up the power Wyatt had at GEI and because of GEI? And as he said - the money. Financially she was comfortable - due to Gemmy's counselling on investments - and now the sale of the flat - and distastefully from the life insurance policies and other death benefits from the Agency. Taxes had taken a chunk, but there were still lots of zeros after numbers in her bank account.

And she had to admit it was generous of Wyatt to sell the factory to the employees. He could have continued reaping profits from the factory - year after year, but instead he sold. Was that all there was to the sale? Rather simplistic when one considered that Wyatt was involved. Was the other shoe going to drop for the factory? Or on the factory - so to speak? He would probably not mention that fact to her - if - and - when it happened.

She was wasting time. She had to tell him. She took the cigar from the file cabinet, slipping it into her pocket.

She took a deep breath and knocked at the door of the library.

"Come in, Gem."

"Good guess," she said hesitantly. "How did you know it was me?" she tried for light humour, but he was frowning as she approached his desk.

"Wild guess." He had wasted enough time away from work the past two days; the interruptions were becoming irritating. "What do you need, my dear?" he strove to force a patient tone.

"It can wait," Gem said uneasily. "You're very busy."

"I usually am. However, you are here. I am here." He leaned back in his chair.

She could tell he was trying to be patient. That was, perhaps, a plus for her.

Gem pulled the cigar out of her pocket and reached over the desk to hand it to him. Wyatt stared at her and Gem forced herself to meet his gaze.

"I see," he said a touch coolly, taking the cigar from her fingers. "Am I to believe there is an actual baby - this time? This is a real pregnancy - this time?"

Gem flushed scarlet. "Yes, of course it is," she replied, stung by his words.

"There is no 'of course' about it. You can hardly be offended by my scepticism - considering your history and flair for lying. Have you seen a doctor?" he said dispassionately.

"Yes," Gem said stiffly, watching his eyes darken to nearly black.

Wyatt's eyebrows lifted. "Indeed. May I see the test report?"

"I don't have one," her voice faltered. "It's a yes or no issue."

"You have a prescription for vitamins for Mr Whitney?"

"I had it filled in London." This was progressing as dreadfully as she had expected.

Wyatt leaned back in his chair. "Well, I must admit I'm not entirely surprised."

"You're not?" Gem said taken aback. She had been stunned at the news!

"No. Were you using birth control?" he asked brusquely.

Gem blushed again. "No," she admitted.

"Well, we both know I wasn't using protection. So there you have it," he continued staring at her, his anger fully evident in his steel grey eyes. "Was there anything else, my dear?"

"No," Gem shook her head. She was obviously being dismissed. She controlled her temper as she walked to the door.

"Gem," Wyatt called after her. She turned to look at him. "Clever touch," he pointed the cigar at her.

She gave a quick nod and left the room, closing the door quietly.

That was bad, but not perhaps as beastly as it might have been. She had expected a reference to James and it had been there, although Wyatt had not mentioned his brother's name. Oh how she despised that man!

She turned to her computer and pulled up the map of the Pacific Ocean, scanning over to the South China Sea, then down to Indonesia, and sank onto the swivel chair.

Blast! Blast! Blast!

Every single day her life seemed to drift more and more out of her control. One might hope for a stretch of time where she could feel like she was on an even keel. But no such luck.

He should have handled the situation more adeptly. He wasn't surprised she was pregnant. It had crossed his mind from time to time the past two months. But - it should have been James's baby, not his.

He had to attempt to be more reasonable. He had to fight to control the constant irritation he felt having her in his home. It had been his decision to bring her here. It was his Game. It would continue to be his Game until it finally played out at the end.

Damn!

He stood up, stared at the cigar in his hand, then with careful deliberation set it down on the desk. Damn! He had to deal with this situation. Yet another interruption to his day because of her.

He tapped at the doorjamb, and Gem spun around to stare at him. Her face was strained. She dragged her fingers through her hair, as he noticed she did when she was frustrated about her thoughts.

"I rather too abruptly ended our conversation," he frowned.

Gem didn't have a reply.

"I must admit I rather wondered if you were pregnant."

"Really?" Gem threw her hands up in the air. "Okay," she shook her head in disbelief.

Wyatt studied her curiously, a thought dawning on him. "You were surprised - stunned - weren't you?" he said in astonishment. "Good Lord, Gem! You need a keeper!"

"I've had other things on my mind," she sighed helplessly.

"Would you like to share those thoughts?" He waited a moment. "No?' he shook his head. "Perhaps I should hire a nanny."

"I'm not due until May," she said awkwardly. Hopefully I won't be here by then!

"I meant for you," Wyatt said dryly. "Honestly, Gem, you shouldn't be allowed out on your own."

"I'm not," her temper flared. "Mr Choate is always with me. And he's not the reason I'm pregnant."

"I am aware of that fact," Wyatt said drolly. "We have spent virtually every night - together - since our wedding night. And you have always been 'available'."

"Yes," Gem said coolly, "except for those few days that you were - extremely angry with me - for suggesting you have an affair." She was beginning to get a headache. "Perhaps you should have had one!"

Wyatt's temper rose. "For your information, sweetheart, you would never know if I was having a liaison. I can fly to Paris on a moment's notice - or Wight - or Inverness - anywhere I damn well choose, actually. I do not need your permission if I do choose to be with other women. However, at that time I found your repeated comments and suggestions extremely galling. Now that should clear away that subject for the future!"

Gem gasped at the cold, clinical remarks. It was disgusting to think of him being with another woman instead of being with her. He had said women! How many had there been since their wedding?

"Disgusting!" she railed at him. "All your women! You are revolting!"

"What?" he scowled.

"You are vile, loathsome! I don't believe you! I simply can't believe what an odious man you are!" Gem stomped away from him.

Wyatt reached out to grab her hand.

"Don't touch me - ever again!" she stormed out of the office, then ran out the kitchen door.

"What?" Wyatt demanded in confusion.

He started after her, then abruptly stopped. She had taken his words at full value - as an admission that he had been having an affair since they married. - Ah ! The text message that one morning about Emerald. She was angry! Furious! She was jealous! That was an interesting new detail in their relationship.

Very interesting. It was a weapon he could use against her. - But no. - That would break the trust he was again trying to foster. God knew it would set the Game back. But he would certainly like to take advantage of her jealousy. It would amuse him. No, setback to the Game. And he had just set it back a bit now with his temper.

He followed her, calling her name, her steps were no match for his long strides.

"It's too cold out here, you don't have a wrap," he caught up with her where the drive met the cobblestone lane. "Come back to the Hall. You can be just as angry in a warm house as out here."

She had to relent. She didn't really have anywhere else to go. She should have grabbed the keys to the Defender. When would she start thinking clearly?

When they entered the house Gem stalked through the kitchen and down the hall, before he caught up with her again, catching her arm.

"You and your damned power! It gets you everything you want, doesn't it? Just snap your fingers - weren't those your words to me?" She turned her back on him again.

"Please look at me when you talk to me, Gem," he ordered gently, but she refused to do so.

Wyatt put his hands on her shoulders. "My words were cruel," he said quietly. "You got angry. I got angry." He turned her around, lifting her chin to force her eyes to meet his. "I have not been with another woman since I met you. I haven't even kissed another woman since I met you. God's truth."

Gem glared at him. "I don't believe you! You and your Games!"

"And what of your games?" he said quietly. "You are still playing them." He was taking a risk here for a future game. "Are you searching for Staunton? He's not in Indonesia, you know. You won't find him."

"I'm not searching for John Staunton! I'm searching for my life!" Gem cried out, then gasped. No slipped cogs!

"What the hell does that mean?" Wyatt demanded, puzzled by the strange admission.

Control! Count to twenty! Control! Count to...

"Gem. Gem," Wyatt said softly.

She slowly opened her eyes.

"What?" she murmured.

"You fainted," he said gently.

He was sitting beside her. Gem looked around. She was lying on the chesterfield in the great room.

"Lie still," he ordered. "I rang Dr Lyndon. He'll be here shortly. Have you ever fainted before?"

"What - are you a doctor now?" she sighed. Blast! Do people babble when they faint? Had she said something she shouldn't have said? Blast!

"Have you ever fainted before?" inquired a voice beyond Wyatt. Gem had not seen him enter the room. "I am a doctor, so I'm allowed to ask that question. And how about an answer, Gem," he said firmly but patiently.

Wyatt stood and moved away to allow the doctor to tend to her." No," Gem shook her head. She realized she was plucking at a blanket. Wyatt must have fetched it from her office to spread it over her. Wasn't he just the thoughtful one, she frowned.

"Any obvious reason that might have caused you to faint?" Lyndon queried as he pulled a chair over to sit by the sofa.

"Gem is pregnant," Wyatt said smoothly.

"Well, congratulations to both of you," the doctor pursed his lips.

"Thank you," Wyatt nodded, acknowledging the sentiment for both of them.

"Hmm. That could be a cause," Lyndon mused patiently, taking Gem's wrist to check her pulse, as he studied his watch. "Pulse a bit fast. How far along are you."

Gem looked at Wyatt who stood at the end of the chesterfield, arms folded across his chest. "A little past two months," she said quietly.

"About nine weeks?" Lyndon queried, and Gem silently nodded, glancing at Wyatt.

"How long have you known?" Lyndon asked.

Gem frowned, avoiding Wyatt's eyes. "A week or so. Why does that matter?"

"Just gathering information. You'll have to start thinking about names for your baby."

"We have a name," Wyatt said firmly.

"Good," Lyndon nodded. "I'm going to take your blood pressure now."

Gem lay quietly as he wrapped the material around her arm and squeezed the bulb.

"A bit high," he stated mildly, reaching into his black bag. "Wyatt, why don't you leave us alone for a few minutes," Lyndon suggested.

Wyatt considered the suggestion. "No, I don't believe I shall," he replied pleasantly, folding his long body into a wingback chair.

Lyndon looked at him. "I would like Gem to be able to speak freely."

Wyatt raised his eyebrows. "I assure you my wife has no difficulty speaking her mind," he said with a touch of humour.

Lyndon frowned at Wyatt who ignored the look. He shook his head slightly then returned his attention to his patient.

"Have you seen a doctor recently?"

"I have," she nodded. Only ever answer the question. Do not volunteer information. Prevent slipped cogs.

"When was you last visit?"

"Two days ago," she glanced at Wyatt, then looked at the doctor.

Wyatt briefly narrowed his eyes as he watched her. He realized the way she was replying to the questions. Where had she learned that technique? Usually people were only too eager to volunteer much more information than was necessary.

"Your regular physician is - ?"

"Hallowell - Davis Hallowell." She could offer the name as he had private patients as well as being the Agency staff's official medical expert.

Lyndon's eyebrows rose sharply. "A most excellent physician," he nodded approvingly. "Why did you see him Friday?"

"I'm exhausted. Every day. I'm so tired I can barely think," she closed her eyes.

"That's not unusual. Did Dr Hallowell explain that to you?" Lyndon's gentle voice said comfortingly, and Gem nodded. "What did he suggest?"

"Rest. Moderate exercise, drink a lot of warm water," she sighed.

"That's a thought." He turned to Wyatt. "Would you please fetch Gem a glass of warm water, Wyatt? Warm, not hot."

Wyatt looked at Lyndon, then at Gem, and left his chair.

"Aren't you the clever one," Gem said wryly.

Lyndon chuckled. He breathed on his stethoscope. "Wyatt's concerned about you."

Indeed! She thought cryptically. Concerned of what you might learn that he doesn't know about me.

"He doesn't like taking orders," Gem said softly.

"Who does," Lyndon chuckled. "I'm going to listen to your baby's heart beat now." And so he did, lifting his eyebrows to Gem. "When do you see Dr Hallowell again?"

"A few weeks," she shrugged.

"Good. I'm going to listen to your heart now. "

She lay quietly while he listened to her heart. Wyatt believed she didn't have one. She was surprised that Dr Lyndon could hear a beat, because she could no longer feel her heart.

"Sounds good," he returned the stethoscope to his bag. "Taking your vitamins?"

Gem nodded. She looked up as Wyatt returned from his errand, handing her the glass. As she sipped the water she mused that she was wasting the doctor's time.

"Did you check the baby's heart beat?" Wyatt frowned.

"Yes. Everything is fine," Lyndon said "How have you been sleeping?" he checked Gem's eyes.

She hesitated, not wanting to be drawn into the subject.

"Gem has insomnia," Wyatt replied for her. "She rarely sleeps more than a few hours a night."

"Hmmm. Is this a recent problem?" Lyndon put the query to Gem. She hesitated again. "A year - two? A few months? Chronic?"

"A matter of a few months," Gem shrugged.

"Early summer?" Wyatt suggested. "May?"

Gem suppressed a smile. Fishing? "Some months," she murmured.

Lyndon caught the play between husband and wife. Wyatt was a force to be reckoned with, to be sure, on anyone's terms, but Gem seemed to be holding her own against him.

"How much sleep are you getting, Wyatt?" he said, a bit amused.

"Less than usual," Wyatt said crisply. He had not returned to the chair, remaining standing at the end of the chesterfield.

"I see. I can't suggest Gem use pills to help her sleep - not in her present condition, but perhaps you might want a prescription, Wyatt," Lyndon said dryly, and Gem couldn't suppress a giggle. He turned his attention to his patient. "Have you considered hypnotism?"

"I don't want to be hypnotized," Gem flatly refused the doctor's suggestion.

"It's a strictly professional situation," Lyndon assured her. "Dr Hallowell could hypnotize you in his office. Or here if you would be more comfortable in your home. Hallowell is quite well known for his expertise with the procedure."

"Dr Hallowell is well aware of my reluctance," Gem informed him. "We have discussed the issue a number of times." She avoided the eyes staring at her from the end of the sofa.

Wyatt's eyebrows rose at her reply. It was news to him that she had talked to a doctor about her insomnia. She was so secretive. Another bit of information he now knew about her. Unless she was lying to Lyndon.

"Dr Hallowell discussed possible influences contributing to insomnia? Unusual stress, depression, sudden life style changes, sudden loss, struggles to cope with grief," Lyndon recited a few issues.

"Indeed," Gem nodded, then scrutinized the man. "Are you a hypnotist?" she asked warily.

"I am not," Lyndon said easily.

"Good," Gem nodded. "I don't appreciate trickery or deceit." She saw Wyatt give her a brief scornful look, and knew exactly what he was thinking: that she was liar herself. "I meant to say I don't want to be hypnotized without my knowledge or consent." The doctor's appointment Wyatt had made for her when they returned from Inverness was her point.

"I highly doubt that could happen, Gem," Lyndon said firmly. "You are very tightly wired. One needs to be able to relax to be hypnotized. It's highly unlikely Hallowell would be successful with you as a subject. I'm going to take your temperature now."

Temperature. Ears. Throat.

"Hallowell checked your blood Friday?" he glanced up from the notes he was writing.

Gem nodded.

After a few minutes of additional note taking, Lyndon closed his medical bag. "You check out, Gem. My best opinion is that the fainting spell was a result of the pregnancy and fatigue. Not unusual. You are exhausted. Follow Dr Hallowell's suggestions, avoid stress if at all possible," he concluded. "My phone number is in your mobile, I believe."

"Indeed," Gem replied.

"I suggest you spoil yourself," the doctor urged. "Stay in bed until noon, if you like, ever if you can't sleep." He paused as a load of fur leaped from the floor behind him to land and sit on his shoulder. Lyndon automatically reached a hand up to scratch feline ears. "Mrs Macgillicudy, my old friend." He smiled at Gem. "I heard she was living with you now."

Gem nodded, smiling at the cat contentedly sitting on the doctor's shoulders. "I thought perhaps she would like to go to the care centre to visit Mrs Moody," Gem suggested. "Is that permitted?"

"A fine idea, but unfortunately too long a drive now," Lyndon deftly lifted the cat off his shoulder to hold on his lap. "Mrs Moody passed last night. Peacefully in her sleep."

"I'm sorry," Gem murmured, reaching out to stroke the late Mrs Moody's furry companion.

Lyndon nodded. "Now, where were we?" He frowned a bit. "Ah yes, rest. Rest and think of baby names."

"James or Jamie," Wyatt said firmly. "Boy or girl."

"Indeed," Lyndon looked from Wyatt to Gem. "Gem, I'll have a chat with Dr Hallowell tomorrow - let him know that I saw you. You might want to check with him in a few days. Especially if your exhaustion increases. At any rate give him a ring."

"Perhaps you should prescribe complete bed rest for Gem," Wyatt firmly suggested.

"If necessary I shall," Lyndon conceded, "however I don't believe we are there quite yet."

Gem lay back against the sofa cushions, trying to decide whether or not to work on Durham while Wyatt saw the physician out of the house. She did want to watch the telly for an update on the Indonesian hot spots. She pushed back the blanket, sitting up, checking to see if she felt light headed.

"Where do you think you're going?" Wyatt demanded, as she stood up.

"My office," Gem declared, startled that he had returned.

"You are going to bed. No arguments," he said. "Shall I carry you upstairs?"

"No," she refused his offer. "I still have two feet. I can manage."

"I'll see that you do," he put his arm around her waist. "Once you're settled, I'll make dinner and a pot of tea. Or hot chocolate."

"Okay, thank you," Gem murmured. She wouldn't argue with him this evening, but she refused to be house-bound. She was going to London tomorrow to chat with Mr Choate. For now, she would watch the news during the dark hours.

Wyatt pulled back the duvet as Gem rummaged through the lowboy, looking for pyjamas.

He sat on the end of the bed. "Would I be in error to suggest you are not very pleased to be pregnant?" he mused.

"You wouldn't understand," she sighed.

"I understand I have never been pregnant and had hormones raging through my body," he said patiently.

"I'm not raging," Gem frowned at him. "And you're the one whose angry that I'm pregnant."

Not raging, but definitely running amok, he thought silently. "This was not an immaculate conception, Gem. If I was adverse to having children, I would have made certain you would not become pregnant. I am not angry."

"You are," she replied, keeping her back to him, not wanting to see his eyes that were no doubt steel grey. "You think it should be James's baby."

Clever girl - woman! "I'll admit I had that exact thought when we spoke in the library," he said quietly. "However, that is not feasible, is it? The Game was scored differently from our wedding night - because you hadn't had sex with James - as I had first believed."

"This is not a Game! It's a baby!" Gem replied softly. Or two!

"Indeed. We, you and I chatted about having children. You broached the subject, as I recall. You stated then that you wanted children."

"That was a lifetime ago. Before -"

James was a lifetime ago, Wyatt frowned. His life. "Before Wight."

"Yes," Gem nodded sadly, still refusing to look at him.

Wyatt considered her words. "As I see it," he said slowly, facing the facts for both of them since she refused to do so, and because the Game must play out, "there is no difference now. We are a family, my dear."

Gem spun about to glare at him. "We are not a family! We are a business arrangement. You can't say in any way that we are a family!"

Wyatt spoke calmly. "We are married. We have a home. We have a cat. We will have a child. One might say that is the perfect family."

"Sheesh!" Gem fumed helplessly. "I'm going to take a shower!" She grabbed a pyjama set and stomped to her bathroom.

Wyatt lazily followed her. "Oh - we should have a dog," he lounged in the dressing room as Gem turned on the shower.

She turned off the tap and stared at him. "A dog! I've never had a dog," she frowned.

"You'd never been married before, or had a cat, or had a baby. First time for everything," he suggested.

"What kind of a dog?" she asked curiously.

"The kind that doesn't eat cats," Wyatt suggested as Mrs Mac wandered past him into the bathroom to snoop out the water drops in the shower.

"Oh, that kind of dog," Gem said doubtfully.

"No," Wyatt said firmly, fetching the cat from the shower, "you can't swim kitty. She'll love a dog - you wait and see. I have meetings through Wednesday. We'll go to a rescue centre on Thursday. No doubt Ms Holton has a list of them."

Gem watched as he expertly tucked the cat under his arm. "We'll prepare dinner, you have your shower and scoot into bed."

"You're frowning," Wyatt said as he set the bed tray across her lap a half hour later.

"I was thinking of painting the bathroom off the office," she replied viewing the tray: steak, salad and a pot of tea.

"You didn't specify so I decided tea," he remarked. "Too late to paint the bathroom, the fumes would make you dizzy and possibly ill."

"I don't mind the odour of paint," Gem protested.

"You didn't previously. You might now," he warned.

"Aren't you going to eat?"

"Later."

"I've been thinking about a dog. Mrs M might not want one in the house," Gem frowned.

"She won't mind," he brushed off her concerns.

"She told me about –" Gem began, then stopped suddenly, realizing she might be treading on dangerous ground.

Wyatt frowned at her abrupt silence. "Ah - Homer the Roamer?" Wyatt said dryly. Mrs M did chat on didn't she; but then she had no reason to believe she shouldn't chat about the Grantham family. "I hate snakes, wouldn't have another one in the house," he gave Gem a brief smile. "I'm going to take a quick shower."

There was a thermos of hot chocolate on the counter next to her computer and the blanket had been returned to her office, draped over an arm of Auntie Jane's comfy chair. Mrs Mac stretched on the other arm of the chair.

Gem turned on the telly, keeping the volume low, although she doubted Wyatt could hear the sound across the entire Hall and up the stairs. The situation in Indonesia had intensified, but government spokespeople insisted the situation would be resolved in a matter of days. News-speak, Gem knew from experience, and inside knowledge of other world calamities with which the Agency had been involved.

Wyatt lay awake, debating whether or not he should have insisted she remain in bed. Gem would have argued and there wasn't a point fighting her resolve. Lyndon's remarks, when Wyatt had walked him out through the kitchen, had been in his mind for much of the evening. "Gem is extremely stressed, Wyatt. And now being pregnant, the stress will compound. She's mentally and physically exhausted, extremely stressed. If those issues do not ease, she might completely collapse. Early stages yet. You don't want to lose the baby. Do as much as you can to relieve her stress. I cannot be more adamant about this."

Stress. Ending their marriage would likely end some of Gem's stress. But he was not about to consider that option. Gem had been tightly wired since the day he met her. She hadn't been so with James in Barcelona. James would have mentioned that.

So! What had happened between the time Gem had left Barcelona in mid-May and appeared at Oscar's Café in early August. Flight. Water. The haunted look. John Staunton? He had only gone missing a few weeks ago. Wyatt reached for his mobile, checking the inter-net for flight problems and distresses at sea. Nothing. Well, she hadn't set a bomb to take down a flight at sea. Thank God! But what had she done?

He could force her to rest. When Mrs M learned of the pregnancy she would constantly mother-hen Gem. Mrs M must set to work immediately in the morning. A few choice words to the older woman and Wyatt wouldn't have to give Gem a thought the rest of his work day. Not that she was ever very far from his mind - but that was for a different reason.

A baby. Gem was less than pleased. A child likely wouldn't suit the life style of her choice. She had managed to hold Baby Erin at the pub. But caring for a child was another matter. He wouldn't really trust Gem with a child. He would hire a nanny.

Children had never completely been out of the question as far as he was concerned. But he had made the decision when Gem had first spoken of children, that he would not allow her sole care of a child. And also at that time he had thought she had destroyed James's baby.

She had been surprised to discover she was pregnant. How the hell could she be surprised? What had she thought would happen if she didn't use the pill? He had never asked her of the matter because he didn't care. She was an extremely intelligent woman but she had no common sense. Thank heavens Choate was with her when she was away from Ticking Bottom.

Surprised! She had had a great deal on her mind! What? Precisely what? Whatever it was, he would discover it. With Lyndon's concerns for Gem, he would have to be much more careful. There were other means to his Game.

He put her from his mind. He had an extremely busy week ahead of him.

Gem switched off the telly, and pushed the start button on the cd player. Wyatt made a lovely cup of hot chocolate.

It was over! She had dreaded telling him. Naturally his first thoughts would have been of James. And her thoughts were of Gemmy. Gem shivered despite the blanket, the hot chocolate, and the electric fires. At least he hadn't ranted at her.

But his following comments about his ability to have an affair, anytime he wished - and she wouldn't know - rankled her. He was disgusting! She couldn't imagine Stuart Holton being unfaithful to Emma! But Wyatt Grantham - Mr Power - Mr GEI - what was it about wealthy and/or powerful men that made them think they had the license to do whatever they wished to do - without impunity?

It wasn't that she was jealous. It was simply disgusting. Ish! She didn't want any images in her mind. And that included Emerald and the other women in the blasted photo album!

Wyatt had said he hadn't been with another woman since he had met her. If she had read his eyes correctly, he had been telling the truth. But she could be losing her touch. She certainly had no reason to trust him.

And to be honest, why should he be faithful to her? A business arrangement. That was all they had. A civil attitude from him was the best she could expect considering how much he hated her because of James.

He wasn't really surprised about the baby(ies). Well, baby - one, for him. - As far as he knew. They had talked of having children - in her previous life - the one she was surviving before she married him. He had never asked if she was on the pill. And because she was a complete idiot she hadn't thought of it. Apparently neither had Gemmy. Two complete idiots. I am sorry, my dear Gemmy, to include you in that label. But you were in love. I was just foolish. But Wyatt hadn't asked. Because he hadn't cared. Just part of the Game? And which Game was that? Russian roulette?

Dr Lyndon had been very kind.

Insomnia. Life style change. Ha! The Hall could be considered that.

Stress: searching for a missing plane hiding the bodies of your family, a dear friend; murdered counter-couriers and counter-agents. Mr Denton. Another master agent in hiding. Harry and Mrs Brown - wherever they were. The passports, the photos. Being married to a man who hated you! Had you followed when you left Ticking Bottom!   Having a baby with a man who hated you! Was she forgetting anything else to cause stress? No? Perhaps not.

Grief. Sudden loss. - Really!

Depression. - Highly likely!

Well. Yes. Sounds like issues to cause insomnia.

Mrs Mac stirred, reaching a tentative paw to touch Gem's chin.

She pulled out her mobile. Mr Cawley was at work.

'Indonesia is a mess.'

'It happens. That's why the term hot spot.'

'So amusing. Blank?'
'Not a clue. Any ideas?'
'No. Harry? Mrs Brown?'
'Him, no. Her, still on 'holiday'.'
'Staff accounted for?'
'Except for the three you mentioned.'
'Odd.'
'Why?'
'Did someone misplace their knife?'
'Sick humour isn't like you. What's up?'
'No recent deaths. Too quiet.'
'True.'
'I'm frustrated.'
'Tell you husband. I'm married.'
Gem nearly dropped her mobile.
'Sorry, Gem. Uncalled for. Think I'm getting punchy.'
'What's up?'
'Concerned re Indonesia, kid.'
'That's why it's called a hot spot.'
'Funny. Blank isn't there. Info we are receiving is so sketchy. I don't trust it.'
'You're worried about Harry.'
'Extremely, Gem.'
'Could he be in contact with Blank?'
'Possibly. I just don't know.'
'Would Mrs Brown know?'
'Perhaps. Unreachable.'
'Lovely.'
'Yes. Are you sorting?'
'Of a sort.'
'Amusing. Go back to work!'
'Nag! Goodnight!'
'Goodnight, Gem!'

She was sorting. But it was Wyatt she was sorting. Actually, she would like to sort him out good!

Mrs Mac touched her chin again. Gem looked at the time on her mobile. Half four. She cleared the messages.

"Okay, Mrs Mac, let's go to bed. Unless Wyatt moved someone into it while we were down here," she muttered.

Monday. Mr Choate. Blast! Gem's brain started clicking before she could force her eyes open.

Mrs Mac stretched and padded her way across the bed to perch on Gem's shoulder.

"Oh no, kitty," Wyatt scooped up the cat and set her on the floor. "Not this morning."

"Indeed," Gem said coolly, pushing off the duvet.

"I was addressing the cat," Wyatt put his arm around her shoulder.

"It works for me too," Gem glared at him.

Wyatt turned her around to look at him. "I meant what I said last night, Gem."

"You said a great deal and made yourself crystal clear - again."

"I see," he pursed his lips. "You are conveniently forgetting what I would consider a rather significant portion of my remarks," he said firmly.

"I don't believe you," Gem said watching his eyes.

"I was being honest when I said I didn't need your permission. That was cruel, but honest. I regret the remarks." The light grey gaze didn't waver, Gem observed. "And regarding the significant portion, I have not been with another woman since I met you," he said again, very firmly.

His gaze was steady, clear, unwavering - and very important, liars look down - he did not. As far as Gem could judge, his words were truthful.

"You haven't had time - too busy," Gem retorted.

"I have made time for you, Gem. I could have made time for another woman, had I wished to. But I didn't," he kissed her, and set the butterflies soaring.

Damn butterflies!

"You made it clear I wouldn't know if you did," she countered, fighting of the winged creatures.

"You are a very astute woman, Gem. You would know." His hands began to wander.

"Emerald."

"Was a long time ago," he brushed her hair back from her forehead. "Mrs M despised her."

"How long ago?"

"You ask me a question, my dear, I'll ask you one in return," he gave her a steady look.

"It's not the same."

"That's the way it will be. Now, no questions, no - no arguing," he insisted as she opened her mouth to dispute, "and no cats," he winked at her.

"Stay in bed until noon," Wyatt urged. "Dr's orders." Wyatt pulled on his dressing gown and checked his mobile for messages.

"It was a suggestion," Gem countered. "I'm going to London," she called after him as he walked into his dressing room. He immediately reappeared.

"I'll have Lyndon prescribe bed rest for you for a week," Wyatt scowled. "Stay in bed. I'll ring Lyndon right now."

"Are you going to threaten him to do so?" Gem said coolly.

Wyatt looked at her in surprise. "What makes you think I threaten people?"

"You threatened me! Passports! Photos!"

"Hah! You made a bargain with me," he countered.

"You blackmailed me!" Gem retorted, shocked at his easy dismissal of his actions.

"I had information about you. You didn't want that information made known. We reached terms. It was a bargain."

"Amazing," Gem shook her head. "You wrote your own dictionary. I'm curious of your definitions of the words 'blackmail' and 'threaten'."

"The definitions are the same. Compromise," he said smoothly.

"Lord! You are insidious!" Gem said, appalled.

"Definitions are different in the Jane Austen world, and the gritty business world."

"You are absolutely frightening," Gem said breathlessly.

"Nonsense, my dear. Mrs Brown may see you as being of Jane's world. But you and I both know you are of my world. You simply do not present the 'real you' to other people. You forget - I know the person you hide."

"Oh, go away!" Gem buried her face in her pillow. "Leave me alone," she moaned miserably.

Damn! Not working well with patience, he silently swore.

He sat on the edge of the bed, leaning across to stroke her hair. "We seem to constantly strike sparks off each other. In bed and out of it," he said ruefully. "I prefer the former," he gently teased. "Why do you need to go to London today?"

"I need clothes. Mine are becoming too tight," she replied, her words muffled by her pillow. Well, it was one of the reasons.

"Ring your friend Ora. Have her send some items to my office. I'll bring them home this evening," he suggested.

"No," she insisted. "I'm not ill, I'm pregnant."

"So I heard," Wyatt teased. "Very well," he relented. "But please, promise me you won't exhaust yourself walking all over the city. Please?" Mrs M would soon take over. He didn't have the patience for this, even if the Game must change direction.

"Okay. I promise," Gem agreed. She didn't have the energy for a long walk, so it was an easy promise to make, and it didn't cost her anything.

Mrs M was delighted when Wyatt made their announcement at breakfast. The housekeeper responded with the joyous enthusiasm the future parents had not shown upon receiving the news of the baby.

Gem was glad to escape the Hall and Mrs M's fussing, which she realized would likely be the older woman's natural state until Gem could get the HELL out of the Hall. Permanently.

She texted Mr Choate.

'Coffee, tea, chat.'

'Howard's now serves coffee and tea.'

'Okay.'

The bookshop was early Monday morning Quiet, and they settled on the sofa at the rear of the shop, where they could watch for customer invasion into their space. Howard remained at the front of the shop to give them privacy.

"Dr Lyndon was at the Hall last night," Choate said pointedly.

"Yes," Gem nodded.

"Anything amiss?" he frowned.

"I fainted," Gem sighed.

"Why?"

"I'm pregnant. It was just that. A bad day."

"Anything else I should know, Gem?"

"I don't know. Did you need to know why Dr Lyndon was at the Hall?" she asked curiously.

"Yes," he nodded firmly. "I protect you. For Mr Grantham and for the Agency. You know, Gem, no one completely retires from the Agency. You are still on staff, you are still working."

"If you knew a doctor was called to Mr Cawley's residence would you question him of the visit?" she protested, but only faintly.

"I wouldn't need to do so. Mr Cawley would report the incident to me."

"Is this a new SOP I haven't heard about?" Gem queried.

"Not quite standard," Choate said gently. "In the past if you were ill, or some circumstance arose, you would have informed Gemmy or your parents. You would have been on a schedule and the Agency would have been aware of your daily activities. This is just a precaution. The Agency always needs to know where you are. We knew you were on Wight and at Inverness."

"How?"

"We knew where Mr Grantham was."

"You track him?"

"Only while you were completely out of contact with the Agency."

"You could have rung my mobile," she said abruptly.

"We could not. We did not have a basis for contact. We do now through T.O., and the fact that Mr Grantham has met Mrs Brown."

"Okay," Gem nodded.

"Are we all right here then?" Choate said patiently.

"Of course," she gave him a smile. "I think your coffee is cold."

He took her cup, "I'll get refills. Congratulations by the way. Inform the Agency as you see fit. Since you aren't actively in the field there is no rush to inform your supervisor."

While she waited for Mr Choate to return, Gem thought of his remarks. She didn't see the need to inform the Agency yet of the baby. It was still early days. Wyatt was the one who absolutely had to know, and that detail had been managed; it was certainly not an occasion for the memory album.

When Mr Choate returned he quickly got down to business.

"Why the chat this morning?" he queried, expecting questions regarding Andriani, Harry, and Mrs Brown.

"Has any Agency staff ever gone rogue?" she asked biting her lower lip. She was treading on eggshells, for Agency employees were extremely proud of their department and record of operations.

"Not the Agency," Choate replied firmly.

"B.I. - Aside from the peculiar Kim Philby character?" she continued.

"Peculiar! A great understatement. The man was a traitor!"

"Yes, I know. He defected to Moscow in '63," Gem agreed. "A traitor yes. But he was peculiar."

"One could say that, I suppose," Choate conceded grudgingly. "The thought of him makes my blood boil."

Gem nodded. "A scourge of investigations in B.I. and the Agency, looking for additional communists and sympathizers."

"The cloud of taint hung over B.I. for years, and would have tainted the Agency also if it wasn't so deeply buried to non-existence in the government."

Choate was passionate of the subject, so passionate that Gem simply had to wonder about the sealed file of his past work.

"Where does your query lead, Gem?" he asked, his voice extremely serious.

"To a mole or a sleeper," she gingerly suggested. "Not wishing to offend either Mr Portermann or you, good Sir."

Choate shook his head. "No offence taken, Gem. You are working. But no. There is no mole or sleeper. Not in B.I., to my knowledge. Not in the Agency."

"SEA Network?"

"Harry scrutinized that part of the Network and it is clean," he said firmly.

There was another tactic to consider, but it was far more sensitive. She couldn't pull back or sugar-coat. Her best efforts were currently stymied by confusion of the next direction which she should be taking.

"Rogue. Philby went rogue. Is it possible someone in B.I. or the Agency has gone rogue?" she queried.

Choate sharply sucked in his breath. "There is no indication that has happened."

"Where is Paul Andriani?" Gem said softly. "No one knows -"

"He was MADE, Gem. He had to leave the field," Choate said with quiet vehemence.

"I realize that," Gem nodded. "He had to leave the field because his contacts were being murdered. He disappeared to protect his contacts."

Choate nodded. "He's not a coward, Gem."

"I would never think him to be a coward," she protested. "I want to know where he is. I want to talk to him," she said urgently.

"If you can find him, you will be able to have your chat," Choate said bluntly.

"Do you know where he is?" Gem pressed.

"Gem, does anyone know where his is?" Choate shrugged.

"Does Harry know?"

"I'm not in contact with Harry. If anyone is it would be Mrs Brown. The less the contact, the better - the safer it is for Harry."

"Where is Mrs Brown?" Gem pressed again.

Choate jerked his head to the window behind the sofa. "Somewhere out there."

"Does she contact you?"

"From time to time."

"Would you tell me, if you knew where she was?"

"No," he said bluntly. "This is not a NTK situation for you, Gem, per Mrs Brown."

It was not an unexpected reply. On to the next question.

"Indonesia."

"Always simmering. A current hot spot," Choate shrugged.

"Many unknowns?"

"Yes. Also not unusual for that area. Cells form, start to boil. Simmer, dissipate, disband, or reorganize into new cells."

"How accurate are the news reports?"

"As accurate as the news media can portray - the usual. They're generally a good sort. It's a dangerous area - currently. Some things the media can just never know," Choate sipped his coffee. "You already know this."

Gem nodded. "As in what is really behind the current roil in Indonesia? Does SEA know? Do you know?"

"Possibly" Choate replied. "If there is any relevance discovered to the Pilos, you will be informed." He let the remark sink in, then asked, "Next?"

Gem thought for a few minutes. "No more questions - today."

"If you have questions for me later, I'll be working very late tonight. Text me. You won't wake me tonight."

"Thank you," Gem smiled gratefully.

"Next then?" he drained his coffee cup.

"Ora & Eda's," she said, following suit with her tea.

"One or two?" he asked curiously as they left the bookshop.

Gem's brows knit as she puzzled through the query. "Oh - I don't know. Dr Hallowell believes possibly two. I told Wyatt only that I am pregnant. I didn't speak of other possibilities," she said in a hushed voice.

"Understood. I would say two," he ventured an opinion.

"Why?" Gem asked in surprise, for the query and for the count.

"Weight gain. Exhaustion. You shouldn't overdo today," he advised.

Another voice heard from the world of fussers.

"I won't," she conceded.

"Don't take the weight comment as criticism," he requested. "Merely an observation."

Gem nodded. "Only that?"

"Your mum and Jane. You and Gem. Stands to reason."

"Dr Hallowell's thoughts, and mine," Gem sighed. "Good heavens!"

"You'll sort it all out, Gem. A few weeks more and your energy will return."

Ora & Eda's Shop was becoming a popular venue, but Ora was eager to design simple maternity clothes for Gem.

"A long sleeve dress, tucked yoke, catch it at the waist with a loose belt, scarf, or a long string of beads caught with a slide," Ora thought out loud. "Soft waist band skirts. I'll run you up two or three pairs of jeans. End of week," she assured Gem.

"Will you have time?" Gem scanned the shop where nearly a dozen customers wandered around the displays.

"We expanded the work shop upstairs. Our mum, cousin, and auntie are also sewing for us now. They all taught me, so we can easily manage. Gran is knitting for us now as well as Eda, so our line is quickly expanding. "We'll expand your expanding wardrobe by the end of the week," Ora smiled.

Gem gave her a grateful smile, then paused. "Put an O&E on everything, on the yokes, the pockets of the jeans - just somewhere it will be noticed."

Ora's eyes lit up. "I shall. And thank you for the suggestion."

"Oh - and I need at least two black skirts, larger turtlenecks, cardigans. Whatever you think," Gem added, giving the young designer her mobile number. "I'll pick up whatever you finish when it's finished."

Her mobile rang as she was leaving the shop. Text message from Wyatt.

'Still in the city?'
'Yes.'
'Lunch possible?'
'Yes. When?'
'Noon? Where, sweetheart?'
'Yes. Chinese?'
'Good. Year of the Tiger?'
'Yes.'
'Late invitation. Don't rush.'

The last text was considerate. Wyatt had made it clear on Wight that she was not ever to keep him waiting. However, she arrived on time. He was relaxed, charming, attentive. He was the man she had fallen in love with in August. The man who no longer existed in real life. No doubt this was another part of his Game. 'Fool me once…' Gem silently reminded herself.

"Did Ora help you with your clothing distress?" he asked, smiling that smile that made her heart flip-flop.

"She'll have some things for me by Friday," Gem replied a touch defensively, gearing for a terse conversation of some sort. But one did not happen.

"Will you please let me pay the bill?" he asked gently.

"That's not necessary," Gem replied.

"I understand that. Accept the offer as an apology for my boorish attitude of this morning." Noting her hesitation he suggested, "Just consider it, please."

Gem nodded, knowing she wouldn't. After lunch he walked her to the Defender, without making a single query as to her plans for the afternoon, and when she intended to return to the Hall. No pressure, she sighed gratefully. And no fussing. Wyatt was not a man to fuss over a woman.

However, Mrs M was apparently well versed in the art of fussing. "You had lunch with Mr W?" the housekeeper demanded as soon as Gem entered the kitchen.

"Yes, ma'am," Gem dutifully replied.

"Then it's time you rested," Mrs M insisted. "The settee in your office or your bed? Which is it?"

"Office," Gem sighed. Best do as Mrs M said because the woman was not one to let go of a notion.

The housekeeper followed Gem into her office. Was she going to stand over Gem while she rested?

"What's this? - I realize it's a rocking chair," she self-edited, so as not to draw an expression from Mrs M suggesting she was furniture-recognition-impaired.

"It was delivered shortly before noon," the housekeeper informed her. "There's a note attached."

Gem slid the white card out of the small white envelope.

'Gem - Rock out until you have energy to pace once more-W.'

"It's from Wyatt," Gem explained to the housekeeper.

"Of course it is," Mrs M smiled. "It's beautifully made."

"It is," Gem agreed, running her hands over the carefully turned spindles of the back and the sides supporting the arm rests. "What's this?" she frowned at a lever near the right runner. She shifted the lever and the chair leaned back. She shifted again and the rocker stopped. "It's a brake!" she marvelled.

"Isn't that something!" Mrs M murmured. "It'll be easy to stand up when you've been rocking the baby!"

"Very clever, indeed," Gem mused.

"You've seen your surprise then. Rest," the housekeeper ordered.

Gem obeyed, relaxing on the settee with a travel book and the blanket Mrs M tucked around her. A few minutes later the housekeeper reappeared with a cup of tea. Gem watched the telly for a few minutes, but there had been no further developments in Indonesia. The government was still attempting to regain control; the insurgents were still out of control. If Harry was there he had his hands full. And she was sure he was there.

She rested for two hours then walked down to the brook and back to the Hall. It was a bit of fresh air and moderate exercise. She sat in the rocker and rocked-out for a few minutes before realizing she should be helping Mrs M prepare dinner.

"There are so many things to do," Mrs M said briskly as Gem took the dinner plates down from the cupboard.

"Tell me what you want me to do," Gem offered.

Mrs M chuckled. "For the baby, dear. She or he will need a nursery."

Blast! Starting already!

"It's months away," Gem protested, "there's really no reason to rush things."

"Rush!" the housekeeper shook her head. "There'll be painting needed, curtains, furniture, clothing. The bedroom is the question. You'll want the baby near you. The room where Jamie's things are. It's a good size room and it has a bathroom."

The thought made Gem very uneasy. She certainly would never put that suggestion to Wyatt. He wasn't pleased as it was that it was his child and not James's.

"No. I don't think that would be a very good idea," Gem said gingerly.

"What wouldn't be a good idea?" Wyatt said casually as he entered the kitchen.

Blast! He was using the Land Rover these days and Gem was still used to the warning of the Jag.

Gem refused to reply, darting a glance at the housekeeper calmly shelling peas into a bowl.

"We were discussing which bedroom should become the nursery," Mrs M said crisply. "It would have to be near the master suite."

"I see," Wyatt replied carefully, noting that Gem refused to look at him. "There's time still before decisions must be made, a good many months in fact."

"Indeed," Gem said firmly. Hopefully she would no longer be at the Hall by the time Mrs M began to sort bedrooms into a nursery. "Many months," she repeated his words.

"You won't have time to spend choosing paint colours or wall coverings," Mrs M pressed on. "Christmas will be here soon, then the New Year. After that the weeks will speed by. Work will have to be done." She rinsed the peas and checked the chicken and potatoes already in the cooker.

Gem stood uneasily, still holding the plates. Wyatt took the dishes from her hand. "You look a touch pale, my dear," Wyatt observed calmly. "Why don't you rest in your office until dinner."

"Okay," Gem agreed, sliding around him and out the door.

Wyatt set the plates down on the island counter and followed her - to Gem's dismay.

She spoke first to attempt to still a tirade from Wyatt.

"I wasn't going to say anything about a nursery," Gem said quietly, relieved to see his eyes were light grey.

"We'll have many matters to discuss in the coming months," he said smoothly. "Mrs M won't make all the decisions," he smiled briefly. "Is the rocking chair comfortable?"

"Lovely. Thank you," Gem smiled. "The lever is brilliant."

"Quite impressive. GEI is working with a new furniture artisan who is quite the inventor. This is her first rocking chair design. The lever brake is rather unusual."

"Brilliant! How is GEI involved?" Gem asked curiously.

"A project researcher is working with the designer to advise business strategies, marketing, financing, procuring the most suitable working space," Wyatt explained.

"And you reap the profit," Gem nodded.

Wyatt sighed. "GEI is donating the researcher's time. There is no profit for GEI. Our contribution is gratis."

"You don't receive anything from the business?" Gem said puzzled.

"I do not," Wyatt replied firmly. "However, you have a new rocking chair. And there is a catch."

"What?" Gem said cautiously.

"You must complete an opinion survey of the design. Quality of the item, aspects of the design, that sort of idea," he eased her down into the chair. "Rock out. I'll lay the table."

"Ms Holton's idea to work with the designer?" Gem asked as he walked to the door.

"Mine actually. Give back to the community. We hope the designer can expand to a half dozen employees this coming year," he winked at Gem and left the room. "Power," he called back over his shoulder.

Hmm, Gem pondered his words. At least he had a few good points. Probably all related to GEI. He was pleasant during dinner, asking her about her day, how she felt, if she had rested. His manner was polite, not critical. He insisted she rest or work on her book while he did the washing up.

Gem worked on the text of Durham; she had barely looked at the cathedral pages in days. But while she tried to concentrate on a massive plan of stone construction in the eleventh century, Wyatt constantly invaded her thoughts, his intrusion underpinned by the rocking chair in her peripheral vision.

She pushed him yet again from her mind and he appeared in reality at her elbow, bearing a cup of tea and a book.

"Another surprise?" she said carefully.

"A book of dogs. I thought you might be interested in the variety of breeds in the canine world," he said as he handed her the book. "I'll be in the library."

"Reading a report?" Gem asked.

"Reading your thesis. I purchased a few copies from the publisher. Mrs M was thrilled to receive a copy, as were Ms Holton and Manton."

Gem shook her head. "I could have given you copies," she sighed, dragging her fingers through her hair.

"But you wouldn't," Wyatt reminded her. "You didn't wish to, and now you have more sales."

He left her office, and Gem was quite relieved to avoid further verbal confrontation.

A book about dogs. "I hope you like dogs, Mrs Mac," Gem said to the cat stretched on her side to the left of the computer. "It looks like you shall be sharing your space with one. It will likely be preferable to sharing space with a snake."

Mrs Mac opened one eye, gazed cryptically at Gem, then slowly closed the eye.

"Better hope it's not a Saint Bernard," Gem murmured, "or there won't be any space for any of us."

Mrs Mac again opened and closed one eye. That was the total of her contribution to the chat.

Gem had progressed to a section delineating specific aspects of the medieval architecture, when she sensed Wyatt behind her. She shot Mrs Mac a narrow look, sending a silent message to the feline that she had neglected to warn of approaching animus.

"It's time for bed, Gem," Wyatt said quietly.

"It's always time for bed for you," she replied, frustrated by the interruption of the flow of words from thought to keyboard. "I'm working!"

"Cantankerous this evening," Wyatt observed dryly. "Yes, you are working, and in a few hours you will be down here again. I'll rephrase my remark: it's bedtime for you, Gem. You need rest."

She glanced at the time on the computer. "It's half eight. And sleep isn't what you have in mind," she retorted.

"Eventually it will be on my mind. However, you always take precedence in my thoughts."

"Bushwa!" Gem scoffed. "Power always takes precedence in your thoughts."

"Bushwa! What does that mean?" Wyatt leaned over her shoulder and clicked the mouse to save, then to turn off the computer.

"I have no idea, but it sounded appropriate."

"Making up words now?" he chuckled.

"Make-believe marriage, make-believe words."

Wyatt spun her chair around so that she had to face him. "We have quite the fantasy life, haven't we," he countered.

"You have the fantasy life. I live the science fiction flick," Gem shot back.

"As you like," Wyatt conceded. "Lyndon said you need rest. I'll relax you until you do rest." He drew her from the swivel chair.

"I knew you weren't referring to sleep."

"'Gem' and 'sleep' are two words rarely used successfully in a coherent sentence. You should realize that, you're a writer. But even you couldn't use those two words factually in a text," he teased, coaxing her into the hall, his arm around her waist.

"Was that a nasty shot at my book?" Gem stopped and stared at him, but he drew her along beside him.

"Indeed not. Your book is quite interesting - watch it - you nearly stepped on Mrs Mac," he pulled Gem aside as the feline scooted ahead up the stairs. "The photos are excellent, the text informative, clear and concise. Well done," he complimented.

Gem thought his words were sincere, however she steeled herself for a 'but' and a critical comment. One did not come, to her surprise.

"Take a shower, relax," he urged her as they reached the bedroom, then walked to his dressing room.

There was a thermos of hot chocolate by her computer when Gem returned to her office hours later. While she had slept, Wyatt had come down to the kitchen to make the beverage for her. Thoughtful. Why? She shook her head as she filled a cup with the steaming brew. Heavens! She was questioning his every move! Good! She had to keep on her toes!

She hadn't received much assistance from Mr Choate, Gem forced her thoughts to work. He was firm in his belief that no mole or sleeper existed in the SEA Network, B.I., or the Agency. And he was very quick to deny any allusion to Paul Andriani as having gone rogue.

Of course, it was only natural for Mr Choate to defend his predecessor, Mr Portermann. And to defend Paul Andriani, the Agency, B.I., and the SEA Network.

Still the logic was there. Someone had murdered the counter-couriers and agents. Someone had brought down the Pilos. Someone had been responsible - had premeditated all the deaths.

Unless the loss of the Pilos was pilot error. That was a loss that had to remain separate from the other events. Until the Pilos was found, and the reason for the 'crash' - it had to have crashed - was determined, it could not be connected to the murders. Except in Gem's mind.

And her mind said MOLE, SLEEPER, or ROGUE AGENT. Or it could be a courier. That was not a totally unreasonable assumption, other than the fact that couriers had the least information of the depth and breadth of Agency operations. As a courier's longevity with the Agency increased so did their information of the department. The Gems' information of the Agency and their advancement into the Agency 'inner circle' had rested a great deal on their parents' Agency association, and because of their photographic memories.

Mr Choate had denied the possibility of traitors in the Agency, B.I., or the SEA Network, but Gem knew he had listened to her ideas, and he would go back and review all personnel files, evidence in the deaths, and SOP in the different agencies Gem had mentioned to him. He had a load of work ahead of him, and she wouldn't add more to his burden by driving to London unless the trip was necessary.

Indonesia. Mr Choate had said a great deal by what he hadn't said. Gem was not NTK. Her best guess on Mr Choate's non-words, and her lack of NTK was the likelihood that the roil was being caused by a completely still unknown faction: a group, feeding unrest to chaos for whatever reason, fuelling passion to dissatisfied hearts and minds. There was no clear cause being supported, or defined. It was simply roiling to disrupt government. Perhaps a bit of a psycho or ego fuelled power play.

Gem pushed the start button again on the cd player, and poured another cup of hot chocolate. Rock-out. She did. She was too tired to pace. It was a lovely rocking chair.

Mr Cawley was awake. Gem pulled her mobile from her dressing gown pocket. She didn't have any questions to put to him, but the connection would be welcomed.

'Any news?'
'No. You working?'
'Yes.'
'Have anything for me?'
'Not yet.'
A thought ticked her brain. Your mum and Jane.
'Was my Auntie Jane a courier for the Agency?'
'Name?'
'Jane Louisa Lawson.'
She waited patiently, sipping hot chocolate, rocking, tickling Mrs Mac beneath her chin.
'Jane Louisa Lawson, B.I. 2003-2008.'
'Previous to 2003?'
'File sealed.'
'What?'
'Curious isn't it?'
'Have you read the file?'
'Only Agency Director and T.O. Director can read sealed files.'
'Was she a courier?'
'No.'
'Agent?'
'No.'
'What?'
'Cryptographer.'
'What?'
'Surprise!'
'No one thought to tell me this information?'
'Did you previously request this information?'
'No!'
'Your error.'
'Oh really!'
'Is it pertinent to current investigation?'
'Probably not.'
'Move on. Back to work, Gem.'

'Fine!'

'Curiosity. Why did you ask about JLL?'

'There was no family money. She never seemed to have a job. But she always had money. She mentioned wages.'

'Okay. Don't tell me.'

'Took a shot in the dark.'

'I'll accept that. But only barely passable.'

Okay, so it was a quick thought. It just wasn't a good one for her search.

A slipped cog from Mr Choate? Had he thought she had put twos together over the years to make the equation? Mr Choate had known both the twins. Your mum and Jane. He had not said 'Your Aunt Jane'. Just 'Jane'.

It was neither here nor there - just another fact she hadn't previously known. But B.I. - not the Agency. Mr Choate - sealed file. Auntie Jane - sealed file. The two probably worked together for B.I. Interesting, but not relevant, unless someone who had a sealed file was now vetting all Agency applicants. Knew all Agency 'secrets', missions, staff members, locations of couriers and agents on a moment's notice, procedures. Knew every damn thing about the Agency!

Mr Choate - who had assigned himself to be her shadow when Wyatt had rung Technical Operations regarding protection for her.

Mr Choate - who knew where she was every minute of the day and night. Who even knew Dr Lyndon had been at the Hall last night and wanted a reason as to why.

Mr Choate - who had seen Gemmy in Barcelona in May. Had seen Gemmy talking to Paul Andriani.

Where had Mr Choate been prior to 2003? File sealed.

Go to London tomorrow for a chat? The long drive. Waste of petrol. She would go for a walk and text him.

Spending a day at the Hall with Mrs M was a daunting proposition. Gem dreaded the thought of constant baby chatter. And she point-blank refused to think of changing James's room to a nursery. She wouldn't be able to bear the constant memory of James every time she walked into the room. It would be the same for Wyatt and Mrs M - at least Gem would think so. She didn't want to still be living at the Hall when the baby was born.

She leaned her head back against the chair and closed her eyes. Rocking. Rocking. It was a lovely chair. She would leave it at the Hall when she moved back to London. Or perhaps to Cambridge. But she would certainly purchase another rocking chair just like this one.

The music ended. Too soon. Gem opened her eyes. Wyatt stood watching her.

"It's nearly five o'clock, my dear. Time to leave your secret world - and rejoin this one - for now," he said quietly.

As Gem stood he lifted her in his arms.

"One day you won't be able to lift me," she sighed. "I'll be too fat."

Wyatt chuckled. "Highly unlikely, sweetheart. Highly unlikely."

Wyatt was very pleased that Gem did not intend to drive to London that morning.

"Don't let Mrs M chat your ears off - about anything," he whispered to Gem at the breakfast table. "And no chores for you. If you see dust and it bothers you, then pretend it's snow."

"Clever!" Gem grinned. She had eggs for breakfast. She could once again look at them and eat them, without feeling queasy. She leaned across the table to whisper, "How does one go about avoiding chatter?"

Wyatt considered the query. "Print off pages and pages of text and pretend you are editing your work," he suggested, also whispering.

"Okay. Good idea," she smiled conspiratorially.

"Don't weary yourself with a long walk. If you do go out -"

"Mobile and hat," Gem sighed.

"Just so. No wild parties," he teased.

"No," she giggled. He could be fun! "Perhaps I'll ask Mrs M to lunch at the Crow."

"An excellent idea. I have told her not to announce to the world about the baby, or you would be inundated with queries and chatter from the locals. Lyndon, of course, won't say a word."

"His office manager?" Gem said cautiously.

"Doesn't have one. He's retired for the most part and only has locals for patients."

That was a comfort to know.

"Do you need anything from London? Anything from Ora & Eda's Shop?" he queried.

"No, thank you," Gem shook her head.

"Then I shall see you at dinner," he kissed her, "mmm, or perhaps before that," he winked at her, then carried their dishes to the kitchen.

Gem was glad to see him leave. The butterflies had already flown that morning and threatened to escape again. Blast! Hormones!

Wyatt's ruse worked perfectly. Gem printed thirty pages of text and whether she was in the office, or stretching her legs wandering through the Hall, pages in hand, Mrs M looked at her, an obvious query on her lips that was quickly stilled. Lunch was another matter, and while Mrs M chatted about the baby on the walk to the pub, immediately as the two women entered the Crow she switched subjects to local gossip.

Despite the walk to the pub and voicing concern that Gem rest, Mrs M did not protest when she went for a brief afternoon stroll. Gem walked the upper cobblestone lane and was well away from the Hall when she pulled out her mobile. There was no one in the upper meadow and field, and if someone walked out of the forest it would take a fast paced hike of a half hour before the person came within listening distance of Gem.   She could easily read the lane and land before her, and to her left and right as she texted Mr Choate.

'How many years did you know Auntie Jane?'

'All her life.'

Whoa! More information new to her.

'Why is her file sealed prior to 2003?'

'It's confidential.'

Amusing! Mr Choate and Mr Cawley were becoming humorists!

'May I please have access to Auntie Jane's file?'
'Yes.'
'When?'
'75 years.'
'Why 75?'
'SOP.'
'And your file?'
'92 years.'
'Why not 75?'
'I'm playing with your mind. 75.'
'Would Mrs Brown or Harry clear me to read Auntie Jane's file?'
'Yes. In 75 years.'
'You are most amusing!'
'You're feeding me the lines.'
'Very frustrating!'
'Sorry, Gem, SOP.'
'I know.'
'If you find the Pilos, Gem, I will personally give you both files any time you request.'
Whoa!
'Deal!'
And it was a hell of a better deal than she had made at Marigold Cottage.

It was the ultimate deal! And Gem was definitely curious about the files. But if she found the Pilos that would be better than reading the mysterious sealed files of two mysterious people.

She spent the afternoon reading the texts for each chapter. There were errors she hadn't noticed before. It was a good afternoon's effort, and she finally had clean copy and clean pages. But Durham was far from finished. An early bedtime last night hadn't helped the Durham chapter, and despite additional hours of sleep she was still exhausted. She simply couldn't be this exhausted until May!

She was mystified that Wyatt had actually made the effort to find her thesis - and she was irritated that he was actually reading it. Sooner or later he would no doubt ask to see the thesis 'completed' this past May. It would be another way to harass her about leaving James.

Mrs M had chatted at lunch about the thesis copy Wyatt had given to her, and she told Gem she and the Mister were going to visit some of the cathedrals on their holiday come spring - before May, of course.

The news of Indonesia indicated a ramp-up of fighting, but government soldiers were gaining ground in controlling the situation. Another few days and the roil would be back to simmering - supposedly.

Wyatt was as pleasant at dinner as he had been the previous night, and although he said he would do the washing up, Gem insisted on doing so. She had spent so many hours sitting and rocking that day that she needed to stand - she also needed exercise and fresh air. Dishes done, Wyatt was the one insisting on accompanying her on a walk; and then insisting Gem go to bed.

The thermos of hot chocolate was again waiting by her computer. Gem settled in Auntie Jane's comfy chair; Mrs Mac settled on her lap for a few minutes then decided to again try perches of different heights.

Gem's brain was dry. Bake a cake. Mrs M always kept the pantry well stocked, and a shelf lined with cookery books, so Gem had the cake in the cooker in fifteen minutes flat. She texted Mr Cawley while she waited for the cake to bake.

'News?'
'No. Quiet night. Indonesia is calming. For now.'
'Harry, Mrs Brown, Blank?'
'No idea. Sorting?'
'Brain is dry.'
'Bake a cake.'
'Working on that.'
'Good. Take the night off.'
'It's morning!'
'Still dark. Night here.'
'I don't know what to do.'
'Rest your brain.'
'Okay. Goodnight.'
'Goodnight, Gem.'

Gem listened to the cd as the cake cooled. Every night. Or was it morning? When did night - at what time - did most people stop referring to night as night and think morning? Midnight? It had to be midnight. But Mr Cawley said it was still night, because it was still dark. Roiling. Simmering. Indonesia was always simmering. Nazis were still simmering.

What had occupied Auntie Jane for years while she was sealed in a file? Mum knew. And dad, of course. Gemmy hadn't known, Gem was certain of that. How curious that with four of them working for the Agency, Gem never knew her Auntie was at B.I. So curious. And working with Mr Choate?

Mr Choate. Mr Choate was as curious as Auntie Jane and Paul Andriani.

She trusted Mr Choate. And Harry, and Mrs Brown.

Gem iced the cake, watching for stray cat hairs floating in the air; that had never previously been a concern of hers, but they were definitely seen now at times in sunlight, floating with dust motes.

Gem put the cover over the cake, turned off the music and followed Mrs Mac back to bed. She lay awake; Wyatt's arms around her, the cat snuggled alongside her, waiting for the dark hours to finally draw to a close - that morning. For only that morning.

Chapter Twenty-Six

"You're going to be late for work," Gem murmured. "And Mrs M will have breakfast ready soon."

Wyatt stretched out next to her. "I rang Mrs M last night and told her not to come over today. I decided the only way you would stay in bed until noon was if I kept you here," he chuckled.

"You have meetings today," Gem reminded him.

"Ms Holton will take the meetings. I'll make you breakfast in bed. Then we'll have a long chat, lunch, and we'll visit a rescue centre and find a dog."

Again the dog. Well, it's his house; he should have a dog if he wanted one. If anyone would be a nay-say factor it should be Mrs M. Gem didn't have an opinion to share; it wasn't her house.

The animal rescue centre was one Ms Holton had suggested to Wyatt. The centre was spacious, clean and the manager, Ed, was easy going and eager to place a canine in a new home.

"Are you interested in a specific breed?" Ed asked, penning notes on a form.

"Gem?" Wyatt asked, and she shook her head.

"Must get along with a cat," she stated firmly.

"And children," Wyatt added.

"Puppy or an older dog?"

"Older," Gem replied. "Two or three years old?"

"Male or female?"

"Female," Gem replied.

"Don't we have enough females in the house now?" Wyatt frowned, but Gem realized he was teasing.

"All the females vote - on any subject - you lose," Gem grinned.

"We'd better have a son then," Wyatt said dryly. "I need another vote on my side."

"Forget it, mate," Ed advised. "Twenty males on your side, you'll still lose to the women." He smiled at Gem, and she nodded. But she and Wyatt both knew he was the only one who would always win. - For now. "One last question. Would the dog be alone quite often or for long periods each day?"

'Not at all," Wyatt stated.

"Right then. I would like to introduce you to Molly. She's two years, a golden lab and something else - or likely part golden lab," he smiled. "She'll bark once when she wants to go outside. I'll fetch her."

He returned almost immediately with a large, golden dog who carried a folded lead in her mouth.

"This is Molly," Ed said. "She's very well trained, as you can see."

Molly wandered over to Gem, sat her feet, and offered a paw. Gem gently shook the paw. "Hello, Molly. You are quite lovely," Gem smiled. She patted Molly gently on the head and the dog leaned against her leg.

"You are a clever girl, aren't you, Molly?" Wyatt said softly. Molly stood, padded over to him, and offered her paw. And after Wyatt shook it, she leaned against his leg and sighed contentedly.

He does that to women, Gem sent the dog a silent message. "Ah the Master's voice," Gem murmured.

Ed carefully watched the exchange. "Molly has been here for nearly a year. We hope to place her soon."

"She's lovely," Gem observed. "I can't imagine no one has taken her before this."

Ed gave them a rueful smile. "Molly has one idiosyncrasy that has put some people off. She refuses to sleep in a crate or to use a doggy pad. She insists on sleeping on furniture and she sheds considerably. I'll leave you three to get acquainted," he smiled and left the room.

"What do you think of her?" Wyatt asked.

"She's very sweet," Gem replied, and as she spoke Molly walked to her and nuzzled her hand. Gem stroked the silky head.

"Indeed," Wyatt agreed, watching the two.

"How do you feel about her sleeping on your furniture?" Gem queried.

"Ah. My furniture. My home. Still having that difficulty with proper pronouns, are you?" he shook his head.

Gem was about to shoot him a glare when Ed entered the room. Before he could speak Wyatt said firmly. "We like her. We'll take her home," and as he said the last word he looked at Gem.

Gem waited with Molly as Wyatt signed the paper work, paid an adoption fee and an additional donation that made Gem blink at the amount.

"I don't think Mrs M will like dog hair on the furniture," Gem said hesitantly as the three left the centre.

"Are you frightened of Mrs M?" Wyatt teased.

"Certainly not. I simply don't want to upset her," Gem protested.

"Mrs M has the premier hoover on the market," Wyatt held Gem's hand as they crossed the car park, Molly walking between them, lead in her mouth. "She'll adore Molly. Hang the hair problem. If Molly is brushed daily there will be less hair on the furniture. And now you will have a walking companion when I'm not home."

"Are you going to put GPS on her name tag?" Gem said pointedly

"Certainly. We wouldn't want Molly to become lost, would we?" He opened the rear door of the Land Rover and Molly immediately leaped to the seat and settled with a sigh. "You are ready to go home, aren't you Molly. So be it. Mr M is going to spirit you away for long walks in the woods."

Wyatt settled Gem in the Land Rover and when he climbed in the driver's seat, Molly put out a paw to him. "No, Molly. You sit there, right behind your mum."

"Mum! And I suppose you're her dad then," Gem groaned.

"That would be so," Wyatt agreed.
"You don't talk that way to Mrs Mac," Gem accused.
"I do. You just don't hear it."
"You are full of it!"

Wyatt reached back to rub the dog's head. "At least you like me, don't you, Molly," he chuckled.

"She doesn't know you yet. She'll like you until you take her out one night and leave her in a field somewhere," Gem said coolly, "and Mrs Mac too, no doubt."

"Why would you say that, Gem? If I didn't dump two snakes out in a field, why would I get rid of Molly and Mrs Mac?" he said, confounded by her remarks.

"The snakes weren't part of your Game," she said pointedly, wondering if he was ever going to engage the engine.

"Nor, precisely, was a baby. Usually women your age are on the pill. But there it is."

"You didn't ask me."

"Because I did not care," Wyatt said smoothly.

"No. You just change the tactics of your Game to suit yourself. I haven't figured out this one yet, but I will. Oh, you are being so kind, so thoughtful! As if you expect me to fall for that malarkey again!"

How brilliant you are, Gem! Almost frightfully so! He engaged the engine and pulled out of the car park.

"You are so suspicious, my dear."

"That's because I know what you are capable of now," Gem gave him a mock sweet smile.

"You think so, do you, sweetheart?" he said dryly. "Don't be too sure of that, Gem."

She fell silent. She knew one thing for certain: she couldn't ever trust him! Ever again!

Wyatt glanced at her. So clever she was! And so accurate in her suspicions. She certainly didn't trust him. No surprise there. But the accusation she made that he would get rid of their pets made him wince. That he would never do!

"Gem, do you truly think I would get rid of Molly and Mrs Mac to hurt you?" he asked seriously. "I promise you, my dear, I most sincerely would not do that. They will be as safe in my care as are you."

"Did you make a bargain with them also?" she said softly and very pointedly.

"Touché! And ouch!" Wyatt said wryly. Heavens she was amusing! And bitter! But not unexpectedly so. "Rest easy, Gem. Mrs Mac and Molly are part of our family now."

Oh how that word stung! The Lawsons and Forresters had been a family! This was not a family! "Family! Ha!" Gem said bitterly.

"What do you have against a lovely family, my dear?" Wyatt focused on the traffic surrounding them. Hormones. Just a touch, he reflected.

"You are not going to draw me into your delusions," Gem scoffed at him.

"What delusion?" he queried in surprised.

Gem raked her fingers through her hair.

"That this insidious relationship is a marriage. That is your fantasy!"

"We are legally married, my dear. We have a cat, a dog, and in the near future, a child. It is not only a marriage, we are a family," he said firmly. "Not a fantasy, my dear."

"It's science fiction then!" she snapped.

"Mind your temper, my sweet. Don't frighten Molly."

"Blast!" Gem groaned. "I want my life back!" She glared out the windscreen, frustrated by her desire to get out of the vehicle and walk for hours, frustrated they were trapped in the car in snarled traffic.

"Which life was that, sweetheart? Living alone in a flat? Did you even know your neighbours? You had no friends, save for Mrs Brown, whom you see infrequently. You had no family. You now have a husband, a proper home in a lovely village, a proper family, and friends: the M's, Mr Becton, Mrs Brown, Mr Choate, the women at the dress shop. You would have friends at Ticking Bottom if you could manage a smile and a chat now and then in the shops, rather than walking hours a day, lost in your secret world," he said candidly. "And what secret world is that, my dear?"

Mr Choate a friend? Wyatt considered Mr Choate to be her friend? Had she slipped a cog to have Wyatt regard her 'bodyguard' as her friend? Which he was - but-?

"You chatted easily enough with Mr Critchley at the car show," Wyatt continued, an edge creeping to his voice. "Was your reaction there because of his car, or the simple fact that he is a man? Was your persona at the car show a means to use him in one of your future misadventures? And a word of warning: Mr Choate is no fool. He won't fall for any of YOUR games, no matter how sweet and innocent you pretend to be. If you thought to play these men, and that other man at the car show, then think again, my dear Gem. I promise you, there will be no future adventures for you with other men."

Gem stewed silently as Wyatt manoeuvred the Land Rover through the dense traffic.

"After you there certainly will not be another man," Gem said icily.

"Thank you for the compliment, sweetheart," Wyatt chuckled sardonically.

"I meant I would rather live in a convent than ever again be involved with another man!"

"Nonsense, my dear. Our child will not be raised in a convent. He or she will be raised at the Hall - our home. Remember, my sweet, I call the shots in our marriage," he warned. "Mind your attitude."

"Didn't your parents ever teach you any manners?" Gem fumed.

"Didn't your parents teach you the meaning of the word veracity?" Wyatt said dryly. "And you will not again be involved with another man."

Gem reflected on his words. No blackmail. No threats. Compromise. His skewed definitions.

"I think you would do anything to anyone if it suited your purpose," Gem said slowly. "I can't believe you weren't married and divorced a dozen times before you MET me. At any rate, you probably have a half dozen children scattered over the landscape of your 'romances'."

"Ouch again! The extremely low opinion you have of me!"

"Do you blame me?" she said harshly.

"Ah, my sweet," his voice oozed charm, "we both know I do."

Gem gasped at his remark.

"However, I can assure you, my dear, that I am not a careless man. - Unlike you I am mindful of how babies are created. The only child I have is the one you are carrying," he said firmly. Then he frowned. "You're still not very pleased to be pregnant are you." It was a statement not a query.

"What?"

"You argue when I want you to go to bed early so that you may get more sleep. You fight resting. You're more concerned about not gaining weight than eating properly. You're out walking when you're exhausted," he frowned. "Don't you want to have our baby?"

Very blunt of him to ask the question. Do I? I have no choice! I have a choice, of course. Yes, she wanted to have this baby(ies) - she again self-edited. Of course she wanted her baby(ies). More than anything - especially now that Gemmy and James could not have theirs. Of course she wanted her own baby(ies)!

"I demand an answer, Gem," he persisted.

"Yes," she finally replied. "Of course I want this baby." Or both of them. Under different circumstances however!

Wyatt couldn't miss the lack of pronoun. "But you would rather the child wasn't mine," he said grimly.

"That's not it," Gem protested, feeling sudden desperation inside. The Agency was her Family. The M's, Mr Becton, only accepted her because she was Wyatt's wife. If they knew the truth about the marriage she would probably be less popular with Mrs M than Emerald. Her thoughts were concerned with locating the Pilos. Gemmy. Her family. She was in limbo. The pregnancy didn't seem real. Because her life wasn't real.

"I just wish it wasn't now," she said quietly, shaking her head miserably. "The marriage is a lie. If the M's and Mr Becton knew that fact they would despise me as much as you do. It doesn't seem real. I can't -"

"Explain," he finished for her. "You can't explain."

"Yes," Gem nodded.

"You never can explain, can you?" Wyatt mused quietly.

"No," Gem shook her head. "No, I can't."

"I see," he replied equally quietly.

The traffic finally thinned and they made progress on their route to Ticking Bottom. "We must stop at the Mercantile for food for Miss Molly," Wyatt finally spoke. "What would you like for dinner, my dear? A perfectly grilled steak and a salad?"

"Yes, thank you," Gem agreed. "I like Miss Molly. It sounds rather Oldie Worldie."

Wyatt chuckled at her words. "Shall I have the pet tag changed then?"

"Yes do," Gem nodded, smiling.

"Gem," Wyatt said thoughtfully, "why did you wait to tell me about the baby?"

"I thought you would be furious," she admitted hesitantly.

"Because of James?" he glanced at her.

"Yes," she nodded. "And - because I was so foolish. I never even thought of birth control. How completely, pitifully stupid is that?"

"I see," Wyatt said carefully. He heard sincerity in all her words. "Well, one could think of this as a learning experience."

"I've had enough of those lately to last me a lifetime," Gem sighed.

Wyatt wanted to ask what experiences she referred to, but he held back; not pressing points, attempting civility. "Gem," he said softly. "With all sincerity, I am not angry about our baby." He reached over to squeeze her hand.

"Okay," she murmured.

"And no convents," he said lightly, patting her hand before he returned his to the steering wheel.

"What? - Oh, okay," she gave him a small smile. A flat in London or Cambridge perhaps?

Miss Molly settled in quickly. She followed Gem and Wyatt into the mudroom, and as they hung their windcheaters on hooks, Miss Molly dropped her lead next to their wellies.

Mrs Mac greeted her new housemate with the requisite hissing and spitting and growling. Miss Molly sniffed the hissing fur bundle, blinked twice and wandered off to survey the domicile. She then followed Gem and Wyatt to the bedroom suite. When Gem finished showering she found the poochie stretched out on the bed.

"The bed is getting smaller," Wyatt chuckled, as he walked out of his dressing room, towel wrapped around his waist.

"So are my pyjamas," Gem groused, tugging at the waistband.

"Don't start on that," Wyatt sternly ordered. "Would you like dinner served in bed?" he queried with an intense gaze.

"No, thank you," Gem parried. "I had breakfast AND lunch in bed. I would prefer to sit on a chair for dinner. Besides, there's no room on the bed," she waved her hand, indicating the snoozing dog.

"I'll arrange something," Wyatt assured her, "but for now, Molly," he said firmly, "here," calling her to the window seat. And Molly obeyed beautifully.

"Dinner's going to be late this evening, isn't it," Gem mused.

"Yes, it is, and then bed for you. I have reports to read this evening," Wyatt said firmly.

Gem sighed quietly as her eyes opened. She took a deep breath, and slipped out from under Wyatt's arm. Mrs Mac jumped down to the floor as Gem pulled on her dressing gown. In the faint glow from the lamp in the sitting room, Gem could see Molly stretched out at the foot of the bed, surprisingly not taking up much room considering her size. Gem skirted the foot of the bed and struck her toe against something very hard.

"Blast!" she clamped her hand over her mouth, hoping she hadn't wakened Wyatt. But she had. And Molly wakened, lifting her head to gaze at Gem.

"Darling? What happened?" Wyatt switched on the bed table lamp.

"A bench," she said in surprise. "I stubbed my toe."

Wyatt walked around the bed, pushing her gently down on the mattress. "Right foot, left foot?" he yawned.

"Right. The toe that should be glowing in the dark by now," she winced.

Wyatt gently manipulated the digit. "Bruised, but not broken," he announced and kissed the throbbing toe. "I'm sorry, sweetheart. You were sleeping when I put the bench there."

Gem poked her finger on the thick pillow stretching the length of the bench. Ah! She recalled seeing it in one of the furniture groupings in the attic.

"Nice bench," she admired. "Brilliant solution. Miss Molly seems appeased."

"More room for us," Wyatt yawned again.

"Oh, Wyatt, I'm sorry I wakened you. Go back to sleep," she said earnestly. As he climbed into bed, Molly jumped down from the bench and started to follow Gem. "No, Molly, stay with daddy," she urged, and Wyatt chuckled. "Now doesn't that sound ridiculous?" Gem stated firmly to him.

"Get use to the sound of it, sweetheart," he chuckled again. "She'll wander back if she wants to," he added.

The hot chocolate thermos was by her computer, and two plush blankets were tucked over the fabric of the comfy chair and the settee. Wyatt thought of everything, including keeping dog hair off Auntie Jane's furniture. Very considerate. Again - what part of his Game was this? Molly wandered through the kitchen and the butler's pantry then curled up on the settee. Mrs Mac eyed the dog with clear disapproval from her perch on the back of the comfy chair. Gem sipped hot chocolate and rocked, keeping an eye on the dog, the cat, and the telly.

The calamity in Indonesia had quieted to what their mum had termed a 'dull roar'; the area was near simmering again. Mr Cawley was awake.

'What news, Mr Cawley?'
'Can't think of a single item. You?'
'Have a dog now.'
'Name? Breed?'
'Miss Molly. Golden lab or something like that. 2 yrs. old.'
'Mazel tov!'
'Thank you.'
'Working?'
'Not yet.'
'Start!'
'Okay!'
'Goodnight!'
'Goodnight!'

Nagging again. She punched start on the cd player, muting the sound on the television. She watched the camera shots, admiring the courage of the reporters and camera crews. She wouldn't have the courage to enter a riot zone; that required a passion she could never feel.

As she watched the news film, something tickled at the farthest reaches of her brain. Something. Something. Something to do with Indonesia. Something to do with the SEA Network? It slipped away. But it HAD been there!

Bless Wyatt for making the hot chocolate!

What?

What was she saying! Thanking him was one thing. Wishing a blessing on him was a completely different matter altogether! Someone else could bless him for something. - The new factory owners! Let them bless him!

Paul Andriani. That something in the back of her mind related to him. She knew it. Something she had heard weeks ago. She couldn't reach the something. Or anything related to when, or who, or what.

Blast!

Miss Molly sighed a long, deep, contented sigh.

What would Wyatt add next to his household? A budgie would not be a good idea. It would only serve as prey for Mrs Mac.

Paul Andriani.

Mr Choate.

Gemmy.

Barcelona.Paul Andriani.

She couldn't reach the thought. And it had that nagging irritation of an ear worm: the strain of a melody playing over and over in your mind; and you can't recall the song, but at times you could even recall the voice singing the song; but not the song itself.

It had to work its way out of the depths of her memory on its own.

She reached again for her mobile.

'Any news regarding Harry or Mrs Brown?'

'No.'

'Blank?'

'No.'

'You're no help.'

'Are you?'

'Ouch!'

'Same here. Get back to work!'

Well, at least her brain was less dry than it had been during the last dark hours. And she had to admit she was a bit less tired physically than she had been for weeks. However, her brain was still weary.

She wiggled her toe. The throbbing had ended, but the digit was still tender. Wyatt had kissed it. What the Hell! What was his Game now? Mr Hyde was apparent more often these days with few appearances of Dr Jekyll. Yet the evil Dr Jekyll still lurked in her peripheral vision.

Wyatt had said he wasn't angry about the baby. But he was still an angry man, admitting so, with his comment about 'blaming her'.

How could she of the Jane Austen world, figure out a game player from the gritty business world? A steel barracuda. She simply had to watch this direction of his Game play out. In a hundred years' time she would not be able to figure out Wyatt Grantham. She had her hands full looking for Gemmy. The best she could hope for was not to be completely destroyed by the man.

Odd. Why was it always Gemmy who took precedence in her thoughts? - And not mum or dad? She missed them as much as she missed Gemmy. Their loss was no less important to her than the loss of Gemmy. But in losing Gemmy, she had lost half of herself. Her life-long confidante, her best friend. Her other half. Half of their Gemini twins.

Where are you Gemmy?

She pulled out her mobile again.

'Any news of search of South China Sea?'

'Pulled off due to chaos in Indonesia. Should resume in or about a fortnight.'
'Blast!'
'Trying to avoid precisely that!'
'Thanks! Goodnight!'
'Goodnight, Gem. Pleasant dreams - when they start!'
'And to you.'

She cleared the messages, slipped the phone into her pocket, turned off the cd player and electric fireplaces, rinsed out the thermos and cup - and shadowed by Miss Molly at her heels, and Mrs Mac from a safe distance ahead, she walked down the long hall to the staircase.

"Back to bed, little ones," she sighed.

Blast! The hormones, she sighed again as she climbed the stairs. The butterflies were again flying. Hopefully the hormones would eventually even out in the next few weeks. She patted the bench and Miss Molly received the message, stretching out full length on the cushion with a deep sigh. Gem stroked the dog for a few minutes before she slipped back into bed.

"If I sigh, will you stroke me?" Wyatt murmured.

"If you sleep on the bench," Gem grinned slightly.

"We wouldn't both fit on the bench," he objected, yawning, slipping his arm around her waist.

"Very well. Allow me a few hours of sleep and then you may sigh," she murmured. And I'll let the butterflies fly.

Miss Molly was warmly welcomed by the M's, and the Mister insisted on taking her for a quick pre-breakfast walk to visit nature. The poochie immediately accepted the M's as part of her new life.

Wyatt's early morning sigh brilliantly curtailed the pesky butterflies, and Gem actually faced the morning with growing energy.

"Interesting," Wyatt reflected as Gem appeared at the breakfast table.

"What?" she asked curiously.

"I actually see the proverbial 'glow'," he admitted in a surprised tone.

"Un-huh," Gem said skeptically.

"Seriously. You look ten times better than you have in weeks," he complimented.

"Good! Then you can cease your constant nagging about rest and sleep," Gem sighed with relief.

"On the contrary, if it's working it shall continue," he countered. "An hour in the morning, two in the afternoon," he ordered.

"You won't be here," Gem challenged.

"I shall be here," Mrs M interjected as she served their breakfasts. "It will be so," she gave Wyatt a firm nod.

Gem put on a pleasant smile, but she was stewing inside. For years she had been capable of managing her own life, aside from the Agency's influence of her career. She had lost that independence with the two fatal words 'I do' this past September. It was frustrating enough having Wyatt telling her what to do; having Mr Choate following her constantly when she left Ticking Bottom. And now Mrs

M had the upper hand. The constraints on her freedom were pushing her to the edge of her patience.

Wyatt said goodbye to her, Mrs M, Mrs Mac, and Molly, in that order. At least, Gem mused, irritated, I am first in his pack order. She cleared the breakfast table, nursing a silent fume, storing the marmalade and butter while Mrs M put the dishes in the dishwasher.

The housekeeper was well aware of the young woman's mood. "Is that steam I see coming out of your ears, dear?" she queried with a touch of amusement.

Gem nodded abruptly. "I refuse to be wrapped in cotton wool," she said firmly. "I do not need cosseting."

"You do not," Mrs M agreed firmly.

"I am an adult!" Gem stated, equally firmly.

"You are. You are a mature, intelligent, responsible young woman."

"Precisely."

"That is your point of view," Mrs M said patiently. "From Mr W's point of view, you are his lovely, young wife, and you are carrying his baby." She folded her arms and leaned against the counter, her back to the sink. "Mr W lost his mother, his father, and dear Jamie. He waited a long time to get married. To make that commitment. And he made it to you, dear. You are his life now."

The thoughts were beautifully and sincerely expressed. Unfortunately Mrs M had bought into the allusion Wyatt had so expertly projected of a 'real' marriage, Gem mused.

"Mr W doesn't easily express his emotions," the housekeeper continued.

He expresses his anger quite easily, Gem did not suggest.

"I believe his past relationships didn't fare well because of that trait. Women wanted more than he was willing to give - but he decided he wanted to share everything to you."

And that again would be anger, Gem winced inwardly.

"He loves you, and Mr M, and Mr Becton," Gem countered.

Mrs M smiled. "We have all been with him since his first day in this world. We grew in his heart naturally. But he risked letting down his defences to take you into his heart. That was truly astounding. Mr Jack said Mr W would never marry - wouldn't give up enough of himself to let a woman into his life. But Mrs Fiona and I always knew Mr W was a one woman man. You are that woman." She fell silent for a moment, then chuckled. "Can you imagine how green that Emerald is knowing how hard she worked to trap Mr W. But he chose you!"

Gem smiled back at the woman. Bought the entire allusion, and the rest of the fantasy life Wyatt had neatly projected. He was a smashing success, wasn't he just! But Emerald turning green was definitely an acceptable image. For some reason she couldn't fathom, that photo in the album in James's room - the snap of Wyatt with his arm around Emerald, absolutely rankled Gem.

"Green, eh?" Gem grinned at Mrs M.

"Through and through - emerald green, pea green, shamrock green, you call it," the housekeeper chuckled.

"Bile?" Gem teased.

"There you have it! And so, my dear, when Mr W attempts to wrap you in cotton wool, please be a bit more tolerant," Mrs M advised.

"Yes, ma'am," Gem nodded politely, reflecting that at least one of them was not delusional. Mrs M could enjoy her delusions for now, and Gem regretted the fact that one day those delusions would roil, then explode. And Gem would greatly miss Mrs M when the fantasy world collided with the real world. Wyatt would have to be the one sweeping up the pieces when Gem permanently left the Hall and Ticking Bottom. And Wyatt would have joint custody of their child, so the M's and Mr Becton would grow naturally in the heart of the next generation of Granthams.

"You go off now and enjoy yourself," Mrs M encouraged her. "I've said my piece and bent your ear long enough."

Gem put the next two hours to good use washing her laundry and putting away the items she wouldn't be wearing again for months.

The laundry task finished, she turned her attention to the dog who had repeatedly, faithfully, followed her from master suite to mudroom and back again.

"Would you like a walk, Miss Molly?" Gem queried to the dog as they walked down the staircase.

Molly trotted off and Gem followed her to the kitchen, arriving as Miss Molly reached the kitchen door, lead in her mouth.

"She is a corker!" Mrs M laughed, watching the dog sitting patiently, eyes focused on the doorknob.

"Staggering!" Gem joined in laughing.

"Mr M gave her a good brushing when he took her out this morning. He said you don't need to use the lead. She won't leave your side unless you say r-e-l-e-a-s-e," she spelled clearly.

"How did Mr M know that?" Gem queried in surprise.

"It's on the instruction form from the animal centre," Mrs M indicated the sheet of paper at the edge of the counter. "When you say that word she knows she can run. When you want to call her back say c-o-m-e M-o-l-l-y."

"R-i-g-h-t," Gem smiled. Miss Molly continued to wait patiently while Gem fetched her windcheater.

"Mobile?" Mrs M queried.

"Yes, ma'am," Gem patted her pocket. It was a grey day so she did not need a hat. She quickly read the instruction form. "Come Molly' was used as a direct tool for the dog so that she wouldn't respond to someone who might try to divert her attention, or try to steal her. Gem noted that Molly also had an identity chip under her skin in the event that she became lost. There was a symbol on her pet tag indicating that she had been chipped, so if found, she could be identified and returned to her family.

Gem closed her eyes briefly, making sure she had the form set in her memory. Yes. "We are off then, Mrs M," she grinned at the housekeeper.

"No longer than a half hour, Mr W insisted," Mrs M warned her.

Miss Molly trotted by Gem's side as if stuck with adhesive. After ten minutes of walking, Gem stepped off the cobblestone lane onto the dormant meadow, and firmly gave the instruction of release to Miss Molly, who instantly dropped the lead and hared off in a flash. Gem looked at her watch. She would give Molly a good run; constantly being patient, quiet, and obedient must store up a great deal of energy under all the fur. The dog bounded back to Gem, crouched down on her front legs, tail wagging, then hared off again across the field, her joy causing Gem to burst out laughing.

"What a delight you are, Miss Molly," Gem said happily, as the dog returned to repeat the front crouch and bolting off game. "Finally one game I can enjoy," Gem mused dryly.

After fifteen minutes, Gem called the order to return and the dog instantly complied, returning to take up the lead in her mouth and again attach herself to Gem's side.

"You are smashing, Molly," Gem patted the dog on the head. "Blast dog hair on the furniture! All the other people who didn't want you were absolute fools! You are marvellous!"

They returned to the Hall within Wyatt's time frame and met Mr M who tied a yellow scarf around Molly's neck and spirited her off for a ramble in the woods.

"Don't let her get hurt," Gem insisted.

"Miss Molly will be fine," the estate manager assured her. "And I believe you are supposed to rest before lunch," he reminded her.

Another member of Team Wyatt heard from; Gem gave him a smile. "Indeed," she entered the kitchen as obediently as Miss Molly had followed Mr M off into the woods. Cotton wool had to eventually wear off. In the short history of their relationship, Wyatt's tolerance threshold of her was exceedingly low. His cotton wool treatment of Gem would return again to indifference and barely concealed contempt, and his interest in the baby would flag. Well, his interest between the sheets would likely remain the same - until she expanded. She knew the 'rules' of his previous Games; she just couldn't yet figure out the scheme of this current one.

Mrs Mac stretched across her lap while Gem rested on the settee. She had not allowed her mind to wander while she was out with Miss Molly, concentrating instead on keeping the poochie safe. However, she could stroke Mrs Mac and reflect. It was mentally exhausting trying to decipher Wyatt's current Game. As difficult, in fact, as trying to locate the Pilos.

That 'something' at the back of her mind was still stuck in limbo, and she well knew that feeling!

Paul Andriani. Where was that man? Barcelona? Or somewhere else in Spain? If she wanted to disappear where would she go to do so? A very populated country - melt into a crowd. Japan, Hong Kong, Indonesia - there was that area again. India. New York City. Rome. Where would it be easiest to find a place to live? That she could not say. Still a highly populated area would be the best bet. Hiding in plain sight.

Mrs M was chatty at lunch - about baby names. "If it's a boy, Mr W will want to name him James, after the baby's uncle," she said confidently.

"I'm sure," Gem agreed, knowing she would have no say in the matter, and she wouldn't have the heart to refuse the tribute to Wyatt's brother.

"And if the baby is a girl, have you thought of a name?" Mrs M queried. "I heard Mr W mention Jamie, which is a pretty little name. But you must have thoughts of your own."

"Anne - with an 'e', is a nice name," Gem suggested, "or Jane." It didn't really matter what she said, she realized. Mrs M merely wanted to chat about the baby. And Wyatt would insist on Jamie. Gem knew she would have to fight for any decision she would be permitted to make concerning the baby(ies).

"Catherine with a 'K' or a 'C'," Mrs M offered, "Elizabeth. What was your mother's name, dear? Perhaps you would like to use her name."

To Gem's relief, Mr M chose that moment to enter the kitchen with Molly. He reminded the Missus of her club meeting that afternoon.

"Oh, that's right!" Mrs M turned to Gem. "I have to leave early. Mr W will be bringing Chinese home for dinner. If you would prefer another choice give him a ring to let him know."

"Chinese is fine," Gem replied. It must be a 'fun' club; Mrs M never missed a meeting. Gem started chatting to the estate manager in an attempt to divert his wife's attention from baby names. "Did Miss Molly enjoy her walk in the woods?"

"She's quite the trooper," he nodded. "She'll have a bit of a rest and will be ready for an afternoon airing."

And baby names indeed slipped Mrs M's thoughts - at least for now, to Gem's relief. She had to find Gemmy and the Pilos!

Mrs M went to her dusting routine, steadfastly refusing to allow Gem to assist with the housework. Gem retreated to her office and pulled up the Durham file on her computer, convincing herself to finish the chapter by the end of the weekend. She turned on the telly, perused the situation on the factions finally calming in Indonesia, then decided to listen to Sibelius instead of the international news. Hot spots might be simmering but none seemed likely to heat to a roil that day.

Flying buttresses, naves, vaults, consumed her until she heard a muted sigh behind her. She turned to discover Miss Molly sitting just inside the doorway, lead in her mouth.

"You're a delight, Miss Molly!" Gem declared laughing; she clicked save and went to fetch her windcheater. She tracked Mrs M down in the library, dusting the book shelves. "Miss Molly had decided we need a walk," she informed the housekeeper.

"You'll never find another one like her," Mrs M smiled. She glanced at her watch. "You must rest when you return," she ordered firmly.

"Yes, ma'am," Gem said respectfully. She couldn't or wouldn't argue with Mrs M. It would be as futile as arguing with Wyatt on any subject.

They walked down the cobblestone lane and Miss Molly behaved perfectly. When they reached the old stone bridge below the Hall, Gem released Miss Molly to run across the meadow. She'd allow the dog to run for a quarter hour, then they would continue to the rail station before returning to the Hall. Gem leaned against the bridge wall, watching Molly run full out until the dog stopped suddenly and stared towards the bridge. Gem turned her head to follow the dog's gaze and saw a man strolling towardss her. Molly bolted back to Gem, putting her body between her mistress and the interloper.

"Good heavens, Molly, you are something else!" Gem said admiringly. "Good Molly." She rested her hand on the dog's head. "It's Dr Lyndon. He's a mate."

"Hello, Gem," the doctor said pleasantly, stopping a bit back from them.

"Good afternoon, Doctor," Gem replied. "This is Miss Molly."

"Hello, Miss Molly," he approached, holding out his hand for the dog to sniff. When she decided he was acceptable she offered her paw which he gently shook. "Where did this beauty come from?"

Gem explained the situation and as she spoke the dog returned to her side, and retrieved her lead.

"She wants to protect you," Lyndon advised. "Only twenty-four hours and she's already well settled in. She's happy."

"So she is," Gem agreed.

The doctor studied her. "And you are looking better than the last time I saw you. Having a bit more rest are you?"

"Yes," Gem assured him.

"Is your insomnia easing?"

"No," Gem shook her head.

"Then rest as best you can," Lyndon suggested. "Did you ring Dr Hallowell this week?"

Gem had forgotten he had suggested she do so. "No, I should, I suppose."

"Next week. I think that would be advisable. Ring me if need me." He said good bye to Molly and continued up the lane.

"Let's walk to the rail station, Miss Molly, then go back to the Hall," she said to the dog, "before Mrs M sends a search party for us."

Mrs M was tapping her foot when they walked into the kitchen. "You are a quarter hour late, young ladies. You can add that on to your rest time," she gave Gem a stern look.

"Yes, ma'am," Gem replied meekly, properly chastised.

Gem rested on the settee, watching with amusement at Miss Molly who sat on the floor at the centre of the room, staring up at Mrs Mac who sat on the counter staring down at the dog.

"You two will be mates one day," Gem advised them. And when that happened she wouldn't be able to take them away from each other. They would both have to remain at the Hall with Wyatt and the M's.

The staring continued even when Mrs M brought Gem a cup of tea. "When did they start that?" Mrs M demanded at the animal tableau.

"First I've seen it," Gem said softly. "I hope they're not preparing to attack."

"I think one of them would be growling by now if that were the case. Just don't step between them if they get riled," Mrs M advised, keeping her voice low.

"Molly is so docile I can't believe she would hurt Mrs Mac," Gem protested.

"Other way around. Mrs Mac has the claws and fangs. Leave them to figure each other out then," she suggested. "I'm off now to my club. I'll see you tomorrow, dear."

"Yes, ma'am."

The animals continued the pose, not moving a muscle even when Ora rang to inform Gem her clothes would be ready the following morning. Gem was relieved she would have looser fitting clothes, and she made a mental note to shop M and S for pyjamas.

As she watched Miss Molly, she remembered the instruction form from the animal centre stated the poochie got along extremely well with felines. So it was Mrs Mac's responsibility, Gem decided, for the cat to accept the dog.

The staring contest was finally broken by the sound of the kitchen door opening and closing, and Molly bounded off to check out the intruder.

"Hello, Miss Molly," the intruder's voice warmly greeted the dog. "Have you been a good dog today?"

Molly trotted back into the office to show Gem the large bone she was carrying in her mouth. "Very nice, sweetie," Gem patted Molly's head.

"You have never once said that to me," Wyatt said teasing, following the dog into the office.

"I don't recall you ever bringing a bone to show me," Gem challenged the remark, adding a grin.

"I brought you this instead of a bone," he handed a shop tote to her.

Gem glanced at him, frowning, then looked in the bag. One, two, four, six. Six sets of pyjamas, she counted pulling a set from the tote.

"They'll stretch a bit," he winked at her.

Gem looked at him, distracted by his smile. The Blasted butterflies were starting to swarm. "Did you send Ms Holton out to shop for you?" Gem bit her lower lip between her teeth.

"Certainly not. I do not expect staff to run private errands for me. You wouldn't expect Dr Hallowell to prune your rose tree simply because you paid him for his services, would you?"

"I would not," Gem agreed. "Thank you."

Wyatt nodded. "Try on a pair, see if they fit, while I set dinner out," he suggested.

Gem slipped into the bathroom. The pyjamas fit perfectly, and had a bit of stretch as Wyatt had said.

"They fit perfectly," Gem joined him in the kitchen.

"As I said before," he teased, "I know every bit of you. How is your toe, by the way?"

"Fine, thank you," Gem replied, still blushing from him previous remark.

Wyatt chuckled, noting the blush. "Will you please feed Miss Molly her dinner? I'll return in a few minutes."

Gem nodded, deciding he was going to change out of his suit. She fed the poochie and checked Mrs Mac's food bowl which had been placed on a wide shelf out of the dog's reach. Mrs Mac seemed to enjoy the view from the high shelf.

Wyatt returned; he had quickly changed his clothes and he was carrying her dressing gown. "It's a bit chilly down here," he said, holding the garment so she could slip her arms into the sleeves.

"Very thoughtful of you," she smiled at him, silently wondering what the HELL he was playing at with the thoughtful manner.

"I do have my moments," he grinned, setting the tea kettle on the cooker.

They ate in the kitchen. Wyatt had ordered all her favourites from the restaurant. Now he was being too obvious, she observed. Did he really think she wouldn't be suspicious of his actions?

`"What is that?" Wyatt waved his fork towardss the kitchen door.

Gem looked across the room. Mrs Mac was sitting on the edge of the counter near the door. Miss Molly was sitting on the floor staring up at the cat staring down at her.

Gem shook her head. "They were doing that just before you came in. I watched then for over two hours. They blink but they don't move."

"An odd way to size up one another," he grinned.

"Perhaps it's a war between pacifists," Gem laughed.

"Would that be considered a war?" Wyatt chuckled. "Or a truce?"

"I have no idea. I just let them be," Gem shrugged.

Wyatt watched the animals as he ate. They blinked but did not move. "Good decision," he agreed.

Gem insisted on doing the washing up. As she started clearing dishes, Miss Molly broke the animal trance, fetched her lead and brought it to Wyatt.

"Well trained, indeed," he murmured. "I believe we are going for a walk."

"Enjoy. She's brilliant," Gem smiled, remembering her outings with Molly that day.

Gem was back in her office in a short time, now with Mrs Mac for company. The animals were a pleasant distraction from the nearly stultifying atmosphere often permeating the Hall. She slipped Queen into the cd player, and read about cat and dog mates on the inter-net. She read a great many articles of multiple animal families but none mentioned the curious stare down that she and Wyatt - and Mrs M - had witnessed of Molly and Mrs Mac. She looked at the time on the computer. Wyatt and Molly had been gone for nearly three quarters of an hour. Mrs M could worry less about Wyatt working himself to an early death now. Molly would see to it that he would be taken from his work each day.

She set aside her work to put her new pyjamas in her lowboy, except for a set to wear after her shower. Wyatt's ploy to project a thoughtful persona! Another lie. And he called her a liar, she groused as she showered and washed her hair. She was braiding her hair when Wyatt, Molly, and Mrs Mac entered the suite; the cat was draped around Wyatt's neck.

"You're wearing a cat," Gem observed with amusement.

"Some people do," Wyatt replied.

"How long has she been doing that?" Gem asked curiously.

"A few days. She wanders down at night when I make hot chocolate for you."

"Ah," Gem replied, chuckling. "Did you enjoy your walk?"

"There was less arguing with her than when I walk with you," Wyatt grinned. "It was a quiet walk. Are you going to bed now?"

"Are you?" she gazed at him. Those Blasted butterflies!

"Quick shower!" he smiled at her, and walked into his dressing room, Mrs Mac still on his shoulder.   Bless those hormones!

Gem did not crack her toe on Molly's bench when the dark hours started, much to her appreciation. The hot chocolate thermos and cup were by the computer. She didn't remember falling asleep, but that didn't matter because the butterflies had been calmed. She slipped Queen out of the cd player and slipped in her constant companion of the dark hours. Mrs Mac stretched out on the counter. Miss Molly curled up on the settee.

Gem chuckled as she recalled Mrs Mac riding high in the air on Wyatt's broad shoulders. He was a very tall man, yet the cat had seemed perfectly relaxed on her perch. Gem checked the inter-net about cats riding on shoulders and found a number of humorous anecdotes regarding the habit. She found a quote that caught her eye: if your boyfriend dislikes your cat, get rid of the boyfriend. If your cat dislikes your boyfriend, get rid of the boyfriend. Amusing! She could only wonder how many women had used cats to navigate romantic relationships using felines to judge the character of their dates. The adage obviously had flaws since Mrs Mac liked Wyatt. Or perhaps she was the one feline who was either a poor judge of character - or she had yet to read the adage.

Mr Cawley was awake, Gem mused as she pulled out her mobile.
'What news have you?'
'Indonesia is quieting.'
'Watched that on the telly.'
'Then nothing.'
'Harry, Mrs Brown. Blank?'
'No information.'
'We're stagnating!'
'Perhaps. Cat accepting dog?'
'So far no tussles.'
'Good start. What do you have for me, Gem?'
'Something at the back of my mind. Can't reach it.'
'Let it fester. Can you pinpoint regarding?'
'Blank.'
'Really! Let it fester then.'
'I shall.'
'Goodnight.'
'Goodnight.'

Paul Andriani. Gemmy. Mr Choate. Barcelona.

The words repeated over and over in her mind, adding no further names, eliminating none. She settled in Auntie Jane's comfy chair, and Mrs Mac decided to join her. Physically Gem was feeling much improved, but mentally she was still exhausted.

Gemmy, where are you? Where are you, Gemmy? After so many months could finding the Pilos be anything other than an unreachable dream?

Harry, Mrs Brown, Mr Choate, Mr Cawley, Mr White. If they couldn't locate the Pilos, then what chance had she to do so? Mr Cawley continued to press. 'What do you have for me, Gem?' he asked so many nights. She had never contributed any item that would have been of any assistance to anyone in the Agency. Odessa. That seemed to be slipping into a flight of fantasy - no pun intended.

She picked up Mrs Mac, left the comfy chair for the thermos, returned to the chair, depositing the cat on her lap and the thermos on the floor by her feet. Best not to have to dislodge kitty again until she restarted the cd player.

In a little over a month the Christmas holiday would arrive. It would be the first Christmas she hadn't spent in Australia since her family had moved there when she and Gemmy were children. Her first Christmas without Gemmy.

Without their parents. Christmas at the Hall with Wyatt. What a dreadfully depressing thought! And it would be Christmas here because she wouldn't have located the Pilos by 25 December.

She would have to purchase a gift for Wyatt. Lovely. Depressing. He had, however, worn the grey sweater she had purchased for him weeks past. He had worn it many times in fact.

She had purchased the sweater for him. He had purchased books, frillies, cds, pyjamas, hats, sunglasses, for her. She had not again worn the Aran sweater he had purchased for her in Inverness, nor had she worn the gifts he had given her before they married. And he had never asked her why she hadn't used his gifts - except that one time he had referred to the pendant watch he had given her on their 'wedding day'. And she never would wear those items. Yet - she wore the frillies, the pyjamas, the sunglasses, the hats, read the books, and played the cds. Was there an invisible dividing line for her there?

Mrs M would expect Gem to purchase gifts for Wyatt. She could push that out of her mind for many weeks yet.

Paul Andriani. Was he the clue to the Pilos? The clue to Geneva?

Where the Blast has Harry been since late August? And Mr Cawley had no news of Mrs Brown even though Indonesia had settled down again to a simmer.

She pulled out her mobile again.

'Any news of underlying cause of roil in Indonesia?'

'None yet reported to me.'

'Okay. Thanks!'

'Pleasant dreams!'

'And to you!'

She cleared the messages on her phone and slipped it back to her pocket.

A headache was creeping in at the nape of her neck, and she toyed with the notion of going to bed to wait for the end of the dark hours. She might disturb Wyatt and he needed his sleep.

The dark hours were still dark, but her new companions made the hours a bit less lonely.

Wyatt didn't argue with her when she said she was going to London to get the clothes from the dress shop. Nor did he caution her against over-exerting herself.

"If you are still in the city at noon, will you join me for lunch?" he requested with considerable politeness.

It was one of the few times he had actually invited her to lunch; usually he told her to meet him for lunch - and where they would meet.

"Yes. Where?"

"Where would you like?"

"Not Jake's," she frowned. "That waitress is a bit irritating. I have no doubt she spits in my food before she serves it."

Wyatt laughed at her reply. "Charley's Pub? The one you visit with Mrs Brown?"

"The service is slow," she lied. "The White Cat?"

"Excellent. Noon. White Cat, if you can manage that time."

Again the decision was up to her? A most interesting direction to his Game.

She was further puzzled by Wyatt's new Game plan when she arrived at the dress shop. Wyatt had visited the shop the past Tuesday, had paid for the clothing Gem had ordered, and had ordered additional items for her: fleece dressing gowns, jumpers, blouses, and a half dozen sets of fleece pyjamas, and skirts with drawstring waist bands.

Gem was less than pleased with his high-handedness, but swallowed her irritation when she saw how pleased the shop owners were to have had Wyatt Grantham as a customer. Well, he was a charming man. Gem had to agree; Wyatt Grantham, if he wished to do so, could charm the skin off an apple with his smile alone. And Gem was pleased for the women because they had made a very large sale.

The clothes fit perfectly and Ora was very pleased that alterations would not be required. As Gem tried on the last skirt she reflected on Wyatt's cold statement weeks back: he didn't have to shower her with gifts, or attention. Yet that was precisely what he was doing as of late. The cds alone had cost a small fortune in her mind. One simply did not make purchases in quantities such as he did! He did enjoy his power and wealth didn't he just!

"How is business?" she asked tongue-in-cheek of Mr Choate as he loaded the bags of clothing in the Defender boot.

"This has been a good day so far," he chuckled, then sobered. "The ladies were quite overwhelmed when Mr Grantham stopped in on Tuesday."

"I hope he was mindful of his manners," Gem said sweetly, drawing an odd look from her Agency co-worker.

"I am certain he was," Choate frowned, thinking Gem was in a bit of an odd mood. "He complimented the ladies on the shop, the merchandise, and stated he was pleased that you had had such pleasant experiences shopping in their establishment. And you are not to know this," his voice lowered, "but Mr Grantham offered the ladies the services of GEI if they ever had any concerns about managing their business. He said GEI would assign a project researcher - gratis - if they felt they would require one. He gave them the number of a Ms Holton to ring if they were interested in the offer."

Gem nodded. The same offer made to the rocking chair designer. "I've heard GEI offers such a program. I think it's an excellent idea, since you certainly don't have the time to spare for the shop," she suggested.

"Bit of a conflict of interest since I'm a silent partner - and your shadow," Choate said uncomfortably.

"Explain the situation to Wyatt - how you got involved in the business. I don't think the facts would put him off," Gem considered the issue.

"I'll think about it. However I can't discuss the issue with the ladies - they regard me as your friend - not your shadow."

"You are my friend, but yes it is an interesting problem," she agreed.

The longer Gem remained at the Hall the more entwined her life became between Wyatt and the Agency, and she didn't want Ora and Eda to suffer because of the necessities of her lies. She thought to mention Mr Choate's conflict to Wyatt at lunch, but decided this was a time she should step back and not interfere in a situation. And perhaps, she thought, the Agency should continue the search without her assistance. It was just possible that her queries and suggestions were making a muddle of the search. Then she thought again. She couldn't step back. Gemmy was depending on her!

Where are you Gemmy!

She had lunch with Mr Hyde. As a matter of fact, De Jekyll hadn't been present for a number of days. However, she knew he was still lurking around the edges of her life. And it was likely Dr Jekyll who paid the bill at the dress shop, and Gem would somehow pay for him having done so.

"You are frowning," Wyatt murmured as she entered the pub. "You're upset that I paid the bill at the dress shop."

"Indeed," Gem replied softly as he guided her to a table. "My clothes. My bill," she insisted.

"Since I participated in your - expansion," he teased, "I insist on contributing to the maintenance." He smiled that smile that caused her heart to flip.

"I wish the hormones would stop surging," she sighed, feeling the butterflies opening their wings. "And I don't wish to argue, but – "

"Excellent! A first step!" he teased.

"First what?" she asked puzzled.

"A first step to fewer arguments. Now what do you think of this?" he queried, drawing a black cloth band from his pocket. "A new collar for Miss Molly."

"With GPS," Gem nodded.

"We don't want her to get lost, do we, sweetheart?"

"No," she agreed. "It's lovely. Good choice."

They ordered the daily special, cottage pie and were quickly served, interrupting Gem's resolve to return to the money issue. She had lost the window of opportunity. "About the clothes -"

"No more discussion regarding that bill," he said firmly. "Have you ever attended an auction?" He watched her scan the room. Why did she do that? Was she worried she would see a former target? How many were there? She did it at every restaurant, pub, shop - even at the Crow in Ticking Bottom.

"I have not. Have you?" she returned her focus to him, realizing he had been watching her. His knitted brows warned her that he was questioning her actions. And she couldn't give away the training that had become second nature to her.

"A few, now and then," Wyatt replied. "Ms Holton suggested you might be interested in an auction at St Albans tomorrow."

"Lovely," Gem agreed. "Ms Holton is a wealth of information, isn't she?"

"Indeed. She's quite indispensable," Wyatt said firmly.

"I thought in business no one was ever indispensable," Gem said in surprise.

"I disagree. I fight to keep excellent staff," he said smoothly. "Ms Holton has an extensive network with her fund-raisers alone. Through her networking she knew of Molly."

"Networks are very important," Gem agreed. "Ms Holton suggested to you that you should get a dog!"

"No. That was my idea. The Hall tends to be a bit dull at times. You must be very bored there day after day," he watched her expressions, reading her as she read rooms.

Not bored, lonely - despite Mrs M's company. "I'm sure many people would relish the quiet of life in the country," she hedged.

He saw her eyes briefly cloud. "But you are used to the noises and activity of London, or Paris, or Rome," he suggested.

Fishing? Turn the tables on him. "Mrs M said the Hall used to be a hive of activity, snakes and all." She would play his Game for awhile. And give him some constant attention.

Wyatt fought to present a pleasant tone. "Indeed. Years ago. Was your home the same when you were growing up?"

Gem smiled wistfully, unaware that her eyes clouded to the haunted look. "It was lovely, but quieter than a hive. I don't recall many snakes," she forced a smile.

His reference to her youth drew the haunted look. How young had she been when she started her life of 'adventure'? - Of targeting men? How had she become so adept at her skill of targeting men?

"I'll wager you had a string of admirers," Wyatt smiled.

"Now and then," she lied. "You?"

"Now and then," he chuckled. "More tea, sweetheart?"

Gem nodded.

"Have you more shopping to finish this afternoon? No?" Gem shook her head. "Shall we take a stroll along the Thames? Have hot chocolate somewhere?"

"Don't you have a full afternoon at the office?" she frowned.

"One phone call to Ms Holton and I am free until Monday," he smiled.

"Power," Gem said lightly.

"Indeed, my dear," he murmured, taking her hand. A pity the London flat wasn't available.

Power. And opportunity. Key words. Opportunity.

"Darling?" he called her back, knowing she had slipped into her secret world.

"A stroll?" he repeated. "Window shopping?"

"Lord! That's how I landed in this mess!" Gem said, gasping, flashing back to Oscar's Café.

Wyatt scowled, his mind racing back to the day he had met her. "Damn! I touched a nerve," he admitted. "I am sorry, darling. Spend the afternoon with me. I promise we will walk a bit briskly - nothing resembling a stroll, and no window shopping," he said, drawing a tiny smile to her lips. "Have you ever watched the otters on the Thames? Clever creatures."

"Yes, I have," her smile increased. She should play his Game, she reminded herself. "Hot chocolate sounds lovely."

"Perhaps a stop at a bookshop?"

"Excellent idea!"

"First we'll look for otters," he suggested.

"I used to name them," Gem said.

"How could you tell them apart?" Wyatt queried.

"I couldn't. I named them all Slick," Gem laughed, then caught her breath, fearful a cog would slip. Gem and Gem. Slowly she forced herself to breathe and to smile. "Charming creatures."

"Indeed! Shall we have dinner at the Crow? I could ask the M's to join us."

Gem nodded, then suggested Foyles Bookshop.

Wyatt's eyebrows rose. "The two of us in Foyles! It's good I have my credit card with me!" he chuckled.

They did not see any otters in the Thames - hadn't expected to - it was, after all, November - and continued on for hot chocolate before stopping and staying at Foyles Bookshop.

"I would like to spend a decade here organizing and cataloguing the books," Wyatt whispered conspiratorially to Gem.

"Yes. Indeed. But then it wouldn't be Foyles Bookshop. It would be Wyatt's Bookshop," Gem giggled.

Wyatt grudgingly agreed. "Better than owning a pub."

"Oh, yes!" Gem laughed.

"See you in an hour or two," he winked at her.

Mr Choate met them at the bookshop, at Wyatt's suggestion, keeping Gem in his view while they all perused the stacks.

Gem forced herself to locate Wyatt twice to see if he had found any tomes to catch his interest. And then she decided she couldn't do it. She couldn't play this part of his Game. She had to lie to him to protect Gemmy, but she wasn't going to prey on him as he had, and still did, prey on her.

Gem continued scanning the book titles of the stacks. One did not go to Foyles to look for a specific title. One went to Foyles to absorb the experience and to chance upon 'finds'. She glanced from time to time to Wyatt, and to Mr Choate, and carefully noted the T.O. Director's raised eyebrows and his location when he discovered a book he thought might interest her. And when he wandered off from the location she strolled to the same section. He had located a book about Hong Kong, the Occupation years 1941-1945, a book on the history of U-boats, one on the occupation of Europe during World War II, and amusingly, a book of braided hair styles. It was easy to locate the books Mr Choate wanted her to find; he turned the books on their spines.

Gem was suddenly struck by a thought as they were paying for their purchases.

"Wyatt! We can't leave Molly alone tonight at the Hall when we go to the Crow - and tomorrow."

"The M's will take her tomorrow," Wyatt mused. "Perhaps we should have take-away from the Crow."

"I'll take Molly for a walk this evening, if you like," Choate offered. "I usually walk for at least an hour every evening."

Wyatt's eyes travelled casually from Mr Choate to Gem before he replied. "Excellent, thank you, Mr Choate." There was something there - something between Gem and Choate. A familiarity that sometimes developed between a client and a bodyguard - or something else? A dependency one to the other? A commitment from him to her. It wouldn't be a physical relationship, naturally. Odd. He couldn't figure it out. But it was there. "Then you must have your dinner at the Crow on my bill."

"Delighted," Choate agreed.

Gem was growing increasingly frustrated. She was completely distrustful of Wyatt's current manner towards her and she simply could not make any headway in her search for the Pilos.

She poured a cup of hot chocolate from the thermos that, as usual, had been sitting by the computer when she went down to the office. Miss Molly and Mrs Mac had dutifully followed her down the staircase, and while Gem watched the telly for hot spots the critters took up their counter/floor staring positions. Mrs M had informed Gem at the Crow that the dog and cat had varied their locations in the house - kitchen, great room, staircase, but the staring competition had continued throughout the day.

There were no hot spots to concern the Agency. So where the Blast were Harry and Mrs Brown? Mr Cawley was awake.

'Any news Mrs Brown, Harry?'
'No.'
'Why?'
'???'
'No hot spots. Where are they?'
'???'
'Is Mrs Brown in contact with you?'
'No.'
'Harry?'
'No.'
'How long?'
'Mrs Brown since Indonesia breached simmer to roil.'
'Frightening.'
'Indeed.'
'Any news SEA Network?'
'Copasetic.'
'Agency?'
'Same.'
'All quiet on the Network Front?'
'Clever! Yes. Ask about the Western Front.'
'Go back to work!'
'Same to you, Gem!'

Another cup of hot chocolate, the Vera Lynn cd, and Gem reached for the book on the occupation of Europe. She settled into the comfy chair, sans cat and dog as they decided to continue their staring - perhaps forming some sort of bond. The further she read into the book, the more she was inclined to text her gratitude to Mr Choate for finding the volume for her. The author had written about the Nazis pillaging of artworks, listing many of the more noteworthy items stolen. Gem booted her computer to check the inter-net for the items listed in the book, and discovered that much on the list was still missing. There was a news article from the previous month stating that the U.S. government had seized a painting - from a museum in the state of Florida, U.S.A. - that had been stolen by the Nazis in World War II. That recent! Gem gasped in astonishment. People were still searching for the pillaged items! And her personal mental equation - there would be people in the world who still wanted to hide the fact that they possessed the stolen art. It was still cooking seventy plus years later.

And then she hit the same wall. So what. There were no new leads.

Break time.

Wyatt had been breathtakingly charming at dinner. How could he turn it off and on as if by a switch? Or was it always on for everyone but her? No! She couldn't believe he was charming at work. At GEI he would be all professional. He only had to smile at someone, to have the light reach his eyes and people were swept away by wonderful Wyatt Grantham. Sickening. And aggravating.

Power. A double dose. It was possible she would never be able to solve that mystery. The mystery of Wyatt Grantham. Perhaps once you suffered the illness you were immune.

She pushed the start button on the cd player again.

Paul Andriani. What was that 'something'? That point she couldn't reach?

It kept repeating in her mind. Mr Choate. Paul Andriani. Gemmy. Barcelona. Geneva.

She felt like her brain was going to explode. Or implode.

She grabbed her mobile.

'I can't do this anymore!'

'Not receiving.'

'I can't.'

'Tell that to Gem!'

'Damn you!!! Go to HELL!'

'Been there. So have you. Get back to work!'

'I hate this!'

'Your point?'

'I am so tired!'

'I am too, Gem.'

'Stop pushing!'

'When our Family comes home. Get to work!'

Sheesh!

Mr Cawley wouldn't let up on the pressure. Nor would Wyatt! But that pressure came from another direction - Gem's not being able to comprehend the direction of his current Game.

Since Miss Molly and Mrs Mac would not end their staring challenge, Gem paced the hall and the great room; there was no clear floor space in the office unless she detoured around the dog who chose to maintain her position towards the middle of the floor. Mrs Mac, on the counter, did not waver her gaze from the dog to Gem, so Gem paced where she could. She retraced her steps to the office to push the start button on the cd player and to pour another cup of hot chocolate.

"You two will likely drive me quite mad one day," Gem said tersely to the animals. They ignored her remarks, so Gem turned, left the office and paced around the kitchen island. Oh how her routine had changed in just a few short days!

She reached for her mobile.

'I quit!'

'So noted! Get back to work!'
'I need to talk to Blank.'
'Thanks for the joke. Get back to work!'
'I don't know the next step!'
'You have said that before. Figure it out! Get back to work!'
'You are no help!'
'I'll help you when you give me something with which to work!'
'Thanks! - receive with sarcasm!'
'So noted. Got anything for me, Gem?'
'No.'
'Go back to work!'
'Goodnight!'
'Goodnight!'

Gem cleared the messages. They certainly had not been worth the effort! To send or to receive!

She felt chilled despite the pyjamas and the dressing gown. She longed for her warm bed and Wyatt's arm around her.

Blast! The butterflies were swarming! When did hormones start settling down? She looked at the ceiling, then at the cup in her hand. She rinsed the thermos and the cup. The long case clock in the main hall chimed half three. She turned off the computer, the cd player and the electric fireplaces.

"Let's go to bed," she urged the non-warring warring factors.

When she slipped into bed, Wyatt snuggled her against him. "Go to sleep, sweetheart," he murmured.

"No," she whispered, turning over, sliding her arms around his neck, rubbing her cheek against his.

Wyatt opened his eyes, and stared into hers. God bless hormones! he silently mused, slipping his arms around her. Take the good hormones with the disgruntled ones. It all evens out in the end. - Hopefully. - He was treading into unknown territory here.

Gem wakened at seven. The moment she opened her eyes Mrs Mac leaped off the bed and Miss Molly raised her head and stared at Wyatt.

"Go back to sleep," Gem said softly.

"Miss Molly or me?" Wyatt yawned, rubbing his face.

"Miss Molly," Gem turned over and stared him directly in his eyes.

"Good Lord! I would like to know which hormones to thank individually," he murmured.

"Hush! You talk too much!" Gem ordered, tracing a finger over the bristles on his chin.

Wyatt took her hand and kissed her fingertips. Best he didn't have a mistress. He would be dead by noon!

"You have been so quiet," Wyatt stated as he pulled the Land Rover into the car park of the auction house. "Where are your thoughts?"

"I should ring Dr Hallowell and ask if I'm normal," Gem sighed.

"I should call my doctor to inquire if my heart is sound," Wyatt drawled. "At any rate, you should be assured I don't have a mistress."

"How would I know that!" Gem demanded, surprised at his words.

"I wouldn't have been able to get out of bed this morning if I had a mistress," Wyatt teased.

"So you say," Gem said a bit huffily.

"Trust me. I wouldn't have. Lord! you are exhausting woman!" Wyatt chuckled.

"It's the Blasted butterflies," Gem sighed.

"What?"

She explained the fluttering and Wyatt laughed. "I'm reminded of the butterfly boxes in Becton's gardens. I will never again be able to look at them without remembering this morning!"

"Stop laughing!" Gem blushed with embarrassment. "You don't understand!"

"In a way I do. You've never been pregnant before. I've never been an expectant father before. You just might frighten the hell out of me," he replied. "Talk to Hallowell, or Lyndon. Talk to Mrs Brown."

"She's on holiday," Gem said automatically. "And she never had children."

"Talk to Willow - she's a professional with pregnancies," Wyatt suggested. "Have lunch and chat with Ms Holton. And I'll have a chat with Mr Becton about putting up more butterfly boxes."

"You are horrid!" Gem groused.

"Yes, sweetheart, but you have known that for some time now," he leaned over and kissed her.

Gem couldn't believe that she had told Wyatt about the butterflies. It was simply another weapon he would manage to use against her. When would she learn? She had made a slip at the pub the previous day mentioning that she had named all the otters the same name, and had then worried he might somehow connect that to twin sisters using the same name. Admittedly that thought was a bit esoteric, but still it had been there.

The thoughts nagged at her brain as she and Wyatt milled through the auction house with the rest of the crowd.

"We don't need furniture," Wyatt murmured as they passed lowboys, highboys, dining sets, settees, "the attic at the Hall is full of it."

"Okay," Gem nodded, not wishing to suggest that she had actually been in the attic.

There were paintings, sculptures, vases, lamps, tables, filling every bit of space in the large warehouse. Wyatt spied the items first. The reason why Ms Holton had thought Gem would be interested in attending the auction: antique cameras. Gem recognized a 1929 Rajah - it was partially made of Bakelite- and a 1948 Agilus Agefold. Other cameras displayed were models she had never heard of - a Lancaster Excelsior circa 1909, and a 1905 Challenge model with red leather bellows. All together there were six cameras from periods ranging from 1905 to 1951.

Wyatt looked on with amusement as Gem studied each of the cameras, reading the details on the description cards. Other women were clustered around the jewellery displays; Gem was fascinated by a 1951 Eight-20 King

Penguin camera, he chuckled. Well, many people were captivated by penguins, he chuckled again to himself.

Wyatt drew her along as the crowd gathered for the start of the auction. Gem found the bidding fascinating and concentrated on trying to see who was bidding on each item.

"Can you tell when someone is bidding?" she whispered to Wyatt.

"Watch eyes and brows," he suggested, also whispering. "Don't move a muscle or we'll have to have that dining set delivered," he teased. "We already have three in the attic."

Gem giggled, thinking there was a fourth set that he had forgotten.

The cameras were among the last items sold. Each went quickly, but Gem couldn't see who had purchased any of them.

"Shall we have tea before we drive back to Ticking Bottom?" she asked.

"Indeed," he agreed. "First we must pay for our purchases."

"Not the dining set?" Gem laughed.

"The cameras," he said smoothly, guiding her across the room, his hand at the small of her back. Mr M can put shelves in your office, and perhaps we can finally set about hanging your artwork. Your walls are bleak despite the slightly more than adequate paint colour."

"You bid on the cameras!" Gem gasped. "That's too much money!"

"It will come out of your decorating budget for your office," Wyatt teased.

"I don't have a decorating budget," Gem protested.

"No. Because it was all spent - on cameras!" he grinned.

Gem laughed. He could be such fun! "I'll pay for the cameras," she insisted.

"Good Lord! You are a difficult woman when it comes to finances," he exhaled sharply. "If you wanted to pay, you should have bid on the items."

"Good Lord! You are a very difficult man when it comes to finances," Gem retorted.

"That's precisely why I have the power and the money, sweetheart," he kissed her.

"You're gloating," she accused, narrowing her eyes at him.

"That I am," he winked at her.

More gifts, Gem mused on the drive back to Ticking Bottom. She had offered to pay for the tea, but he had refused.

"Why don't you close your eyes and rest awhile," Wyatt suggested. "Are you warm, or shall we have some heat?"

"Perfectly warm, thank you," she murmured, doing as he suggested.

Thoughtful, pleasant, kind, generous. It couldn't last, she decided. He was fighting against his deep dislike for her. But it would surface again soon.

"The cameras are extraordinary," Gem opened her eyes and looked at him. "Thank you for bidding on them, they are history."

"You are most welcome, my dear," Wyatt reached over to give her hand a squeeze.

She closed her eyes again, relaxing, enjoying the outing and the pleasant, if temporary, truce they were sharing for a few hours.

Diamonds. Rubies. Cameras! Wyatt reflected. She certainly wasn't demanding; he had not received a single bill for her purchases other than the one from the Crow when she and Mrs M had lunched there while he was in Paris. He would never have seen the bill from the dress shop if he hadn't stopped in to pay it. She didn't make demands, and she didn't lavishly spend money. Other than the pitched battles they had had she rarely was even a blip in his daily life. And although he tried to, he could not find fault with her behaviour. And other than a rather startling jealousy of Emerald, Gem didn't pry into his private life. She didn't flaunt her position as his wife over GEI staff. She did not meddle in his life.

She had quickly sunk her claws into James, but had not taken advantage of their marriage. Was the knowledge of the passports and the photos keeping her in check?

And oh, how she fascinated him! He had known her for three and a half months and she was still such a mystery to him!

"Shall we have a late lunch at the Crow?" he suggested.

"Mmm, lovely," Gem agreed, keeping her eyes closed.

"Then a walk with Miss Molly?"

"Yes, please."

"Then hot chocolate and biscuits by the fire in the sitting room?"

"Will you be wearing a cat?"

"Possibly."

"Okay then," Gem giggled.

Miss Molly returned happily to the Hall and resumed her position on the floor in the kitchen staring up as Mrs Mac stared down at her; Wyatt watched the critters as he filled a thermos of hot chocolate for Gem, and opened a bottle of wine for himself. While Gem had showered and changed into pyjamas, Wyatt had showered and had pulled on his dressing gown. The fire glowed in the grate in the sitting room where the hot chocolate and wine awaited them. Miss Molly curled up on the rug on the hearth; Mrs Mac stretched out full-length, tummy down on the back of the settee.

Gem propped her feet up on the coffee table, a thought tingling in her brain. Not the lost thought - another one. Dr Hallowell. He was not equipment impaired at the Agency clinic. He had been capable on her first visit with Mrs Brown to listen to the baby's heartbeat. He could have told her that day if she was carrying twins - but he hadn't. Was that why Dr Lyndon had told her to ring Dr Hallowell? Had he heard two heartbeats? But she and Wyatt only referred to one baby. Patient confidentiality. Dr Lyndon couldn't say anything to Wyatt about what he had learned last Sunday night when he had listened to the baby's heartbeat. And he hadn't said anything to Gem except to advise her to speak to Hallowell.

Oh-oh-oh.

Monday! She would get an answer from Dr Hallowell on Monday! At least one issue could be addressed! She had nearly thought 'problem'. But the baby or twins would not be a problem. He/she/they would be a concrete acknowledgement of her future. The only one she had for certain - so far.

Wyatt handed her a cup of hot chocolate, and poured a glass of wine for himself.

"I'd offer you a sip - but -"

"No. I would like a beer but -" she sighed, sipping her beverage.

"Did today exhaust you?" he asked gently.

"Not at all," Gem assured him. "The hand swung high on the pleasameter dial."

"I'm not familiar with that specific dial," he raised a brow.

"Similar to butterflies," she sighed, wiggling her toes before the flames. "Fires are brilliant," she murmured, confident and relaxed in the knowledge that she would have a bit of resolution in less than forty-eight hours. It would be one question of many that would have a proper answer!

"We need to address a subject," Wyatt said thoughtfully.

"Mmm, what would that be?" Gem snuggled back into the cushions of the settee, letting her mind wander.

"The nursery," Wyatt said quietly.

Blast! She had dropped her guard a bit there, not having heeded his words and the tone in his voice. This was a subject she had wanted to put off for a few months yet. "No rush is there?" she sipped her hot chocolate, and steeled herself for the pleasameter to take a deep swing to low.

"Is there a reason not to discuss the subject?" he asked, narrowing his gaze slightly.

Perhaps because it will start an argument. "If you wish," Gem said grudgingly.

"Mrs M has suggested James's room," Wyatt said, his voice still quiet. "For the first few months the baby will be in our room, of course."

"If the baby," she mentally added - ies - "is fussy, you won't get any sleep at night. You'll be dazed for work each morning," Gem pointed out an obvious obstacle to his suggestion.

"I'll go in late to the office," he countered.

"Okay," Gem conceded. She had no answers or suggestions because she wasn't mentally committing to imagine herself and the baby(ies) ever living at the Hall.

"James's room is the most logical choice, as Mrs M suggested," Wyatt said calmly.

"No," Gem said firmly. "There are other bedrooms." And hopefully a flat in London.

"It wasn't James's bedroom," Wyatt informed her. "It was mine. I had the master suite re-configured after James died, adding the other bathroom, dressing room, and the sitting room. I moved James's things into that bedroom in late July. His original bedroom was down the hall. The bedroom of choice is very large and receives excellent light during the day."

"You're a visionary, aren't you," Gem murmured thinking of the work he had had done in the master suite. She was no longer relaxed. And the pleasameter had dipped to zero.

"Power. I knew I would eventually track you down and one way or another -"

"Did you assign a project researcher to that idea?" she queried sarcastically.

"You know I wouldn't do that. You were my own private project," he forced himself to remain calm.

Gem stared at the flames, the hot chocolate in her cup turned cold. Dr Jekyll had returned. As she had known he would. "Mrs Brown was so very wrong. She said you were a man of ethics," Gem said coldly.

"I married you, didn't I? I didn't have to Gem. I could simply have used you, then destroyed you with the photos and passports. Compromise, my dear," Wyatt said casually.

Definitely not the pleasant chat she had expected that evening. The hand on the pleasameter slipped completely off the dial and disappeared into oblivion. "You must know a great deal of wealthy, powerful people," Gem mused.

"I do," Wyatt agreed, wondering at the statement.

"Do any of them have a conscience?"

"And I do not?" Wyatt challenged. "You do not possess one. Why should I?"

Gem picked up her cup and the thermos of hot chocolate and walked out of the suite. She had had enough of his company for the evening. Mrs Mac lifted her head, jumped down to the cushion then to the floor and swiftly followed Gem. Molly raised her head, watched the tail disappear out the door and trotted after it.

Damn! Wyatt muttered. He had approached the subject badly. He had set her off again! She had set him off again! His most difficult take-over to date had progressed more smoothly than this relationship. He could manage a boardroom full of adversaries, but he couldn't manage his own wife. His own target. It was no surprise that divorces were often so contentious, that divorce court agendas were so crowded! Wives!

He reached for the bottle of wine, and bottle in hand he followed the trio downstairs.

Gem turned on the computer and the telly. No new hot spots she observed, watching the international news. The only hot spot she currently knew of was in the master suite - and tonight butterflies were not involved in any way.

Wyatt filled his wine glass, set the bottle on the kitchen island and went to Gem's office, knocking on the open door.

"What?" she said coldly, not looking up from the computer screen.

"I suggest that James's things be moved to the bedroom across the hall," he said calmly.

"That is full of furniture," Gem said, clicking the mouse on the Durham file.

"There's still a bit of space in the attic for yet another bedroom set," he suggested. "Space, good light, and close to our bedroom. And as you said, there's no immediate rush. But please consider the idea."

"Okay," Gem nodded, still refusing to look at him.

"And as a side-note, Gem," he said candidly, "I never brought another woman home to spend the night here. - If that was a question in your mind about that bedroom."

"Okay," she replied. It had not been a question in her mind. But oddly, she was pleased to know that information.

"I'm going to prepare chicken for dinner. Would you like a salad?"

"No, thank you," she shook her head, wondering why he had made the remark about other women. The only logical reason for doing so was that he was attempting to regain her trust. And that would not happen a second time!

Gem wandered from room to room, sipping the hot chocolate from the thermos Wyatt had left by her computer. She was tired of thinking. She couldn't retrieve that 'something' from the back of her mind, and Wyatt's attentive manner was slowly driving her closer to the edge of her sanity. That could actually be his plan, she decided dryly. She wondered if he had ever lost on a business venture. If he hadn't she could be in very deep trouble.

Her thoughts turned, as had become habit, to Mr Cawley. She pulled her mobile from her dressing gown pocket.

'Any news?'

'No.'

'Mrs Brown, Harry, Blank?'

'Same reply as first query.'

'What are you doing now?'

'Reviewing files of applicants for courier positions.'

'Any possible?'

'Not likely. Sorting?'

'Trying to retrieve.'

'How are the dog and cat relating?'

'They constantly stare at each other.'

'Odd that.'

'They're furry statues.'

'Don't let them distract you.'

'Too much pressure from you!'

'Complain to Mrs Brown.'

'How amusing you are!'

'Get to work!'

'Okay. Goodnight.'

'Goodnight.'

She went over the names again, trying to spark Paul Andriani to another connection, but there was too much to sort through in her brain. She pressed the start button on the cd player, filled her cup with the hot liquid brew, and stared at the dog staring at the cat. There was a slight alteration of the position of the animals. Mrs Mac had taken her position on the arm of Auntie Jane's comfy chair; Miss Molly sat on the floor just out of reach of the cat's claws.

Germ refused to think of Wyatt. They had had a pleasant day until he had ruined it with his remarks of the alterations to the master suite - and the reason for the changes. And he could do whatever he pleased with James's room. She refused to be involved with his plans for the nursery.

Where are you Gemmy? Why can't we find you?

Ping

'Search resumed in South China Sea. Clear so far.'

'Thanks!'

Coincidence that. Mr Cawley's text received as she had put the query to Gemmy. She hoped that was a sign that her search would finally make progress.

She cleared the messages on her mobile and slipped it into her pocket.

She dreaded Sunday, being alone at the Hall with Wyatt all day. Hopefully he would spend the day reading reports in the library. He must be a bit behind in his reading considering the time he had spent with her at the auction, and then the walk with Molly in the afternoon.

She wandered through the rooms, listening to the cd; she had long ago memorized all the lyrics to all the songs. She wandered back to the office for hot chocolate and to stare at the cat staring at the dog. She shook her head in wonder, retracing her path over and over again until the dark hours drew to a close. Her brain was a jumble of information. Nothing shifted to allow her mind to sort. And there was no new information to cause a spark, a catalyst to propel her forward in her search.

Chapter Twenty-Seven

Wyatt jerked awake as his mobile rang. He grabbed the phone and ducked into his dressing room.

Gem struggled awake to hear him ask, "What? When?"

She sat up and listened, worried at the startled tone of his voice. "What the hell? - I'm on my way." A minute later she heard beeping as he scrolled down his mobile contact list. "Grantham here. We're going to Paris. I'll meet you at the plane."

Gem sprawled across the bed to switch on the lamp on his bedside table. He came out of his dressing room in jeans, pulling a sweater over his head.

"Darling, I'm sorry you wakened," he sat on the edge of the bed and tucked the duvet around her.

"What happened? Why do you have to go Paris?" She yawned.

"Manton got mugged."

"Manton? Jogging?" she frowned, sitting up.

"Yes. I'll likely be back tonight. I'll ring Mrs M to come spend the day with you," he leaned over to kiss her.

"That's not necessary. I don't need a nanny," she protested. "When did it happen?" She looked at her watch. Half six.

"An hour ago. Go back to sleep, darling. I'll give you a ring later."

Gem could see that he was visibly upset. "One incident - understandable. Two - no - not when he was jogging both times," Gem thought out loud, as Wyatt pulled on his socks. "He's being targeted," she said seriously.

Wyatt exhaled sharply. "What? No! That's not likely. There's no possible - nothing that could put Manton in danger because of GEI. He's very low profile -"

Gem shook her head. "Perhaps nothing to do with GEI," she mused. "Put Mr Choate on the case," she firmly suggested.

"Choate?" Wyatt said sharply.

"Eyes and Ears of Britain," Gem reminded him. "He knows his profession." And the Agency knows even more! "Put the information to Mr Choate. Perhaps it is nothing to do with GEI - perhaps it is." She tried to assist without being a courier on assignment - without Agency training and knowledge. "Oh Lord! Peter was at the Paris office!" she gasped.

"Oh Lord! Not him again!" Wyatt grimaced at the thought. "You don't think?" he scowled.

"That lad might need a libido adjustment," Gem suggested, raising her eyebrows.

Wyatt shook his head doubtfully. "Young Peter has been gone from Paris for weeks. I'll see how the police report reads. I have a plane waiting. You go back to sleep."

"That is not going to happen," Gem pushed back the duvet. "It's quarter to seven. I'll be awake in fifteen minutes. I might as well be awake now. I'll walk you down and take Molly out," she pulled on her dressing gown.

"Not dressed like that you won't!" Wyatt retorted sharply.

"Very well," Gem pulled on jeans, a jumper and slippers.

Molly trotted ahead of them down the stairs, and fetched her lead from the mudroom.

"I'll ring you later, sweetheart," Wyatt gave her a long kiss. "Mmm. Damn!" he groaned. "Rest today!" he ordered.

"I shall."

He gave her a quick kiss then hurried off to the old stables.

Molly waited patiently, watching as Wyatt drove past them to turn onto the cobblestone lane, then she answered the call of nature and returned to Gem's side. "Breakfast," Gem led the dog inside.

She waited until the clock struck seven, then rang Mr Choate, putting the information to him.

"I won't get involved in GEI, Gem," he protested.

"Please, Mr Choate!"

"T.O.'s contract is with Mr Grantham and only regards you. The situation with Mr Manton is police business. Civilian," he point blank refused.

"May I plead on Agency Family grounds?" She would not wheedle, but it was an honest, legitimate request. "T.O. must have contacts in France. And it does take civilian cases."

"You do not, in any way, legally represent GEI."

Gem couldn't refute that remark. "Please, Mr Choate?"

The line was quiet for a minute. "I will investigate, Gem, but only if Mr Grantham makes the request. Suggest that he ring me."

"I did, but he didn't take me seriously," she admitted.

"Then my hands are tied," Choate said firmly. "Now I have phone calls to make. When are you going to walk Molly this morning?"

"Probably about ten o'clock," she replied, her voice betraying her disappointment.

"Ten o'clock then. Walk to the bridge," he ordered and rang off.

"Fine," Gem replied to thin air.

Ten o'clock was hours away, time filled with laundry, cleaning her bathrooms, brushing Miss Molly who sat perfectly still through the process - staring at Mrs Mac.

"Are you two playing a game?" Gem queried of her companions. "I should warn both of you that there are already enough Games being played in this house. And the four of us - perhaps five - are not likely to win any of the Games. Power trumps good intentions. Power trumps everything," she sighed. "Perhaps Wyatt and I should learn from the two of you - no conversations - no arguments - just a silent staring contest. Suggestion revisited - staring into his eyes would only keep the butterflies in constant flight," she sighed again. And as she sighed, Molly leaned against her.

She had an entire day to herself. And what should she do with her time? Odd, she thought. Mrs Brown was away. Mr Cawley would be sleeping by now. Who was in command at the Agency? Mr White? A skeleton crew. No wonder Mr Cawley had been a bit agitated with his text replies lately. Or perhaps Mr Choate was in charge. He could dispatch messages through one of his operatives at T.O. Odd. That was very likely the case. - He had delegated a T.O. staffer to dispatch. Curious. But perhaps not. Mr Choate would need a second in command. And that person would have to be from the Agency. Or perhaps from B.I. Requests for staff could be made to B.I., if the need was warranted; and Mr White could simply not work 24/7. Even Mr Choate could not keep that gruelling schedule.

Gem put away the dog brush and wandered to the library, scanning the shelves, wondering the location of Wyatt's safe. Of course he had one. A structure such as Grantham Hall always had a safe. And logically it was behind the bookcases behind Wyatt's desk. The woodwork was flush and of exceptional quality, either original because it perfectly matched all the bookcases in the room - or it had been created by a master carpenter.

Gem jumped as her mobile rang and she caught her breath relieved that Mrs M was on the other end of the call - and not in the house watching Gem in her surreptitious activities.

"Good morning, dear, are you managing, or shall I come to the house?" the woman's voice was cheery as usual.

"I am managing quite well. You enjoy your day off," Gem insisted. "If I have any concerns I'll ring you immediately," she assured the house manager.

Mrs M chatted for a few minutes, then rang off and Gem left the library. She would ponder the safe situation and return to the room later if she felt a eureka.

She went up the stairs to James's room. Wyatt had suggested it for the nursery, and she was to consider the idea, so she accepted that as his permission for her to enter the room. She had to look at the room to give it every consideration.

The bedroom was indeed very large, the light from the windows was bright. The stone floor would require a thick carpet. The walls were a soft grey which was splendid against the cherry woodwork. That was it. She couldn't imagine the room a nursery because she wanted to be quit of the Hall.

She could search the room to her heart's content, with no one being the wiser. And so she did; but she didn't notice anything she had not previously seen. If there had been any of Gemmy's possessions left at the Barcelona flat - other than the items with which Wyatt taunted her - then he must have put them in the safe. But then Gemmy wouldn't have been likely to leave anything in the flat at Barcelona.

Gem was due at the bridge in a half hour. Miss Molly was still seeing eye to eye with Mrs Mac but one word diverted her attention.

"Walk," Gem said crisply and the poochie darted off to the mudroom for her lead.

Gem grabbed her camera bag, her windcheater and they were off. Miss Molly sat patiently on the cobblestone lane while Gem snapped some shots of her, and then again at the old stone bridge. They were early to their meeting with Mr Choate, so Gem released Molly to run across the meadow. The camera had a full roll of film and Gem shot snap after snap, using her various lenses as the dog ran, bolted, stopped dead in her tracks, sniffed cautiously at the burbling brook, then hared off again, turning to search for her mum, and once having located Gem, she raced off in the opposite direction.

Gem lowered the camera as Mr Choate approached.

"It's difficult to wear her out," Choate gazed at the golden bullet streaking across the bleak fall remains of what was likely a vibrant meadow in summer.

"That she is!" Gem laughed. "It's a joy to see her running free."

Since her co-conspirator did not immediately offer conversation, Gem put to him a query of her earlier thoughts.

"Mr Cawley is likely sleeping," she observed. "Who is commanding the Agency as we speak?"

"T.O.," Choate responded, not taking his eyes of the golden dog. "Why do you ask?"

"No Mrs Brown, no Harry. Mr White can't work around the clock," Gem shrugged.

"At times he does. We all do."

Gem realized that fact, having had back-to-back-to-back assignments when the Pilos had gone missing. "Indeed," she nodded. "You're in charge now then," she suggested.

"An operator is at the T.O. office," he replied in clipped tones.

"A transfer from B.I.? I know Agency staff is paper thin."

"Indeed it is," Choate nodded.

"And I am taking you from your work," Gem said apologetically. She turned to look at him, resting her arms on the stone cap of the old stone bridge.

Choate gave her a quick nod. "I needed air," he replied graciously. "As you can imagine, I am not used to occupying a desk in an office."

"Nor am I," Gem chuckled. "I rather miss the hustle through an airport to catch a flight, tripping over a traveller's carelessly placed luggage."

"I don't miss attempting to locate a loo from four different language signs in four different airports in a single day," he muttered dryly.

"And at least two of them out of order in every airport, in every country, every day," Gem suggested, drawing a laugh from him.

"Indeed. The glories of travel," then wishing to avoid dredging up sad memories for her, he changed the subject. "Is your walk time limited today?"

"No," she said firmly. "I am without supervision."

She turned her head, listening to what sounded like a sharp dull echo. It repeated and moments later sounded again. "What was that? Was that a gunshot?" she demanded of Choate.

"Skeet shooting," he replied without hesitation. "Some of the locals meet on Sunday mornings for sheet shooting."

"Oh," Gem replied. "I thought it was T.B. security terminating an intruder."

Choate raised his eyebrows. "They prevent, they do not terminate," he eyed her steadily. "There are thickets surrounding the entire scope of T.B. It's not an easy area to breach I assure you."

"Skeet shooting?" Gem said, surprised at the information.

"There are a number of the clubs in this area," Choate advised.

"Excellent. Skeet aren't endangered as far as I have heard," Gem smiled.

"Oh, they are in Ticking Bottom," he jested.

"I don't understand. The perimeter is well protected but anyone can just drive into T.B. No gates," Gem mused.

"One would have to be quite lost to find this village, wouldn't you say?" he chuckled.

"Rather," Gem laughed.

"Seriously, Gem, this village is well protected, without being obviously so."

Gem nodded. "So it would seem."

Choate watched Molly running free back and forth across the meadow. "Did Mrs Macinski ring you? Mr Grantham said she would be doing so."

"She did. You spoke to Wyatt?" Gem said eagerly.

"He rang me before he left Ticking Bottom - before I spoke with you. He didn't mention the Paris incident, only that he had to fly over for the day, and that you would be alone. I was to contact you to see how your day was progressing."

"That's the reason for this meeting?" she queried dejectedly.

"No," Choate grew serious. "Suggest again to Mr Grantham that he should ring me about the Manton case."

"It is a case then!" Gem said eagerly.

"Your instincts are good, Gem. However, the Paris police believe the act was a random mugging."

"But you don't think so!" Gem said with growing excitement and alarm.

"It was not random. As you believed, Mr Manton is being targeted," Choate advised her. "And it is sure to happen again."

Gem looked about them, as had Choate. Even in Ticking Bottom he scanned the territory. "What did you learn from your phone calls?" He had stated earlier that he had phone calls to make.

"Private information, Gem," he refused to elucidate.

"But Mr Manton could be seriously injured if he isn't warned!"

"Then ring your husband, Gem."

"Mr Choate -"

"Back off, Gem. Let me do my job," he firmly warned her. "I stepped over the line for you. There will not be a second time where GEI is involved."

"You used Agency contacts not T.O. operatives," Gem realized the facts.

"Sometimes they are one in the same. This time not. Do as I say, please. This is not a request that can be hedged."

"Yes, Mr Choate. I just hope Wyatt will listen to me," she sighed.

"That may be a problem. He isn't aware of your background, your special insight at times," Choate nodded. "Do the best you can, Gem. If he declines to listen to you, I might be able to put a shadow on Manton to protect him, but that bill must be paid to T.O. Family cannot cover the cost there."

"I understand," Gem said seriously. If it came to that, she could pay the bill to T.O. Wyatt would never know. She had her own money. And how was she going to convince Wyatt? When had he ever listened to her? She thought long and hard. No, never, that she could recall.

"Shall we go to the Crow for a cup of tea?" Choate suggested.

"How could we manage that," Gem sighed. "The locals gossip."

"They do, indeed. But it's a rare person in T.B. who doesn't know that I'm your bodyguard - in their vernacular," he drawled.

"Seriously?" Gem queried in astonishment.

"Think, Gem. Wyatt Grantham secured the suite for me at the inn. When the Defender leaves the village I am always seen following you. It is well known in T.B. that I am in Mr Grantham's employ."

"So it would seem," Gem nodded in agreement. "But what about Molly?"

"Mr Grantham owns the building," Choate chuckled. "Do you think Mike Morgan is going to refuse entrance to the Crow to his landlord's dog?"

Gem laughed. "Highly unlikely he would."

"Just so."

"Then I would prefer hot chocolate."

"Very well," Choate nodded."

They were waiting for their beverages when Gem's mobile rang. Wyatt! She left the table she and Mr Choate had taken, and moved to the opposite end of the room, where her phone conversation could not be overheard.

"Are you working on your book, sweetheart?" his deep voice caused the butterflies to start swarming.

"I'm at the Crow with Mr Choate," she replied. "Molly and I were out for a walk and we met up with him."

"Excellent," he seemed pleased that she was with her shadow. "Did Mrs M ring you?"

"She did," Gem confirmed. "How is Mr Manton?"

"Bruised. The doctor first suspected a concussion, but decided not."

"Thank heavens!" Gem murmured, then went for a direct plea. "Wyatt, please, please, ask Mr Choate to investigate. Please! For Mr Manton's sake!"

"Gem, I have spoken to the police, and they concluded this was a random attack," he firmly insisted.

"Then they didn't do a proper investigation," she retorted. "GEI is not a small, local company, Wyatt. It's major. Mr Manton is the Director of the Paris Office. He's major. No one is going to mistake him for a hapless tourist. He may keep a low profile, but he is well known in the European business world in his own right, and as your second in command at GEI. One accident the percentages are with him. Two in two months the percentages are against him."

"This is not your concern, Gem. You are overreacting, and overreaching yourself," Wyatt said coolly.

"Well, apparently Mr Manton is not your concern either, or you would get your Blasted head out of the sand. Perhaps next time something happens to him you'll realize that it's more than just an accident. And you had best pray he survives the next attempt. But then for you he's just an employee!" she snapped the phone shut and returned it to her pocket.

He rang back immediately, and Gem refused to answer her mobile. He would be furious! She was always to answer when he rang her mobile! She sent him a text message.

'I can't hear you through the sand!'

And she returned to her table to sip her hot chocolate.

It was less than five minutes later that Mr Choate's mobile rang.

"Your husband," Choate mouthed to her, and he moved across the room to take the call in the same area where Gem had sought privacy.

Gem waited impatiently for their conversation to end. It went on for at least ten minutes, and she signalled Mike Morgan for another round: one tea, one hot chocolate. The beverages were served shortly before Mr Choate returned to the table. He gave her a thumbs up signal.

And Gem received a text.

'Answer your phone DAMN IT!'

She complied as soon as it rang, staying seated.

"Don't ever ring off again, darling, do you understand!" he ground out his words.

"Absolutely," Gem agreed smiling, her voice completely sincere. "Will you be back for dinner?" she queried for effect of the publican and others who might be listening to her.

"I'll be home late. You'll probably be in bed by that time. Do you understand?"

"Indeed I do," she said complacently.

"How are the furred ones doing?" his voice softened a touch.

Gem laughed easily. "They stared at each other for nearly three hours this morning."

Wyatt chuckled in return. "I have to get back," he said quietly.

"Give Mr Manton a hug for me!" she said impulsively.

"I don't believe I shall!" Wyatt replied firmly, and Gem could imagine him frowning.

"Okay," she said breathlessly.

"Are the butterflies swarming?" he teased.

"Yes!" she said blushing.

"You're blushing aren't you?" he teased.

"Yes! Ring off!" she laughed.

"Later, darling!"

"Yes!"

As Gem returned her mobile to her pocket, she avoided Mr Choate's eyes, but still drew a comment from him.

"You're blushing," he chuckled.

"Oh, hush!" she groused, then asked curiously. "Have you ever been married, Mr Choate?"

"I have not," he shook his head wistfully. "But one day I hope to be. But that's a long time in the future. In a different world."

When he retired, no doubt, and didn't have to devote his life to the Agency. And what had been between Auntie Jane and Mr Choate? she wondered.

"I must be off Mrs Grantham, but Mr Grantham asked me to walk you to the bridge. Mr Macinski will be waiting for you there - something to do about shelves for your office and an auction," he informed her.

"Oh! Wyatt purchased antique cameras for me at an auction yesterday," she explained. "They should look smashing in my office. I had never been to an auction before."

"Indeed," he replied. "Is a Rajah involved?"

"Yes," Gem replied, signing the beverage tab. "Wyatt said beverages were on him," she said for the benefit of the publican. Wyatt always insisted on paying the bill so he could have this one, she decided.

Mr Choate filled her in on his conversation as they slowly walked to the bridge.

"Whatever you said to Mr Grantham worked," Choate said strongly.

Gem couldn't recall her exact words - and something she had said had slipped to the back of her mind - where she couldn't retrieve it. "I mentioned percentages," she frowned. What had she lost? "Twice in two months - there would be a third time and he'd better hope Mr Manton survived the next attack. Three times you're IT!" Where had she heard that? A snowball fight in Chicago? She shook off the fading memory.

"How soon before you have information for Wyatt?" she pressed. She could see Mr M waiting at the bridge. "Release," she said to Miss Molly, and the dog bounded off to the estate manager.

"I have the information. I'll wait until mid-afternoon to ring Mr Grantham," Choate held back a smile.

"Well done, Mr Choate," Gem murmured.

"Well done, Gem. You are brilliant." He wanted to say that she was one in a million, but he knew that would strike at her heart with overwhelming pain, for there had once been two of them, and not so very long ago. Pain still so recent it could not be assuaged.

"Thank you, Mr Choate," Gem held out her hand to him, for with Mr M watching she could not give him the hug she so wanted to give.

"My honour, Mrs Grantham," he shook her hand, then raised his eyebrows a touch. "London tomorrow?"

"Most assuredly!" She had words to say to Dr Hallowell!

Gem and Mr M sorted out the question of the shelves for her office: length, width, where to put them, and he would paint them the same pearl grey of the ceiling. Mrs M had sent over a turkey breast and mixed vegetables for dinner. Miss Molly took a long nap, stretched out on Auntie Jane's settee, and Mrs Mac spent time sitting on the back of the comfy chair - staring down at the dog. Gem and Miss Molly had an early afternoon, and early evening walk and Gem went to bed to read of Lizzie Bennett arguing with Mr Darcy.

Gem stirred as Wyatt quietly slipped into bed. "What time is it?" she murmured drowsily.

"I had hoped not to waken you, sweetheart," Wyatt said softly.

Gem glanced at her watch. Four hours until the dark hours would come. She snapped on her bedside lamp. "Did you have dinner?" she asked, yawning.

"At the airport," he kissed her.

"That's not proper food," she protested.

"It will do," he said firmly, lying back against the pillow.

Gem sat up to look at him. "How is Mr Manton?" she frowned.

"Out of hospital. He will be at the office tomorrow," Wyatt said hesitantly. "Mr Choate is a marvel at his profession," Wyatt continued.

"Did he find out any information?" Gem held her breath. He had! And would Wyatt share? She knew she wouldn't be able to pry the facts out of Mr Choate. The man was being so SOP on the Manton business!

"He did," Wyatt admitted, shaking his head. "And you were correct, my dear. Manton was a target both times."

"Heavens!" Gem gasped. "But why?"

"It seems that a young woman is pregnant," Wyatt said crisply.

"Mr Manton!" Gem was nearly speechless.

"No," Wyatt chuckled, and gave her a quick frown. "The fact is, Manton shares the same first name as his son, Peter."

"Good Lord! It WAS Peter!" Gem stared at Wyatt.

"Indeed. However, the young woman's father did not know there was a father and son." Wyatt exhaled sharply. "I'll start over, shall I?"

"Please," Gem waited impatiently.

"Young Peter met a young woman, Mademoiselle Celine, at a bar. Dated, dated, got involved. And young Peter was sent to Greece. He dropped his mobile in the bath, lost her number. Wrote to her, misspelled her street address, and his letters were returned. He thought she had rejected him. She thought he had lost interest in her. Mademoiselle discovered she was pregnant. Told her papa who rang Peter Manton at GEI Paris. Manton did not recognize the name, passed it on to a researcher, thinking the caller was interested in a business project. Papa was livid at being pushed on to a lesser employee. Mademoiselle's two brothers decided to take matters into their own hands," he concluded, holding up his hands.

"The 'accidents'," Gem nodded. "And so -" she urged him to continue.

"Mr Choate investigated," Wyatt looked pointedly at Gem, and she looked at him, wide-eyed, nodding for him to continue. "He gave me the information which I relayed to Manton, who relayed the information to young Peter."

"And!" Gem slapped the duvet with her hands.

"Young Peter is desperate to see Mademoiselle again. She to see him," Wyatt shook his head in disbelief. "They are in love. There will be a wedding midweek in Paris. Manton is in shock but hopes his future daughter-in-law will settle Peter down. Papa is thrilled his daughter will have a husband and a father for her child. Papa is furious with his sons who are most repentant for their actions against the most notable Director of GEI. Peter is flying in from Canada as we speak. The couple will be honeymooning in Toronto. End of story," he said in clipped tones.

"Wow!" Gem said in amazement. "What an odd story. And an odd day. Especially for Mr Manton."

"Indeed," Wyatt said abruptly. "And now, my dear, you must tell me how you knew!"

"I didn't know anything," Gem protested, frowning. "It just didn't feel right. It just didn't. Mr Manton is no fool. He wouldn't take the same jogging route every day. Law of averages: two accidents in two months. It just didn't feel right," she repeated.

Wyatt reached out his hand to twine a lock of her hair around his finger. "Your 'feeling' was right on the mark. Mr Choate had information for me in less than four hours. He is, indeed, remarkable at his profession." He gazed at his finger, twirling the lock over and over again, then he looked up into Gem's eyes. "I think you saved Manton's life. The brothers were out for his blood."

"Best keep young Mr and Mrs Peter Manton in Canada for a long time," Gem advised, unsmiling.

"For now at any rate," Wyatt agreed. "Manton, by the way, sends his gratitude."

"He is most welcome," she replied, watching his fingers curling the lock of her hair, and then he tugged on it.

"Do not ever – EVER - again ring off when I am talking to you, darling," Wyatt said sternly, his eyes locking hers in a dark steel grey gaze.

"I won't," Gem promised, unable to break the gaze.

"And," Wyatt continued, his tone again stern, "I shall never ring off when I am talking to you," he finished, and released the curl.

Gem nodded, finding it very strange that he would return the promise. It was likely some sort of a future trap. And she would deal with that when the trap snapped.

"And the butterflies?" his voice softened, his grey eyes lightened. He traced his finger across her cheek.

"Butterflies - or hormones - raging," she said confidingly.

"I'll accept either," he smiled, slipping his hand to the nape of her neck and drawing her head down, her lips to his.

Gem's brain pounded as she wakened. Three points! Three points that she could not retrieve from the furthest reaches of her mind.

The thermos of hot chocolate sat next to her computer. Tired as he had been returning from his tenuous day in Paris, Wyatt had remembered to prepare hot chocolate for her. Habit? Kindness? Ploy? Gem decided on the last as fact.

It had been a very long day! But Mr Manton had been sorted. Gem was still rather surprised that most of T.B knew that Mr Choate was her bodyguard - a situation completely unusual to her, but apparently not so unusual to the residents of the small village - who were used to the wealthy and powerful Wyatt Grantham.

Gem felt a bit of a thrill that Wyatt had actually listened to her, and had asked Mr Choate to investigation Mr Manton's 'accidents'.

Ha! She could solve something as esoteric as Mr Manton's 'accidents' but she couldn't find Gemmy! She couldn't find the Pilos!

Gem pressed the start button on the cd player. She pushed all thoughts from her mind and listened to every word Vera Lynn sang - every word of every song. There were nine songs and medleys before the song came: I'll Be Seeing You...Every word, every nuance of the silky vocals seared into Gem's brain. And the cd continued to the last song, Land of Hope and Glory. Over the past five and a half months, Gem had listened endlessly to the songs, letting the music flow over her when she couldn't bear to let herself think. When she couldn't bear to accept the facts of what had happened. When she needed the music as comfort background as she scoured computer web-sites for information. When she read book after book, watched dvds of the Second World War, trying to find a connection to Gemmy, the Pilos, to the murders of the counter-couriers and agents.

And she had the information. She knew it. She had every single piece of information that she needed - or had that 'something' that could make the connection. Three 'somethings'. Far, far away at the furthest recesses of her mind. As lost as Gemmy. As lost as the Pilos.

But! But! But! She could retrieve them. The 'somethings' were there. But God only knew how long it would take to retrieve them. And where it would lead her. And the most important fact was the one most difficult to retrieve. But she had it. She knew she had it. And she would have to fight to retrieve it. Because it was fighting to keep from her grasp.

Mr Cawley was awake. Gem pulled her mobile from the pocket of her dressing gown.

'What news have you, my friend?'

'Give it over, Gem!'

'I can't.'

'Why not, damn it?'

'I can't reach it.'

'Damn!'

'How do you think I feel?'

'A bit frustrated.'

'A total understatement!'

'How can I help?'

'You can't. Except -'

'Except what???'

'Don't say a word to anyone. I have to do this on my own.'

'Understood.'

'If you say a word - if I get an inkling, I will bail! I'll quit the Agency and disappear!'

'Whoa!'

'I am serious! Not a single word!'

'I promise, Gem. On my honour and on my life!'

'Thank you.'

'I doubt your husband would appreciate if you up and disappeared.'

Wyatt would explode.

'He probably wouldn't.'

'Understatement there! How can I help you, Gem?'

'I don't know yet.'

'I'm here, Gem, Anytime. Day or night. I am here!'

'Thank you.'

'You are most welcome, Gem. Not get back to work!'

'Thanks! I need more pressure! - HA!'

'I won't let up!'

'Okay.'

She cleared the messages.

Gem pressed the start button again on the cd player. She had not been alone for months now. She had Mr Cawley with her. And Vera Lynn. And now she had two furred ones who constantly stared at each other.

She turned to look at Mrs Mac and Miss Molly. Mrs Mac sat on the seat cushion of the comfy chair. Molly sat on the floor. And they stared at each.

"What exactly do you see?" Gem sank to her knees at the side of the chair? "A melding of minds? A means to gain a compromise of sorts? A means to be able to tolerate one another?"

They did not look at her. They did not speak to her.

"Well," Gem said patiently. "Carry on."

And so would she.

As they walked up the stairs to bed, Gem mused on Peter Manton's new life. What a lovely future he would have with his Celine, and she with him. Brilliant.

Chapter Twenty-Eight

Gem walked out of Dr Hallowell's office, exhausted mentally, and filled with a new resolve.

Twins.

"Why didn't you tell me when I was here the first time?" she had asked quietly. "You could hear the heartbeats."

"You could barely accept the fact that you were pregnant, Gem," Dr Hallowell had said matter-of-factly. "You knew it was a likely possibility. You are a twin. Your mother was a twin. You were physically and mentally exhausted. I thought waiting a month was an acceptable hedging point. It has been less than a month, but you are better physically. And now you know for certain."

Gem had reflected on his words. "Is hedging part of the Hippocratic Oath?" she had mildly challenged his previous decision.

"Hedging yes, lying no," he had said firmly. "Your babies are healthy and are progressing as they should. I want to see you at your scheduled appointment at the end of this month. Give me a ring if you have any questions, or come in whenever you like."

She had her answer. She couldn't fault him for not stating twins at her previous visits. One or two. Two. She HAD been exhausted. And now she felt better.

Mr Choate was waiting on the pavement at the bottom of the steps.

"I need a beer," she sighed.

"Too bad. Not allowed," he point blank refused her remark.

"Two," she said, shaking her head.

"Two it is then," he nodded. "Not a great surprise."

"I suppose not," she said grudgingly.

"Still your own information," he assured her. "Yours alone to tell to whomever, and in your own time."

"Not Wyatt," she said firmly. "Not yet."

"As you say, Gem," he nodded. "Ticking Bottom?"

"Hot chocolate."

"Charley's?"

"Perfect," Gem nodded.

Gem had had lunch at Charley's Pub with Mr Choate insisting on paying the bill. She had rung Mrs M to notify her that she was lunching in the city - one of Wyatt's steadfast rules - notify Mrs M.

She and Mr Choate had quietly discussed the Manton situation, and Mr Choate had informed Gem that a check from GEI had been delivered to Technical

Operations that very morning, with a note of thanks for a job 'swiftly and professionally resolved'. The note had been signed WG.

"Thank you again, Mr Choate," Gem had smiled.

"It was your call, Gem. I simply checked with a few contacts," Choate had replied.

After lunch it was back to Ticking Bottom. Mrs M was concentrating on a new chicken recipe, and Miss Molly was more than ready for a walk.

Miss Molly ran across the fields as Gem patiently waited and watched from the cobblestone lane.

Another item resolved. Babies. Plural. Now she had to find Gemmy and the Pilos. And soon! How long could she put off telling Wyatt about the twins? And when she told him, if she had to tell him without having found the Pilos, he would likely guess that she had a twin. He would want to know if she had been with James or had her twin deserted his brother? And, of course, John Staunton would be mentioned. And Gem's lies. And why she had lied.

It was too much to address without telling Wyatt everything. Mrs Brown had given her approval to do so. Harry had not given his approval. It was against all Agency SOP. Wyatt was a civilian.

It was a muddle.

She had to reach three 'somethings'. Three of them.

Miss Molly darted across the field for nearly twenty minutes before Gem called her to return. It was time for a walk for Molly's human unit. Gem cleared her mind, enjoying the walk and a chat with Molly who didn't feel pressured to engage in an in-depth conversation of any subject.

Mrs M was still perusing cookery books when Gem and Molly returned to the Hall, so Gem pulled up the Durham file on her computer, turning on the telly to attempt a guess as to why Mrs Brown and Harry were still not available to the Agency. She had no doubt that they were working - and not lounging at a resort in the Mediterranean. But she could not glean an idea of what was consuming their efforts in the Agency Network world.

She couldn't concentrate on Durham, deciding instead to use reading the book of the Hong Kong occupation as a cover, as she attempted to solve the riddle of the three - what were they -? Keys! They were three missing Keys! Perhaps if she could get one of the Keys the others would soon surface at the front of her brain. She snuggled on Auntie Jane's settee, with Mrs Mac draped across her knees; Molly stretched out at her feet for a long nap.

However, despite her effort, in an hour she had not read a single page in her book, nor had the Keys progressed as much as an iota from hiding. Three Keys and not one to be grasped. Gem heard Mrs M rooting through cupboards for cooking pans, and set aside her book and thoughts to offer her assistance in the kitchen.

Dinner would be chicken marinated in Italian dressing, potatoes in jackets, and of course, salad. Mrs M did not need assistance.

Gem sipped a cup of tea while the cook chatted about the new people interested in renting Mrs Moody's cottage. "They would prefer to purchase the cottage, however since that is not an option they will rent," Mrs M said matter-of-factly.

Naturally, they could not purchase the cottage, Gem silently mused. Wyatt would prefer having the control of his Kingdom. She was relieved that she hadn't made the remark aloud. She was probably the only person who resented his compulsion to control everything in his wake. And indeed, she was resentful. All she had control of was her secret about the twins.

Gem walked to her office, tea cup in hand. She had pushed the fact from her mind since she had told Mr Choate the news - the confirmation - and then the few minutes when she was watching Molly running across the field.

Twins, a cat, a dog. Wouldn't her life just be full!! Wyatt insisted they were a 'family'.

Family.

He had repeatedly used that word. His parents and James were dead. Gemmy and their parents were dead. Wyatt had the M's.

He insisted on family. Gem, a baby, Miss Molly, Mrs Mac. Did he actually want a family? Did he actually want or need a family to add to the M's? Or was he simply gathering 'items' for a composite family? A family who existed by his power, to be within his control, to exist at his whim, for as long as it suited his Game?

Back to the Game. It always tracked back to his Game. To James.

Miss Molly stretched, sighed one of her long sighs, lifting her head to look about, searching for -, Gem grinned as Mrs Mac shot into the room, leaping up to the counter, taking her place to stare down at the dog.

"Unbelievable," Gem grinned, sitting down on the swivel chair, the furred ones clear in her peripheral vision. She keyed in a word here and there in the Durham text, but her thoughts were consumed by the twins. Girls, boys, one of each? It would be at least another month before Dr Hallowell could give her that information. If she wanted to know. And she did want to know. She already had too many unknowns in her life.

Gem corrected a misspelling and reversed digits in a glaring error of date. And she jumped as a camera flashed in her peripheral vision. Mrs Mac scattered, and Molly exuberantly raced to Wyatt who stood by the bathroom door, camera in hand.

"I didn't realize you were here," Gem said in surprise.

Wyatt grinned at her. "I thought I could sneak in the front door to get a photo of the three of you."

"I forgot you had a camera."

"Surprise," he scrolled the snaps on the camera to show her the shot. "You were deep in thought and the little ones entranced in each other."

"A good shot," Gem complimented.

"Thank you, my dear," he leaned down to kiss her. "How goes Durham?"

"Still standing after all these centuries," Gem shrugged. "How is Mr Manton?" "Truly amazed at the change in young Peter, who is masterfully, according to his father, organizing a quiet, simple, yet meaningful ceremony to be held this Wednesday."

"Are you flying over for the day?" Gem queried.

"Family only. The bride is very shy," Wyatt replied, then frowned. "I still don't understand how you figured out the accidents - and that young Peter was involved."

Gem couldn't explain. "It just came to me."

"Eureka," Wyatt murmured, stroking her cheek.

"Precisely."

He moved his hands to massage her shoulders.

"Lovely," Gem sighed, closing her eyes, bending her head forward.

"Have you had a chance to consider the room for the nursery?" he said casually, then frowned, feeling her tense beneath his hands. "Or shall we discuss that another time?"

"Another time, yes," Gem said carefully.

He didn't mention the subject again that day, but Gem considered the fact that James's room would be adequate for a nursery for infants, but not for growing twins. She and Gemmy had shared a room in Brisbane, but that home had been a rambling structure, and their bedroom nearly as large as the master suite at the Hall. It had been too large for Gemmy when Gem moved back to England with their mum. She couldn't think of the nursery problem now. She had more pressing problems on her mind.

They took Molly for a long walk after dinner and Gem went to bed early, without Wyatt insisting she did. Her exhaustion was definitely waning, but she was learning to pace herself. And the butterflies had wanted gathering.

Gem filled her cup with the hot chocolate from the thermos. She watched the international news on the telly, looking for glints of hot spots, but saw none. Not ever a flicker. She pushed the start button on the cd player.

She paced the hall through the great room and back to the kitchen, her path through the office again impeded by Miss Molly and Mrs Mac. As she again reached the office she pulled out her mobile. Mr Cawley was awake.

'Any news?'

'No. What do you have for me, Gem?'

'Queries. Why haven't Mrs Brown, and Harry returned?'

'Damned if I know.'

Blast! Where were they and what were they doing?

'Search in SCS?'

'No reports yet.'

'Couriers and agents?'

'All accounted for as of midnight.'

'Blank?'

'No information.'

'Stalemate.'

'You have answers.'

'I can't reach them! I just can't.'

'Tell that to Gem!'

'Damn you!'

'You can't say that to your parents! To Portermann! There are dead agents and couriers!'

'Stop the pressure!'
'It's my job to keep the pressure on you. Get to work!'
'Mrs Brown is nicer than you!'
'She's not available, is she? Nor is Harry! Don't let down your Family, Gem!'
'Harsh!'
'Face the truth, Gem! Do the work! Goodnight!'
'Goodnight!'

Face the truth! She did every waking hour of every waking day and night!

The truth was she was failing. And the dark hours would never end. She was as alone as Gemmy in her search. But Gemmy wasn't alone. Gem was. And she would always be alone.

I'll Be Seeing You drifted from the cd player. Every time she and Gemmy said goodbye to their dad…he sang the words…the hug goodbye…

She was so alone.

Gem set the cup on the counter, turned off the cd player, the lights, the electric fireplaces and went up the stairs. The furred ones followed, Mrs Mac settling on the bed, Molly on her bench.

As she slipped between the sheets, Wyatt reached over to draw her close against him. Gem turned to lay her head on his shoulder, resting her cheek against his chin.

Wyatt wrapped his arms around her, stroking her hair. She always slept with her back to him, he puzzled.

Gem lay quietly, listening to Molly's contented sighing, and feeling Wyatt's heart beating beneath her hand.

"This is too very sad," she choked, pulling away, slipping from the bed to retreat to her office.

She pushed start on the cd player, and sat in Auntie Jane's comfy chair, drawing her feet up to the cushion, resting her head upon and wrapping her arms around her knees. Mrs Mac leaped to the top of the chair, her tail swinging and brushing the top of Gem's hair. Molly wandered about the room, finally curling up in a ball on the settee, sighing again the contentment Gem could not feel.

I'll Be Seeing You continued to play. Wyatt listened to the words from the doorway. Why this cd early every morning? He had the copy of the same cd that he had found in James's flat in Barcelona. On the case was 'Gem' written in a black ink marker. He had known before he saw the name that it wasn't his brother's cd. World War II songs. Was this the reason for Gem's insomnia? I'll Be Seeing You…Why had she come to him?

He pulled the rocking chair over to sit by the edge of her chair. "Gem," he said softly, taking her hands. "Gem, please look at me."

She slowly raised her head and he was shocked by the despair in the clouded violet eyes. Did she even see him or were her thoughts so lost in her secret world?

"You came to bed because you needed to be held, didn't you?" he gently queried.

Gem shook her head, and lowered it, resting her forehead on her knees.

Wyatt sat quietly, pondering her action, and the pain he had seen in her eyes. Before, when her eyes had clouded, he had thought the looked was haunted - from guilt. Now he realized the look was one of such pain and sadness so deep, in fact, that there was no word to describe it. What was the word? He searched his memory. - Han. That was the word. Pain and sadness so deep -

"You came to bed because you needed to be held, and I was the only one here - but I could never understand how devastated you feel. 'This is too very sad'," he said softly.

Gem slowly raised her head. "Yes," she whispered.

He nodded. This was the second time she had come to him when she needed him.

"Come." Wyatt drew her to her feet, as he stood and moved back the rocking chair. He sat down again, drawing her on to his lap, folding his arms around her. She laid her head on his shoulder, and he began rocking, holding her securely in his arms.

He didn't speak. He couldn't. The haunted look. It had been in the lovely violet eyes the day they met at Oscar's Café. She had been polite to the tourists from San Francisco. But the look had been in her eyes. The haunted look. It wasn't guilt for something she had done, he sensed. It was nothing to do with James. At Wight, she hadn't ever known James had died. 'It' - whatever 'it' was, had happened between the time she had left Barcelona - no after that - Geneva - and the day he had met her at Oscar's Café.

Something that had caused pain, sadness, and deep despair.

Something she couldn't - Could Not - speak of. Not wouldn't. Could Not. Something she had to keep secret. She would give him the third passport - if she could.

'I can't.'
'You won't.'
'Have it your way.'
Again 'Can't'.

Gem was not at liberty to tell him. To explain. She 'couldn't' tell him what she knew. Or - was it something illegal - she didn't dare tell him? Or, it was so horrifying she simply 'couldn't' bear to speak of what had happened?

A flight. Water. He had found nothing on the computer referring to either or both. A private flight? A private airstrip? Again illegal?

He could make no sense of it. Of her. The M's adored her. Mr Choate's reports of Gem were clean to the point of boring. Ms Holton, an extremely astute business woman, was very impressed with Gem. And Gem knew that Manton was being targeted. It made no sense.

James! It was still there! The anger he felt! No - it was rage! The pain he felt! No. He couldn't forgive Gem.

Yet, he couldn't believe this was the same woman who had deserted James! What had happened to her in those few months to have so changed her? She was simply not the same woman who could so badly have hurt James.

"Gem," he said softly.

"Yes," she stirred.

"Let's go to bed, sweetheart."

"Yes. Thank you."

She gazed up at him and he saw lovely, clear violet eyes.

He held her in his arms, her arm stretched across his chest. Wyatt exhaled slowly, feeling the tight band around his heart ease just a bit.

"Thank you," she whispered.

"You are welcome, my sweet. Go to sleep," he said gently.

Gem wakened slowly. Seven o'clock. Her arm still stretched across Wyatt's chest, her face was buried in his neck, his arms held her as they had during the dark hours.

Molly raised her head, listening to movement downstairs. She jumped down from her bench and padded out of the suite.

"Hmmm," Gem said drowsily. "I could spend all day like this," she sighed.

"Done!" Wyatt said instantly, reaching for his mobile, and texting two messages. "I told Mrs M to go home and take Miss Molly with her."

"How can you simply not go to the office?" Gem protested.

"Ms Holton and Ms Wexton," he replied, shifting to lean over her. "The perks of having an excellent staff. Are you hungry?"

"Yes," Gem wrapped her arms around his neck.

"I'll serve you breakfast in bed."

"I'm ready," Gem teased.

Wyatt grinned at her. "Breakfast in bed, then brunch later," he murmured.

"As you say," Gem agreed.

It was breakfast in bed, then shower, then brunch in the kitchen. Gem watched as Wyatt prepared bacon and omelettes. His deep blue silk dressing gown accentuated the blue rim around his grey eyes. He gave her a dazzling smile as he handed her a plate. Her heart flipped, her pulse started to race. He was too handsome for words! This man was different than the man she had met in August. There was something different about him now. Perhaps something in his eyes? Gem couldn't figure out what it was.

"You look positively luscious this morning," he reached across the counter to stroke the soft skin between the folds of her dressing gown.

"There's not much remaining of morning," Gem grinned, tucking into her food.

"Finish your breakfast," he ordered. "There's too much dressing gown on you."

"One track mind," Gem teased.

"At least today we are on the same track," he winked.

"Indeed," Gem murmured. Her skin tingled from his caress. What was the matter with her today? She couldn't get enough of him. "Ms Holton and Mrs M must be scandalized by your abrupt texts this morning. Don't you wonder what they are thinking?" she blushed.

"Mrs M is enjoying her day off and is very likely spoiling Miss Molly. Ms Holton is thinking again how excellent you are for the advancement of her career - which is a fact. You occupy my attention - she directs GEI London."

"Don't you worry about a take-over?" Gem puzzled.

"Not possible. I own GEI outright. Remember? No shareholders, no stockholders, no board of directors, no other finger in the till. I sink or swim on my own."

"That must be overwhelming," Gem observed.

Wyatt shook his head. "I have good staff. I allow them to develop their talents, and they shine at their jobs. However, if need be, I can have a heavy hand," he said casually, but Gem heard a thread of steel in his voice. And she knew that steel so well from her own experiences with him.

Gem ate slowly, reflecting on their relationship. She knew many women were drawn to powerful men. She was not. She had to admit that she felt an underlying thread of fear within her of Wyatt - aside from the passports and photos. Yet while she felt that fear of him - as the man in control of their legal relationship - she still couldn't wait to get her hands on him in bed. Oh, how she would miss this part of their relationship when she left the Hall. And she had to leave. Soon. That thought brought a frown to her brow.

Wyatt watched as the violet eyes began to cloud.

"Look at me, Gem," he gently ordered.

"What?" she raised her head, looking into the light grey eyes.

As he gazed at her the clouded look disappeared. "Just checking," he gave her a gentle smile. "Food. Eat," he ordered. "Bed."

"Indeed," she smiled. He had been so gentle with her during the dark hours. It had been lovely to be held in his arms. By this man. The butterflies were swarming. But she didn't trust him. She couldn't trust him.

They spent the rest of the day in bed, and Wyatt was pleased that she was able to fall asleep in late afternoon after a cheese sandwich and hot chocolate. He read reports in the library, filled the thermos with hot chocolate, and went to bed without waking her. Mr M had delivered Miss Molly home after dinner and the poochie settled down on her bed as Wyatt pulled back the duvet to slide in next to Gem.

But sleep escaped him, and he pondered Gem's desire to spend the entire day in bed - with him. It was definitely out of character for her - to his delight. Usually she would rather he wasn't in her view. She certainly was no longer shy in bed, and yet as well as he knew her physically, she was confounding him more every day.

He had held her during early morning and most of this day. And for the first time since he met her he was very pleased to have her in his life. It was no longer an effort to look at her. To speak to her. To spend time with her. It was a pleasure.

He knew why James had been captivated by her. There was no other woman in the world like her!

And she didn't trust him. That would have to change. He would manage it. He still had to know why she had used James. Why she had deserted him. What her game was. What had happened during those few months this past summer that had so changed her. He knew what would be her future - it would be with him - he could control her, prevent her from resuming her past life, but he had to know her past; all of it.

Gem sipped the hot chocolate as she watched the international news - checking yet again for hot spots, and again not finding a single one. Harry and Mrs Brown weren't involved in a hot spot then. Perhaps working underground in an area that had yet to even begin to simmer. Perhaps Harry had noticed a barely beating pulse and was trying to diffuse a surge to simmering. He had managed that a few times in his past at the Agency.

She pulled out her mobile. Mr Cawley was awake.

'News?'

'Only if you have some for me.'

'I do not.'

'The ball is in your court, Gem.'

'I understand.'

'Are you sorting?'

'Yes.'

'Then get back to work.'

'Couriers and agents?'

'Tracking one.'

'Oh dear. Good luck!'

'May need more than that.'

'New courier?'

'Yes. Might be lost in Russia.'

'Preferable to SEA.'

'Quite.'

'I was lost on assignment once.'

'New York City. Your third assignment.'

'Gem was lost in Tokyo once.'

'She neglected to text message delivered code, neglected to charge her mobile, thus was unable to text cleared when she left Tokyo air space. We couldn't track her.'

Gem waited for the entire message, which came in two parts because of its length. She recalled the incident with Gemmy. 'Clear' meant the courier was on the way back to their base country.

'Harry was furious.'

'Almost as much as the missing passport.'

'Hopefully new courier made SOP error.'

'Indeed. Get back to work, Gem. You're wasting time. Goodnight.'

'Yes, Sir! Goodnight.'

Mr Cawley's texts indicated a fair degree of frustration, Gem mused as she cleared her messages. Coping with his regular routine and then adding a missing courier to his list of duties must be giving him a lovely headache.

Gem had literally been lost in NYC - confusion - hers - of an address. Gemmy, however, had caused Harry great consternation with her carelessness of not charging her mobile. Gem had had that problem on paint day - non-working mobile. Agency staff relied greatly on their mobiles for SOP when on assignments. Couriers who repeatedly had mobile SOP errors were reassigned to every day government office positions, sometimes mundane, and never involving travelling, other than possibly from one floor to another via a lift.

Mr Cawley hadn't given her any information to spur one of the Keys to shift position.

Gem looked to her left to watch Miss Molly staring at Mrs Mac who, as usual, was staring back at the dog. But there was a difference now. Each furred one had her eyes closed and was gently sniffing the air. A new aspect to their game? Or was it a new game? One involving trust?

Gem could think the same of Wyatt's new Game, or rather a direction change in this current Game. Was he attempting to get her to trust him again? That was all she could think of to explain his behaviour.

Wyatt had been so kind during the dark hours. She had needed to be held, to be comforted. And he had realized why she had gone to him - there was no one else from whom she could seek comfort. And he had comforted her. And she had wanted the comfort to continue, because it had been lovely to be held. And it would have been perfect if he didn't hate her so. It would have been real.

She shook her head sadly. Because of Gemmy and James, Wyatt and Gem had been brought together. And because of Gemmy and James, Wyatt and Gem would always be divided.

She pushed start on the cd player again.

Their parents had been separated for months at a time, but it had been a separation only of distance - not of heart. The Lawsons and Forresters, while a family of different names, had been a loving family.

Wyatt and Gem's twins would share the same surname, but would be part of two different loving families. Loved by each parent, but still they would be of two families.

And Gem had to work to make two loving families instead of one sham family. It would be very sad to have the two families - but it was critical for Gem to be able to survive and to stay sane.

It was strange to think of being pregnant. It did not seem real to her. Other than the weight gain - and the often rampant hormones - she didn't feel any different than usual - well now that she was no longer exhausted.

Gem closed her eyes and leaned her head back. Gemmy might have had her baby by now. Gem would have met Wyatt under different circumstances. And what joy they would have shared! She couldn't imagine how the emotions would flow come May.

Gemmy! She had told James she was pregnant. She hadn't said she might be but rather that she was! Had she seen a doctor? Had she seen Dr Hallowell? If she had, he couldn't give that information to Gem. Nor could he inform Harry, Mrs Brown, Mr Cawley, Mr Choate, or Paul Andriani. She couldn't even ask Dr Hallowell of Gemmy's last appointment with him. Or had Gemmy seen a physician in Spain?

Her brain was overwhelmed. She pushed start on the cd player, filled her cup with hot chocolate, and started to pace. Miss Molly had opened her eyes; Mrs Mac had not. The contest continued.

Gem pushed thoughts of the Pilos from her mind when they tried to creep in and drain mental energy. And thoughts of Wyatt drifted in. When he hadn't been occupied corralling her butterflies that day, they had spoken very little, each seemingly consumed with their own thoughts. Neither had mentioned the 'baby' but both had offered observations of the furred ones.

Days before, when he had asked Gem if she wanted the 'baby' he hadn't said how he felt or what he thought about her pregnancy, other than saying he was not angry that she was pregnant.

Gem paced until she realized she would not make any progress on any issues. She shut down the office, and Miss Molly and Mrs Mac followed her up to bed.

And as Wyatt put his arms around her, drawing her close to him, as he stroked her hair, Gem felt two Keys slip. She closed her eyes, relieved to know that there was still hope.

Gem had thought Mrs M would make little surreptitious remarks about the previous day, but the housekeeper did not. In fact, Mrs M was very much occupied with a cookery book. Gem glanced at the book while she made tea for them. And wished then that she hadn't seen the book. It was a cookery book for baby food.

That was it! Gem needed a long walk. She hurriedly finished her tea, said, "Molly walk," and they were on their way. She concentrated on Miss Molly until she released her into the meadow for a long run. Gem surveyed the area; there was no one about who would surprise her, so she let her mind wander.

Two Keys had slipped - just a touch as the dark hours were ending that morning. Which two? She didn't know- there was so much information in her mind - but she knew there were two. - No wait. She did know one Key. Paul Andriani.

Paul Andriani had disappeared. But it was possible that he was with Harry and/or Mrs Brown - unbeknownst to the Agency. Harry was underground; Paul Andriani was, so to speak, off the radar - ouch! Gem was stung by the surging reminder of the Pilos being off radar. Paul Andriani could still easily be in South East Asia. - Hiding in plain sight in Indonesia, Hong Kong, Malaysia. He still could be working for the Agency on an assignment of which only Harry was aware. And Mrs Brown? Then why had she informed Gem that Paul Andriani had disappeared? A red herring from the Agency? Possible.

Or he was so deeply underground no one could find him. Would Harry or Mrs Brown attempt to find Paul Andriani now that Indonesia was no longer simmering? Did the Agency ever try to find agents who had disappeared for their own safety? No. That would be foolish and could cause cogs to slip one after another. They would damn well try to find an agent if they thought he/she had been involved in murder.

Yes. Paul Andriani was one of the Keys that had slipped. What was the second Key? Still unknown, she shook her head, and called Miss Molly back. They walked along the upper cobblestone lane, down, around, through the village, greeting the locals with a nod and a smile. When they reached the old stone bridge below the Hall, Gem released Molly to run again across the meadow and brook. She glanced at her watch from time to time, finally calling the dog back after a good half hour run, and they slowly continued on to the Hall.

Mrs M gave her a frown when Gem and Molly entered the kitchen. "I was just about to send out the Mister to find you."

"I was letting Miss Molly have a proper run," Gem smiled. "It's a dog's life. Run, sleep, stare at the cat, repeat endlessly."

The housekeeper chuckled. "Well lunch will be ready soon. I have a club meeting late this afternoon so I will prepare dinner and you keep an eye on it until Mr W comes home. He knows about the meeting," she assured Gem, who did not need reassuring.

Gem didn't consider that she was responsible for reporting to Wyatt on Mrs M's activities, or the time the housekeeper came and left the Hall. As far as Gem was concerned, Mrs M was the manager of the Hall and was her own free agent in regard to her job. It was Wyatt's home, after all, not Gem's.

"Just tell me what to do about dinner and I shall do it," she nodded.

She was at loose ends during the afternoon. The first Key seemed to slip once again, but Gem simply could not hasten it to within her ability to process the thought. She stared at the Durham text for hours, watched a dvd episode of Dr Who, envious that she did not have a blue police public call box in which to travel back in time to stop the Pilos from flying off into the netherworld; she wouldn't mind travelling forward in time - past this coming May to see where in the world she would be. And while she escaped on the Tardis on the telly, she glanced from time to time, watching the silent, closed eyes contest of the furred ones.

When she finally returned to her work on the computer, she wondered if young Peter Manton had by now pledged his troth to his Celine. She wished them happiness and good luck with their fathers-in-law, an unknown entity that they hadn't before had to face.

Miss Molly opened her eyes and sighed. Mrs Mac opened her eyes, sailed across the room to land on the back of the comfy chair and Miss Molly retrieved her lead.

"Again?" Gem marvelled in surprise. No wonder Miss Molly slept so soundly at night! Well, except for the dark hours when she was staring at the cat in Gem's office.

Gem put on her wellies for this walk, got last minute dinner prep instructions from Mrs M, then headed off across the fields with Molly, leash in the dog's mouth, camera in the human unit's hand. Gem released Molly and then she snapped roll after roll of film of the dog running and investigating the terrain. Gem was so focused on her camera work she literally jumped when her mobile rang. She rarely had phone calls. Even Wyatt usually texted her - except when he had rung her from Paris on Sunday.

"Hello?" she said warily.

"Darling, are you out with Miss Molly?"

"I am," she felt awkward. "How is your day going?"

Wyatt paused, startled by the query. "Busy. It looks that I will be late for dinner. An hour or so."

"I'll set dinner back," Gem said calmly.

"Thank you. Don't overtire yourself, sweetheart," he gently ordered.

"I won't. Don't overwork," she countered.

"I won't," he chuckled. "Later, darling."

"Later."

Wyatt slipped his mobile into his pocket. That was managed cordially, and without the usual forced effort on his part when he had to speak to her. And she didn't argue or protest that dinner would be ruined if he was late. She reacted as Mrs M always had. Again, Gem was not demanding.

Gem sighed as she slipped her mobile into the pocket of her windcheater, wishing Wyatt was the man she had thought she had married. If wishes were fishes...she sighed again. And wondered if it was possible to actually wear off all of Miss Molly's energy.

They tramped the fields until the sun began to set, slowly walking back to the Hall. It was dark by the time they entered the kitchen. Mrs M had left for the day, and Gem had forgotten to set the dinner prep back an hour. She turned down the heat on the cooker, then took Molly into the mudroom and cleaned and dried her paws so she wouldn't track mud through the house. By the time she returned to the kitchen to check on dinner it had burned. Gem pulled the cottage pie out of the cooker and set it in the sink.

"Blast!" she dragged her fingers through her hair.

"Blast what?" Wyatt queried as he walked in the door.

Gem spun around moaning," I forgot to set dinner back. I ruined Mrs M's pie," she said guiltily. "It's a disaster. I was out with Molly and forgot about the time."

Wyatt walked over to the sink. "A minor disaster, sweetheart. A happy Molly is more important than dinner."

"Mrs M will be offended that her work was ruined - all the time she spent making the pie was wasted," Gem frowned.

"Darling, Mrs M has scorched many a dinner herself," Wyatt soothed. "I'll change, then make you steak and chips," he kissed her.

"You already worked all day and have reports to read, I'll prepare something," she offered.

"Let's do the pub," he countered. "No washing up."

"Lovely," Gem smiled. "I'd best change so I don't look like something the cat wouldn't dare drag in," she looked down at her mud stained jeans.

"You always look beautiful, Gem," he hugged her. "Covered in paint or mud, always beautiful."

He coaxed her along the hall towards the staircase.

"Did you send the newlyweds a gift?" she queried.

"You and I sent a monetary gift to help fund their new flat," Wyatt replied, kissing her. "Now let us provide another reason for a scorched dinner," he teased.

Gem filled her cup with hot chocolate from the thermos at the right of her computer. She pulled out her mobile and thought twice about texting Mr Cawley. He was becoming a tad bit grumpy as of late. His badgering was compounding her stress. But she was curious to learn if the new courier had been located.

'New courier?'

'Safe. Neglected to send delivered code. As you did once.'

'Okay. Any other news?'

'Mrs Brown may return by the weekend. Have you news for me?'

'I am working.'

'Ramp it up.'
'Okay.'
'Goodnight.'
'Goodnight.'

A bit more difficult every day or rather the dark hours. And still she couldn't fault him; Mr Cawley was working in the dark - so to speak - without information from Harry and Mrs Brown. And she herself was also working in the dark.

The furred ones were staring at each other but had moved to the kitchen, thus freeing pacing space for Gem. She paced as she watched the international news, and could not find any area of interest to Mrs Brown or to Harry that would detain them on 'holiday'.

She pushed the start button on the cd player, letting her mind wander as she paced. The Keys were still stationary, so she didn't try to force what had to happen naturally. Thoughts came randomly to the fore: flight nautical miles, Geneva, Paul Andriani, the murdered couriers and agents, Gemmy, the Pilos, Mr Portermann. Gemmy in Tokyo.

That was new. Gemmy in Tokyo. Just a code SOP error. A memory juggled loose by the new courier dispatched to Russia.

Another cup of hot chocolate and pacing only helped Gem to realize that her feet were cold despite the electric fireplaces. A thick carpet would be preferable to the rugs. She should suggest that to the next person who used this room - perhaps Wyatt's next wife - despite Mrs M's delusions that he was a one woman man, and that Gem was that woman. Wyatt Grantham was obviously a man who would constantly have a woman in his life - or rather in his bed. Here or at the London flat.

Oh, Gem sighed, her frustration increasing. Where are you, Gemmy?

She finally settled in Auntie Jane's comfy chair drawing her feet up to the cushion to keep them warm.

Hopeless. It was all hopeless unless she could get one of the Keys to slip, or if another one would appear. Until then she was simply again treading water. And she hated water!

She longed for the nice, cosy, warm bed. With or without Wyatt. - He certainly had been patient when she had burned dinner. Mr Hyde was currently in residence at Grantham Hall. Perhaps Dr Jekyll was terrorizing the GEI staff in London. Wyatt confused Gem when he was being patient and generous. She had been getting used to his curt attitude and when he was pleasant she had to regroup her mental defences against him - because his smile and his beautiful eyes were too mesmerizing for her to easily fight. Oh, that handsome man! If one of the twins was a boy, females in the future would swarm with butterflies. And God help them!

Gem gave up trying to make any sense of any part of her life. She would lie awake in a warm bed and wait for the dark hours to end.

"Heavens, Gem, you are ice," Wyatt murmured when he put his arm around her. "Another electric fireplace and warmer dressing gowns for you," he insisted. "Good Lord, warmer slippers," he exhaled sharply as his feet touched hers. "We must put carpet in your office. I'll chat with Mr M about it tomorrow. Start thinking about a colour you would like. For now, I'll keep you warm."

"Mmm," Gem nodded. "Lovely."
And she realized a Key had slipped.

Wyatt left before breakfast for an early morning meeting. Gem hadn't intended to go to London, but Wyatt had insisted she choose a colour and carpet as soon as possible. She rang Mr Choate who replied that he would be prepared to leave Ticking Bottom in a quarter hour. Gem hastily gathered her windcheater, shoulder bag, mobile, and camera bag, thinking to purchase another lens that had recently come on the market; it was compatible with her camera and she was already going to the city. Add lens to list. She told Mrs M that she wouldn't be in for lunch, not knowing how long it would take her to decide on carpet - it had taken her weeks to select the paint colour for her office! She patted Miss Molly and was assured the poochie would have her morning walk.

Mr Choate's dark blue Range Rover pulled onto the cobblestone lane behind the Defender as Gem passed the inn.

And a Key dislodged.

And it fell.

Gem smacked her forehead. How could she have missed such obvious signs! As the Defender crossed the last old stone bridge Gem pulled the vehicle to the side of the road. She disengaged the engine, stepped from the Defender and walked back to Mr Choate's Range Rover.

"Something amiss, Gem?" Choate frowned as he got out of his vehicle.

"Indeed! For sometime now, Mr Choate," she said firmly. "I want to see Paul Andriani! Today! It's nine o'clock now. Shall we say half ten!" It was not a query but a demand.

"He is missing, Gem," Choate said mechanically.

"He's sleeping."

"So it would seem," Choate nodded.

"And very comfortably, I am sure - at Wyatt's flat in London!" she said triumphantly. "And I wager it is a very high security building!"

"It is completely secure," Choate began, "but -"

"Half ten, Mr Choate," Gem insisted strongly. "Ring me with the location. I leave that to you and Paul Andriani." Without another word she strode back to the Defender, snapped on her seatbelt, engaged the engine and sped away, leaving Choate to scramble into his vehicle to catch up with her.

Traitor's Gate came into view as Gem's mobile rang. Interesting...Symbolic?

"Speak," Gem ordered abruptly into her phone.

"St George's Cathedral. You will be shooting the front facade," Choate stated.

"Done," Gem broke the connection. She patted her constant companion sitting on the passenger seat. Always carry a camera!

St George's! 1848? If her memory served her correctly. Hardly medieval. A poke of fun from Paul Andriani - Master Criminal and Agent, and what else? - she wondered.

Gem arrived a few minutes early and immediately began shooting the cathedral. It was a very impressive structure.

A priest in a black cassock and elbow length cape, watching her from the steps, descended and walked over to her. "St George's Cathedral is a striking example of the work of architect Augustus Pugin. He also designed St. Frances Xavier's Church in Berrema, New South Wales. St George's Cathedral was the first Catholic Church built in the U.K. following the Reformation. It is of the gothic revival style. Exceedingly striking," the priest admired. "It was heavily bombed by the Nazis in 1941, and with extreme dedication of generous souls was rebuilt, opening again in 1958," he nodded. "Pugin also designed Anglican churches, bless his soul."

"Cut the poppycock, 'father'," Gem pointedly said the last word. "And FYI, you missed a button on your cassock."

"That was your clue, my child," the man said quietly, continuing to gaze at the cathedral.

"I didn't need a clue," Gem said coldly. "You'll probably go to hell for impersonating a priest," she advised.

"I already have a foot down there," Paul Andriani replied dryly. "I don't remember you being so hostile."

"I want answers!" she said emphatically, but quietly.

"If I have answers, they are yours, Gem."

"Why did you disappear?" she said bluntly.

"I got made, Gem," he scowled.

"By whom?"

"I do not know," he said, his voice hollow.

"Then how do you know you were made?" she countered.

"My counter-couriers and agents started showing up dead at our contact points," he said crisply. "I'd show up at a destination and - no contact. Days later a body would be found in the area. Never a good sign to an agent."

"Why wasn't another agent sent in your place to make the contact?" Gem protested, puzzled.

"They knew me. They trusted me," he frowned.

"Which contacts were yours?"

"Thai, Philippine, Malaysian, the latest from China, your mum at times, Gem twice," he sighed.

"You're the Proverbial Finger of Death," she said, her voice barely above a whisper.

"I'm not familiar with that proverb," Paul Andriani rubbed his eyes.

"My creation. How do you know it wasn't the SEA Network that was made?" Gem insisted.

"Too much coincidence. And then there was your mum and Gem. The others were regular contacts. Your mum was only two or three times a year. Gemmy twice in the past year."

Gem nodded. She hadn't properly prepared her questions for this meeting.

Paul looked at her wrist as she focused her lens, still shooting every few minutes. "You're wearing Gem's bracelet. That one was her favourite," he murmured. "And you're wearing her ring."

"Yes," Gem nodded, slightly stung by his references to Gemmy.

"It was an engagement ring," he said gently.

"How do you know?" she asked, so startled she nearly dropped her camera. He couldn't know that she knew! Not yet!

"She was so like you, Gem," he chuckled. "She never wore a ring on that finger before. Just like you - until you married. Were any twins ever as alike as you and Gem!"

"Were you in love with her?" Gem queried, no longer able to restrain her curiosity of Gemmy's connection to him.

"I loved her," he admitted after a momentary pause. "But I was not in love with her. I love you too, Gem," he said kindly. "You are my Family. As is Choate, Mrs Brown, Harry, Cawley, White, your parents, Portermann, and all the rest in the Agency. The Agency is all I have."

Without the Agency, he would be as much adrift as am I, Gem mused sadly.

"You saw Gem in Barcelona."

"How did you know that?" It was Paul's turn to be surprised.

Oops! Watch for slipped cogs. "You saw the ring. She got it in Barcelona - just before she flew to Brisbane for - the - last assignment. I thought she bought it there. She wasn't wearing it when I saw her at home. And Mr Choate said you had seen her there."

Paul Andriani indicated that she should move to her left to alter her perspective for her camera shots.

"Yes," he admitted grudgingly. "I saw her in Barcelona."

Careful. Careful, Gem, she coached herself. "Did she tell you her fiancé's name?"

He shook his head. "Didn't even mention she was engaged. I saw the ring, and I knew. She wouldn't have said anything to anyone before she told you and your parents. And since you didn't know, she took her secret with her," there was a catch in his voice. "Whoever he is, he doesn't know what happened to her. What can he be thinking? What can he be feeling? She simply disappeared from his life." She heard the wrenching emotion in his voice and it tore at her heart. She couldn't hug a priest - could she? "That cuts into my thoughts every day, Gem. Yes," he said softly, "I loved her. But HE was in love with her, and SHE with him."

Gem nodded. "If you knew his name - would you find him? Would you tell him what had happened?" she asked curiously, holding her breath, wondering.

Paul stared at the cathedral. "I've thought about that - all these many months, Gem. And - yes I would. If Gem loved him, that meant she trusted him. She couldn't have told him about her work - not without clearance from Harry. But damn! Yes! I would have told him!"

"Yes," Gem nodded, grateful that Paul would have tried to ease James's pain. "Why did you meet her in Barcelona? She wasn't on assignment."

Paul chuckled dryly. "It was a fluke. I was at the gardens to - meet - someone. She wasn't on assignment, so it was likely she was waiting for her fiancé. I just turned around and there she was."

"Were - you on the job - so to speak?"

"No," he exhaled sharply. "Oh, hell, Gem," he shook his head. "I was there to meet my lover," he said slowly.

"Oh," Gem nodded. "Oh -oh..."

"Yes," Paul Andriani smiled briefly. "We have been together for many years."

"Oh! The flat! Mr Choate!" she whispered, recognition of his words finally dawning.

"Yes," he nodded firmly.

"Did Gemmy know? Not that it matters," Gem said embarrassed. "I just wondered."

"She knew that day. She saw me - then Choate - and she sensed that neither of us were on assignment. She put two and two together and -"

"Got eight," Gem protested. "That's not a logical sum. He could have been on assignment."

"She just knew, Gem. Just like you just knew 30 May."

Gem nodded, mentally ticking off her queries. "May I ask what you chatted about with Gem?"

"She chatted about going home to Brisbane. About seeing you and your parents. And she was very, very happy. She was glowing," he smiled sadly.

Yes she was glowing! Gemmy had been pregnant! But Paul didn't know that.

Photographs of nothing. A casual meeting between friends, which could have been taken as a casual verbal exchange between strangers. It was a cog that had slipped because of shutterbug James, and Wyatt being able to recognize John Staunton. Totally absurd reality! And she was the one who had been stung by the shutterbug!

"That was it? Nothing else?" Gem pressed.

"She was having trouble with her mobile. A new one was going to be drop shipped to her in Brisbane. It takes quite a bit of effort to program Agency mobiles, to properly place the special tracking chip, satellite blocks, Agency numbers, and the blocks for those. That sort of thing."

"Okay," Gem said dispirited, and feeling very guilty that she had suspected Paul Andriani of wanting to hurt Gem.

"She was chagrined about the phone business since Harry had had to replace her passport the month before - and that is as involved as replacing an Agency mobile. She worried that Harry would think she was being careless."

"I can see her point," Gem winced. "We had all received new mobiles in January - well, not you," Gem excepted Paul. "You haven't used one for a while?" she queried knowing the answer.

"I used them for a time. However, a mobile ringing at an inopportune moment could have got me my throat slit. I didn't want to be tracked in the event I was involved in an acutely dicey meeting. I couldn't chance an Agency mobile being stolen," he shrugged, pointing to her to again refocus her camera perspective on the cathedral.

"A hassle, indeed," Gem agreed.

"There are too many codes on an Agency mobile to suit my needs. Codes I needed blocked might accidentally be dropped if an unfriendly nation was playing with satellite disruption. I didn't want the access codes that would activate Agency computer tracking of my mobile. Courier and agent mobiles have those codes - as you know."

Gem puzzled about the differences in her current mobile and his previous Agency mobiles, storing it for future consideration. "So you used disposable mobiles," Gem nodded.

"I was underground, Gem. I needed the ability to be anonymous when I wasn't Staunton. I couldn't depend on the Agency mobile safety programming not being disabled by some satellites - which does happen in South East Asia."

"North Korea." Gem volunteered.

"It has been said," Paul Andriani smiled wryly. "I use the disposable mobiles for a short time. A day or two, then dump them in an incinerator."

"You were so careful. How did you get made?" Gem frowned. "It doesn't make sense."

"I do not know, Gem," he shook his head. "How the hell can an Agency plane with four accomplished Agency staff disappear without a trace?"

"There's a mole or a sleeper," Gem said quietly.

"Has to be," he nodded. "But everyone - every staffer - had been cleared in all the Networks. It's frustrating as hell!"

"One dressed such as you should not swear," Gem said serenely.

"It's another foot down," he said dryly.

"Why did you agree to meet me?" Gem asked curiously.

He chuckled. "You made me. You are good, Gem. No one else in the Agency made me. But you did. Very impressive! And I agreed to meet you because I trust you, Gem," he grew serious for a moment.

The dangerous life of an undercover agent. An undercover agent James just happened to catch on film.

Gem shook her head in amazement. "You just happened to be in Barcelona."

"Our holiday destination for years. It should have been safe - Choate was courier to Barcelona. We had never run into Agency staff before last May," he said wryly.

"Oops," Gem winced. Then a thought struck her. "When you were in Barcelona in May, were you John Staunton or Paul Andriani?"

"We were one and the same," he smiled.

"I thought you used disguises - such as," she looked at his cassock.

"I ran into Gem shortly after a meeting. I hadn't had time to alter my appearance. It could have caused a cog to slip, but fortunately it did not."

On the contrary! A cog did slip! A giant cog! And it landed on me! And THAT thought she would reflect on later. And quite often, she knew.

"What are you going to do when you leave the priesthood?" she queried lightly, her tone much different than when he walked down the cathedral steps to meet her.

"Have lunch," he chuckled.

"Thank you for meeting me. You could have done a mid-morning flit," she smiled.

"As I said before, Gem, I trust you."

She realized he was asking for her trust. "You can," she agreed. "I've never been to Wyatt's flat. Is it lush?"

"Comfortable. Practical. Mr Grantham doesn't slash it around, does he? He's not ostentatious," Paul glanced at her, briefly taking his eyes off the cathedral.

"No, he doesn't," she agreed. "I'm pregnant - he has to save for university fees," she tried to inject a bit of humour.

"Kudos, Gem!"

"Magical glory," she murmured.

"Just so," he grinned. "Lord, Gem, you should be glowing, but you look like you rarely sleep."

"Still the silver tongued devil, aren't you!"

"Not the proper word to call someone in this get-up," he warned her. "You've gained a bit of weight - which you needed - since the last time I saw you. But you're still a shadow of your former self," he insisted.

The last time they had met was at an emergency Agency meeting in mid-June.

"I'm only half of my former self," she agreed. "Not even half, at that," she sighed.

Paul shook his head, suggesting with his eyes that they move to the far right of the cathedral to yet another perspective of the structure.

"If you mean you're only half a person - or less - because Gem isn't here, then, dear girl, you are so phenomenally wrong in that thought. You are so wrong. Remember looks aren't everything. You and Gem may have used the same name, you may have looked and sounded like one another, but twins means two - not one. Margaret gave birth to two daughters - not just one," he gently reminded her. "And I don't see you in your eyes anymore."

"But Gem doesn't exist," Gem's throat tightened. "I can't even grieve for her. I can't mourn losing her. She doesn't exist," she repeated.

"Not now perhaps. And that's the ultimate cruelty. But she will exist again one day. All four of our loved ones will. We all mourn them in our hearts. God, Gem, you're not alone. We all grieve with you. Our hearts are also broken. You just feel the pain the most - and the deepest."

"Thank you, father," she attempted a bit of humour to shake off breaking down and giving into her emotions.

"Bless you, my child. Now I'm three feet down, and that's only from our chat today," he shook his head wryly. "Now, my dear friend, separate yourself from Gemmy. Uncloud your brain. You were summa cum laude - keep putting your brilliant brain to work and solve this mystery. You made me. Find the Pilos. And for God's sake get some sleep. Wyatt Grantham should take better care of you!"

"He tries," Gem protested. And he did, because how she appeared reflected back on him, no doubt. "I do sleep."

"Not enough, girl. Now I've been here too long. If you need to chat again notify Choate. But do not disturb me during vespers," he grinned. "I have to go hear confessions now."

"Four feet down," she stifled a giggle. Gem watched as he entered the church. Hear confessions? Would he? No! - NO! Clear your head, Gem!

She snapped another half dozen shots of the cathedral. Not medieval, but still riveting, she reflected, glancing at her watch. Nearly half eleven. She took a chance and texted Wyatt.

'Lunch?'

She waited patiently. Perhaps he was in a meeting.

'One hour?'

'Yes. Jake's?'

'If you like.'

'Regards to Ms Holton.'

There was another pause.

'Sends same. One hour then.'

'Yes.'

She slipped her mobile into her pocket and walked back to the Defender where Choate had patiently waited for her.

"Thank you, Mr Choate," she smiled at him.

"You are very welcome, Gem. Are you going to mention to Mr Grantham about the flat?" he frowned slightly.

"The flat?" she gave him a blank look. "I don't anything about the flat. I've never even been there. I heard it is currently occupied, but that's all I know about it," she shrugged.

"Thank you, Gem," he nodded, and she gave him a quick smile.

"I'm going to meet Wyatt for lunch at Jake's in an hour," she informed him, "but I have a query."

"Yes?"

"Can anyone intercept or hack into messages I text to you or Mr Cawley?"

"No," he shook his head. "Agency mobiles are blocked to prevent hacking, and the block cannot be removed or challenged by any method."

"Okay. Not even by Ticking Bottom Security?"

Choate chuckled. "I am now T.B. Security."

Gem did a double take. "Well! Aren't you just handy to have around!"

"I am indeed," he grinned.

"Don't spread yourself too thin," she warned.

"I won't. It's a temporary position. I'm reviewing all T.B. SOP. Actually I recently hired a new employee at Technical Operations to take over some of my work load."

"Good," Gem nodded. "And you're certain you can trust this person?" she queried, getting a feeling…

"I have absolute confidence of that. I've known him for a long time. He's a former priest, you see," Choate said with a straight face.

"That must mean he's finished hearing confessions." Her feeling had been correct.

"Long finished and no doubt back at the office by now."

"Does the Agency know of this new employee?" Gem asked curiously.

"Only you know, Gem. No one else in the Agency," he said very seriously.

"I understand," she nodded. "There's a sleeper, you know," she said equally seriously. "Or a mole."

Choate nodded pensively. "So it would seem." He glanced at his watch. "You don't want to keep Mr Grantham waiting, Gem."

"Omigosh!" Gem looked at her watch, and pulled her keys from her shoulder bag.

"You go girl," Choate laughed suddenly.

Gem was startled. Had she ever heard him actually laugh before?

She gave him a quick wave, and blessed Mr Critchley for counselling her on driving route techniques on crowded streets. She arrived at Jake's as Wyatt reached the door of the pub.

Gem gave Wyatt a dazzling smile, put her arms around his neck and gave him a passionate kiss. He returned the kiss with full measure, then grinned down at her.

"Someone's hormones are raging today," he laughed. "Or are you actually pleased to see me?"

"Hormones," she teased, laughing. "You're not the only one who has them."

"I was beginning to wonder about that," he chuckled.

"They come and they go," she laughed as he ushered her into the pub.

"Then I'd best enjoy them while they are here!"

"Just for that, you're paying for lunch!" Gem tapped his chest with her finger.

"My pleasure," he raised a brow. "Now and later," he chuckled again, emphasizing the last word.

"Back to your hormones," Gem sighed mockingly.

"Sass!" Wyatt laughed.

Chapter Twenty-Nine

"I'm rather surprised you suggested Jake's, my dear," Wyatt whispered. "The same waitress is here."

"I thought this pub would be the most convenient for you if your day is frightfully busy," Gem whispered in return. "I'll have to chance the food," she grinned.

When the waitress came to take their order she only addressed Wyatt. "You haven't been in for weeks," she gave him a provocative smile and lowered her eyelids.

Gem raised her eyebrows and pursed her lips forcing Wyatt to suppress a grin. "My wife is recovering from a severe case of morning sickness," he replied smoothly to the blatant young woman. "But she is feeling better now, and this is her favourite pub, so we are both very pleased to be here today."

"Oh," the waitress was a bit taken back, and altered her pose a touch while she took their order.

"She'll spit in your food now also," Gem grinned at Wyatt.

"I'll have that image in my mind the rest of the day, thank you," he replied dryly. "Henceforth it will be the White Rose or Cat for us!"

"I think so," Gem laughed.

"Did you have a pleasant morning looking at carpet?" Wyatt changed the subject.

"Yes," she replied. "But I wasn't looking at carpet. I was photographing St George's Cathedral."

"Hardly medieval," Wyatt returned with an expectant gaze. "Ah! The destruction - early War years," he nodded. "I'd forgotten your obsession with cathedrals bombed during the war."

Gem nodded, not about to disagree with his conclusion. "Carpet this afternoon."

"And dressing gowns and warm slippers," he reminded her. "I wish I could spend the afternoon with you, but Ms Holton is currently in a meeting, and I have a conference call this afternoon. I did ring Ora this morning to suggest you might stop by the shop this afternoon."

"My how organized you are," Gem mused, scanning the food for unusual wet spots when it was served.

"You have frightfully cold feed in bed," he teased. "Mr M installed the shelves in your office and purchased another electric fireplace," he added.

"Busy morning for you. Thank you," Gem smiled. I tracked down a master undercover agent who was impersonating a priest, AND who is, by the way, currently residing in your London flat. My entire life is a lie, and I am going to go mad if I have to continue living in two separate worlds.

Wyatt watched the haunted look begin to cloud her eyes, realizing her smile was forced.

Gem was suddenly overwhelmed with the reality of her meeting with Paul Andriani. Intense memories threatened to flashback at her. It could all start to come together. And the pressure from Mr Cawley would be unbearable. She had to get this right!

"Gem," Wyatt said gently. When she looked at him he saw that the colour had drained from her face. "Darling -"

"I hate shopping. I have no idea what carpet to purchase, and I don't know what colour to choose," Gem said. "I don't know what clothes you want me to wear, what I should buy," she said breathlessly.

Wyatt stared at her in astonishment. He took her hand, gently squeezing it. "Very well, darling," he said smoothly. "Request that Ora and Eda take over the responsibility of your wardrobe. I shall direct Mr M to select the carpet. Now take a deep breath and relax," he coaxed gently.

Gem did as he said, and after a few minutes she began to relax. "Thank you," Gem sighed, looking up to his face, getting lost in his eyes.

"You needn't think about anything that will cause you additional stress," Wyatt assured her. "You might be required to make decisions now and then regarding the baby, but only when you feel able to do so." He watched her manner slowly alter.

"I can manage that," Gem assured him carefully.

What the devil so consumed her thoughts that she had to fight to keep her equilibrium to manage through each day? And why had he not noticed that trouble of hers before this? He had been so oblivious to so many of her needs and concerns since they had met. He had been insensitive of her needs because he only regarded her as a target. But she was carrying his child, and he would have to be more concerned about her needs other than rest and making sure she had a proper diet. And there was the stress issue that Lyndon had addressed.

He watched her as they ate, noting again her habit of scanning their surroundings. Still that habit. She was so difficult to figure. It wasn't that she didn't think the Hall needing redecorating, but rather that she wasn't interested in the project. The women he had previously been involved with had thoroughly enjoyed spending money, suiting their surroundings specifically to themselves. Nothing was ever good enough for them.

He had warned her at Wight that he would not shower her with gifts and attention. And he realized now that that was not the reason she did not make demands on him. She didn't make demands on him because she didn't expect anything from him. And not because of his remarks; simply because she did not expect anything from him. There was no sly coaxing, no wheedling, no artful pouting, no demands. She was not a demanding woman. And he did not believe her lack of expectations was contrived.

But she had insisted on the flat in Barcelona. And James had purchased it for her. James had not mentioned any other demands, but that doesn't mean she hadn't made any. Damn! She was a puzzle.

Wyatt pulled out his mobile to check the weather forecast for Saturday and then he sent a message.

"Do you have to return to your office now?" Gem asked quietly.

"Not quite yet, my dear," he smiled, signalling the waitress for more tea. "Shall we take a day trip this Saturday? Perhaps Stonehenge? The weather forecast is sun and a mild temperature. You can use your cameras and decide if you prefer one to the other."

"But Molly," Gem winced.

Wyatt's mobile indicated a text message.

"Mr M," he read, "will order the carpet and will also take Miss Molly on Saturday. Would you like to have a day-trip?"

"Yes!" Gem said eagerly. She didn't have enough to occupy her time since Mrs M would no longer allow her to assist with the housework. She couldn't concentrate on her book for more than a few minutes at a time. She would dearly love the distraction from her search. And she was thrilled to be rid of one of her Keys. There were two additional Keys to retrieve, and perhaps today's chat with the fabricated priest would help loosen another Key. "Perhaps you would like to try the Canon," she offered.

"Thank you, sweetheart, but I'm comfortable with my camera. You search out pubs or restaurants for our meals, if you have the time, otherwise we will see what comes our way on Saturday," he suggested, smiling.

"No seafood or lamb," she grinned, the butterflies waking.

"Or mutton," he winked. "And now I fear I must go back to the office, darling."

With a warning to rest later, Wyatt returned to the office, and Gem and Choate continued with errands, stopping first at the photo shop to drop films off of Molly and two rolls of St. George's Cathedral. Ora and Eda were delighted by Gem's request to handle her wardrobe needs, and their mother had already managed to sew a thick, warm dressing gown for her. Their auntie had scouted two shops and presented Gem with lined slippers guaranteed to keep the wearer warm.

Gem was surprised to be introduced again to Ms Ames from GEI Research and Development, who was studying the shop to offer advice on improving the profit line. Apparently Wyatt had not seen a conflict of interest of Mr Choate's involvement as a silent partner in the shop. Ms Ames was very pleasant and was obviously pleased to have been selected for this particular project.

Eda confided to Gem that Ms Ames had purchased three outfits and had brought in four new customers by wearing Ora's designs. She also informed Gem that Ms Holton was now a regular customer at the shop.

As Gem finally left the shop with her purchases she realized she had a query for Paul Andriani. She put the matter to Choate who quickly gave her the former agent's mobile number. Wouldn't Wyatt just pitch a battle if he knew John Staunton's mobile number was on her phone! She keyed the number into her Agency contact list that was accessed only by agency code. John Staunton's new identity according to Mr Choate, was Glynn Harper. She had no doubt Mr Harper was very credentialed in the field of his new career, private investigator, Technical Operations.

"Mr Harper," Gem said politely, "have you any idea why Gem stopped over at Geneva on her way from Barcelona to Brisbane?"

"She didn't mention Geneva to me," he relied, puzzled. "Geneva was Choate's territory at that time. Engagement gift for her fiancé, perhaps?"

"My thought, but there wasn't a receipt found at the Agency warehouse," Gem sighed.

"Perhaps it is with her," he said gently.

"Perhaps," Gem concurred. She couldn't tell him about James or the fact she had searched his possessions hoping to discover something that might have been a gift.

"Add it to the list of 'unknowns'," Paul Andriani, a.k.a. John Staunton, a.k.a. Glynn Harper, suggested.

As Gem ended the call she realized that a Key had slipped just a touch. But which Key it was, she could not discern.

When she returned to the Hall she walked Molly, refusing to let her concentration of the dog waiver. She rarely saw the Ticking Bottom Security Force at the edge of the woods but she wanted to be certain if she did see anyone with a firearm, she would know exactly Miss Molly's location.

Mrs M did not make reference to the scorched dinner of the previous evening and was yet again studying cookery books.

"Are you looking for a specific recipe?" Gem asked the cook.

"I am trying to decide a menu for the Christmas holidays for your approval - and a list of treats," Mrs M sighed. "Have you any suggestions, dear?"

"Ham," Gem replied, "if Wyatt agrees to that." Unable to think of any additional suggestions, Gem went to her office.

She should have asked Paul Andriani if he knew any reason why Harry and Mrs Brown had not returned to the Agency. She debated texting him with Mrs M just around the corner in the kitchen. She wouldn't text him during the dark hours for he would be sleeping. It would be now, but up in her bathroom. She told Mrs M she was going to take a shower and before she did, she sent the text query to Glynn Harper. His reply came quickly.

'Have not been able to contact Harry for weeks. Mrs Brown due back within a fortnight is my understanding.'

'Thanks!'

Very odd. Had Harry been in contact with Mrs Brown?

She quickly sent another text to him.

'Have you been in contact with Mrs Brown?'

'No.'

'Why?'

'Hiding is safer with few people knowing your location.'

But Mrs Brown?

'Are you going to contact her when she returns?'

'Perhaps. Will play by ear.'

'Okay.'

'The fewer people who know, the safer I am.'

'Okay.'

'Please trust me, Gem.'

'I will.'

'Thanks. I trust you.'

That was the end of his text, and Gem was out of questions - for the time being. She deleted the messages, showered, and washed and braided her hair.

She had learned very little from Paul Andriani that she didn't already know. He had known Gemmy was engaged when the plane went missing, but he hadn't told her at the Agency meeting in mid-June. She grabbed her mobile.

'Why didn't you tell me in June that Gem was engaged?'

There was a long pause this time before he replied.

'You were dealing with raw emotion. Guess on my part then. Since then decided it was fact. Thought you could accept the fact today.'

'Okay.'

'Thought if you knew you would have said so at meeting. If you didn't know - what could you have done?'

'Okay.'

'It was a quandary.'

'I understand.'

'Thanks.'

She well understood his quandary of mid-June. It was a month after that strategy meeting that she had been approached by James at the Barcelona airport. If Paul had mentioned what he thought to Gem in mid-June she would have gone to Barcelona while she could still fly. She wouldn't have recognized the fiancé, but she could have tried somehow to contact him. Instead there had been the confusion at the airport in July and she had muddled things so horribly.

And if she had known in mid-June she would not be at the Hall today! She didn't blame Paul. She only blamed herself for not thinking clearly for months. Setting aside blame, she reminded herself that she had two additional Keys to retrieve.

Gem watched the international news, well aware that there wouldn't be anything to alert her to Harry and Mrs Brown.

The furred ones were in the great room continuing the staring contest; Miss Molly was sitting on the floor and Mrs Mac had taken a position on one of the coffee tables. Not a terribly safe distance between them, Gem mused, if one of them needed protection from the other.

Gem pretended to read the book of the Hong Kong occupation while she 'relaxed' on Auntie Jane's settee. She wasn't relaxing, but rather was pondering Paul Andriani's residing at Wyatt's flat. Another brilliant deception on her part of her pack of lies to Wyatt. She was likely four feet down with Paul Andriani. And as he had said - that was just for today.

Mr Choate and Paul Andriani had long been a couple. She wondered if Paul knew the information of Mr Choate's sealed file. If he didn't already know, he could read the file in seventy-five years with Gem. They could read together over a cup of tea, Gem chuckled to herself. Day by day her life became more and more bizarre.

She no longer had to wonder if Paul Andriani had been in love with Gemmy. She was curious of the cause of the fire that put Mr Choate out of his flat and in Ticking Bottom. She didn't believe he would start the fire to have an excuse for needing a flat for either himself or for Paul. Still, she checked the news story of the fire on the inter-net. Candles left burning by young romantic couple; young woman slightly injured. It was an honest and credible reason for Mr Choate and Paul to require temporary digs. Well done, Mr Choate!

My brain is so tired, Gem sighed. She had the information she had wished for for months, yet she was no closer to solving the problem of the Pilos - and Gemmy.

Geneva! Gemmy would not have stopped over in Geneva without a good reason to do so! What was the Blasted reason?

A day in Geneva.

Gemmy was pregnant. She was engaged to be married. She was flying home to finish her thesis, to complete that which she considered her last assignment for the Agency, and to have a holiday with her family.

A full plate.

A day in Geneva.

A day in Geneva to relax. To take everything in. To be by herself. To sit at a café with a cup of tea - or coffee - and sketch. To think about her lovely future.

That was the best reason Gem could think of for Gemmy to stop in Geneva. And it would do for now - unless another logical reason came to mind.

She had talked to Paul Andriani, but she had no new information.

One Key down.

And it solved? The location of Paul Andriani. That was it. Plain and simple.

All this sorting, the wondering. No help.

No. That wasn't true. Another Key had slipped!

She had forgotten another Key had slipped! What else was she forgetting? Hopefully not very much.

Gem leaned her head back against the cushion and looked at the ceiling - and noticed the shelves Mr M had hung. She hadn't noticed them earlier and Wyatt had told her Mr M had hung the shelves that morning. What else was she not seeing? Ah! Another electric fireplace!

The kitchen door opened and she heard Mr M's voice. She hurried to thank him for the shelves, and the electric fireplace, and he showed her a sample of the carpet; stone grey colour, deep pile - which would be installed the following day. Wyatt's power certainly could be effective!

And as she thought of him, Wyatt walked into the kitchen. He greeted all, Gem with a long hug and a quick kiss, then he immediately began discussing the carpet particulars with Mr M. Mrs M had dinner well in hand, so Gem went upstairs to gather her laundry to wash. In another month, hopefully not weeks, she would need another size of frillies. She needed to research twin pregnancies. Being a twin could in no way prepare her for the next few months and Blast - she couldn't get advice from mum or Auntie Jane. Since her office would be occupied tomorrow, she would spend time at Howard's Bookshop, reading whatever materials he had, and she would take her laptop with her to research the inter-net. More subterfuge. She couldn't wait for the day when her every action and word would be honest and not one lie compounding yet another lie.

She carried the laundry basket out of the dressing room and heard Wyatt's sharp order, "Put that down!"

"What?" Gem demanded, startled.

"You shouldn't be lifting anything heavy," he said firmly, taking the basket from her hands.

"Real world," Gem crisply informed him. "Women are not made of glass."

"Consider yourself to be so," he said sternly.

Gem put her hands on her hips and glared at him. "Do you honestly believe your father coddled your mum when she was pregnant?" she demanded.

"James was ten years younger than I. I know he did," Wyatt retorted.

"And your mum hated it," Gem surmised confidently.

"Indeed," Wyatt suddenly grinned. "But he didn't back down," he added, leaving the suite with the basket.

Gem followed him, her feathers still ruffled. He had just clearly defined the next battleground between them. How Fiona Grantham must have had her hands full with three Grantham men in the house! And two snakes - at least they were consecutive and not concurrent.

Wyatt did allow her to sort her laundry and proceed with its washing. And having filled the machine she sought peace and quiet in her office.

The moment she walked into the room she saw the delicate white vase with six perfect pink roses."

"What?" Gem said, puzzled.

"Pink roses," Wyatt said, behind her. "Gratitude and appreciation."

"For?" Gem turned to look at him.

"For inviting me to lunch," Wyatt gave her a small hug.

"You paid the bill," Gem protested.

"Naturally," he gave another nod. "But a lunch invitation from you is a rarity. A text from you is also rare."

Gem drew a blank. She couldn't even understand why she had texted him that day. Wait! She had a thought of another lunch. The day she had gone to his office not splattered in paint.

"A month ago," she said firmly, "when I was not covered in paint. I invited you to lunch."

"Ah," Wyatt grinned again, "but you had an agenda that day - appearing at my office looking stunning. Or - did you also have an agenda today?"

"No," she protested quickly.

Wyatt's grin slowly changed to the smashing smile that freed butterflies. "So! You thought of me today!" he teased softly.

Gem frowned slightly, looking beyond him to the open door.

"Mrs M has left for the day," he informed her. "An unscheduled meeting. You thought of me," he repeated.

Gem hesitated before replying, turning her back on him to seek protection from his smile. "I don't understand," she said wearily, dragging her fingers through her hair.

Wyatt frowned. "What don't you understand, sweetheart?"

Gem spun around. "This change in your Game. I know the others. I have to play by your rules. I had to accept that and I did. But why," she stared at him, "why do you think I would trust you again? That is this new change in your Game, isn't it? Do you consider me so dull-witted that I would be idiotic enough again to trust you?" she demanded painfully. "You won your Game! You won it the day you tricked me into marrying you! You have won over and over again! When is it going to be enough for you?"

The haunted look wasn't here, but the sheer pain in the violet eyes tore at Wyatt's heart. "Gem!" he said urgently.

"No! Leave me alone!" she cried and ran to the mudroom to grab her windcheater off its peg. Molly trotted after her and picked up her lead.

"No, Molly, stay with daddy," Gem said firmly and rushed out the kitchen door before Wyatt could stop her.

Wyatt grabbed his Mac, pulling it on. "No, Molly, stay with Mrs Mac," he ordered to the poochie waiting patiently at the door.

"Gem," he called after her, but she refused to stop, and he lengthened his stride to catch her. "Leave me alone!" she glared at him as he caught her arm to stop her.

"Walk with me," was all he said. And she did, refusing to look at him again. He slipped her arm through his. "Slow down, you'll wear yourself out at this pace."

Gem reluctantly complied. "Oh Blast! Dinner! It's probably burned again!"

"I turned down the temperature dial when Mrs M left," he said quietly.

"Always planning ahead," she said coldly.

"Force of habit," he conceded. "Gem, the roses were intended as a thank you - simple as that. It was a very pleasant surprise when you texted me this morning, and I wanted to surprise you in return - not upset you," he said sincerely, slipping his arm free to put it around her shoulders. "The wind is stiffening. Are you becoming chilled?"

"No," she shook her head, but she didn't mind his arm around her.

"Are you hungry?"

"No."

"Shall we repaint your office a darker colour?"

"No," Gem frowned, still refusing to look at him.

"Are the butterflies fluttering?"

"No."

"Do you trust me?"

"No."

"Are you still angry with me?"

"No."

"Are you actually listening to me?"

"Yes."

"Really?" He stopped walking, holding her to cup her chin with his fingers. The violet eyes staring back at him were cold.

"Yes."

"I do want you to trust me, Gem," he said sincerely.

"So you can pry into my life," she said bluntly.

"So that I can help you ease your stress, Gem," he said steadily.

Gem searched his eyes. "You are a very adept liar," Gem replied still bluntly, although his eyes said he was telling the truth. She was losing her ability to read people. "Fool me once - and you certainly did!"

"I don't believe I have ever lied to you, Gem," he said clearly.

Gem stepped back and out of his grasp.

"I manipulated you, but I didn't lie to you," he admitted easily.

"Oh, you are so brilliant at blurring the edges. You should publish your own dictionary. You'd make a fortune!" she said in astonishment.

"I already have a fortune. I don't need another," he put his hands in his pockets.

"What you need is a conscience," Gem said pointedly.

"Darling," he smiled his exquisite smile, "may we please argue at home? I don't want our child to be born with your cold feet."

"I don't want to argue -"

"Darling, may we please not argue at home, for the same reason I previously stated?" he coaxed, still smiling.

"Oh very well," Gem said wearily. "I still don't trust you," she added.

"I understand," Wyatt replied, and he was no longer smiling.

"I will never trust you again," Gem said bluntly.

Wyatt nodded slowly. "I understand." But you will, he thought to himself. He reached out to take her hand as they walked to the Hall.

"And you needn't give me any more gifts. You can't buy me. I won't ever love you again," she said bluntly.

"Ah Gem, you still do love me," he said smoothly.

She jerked her hand from his and ran to the kitchen door, slamming it shut behind her. He caught up with her in the mudroom, and as she shrugged off her windcheater he took it from her hands, hanging it on a peg and his Mac alongside it.

"No reply, my sweet?" he queried, raising his eyebrows.

Gem turned to face him. "You are frightfully egotistical, Mr Grantham. And very, very wrong," she said, her voice deadly calm. She walked into the kitchen checked on the dinner in the cooker and turned up the temperature.

Wyatt followed and leaned against the counter.

"I believe we need a chat, my dear," he said quietly.

Gem gave him a cold stare then wordlessly walked around the counter, out of the kitchen and down the hall. He caught up with her as she passed the great room, took her arm and gently turned her around to face him. "Cat got your tongue?" he queried teasing.

"I refuse to speak to you," she replied coldly.

"Did that cat give you distemper?" he queried patiently.

Gem continued to glare at him.

"Perhaps we'll chat another time," he relented and let go of her arm. "I'm going to shower. Would you please finish dinner prep?"

"I shall," Gem agreed, walking back to the kitchen.

"If you scorch dinner we'll walk to the pub," he advised her.

"Too, too amusing for words," Gem retorted without turning around.

Gem's annoyance with Wyatt simmered while she laid the table in the breakfast room and put Mrs M's dinner rolls in the cooker, setting the brisket on the island to rest.

"I'll carve," Wyatt said as he entered the kitchen. "I don't think in your mood that you should handle knives this evening."

"More of your clever wit!" Gem snapped.

Wyatt let her remark pass without further comment from him.

Dinner was extremely quiet and Gem only picked at the excellent food Mrs M had prepared. Not only was she annoyed with Wyatt for his damned Games, but also with him for insisting she was still in love with him. She couldn't bear his extraordinary ego. And the thought of her being in this relationship because Paul Andriani had kept silent in mid-June, was fraying her nerves to the thinnest of filaments. Wyatt Grantham, Paul Andriani, and hormones. She needed another Key to slip. And quickly!

"If you've finished eating, I'll clear and do the washing up," Wyatt said quietly.

"Thank you," Gem managed a cool reply and left the table without looking at him.

She had forgotten her laundry in the washer; she tended to that chore, then sought refuge in her office. She tried to concentrate on Durham Cathedral, but the more she edited the text the more she felt she would never finish the chapter. She turned on the telly, watching the international news for the faintest hot spot for a clue to Mrs Brown and Harry. Despite Agency staffers' assurance, she again felt terribly alone.

Mrs M was studiously planning her holiday recipes and Gem couldn't bear the thought of spending Christmas at Grantham Hall. She couldn't bear the thought of enduring cheery 'family' holiday celebrations when she didn't know where the HELL her family was!

She couldn't remember celebrating Christmas in England. Even Auntie Jane had joined the Lawson-Forrester holidays in Brisbane.

"It's time for bed, Gem," Wyatt said as he walked into her office.

"No, thank you," she replied curtly.

"That was not a suggestion," he frowned, growing weary of her mood.

"It's a matter of choice," Gem argued. "I'm not given the courtesy of choice."

"Harking back to tired arguments?" he scowled. "No more arguments tonight."

"More of your orders! Your terms! Always your Blasted terms!" Gem glared at him.

"You are tired -"

"Your Games! Always your Blasted Games! And your Blasted terms!"

"You don't like the terms? You should have been a better negotiator. To appease you, let's review your bargaining chips. Hmm. No. No. I don't recall that you had any bargaining chips. Do you recall having any? No? And, my dear, you still lack a single one," he said calmly. "Weeks past you promised no more pitched battles. I am attempting to be patient with you -"

"Being patient with me!" Gem folded her arms and leaned against the counter. "That's your latest Game! Being kind, being patient, being thoughtful! Good Lord! What can I say! - You certainly challenge my mind!" She threw up her hands in frustration.

"Thank you - yet another compliment from you." Wyatt gave her a slight bow. "Now, my dear, are you just stewing for a fight, or is there an actual point to this evening's verbal fencing match?" he said crisply.

"Oh, how very clever of you!" Gem folded her arms again, her eyes narrowing. "Two game references in one sentence! Clever, clever! For your future reference, Mr Oh-So-Wealthy-Powerful-Charming-Shockingly-Conceited-Wyatt-Grantham, a woman likes to be asked - not told - not ordered about like some pitiful lackey!" Gem said haughtily.

"You were 'asked', my sweet, twice, I believe, which is why you are obligated to follow the terms of the Games," he said crisply.

His words struck hard. Paul Andriani, mid-June. "Touché," she replied stunned by an unexpected direct hit. "Never one to lose the upper hand are you?" she gasped.

"No, my dear," Wyatt shook his head. "You should well know that by now," he said quietly. "When I am attacked, I strike back."

"I was wondering how Emerald ever let the magnificent Wyatt Grantham escape her. It's more likely she was chased off by your cold charm and caustic wit!"

Wyatt's brows rose in astonishment. "How the hell does Emerald come into to this debate?" he queried in confusion.

"The beautiful Emerald, tall, reed thin, gorgeous," Gem said bitterly. "How long did she fascinate you? Why didn't she marry you?" Gem demanded.

Hormones? He would have to ask Lyndon how long they were likely to rage.

"Emerald didn't marry me, because I did not ask her to marry me," he said patiently.

"I just bet she hinted at it!"

"Two or three times," he admitted. "Emerald doesn't like children. Can you imagine that?" he frowned, perplexed. "I can understand people not wishing to have children," he said pensively. "But can you imagine simply not liking children?"

Gem gazed at the puzzled expression on his face. "You like children?" she queried in surprise.

"Certainly I do, Gem. We did discuss having children," he reminded her - again.

"But that was part of your Game," she protested.

"I told you before, Gem, that if I hadn't wanted children I would have prevented having them. I've told you again tonight. I will repeat the words as often as you need to hear them" he said smoothly.

"Would you have married Emerald if she had wanted children?" Gem asked curiously.

"No," Wyatt said firmly. "And I do not wish to ever discuss her again. Put her out of your mind, for heaven's sake. She is never in mine."

"Then who is in your mind?" Gem demanded.

"Other women?" Wyatt frowned.

Gem nodded.

Wyatt wearily shook his head. "Mrs M, Ms Holton, Ms Wexton - GEI employs many women."

"That's not what I mean," Gem said crossly.

Wyatt grinned. "You want me to say only you. And so I shall. Only you, Gem. You are the only woman ever in my thoughts."

"I don't believe you," Gem protested.

"Come to bed, darling, and we'll chat," Wyatt smiled at her, and Gem watched as the smile reached his eyes.

"We never chat in bed," she protested, butterflies flying.

"I promise we shall," Wyatt coaxed her with a velvet voice.

Gem frowned, hesitating, then stared at the floor. Wyatt gazed at her. When she raised her eyes to meet his gaze she looked defeated. The look of pain the other night. Now the look of defeat. She was a fighter, but the will to fight was gone. She no longer had the strength or the will to fight him. There would be no more battles. She looked like a wounded doe. The hair on the back of his neck prickled.

He had Won.

And he would take his time deciding the future for the three of them. Every decision would be his.

"Gem," he said gently. "Will you please come to bed. You are exhausted. Please," he repeated.

The dynamics had changed somehow, Gem realized, but she didn't know in what way. His eyes were so different.

"I'll confess, my dear," he smiled gently, "there is a thermos of hot chocolate in the bedroom. Would you please join me in an evening of hot chocolate, bacchanalia, and debauchery?" he gently teased. He held out his hand to her.

A smile crept to her lips. "Hmm," she nodded. "Now was that so difficult, Wyatt? A simple request, eloquently phrased." She placed her hand in his. "Good manners are so important, you know."

"Sage words of advice," Wyatt laughed at her clever words.

Lord she was so tired! And not because of the trapped butterflies. She was mentally burned out. If only Paul Andriani had spoken to her in mid-June the past months would have been so different. Hellish beyond belief, but still not as horrid as they had been! She would have looked for Gemmy's fiancé. She would likely be able to fly - to have more flexibility in her search, instead of furtive searches, instead of hiding from prying eyes, instead of having to lie to people - the M's, Wyatt - instead of being forced into this sham marriage!

Wyatt watched the violet eyes cloud. Hormones, yes. But hormones weren't entirely to blame for her outbursts this evening. His gift of roses weren't to blame, but they were perhaps a catalyst - or one of them. Terms. Games. Trust. Love. Emerald -for God's sake! Children.

Gem was jealous of Emerald, which was ridiculous. He had never had any emotional ties to Emerald. Why would Gem be jealous of the other woman unless she was still in love with him? He wasn't conceited as she believed him to be. However, as comfortable as he was with his attributes, he had only ever used them as a weapon against Gem. He had purposely charmed her as she had charmed James. He had manipulated her into falling in love with him. Part of his Game. He had smashed her heart without feeling any remorse, or guilt for having done so. And she had hated him for all his actions. He had intended to break her spirit, to destroy her will to fight. He had intended to crush her, and then to make her realize that she still loved him. And to get her to trust him again. He would learn everything he wanted to know about her and then he would use it against her. And then he would have given the photos and the passports to the tabloids.

She no longer had the spirit to fight him.

She was still in love with him.

He had to get her to trust him again.

And then he would learn everything he wanted to know about her. He had never before quit before reaching a goal. He would not do so now.

But now there was the child.

The passports and photos would remain secured. They would always be a handy weapon in the future.

Win the final Game. Trust. And then proceed on to deciding their futures. He could tolerate continuing the marriage. At least for a time. And considering her past association with Staunton, he could never trust her with their child without constant supervision. And although Staunton was apparently no longer of this world, Wyatt had not been able to discover any other past associates Gem had had. And if he decided not to continue the marriage, he would not have any difficulty obtaining full custody of the child. If. If...

The end of the Game. The final Game.

"Gem, darling," he coaxed her return from her secret world. "We need to have a chat," he said smoothly.

Gem frowned at the sound of his voice. "What?" She tried to shake off her thoughts, and as she met his eyes she saw again the look that had been in his gaze earlier - in the office.

"Darling," he repeated again, "we need to chat."

"No," she shook her head in confusion. "I've had enough chats for today," she said wearily, pushing back the duvet. "Would you please move your leg? I want to get out of bed."

He did not move his leg; he propped himself up on his left elbow to learn over her. He gazed into her eyes as his right hand reached up to gently stroke her hair.

"First we chat," he insisted, his voice as smooth as silk.

"What?" she sighed, completely unable to marshal any further defences against him.

"The Game is Over, my sweet."

"What?" Gem frowned warily. "What does that mean? You'll give me the photos and the passports? A divorce?"

"No," Wyatt shook his head. "That will never happen."

"Then what do you mean?" she demanded wearily.

"From now on you needn't search my words or actions for false meanings. I will make no attempts to manipulate you or to pry into your private world."

"And Mr Choate?" Gem queried, going into information gathering mode. "Will he disappear?" She hoped she wouldn't lose that easy means of contact with the Agency.

"No. Choate is necessary for your protection," Wyatt said easily. "However I will no longer require daily reports of your activities. Technical Operations will keep a file of your activities solely in the event of a protection crisis."

"Okay," Gem nodded. That would give her a bit more flexibility - if she needed it. And Mr Choate would not have to fudge reports for her benefit. "Will you remove the GPS tracking from my mobile and the Defender?" she queried.

"No. That again is for your protection, my dear."

Gem frowned. Not pleased by his refusal of that issue.

"In the future if I give you gifts, you should simply accept them as such - and not regard them as a ploy in a Game. A gift will be a gift, not a secret agenda."

"I don't want gifts from you," Gem insisted.

"Be that as it may, please accept the gift," Wyatt also insisted firmly. "Husbands do, from time to time, bestow gifts upon their wives."

"Out of guilt?" Gem suggested.

"If that is a veiled reference to other women, we have had that discussion in the past," Wyatt replied, his voice still firm. "And not intending to sound crass or intentionally cruel, if in the unlikely event I do become involved with another woman, I shall make a promise to you at this time, that I shall inform you of the other woman, and my relationship with you will be dissolved."

"You could decide not to tell me and I wouldn't know," Gem scoffed. "You have already made that quite clear."

"You would know, Gem," Wyatt kept his gaze steady. "I know what I said previously, and now I have made a promise to you."

Gem shrugged, lowering her eyes to the duvet as she plucked at the fabric with her fingers. "I don't believe your promise," she countered quietly.

Wyatt made a brief nod. "I understand your refusal, but I believe you will come to change your mind."

Gem absorbed his remarks. "Well," she sighed wearily, "I have gained a bit from the end of your Game."

"I am not finished, my dear," he said, hesitating a moment. "I promise I will no longer search your possessions on a regular basis," he said bluntly.

Gem's head snapped back and she gasped in astonishment. "What?" she demanded, suddenly incensed. "You search my things? How dare you!" She tried to scramble from the bed, but Wyatt grabbed her and held her back, his hold gentle, but as unrelenting as his voice. "I dare a great deal, Gem. Don't ever underestimate me."

"You're threatening me!"

"I'm warning you."

Gem lay still, watching his eyes; they were light grey. He wasn't angry. Yet.

"Damn you! How could you search my things?" This knowledge stung her as deeply as any of his words ever had.

"Calm down, sweetheart," he kept his hold on her, despite her attempt to pull away. "Why would I not search your possessions?" he demanded. "When James died I did not request an autopsy, but the blood work at the hospital didn't show any drugs in his system, other than the alcohol he had ingested that night. But he had been involved with you and you were involved with a known drug lord." Gem held her breath as he referred to John Staunton a.k.a. Paul Andriani. "And James was a recovering addict. He had told you that on your second date." And that was new information for Gem. Nothing to influence her search, but something that Wyatt might try to hold over her as 'Gem' in the future.

"Your behaviour suggests drug use. You go off mentally into your private world, you frequently self-edit, worrying if you have said a remark you dare not say. There is your insomnia. Your constant pacing at night. Perhaps you are unaware of fleeting, desperate looks in your eyes from time to time." She WAS unaware of that fact. "You are quite easily distracted. You were exhausted, even when I first met you. Being pregnant has exacerbated that exhaustion. You are an extremely secretive woman. You refuse to speak of your past. You lie constantly. You constantly read your surroundings wherever you are. It is Choate's job to do so as a private investigator to protect you. Your habit is one of searching to hide your identity, to hide an addiction, to look for a source for your habit."

"I am not a drug addict!" Gem seethed.

"As I said once or twice I know every millimetre of your body," Wyatt nodded.

"You look for needle marks!" Gem gasped. How could he speak so damned deliberately, so calmly of his actions!

"Indeed. Needle marks and pills, whatever I might find," he said firmly.

Gem laughed harshly. "I do have the locked cabinet in my office. You can't break the combination!" she said triumphantly.

"I would have had the cabinet opened, but you rarely opened it. I checked it often for dust. You never clean the keypad," he said with a touch of a bemused smile. "First week of November there were fingerprints on the keypad. I concluded you kept your vitamins from Hallowell in the cabinet until you informed me that you were pregnant."

"My heavens, aren't you just brilliant!" Gem said sarcastically. She couldn't dispute any of his words.

"I had to be clever, my dear," Wyatt said sternly. "I am extremely adept at searching for drugs. I had to learn that ability because James was a master at hiding them. I vowed that I would not lose him too. To anything. But I did lose him. Not to drugs. And I don't think I would have to alcohol - except -" he didn't finish the remark.

Gem covered her face with her hands. "You had no right!" she retorted. "No right at all!"

"I disagree, Gem," he said firmly. "By marrying you, I was bringing you into my life, my world. GEI. Ticking Bottom. I have many people to protect. I wasn't about to then, nor shall I ever, allow you to place other people in harm's way."

Gem shook her head in disbelief, then lowered her hands to her lap. "Foolish error," she said pointedly. "Ms Jones and Ms Carton allowed me access to your office."

Wyatt smiled briefly. "You passed through metal detectors, my dear, and you were monitored by security from the front door of the Grantham Building to Research and Development," he said dryly. "I knew you were in the building, sweetheart. Your mobile wasn't charged, but the GPS was still sending a signal. I monitor my phone frequently when you are out of my sight."

His remark caught one of the Keys in her brain. "Wyatt," she asked curiously, her anger suddenly fading, the rest of the chat pushed aside. "Wyatt - if a mobile isn't charged - how could the GPS continue to work?"

Wyatt drew back, releasing her, puzzled by her query and sudden change in temper. "What?"

Gem dragged her fingers through her hair. "If," she paused, gathering her thoughts, "if a mobile hasn't been charged - the battery isn't working. Correct?" her eyes entreated him for a reply.

"Yes," he nodded, propping himself up against the pillows.

"If the battery isn't working, the mobile doesn't work," she puzzled, then sought his eyes with her own. "How could the GPS still be sending a signal? I don't understand."

Wyatt felt chills creep up his spine. What the hell was she searching for? he frowned. She completely disregarded a subject that had caused her to become incensed, and was now consumed by a query of mobile phones and GPS signals!

"I added the chip to your phone," he admitted quietly. "Your mobile likely came with GPS. I didn't use that system. I placed a chip on your phone the night of the art show, and keyed in the activation code. It connected immediately and started tracking your phone. The chip is so tiny you wouldn't see it if you weren't specifically looking for it."

Gem nodded, considering his words. "How long does such a chip work? Six months? A year?" she asked, searching his eyes.

"The chip in your phone is guaranteed to last two years," he replied, watching her expression, trying to glean the faintest reason for her urgent query.

"Okay," Gem nodded, "okay."

"Does that help?" he asked softly.

"I don't know," Gem raked her fingers through her hair. "I don't know."

He watched her quietly as she mentally processed the information; her lips were pursed as if she was gently blowing air from her lungs. The lovely violet eyes were fleetingly marred by devastating pain before they clouded with the haunted look. He remained silent, willing his body not to move, as he watched her disappear into her secret world. How long would she be unaware of anything but the thoughts into which she had been drawn.

Gem jerked back quickly as Mrs Mac sailed over her, landed on Wyatt's chest, lost her balance and slid down his body, all claws grabbing for traction as they raked bare flesh.

"Damn! Mac!" Wyatt erupted in pain, frightening the feline.

"Heavens!" Gem winced with phantom pain as he attempted to pull the cat from his body. "No! No!" she advised Wyatt softly, then cooed to the startled cat. "Easy, Mrs Mac, easy, baby, relax," she spoke gently, cooing, coaxing the cat to calm. She frowned, squinting her eyes, catching her lip between her teeth as she quickly searched her brain for the pages she had read about cats, cat claws and frightened cats. "Retract sweetie," she slipped her hand under Mrs Mac's tummy, speaking in a comforting tone, gently pressing each paw to encourage the feline to retract her claws as she disengaged the furry body from Wyatt's chest.

"Aah," Gem sighed heavily, as she gathered Mrs Mac against her breasts, and gently leaned across the bed to set the cat on the floor. "Run along then, sweetie, daddy's in a snit," she gently tapped the cat on the bottom and Mrs Mac shot across the room.

"A snit!" Wyatt growled, and Gem turned her attention to him.

"Ouch," she winced. "I'll get the antiseptic and cotton wool," she murmured, dashing to her bathroom, grabbing also, an ointment and bin liner, as an afterthought.

"This won't hurt," she said calmly, soaking the cotton wool with the cool liquid.

"I know," Wyatt growled again, as she carefully cleansed the wounds, starting at the top of the red scratch line and deftly working down the first stretch of wounds.

"How is your immune system?" she asked, glancing up at his face as she dabbed at the marks.

"Excellent," Wyatt ground out between clenched teeth. "Yours?"

"A bit compromised, I would imagine," Gem replied methodically. "The puncture wounds might be painful, but I don't think they are deep enough to be a health concern."

Wyatt watched her pause in her tender ministrations, concentrate, her eyes narrowing as she apparently searched her thoughts.

"Painful, but not deep," Gem resumed gently dabbing the wounds, tossing cotton wool into the bin liner and taking a fresh one from the pack. "If you begin feeling a bit off you should consult Dr Lyndon in the event you contracted cat scratch fever," she advised calmly. "I rather think Mrs Mac has had the required immunizations, she's healthy, so you probably needn't worry. But if you notice any swelling of lymph nodes you should definitely talk to the doctor."

"What were you doing?" Wyatt asked curiously. "The look on your face when you were thinking just then?"

Gem frowned at him, then realized he was referring to her mentally reading the pages she had read from the books on cats. "Trying to remember what I had read on the computer - and a couple of books about cats," she concentrated on the wounds, refusing to meet his eyes. She had been sorting through her lengthy memory recalling with nearly one hundred percent accuracy.

"Is that what you call it?" Wyatt said with veiled interest.

Gem stayed calm, not wanting a cog to slip. "Don't you remember some of what you read?" she turned the defensive over to him.

"Generally a great deal of it," Wyatt nodded. "And you?"

"I have a fairly adequate memory," Gem replied smoothly, tossing cotton wool one after another into the bin liner. "One side is finished," she advised him, glancing up at his face. There needed to be a change of subject. "Have you finished your chat?"

Wyatt studied her carefully. 'Our' chat, but she had again refused to use a plural pronoun. And why? It was always singular with Gem. Why was it so difficult for her to think one plus? 'Your' chat. 'Your' home. Singular was so disconnected. So alone.

"Did you have further questions about mobile phones and GPS chips?" he queried, suddenly wincing.

"Sorry," Gem apologized. "I think the surrounding tissue is receiving alerts of tissue damage: 'Be Prepared to Ache Also'," she said with a sympathetic grimace. "What?" she had forgotten his query.

"Questions? Mobiles? GPS chips?" Wyatt repeated, watching her intense focus on his wounds. She was being so gentle. She had immediately come to his assistance tonight as she had the other time Mrs Mac had clawed him. Was this sensitive manner an act? Yet another part of her he hadn't previously noticed?

Gem paused, pondering his query. "I don't think so," she shook her head, and began swabbing the second long red line of scratches.

"Then," Wyatt said crisply, "we will continue on with the original chat."

Gem sighed. His pointed remarks of the end of the Game - which she knew had not really ended. He was still in complete control. Master of all the rules. Always his terms. "GEI, metal detectors, Ticking Bottom, people to protect," she quickly summarized the last facts of Wyatt's Game List - another fantasy of his Game Over announcement.

"Ticking Bottom," Wyatt repeated.

She hadn't known about the security devices at GEI, but she wasn't really surprised. Why he had mentioned the GEI security to Gem she could not imagine.

"I'm listening," she glanced up at him, then back down to his wounds.

"Ticking Bottom," Wyatt frowned, stepping over his own guard line in pursuit of the actual end of the Game, "is not precisely a village."

Gem paused. No slipped cogs. "Oh yes?" she looked up warily, then continued attending the scratches.

"It's a gated community," he said finally.

"What?" she asked, surprised he had actually shared truth with her. She was growing very suspicious of his sudden bout of veracity.

"Ticking Bottom has been a gated community for nearly ten years," Wyatt replied. "Locals couldn't afford to keep up with maintenance on their homes and shops. I purchased one then another, and finally all the structures in the village. Most of the residents are retired and appreciate not having the responsibility of owning their homes."

"And the shops?" she frowned, listening but steadily working to cleanse the last of the punctures and scratches.

"I own the buildings, the merchants own the product."

Gem tossed the last blood stained cotton wool into the bin liner. She looked up and stared at him. "Why did you tell me this? About GEI and T.B.?" she quietly asked.

"Game Over, darling, as I said," Wyatt held her eyes with his steady gaze. "If our marriage had begun under different circumstances, I would have told you about T.B. months ago."

Gem sat silently. He could tell her anything he wished, but she wasn't going to ask further questions until she figured out this part of his Game. Game Over - HA!

She gently spread the ointment over the scratches. "Best use a cream instead of an ointment in the morning so your lovely shirts aren't ruined," Gem advised.

Wyatt took her hands in his and kissed the tips of her fingers. "Thank you, darling. You are a most excellent nurse. Have you any questions regarding our chat?"

"No," Gem shook her head.

"Really?" Wyatt replied.

"Really," she nodded. "Your Game isn't over. You can't entice me to love you again. And you can't convince me to trust you again. No matter how hard you try. Now, if your evening of debauchery and bacchanalia is over, I am going to have a cup of the lovely hot chocolate you prepared. Shall I pour a cup for you?"

"My God, Gem! You are brilliant!" he marvelled with a slight smile. He gently squeezed her hands. "Hot chocolate, please."

As they sipped the beverage, Gem sat cross legged in the centre of the bed, facing him. "You look as though you were shredded by a lion," she winced, looking at his taut chest.

"Indeed. Where is the little beastie?" Wyatt said dryly.

"Coffee table, sitting room, alongside the thermos," Gem suppressed a smile. "She's winged you twice now. You must be more cautious of felines with claws."

Wyatt studied her, his eyes narrowing, and an uneasy thought struck him. "You don't have claws, do you, Gem?" he said quietly.

"Everyone has claws if they are needed," she looked down at her cup. "If I need claws, I could use them," she admitted.

No, you couldn't, my dear. What game are you playing? What game have you been playing?

Gem raised her eyes to him. "You made a number of promises to me tonight. I do not trust you to keep them. And although you do not trust me, I promise you that I have never been involved with drugs," she said softly. Nor have I ever been involved with anything illegal in my life, she did not say aloud.

Wyatt nodded. "I believe you," he forced himself to say.

"No, you don't," Gem replied with a half-smile. "Quite a tainted relationship. You don't trust me and I don't trust you. You don't love me and I don't love you. Not a healthy environment in which to raise a child." Children!

"We'll work on that," Wyatt quietly assured her. "A healthy environment is critical," he nodded. He would make sure the atmosphere at the Hall was stable. With or without her. Without her? he frowned.

The thermos was by her computer. Practiced thoughtfulness. Gem's mind fairly reeled with the events of the day. She WAS angry with Paul Andriani for not telling her in June about Gemmy's engagement. It was absurd and fruitless to be angry. Paul would never have done anything to hurt her any more than he would have hurt Gemmy.

And it had been Gem who had made the error to marry Wyatt. It was her decision to agree to his terms of blackmail - her word, if not Wyatt's. She had made the decision to protect James and Gemmy. An incredibly senseless decision influenced by grief and extremely fuzzy thinking.

No she did not blame Paul Andriani.

And she was grateful now to have yet another Agency contact to text or call with queries. Text. Mr Cawley would be awake. It was odd to think that only she and Mr Choate knew the precise location of the master undercover agent!

'News?'

'A quiet day. A quiet night.'

'Mrs Brown? Harry?'

'No word.'

'Blank?'
'No word.'
'Staff safe?'
'As of midnight. What news have you, Gem?'
'Dry.'

That was a lie. Who hadn't she lied to in the past few months? It was quite the habit for her now. And she had to ask about Blank, or Mr Cawley would be suspicious of her not asking of Paul Andriani.

'Ramp it up, Gem! Time is passing quickly!'
'As if I didn't know that! Any news SCS search?'
'No reports twenty-four hours.'
'Mrs Brown due back - weekend?'
'Possibly. Get to work, Gem! Give me some support here!'
'Will try!'
'Try harder!'
'Yes, Sir! - sarcasm intended!'
'Sarcasm noted. Goodnight!'
'Goodnight!'

He was still crotchety. He needed relief - Mrs Brown, or Harry.

Gem felt a sudden chill course through her body despite the electric fire places and the plush new robe and slippers.

Harry wasn't coming back. She didn't know how she knew - but she did. Harry would never return to the Agency. Perhaps he had had to go the route of disappearing as had Paul Andriani. She would never see Harry again.

It was all too much to think about, to sort. And if it wasn't difficult enough sorting, searching for the Pilos, she now had Wyatt's Games again coursing through her mind.

Game Over. HA! Perhaps she shouldn't have told him she recognized his newest Game. Trust him? Never!

The roses caught her eye. Gifts. Promises. "HA!" she said aloud, startling Mrs Mac who was sleeping on the counter alongside the flowers. Miss Molly had decided to remain in the bedroom. When Gem left the room she saw the poochie sleeping on the edge of the bed, smack up against Wyatt's back. Hopefully he didn't roll over or Molly would be pushed to the floor.

She winced, thinking of the scratches Mrs Mac had bestowed upon Wyatt, and she was grateful that he had not exhibited any ill will to the cat when the feline eventually settled across Gem's knees to sleep.

Gem was very weary of fighting Wyatt. Why he had spoken so freely hours ago, Gem could not say. He had spoken, not fondly, of Emerald. Why had he told her of the security at GEI and of Ticking Bottom? She was appalled that he had actually searched her possessions.

And why was there the change in his eyes? Revelation? That's what it was! Of what? But she could not be bothered with that now. The information about the GPS chip in her mobile was very interesting knowledge to store in her memory. She pulled the phone from her pocket and searched for the chip. She couldn't see it. How tiny was it? She slipped the phone back into her pocket. It didn't matter whether or not the chip was contacting Wyatt. When she left Wyatt and

Grantham Hall, she would request a new mobile from the Agency. And when she left Wyatt and the Hall, she would again 'retire' from the Agency - as much as one ever truly was 'retired' from the Agency. - However - when Wyatt would have the children - hmmm. Assignments?

A healthy environment for a child. Not their marriage. That was painfully tainted. She would, however, trust Wyatt with the children. He had no love for her, but she knew he would love the twins and he would be a good father to them. He had, after all, been a great brother to James.

Gem started pacing. Her mind was too full to sort; too much coming too quickly, colliding and mushing together.

Paul Andriani got made. And he had no idea who had made him. Wouldn't that be just too terrifying for words! Not knowing whom he could trust. Network? Agency? Counter Agencies? Former contacts? New contacts?

Gem had made him. That Key, once as unrecognisable as the others, could now be labelled Paul Andriani. And what were the labels of the other Keys?

What the devil had prompted her to text Wyatt to ask him to lunch? Chalk it up to Blasted hormones. It was going to be a mad ride in the future unless the hormones settled down a touch.

A Key slipped.

But still it was so thoroughly hidden by other information she could not mentally sort her way to it.

Her head began to ache. She pushed start on the cd player again and filled the cup with hot chocolate.

Wyatt wanted her to trust him. How could he be so daft to think that would happen again in his lifetime? It would not!

And love him! Again daft! Never again!

She paced. Wondering why Harry would never return to the Agency. She could not put that feeling to anyone else. No one would believe her. It sounded a ridiculous notion. Yet, still it was there. She had no doubt he was still alive, for if he wasn't, Agency staff would likely be informed. Unless he was missing - and not of his own free will. That - that was the terrifying part of a theory. Hopefully theory was not fact.

Love Wyatt Grantham! How egotistical the man was! But it was soothing - perhaps relief - would be a better word choice - to know that he wasn't still charmed by Emerald. That woman grated on her already frayed nerves.

Gem sank into Auntie Jane's comfy chair. It had been a Blasted long day. And she was done. She couldn't fight Wyatt any longer. Just thinking of having another battle with him made her head ache more.

She rinsed the thermos and cup, shut down the office machines and climbed the stairs.

Wyatt glanced at his watch as she slipped into bed. Half three.

"Are you cold, sweetheart?" he asked softly.

"My head aches," she moaned.

"Molly move please," he gently ordered the dog to shift.

In a minute he was gently ordering her to drink the glass of warm water he held for her. Then he placed a warm cloth across her brow.

"Thank you," Gem whispered.

"My pleasure, sweetheart. A fair trade for tended scratches," Wyatt said softly.

There was another cloth and another glass of warm water, and Gem waited for the dark hours to end, steadfastly refusing to allow any thoughts to enter her mind.

Chapter Thirty

"You are going to the city today?" Wyatt queried at breakfast.

Gem nodded.

"Will you have time to have lunch with me?" he inquired politely. "Chinese perhaps?"

"Chinese, lovely!" Gem agreed. "Not Jake's?"

"I doubt I will be able to eat there again," he frowned. "As long as that same waitress is employed there."

"GEI could hire her," Gem teased. "She could still make passes at you."

"God forbid!" Wyatt choked on his eggs.

Gem laughed at the appalled look on his face. "Chinese," she said with a grin.

"The GEI holiday party is scheduled for the twentieth," Wyatt informed her. "I alerted Ora yesterday afternoon that you will require a casual outfit - hopefully something that shows your lovely legs -"

"You didn't say that!" Gem gasped.

"Not put quite that way," he teased. "I also suggested a sapphire colour - if that appeals to you. Ora will consult with you on the design and the colour. You will have a fitting on the sixteenth to allow her time for alterations. She will change that date to suit you."

Gem stared at her food, absorbing his remarks. She had mentioned at lunch the previous day that she hated shopping, and he had assumed the responsibility for her wardrobe. It was a blessed relief. "I will leave the details to Ora," she nodded.

"She will ring you with time and date reminders," he added. "Also," he stated carefully, "with your approval I will have the bedroom next to the master suite cleared of furniture and items, so that alterations can begin for a nursery. I suggest a medium sage green colour as an alternative to the traditional blue for boys, pink for girls."

"At one time those colours were reversed," Gem stated, thoughts from mental sorting surging to the fore. "If I recall correctly."

Wyatt considered her words. "I am certain you do, Gem," he said thoughtfully. "Mr M will select paint colour samples for your approval, or if you wish I'll decide the colour."

Gem thought for a moment. "I would like to see the colours," she decided, then realized that it was her goal to leave the Hall before a nursery was used. She shook her head. "No, you decide," she said quietly. And then there was a new hurt. Gem could not bring a reason to mind for the new emotion. "You decide," she frowned.

Why the abrupt change of thought? Wyatt puzzled. In his experience in a non-business decision one should go with the first impulsive reaction. He would have Gem look at the paint colours. "If you have a diagram of the arrangement of art for your office, Mr M will hang the items after the carpet is installed."

"I do have a diagram," Gem replied enthusiastically. "That would be lovely!"

"Have you definite plans for this morning?" he asked casually.

"I do," Gem nodded. "Why?" she became suspicious.

"Just curious," Wyatt shrugged. "Your morning will no doubt be much more interesting than mine. - Meetings."

"A bookshop," Gem said hesitantly. "I thought I would do some research on babies," she said, exhaling softly. It wasn't a lie - and plural fit nicely.

"Research?" Wyatt puzzled.

Gem shrugged. "I know very little about infants. My memory doesn't stretch that far," she admitted hesitantly.

Wyatt suppressed a smile. She had no younger siblings, if her words were honest, and by her rueful smile he believed they were. He had been ten when James was born, so he was not completely inexperienced with infants. "Valuable information, indeed," he agreed. "Changing nappies is one matter," he chuckled," what they hold is another matter still."

"Unseemly breakfast thoughts," Gem burst out laughing. "An image I hope does not remain with me through lunch!"

Wyatt saw her place her laptop on the passenger seat of the Defender, but he made no reference to it. He had to trust her, he thought, then stopped short. When had that possibility entered his mind? He did NOT trust her. And now - he HAD to trust her?

Wyatt stepped back abruptly from the vehicle.

"What?" Gem smiled curiously at his sudden move.

"What?" he replied, gazing at her, perplexed by the unconscious prompting that he had to trust her.

And as he looked at her his mind saw a different woman. Gem gazed up at him, relaxed. The violet eyes sparkled. Her skin glowed. Her lips, barely parted, were sweet and inviting.

What the hell?

Gem was - what was the saying? - Bonny and blithe, and good and gay...As his grandfather had so often described Wyatt's grandmother. Wyatt had never completely understood the vision his grandfather had described - until this very moment: Gem WAS in love! And it had better be with him!

"What?" Gem laughed.

The sound of her voice was - oh so - tritely - like music - he grudgingly admitted.

"You look - lovely," was his gentle reply.

"You are very easy to please," Gem protested, artlessly shaking her head.

"On the contrary," Wyatt firmly shook his head. "Grantham men, as you should know by now, are extremely difficult to please!" He gently kissed her lips. "Lunch. Chinese."

"Yes," Gem said breathlessly, truth creeping into her mind. She refused to address it!

She did finally address the issue, however, as she sat on the sofa at the bookshop, and waited for her laptop to connect to the server.

Wyatt had won nearly all of his Games. She did not trust him. But she was a fool. Twice. She WAS in love with him. Again. Without reason. Without logic.

It was superficial, she could only conclude. How could one look at Wyatt and NOT be absolutely staggered! His smile, his eyes. His smashing body! She was as 'star struck' as a teen in love with the latest, hottest rock star.

But no. It was more than that. She was, to her fervent dismay, completely and unequivocally in love with him. He was hateful, domineering, egotistical, an ogre, and breathtaking, charming. And she was not pleased to have to face the fact! She did NOT want to be in love with him. The first time had ruined her life! She REFUSED to waste any more time on love! Or on Wyatt Grantham! Particularly on Wyatt Grantham!

She focused her thoughts on twins, and read little that she already knew. She had come to realize she would need a nanny to assist her when she left the Hall.

She refused to think of Wyatt and the feelings she had for him. And if he realized her feelings he would use them against her, trying to manipulate her to trust him. It was a quest for him, she decided. Simply a goal. An amusing pastime to divert his thoughts when he was bored at the office, or weary from reading reports at the Hall.

Blast! She put him from her mind, and he insisted on breaching her defences!

Mr Choate sat down on the sofa, draining his third cup of coffee, Gem judged by the way he tapped his fingers on the cup. He usually did not tap his fingers.

"Work satisfactory?" she murmured, quickly scanning the aura surrounding the sofa.

"Indeed," he nodded. "My work load has been halved."

"Excellent," Gem glanced up from the computer screen. "What troubles have you, my friend?" she queried, then wondered at her own question.

"I do not know," he scowled. "Can't put my finger on it."

"That's because you're tapping it," she said with failed humour. "It's about Harry, isn't it?" she asked, barely above a whisper.

"Is it?" he puzzled. "I don't know," he shook his head, glancing out the window behind them, then scanning the bookshop and customers.

"He's not returning to the Agency," Gem said, her teeth tugging at her bottom lip.

Choate broke his concentration to stare at her. "How do you know that?" he frowned again. "What have you heard?" He was obviously confused by her statement.

"I haven't heard anything," Gem protested. "I don't know," she sighed. "It's just a feeling." She followed his habit of scanning.

"How long have you felt this way?" he asked thoughtfully. He had learned not to disregard Gem's 'feelings'.

"Just a few hours," Gem conceded. "It's just - there," she said, her voice void of emotion.

"I see," Choate nodded shortly, absorbing her remarks.

"Please don't tell anyone what I said," Gem asked plaintively.

"Not a word," Choate shook his head. "Please let me know whatever else you sense, Gem."

"I shall," she nodded.

A few minutes later, Gem's mobile alerted her of a text. Likely Wyatt, for it was not the Agency ping.

'Carpet installed. Art on walls.'

'Lovely! I shall deliver bottles of wine in appreciation.'

'Add a bottle or two of beer for me, please.'

'So noted. Good morning?'

'Long, exceedingly dull meeting. Please rescue me!'

Gem chuckled.

'Did you tell Ms Holton of your scratches?'

'A bit personal to relate to staff. We were between the sheets!'

'True.'

Gem grinned at his remark.

'Studying infants?'

'Yes. You?'

'Listening to presentation of winery. Looks exceedingly profitable. Fighting to stay awake.'

Gem glanced at her watch. Half ten.

'Early lunch? One hour?'

'Please!'

'Later then.'

'Later indeed, Gem!'

Gem smiled to herself. She didn't have to love him - or trust him - to enjoy texting him.

Gem allowed Miss Molly to run for twenty minutes, as she waited patiently at the old stone bridge below the Hall.

Molly bolted, stopped dead in her tracks to sniff the breeze, then darted off again, stopping abruptly to search the landscape for her human unit's location, and thus assured, bolted off again. She was a happy dog, Gem laughed to herself.

She took a deep breath, and reflected that she had become one of Molly's anchors. Well, furred ones needed anchors as much as did humans. And Gem had the Agency to ground her. She held her thoughts of all but Miss Molly until they returned to the Hall.

The carpet on the office floor was luscious beneath her feet, and would keep her warm during the dark hours. Amazing. Wyatt decided the office required carpet - and the work was done. Shelves would be advantageous - and shelves were installed. Mrs M suggested to Wyatt that Gem needed a friend - and Mrs Mac arrived. Then Miss Molly. Mrs M informed Wyatt that Gem needed a variety of cds, and Gem soon had a stack of the discs. Hmmm. And now her art items had been properly hung. Gem settled into Auntie Jane's comfy chair with a cup of tea. Despite Wyatt's cold pronouncements at Marigold Cottage - no gifts, no attention - he had provided much for her nonetheless.

Why?

A whim, no doubt. And, of course, if Mrs M suggested something Wyatt had to act upon her words, or suffer 'certain looks' that associates of long time standing used against one another. He couldn't disregard Mrs M's suggestions or she would expect a reason for his doing so. And he couldn't admit to Mrs M that he loathed his wife.

And if Gem had to admit so, Wyatt hadn't been the tyrant she had expected him to be from his tirade at Marigold Cottage. She had had two professors at university who made Wyatt Grantham appear to be an entirely reasonable and gentle person. Which he definitely was NOT in any definition of those words. But then he had written his own dictionary - hadn't he! According to Wyatt Grantham's dictionary he would probably be defined as Saint Wyatt Grantham. Blast! She had to get him from her thoughts. Butterflies were threatening to stampede!

Gem turned on the telly, hoping against hope to see a hot spot steaming in ANY region of the world. Her hope against hope was again in vain, so she turned her attention to Durham Cathedral and lo and behold! she finished the text! And having done so, she rewarded herself with a relaxing shower.

Mrs M was leaving early again that day - another club meeting. It must be a worthy club, for Wyatt never questioned his housekeeper's necessity to leave early for a meeting. Actually, if Gem really considered the Hall staff - which was solely Mrs M - Wyatt was considerably lax regarding her work hours. And perhaps because of his attitude there was a certain calm atmosphere at the Hall - except when she and Wyatt were arguing.

Gem washed and rinsed her hair, deciding to braid it; the effort would occupy a bit of her time. Chapter complete, she had to decide which cathedral would be next. Glasgow Cathedral or Aachen Cathedral - a European cathedral for a change - just for a breather. Photos of either were complete and she was extremely satisfied with every single shot of each structure. Glasgow, she decided, sighing. Cathedral, Pilos, Cathedral. Pilos. And she was finding it very difficult to focus on her book. She was eager for the day trip to Stonehenge the following day.

Blast! She had forgotten to select the restaurants for their day trip. She returned to the office for the book of English villages she had purchased weeks past. She hadn't finished reading the book and only could sort villages north of London, and they would be motoring south.

"What?" she stopped as she walked into her office.

A second vase of flowers!

"Purple hyacinths," Wyatt said from the doorway. "The meaning is 'I'm sorry'."

"I am aware of the meaning," Gem said, confused. "Why the apology?" she asked warily.

"I apologize for upsetting you with the pink roses," Wyatt grinned, winking at her.

Gem laughed. "They are lovely. Thank you."

"Have you decided on pubs for tomorrow?" he queried, giving her a quick kiss and long hug.

"Next on my list."

Miss Molly padded into the room, her lead in her mouth.

Wyatt chuckled. "I believe I'm going for a walk," he grinned. "I told Mrs M not to bother with dinner. I thought we would go to the Crow if that suits you."

"Yes," she nodded.

Gem made a cup of tea then snuggled in the comfy chair, Mrs Mac stretched across her lap. By the time the walkers had returned, Gem had selected pubs for lunch and dinner. Mrs Mac glided to the counter to sit by the computer and Molly took her position on the floor to stare up at the cat looking down at her.

"Since they are occupied, shall we go to the Crow?" Wyatt laughed.

Gem agreed.

"Your office looks properly finished," Wyatt observed before they left the room.

"Indeed," Gem nodded.

Gem pushed the start button on the cd player and filled her cup from the thermos.

Mr Choate hadn't offered any further comments of her suggestion that Harry wouldn't be returning to the Agency, Gem mused as she sipped her beverage. She still had no logical reason for believing Harry wouldn't return. She dearly hoped she was wrong. It would be terribly frightening if she wasn't. It could mean Harry had also been another victim of the skin-heads. Perhaps Mrs Brown would be able to share information when she returned.

Gem pulled out her mobile.

'News regarding skin-head who murdered last agent?'

'No. No leads.'

'Staff safe?'

'As of midnight. Are you working?'

'Yes.'

'Have you any information for me, Gem?'

'No.'

'Go back to work. I know you'll find something.'

'Okay. Goodnight.'

'Goodnight, Gem.'

His mood was a bit less grumpy, and a touch encouraging.

Gem started sorting. The Pilos, flight times, nautical miles. Couriers and agents murdered. She again included Mr Denton. She had sorted the information countless times, and could not find a single fresh perspective.

She sorted, sipped hot chocolate, pressed the start button on the cd player, and paced for three hours, grateful as the dark hours drew to a close for her.

Gem filled her cup from the thermos. Her actions were becoming rote. Hot chocolate, start button, pace, sorting. Running smack into the same brick wall of no progress.

Mr Cawley was awake.

'Mrs Brown return?'

'No.'

'Blast!'

'Agreed.'

'News of SCS search?'
'Ended. No resolution.'
'Blast!'
'Agreed!'
'Word of Harry?'
'No.'
'Blank?'
'No. Have you any information for me, Gem?'
'No.'
'Ramp it up, Gem! You have to give me something.'
'A headache?'
'Have one already. Get to work!'
'Okay. Goodnight.'
'Goodnight.'

She had to ask still about Paul Andriani or Mr Cawley would wonder why she hadn't.

The search in the South China Sea had been wasted effort. Where to go now? Where to go now?

Gemmy. Geneva. Nothing.

Gem filled her cup. It was very thoughtful of Wyatt to prepare the hot chocolate for her every night. And he had been very considerate throughout their day-trip to Stonehenge. He had taken her up on the offer to use her new camera, and she had shot photos of him snapping photos of the monoliths.

Stonehenge reminded her of something, but as was becoming a frustrating habit, she couldn't think of the Blasted 'something'.

And then a Key slipped. Yet it was still out of reach. And still she could not identify the Key.

Gemmy. Geneva. Stonehenge.

And the same Key slipped again.

Gem started pacing. Miss Molly was sleeping on Wyatt's left side. Mrs Mac was curved around the computer monitor. She had clear pacing space and she was comfortably warm: carpet, warm slippers, snugly dressing gown, electric fireplaces. And she paced, hour after hour. The Key did not slip again. Gem dragged her fingers through her hair, becoming more frustrated and weary with every passing minute. She had been acquiring information for months without getting any closer to finding Gemmy and the Pilos. Day after day, week after week. It was too likely now that the Pilos would never be found. - Unless Mrs Brown had information to share when she returned. And when the HELL would that be?

No new information. Stalemate again, she moaned as she dragged herself off to bed. Mrs Mac followed.

Wyatt moved close to her as she slipped into bed. "The two of us, cat, dog, add a child and we need a larger bed," he kissed her shoulder.

Add two children, Gem replied silently. "Miss Molly has her own bench," she murmured.

"You explain that to her. Let me know how it goes," he yawned. "Time for you to sleep, darling."

The work on Glasgow Cathedral progressed at a snail's speed. The Keys nagged at Gem's thoughts. Out of habit, she watched the international news but again drew a blank on hot spots. She was tempted to inquire of Mr Cawley if he had information on skin-head activity in SEA. She knew it was being monitored after the latest victim's final text. But she couldn't text Mr Cawley because Wyatt was reading reports in the great room. If he walked into the office while she was texting or receiving a message he would naturally be suspicious. And she didn't believe for one minute that he wouldn't attempt to find out about a text. And logically, if Mr Cawley had information he would have texted it during the dark hours.

Gem paced the floor, a much more pleasant exercise with the lush carpet. She had ample space for pacing since Miss Molly and Mrs Mac were holding their staring contest in the great room - much to Wyatt's amusement.

As she paced, trying to concentrate on the Pilos, Wyatt drifted into her thoughts. He had seemed much more real the past two days. And despite her scepticism of his remarks during their war of the roses, his manner was decidedly different towardss her, less forced, less critical, less subtlety suspicious.

It still grated on her that he had searched her possessions. She could understand why he had done so, but she could not accept the fact that he had. She hated the invasion of her privacy. He admitted what he had done, then wanted her to trust him! His code of ethics was as creative as his personal dictionary!

She dragged her fingers through her hair. Geneva! That had to be one of the two remaining Keys. Geneva. Gemmy. Stonehenge. Blast! Why that combination?

Gem paced on. Nautical miles. Skinheads. Nazis. Pillaged museums and homes. Three submarines at the bottom of the South China Sea. She sorted, sub-sorted, cross checked facts in her mind, victims. Missing Nazi files. Odessa.

"Trouble in Glasgow?" Wyatt quipped from the doorway.

"What?" Gem glanced at him, startled by his voice, so lost had she been in her 'secret world' - as Wyatt referred to her private thoughts.

"Pacing, furrowed brow," he suggested nodding to the computer screen. "That is the Glasgow Cathedral, isn't it?"

Gem glanced at the computer. "Oh, yes," she confirmed his guess. "Texts can be so very frustrating," she replied. "Fact checking, dates, architectural details."

Wyatt nodded, not believing a word she had said. Her eyes were not clear violet. They were clouded. Gem had been in her office physically. Her thoughts were a great distance away.

"Break time," he announced, without refuting her words. "Hot chocolate, marshmallows in the great room." He caught her hand, coaxing her along. "The cameras are quite striking on the shelves," he complimented.

Gem sighed inwardly. Mr M must have unpacked the box sitting next to the student's watercolours. She hadn't noticed the cameras. She probably hadn't noticed half of what she had seen the past week - or even before that. She suppressed another sigh.

She hadn't been aware that Wyatt had been in the kitchen preparing the hot chocolate in the thermos on the coffee table. There were also sliced cheeses, apples and bananas, and various meats.

"A feast," she acknowledged his effort. "Lovely, thank you. Tired of reading?" she teased.

"Reports, yes," he sat on the chesterfield and pulled her down next to him, spreading a blanket across her lap, before reaching for a book on the table. "You have been working for hours. Time to relax. I'm shall read to you of the Etruscans," he informed her.

"Oh- the book I gave you," Gem murmured. She couldn't remember when she had given it to him. Before Wight? Wight. The disastrous dividing line between them. Their Maginot Line so to speak.

"It is fascinating, and I wanted to share it with you - history," Wyatt said firmly. He filled a cup with hot chocolate and handed it to her. "Relax, Gem."

She realized he had been using her name more frequently, the sham terms of endearment less frequently. That change felt odd to her. She had become used to the other words.

"You're frowning. Are you not interested in the book?" he observed.

"Oh, but I am!" Gem insisted, then sighed.

"Then what?"

"You use my name more frequently," she said pensively.

"You dislike terms of endearment, and Bloody Mary does seem a bit crass," he replied smoothly.

"Since when did you start listening to me?" she challenged.

"I always listen to you, Gem. I do not always agree with you. But I always listen. Now, chapter one," he opened the book. "Nod every once in a while if you wish to pretend you're listening," he teased.

Gem did listen, but she also recalled that shortly after their marriage she had come to realize that he always used her name when he was being forthright with her. Did he realize that was his habit? "Please begin," she requested. She did want to hear what he was reading.

"Certainly," he replied, doing as she requested, "Chapter One."

"Too, too clever," Gem chuckled, leaning against his shoulder as he read.

It was heaven - or a vision of heaven that suited Gem: his voice soothing and clear, reading chapter after chapter, re-filling her cup with hot chocolate, handing her a plate of cheeses, meat, fruit - some of the apples and bananas dusted with a touch of cinnamon, some with brown sugar. His voice entranced her as completely as his smile and intense gaze. He read until dinner, prepared bacon, eggs and toast for them, then read again until they were ready to retire for the evening.

"A lovely time, thank you," Gem wrapped her arms around his neck, lightly rubbing her nose against his.

"Indeed. Perhaps another time you will read to me," he suggested, his hands smoothing her hair.

"You select the book and it's a deal," she smiled.

"I selected this book. The next choice is yours," he countered. "Whatever and whenever."

Her choice. Another reference to his chat of the previous evening? she frowned.

Wyatt sensed her thoughts. "Oh no, Gem, cease errant thoughts," he ordered, deciding it was best to free and then wrangle butterflies to divert her from going into her secret world.

Gem sighed quietly as the dark hours started. She hated the thought of leaving Wyatt's arms and the warmth of his body to pace the office floor. Mrs Mac followed her down the steps; Miss Molly was more inclined to gain territory of the bed. Gem waited until she reached her office to give into the impulse to laugh at Miss Molly and her love of furniture. "Oh the silly people who chose furniture over Molly," she laughed, hugging the cat. "You like her also, you must admit!"

Mrs Mac declined to reply, squirming to be released to jump to the counter.

She could have sworn Wyatt had fallen asleep when she had, yet there was a thermos of hot chocolate to the right of her computer.

And a new mug bearing the photo Wyatt had snapped of Molly, Mrs Mac and Gem, that day in the office. Gem felt a lump come to her throat and she forced it down.

Clever. The current part of his Game. The love part, not the trust part. She didn't know whether to resent or to be pleased with the gift. The photo was delightful: Gem was sitting in her swivel chair staring at the computer screen; Mrs Mac was on the counter staring down at the dog sitting on the floor staring up at the cat. Wyatt had shot the photo, had it processed, then had ordered the mug. An effort he had made especially for her. Just accept gifts, he had said, without looking for a ploy or hidden agenda. But it was so difficult to believe those words. There was the trust part.

Blast! She was confusing the love and the trust parts of the game.

She refused to trust him again! She repeated three times to herself to further ingrain it into her mind.

And she refused to love him again! She refused to be hurt and humiliated - especially by Wyatt Grantham!

Gem suddenly sank into the comfy chair, struck by a devastating realization. She wasn't star struck. She was still totally, completely, in love with him! She felt at that moment, as betrayed as she had felt that hideous night at Marigold Cottage!

She groaned, pounding her temples with her fists. Stupid! Stupid! Stupid! She had enough on her plate with which to deal!

Oh, and wouldn't he just jolly well be pleased!

He had Won again!

This time he had not let her down. She had let herself down.

But while she had to admit the fact to herself, she would NEVER let him know she loved him!

Fool me twice; I am the stupidest person in the world!

He did know! She groaned again. Was that the different look in his eyes, the difference in his demeanour? He knew? She would never let him know that she knew that he knew. A convoluted Game. So Blasted frustrating!

I have too much to sort tonight, Mr Wyatt Grantham! You will not constantly invade my thoughts! I don't want to love you. So it will not truly exist.

Hearts were exceedingly poor judges of character. Squelch the heart! Strive to control the mind!

Gem took three breaths and counted to twenty six times.

Then she reached for her mobile. Mr Cawley was awake. She slipped the mobile back into the pocket of her dressing gown.

How could she love Wyatt? She hated him! She had heard of love-hate relationships but she had never expected such a battle in her own mind.

Be gone, Dark Lord! She silently fumed.

She texted Mr Cawley.

'Skinhead activity in SEA?'

'Always just below simmering.'

He had certainly quickly responded!

'On radar?'

She winced at her choice of words. Flying under radar - the Pilos.

'No. Just simmering. Many aliases used in different factions.'

'Any incidents traceable to factions?'

'No evidence, but possibly 5 small bombings as of late. Unconfirmed reports: 4 minor injuries. 1 serious. No witnesses.'

'Investigations complete?'

'Open cases. No leads.'

'Mrs Brown return?'

'No. Not likely soon.'

'Blast!'

'I assume no pun intended to previous messages.'

'Indeed! Very sorry - poor choice of exclamation.'

'What information have you for me, Gem?'

'Sorry.'

'Not what I wanted.'

'Harry? Blank?'

'No news.'

'Okay.'

'I need help, Gem.'

'I understand.'

'Get to work! Goodnight!'

'Okay. Goodnight.'

A bit of information. She would have classified small bombings as more than just below simmering. How many casualties were necessary to reach simmering? she mused.

She pushed the start button again on the cd player and refilled her thoughtful, delightful, completely annoying new mug.

No Mrs Brown. No Harry. She had Paul Andriani. She needed the others. She needed any information they could supply to help the Keys shift!

Gem paced constantly, stopping only to fill her mug and to press the start button.

No matter how many times she sorted the information in her brain, she arrived at the same conclusion. Gemmy. Geneva. Stonehenge. Gemmy. Geneva. Stonehenge. Harry.

Harry!

Why Harry?

Gemmy. Geneva. Stonehenge. Harry.

Blast! Gem let her mind wander, then returned to sorting.

Gemmy. Geneva. Stonehenge. Harry. Mrs Brown.

Blast!

She stopped sorting and went to bed. The more she sorted, the more turmoil simmered in her brain. Her thoughts, the sorting, the simmering, were all blurring together.

Gem had no reason to go to London that day. Mr Choate could have the day to his more important work, she decided as she cleaned her office.

She had thanked Wyatt for the mug that morning after the butterflies were quelled. And she would continue to use it although it grated on her nerves - a constant reminder of his egotistical belief that she was again in love with him.

Miss Molly was spirited away for the day by Mr M who was spending the week walking the boundaries of Ticking Bottom. She would spend her nights at the Hall, and days as a constant companion to granddad as Mrs M referred to her husband where the poochie was involved. Mr M referred to the Missus as the furred ones grandmum. Gem was beginning to consider the Hall estate staff borderline eccentric.

Without Molly at her side and to let run, Gem walked Ticking Bottom on her own, allowing her mind to wander at times, then focused sorting until she thought her head would explode. No Keys slipped. And try as she might, she could not see a connection between Gemmy, Geneva, Stonehenge, Mrs Brown, and Harry.

She walked all the cobblestone lanes of Ticking Bottom, returning to the Hall for lunch with Mrs M, who wanted to discuss holiday menus. Gem heard all the housekeeper's suggestions, and having listened to the inflection in the older woman's voice, suggested items on the list that Mrs M favoured. It was a sneaky way to manage the discussions, but Mrs M seemed very pleased at Gem's decisions. And the menu was ready for Wyatt's approval.

Gem went out again in the afternoon, walking the narrow path between fields and meadows and the forest. She was no more successful in the afternoon sunlight than she had been in the morning sunlight. Great exercise, but a complete waste of mental effort.

And she grew more frustrated by the hour.

Wyatt's scratches were healing and showed no permanent damage to his smashing body. He wasn't showing any ill effects of the wounds, other than being a touch wary of Mrs Mac when there was nothing but air between bare flesh and claws. Gem had laughed until she was exhausted, when Mrs Mac tried to climb Wyatt's leg, as if it were a tree, when he emerged from the shower before breakfast.

Late afternoon two carpeted cat trees with hidey holes and climbing limbs were delivered to the Hall by the T.B. blacksmith/carpenter; one tree was placed to the right of the fireplace in the master suite, the other was placed in the downstairs main hall overlooking the back gardens, an area bathed in light on sunny days. Wyatt was certainly one to indulge the furred ones. Gem would have to make sure he did not overindulge their children.

Gem was not warned by either Mrs M or Wyatt to rest; apparently he was relinquishing a bit of his control over her. But she did rest that day, watching the international news and 'reading' a book about dogs as she mentally sorted and re-sorted information. By dinner time her mind was burned with exhaustion, and she had no desire to walk another yard of Ticking Bottom.

Gem paced the office, repeating the previous day's dark hours of hot chocolate and Vera Lynn. Miss Molly slept alongside Wyatt; Mrs Mac slept in a hidey hole in the bedroom cat tree.

She automatically reached for her mobile to text Mr Cawley, doubting that he would have new information for her. She was correct. Mrs Brown had not returned, nor had Harry. Mr Choate and Gem were still the only people who knew Paul Andriani was living and working in London.

Gem's sorting resulted in conclusions which were always the same: Gemmy, Geneva, Stonehenge, Mrs Brown, Harry.

She printed sheets of information of Stonehenge, committing the reference material to memory. At one point she feared an additional sentence crammed into her mind would cause an overload and words would start leaking from her ears. She swore to herself that she would not read a single word on Tuesday.

Mrs Mac strolled into the room, vocalizing demands that Gem decided were requests for kitty crunchies, and once the treats were served and chewed, the feline strolled out of the office.

Gem paced again, filled her mug with hot chocolate, and pressed the start button on the cd player. She wished she could travel in time, not as a regular habit - but just once. Just a one-time journey back to 29 May. To delay the last flight of the Pilos.

She collapsed into Auntie Jane's comfy chair, unable to put one foot in front of the other, and had to drag herself to bed as the dark hours ended. Again no progress had been accomplished. No Keys had slipped even the tiniest slip.

Tuesday was a virtual repeat of Monday except that cat trees were not delivered. Gem walked the fields and meadows of Ticking Bottom, organized the books, dvds, and cds in her office. Wyatt declined to offer an opinion on any holiday menus other than agreeing with Gem on ham.

In the afternoon, Mrs Mac slept hours on end on a cat tree limb in the downstairs hall, her fur glistening in the sun. Miss Molly had eagerly left with Mr M after her breakfast, returned for lunch and a brief rest, and was out the kitchen door again in early afternoon.

Gem walked the cobblestone lanes in the afternoon, sorting and re-sorting until she had to take a forced break when her head began to ache.

Mrs M frowned at her when Gem returned to the Hall. "Any more walking and that child will be born wearing hiking boots," she said pointedly. "Mr W said I wasn't to vex you with concern, but you are beginning to look thoroughly worn."

Gem nodded. She was beginning to feel thoroughly worn. Day after day, the dark hours - and no progress. At the end of this week another month would have progressed with hundreds of hours of searching by many people. Hundreds of hours with not a single result. - Other than the knowledge that Paul Andriani had not been in love with Gemmy and that he was living in Wyatt's London flat. Little results for all the time spent searching.

Mrs Brown had assured Gem that the Agency would never stop searching for Gemmy and their parents, for Mr Portermann. And justice would be sought for the murderer of the SEA Network counter-couriers and agents. And for Mr Denton. Gem always insisted on including him as a victim of this plot - whatever plot it was.

Mrs M had to leave early for her meeting and Wyatt was bringing Chinese take-away with him for dinner.

Gem rested on Auntie Jane's settee in late afternoon. She looked at the photos of canines in the dog book, but did not read words. She watched the international news - no news of vital importance to her search - and finally wandered upstairs to shower, washing and braiding her hair. Wyatt arrived while she was upstairs and had plates at the ready to serve her dinner.

Wyatt gazed at her, pondering a way to mention that she looked weary - without raising her ire. "If you're too tired to eat, I'll blend the food and you can drink it," he teased.

Gem laughed, shaking her head. "I can manage," she replied with no animosity - to Wyatt's relief.

He insisted on doing the washing up and Gem wandered listlessly back to her office. Every thought was a struggle. And every thought revolved around the Pilos and the seemingly endless, futile search.

After the dishes were put away, Wyatt brought her a cup of tea. "I thought you might enjoy a change from hot chocolate," he smiled.

"Lovely, thank you," Gem nodded.

"My pleasure," he replied. "Is Glasgow still trying?"

"I would have to place the onerous on me, not on the cathedral," Gem admitted.

"Perhaps you need a holiday from composing text. Mrs M would be happy to teach you to knit," he smiled.

"I should like that - but not now," she sighed.

Wyatt looked around the office. "A proper office for you, Gem. Is there anything else you need or wish to change?"

"I think not. The work has been beautifully done. Thank you. It's a lovely place to work," she smiled.

Wyatt continued looking about and noticed the case at the top of the cd stack. The Vera Lynn cd.

"I'm going to shower. Mr M is going out early in the morning and will keep Miss Molly overnight," he informed her.

Gem's eyes narrowed at his words. "Just for tonight?" she asked him warily.

Wyatt turned quickly to look at her. "I'll go this very minute to bring her home if you're concerned for her safety, Gem. You saw Molly this afternoon," he reminded her.

"I did," she nodded.

"Will you at least trust me for one night?" he asked, frowning. "Molly is with the M's."

Gem searched his eyes, deciding that he was being honest with her. She would trust him - for just one night.

"Yes," she agreed.

"Okay," Wyatt nodded. "One night. If you change your mind, I'll fetch her after my shower," he gave her a brief smile. "And now, if you will excuse me, I hope to spend some of this evening with an incredibly lovely, young woman, and I need to wash away the day," he winked at her.

"Very well," Gem agreed, smiling at him.

"See if you can stir up a few butterflies that need rounding up," he teased.

"They are already stirred," Gem smiled.

He was different, Gem mused as she returned her focus to the computer screen. Glasgow Cathedral was before her eyes, but no work was accomplished on the text.

She needn't have fussed about Miss Molly, she realized. The M's adored the dog, and Gem could not believe that they would harm her. She trusted the M's. It was Wyatt she didn't trust.

While he showered, Wyatt thought about the cd case. Vera Lynn. After his shower he retrieved the cd. Had Gem not realized she had left the cd at the flat in Barcelona? He would not hand over the passports or the photos, but there was no reason why she shouldn't have the cd. He slipped it into the pocket of his dressing gown.

Gem heard his step behind her, and there was the light scent of his cologne. When had he stopped using the cologne he had worn at Marigold Cottage and for weeks after - how many weeks? Her senses were so dull she couldn't find the answer to her own query. But - he was no longer wearing the cologne that Gemmy had given to James.

Wyatt pressed the start button on the cd player. Vera Lynn's voice filled the office. "You must be very fond of this cd," he said gently.

"It's a good one," she shrugged, preferring to look at the computer screen and not into his eyes.

He walked over to her and pulled the cd case from his pocket. "This is your other copy. I found it at the Barcelona flat," he purposely did not mention James's name. He set the case on the counter.

Gem quickly counted to twenty. Control. Control. No slipped cogs. She looked at the case. This was the cd their father had given to Gemmy last Christmas. It was a small thing to have left at James's flat, but it was NOT a small thing: 'Gem' was written on the case in black marker ink. A cd. Was there anything else Gemmy had left behind so carelessly?

The song playing ended and 'Yours' began.

"Very romantic songs," Wyatt said, his voice gentle.

Gem listened to the lyrics, then left her chair to push the stop button.

"You're a romantic, aren't you?" Wyatt said softly.

Gem shook her head, still refusing to look at him. "I'm just a fool - as you well know," she said tonelessly.

"I don't believe you're a fool, Gem. For some reason you let down your guard. You were too trusting. And you shouldn't be ashamed of that." He pushed the button to start the song playing again. "I wonder whom you have loved," he paraphrased the words. "But that isn't my business to know, is it?'

Gem stopped the player, replaced the cd with the Brandenburg concerto, and pressed the start button, all the while keeping her back to him.

"How you fascinate me, Gem!" He slipped his arms around her waist, resting his cheek against the top of her head.

"Not likely," she said coolly, staring at the curtains, wondering what his ploy was this evening.

"But you do, Gem. And cds become scratched - ruined. I thought you would like to have your other copy," he murmured. "Would you like a cup of tea?"

Gem shook her head.

"Hot chocolate?"

Gem shook her head.

"Wine?"

"I can't drink wine," she turned around to scowl at him, and saw his teasing eyes.

"Beer?"

Her reply was cut short by a leisurely kiss.

"Would you like to come to bed. I'll give you a massage," he murmured. "Or shall I fetch Molly?"

"Massage," Gem whispered. She had been very annoyed with him, but butterflies were storming. She reached over to click the mouse to save her files then clicked again to shut down her computer.

The hot chocolate thermos, the cd - now she had two - and a lovely warm office. How could she possibly trust him? Oh what a brilliant Game he played! And, oh, how excellent he was at giving a massage! And then the butterfly gathering.

Gem's brain was burning. She had to find Gemmy! To find the Pilos! And then hopefully everything would fall into place. A murderer would be caught.

And then there was Wyatt, dividing her attention. Fighting his love/trust Game.

Her concentration was skewered by the division between Gemmy and the Pilos, and Wyatt and his Game. The former won out. She couldn't afford to miss a slip of a Key because she was trying to decipher Wyatt's Game of revenge. First one issue then the other.

The one bright point of her mental turmoil was the cd Wyatt had given to her. Gem had assumed the cd was at the Agency warehouse - packed last 30 May as she stared, eyes glazed by the turmoil of having her family memories packed away in bubble wrap sheets for God only knew how long - months, years, decades.

She had to ring Ora later and request another dressing gown, for this one was superbly warm; it was like snuggling into two dozen furry cats. Weird thought. "Sorry, Mrs Mac," she murmured to the feline who had commandeered the cushion of the comfy chair.

Gem paced, sipping the hot chocolate, then set the mug down and reached into her pocket for her mobile to endure the nightly text with Mr Cawley. She tried a different style of query.

'Faring well this morning?'

'What do you have for me, Gem?'

'Still sorting.'

Her new style of query hadn't worked. There was a lengthy pause before she received a reply. She paced and finished another mug of hot chocolate.

'Shall I forward that comment to Gem in my Christmas card to her?'

Gem gasped at the remark.

'Could you be more heartless?!' she texted, her fingers shaking.

'Sorry. How many months shall we drag out this investigation?'

Gem was tempted to pitch the Agency mobile across the room, but Mr White's likely chastising frown crept into her mind. Mobiles were Agency property and must be respected as vital government property. She counted to twenty, over and over again.

Ping

'How many times did you count to twenty?'

'Seven!'

'Slow counting. No wonder you are slow at sorting!'

'Reverse psychology. Not very original.'

'And not successful apparently. Get back to work! I am buried in time taken up by the search for the Pilos!'

'Whatever the step lower than coal - that is your Christmas gift from Santa this year!'

'What is Gemmy giving you this year? Your mum? Your dad? Did you find a gift for Portermann or are you waiting a few weeks to begin your shopping?'

'You BASTARD!' Her fingers flew over the letters on her mobile key pad.

'I am out of patience, Gem! You have one month to give me a solution to the Pilos. After thirty days I will permanently end all the search funding.'

'Good inspiration! Your threats won't work! Mrs Brown said we never forget our own!'

'She is not currently your supervisor. She is not currently Acting Director of the Agency.'

'You cannot supersede her orders!'

'I can. I will.'

'She can countermand you when she returns!'

'When will she return? FYI-Agency Directors rarely countermand Acting Director's orders. Thirty days and Gemmy and the Pilos go into agency Unsolved Files.'

'What of the murdered SEA couriers and agents?'

'That query will be relegated to the SEA Network for their resolution.'

'You BASTARD!'

'I climbed a mountain for you, Gem, and became deathly ill. What have you done for me in the past few months?'

'Goodnight!'

'In the event you are interested: no news, Harry, Mrs Brown, or Blank!'

Well I could give you Paul Andriani, but I shan't because you make my blood boil! Gem fumed.

She quickly cleared the messages, then quickly sorted, mentally reviewing the Agency SOP sheets she had read over the years. She hated the conclusion she had to draw.

Mr Cawley could end the investigation - the search for Gemmy and the Pilos at any time - at his sole discretion - as Acting Director - the Agency. He could. And he would. Really? If his words had been meant to spur her on, to increase the pressure she already suffered - did she really need to feel additional pressure? - No, she did not!

But he was her supervisor, and she couldn't fight him! Even if she had the energy to do so. Which she didn't.

Zounds! Fireworks emblazoning Wyatt's name exploded in her brain. Now she had to fight Wyatt and Mr Cawley! Well, if that wasn't a day brightener what was!

She knew - KNEW -Mr Cawley wouldn't end the search! But he could! And if he did where would that leave the passengers of the Pilos? Gemmy! And where would that leave Gem? She would be stuck with Wyatt Grantham forever!

She turned on her computer and pulled up the screen of the Pacific Ocean, staring at the expanse, scrolling over to South East Asia. Damn and Blast! She had spent hours on the computer, researching information, and hours with a calculator figuring out nautical miles and fuel supply. She didn't know what else to do. She couldn't figure out what to do next!

And another Key slipped. Damn! She couldn't reach it. And then she realized it was a third Key. She just knew it was a third Key. That would make four total. She started pacing again. She had one Key: Paul Andriani. But there were now, again, still three Keys. She hoped if she retrieved a second Key that yet another one would NOT pop up to be equally annoying and frustrating.

She pressed the start button again on the cd player. She was not becoming sick of Vera Lynn. She hoped the reverse sentiment was the same.

The hot chocolate was gone, and still there was an hour left until her brain would sleep with or without her consent. She made another pot of hot chocolate.

Where else could she go? Brick wall no matter how she sorted.

Gemmy. Stonehenge. Geneva. Harry. Mrs Brown. Had Stonehenge shifted? Did she care? It was involved. She would not place drama on position in her sorting. She paced continually, expanding her route to the kitchen, down the hall, through the great room, then to the main hall, and back to the office.

Finally the pacing became too monotonous to continue. She attempted to shift Mrs Mac, but claws digging into the cushion of the comfy chair warned Gem that a stubborn cat should probably not be shifted against her will. Gem settled for Auntie Jane's settee. The cd had stopped playing. She would press the start button in a minute.

Wyatt gazed down at her - sitting, yet sleeping on the settee. He would risk waking her if only to prevent a damned uncomfortable stiff neck for her when she again wakened in an hour.

How could she manage with so little sleep? She could simply not keep burning the candle at both ends.

Gem didn't remember going to bed, she realized as her brain wakened at seven o'clock; she stretched, dislodging Mrs Mac from her knees, and bringing Wyatt awake to scatter, then gather butterflies.

It wasn't until she had stopped on her walk that morning at the old stone bridge below the Hall, that she realized she must have fallen asleep on the settee as the dark hours ended.

She pulled out her mobile to text Wyatt.

'Did you carry me to bed this morning?'

His reply was immediate. Well -she couldn't accuse him of ignoring her.

'Yes.'

'Thank you. I don't remember you doing so.'

'Not surprising. You were asleep. Shall I do that again this evening?'

'You had best save your back. You might be required to dig a garden pool next summer.'

There was a long pause and Gem thought he had ceased texting.

'Checked w/Ms Wexton, my scheduler. She said I am booked all summer to push a pram. No time for digging. Back will be fine. For carrying you and doing other things to and w/you!'

Gem burst out laughing. Then quickly texted.

'Banter!'

'Hereditary. Dad was a writer for Benny Hill.'

'What?'

'Banter! Keep up w/me!'

'Don't think I can!'

'If you can't, Gem, no one can!'

'Complete and udder tripe!'

'Let me ruminate on that!'

'How mammalian of you!'

'Try again, Gem!'

'Ah! The inadequate facetiousness of an indelicate mind!'

'Score! Exceedingly brilliant!'

'Banter!'

'Sass! Please come have lunch w/me!'

'One hour. Where?'

'You say, Gem.'

'White Rose.'

'One hour, Gem!'

'Okay.'

'Until then!'

Mrs M was not put out, to Gem's relief, when she burst into the kitchen, grabbed the keys to the Defender and rushed out again saying only three words. "Lunch. Wyatt. London."

Mrs M raced after her, grabbing the hem of her windcheater, stating two words. "Mr Choate!"

Down to one word for Gem. "Blast!" she muttered, scrolling down to his contact number on her phone.

"Five minutes," he stated firmly.

Lunch was perfect and neither of them had a second thought of fear of spit in their food. Wyatt was charming, witty, and attentive. Gem assured herself that she could be excused for having fallen in love with him again. What woman wouldn't fall in love with him! Really! But this was a different man than the one she had met in August. He had changed, and she was tempted - logic aside - to trust him. Tempted, yes. Foolish? No! Okay. A seemingly different man, yes. But still the Game player. And with this information seared into her brain, she could thoroughly enjoy his company. She had her guard up. Now she had her guard up.

Wyatt returned to his office, Gem to the Hall, and Mr Choate to whatever mysterious action occupied his time when his efforts were not devoted to Gem.

Mrs M was again sitting at the kitchen island; she snapped shut the cookery book that was in front of her on the counter. "Did you have a pleasant lunch, dear?" she queried. She smiled, but Gem noted it was wistful and a touch sad.

"Lovely," Gem smiled. "And how was your day?"

"About the same," Mrs M replied, forcing a brighter smile. "I have written a few thoughts," she shuffled papers beside the cookery book.

The coming holidays seemed to be at the forefront of Mrs M's thoughts of late, Gem mused. And then she realized it must have been years since Christmas had been celebrated at Grantham Hall. Hadn't Mrs M said weeks back that Wyatt and James had moved to the London flat after James had been released from hospital?

"The holidays must have been quiet here for the last few years," Gem ventured her thoughts.

"Many years," Mrs M nodded. "Jamie was in hospital the first year after the Seniors died. Then in and out of treatment centres. Mr W took him to Marigold Cottage one year, then another year to Inverness - places Mr W could keep a strict eye on him - where Jamie couldn't buy what he shouldn't have."

Gem couldn't imagine the struggles Wyatt had had working to help his brother accomplish sober and clean.

"Did Mrs Fiona decorate the entire Hall?"

"Indeed," the housekeeper's voice and face brightened. "There were always huge trees in the great room and the living room, and a smaller one in the dining room."

Gem prepared a pot of tea while Mrs M reminisced. "There were banks of red poinsettias and white trumpet flowers in the main hall and the solarium - now your office. Oh - they were throughout the house. And lovely fir boughs with ribbons, holly and mistletoe balls everywhere," Mrs M sipped her tea, a dreamy look in her eyes.

"It was splendid. We would decorate every day for a fortnight and bake long into each night. The Seniors would invite the entire village for an afternoon buffet the Sunday before Christmas. The lads pitched in when they could, but they had their studies, and friends and parties to occupy some of their time. But even Mr Jack, as busy as he was, would be here to trim the trees, and they would all be home Christmas week then through the New Year. New Year's Day the locals would stop in for Mrs Fiona's special eggnog, and Mr Jack's mulled wine. The lads were always on hand during the holidays to see that those who over indulged, so to say, made it home safely without mishap. Oh, there were treats too, pies, ham sandwiches, crisps, cakes, biscuits. It was always congenial and so festive. But Christmas was the full buffet."

A lump rose in Gem's throat as memories came to mind of her family's celebrations at their home in Brisbane.

Mrs M shook herself. "Not everyone celebrates the same way, naturally," she said, as she noted a sad look enter Gem's eyes. "Some people prefer a quiet time over the season," she suggested in the event that Mrs Grantham's family holidays had been more subdued.

"Do you think Wyatt misses the Hall festivities?" Gem inquired, thinking it was more likely Mrs M and the village who longed for the Hall Christmases of the past.

Mrs M shook her head, puzzled. "He hasn't mentioned the holidays but to say he'll agree to menus," she frowned.

Gem poured another cup for each of them, and thought of Wyatt's feelings. "This will be Wyatt's first Christmas without his brother. It will likely be extremely difficult for him - so many memories," she projected her own emotions to his feelings.

"Yes," Mrs M sighed.

Gem shook her head. "I'm not certain Wyatt would wish to make polite chat with a house full of people this year," she observed. "A Christmas tree, naturally," she thought aloud. She didn't want to celebrate the holidays this year. She could certainly understand that Wyatt might have similar feelings - especially if he had so far only agreed to menus. "Perhaps we'll know better in a week or so how he feels," she advised. "But I think it would be fun to try new recipes - perhaps to ease him a bit towards a holiday mood." If that was possible.

Mrs M brightened further at the suggestion. "Subtle," she nodded a touch conspiratorially. "Perhaps a honey glazed ham and marinated tomatoes for dinner one night soon."

"Sounds heavenly," Gem agreed. And she would broach the subject with Wyatt for Mrs M's sake. Eventually Wyatt would have to acknowledge the holidays in some way with their children.

In the meantime she pulled on her anorak to do another long foot tour of Ticking Bottom. She scanned the fields and meadows wondering if Miss Molly was bounding through the trees or tramping quietly alongside Mr M. He couldn't have a better companion than Miss Molly for his hiking days.

Gem was not any more adept at sorting while walking the cobblestone lanes than she was pacing inside at the Hall.

She could not believe deep in her heart that Mr Cawley would end the search for the Pilos. Wasn't it the Agency's responsibility - and duty - to bring home lost staff when possible?

Perhaps if Mr Cawley was so buried in work he should hire an assistant for himself. Perhaps transfer an operative from T.O. to the Agency. T.O. was a person extra now with Paul Andriani on staff - although Mr Cawley was not aware of that hire. If he was desperate he could ask for a temporary aide from B.I. However, the Agency disliked any influence of B.I. in their ranks, Gem, had to admit. She could sympathize with Mr Cawley, but after all, he had to do his job just as did every other Agency staff member.

And she did not need or appreciate the constant pressure he put on her!

She walked for over two hours, no closer to finding the Pilos, but no further away from it either, she sighed as she returned to the Hall.

As she entered the kitchen she realized one of the Keys had slipped. It was still out of reach, but it was still moving. Keys were still moving.

It was odd about Keys and cogs. A slipped cog could cause a disastrous situation. A slipped Key could resolve a disastrous situation. Very odd!

Wyatt's pleasant mood at lunch extended into the evening. He had settled to read on the chesterfield in front of the fireplace in the great room, and Gem took a chance that he might be receptive to a chat about the coming holidays. Dr Jekyll had not appeared for a few days, and Gem hoped he would not choose to make an abrupt appearance that night.

Wyatt smiled when she entered the room and he set aside his book.

"Butterflies out of control?" he teased.

"A bit," Gem admitted, "but actually I wanted to have a chat with you," she said uneasily.

"Certainly, Gem," he patted the cushion next to him, but Gem remained standing. "If it's about Miss Molly, she'll be home in an hour or so. She's having a play date with a collie in Crispin."

Gem nodded. "It's not Molly. It's regarding Christmas," she said hesitantly.

"Go on," his smile faded a bit.

Gem frowned. "Mrs M was chatting today about the holidays," Gem caught her bottom lip between her teeth. "She was chatting of the Hall Christmas parties."

"Ye merry old traditional Christmas festivities. The ghosts of Christmas past. Well there are certainly enough ghosts now. How Dickensian," he said dryly. He instantly regretted his words as Gem visibly stiffened. "I'm sorry, Gem. That was cruel of me," he scowled. "Come sit for a moment."

She sat beside him, carefully choosing her words. "I do understand why you said that. It's just that Mrs M seemed rather hopeful that you might want to decorate the Hall - make it a bit festive," she faltered, knowing she was making a hash of the subject.

Wyatt shook his head in disbelief. "We should hark back to the past to brighten Mrs M's holidays?" he said with a perplexed smile.

"You were away from the Hall for so many years," Gem tried to explain. "I think Mrs M simply wants to make this a lovely Christmas for you."

Wyatt considered her words. "There is the holiday party at GEI, the party at the Crow. Personally that will be enough holiday for me. But you and Mrs M do whatever you like here. Decorate, party your hearts out. I'll drive the inebriated home as in days of yore," he said resignedly. "However, I will not help or plan or decorate. Hire someone from the village if you require assistance."

"Very well," Gem sighed. She didn't think Wyatt avoiding the particulars was exactly what Mrs M had in mind. And she didn't blame Wyatt for a moment for his disinterest.

"What now?" he demanded, again with the resigned tone.

"I believe Mrs M wants an old fashioned Christmas," Gem winced.

"Dickensian, Elizabethan, Victorian? How old is old fashioned?" he exhaled sharply.

"More like an old fashioned Grantham family Christmas. Banks of poinsettias, angel trumpets, holly, Christmas trees - plural, etcetera, etcetera," Gem said gingerly.

"I see. Do you realize you said 'family' without your eyes shooting daggers at me?" he observed, a bit of tease in his voice.

"I choked on the inside," Gem admitted, but without even a bit of nasty or cool in her voice.

"Still, it might be progress," he gave a brief nod.

The first Christmas without James since his brother was born. The first Christmas with Gem - the reason this would be the first Christmas without James. He thought about the other first Christmas in his life - the one he and James had suffered through the year their parents had died.

"I don't know, Gem," he grew serious.

"Blast!" she jumped to her feet. "I will be here for the holidays because James is not here. I'm sorry!" she spun around to face him. "I should never have begun this conversation. I just wanted Mrs M to be able to look forward to Christmas. A foolish, insensitive idea. I'll try to explain to her that the other holiday parties would be one matter, but quiet holidays here would be preferable this year. I'll handle the matter with Mrs M," she repeated, and hurried from the room.

Gem slumped in Auntie Jane's comfy chair, covering her face with her hands. Stupid! Insensitive!

"Gem," Wyatt said pensively, standing in front of her.

She looked up to see his gazing down at her, his light grey eyes patient.

"Why didn't I simply shoot an arrow through your heart!" she exclaimed, completely appalled that she had thought to convince him to celebrate the holiday season.

"It was sweet of you to care about Mrs M's feelings," he soothed.

"Skewering your feelings by doing so," Gem shook her head in disgust with herself.

"A bit awkward there," Wyatt admitted wryly. "Why don't you make me a cup of tea and we'll pretend our chat never happened."

"You have a remarkable fantasy life if you can imagine it never happened," Gem said in amazement, leaving the comfy chair.

"I do indeed," Wyatt chuckled. "And you are a big part of the fantasy," he added, teasing. "Now, Miss Molly will be home soon. Don't let her see that you're upset of she won't go off to keep Mr M company tomorrow. And he needs her. Walking the boundaries of T.B. is an exhausting job."

"Why is he doing it?" Gem asked curiously.

"He's checking for anomalies. He walks the boundary once a year. Actually he enjoys the project, and Miss Molly is learning the lie of the land."

Anomaly.

Wyatt saw the violet eyes cloud. What had he said to cause her to retreat into her secret world? He went over every word but could only guess at anomalies.

Anomaly. Gem latched onto the word.

Geneva was an anomaly.

A Key lurched.

Geneva was definitely one of the Keys. Or a Key to one of the Keys.

"What?" Gem spun around as Wyatt tapped her shoulder.

"You owe me a cup of tea, Gem," he reminded her.

Her eyes cleared and the cloud did not return as long as she was with him that night.

Gem sipped the hot chocolate, as she pushed the start button on the cd player. Geneva.

Wyatt hadn't allowed her any time to sort during the remainder of the evening. He completely occupied her attention, chatting, teasing, wrangling butterflies, insisting she listen carefully while Miss Molly described her day. And since Miss Molly was silent ninety-nine percent of her daily life, her tales of adventures walking the boundaries of T.B. left much to be desired.

Wyatt had been witty, charming, mesmerizing. He was ten times more him than he was the entire month of August; Gem pondered the difference in the man.

Gem actually began to believe she was seeing the true Wyatt Grantham. Another Game, she surmised. Another way to keep her off balance. How brilliant he was at his Games!

She had felt sickened by her attempt to convince Wyatt to plaster Christmas all over the Hall. She had tried once more to apologize to him, but he said the subject was invading fantasy space life. And he snapped his fingers and announced the subject had magically disappeared. The children were going to adore his imagination.

Gem shook her head.

Geneva. Key.

Geneva had not just been an escape day for Gemmy.

And Gem needed to find the reason for Geneva. She paced, sipped her beverage, and pressed start again and again and again on the cd player.

She thought to text Mr Cawley, but she was still very angry with him for his cruel remarks during the previous dark hours. He didn't have information for her and she didn't have information for him. Texting would be a waste of her patience.

Mrs Mac strolled into the office, gazed at Gem, then strolled into the kitchen. Cat silently scolding for kitty crunchies, Gem surmised - and accurately so, for having been provided treats, Mrs Mac crunched and then strolled off down the hall. Life at the Hall definitely had more colour in it now with the furred ones!

Gem paced again, sorting from the beginning: two o'clock, 30 May. She had mentally sorted through the flight and fuel calculations when her brain began to scorch. How many times would she have to sort and re-sort before the next Key would shift? She felt like a calculator - no - a computer. Over and over again Geneva would dart through her brain.

Blast! She sighed, trudging up to bed.

A Key had shifted, she suddenly realized.

"I'll tell Mrs M it would be best to have a quiet Christmas at the Hall this year," Gem assured Wyatt before they went down to breakfast.

"You and Mrs M do as you please," Wyatt countered. "If you want to have a party, have one."

"And you would arrange to be away on business that day?" Gem frowned, knowing that would be his wish.

"That could be arranged," he nodded. "Or I could be the taxi service."

"Your heart wouldn't be in the day. It would be too difficult for you, and Mrs M will understand," Gem said firmly.

"But you will be disappointed," Wyatt suggested as he tied his tie.

"Not in the least," Gem protested. "I have less than no interest in Christmas. The date could fall off the calendar and I wouldn't care or even notice."

Wyatt was taken aback by her complete apathy. "Why?"

Gem turned her attention to straightening the bedcovers.

"You have your reasons, I have mine," she refused to elaborate.

"Because you will not be with Staunton?" Wyatt asked crisply.

"No!" Gem exclaimed in surprise.

"Very well," Wyatt did not want to press the issue. From her behaviour, he observed, as he attempted to ease her stress, her stress only seemed to compound. If he was not the cause of her stress, then what outside influences were affecting her? By her look of surprise, Staunton was not one of the influences.

She never let down her guard protecting her secret world. And who was she protecting in her secret world? Staunton? Others? Or herself alone? More likely she was protecting more people that just herself.

"What are your plans for today, Gem?"

"Glasgow," she shrugged. "Go for a walk."

"Why don't we spend the day together? We could go for a drive, stop somewhere for lunch, visit a few shops," Wyatt suggested.

"What shops?" Gem queried, suddenly suspicious.

"Paint, carpet, furniture -"

"Baby," Gem winced.

"You can shop without having to make decisions," he coaxed.

"It's too early," Gem protested. "Three months is too early. In another month - after the holidays," she suggested. Another month would buy her more time. If the Pilos wasn't found by then - if Mr Cawley - or Mrs Brown, ended the search, she would have to tell Wyatt about the twins.

"In another few weeks, Dr Hallowell should be able to determine girl or boy," she hedged. "It will be easier to plan, to shop."

"I realize it's popular to learn the gender before birth," he frowned, "but wouldn't you rather be surprised, Gem?"

"I've had enough surprises to last my entire life," Gem sighed. "If you don't want to know, I won't tell you."

Wyatt nodded. "Might we have this chat another time? We could go antiquing, go to an art gallery."

"Don't you have meetings today?" she queried, quickly braiding her hair. "Mrs M will have breakfast ready soon."

"My next meeting is Monday morning. Mrs M is flexible. Would you like to go away for a few days, Gem?" Wyatt suggested. "A bed and breakfast perhaps? There's a charming one near Tiverton -"

"Is there?" Gem said pointedly.

"According to Ms Wexton," he grinned. "Whatever you are thinking - stop it!"

"I wasn't going to say any names," Gem smiled ruefully, then shook her head. "I'd rather not go away right now." If they went to a B and B she wouldn't have the privacy during the dark hours - Wyatt would be in the room or suite. He would be with her most of the time they were away. She needed to divert him from Tiverton. "Lunch and a gallery sound lovely. A bit of window shop. Paint, carpet, no furniture."

"Deal!" Wyatt smiled. "I'll change to something more comfortable."

"First time anyone has spoken those words when sex didn't follow," Gem teased.

"If you don't scamper off it will," he laughed.

The weather was sunny, the breeze was mild, very conducive to a day out and about in London. Wyatt selected a light sage green for the baby's room, and Gem, only had to approve or disapprove; she approved. She approved the carpet and colour - not even sure of what the actual colour was - green, grey? - something. And that was it for the shopping as no furniture was part of the day.

"It will show every piece of lint and fluff," she warned of the carpet.

"We have an excellent hoover," he reminded her.

She truly didn't care what Wyatt selected; she would have approved any choice. The Hall was his home; he should have what he wanted.

He suggested Jake's for lunch.

"Are you daft?" Gem vehemently protested.

"A happy change," Wyatt said smoothly. "Ms Jones informed me yesterday that one particular waitress at Jake's has sought employment in Birmingham - where her new fiancé manages a café."

"Avoid all Birmingham cafés in the future," Gem giggled.

They visited three art galleries and ended their day trip at the Crow, joining the M's for dinner, then stayed the evening for the live music.

Gem should have felt refreshed from an entire day not thinking of the Agency, but she had to drag herself from bed as the dark hours began. She had closed her eyes, willing herself to fall back to sleep, but naturally, that did not happen. And wouldn't until she found the Pilos.

She filled her mug with hot chocolate, pressed start on the cd player, and began to pace. Then she stopped, turned on her computer and switched to the screen of the Pacific Ocean, looking for inspiration. It did not come.

Mr Cawley was awake but she still wasn't ready to communicate with him. And she should since he was her current supervisor.

She pulled out her mobile.

'News?'

'Are you still pouting?'

'Anger is not pouting!'

'It's also no help.'

'Do you have any news? Mrs Brown?'

'Returned. On leave.'

'What?'

'Returned. On leave.'

'Not amusing. Why on leave?'

'No reason given.'

'This is becoming absurd!'

'Did you just notice that?'

'What is current status of the investigation?'

'No change.'

'Harry?'

'???'

'Is any one working on this project?'

'You are. What news have you for me?'

'I am dry.'

'Get back to work. Goodnight.'

'Goodnight.'

Harry was whereabouts unknown. Mrs Brown was now on leave. The small Agency department was dwindling. How long would this status be quo? she groaned.

She paced: from her office to the library, from the library to the kitchen, back and forth, stopping to fill her mug, or to push the start button on the cd player to waken Vera Lynn. She could not make progress. She sat in front of her computer staring at Brisbane, Papua New Guinea, Jakarta, Hong Kong, the South China Sea, the Banda, Timor, and Arafura Seas.

Mrs Brown, months ago, suggested air piracy. Was that such a strange idea now? Drugs? Gun running? If that had been the case, Paul Andriani would have tripped to the information. There would have been rumours - the 'no honour among thieves' bit.

She crossed her arms and put her head down on them, staring unseeing at the wood counter.

Wyatt gazed at her from the doorway. He had a clear view of the maps on the computer screen until it went to a screen saver black. She was searching. Searching for something which caused her to be desperately sad, and, he realized, desperately lonely.

"I am so tired," she moaned. "I can't do this any longer. I can't figure it out. It's there! Somewhere! I can't find it!"

Wyatt knelt on one knee, slipping his arm around her shoulder.

"Gem - please - tell me - how I can help you," he said quietly.

She raised her head, letting it rest on his shoulder. "Truly, I wish I could tell you," she whispered. "But I just can't tell you."

Again 'Can't'. Not 'Won't'. She wasn't refusing to tell him.

Wyatt stroked her hair. "You aren't at liberty to speak," he soothed.

She turned to look him directly in the eyes. "Correct," she said helplessly.

And she had won a major part of the Game, Wyatt suddenly realized. He trusted her. He had no reason to do so. And why the hell he did, he could not say. But he did trust her.

Wyatt reflected back through the months to the day he had met her at Oscar's Café. And he could not for a moment think of a single incident where he could find fault with her actions. Oh, he knew she had lied to him - repeatedly - so many times he had stopped keeping track of the lies. Lies, or subtle evasions of the truth - made because, again, she was not at liberty to take him into her confidence. And he had certainly never given her a reason to be able to confide in him - to trust him.

He had so neatly played her. But it wasn't his Game that was driving her to the edge - where he had wanted her to be - because of James's death. What was driving her to the edge was her search. While he was tormenting her out of revenge - her words at Wight had been correct, revenge - she had been facing him with silent courage and strength, and graciousness despite her anger and hatred of him.

He'd be damned to know why - after what happened to James - but he did trust her.

Game well and truly Over. But she would never believe him. Or trust him. She once had, months ago. But a trust so thoroughly profaned, could never be regained.

"Come to bed, Gem," he coaxed.

"Oh, Wyatt. Is that your answer to everything?" she attempted a faint smile.

"Ninety-nine percent of everything," he gently teased, as she shut down her computer. He turned off the cd player and the electric fireplaces.

As they climbed the stairs, Gem felt butterflies rebelling.

He pulled back the duvet. "Take off your dressing gown and lie down," he ordered.

"You always take it off for me, Dark Lord," she replied. "Getting lazy are you?" she slipped her arms around his neck.

"Rein in, darling," he extricated himself from her hold. "You need a massage - the other one percent of everything."

"Is there anything you cannot do?" Gem murmured, sighing, relaxing beneath his expert manipulations.

"Unfortunately, I cannot help you, love," he replied regretfully.

"Through no fault of your own," she admitted, grateful not to be pacing and mentally sorting.

"And no fault on your part, I am sure," he tried to comfort her. "Now hush, my sweet. Relax."

The words of endearment didn't irritate her now. Even if he didn't mean them, the words were still pleasant. And she desperately wanted them to be sincere. For the first time since she had met him - could the words please be sincere?

Gem heard the long case clock in the main hall strike five times.

Chapter Thirty-One

Gem opened her eyes. Seven o'clock. She heard the clock in the main hall strike seven times. Blast! She longed to sleep another hour or two. But her brain would not permit it.

"How lovely it would be to be able to sleep when I wished to sleep, and for as long as I wished," she murmured.

"I can't help you with that, sweetheart," Wyatt murmured, stroking her stomach. "Hmmm. What have we here? A bit of a change."

"Stop that!" Gem blushed and pushed his hand away.

"I hope you never stop blushing. It is so becoming on you."

"Stop teasing! I've never been in this situation before," Gem frowned.

"Nor have I. Two novices for parents. Poor child," Wyatt concurred. "We'll read a book together. Something on the order of Parenthood for Dummies - or - Motherhood For Those Who Frequently Blush When Embarrassed."

Gem slipped away from him and reached for her dressing gown. "Shower!" she declared.

"Not yet, my dear," he chuckled. "I am taking you up on the offer you made two hours ago. And I am not - repeat - not lazy."

"The massage was brilliant," Gem stroked his brow. "You are a man of many hidden talents. Where ever did you learn -"

Wyatt took her hand, turning it over to kiss her palm. "I am not going to ask you questions, sweetheart, and you shall not ask me any," he said firmly.

"I don't have that sort of past!" she protested.

"And it's too late now to have one," Wyatt teased.

A long while later, Gem sighed, nestling in his arms. "Mrs M must be fuming over cold breakfasts."

"I texted her not to come to the Hall today," Wyatt replied.

"When did you?" Gem asked, surprised.

"After you fell asleep. I'll prepare breakfast for you. Baby must be nourished."

Gem frowned. Too many thoughts began surfacing in her mind. Too many thoughts threatened to rampage.

Wyatt fell silent absorbing the emotions slowly coursing through his body. As rage dissipated – compassion - an emotion he hadn't felt for months - began to emerge. Compassion had appeared at one time or another the past few months, but he had managed to suppress it. Now it was fully released and was becoming extremely painful.

The Game was Over. Well and truly Over. He confirmed that in his own mind. But there were too many unknowns to be explained before he could let down his guard. He had to trust Gem if he was ever going to learn of her secret world.

He couldn't decide their futures and that of their child if he didn't know exactly the world in which she truly existed. Her true nature might have been of the Jane Austen world at one time, but other catalysts influencing the world she had grown into were far from the scope of a 'genteel, gracious society'.

He realized that Gem was fighting for emotional survival. In her secret world, Wyatt doubted that a Mr Darcy existed.

He fought an overwhelming urge to protect her from the world. She couldn't fight whatever demon she had to battle if he wrapped her in cotton wool. He could only assist her by stepping back, by letting her battle as she could on her own, by supporting her when he could, when she needed him to do so. But she needed to be able to trust him. She needed to believe that she could trust him.

"Do you still hate me?" Wyatt asked softly, his heart skipping a beat, as he waited for a reply. Did he actually want to hear her answer?

His query astonished her. She was confused by his reason for asking the question. Who was asking the query? Dr Jekyll? - No; she hadn't really seen him for a matter of weeks, but she had no doubt that he still existed. Mr Hyde? No. He was simply a milder, less aggressive persona of Dr Jekyll. And neither of them was the man within whose arms she lay. And this man was not the one who had beguiled her in August. This man had to be - could he be - the actual Wyatt Grantham? The man who had rushed to Barcelona to hold James in his arms as he lay dying?

Was there one of any of Wyatt's personas whom she could trust? If there was, it would be this Wyatt. There was that 'something' different in his eyes. - A touch of his soul perhaps? That would be a marvel since the other personas had not possessed a soul - at least as far as she was concerned.

But trust wasn't the question. Hatred was. It was a very fierce word. Gem had hated him that first night at Marigold Cottage. She had hated him for deceiving her. He had tricked her, then crushed the love she had felt for him, had wanted to give to him.

And she loved him. Again.

Still there was resentment, anger. However, she did not feel the hatred she had felt when she had first learned of his deceitful Games.

"Just around the edged, perhaps," she said truthfully. "But you still hate me." She steeled herself for verbal backlash at which he was so accomplished. And what Game was this? she sighed inwardly. Oh how adept he was at ruining a decent moment.

"I never hated you, Gem," Wyatt said quietly.

"Perhaps loathe is a better choice of words then," she nodded. "You still loathe me."

Wyatt faced his own truths. "Yes. But just a bit around the edges," he admitted. "Add to list of goals for today - work on edges."

"Yes," Gem agreed to that goal. She was no longer going to think about his Games.

"What else is on your list for today?" he queried.

"Visit the IWM," she replied without thinking. What brought that idea to mind?

"Again?" However he did not press for a reason.

"History fascinates me. Walking through the IWM inspires me. And perhaps a walk along the Thames."

"You are a great walker!"

"Walking relaxes me."

"I relax you," he countered.

"Indeed you do," Gem nodded firmly.

"I'm going to relax you now."

"Yes, oh Dark Lord!" she said commandingly.

"You are a very demanding woman," he growled. "Breakfast will be brunch. May I escort you to the IWM?"

"When I am relaxed," she replied, as he gently shifted Miss Molly off the bed.

There wasn't any harm in Wyatt accompanying her to the museum. She had no idea why the thought of the visit had come to her mind. She hadn't been there in weeks, but her previous visits hadn't produced any information for resolving the plight of the Pilos.

I'm still trying, Gemmy, she sent the silent message into the atmosphere.

Wyatt broke into her thoughts. "I don't know what your search involves, Gem, but may I say - without offending - that it doesn't seem to be progressing."

Not offending, but discouraging. "No," she admitted with a sigh.

"And having no information, I can only wonder if you are searching logically or at random," Wyatt said thoughtfully. "At times - when one is working to resolve an issue, information flows in randomly. One might be compelled then to review information randomly."

Gem was wary about the reason for his remarks. Was he fishing or merely offering advice?

"You are overwhelmed," he observed, his tone matter-of-fact.

"Yes," she admitted.

"Are the flashbacks also coming at random?" he glanced at her, then returned his gaze to the road ahead.

"Flashbacks?" Gem said cautiously.

"There's no point in denying them, Gem. I know when they occur," he said firmly.

"How?" she demanded in surprise.

"I see it in your eyes, my dear," he reached over to give her hand a squeeze. "I admit it took me awhile to recognize them, but I do know them now. So we will accept the fact that you have flashbacks, shall we?" he requested.

Gem grudgingly agreed. "Yes." Prying, she decided, but since they were in the Jag she could hardly ignore the conversation and walk away from him as she could have done at the Hall.

"Very well," Wyatt continued. "Do you have substantial information to reach a conclusion or are you still seeking information?"

Gem reflected on the query to such a length that Wyatt was beginning to wonder if she had decided not to continue their chat.

"I believe I am close," she said pondering the query, "I have a great deal of information - if not all of it. Now I wonder if there is something I missed. I simply cannot solve the puzzle."

"Go with your first impulse, yes or no," Wyatt directed.

"Yes. I have all the information," she said firmly. "But I can't SEE it."

"Is it being obscured by the amount of information?" he suggested. "Take what you have, sort through it and find Square One, capital S capital O. Sort again until you have Square Two. Logical progression. Set your squares, filter information as to vital or superfluous information. Set aside, but do NOT completely discard information. Then filter information to possible or improbable, true or false. If is possible, is it true. If so, what is the next logical progression."

Gem nodded. It certainly was worth a try. "But what if I reach - Square Four - Capital S Capital F," she offered the slightest tease, "and I can't find the fifth square?"

"Then there is perhaps additional information to gather and sort after Square Three."

He turned the Jag into the car park and disengaged the engine.

"I realize now why you are so successful in business," Gem said.

"I can't honestly take all the credit for my success. I do not work alone. And I inherited a very large, very stable company."

Gem nodded. "Excellent employees. Let them use their expertise and follow their passion." He had suggested such remarks in the past. She thought of Harry and Mrs Brown, allowing their staff to do their jobs - such as Paul Andriani - they let him soar.

"We have arrived, my dear," Wyatt caught her attention, and took her hand. "May I request a favour, Gem?"

"You want me to drive the Jag back to Ticking Bottom?" she queried lightly.

Wyatt cringed at the suggestion, then conceded with a nod. "You may if you wish, but I shall have to wear a blindfold."

"You'll also have to be anaesthetised," she laughed. "Would three pints do?"

"Double that," he grimaced.

"The favour," she prompted, growing serious, and very uneasy.

"Okay," Wyatt also grew serious. "I'll do whatever I can to help you, Gem," he said quietly, "without asking questions, I promise. But would you please promise in return not to lie to me again? If I make a false step into your private world, just state 'I can't' and we will move on. Please?"

The skin at the nape of her neck tingled, and she suddenly felt overwhelmed, yet again. His words would definitely suggest that he was trying to show her that HE trusted HER.

"Please?" he requested again.

"Yes," Gem hesitantly agreed. "I promise," she slowly exhaled.

"Do you realize that you're relaxing again, my dear?"

Gem nodded. "Yes," she admitted slowly. "I am." And she actually felt a bit less alone.

"Then on to the front - which ever war you choose today," Wyatt stepped from the Jag, walking around to assist her from the sports car. "Do you truly want to drive home?" he frowned.

"Drive your Jag? Not in a million years. And now you can relax," Gem laughed.

Wyatt laughed heartily. "You minx!" He slipped his arm around her waist. "However, I am certain Mr Critchley would deem you extremely competent."

"He would," she agreed "But he wouldn't let me drive his Silver Dawn. I already asked him," she laughed. "He said NEVER!"

"You charmed him," Wyatt observed as they reached the entrance to the IWM."

"No," Gem protested. "He's just a very nice man." We are very old friends!

"You still don't realize the affect you have on men," Wyatt shook his head.

"You are full of beans!" Gem laughed, completely enjoying his company. "And for that absurd remark, you must pay the bill for lunch!"

"We just had brunch," it was his turn to protest.

"Hot chocolate then, after the museum. And a pint for you."

"Agreed."

Inside the building, Wyatt gave her a quick kiss. "You are on your own, my love. Please don't charm any men here!" he crisply ordered.

Gem laughed again as he walked away, marvelling how much she could enjoy his company when he wasn't being the man who had raged at her at Marigold Cottage. She didn't expect to experience an epiphany at the museum; she was touching base of one of Wyatt's future squares. The Second World War, she simply knew, was involved.

Two hours later Gem caught up with Wyatt in Korea.

"I haven't been here for years," he admitted to her. "Thank you for suggesting this visit. Hot chocolate then?"

She nodded and they left the museum. He kept his promise and did not ask if the purpose of the visit was met. No probing, no queries, to Gem's relief. On this occasion he had been a man of his word. How long would he keep his promise? she wondered skeptically.

Their next destination was the White Rose and they did not rush their break, deciding to stay for lunch, and then it was a stroll along the Thames. No otters were sighted.

"The Jag is magnificent," Gem harkened back to her earlier tease. "A brilliant set of wheels! It was a lovely inheritance."

Wyatt nodded. "The Jag, Grantham Hall, Grantham Enterprises. The maintenance, the taxes, the entire load."

Gem quickly sobered. "Extraordinary responsibility."

"Mr M is a great help," Wyatt replied. He frowned, then continued his thoughts. "James inherited our mother's '52 Morgan."

"A Morgan! They're brilliant!"

"Indeed," Wyatt grinned. "I noticed you were quite taken with them at the car show."

Gem laughed. "I've always been taken with them." Then she quickly grew thoughtful. "He also inherited Marigold Cottage," she said softly, then felt dismayed that she had brought up the subject. It had been such a pleasant day and now memories would likely dredge up Dr Jekyll who would rail at her for weeks. "I'm sorry - I shouldn't have mentioned that." She turned to stare at the river.

"Yes, he did," Wyatt nodded, and scowled, and Gem waited for caustic words. But they did not come. "That was dastardly of me," he admitted. "I'm astonished, I must say, that the edges don't permeate all the way to the core."

Gem put her hand on his. "Wyatt," she said quietly. "While I consider your actions, your Games, reprehensible, contemptible, in fact, I do understand. I can't explain anything - I desperately wish I could - and you won't believe me, but I truly understand the reasons for your actions."

Wyatt put his arm around her shoulder. "Words accepted. You can't. And I hope someday that you will be able to consider accepting my apology for my actions."

Gem silently gazed at the river. She already had enough to think about - the search, fighting his Games - she couldn't consider it at this time. "I shall consider it," she said softly. She would consider the issue when she was living in her own flat - when she was free again.

"Thank you," he murmured. "We have a great deal to sort out Gem. The Games were cruel - unethical. I do regret them."

Gem held her breath as he spoke. His voice sounded so sincere. Yet she had thought him to be so in August. He wanted her to trust him, but she simply could not actually make that commitment.

Wyatt stared at the Thames. He had so much work ahead of him to try to redress his actions. "I asked Mr M to have the Morgan serviced. I have signed the Morgan and Marigold Cottage over to you. You will own both outright - no strings. Despite whatever happened between you and James, I believe he would have wanted you to have both. He loved you, Gem," Wyatt finished, his voice deathly quiet.

"No!" Gem gasped. "I couldn't accept either! Hopefully one day I can tell you why," she shook her head. Mrs Brown had given her permission to do so, but Gem was not ready to speak to anyone outside the Agency about what had happened. She had no evidence to show that Gemmy had ever existed. There was no evidence of the Pilos or of any of the murders. Wyatt didn't want to hear any more lies, and he could only think of her explanation as the greatest lie ever told. It was all Agency and SEA Network hush. Mrs Brown was on leave and not available to support any words Gem spoke to Wyatt. And no one in the Agency had the authority or permission to back Gem's 'story' - except for Mrs Brown - who was on leave! Only Mrs Brown and Gem knew that Gem had been cleared to speak of the matter. Without Mrs Brown, Gem's head would be on the proverbial legal platter if she violated Agency law.

Wyatt leaned forward to look at Gem's eyes. Clouded. Haunted. "Gem," he said softly, attempting to draw her out of her secret world.

Gem shook herself. "What?"

He gave her a wistful smile. "As you say, Gem, but my decision stands," he said firmly. "The Morgan and the cottage are yours." He shook his head. "I can't believe I am saying this now, but I do trust you. I swear I don't know why, but I do. And perhaps one day you might begin again to trust me. But to be honest, I won't hold my breath on that possibility."

Gem nodded. She listened with an open heart, but she would not consider trusting him. – Yet.

"Hot chocolate?" he queried.

"Yes," she quickly agreed.

They settled by a blazing fire in a cosy pub.

"Now what precisely," he began, stretching his long legs before the fire, "does Mrs M require this year to have a happy old fashioned Christmas at the Hall?"

Gem splashed her beverage in surprise at his query. "Well, she mentioned Christmas trees - plural."

"Great room, living room, dining room," Wyatt nodded. "My mother had a penchant for lavishly trimmed trees. Next?"

"Banks of poinsettia's and trumpet flowers, pine boughs." Gem's brows knitted as she recalled the conversation. "Decorating the Hall by day, baking at night."

"Sumptuous aromas, hams, turkeys, cakes, pies, biscuits, mulled wine, one hundred proof eggnog," Wyatt chuckled.

"That sort of thing," Gem agreed.

"The Hall Holiday Buffet for the locals, Sunday prior to Christmas Day," Wyatt nodded. "I scheduled the T.B. holiday parties at the Crow in lieu of the Hall gala," Wyatt explained, "after the plane crash. James was in hospital in Geneva, then London. I rarely made the drive to T.B. during that time. I moved to the London flat to be near James, then to keep him on a short lead when he fell to his addictions. The locals weren't cheated of their holiday treat, and to be honest, I hadn't thought of the Hall parties until you reminded me of them."

"I haven't had a chance to speak to Mrs M, but I know she won't mind not having a Hall party this year," Gem assured him. "She may be a bit disappointed, but she won't fuss."

"Hmm," Wyatt pondered her words. "It's not wise to disappoint the head of the household," he said with a frown.

"You are head of the household," Gem protested.

"Don't you believe it," Wyatt chuckled. "I hold the power at GEI, but Mrs M holds the power at the Hall. You greet her at breakfast on Monday morning, and she will inform you that she has already selected a half dozen invitations for you to choose from for the party. And she has a list of all the proper names of every resident in T.B. The invitations shall be engraved - probably in gold lettering - she prefers that to silver - and the envelopes will be addressed in fine script by the engraver's wife in Crispin."

"No!" Gem gasped in astonishment.

"Indeed," Wyatt countered. "The butcher will already have the order for three hams, two turkeys, and the finest roast beef to which he has access."

"The party will cost you a small fortune," Gem said breathlessly.

"Mrs M will manage at a pittance compared to a caterer's bid. And you needn't worry about baking all night. Mrs M will hire a girl from the village to assist her."

"But you don't want a party this year," Gem protested yet again.

"We have no choice now," Wyatt shook his head. "Mrs M has her mind set and there it is. I'll make it clear to her that you are not up to the effort, so she won't take time from your work."

"Poor you," Gem said sympathetically, patting his arm. "But won't the locals be disappointed that the party won't be at the Crow?"

"I shouldn't think so. There's more room at the Hall. I'll ask Mike Morgan to hire music for us. He'll suggest his son, who will have a paying gig, and Mike will have a day off work, because Mr M will bartend."

"It's settled then?" Gem asked in amazement.

"It was settled the moment Mrs M started chattering to you about it," Wyatt laughed. "She has it in her mind to make the holidays sparkle for you, Gem. Let her," he suggested. "She wants you to see the sparkle."

"I don't need or want sparkle," Gem shook her head.

"You shall have it all the same. I'll inform Ora that you will need something to wear - comfortable, a bit less than semi-formal. Arrange the fittings with her, will you please?"

Gem sighed and nodded. The holidays were going to be extremely difficult this year!

Gem sipped the hot chocolate, listened to the cd and reflected on the day.

The day had been wonderful. Lord! she was in love with him! Just hearing his voice, gazing into his smashing eyes, watching him smile. She was a puddle of fool drool.

She did love him! For some reason - known only to him - he had decided to trust her. That was a very poor decision on his part. First he had thought that she - as Gemmy - had caused James's death. He had reacted viciously to that concept. She couldn't imagine how he would react when he learned that she AND Gemmy had devastated James. One sister hurting James was bad enough - but two! The episode at Marigold Cottage had been hideous. The next time she had to 'chat' with Wyatt about James - and this time tell him the truth - he would be in a rage incomparable to the one he experienced at Marigold Cottage.

He had signed James's Morgan and the cottage over to her. Why? Why? Why? Another Game! He had admitted and apologized for his cruelty in trapping her in his Games. Then why play yet another Game?

She had had enough. No Games. No thinking about them until she had found the Pilos. She wasn't going to think about trusting Wyatt - or of being in love with him until she could actually have logical, coherent thoughts of the subjects. Yes, the end of all Games! She was only going to focus on Gemmy and the Pilos!

She filled her mug with hot chocolate and pushed the start button on the cd player.

Square One: But what was the first square? The night the Pilos was lost? The three submarines that were listed as lost in January 1945, in the South China Sea? The pillaging by the Nazis in war torn Europe?

Square One: The pillaging of Europe.

Square Two: Odessa and U-1408.

U-1408 was supposition, but would remain as the second square.

I'm wagering on agents - i.e. spies, and other evacuated Nazi personnel - SS officers filtering out of Germany with as much pillaged museum and privately owned art as could fit in a U-boat. The purpose - to trade on the Hong Kong black market to finance a future secret underground Nazi community in the event the Axis powers succumbed to the Allies.

Gem pulled out her mobile. Paul Andriani would forgive her for texting at this hour. She needed clear answers and Mrs Brown had accepted Gem's theories, but had never confirmed them as a likely possibility. However, if Mrs Brown hadn't been able to refer the queries to the master spy, it would have been difficult to confirm to Gem. She wanted a Yes or No confirmation and worded her question accordingly.

'Does Odessa - as a Nazi community exist in Hong Kong?'

She didn't expect a reply until the sun had risen. She and Mr Cawley were the only Agency staff awake at this hour.

She continued sorting the information, or information she had surmised from the basics she had read in the various books of the War in SEA.

U-1408 had likely been at the Singapore docks on a government mission - or for repairs - in mid-December 1944. The U-boat probably continued on, docking at Hong Kong - it was logical that it had stopped for supplies since U-boats did not have a great amount of storage space -then had continued on to destination unknown. The Coventry and Seahawk were reported missing first week of January 1945.

Gem, decided U-1408 had docked in Hong Kong by the last week of December1944, to discharge Odessa officers and art, and had returned to sea and to a fatal, unexpected rendezvous with the Coventry and the Seahawk. It was only logical that U-1408 would have sent a coded message to Berlin stating that the 'cargo' had been delivered.

Ping

'I believe Nazi. Likely Odessa. Never able to confirm Axis underground network HK. Buried too deep. I believe it flourishes in HK and SEA. Gut feeling DEFINITELY!'

'Possible skinhead connection?'

'Likely. Could never confirm.'

'Thank you. Sorry to wake you.'

'Wasn't asleep. Watching telly. Haven't been able to do so in yrs.'

'Enjoying your new life?'

'Indeed. But I miss confessions.'

'Another step down?'

'Probably free fall now. You holding up?'

'For now.'

'Good. Here if you need me. Ciao!'

'Ciao!'

Confirmation enough for her!

Gem filled her mug, pushed the start button, and wrote notes on a sheet of paper.

Square Three: had to be Geneva

Square Four: 29/30 May - the Pilos

Square Five: Mr Denton's NOT accidental death
Square Six: the murders of the SEA couriers and agents (counter)
Square Seven: Harry goes underground
Square Eight: Paul Andriani 'disappeared'
That was all she had. Possible, improbable, true, Wyatt had stated.

One: true - Europe was pillaged. Two: possible and very likely - Paul Andriani confirmed gut feeling. Three: Gemmy was there so it was true, and the reason why was still a mystery. Four: true- the Pilos was airborne and went missing. Five: she felt in her heart that Mr Denton was murdered. Six: murders confirmed. Seven: true. Eight; true.

Nazis, skinheads. She imagined their networks were as efficient and subtle as the Agency and the SEA Networks. Somehow the Nazi network had learned that the U-1408 had been found and did not want it recovered or at the very least searched. But Gem couldn't believe that any water-tight containers bearing files or other information would have survived sixty plus years in the U-boat.

All files of U-1408 were missing, most likely destroyed when the submarine disappeared. The only surviving references to U-1408 would be codes. In a massive volume of undeciphered codes. The book her father had had.

She pulled out her mobile again. Mr Cawley was awake.

'Who has the massive WWII German code book my dad was deciphering?'

'Unsure. Will send query to warehouse.'

'Thanks! Put query to Mrs Brown months back of print backup dad sent to Harry re: codes dad had deciphered. Who has the print backup?'

'Will check.'

Gem cleared her messages, filled her mug, pushed the start button, and paced. She hadn't thought of the codes in weeks. She was certainly failing at her task. Why hadn't Mrs Brown ever replied to her query? Gem had made the query in August? Wasn't it August?

It was a full thirty minutes of pacing before she had a reply.

Ping

'Checked Mrs B's files. Query put to Harry in August - can't read date. No response noted. Checked Harry's files. No print backup.'

'Dad would have sent backup.'

'I have no answer for you.'

'Obviously. Who processes Harry's correspondence while he is away?'

'First Mrs Brown. Now I do.'

'Mrs Brown's files?'

'No backup print.'

'I don't understand.'

'Will request warehouse check your dad's files.'

'Thank you!'

'Information for me, Gem?'

'Not at this time.'

'Don't continue treading water.'

'I'm not!'

'Very well. Goodnight.'

'Goodnight!'

Mr Cawley was not pleased, but she could not give what she did not have! Her head began to ache. She glanced over to Mrs Mac, curled up in a tight ball, sleeping peacefully by Gem's computer. She would love to go to sleep. But since she couldn't, she would accept the second best thing. She read her notes. Cut them in small squares and shredded the paper. Only four o'clock, but she shut down her office and went to bed.

Wyatt stirred as she climbed in beside him. He glanced at his watch. "You're early," he murmured.

"Hold me, please," she whispered.

"Forever, darling," he murmured, startled by his own words. He sincerely meant them. And again he was startled by that knowledge. He had put up so many defences against her, but she had destroyed each one in its turn. No wonder she had so easily captivated James! And knowing what she was, and keeping his guard up against her, he himself had been lost to her! Wasn't there something about loving well, but not wisely? Ouch! And Damn!

It would be a full hour before she could sleep. "Frustrating hours?" He snuggled her closely against his body.

"Pegged squares. Information is missing. My brain is so full it aches," she moaned, "but I can't stop thinking."

"I'd sing you a lullaby, but I can't sing a note," Wyatt soothed.

"I thought you were capable of doing absolutely everything," Gem teased lightly.

"Don't believe that, sweetheart, or you will become greatly disappointed with me - if you aren't already. Or shall I say disenchanted with me," he replied. "But then that has already happened, hasn't it." It was not a question.

Gem rubbed her cheek against his breast, and contemplated his remarks. "I must agree that I no longer believe you to be the perfect man, as I did when we met," she admitted.

"Timber - shining knight falling off white steed. Ouch. And good. I am not, nor have I ever been perfect," he admitted sincerely.

"You dress well," Gem conceded.

"My tailor thanks you. I thank you," Wyatt chuckled.

"You are a competent driver."

"Only competent?" he growled

"Adequate then," she giggled. "You speed too often."

"I'll concede the speed habit."

"Regarding butterfly gathering -"

"Since you have no previous experience on that subject, I doubt you to be a decent judge of the matter," he said dryly.

"I should be allowed to voice an opinion," Gem insisted.

"Perhaps you need a current demonstration before you make your decision," he growled.

"Perhaps I do," Gem giggled again.

And awhile later Gem murmured her decision, "Acceptable."

"What?" Wyatt demanded.

"As you say, I am lacking experience to voice a decent judgment," she laughed. "If it will soothe your ego, I shall say perfectly adequate."

"Go to sleep," he chuckled. "We'll have words later, sweetheart," he added, as the long case clock struck five chimes.

Sunday was the same as Saturday. Miss Molly was home and required long walks and runs in the fields and meadows. Both her human units accompanied her on the excursions. Breakfasts were contributed by Wyatt, lunches and dinners were served at the Crow, along with Rock-a-Billy music both nights, drawing a full house of customers. Wyatt read in the library while Gem prowled the house contemplating squares and growing more frustrated with absolutely no progress on her search.

The dark hours, early Sunday morning, dragged endlessly until Gem was ready to pull out her hair in frustration. Mr Cawley had no information for Gem, and there had not been a response from the warehouse regarding Gerald Forrester's backup print.

Gem felt the entire process of the search was being blocked by the absences of Harry and Mrs Brown. Mr Cawley continued to press Gem for information which she did not have in her brain.

By early Sunday afternoon, Gem desperately needed a break from concentrating on complete futility. She went to the library to spirit Wyatt away from his reports but discovered the room to be vacant. She looked in the study, den, and sitting room, but did not find him.

Miss Molly's toenails clicking on the floor in the upstairs hall alerted Gem, and she found Wyatt in James's room packing his brother's possessions into boxes.

Wyatt looked up to see her staring at him, her expression one of stony silence.

"What?"

"I thought we weren't going to discuss baby subjects until after the New Year," she said abruptly.

"We shall not," Wyatt nodded in agreement. "We are not discussing. I am merely packing to clear the room," he said smoothly.

"You're splitting hairs," Gem said quietly.

"We do not need to chat about this, my dear. It is the only logical decision. I do not need your input or your assistance for this project. You have your work to do. I'll manage this."

Gem miserably shook her head. "It's all my fault," she murmured.

"That's absurd, Gem," Wyatt said firmly. "Yours was not an immaculate conception - remember? I was most definitely there. Our - I stress the word 'our' - baby will require a nursery. End of discussion regarding this room," his voice was still firm. "Now what do you require - butterflies need netting, or did you just miss me?" he teased.

"A walk?" Gem lifted her hands helplessly.

"We had a morning walk with Miss Molly, and we walked to and from the Crow for lunch just a short time ago," he reminded her. "Perhaps a drive - a change of scene," he suggested.

Molly disappeared from the room and reappeared almost immediately, lead in her mouth.

"Ahuh," Wyatt chuckled. "Shall we take Molly for a drive in the country?"

The notion struck Gem as oddly funny. "No speeding," Gem laughed.

"No doubt I shall. You remind me to slow," Wyatt chuckled. "And later, I'll corral butterflies and you can tell me again that I'm perfect," he teased, winking at her.

"Power and ego," Gem grinned. "Must go hand in hand, eh?"

"Ouch! Sass!"

"Banter" Gem sighed, and smiled. She would forget the Pilos for a few hours. Perhaps if her brain was refreshed, squares would all become true, and all Keys would slip. It must have been days since any of the Keys had slipped.

Gem's eyes widened as she sipped the hot chocolate. Mint hot chocolate. Lovely! A very thoughtful surprise from Wyatt! She wasn't going to dwell on why he was being so kind. Thank him and move on. She would sort out why's when her other questions were answered.

She pulled out her mobile to put queries to Mr Cawley.

'Code book found?'

'Not at warehouse.'

'Dad's files warehouse?'

'No files on codes.'

'Blast!'

'Indeed.'

'Mr Denton's possessions at warehouse?'

'Yes. Daft question.'

'Rude reply. Could warehouse staff check Mr Denton's possessions for print of deciphered codes?'

'Denton was not a cryptographer.'

'I realize that.'

'Very well. I will make request.'

'Mrs Brown available?'

'No.'

'Harry? Blank?'

'???'

'When will Mrs Brown be available?'

'???. What news have you for me?'

'Not a word.'

'Get back to work. Goodnight.'

'Not done yet. Who of Agency staff has access to warehouse other than warehouse staff?'

'All Agency Directors.'

'Anyone else?'

'Did I suggest anyone else?'

'No.'

'There is your answer. Goodnight again!'

'Goodnight!'

He certainly was grumpy!

She was drifting away from the squares, but she still needed information. She felt as if someone was purposely blocking her from obtaining the necessary information to find the Pilos. She had asked Mrs Brown about the backup print in August. Then Mrs Brown and Harry had gone on 'holiday', and the SEA Network had gone into crisis. It was actually not surprising that Mrs Brown had not received an answer from Harry about Gem's request. Mrs Brown had otherwise answered Gem's queries when she had the information. Mr Cawley had answered her queries when he had information. Mr Choate and Paul Andriani had answered her questions, save for Mr Choate and Auntie Jane's activities for a number of years. But still - Gem felt she was being blocked. Evidence was perhaps to the contrary. Just a feeling then.

Gem had no idea how to proceed other than to let her thoughts roam randomly to clear her mind. She didn't sort, she simply let thoughts float.

Ping

She jumped, not expecting another text message from Mr Cawley. It was from Paul Andriani!

'How goes the night?'

'Long!'

'Making progress?'

'No!'

'It will come.'

'Do you ever sleep?'

'In fits and starts. Have for years. Regular life is an adjustment.'

'Indeed!'

'Any way I can help?'

'Not yet. Thanks for asking.'

'Anything I can do to help, I will! Ciao!'

'Thanks! Ciao!'

Mr Cawley had once brought cheer to the dark hours. Now Paul Andriani was providing the cheer. What a dear man! Her spirits were buoyed, but still she made no progress.

She longed to go to bed, but she didn't want to disturb Wyatt. He had meetings later that morning. And as much as she wanted him to comfort her, she needed just as much not to depend on the comfort he offered - and so brilliantly - provided. Once she had found Gemmy and the Pilos, Wyatt would no longer want to offer or provide comfort. She would be alone again, just when she was finally not feeling completely alone.

Gem finished the hot chocolate, and switched off everything in the office that required to be switched off. She wandered slowly along the hall, stopping to look into the great room which was faintly lit by the hall lights. She could imagine a huge Christmas tree, gloriously trimmed, fairy lights twinkling in the depths of the boughs, glowing magically in the darkened room. Her family had always had a tree at Christmas. And if Mrs M got her way there would be three trees at Grantham Hall this year. Gem actually looked forward to helping Mrs M trim the trees - certainly Wyatt wouldn't be interested in doing so - he had made that very plain. And she certainly did not blame him for stepping back from the holiday preparations.

Mrs Mac had followed her from the office and wreathed her slim body around Gem's legs. Kitty! Gem exhaled sharply, grimacing, imagining Mrs Mac scaling the tree trunk and possibly felling the tree as it would be done in the woods. Best put that concern to Wyatt and the M's, she decided.

Wyatt awakened to take her in his arms, kiss her forehead as she laid her head on his shoulder, and murmur, "Sleep, my dear."

Gem closed her eyes as the clock chimed five. And she slept.

It seemed like weeks since Gem had stopped at Ora and Eda's Shop. Ora had received a message from Wyatt Sunday morning, stating that Gem needed an outfit for the Hall Holiday party. Ora already had three designs for Gem's consideration. Since Gem liked all the designs she selected the second one and left the fabric and colour choice to Ora to decide. Gem didn't need any clothes, but she wandered the shop, looking at items that had arrived since her last visit. Ora had three new warm dressing gowns and matching slippers ready for her to take with her. Eda gave her a surprised look as Gem pulled her credit card from her shoulder bag.

"You have an account here," the shop partner advised her. "Bills are sent to Mr Macinski."

"Yes, of course," Gem forced a smile. High-handed of Wyatt, but then he always was where money was concerned.

Ms Ames came down the stairs from the office on the first floor, invoices in hand and a query for Eda; and upon seeing Gem she gave her a big smile and a cheery wave. Gem returned both, and continued looking around the shop. She was amazed to realize how many people she had met in London and Ticking Bottom since she had married Wyatt. Perhaps it wasn't a lot of people by someone else's count, but it was a lot to her.

Ms Ames received the needed response from Eda and returned to the office. GEI staff were friendly but didn't waste time away from their work.

As Gem was signing the account slip for her purchases a man wearing a remarkably ordinary business suit and hat entered the store. Gem glanced at him, then turned to examine a display of earrings to the left of the counter. Paul Andriani.

"Good morning, Mr Harper," Eda warmly greeted the man. "Ms Ames is waiting for you in the office."

Mr Harper made a quick remark to Eda and climbed the stairs to the first floor.

"It's busy here this morning," Gem smiled at Eda as three customers entered the shop.

"It is," Eda grinned. "Ms Ames never seems to stop for a moment. Mr Harper is going to install a new security system in the shop. Mr Grantham suggested we use Mr Harper's company, although I don't believe he owns the security company. He's a manager I believe."

"Indeed," Gem murmured, and after a few more pleasantries she left the shop. She texted Mr Choate for tea and coffee.

"Is T.O. bugging the shop for Agency use?" she bluntly asked her personal security guard as they sat at a table in the corner tea shop.

"Certainly not," Choate replied, frowning. "The shop needs a new system, and Ms Ames stated the necessity in her weekly report to Mr Grantham. It was he who suggested the shop use T.O. We do not 'bug' - as you say - private businesses - unless we have clear evidence for doing so. Mr Grantham was impressed with T.O.'s expeditious solution to the Manton incident, and thus made the recommendation to Ms Ames. YOU were the one who insisted Mr Grantham call T.O. - if YOU recall. And we need money coming into T.O. because we do not operate at taxpayers' expense."

"Except for your salary," Gem murmured.

"No, indeed. T.O. pays my salary," Choate replied.

"Must be very confusing since you are Agency staff," Gem frowned.

"It takes a bit of mental juggling," Choate agreed. "But then the Agency exists as a department of government statistics. Which you would notice from your pay-packet if it wasn't directed via computer to your bank instead of coming on paper."

"Okay," Gem nodded. "I was just curious."

"I understand your concern, Gem, but I assure you T.O.'s business dealings with GEI are strictly ethical. Now if you are finished with your tea, where next?"

"I don't know," she sighed. "I'm not ready to go back to the Hall, but I do not need to shop."

"IWM?"

"I was there last week."

"Howard's Bookshop?"

Gem thought of the suggestion and then agreed. Shopping was one matter, bookshops were her passion.

"And the photo shop. I dropped off film quite a while ago - and forgot it," Gem grimaced at her error.

"Right then."

"Isn't it a bit risky to have Mr Harper out of the office? Someone might recognize him," Gem suggested.

"You are used to recognizing him in various personas because of practise in doing so. In his previous world J.S. is presumed dead - murdered in a drug deal in SEA," Choate whispered at they left the tea shop.

"Ah, the details come."

"And are quickly forgotten," Choate replied.

"Naturally," she pursed her lips. "The ordinary man. He's wearing blue contact lenses, his eyebrows are a different shape. Did he get his ears tucked?"

"Just a bit."

"His nose it slightly narrower. And the glasses."

"He was always disappointed with his nose. Not bad detailing for a glance," Choate observed.

"Thank you," Gem smiled to herself.

"However, would you have made him had you not known he was in London? That is the question?"

Gem thought seriously as she considered the query. "I don't think I would," she concluded. "His voice is different. Less generic."

"The voice and accent God gave him."

"I especially wouldn't recognize him if I thought he was dead," Gem offered. "Hiding in plain sight in a large city."

"He's not hiding, Gem."

"Is Harry following suit?" she wondered.

"Possibly," Choate replied. "We may never know - especially if you are correct that he won't be returning to us."

"Would Mrs Brown know?"

"I believe so. Agents who disappear for self-preservation never sign Agency separation forms. It's possible Harry has been in contact with Mrs Brown. It's wait and see."

"Mr Cawley is completely in charge of the Agency," Gem thought aloud. "You are covering his job when you aren't with me. When will Mr Cawley be off the night shift?"

"Mrs Brown will return at the end of this month - supposedly. An agent is coming out of 'retirement' to train for Cawley's position. She is currently in the process of relocating from Florence. Mr Harper has cleared two applicants for courier training and another to train as assistant to Gordon White - he's burning out. The past six months have been very difficult for him - not only because of Gemmy, your parents, and Portermann, but also Denton. White and Denton had known each other since university days. White agrees with you that Denton was murdered, and he has told the investigators they are incompetent. I believe he's been investigating on his own since Denton's accident."

That information was a comfort to Gem. Mr White was verifying her opinion! "Perhaps I should talk to him," she mused.

"Don't, Gem," Choate quietly warned. "White is so very close to the edge. Talking to you might push him over. It took him weeks to be able to keep his composure after he saw you at the Agency in July - the day you ended your courier position. Wait until his assistant is trained in. The Agency simply cannot afford to lose another Director at this time."

"Mr White won't like having an assistant," Gem said, frowning.

"He will have no choice in the matter."

"Harsh," Gem murmured.

"Not at all. He insists on working 24/7. Once he has an assistant, Mrs Brown can suggest White concentrate solely on writing computer programs for the Agency, and investigating Denton's death. The assistant can manage the Agency computer lab, which will enable White to have more flexibility in his work hours. Harry and Mrs Brown used to cover many of White's non-vital responsibilities."

"Okay," Gem hesitated again, deciding she didn't really need to chat with Mr White about Mr Denton, since she already had the late agent on her list of murder victims. And she didn't want to add to Mr White's emotional burdens.

She browsed at Howard's Bookshop after a quick stop for her photos. Mr Choate wandered the bookshop, chatting with the shopkeeper and continually reading the room. Gem had thought to look for a book to read to Wyatt as he had read of Etruscans to her, but nothing caught her attention.

She couldn't push the Agency from her mind. And poor Mr White! And Harry and Mrs Brown also. They had all worked together for so many years, knew more about each other than their friends and relatives knew about them. And include Paul Andriani in that mix. Not, however, Mr Cawley, who hadn't been posted at any time to the Hong Kong embassy. Mr Choate was not included in the original group from the embassy. Who knew where he had been that caused his files to be sealed!

Gem redoubled her focus on the book shelves. Her brain was too tired to think. Christmas was coming, then there would be the nursery to sort. She had to tell Wyatt about the twins before that project began. Mr Cawley had threatened to end the search for the Pilos. She had to concentrate on Gemmy and bury her head in the sand on the other subjects. As Wyatt had said, Mrs M could handle the holidays.

Find a book, go back to Ticking Bottom, walk Miss Molly, Gem silently groaned. Wyatt was not available for lunch, but would bring Chinese for dinner as Mrs M was leaving early to pick up the invitations for Gem to choose for the engravers. Wyatt had been absolutely correct that Mrs M would be in party mode by this morning. Mr M had been charged with searching the woods behind the Hall for three trees of various sizes - of which his spouse would give final approval.

Gem felt her heart start racing as she recalled the housekeeper's current update at breakfast that morning of the ambitious holiday festivity plans. Mr Cawley would be hammering at her during the dark hours for information - for a solution she could not reach. She couldn't do this - not any of it. Gem couldn't catch her breath.

Choate grabbed her arm, pushing her down to a nearby chair.

"Drink this - all of it," he quietly ordered, forcing a cup of tea in her hand.

Gem nearly choked on the liquid heavily laced with sugar.

He leaned over her. "You're having a panic attack," he advised her. "Do you have them often?"

"Never," Gem shook her head.

"You were due one then," he replied, handing her another cup of the sugary tea.

"Please, don't tell Wyatt," she pleaded.

Choate hesitated before replying. "I won't - under one condition," he frowned.

"What's the condition?"

"Lunch at Charley's - on me," he said firmly.

"Deal," Gem gave him a grateful smile. Mrs M wasn't expecting her at the Hall for lunch.

It wasn't an Agency meeting, so civilian customers were at Charley's, but their host seated them in a quiet corner of the pub.

"Give over, Gem," Choate quietly ordered when their food arrived. "You're stressing out major again."

"The search. I'm not making any progress," she said dispiritedly.

"It will happen."

"Wyatt wants to begin work on the nursery in January. I can't tell him yet about the twins. I can't explain them."

"That's a month in the future. A lot can happen in a month."

"Mrs M wants to have a festive family Christmas at the Hall because this will be the first Christmas Wyatt has spent there in ten years. All the trimmings, a huge party for the locals, blah, blah, blah," Gem sighed. "It's Wyatt's first Christmas since his brother died, and I want the holidays to disappear."

Choate drew back, surprised at her remarks. "Why doesn't Grantham simply reject the holiday hoopla?"

"He did at first," Gem puzzled, "and seemed to change his mind. I think he decided Mrs M expects cheery holidays because it is our first Christmas as a married couple." Odd hearing Mr Choate use the word 'hoopla', she silently mused. "I don't know. It's all just too much." She frowned then had a pleasant thought. "You'll have a lovely Christmas this year," she murmured, smiling at her companion.

"First together in many years," he agreed, his voice barely above a whisper. "However, that is not my concern at the moment. You are. I know you won't stop working for a month. Perhaps you can convince Mr Grantham that you simply would rather have a quiet holiday season. Talk with him before Mrs Macinski's plans go forward."

"She's already full steam ahead," Gem sighed. "An old fashioned family Christmas. I don't want her to be disappointed."

Choate choked on his food and then laughed, but there was no humour in his voice. "You're stressing over holiday fuss to please the housekeeper? You ARE a push-over, Gem!"

"Good house managers are hard to come by," she said firmly.

"Not that hard," Choate scoffed. He shook his head. "I had hoped to be able to ease your burden, lessen your stress, but I don't see a way in which I can help."

"At least I can talk to you about all the hassles. And that is helpful. I know it will all sort out, one at a time. I just don't know in what order."

Gem felt a few degrees better by the time she returned to the Hall. She had been well-fed, and the chat with Mr Choate had lifted her spirits. Miss Molly met her at the kitchen door, lead in her mouth. Gem greeted Mrs M - who sat at the kitchen counter writing lists, then set her purchases in her office and acquiesced to the poochie's request.

They had reached the old stone bridge below the Hall when Gem realized a Key had slipped. It was still - Blast It- out of reach. But one had definitely slipped.

As she put away the items from the dress shop, Gem reflected back on her conversations of the morning in an attempt to recognize the Key that had slipped. The most logical thought would be Paul Andriani, but blue eyes, glasses, a narrower nose, ears tucked back, and differently shaped eye brows did not set bells clanging. She showered, washed and braided her hair, and retreated to her office to watch the international news. Turmoil in Egypt, Syria - that was constant - but SEA was still only simmering.

Gem curled up on Auntie Jane's settee with a book and a cup of tea, but her attention was drawn to Mrs Mac, sitting on the seat of the swivel chair, staring down at Miss Molly staring up at her. The height difference between the two had been greatly reduced, each very much within striking distance of the other.

Striking distance. An interesting term.

And a Key slipped.

Blast!

She wished she knew which Keys had slipped. There were still three. One down, three to go - week after week after week.

At dinner Wyatt inquired if she had had a pleasant day but he did not ask particulars other than of her opinion of Ora's designs for Gem's holiday outfits.

"She had three sketches, I selected one of them" Gem informed him, as Wyatt filled her plate with fried rice and egg foo young. "That's too much food, Wyatt," she protested.

"Eat what you want, my dear," Wyatt handed over the plate. "I told Ora to make all three of the designs."

"When? Why?" she demanded in surprise.

"This afternoon. You may change your mind when the outfit you selected is finished. Now you will have more choices," he replied. "Enjoy the flexibility, my dear. Did you have lunch?"

"Yes," she nodded. He did not ask further questions on that subject either.

"Have you found a book to read to me?" he teased.

Gem sighed. "I looked today at a bookshop but couldn't decide."

"No rush, sweetheart. We do have an excellent library here if you wish to peruse the stacks. I have reports to read this evening. You could look at the books and keep me company."

"You'll be reading - not much company for you there."

"I can look up and fill my eyes with your beauty," he countered.

"You are full of -"

"Chinese food," he finished for her, smiling.

"Just so," Gem laughed. "Okay. Your library," she agreed.

Your library. Still the problem with pronouns. "You realize, Gem, you can use the library any time you wish," he suggested.

"It's your office," she gave a shake of her head. "I don't want to intrude."

"Nonsense, there would be no intrusion."

Gem thought of the unused study and den. "Wyatt," she thought aloud, "Mrs M spends much time in the kitchen preparing menus, keeping the Hall budgets - perhaps she should have an office here," she suggested.

Wyatt stared at her. "I should have thought of that years ago!" he exclaimed. "I'll suggest it to her tomorrow. She'll be very pleased that you thought of it for her."

They did the washing up together, then took thermoses of tea and hot chocolate to the library. Gem whiled away two hours, studying each shelf of books, considering one then deciding against it, and selecting another then returning that one to the shelf.

She heard Wyatt chuckle and looked his way. He was watching her with obvious amusement.

"What?" she demanded.

Wyatt chuckled. "You will choose a dress in three minutes but spend hours looking for a book to read."

"It has to be the right book," Gem insisted.

"Sweetheart, I don't give a damn if it's a guide to London pubs. It's the time spent with you that is important to me," he smiled, freeing butterflies.

"You are full of -"

"Still Chinese food," he teased, standing and walking around the desk towardss her.

"I'll find a book," she assured him.

"Too late," he pulled her down on the sofa, "time to gather butterflies. I see it in your eyes."

Gem giggled. "I don't believe this sofa is conducive to gatherings - of the kind you mean, and you have reports to read," she reminded him.

He took the band from her braid and stroked his fingers through the plait to free her hair.

"You are very sexy with your hair crimped," he murmured.

"Reports."

"Done." He buried his fingers in her hair.

Mint hot chocolate and a plate of biscuits waited for Gem by her computer. She pushed the start button on the cd player and texted Mr Cawley.

'What is new?'

'No Harry, Mrs Brown still on leave. No Blank.'

'None of that is new.'

'What do you have for me?'

'Can't think of a single thing.'

'That is not new.'

'Sarcasm!'

'What did you expect? Champagne and roses?'

She ignored his last message.

'Reply from warehouse?'

'Not yet.'

'Why? Isn't there a list of Mr Denton's possessions?'

'Electrical snap. Computers at warehouse down. Entire neighbourhood down since early morning.'

'Blast!'

'Don't you listen to news?'

'I don't know the location of the warehouse.'

She had not heard of the electrical problem, but she took a convenient - but true - excuse.

'Should have reply in 24 hours.'

'Okay.'

'Get back to work. Time is wasting.'

'Goodnight!'

'Make it one, Gem!'

He never let up. She would have shared Mr Cawley's attitude with Mr Choate at lunch, but she couldn't complain of her supervisor to another Director. It just wasn't done. Mr Cawley was correct, after all; she was being paid to do a job - the end result of which meant more to her than anyone else at the Agency. No excuses! Do your job! But Mr Cawley's attitude could be a bit less harsh.

And Mr Choate never demanded information from her as did Mr Cawley. Every night for weeks he demanded information of her. Did he think she was hiding information from him? Well, she was withholding information from Mr Cawley regarding Paul Andriani. But she could not - would not - betray his confidence.

Thank heavens Wyatt was no longer aggravating her for information about James - or anything she couldn't explain to him.

Blast! She was so irritated with Mr Cawley she had neglected to clear her messages from her mobile.

She wandered the rooms of the Hall, sipping hot chocolate, but not moving beyond the sound of the cd player.

Christmas without Gemmy and their parents. No one needed anoraks at Christmas in Brisbane; it was sunglasses and sun cream; Christmas dinner was served by the pool; the tree was artificial but the family trimmed it every year - not just draped a tarp over it and rolled it into a storage room.

The dull pain in her heart had eased the past few weeks, but it returned now with renewed vengeance. She had no doubt Wyatt had a similar dull ache. Put on a cheery smile, keep your mouth shut, and suffer silently through the horrid holidays, she ordered herself.

The dark hours had been a refuge from Wyatt until the past few weeks. Now he was a refuge during the days from the dark hours.

Another Key had slipped.

And she just realized so. And this time is seemed so within her grasp. And try as she might she could not find a reference in her previous thoughts to give her a clue to the identity of the Key.

Gem put the details of the search from her mind and returned to her office to press the start button again. She listened carefully to every lyric of every song, wondering again how the people of the U.K. had found the tremendous strength and courage to survive the War years - and still have an indomitable spirit yet today. Gemmy and their parents had had courage, as had Mr Portermann - and the other victims in the SEA Network.

Wyatt stood watching her from just beyond the doorway. Her back was to him; she stood stock still, facing the roman shades. And as the next song began, she buried her face in her hands and slowly shook her head.

Wyatt walked to her, and, gently taking her in his arms, he swayed ever so slowly with the music.

I'll Be Seeing You - Wyatt listened to the lyrics, hearing Gem sigh as Vera Lynn's velvet voice caressed the heart rending words.

Gem melted against his body, resting her cheek against his shoulder, lost in the song and the memory of her parents, totally absorbed in each other - dancing to this song last Christmas Eve.

When the song ended, Gem clung to him. Wyatt held his breath, certain her thoughts were not of another man, but yet of memories of her past - memories that were crushing her heart.

Wyatt reached over and pressed the stop button on the cd player, then swept her up in his arms and silently carried her to bed.

As the long case clock in the main hall struck five chimes, Gem fell asleep in Wyatt's arms.

Wyatt did not sleep. She listened to the same cd every morning when she left their bed. Every morning the same songs. He had purchased nearly two dozen cds for her, which she did listen to during the day - yet every morning she listened to the Vera Lynn cd. And only that cd.

He had watched her listen to a half dozen songs just now, but it was that specific song that had wrenched her heart. I'll Be Seeing You. The words played over and over in his mind. He could not begin to fathom the memory chord the words struck within her mind. But whatever it was, it was as devastating to her, as losing James had been to him. He had searched for months for information on her, and had only found basic information. What the hell had happened to her?!

He stroked her hair as she slept, and she rubbed her cheek against his chest - and sighed in her sleep. His breath caught in his throat, and he tightened his arms around her. Whatever the hell had happened in the past, he would make damned sure that she wasn't ever hurt again.

Wyatt gently shook his head in amazement. He had first sought her out to destroy her. Now his only thought was to protect her.

Damn! How intentions change!

Chapter Thirty-Two

Gem slowly opened her eye, and watched Wyatt's chest rise and fall as he slept. She didn't move a muscle, not wishing to waken him. She loved that he had held her for those moments during the dark hours, during the song, as her father had held her mother. She hoped at one time Gemmy had shared the song with James. At least they were together now, and James knew what had happened to his beloved Gemmy. James knew - but Gem did not.

Yet for the first time in months, Gem truly believed she would have resolution to Gemmy and the Pilos. And hopefully the murders of Mr Denton and the SEA Network couriers and agents would be resolved at the same time.

Her thoughts were disturbed by Wyatt chuckling and she raised her head to look at him.

"What?" she asked curiously.

"Your eyelashes tickled when you blinked, my dear. Soft as butterfly wings," he teased.

"Well, since you mentioned them," she teased back with a smile, and then grew thoughtful. "Thank you for -" she shook her head looking for the words - "for the song," she said awkwardly.

"You are welcome, my dear," he kissed her forehead.

Gem smiled as she looked into his eyes, gentle and warm. And real.

And then the butterflies were gathered.

Mrs M was delighted with the suggestion of an office and after Wyatt left for London, she decided on the study, since it already had a desk. Gem helped her arrange the space, emptying drawer contents and books from the shelves into boxes, which they shifted to the den.

"New curtains, definitely," Gem said crisply, frowning at the drab brown fabric at the windows. "Or roman shades. A bright area rug," she grimaced with distaste at the brown square of carpet.

"It will suit me just fine for now," Mrs M said firmly.

"Nonsense!" Gem protested. "You insisted my office be finished for me, and I insist the same for you."

"Well," the house manager said doubtfully, but Gem would not let the matter drop.

"Road trip - London, shopping, lunch!" Gem declared. "I'll alert Mr Choate."

Gem discovered again that it was much more pleasurable to shop when someone else was making decisions. And it was easier to shop for curtains and rugs with Mrs M than it had been shopping with Wyatt for nursery paint and carpet.

She had suggested a different type desk but the housekeeper insisted she like the old walnut stained desk that had been in the office for years.

"Perhaps there are other desks in the attic," Gem suggested, knowing full well there were five of different periods amongst the 'rooms' of furniture.

"I've polished the one in the study for years," Mrs M replied. "It's an old friend."

"So be it," Gem relented.

Mrs M hadn't been to the White Cat before, so Gem took her there for lunch and two pints - hot chocolate for Gem - returning then to the Hall to hang the new curtains. Mr M would be over the following day to shift furniture so the new rug could be rolled out on the floor.

Mrs M had to leave early for her club meeting, but remembered before she left to give Gem the invitation samples for the Hall Holiday Party.

"Which do you think would be best?" Gem stared blankly at the styles, only one of which she liked: red, trimmed in green and gold bands, lettering in gold.

"The red," Mrs M suggested.

"Agreed," Gem breathed easily. "Check it off your list!"

Dinner was in the oven and Gem was at loose ends until Wyatt arrived at the Hall.

Mr M had taken Molly for a long walk in the morning, and the poochie was ready for her afternoon excursion. They turned left at the end of the drive. After ten minutes of walking, Gem released Molly for a solid twenty minute run. If they continued down the lane, around the curve and past the shops, following the cobblestone lane curving up across the old stone bridge, they should be foot and paw weary by the time Wyatt arrived at the Hall.

As they continued the walk Gem saw people here and there scattered across the distant fields, and as they waved she returned their greeting. It was a lovely walk and Gem felt stress fall away from her tense muscles and clouded mind.

She liked Ticking Bottom. It was the perfect English village, snuggled and wrapped in a lush forest. As the sun faded, lights began to glow in one window and then another in the cosy thatched cottages; smoke curled and drifted from chimney stacks. As she and Miss Molly walked past the shops, cheery faces appeared at the windows and the shop owners and assistants waved and gave her a friendly smile.

She hadn't known many of her family's neighbours in Brisbane - the houses were far apart in the country; she recognized her neighbours in the flat above and below hers in London, but knew them only to say a brief 'hello'.

She knew many of the locals in Ticking Bottom by name, from her visits to the Crow with Wyatt and the M's. And she knew quite a bit about the families from her chats with Mrs M over lunch at the Hall. Now when Mrs M mentioned that Mrs Webb's grandson had decided to leave the law to study architecture, Gem knew precisely that Mrs Webb was the tall, thin woman with the iron grey hair, who always wore pearls whether she was wearing a denim shirt while raking her lawn, or dressed in a sharp twin set and skirt for buffet Sunday at the Crow.

Gem waved to Mrs Hewes as the woman turned up the lane to cross over the rail tracks. Mrs Hewes had two sons in the Royal Air Force and she was bursting with pride at that fact.

And little Erin was getting her second tooth, her mother already looking forward to starting baby number two, but starting wouldn't be until March.

Gem caught up short as the names and faces came unbidden to her mind. She hadn't even realized how much she had listened during Mrs M's lunch chats and over the afternoon cups of tea in the Hall kitchen.

Yes. She definitely liked Ticking Bottom.

And she wouldn't be here but for Wyatt Grantham.

Gem released Miss Molly when they reached the old stone bridge; she stepped off the cobblestone lane onto the brown meadow. She could just see the poochie as the sun shed its last rays of the day.

She should still be furious with Wyatt. But she wasn't. She wondered if she would have been able to manage her life during the past few months had she still been living alone in her London flat. Before she had met him she was floundering in her grief. She had wandered aimlessly across London day after day, skipping breakfast because she would have an early lunch, forgetting lunch then, finally eating a scratch dinner day after day. She hadn't been able to focus on anything other than Gemmy and the Pilos. Her only real conversations had been with Mrs Brown during their infrequent meetings.

Oh, how she had hated Wyatt! And with damned good reason! But she no longer felt even a shred of that emotion now. She had thought early on that Wyatt and his vile Games would drive her over the edge. But now, she mused, he had probably saved her from that very same edge.

And she was no longer a completely befuddled twit. She didn't feel lost. And while at times she still felt dreadfully alone without her family, she did not feel lonely.

And she felt - to some extent - that she could trust Wyatt.

Gem winced as she thought of him packing up James's possessions so that the bedroom could become a nursery for their baby. She had to address the issue of the twins soon. Twins - now that still didn't seem real. But at least Wyatt hadn't expressed - not even for a moment that she knew - regrets about the baby - change 'y' to 'ies' she mentally added.

If she was still at the flat she would never have had the joy of Miss Molly, Mrs Mac, or the company of the M's, and Mr Becton.

It would all end, she knew, when Wyatt learned the truth of James and Gemmy. Her current world would abruptly end. Dr Jekyll would return - Full Force. And Wyatt had the wealth and power to make her life miserable again. But when this current Ticking Bottom world ended, Gem would have the Agency behind her - Full Force. He might put up a brilliant fight against the Agency, but this time it wouldn't be a winner takes all for Wyatt Grantham.

And she would hate it when this world ended. She didn't want to leave Ticking Bottom, the M's, Mr Becton or the furred ones. She didn't want to leave Wyatt.

Gem sighed and gave the order to Miss Molly to return. She turned to survey the cosy village; holiday lights were already brightening the exteriors of some of the cottages; the Yellow Crow fairly glowed with streams of lights.

She sighed as she thought again of Wyatt and the dark hours of that morning. He had held her so gently; his arms had felt so safe and strong. She hadn't wanted him to ever let her go. His strength - and gentleness had lessened the pain in her heart as the lyrics filled her mind.

She saw the headlights of the Land Rover sweep the fields below the bridge, then swing up to capture Gem and Molly and on towards the Hall as Wyatt stopped the vehicle.

His eyes twinkled as he lowered the window and leaned across the passenger seat.

"Long walk, my love?" he smiled.

"Lovely long walk," she smiled back, butterflies moving.

"Dinner scorched?" he teased.

"Blast!" Gem exclaimed. "I forgot the time!"

He got out of the vehicle, came around to settle Molly in the back and Gem in the passenger seat.

"I hope dinner isn't ruined again," Gem groaned. "Mrs M will lose her patience with me."

"Never!" Wyatt laughed. "She chuckles at scorched dinners. Mrs M is a very passionate soul, you know," he informed her as he drove the Land Rover to the Hall.

Dinner was served at the Crow that evening, and Gem completely relaxed in the warm ambience of the friendly pub, and the even friendlier chatter of the locals - all eager for the holiday banquet to be held at the Hall later that month.

"We are in it now," Wyatt grinned at Gem.

"I hope you won't hate it," she said hesitantly.

"It will be lovely," he assured her, taking her hand and gently squeezing it. "It will be most fine - you'll see."

"You're very patient at times," she smiled.

"I shall endeavour to improve on that, I promise," he smiled. "Another hot chocolate?"

Gem nodded, sighing contentedly.

There was no point texting Mr Cawley, Gem decided as she sipped mint hot chocolate. She had no news for him, nor would he have news for her. She wasn't required to text him every morning. It wasn't SOP. It merely had become habit when Mrs Brown had gone on holiday after Gem had moved into the Hall - and Gem had had a query - and only Mr Cawley had been awake that night - and then other nights. He had been much cheerier then, much less stressed. She didn't need to add to his stress each morning with futile texts.

Keys, she muttered as she listened to the cd. Keys. So close. Yet still out of her reach.

She wished she could feel Gemmy - sense her.

Gem absent mindedly rubbed her tummy, and was startled by the gesture. She hadn't done that before!

Suddenly the babies seemed real. Wyatt wanted to be surprised. She didn't. Perhaps he would wish to know the gender when he learned there would be two of them.

'Margaret didn't have one baby - she had two', Paul Andriani had said at St. George's Cathedral.

She and Gemmy had always been One. That was how they had wanted to be. Even half a world apart from the age of twelve, they were still One.

And now she really was One.

If the twins were girls and identical would they be One? Or two?

Their mum and dad had never reinforced their twin identity - nor attempted a forced pattern of individualism. The Gems had made their One decision as early as either of them could remember. And it had worked for them as far as they had been concerned.

It would certainly be interesting raising twins!

She had an appointment with Dr Hallowell on Friday. Perhaps he could tell her then what the babies would be.

Blast! She had to text Mr Cawley about her query to the warehouse. She filled her mug with mint chocolate comfort.

'News from warehouse?'

'Not good news.'

'What?'

'All warehouse computer files are lost. The entire system crashed.'

'Why?'

'It happens sometimes with power failures. Mr White and the warehouse manager are trying to retrieve what files they can salvage.'

'Print backup?'

'Definitely. Excruciatingly detailed.'

'And? Any print copy of deciphered codes?'

'Not listed. Warehouse staff will fact check Denton's files later today in the event inventory staff made error.'

'I doubt it.'

'As do I.'

'Who has the book?'

'Don't know.'

'The code book should have been packed with dad's possessions.'

'Yes.'

'Or Harry or Mrs Brown removed it from our home before the packers arrived.'

'Against SOP, Gem.'

'Then it was removed from the warehouse.'

'Possible.'

'Who has the authority to remove items from the warehouse?'

'Only Harry and Mrs Brown.'

'Not you as Acting Director?'

'Well yes, there is that. But it is very wavy territory. Harry or Mrs Brown could pin my ears back good when they return, if I did remove an item.'

'Not worth the risk?'

'I can enter the warehouse, Gem. I can do a search of items. That is my only authority. It's a very fine line.'

'But you could remove an item.'

'Checks and balances, Gem. Do you want just anyone removing items from your family's possessions?'

'Definitely not!'
'There you have it.'
'But you could.'
'Damn it, Gem. What do you want me to take from the warehouse for you?'
'Gemmy's thesis. I want to read it.'
'Then find the Pilos. Find Gemmy!'
'Would you retrieve something else for me?'
'No!'
'Goodnight!'

Well, not concrete evidence, but she didn't think Mr Cawley would step over the fine line to take the code book from the warehouse, she mused as she cleared her messages.

He was still a bit grumpy, Gem reflected as she filled her mug and pushed the start button on the cd player.

Would Mr Choate remove the code book? She trusted him completely. Mr White? Did he ever have a thought in his brain that didn't relate strictly to computers?

Paul Andriani. He would have known of the code book! He was trying to track down Nazis in Hong Kong. He was in Hong Kong on 30 May - according to Mrs Brown. But she would only know the location he had stated to her. He could easily have been in Brisbane.

But why would he want the code book? He could have been bought off by the Nazis - or skinheads. Four of the murdered SEA Network counter-couriers and agents had been his regular contacts.

Nice frame job! No wonder he had disappeared!

Or - or Harry or Mrs Brown could simply have removed the book to a secure site as evidence - along with the print backup. Either of them could have deleted the item on the computer list, then printed a new copy for the warehouse files. Mrs Brown could have managed that neat trick after the last agent had texted her dying message: skinhead. Harry could be in this country for all any of us know, Gem concluded.

Keep the code book and print copy in mind, Gem told herself.

Move on to bed and sleeping in Wyatt's arms. Enjoy the luxury while she still could.

Rain drummed on the roof as Gem opened her eyes. It would be a soggy day. Miss Molly would require a shower after her walks.

"Too beautiful to be ignored," Wyatt rubbed his eyes with one hand and stroked her hand with his other. "How are the butterflies?"

"Hmm," Gem rose and leaned over him, her lips close to his. "As you likely know, butterflies rarely ever rest."

Mrs M served breakfast, then went to her office to decide if she wanted the room painted.

"A most brilliant suggestion, sweetheart," Wyatt smiled. "Mrs M is a bundle of energy this morning."

"The woman loves a project," Gem grinned. "How many can she juggle at a time?"

"As many as needed. I offered her a position at GEI five years ago, but she declined," he frowned, suddenly focusing his gaze on Gem as she sipped her tea.

"What?" she asked curiously. She looked down at her jumper. It was hers, not Gemmy's, so she couldn't figure out what distracted him.

"You're very fond of that bracelet," he shrugged.

Gem looked at her wrist. The silver filigree bracelet. She had been wearing it for weeks, but it was usually covered by her sleeve.

"You wore it in Barcelona," Wyatt shook his head. "Sorry I mentioned it." He stabbed his eggs with his fork, determined not to dredge up memories or accusations.

"How do you know?" Gem demanded, feeling a Key poised to slip, but she didn't know why.

"You were wearing it in one of the photos," Wyatt frowned, puzzled by the confused look in her eyes. "It was probably the first photo James shot. You were holding your mobile. The bracelet had slid down your wrist," his voice took a hard edge.

Gem paled. "Truly?"

"Yes. I've seen the photos a hundred times," he ground out.

"You're certain? No doubt?" Gem pressed insistently.

"I've studied the photos. I've memorized every shot."

Gem sat back in her chair. "It's there," she murmured. "That's it! Or one of the 'its'. I don't understand," she puzzled.

"What 'it'? What's to understand?" Wyatt demanded, watching a veil descend over her eyes. He realized she wasn't hearing a word he said.

Gemmy had been talking on her mobile when she just happened to meet Paul Andriani. He said she had been having difficulties with her mobile. One was being programmed and would be drop shipped to Brisbane.

"Oh my God!" Gem gasped.

And another Key slipped.

"Geneva!" she whispered.

"What the hell about Geneva?" Wyatt demanded. "Gem!" He reached over to gently shake her.

Gem was suddenly aware of him. "It falls into place," she stared at him in amazement, then jumped up from her chair and ran to her office. She had to think. She had to sort.

Gemmy's mobile wasn't working properly. That could be a disaster for a courier who had to transmit codes confirming delivery of a message, then the next code confirming returning to home base. Gemmy had needed her mobile for her assignment to Singapore.

She needed more information. She needed to talk to Mr Cawley. Now. She couldn't wait until the dark hours. Gem reached into her pocket for her mobile.

Wyatt watched her from the doorway, confounded by her reaction to his comment about the bracelet. She hadn't remembered wearing it in Barcelona. So?

Her mobile wasn't in her pocket! Blast! Where was it? She turned to scan the counter, the comfy chair - and saw Wyatt watching her.

"Eureka?" he queried quietly.

"Yes! Why do they have to be so blasted far apart?" she demanded, highly frustrated.

"What about the bracelet?" he queried.

"I can't explain!" Gem exclaimed. "Where the Blast is my mobile?" she searched the cushion of the comfy chair.

"Use mine," Wyatt reached into his pocket handing over his phone.

Gem shook her head. "I need mine!"

Wyatt frowned. "Your dressing gown?" he suggested.

"Yes!" Gem stabbed the air with a clenched fist and ran from the office, down the hall, taking the steps two at a time to the master suite. Her hands shook as she searched one pocket then the other, gratefully closing her hand around her mobile.

She needed to be alone! And she needed Gemmy with her! She ran to the dressing room. She had to have it! She hadn't discarded any of Gemmy's clothes. She ripped the hangers along the pole until she found it - hanging in the corner, lost and neglected. Gemmy's trench coat, found in a vintage shop in New York City three years ago. Gem pulled on the long black coat. Gemmy had laughed hilariously when she had tried on the coat, saying it made her feel like a seedy private eye in an old B black and white mystery film.

Wyatt was standing at the foot of the stairs as Gem ran down the steps. "For God's sake be careful on the steps!" he sharply ordered. "You can't be careless of the baby!"

"No! Yes! Whatever you say!" she agreed, racing to the entrance double doors. "Damn!" It was locked.

Wyatt placed his hand over hers, as she fumbled with the lock. "Where are you going?"

"Out!"

"Where?"

"Wyatt! Please! I need to be alone!"

He twisted the lock, turned the doorknob, pulled open the door, and she pushed out past him.

The air struck her face, coolly refreshing, invigorating her senses - exactly what she needed to keep her mind sorting.

The rain had faded to a fine mist. Gem pulled the hood of the trench coat over her head; the protection would have to suffice since she had neglected to grab an umbrella from the mudroom.

She scanned the landscape. Privacy. The huge beech tree on the lawn would provide a bit of shelter. She could go sit in the Defender but her keys were in her office.

Impulses! Blast!

She pulled out her mobile, scrolled the contacts to Mr Cawley and pressed the key to connect.

"What is it, Gem?" Cawley's voice demanded.

"Are you sleeping?" she asked breathlessly.

"I don't talk in my sleep! I was tested, same as you. Remember? What?"

"Mrs Brown is much nicer than you!"

"You RANG me to tell me that? Are you pissed?"

"Certainly not!" Gem snapped, glancing towards the house. Wyatt was standing on the steps watching her.

"What is your question? It must be a corker if you rang me - AND at this hour of the day. It's morning, you know," he said sharply.

"Of course I know that it's morning! Mr Cawley," she tried to focus her thoughts and ignore his attitude at the same time, "can my mobile be monitored at Ticking Bottom?"

"Agency mobile?"

"Of course! It's the only one I have!"

"Monitored only by the Agency."

"That's a plus," she nodded to herself. – Except for Wyatt's GPS tracking chip on her phone, she mentally added.

"Is that the monumental query? You're wasting my time," Cawley growled.

"Damn it, Cawley! I may shoot you!" she declared, infuriated by his cavalier attitude.

"Don't threaten Family, Gem. This call is being recorded!"

"What! Really?"

There was a lengthy pause.

"This is a mobile, Gem," he said sharply. "What the hell are you thinking! Snap out of it!"

"Stop the attitude! I am fed up with it!"

"Start thinking then girl! Harry is unavailable. Mrs Brown is unavailable. Andriani has done a flit. Choate is tied up shadowing you all over London. I have my hands full here and now you have gone non compos mentis! Get your blinking act together, Gem, and give me some damned help! Now take deep breaths and count to twenty four times before uttering another word," he crisply ordered.

Gem slumped against the trunk of the tree, breathing and counting. How many times had Mrs Brown ordered Mr Cawley to practice the same control method?

After a few minutes he spoke again. "Now speak calmly," he ordered.

"Good morning, Mr Cawley," she held her voice steady. "How is the family?"

"In flux. How may I help you, Gem, so that you might assist me?" he said quietly.

"How many couriers are active?" she asked curiously.

"Three. Two have flu."

"Three! Good Lord!" Gem gasped.

"Want my job?"

"No!"

"Can you fly yet?" his voice sounded hopeful.

"No and I'm pregnant," she informed him. It was so good to be able to talk to him, to hear his voice. And he would, hopefully, have answers for her.

"Really! Mazel tov!"

Neither Mrs Brown or Mr Choate had apprised her superior of the fact. She could not take an assignment overseas if she was pregnant. But Gemmy had known she was pregnant, and had taken the assignment which she had told Gem would be her last for the Agency. Huge violation of Agency SOP!

"Thank you." A notion was teasing her brain. "Are you in your office at the Agency?"

"No. I just arrived home. No one is here and the house is not wired. Speak freely."

"This call is not being recorded?" she pressed.

"No."

"It is being monitored?" she puzzled, trying to connect dots.

"The signal is, yes."

"Who is monitoring this call?"

"A computer."

"Who is monitoring the computer."

"The Director of Computer Communications."

Mr White, Gem mused.

"When I am in my office, I can switch computer screens to access the mobile monitor."

"Is anyone else able to monitor our mobiles?"

"Mrs Brown and Harry when they are in their offices."

"Of course." Gem wasn't sure precisely what information would further her sorting. Ask questions and glean whatever information came her way. "How does the monitoring work?"

"The mobile is monitored to show your location. For example, where are you at this moment?"

"Standing beneath a beech tree at Grantham Hall."

"Then at the Agency the computer screen is registering the area of Ticking Bottom, and is registering a notation next to your mobile number."

"It's not shown on a map?"

"The staff member monitoring can switch to a map screen, where your phone is indicated by a blinking light yellow dot. All staff mobiles have different colours."

"What was Gemmy's colour?"

"Medium green."

"But what you're saying is that the location is not precise?"

"Not at Ticking Bottom. It's private property and can't be entered onto a grid. Were you in, for instance, London, the computer could place you within a city block," he further explained.

"Oh! Very handy. If Paul Andriani still had an Agency mobile, you could find him today," she thought aloud.

"Indeed we could, but he had good reasons to stop using our mobiles. It became a safety hazard for him when hackers honed their skills to today's levels."

"Can hackers breach Agency security?" Gem queried, frightened at the consequences for Agency staff by such actions.

"White is constantly updating security - hour by hour, in fact. The man is exhausted by his efforts. Hackers terrify him."

Gem looked towardss the Hall. Wyatt was casually leaning against the front door, his arms crossed, his face expressionless, so hopefully he wasn't growing impatient with her insistence of staying away from the house.

"Good," Gem murmured. "Does the computer register that the mobile is in use?"

"That is the blinking. If the mobile is not in use the dot is static. The computer also registers start and end times of each call and is marked by a single asterisk," Cawley continued patiently.

"So when I rang you, the computer registered the call and time."

"Affirmative."

"Does it register your number as receiving the call?"

"Yes. It's similar to a regular phone bill, time and phone number. But you probably have never seen a phone bill because you have always had an Agency mobile - no bill."

Well, she had had a phone at her flat.

"Did the computer register Paul Andriani's mobile number when he switched to disposable phones?" she mentally sorted her thoughts.

"That's a problem. The computer can register public phones and hard wired private phones but not disposable."

"Why not?" Gem demanded. The information was probably not vital to her search, but the information was puzzling.

"Users pay for minutes and are given an access code to activate the phone. There is a near infinite set of numbers that can be used for the access codes. Mobile companies sell the minutes and keep a record of the code number and the consumer also has the number. Consumers would likely toss their copy after activation. If an Agency mobile rings a disposable mobile the computer does not register the call. There is no indication the Agency mobile is in use. Disposable is the key word." The word Key distracted Gem, but only for a second. "They are less expensive and most do not have all the bells and whistles of expensive contract phones. They are a good option for people who are careless, lose their mobiles, drop them, or don't frequently use phones."

"I see," Gem nodded, mentally storing and sorting his remarks. "So," she thought aloud, "two Agency mobiles are being monitored at this very moment."

"I'm sorry, Gem," he said softly. "No mobiles registered on the computer after take-off."

He had seen that query coming.

"But didn't the computer register that as an anomaly? Four mobiles not registering. Didn't the computer send up some sort of alert?"

"It did indeed. The computer made a ringing tone, to alert the person monitoring the computer. We check the computer every half hour, but the computer alerted the staff monitoring that night. Anomalies can occur with satellite interference, and a certain country in that part of the world has been known to disrupt satellites on a regular basis."

"No disruption was noted that night by other pilots in the area," Gem protested firmly. "That was fact checked."

"It's possible that the disruption did not impair flight instrument panels. Satellites could still have disrupted mobiles. It can and has happened, I assure you." Mr Cawley's voice was sincere and sympathetic.

"Why that night! Blast it!" she sighed.

"Indeed."

Gem forced a difficult question. "If I dropped my mobile in a bucket of water, would it still register on the computer?"

"No. Agency mobiles are not waterproof. Gordon is working on that problem, but that is no consolation to you."

"I see," Gem murmured, shifting around the tree to avoid her mobile taking on damp as the wind shifted the leaves sheltering her.

Cawley waited patiently.

"Is Harry's mobile registering on the computer?"

"No. Hasn't for some time now."

"Mrs Brown's?"

"No."

"Do text messages register?"

"Text messages register as a phone call, but with a double asterisk."

"Okay...okay," Gem continued mentally sorting for other questions.

"Excellent questions, Gem," Cawley praised. "Remember, deep breaths and counting to twenty if you start becoming anxious."

Gem sighed. "The Agency already thought of all my questions."

"That is our job. May I ask the reason for the queries? Do you have something for me? Or is there anything I can do for you? Requests for other information? Any searches? Anything at all I can work on for you?"

Gem turned to look at Wyatt - still watching her, his arms still folded, still leaning against the front door.

"I have to think about that. It's just a spark in my mind. I can't get a clear read on it right now."

"You're holding out on me, Gem," he scolded. "It's more than a spark. I am your supervisor. Your first line of defence at the Agency. Your first contact with any information about Gemmy and the Pilos. You memorized SOP. Do not forget it!"

"I know," she replied thoughtfully.

"Anything at all, Gem. I can't be more serious about this issue," he repeated his warning.

"I know," Gem repeated. "Thank you for the information. For talking to me. I know you're way past your work hours. You need sleep."

"Screw sleep. 24/7, Gem. Family. I want everyone home. Ring me, text me, any time day or night. Promise!" he demanded.

"Promise!" she replied firmly. "Bye."

"Bye, Gem."

She slipped her mobile into her pocket, turned to look at Wyatt, and reached again for her phone.

"Yes, Gem," Cawley answered immediately.

"Who programs the Agency mobiles?"

"White. Harry. Mrs Brown. Choate now. I can manage it as long as it's the standard program. The others can do the mobiles that require special procedures."

"What special procedures?" Gem asked.

"All Agency mobiles have the same ring and text tones, except for agents' mobiles which now only vibrate instead of ring. Harry and Mrs Brown have one of each of the mobiles, to use depending on where they are travelling. If they are in a foreign country which is - shall we say - not particularly friendly to the U.K. - they will use the mobile that vibrates."

"Who programs the mobiles we each receive every January?"

"The mobile exchange requires programming many phones. We generally all do a few, since White is always swamped with other computer work."

"Who would program a mobile for a staff member who needed a replacement during the year? To whom does one make the request?" Gem persisted with the same line of thought.

"The request can be made to any of the Directors. Are you having difficulty with your mobile, Gem?"

"No. Information gathering," she frowned. She was not getting specifics which was what she wanted. "Who would most likely program a new mobile?" she pressed.

"White or Harry. They would process the mobile more quickly than say, Mrs Brown or I would, basically because Mrs B is often in transit and not often in the office. I am on the night shift generally, so I would be less likely to get a request."

"How many replacement mobiles were programmed since last January" Gem queried, the hairs at the nape of her neck tingling in anticipation. "Is there a list you can check?"

"I don't need to check the list. Mr Denton requested a new mobile late last June. He dropped his in a creek while he was fishing. Harry programmed the phone for him."

"That was the only new mobile programmed?"

"Yes. There's a clipboard hanging on the wall by the door in the computer lab. It's on my daily routine to check the list. I do it beginning and end of shift."

"The agency must have a supply of basic mobiles on hand in the event a request is made for a new one."

"We have a dozen cases at all times, but the mobiles are virtually built at the Agency. A phone is programmed, a new case in put into the box, and the request is noted on the list with date requested, name of staff requesting the mobile, and the list is signed by the person who programmed the mobile."

"There are no checks and balances there. You could program a phone and replace the case and no one would know," she protested.

"There are two keys for the box containing the cases. Harry has a key. White has a key," Mr Cawley said crisply.

"Does Harry still have his key?" Gem pressed.

"I have it."

"Okay," Gem murmured. "Then the mobile cases are secure."

"They are," Cawley assured her.

"Good. That eases my mind," Gem said firmly.

"Anything else, Gem?"

"No. Thank you, Mr Cawley. I won't disturb you again for hours," Gem assured him.

"Okay. You had best go inside and get dry. Beech trees are not known for being as waterproof as umbrellas. You don't want to ruin your mobile," he chuckled.

"Correct," Gem laughed, and flipped her mobile shut, and slipped it into her pocket. As she walked to the house she steeled herself for a barrage of questions from Wyatt.

Wyatt wrapped his arms around her, briefly holding her tightly.

"You are decidedly damp, sweetheart," he declared.

Gem tilted her face up to look into his eyes for warning signs. The grey in his eyes was light.

"You need a warm shower," he bent his head to kiss her. "Ouch! Cold lips! You need hot chocolate!"

"You need to go to work," she insisted as he guided her into the Hall.

"I'm not going to the office today. Mr M has dragooned me into moving furniture in the Missus's office in order to lay the new rug." He walked her up the stairs, his arm still about her waist. "I have dragooned him to shift furniture to the attic with me."

He halted at the top of the stairs. "No more taking steps two at a time. No more running down the steps. This is a handrail," he firmly smacked the wood. "Use it!" he ordered sternly.

"Yes, Sir," Gem said meekly, as he urged her into the master suite. She had too much on her mind to have her thoughts diverted by an argument with Wyatt.

"And don't leave your mobile in your pocket- your coat is damp." he slipped the garment from her shoulders, then held it out so she could reach into the pocket. After she had retrieved her phone, Wyatt kept the coat. "Wherever did you get this article?" he queried with a wry smile.

"Vintage clothing shop. I think it is stunning. Apropos of vintage black and white detective films," she said firmly, not adding the shop was in NYC.

"Indeed," Wyatt said dryly, his eyebrows rising. "I'll hang it to dry in my shower since you are supposed to be occupying yours," he said pointedly.

"I'm going," she laughed, walking towardss her dressing room, stopping, then turning to look at him. "Thank you - for not asking questions," she said simply.

"I'm giving it my best shot," he replied with a slight frown.

Wyatt shook his head, puzzling over her earlier reactions, as he set the tea kettle on the cooker. He would keep his promise to not ask questions of her. But he would damned well like to know the recipient of the phone call. With whom was she involved? Practise patience. Trust her. That was his only recourse. And from the puzzled look on her face, he was very certain that she had been gathering information in her secret world. He shook his head again. No. He would not ask questions.

Thoughts cascaded through her mind as thoroughly as the water drenching her from the shower head.

James must have had a disposable mobile or the Agency would have traced his number from the computer record when Gemmy rang him - which of course she had done. How could she finagle a reply of that query from Wyatt? She could only think to ask him if he knew anything about those specific mobiles, hoping he would use James as reference to any knowledge he had.

Gem sighed contentedly as the water warmed her. Shampoo, rinse. She was not eager to leave the drumming water and the aloneness of the bathroom. Wyatt would be attending furniture, so her time would be her own.

She had two Keys. Paul Andriani was the first Key. Gemmy's mobile phone and Geneva were the second Key. (Amazing how the monoliths at Stonehenge looked like Agency courier mobiles when the mobiles were flipped open!) Gemmy was having problems with her mobile. A new one was being drop shipped to her in Brisbane. And what if Gemmy had rung the Agency again to ask that the mobile be shipped over night to Geneva. She might beat the phone to Brisbane and she wouldn't want to be without Agency connection for any great length of time. Why Geneva? She was already leaving Barcelona. She had never been to Switzerland. Why not go to Switzerland? Or perhaps the person who was shipping the phone had suggested Geneva? Did it really matter? Gem didn't think Geneva as a destination was a huge question. Or perhaps it entailed flight connections to Brisbane. Questions that so far, had no answers.

However - and this was a HUGE - HOWEVER -Mr Cawley said only one replacement mobile had been programmed so far this year. Either he was lying to her, or someone had programmed the mobile, shipped it to Gemmy and had not noted that information on the Agency mobile phone recording list.

Gemmy had sent the all clear that night from the Pilos as it left the private landing strip.

Gem wasn't going to entertain any flimsy excuses for the new mobile not being on the list. There were only two reasons: the person who had programmed the mobile had forgotten to make the notation - which was highly unlikely that a senior Agency staffer would simply forget SOP; or - the person had purposely not indicated a mobile had been programmed and shipped.

A mole.

Gem wouldn't have this information if Gemmy hadn't fallen in love with James; if James hadn't snapped the photos; if Wyatt hadn't found the photos and set about to trap and torment Gem because of James's death; because Paul Andriani wouldn't be living in Wyatt's London flat; if Paul Andriani wasn't living in Wyatt's flat, Gem would never have chatted to him about Gemmy and Barcelona, and Gemmy's mobile.

If this was fate it was damned peculiar!

Gem towelled dry and quickly pulled on jeans, a turtleneck sweater, and a cardigan, then went to sit on the bed to braid her hair. Wyatt was waiting for her with a thermos of hot chocolate and a plate of scones.

"You didn't finish your breakfast, young lady," he reminded her. "The baby cannot be neglected - even for Eurekas - no matter how vital they are."

Gem nodded, not wanting to upset his pleasant mood. "Indeed. I shall make note of that." She sat cross legged on the bed.

They chatted while she ate, discussing Mrs M's sudden decision to have the office painted - a heavy crème colour.

"Another reason to clear out the room. Then Mr M will paint," Wyatt informed her.

"And your plans for the remainder of the day?" she queried. Having finished her food, she brushed her hair, dividing it into sections.

"First I am going to watch you braid your hair," he stretched out on the bed, resting on his left elbow. "You make it a work of art."

"You are full of -"

"Ham and eggs," he concluded for her.

Gem laughed. If only he could remain this pleasant with her for the rest of his life! It was not to be.

"Lunch at the Crow with you," he ventured. "Just you and me at the table by the fireplace. Hot chocolate for you a pint or two for me. We'll listen to the rain drumming on the roof, and gaze longingly into each other's eyes," he teased.

"You are absurd," Gem grinned, finished her braid, then stretched on the bed to face him, propping herself on her right elbow. "What do you know about disposable mobiles? The ones for which people have to purchase minutes and codes to activate the mobiles before use."

Wyatt frowned slightly. "Just what you said. Purchase minutes, key in a code, mobile works," he shrugged.

"Oh," Gem nodded, trying not to show her disappointment that he didn't offer more information.

"Not to hit a sour note," he said hesitantly, "when James was whacked on whatever caught his fancy years back, I always made sure he had a mobile with GPS, so I could find him when he had bolted from the flat - between recovery centres, that is."

Gem held her breath as he spoke. His voice was gentle, not accusatory of her in any way.

"When he had stabilized, was C and S, he started using minutes mobiles. He could not keep track of a mobile. One fell in the loo," he winced, "he dropped one in the sand on Wight - never could find that one. A week later he dropped one in a can of paint when we painted the shutters at Marigold. He lost two in cafés in London, two in Paris, and three in Barcelona. After he met you he never lost another phone, but he still used the minutes mobile - as he called them," Wyatt concluded.

His gaze had not wavered from hers, and while the grey of his eyes deepened slightly, the tone of his voice did not alter. Gem didn't know what to say to break the silence. But she had her answer.

"Is that what you wanted to hear?" he asked gently, his voice still clear of tension.

"It's good information," she replied softly. "Thank you."

"Very well," Wyatt nodded. "Shall we go down to see what the true Lord and Lady of the Manor are up to now?"

Gem burst out laughing, despite her apprehension of what could be a brittle mood for him. "You are so apathetic about that!" Gem exclaimed of his title.

"I have a title," he shrugged. "Does the title impress you, Gem?" he queried.

"I never think about titles," she admitted.

"Nor do I. It was inherited, not earned. However, I did earn a title from you," he teased.

"Dark Lord. You deserve that title at times," she retorted loftily.

"And I like it," Wyatt chuckled. "It's emblematic of your passion for me."

"You are delusional!" she laughed, reaching above her head for a pillow which she crashed down on his head.

"And I am enjoying every minute of it!" he responded with his own pillow.

The pillow fight was eventually called a draw.

"Your braid is a mess," Wyatt informed her.

"Your fault!" Gem pulled off the band and brushed her hair.

"Sooner or later everything will be my fault," Wyatt chuckled, straightening the bedclothes.

I don't think so, Gem mused silently. "We'd best check on the M's," she replied aloud. "They'll be wondering where you are hiding your muscles."

"I'll show you later," he winked at her.

"Outrageous," Gem giggled.

"I can manage that also," he teased.

As they walked down the steps - Gem holding the railing - a Key slipped.

Blast! Which Key?

Only two Keys remained. But they were still far from her grasp.

And another Key slipped ever so slightly. She realized it had earlier - while she had chatted with Mr Cawley - but she only now noticed it had moved.

Wyatt was occupied with the M's until past noon, the men moving the furniture, Mrs M instructing them on how the furniture should be moved and - nicely - where they should put it.

Gem paced her office, continuing to sort the information she had obtained from Mr Cawley and from Wyatt.

James had had a minutes mobile, so there was no way the Agency would have known he was ringing Gemmy, or that she was ringing him. If Wyatt still had James mobile, and very likely he did - but it had not been in James's room - then there was no way Wyatt could have connected with Gemmy no matter how hard he had tried to do. And of course, James could not have connected to Gemmy no matter how many times he had tried to ring her. This had nothing to do with the Pilos, but it cleared up some queries she had formulated while probing Mr Cawley for information.

And she could conclude that Gemmy had stopped over in Geneva to wait for a new Agency mobile. It was logical. Why Gemmy hadn't waited in Barcelona for another day was beyond Gem to decide. Perhaps, after all, she needed a -. How silly of her. Stupid! Stupid! Stupid! The Lausanne Cathedral. Gemmy had likely thought of it, spur of the moment, and had taken the advantage to visit it. If Gem ever travelled to Switzerland that would be top of the list of what she wished to see. Gemmy was leaving Barcelona; if she had stayed another day, she would have had to make excuses to James. Why not take a quick trip to Geneva! - Or the person who was sending the phone had suggested Geneva. No answer there yet, after all.

Gem thought back to those weeks in May. The week Gemmy had flown to Brisbane was very clear to Gem. She had had multiple assignments all originating at the Agency, and all Directors had been at the office: Harry, Mrs Brown, Mr White, and Mr Cawley as Assistant Director, because Mrs Brown was 'retired' and was planting her gardens; yet she had stopped at the office every day.

Odd that Mr Cawley, as the Director currently in charge, had not been instructed in programming the special procedures into the agents' mobiles. Gem wondered if Mr White was hesitant to teach Mr Cawley the procedures - Mr Cawley had only mentioned one procedure, but had used plural - because Acting was only a temporary title; when Mrs Brown returned - or Harry, not likely to return, she sensed - Mr Cawley would likely revert to Assistant.

There was no record that Gemmy had requested a new mobile - other than Paul Andriani mentioning that information to Gem. There was no evidence that a new mobile had been shipped to her. And now the - why. Gem had already considered that query in the shower and she stood by her two thoughts. Neglected SOP - negligence. Ignored SOP.

Did Gemmy actually get the new mobile? - Had to - that's why Geneva. What had she done with the mobile that was being replaced? SOP, Gem searched her brain. Ah - return to the Agency. Gemmy would have posted it from Geneva, when she received the new mobile. And to whom had she posted it? Another question for which she would have to wait for an answer.

A mole. Harry. Mrs Brown. Mr Cawley. Mr White.

Harry and Mrs Brown. Completely unavailable. But Mrs Brown was on leave now, which was an indication she would be returning to the Agency - especially if Harry was still 'whereabouts unknown'.

Mr Cawley and Mr White were always available 24/7.

Gem didn't doubt for a minute that Paul Andriani could program an Agency mobile - without Agency knowledge of that fact. But he was in Barcelona, and when he met her at the gardens she was on her mobile - likely requesting the new phone.

It was all a bit of guesswork, but she had no one with whom she could check facts. She had a premise and she would go with it. Her only premise/theory was a shot in the dark.

She continued pacing, but the Keys did not slip again. She needed to clear her mind, and Wyatt appeared and provided the opportunity to do so - outside the bedroom.

"Lunch. Crow. Walk or ride?" he shot out the questions as if from a pistol.

Shades of Gem's last thought of a shot in the dark!

"Walk!" she quickly decided.

"When are the M's going to purchase the paint?" she asked as they walked down the cobblestone lane.

"June," Wyatt replied.

"June? Why not until then?" she demanded.

"Mrs M remembered that paint fumes might make you feel ill. She thought to opt for a wall covering instead, but decided to wait. We'll move in the furniture she wants to use this afternoon."

"I feel bad about the paint," Gem protested. "The Hall is so large, I doubt I would smell the odour."

"Mrs M has her mind set. She and the Mister are going to Crispin to order the invitations for the party then have lunch out somewhere. We are on our own for a few hours, my dear," Wyatt ended all arguments about paint. "Mrs M will have little time for the next few weeks to worry about the colour of her office walls. She will need to be in full party planning mode. Now no more worries about Mrs M - she is quite capable of making her own decisions. We are going to have a pleasant, relaxing lunch," he ordered.

"And a lovely afternoon for you," Gem teased.

"And a lovely evening for us," Wyatt pulled her close to him as they crossed the old stone bridge.

Gem, where are you? Help me Gem!

Gem bolted upright, gasping for breath. Wyatt switched on the lamp on the bedside table.

"I can't - breathe," she gasped.

He sat up and put his hands on her shoulders. "Concentrate," he said gently, then gave her right shoulder a sharp pinch.

"Ow! Why did you do that?" she demanded, turning to face him.

"I hoped it would distract you. And it did. Now breathe slowly, concentrate," he ordered firmly, grasping her upper arms. "Look at me! Slowly. Slowly. Keep your breathing shallow. Slowly," he repeated until she could breathe normally. He brushed her hair back from her face. "Better, my sweet?" his eyes searched hers.

Gem nodded, then covered her face with her hands. "I hate that feeling!" she groaned.

"Twice now that I've seen you awakened like that. Were there other times - before we met?" he asked gently.

Gem shook her head. Wyatt took her hands from her face and held them.

"Were you dreaming?"

"I never dream - I know I do - but I can't remember my dreams," Gem shook her head.

"You shot out of my arms. What did you feel?" he softly coaxed.

"I felt like I was drowning. I couldn't breathe," was all she could explain.

"Okay, sweetheart, don't force any thoughts, just relax," he gently encouraged.

"How did you know to pinch me?" she queried. "It helped."

"Desperation," Wyatt admitted seriously. "I didn't know how else to distract you - to disrupt you gasping for breath."

"Clever. Thank you," Gem murmured.

"You won't thank me for the bruise you'll have later," he said, gently touching the reddened area of her skin. "Yes, it's already coming black and blue." He frowned. "I had promised not to do that again."

Gem wrapped her arms around his neck. "I appreciate this bruise," she rubbed her nose against his.

"Good Lord, your nose is cold," he chuckled.

"Cold nose - means I'm still breathing," she laughed.

"Got your feet warm, now your nose is cold," he teased. He gently rubbed her nose with his finger. "Better now," he touched his nose to hers. "Are you feeling better?"

Gem nodded, then realized the time. "Oh, Wyatt, you need to sleep! You have to work in the morning!"

"I don't have to go to the office early," he replied.

"I'll go down to the office so you can go back to sleep," she started to move to the side of the bed.

"I'm going to the kitchen," Wyatt announced, tossing back the covers, reaching for his dressing gown. He noticed Molly sitting on the floor, staring at him. "Oh, Molly, I brushed you off the bed, didn't I," he gave her a pat of apology. "I'm going to prepare bacon and eggs and you shall have a special treat."

"Breakfast?"

"Indeed. Hungry?" Wyatt teased. "For food?"

"Definitely," Gem pulled on her dressing gown. "When are you going to sleep?"

"I'll sleep late," he assured her, "although I know you won't."

Gem sat at the counter while he fried the bacon and eggs, gave Miss Molly a treat, and fed Mrs Mac her kitty crunchies.

"You are most capable in the kitchen," Gem complimented. "I enjoy watching a handsome man cook for me," she teased.

"That remark had better be limited solely to me, now and in the future," Wyatt warned firmly.

"It shall," Gem nodded. But that would be up to him.

As she ate, Gem thought again of the fright she had had earlier. "Wyatt, thank you again," she murmured. "And I'm sorry I wakened you."

"You are welcome and you have no reason to apologize, my dear," he replied casually. "But perhaps you should talk to Dr Hallowell about the incidents. Get his input into the matter."

Gem shook her head. "I know the problem - issue - I can't explain," she said helplessly.

"I understand," Wyatt replied. "You can't." He thought for a moment. "I promise you, Gem, I will never again leave you alone when you are sleeping. I need you to promise me you won't fall asleep again in your office."

"Promise," Gem readily agreed.

After they did the washing up, Wyatt went up to bed with Miss Molly, and Gem and Mrs Mac went to her office. It was only half three - for her half way through the dark hours, but it was definitely a lack of sleep that would hurt Wyatt during the day if he didn't sleep late.

The thermos of hot chocolate was sitting to the right of her computer. When had Wyatt made that? Gem shook her head. A very competent man, she smiled to herself.

She pulled out her mobile, debating whether or not to text Mr Cawley, but she wasn't up to doing so this morning. And she had thoughts to occupy her mind. She pushed the start button on the cd player.

The 'attack' - whatever it was, was different this time. It was like drowning, but unlike drowning. She touched the bruise on her shoulder. It was definitely painful, but it was better than not being able to breathe. Wyatt was certainly a clever man!

She didn't think she could squeeze out any additional brain power for hours. And then she realized a Key had slipped - just a touch.

Blast! If only she could identify the rest of the Keys. Paul Andriani. Gemmy's mobile. Two Keys. She needed another point of reference.

She wandered out of the office and into the dining room then through the great room, imagining what the rooms would look like when Mrs M had finished her decorating plans for the holiday. She knew the Hall would look brilliant. Mrs Mac followed her for a few minutes then made a detour through the kitchen to the food bowl in the mudroom. Gem watched the cat disappear into the dark room at the end of the hall.

What a lovely cat. Molly was a lovely dog. Wyatt had provided her with so much!

'Is that what you wanted to hear?' Wyatt had said, after he told her about James's mobile issues.

It was the information she had wanted. She hadn't couched her query of disposable mobiles to be directed to James. But Wyatt had included James in his reply. Didn't he think she should have known already about his brother's mobile problems if she had been engaged to James?

She couldn't puzzle out the conversation. She simply couldn't believe that Wyatt hadn't demanded - or at least requested - why she had asked about the mobiles, or why she hadn't been affronted when he had mentioned James.

No questions. No pressure. He had promised to help any way he could. And he was helping her.

The new Game? Gem just couldn't believe that. She didn't want to believe this was all another Game for him! He wanted her to trust him. And she would - for now. She would forget about Games - bury her head in the sand - let Mrs M have a lovely time planning a brilliant Christmas at the Hall. Thank heavens there were weeks still ahead to shop for gifts. She would manage that. Her one and only Christmas at Grantham Hall. Her one and only Christmas with Wyatt!

Blast!

She wanted more than one!

Gem wandered back to the office and filled her mug with hot chocolate. She would not sit on any comfortable furniture. She would not fall asleep in the office. She had promised Wyatt. She had to keep her promise to him. He was keeping the promises he had made to her.

Mrs M wouldn't have her new office painted because of the baby - add ies - Gem mused silently.

When she found the Pilos - when she found Gemmy, she would be leaving the Hall. Then Mrs M could paint. Next week. Next month. Two months. It was going to happen.

I'll find you, Gemmy. I know I will!

She wandered the room, returning for hot chocolate and to push the start button on the cd player until the long case clock in the main hall struck three quarters of an hour.

Gem switched off everything in the office requiring switching, and climbed the stairs, holding on to the hand rail. As she walked quietly through the sitting room she stopped suddenly.

A Key had slipped.

The Keys were starting to move. Two Keys had slipped free so far. The two remaining Keys were already slipping today.

Gem didn't accomplish anything the entire day. Her thoughts were constantly interrupted by 'outside' issues swirling around her head like annoying fruit flies.

She had managed to slip out of bed at seven o'clock without waking Wyatt. She went down to the kitchen in her pyjamas and dressing gown to warn Mrs M not to start breakfast as Wyatt was sleeping in a bit; and she managed to convince the housekeeper that she could wait for her own breakfast until Mr W was ready for his.

Once convinced, Mrs M launched into a chat about the holiday party and would Gem like other than red poinsettias and white trumpet flowers for the Hall floral decorations? Perhaps white and or pink poinsettias? The different colours look 'so beautiful together'. Mrs M had seen arrangements of the three colours of the poinsettias at a florist at Crispin. Gem nodded that the colours sounded brilliant. A lovely idea.

Mrs M chatted on that the hams and turkeys had been ordered, and of course, the roast beef - probably one would do - ham would be the most preferred meat with the locals, but 'we' really should serve all three. Tomatoes with rosemary would be a nice taste - and would add colour to the buffet table. There would be turkey gravy with cider - she had written down the recipe - it was somewhere in one of the cookery books, if she couldn't find her copy.

Mrs M chatted on. Gem was beginning to worry that her eyes would glaze over and that her brain would start to melt and leak out her ears - Keys would fall to the floor with a tremendous clink - and then shatter into a million pieces.

"Mulled wine," Wyatt's smooth voice interjected from behind Gem. "Eggnog laced with - I don't recall what," he admitted, smiling at Gem as she turned to him. He winked at her and she returned the smile. "You missed your shower this morning to let me sleep," he drew Gem off the kitchen stool and out of the kitchen. "Forget breakfast, Mrs M, we're going to London for brunch."

"We are?" Gem asked in surprise.

"We will - only way I could think to rescue you," Wyatt chuckled as they climbed the stairs.

"You have to work!"

"I shall! What? Are you worried about my pay packet? I put in the hours, I assure you," he teased. "Your side of the bed was very cold when I wakened. I warmed it up for you," he whispered in her ear, causing her to giggle. "After you have enjoyed a warm bed, and a lovely shower, we'll brunch in the city. You will have a fitting with Ora. She just rang me."

"Why didn't she ring me? She shouldn't disturb you," Gem protested.

"I told her to ring me. You don't want details, so I'll handle them. But if you wish, I'll inform Ora to ring you in the future," he conceded. "Just let me know when you feel overwhelmed."

"I shall," Gem said firmly.

Mr Choate met Gem at the café after her brunch with Wyatt, and walked with her to the dress shop. Wyatt had specifically chosen a café close to the shop so that Gem wouldn't have to find another parking space for the Defender after they left the café. His thoughtfulness amazed Gem. She winced, thinking of how she was going to express her gratitude to him in the future when she explained James had needlessly died because of her.

She had the fittings - for the holiday party outfits, and then for other clothes Wyatt had ordered for her. Ora and Eda were so excited for Gem for the additions to her wardrobe. If only it had been Gemmy receiving the new clothes. She would have been thrilled with the designs - and more clothes than she could ever wear. But in one respect, the clothes were extremely acceptable, for Ora was a brilliant designer. The clothes would see Gem to spring as she expanded with the twins.

Blast! How soon before she had to tell Wyatt? The first week of December was nearly gone. When? Perhaps two weeks? Perhaps three? A little dicey at three.

She greeted Ms Ames but did not see a sign of Mr Harper. Mr Choate wandered around the shop and the shop staff didn't seem to think it was odd that he always came into the shop with her. When Gem had first starting visiting the shop he had waited outside on the pavement. Now Mr Choate entered the shop after she did, but never entered into discussions between Gem and the other shop owners and staff when they happened to come down from the workshop on the first floor.

Gem was pleased to see that the shop was busy with a steady stream of customers who were making substantial purchases. And she was just as pleased to escape from the shop after the fitting, eager to return to the Hall and enjoy a long walk with Molly before the sun faded. She didn't have to worry about keeping an eye on dinner - and then sighing when it was scorched because she hadn't kept an eye on it. Mrs M had her club meeting that day and Wyatt had told the housekeeper that he was bringing Chinese home for dinner.

Gem chuckled to herself as she steered the Defender over the old stone bridge below the Hall. Wyatt had removed another detail from the list of issues with which she might not wish to deal. He was certainly attempting to make her life easier - to relieve her stress. And his efforts were helping.

Miss Molly was waiting for Gem at the kitchen door. "Give me five minutes to change, sweetie, and I'll take you out," she patted the dog.

"Mrs M," she called, and listened for a reply, tracking the housekeeper to her new office.

"Yes, dear," the older woman looked up from her lists, gratified to see the bride wearing a bit of spirit for a change.

"Tarts. I love tarts - for the party," Gem suggested.

"Strawberry or raspberry?" Mrs M queried.

"Oh -," Gem frowned.

"Both!" the house manager declared, adding the items to the list at the right side of the desk.

"Brilliant! I'm going to change and take Miss Molly out for a ramble," Gem called over her shoulder as she ran, then stopped herself, and walked up the stairs.

Mrs M, satisfied smile spreading over her face, sat back in her chair. It would all come together. And Mr W would help trim at least one tree - if she had anything to say about it!

Molly ran full out across the fields, then darted across the adjoining meadow, bolting back to Gem to race away again.

"Blast! Furniture!" Gem smiled to herself. Molly was worth more than any chair or sofa - or bed in the house. And as much as Gem and Wyatt had tried to coax the golden dog to sleep on her special padded bench, Miss Molly insisted on sleeping at the edge of the bed near Wyatt. Wyatt insisted again that they needed a larger bed, but Gem highly doubted he would need one when -

And 'when' would happen, she mused, the smile fading from her face. She pushed the thought from her mind, and focused on enjoying Molly's burst of energy. After twenty minutes, Gem called Molly back and they continued on their amble, down around the curving cobblestone lane, past the churchyard, and past the colourfully lighted shops, more of the stone buildings sporting Christmas trimmings. Apparently the holiday spirit came very early to Ticking Bottom, she smiled. She wondered if Mrs M had planned exterior decorations for the Hall. Best not to voice that query aloud, in the event that idea had not already been added to one of the housekeepers many party lists.

The M's, in one of the Hall Land Rover's passed the pair as Gem and Molly crossed the old stone bridge. The humans waved, and Molly voiced a single woof as the vehicle passed by. When the Land Rover was out of view, Gem released Molly again for a final run of the day. After twenty more minutes, the poochie was ready to return to a sofa or chair of her choice at the Hall, and Gem was ready for a pot of tea. She had a cup, then while Miss Molly snoozed on Auntie Jane's settee, Gem went to the library to again peruse the book shelves. And within a half hour she had selected a book - a biography of David Livingston. It appealed to her and she hoped Wyatt hadn't recently read the book. She had always been interested in reading about the Scotsman who had explored Africa, but had not previously made the time to do so.

She presented the book to Wyatt at dinner and he whole heartedly approved.

"Hot chocolate and tea by a cosy fire in the great room," Wyatt declared. "We could go upstairs to the sitting room, but Miss Molly has declared a preference for the chairs down here."

"Indeed!" Gem laughed. "Just look for the dog hair!"

Gem watched the international news, only because she hadn't heard any news for a good twenty-four hours. She learned that the world had survived very nicely without her avid attention. Simmering continued with only a few hot spots, but none in SEA.

She felt it still in her bones that Harry would never return to the Agency. Why? What had happened when Harry had gone underground? He was head of a government 'statistics department' - he simply couldn't disappear into oblivion! His Agency cover wasn't an actual job, but people knew him. He had a home in a

London suburb; he had neighbours. He simply couldn't disappear as had the Lawsons and Forresters. He was much more visible for having lived in an area where people noticed you on a daily basis.

She filled her mug, pushed the start button to release Vera Lynn's melodic voice, and Gem smiled softly as she recalled Wyatt's arms around her the other night when he had comforted her through her parents' song.

I'll Be Seeing You - I'll find you - I promise I will find you Gemmy! I'll find all of you! mum, dad, Mr Portermann!

She pulled her mobile from her pocket.
'What's new?'
'Can't think of a thing, Gem. You?'
'No.'
'Still stalemate then?'
'It appears so. Long dark hours.'
'Indeed.'
'You need an assistant.'
'I shall have one soon. Any additional queries re: mobiles?'
'No.'
'Working or dry?'
She hesitated before replying.'
'Dry.'
'Damn. Keep trying. I need your help, Gem.'
'Will you terminate the search at the end of this month?'
'If there is no progress I would say yes. End of this month.'
'You don't need Mrs Brown's or Harry's approval?'
'No. Give me something, Gem, and the Agency will continue the search.'
'Any reply from the warehouse?'
'Not yet.'
'Okay. Goodnight.'
'Goodnight.'
What took so long at the warehouse to complete a request?

And she was working. And she wasn't dry. Why had she told him she was dry? She had hesitated - because she was beginning to feel she couldn't trust him? Why?

Because Mr Cawley was her only source now. She couldn't cross check with anyone else. The mobile issue alone filled her mind with doubt. The checks and balances had been corrupted.

What was it about Gemmy's replacement mobile? Had the programmer made an error in the phone? Ah! Had she been sent an agent's phone in error? Oh - that could have been a problem.

She texted Paul Andriani, hoping the former agent was still delighted with telly.

'Good morning, Gem!'
'Did I wake you?'
'No. Having difficulty getting used to a regular daily schedule.'
'Insomnia?'

'No. Just not used to sleeping more than four hours at a click. What can I do for you?'

'What are the differences between a courier's mobile and that of an agent?'

'No assignment completed code. No returning to base code. Agents can time delay texts. Agents' mobiles are mini recorders and can transmit data at any time. Can time delay transmission of photos.'

The text came in two parts because of the long message. Gem waited for the entire message before she replied.

'Very cool!'

'Yes. White may have added a few tweaks since I had my last Agency mobile.'

'Could you program an agent's mobile?'

'The old ones yes. I heard White was trying to install an alert the agent could send when in crisis.'

'Sounds great!'

'Yes. A sort of SOS or Mayday idea. Not sure if it would be successful other than in large cities. It was to send a direct signal to the nearest police centre with the agent's precise location.'

Another long message that had Gem waiting.

"Is it in use now?"

'Think two agents are using a prototype. It's a special mobile case. A bit thicker.'

'You ARE using a disposable mobile now, aren't you?'

'Absolutely. The Agency isn't aware you are using your mobile.'

'Good!' she needed that assurance.

'If the Agency could track your mobile to mine, Choate would have given you a disposable to contact me.'

'Okay.'

'Are you good for now?'

'Yes. Thanks.'

'Anytime, Gem. Choate or me, anytime. The Agency can track your calls and texts to Choate, but he is your shadow, per WG, and that is Agency approved.'

'Thanks for the reminder. Bye!'

'Ciao, Gem!'

What a dear man. And hadn't Wyatt just done her a very good deed by connecting her with reason to Mr Choate! And then the offshoot connection to Paul Andriani!

There was a mole in the Agency. But she did trust Paul Andriani and Mr Choate.

Did she trust Mr Cawley? Why did he constantly insist he was the first person to receive any information she could discover about the Pilos? That was beginning to grate on her nerves. Why couldn't she tell Mr Choate or Mr White? Acting Director. All the power. Well, if Mrs Brown thought there was a problem with the Agency she wouldn't have gone on leave. So Mr Cawley it was. But she still wasn't going to give him any information until she had more pieces of the puzzle.

She filled her mug with the last of the hot chocolate and pushed the start button. Hot chocolate every morning. And every evening. She had read to Wyatt for hours. It had been so peaceful; she had snuggled against him on the chesterfield, the crackling fire - Gem shook off the feeling. Then decided to keep it.

She finished the beverage, rinsed the thermos and mug, shut down the office and went to bed. To snuggle until the dark hours were over.

Gem had lunch with Mr Choate at Charley's Pub after her appointment with Dr Hallowell. Wyatt had meetings throughout the day and wasn't able to have lunch with her, but she and Mr Choate were hungry.

"Everything good with the - " Choate hesitated.

"Good," Gem replied.

"Too early to tell?" He raised his eyebrows.

"Dr Hallowell was very willing to hazard a guess," she stabbed a fork at her salad. "One of each."

"Have you told Mr Grantham twins?" Choate took a bite of his steak. "Oh, this is good. Give yours a try. Glynn also makes a proper steak."

"Does he?" Gem smiled, then shook her head. "I haven't told Wyatt."

"You have awhile yet. More accurate read at twenty weeks," Choate advised.

"How do you know?" Gem asked curiously.

"Common knowledge," Choate shrugged. He looked at her and frowned. "Cawley's worried about you."

"Why?"

Choate savoured more of his steak before he replied. "He thinks you're being less than honest with him - that you don't trust him," Choate advised her.

"Oh," Gem frowned.

"Don't you trust him?" Choate pressed.

Gem reflected on her words before she replied. "Do you trust him?" she asked bluntly.

"I've never had reason not to trust him. I was never in the field with him. Mrs Brown was," Choate relied thoughtfully. "She's the one suggested him for Assistant. And she's no fool."

"I know," Gem sighed, stabbing a bit of steak, biding her time of replying by focusing on her food.

She trusted Mr Choate, but she hadn't told HIM about the Keys - the mobile - Geneva. He didn't press her to talk and she finished lunch in silence. However he revisited the subject when dessert - Charley's 'famous' cheesecake was served.

"Do you have a reason not to trust Cawley?" Choate frowned.

Gem shook her head. "I don't believe so."

"Is it a 'feeling'?" He was serious, not making light of her 'intuition'.

"No," she admitted. "It's -" she hesitated. It wasn't the thing to do to complain of one's supervisor to another. She didn't feel she had the right to violate that practise.

"He's always pressing me, reminding me he is my first contact if I can think of anything. He keeps pressuring me," she murmured. "And not very nicely," she added, but refrained from repeating the nasty comments her supervisor had made to her as of late.

"That's his job, Gem. He wants you to stay sharp," Choate explained.

"But I'm not sharp, Mr Choate," she sighed. "It's been nearly six months. Mr Cawley has threatened to terminate the search at the end of the month."

Choate nodded thoughtfully. "He has the authority to do so."

"I request information from the warehouse - it takes days for a reply, and I haven't had a reply on the last query," she complained.

"Down to a skeleton crew there. Two staff are in courier training," Choate informed her.

"Who is training them?"

"Cawley. Me. There is no one else. Cawley's back is against the wall," he frowned. "But - look, Gem, if you don't feel you are able to trust Cawley, ring me, or Glynn - we don't have to report to him."

"I should THINK Mr Harper would not have to report to Mr Cawley," Gem stifled a smile.

Choate also grinned. "Bit awkward that would be," he admitted. "Don't ring Gordon White. He's a step down on the rung from Cawley and he does have to report to Cawley. You don't want to get him in Dutch with the AD."

"Okay," Gem nodded. "Why, if Mr White has to report to Mr Cawley, you do not?"

"White is Agency. T.O. is Agency but a separate division. Makes all the difference."

"Confusing," Gem protested. "To whom do you answer?"

"I do not answer to, I confer with."

Gem considered the difference - which was considerable. She scanned the room as she sipped hot chocolate. "Is this building wired?" she asked, mindful of the other customers.

Choate shook his head.

"How do you know?"

"Who would wire it but the Agency, T.O., or B.I. - That could always be a possibility, but Charley sweeps the building three times a day to make sure it's clean."

"Okay," Gem nodded. "Can we go somewhere to chat?"

"Park?" he suggested. Gem agreed with a nod.

They needn't be concerned to be overheard in the park; they virtually had the entire area to themselves.

"Questions, Gem?"

"Mr M walked the perimeter of Ticking Bottom last week," she said.

"Indeed," Choate nodded.

"Is a new security system being installed?"

"You would have to put that query to Mr Macinski or to Mr Grantham," Choate deflected the question.

"But you are T.B. Security."

"I am. However I am not at liberty to discuss T.B. security with you. I can tell you that Mr Macinski walks the boundary every year."

The same story Wyatt had told her. She didn't really require an answer, but rather was wondering if Mr Choate would violate Wyatt's confidence. "You told me private information about Wyatt's businesses."

"You had a legal right to know that information, Gem. You are his wife. That information did not relate to T.B. security."

"Fair enough," Gem agreed. She scanned the park behind Mr Choate as he scanned the area behind her. "Is the main T.O. computer linked to the main Agency computer?"

"No. Entirely different systems."

"Are Mr Cawley and Mr White able to access the T.O. computer system?"

"No."

"Why? Because T.O. is a separate entity? Yet T.O. is still a part of the Agency."

"T.O. has privacy data that is only available to T.O. as we have a public customer base as well as our major customer - the Agency."

"Can you access the Agency computer?"

"I am a Director – yes - I have access."

"You did background investigations on applicants for the Agency." Gem puzzled the aspects of each department.

"Indeed. That information is in the T.O. computer, and was forwarded to the Agency system."

"You can access the Agency computer. Does Mr Harper have access to that computer?"

"He does not," Choate admitted. "That would require Harper meeting with Cawley and White."

"Does Mrs Brown now know of Mr Harper's alter ego?"

"No. She is on leave. Perhaps when she returns to the Agency," Choate shrugged. "But the murders of the SEA Network must be solved before Harper can be relieved of his current identity."

Computers. Computers. Computers, Gem mused silently. Did she have any other queries? Basically she was just interested in learning everything she could of the 'insides' of the Agency.

"Are you of the same calibre with computers as Mr White?"

"Definitely not," Choate chuckled.

"Mr Cawley? Harry? Mrs Brown?"

"Harry would be the closest in ability to White. White is a wonk, but Harry is damn close. White eats, sleeps, breathes, computer technology. Harry is a geek."

"Mr Cawley?"

"He and I are comparable."

"The agents' mobiles - SOS - whose idea was that?"

The query caught Choate off guard and he choked in surprise. "Who told you about that?" he demanded.

Gem looked at him and raised her eyebrows, then lowered them, and did not reply.

"I see," Choate relaxed, and Gem realized he knew where the information originated - and that her source was secure. "The idea and designs were Harry's. The prototypes are seriously flawed, but White is trying to correct the problems."

"What is the difference in the cases of the prototype mobiles and say - a courier's mobile."

"A tad thicker, not by much. The first prototypes were noticeably thicker."

Gem turned to scan the horizon. She couldn't think of additional questions. She had enough information to sort later when the dark hours descended. Would they ever end?

"Questions?"

Gem shook her head. "I'm still sorting," she admitted. "When will it end?" she wondered as they walked across the park to their vehicles.

"Only you know, Gem," Choate murmured.

Another thought struck her and she stopped walking to face her companion. "Mr Choate - the book of Nazi codes my father was working on - it's missing."

"Go on," he frowned.

"It should have been packed with my father's possessions at Brisbane. It should be at the warehouse. It's not there," Gem said, her tone accusatory.

"You had the computer inventory list checked?"

"Mr Cawley checked it. Yes. It wasn't on the list."

"Print copy?"

"Negative print copy, negative computer," Gem firmly replied.

"Where is it then?" Choate demanded, clearly perturbed. He scowled, scanning the landscape.

"Gem, did you watch the crew packing at Brisbane?" he asked slowly, considering the problem.

"Not really," she admitted. "Mrs Brown and I were sorting Gemmy's things - what I could take - so I would have something of hers."

Choate nodded his understanding. It had been a horrible twenty-four hours for her.

"It's the process I'm considering. The transfer crew used a computer. Each item packed was first scanned into the computer. There was a master list and a separate list in each box stating the exact contents and count of each item. The master list was transmitted to the Agency. A print copy was given to the Director in charge of the Property Clearance."

"Okay," Gem nodded, her heart fluttering a bit at a thin line of hope.

"The print copy would have been sealed in a large envelope and handed to the Director as the house was sealed."

Gem nodded.

"Who was the Director who sealed the house?" he stared at her, his gaze steady.

"Mrs Brown was with me from the moment she and Harry first arrived. They flew in from Sydney," Gem thought aloud. "Harry stayed for a few hours, then left for a meeting about the search." She fell silent, forcing her memory back to the first dark hours and the subsequent remainder of that day.

"The packing crew arrived about nine o'clock that morning. It seemed like a swarm of people but was probably only a dozen. I tried not to watch, but I did notice they were extremely quick and professional." She took a deep breath and continued. "A sticker was placed on each item," she stopped the thoughts of particulars and thought ahead to late afternoon. "Harry returned. Mrs Brown and I walked out the door, Harry was behind us." She paused, frowning. "The crew chief handed an envelope to Harry. Harry then locked the door and put a small strip of sealing adhesive by the doorlatch."

"The cartons were shipped on a government jet, then delivered directly to the warehouse. The crew chief's count matched the shipment manifest at the airport, which matched the count that arrived at the Heathrow, and then again at the warehouse."

"How do you know all of this?" Gem queried breathlessly.

"I was in Cairo. Mrs Brown dispatched me to the warehouse and instructed me to assume Portermann's duties as Agency Security and T.O. Receiving the inventory at the warehouse was my first duty as Director of T.O.," he explained. "The contents of each box were inventoried and certified and accepted as Property Clearance Complete."

"Where is the damn book then?" Gem demanded.

"Harry or Mrs Brown took it," Choate said crisply. "By the way, Harry was not at search meetings that day. He was at an Agency computer removing your family - temporarily - from history."

"Oh." Gem felt totally exhausted and deflated from the memories and Mr Choate's analysis of her query.

"Or someone entered the warehouse, took the book and altered the lists - computer and print."

"Harry had the master print copy," Gem whispered to herself.

"Indeed. Someone should search for that list," Choate said dryly.

"Who has the keys to Harry's office?" Gem queried, biting her lower lip between her teeth.

"Cawley has Harry's keys, and I also have a set - and the authority to enter Harry's office - Agency security," Choate said loftily.

"Don't you need a reason to enter?" Gem said doubtfully. "Without raising suspicions, I mean."

"We'd best think of one, hadn't we?"

Gem thought of the locations of the offices at the Agency. The building was narrow and occupied the second floor of the structure. The ground floor, a small shop with dirty windows, had been vacant for years - solely because the rent was so exorbitant - so no one would consider renting the space. The first floor was storage - empty boxes. The second floor was the Bureau of Statistics. There were six offices, three on each side of the corridor; Mrs Brown, Mr Cawley, Harry, were on one side of the corridor; two offices opposite were vacant and used for lunches, meetings and cat naps, the third office was that of Mr White's, but he virtually lived in the computer labs which covered the last third of the building at the end of the corridor.

"Power snap?" Gem ventured. "The offices have security alarms, don't they?"

Choate nodded. "When alarms sound, each office must be thoroughly checked." He gave her a stern look. "Couriers should NOT have devious minds!"

"I'm no longer a courier," she reminded him with a grin.

"As you say," he agreed. "I'll manage the search. Power failure would work. The computers are all on backup power and back up to that, so there wouldn't be any issues with White's communications department. Are you ready to return to T.B.?"

"I am," Gem firmly nodded.

Wyatt texted as Gem was about to engage the Defender's engine.

'Mrs M has meeting today. Pub, Chinese, Italian take-away?'
'Pub.'
'Later!'
'Yes!'

Gem cleared her mind of thoughts as she drove to the village. Mr Critchley had always insisted on his drivers being completely focused only on driving. But as Gem crossed the third old stone bridge below the Hall, she relaxed and thought of the weekend. She wondered if Wyatt had plans for the days - he always had plans for the evenings. Her anticipation took a sharp dip when she entered the kitchen.

Miss Molly was sitting at the door, lead in hand, waiting for her human unit. Mrs M was staring at Gem with obvious concern.

"What?" Gem said, suddenly worried.

"I'm afraid you might be a bit upset," the house manager winced.

"What?" Gem pressed for a response.

"I'll show you," she walked around the island and down the hall as she spoke. "Mr W suggested the Mister bring over the boxes of Christmas trimmings from the carriage house store room. I don't think Mr W realized how many boxes there are."

Gem followed and gasped as Mrs M stopped at the door of the formal dining room. There were at least thirty boxes, all very large, lined on the floor.

"Oh my!" Gem couldn't believe her eyes.

"In his defence, Mr W was always at school, then at work, when the boxes were packed each year," Mrs M observed.

The boxes were neatly marked: plateware, glasses, serving trays, trim G.R. tree, trim D.R. tree, trim L.R. tree, tablecloths, serviettes, tree skirts, on and on.

"I don't know what you will want to use," Mrs M shook her head in dismay.

"Uh-huh," Gem's eyes grew wide at the thought of the Christmas challenge. "Perhaps," she grimaced "I'll take a peek in the boxes this weekend."

"Or when you can't sleep," Mrs M suggested.

Gem was startled by the remark. It was the first time Mrs M had referred to her insomnia.

"We'll handle it," Gem assured the woman. "But for now, Miss Molly requires a walk."

She quickly changed, eager to escape the frightful sight in the dining room. Wyatt would probably pitch a fit at the holiday invasion, she fretted, as she and Molly strolled the cobblestone lane.

One of these days she would inquire of Mrs M of her club meetings. It must be great fun because the house manager apparently never missed a meeting. And Wyatt still did not seem to resent the fact that Mrs M left early two or three days a week. Gem smiled. She liked Wyatt's flexible attitude towards life. He was not stuck with adhesive to schedules. She sorely wished she could have known Mrs Fiona and Mr Jack; and she could not help wondering how much influence they had had on their eldest son's personality and manner, because Wyatt could be a very kind person. He could also be an insidious nightmare. Which was the true Wyatt Grantham? Perhaps a blend - as all people were.

They didn't meet anyone on their walk, taking the route that had become habit, to the left of the drive, down and around the curve and through the village before returning across the old stone bridge to the Hall. Molly was released twice for a run and was eager for her dinner when they returned to the house.

Wyatt was stunned at the quantity of Christmas to be sorted through.

"Leave it for Mrs M," he ordered, frowning. "She'll have someone from the village in to help her unpack and sort what she wants to use this year. Most of this can likely be sent back to storage or Mrs M can discard it."

Gem didn't think that was what Mrs M had in mind, but she didn't press the issue.

They walked to the Crow for dinner and were early enough to get one of the tables by the fireplace.

"I've discovered an error in our nursery plans," Wyatt advised her after their food had arrived.

"What?" Gem asked warily. She already knew an error of which he was not aware.

"A simple matter of painting the room."

"Oh, yes," Gem nodded.

"I suggest we rent a cottage somewhere for a fortnight. Mr M will have the nursery painted and Mrs M shall have her crème coloured walls in her office."

"Okay," Gem nodded. He would likely have tossed her out of the Hall by then. He could cancel the cottage and not have to be concerned about the painting of either room. "It is definitely an option," she agreed.

Wyatt watched her eyes cloud over. He had touched a nerve, and he could see she was trying to hide her uneasiness at his suggestion.

"Did your appointment go well with Dr Hallowell?" he asked casually.

"Yes," Gem replied. "No issues." *That you need to know this evening.* "Did your meetings go well today?"

"Very well. But I have a great deal of reading for this weekend. I won't be much company for you. Ms Holton has suggested that GEI purchase a brewery. The stats look extremely good, but I don't know if I want to acquire another business."

"Really!" Gem said in surprise.

"GEI purchased three businesses this year, sold one," he said pensively.

"Buy the brewery and you'll be back to three," she teased. "A brewery, Wyatt! You love beer! You could drink your own beer!"

"And you love beer," he chuckled. "Perhaps I'll buy the brewery for you for a Christmas gift," he teased.

"Nonsense," Gem protested. "I do not need a single thing!" Then she relented. "Well perhaps a book."

"I'll consider a book," he agreed.

"Good! Where is the brewery located?" He had definitely peaked her interest. Imagine simply deciding whether or not to purchase a business!

"Penzance. Have you been there?"

Gem shook her head.

"Perhaps we should spend a fortnight there in January."

"What is your time frame for purchasing the business?"

"Late January. The current owners are still considering their demands. Staff is batting about the idea of employee purchasing," he shrugged. "No one is ready to meet at the table just quite yet."

"Like the factory you sold this fall," Gem mused the subject.

"Indeed. But do consider Penzance as an escape from paint odour," he smiled.

"Yes," Gem agreed, as she ate.

Her eyes had cleared, Wyatt noticed and he switched the conversation to Molly as a neutral topic of conversation. Her eyes sparkled as she described their afternoon ramble and Molly's ability to instantly turn direction as she bolted across fields. Wyatt listened and relaxed, letting the issues of the business world ebb away as she chatted.

"I have a suggestion for this evening," Wyatt remarked as they left the pub and walked up the cobblestone lane to the Hall.

"You usually do!" Gem laughed.

"Ah - wait for it," Wyatt teasingly chided. "A cosy fire, hot chocolate for you, tea for me, and you read to me."

"Lovely," Gem agreed.

"In bed," he added.

"You won't last two pages," Gem scoffed.

"I will," Wyatt said firmly.

He managed to listen through an entire chapter much, to Gem's surprise.

Hot chocolate - mint - of course, and Vera Lynn. Gem wandered down the hall and back to her office, stopping short when she passed the dining room. She thought to close the doors but it wasn't worth the effort to move three boxes to do so. She couldn't block the boxes from her mind anyway. Wyatt had to spend most of the weekend reading; she would investigate the boxes.

Ping

Gem hurried to the office to read the text and fill her mug. Mr Choate was awake!

'Book not listed on inventory master.'

'Okay. How did you manage the mission?'

'I cover for Cawley when I'm not with you. Took White a huge turkey sandwich and three beers for a late lunch. He fell asleep in his lab.'

'Excellent! Where is the book?'

'Harry must have taken it when he arrived your home Brisbane early 30 May.'

'Why?'

'Only copy of book in U.K. Still a security interest.'

'Where is the book?'

'Perhaps Harry's safe. Only he has combination.'

'Print copy of dad's deciphered codes? Harry should have copy.'

'Likely in Harry's safe with book.'

'Blast!'

'Blast proof.'

'Funny!'

'One can only try.'

'How can you cover for Mr Cawley when you are in T.B. afternoons?'
'Excellent computer system. Few in the world can beat the Agency system.'
'What about the mobile monitoring computer?'
'I have one here.'
'How many hours a day do you work?'
'Cawley does at least 12. I do 16. Cawley's new assistant starts Monday. She's able to start sooner than expected. White's new assistant starts Monday also. White is morose to have to train the young man.'
'Why?'
'White isn't one for chatting, and is loathe to sharing Agency info.'
'Best of luck to new assistant then.'
'Got to go. Glynn is texting.'
'Bye.'
'Bye.'
Glynn! Brilliant!
She thought she should text Mr Cawley since Mr Choate mentioned the A.D. thought she was avoiding him.
A refill of hot chocolate and time to press the start button on the cd player.
'Any news?'
'No book on paper copy at warehouse.'
'Blast!'
She didn't want him to know that Mr Choate had resolved that issue.
'Sorry, Gem.'
'Thanks for the effort. Will try another idea.'
'Okay. Let me know if I can help you.'
'Indeed I shall.'
'Sorting?'
'Yes.'
'Dry?'
'Getting better.'
'Okay. Goodnight.'
'Goodnight.'
He was not brittle this morning.
And a Key slipped.
It was just barely out of reach.

Gem thought she could recognize the Key. But she would not try to reach it just yet. She had sorting to do, and that would take the weekend. She could sort her thoughts while she sorted Mrs M's Christmas boxes.

She wandered the downstairs, staying within hearing of the music. She thought of the brewery in Penzance and of a fortnight's holiday in January. When was the last time she had had a proper holiday? She certainly couldn't regard the ghastly visits to Wight and Inverness as 'holidays' in any way.

Well, she knew one thing for certain. If she was ever going to visit Penzance she would have to do it alone. She fought off gloomy thoughts of losing Wyatt; of leaving the Hall.

When she told Wyatt the truth she would also warn him that he could not turn the photos and passports over to the tabloids. The Agency would squash him like a bug smashed against a windscreen. He could choose whatever reason he liked for a divorce, but he couldn't use slander or libel against her. The Agency would not tolerate that. And she would keep her mouth shut. Irreconcilable differences would be best. Shared custody of the children.

Damn! Blast! She was planning a divorce she didn't want from a man she wanted to waken this very minute to kiss him senseless.

She glanced at the long case clock in the main hall. Half four. What the hell! He could sleep in for a few hours this morning. She shut down everything in the office that needed shutting down, rinsed out her hot chocolate vessels and went up the stairs - holding the hand rail.

"Hello, sweetheart," he murmured as she laid her head on his shoulder.

"Are you very sleepy now?" she whispered.

"Molly, honey, move to the floor," Wyatt patted the dog.

That was the only answer Gem needed.

Gem took Molly for a brisk walk, served Wyatt breakfast in bed, to his surprise, did the washing up and sent him off to the library to read. She took paper and pen to the dining room, and opened the first box marked plates: the pattern was called Christmas roses - red roses circled around the rim of stark white plates banded in gold above and below the pattern. She counted forty-eight; a second set of plateware in another box were similar with red poinsettias instead of roses. Forty-eight; matching tea cups, saucers, glasses, serving dishes. - Who the hell had place settings for forty-eight? - And two sets at that! Margaret Lawson would have been shocked at the Grantham Hall holiday dinner service. Gem certainly was. She carefully set the items on the dining room table and flatted the boxes for storage. Two boxes down.

Gem made a pot of tea and carried the pot and cups on a tray to the library. "Tea time," she announced and won a grateful smile from Wyatt. "And what do you desire for lunch, Dark Lord?" she teased as she served him his tea.

"That which I missed this morning because I couldn't waken at seven when you did."

"Ah, that would be dessert. You must have a proper lunch prior to dessert."

"A stroll to the pub," he declared.

"Well, you certainly cannot have dessert there!" Gem laughed. "But pub grub it is!"

"You know, love, I rarely ate in pubs before I met you. Now pub grub is my usual diet," he chuckled.

"And you have managed to keep your smashing figure," Gem declared with a suggestive look.

"I have a wife and a dog who constantly nag me to go for walks!" Wyatt set down his tea cup. "I think it's time for dessert now."

"I should say not. You have work to do. Lunch in one hour. Followed then by dessert," she said firmly, taking her cup with her as she left the library.

Gem unpacked serving trays, red and green linens, adding counts to her list, and flattened another box. The next box held beautifully woven gold rope garlands. She decided that if she laid them end to end the rope garlands would stretch from the kitchen door of the Hall to the Crow and back. Lovely. What the hell would someone do with all the garland rope? She carried the lighter items to the counters in the butler's pantry. By the time she quit for lunch she had made a path through the boxes to the breakfast room.

She knocked at the library door, opened it and smiled at Wyatt. "Lunch, Dark Lord. Pub grub time."

He came willingly, but caught her hand as they passed the dining room. "What's this?" he demanded, scowling.

"Clearing my brain," Gem said firmly. "Mental holiday. Please don't go all grim and ruin the day."

"As you wish. But no heavy lifting," he relaxed and changed his tone. "And you best not be too tired for dessert!"

"Never," she smiled. "Not as long as you're serving it."

Wyatt kissed her and sent silent words of gratitude to her hormones.

Gem pushed all thoughts of sorting from her brain when they tried to invade. Holiday colours and trimmings distracted for a time and then the assault on her mind returned. She didn't want to admit what she dreaded would be the truth of her search. And the thoughts were still germinating; she couldn't decide precisely how to proceed until she was ready to retrieve the next Key.

Wyatt read until he stated that his eyes were blurry, and they should take Molly for a long walk and run. He made dinner that night and Gem managed to read aloud two chapters in the book before his attention wandered - as did his hands.

Mint hot chocolate, the music from the cd, Mrs Mac sleeping soundly on the cushion of Auntie Jane's comfy chair. Gem surveyed the office and raked her fingers through her hair.

Harry, Mrs Brown, Mr Cawley, Mr White. A mole.

She couldn't ignore the fact that the mole was likely in the Agency and not the SEA Network.

Harry hadn't been available for months. And she simply knew he would not be returning to the Agency. He knew nearly as much about the Agency computer system as did Mr White. Wherever Harry was he could be tracking the Agency and the SEA Network from another computer.

Mr Choate's deductions were logical and likely true. Harry had the code book, and the printed copies of the Nazi codes that her dad had been able to decipher. The information she had been looking for had been in Harry's safe for months - or somewhere in Harry's possession. And where was Mrs Brown in all of this? Did she actually know where Harry was? Was she looking for him? Harry's last known location was in South East Asia. Mrs Brown had been on 'holiday' for weeks at a time. Was she searching for him?

No agency staffer had ever gone rogue - according to Mr Choate. What of Harry? If he hadn't gone rogue, where the HELL was he?

Not an adequate correlation. Paul Andriani had disappeared, but he had not gone rogue. That was a fact even if only the three of them knew where Paul was.

Gem pulled out her mobile. At least Mr Cawley would know she wasn't avoiding him.

'Do you think Blank has gone rogue?'

'Soldier of Fortune so to speak?'
'Yes.'
'I doubt it. But it is possible.'
'Do you think he will ever return to the Agency?'
'No.'
'Would you trust him again if he did want to return?'
'Depends where he had been - his activities.'
'What of Harry?'
'What about Harry?'
'He disappeared. Same as Blank.'
'Harry didn't leave a trail of bodies behind him.'
That was a huge slap!
'Do you think Blank killed the c-couriers and c-agents?'
'Not for a minute.'
'Then why different?'
'Bodies. No bodies. Blank couldn't go out into the field again.'
'True.'
That definitely made sense.
'Okay. Just curious of your thoughts.'
'I'm curious of your work. What have you for me?'
'Not sure. But something is cooking.'
She might as well admit it. After all, Mr Choate trusted Mr Cawley. Gem just hoped he was right to do so.
'Turn up the heat. Ring me first, Gem! Night or day!'
'Yes.'
'Goodnight, Gem.'
'Goodnight.'
But would she ring him first? Or would she ring Mr Choate? Or Mr Harper?"
Harry hadn't left a trail of bodies, Gem mused as she filled her mug. Definitely true, Gem agreed, pressing the start button again on the cd player. But Mr Cawley didn't know Paul Andriani had resurfaced quickly - and was in London working for T.O.
She pulled out her mobile again.
'Why don't you go back to the Agency?'
'I don't want my file closed.'
'Why?'
'I want doubt in the world as to my existence - where I might be.'
'Word is JS is dead.'
'But not confirmed.'
'Who would know if you returned to the Agency?'
Agency staff would!
'That is the question.'
'Mole.'
'Yes.'
'Mole may be in SEA Network.'
'Possibly, Gem. Most agents who disappear never resurface, never return to the Agency. Safer for Agency and staff.'

'Who is the mole?'
'You tell me, Gem.'
'I don't know.'
'Same here.'
'Okay. Bye.'
'Ciao, Gem!'

She could hardly say that Harry was her first guess. Paul wouldn't believe her. She didn't believe herself. She didn't want to believe it. She simply did not want to believe anyone in the Agency would murder Gemmy, their parents, Mr Portermann, the counter-couriers and agents. Harry wasn't cold-blooded. In fact, she didn't know anyone who was capable of committing all those crimes.

Enough. She rubbed her eyes. She needed sleep. It was an escape from the Key that demanded to be retrieved. The long case clock in the main hall chimed thee quarter hour. She completed her second bedtime routine: thermos, electric fires, cd player, mug, and went to bed.

Wyatt was awake and waiting for her.

Gem was amused by how Sunday nearly completely replicated Saturday. And Wyatt was amused by being served breakfast in bed again, tea in his office, and dessert in bed after lunch at the pub. Gem unpacked Christmas boxes, setting aside worn and damaged trimmings. Mr M claimed Miss Molly for a long walk and a thorough brushing.

The weather was clear and pleasantly cool, requiring only a thick cardigan. Gem wore the one Wyatt had purchased for her in Oslo, for their walk to the Crow for lunch.

"It's perfect on you," Wyatt smiled, freeing butterflies. "Do you ski? - Oh sorry - thoughtless question," he quickly apologized.

Ah yes, the broken arm.

"Not much of a skier," she murmured. "You?"

"Not bad," he admitted.

"You scorch the trails don't you," she replied, a statement, not a query. He owns ski resorts, she recalled Mr Choate saying.

Wyatt nodded. "I have been known to do so. GEI owns four ski resorts. I thought it best to know all the trails."

Gem nodded and he changed the subject to lunch and hurried them on their way.

"Mike's trying a new pasta sauce at the Crow - we're to be taste testers today," he informed her. "Don't make faces if you don't like it," he teased.

"I would never do that!" Gem laughed. "He might spit in my food if I requested something else."

"Thank you for that image," Wyatt groaned. "I may opt for a liquid lunch."

Wyatt read reports the remainder of the afternoon - after a delicious dessert - and Gem finished unpacking the Christmas boxes, rearranged all the items for Mrs M's careful inspection, then washed her hands of the rest of the holiday preparations. The remainder of the work would be in Mrs M's capable hands. Once the work was accomplished, the dread of the holidays returned to Gem. By the time Mrs M, and her assistant from the village, had the Hall decorated, Gem would probably hate gold, green and red. And poinsettias.

She wandered to her office and watched the international news. There was not a single story of interest to her. She slipped a Dr Who dvd into the player, and decided to settle into Auntie Jane's comfy chair to divert her thoughts.

"Still travelling in time and space?" Wyatt walked into the office, bearing a mug of hot chocolate and a plate of biscuits.

"Trying not to actually," Gem sighed.

"Interesting tool of avoidance," he observed mildly. "Molly has requested a walk, and Mr M has again requested her company.

"He is so kind to her."

"Indeed," Wyatt nodded. "Would you like to chat with me while I grill you a perfect steak and chips for dinner?" he queried.

"Hmm," Gem smiled.

"Then I have other avoidance ideas for you," he teased.

"You always do," Gem laughed.

Hot chocolate, tea, and an additional chapter of the biography of David Livingston, explorer extraordinaire. But only one chapter.

Gem sipped the hot chocolate, trying to decide the flavour - a hint of raspberry, perhaps. Wyatt was full of surprises.

Oh! how she did want to continue to live in his world with him. But now she had to work to leave his world.

Gem let the third Key slip. Computers.

Harry. Mr White. Mrs Brown. Mr Cawley.

Mr Choate had an Agency computer in his suite at the inn in Ticking Bottom. And he had a mobile phone monitoring computer. Harry could have managed the same computer set-up wherever he was. Mr White had the Agency computers. Mr Cawley had access to all computers in his office. Mrs Brown was not equal to Harry or Mr White's calibre, but who knew what she had learned over the years - unawares to the others.

Gem pulled out her mobile. Mr Cawley was awake.

'Where is Mrs Brown?'

'Don't know.'

'Can you contact her?'

'In case of emergency only.'

'Can you contact Harry?'

'No.'

'Can Mr White contact either?'

Should be no since Mr White had to answer to Mr Cawley, according to Mr Choate.

'No.'

'Are you positive?'

'Yes.'

'Okay. Goodnight.'

'Goodnight.'

She cleared the messages and texted again - this time to Mr Choate.

'Where is Mrs Brown?'
'Not certain. Possibly in country.'
'At her home?'
'No.'
'Can you contact her?'
'In emergency only.'
'Something very serious has happened.'
'An understatement!'
'Something else! Are you playing with me?'
'No! Absolutely not! Haven't a clue to your queries!'
'Is Harry still alive?'
'I have no reason to believe otherwise! Seriously, Gem! If I had information I would share with you!'
'Okay.'
'Can you share your thoughts?'
'Not at this time.'
'Very well. I'm here if you need me!'
'Thanks! Bye!'
'Bye, Gem!'

Mr Cawley and Mr Choate could call Mrs Brown in case of emergency. Something had happened to Harry and Mrs Brown was with him. Or she was providing cover for him.

Mr Choate thought Mrs Brown was possibly in this country.

She pulled out her mobile again.

'Can you track Mrs Brown's mobile?'
'No.'
'How do you know she went on leave?'
'She called and said she was on leave. Then turned off her mobile.'
'Okay. I won't bother you again tonight. Go back to sleep.'
'Not sleeping. Reviewing applicants.'
'Good luck!'
'Have some good ones. Agency should be full force by end of year.'
'Good. - Can you hack into SEA Network computer?'
'No.'
'Could Harry, Mr White?'
'Probably.'
'Okay. Bye!'
'Bye. Gem.'

Did she have any other questions? She thought not. She thought again and texted Mr Choate.

'How can you contact Mrs Brown if she turned off her mobile?'
'She has a pager.'
'Okay. Goodnight.'
'Goodnight, Gem.'

A hot chocolate refill, and more music. Mrs Mac wanted kitty crunchies.

Gem stared at her computer. She was well versed in her computer programs, and with her laptop, but they were the only types of computers she had ever used.

She had no idea what a wonk and a geek could do with computers. Obviously track mobile connections and text messages. Her father had used a twenty-first century computer model of a cryptograph for encoding and decoding messages, which he had e-mailed to the Agency. Which he had also used to decipher the Nazi code book.

Mr White had her father's code computer to attempt to find the glitch that had scrambled the last message he had sent regarding their flight plan. Harry had been in Sydney. Could he have scrambled the message using another computer? All Agency computers were supposed to be protected. Mr White worked tirelessly at that purpose. Perhaps the code computer had never had a glitch. Perhaps Mr White had spent - no wasted - hundreds of hours, countless sleepless nights searching for a glitch that never existed.

Her father had sent the cryptogram to Harry; Harry had been in Sydney. Harry could not decipher the message. Her dad had never made errors.

Gem's head spun. She turned off switches, rinsed items and went to bed.

Wyatt roused for a few moments, folding his arms around her when she slipped into bed beside him. She listened to his quiet breathing, forcing thoughts from her mind. Her mind would be clearer in a few hours. Perhaps then she would know the next step she should take.

Chapter Thirty-Three

"You are very quiet this morning, sweetheart," Wyatt frowned with concern at breakfast. Quiet, distracted, a bit agitated.

"I'm sorry," Gem winced. Wyatt had gathered the butterflies and she had been relaxed until she showered and dressed. Then her thoughts started ambushing her. By the time she reached the breakfast table she was sick of the word 'computer'. "I have a bit of a headache," she forced a smile. "Perhaps a walk with Molly this morning will clear my head."

"Try a rest if the fresh air doesn't help," he suggested.

"I shall," she nodded.

Gem and Molly walked Wyatt to the Land Rover in the old stable, and waved him on his way.

She followed Miss Molly into the field and broke her own rule. While the golden dog raced about the countryside, Gem took her thoughts away from Molly.

She needed help, but she couldn't ask anyone from the Agency. She needed a completely uninvolved person. Someone she could trust - without question - to answer her queries, but not ask questions in return. Someone to answer her questions and to keep their mouth shut.

She needed a computer wonk. Someone with Agency calibre.

She pulled out her mobile and texted Mr Choate.

'Aside from Agency and B.I., who has best computer wonk in G.B. who keeps mouth shut?'

It was a few minutes before the reply came and Gem groaned at the reply.

'GEI.'

Damn and Blast! Blast! Blast!

'Next?'

'None!'

'Not possible!'

'GEI best wonk. Wonk is silent as the grave. GEI can't afford wonk that chats. WG hires the best!'

'Okay. Thanks.'

'Sorry it wasn't the reply you wanted.'

'It's an answer. Bye.'

'Bye. You know where I am if you need me.'

Blast! It would have to be Grantham Enterprises International! How did Wyatt Grantham manage to invade every aspect of her life!

But she had no other choice! She needed information that she did not want to share at this time with Agency staff!

And Wyatt had offered his assistance. He wanted her to trust him. He had to trust her.

She couldn't do it! She couldn't ask him!

Mrs Brown trusted Wyatt. Mr Choate trusted him. But the GEI wonk was a step away from Wyatt. A wonk 'silent as the grave', Mr Choate had insisted. But Gem's queries were beyond a business security matter. It was a question of deaths.

Gem couldn't afford to let any cogs slip. This particular cog slipping would go crashing into international space at a terrifying, uncontrollable speed, and into an inconceivably destructive end.

Definitely not good to let this cog slip!

Gem paced the field, keeping an eye to Molly, deciding her options. It was a quick thought. She had only one.

She made her decision.

She gave Molly the command to return and hurried to the Hall.

Mrs M had been stunned that morning when she entered the house, by the array of Christmas ready for her ministrations; and she was still chattering about it when Gem and Molly returned from their walk. Gem gave the house manager two thumbs up to proceed with her holiday preparations, then dashed to her office to search the computer for a phone number to a restaurant which she knew Wyatt would enjoy. The Cumbria. Bad memory for her, but he favoured the establishment. She rang the number and set her day in motion, next ringing Mr Choate to advise him that she would like to drive to GEI in a half hour. He assured her he would be ready to leave at that time.

The she pulled out the big guns. The long black skirt- which still fit having an elastic waistband - black turtleneck, black knee length cardigan, black knee length lace up boots. She carefully brushed and braided her hair, slipped her mobile into the pocket of her skirt and hurried down the staircase - careful to use the hand rail.

Mrs M stepped back, nearly dropping her tea cup, as Gem entered the kitchen.

"You look to be a statue of death," she said with uncharacteristic bluntness.

"New clothes wanting to escape the wardrobe," Gem said with a forced smile.

"Wanting to hide more like it," Mrs M protested.

"Too fierce?" Gem frowned.

"Depends on whom you wish to kill. But it's very striking and sleek, particularly with your hair colour."

"That's what I want," Gem replied, but thought a moment and dashed upstairs to grab a very long white scarf, which she drew around her neck to hang free and very nearly down to the hem of the long cardi.

"Better?" she asked the housekeeper.

"A touch. But there won't be any survivors," Mrs M replied, again bluntly.

"No," Gem agreed, but her reply had a double meaning for her. No one on the Pilos had survived.

Mr Choate was waiting to pull out behind her as she drove past the inn. She concentrated on her driving, breathing steadily to control her nerves. Luck was with her to find a space for the Defender, Mr Choate one for his vehicle, in a car park two blocks from the Grantham building.

Choate's eyebrows shot up as Gem stepped out of the Defender.

"Are you going to make a request, or just try to frighten the hell out of your husband?" he asked dryly.

"We'll see how that goes," Gem gave him a steady gaze. "Wyatt is not easily frightened."

"You must share with me later, Gem. I've never seen this side of you before."

"I'm on edge," she said defensively.

"Well, don't show it," he ordered. "Your man, your plan. Good luck!"

"Thank you," she slipped her keys into her shoulder bag, patted her mobile in her pocket, and started the walk to the Grantham Building, Mr Choate a short distance behind her.

There was a new receptionist at the front desk. The young woman smiled when Gem approached her.

"Mrs Grantham," she said formally, "I'll notify Mr Grantham that you are here." She reached for the telephone on her desk.

"Please don't," Gem smiled, "Ms Meyers," she read the name plate on the desk.

"Yes, ma'am," the young woman replied.

"How did you know my name?" Gem asked curiously.

"I saw you with Mr Grantham at the rescue centre," the young woman smiled. "I volunteer there. I trained Molly. Ms Holton volunteers at the shelter also. She suggested I apply for a position here."

Ms Holton. Molly. Of course. "It's a pleasure to meet you, Ms Meyers. Thank you for Molly. She's lovely," Gem shook the receptionist's hand then walked to the lift.

When Gem stepped off the lift she discovered Ms Carton had also been replaced by a Mr Reed who stood and offered assistance.

"Research and Development," Gem replied, "I know the way, thank you."

"Yes, ma'am," he nodded, his eyes growing wide.

Gem felt his eyes on her as she walked along the corridor. She glanced back. He had reached for the phone on his desk. Probably ringing Ms Meyers for information, Gem mused.

When she entered the R and D office, all eyes turned to her as they had before when she had visited Wyatt. Ms Jones and Ms Carton now had desks in the large room and both women smiled and nodded to her.

Ms Holton had been speaking to the staff, but immediately approached Gem.

"Mrs Grantham, Mr Grantham is in his office," she smiled, holding her hand for Gem to precede her to the far double doors.

And beyond the doors, was an office, smaller than the R and D office, but impressive nonetheless; the upper half of the walls were richly panelled in mahogany, the lower sections were old mahogany book cabinets with glass lift up doors.

There was a single beautifully polished desk below the bank of windows to the left, at which sat a pretty young woman with a mass of short golden curls.

"Mrs Grantham, this is Ms Wexton," Ms Holton graciously made the introductions. "Ms Wexton is Mr Grantham's Personal Assistant."

Gem shook hands with Wyatt's assistant and they each said a brief greeting with a smile.

"This way, Mrs Grantham," Ms Holton spoke again, and tapped gently at another set of double doors. A burnished gold name plate on the wall to the right of the door said 'Wyatt Grantham' in subtle letters. Not ostentatious - as Paul Andriani had said at St George's Cathedral.

Ms Holton immediately opened the door and as Gem entered Wyatt's office he stood up from the chair behind his desk, his jaw dropping as he saw her. Ms Holton closed the door leaving the two Granthams alone.

"Too intense?" she queried, slightly raising her eyebrows.

"Depends," Wyatt said slowly. "Was your intention to stun my staff, or to frighten the hell out of me?"

"Mr Choate made a similar remark," Gem smiled. "I told him you aren't easily frightened."

"There's always a first time," Wyatt countered.

"It's a new outfit," Gem said simply.

"Well, it certainly is striking with your fair hair," he observed. "Thank heavens you don't have black hair or I might be running for my life."

Before Gem could reply, the telephone on Wyatt's desk beeped. While he answered the ring, she glanced around the office. It was very similar to Ms Wexton's office, but was much larger and there were seascape paintings on the walls- paintings that Gem recognized as James's. She was now very familiar with James's style and brush stroke. Ms Weston's office had pastoral paintings, which had not been painted by James.

Wyatt's desk was very large and held many framed photos. She couldn't see the subjects, but she could see a mug on his desk - the same mug Gem used for hot chocolate every day and during the dark hours. She couldn't believe Wyatt would want a mug with a photo of Molly, Mrs Mac and her on his desk.

"Very well, hold please," Wyatt said and looked at Gem. "Ms Holton wishes to know if she can use your 'look' for a meeting tomorrow?" he shook his head, puzzled.

"It would be my honour," Gem smiled.

Wyatt repeated the remark into the telephone then replaced the receiver. He looked at her, shook his head again, then walked around his desk, gently placing his hands on her shoulders. He kissed her, then slid his hands down her arms to hold her hands.

"Oh dear," Gem suddenly murmured. "I should have rung to see if you were able to see me today - I didn't think - I'm sorry. It was very rude of me to just come by like this."

"Good Lord, sweetheart!" Wyatt scowled. "I don't want you to ever think you need to schedule an appointment to see me!"

Gem sighed. "I wanted to ask you to have lunch with me. I booked a table at the Cumbria for half noon. I used your name, by the way. I hope that was alright to do," she said hesitantly. The last thing she wanted was to annoy him.

"Your name would have achieved the same result, my dear. You are known there," he gently informed her, but did not refer to the two occasions when she had previously dined there. "Sweetheart, you do not enjoy the Cumbria."

"You do," she countered firmly. She took a deep breath. "And when one requests a favour, one should return in kind," she looked at him steadily.

"Must be a HELL of a favour," Wyatt observed with amusement. "Hold the thought," he kissed her. "I'll be back in a few minutes. Look around if you like. This is the first time you have been in my office."

He closed the door behind him as he stepped into Ms Wexton's office, and Gem quickly walked around to look at the photos on his desk: his parents, James, four of her: one taken after their wedding ceremony, one of her taking photos of Fortrose, one he had taken of her that day in her office when he had tried her new camera; the fourth was one of her standing on the old stone bridge below the Hall; she was gazing down at the village. She walked over to look out the windows to the cityscape of London. She didn't want him to think that she was snooping at the photos on his desk - nor did she want to be seen studying James's paintings. She didn't want James to be at the front of Wyatt's mind when she asked her favour of him. She stared down at the street below, wondering when Wyatt had taken the photo of her on the bridge.

Wyatt returned. "We are off, my dear, a taxi is waiting for us."

"A taxi," Gem protested, as he ushered her through the various offices. "We can take the Defender."

"I want to relax and enjoy your company, so I will be ready to be asked the favour," he teased.

Ten minutes later Gem whispered to Wyatt. "We are going in the wrong direction."

He put his finger to her lips. "Hush." He reinforced the order with a long kiss.

Gem did not argue, and didn't have time to question the change in her plans. She was occupied.

"What?" she laughed as they finally arrived at their destination. The British Museum.

"The Court Restaurant. I believe comfortable for both of us," he assisted her from the taxi.

Gem grinned at him as they entered the museum. "Always full of surprises!"

"I am growing quiet fond of pub grub. One can't argue with good cooking. But this should do us today."

"But the booking at the Cumbria," Gem protested uneasily.

"Ms Holton and Ms Wexton were delighted to stand in for us at the Cumbria on my tab."

Wyatt waited patiently through their lunch, allowing Gem to request the favour in her own time. She had insisted on paying for lunch, but he could divert her attention from that when the bill came.

Gem waited until after they had finished their dessert, biding her time, regularly reading the room. There were no other customers seated near them; in fact the restaurant was rather sparsely filled, and no one was lounging over their food.

Finally she set down her fork and quietly addressed Wyatt. "I need a favour."

Wyatt leaned forward to hear her soft voice. "However, I can assist you, my dear, I shall," he gently assured her.

Gem took a deep breath. "I need a computer wonk. And you have the best computer wonk in this country," she said abruptly.

"How do you know that?" Wyatt said skeptically.

Gem took another deep breath and looked directly into his eyes. "I just know," she replied, her voice quiet but firm. "I need a computer wonk who will not divulge what I ask - to anyone. Not even to you," she had to struggle now to meet his eyes. "That person is your computer wonk."

"Oh. I see." Wyatt leaned back in his chair, pondering her words. Whatever he could have imagined the favour to be, this would never have been considered.

"You told me a few weeks past that you trust me," Gem pressed, not wanting to lose her nerve.

Wyatt nodded, but remained silent. He had made that statement a number of times. Before he had ended the Game. And then again after he had ended the Game.

And Gem lost her nerve. She could see the skepticism in his eyes. He didn't trust her, and this was a very great favour, indeed, to request. But it was too much to ask she could clearly see.

"Oh, Lord, Wyatt. I wouldn't have asked you - but there's no one else I could go to," she faltered in dismay.

Wyatt nodded, frowning. "You are in dire straits, Gem."

"I haven't done anything illegal, Wyatt - never in my entire life," she promised with quiet intensity. "Nor will I, I swear to you."

Gem sat back in her chair and stared at the empty dessert plate. How could she convince him? It was difficult to plead to him to 'please trust me' when she could give him no reason as to why he should.

She leaned forward again and Wyatt watched the pain and haunted look cloud her eyes. She looked deathly pale, all colour drained from her face.

"Something monstrous happened awhile back - before I met you. I can't tell you what happened," she whispered. "I simply can't tell you. But I think I know how it happened. I think I know why it happened," Gem's voice shook with desperation. "I need a computer wonk who could validate my suspicions. There's no one else I could -" she shut down. She covered her face with her hands, then lowered them to look at him.

"This was a huge mistake - I'm sorry." Gem grabbed her shoulder bag from the back of her chair and suddenly stood and rushed off.

Wyatt was shocked by her words, and then again that she had run off. Well, he thought as he reached for his wallet, he had arranged after all to pay the lunch bill.

Damn! Either he trusted her now, or he would have to spend the remainder of his life doubting her.

Wyatt caught up with her at the top of the museum steps.

"Gem!" he caught her arm, pulling her beside a pillar. He stared into her eyes, and the pain he saw there tore at his heart. "Sondra Blessington. She has been with GEI for over ten years. She is a virtual clam. She minutely follows Need-To-Know, which is a law written in granite at GEI. I shall tell her no one but you are Need-To-Know. I will not ask her a single question about this - ever. Nor shall I ever ask questions of you."

"Thank you, Wyatt," she whispered, then leaned against his shoulder. "I'm not sure I want to know if what I think is true. But I have to know." I don't want to know, because if I am right, I will soon be losing you. And you will soon be hating me again. And I have to use you to hurt you. I am as horrid as you accused me to be at Marigold Cottage.

Wyatt held her in his arms, resting his cheek against her hair. "Do you wish to meet Ms Blessington at her lab - or?" he gently asked.

Gem thought a moment of a place that should not be too busy on a Tuesday in December. A past assignment delivery site. "Tomorrow at eleven o'clock. The Milkshake Bar, Barclay Court, London Zoo."

"As you wish." He released her, pulled his mobile from his pocket and stepped away from her.

Gem watched him as he spoke crisply, quietly into his phone. Her heart ached so deeply for him, for Gemmy and James and their baby, mum, dad, Mr Portermann and all the others. It ached so deeply she couldn't imagine her heart would ever again be free of the hurt.

Wyatt returned the mobile to his pocket and walked back to her. "It's set," he nodded. "You won't be able to miss her - short, flaming red hair, porcelain white skin, very petite, piercing blue eyes that can cut right through you."

"She sounds terrifying," Gem said faintly.

"You can decide that when you meet her," Wyatt chuckled, taking her hands in his.

"Thank you, thank you," Gem sighed deeply. It was not a sigh of relief, but rather one of sadness - of questions to come in the near future. She hoped she was wrong. Hopefully Ms Blessington could clear her vision.

"Oh, Wyatt! I forgot to pay the bill for lunch!"

"I settled it," Wyatt laughed suddenly. "You can spot me dinner at the Crow this evening."

"Really?" she smiled eagerly.

"Certainly not," Wyatt gently scoffed. He pulled her against him, staring down into her trouble eyes. "But I wouldn't mind breakfast and dessert in bed this weekend."

"As you wish, Dark Lord," she slipped her arms around his neck and kissed him.

"I believe I shall have that title added to all my personal stationery," he chuckled.

"And just how do you intend to explain that to whomever receives your correspondence?" Gem teased.

"I'll just let the reader's imagination soar with it," he laughed.

On the taxi ride back to the Grantham Building, Wyatt laced his fingers through hers. "Are you okay to drive to Ticking Bottom, or shall I take you home, my dear?" he frowned.

"I am okay," Gem assured him. "Thank you for asking," she rested her head on his shoulder, wishing the taxi driver would get lost in the city traffic.

"Very well, dinner at the Crow then. I'll text Mrs M not to prepare dinner," he kissed her.

"Perfect."

Mr Choate was waiting for Gem as they stepped from the taxi.

"Mr Choate, how do you know when to so promptly appear?" Gem queried.

"Mr Grantham rang me with the time and location," Choate grinned.

Ah - on the museum steps after Wyatt had rung Ms Blessington. After another quick kiss, Wyatt entered the building bearing his name and that of his ancestors.

Gem spoke softly to her steady companion and co-worker. "I need a cup of tea."

"Howard's?" Choate replied barely moving his lips.

"Yes."

"You lead, I follow," Choate ordered.

Howard's was very quiet, after what he said had been a phenomenally busy morning. Gem collapsed on the sofa at the rear of the shop.

"Did your outfit startle Mr Grantham?" Choate queried as he sat down beside her and handed her a cup of tea.

"He said the same thing you said," Gem replied, blowing on the steaming brew. "Did you text him what to say?"

"Didn't think it was necessary. Only way he could react. You stormed his office."

"I did in a way," Gem mused.

"Gem," Choate began slowly, "do you wish to talk about all your queries of late? I have two ears - both willing to listen."

Gem shook her head. "I'm still working on something. I'll let you know as soon as I know if my thoughts are solid."

"Very well. I can be patient when needs be," he nodded.

"You're very patient with me," Gem said gratefully.

"Family, Gem," was all he said in reply.

Gem was emotionally drained by the time she returned to the Hall. Mrs M had received Wyatt's text and had diverted dinner preparation time to Christmas preparation time. Gem changed to jeans and a jumper, and had a cup of tea with the house manager, listening to chat about which ornaments went to which tree. Mr M had selected three trees for the Hall, had gone back to the woods to review his choices, decided against the one for the dining room, fearing it would be too wide, and had selected an alternate tree. Mrs M would go out with him Saturday to approve his decisions.

Molly finally interrupted the chat with her lead in her mouth and a single bark at the kitchen door.

Gem gratefully escaped the Hall, letting the poochie roam the fields and meadows while she walked the cobblestone lane. Before her drive to London, Gem had greatly doubted that Wyatt would grant her favour. She still couldn't believe he had done so. He had assured her he would never ask Ms Blessington - his own employee - of Gem's questions to her. Mr Choate trusted Sondra Blessington. Wyatt trusted her. Now Gem had to trust her, and hope Wyatt would be true to his word.

She forced the thoughts out of her mind for the duration of her walk with Miss Molly. Mrs M was completely enthralled in her holiday plans and Gem gladly escaped to a shower and fresh jeans, turtleneck, and the sweater Wyatt had purchased for her in Inverness. She could at least show him she appreciated his gifts before she skewered his heart again.

Gem went down to her office and watched the telly. There was no international news to catch her thoughts, and nothing on the local news to occupy her mind. She pulled up her computer file on Glasgow Cathedral, but couldn't focus on the text. She paced the floor, watched a Dr Who dvd, watched the news, listened to the Sibelius cd, brushed Miss Molly, and wished she had taken up the habit of chewing her nails, because that might be a way to still her splitting nerves.

Wyatt arrived at the Hall and showered before they walked to the Crow for dinner. And while they chatted about Gem's visit to Wyatt's office that day, neither of them referred to their lunch or the subsequent conversation.

"I fear you have started a new trend at GEI," he said with a raised brow. "Office chatter is of Mrs Grantham's 'power look'," he put air quotes around the last two words.

"It's a very common look," Gem countered.

"Not used before at GEI," Wyatt laughed. "I'll let you know how it affects business."

When they returned to the Hall, Wyatt had a phone call that lasted most of the evening. Gem couldn't focus on the cathedral, so she switched on the telly and perused viewing options. Still no international events that hinted of Harry's whereabouts; the U.K. was on an even keel. Everything was copasetic. But her life might soon disintegrate.

She paced the downstairs, made a pot of tea, and carried it to Wyatt in the library. He blew her a kiss and gave her a quick smile. Must have been quite a chatterbox at the other end of the mobile call. She had already started getting ready for bed when Wyatt finally finished his call and tracked her down to the bedroom.

"You are very distracted," Wyatt murmured a few minutes later, stroking her cheek.

"I'm sorry," Gem apologized, sighing.

"No need to apologize, my sweet," he soothed. "I think you need a massage. It will help you relax and ease you to sleep."

Wyatt's massages were better than a sleeping pill - she would imagine - never having taken one. She filled the mug with hot chocolate. She still found it odd that Wyatt had a matching mug on his desk. That was very sweet. She pushed the start button on the cd player, and paced.

Perhaps Gemmy, perhaps I know what happened. There is another issue. Gemmy! Gemmy! Gemmy! I'm afraid I know what happened!

She paced the office, the great room, the living room, the kitchen, the butler's pantry, through the breakfast room and through the dining room, then past the library to the sitting room and den. She would not enter Mrs M's new domain. The sitting room or den would make a lovely playroom for the twins.

Twins! Lord! She so often quite forgot she was pregnant. She was going to be a horrible mum. Gemmy would have been a brilliant mum!

Right after the delivery she was going to have a beer - if only to share a half pint; but it wouldn't be shared with Wyatt.

Wyatt would be an excellent father. She would probably forget she had children and forget to feed them.

Ms Blessington! Eleven o'clock. Eight hours.

She filled her mug and pressed the start button and paced.

If Ms Blessington confirmed Gem's theory, the Agency would have a much better chance of finding the Pilos.

Her thoughts roamed back and forth, to the Pilos, to her conversation with Wyatt at lunch. He had not wanted to trust her. But he had. He could have refused unless she explained her request. But he hadn't asked questions. And he hadn't refused her request. She had told him more than she probably should have. But he had listened and he had agreed.

Wyatt lay awake for an hour after she slipped from their bed. Something monstrous had happened, Gem had said by way of explanation of her request to meet the GEI wonk. Perhaps he would finally have information of Gem's past. Perhaps a reason as to why she had deserted James. He had to trust her. And so he would, he yawned. Then he closed his eyes to sleep.

Gem counted the hours. Seven hours. She finally went to bed, hoping she could sleep, hoping the dark hours would not lengthen that morning. She needed sleep to be able to speak coherently to a blue-eyed, flaming red-haired, clam-like computer wonk, in just a few hours' time.

When Wyatt's arms encircled her, holding her close to him, she did indeed sleep as the long case clock chimed five times.

Chapter Thirty-Four

Gem arrived ten minutes early at the Milkshake Bar and waited nervously, repeatedly glancing at her wrist watch, hoping time would speed by. But it did not. However, Ms Blessington was apparently not a procrastinator. She arrived five minutes ahead of time, and Gem instantly recognized her from Wyatt's description. Flaming red hair, lovely porcelain skin, piercing blue eyes. Gorgeous! She was a little off-putting, her manner confident, her spine straight, shoulders back. Gem was a bit afraid to confide in the woman. And then Ms Blessington smiled. A wide warm smile.

"Are you, Gem?" the young woman queried, still smiling.

Gem nodded.

"Mr Grantham told me to call you, Gem - said you're not a toff, that you're already on pins and needles about whatever it is we're here to chat about. I'm Sondra Blessington," she stuck out her hand.

"Gem Grantham," she replied as she shook the other woman's hand. The surname no longer made her cringe.

"I'm in no hurry today, Gem, so do you mind if I get a milkshake before we start?" Sondra grinned. "Pineapple. Used to hate the taste, but now I can't get enough of them." She didn't wait for a reply and placed her order. "I'm pregnant. Cravings."

"Same," Gem nodded. "Hot chocolate, but I'll definitely try a pineapple shake."

Sondra gave her another wide smile. "Congratulations! Poor Mr Grantham! Surrounded by pregnant women!"

"Surrounded?" Gem puzzled.

"Clover - my partner - Clover Wexton - Mr Grantham's P.A."

"Ah! I thought you owned a horse ranch. I didn't know you both worked for GEI."

"We do." Sondra sipped her shake. "My brother and his wife do the daily chores at the farm. Clover and I bring home the pay packets."

"So all three of us," Gem grinned.

"Four - Emma Holton found out yesterday. A surprise for her - number four. She is probably breaking the news to Mr Grantham right about now," she glanced at her watch. "They have an eleven o'clock meeting today."

"Oh dear! A shock to the boss - he relies on her so," Gem winced.

"He'll still be able to - Emma's a wonderful mum, but she has the babies and hands them over to her husband. Stuart dotes on the kids. He's self-employed, and tells Emma to return to work any time she likes. GEI has great maternity benefits, but Emma can't stay away from the challenges of GEI. Stuart could give parenting courses. You have a query - he's the man with the answers."

"You AND Ms Wexton?" Gem was amazed.

"Really poor timing that," Sondra admitted. "I couldn't get pregnant, so when my last test was negative, we decided Clover should give it a try. She did and it took first time. Then my last test was proved rubbish, so both of us - three months apart. Mr Grantham's former P.A. will cover for Clover for a time. He's a project manager now but he'll take up the reins for Mr Grantham for a few months."

"Lovely," Gem smiled, as she sipped the shake, deciding it was a decent alternative to hot chocolate.

Then there was the awkward moment. Someone had to refer to the subject of the meeting.

"The time has come the Walrus said to talk of computer things," Ms Blessington seemed to sense Gem's thoughts. She drew Gem away from the Milkshake Bar to an area where no one could overhear them without being seen.

"And not of shoes, ships, sealing wax or cabbages, or kings, or boiling seas," Gem twisted the lines of the poem, and surveyed the area around them.

She drew a deep breath. This was as difficult as she feared it would be. Violating Agency law - going outside the Family.

"Between you and me, Gem," Sondra wagged a finger from Gem to herself. "Just us, for as long as you say - or forever. And if you are in any way concerned: I never drink alcohol - or smoke anything. I do not talk."

Gem gave a quick nod. "Mobiles have inter-net connection," she began.

"Most do these days if you want to pay a big bill," Sondra nodded.

Gem took another deep breath. "Could a computer use a mobile to send a signal to - disrupt something?" she said hesitantly.

Sondra's brows shot up.

Gem hastened to assure her. "I'm not involved in anything illegal! I swear!" she used the same words she had spoken to Wyatt.

"I am certain of that," the wonk replied. "If you were involved in something illegal, you would be nervous guilty. You aren't really nervous - you're in pain. I can see it in your eyes. The pain so deep - the Chinese have a word for it -" she frowned, tying to recall the word.

"Han," Gem said.

"Yes," Ms Blessington nodded. "Go on."

Gem covered her face with her hands, then shook her head, lowering her hands to look Sondra straight in the eyes.

"Could a computer send a signal to a mobile phone to disrupt the electrical mechanics of say - a plane?" Gem said in a rush.

"Lordy! Mrs Grantham. You know something about something?" Sondra's eyes opened wide.

Gem casually glanced around. No one was near them. "Or at least I think I do. I can't explain. What I say to you - you couldn't try to track - to find out anything. It is buried so deep - you just couldn't."

"Nor would I wish to, I am certain of that," Sondra firmly replied. "Go on - a plane - a commercial jet - 747?"

"Small. Say a prop."

"A nice shiny new one with all the computer bells and whistles?"

Gem nodded. "Say within a year or so new."

"You will probably dislike my answer," Sondra pursed her lips. "Let me think on this for a few minutes. Refill, please" she handed her cup to Gem.

She was ready to speak when her beverage was handed over.

"Private plane?"

"Yes."

"Pilot owner?"

"Yes."

"Did all the maintenance work - only person to do so, and to fly the plane - knew the plane inside and out?"

"Yes."

"Let's go to take-off. Passengers - I don't need to know how many."

"Yes."

"And one had a mobile."

"Yes."

"That someone else - someone trusted - had access to."

"Yes." Gem said, the word catching in her throat. "I know that's true. That is a fact."

"Positively diabolical," Ms Blessington grimaced. "Yes, it could be done. Someone put a chip in the mobile. That same someone programmed a computer to send a signal to the chip, which in turn sent a signal to disrupt all the electrical components - perhaps even recalibrating the components to send false readings to the pilot."

"My thoughts," Gem said firmly. "Cloudy skies, rain, pilot couldn't use dead reckoning even if he suspected a problem."

"Well, the programmer lucked out there," Sondra frowned. "Clear skies, would have him - her?" she looked at Gem for confirmation. "Easier to be specific - don't always have to mentally keep shifting pronouns."

"Him."

"Clear skies would have had pilot questioning the instrument panel, especially since he did all the maintenance. He knew his plane. Pilots do," she thought aloud. "Cloudy skies, rain, he trusted his instrument panel. Clear skies, the programmer probably would have had an alternate plan."

"No doubt," Gem nodded.

"Flight plan?"

"Sent by a computer to another computer. Receiving computer scrambled the message. Unreadable."

"Easily done," Sondra nodded. "Pilot clean and sober?"

"As the day he was born!"

Sondra gave her a steady look as Gem quickly looked about them.

"Pilot flying under radar?"

Gem nodded. "At take-off. Not confirmed. Likely. Okay. Yes. But it wasn't in an area which crossed commercial airfield traffic pattern."

"Quite a mouthful that," the other woman observed with a grim smile.

Gem was feeling better chatting to the computer genius. "How would one prove all of this - or any of it?"

"Your programmer is a wonk?"

"Yes. Or a geek," Gem, dragged her fingers through her hair.

Sondra nodded. "He or she will NOT permit you access to his/her computer. And the computer could be anywhere," she thought aloud. "You don't have the mobile phone?"

"No."

"The plane?"

Gem raked her fingers through her hair again.

"Oh dear God," Sondra Blessington sighed, shaking her head sadly. "You're searching for a missing plane, Gem."

"I didn't say that!" Gem protested fiercely, frightened of cogs suddenly slipping all over the world.

Sondra looked at her and shook her head again. "I did NOT hear you make such a remark," she exhaled sharply.

Gem casually scanned the landscape again. For the first time since she had arrived at the Milkshake Bar she clearly saw Mr Choate. He was far enough away as to not overhear the conversation. He was smoking a cigarette. Gem frowned briefly. Mr Choate never smoked - at least that she knew. He turned and looked beyond her, directly across from his position. Gem turned slightly to her right to see a priest, also smoking a cigarette. Family. Letting her know she was safe and to talk freely. Two men, definitely not computer wonks or geeks.

Gem looked back to Ms Blessington who was carefully watching her.

"You are in a hellish limbo, aren't you, Gem? And have been for some time," she observed quietly.

"Yes," Gem nodded, her voice cracking.

"Mr Grantham doesn't know. I realize that now. But is there someone else who knows? Are you alone in your search?" Sondra quietly asked.

"Not completely alone. But I can't say more than that. Saying anything right now to anyone could have disastrous consequences," Gem admitted. "I needed an expert - you."

"No need to say any more," Sondra replied. "If you have further questions, problems, ring me, text me." She wrote her mobile number on a slip of paper from her purse.

"Is your mobile secure?"

"It is. I built it. And Mr Grantham's, Emma's. All the executives' mobiles. They cannot be breached."

Oh yes they can. Someone breached Wyatt's mobile. Gem had to find out who had done so. Mrs Brown, Harry, or Gordon White. Or - had Mr Choate provided Wyatt's mobile number to Mrs Brown. She would soon find out that answer!

"Thank you, thank you," Gem sighed, forcing a small smile to Wyatt's computer wonk. "The programmer built the mobile in question."

"I thought so," Sondra murmured. "Did that same programmer build your mobile?"

Gem suddenly frowned. "I don't know."

"Is there a way you can check - just find out for sure?" Sondra took two steps to toss her shake container into a waste bin.

"Possibly." Gem thought of the list Mr Cawley checked at the beginning and end of each shift. She couldn't imagine the Agency would shred the log sheets.

"If not, I could take your mobile apart - put it back together in a couple of hours, at my lab," she offered.

"I'll let you know either way," Gem nodded.

Sondra glanced at the sky. "Weather is moving in - rain soon," she observed. "Perhaps the three of us soon-to-be mums could get together - chat babies with Emma. It might be helpful to get advice from a pro."

Gem winced. "Most of the time I forget I'm pregnant. That's a horrid thing to admit."

"You have other issues on your mind. I can't believe you're still sane. I don't think I would be," Ms Blessington said matter-of-factly. "You know you're being followed by a priest and that other chap, don't you?" She nodded in Choate's direction.

"My bodyguard and his trainee," Gem explained wryly. "Wyatt thinks I'm an airhead in need of a nanny." She had to have some way to explain the men and half the explanation was fact.

Sondra's eyes widened in amazement. "Heavens, Gem, the man is mad about you. Of course he wants to protect you. He's very protective of all his employees too. Whenever any of us work late, security escorts us to our vehicles to make sure we are safely on our way. Staff who work late and don't have vehicles are sent home in taxis. We have to ring security to give a code when we arrive home," she offered.

"Really!" It was Gem's turn to be amazed

Sondra grimaced. "An employee was murdered in the tube years back on her way home from work one night. Mr Grantham made sure that would never happen again."

The sounded just like Wyatt, Gem mused. Always in control of everything. Except for her. Now.

"The fake priest will probably go to hell for his impersonation," Sondra quickly changed the tone of the conversation.

"He's already booked a room there, according to him," Gem chuckled. "He's about five feet down now. Puts one foot down, then another. Standing on quicksand he is." Gem kept Mr Harper in her peripheral field. "I'd best let you get back to your work. You're on the clock," she sighed.

"I haven't been on the clock for years," Sondra laughed. "I often sleep at the lab. I'm going to put a nursery area in one corner come spring."

"Who will spell you when you have your baby?"

"I have a lab assistant, but I won't be out long. I'll just bring the baby to work with me."

"You're very dedicated," Gem said with surprise.

"I love my job," Sondra said firmly. "Did you ever have a job you loved?"

"Once," Gem admitted, the word catching in her throat. "A time ago," she murmured.

"Ah, that's how it is," Sondra said softly. "Well, you have your information now. My silence forever. My mobile number. Good luck on your search, and I'm on your team now," she put out her hand.

"Thank you again," Gem managed to say as she shook the wonk's hand.

Once back in the Defender, Gem drove to the park and texted Mr Choate.

'Chat.'

'Okay.'

He was alone. Perhaps the priest had to listen to confessions, Gem thought wryly.

"Why the priest?" she demanded, trying to suppress a grin, when he joined her at the centre of the park.

"He needs practise shadowing people," Choate suggested.

"He's an agent, for God's sake, he knows how to shadow people!" Gem protested laughing, then fell into the habit of scanning the landscape. "You two stuck out like a sore thumb."

"Only when you saw us - that was deliberate. Glynn wanted to make sure you knew you had our full support - in everything," Choate grew serious. "You broke Agency law today, Gem. I don't have to remind you how serious were your actions."

She well knew what she had done. "Are you going to tell Mr Cawley?" she queried apprehensively.

Choate drew a cigarette from his pocket, looked at Gem and put it away. "I'm Agency Security Director," he reminded her, and her heart plummeted. "I don't have to tell Cawley a damned thing," he replied bluntly. He gave her a stern look. "But don't get over your head, young lady," he warned. "I have told you, you aren't alone in this. Get it into your brilliant mind that I am not your enemy. Neither is Glynn. You have to trust us."

Gem heard the words and knew them to be sincere. But there was so much subterfuge, so much rubbish, her mind could not sort all the deceptions.

She scanned the landscape again then looked him directly in the eyes. "Where were you and Auntie Jane before you 'joined' -" she used air quotes around the word, "the Agency?"

"Seventy -five years - or find the Pilos - as I told you before," he remained implacable on the subject.

Gem folded her arms across her chest and continued to stare at him, refusing to back down.

"Oh, very well," Choate brushed the air with his hand. "Your Auntie Jane and I took out a dictator. The mission was not Agency sanctioned. It was a small country, a righteous uprising of the people. Jane and I were there as unofficial observers for the Agency."

"You got swept up in the moment," Gem quietly suggested, watching his eyes. He was telling the truth as far as she could discern.

"Hell no!" Choate frowned. "But we realized there was going to be a blood bath. The dictator and his general had to go."

Gem watched him, realizing the struggle he was going through remembering the event.

"The general took out the dictator, general committed suicide - as the army revolted and collapsed. The leader of the uprising came to power. Stabile government ensued," he capsulated the episode.

"How did you manage the murder/suicide?" Gem marvelled.

"That was Jane's plan and I managed the execution - no pun intended. I shall not tell you how," Choate steadfastly refused. "The Agency was extremely pleased with the outcome of the situation, but not being sanctioned has its penalties."

"Which were?" Gem held her breath as he spoke. Quiet mannered, gracious Auntie Jane! Good grief!

"Jane retired to a village for a few years and helped your mum raise you. I was sent to manage a vegetable farm," he replied wryly.

"Do you enjoy gardening?" Gem teased, breaking the tension.

"It's brilliant. Glynn is looking for a cottage for us. We want land, to hopefully become weekend gentlemen farmers" he grinned.

She couldn't suggest that they contact Wyatt about one of his sixty some thatched cottages, because he would likely soon cast her from the Hall. And he would most definitely not want to assist anyone she knew. Mr Choate would no longer be needed, and Glynn would become collateral damage.

"Are you reassured now, Gem?" Choate queried, exhaling long and deeply.

"I am," she admitted.

"Then - what can you tell me?" he frowned.

"I have to think," Gem murmured. Their chat had been a gratifying break, but now she was again plunged into the horror film starting to roll in her mind. "I think I want to go back to the Hall." While she was still welcome there.

"Okay," Choate reluctantly accepted her remarks. "But - have we an understanding?" he asked hopefully.

Gem looked at him, unsmiling. "Oh, Mr Choate, I do trust you," she said grimly. "You and your completely mad priest mate," she added. "He seems to be happy," she suggested as an afterthought.

"He is! He doesn't have to worry every day that some psycho radical is going to take him out," Choate nodded. "The life expectancy of an undercover agent is just a bit better than that of an RAF pilot in the opening years of the War. Not real good. Five missions for the pilot, a bit more than that for an agent of Glynn's line. He beat the odds repeatedly, but his time was coming. It's a deadly job."

Gem nodded. Now she had to find another agent who had also been a pilot.

Gem had to struggle to focus on her driving on her return to Ticking Bottom. A feeling of dread crept into her heart as she turned onto Litton Lane. The fields and meadows bordering the tarmac were drained of life by the cool winter temperatures, but she would miss the drive, she mused as she then directed the Defender on to Sedgely Lane. Thorne Lane was her favourite with the wide expanse of meadows - gold in September - when she had first seen them.

She would miss the old stone bridges over the brooks, the first one at the turn onto Sedgely, the second on the turn to Thorne, then abrupt curve down into Ticking Bottom proper. Wyatt could have ploughed under the wide expanses of meadows and the fields, to construct additional thatched cottages, to increase his rental base, but he had not done so. She did want to see Ticking Bottom in summer to know and remember its full beauty.

Mrs M hounded her the instant she walked into the kitchen.

"Mr W said you might not have stopped for lunch," the woman demanded.

"I did not even think about it," Gem admitted. Her appetite was dulled by nerves, but that would not do for Mrs M.

"Tea or hot chocolate?"

"Tea, please," she said politely.

"Sit yourself down then and I'll make you a sandwich. Turkey or ham?" the cook queried.

"Ham, please," Gem murmured, suddenly overwhelmed by the feeling of dread that had touched her on the drive to T.B. "Cheese, mustard," she automatically suggested. The same sandwiches Wyatt had, at times, prepared for her.

"What?" Mrs M stated.

"What?" Gem replied startled.

"You look as though someone has just walked over your grave," Mrs M said bluntly.

"Odd statement!" Gem frowned.

"I don't know how odd, I'm sure," the cook replied firmly, "but that's the look. I'm leaving early today for my club. Mr W is bringing Chinese food home for dinner, unless you want otherwise. Ring him if you do," she informed the young woman. "Miss Molly was out with the Mister all the morning, so you needn't worry yourself about a walk for her. I think you should have a rest, young lady," she said sternly. "Three and a half months soon. You need to be taking better care of yourself!"

"I am," Gem countered. "Truly. What do you want me to do?"

Mrs M sliced the sandwich into quarters, set the squares neatly on a plate in front of Gem, then put her hands on her hips. "I have not heard you mention one word of the nursery. Not one word of a name," she announced firmly. "James, naturally, if it's a boy - but if you don't want that name, Mr W will probably settle it for a middle name. A girl? What?"

"I have no idea," Gem replied with a sigh. Gemmy! Only Gemmy!

"Fiona would be my suggestion, if only as a middle name," Mrs M's stern attitude faded a bit.

Margaret, Gem mused. Gemmy Margaret was gummy on her tongue, she frowned. "Fiona would be prefect for a second name," Gem admitted. Gemmy - no - Gemma Margaret Grantham, she nodded. My daughter's name has been decided. And James Jack Grantham. "This sandwich is absolutely brilliant," Gem sighed "Oh how I would love a beer to go with it."

"Months away," the older woman chuckled. "Christmas invitations have been posted. Mr W made sure to include Mr Choate. I have someone in mind for him, but he may already have a special person," Mrs M frowned as she thought aloud.

"I believe he has," Gem nodded, speaking around her mouth full of ham and cheese and mustard.

"Well it's no never mind to me then," Mrs M said pleasantly. "Everyone has the right to their own happiness. Perhaps they can adopt. Mr Choate would make a fine father."

Gem nearly choked on her food. Well - Mrs M knew. Lord! The woman knew things! "Yes. I agree. He would make a lovely father." She quickly finished her lunch, chips and all, and went upstairs to change her clothes. She needed a walk and discovered that Miss Molly, while not interested in a run, was willing to amble the cobblestone lanes with her.

At one point at the beginning of the walk, Gem stopped and gazed down at the golden dog.

"You are absolutely perfect, Molly," she said, then bent down on one knee to hug the poochie. Molly leaned into her human unit and sighed deeply.

"What?" Gem stood as her mobile rang. That was a rarity. Whenever did she actually have a call instead of a text! "Yes, Mr Choate?" she said anxiously.

"Everything all right?" His voice was tense.

"Fine, yes. Why?"

"First time I've seen you stop and hug Molly," he replied.

Gem turned and looked down towards the village. "Can you see me?" she asked in surprise.

"My suite is the entire second floor of the inn. The attic. I see all sides of T.B.," he informed her.

Gem could see the hint of a shadow in the left window on the top floor of the inn. She raised a hand and waved, and saw the shadow return the gesture.

"I was just telling Miss Molly that she is absolutely brilliant," Gem smiled as she assured her watcher.

"Absolutely. Hug her for me."

"I shall. Bye."

"I'm here, Gem."

"Thank you!"

Gem slipped the mobile into her pocket. Family. At least she would have the Agency.

Mrs M left early as had been her habit on Tuesdays since mid-fall. I'll have to inquire of her club, Gem reminded herself again as the house manager left the Hall.

Gem walked around the rooms, noting that Mrs M had set various groupings of Christmas trimmings in the various rooms. Thus Gem had a pretty clear idea of how each of the three trees would be trimmed. All decorations no doubt placed where Mrs Fiona had once decided they should be hung, Gem realized.

She made a pot of tea and settled in the now notorious Auntie Jane's comfy chair, to watch the telly. She simply could not shake the feeling of dread that had now completely filled her. She clicked from one network to another, watching the international news for a half hour. There was not a single news item that could in any way affect the Agency. She mentally reviewed her long, informative chat with Ms Blessington, finally feeling capable of accepting the facts the computer wonk had expressed. Gem had tried to avoid the truths for as long as possible. Escape was no longer possible.

Harry or Mr White - she held her breath as the facts smacked her brain - had managed to scramble the electrical on the Pilos. One of them had managed to program a computer - Agency's or personal - to direct the Pilos off course. Harry or Mr White had, with vicious premeditation, programmed a computer to fly a plane with four passengers into oblivion.

Chat with Sondra. Chat with Mr Choate. Chat with Mrs M. Her brain was tired.

Now she could no longer push off the truth. It was right in front of her. The final steps of how the Pilos disappeared. The final realization of the facts that the loss of the Pilos was not accidental. Harry or Mr White had intentionally murdered her family and Mr Portermann. She had the how. She did not have the why. Just a guess on that. She still did not know the location of the Pilos.

And she realized the other Key had slipped. But what was the Key? She could not reach it enough to recognize it. It still was not within her grasp.

And still the feeling of dread grew stronger. It was not of the facts. It was something else.

Gem drank cup after cup of tea and watched the news broadcasts. Thank heavens there was a bathroom close to her office!

It was there! It should be there - on the news! She knew it should be there.

Thoughts of the Pilos hammered at her brain. Gemmy. Mum. Dad. Mr Portermann. The murdered staff of the SEA Network. Mr Denton. She knew Mr Denton's death was not an accident. He was to be included in the body count.

Gem felt a film of defilement creep over her flesh. Keep your sanity, she urged herself. Regular habits - she grasped for help - deep breaths, counting to twenty repeatedly. She took a shower, washed and braided her hair. She forced herself to select jeans, a pumpkin coloured boat neck jumper and a dark brown cardigan. She took off the silver filigree bracelet and put it in her jewellery box. Wyatt had noticed it, prompting her to ring Mr Cawley, that Eureka morning. She would not wear it again until after she left Grantham Hall. And that day was very nearly in sight. She had to begin to separate herself from Wyatt. She had to return to her previous life. She would still have the Agency. She would have her children. She would have a very different life. And that she had had for the past six months. One change after another. And now - yet another change.

"You're here!" Wyatt said rather surprised. "The telly was on in your office, but no you." His eyes searched hers. The clouded veil was there.

"I am," Gem forced a smile.

"Dinner, Chinese," Wyatt said casually. He had to allow her to proceed as she could. Sondra Blessington had confirmed with Wyatt that the meeting had occurred, and no other words had been exchanged of the subject.

He could tell it had been a draining day for Gem. It had been a draining day for him, hearing that a third employee would be welcoming an addition to their family, causing him to consider having the water at the Grantham Building screened for aphrodisiacs.

Gem tried to divert her attention to their dinner. She desperately needed to escape wondering if Harry or Mr White had murdered her family and many others.

"Ms Blessington is a marvel," she said matter-of-factly. "I can't imagine people who are so staggeringly brilliant. What a gift she has!"

Wyatt choked on his food. "God, woman! Do you ever look in a mirror!" He reached over and touched his finger to her nose.

"Do I have smut on my nose?" she exclaimed, dabbing at the offending part of her face with her serviette.

"No, Gem!" he toned his voice down. "I only meant to suggest that you are as remarkable as Ms Blessington. Also as pregnant might I add," he shook his head. "I am surrounded by -"

"Choose your words carefully," Gem attempted levity she truly did not feel.

"Mums to be - and be again," he replied, raising one eyebrow. "Ms Blessington, Ms Wexton, my sweetheart, and now Ms Holton," he exhaled slowly.

"What DO you put in the water at GEI?" she suddenly laughed.

Wyatt dropped his fork. "My thoughts exactly," he eyed her suspiciously. "Are you now able to read my thoughts?"

"Since ninety-nine percent of your thoughts involve chasing butterflies between sheets, I would say yes," Gem replied easily.

Wyatt gazed at her. She was quick witted, but her eyes were tortured. Things were going to become very difficult, he realized. At her own speed. He trusted her. He had to do so. She was his life now. And when the hell DID everything change? When DID she become so important to him?

When did everything change? When James died in his arms, he could literally have killed Gem - without a single thought or second of regret. He had wanted to do so that first day he had seen her at Oscar's Café. He had endured her company the entire month of August. He had still felt like killing her that first night at Marigold Cottage.

How it had all changed!

And now, what did the future hold for them? He had no idea of what she had been searching for since he had met her. How long before that had she been in this battle unknown to him? He had to keep his mouth shut - to be a clam like Ms Blessington. He had to trust her. He did trust her.

"Do you have reports to read this evening?" Gem asked casually. He had obviously been diverted by something other than butterflies.

"I'm sorry, my dear, I do in fact," Wyatt admitted. "The brewery owners are pressing for a sale. The employees wish to purchase the business. Ms Holton wants GEI to purchase, and reorganize with the intent of employee owned in the future. With a tidy profit, yes," he conceded to her.

"If the employees are serious, they will meet your terms," Gem smiled warmly at him. Not the perfect man, but a damned decent one. "It sounds like a good investment. Beer," she gave his a teasing smile.

"Perhaps," Wyatt smiled briefly.

Gem did the washing up, not a difficult process with take-out, while Wyatt settled in the library with his work. She made him a pot of tea, which brought her a kiss when she set the tea tray on his desk. And then she went to her office to think - or to try not to think. Thinking won out.

Her thoughts had not changed. Harry or Mr White. She had no evidence. Only conjecture. She had no proof. Only accusations. She couldn't face Harry with her accusations. No one knew where the hell he was! Except, perhaps, for Mrs Brown. Gem couldn't face Mr White. He could simply deny whatever she said to him. She could tell Mr Choate and Mr Harper her thoughts. They could agree with her, accept her theory. And there would again be stalemate. No proof. No evidence. No Harry.

One serious.

One serious what?

She couldn't remember. Someone had told her something. But she couldn't remember.

'Did the same programmer build your mobile?' Ms Blessington's words.

Good question!

Gem pulled out her mobile and texted the query to Mr Choate. She didn't worry that Wyatt would walk in while she was using her mobile. He no longer asked questions of her actions.

'Who built my mobile last January?'

Mr Choate must have had his mobile close at hand.

'Mrs Brown did courier phones as she was their supervisor. Harry and Mr White did agent mobiles.'

'How do you know that?'

'No assignments most of that month. Spent a lot of time in the office reviewing old SOP forms with Harry.'

'Okay. Thanks.'

'Still here, Gem.'

'I know. Soon. I promise!'

'When you are ready.'

She cleared her messages, and sent a text to Ms Blessington that her phone was clear. Then she sank into the comfy chair - previously owned by the Agency infamous Auntie Jane.

Imagine! Auntie Jane and Mr Choate redirecting the future of a country by eliminating a dictator and his general. Amazing! Brilliant! Frightening! At least Mr Choate was on her team. She wouldn't want Mr Choate for an adversary. And Ms Blessington was on her team. Lovely! And sweet!

Gem watched the telly, switching the channels, watching, switching channels. It was there. The feeling of dread. Something had happened.

Wyatt tossed the report to the desk. He didn't have to read the report this evening. He could put it off until morning; read it at the office. But he realized Gem had to be on her own. It was obvious that whatever she had conferred of with Sondra Blessington was occupying her thoughts. He had complied with her wishes. She had met with GEI's computer wonk. He had to wait until Gem asked him again for help.

Chapter Thirty-Five

Wyatt scowled as his mobile rang. He wasn't in the mood for business discussions this evening. He glanced at the number:
Mrs Brown.
What the HELL!
"Yes?" he answered, perplexed by the call. Gem hadn't mentioned the woman in weeks.
"Wyatt, this is Mrs Brown," the voice said brusquely. "Do not allow Gem to watch the evening news."
"I beg your pardon?" Wyatt countered, bewildered at the order.
"Please do not waste time, Wyatt! Do as I say!" The call abruptly ended.
Wyatt stared at his mobile, then snapped it shut and quickly strode to Gem's office. She was standing in front of the telly, staring at the screen. Wyatt listened to the news story:

Harry Breckett, Director of the Bureau of Statistics, for the past fourteen years, passed away today of a heart attack, at the age of fifty-five. Mr Breckett had no survivors. There will not be a memorial service.

Wyatt stared at Gem watching as the blood drained from her face.
"Gem!" he said sharply, switching off the telly.
His mobile rang again. "It's Mrs Brown," he quietly informed her, holding out the mobile to her.
"Too late," Gem said tonelessly. "Tell her I have already seen the story."
She walked away from him and leaned her back against the wall, her eyes closed.
"Wyatt," Mrs Brown spoke firmly, "put her to bed. Watch her every minute. Do not leave her alone. When she is lucid, tell her that I order her to speak to you. She needs to tell you everything. Otherwise, I am afraid she will have a complete mental breakdown."
The connection ended as abruptly as had the first call.
Wyatt turned to see Gem wander out of the room. He followed her along the hall. She walked as if in a dream - up the staircase, through the sitting room and into the bedroom. She crawled into bed, clothes, shoes, and pulled the duvet up to her neck.
Gem turned her face into the pillow, squeezing it repeatedly with her hands.
Wyatt sat on the edge of the bed. Her eyes were open, blank, unseeing. He sat beside her, waiting. He had no idea what was going through her mind.

Who the HELL was Harry Breckett? What the HELL connection did Gem have to someone who had worked at the Bureau of Statistics? He had never heard of the bureau. Gem had never mentioned the name Harry to him. Was this Harry Breckett related to her?

Wyatt reached out his hand to stroke her hair. She didn't react to his touch. He gazed down at her; his only option was to wait as Mrs Brown had advised him. Wait until she was lucid. Who the HELL was Mrs Brown to realize how the announcement of Breckett's death would affect Gem? What the HELL was happening?

He gently placed his hand on her shoulder, wanting her to know he was beside her, yet not wishing to push her into responding, to connecting to reality until she was able to do so.

She didn't speak. She didn't close her eyes. Wyatt sat beside her and waited as the long case clock in the main hall ticked away the time.

Gem squeezed the pillow, as thoughts careened out of control. Harry... Gemmy... the Pilos... Marigold Cottage... nautical flight miles... fuel consumption... Timor Sea... Wyatt... Barcelona airport... Gemmy... I'll Be Seeing You...mum...Paul Andriani...Mrs Brown... thoughts swirled repeating...Nazis...couriers...her head throbbed...dad...Gemmy...Wyatt...tell Wyatt everything...over. It was over. I'll find you Gemmy! So close...

Her hands stopped squeezing the pillow and Wyatt gently stroked her right shoulder. She jerked at his touch and stared at him. She shook her head as he gently touched her hand.

"Oh, Wyatt," she said, her voice sweet, and unbearably sad.

"Mrs Brown ordered you to talk to me," he said softly.

"But she doesn't know all of it," Gem said, her voice breaking. "I am so sorry."

"Sweetheart," he murmured, "please talk to me."

Gem nodded. She pushed back the duvet, dragged herself from the bed, and took his hand to lead him to the sitting room. "Sit," she pointed to the settee. "I will be back in a minute or two."

She went directly down to the kitchen, her brain on automatic pilot. Too bad Mr Portermann hadn't been able to use that switch. Or had he? It didn't matter; it would have been useless.

She took three bottles of beer from the fridge and carried them to the master suite. "I can't drink these now, but you can," she handed one bottle to Wyatt. "Just pour it down your throat," she said tonelessly. "Here are two more for when you need them."

Wyatt set the bottles on the coffee table in front of him.

Gem pulled her mobile from her pocket, turned it off, and set it on the table. "No interruptions."

Wyatt stared at her in disbelief, wondering if he had just been handed the end of the world in a damned beer bottle.

She put a match to the logs in the fire grate. Whenever did Mrs M have time to tend to fireplaces? she wondered.

Gem turned to face him. Wyatt Grantham. The man she had loved with all her heart - twice. In August. And again, now.

And now it would end.

"I need to tell you a very, very long story," Gem said, her voice composed, but weary.

He set the beer on the table. She picked up a bottle, removed the cap and handed the beer to him, capturing his gaze with her eyes until he took the brew from her grasp.

"Please let me talk, and then I will answer all of your questions - or as many as I have information to answer. As many as I can answer without putting other people in danger. You will have a great many questions."

She spoke quietly, wistfully, Wyatt thought, holding fast to the beer bottle that her manner suggested he might indeed require.

Gem drew a deep breath and began to speak.

"My mum was Margaret Louisa Lawson. My dad was Gerald Henry Forrester," Gem looked at Wyatt, then pulled the band from her braid, raking out her hair with her fingers and shaking it free. It was a habit she needed. "We lived in a lovely house outside of Brisbane, Australia - our home base. Mum and dad were travel writers. Mum actually did the travelling while dad kept the home fires burning, so to speak. They wrote travel books together. That's a cosy enough picture isn't it?" She looked at Wyatt then shook her head. She started to pace the floor as she spoke.

"In actuality - curious word that if you think about it - actually - Mum was a secret government courier for Great Britain - Land of Hope and Glory – that's the ring for outside texts on my mobile." Gem shook her head, trying to focus her thoughts. "Dad was a cryptanalyst for our government. They were employed by the Agency - that's the name of it - the Agency. You can search all you like for it," she glanced at Wyatt, "but you will never find a shred of evidence that the Agency exists. It's not loud like British Intelligence or the CIA."

She looked at him. "Better take a drink now, as this will be a shocker to you - it all will be from now on," she advised him.

"My name is Gemimah Louisa Forrester. My identical twin sister is Gemma Louisa Lawson. Take a drink now, Wyatt. It only gets worse from here," she urged. She didn't dare look at him, but continued to pace as she spoke.

Wyatt exhaled sharply as if she had punched him a horrendous blow to his chest.

Gem didn't want to look at him, but she did and she would have to continue to face him. "I don't want to hurt you, but I don't know how else to say all that I have to say."

Wyatt nodded and remained silent.

"By the way, I am carrying twins - not a huge shock to me - but likely a shock to you." He nodded and stayed silent.

She paused, gathering her thoughts.

"Gemma and I are so twin that little other than fingerprints separate us. We called each other 'Gem'. That is our name. We are beyond sisters. We are totally devoted to each other. We are One."

"We have different surnames - our parents' decision to help us establish our own identities. It was also a safety measure to protect us because of our parents' careers."

"Mum was needed more and more out of the Agency's London base. I moved here with her, and we lived in the country with my Auntie Jane - mum's twin sister." She did not elaborate on Auntie Jane! "Gemma stayed in Brisbane with dad. Mum and I travelled to Australia many times each year. Gemmy and I were actually born in London - but that is neither here nor there at this time."

"Gemma and I never went to school, we were parent and self-educated. If you tried to trace me through school records that wouldn't have been of any help to you."

"Here's an interesting fact for you - we both have photographic memories. Well, that's what some people call it. More accurate - we can remember everything we read."

Wyatt nodded, but otherwise did not move a muscle.

"Gemma and I sailed through our studies - I went to Cambridge, Gemma studied at Melbourne. We both read art history."

"We were hired by the Agency when we were eighteen - as couriers - same as mum. Oh, by the way, the Bureau of Statistics does not exist. Harry was the Director of the Agency," Gem said wearily. She stopped pacing to drag her fingers through her hair. If she stopped speaking now she would never be able to continue. "Mrs Brown is also a Director of the Agency, she is our supervisor, and is also an excellent gardener."

"I was based out of London, Gemma usually out of Melbourne, sometimes out of Paris. South East Asia is sometimes too hot for couriers, and agents sometimes have to take over courier assignments there. But not always too hot," she sighed.

"I completed my PHD a year ago. Gemma completed hers last May. I haven't had a chance to read hers, but I'm sure it's most excellent."

"We travelled for the government - on very special, micro-chipped passports. I can explain those later. We also have lovely, special mobile phones," she pointed to hers on the coffee table.

"But I am digressing. And I hadn't intended to tell you the rest of this so soon - within the next few weeks - yes - because you needed to know about the twins."

"Gemma and I have always been Gem - to family as small as it is - and to our co-workers at the Agency. Since we are identical, it was just easier for our contacts to know us as Gem. That's what we call each other. The counter-couriers we delivered to probably never knew which one of us they were meeting - they might not have even known we were two people."

"Please take a drink, Wyatt," she begged.

Wyatt did as she suggested, his eyes never leaving her face. He didn't dare let his thoughts waver for as much as a second.

"Now on to the sad parts of my tale. I am telling you because Mrs Brown ordered me to tell you. But you see, she doesn't know all about you and me. I was going to tell you about this soon, because it is foolish to prepare a nursery for one child when you will have two. I didn't want to tell you about twins, because then I would have to tell you that I was a twin. And then I would have to tell you the entire story."

"The sad part: as I knew it before I met you, that is."

"Gem - Gemma finally had the time to finish her thesis. I travelled as much as she, but her assignments were further distanced than mine. In mid-May she returned to Australia to complete her thesis, and she worked extremely hard to finish her work. She had an assignment, along with mum - a routine assignment. Dad went along for cover as a travel writer. I had just finished a half dozen back-to back assignments. I arrived home a half hour before Gem, mum and dad were to leave on assignment to Singapore. Gem was packing. She was so excited because she had decided this would be her last assignment. She had sold her stocks and bonds to buy a flat in Barcelona. She is a wiz at the stock market - helped me get my flat with the investments she made for me - another story."

"She showed me a stunning ring - over two hundred years old! She told me she got it in lovely Barcelona. She asked me to take care of the ring for her until she returned from her trip."

"Gemmy, mum, dad, and the pilot, Mr Portermann, an agent, left from a small private air strip at eight o'clock that night - 29 May. I was exhausted. I went to bed at midnight."

"At two o'clock in the morning I sat straight up in bed."

Wyatt's blood ran cold.

"I could swear I heard Gemmy's voice calling to me - 'Gem, where are you? Where are you? Help - please dear God! Gem!' Then the feeling ended. I knew she was dead. I knew they were all dead. Gemmy, mum, dad, Mr Portermann."

"I rang Mrs Brown and Harry. They were in Sydney for meetings. They came as quickly as they could. Harry tried to get information about the flight and then the confirmation came that the plane was lost."

"At five o'clock in the morning," Wyatt said hoarsely.

Gem nodded. She looked at Wyatt, her eyes glazed with pain.

"It was a secret government flight. All passengers aboard were either couriers or agents. The location of the crash site was unknown."

Still unknown. Wyatt could barely grasp what he was hearing.

"In less than twenty-four hours their possessions were packed and cleared from our home, and transported to the Agency warehouse - somewhere in London. Neighbours were told that mum and dad had relocated to the States. Harry worked all that day using his government expertise to erase all information of Gemmy, our parents, and Mr Portermann. They ceased to exist. I was allowed to keep Gemmy's personal items - nothing bearing the name Gemma or Lawson. I have her jewellery and her clothes."

Wyatt took a long pull from the beer bottle. And then another.

"I returned to London and had to go about my 'normal life'. I had to send all my family computer files to the Agency warehouse. Everything my family owned is now there. Their computers are there - monitored - hoping someone will send a message - but there won't ever be any. It's just Agency SOP."

"Before I left Brisbane, as I was packing Gemmy's jewellery, I saw the ring - the ring that had so captivated her. Honestly - I thought she had bought it as a reward for finally finishing her thesis. She loved jewellery. I used to call her Crow as a nickname. Anyway - I put on the ring because I wanted to have her close to me."

"I continued as a courier for the Agency. I went to work, and carried on as if nothing had happened. I couldn't tell anyone what had happened. You can't lose a sister and parents who never existed. You can't grieve for people who never existed."

"Four people died in an air crash. The cause of the crash was unknown. There were secret government documents - messages on that plane - the Pilos."

"In mid-July I had an assignment to Milan. I flew from London to Barcelona, and had to catch a connecting flight to Milan. The flight from London was delayed, so by the time I reached Barcelona I had barely ten minutes to catch my next flight."

Gem continued pacing, dragging her fingers through her hair. Wyatt watched her, barely able to breathe, his mind numb from seeing the pain she suffered as she spoke.

"I was shocked to the core when a young man ran after me at the airport - he was calling me Gem! I was so confused. I'd never been in Barcelona before. I'd never seen him before. And then he was asking me where I had been. What had I done to his baby? I was still wearing his ring!"

Gem stopped and turned to look at Wyatt.

"Wyatt, I had no idea who he was! I didn't even know Gemmy was pregnant!"

"I had to catch the flight to Milan. I had to deliver a message to an agent there, warning of a likely assassination attempt of a President in a small African country."

"I begged the young man to meet me the next day at the airport. I didn't know what I was going to say to him, but I knew I would have to tell him that Gemmy had died - as gently as I could tell him. I was on the plane before I realized that I didn't know his name. I know Gemmy hadn't told him she had a twin. Our family had such a secret life. But I knew she would have told him as much as she could - after she had told family she was going to get married. When I was growing up in this country I never told anyone I had a twin sister. We kept our lives so very separate and quiet because of the Agency - especially after Gemmy and I became couriers. But I know we would dearly have loved to have had James in our family. I don't know - perhaps James wouldn't have believed that I wasn't Gemmy. I just don't know."

Gem sighed. "I couldn't get out of Milan for two days because of the fog," she returned to her story and her pacing. "I waited at the airport for ten hours, but he didn't come. I had to fly back to London and report my mission end to Mrs Brown at the Agency. I decided I would immediately fly back to Barcelona to look for Gemmy's young man. But when I got off the plane at Heathrow that day, I went blank. I couldn't fly again. I couldn't bear the sight of oceans - the likely location of the Pilos and Gemmy - everyone. I put adverts in the newspapers in Barcelona asking for the 'handsome, young man at the airport, and the time and the date' - but there was never a reply."

"I knew he was British. Gemmy had been in London last spring. I took her assignments while she stayed at my flat, recovering from her broken arm. I wondered if she had possibly met the man at Oscar's Café. That was her favourite café when she was in the city. I never went there, because I didn't want to be mistaken for her. I started going to Oscar's in hopes that I would see him. The day I met you was the first time I had been there. I sat there every day for hours during the entire month of August. And I met you there instead of the young man from Barcelona."

"You had asked me questions about James that I couldn't answer, because I had only met him for a very few minutes. I think about Gemmy and James constantly. She would have had their baby by now."

"Damn! She shouldn't have taken that assignment! It's against Agency SOP to fly when you're pregnant. I would have taken that assignment for her. But she wouldn't have asked me to do so, because she knew I had taken my assignments and those of two other couriers who had been out with flu. I was exhausted. She had always wanted to go to Singapore. And it would be a special time for her to be with mum and dad. She probably planned to tell them about James. I don't know. I just don't know. I do know that Gemmy was going to buy the flat in Barcelona. I know she loved James. I just know she did."

"I quit my job as a courier that day I returned from Barcelona. I couldn't fly, but I could have taken local assignments which didn't involve flying. But I had bungled meeting Gemmy's sweetheart. And I had lost contact with him. I realized I couldn't trust my judgment anymore. All I could do was to look for the Pilos - try to figure out what had happened. That's been my Agency assignment for the past months."

Gem walked over to Wyatt and knelt down beside him.

"I would give anything to go back to that day in Barcelona. I will forever regret going on to Milan that day," she said hoarsely. "There is nothing I can ever say or do to apologize for what happened to James. It was my fault that he died. I was trying to save one person's life. And then I was responsible for another person dying."

She laid her head on his shoulder.

"I know how devastated you were, still are to have lost James. I pray that there is a heaven and that Gemmy and James are together.

She stood up. "And now you hate me again," she said sadly. "If you ever really stopped doing so. I'm so very, very sorry, Wyatt."

He remained silent for a long time and Gem did not move. She had told her story, and she had to take what he had to say to her. She steeled herself for his anger, recriminations, and accusations.

To Gem's astonishment, when he finally did speak, his voice was quiet. "You were doing your job. You couldn't have known what was going to happen to James. You left him that day because you had to, not because you didn't care."

"It was the worst decision I have ever made in my life," Gem said sadly.

"It wasn't your fault, Gem," Wyatt said quietly. "I hate what happened." He looked up at her and Gem could see there was no anger in his eyes. "But I don't blame you. And I don't hate you. You simply couldn't have known."

Gem shook her head.

"All this time," he forced himself to speak, "all this time you had to be two people because Gemma never existed."

Gem nodded.

"Have you ever been to San Francisco?"

"No."

"Or Geneva?"

"No."

"All this time," he thought aloud, "you've been searching for the - Pilos?" Gem nodded that the name was correct. "You've been looking for Gemmy - and the others." He ran his fingers through his hair, shaking his head. "I lost James. You lost your entire family." He stood up, and looked into the violet eyes filled with so much pain. "You couldn't share your loss with anyone other than the staff at the Agency. How could you bear it?" he asked, his eyes filled with sympathy for her.

Gem simply shook her head. "It's just there," she said numbly. "But - you have - questions. I owe you every answer that I have to give you."

"My God, you're exhausted," Wyatt studied her face and worried at the glazed look in the lovely violet eyes. For all the effort she had put into telling her story, she was little better than she was upon hearing of Harry Breckett's death. "I'm putting you to bed - now. I'm going to make you a cup of strong, sweet tea, and then you are going to sleep." He guided her into the bedroom as he spoke.

"But we have to talk," Gem protested.

"We will talk tomorrow - for as long as you like," he soothed as he removed her clothes and helped her into her pyjamas.

"In bed," he ordered. "I'll be back very soon with the tea."

He was right. She was so tired. And he was in shock, she thought numbly. They would chat tomorrow and she imagined his reactions to her confession would greatly differ from his attitude tonight. She had made a muddle of her words. Tomorrow would be a time for explanations.

Wyatt returned with the tea, and Gem quickly drank it. In a few minutes he was in bed, propped against the pillows, holding her in his arms. Gem sighed deeply and fell asleep. Oh how she would miss his strong arms around her.

Wyatt did not sleep. His mind was in such turmoil he doubted he would sleep at all that night. He had many questions for her, indeed.

He knew now why he couldn't trace Gemma Louisa Lawson. And there were still the questions of Gemma and John Staunton. He knew now why Gem hadn't returned to James. He knew she hadn't deserted James.

He was confounded that there had been two Gems. The ring. Gem had known about the flat in Barcelona. Gemma was going to sell her stocks and bonds to purchase the flat. Gemma was going to start a new life in Barcelona, Gem had said. With James.

A special micro-chipped passport. No wonder Gem had been devastated on their 'wedding night' when he had mentioned the passport with the name Gemma Louisa Lawson. A passport of a woman who did not exist. Not a forged passport. He could understand the Agency not admitting to an air crash - government papers. But there had to be more to the secrecy that Gem had mentioned. And he would like to know the full story when Gem could speak of it. But perhaps she would never be able to do so.

He went over in his mind meeting her at Oscar's that day. Oscar's Café. James's favourite café. The café where James had met Gemmy.

No wonder Gem had acted vague with the couple from good Old San Francisco. It had been Gemma who had met the men in the States. It had been Gemma, he now knew, who had sketched the dying child in Geneva. Gem couldn't give him the third passport. It was with Gemma on the Pilos. God! How confusing her life had been since 30 May. Gem had had to pretend to be her sister, because Gemma had never 'existed'.

Good Lord! What had he done! He must have been out of his mind with rage! The Games. How he had finessed her, tricked her. Trapped her. No wonder they were both so shocked on their 'wedding night'! He couldn't wrap his mind around all that he had done to Gem. How had she kept her sanity? Grieving for her family and enduring his deceit and anger. No wonder she had become hysterical when he had called her Gemma that day she had avoided the doctor's appointment. Gem didn't want a doctor to examine her. She was afraid the broken arm might have been mentioned - it wasn't likely, but she couldn't risk the issue. And he had mentioned the broken arm to the physician when he had made the appointment.

All the times he had accused her of lying. She couldn't be blamed for lying. She had had no choice but to lie.

The times he had asked her about James and she had refused to answer him. She'd barely met James. How could she answer questions about a person she had only briefly met?

The Grantham family jewellery. Wyatt hadn't believed that Gem couldn't tell the difference between diamonds and cubic zirconium. She hadn't been aware that James had given the jewellery to Gemma. Gem hadn't been interested in the diamond and ruby jewellery at the auction - she had only been interested in the antique cameras. Her head wasn't turned by fine jewellery and expensive frills - her head was turned by bookshops - and cathedrals.

And Gemma's thesis was at the Agency warehouse. Gem hadn't even had the chance to read her sister's work.

Poor Gemma. She hadn't had the chance to tell her family that she was pregnant He felt sick at heart. Gemma would have had their baby a few weeks ago - due mid-November, according to James.

Poor Gem. She was pregnant because of his vicious Games. And twins. And she had known she would have to tell him her story soon because she had to explain twins. And how do you explain a sister who had never existed? Unbelievable - unless one had photos and a passport - of which Gem had been unaware he had – until Wight. Those questions would be for tomorrow.

Her meeting with Sondra Blessington. She had needed a computer wonk to help her solve the mystery of the missing plane.

God! How could she bear the pain?

Her reference books to South East Asia, he now understood. Her fervid studies of the Second World War he did not understand, but perhaps for some odd reason she thought it connected to the Pilos.

It was hardly surprising now that she had no interest in celebrating Christmas. It would be her first Christmas without her family - as it would be his first without James.

Odd how plane crashes had so disastrously altered both their lives, their families.

Saying the word family was so difficult for her.

His mind went over and over the events of the past months - and how he had hurt her. And how he hadn't cared until recently if he had hurt her. She had had to bite her tongue so often not to let her secrets slip. Her self-editing - fear of saying something that might give away her secret in some way.

She had gone to James's grave because James's had loved Gemma and Gemma had loved James. And Gem hadn't been able to tell James why Gemma had 'deserted' him.

Hell!

Her insomnia. Hell again! She had refused to see the doctor he had suggested because she knew damn well why she couldn't sleep for the exact same three hours every morning. Seven o'clock also had some significance to 30 May. Dr Hallowell was probably an Agency physician. She had told Lyndon that she had talked to Hallowell about the insomnia. Hallowell knew it was a condition that could not be easily resolved.

It was staggering that Gem had wakened, sensing the plane had been lost. A psychic link to Gemma? Stranger things had happened in the world. Why shouldn't the sisters have a link no one could explain? The two attacks she had suffered. She had felt she was drowning. Another link to Gemma. The plane crashing into the sea. There were certainly enough seas in South East Asia.

Was anyone at the Agency other than Gem searching for the Pilos? Another question for her. But he had no right to know that information unless she was willing to share it. And it was no wonder he had not been able to find references to a water/air crash in the months since Gemma had left Barcelona to finish her thesis.

A 'photographic memory'. He had long known she was an incredibly amazing woman.

He had so many thoughts; he would be unable to sleep. Nor did he wish to sleep. Gem had been alone for too long during her 'dark hours'. She would never be alone again until the 'insomnia' ended.

His mind wondered to the future. She had insisted on a divorce many times, had argued for one, had pleaded for one. He didn't want to let her go. But he wouldn't force her to stay married to him. There was no pre-nup. He had never conceived that he would need one. He had been out to control her - destroy her. He couldn't believe now that he had ever felt such thoughts. He had excellent solicitors. He would see that she had the same.

He would hate his life without her.

There were a great many questions he would have for her in the morning. There were many issues to discuss of her future and that of their children.

The minutes ticked by and Gem slept. Wyatt heard the long case clock in the main hall strike three quarters hour. He glanced at his wrist watch. It would soon be two o'clock. She slept soundly, and he wondered what the trigger was in her brain that made her sense the hour early each morning. Something in her brilliant mind!

Gem wakened and slowly sat up. Wyatt pushed himself up against the pillows. She buried her face in her hands and Wyatt realized she was weeping. He hadn't seen her shed a tear since that first night - that first night at Marigold Cottage.

Wyatt put his arms around her. Gem laid her head against his chest and wept inconsolably - as she had the night on Wight. The flood was unleashed.

"Cry it out, love," he murmured.

Gem wept until she was exhausted and no tears remained - as she had that night on Wight.

Wyatt stroked her hair. "Sleep, my love, sleep. I'll take care of you, and hold you forever," he whispered.

Gem heard the words, and she snuggled her cheek against his chest. And she slept.

Wyatt held her as he listened to the ticking of the long case clock. The clock chimed three times, then four times. And Gem slept. When the clock chimed five times, Wyatt closed his eyes and he slept, still sheltering her in his arms.

Chapter Thirty-Six

Gem slowly opened her eyes, and sighed. Wyatt's arms tightened around her, warning her that he was also awake.

Last night!

She had told him a great deal of information - on Mrs Brown's orders. So Gem had violated Agency SOP - again - this time with permission. Wyatt now knew everything about her family, about Gemmy and James. How much he actually believed troubled her. She could give him no proof. He had to believe she had had a twin - Gemma - after all, he was going to be the father of twins.

Wyatt had been so very kind last night. But this was morning and he would have had time to absorb what she had told him. His reaction might very well be much different today. He had had time to think about everything. And he would have queries she would have to answer, she mused, then noticed the bright sky beyond the windows.

What? She remembered waking as usual at two o'clock. She remembered Wyatt holding her as she wept. She remembered he had comforted her. She didn't remember the rest of the night - the dark hours.

"What is the time?" she murmured.

"Half eight," Wyatt said quietly.

"What?" she gasped. "The dark hours!"

"Yes, the dark hours. Very aptly named." He didn't move a muscle, allowing her to gather her thoughts. "You slept."

Gem sat up and turned to look at him. "You didn't sleep much, did you then?" she saw the shadows under his eyes.

"A few hours," he admitted. "I had a great deal to think about. A very great deal."

"Indeed," Gem replied hesitantly. "Breakfast - Mrs M," she suddenly frowned.

"Will not be coming to the Hall today. You and I need to have a long chat," he rubbed his eyes and frowned.

No butterflies would be corralled this morning, Gem realized, seeing his eyes darken a bit.

His manner was off-putting, matter-of-fact.

He leaned to his right to coax Miss Molly to the floor, and to reach for his dressing gown at the foot of the bed.

"Have a shower," he suggested. "I'll make breakfast when I'm dressed," he said with a short smile; the smile did not reach to his eyes.

Gem nodded, dreading confronting the day. She didn't dawdle in the shower or at dressing; there was no point in doing so. She had to face him. He had been more than patient with her and she owed him the same courtesy. She anticipated breakfast being a frosty affair, but he kept his tone even as he served her a plate of scrambled eggs and bacon, and sat on a kitchen stool to tuck into his own food.

"Does Dr Hallowell have an opinion on the gender of the twins?" he asked quietly.

"He has suggested," Gem murmured, eating her eggs, keeping her eyes on her plate. "He'll know more clearly eighteen to twenty weeks. I'm about fourteen. However, he was quite certain," she said uneasily. "Do you want to know what he said?" she glanced up at him.

Wyatt gave a shake of his head. "Not right now." He frowned. "I made you tea. Would you prefer hot chocolate?"

"Tea is fine, thank you," she replied politely. She forced herself to eat, becoming consumed by the horrible hollow feeling. Perhaps she had imagined the words she had thought he had spoken last night.

'Sleep, my love, sleep - I'll take care of you - hold you forever'.

But then those words could have a very ominous meaning - and not one of comfort.

Or perhaps the words had been a dream. But she didn't remember her dreams. But then she hadn't slept through the dark hours until this morning.

He didn't want to know if he was going to have sons, or daughters, or one of each. Well, she certainly couldn't blame him for being distant about plural babies. She had known the fact for some time. The information was no doubt a stunning blow to him.

He reached over to fill her tea cup.

"Where's Molly?" Gem suddenly realized the dog was not in the kitchen with them. She usually waited for treats when Wyatt cooked.

"She's spending the day with the M's. Mrs M is approving Christmas trees today. Molly will have a lovely romp in the woods," he said, his voice still even, not betraying his underlying mood. But his eyes were very dark.

"Oh," Gem murmured. She had taken the lead last night. It was his turn to direct the conversation today.

However he did not take the lead and remained silent while they finished the meal.

"I'll do the washing up," Gem suggested quietly.

"Dishwasher," Wyatt said crisply. "You didn't have one in Brisbane, did you? You rarely remember to use this one."

He had started referencing. "We did not," she concurred. "We lived rather a simple life. I rarely remember how to use this one," she admitted.

Brilliant mind! But can't remember how to use a dishwasher, Wyatt silently mused. She was fascinating!

"You didn't date much, did you?" Wyatt queried, filling the tea pot with water, setting it on the cooker.

"No. Gem -" she stumbled over words, "we were too busy studying, reading, working," she self-edited, being extremely cautious of her words.

"Memorizing," Wyatt reflected. "I imagine you are quite a walking encyclopaedia."

"Not quite that," Gem protested uncomfortably. "There are too few dishes to load in the dishwasher." she observed.

"Let the damned things sit," Wyatt ordered.

Gem waited for his next word or action, wary of the tension building within him. She watched him rinse two thermos bottles with hot water, filling one with tea, the other with hot chocolate, placing them and two cups on a tray.

"We need to talk," he said grimly.

Gem nodded, and followed him as he carried the tray to the library.

"Make yourself comfortable," he waved his hand at the sofa. "We may be here awhile." He handed her a cup of hot chocolate and took one of tea for himself.

"You're not going to your office today," she murmured.

Wyatt raised an eyebrow. "No," he said firmly. "Ms Holton manages extremely well whenever you are driving me to distraction. She'll manage without me today." He gazed at Gem. The look of pain had been replaced by one of fear. "I'm not going to bite you," he scowled, but his voice softened. He remained standing, knowing he would now be pacing instead of her.

"You said last night that you would answer my questions. And I do have many," he began.

Gem nodded stiffly. "I was incoherent last night. I realize I probably didn't make a great deal of sense," she frowned.

"On the contrary. What you said was quite understandable," he countered. "And quite shocking."

Gem nodded, holding her tongue. This was his time to speak.

"You spoke quite clearly of your parents, Gemma, your careers with the - Agency," he stopped pacing to look at her and she confirmed the name. "Of the Pilos," he scowled again. "Of Gemma and James." Her words of the previous night came back to him in a rush, and he strove to control his emotions. "My first query would be -" he looked at her, shaking his head. "Why the HELL didn't you tell me that first night at Marigold Cottage?"

"I couldn't," Gem sighed. "Gem - Gemma - no longer existed. You had tried to find her, and you couldn't. How could I explain someone who had no paper trail. She had been filtered out of all records - birth, university. You had the only evidence of a person named Gemma Louisa Lawson. You had the passport she had lost last April. Harry had made her a new one. He monitored the first passport, wondering if someone else had found it - was using it. It was never used, and had been thought destroyed somehow. You had photos of Gemma. If I had told you that night that Gemma was my twin sister, would you have believed me? I had the ring James had given to Gemma. I had the other pieces of jewellery he had given to her. I admitted seeing the young man at the airport in Barcelona. I am called Gem just as surely as was Gemma."

"I was searching for Gemmy and the Pilos. I couldn't risk you not believing me, and throwing the passports and photos to the tabloids before I could manage damage control. And the Agency hadn't known about James and Gemmy. The photos James had taken at the gardens at Barcelona! There was too much muddle out of control."

Wyatt nodded, pondering her words.

"The photos," he said, staring straight at her.

Gem sighed, running her fingers through her hair. This was information even Mrs Brown didn't know.

"You can't tell me," he said, frowning. "Gem - I swear you can trust me. You've trusted me this far."

Gem sprang up from the sofa and paced. Barcelona! Information no one knew but Paul Andriani, Mr Choate and herself. She took three deep breaths and counted to twenty four times, as Wyatt curiously watched her.

"A special mantra?" he asked as she turned to face him.

"Orders from Mrs Brown on the first day of courier training. When in a dire situation, take deep breaths and count to twenty before continuing - whatever it is you are doing," she explained.

"I would like to use that technique at GEI - but I won't," he assured her.

Gem shook her head to clear her thoughts. "The photos," she looked apprehensively at Wyatt. "Only you and I know of the photos. If Mrs Brown knew she would have apoplexy."

Wyatt gazed at her. "You have my silence, Gem."

She could tell by his eyes that he was sincere. Yet his eyes were still very dark.

"Okay." Gem took the plunge. "The photos of Gemmy and John Staunton. Lord! Gemmy would have been petrified if she had known of them!" Gem looked at Wyatt, shaking her head. "Gemmy literally bumped into him at the gardens - out of the blue!"

"How can you say that?" Wyatt demanded. "You didn't know about the photos until I told you at the cottage!"

Gem laughed whimsically, again shaking her head. "John Staunton is the alias of Paul Andriani, Agency master underground agent. He was actually on holiday in Barcelona, waiting for his - oh what the hell - his lover - when he ran into Gemmy. They were both quite startled to see one another that day," Gem admitted with a sigh.

"You've talked to him?" Wyatt asked brusquely.

Gem nodded. "A few weeks ago," she admitted. She might as well tell him all of 'everything'.

"I checked with the Agency because I couldn't understand the photos. You said Gemmy was wearing the ring in the photos. We never wore jewellery on assignments except for our watches - which of course matched because we were 'one person'," she used air quotes. "Gemmy shouldn't have been on assignment to Barcelona - it wasn't her territory. There was no reason for her to be there other than to be with James."

Wyatt listened to her words still puzzled. "How did you contact this - Paul Andriani?" he frowned.

"Also interesting - but another very long story," Gem winced. "Can we let it suffice to say that Paul Andriani had to go into hiding to protect his life?" Gem paused, and frowned. "Wyatt, I know you hate spies - but -"

"Good Lord, Gem! Industrial espionage is a great deal different from national security. I do realize that!" he exclaimed.

"Well, good then." She took a deep breath. "Paul Andriani went into hiding. The Agency still doesn't know where he is."

"But you do!" Wyatt said in amazement.

"I figured it out," she nodded. "Between you and me?" she queried, her eyes pleading.

"For life," he solemnly agreed.

"Okay," Gem nodded, confident of his promise. "A flat block fire, a chat in Jake's, a friend who needed a place to live, a former courier now Director of Technical Operations. Paul Andriani is living in your London flat."

"The HELL you say!" Wyatt erupted in astonishment. "This is too much!" He considered her words. "Choate is a former courier?" he demanded.

"Yes," Gem nodded. "His former courier territory was Barcelona."

Wyatt scowled at her, not in a rage but considering all the information she was giving to him. "Ah! A holiday - Barcelona!"

"Exactly." Gem agreed.

"Good Lord, Gem! How could you figure all this out?" he asked in amazement. "You think Sondra Blessington is a marvel. You're bloody brilliant!' He paced the floor. "Choate! Then - Critchley?" He stopped to send her a questioning look.

"Yes," Gem nodded.

Wyatt exhaled sharply. "So! How many times have you taken that damned defensive driving course?"

"Every year. Twice this year," Gem sighed.

"Wait here!" Wyatt ordered, and left the room returning with a beer. He took a long drink, then stared at her. "I'm surrounded by the Agency," he said pointedly.

"Rather - but just a bit around the edges," she admitted.

"Has GEI been infiltrated?" he demanded.

Gem shook her head. "The Agency doesn't work that way - well, it might, if it was thought you were selling drugs, or running guns - if they thought you were a traitor to this country," she admitted. "But Mrs Brown," she pushed a thought from her mind, "thinks very highly of you. You're clean in Agency specs."

"Thank God for that!" he muttered. Then he looked at her again in wonder. "Choate!"

"And Charley's Pub, my favourite bookshop, etcetera, etcetera."

"Quite the organization this Agency."

"Very quite."

Wyatt drained his beer and fetched another before continuing his questions.

"And Ms Blessington?" he finally had his thoughts secured.

"I asked her for information - about my search for the Pilos - for Gemmy, and our family, for Mr Portermann - the pilot," she exhaled sharply, her mood instantly changing.

Wyatt nodded slowly. "You're not ready to talk about that."

"I can't. I haven't told Mr Choate or Mr Harper yet of my thoughts," she said quietly.

"Harper?" Wyatt frowned. "Who is he and where does he come into all of this?"

"Paul Andriani is now Mr Harper. He's also in hiding from the Agency," Gem sighed. "I will tell you this - because I need you to continue to trust me - and Mr Choate. It involves murders of counter-couriers and agents as well as the Pilos."

"I think I'm hallucinating," Wyatt said, rubbing the back of his neck.

Gem nodded. "I feel that way every day."

Wyatt stared at her. "I can well believe that!"

Gem dragged her fingers through her hair. "Gemmy was not only my twin sister. She was the dearest person in the world to me," Gem said sadly. "I can't even acknowledge that she existed. I don't have a mum or dad. I never did. - I can't find the Pilos. Until we - the Agency - knows why it disappeared - until we know who destroyed the Pilos - and my family. Until we know what government papers are aboard the plane. Until we know who committed all the murders my family remains non-existent."

Wyatt didn't speak for a long time. Gem poured a cup of hot chocolate, sipped the beverage and refilled her cup before he spoke again. He considered all the astonishing information she had confided to him. And he believed every word she spoke. And it made him feel all the worse for how he had played her.

Finally Gem could no longer bear his silence. Her nerves were frayed to filaments. She could not bear another argument with him or recriminations of her actions - what she had thought she had to do.

"This is all difficult to believe - I know," she started to say.

"It damned well is!" Wyatt shot back firmly.

"I can't prove any of what I have said."

"I'm not asking you to prove it!" Wyatt exhaled sharply. "The damned thing is I do believe you, Gem."

Gem collapsed in relief on the sofa.

"But you are right about one thing. I wouldn't have believed you that night at the cottage," he admitted. "I won't press you about what you still can't tell me," he frowned. "But are you safe? Someone brought down the Pilos - and the other murders you referred to," he queried worriedly.

Gem nodded. "You made certain I am safe," she reminded him. "And no one knows what I think happened. - Well - except for Ms Blessington. - And I asked Mr Choate about a computer wonk. It was he who suggested GEI."

"You trust Choate?" Wyatt demanded.

"Indeed, I do," Gem smiled confidently. "I trust him with my life - and Mr Harper."

"Okay," Wyatt said grudgingly.

She could understand Wyatt's doubt, but he was not the one who did not have to wait seventy- five years to read a file. And she had looked into Mr Choate's eyes.

Wyatt shook his head in amazement. "Agency training. The way you always scanned the pubs, restaurant, shops, museums - wherever we went."

"Indeed," Gem agreed.

He fell silent again, pacing, then abruptly turned to her. "Why?" he demanded.

"Why what specifically, Wyatt?" It was her turn to be puzzled.

"Alliteration aside, why did you let me blackmail you into staying married to me? I realized last night that you only had to make a phone call - that night at Marigold. You could have rung Mrs Brown - and what? Would I have conveniently disappeared? Been charged on some trumped up issue of treason? Stood back to watch GEI be destroyed."

Gem held her breath. She did not want flashbacks of that horrid night. "I don't know - but, yes. That's likely what would have happened," she admitted hesitantly.

He stared at her and Gem didn't want to meet his eyes. Well, the Agency had power.

"Why didn't you make that call, Gem? HELL! You could have rung Mrs Brown any time during the past - fourteen - weeks!" he said hoarsely. "Why did you protect me?" he demanded.

Gem raked her fingers through her hair. "I wasn't only protecting you, Wyatt. I was also protecting Paul Andriani. From you."

Wyatt held his silence, knowing she was struggling with her thoughts as much as he was.

"Before I went on my first courier assignment, Mrs Brown gave me stern advice, and it frightened the hell out of me," Gem said softly. "She said to always think as carefully as I could because one misstep and I could die. Or someone I loved could die. Or perhaps someone I had never met could die. One misstep meant death for someone. Did the Pilos go down because of one misstep? I don't know," she sadly shook her head. "James -" she took a deep breath, "James died because of my misstep." Gem stared down at her hands clenched in her lap. "I had done enough damage to your family, Wyatt. I wasn't going to see you - and others who rely - depend on you - be destroyed by circumstances over which you had no control or knowledge."

He stared at her dumfounded.

"You are a civilian. The Agency protects civilians," Gem continued. The room was deadly silent. "No one but you and I knew about James and Gemmy - of the photos of Gemmy and Paul Andriani, a.k.a. John Staunton; only you and I knew Gemma's passport still existed. You - warned me - that no one, but you, could get to the photos and passports. I had to trust you on that. I believed you when you said you would make me miserable if I crossed you. I believed you when you threatened to turn the passports and photos over to the tabloids if I crossed you. So I believed the items were safe with you."

Wyatt was speechless.

"Two gunfighters at a shootout," she continued. "The one who blinks first loses. You had the Game. And I had to blink. I didn't want anyone else hurt."

Wyatt listened to her, then set the beer bottle on the table with a smack that made her jump and raise her head. She watched him walk to the book case behind the desk and push something with his finger. Gem gasped slightly as the upper half of the bookshelves swung back into the room, revealing a streamlined safe with touch pad combination. As he pressed the key pad she looked away.

"So now you know the combination," Wyatt said bluntly turning to look at her, but saw that she was staring at the fireplace.

"I didn't watch," Gem shook her head. "I wouldn't."

"No," Wyatt exhaled sharply. "You wouldn't then, would you?"

Gem turned her head now, as he spoke.

"This is the safe James opened to get the ring and the other jewellery he gave to Gemma. Now I am the only one who can open it." She watched him reach in and pull out three items, close the safe and cross to stand before her.

"The photos, negatives, and the passports. Yours is on top," he handed the slim blue folders and the photo packet to her.

Gem took the bundle, groaning as she sifted through the photos. "As bad as I had thought," she winced. "Excellent shots of Gemmy and Paul Andriani. Gemmy would have been terrified had she known these existed," she scowled. "Oh Lord!"

She set the photos on her lap and opened Gemmy's passport. "Looks like any other British passport, but oh how it is not!" she looked at Wyatt. "There's a nifty little chip in here that can get one immediately through customers in most airports in the world! No search! No questions asked!"

Gem gazed at the passport, staring at the photo of Gemmy, and gently touched the image.

"We have to burn the photos and the negatives. The Agency can never know they existed. I'll have to give the passport to the Agency. I'll tell them - I don't know - that I found it when I was sorting through old magazines - cleaning my office. I'll get a scalding for not having found it sooner, but it will be okay."

Gem sighed as she again looked at the passport photo. "I hope this isn't the last time I ever see her. If I can't find the Pilos, my dear Gemmy, and our family, may vanish forever. I'll never be able to retrieve my family's possessions from the Agency warehouse. Our photo albums, Gemmy's thesis - books - everything."

Wyatt sharply sucked in his breath. He walked over to sit beside her on the sofa. He touched the ring on her right hand. "You will always have her with you. Just look at the ring and remember all that she ever shared with you. She asked you to take care of this ring for her. And you always will," he said gently.

"The ring belongs to you, Wyatt," she started to take it off her finger, but he stopped her, placing his hand over hers.

"James gave it with love to Gemmy. She gave it to you to take care of for her. You wear it for both of them," he insisted.

Gem nodded solemnly. "Then I shall. Thank you." Tears stung her eyes, but she forced them back.

Wyatt slipped his hand into his pocket for the photo he had taken from his wallet that morning.

"The Agency doesn't know about this photo either," he handed her the snap she had found in James's photo album the day he had found her searching his brother's room. "Gemmy in the black dress you wore that night in Inverness. Her hair was braided as you often wear yours. It's unlikely anyone could ever identify where the photo was taken. It could easily be a photo or you. Only you and I know it's Gemmy. And you will have it as a memory of her."

Gem nodded. Tears slipped down her cheeks. "Thank you," she whispered, brushing away the tears. She took a deep breath and focused her thoughts. "And now - your next question?"

"I haven't any at the moment," he said quietly. "Perhaps tomorrow. The next day." He abruptly stood and paced the floor, then stopped to stand in front of her.

"I am the world's bloodiest bastard!" he said bluntly, and Gem started at the vehemence in his voice. "I hunted you. Trapped you. There was no excuse for what I did. None." He shook his head, staring into the soft violet eyes." And you are an astounding woman, Gem. Sweet. Kind. A gentle spirit. Exquisitely beautiful. Brilliant. Definitely not deserving of the cruelty I inflicted on you."

Gem gazed up at him, wary of the direction of his thoughts and she held her breath as he spoke.

"We have a great deal to sort. I'll move to a hotel in the city - as it sounds like the current tenant in the London flat requires the security of that residence. You shall remain here - if you like - until you find a flat - or perhaps you would prefer a house of your own. City, country, whichever you choose. I can't legally give you Grantham Hall as it is entailed to the first born of each generation, but if you choose to live here, you may for as long as you like - or until you remarry."

Gem felt a rushing sound in her brain. And, so here it was. The end of the life she had come to love. The end of her life with Wyatt Grantham.

"Naturally I will provide for you and the children. I will arrange for a quiet divorce. I am at fault and I will admit it. Not having a pre-nup will be greatly to your advantage. And I won't fight that. I was in the wrong all along from the day we met."

Wyatt forced himself to look at her and she saw the pain in his eyes.

And he wouldn't fight not having a pre-nup? She could get half of everything he owned. He could likely lose half of GEI in a divorce. Half of everything the Grantham family had worked for, for over a hundred years! Everything Wyatt had worked for – 29/7 for a decade and no doubt long before that!

That was totally and completely mad!

The Game was hers now.

And she damned well knew it!

His Game had ended when he said it had.

And now she damned well knew it!

The Game was hers!

"Your mea culpa," Gem said slowly, relishing dawn brilliantly smashing into her life. "Oh, yes Wyatt, you are most absolutely at fault," she said firmly. "I wouldn't be in this house if it wasn't for you. We both definitely know I wouldn't be pregnant if it wasn't for you." She stood, slipping Gemmy's passport and the photos into the pocket of her cardigan.

"If you think you are going to leave our children and me here at Grantham Hall, or stick us in a flat in London, or a cottage in - Ely - or somewhere, and then go merrily on your way to your next woman - well you have another think coming," she clipped out her words. "For the past six months I have been smashing into one damned brick wall after another - and you were one of those damned brick walls. I was a fool twice, but I am not a fool now!" She looked at her watch.

"We have been talking a long time. The children and I are hungry. You should prepare lunch for us," she picked up the tea tray and walked out of the library. "Bring your beer bottles. Can't just leave stuff lying around you know. Mrs M is off for the day and she doesn't have time any day to pick up after you," she called over her shoulder.

"What the HELL!" Wyatt swore but he picked up the bottles and followed her.

Gem counted quickly to twenty to keep her control. She only had enough time to count once. She had to get this particular issue settled because she had to sort out a killer whether he was dead or alive.

Gem turned to face Wyatt across the island. "Wyatt Grantham," she firmly announced. "You are in serious trouble." She slapped the passport and photo pack on the counter.

He stared at her confounded.

"I found these in your safe," Gem continued. "Having these items in your possession could be considered treason by our government. This passport is obviously a forgery as there is no such person with this name. These photos are of a government undercover agent. You have obviously been hiding secret government documents."

Wyatt stared at her, wondering what the HELL she was playing.

"And now, so you see, I have won the Game. If you think you are going to blithely escape from your responsibilities of being a damned attentive husband to me, and a blasted good father to our children, to Miss Molly and to Mrs Mac - then, again, you have another think coming." She enforced her words with a firm smile. "The children, Molly, Mrs Mac, and I will not be leaving Grantham Hall - ever. Nor will you leave. If you attempt to leave, I will hand this information over to government officials. Do you understand?"

Wyatt stood watching her, stunned into complete silence.

Gem held up her left hand and pointed to the diamonds glittering on her third finger. "Wedding ring, remember? Symbol of eternity? You are bound to me for life, Wyatt Grantham," she parroted the words he spoke on their wedding night. "You promised me last night that you would hold me forever. Forever isn't over yet! I don't want your money, or your heirloom jewellery. I just want you."

She had heard him last night. Wyatt sucked in his breath.

Gem held up the passport in one hand, the photos in the other.

"I Win, Mr Wyatt Grantham. Game. Set. Match. Win," she said triumphantly.

Wyatt shook his head in disbelief, then smiled the smile that freed butterflies. And the smile reached his eyes.

"Yes, my darling. Game. Set. Match. You win," he repeated. "You no longer hate me around the edges?"

"No. And you no longer loathe me around the edges," she said confidently.

"I do not. You indeed Win," Wyatt nodded, again smiling.

"And again and again and again," Gem said firmly. "You are going to have your hands full, Dark Lord!"

"I relish the challenge. I would like to have my hands full of you right now," Wyatt teased, then sighed deeply. "I thought this was going to be a terrible day. I feared I would lose you." He suddenly laughed with relief. "Shall we go upstairs and celebrate our non-divorce?" He walked around the counter to kiss her.

"Oh, yes! Butterflies are surging out of control," Gem kissed him in return. "Oh! But first we must burn the photos and the negatives! And please put this passport back into your safe until I can give it to Mr Choate. He is Agency Security as well as Director of Technical Operations."

"Damned busy man!" Wyatt marvelled, slipping his arm around her waist as they walked to the library so that Wyatt could again open the safe.

"Indeed," Gem agreed. "Wyatt, we really must clean up our language. We swear too much. Bad influence on our children."

"Agreed. My God! Twins!" he chuckled. "Sorry, darling," he laughed. "We'll burn the photos and negatives in the fireplace in our bedroom. But wait! I thought you and the children were hungry."

"We'll last a bit longer," she assured him. "Butterflies, lunch, than I have to get back to tracking a killer," she said, sobering a bit.

"Is there any way I can help you, Gem?"

"You did already. Ms Blessington," she reached up her hand to stroke his cheek.

After dessert and lunch, they picked up Miss Molly from the M's and took a long walk around Ticking Bottom. Wyatt kept his eyes on Gem, and she turned her thoughts to the Pilos.

If Harry was dead, how was she ever going to prove that he was responsible for the Pilos and the other murders? If he was, indeed, responsible. And what of Mrs Brown? She had broken her 'silence' to call Wyatt.

A thought struck Gem and she pulled out her mobile. She saw Wyatt glance at her but he did not say a word. She could easily step away from him to ring Mr Choate, but decided to text instead.

'Did you give Wyatt's mobile number to Mrs Brown earlier this fall?'

'Yes. Agency request had to trump T.O. that time.'

'Okay. Just wondering.'

'Everything okay with you, Gem?'

'Indeed. Chat to you soon.'

'When you are ready.'

Was there a point in mentioning the issue to Wyatt? She could still take the blame for that incident. And she was now assured that Ms Blessington's ability with GEI execs' mobiles was still solid.

Let it pass for now. Wyatt had never pressed the issue. Not even last night.

Harry! He had been part of her life for as long as she could remember. She couldn't make her mind to accept Harry as a killer. Or Mr White. And where did she go from here? Gemmy. Mobile. Pilos.

Harry had been away for months. There hadn't been another murder for quite some time. Mrs Brown had been on holiday or leave off and on for months, and she had been away the entire month of November. When had Harry died? Yesterday? Or months ago? And the Agency or the 'Bureau of Statistics' was just releasing the information now? Had Mrs Brown first had to find him and then confirm his death?

Perhaps it was best to think of Gemmy and the Pilos right now.

At least half of her life was sorted now. She watched Wyatt as he threw a stick for Molly to retrieve. Three months of gathering and sorting information to find the Pilos so she could escape from him, to leave the Hall and return to her old life in London. Now Grantham Hall would be her home.

Wyatt turned to look at her, then held out his hand to her. Gem walked slowly over to put her hand in his, marvelling at how much her life had altered in less than twenty-four hours. And much of the stress she had felt had dissipated.

"Hot chocolate at the Crow?" Wyatt suggested.

"Brilliant. What about Molly?"

"There won't be a problem. Mike likes Molly. Now are you thinking or relaxing?"

"Thinking about you," Gem admitted.

"In what way?" he frowned. "Good or bad thoughts?"

"Good," Gem smiled. "And, I think Penzance in January is a lovely idea."

"Excellent!" Wyatt smiled. "I told Ms Holton to buy the brewery."

"You did! What about the employees?"

"They decided against taking on the responsibility. I bought it for you. The brewery will be in your name," Wyatt replied.

"No!" Gem gasped. "Wyatt, you can't simply give someone a brewery," she protested.

"You're not someone, Gem, you are my wife. The mother of my soon-to-be children."

"Not that soon," she teased.

"What did Dr Hallowell think by the way?" Wyatt slipped her arm through his.

"You want to be surprised."

"I do - and I don't. I am curious," he admitted, grinning.

"Dr Hallowell might be wrong. Best wait for another month or so," Gem parried.

"I won't be disappointed, sweetheart," Wyatt shook his head, "But I'll wait to ease your mind." He chuckled. "Think how delighted the M's will be. Naught to two, first time. A house full of children would be wonderful!"

"It would," Gem agreed. What lovely thoughts.

The M's were at the Crow for a midafternoon libation and were indeed thrilled to hear of twins; Mrs M insisted the room chosen for the nursery would easily suffice for the babies for the next two to three years.

Gem sipped her hot chocolate, smiling at the M's and Wyatt, and relaxing. They were her Family now. Grantham Hall was her home. Ticking Bottom was her village - so to speak. She leaned over, slipped her arm through Wyatt's, laid her head on his shoulder, and sighed contentedly, letting the conversation drift around her. Wyatt's hearty laughter at one of Mr M's remarks warmed her heart. He sounded so happy!

And she had her Agency Family. But one of them was or had been a murderer.

Try as she did the remainder of the day, she could not figure out what her next step would be. Should she talk to Mr Choate? To Mr Cawley. Tell them her suspicions? Concentrate on finding the Pilos? And just how the HELL should she do that? What more could she do there? Wait until another charter pilot spotted a plane crashed into a mountainside in Indonesia?

She read to Wyatt in the great room that evening. Fire in the fireplace, hot chocolate for her, tea for him, Miss Molly sleeping on one of her favourite chairs, Mrs Mac stretched across the back of the chesterfield.

And the last Key slipped. But it was still out of reach.

While Gem and Wyatt each wondered if the dark hours would continue in the early morning, neither mentioned it to the other. Gem had been grateful for only briefly waking that morning, but she resolved to expect that was only an aberration. Wyatt knew that if she awakened again at two o'clock, he would rise with her, and never leave her alone again for those three hours each night.

Surprisingly it was Wyatt who wakened at the dreaded hour, while Gem slept. He listened to the clock ticking in the main hall, then closed his eyes, hopeful that the cycle of Gem's insomnia had been broken - and resolved.

Gem bolted up from her pillow, gasping for breath. "I know!"

Damn! Wyatt silently swore. "Gem!" he said sharply. "Is it the same feeling?"

She caught her breath, shaking her head. "Not drowning," she gasped, grabbing for her dressing gown to retrieve her mobile in its pocket.

Wyatt rubbed his eyes. When would her torment end? He glanced at his watch, then heard the long case clock chime five times. The end of the dark hours, he frowned. The pattern had changed.

Gem waited impatiently for her contact to answer his mobile.

"Yes, Gem!" Choate's voice was sharp.

"Meet me at the old stone bridge below the Hall!" she ordered. "Twenty minutes!"

"Tell Mr Grantham to bring Molly," he ordered and rang off.

"What?" Gem stared at Wyatt. "You're supposed to bring Molly."

"Of course," Wyatt replied crisply.

"What?" Gem stared at Wyatt who was already pulling on his jeans.

"Choate knew I wouldn't let you go out alone at this hour."

He was nearly dressed and Gem had to jump to get ready.

Face washed, teeth cleaned, jeans, jumper.

"Fetch your lead, Molly," Wyatt said firmly, pulling on a sweater.

Molly waited for them as Wyatt fetched anoraks for the dog's human units.

Gem's thoughts raced as they went out into the brisk early morning air. She hadn't realized the last Key had completely slipped. She couldn't solve the entire mystery but she had a major part of it.

Her heart pounded furiously as they left the drive and turned right onto the cobblestone lane. Mr Choate was approaching the old stone bridge - Gem could see the red tip of his lighted cigarette.

"Why Molly?" Gem whispered, puzzled.

"Cover. We're walking Molly; Mr Choate usually walks at this time of morning."

"How do you know that?" Gem quietly demanded.

"He told me when he moved into the inn," Wyatt grinned.

"Really! I didn't even know he smokes! You know he walks every morning!"

"To smoke," Wyatt chuckled.

"Ah!" Gem murmured, then looked up at the early morning sky. "Such different stars," she gulped, choking back a sob.

Wyatt stopped suddenly and grabbed her, holding her tight. "You aren't alone, darling. I swear you will never be alone again. I love you!"

Gem looked up at him. "I know. I love you too," she whispered.

Wyatt leaned down to kiss her. "That's the first time we have said that to each other," he whispered.

"Brilliant!" Gem whispered back, giving him a quick kiss. "Best not to keep Mr Choate waiting. He has a lot of work ahead of him today."

When they reached the old stone bridge, Mr Choate silently handed Wyatt a beer from his Mac, pulled one out for himself, and handed Gem a thermos which she discovered contained hot chocolate.

"Lord, I want a beer!" Gem groaned.

"Not now!" the men exclaimed in unison.

Then Choate ordered, "Talk to me, Gem!"

Familiar words! From Mr Choate, from Mr Cawley. She couldn't recall which. It didn't matter.

Wyatt stepped back to walk up the cobblestone lane, but Gem and Choate called him back.

"You're part of this now," Gem said evenly. "If I trust you, Mr Choate trusts you."

Choate nodded as he sipped his beer.

Wyatt released Miss Molly to run.

Gem looked at the men then started talking, starting with her conversation with Ms Blessington. At one point Mr Choate choked on his beer, and Wyatt swore vehemently. Bottles emptied, Mr Choate, pulled two more from his pockets.

"And now," Gem said, weary of her dissertation, "I know. I think my brain continues sorting when I can no longer concentrate."

"It's your subconscious, darling, and your instincts," Wyatt stated. "All the years of reading, your mind storing more information than you can imagine. Storing, sorting, reading."

"You too?" Choate demanded.

Wyatt nodded. "You can't forget. It's always there. Percolating."

"You could have told me," Gem said irritably.

"You could have told me!" Wyatt replied humorously.

"Settle down you two! I can tell you both right now, I refuse to baby-sit your children. Gem," he said crisply, "continue when you are ready."

Children. Gemmy. James. Mum. Dad. Mr Portermann. The murdered couriers and agents. Mr Denton. All someone's children.

"The instrument panel of the Pilos was corrupted," she took a deep breath. "Mr Portermann continued according to his readings. Rain. Dark skies. Rain ended. I am surmising here," she nodded to the men. "I read - somewhere - that flying over water at night is almost like flying blind at times. There are no reference points. Flying over desert is the same sensation. No ref -"

Before Gem had finished her sentence Choate was on his mobile. She didn't know to whom he was speaking, but she heard the words. "Secret. Alert all bush pilots, charter pilots -" he broke away to look at Gem. "Instinct?"

"I don't know," she shook her head. Gem where are you? Gem help? - "Kimberly region?" she shot back to Mr Choate.

"Concentrate first Kimberly," he snapped his phone shut. "Why Kimberly?"

"Pure instinct," Gem said, then suddenly had to gasp for breath. "They didn't crash into water. Gemmy wasn't drowning: she was smothering in sand pouring over her."

Stick your head in the sand. Keep my head in the sand - the references to sand - the past month - the last Key. One of the many Australian deserts.

"Gem." She realized Wyatt was holding her. She looked past him to Mr Choate who was scowling.

"Snap out of it, Gem!" Choate ordered. "You're a courier. Buck up!"

Gem pulled away from Wyatt. "I am retired!" she shot back.

Mr Choate glared at her. "Gem, no one -"

"-ever really truly retires from the Agency," she parroted as all staffers had done over the years.

Wyatt watched the scene unfold; confounded by his reserved wife's continuing transformation into a woman he had been married to for months - but whom he had never truly known.

"What else can you give me?" Choate demanded.

Gem shook her head. "Harry went underground. He disappeared. Murders stopped. - Mr Denton was murdered. I know he was!"

Wyatt scanned the landscape as he had so often seen Gem do.

"Mrs Brown knows something," Gem puzzled, then raked her fingers through her hair. "I can't sort that. I don't have the information. - No. I do. But I seem to have lost what that 'something' is."

Choate checked his mobile then turned away.

Gem could hear him talking to someone about pulling in Mrs Brown from leave, but she knew that wouldn't do. Mrs Brown was never told what to do. She was the Agency Director when Harry wasn't available. She wouldn't respond to queries. She was above it all.

"Lights are coming on," Wyatt said crisply, turning to look at the horizon. He called Molly to return.

Choate scanned the area. "We're done here," he announced. "Go home. Gem, any feelings - instinct - ring me."

"Do you ever sleep?" Gem demanded in amazement.

Choate looked at her, and Wyatt saw in the other man's eyes the commitment the detective had made to Gem.

"I'll sleep when our Family is home, Gem," Choate said solemnly. "Wyatt," he looked beyond the young woman, "feed her. She's hungry," he ordered.

"Husband, we are all hungry," Gem smiled.

"Twins," Wyatt said to the other man, but realized Choate already knew. He wasn't angry that Gem had confided to Choate of the twins. She had needed someone - and she had not been able to confide in him at that time.

And Choate backed Gem as he would always do.

"Congratulations! Twins!" He smiled at the couple.

Wyatt wondered as they walked back to the Hall, if he would ever know everything of Gem and her time with the Agency - of the confidences she had shared with Choate. But, he realized, if he didn't, it would never alter his love for Gem. After all, the Agency had been her career. And after all, he wouldn't be jealous of Choate. Mr Choate had Mr Andriani - or Staunton - Harper - whoever the man was this month.

Wyatt put his arm around her shoulders as they climbed the drive to the Hall. Gem had decided on her own, had insisted, that she wanted to be with him. And that was all he ever really needed to know. That was all he really wanted.

"Eggs, bacon, ham? What would you like?" he kissed the top of her head as they walked into the kitchen.

"I want a beer," Gem sighed.

Wyatt looked at her, then pulled his mobile from his pocket and sent a text message.

Gem stared at him, wondering who was the recipient of the message at this time of the morning.

"Okay," Wyatt announced. "Lyndon says you may have a light beer as long as you have a full breakfast first," he smiled at her. "Take a shower, my love; we're starting our day early!"

"All of it," Gem decided. "Eggs, bacon, ham - you -"

"Later," Wyatt raised an eyebrow, "much later. We need to see how this day will flow."

"Indeed," Gem agreed solemnly, before she went off to take her shower.

It was a lovely breakfast. After a sip of beer she was satisfied, and Wyatt finished the bottle for her.

"Beer at half five in the morning and again now," he chuckled. 'What a way to start a day!"

"Indeed," Gem said, wide eyed. At least she was getting more sleep at night.

Chapter Thirty-Seven

Gem listlessly pushed the hangers from left to right, sighing at Ora's new designs on her displays. It would be months and months before she would be trim enough to fit into the outfits.

She waited patiently as the designer finished the final stitching on the hem of the dress Gem would wear to the GEI holiday party - London office. The outfit for the Hall party was finished, and hanging in her dressing room at the Hall. New clothes Wyatt had ordered, unbeknownst to Gem, were finished and were also in her dressing room.

She couldn't really complain about all the clothes Wyatt had ordered for her, Gem admitted. Wyatt had taken decisions she had hated off her hands, as she had desired. She was still grateful for his help. Her nerves were fraying a bit but it was just the Blasted waiting to hear about the Pilos that was causing her distress. Not clothes, not Ora, and never Wyatt - now.

Ms Ames came down the stairs to greet Gem, and to say how excited she was for this year's holiday party. Gem learned that Wyatt's habit had been to stay only a few minutes at the party each year. This year his staff was hoping he would stay longer - now that Mrs Grantham would also be attending the festivities. Gem smiled and nodded. She would make sure Wyatt would actually, visibly, attend the celebration he gave his staff. And she looked forward to seeing Ms Holton, Ms Jones and Ms Blessington again.

Gem sighed silently, eager to return to the Hall. After breakfast, and a sip of Wyatt's beer, they had decided to continue on with their day. Mr Choate had set the wheels in motion. He would give them information when he had information. But Gem knew the search for the Pilos in the Australian deserts - starting with the Kimberly - could take months or years. Australia was a continent - not an island. The Kimberly area of the Great Sandy Desert, she mused. The Great Sandy encompassed nearly three hundred thousand square miles. The Gibson Desert. The Tanami Desert. Years, if ever, Gem silently groaned.

She had insisted Wyatt go to his office. A full breakfast, shower, and they were ready to leave the Hall at ten o'clock. He had his own life - and GEI. There would be no word from Australia today.

Ora had rung Gem on a final fitting for the GEI dress, and Gem had shrugged why not. Her brain was at a stalemate over computers and mobile phones. She just hoped she wouldn't have to wait until the Pilos was found, to have an iota of information to continue the search for the person who had brought down the plane - and murdered the agents and couriers.

Gem glanced to her left. Mr Choate was monitoring his mobile and frowning. She didn't ask him questions. He was in charge now - until she could think of something else to aid the search for the Pilos.

The fittings were done. She couldn't think of any other errands in the city. She was free to go back to Ticking Bottom. Ringing Wyatt to have lunch with her was a thought, but he had spent the entire previous day with her and he had business that needed his attention. Mr Choate put her parcels in the Defender and Gem buckled her seat belt. As he stepped away from her vehicle his mobile rang.

"I'm going to take this," he told her. "But I will be right behind you." He walked towards his Range Rover.

Gem nodded keeping her eyes on the wing and rear view mirrors then pulled out into traffic, eager to return to the Hall to lunch with Mrs M and to chat about Christmas preparations.

Choate walked to his vehicle, swearing under his breath that Gem hadn't waited until he had reached his Range Rover.

He felt a sharp pain in his back, then staggered, falling to the pavement. Damn! He dragged himself to his feet, keeping his eyes on the door of the shop. Gem was alone!

Eda looked at the shop door as it opened. Mr Choate, she frowned. He had left with Mrs Grantham. Then she looked on in horror as he plunged to the floor.

"Ora! Help!" she shrieked, rushing to their angel.

Ora looked, then hurried to the front of the shop. Ms Ames, tripping down the stairs, invoices in hand, threw the papers on the counter by the register and ran to the front of the shop to investigate the crisis.

Choate handed his mobile to Eda. "Ring Harper," he gasped. "Gem is alone. - Driving to -"

Eda scrolled down the contact list and hit the key to connect.

Ora, seeing the blood seeping across the back of the man's suit, reached for her mobile and rang for emergency services. Ms Ames raced to the back of the shop and up the stairs.

"Cawley," Choate murmured to Eda. "Tell him rogue - ." He tried to repeat his words as he lost consciousness.

Blast! the traffic, Gem drummed her fingers on the steering wheel. Stop and start for miles until she finally hit the A1. She looked in her wing mirror for Mr Choate.

Where the devil was Mr Choate? She waited until traffic slowed to a stop, then rang his mobile. No reply. NO REPLY? Damn! When was the last time she had charged her mobile? No. Her bars were good. Blast! She rang Wyatt. No reply. Damn!

Now was not the day to try to stop swearing!

As traffic moved, her mobile rang. She heard a voice but couldn't understand the words.

"I can't hear you, whoever you are," she said crisply.

Gem was stuck in the flow of the traffic, repeatedly scanning her mirrors to spot Mr Choate's Agency/T.O. blue Range Rover. He was not behind her. There was a grey sedan following her, or so she thought, but then it hung back. She didn't see any vehicles behind her that could be Mr Choate. She had well and truly lost him. Blast! She certainly could make it to Ticking Bottom on her own. She hoped her shadow hadn't got stuck in traffic with vehicle issues. She turned on to Dryden, trying Mr Choate's mobile again. He was going to scald her for not waiting for him! She could turn off, double back to look for him, but never double back. Mr Critchley's orders. You could be a sitting duck. And a sitting duck was a target!

Blast!

She was a target! She scanned her mirrors. The grey sedan was again behind her, and keeping a steady speed, hanging back just enough so that she couldn't get a glimpse of the driver. She couldn't tell if the driver was male or female.

She took three deep breaths and quickly counted to twenty twice. Then slowing a bit she quickly scanned her mobile contact list for Sondra Blessington.

"Who is this?" the voice demanded, puzzled.

"Gem - my mobile is bad -"

"What do you need?"

"Choate is gone - my bodyguard. I can't get a hold of Wyatt!"

"Wyatt...Emma -"

Gem lost the connection. She scanned her mirrors. The grey sedan was right behind her. She hit the pedal and pulled ahead of him and her mobile rang.

"Gem - where are you?" Paul Andriani's voice demanded.

"Dryden-"

Damn! Lost connection! Dead spot?

Damn! She had to stay on Dryden. Turning off she might get lost. She knew the lanes to Ticking Bottom.

Her mobile rang.

"What?"

"Rogue - rogue -" was all she could make out between the static.

Lovely! Rogue ! Who? Who had gone rogue?

Static.

If she pulled ahead she could hear on her mobile.

Scrambling reception.

There could only be one choice. Gordon White.

Dryden to Litton to Sedgely to Thorne.

The grey car sped up, Gem pressed down on the pedal, and swerved to cover the road. She slowed just briefly to scroll down her mobile contact list, finding the name, then as she pressed the key to connect she pressed down on the pedal.

"Crow! Gem! Can you hear me?"

"Yes! Choate is down. I can't reach Wyatt. I'm in trouble!"

"I know! Got you on GPS, but it's off and on."

"Being followed. Grey sedan."

"Speed ?"

"Mine 50, his 40."

"Keep coming, watch your mirrors."

Shift - check - shift - swerve -

"Keep coming. Keep your speed best you can."

"Yes."

She lost the signal.

Blast!

But Mike knew!

And now she only had to concentrate on her driving.

She increased her speed, slowing only to turn on to Litton. His speed increased. He tried to cut her off but she swerved and stomped on the pedal. She covered the road, swerving. She couldn't let him pass her. He sped up to ram the back of the Defender, but she neatly swerved, hoping he would shoot into the ditch as he lost control of his car, but he quickly recovered.

Did she have the advantage? She had driven the route at least twice a week, to and from London, for the past three months. Did he know the route - the curves?

She covered the road, speeding, then slowing, hoping he would swerve the wrong way and plough off the tarmac into the hedgerow. But he didn't.

Swerve. Cover the road.

Control.

Shift.

Concentrate.

Mirrors.

Petrol check. Good.

Shift.

Stomp the pedal.

Don't think of Wyatt, the babies, or Mr Choate.

Shift.

Speed. Swerve. Cover the road.

Perfect Defender. Take the curve.

It all became automatic.

Hug the curve, Sedgely ahead, at this speed a sharp turn left, and across the first old stone bridge.

She crimped the wheel. He overshot, but quickly corrected. Damn! She couldn't shake him.

She knew it was him.

Mirrors.

Shift. Speed. Control.

She had to ease up on the pedal to make the next curve and as she straightened the car, he hit her from behind, coming in again for another direct hit, but Gem pressed the pedal to the mat.

Hairpin curve ahead. She had to time it perfectly. She eased up a bit or the Defender would catch air. He saw the hairpin coming, hitting his brakes, Gem eased on the pedal, crimping the wheel to the right, then hitting the pedal as she pulled out of the curve.

Swerve. Cover the road, swinging from one side of the tarmac to the other. Keep steady. He was right on her tail, and she had to avoid him hitting her again. Swerve. Cover the road. Hope he hits the ditch!

Thank God there was no other traffic or they would all instantly be dead.

She increased her speed. At one time he HAD read the road.

Not too far to go now, she soothed herself. The next turn on to Thorne and the second old stone bridge were ahead, then over the rise and curve into Ticking Bottom proper.

What was that sound? Faint. Growing louder.

Mirrors!

Shift!

Swerve!

Gem saw it. A vehicle behind the grey sedan. Stay back! Don't get hurt, she silently willed the third driver.

Wait!

It was a Range Rover. Dark blue. Agency?

They had him pinned between them.

She made the turn onto Thorne, the caravan still behind her coming fast. Beyond the curve, beyond the bridge would be Ticking Bottom and Mike. He knew they were coming.

He hit her again.

Damn! Concentrate!

Swerve! He nearly went off the tarmac. Even Gordon White had to take Mr Critchley's course.

He hit her again. Thank God for seat belts!

She swerved, covering the road, keeping her speed. Over the rise, down the other side, around the curve, another rise, and - Gem's jaw dropped. Both sides of the tarmac, just before the bridge, were lined with Ticking Bottom Security - rifles raised! There were at least two dozen of them!

She heard a crack, and the sedan swerved to the right, to the left and then skidded to a stop.

Gem shifted, crossed the bridge and hit the brake. All rifles held steady on the sedan.

Gem jumped out of the Defender and turned to see the driver of the blue Range Rover, a priest in full black cassock, leap from his vehicle, then move slowly to the sedan, rifle barrel trained on his quarry.

Another faint sound. Whapping. Gem looked up to scan the sky, shading her eyes from the sun as a helicopter, whooshing dust over the entire scene, landed in the winter worn meadow bordering the tarmac. The blades were still chopping the air as Mr Cawley jumped down from the helicopter.

Gem turned her attention to the sedan as the driver of the Range Rover tossed his rifle to Mr Cawley, then dragged Gordon White from his vehicle, slammed him over the bonnet and handcuffed him.

Mr Cawley did a double take as he looked at the priest holding Gordon White. And a second helicopter filled the sky with noise and another wave of dust as it landed on the field beyond the sedan. Gem thrilled to see Wyatt climb down. She waved wildly as he hurried to the Defender and yanked her into his arms.

"I'm all right," she gasped, feeling his heart pounding as fiercely as hers.

"Oh my God!" Wyatt choked, holding her tight.

Mike Morgan walked over to them. "Handcuffed, under guard - he's not going anywhere," the publican assured them.

Gem pulled free of Wyatt and flung herself at the pub owner, kissing him on both cheeks. "You were smashing!" she exclaimed. "I knew you would be here!"

Mike held her back at arm's length, turning her towardss Wyatt. "You have a lot of courage, Gem! Most excellent job!"

"Thank you! Thank you!" Gem said breathlessly, hearing Wyatt exhale sharply.

"You are most welcome, Gem!" He gave her a brief nod and strode back to talk to the T.B. security force.

Gem gave Wyatt a quick kiss then hurried over to Mr Cawley. "Mr White did it! He took down the Pilos. Let me know when you find out exactly why. I know how. All I can guess it that he got involved with some rancid old Nazi's when he was posted to Hong Kong. CSU must have got them all unhinged. Or dad successfully deciphering the old Nazi codes," she said breathlessly.

"We'll get on it right away, Gem," he nodded. "You did it! You solved IT!" He smiled then winced. "Who the hell is the priest?" he demanded, pointing at the driver of the third vehicle.

"My cousin?" she said sheepishly. "No one you know, right?"

Cawley looked from her to the priest and back to Gem. "Never saw him before in my life," Cawley drawled, after a moment's hesitation. He shook his head, knowing he would not get another explanation from her - or the priest. His mobile rang. "Mrs Brown," he mouthed to Gem. "Yes, ma'am, we got him!"

Gem stopped listening to his remarks, and turned to face Gordon White, held between two Ticking Bottom security officers. She had a great deal to say to him, but was too filled with rage to say more than a few words to the man who had destroyed her family and had shattered so many other lives. "The Family disowns you, you bastard," she said with quiet disgust, then turned to walk to the priest.

"Another foot down," Glynn Harper grinned at her.

"I think you'll definitely get a pass on this one, my dear friend!" she laughed, hugging him and kissing him on both cheeks. "God bless you!" She shook her head. "Why the cassock?"

"Working on a case." Paul Andriani a.k.a. John Staunton a.k.a. Glynn Harper hugged her tight. "Search planes out in Australia. They'll find Gemmy. They'll find the Pilos. The Aussies are brilliant, as you damned well know from your years of living there."

"I do indeed," she solemnly nodded. "Mr Choate?" she said anxiously.

"Stabbed in the back- double entendre just perverse humour," Paul said, his face suddenly grim. "As he walked to his vehicle. Probably White. But he managed to make it back to the shop. He's in hospital. I'll just finish here and go to him. I'll let you know how he's doing."

"When you see him, give him my love," she said, her eyes misting.

"I shall," Paul gave her a gentle smile. "Go back to your husband. He looks ready to spout lava."

Gem half chuckled. "I love you - you mad priest!" she gave him another hug and a kiss.

"I love you too, Gem!" He gave her a quick hug and then walked back to his vehicle.

Gem turned and slowly walked back to Wyatt, glimpsing the faces of the armed guards still training their rifles on Gordon White, despite his guards. Mr Cawley, ruffling his hair with his hand, was still on his mobile, likely still sorting particulars with Mrs Brown.

"Can I shoot him now, Wyatt?" a familiar voice demanded.

Wyatt sent a questioning look to Cawley who had caught the query. Cawley frowned, quickly considering the request, then hesitantly shook his head.

Wyatt, his face taut with tension, sharply exhaled. "No. Were it only so!"

Gem wearily leaned against her husband, who asked, "Who the HELL is the priest?"

"John Staunton, Paul Andriani, Glynn Harper," she whispered. "Your tenant."

Wyatt shook his head in amazement. "We won't need to read any books for a long time. You have enough of your own tales to tell me."

"I do," she sighed, leaning against him, glancing at the T.B. security team. She recognized Dr. Lyndon, Royce Harwood - the T.B. dentist, Daniel Whitney - the chemist, Bert Shaw - the greengrocer. All the men she had met the day Wyatt had first taken her to the Yellow Crow for a pint. She didn't recognize the others, their faces hidden by the wide brims of their hats.

"Take Gem home, Wyatt," Mike Morgan firmly suggested.

Gem waved to the mad priest as he locked his weapon in the boot of his Range Rover, and watched as he backed the vehicle around and drove up Thorne Road, heading to the hospital. Gordon White still in the hands of T.B. security, Mr Cawley following behind, was hustled to the Agency helicopter. Only guards would ever again see the Agency's former computer wonk. Wyatt's helicopter took off shortly after the Agency bird flew out of sight.

As Wyatt put Gem in the passenger seat of the Defender, she heard Mike Morgan call out to the remaining security force.

"Back to your posts. Beer and food at the Crow for all at the end of your shifts. Wyatt's picking up the tab."

Gem laughed wearily at the publican's remarks, then patted the dashboard of the vehicle, as Wyatt engaged the engine. "This is a very good Defender," she said simply. "Very good Defender."

Wyatt remained silent as he drove through the village, past the shops, across the old stone bridge, and on to the drive of Grantham Hall.

Miss Molly greeted her human units with her usual placid manner, tail whacking the fridge, as they walked into the kitchen. Gem collapsed on a stool at the centre island and watched Wyatt fill the tea kettle then set it on top of the cooker.

He turned to stare at her, his face still grim. "When I think what could have happened today!" he helplessly shook his head.

"It got a bit out of control - and so quickly," Gem sighed. "I thought Mr Choate was right behind me. Paul - Glynn - whoever, said Mr Choate had been stabbed in the back on his way to his vehicle. When I noticed I was alone I was caught in traffic and got swept along. I tried to call him, then you, but my mobile kept cutting out. I called Sondra Blessington, and lost her too." She shook her head.

"I heard Cawley say that White had a device in his car. He was scrambling signals. Probably caused much of London to wonder what the hell was wrong with their mobiles. I was in a meeting when Ms Ames rang me to tell me that Choate was down and that you were alone. Then Ms Blessington rushed in. Harper from T.O. rang my mobile to say he was going after you, and to give me a head's up on what he thought was going down. Ms Holton arranged the helicopter for me. Harper thought White was jamming signals. He spotted you on the A1, kept his distance not wanting to tip his hand to White. Then I lost his signal, and had to hope to hell that he could take control of the situation."

Wyatt's mobile buzzed a text alert. He quickly replied, letting Ms Holton know that everything was settled. He filled tea cups, adding spoonfuls of sugar to Gem's. "I got a hold of Mike at the Crow. He said he had you on GPS and said the T.B. security was coming in and would be ready for you."

Gem nodded slowly. There was so much to take in. Her heart was just beginning to ease off pounding to a dull thumping. She suddenly gasped. "Was that Mrs M with a rifle? The one who wanted to shoot Gordon White?"

"Drink your tea," Wyatt ordered. "Dead shot. Her passion, other than the Mister, is American westerns. Where you are concerned she completely believes in shoot first, ask questions if the perp survives," Wyatt grimly chuckled, then re-filled Gem's cup with tea and sugar. "She terrifies Amos. From my view from the copter, she's the one who took out the tire on the sedan."

"Mrs M and guns!" Gem muttered as she sipped her tea.

"Her club meetings - skeet shooting, target practise," Wyatt explained. "I always thought her expertise would come in handy one day. Hopefully today is the only time it will be required."

"Lunch is going to be late today," Gem murmured.

"Yes, Mrs M has to clean her rifle," Wyatt chuckled dryly, his tension was easing a bit.

"Amusing," Gem said half-heartedly. "Thank God I'm home!"

Wyatt's mood eased considerably with her words. She had finally referred to the Hall as 'home'.

"Have you ever been terrified of anything?" Gem asked wearily.

"Absolutely," Wyatt nodded, his tone extremely serious.

"Of what?"

"For God's sake Gem - of losing you!" he replied in astonishment. "I thought that maniac was going to kill you! He had two guns in his car! I thought Cawley was going to lose his breakfast when T.B security pulled the weapons from the sedan."

"I didn't see any of that," Gem looked at him in surprise.

"Mike turned you so that you wouldn't see."

"Ah, that move. Very adroit," Gem nodded, then sighed as her mobile rang until she saw the caller's number. "Paul" she mouthed to Wyatt. She answered her mobile, listening carefully, and glanced up as Wyatt's phone rang. She talked to her mad priest, then rang off and waited for Wyatt to finish with his call.

"Mr Choate is stable, looks good for him," she sighed gratefully.

"Ms Wexton is taking Ora, Eda, and Ms Ames to the farm for a week to recover from shock. Ora and Eda's mum will run the shop during that time," he informed her.

Gem sipped her tea, a bit shocked herself from their very early morning start of the day to the current moment.

"Mike will ring me when he sorts matters with your co-workers. Lord - you have a dangerous career," he muttered. "I'm staggered by your courage, Gem!"

"I have to have it," Gem replied, a light smile touching her lips. "I'm married to you," she teased.

"Ouch!" Wyatt grimaced.

"Sorry darling, it just slipped out. A bit of a flashback," she said apologetically.

Wyatt nodded. "We'll have to work on that. The only flashbacks I want you to have from now on are pleasant ones."

Gem nodded, desiring the same. "Mrs Brown and Harry trained us well, Wyatt," she referred back to remarks of her career. "And mum and dad added advice from their experiences. Gemmy and I always followed SOP to the letter - except for her last flight," she caught her lower lip between her teeth. "You know - I was never worried - always cautious, however - until the Pilos was lost."

She frowned, thinking over the past months. "I should never have become involved with you - you being a civilian - but I wanted you desperately. I am retired from the Agency, as a courier - but staff never really retires - our motto. I was assigned to search for the plane. I never thought I would endanger you - not even the past few days. And you have T.B. Security. I just haven't thought clearly since the Pilos went missing. I am, after all, the idiot who didn't even know she was pregnant. Mrs Brown is the one who tumbled to that," Gem said, chagrined. "Well, and you even had thoughts about that. But I didn't."

"You were thinking clearly, my love, just not of yourself. I was thinking like a mad man," he scowled.

"Do you realize, Wyatt," she held up her cup for more tea, "if the Pilos hadn't gone down, I would have met you at James and Gemmy's wedding - if not before. I would have sparkled like Gemmy, I would have been lucid. And you would likely have had some stunning actress or model hanging on your arm."

"Not after I met you," he smiled gently. "And I would have swept you off your feet - properly - not with malice." He looked at her cup. "Hot chocolate this time, love?"

"Yes, please," she accepted.

"A query, Gem," he frowned. "Why the song - I'll Be Seeing You - that is the one - the reason you play the cd over and over - isn't it?"

Gem smiled wistfully. "It was our mum and dad's favourite song. They always danced to it. I'll never forget that. Dad gave us the cds. Whenever we left the house, even just to go into town to shop, he would always hug us and say, 'I'll Be Seeing You', and give us another hug and a kiss goodbye. It is the only thing I have left of my parents."

Wyatt handed a cup of hot chocolate to her. "You solved the mystery, Gem," he reminded her gently. "When the Pilos is found, all your family possessions will be returned to you."

Gem sighed sadly. "Planes go missing in the deserts in Australia, and aren't found for years, sometimes never."

"I'll buy a charter service in Australia, if necessary, my love. I already told Choate I'll pay for civilian charter planes to search as long as necessary. I offered to pick up the tab for the RAAF search, but he said that wasn't necessary."

"There'll be an Agency trade-off there somewhere," she knew from experience. "Thank you, Wyatt. You are so very kind and generous."

"You'll have everything soon, Gem. I know you will. You have the Agency on your side," he said gently. "And perhaps your parents wouldn't mind if we continued the song for our family," he suggested.

Gem smiled. "Mum and dad would be delighted."

A tap at the door announced Dr Lyndon, who simply walked into the kitchen, as if it were a long standing habit to simply tap and walk in.

"Thank you, Dr Lyndon," Gem said warmly, giving him a grateful hug, and Wyatt echoed her words.

"It's about time you call me Miles, Gem," the doctor suggested. "I still make house calls - flu, colds, teething. I'm not your physician, but I wouldn't feel comfortable if you didn't have just a brief check after your harrowing experience. I rang Hallowell to suggest he come out to see you, but he is with Mr Choate."

"You will do very nicely."

"Does he know yet?" Lyndon jerked his head towardss Wyatt.

"Twins - yes he knows," Gem laughed, remembering the doctor's insistence that she see Hallowell after she had fainted. She and Wyatt had referred to a baby. Dr Lyndon, Gem realized, had heard two heart beats and had wanted her to see her own physician, to learn of the facts from him. And he had kept his silence.

There was another tap at the door and Mike Morgan sauntered in along with the M's.

"Does anyone ever use the front entrance?" Gem demanded curiously.

"Only delivery people, funny enough," Wyatt grinned. "The double doors, you see." He leaned over to whisper. "Such as our new bed, straight up the staircase. Space for all of us - twins, you know!"

Gem smiled and shook her head in amusement.

"I'll handle this lot - you take Miles into your office," Wyatt suggested.

The kitchen confab was still in session after Gem's vitals had been checked to Dr Lyndon's satisfaction. She learned that Gordon White's sedan had been impounded and spirited away by Agency representatives - as easily as Gordon White had been spirited away to his new oblivion.

"White is definitely a broken man," Mike Morgan observed. "He was terrified when Cawley led him away."

"He's a murderer many times over," Wyatt said, his voice deadly cold. Gordon White. The man who had ripped Gemmy's love from his dear brother, and Gem's family from her.

"White started talking, babbling to Cawley, saying more than he should of for our ears to hear," Mike agreed. "White will be dealt with according to Cawley. It is for us to forget the incident. For public knowledge, Gem had been chased by a stalker. It's not an unusual incident in today's world. The situation is over. Closed."

Mrs M took the next current situation in hand. "Wyatt - put Gem to bed - no protests, young lady. You need rest. We have a house to decorate for Christmas!" she gave Gem a stern look. "I'll have lunch ready for you in a half hour."

"Yes, ma'am," Gem replied as Wyatt propelled her from the kitchen. She was not foolish enough to argue with a woman who was a crack shot. "Mrs M is so fierce!" she whispered to Wyatt as they walked along the hall to the staircase.

"Her true colours," Wyatt whispered back. "Let the tire be a clear warning to you!"

"She's on the T.B. Security Force!" Gem said in amazement.

"No. She just likes to fire weapons. Why do you think Amos is terrified," Wyatt chuckled. "Jesting a bit there. Amos is extremely proud of her abilities, but he doesn't allow weapons in the house - other than knives in the kitchen. Mike rang Mrs M for assistance because she's a dead shot."

He pulled back the duvet, then fetched her dressing gown. "Normally Mrs M wouldn't hurt a fly," he said as he assisted her out of her clothes, wrapping a dressing gown around her. "But Mrs M would have put a bullet through White's damned head to protect you, my darling," he said seriously. "She thinks of you as her daughter - has since the first day you walked into the kitchen to have a glass of wine with her - instead of insisting on being treated as Lady of the Manor."

"Ah - the threshold bit," Gem giggled. "Cameras."

"Yes - there was that. Then you settled in the kitchen to have a glass of wine with her, and served her, instead of expecting to be waited on. Mrs M is a rare type of house manager."

"She's not off-putting or formal," Gem laughed, and watched as Wyatt sorted through the lowboy for her pyjamas, as Mrs Mac attempted to crawl into the drawers.

"And she's waiting to be a gran. Amos is itching to purchase cigars with pink or blue bands to hand out around Ticking Bottom. They never had children of their own, Gem. We are their Family." He gently set the cat on the bed. "No, Mrs Mac, cats don't need to wear pyjamas or frillies."

Gem giggled again.

"Warm shower," Wyatt ordered, leading Gem by the hand to her bathroom and turning on the tap.

"Mr M would love a grandson," Wyatt teased, obviously hinting.

"Wyatt, if I say anything you could be very disappointed," Gem protested, as he removed her dressing gown and put her in the shower.

He fetched the pyjamas, towelled her dry and put her to bed.

"I wouldn't be disappointed, darling," he assured her. "All boys, all girls, some of each - a dozen daughters - I'll never be disappointed. Nor will Mr M be," he kissed her as Mrs M arrived carrying a tray of lunch for both of them.

"Grandmum M and I shall have great fun shopping for babies," Gem grinned at the housekeeper.

"So we shall, dear. After Christmas," Mrs M said firmly.

"You can help us shop, Wyatt," Gem teased.

"I shall be the chauffer, carry the camera, tote parcels, fetch pub grub - dad in training."

Mrs M smiled at the couple, then quickly left the room.

"Stop chatting and eat," Wyatt ordered. "Then perhaps a nap."

"Sounds lovely - if dessert is before a nap," Gem smiled. "Oh, Dark Lord, I am so happy. So very Happy! I never thought I would ever be happy again. I have two families now - the Agency - and our family," she smiled at Wyatt. "I have you. I have a home. Are you happy?" she searched his eyes.

"As long as I have you, sweetheart," he leaned over to kiss her. "Eat," he insisted as she chatted.

A long time later Gem said thoughtfully, "I want to see Mr Choate as soon as he is able to have visitors," she yawned.

"I'll ring Paul - Glynn - whatever his name is going to be," he agreed. "Now I think it's time for you to nap."

"Oh, Wyatt, I can't sleep during the day," she protested, yawning again.

"You can sleep at night now, Gem. You'll sleep during the day," he assured her. "I'll hold you and you will sleep."

And to her amazement she did sleep.

The Christmas trees arrived the following day, cut down by Wyatt and Glynn, while Mr M moved furniture to make room for the trees. Glynn moved temporarily to the Killingstoke Inn to cover Choate's work while the T.O. Director was in hospital. Mr M and Wyatt were of very little help with the holiday decorating other than assisting with the trimming of trees. But Glynn was a marvel, assisting Mrs M and Gem in decorating the entire Hall when he wasn't at his 'day job'.

Mr Critchley pulled Gem's license - which was a special Agency license - until she had again completed his defensive driving course. She was retired from the Agency, but as every staff member knew - no one ever completely retired. Critchley insisted that Gem should have immediately been aware that Choate was not behind her in the city traffic. She should have spotted Gordon White while she was still in the city, that being doubly-reinforced when her mobile suddenly developed interference. Not being allowed to drive was not an immediate issue to Gem as Glynn was her shadow and driver with Mr Choate indisposed for a month.

The first annual Grantham Hall Holiday Party in ten years was a roaring and glittering success, and Mr Choate was well enough to attend. Mrs Brown, Mr Cawley, the Critchley's and Mr Harper all attended - as Gem's 'cousins'. They were, after all, Family.

Mrs Brown made frequent appearances at the Agency until Mr Cawley's new assistant was completely trained in as Agency Assistant, and Mr Cawley became the new Director of the Agency. He received a rise in pay commensurate with a title of 'Executive in Charge of all European Accounts' for his 'accounting firm'. He now slept at night - unless South East Asia or some other area was beginning to roil. Mrs Brown was again, semi-retired, as much as anyone -. Gordon White's new assistant proved to be a wonk and immediately became Director of Agency Computer Communications - when Mr White had to leave the firm with sudden 'health complications'. A new assistant was hired to aid the new DACC.

A thatched cottage became available at the first of the New Year, and Mr Choate and Mr Harper became Ticking Bottom's newest residents.

Gem eventually had a new shadow, so well trained by Mr Choate and Mr Harper it took her a fortnight to make him. She never did get a really good look at him, but she always knew he was behind her.

The nursery was ready by the time the expectant parents had returned from a holiday in Penzance where Gem toured her new brewery.

Mrs M's new office was painted and she was thrilled with her new quarters. She hired Dr Lyndon's granddaughter as an assistant housekeeper.

Mr Choate remained Director of Technical Operations, and Mr Harper remained his assistant for a matter of months.

Everything had fallen quickly and brilliantly into place, Gem mused at the end of January - except for one issue. While the search continued for the Pilos, the prop plane had still not been found - to her great sadness.

Mr White had very quietly disappeared into nonexistence after admitting to planning and executing - his words - the demise of the Pilos and to being involved with the deaths of the SEA Network's counter-couriers and agents.

Gordon White's infamous adventure into murder and mayhem was indeed the result of Gerald Forrester's persistence of deciphering the old Nazi codes. Mr White, while being posted to the Hong Kong embassy, had become involved in the black market which led him into the underground world of many surviving members of Odessa - and their flourishing families. This new world was a break from his rigid world of computers. He enjoyed the intrigue, a bit of power, and many, many gifts for his use of computers in protecting the underground Nazi network. His home in London, thoroughly searched by Mr Cawley, Mrs Brown and the new Agency AD was a mini treasure trove of European art items long ago pillaged by the psychotic Nazi lunatics. The art items were quietly returned to their legal and rightful owners.

Mr White had intercepted Gerald Forrester's print copy of deciphered Nazi codes and recognized the names of many of his cohorts of the HK Nazi underground; there were also names of Odessa members who had fled to Mexico and South America, Indonesia, Malaysia, and the Philippines. Agency couriers delivered the names to certain groups who were interested in tracking down the aging Nazi criminals.

White had alerted his contacts in Hong Kong and had set in motion the plan to kill Gerald Forrester. White had killed Mr Denton because the print copy of the deciphered codes sent to Harry - intercepted by White - had indicated a second print copy had been sent to Mr Denton - formerly posted to the Hong Kong embassy, Second World War buff, 'retired' Agency staff, and a dear friend of Gerald Forrester. But White didn't find print copies he was looking for in Denton's possessions, so perhaps none had been sent to him by Gerald Forrester. The deciphered codes indicated not only the names of the Nazi officers but also the names of U-boats which had transported the Nazi's to the various countries: dates, time, and country. White had destroyed the print copies, and the computer transmissions to Harry. Gemma and Margaret Lawson, and Eric Portermann were collateral damaged in White's mission to eliminate Gerald Forrester. The SEA Network couriers and agents were murdered, first as a red herring to divert focus from the Pilos, then to implicate Paul Andriani who had over the years tried to infiltrate the Nazi underground network in Hong Kong. Paul's inability to crack the Nazi underground network was due to White's warning the Nazi's as to a possible mole invading their group. Gem's suggestion to Mrs Brown of Nazi involvement in the disappearance of the Pilos, further inspired White to continue implicating Paul Andriani. White had scrambled Gemmy's mobile signals prompting her to request a new mobile. White had anticipated the phone call and managed to take the request. He had offered to overnight drop ship the phone to Brisbane. Gemmy had rung back to request he ship the mobile to Geneva. There was a cathedral there that she wanted to visit.

Mr Cawley had explained Gordon White's scheme to Gem and Wyatt at Grantham Hall shortly after Christmas. Wyatt had held Gem gently as Cawley peeled back the layers of the crimes, drawing a gasp from Gem that a man she had trusted at the Agency had not only planned to murder her father, but had consciously considered Gemmy, their mum, and Mr Portermann as nothing more than detritus; dandelion fluff on a breeze.

Gordon White, monitoring the mobiles grouped at Ticking Bottom that one early morning, then Mr Choate's subsequent calls to Mrs Brown and Mr Cawley, then Mrs Brown's immediate call to the RAAF, alerted White that Gem had likely redirected the Agency search from the seas of South East Asia to the deserts of Australia. He had decided he was correct when no one had spoken to him of any issues that could possibly have related to the early morning mobile calls - especially the crisis only call to Mrs Brown. White decided Gem had tripped to the computer connection to the missing Pilos. He then began his plan of retaliation against Gem for attempting to ruin his settled, perfect life. He had expected to be able to run her off the road along the route between Litton and Thorne - or to put a clear shot through the rear window of the Defender to take her out. He hadn't anticipated Gem's personal network that came to her aid after he had put the knife in Mr Choate's back - again the cruel double entendre.

While Mr Cawley spoke, a thought grew in Gem's brain, and she caught her breath before she spoke the thought aloud. "Gordon White was protecting Nazi's," she murmured, and Wyatt and Mr Cawley leaned forward, listening, Wyatt eager to 'watch' her most brilliant mind in action. "Dad and Mr Denton with one exceptional common interest. The Second World War - interesting since neither of them had been born until the '60's."

"Go on," Cawley was also fascinated to watch Gem sort - as she called the process.

"It's likely that they read the same history books, biographies, autobiographies, the like - and had chatted via e-mail or by mobile. Dad was a cryptanalyst."

"Puzzles," Wyatt suggested.

"Yes," Gem nodded. "Mr Denton was Agency - he was aware that we all considered the Pilos missing was not pilot error - but something Agency related. He had received print copies of the codes from dad. He cut out the vital information - names, dates, etcetera and hid them in a book - on the War. Perhaps he slipped it into the spine of a book," she nodded.

"But why?" Cawley demanded. "You didn't even make a connection to the Nazi's until early September.

"At Fortrose Cathedral," Wyatt exhaled sharply. "Your Eureka moment! You said - why do they have to come so far apart - my God you are amazing!"

"Isn't she just!" Cawley demanded.

Gem didn't even hear their words of compliments. "Dad was dead. What had he been concentrating on for months. The Nazi codes. And Mr Denton knew it. Perhaps he had a 'feeling'. Check the warehouse. Compare the titles of books dad and Mr Denton had on the War. Look for same titles. Check the spines of Mr Denton's books. If I wanted to hide a list bearing specific names of Nazi's - Odessa - well that's where I would put the list - hoping someday someone would find it," Gem rubbed the bridge of her nose.

"Denton hoping that if his suspicions were true – if something happened to him - that you would figure out this puzzle, Gem," Wyatt murmured.

"Very likely that is exactly what he thought," Cawley was immediately on his mobile to the warehouse.

"I'm tired of thinking about Nazi's and their White Devil," Gem sighed, dragging her fingers through her hair.

"Time for a walk to the Crow for hot chocolate, darling," Wyatt firmly suggested.

"Lovely," Gem agreed, making a detour up to the master suite for a cardigan in case the Crow was a bit chilly. Wyatt saw Mr Cawley on his way, and Gem put the Agency Director out of her mind, quickly braiding her hair, and reaching into her jewellery box for the pendant watch Wyatt had given her on their wedding day. She had started wearing the watch the day Gordon White had been spirited away to his own private netherworld.

As she walked down the stairs she saw Miss Molly and Mrs Mac sitting at the bottom of the steps, staring at each other, very nearly eye to eye.

"You two will drive me positively mad one day," she said, shaking her head.

"And then it will be two other children driving us both mad," Wyatt laughed. "I'm glad to see you're wearing the watch," he smiled.

"Oh gosh!" Gem gasped. "My jewellery box! I never did give it to you to look for anything else James might have given Gemmy!"

Wyatt chuckled. "You're the only Grantham Gem I'm interested in now, sweetheart."

"Wyatt," she kissed him, "that is so hokey," she laughed.

"But true, and it made you laugh," he kissed her squarely on the lips.

Chapter Thirty-Eight

Gem stared at the engraved card in her hand, puzzled and surprised at its message.

"What have you there, darling?" Wyatt queried, as he walked into the kitchen. "An invitation to Buckingham Palace?"

"Better," she stared at him in disbelief, while she read the message to him. "You are cordially invited to tea at the home of Mrs Ardatha Brown, at eleven o'clock, the twenty-fourth of February."

"Gadzooks!" Wyatt exclaimed. "Seriously?"

"I believe so. It must be a real invitation. It actually bears an address and driving instructions."

"Gadzooks again!" he exclaimed.

"Really, darling, I think I would actually prefer that you curse rather than use gadzooks. To use that word a bubble must appear over your head," Gem teased.

"Blast!" Wyatt replied. "Is that better?"

"It will suffice nicely," Gem agreed. "You know, I don't believe I ever knew Mrs Brown's first name until now," she pondered aloud. "And I don't know Mr Choate's first name!" she said in amazement. "And I've known him for years!"

"George," Wyatt replied crisply. "But he never uses it. He was named after an uncle he absolutely detested."

"Seriously!" Gem marvelled. "How do you know all this?"

"Pints at the Crow when he was on medical leave. You and Mrs M were off baby shopping with Glynn. He, by the way, insists on freshening the décor of the dining room. I told him you wouldn't mind. It will include a wine 'cellar'," Wyatt used air quotes.

"Lovely!" Gem smiled.

"Don't forget to mark the twenty-fourth on our calendar," he said firmly. "Hmm. Ardatha," he said thoughtfully. "Interesting. Perhaps for our second daughter."

"She will be Fiona Jane," Gem countered. "And Mrs M would like to add Elizabeth after her mum.

"Brilliant," Wyatt agreed. "We'd best see how we get on with the first batch of kids though," he suggested.

"So true," she murmured, marking the calendar.

"Good it's not the twenty-third. We have the baby showers, for Ms Holton, Ms Wexton, Ms Blessington, and Ms Grantham. That will be a day! Who the hell ever heard of inviting men to a baby shower?" he demanded, frowning.

"I don't know," Gem said helplessly. "Perhaps it's a new thing. The women will sip tea and gush over the gifts. The men will drink beer and get fathering advice from Stuart Holton. I think it was Ms Blessington's idea."

"Okay. I'll be there," Wyatt assured her.

"Of course you will. Glynn is making the food for both gatherings. And you are bringing the beer!" Gem reminded him.

Gem had barely thought of the Agency proper in weeks. Mr Choate and Mr Harper had wired a baby monitor from the nursery to most of the rooms in the house. Mr Harper referred to it as his 'baby spying device'.

Mrs M had spent a great deal of time shopping for baby items, until Gem had to finally curtail the purchasing, because no two children would ever be able to wear all the clothes the M's had insisted were necessary for all types of weather - from monsoons to a visit to Santa at the North Pole.

Mr Becton had decided not to put in a garden pool as it would be a hazard to small children. He decided on a series of tall fountains instead. Mr M was still arguing that project with the gardener. Mr Becton had obtained clearance from the estate manager, however, for a future children's garden where he could raise a generation of Grantham gardeners at the Hall - having totally missed that opportunity when Wyatt and James steadfastly refused to use the soil for anything other than mud ball missals.

Gem thought over the past weeks as she made tea for Wyatt who had returned to the library to read yet another report.

It had been Mr Choate, not Mr Cawley who had informed Gem and Wyatt, that a slip of paper bearing the names of Odessa officers had been found in the spine of a book about the invasion of Hong Kong by the Japanese in 1941.The exact same book Gem has read last fall. When Gem retrieved the book from her office both Choate and Wyatt had visibly shivered at the strange coincidence. "Staggering!" Mr Choate had muttered. Wyatt merely shook his head, stating that nothing really shocked him about Gem any longer. He was still peeling back layers of her as one peeled back the layers of an artichoke. He realized the layers were infinite.

It had also been Mr Choate who had informed them at the beginning of February, that Gordon White had pleaded guilty to all charges of treason and espionage, and all the counts of murder. He would forever be incarcerated in his own netherworld, and would never again be allowed access to electronic devices - not so much as a table lamp.

Gem had completed her book of medieval cathedrals of the U.K. It would be published in early summer. She hoped to start the next volume after she was certain she wasn't making a mess of motherhood.

She missed Harry terribly and thought of him every day, as she did of Gemmy, mum, dad, and Mr Portermann.

Everything was sorting out. Thus the invitation to tea with Mrs Brown was rather a flashback of sorts to a previous life.

And to Gem's knowledge, no Agency Family had previously been invited to Mrs Brown's country sanctuary.

It was nearly as difficult to find Mrs Brown's cottage as it had been finding Ticking Bottom when Gem had first moved to Grantham Hall. England was a relatively small island, comparatively speaking, so how one managed to find intricate hiding spaces in secluded forested areas was a query that often perplexed her.

There were four Range Rovers already parked at the thatched cottage, when Wyatt drove the Defender into a corner parking space near a meticulously maintained stone garden wall. The wall surrounded the cottage then extended down to an old stable quite similar to the stable at Grantham Hall.

Wyatt had to drive as Gem still had not arranged to take Mr Critchley's defensive driving course. However, she wasn't interested to often leave Ticking Bottom, shopping in the village for her needs as much as possible. She would, however, work again with Mr Critchley because she wanted to drive James's Morgan - Wyatt's gift to her - a gift she would one day share with her daughter as their son would have Wyatt's Jag. And one child would, in the future, receive the Defender. Heaven only knew what ideas Wyatt would come up with to gift any children after the third one.

Mrs Brown welcomed them warmly, and Gem and Wyatt were delighted to also be greeted by Mr's Cawley, Critchley, Choate, and Harper. Mr Harper! Now that was a splendid, and shocking, surprise! He was truly back in the Agency Family. Everyone was together again!

"A reunion," Gem smiled, her eyes misting at seeing all her dear friends together.

"Indeed," Mrs Brown smiled at her. "And, Gem, Wyatt, I would like to introduce you to my husband, Arthur Palmer."

Gem shook hands with Arthur, then frowned, puzzled by the sparkle in the man's eyes, and then Wyatt was stunned when she threw herself into the man's arms.

"Harry! Blast you! You damn well broke my heart!" she gasped, tears streaming down her cheeks.

"Hello, my dear. A delight not a fright?" he chuckled. "How did you recognize me?"

Gem studied his face. Scars of surgery were still red, but would likely fade with time. "Your eyes. I can still see you in your eyes. What the hell happened - or that a query not to be ventured?"

Harry - the man now known as Arthur, winced slightly. "A mad man with a match and a petrol can. You know how Indonesia oft times flares to a boil."

"Dear God!" Gem gasped. "One seriously injured!"

"Indeed," Mr Cawley nodded to her, remembering the text they had share so many months ago now.

"And thank God for dear Mrs Brown, now Mrs Palmer," Harry/Arthur smiled at his wife. "I went underground and got into a bit of hot water - no horrid pun intended. I yelled to her for help and she flew out, arriving about an hour after the match hit the petrol. She connected with an SEA agent I was with, and then they both managed to get me to the adult burn centre in Adelaide."

"He couldn't continue to be Harry as Mr Harper well knows," Mrs Brown/Palmer explained. "Skin grafts, healing. And for his own safety he had to disappear permanently."

"You broke my heart," Gem chided her 'late' friend, "and now I am so happy to see you!"

"The newscaster was supposed to hold the story a day, so that I could warn you," Mrs Brown interjected, "but he altered 'yesterday' to 'today' and aired the news item. He rang me to say he was doing so, and didn't give me a chance to tell him not to do that," Mrs Brown grimaced. "Hence, my urgent call to Wyatt. I am sorry it caused you and everyone else in the Agency such distress, my dear."

"Actually, I think it helped," Gem replied thoughtfully. "I explained everything to Wyatt, as you ordered me to do, and things started falling into place in my mind."

"A catalyst," Wyatt murmured.

"Yes," Gem nodded gently.

"And you sleep at night?" Harry/Arthur asked.

"Thank God, she does!" Wyatt exclaimed.

Gem nodded. "And now we all can have a lovely reunion."

Mrs Brown/Palmer looked hesitantly at her husband and replied. "Not quite, my dear," she said taking Gem's hand to lead her to the sofa.

Gem finally scanned the room, the buffet on a table in the dining room, the kitchen beyond, a library and a staircase to the left of the central living room. And then she saw an oblong box on the coffee table in front of the sofa.

"Sit, my dear," Mrs Brown/Palmer said quietly, and Gem looked up at the six most important men in her life. She caught Wyatt in her peripheral vision and he gave her the slightest of puzzled looks.

"Gem, my dear," the woman said softly, "the RAAF has found the Pilos. - Everyone has been recovered."

Tears started streaming down Gem's face, and she reached out a hand to Wyatt. He sat down beside her and put his arm around her shoulders.

Mrs Brown/Palmer continued softly. "Harry and I escorted our Family home yesterday. There will be a small notice in the newspaper tomorrow." She cleared her throat and read from a sheet of paper:

Gemma Louisa Lawson, 24 years
Brisbane, Australia

Margaret Louisa Lawson, 52 years
Brisbane, Australia

Gerald Henry Forrester, 52 years
Brisbane, Australia

Eric Anthony Portermann, 52 years
Brisbane, Australia

30 May, 2011
Small plane crash, Kimberly Mountains, Australia

"We need to discuss burial arrangements," Mrs Brown/Palmer said softly.

"Ticking Bottom," Wyatt said firmly, but softly, and Gem nodded. "Grantham Family plot."

"Could that please include Eric?" Harry/Arthur asked. "He has no family to mourn him, aside from the Agency."

"He has now," Wyatt said quietly.

"So it is over," Gem said, not believing the words that came from her mouth. Not believing these moments were happening. "It is finally, well and truly over."

"Indeed," Mrs Brown/Palmer agreed. She reached for the long box on the coffee table, and handed it to Harry/Arthur, then drew Gem to her feet.

Harry stood straight and tall, squared his shoulder, and said in a clear, steady voice, "Gemimah Louisa Forrester Grantham, the British Government wishes to present to you the Agency Memorial Medal in honour of Gemma Louisa Lawson, Margaret Louisa Lawson, Gerald Henry Forrester, and Eric Anthony Portermann, in gratitude for their unwavering courage and service to their country."

Gem took the box and opened it to see the four beautiful medals on deep purple ribbons. 'In Memory of Service' was on the front of each of the medals. On the back was the name etched in gold of each of her loved ones.

"Thank you," Gem said, refusing to let her voice falter. "I believe these had best go in Wyatt's safe."

"Indeed," Arthur Palmer said firmly.

"The Agency does not exist," Gem smiled. "But my family does. All my Families." She smiled gratefully at each person in the room.

Mrs Palmer shook Gem's hand, then Arthur, Mr Choate, Mr Harper, Mr Cawley, and Mr Critchley, came forward to do so.

Mrs Palmer eased her guests to the buffet and away from Gem, allowing her to absorb the day's event. Gem had Wyatt at her side, where he always would be, Mrs Palmer thought with great confidence. She had been concerned of the match, but could see now she needn't have worried about a girl from a Jane Austen World and a man from the Shark-Infested, Gritty Business World.

As the group began to chat softly, then more casually, Gem slipped the box into her shoulder bag and walked over to join the others.

"Girls, boys?" Critchley asked Wyatt as he filled his plate from the buffet.

"One of each," Wyatt grinned, "and both are proper kickers!"

"You two are going to have your hands full," Critchley laughed heartily. "Don't plan on getting any sleep for eighteen or nineteen years. You'll both be exhausted - especially the first six months."

"They will not," Glynn Harper said firmly. "I'm taking a leave of absence from T.O. to take charge at Grantham Hall. Nanny in residence."

"Since when?" Gem demanded in astonishment.

"Since yesterday," he said firmly. "I already settled it with Wyatt and Choate, and the M's. I'm ready to go when you do, love!"

"Lovely!" Gem exclaimed, giving him a kiss on the cheek, then one to Wyatt. "But Mr Choate will be down an employee."

Choate glanced at Wyatt. "I hired Ms Jones. She starts Monday."

"She breaks things!" Gem laughed. "She told me so."

"She sets hot coffee cups on cds," Choate grinned. "Sound familiar, Gem?" He shook his head and became a bit more serious. "She's got an eye. Ms Jones walked into O and E's shop to purchase a scarf, and caught a shoplifter in thirty seconds flat. Wyatt recommended her."

"I did indeed," Wyatt agreed. "One of the sharpest employees GEI has ever had."

"Ms Jones wants to be an agent, and T.O. will train her," Choate said firmly.

"The Agency will welcome her with open arms when she's ready," Cawley nodded.

"Life is so bizarre sometimes," Gem shook her head smiling. "What a lovely Family we have, Wyatt!"

"Indeed!" he smiled that wonderful smile that loosened butterflies.

"The Palmers expect to be Auntie and Uncle," Arthur Palmer stated, reaching for a glass of wine.

"Uncle," Choate held up a hand.

"Uncle," Critchley held up his hand.

"Uncle," Cawley extended his hand.

"The Power!" Glynn Harper held up his hand. "The one who says 'no' when everyone else is fawning and cooing ad nauseum."

Gem and Wyatt look at each other. "Brilliant!" they said in unison.

"Names?" Mrs Palmer queried.

Wyatt smiled at Gem. "Gemma Margaret Louisa Grantham."

Gem smiled at him in return. "James Gerald Eric Grantham."

"Hear! Hear!" the call was made around.

"Gemma and James," Wyatt whispered to Gem, "after their auntie and uncle. They may never know the entire story of their namesakes. The two people who brought us together," he leaned down to kiss her.

"Indeed," Gem smiled.

"Thank God you believe in forgiveness, my love," Wyatt whispered.

"I'm still deciding on that, Dark Lord," she teased, grinning.

Gemma Louisa Lawson, Margaret Louisa Lawson, Gerald Henry Forrester, and Eric Anthony Portermann, were finally laid to rest in the Grantham Family plot at Ticking Bottom Church cemetery, the following Saturday. The entire village attended the memorial service, as well as Gem's Agency Family, and Ms Blessington, Ms Wexton, Ms Ames, Ora and Eda - their mum ran the shop that day - Emma and Stuart Holton, and Mr Manton. A single line was printed on the memorial program: Died in a plane crash, 30 May 2011, recovered February 2012.

The following Saturday, Gem and Wyatt watched as the headstones were set in place over the graves at Ticking Bottom Church cemetery; and James's headstone was reset.

Gem studied the words written below the dates on Gemmy's headstone. 'Beloved - JGS', and the inscription that had been added to James's headstone: 'Beloved- GLL'.

"Wyatt, darling," Gem mused, "someone is going to have questions about -"

"People are only interested in information of their own family," he said smoothly.

"Well, our children are going to ask questions someday," she persisted.

"When that time comes only Gemmy and James will be told the truth. When they are old enough to know and old enough to respect that some Family matters are kept private," Wyatt said quietly.

"Agreed," Gem nodded. "But we won't tell them about us - about how we met-"

"Hell no!" Wyatt said firmly. "Only the very basics of Gemmy and James."

"Shall I write down the story so that we keep it straight?"

"Good idea," he nodded. "We'll read, memorize, and then put the copy in the safe."

"Agreed," she smiled.

Gem read the café scene. It had been months since she had stopped at Oscar's Café. She and Wyatt spoke now and then of the marvel that Gemmy and James had met at Oscar's, and had fallen in love. And that they, Gem and Wyatt had met at Oscar's Cafe and had eventually fallen in love - well and truly - despite a rather rude and rocky beginning to their relationship - marriage, Gem smiled to herself, as she savoured that last word.

Gem thought of the hours she had spent the previous summer, watching, hoping, that a handsome young man would appear so that she could explain herself.

She sighed happily at her companion. "You are a handsome, young man," she smiled, and sipped her tea.

"It can be dangerous to speak to strangers," a voice warned from her left.

"He's no stranger than his father," she said crisply, handing over her companion. "You are rather strange, you know," she teased.

Wyatt accepted the bundle, leaned down to kiss her, then took the chair next to hers.

"Thank you, darling," she smiled. "You're early."

"Gemmy is sleeping, but we finished our errand." He handed her a very large box, and adjusted both prams closer to him.

"And what can this be?" Gem smiled curiously at the plain white box.

"Open it," he quietly urged.

Gem took off the lid and spread the tissue surrounding the gift. "Oh, Wyatt!" she gasped. "I just thought you were reading it," she lifted the book from the box.

"I wanted to surprise you," he said softly.

Gem ran her fingers lovingly over the cover of the very large, very handsome book, and read the title: "Cathedral Art Glass of the Medieval Ages, by Gemma Louisa Lawson." She opened the cover and gently turned pages, stopping at the inscription page, and read: "Published by Gemimah Forrester Grantham in loving memory of the author: Gemma Louisa Lawson, June 1987 - May 2011," she said softly, her eyes brimming with tears. "It's a lovely surprise," she leaned over to kiss him.

"I ordered two thousand copies printed. The publisher has already had requests for fourteen hundred copies from universities, libraries and museums, art dealers, all over the world. I talked to Ms Carton this morning. The two thousand copies of your new book that you donated to the cathedrals have all sold. GEI has ordered another two thousand for the cathedrals. Of the two thousand ordered for bookshops, nine hundred have been sold. Not bad at all for a reference book, darling."

"Cash for the cathedrals," she grinned, then thought of Gemmy's book. "Will Ms Carton take on Gemmy's book for the cathedrals and the bookshops?"

"Whatever you wish, my dear," he said gently. "And the publisher is already asking about your work on medieval European cathedrals," Wyatt informed her.

"Well, since Glynn has us so well organized, I may start on the next book at this end of this month," Gem laughed.

"You realize he's going to be with us until the last child goes off to university," Wyatt said dryly.

"Fine with me," Gem sighed happily, "but Mr Choate may have something to say about that."

Wyatt chuckled. "Lunch here or at home?" he moved the subject on to current matters.

"Home! Grandparents are babysitting this afternoon," Gem grinned. "We have the entire afternoon together. Alone!"

"Lovely to have grandparents in the carriage house." Wyatt gazed into the lovely violet eyes. They very rarely ever clouded these days. And when they did, Wyatt realized it would still take a very long time before she could have her memories without the pain. "Where is the Power today?"

"Preparing for tonight's picnic," Gem reminded him. "Auntie Palmer and all the uncles are coming. Remember?"

"Oh, yes." Wyatt leaned over to kiss her again. "God bless our Family!"

"Indeed," Gem stared into the beautiful grey eyes. Butterflies were beginning to swarm. She knew they would never settle for long.

He wasn't the perfect man that she had believed him to be a year ago - when they had first met. But he is perfect for me, Gem sighed happily.

He leaned over to kiss her yet again. "Svengali," Gem murmured.

"Trilby," Wyatt kissed her gently.

The End

CPSIA information can be obtained at www.ICGtesting.com
Printed in the USA
LVOW10s0522260716

497751LV00018B/139/P

9 781622 872626